LE CHIEN D'OR / THE GOLDEN DOG

The Centre for Editing Early Canadian Texts (CEECT) is engaged in the preparation of scholarly editions of selected works of early English-Canadian prose. *Le Chien d'or / The Golden Dog: A Legend of Quebec* is the twelfth—and final—text in the CEECT series.

Portrait of William Kirby

Le
Chien d'or

The
Golden Dog

A Legend of Quebec

William Kirby

Edited by
Mary Jane Edwards

McGill-Queen's University Press
Montreal & Kingston • London • Ithaca

b4/35 80 28

ISBN 978-0-7735-4030-9 (cloth)
ISBN 978-0-7735-4016-3 (paper)

Legal deposit second quarter 2012
Bibliotheque nationale du Quebec
Printed in Canada on acid-free paper.

Library and Archives Canada Cataloguing in Publication
  Kirby, William, 1817–1906
    Le Chien d'or = The golden dog : a legend of Quebec / William Kirby ; edited by Mary Jane Edwards.

(Centre for Editing Early Canadian Texts series ; 12)
ISBN 978-0-7735-4030-9 (bound). –ISBN 978-0-7735-4016-3 (pbk.)

    I. Edwards, Mary Jane, 1939– II. Centre for Editing Early Canadian Texts III. Title. IV. Title: Golden dog. V. Series: Centre for Editing Early Canadian Texts series ; 12.

PS8471.I73G6 2012   C813'.4   C2011-908470-8

Published and distributed by McGill-Queen's University Press.

ACKNOWLEDGEMENT

This book has been published with the help of a grant from the Canadian Federation for the Humanities and Social Sciences, through the Aid to Scholarly Publications Program, using funds provided by the Social Sciences and Humanities Research Council of Canada.
McGill-Queen's University Press acknowledges the support of the Canada Council for the Arts for our publishing program. We also acknowledge the financial support of the Government of Canada through the Canada Book Fund for our publishing activities. McGill-Queen's University Press and the Centre for Editing Early Canadian Texts gratefully acknowledge the support of Carleton University and the Social Sciences and Humanities Research Council of Canada in the preparation of this edition.

Cover illustration: OTAR, Kirby, F-1076, Photographs, MU1665, K-162, Le Chien d'Or Tablet (close up). Courtesy of the Archives of Ontario.

Contents

CONTENTS

Abbreviations

AEU	University of Alberta Library, Edmonton, Alberta
AL	Autograph letter
ALS	Autograph letter signed
ANB	*American National Biography.* New York and Oxford: Oxford University Press, 1999.
Bell	Andrew Bell. *History Of Canada ... Translated From "L'Histoire Du Canada." Of F.-X. Garneau ... In Three Volumes.* Montreal: Printed And Published By John Lovell, 1860.
BU	*Biographie Universelle (Michaud) Ancienne Et Moderne ... Nouvelle Edition.* Paris: Chez Madame C. Desplaces, and Leipzig: Librairie De F. A. Brockhaus, 1843 ff.
BVAU	University of British Columbia Library, Vancouver, British Columbia
Catholic	*The Catholic Encyclopedia.* New York: Robert Appleton, 1907 ff.
CEECT	Centre for Editing Early Canadian Texts
Chansons	Ernest Gagnon. *Chansons Populaires Du Canada Recueillies Et Publiées Avec Annotations, Etc..* Québec: Bureaux De "Foyer Canadien," 1865.
DBF	*Dictionnaire De Biographie Française*
DCB	*Dictionary of Canadian Biography*
DLB	*Dictionary of Literary Biography.* Detroit: Gale Research Company.
Grove's	Grove's *Dictionary of Art.* Ed. Jane Turner. London: Macmillan, 1996.
IB	*Interpreter's Bible.* New York and Nashville: Abingdon Press, 1951 ff.
Kirby	William Kirby Collection
Maple Leaves	James MacPherson Le Moine. *Maple Leaves: A Budget Of Legendary, Historical, Critical, And Sporting Intelligence.* Quebec: Printed, For The Author, By Hunter, Rose & Co., 1863.
Memoirs	Charles Mackay. *Memoirs Of Extraordinary Popular Delusions.* London: Richard Bentley, 1841.

Molière	Jean-Baptiste Poquelin *dit* Molière. *Oeuvres De Molière.* Ed. Eugène Despois and Paul Mesnard. Paris: Librairie Hachette, 1873 ff.
Odes And Epodes	Horace. *Odes And Epodes.* Ed. and Trans. Niall Rudd. Cambridge and London: Harvard University Press, 2004.
ODNB	*Oxford Dictionary of National Biography.* Oxford: Oxford University Press, 2004.
OHM	McMaster University Library, Hamilton, Ontario
OKQ	Queen's University, Kingston, Ontario
OKR	Library, Royal Military College of Canada, Kingston, Ontario
OONA	Library and Archives Canada (Archives), Ottawa, Ontario
OONL	Library and Archives Canada (Library), Ottawa, Ontario
OOP	Library of Parliament, Ottawa, Ontario
OPET	Trent University Library, Peterborough, Ontario
OTAR	Archives of Ontario, Toronto, Ontario
OTMCL	Metropolitan Toronto Central Library, Toronto, Ontario
OTU-F	Thomas Fisher Rare Book Library, University of Toronto, Toronto, Ontario
Rabelais	François Rabelais. *The Works of Francis Rabelais.* Trans. Sir Thomas Urquhart and Motteux. 1693. A New Edition. London: H. G. Bohn, 1849.
Ready	William Ready Division of Archives and Research Collections
Shakespeare	William Shakespeare. *The Riverside Shakespeare.* Boston: Houghton Mifflin Company, 1974.
Siècle	François-Marie Arouet de Voltaire. *Siècle De Louis XIV.* Paris: Chez Mme Veuve Dabo, 1823.
TL-C	Copy of typed letter
TLS	Typed letter signed
Ursulines	Catherine Burke, dite de Saint-Thomas. *Les Ursulines De Québec, Depuis Leur Établissement Jusqu'à Nos Jours.* 4 Vols. Québec: Des Presses de C. Darveau, 1863–66.
Vie Privée	Mouffle d'Angerville. *Vie Privée De Louis XV; Ou Principaux Événemens, Particularités Et Anecdotes De Son Règne.* London: John Peter Lyton, 1781.

Foreword

The Centre for Editing Early Canadian Texts (CEECT) at Carleton University was established to prepare for publication scholarly editions of major works of early English-Canadian prose that were either out of print or available only in corrupt reprints. Eleven of these editions—Frances Brooke's *The History of Emily Montague,* James De Mille's *A Strange Manuscript Found in a Copper Cylinder,* Thomas Chandler Haliburton's *The Clockmaker, Series One, Two, and Three,* Julia Catherine Beckwith Hart's *St. Ursula's Convent,* Rosanna Leprohon's *Antoinette De Mirecourt,* Thomas McCulloch's *The Mephibosheth Stepsure Letters,* Susanna Moodie's *Roughing It in the Bush,* John Richardson's *The Canadian Brothers* and *Wacousta,* and Catharine Parr Traill's *The Backwoods of Canada* and *Canadian Crusoes*—have been published. William Kirby's *Le Chien d'or / The Golden Dog: A Legend of Quebec,* the enormously popular historical novel set in eighteenth-century Quebec that helped to define an identity for the new nineteenth-century Dominion of Canada, is the twelfth—and final—edition in the CEECT series.

In the preparation of these editions advice and guidance have been sought from a broad range of international scholarship, and contemporary principles and procedures for the scholarly editing of literary texts have been adopted. They have been adapted, however, to suit the special circumstances of English-Canadian literature and the particular needs of each work in the CEECT series.

The text of each scholarly edition in this series has been critically established after the history of the composition and first publication of the work has been researched and its versions analysed and compared. The critical text is clear, with only authorial notes, if any, appearing in the body of the book. Each of these editions also has an editor's introduction with a separate section on the text, and, as concluding apparatus, explanatory notes, a description of the copy-text(s), and, when relevant, of other authoritative versions, a list of published versions of the work, a record of emendations made to the copy-text(s), a list of line-end hyphenated compounds in the copy-text(s) as they are resolved in the CEECT edition, and a list of line-end hyphenated compounds in the CEECT edition as they should be resolved in quotations from it. An historical collation is included when more than one version has authority, and, as necessary, other apparatus and appendices containing material directly relevant to the work.

In the preparation of these CEECT editions for publication, identical procedures, in so far as the particular history of each work allowed, have been followed. An attempt has been made to find and analyse every unpublished version of the work known to exist. At least five copies of each published version that was a possible choice for copy-text have been examined, as have at least three copies of each of the other published versions that the author might have revised. Every published version of the work has been subjected to several collations of various kinds. Specialists from Carleton University's Computing and Communications Services have developed programs to help in the proofreading and comparison of texts, to perform word-searches, and to compile and store much of the information for the concluding apparatus. The edited text has been proofread against its copy-text(s) at all appropriate stages.

Editor's Preface

My close connections with William Kirby's *Le Chien d'or* began many decades ago, in a way even before I was born. In 1911 my mother emigrated with her family from London, England, to St. Thomas, Ontario. She attended high school in that county town in the 1920s, a time when Canadians were especially proud of their country because of its role in World War One, in which her father and her two older brothers served. At the St. Thomas Collegiate Institute and Vocational School she not only learned a good deal about her adopted homeland, but she also read the fiction and poetry of many Canadian authors, including Kirby's majestic historical novel.

I do not know which version of *Le Chien d'or* formed part of my mother's syllabus—in the 1920s there were at least four versions available, including two that were published by the Musson Book Company, Limited, of Toronto. I do know that she loved this novel very much, that at one time or another there were several copies around our house, that she re-read it in all or in part at least once a year until she died, and that she passed her enthusiasm for it on to her daughter. It is not really surprising, therefore, that when, aged nine or ten, I visited the old city of Quebec on a school excursion from Montreal, the site that impressed me most was not the Plains of Abraham, but the tablet of the Golden Dog with which Kirby's novel was so closely associated.

Many years passed, however, before I became professionally involved with this tablet over the principal entrance to the main post office in Quebec, the traditions attached to its legend, and the work of prose fiction that Kirby composed about it. By then I had received an MA in Canadian literature from Queen's University (Kingston, Ontario). I had earned my doctorate at the University of Toronto with a thesis on nineteenth-century English- and French-Canadian fiction. I had taught Canadian Literature at the University of British Columbia and at Carleton University. And I had recognized three problems that pertained in particular to early Canadian literature in both English and French. Many important works were not in print. Many of those that were available represented a version that was shortened and that used as its copy-text an unauthorized edition. Much of the scholarship on these nineteenth-century works was based on these imperfect productions and, thus, was more or less inaccurate. I was not alone in making these observations, of course. It was inevitable, therefore, that a project to prepare a series of scholarly editions of major works of early English-Canadian prose should be developed.

Le Chien d'or was unfailingly among the first works suggested when, in the early 1980s, the Centre for Editing Early Canadian Texts (CEECT) asked professors of Canadian literature and other members of the academic community in Canada and abroad what works they deemed to deserve what we described as "a full editorial treatment." Of these early cultural productions, moreover, Kirby's novel was also one of the few to have a descriptive bibliography, Elizabeth Brady's "A Bibliographical Essay On William Kirby's *The Golden Dog* 1877–1977" (*Papers of the Bibliographical Society of Canada* 15 [1976], 24–48). It was she whom CEECT asked to prepare its scholarly edition of Kirby's work.

Elizabeth responded enthusiastically to this invitation. It was only in 1986, however, when the project received a Major Research Grant, its second five-year grant from the Social Sciences and Humanities Research Council of Canada, that the CEECT edition of *Le Chien d'or* got underway. And shortly thereafter Elizabeth had to withdraw as editor. When this happened, although I did not fully realize it, most of the construction of the CEECT edition was still to be accomplished. We had, nevertheless, poured its foundation, and we were beginning to build its scaffolding. For her preparatory work on the edition, therefore, as well as for her important contribution to the bibliography of Kirby's novel, I should especially like to acknowledge and to thank Elizabeth Brady.

I am ultimately responsible, however, for *Le Chien d'or / The Golden Dog: A Legend of Quebec*, the CEECT version of Kirby's sad tale. Despite my extensive editorial experience, its achievement has taken many years. Some of this is due to other academic endeavours, including my editorship of five volumes (1998–2002) of *English Studies in Canada*. Most of it is due to the nature of both scholarly editing and the work being edited. I underestimated, for example, the time that would be necessary to perfect the CEECT transcription of the manuscript, to establish the text, and to research the explanatory notes. The tortuous history of the novel's creation and publication, the nature of the vision that Kirby expressed in it, and the breadth and depth of his knowledge, furthermore, required much reading and extensive travelling. These journeys, literal and figurative, have, nevertheless, allowed me to revisit aspects not only of my historical and literary education but also of my religious training. Likewise they have permitted me to refine my ideas both about Kirby and about notions of civility and culture that helped shape nineteenth-century Canada and that in many ways still inform the country that Canada has become in the twenty-first century.

Because I have spent many years with *Le Chien d'or*, I have also had the opportunity to take account of new developments that have influenced theories and practices of scholarly editing. When we first discussed how to prepare our editions, it was with some difficulty that we were convinced to use computers as much as possible. Since then we have migrated from main frames to personal computers, laptops, notebooks, and net books; through numerous computer languages and programs; and through magnetic tapes, disks of various sizes, CDs, memory sticks, and files attached to e-mails. These media have not necessarily changed the message of this edition, but they have altered the way it was prepared. Although they did not hasten the process, electronic databases, for example, aided the compilation of this edition's explanatory notes.

CEECT has always claimed that it produced "reliable" rather than "definitive" editions. Such an edition is, furthermore, both a critical and a creative endeavour shaped by such matters as its compiler's sense of the author and his or her work, the material included in the edition as well as the manner of its presentation therein, and the time and place of its preparation, printing, and publishing. In the case of *Le Chien d'or / The Golden Dog: A Legend of Quebec*, I have incorporated into my "Editor's Introduction" a good deal of information—much of it previously unpublished—about the novel's production and reception from its first publication to the present day. In so doing I have benefitted from the rapprochement of scholarly editing and the history of the book and from the ideas of the latter about the importance of material artifacts in cultural studies.

If it takes a village to raise a child, it also requires many kinds of support to produce a scholarly edition. I am particularly grateful to Carleton University and to the Social Sciences and Humanities Research Council of Canada for their financial contributions for both CEECT in general and for *Le Chien d'or* in particular, and to the Canadian Federation for the Humanities and Social Sciences, through the Aid to Scholarly

Publications Program, for its grant to help cover the cost of publishing the CEECT version of Kirby's novel. Likewise I wish to recognize the Institute of Commonwealth Studies at the University of London, where in 1996–97 I held a Henry Charles Chapman Fellowship. This sojourn allowed me to explore many British repositories that held material relevant to Kirby and his work, especially in the context of nineteenth-century English publishing.

In addition to those I have already mentioned, many institutions in several countries have contributed to the preparation of this edition. In Canada these include the Archives of Ontario, Laval University, Library and Archives Canada, McGill University, McMaster University, the Metropolitan Toronto Central Library, the National Library and Archives of Quebec (Montreal), the Niagara-on-the-Lake Public Library, the North York Public Library, the Ottawa Public Library, the Quebec Literary and Historical Society, Queen's University, the Royal Military College of Canada, Simon Fraser University, Trent University, the University of Alberta, the University of British Columbia, the University of Ottawa, the Thomas Fisher Rare Book Library and the Victoria University Archives at the University of Toronto, and the Ursulines of Quebec. In England they are the Bodleian Library, the Bristol Central Library, the British Library, the Harris Library (Preston, Lancashire), the Hull Local Studies Library, the Humberside County Record Office, the archives of Jarrold and Sons Limited, the Kingston Upon Hull Record Office, the Lancashire Record Office, the Northallerton Library, the North Yorkshire County Record Office, the Royal Commission on Historical Manuscripts, the Sheffield Central Library, the St. Bride Printing Library, University College (London), and the University of Hull. Elsewhere they are, in Australia, the Australian Defence Force Academy, the Australian National University, the Mitchell Library (State Library of New South Wales), Monash University, the National Library of Australia, the State Library of Tasmania, the State Library of Victoria, the University of Melbourne, the University of Sydney, and the University of Tasmania; in France, the Académie Française and the Bibliothèque Nationale de France; in South Africa, Rhodes University; in Sweden, The Royal Library (National Library of Sweden); and in the United States, the Feinberg Library at the State University of New York (Plattsburgh), the Plattsburgh Public Library, and the Princeton University Library. As well as these institutions that I visited, there are many that lent books, newspapers, and other periodicals through Interlibrary Loans at Carleton's MacOdrum Library. I owe a good deal to the staff of this division. I thank them especially for their unfailing cheerfulness and cooperation.

Many editorial assistants and other members of the CEECT team as well as numerous students have helped with aspects of this edition. They include Lee Ann Astophen, Heather Avery, John Baillieul, Annette Berndt, Micheline Besner, David Bieber, Joseph L. Black, Christina Boyd, Nicolas Campeau, Erica Charters, Robert Chamberlain, Linda Collier, Karen Colvin, Mary Comfort, Cheryl Cundell, Rosemary Daniels, Brenda Di Luca, Larissa Douglass, Andrew Elliott, Cindy Elphick, Allison Fillmore, Michelle Glennie, Michelle Gonsalves, Lorraine Goulden, Paul Griffin, Ray Hachey, Vaughn Hambley, Sharon Hamilton, Dallas Harrison, Blaine Hertz, Susan Hillabold, Nicole Honderich, Janice Isaac, Michelle Kelly, Andrew Kerr-Wilson, Nancy Kerr-Wilson, Suzanne Kiely, Lydia MacLaren, Victor Mallet, Rachel Maloy, Brenda McPhail, Amanda Mullen, Dianne Payne, Dana Patrascu, Margaret Poetschke, Noreen Poetschke, Karen Reynolds, Erin Robinson, Randy Schmidt, Kevin Stinson, Patrick Toner, Deborah Wills, Daniel Wilson, and Kenneth C. Wilson. S. F. (Syd) Wise, acting as my general editor, cast a keen historical eye over the explanatory notes, most of which he had read and approved before he died. Robert G. (Bob) Laird, who took over as my general editor, has not only carried on Syd's critical care, but he has also brought his penchant for clear thinking and concise expression to my aid. We have also worked closely with Christina Thiele, who prepared the pages of this final CEECT volume, and with Mark Abley, the editor at McGill-Queen's University Press, who shepherded it through the various stages of its publication. We are grateful for their enthusiasm, expertise, and, above all, patience.

No work of this complexity is accomplished without the help and support of colleagues, family, and friends. In addition to those already named, I wish to thank Hilda and Len Barlow, Jack Billingsley, Winnifred M. Bogaards, Marian and Norman Cook, Gwendolyn Davies, Marion Diamond, Walter Dietrich, Brenda, Paul, Peter, and Wendy Doye, Paul Eggert, Ian and Maureen Gunn, J. A. W. (Jock) Gunn, Ted and Louise Gunn, David M. Hayne, Wallace and Joan Kirsop, Margaret Wade Labarge, Geri Laird, Carrol Lunau, Charlotte and Ivan McWilliam, Joan Melvin, A. P. A. Milaire, Elizabeth Morrison, David J. Nordloh, Jane Oulton, George L. Parker, Bettina Tate Pedersen, Gordon H. Roper, Rupert Schieder, Peter L. Shillingsburg, Gregory Snell, Carl Spadoni, Thomas B. Vincent, Leon Warmski, J. B. (Jake) Warren, Elizabeth Webby, Anneke de Zeeuw, and Elaine Zinkham.

I dedicate *Le Chien d'or / The Golden Dog: A Legend of Quebec* to my mother, Winnifred Idette Billingsley Edwards. She did not live to see one of her favourite books produced in a scholarly edition, but she would be delighted that the CEECT version of Kirby's novel is published at last.

Mary Jane Edwards
Carleton University
July 2011

Editor's Introduction:
The Anatomy of a Novel

One of the curiosities of the city of Quebec is a tablet that features a carving of a dog gnawing a bone and the words:

JE SUIS UN CHIEN QUI RONGE LO
EN LE RONGEANT JE PREND MON REPOS
UN TEMS VIENDRA QUI NEST PAS VENU
QUE JE MORDERAI QUI M'AURA MORDU,[1]

or, in a well-known English translation:

"I am a dog that gnaws his bone,
I couch and gnaw it all alone.
A time will come which is not yet,
When I'll bite him, by whom I'm bit."[2]

In the early twentieth century it was established that Timothée Roussel, a surgeon who emigrated from France to Quebec in the 1660s, had the carving on a wall just outside Pézenas, a town in the Hérault district of Languedoc-Roussillon, replicated and placed on the stone house that he had built on Buade Street in 1688. Roussel, who came from the same region in the south of France, had most likely seen this bas-relief before he left for Canada. For most of the nineteenth century, however, the tablet of the Golden Dog—the dog was gilded—was connected to Nicolas Jacquin *dit* Philibert, the merchant who bought Roussel's house in 1734, and his fatal stabbing in 1748 by Pierre-Jean-Baptiste-François-Xavier Legardeur de Repentigny, a member of one of the first families of New France.

It was from this nineteenth-century tradition that William Kirby (1817–1906) developed *Le Chien d'or*, the work of historical fiction that provided Canadians with a prose version of their heroic past and that became an icon in the literature and culture of both English and French Canada.[3] Originally published in 1877, this novel reappeared in English in new typesettings five more times in the nineteenth and twentieth centuries. Its translation into French was also issued in two editions, the second a corrected and revised version of the first. Since its first publication, in fact, *Le Chien d'or* has been reprinted many times in English in Canada, England, and the United States and in French in Canada. It presents, thus, a complicated case study in international publishing history involving authors, editors, publishers, reviewers, and translators, many of whom were—and still are—well-known figures in American and British as well as Canadian literary culture.

Despite its importance as a Canadian artifact, its numerous issues in each of Canada's two official languages, and its wide distribution, few people have read the work that Kirby meant to see in print when he submitted his albeit messy manuscript for publication. Only two of the six editions in English come close to representing his intended text, and neither is the one that claimed to be authorized. The other four are abridgments, each done by a different editor who cut the cloth of Kirby's novel to suit his interpretation of what it meant. The French translation, too, wanders in its vision of a Canadian nation from that imagined by Kirby. Because of these transformations, the preparation of a scholarly edition of *Le Chien d'or* is both particularly necessary, and particularly challenging. The aim of this volume is, nevertheless, to provide the reader with an edition that contains a critically reliable text of Kirby's iconic work and that places this text in as complete an historical context as possible.

Coming to Canada

Kirby, "author, tanner, journalist, teacher, and public servant,"[4] the son of John Kirby, a currier, and his wife Charlotte Parker Kirby, was born on 13 October 1817 in Kingston Upon Hull, England, then a thriving port on the Humber River. From his father's residence Kirby would not only have been able to see the sailing ships but also to play among their goods on the docks. Hull, then, provided both a lively embodiment of British mercantilism and alluring glimpses of other cultures across the seas.

The heroism and romance as well as the tragedy and violence that lay behind Hull's achievements were further ingrained in the young boy by family traditions. One was that the Kirbys, who were associated with several villages near Northallerton, including Kirby Wiske and Newby Wiske, where Kirby, staying with his paternal grandparents, took his "first lessons" in 1825,[5] were descended from the Vikings who settled in Yorkshire in the ninth and tenth centuries. Another concerned the part that members of the Watson family, who were related to his mother, played as prominent Royalists during the Civil War in England in the seventeenth century. Yet another was that a great-grandmother and her family were forced to leave Virginia and return to England because of their support of the British during the American Revolution in the eighteenth century. According to her great-grandson, who heard "of her through tradition," she particularly "hated" George Washington "for his disloyalty."[6]

The family's earlier misfortunes in North America notwithstanding, it participated in what Edwin C. Guillet described as the third "great" migration of history, that is, "the Atlantic Migration to the New World ... between 1770 and 1890, when eleven million people came from the British Isles to North America."[7] In 1832 John and Charlotte, accompanied by Kirby and his four sisters, immigrated to Cincinnati, Ohio, which was then "the fastest growing city"[8] in the mid-western United States. Kirby worked there as a tanner. He also attended the Classical and Philosophical Academy, a school established in 1827 by Alexander Kinmont. A native of Scotland who had arrived in the United States in 1823, he instructed his "scholars" in "the various branches of a Classical, Mathematical, and English education"; he was particularly keen on teaching them ancient and modern languages, on encouraging them to do translation, which he believed was an extremely "beneficial ... mental discipline," and on pushing them to read "the widest possible range of authors of all ages."[9] Under his guidance Kirby learned to read and write in Latin and French, studied German and Swedish, developed a taste for reading many books on a variety of subjects, and acquired a lifelong interest in the philosophical and religious principles of Emanuel Swedenborg and in Swedish culture generally. Kirby later described this "old friend and teacher" as "the noblest character and most gifted, both in intellect and power of expression," that he had ever met.[10] Certainly Kinmont's influence can be felt in the broad range of cultural allusions that help shape *Le Chien d'or*.

Kirby, however, never really adapted to life in the United States, and in the late 1830s several events occurred that caused him to abandon the republic. In May 1837 an economic depression began in Cincinnati that "ate away at the savings and independence of thousands of men and women."[11] In September 1838 Kinmont died aged thirty-nine, and his school, at which Kirby seems to have been teaching,[12] closed. In 1837–38 there were rebellions in the British North American provinces of Lower and Upper Canada. As Kirby later remembered,[13] although these uprisings were "suppressed, ... the United States were seething with sympathy and help for the rebel cause." As a result, "British residents in the States were profoundly agitated by this state of things," and "War was expected." Kirby, therefore, like "many British born" in the United States, "came to a resolution to go to Canada and aid in the defence of the Provinces." In July 1839 he "set foot in dear old Upper Canada, being the last, almost, ... of the U[nited] E[mpire] Loyalists who came in."

Visiting Quebec

Kirby crossed the border at Niagara Falls. After several days there and in Toronto he decided "to go down to Quebec." In late July 1839 Kirby stayed for two days in this "incomparable city," which he toured assiduously, and with which he fell "in love." One of the sites was "the tablet of the Chien d'Or on the façade of the old Philibert House" on Buade Street. Kirby's attention might have been drawn to the sculpture because in 1839 the ground floor of the building, which had been once owned by the Masons and, thus, was also known as Freemasons' Hall, was at least partly occupied by Thomas Cary and Company, the printer and publisher of the *Quebec Mercury*. Kirby "gazed up wonderingly" at the bas-relief and asked questions about its source.

The "tale"[14] connecting the tablet to Nicolas Jacquin *dit* Philibert and his stabbing by Legardeur de Repentigny had already been related at least three times: in *Picture Of Quebec* (1829) by George Bourne, the Protestant minister who was later one of those responsible for the notorious anti-Roman Catholic writings attributed to Maria Monk; in *Quebec And Its Environs; Being A Picturesque Guide To The Stranger* (1831) by James Pattison Cockburn, the "army officer and water-colourist" who, as commander "of the Royal Artillery in the Canadas," spent from 1826 to 1832 in Quebec;[15] and, with one variation, in *Hawkins's Picture Of Quebec: With Historical Recollections* (1834) by Alfred Hawkins, who from 1818 to 1820 had operated the "firm of Hawkins and Maquay, wine and brandy merchants," out of "the office and vaults" of the old house.[16] Nevertheless, Kirby "found no one able to tell" him about the tablet's "origin or meaning." Looking back from a distance of over sixty years, he reminisced, "I did not think that day that I should ever help to solve the mystery of 'The Golden Dog.'"

After his visit to Quebec, Kirby returned to Montreal "for about six weeks." During this time he tried to decide where he should settle. Montreal was an exciting city, but it did not "win" his "love like Quebec." There was also Upper Canada, which "pulled hard" for his return. Finally, he recalled,

"I tossed up a coin, with heads I go to Upper Canada, with tails I return to Quebec,—and heads won. I was perfectly satisfied, and ... I returned to Upper Canada and cast anchor in old Niagara."

Settling in Niagara

Kirby not only earned his living in Niagara, but he also took part in public activities. After returning to the region in late September 1839, he worked as a tanner, first at St. Davids, and then at Four Mile Creek. This career ended in the mid 1840s, however, when his partner absconded, and Kirby, unable to pay their debts, had to declare bankruptcy. He taught school in Hamilton in 1846 and 1847 until he settled permanently in Niagara shortly after his marriage on 23 November 1847 to Eliza Magdalene Whitmore, the granddaughter of one of the original United Empire Loyalists in the area. In 1850 Kirby became the editor of the *Niagara Mail*, which he bought in 1853, and with which he remained actively associated until the 1860s. His position as the owner of a local newspaper led to his playing other roles in the community. In 1856, for example, he was made a magistrate for Lincoln County and in 1861, reeve of Niagara. In 1863 he became curator of the military reserve at Niagara. For several years he helped lead the campaign against the proposal to move the county town from Niagara to St. Catharines. It has been reported as well that, as a result of the so-called "Niagara Affair," a controversy that occurred in 1855–56 over the conduct of Thomas Creen, the rector of St. Mark's Anglican Church in Niagara, Kirby, a devout member of the Church of England, "refused to attend church for the next fifteen years and according to popular mythology picketed St. Mark's weekly."[17]

These occupations notwithstanding, Kirby also found time to begin his career as an author, especially one who wrote about British subjects. One early publication was "Monody, On The Sickness And Retirement Of His Excellency Lord Metcalfe From The Government Of Canada, Nov. 1845," an occasional poem that appeared unsigned in the 31 December 1845 issue of the *Niagara Chronicle*. Charles Theophilus Metcalfe, first Baron Metcalfe, was "governor-in-chief of the province of Canada" from 1843 to 1845.[18] Another early work was "Counter Manifesto To The Annexationists Of Montreal," in which Kirby, using the pseudonym "Britannicus," inveighed against the Montreal merchants who had proposed that the former British North American provinces of Lower and Upper Canada, now united as Canada East and Canada West or Canada, should join with the United

States. First published as a letter in the *Niagara Mail* on 31 October 1849, several thousand copies of the manifesto were immediately reprinted in pamphlet form for the Canadian government.

Kirby's first full-length literary work was *The U. E. A Tale Of Upper Canada.* A long poem written in rhyming couplets and presented in twelve cantos, it tells the story of Walwyn and his sons Ethwald and Eric, who come to Upper Canada from Yorkshire in the late 1820s, and the United Empire Loyalist Ranger John and his sons Herman, Hendrick, Simcoe, and Hugh. The poem reaches its climax during the rebellions of 1837–38 when Hugh returns from the United States as a leader of a band of Americans intent on helping the rebels. After unknowingly killing his brother Herman in an encounter on the Niagara frontier, he as well as Ethwald and Hendrick are killed near Prescott. Eric and Simcoe survive, and Walwyn and Ranger John live to be old men. The final lines of the poem depict Ranger John surrounded by his grandchildren, who are "Filled with the spirit of the old U. E." and "Learning to guard, like him, in days of yore / England's proud Empire, One, for ever more."[19] Kirby completed his "epic song"[20] in 1846, but it was not published until 1859 when he printed it himself and issued it from the office of the *Niagara Mail.* Although in 1903 Kirby called *The U. E.* a "bantling ... full of juvenile faults,"[21] two selections from it appeared in the first anthology of Canadian poems, Edward Hartley Dewart's *Selections From Canadian Poets; With Occasional Critical And Biographical Notes, And An Introductory Essay on Canadian Poetry* published in 1864. By then several major themes of Kirby's life and works—his distrust of the United States, his love of the British monarchy and empire, and his interest in Canada's past, present, and future—were firmly established. He was ready, in other words, for the events that led to the confederation of the British North American provinces of Canada (Ontario and Quebec), New Brunswick, and Nova Scotia in 1867 and for the creation of *Le Chien d'or.*

Beginning Le Chien d'or

On 25 July 1865 Kirby wrote in his diary, "Appointed by Council to go to Quebec."[22] The day before Kirby had answered a letter dated 14 July 1865 from Benjamin Sulte; he had met this "clever French Canadian"[23] earlier that year when this "journalist, writer, office holder, and historian"[24] was serving in the Canadian militia in Niagara. In his response Kirby, who frequently wrote in French, explained that he was going "à Quebec à l'ouverture du Parliament pour y faire attention à un projet de loi qu'on doit amener devant la chambre."[25] Kirby left Niagara on 4 August 1865 and arrived in the capital of Canada two days later. There, as well as lobbying his bill and seeing Sulte, who had moved to Quebec from his native Trois-Rivières, he toured the city and its surrounding area. He, thus, saw again the tablet of the Golden Dog on the house built by Timothée Roussel, which in the 1860s was the main post office.

Kirby also read a copy of *Maple Leaves: A Budget Of Legendary, Historical, Critical, And Sporting Intelligence*, a collection of essays published in 1863 and written by James MacPherson Le Moine, a Quebec "lawyer, office holder, and author,"[26] who took a lively interest in local history. Three of these sketches in particular caught Kirby's attention. One was "A Visit to Chateau-Bigot. 4th June, 1863," the description of an excursion to "an antique and massive ruin ... some five miles from Quebec."[27] The remains of the country residence of François Bigot, the last intendant of New France, it was the place where supposedly he kept Caroline, his half-French and half-Algonquin mistress, and where she was murdered. Another was "Marie Josephte Corriveau,— A Canadian Lafarge," an account of the murderess, popularly known as La Corriveau, who was hanged in 1763, and whose bones were supposed to have been exhibited in an iron cage in Lévis, the town across the St. Lawrence River from Quebec. Still another was "Le Chien d'Or—The Golden Dog." In this sketch Le Moine mentioned the "meager account of the tragedy enacted ... about one hundred and fourteen years ago" given by each of George Bourne and James Pattison Cockburn and "the elegant French sketch" on the subject written by Auguste Soulard, a Quebec lawyer, that was first published in the *Canadien*, a Quebec newspaper, on 20 November 1839. Taking details from all three authors, in his sketch Le Moine linked the carving to "Nicolas Jacquin Philibert, a Quebec merchant" who owned the house on Buade Street in the mid-eighteenth century; his quarrel with "the Intendant (Bigot), perhaps for refusing to aid him in his peculations and extortions"; "the deadly thrust" given to him in 1748 by "Pierre Legardeur, Sieur de Repentigny," the "French lieutenant" whom Bigot, "to annoy Philibert," had ordered billeted at his house; and, despite his "pardon," Legardeur's eventual death in a duel "at Pondicherry, in the East Indies" at the hands of Pierre Nicolas Philibert, the "young man" with "a sombre expression" on "his austere but beautiful face" who had thereby avenged his father's "untimely end."[28]

As he explained in a letter to Le Moine written in April 1877 shortly after the publication of the first edition of *Le Chien d'or*, Kirby, "sitting ... one day in the window of the St Louis Hotel" while he was still in Quebec, read "portions" of *Maple Leaves* to Sulte and remarked "that here was the finest subject for a romance that" he "knew of." The two friends then "talked much of Chateau Bigot and the Chien d'or." "I wanted," Kirby added, "Sulte ... to write the story, and finally half in jest, half in earnest, threatened him, that if he would not write the story of the Chien d'or I would—!—That was the beginning of it—the planting of the grain of mustard seed that has grown into the big tree full of leaves, or rather book full of leaves, that you see."[29] The twelve years between the planting of the seed and the publication of the book were arduous, however, both for Kirby and his novel.

Envisioning the New Dominion

Kirby left Quebec on 9 September 1865 and was back in Niagara four days later. There he continued to lead a busy life. In 1866 he helped organize a home guard to defend Fort Erie against the Fenians, the Irish Americans who had crossed into Canada with the intention of liberating the country from the British crown. In 1867 he worked for the local Conservative candidates in the federal election that followed Confederation. In 1869 he chaired a committee on education in Lincoln County. In 1873 he became president of the Niagara Mechanics' Institute; he remained president of its library, which became the Niagara Public Library in 1895, until 1903. His most important—and most lucrative—appointment was that of "a Collector in Her Majestys Customs" at Niagara.[30] He took up this post, which was at least partly a reward for his services to John A. Macdonald and the Conservatives who were then in power in Ottawa, on 1 July 1871 and kept it until he was forced to retire in 1895. Janet Carnochan, the "educator and historian"[31] who worked with Kirby on the library, later offered a glimpse of his daily routine. He arrived at the Custom House promptly at nine in the morning; "at noon he was gone to lunch, and at four the office was closed."[32]

In addition to these activities, Kirby kept up with both his correspondence and his creative writing. One subject that fascinated him was the nature of the nation that was being created in the northern half of North America as a result of the 1867 union. One of his earliest efforts to articulate an identity for the new dominion was a poem published as a broadsheet and dated "Niagara, Ontario, Sep. 24, 1867." Entitled "Canadians Forever. A National Song" and written in the form of an ode with the chorus "Our glorious dominion— / God bless it forever," it set out several characteristics, actual and proposed, of the country. It stretched

"From sea to sea," beginning in "Newfoundland at break of day" and continuing "Westward"; Niagara Falls was "midway thundering down." It was a land of oceans, rivers, and lakes and of fields and forests with "spreading oaks and towering pines" that experienced "summer's glow" and "winter's snow." Founded by the warrior heroes "Of France and England's martial race," it was populated by hunters, boatmen, and "loyal yeomen." It was a constitutional monarchy under "Victoria's regal throne" and an integral— and equal—part of "her Empire." Above all, as enunciated from the poem's first line to its last, it was a Christian nation under God with the graces, and responsibilities, "Bestowed by His Almighty hand."[33] A copy of this poem sent to Alfred Tennyson led to a correspondence with the British poet laureate. In the 1870s this exchange centered on such subjects as the need for Canada to remain within the British Empire and, if it did not, the danger of the country's "immediate annexation to the United States."[34]

Kirby further defined Canadian identity in a letter that he wrote to Benjamin Sulte in November 1867. Sulte had had a conversation "un peu vive" with an Englishman who had refused to recognize that "la race française du Canada" had an incontestable right to conserve its own nationality.[35] As a result, in June 1867 he had composed "Le Canada Français A L'Angleterre," in which he outlined the value of French Canada and its equality with English Canada. "L'érable et le rosier sont nobles tous les deux," the poem concluded, and, therefore, "Nul n'abdique ses droits, nul ne se mésallie."[36] In his response to Sulte, who had sent him a copy of this defense of the rights of French Canadians, Kirby commented that there was "trop de méfiance et d'éloignement entre les deux races." The duty of "un homme de coeur et de vrai patriotisme" was, therefore, to work to remove these prejudices. A wise man, he continued, "verrait que dans ses deux races, le Canada possède un trésor double: ses deux langues, ses deux litteratures, ses deux histoires, avec sa double mémoire de grands hommes et de grands faits qui roulent ensemble comme deux fleuves et se joignent dans les eaux de notre St. Laurent." This union, Kirby concluded, would make "un jour la gloire de notre pays."[37] To enhance the understanding between the French and the English of Canada by providing an epic narrative that united their two histories became Kirby's goal as he prepared his novel.

Gathering the Material

Kirby always emphasized that *Le Chien d'or* "originated" with James MacPherson Le Moine's 1863 collection of *Maple Leaves*.[38] He consulted many other works during the composition of the novel, however. One was Auguste Soulard's "Le Chien D'Or, A Québec," from which he likely took the idea that it was a "démon, sous la figure d'une femme," who whispered in the ears of Legardeur de Repentigny that he was carrying his sword "en vain" if he endured the insults that Nicolas Jacquin *dit* Philibert was allegedly hurling at him;[39] Le Moine had not repeated this detail in "Le Chien d'Or—The Golden Dog." Some were volumes that dealt with French-Canadian history and society. These included Philippe-Joseph Aubert de Gaspé's *Les Anciens Canadiens* (1864) and his *Mémoires* (1866), Catherine Burke, dite de Saint-Thomas' *Les Ursulines De Québec, Depuis Leur Établissement Jusqu'à Nos Jours* (1863–66), Ernest Gagnon's *Chansons Populaires Du Canada Receuillies Et Publiées Avec Annotations, Etc.* (1865), and François-Xavier Garneau's *Histoire Du Canada* (1845 ff.). Others like François-Marie Arouet de Voltaire's *Siècle De Louis XIV* (1751) and Mouffle d'Angerville's *Vie Privée De Louis XV* (1781) covered seventeenth- and eighteenth-century French history. Kirby also drew on a wide range of American, British, French, German, Greek, Roman, and Swedish authors as well as the Bible for allusions in the text and for titles of the chapters of his novel.

Kirby collected his material in various ways. He acquired a copy of each of Aubert de Gaspé's, Gagnon's, and Voltaire's volumes. His library also contained *History Of Canada* (1860), Andrew Bell's translation of the third edition of Garneau's influential work. In September 1866 Kirby borrowed from the library of the Niagara Mechanics' Institute *The Englishwoman In Russia* (1855), the probable source for his comment about "the man followed by wolves who cast out of his sledge, one child after another" (477). In August 1872 Benjamin Sulte sent him a copy of Joseph Marmette's "Roman Canadien" *L'Intendant Bigot*, which had just appeared.[40] The Library of Parliament in Ottawa supplied him with a handwritten copy of several pages from an edition of *Vie Privée De Louis XV* published in 1788 that described the "déplorable état"[41] of Canada and the excesses of Bigot and his associates in Quebec in the years before its conquest by the British. Kirby copied passages from this work and others into his notebooks.

When the volumes he consulted did not provide him with the details about the history and topography of Quebec that he required, Kirby asked various people for help. On 17 March 1869 Josephine Amelia Lowe, a young woman from Niagara who was attending school at the Ursuline Convent in Quebec, added in a postscript to her letter to Kirby that "La Superior en 1740 était La Mère de la Nativité," that "Mad. de Repentigny quitta la

Couvent en 1738," and that "Mad. Angelique de Meloise" left it in 1739.[42] The next month Josephine sent him a list of the paintings in the "Church of the Ursuline Convent"; they were, she noted, "for the most part bought in France about 1815."[43] In 1872 Kirby requested information from Hannah Catharine Lowe, Josephine's older sister, who was visiting Quebec. In a letter to his "dear Sister" written on 19 July 1872, Kirby, signing himself "Your loving Brother," asked her to "visit ... Beaumanoir that is Chateau Bigot" and to provide him with "a description of the place & its surroundings. See if any remains of the old watch tower be left, and the direction of the little brook with respect to the house." He also asked her to try to find "any remains of the Palace of the Intendant" in the city.[44] The next month Hannah sent Kirby a sketch of the "Ruins of Chateau Bigot"; on it she recorded, among other data, that there was a distance of about twenty-four meters "from the tower to the Castle."[45] The same month Kirby received a response to his query about the circumstances of the death of Bigot. According to Marmette, there were three possibilities: Bigot had died in the Bastile, he had died at Bordeaux, or he had died "à l'etranger."[46] Marmette provided this explanation at the request of Benjamin Sulte. In 1869 this friend had also consulted Narcisse-Henri-Édouard Faucher de Saint Maurice, who was then regularly publishing "short stories, essays, and accounts of his travels,"[47] about "la Porte Prescott de Québec."[48]

People and events from Kirby's life also helped shape *Le Chien d'or*. In his article "Le Chien D'Or Son Origine—Son Histoire" dated "Québec, le 8 janvier 1886," Le Moine revealed that the model for the Bourgeois Philibert was Sir Henry Etherington, a rich merchant who was mayor of Hull in 1769 and 1785. Known in the early nineteenth century as the "Father of Hull," he himself lived simply, but "he provided in the most princely manner for his servants" and his "numerous dependants,"[49] and "he was a patron of every charitable and religious institution in the town."[50] "Sir Henry," Le Moine explained, "faisait chaque jour préparer pour douze convives une table à dîner, bien pourvue de mets qu'il allait lui même acheter au marché." Etherington, aged eighty-eight, died in 1819. While Kirby was growing up, however, he would have heard about this man's benevolence, and he would have walked past his handsome house on Hull's High Street.

In the same article Le Moine also confirmed, "Au physique et au moral, Amélie de Repentigny" was modeled on Josephine Lowe, who often signed her letters to Kirby "Amelie," and that Louise Roy "personnifiait une charmante Demoiselle King," who had become "une grande dame."[51] In

1874 Marie-Louise King, a friend of Josephine from their days as students at the Ursuline Convent in Quebec, had married Joseph-Adolphe Chapleau; he served as premier of Quebec from 1879 to 1882 and as its lieutenant-governor from 1892 to 1897. Much later Launcelot Cressy Servos, the son of Hannah Lowe, who had married John Dease Servos in 1878, claimed that "Miss King ... a beautiful girl, with a most wonderful head of hair which when she let it down fell to her knees,"[52] was also the model for Angelique des Meloises. Among the photographs Kirby possessed were not only ones of Josephine and Marie-Louise but also one of "Mrs. Hope Sewell, Quebec, 'The Charming Josephine' of The Golden Dog."[53]

Transforming "Raw Material ... into ... Art"

Kirby, however, was writing neither history nor biography. He was creating historical fiction after the manner of such writers as Sir Walter Scott and Alessandro Manzoni. He was, thus, taking "historical facts, legends & traditions" and, "like every writer who is worth reading," forming this "raw material ... into works of art and things of beauty." In this process he made changes to his "brute matter."[54] Nicolas Jacquin *dit* Philibert, for example, died in January 1748, a fact repeated by James MacPherson Le Moine in "Le Chien d'Or—The Golden Dog"; Kirby has him murdered in November of that year. Caroline, François Bigot's half-French, half-Algonquin mistress in Le Moine's "A Visit to Chateau-Bigot. 4th June, 1863," became Caroline de St Castin, "an Acadienne of ancient and noble family" (78).

Set in Quebec and its environs in a few weeks in the autumn of 1748, the plot of *Le Chien d'or* involves three love stories, each of which is more or less developed in the form of a love triangle. François Bigot is flirting with Angelique des Meloises while he is hiding at his country residence Caroline de St Castin, to whom he is betrothed. Le Gardeur de Repentigny is pursuing Angelique, who is actively encouraging Bigot's suit; Bigot himself is challenging his henchman De Pean to marry Angelique. Pierre Philibert is courting Amelie de Repentigny, Le Gardeur's sister, with whom he has long been in love; her hand is also being sought, albeit languidly, by Angelique's brother.

Through such aspects as their positions and professions, these personae, most of whom are based on historical figures, allow Kirby to describe the social and religious customs of eighteenth-century New France and to introduce legends about it. The aunt and guardian of Le Gardeur and Amelie, for instance, is the widowed Lady de Tilly, who runs both a large house in Quebec and an important seigneury in the colony. These three, as well as Angelique, her brother, and her suitor De Pean, have relatives who are nuns in the Ursuline Convent in Quebec, where both Amelie and Angelique have been educated. The aunt of Fanchon Dodier, who becomes one of Angelique's maids, is La Corriveau. Not only does Kirby use his characters and their connections to depict the culture of New France, but he also employs them to sketch its political problems. The father of Pierre Philibert, the Bourgeois Philibert, is the leader of the so-called *Honnêtes Gens* and the one merchant in Quebec powerful enough to withstand the machinations of Bigot, who with his associates is ruining New France in the same way as his supporters at the French court, most notably Madame La Pompadour, the mistress of Louis XV, are plundering the mother country.

The private narratives are both embedded in and shaped by their public counterparts. The story begins in Quebec when its defenses are being prepared for what "his Excellency Count de la Galissoniere Governor of New France" (3) and his advisors see as the inevitable consequences of the recent peace in Europe between Great Britain and France: increased tensions in North America between the British and their American colonies, on the one hand, and between them and the French and New France, on the other. The last scene in the novel occurs in 1777, when, as a direct result of their help in defeating the French in North America during the Seven Years' War (1756–63), the Thirteen Colonies are "in rebellion against the King" (747).

In his novel, however, Kirby did more than relate a story in the best traditions of sentimental and sensational melodrama and describe the history and legends of New France. He also linked the French-Canadian nation of New France, which included aboriginals, to its Greek, Roman, Viking, and Norman heritage and, thereby, united its history with that of Canada's British settlers. Writing, thus, an epic narrative, he created for the Dominion of Canada a national identity that recognized the First Nations, but that was fundamentally bicultural, bilingual, Christian, conservative, European, imperial, and northern. This constitutional monarchy was to act as a counterweight to the United States of America, the republic so distrusted by Kirby.

Composing and Copying

In his letter to James MacPherson Le Moine dated 13 April 1877, Kirby explained that, given that his "hands" were "full of other business," he had written "the Chien d'or in 1868—69—70—at intervals" as he "found time."[55] A slightly different period of composition is suggested by the dates that Kirby recorded in one of the two extant fragments of a holograph manuscript of what was certainly an early, and may well have been the first, complete draft of his novel. The first fragment, which corresponds roughly to Chapters 1 to 34 or pages 1 to 403 of the CEECT text, consists of 549 numbered leaves measuring approximately 339 mm. in length by 210 mm. in width and sewn together in a series of twenty-two notebooks. On the recto of the first leaf, Kirby wrote, "The / Golden Dog / A Legend of Quebec";[56] he dated this recto 15 April 1869. Several leaves bear 1871 dates. The recto of the leaf numbered 392, for example, is dated 1 February 1871; the recto of the leaf numbered 433, "3 p.m.—Feb 24, 1871."[57] The second fragment of this holograph manuscript, which corresponds roughly to Chapters 38 and 39, or pages 444 to 481 of the CEECT text, consists of leaves numbered 576 to 598. None bears a date, but the verso of leaf 576 begins with "Chapter XXVIII" in Kirby's hand.[58] According to a note in one of his scrapbooks, Kirby composed this chapter between the "2nd" and "16th" January 1872.[59]

The probability that Kirby created the first complete draft of his novel between 1869 and 1872 is strengthened by other documentation. It is not clear that Benjamin Sulte knew precisely what Kirby was writing in 1869. In his letter of 6 May, however, in which he promised to get Kirby the information that he had requested on "la Porte Prescott de Québec," Sulte applauded his friend's return "à la Littérature."[60] On 1 November 1870, when Kirby announced to Sulte that he was "dans le piège d'ecrire un roman ... en prose," he stated that this "oeuvre" was "à moitie faite." "Dieu sait," he added, "quand j'aurai le temps de la finir."[61] On 2 June 1872 Kirby, writing to Hannah Lowe in Quebec, told her that he was working on "the last chapter of the book."[62] But since he was still collecting material for his novel throughout the summer, the draft may not have been finished until the fall.

In this letter Kirby also reported that Hannah's sister Josephine wished to transcribe his holograph manuscript. This was a difficult task. His handwriting may not be quite as bad as the "combination of the running hand of the early Egyptians, [Arabic], and Hebrew" that Launcelot Cressy Servos described in a letter that he wrote in 1956 to Lorne Pierce, the editor of Ryerson Press, when they were negotiating the acquisition of the fragments of Kirby's manuscript by Queen's University (Kingston, Ontario).[63] His penmanship is, however, certainly not easy to decipher. Such characteristics as the capitalization or non-capitalization of nouns and the use of dashes of different lengths to indicate various marks of punctuation pose one set of problems. The way Kirby composed his manuscript creates another. He wrote the main text of *Le Chien d'or* on the verso of a leaf. He would then often revise his text by crossing out passages and either adding new text over the deleted words on the verso or penning his replacement passages on the recto of the next leaf. In this case he would mark an "X" on the relevant verso beside where the text on the recto was to go; sometimes he would place a corresponding "X" on the recto as well.

According to Servos, Kirby's manuscript often baffled Josephine. Hannah, therefore, whose copying the author apparently preferred, and Mary (or Mercy) Webster Lowe, the sisters' widowed mother, also helped. Their progress is recorded by various marks in the extant fragments of the holograph manuscript. On the recto of leaf 546, for example, there is a pencil drawing of an older woman in a bonnet; "M. W. Lowe" (Mary Webster Lowe) is written underneath it.[64] On the recto of leaf 373, apparently Kirby noted "H C L & Co—novelists" and "J A L & Co—novelists," the initials standing for Hannah Catharine Lowe and Josephine Amelia Lowe. This recto also has a pen sketch of "Lizette," Angelique des Meloises' maid, and "Jan 21, 1871."[65] If this date was inscribed on the leaf when Hannah and Josephine were copying the manuscript, then this enterprise may well have begun before Kirby had finished composing the first draft of the novel. In his 1956 letter Servos also stated that occasionally neither Josephine, nor Hannah, nor their mother could "make out just how his words were to follow one another," and, thus, they "had to wait" until Kirby "came again to get him to explain them." Despite these delays, Servos' account implies that by the end of 1872 one copy of the holograph draft of Kirby's novel had been completed.

In the same letter Servos described another problem. Kirby's frequent visits to the Lowes caused gossip in Niagara and roused his wife's suspicions. She and Mrs. Lowe "had a long conversation," the result of which was that Kirby had to find another amanuensis.[66] Although Mrs. Kirby herself helped in the transcribing of Kirby's prose, it was Mary Torrance, a young woman who also lived in Niagara, who came to Kirby's aid.

That these two women copied part of a version of *Le Chien d'or* is certain. What is not so clear is what version they replicated. In the mid 1920s, when Kirby's books and manuscripts were being either sold or distributed to various institutions, Janet Carnochan, signing herself "Secretary of the

Niagara Historical Society," stated that the manuscript of the novel "was copied in Niagara by different young people for him, as he told me he had three copies made, one for publication, one for the Archives, retaining one for himself."[67] That several copies were made is confirmed by the correspondence that details his efforts to get his work published as well as by a letter that he wrote many years later to Hannah. In this document, dated 1 November 1905, he remarked on his "long and severe illness" and lamented, "I am no longer as I was Thirty years ago when I was writing The Golden Dog and you and Josie worked hard, late & early copying my MS. for revision & correction more twice over while I prepared it for the printer."[68] It seems, thus, that Kirby revised the first copy of his holograph manuscript and had this new version copied. Most likely he also revised this version and had it re-transcribed. Some of the last transcription, which contains leaves copied by the three Lowes as well as by Mrs. Kirby and Mary Torrance, forms part of the manuscript that became the copy-text for the first edition of the novel.

Finding a Publisher

Kirby began the long and complicated search to find a publisher for his work in 1873. On 2 January of that year William Henry Withrow, the "Methodist minister, journalist, and author"[69] whose "volume on the Catacombs of Rome" was about to be issued by another New York publisher, wrote a letter to Harper and Brothers "to recommend" its "favorable consideration" of *Le Chien d'or*.[70] Withrow, who had spent time enjoying "golden leisure" at Niagara,[71] had read "the whole of the Ms." and had a "high sense of its literary merits." It would, he predicted, "prove one of the most important contributions to current fictitious literatures." He had, therefore, urged his friend to submit "some average specimen pages" to Harper "rather than to any other publishing firm" so that "an adequate judgment" of the novel's qualities could be made.[72] Following Withrow's advice, Kirby sent, along with his friend's letter, sample pages of his work to this New York publisher. On 14 March 1873, however, Harper rejected " 'The Chien d'Or.' " The firm would "accordingly hold the MS. subject to" Kirby's "order" for its return.[73]

Most likely even before he received this letter, Kirby approached a second American publisher. On 15 March 1873 he offered his work to James R. Osgood and Company of Boston and New York. Writing from Boston, the firm acknowledged his letter and announced that it would "take pleasure in receiving for examination the MS to which" Kirby had referred.[74] On

12 June 1873, however, this company also rejected "'The Chien d'Or'" because it did "not find it available for" its "channels of publication." The publisher would "return the Ms. by mail."[75]

The same spring Kirby tried his luck in England. On 31 March 1873 he enclosed "copy of a few detatched chapters" of his novel in a letter that he wrote to Trübner and Company of London. In the letter he explained that he lived "in a part of the world remote from any center of literary activity," and, therefore, that he was asking the firm's "opinion and advice, respecting the publication in England of a Canadian work" that he had "ready for the press." Canada, he continued, "is an old country for America. Its annals under the French regime furnish some of the most striking and romantic incidents of any portion of the New World." It was some of these "National traditions" that he had "endeavoured to reproduce" in "a historical novel of the Chien d'or," which was "the name of a famous tablet and legend in the city of Quebec." He did not know how "literary business" was "transacted in England." He had not enclosed "stamps for return postage" because he had "no English ones," although he would "remit any expence" that returning his manuscript might entail. He requested Trübner, nevertheless, "to be kind enough to peruse" what he had submitted "with a view to publishing," and, he asked again, "let me know, your opinion whether a Canadian work of that kind would be worth publishing in England."[76]

Trübner, describing itself as an "American, Continental And Oriental Literary Agency," replied on 5 May 1873. It explained, "unfortunately works relating to Canada meet with such an unfavourable reception as regards sale at the hands of the English public that we could not recommend you to print it unless you are certain of its success in Canada alone. However interesting the work might be we should not like to guarantee a sale of even twenty copies in this country." The company, nevertheless, was willing to give the author "an estimate of the probable cost" to print the work, or, "If you print it in Canada and like to send us a few copies on sale we shall be happy to do our best for it."[77] Kirby remembered—and resented—this response for the rest of his life.

In the years that followed, Kirby explored other publishing possibilities. In November 1874 he offered his "Canadian historical novel" for serialization in the Toronto *Mail.* In his reply of 3 December of the same year, John Webb, the "News Editor," responding on behalf of the newspaper's manager, explained that the latter was "not at present prepared to arrange for any such publication … as in all probability no new story will be commenced until the close of the local and Dominion Houses, and a selection has already been made which will occupy several months after that period." In a handwritten note attached to this letter, Kirby recorded, "I also made an offer of the MS to the Toronto Globe but they did not even acknowledge my letter."[78]

On 7 October 1875 the author contacted James Campbell and Son of Toronto "regarding MS of Canadian novel." Rejecting the proposal the next day because its hands were "full ... consequent on changes introduced by the Council of Public Instruction," it advised Kirby to "correspond with Messrs Routledge, McMillan and Scribner all of New York." Any one of these publishers, it continued, would be "better able to do justice to" *Le Chien d'or* "than any Canadian publisher."[79] In December 1875 Withrow, "regretting the delay in its appearance," gave his favourable "opinion" of Kirby's "book" to Belford Brothers of Toronto.[80] Kirby, therefore, submitted his manuscript to this publisher. Its decision came quickly. On 27 December it announced that it was "afraid to risk so much at present." Times, the publisher explained, "are so dull; to be stuck on a book the size yours would make, would ruin us." His "best plan" was to place the novel with "an English house," for the "Story" was "a good one and ought to have a good sale in England."[81]

Kirby did try again to have his novel published in London. This time his agent was Maria Susan Rye. An English "social reformer," she operated "Our Western Home," "the reception centre ... in a converted court-house and jail at Niagara" for the poor and orphaned English girls that she brought to Canada.[82] A friend and an admirer, Kirby sent Rye, who had returned to England, a section of his manuscript in April 1876, and she took it to Daldy, Isbister and Company. On 29 May 1876 this firm responded. It was "very favourably impressed" with the "ability" of the chapters that she had "kindly left with" it, but, the letter continued, "At the same time the interest of the story seems so exclusively confined to Canada & its past history that we fear it would fail to secure the favour of many English readers. Judging by this portion we could anticipate favourable opinions from the press, but not a remunerative sale with the public. We are therefore unable to undertake the risk of its publication."[83] When Rye sent this letter to Kirby, she attached a note to say that she regretted this outcome, but that she would "try else where—there are lots of other places in London."[84] By May 1876, however, the publication of *Le Chien d'or* in England was becoming less urgent.

In May 1873, his manuscript having been rejected in both the United

States and England, Kirby wrote to Adam, Stevenson and Company, "*Importers & Wholesale Booksellers*," of Toronto. In its reply of 19 May, the company acknowledged Kirby's "favour in regard to" his "Historical novel" about which it had already "heard from the Rev. W. Withrow." Given his "high opinion" of the work, it would "be pleased to have the ms submitted" and "to arrange for its publication if, on examination," it was as good as the minister had suggested. Although it wondered about the novel's serialization in the *Canadian Monthly and National Review*, the periodical that the firm had begun the previous year, it understood that it was probably too long for this purpose. Adam, Stevenson proposed instead to arrange "a simultaneous copyright publication" in Canada and in England with one of "the more important" English houses "who publish 'novel' literature." It asked Kirby, therefore, to state the "price" that he "put on the Copyright," and to indicate whether he intended "to dispose of it finally in some <u>bloc</u> amount" or "to accept a royalty on the extent of sale the various Editions might achieve." Finally, it requested Kirby to submit part or all of the manuscript. If he did not send "the whole," he should let the firm know "the bulk of the work as to the entire number of pages."[85] Thus began Kirby's mostly beneficial connection with Graeme Mercer Adam, one of the principals of the company and an "influential literary figure" in post-Confederation Canada.[86]

Adam, Stevenson contacted Kirby again on 8 July 1873. This time William Whitelaw, writing on behalf of Adam, reported that the latter and Goldwin Smith, the English "writer, journalist, and controversialist"[87] who had recently moved to Toronto, had been "reading the manuscript jointly." Both were "<u>more than pleased</u>" with it and "would like Exceedingly to see it brought to light." Whitelaw, therefore, asked Kirby to forward "<u>immediately</u> if possible … another and more distinct copy" of the manuscript that Adam "could take home to England." Perhaps Kirby could even "succeed in obtaining the copy sent to New York, which" was, Whitelaw believed, "never returned." However Kirby arranged to get the manuscript to Adam, there was no doubt "that it would be readily taken hold of" in England, and that "all arrangements could be made as to style—price etc." The letter concluded with an invitation to Kirby "to run over" to Toronto before Adam's departure in a few days for London in order to make "any arrangement satisfactory to both Parties."[88]

This search for an English publisher was protracted. In December 1873 Withrow had heard that the " 'Chien d'or' " was "likely soon to be unmuzzled."[89] In the early months of the new year Kirby wrote Adam, Stevenson twice to inquire about its fate. And Adam in turn asked Henry S. King and Company of London, to whom he had submitted Kirby's work, about its progress. On 14 February 1874 Adam informed the author, "I am keeping them up to the mark & have heard recently from them that having got over their busy holiday trade they will now address themselves to the story."[90] In June 1874 the answer finally came. When the English publisher had "at length received the completion of the Ms of 'Le Chien D'Or,' " it put "it in the hands" of its reader. He gave the work "a careful consideration," but "on his advice" the firm came "to the conclusion that it" was "impossible to publish it with any chance of pecuniary success." Because the novel was "far too long, and too slow in its action," it did not see that it was "possible to make any alteration in it which would make it more acceptable." King was "very sorry."[91] On 22 June 1874 Adam enclosed this letter in one to Kirby. He regretted both the result and the time that it had taken to come to a decision. Adam, Stevenson, however, "must be held free from" blame for the delay. In the same letter Adam asked Kirby to decide whether the manuscript submitted to King or an "original" should be "handed to another publisher in England."[92]

Over the course of the next year various misadventures beset Kirby's novel. The manuscript of *Le Chien d'or* that had been sent to England was shipped back in November 1874, but did not turn up until January 1876 when Adam found "a missing Case from London" at the post office in Toronto.[93] The "representative" of Adam, Stevenson in England continued to try to interest publishers there in the work, "but without success." Adam reported to Kirby on 25 May 1875 that when this man returned to Canada, he brought "back the old story of the plethora of material in their hands & the almost impossibility of getting an audience among English readers for Canadian literature."[94] As early as December 1874 Adam, Stevenson contemplated publishing the novel either itself or jointly with Hunter, Rose and Company of Toronto. In the early 1870s this firm, which had been in business under this name since 1861, had begun "to expand its activities by publishing ... works in the fields of history and literature by Canadian authors."[95] Adam also seems to have considered once again serializing Kirby's work in the *Canadian Monthly and National Review*, which he was proposing to enlarge. In June 1875 Kirby told Adam that he had "no objection" to this proposal, "you can allow me what is usual for the Magazine and if published in Book form I waive my claim to royalty or what not until sufficient copies are sold to reimburse you in cost of Edition."[96] On 12 July 1875, however, Adam, Stevenson announced that it was not able "to effect the publ[icatio]n" itself due to its "crippled" financial position. And, Adam informed Kirby, while Hunter, Rose was willing to print and bind "2500" copies for "$1800.00," it would "only set the work" if Adam, Stevenson took full "responsibility" for it. Hunter, Rose had decided, according to Adam, that "at present" it would "not take any risk" in the novel.

Apparently undeterred, in the same letter Adam suggested four other possibilities. One was that Kirby himself help finance the publication by paying a larger "proportion" of the cost than had been previously discussed. A second was that the author request his friends to "take some stock in it." A third was "to set up some portion" of the work, issue it with an "analysis" in a "prospectus," and thereby "secure orders in advance of publication." Adam thought that if his company could sell a thousand copies by way of this subscription, it "might go ahead safely." The fourth—and the only other "alternative"—was "to make another effort with Mr. Lovell at his Rouses Point office." Adam was going there shortly, and he promised, "I will try all I can to make some arrangement with him."[97]

In response Kirby not only continued his own search for a publisher, but he also carried on discussions about Adam's suggestions. On 8 April 1876, for example, Withrow told Kirby that he was "right in not risking anything on" his novel "beyond" his work. "You should," he added, "have 10% on retail price, at least after the first thousand." Regarding it "as a national calamity from a literary point of view that" its appearance had been "so long delayed," Withrow regretted that *Le Chien d'or* was not suitable for serialization in the *Christian Guardian and Evangelical Witness*, the Methodist magazine he was then editing in Toronto. Probably responding as well to Adam's suggestion that part of the novel be set and subscriptions be sought, Withrow wondered if Kirby should "adapt a chapter" for the *Canadian Monthly and National Review*; his choice would be "that on the Voyageurs boat songs, where the Tilly family sail up the river from Quebec to their estate." Withrow, his faith still firm in the quality of the novel, concluded, "It is sure to make a sensation yet, if you can only get it befor[e] the public."[98]

Landing the Lovells

As 1875 turned into 1876, Kirby himself seemed to favour the possibility of his work being published by the firm established in Montreal by the "printer and publisher" John Lovell. From 1838 to 1851, as Lovell and Gibson—John

Gibson was Lovell's brother-in-law—it had issued the *Literary Garland,* the "first successful literary magazine in British North America," and in 1864, as John Lovell, it had published Edward Hartley Dewart's *Selections From Canadian Poets,* the anthology in which passages from Kirby's *The U. E.* had appeared.[99] Called in 1875 Lovell Printing and Publishing Company, it had an office in Montreal as well as the Lake Shore, or Lake Champlain, Press in Rouses Point, New York. John Lovell, the "Managing Director" of the firm, had his "residence" in Rouses Point, although he spent "considerable of his time at the Montreal office." John Wurtele Lovell, his eldest son, had "the Superintendence of the 'Lake Shore Press.' "[100]

Graeme Mercer Adam, who had married John Gibson's daughter in 1863, had proposed in July 1875 that this firm publish *Le Chien d'or.* At the same time Adam himself was negotiating with the Lovells a possible partnership in a publishing firm that would have an office in New York City. In the fall of 1875 and the winter of 1876, Adam reported to Kirby on both these initiatives. Answering a letter the latter had written on 1 October 1875, Adam announced that he had "been quite deterred from" visiting New York because of "the accounts received from there of the utter prostration in trade, & the continued business depression ... every where." If there were "a revival in trade," however, he hoped "to be in a position to take advantage of it to push on" his "proposed place in N. Y." as well as their "project" of Kirby's novel. On that subject he was "waiting letters from Rouse's Point," and he was hoping "to get away to see Mr. Lovell at an early day."[101] On 20 January 1876, again responding to a letter from Kirby, Adam not only announced the appearance of "the lost MS. of Le Chien d'or" and discussed books that Kirby might order for the library of the Niagara Mechanics' Institute. He also explained that since "the depression of trade in the States" continued, it would "be very imprudent ... to make any step New York wards." Nevertheless, he intended to "make every possible effort" to get the novel published unless Kirby were "fortunate enough to get this secured else where."[102]

Events took a turn for the better that spring. On 24 May 1876 Adam wrote "hastily" from Rouses Point. He was on his way to New York City and London, England, where he could be reached "care of" Daldy, Isbister and Company. In the meantime, he had persuaded John Lovell to submit "100 pages" of Kirby's manuscript "to a Montreal gentleman of some literary competence." He was both "to satisfy Mr. L. of the character of the work" and to "put the M.s. in some better shape" for printing. It needed, according to

Adam, "punctuation & some mechanical touching up." Thinking it "highly probable" that the publisher would accept the novel, Adam instructed, "Please send Mr. Lovell to Montreal the balance of the M.s. as you have it ready, & kindly finish it as far as you can for the printer so that it may entail as little revision as possible." Proofs, he expected, would be sent to Kirby "early in June & from then steadily on until the work is turned out." Kirby was to give these "proofs a careful perusal, but without altering the structure of sentences or anything entailing serious alteration." Adam, who wished the work "to appear in creditable literary shape," regretted "in this respect" that he could not "supervise it in the press."[103]

Adam's confidence in the manuscript's acceptance was confirmed in the letter that John Lovell wrote Kirby from Montreal on 12 July 1876. "The delay" in reporting on the novel was caused partly by "the illness of the gentleman who undertook to read it, and partly" to Lovell's "own absence." The assessor spoke "highly of it." Although there is no evidence that he altered the manuscript in any way, he did point out that there were no quotation marks around "the conversational parts," and that "the author" of each speech was not identified. Kirby, therefore, should "attend" to these matters both in the "part of the copy" that Lovell was returning in the same mail as his letter and in the part that he had not seen. These changes made, the publisher would "put the MS. in hand, make Stereotype Plates of it, and be ready to pull off an edition on Mr Adam's return" from England in August. Lovell had "no doubt the work" would "have a good sale."[104] When Kirby received this letter two days later, he entered in his diary, "Bonnes Nouvelles de C d'O."[105] Good news indeed!

Lovell, Adam, Wesson and Company Edition

The version of *Le Chien d'or* that the Montreal gentleman read, that John Lovell accepted for publication, and that Kirby was asked to perfect in 1876 differed substantially both from the one in the early holograph manuscript and the ones that Josephine, Hannah, and Mary Webster Lowe, Mary Torrance, and Mrs. Kirby copied in the early 1870s. Its oldest portion, however, represented part of a copy that the women had made from Kirby's revised and corrected version of their original copy. According to Kirby, this manuscript consisted "of about 1600 pages foolscap."[106]

Kirby continued to correct, revise, and compress this version of his novel while it was being considered for publication between 1873 and 1876. In June 1875, for example, he informed Graeme Mercer Adam, who had requested Kirby to shorten his story after it was rejected by Henry S. King and Company in 1874, that he had "gone through the Chien d'or." Kirby had "reduced" the manuscript "from 1600 to about 1300 pages." In "consequence of this evisceration," he had "recast a portion of it." This portion, the last two chapters of the novel (733–55), was, he decided, "altogether" an improvement. He added, furthermore, "I never read it over before, since I wrote it. If I might be allowed to speak as a critic on my own work, I must say it is a better book than the author thought it was."[107] In his letter of 12 July 1875, Adam asked Kirby to send him the new section, for he was "going over" the manuscript himself "so as to form a new, intelligent idea of the merits & character of the story."[108]

By the time Adam left the manuscript with John Lovell in May 1876, Kirby had reduced it further by compressing the text on roughly the first 742 leaves of the 1600-page manuscript to just over 400 leaves (3–305). He also worked on the leaves that he was keeping from this version (306–732). He corrected mistakes made by his five amanuenses; he added, deleted, and recast sections; and he renumbered these leaves to make them sequential to the shortened text that preceded them. He also renumbered the leaves that held the shortened conclusion. The 1876 manuscript, thus, had about 1035 leaves that contained about 1038 pages of text.[109]

After the manuscript had been accepted for publication, Kirby made other changes, including the improvements to the punctuation mentioned by Adam and the alterations to the conversations required by John Lovell. The speed with which the author complied with these demands can be traced through entries that he made in his diary for 1876. By 17 July, three days after he had received the letter from Lovell accepting *Le Chien d'or* for publication, Kirby had worked over the first 100 pages. He mailed them to the publisher the next day. By 24 July another 200 pages were ready; sent to Montreal the same day, they were "received" and acknowledged on 27 July.[110] By 22 August 1876 he had completed correcting the entire manuscript. On the last 137 leaves (662–755), which he worked on between 17 and 22 August, Kirby wrote in "a subject heading for each chapter";[111] John Wurtele Lovell had asked for these additions in his letter to Kirby dated 17 August 1876. Because this request came after the bulk of the manuscript had been returned to the publisher, Kirby most likely added a title for each of the other chapters on the set of galley proofs that he corrected. Sometime during this process he crafted the dedication of the novel to Maria Susan Rye. Possibly at this time Kirby also prepared the preface from Alessandro

Manzoni's novel *I Promessi Sposi* (1827 ff.), which he later claimed had been omitted when *Le Chien d'or* was being typeset at Rouses Point.

On 17 August 1876 Kirby entered in his diary that the "1st proofs Chien d'or"[112] had arrived. He received, corrected, and returned the 203 galleys on which the text was printed from then until December 1876. He mailed proofs, for example, on 11 September and on 25 September. The receipt of the first set in Rouses Point was acknowledged by John Wurtele Lovell on 18 September; the receipt of the second, on 29 September. On 7 December Lovell wrote that "galley proofs 151 to 159" had come;[113] Kirby had sent them on 4 December. On 8 December he finished, and probably returned, the galleys that contained the text of Chapter 59, the last in the novel. The Lake Shore Press "completed the printing of The Chien d'or" on 12 January 1877.[114]

During this time at least twenty-three employees of the Press set the manuscript in type and adjusted the standing type to accommodate changes. In his letter of 18 September 1876, for example, John Wurtele Lovell reported to the author that "the correction" he "desired 1742 to 1748,"[115] presumably in the phrase "in the year of grace 1748" on the opening page of the novel (3), had been made. Lovell would not, however, accede to Kirby's request to change "The" in the title and running titles of the novel to "Le" so that these read "Le Chien d'or." In his letter of 7 December 1876, replying to Kirby's of 4 December, Lovell affirmed, "The title will have to be 'The Chien d'or' as we have made the running title in the plates all through in this way." Perhaps to justify his or a compositor's possible misreading of Kirby's handwritten "Le" as "The," he added, "In your early letters you expressed a wish to have it this way and we complied."[116] Despite these statements, Lovell did have the title on both the spine and the front of the casing printed as *Le Chien D'Or*. He did not, however, send Kirby "a revise proof,"[117] even though, as Kirby later noted in a letter to John Colborne Kirby, his younger son, the publisher had "thousand of time to do it." There were, therefore, "a number of errors" in the body of the edition that the author had not been able to correct.[118]

In his letter of 27 July 1876, John Lovell assured Kirby that the Lake Shore Press would begin the process of "putting" his manuscript "in type in two or three days," and that "the matter" would "be pushed on" under the "superintendence" of Adam.[119] In his letter of 17 August John Wurtele Lovell informed the author that Adam, who had "just returned from England," thought that "the book ought to be issued on the 15th

September."[120] Except for the "cut of The Chien d'or" for the title-page, which the company was "having made in Montreal,"[121] the composing, the in-house proofing and correcting of the standing type, the printing, and the preparation of the stereotype plates of the first edition of Kirby's novel were all carried out at the Lovells' "great printing establishment" at Rouses Point that contained many facilities that should have streamlined its production. There were, for example, "a separate room" for "each proof reader and his assistant" and a "Press Room" that held "some six or eight large Hoe and Adams Presses, capable of turning out an immense amount of work."[122] Still, there were several factors that delayed the issue of *The Chien D'Or / The Golden Dog / A Legend of Quebec*.

Some had to do with the production process. The manuscript was longer than had been calculated when it was cast off. In mid August 1876, when he sent Kirby "a lot of proof," John Wurtele Lovell informed him that in order that "the book" might "make fewer pages," he had ordered that "three lines" be added "to each page of print."[123] Perhaps because the Rouses Point plant was doing many printing jobs at the same time, its "font of type" for Kirby's work was "not very large." The type was, nevertheless, left standing until Kirby returned his proofs. It took, Lovell calculated in his letter of 18 September 1876, "about 10 days for proofs to get back" to Rouses Point from the time they left. It would, therefore, "be better to send proofs direct to" the firm's Rouses Point address "marking them via Montreal as one day" would "be saved by that means."[124] In the same letter he also hinted that the typesetting would proceed more quickly if Kirby travelled to the plant, where there were rooms "intended for the use of authors, who come to Rouses Point to supervise the printing of their works."[125] "If you were here to read proof," Lovell advised, "we could complete the work in from three to four weeks at most. As it is it will be probably ten weeks before it is completed."[126] In reality it took almost another four months, and even then *The Chien D'Or* was not ready to be issued.

One further problem was the casing. In his letter of 7 December 1876, John Wurtele Lovell informed Kirby, "We thought of working in the picture of The Chien d'or in the design for the cover and printing this in black and gold. We wish to make an attractive cover and at the same time something neat."[127] This plan was carried out, but there were complications. "The binding," Lovell reported when he sent Kirby his "advance copy in sheets" on 12 January 1877, was "waiting for brass dies for stamping." He hoped, nevertheless, "to issue the work next week."[128] Four days later, in answer to a letter that Kirby had written to the publisher's Montreal office on 10 January 1877, Robert Kurczyn Lovell, another of John Lovell's sons, reassured the anxious author that "the only thing now delaying" the issue of his work was the "die for the cover." It would, however, "be ready in a few days."[129] On 29 January Adam, writing from New York City, informed Kirby that he was waiting "daily for bound copies" of *The Chien D'Or*, although "Mr. Lovell" had told him "that the dies for binding" were still not "ready."[130]

Since shortly after his return in August 1876, Adam had been "the resident partner" in "the publishing firm" that John Lovell, John Wurtele Lovell, and he had established in New York.[131] First called Lovell, Adam and Company, the three were soon joined by Frank L. Wesson, a son of Daniel Baird Wesson, who in 1874 had become the sole proprietor of Smith and Wesson Company Limited of Springfield, Massachusetts, the firm that became famous for manufacturing guns. Frank had married John Lovell's daughter Sarah. Lovell, Adam, Wesson and Company of New York and Montreal was the publisher of Kirby's novel when it was "issued at last"[132] in late February 1877.

Copyright and the Lovell, Adam, Wesson and Company Edition

Responding to James MacPherson Le Moine's comment in his letter of 22 March 1877 that Kirby was "lucky to have had" his novel "published with such elegance,"[133] the latter explained, "You must credit my publishers with the handsome style of workmanship in printing & binding the volume. They accepted my MS and have published it at their own risk & cost, so I have nothing to do with their business arrangements in the mode of issuing the work." He trusted, however, that they would "not lose by their enterprise in opening a new vein in Canadian literature." Indeed, Kirby, apparently determined to test "the value" of his work, seems to have taken no interest in the business aspects of its publishing.[134] He certainly ignored Adam's request in his 29 January 1877 letter for "one or two hundred dollars" to help defray the publisher's expenses "in getting the work out," the amount "to be returned from sales or to be accounted for against supplies of the book."[135] In "Brief Of The Publications Of William Kirby's Novel 'Le Chien D'Or' (The Golden Dog) to Dr. Lorne Pierce" written in 1925, Kirby's grandson and namesake stated that the "arrangements of Kirby" with Adam and the Lovells were that they were "to protect this work for Kirby by copyright at the time of publication, paying Kirby a stipulated royalty after reimbursement of half of the cost of publishing this edition."[136] The letters between Kirby and various members of the Lovell enterprises, however, are silent on both copyright and royalties. Moreover, even though Kirby kept precise records, and his papers were well preserved, they contain no contract between him and the publisher of *The Chien D'Or*.

In 1880 Graeme Mercer Adam told Kirby that "There was no U.S. copyright secured"[137] for *The Chien D'Or*. According to George L. Parker, the novel was, nevertheless, "protected" in the United States "inasmuch as the proprietor of the plates could control its distribution" both there and in Canada.[138] As it turned out, no Canadian copyright was obtained either. The reasons for this are less clear. On the one hand, the University of British Columbia owns a copy of *The Chien D'Or* that contains on the verso of its title-page a version of the copyright statement required to be inserted in every copy in accordance with the "Act respecting Copyrights" passed by the Dominion of Canada in 1875. This statement, which assigned copyright to "WILLIAM KIRBY," registered the novel's year of entry as "one thousand and seventy-seven."[139] Although the notice seems to be spurious, it is possible that it was added by a compositor at the Lake Shore Press sometime during the production of the novel and signals the Lovells' intention to copyright the novel in Canada. Adam, who, like John Lovell, was something of an expert on copyright, certainly thought that a Canadian copyright had been obtained. In July 1878, when he and Kirby were wrestling with the legality of another story based on the tablet of the Golden Dog, he pointed out that "the Canada" copyright of *The Chien D'Or* did not protect the "work ... in England."[140] And in March 1880 Adam reaffirmed, in answer to Kirby's query on the subject, that it was his "impression" that "Mr Lovell" had "secured Canadian copyright."[141]

On the other hand, the two copies of *The Chien D'Or* required by the Canadian copyright act of 1875 to be "deposited in the office of the Minister of Agriculture" in Ottawa were never received.[142] On 11 April 1878 John Wurtele Lovell, writing from New York where he was in the process of establishing yet another in the succession of publishing companies with which he was involved for the next two decades, explained to Kirby, "The not having copyright in Canada makes but little difference as the book is too expensive a one for anybody to go to the expence of making a second set of plates knowing one set to be already in the market." "The plates," he added, "cost about $750" to produce.[143] Finally, Joseph-Charles Taché, Deputy of the Minister of Agriculture, reported on 10 March 1880 to Josiah Burr Plumb, Kirby's friend and the federal Member of Parliament "for the

county of Niagara,"[144] "In answer to your note about Mr. Kirby's work, ...
I have to state that this Book is not copyrighted in Canada, and that it
can only be so copyrighted by reprinting and republishing it in Canada."
He added, "The first printing and publication of the Book having been
made in the United States, the author had no right to Registration in
Canada, on that first publication."[145] Perhaps, then, John Lovell had tried
to copyright Kirby's work and been refused. Perhaps the failure to secure
copyright for *The Chien D'Or* in Canada had been an "oversight"[146] caused
by the management structure of Lovell Printing and Publishing and its
various associates. Or perhaps, as Parker has also suggested, John Wurtele
Lovell, who became "the most cunning publisher of the day," deliberately
slipped up because "he foresaw that without registration, the author would
be powerless to collect royalties."[147]

Marketing The Chien D'Or

The marketing of Kirby's work went smoothly enough, although there were
signs of confusion between Graeme Mercer Adam representing Lovell,
Adam, Wesson and Company in New York and Robert Kurczyn Lovell
representing its Montreal branch. In his letter to Kirby of 29 January
1877, Adam outlined his plans for *The Chien D'Or*. While he was waiting
for the book to be issued, he had "sent advance sheets" to Francis Parkman,
who had promised "to give the book audience & to write some critique
upon it."[148] This American historian had already published such works as
Pioneers Of France In The New World (1865) and *The Old Régime In Canada*
(1874), and "his interpretation of the French and British experience in
colonial times" was beginning to be widely accepted.[149] An endorsement
from Parkman, therefore, would, in the opinion of Adam, "prove most
serviceable in furthering" the sales of Kirby's novel.[150] Although in his
response Parkman commented on the "many blemishes" in *The Chien
D'Or*—it was "impaired by diffuseness and repetitions," and "Parts of it" were
"overstrained and sensational"—he was, on the whole, impressed. He would
"be surprised," thus, if the work did "not attract a good deal of attention."[151]
Adam included a copy of Parkman's review in his letter to Kirby of 20
February 1877. Except for the sentence about its "blemishes," the entire
review was repeated in the advertisement for the recently published "Great
Canadian Romance" that Lovell, Adam, Wesson placed the following month
in North American newspapers.[152] Adam also "sent advance sheets to some
of the best reviewers" in the United States.[153] He distributed actual copies

of the novel when he received his consignment of Kirby's book in late February. And on 1 June 1877 he reported to Kirby that he was planning to issue "a neat Circular" that contained American and Canadian reviews for distribution in the United States and Canada; he would send the author a "supply" when it was ready as it would "doubtless be useful" in increasing the sales of his novel.[154]

In Canada, in addition to these arrangements, there were others made for the work's advertising, distributing, and reviewing, and, in the words of Adam, for assessing Canadian loyalty. "If there is anything living & earnest in Canadian patriotism," he wrote to Kirby on 29 January 1877, "now is the time to test it—in patronizing an important Canadian historical romance." In the same letter he reported that William Raby (or Raley) Burrage, a "Subscription and general book agent" in Toronto,[155] was expected to handle that city and the larger towns in western Ontario. Dawson Brothers of Montreal and a Montreal canvassing firm would "work Montreal Quebec & the Lower Provinces." Adam hoped that Kirby himself would be able to canvass in Niagara, St. Catharines, and "round the lakes where" he was "doubtless known."[156] In his letter of 20 February 1877, Adam confirmed that Burrage would supply Toronto and southwestern Ontario; the novel was to sell "retail" for "$2.00."[157] And on 1 June 1877 Adam promised Kirby, whose efforts at publicizing his book in his home region had apparently not been too rewarding, that he would "see to pushing the canvass" in the district of Niagara "more actively as well as elsewhere."[158]

On 12 March, the day that Lovell, Adam, Wesson dated its advertisement for this "Novel founded on a Legend of Quebec,"[159] Robert Kurczyn Lovell informed Kirby that the publisher was proposing "to issue the work as a subscription book instead of through the book-stores, hoping in this way to dispose of a larger number of copies." In this regard Adam would "look after Toronto," and the Lovell Printing and Publishing Company would "take Quebec and Montreal." Lovell reported, however, that "three different canvasses in Montreal" had not been successful. "The state of trade" there, he added, "could not be worse." It was, therefore, "almost useless to push the book until things" improved.[160] On 14 April 1877 Lovell, answering another of the several letters that he had received from Kirby in the previous month, reported that the Montreal office of Lovell, Adam, Wesson was "finishing some posters for the book." It was also planning to send "a man" to Quebec to give the city "a thorough canvass."[161] This "agent for Mr. Kirby's famous work" was likely "Captain Cowan, teacher of navigation in Montreal," for on 11 May 1877 an announcement in the *Quebec Daily Evening Mercury* stated that he was "now residing" in Quebec and taking orders for "'LE CHIEN D'OR.'" The newspaper, therefore, recommended that its readers "send in their orders for the work as there is only a limited number."[162]

These strategies resulted in Kirby's novel being available for sale throughout the Dominion in the spring of 1877. On 2 April Dawson Brothers advertised in the Montreal *Gazette* that "The Chien d'Or, a Legend of Quebec" was one of the "NEW BOOKS" at its store on St. James Street.[163] Two days later the same firm announced in both the Quebec *Morning Chronicle* and the *Quebec Daily Evening Mercury* that the work was for sale in its store at the "Foot of Mountain Hill" in that city.[164] On 5 April it could be bought in Halifax, Nova Scotia, from "W. Gossip, 103 Granville Street."[165] And on 11 April it was advertised in the *Saint John Daily News* as being "For sale by J. & A. McMILLAN" in that New Brunswick city.[166] This bookseller was still selling it as one of its "New Books" at the end of May.[167] "Willing & Williamson BOOKSELLERS,"[168] located on King Street East, Toronto, advertised it in late April; Robert Burns Willing and William Williamson, both former employees of Adam, Stevenson and Company, had purchased its "retail store in 1872."[169] "R. Wilkinson,"[170] that is, Russell Wilkinson, whose store was on the corner of Toronto and Adelaide in Toronto, announced it in early May, as did "JAMES CAMPBELL & SON,"[171] a bookseller in the same city. In April it could also be bought at the bookstore of "J. DURIE & SON" in Ottawa;[172] in May, at "E. A. TAYLOR & CO." in London[173] and at S. Woods' "NEW BOOK STORE" in Kingston.[174]

Copies of *The Chien D'Or* were also distributed to Canadian newspapers and periodicals. On 12 March 1877, for example, Robert Kurczyn Lovell informed Kirby that he had provided "copies to the Press both" in Montreal and "in the cities of Ottawa Toronto and Quebec."[175] In his letter of 14 April 1877, he further assured the author that among the serials sent copies were *Belford's Monthly Magazine* and the *Canadian Monthly and National Review*. Lovell had also arranged for two copies "for the 'Press'" of St. Catharines.[176] The press, in fact, had been receiving material since February 1877.

Notices and Reviews

Although they took some time, notices and reviews appeared in the United States that spring. "*Le Chien d'Or (The Golden Dog): A Legend of Quebec. By WILLIAM KIRBY*. New York and Montreal: Lo[v]ell, Adam, Wesson, &

Co. 12mo. pp. 678," for example, was the first item listed in "Publications Received" in the May–June 1877 issue of the *North American Review*.[177] And on 4 May 1877 a reviewer in the *New York Evening Mail* praised the novel in general as a work "rich in historic reminiscences" and the chapter entitled "Olympic Chariots And Much Learned Dust" in particular for its "very interesting" scientific theories. The work had "faults," but these were much outweighed by its "merits." It was especially commended to those who had "sufficient maturity of mind to read unvarnished truths" about the court of Louis XV of France, "the most dissolute court in Europe." The review concluded by pointing out that "the tablet of the Golden Dog" was "still to be seen" in Quebec, "the sole sad memorial of the tragedy to which it gives name."[178]

The distribution of Kirby's novel in Canada produced notices and reviews throughout the country. On 21 February, the day that Robert Kurczyn Lovell informed Kirby that *The Chien D'Or* was issued, a notice appeared in the Montreal *Gazette*. Advising its "readers to subscribe," it paid particular attention to the dedication "to Miss Rye, that well-known philanthropic lady," who had "done so much to rescue poor children in England from vice and degradation, and make them the happy inmates of many a contented and virtuous home in Canada." The novel itself was "purely Canadian ... full of historical facts and references ... and ... well-written." It was also printed and bound in the "well-known tasteful style" of "the Lovell Publishing Company."[179] In March 1877 both the Montreal *Daily Witness* and the *Montreal Herald* published short notices. The first allowed that this "romance founded on an old Quebec legend" afforded "many a graphic picture of Canada and Canadian society in the corrupt days of Louis the Fifteenth, and the Intendant Bigot who, in his chateau in New France, held revels that matched in bacchanalian frenzy, the wild orgies of the Regency";[180] the second, that the "romance" was "well worthy of perusal." "Every body who has been to Quebec," it stated, "will remember the 'Golden Dog,' which gives its name to the book."[181]

These notices and reviews continued to appear in the Canadian press throughout 1877, particularly in Ontario publications. The *Canadian Monthly and National Review* listed "LE CHIEN D'OR" among its "Books Received" in its April 1877 issue;[182] it reviewed it in its next. "The style is flowing and often extremely beautiful," this item concluded, "and, as a whole, the work deserves to be attentively read by all who relish an interesting book, but more especially by those who love Canada and her traditions, and desire to foster and encourage native literature."[183] On 5 July 1877 the St. Catharines *Daily News* was also complimentary. The author, it noted, was "formerly editor of the *Niagara Mail*"; his work not only spoke "well for Canadian ability in the region of fiction," but it could also serve as a travel guide. "How we should enjoy reading it sitting upon the ramparts of the Citadel," the review enthused. "We would advise," it continued, "those intending to make the St. Lawrence tour, to buy the book, it would be a delightful companion on the journey."[184]

Most of the reviews, including the one by Pantaléon Hudon in the March 1877 issue of the *Revue Canadienne* that called *The Chien D'Or* a book that would have "un beau succès,"[185] were equally positive. One negative commentary, however, appeared in the Halifax *Morning Chronicle*. " 'Le Chien d'Or' " was, in the opinion of this Nova Scotian publication, "a terribly long novel, half historical, half something else." The "whole thing" read "like a weak attempt to imitate Scott's 'Waverley' and Dumas' 'Three Musketeers.' " "Had the author cut his book down to one-third," the notice ended, "he would have produced a good novel; as it is the search after the points of interest is about as amusing as looking for a needle in a haystack."[186]

It was William Henry Withrow, James MacPherson Le Moine, and Benjamin Sulte who were most active in promoting Kirby's novel. On 24 February 1877 Withrow, responding to Kirby who had apparently announced the imminent publication of his novel, offered his friend "congratulations on the fame" that was "in store for" him. In the same letter he also promised to review the "Chien d'Or" in the *Canadian Methodist Magazine*, which he edited.[187] When he received his copy in the first week of March, Withrow "fell upon it and devoured it in a few hours." His one concern was "the parlour oaths" of the "villains and their rather free talk." William Makepeace Thackeray would have used a blank line for "those strong words." Otherwise, although Withrow thought that Kirby had been "wise to condense" his work, there was nothing to criticize. "Amelie" especially was "an angel." "I nearly cried my eyes out over her," the minister confessed. Most importantly, he would have "a good notice" for Kirby.[188]

In his review, which appeared in the April 1877 issue of the *Canadian Methodist Magazine*, Withrow, admitting that he had "had the privilege of reading this remarkable book in MS.," claimed that Kirby had "accomplished for Quebec" what Sir Walter Scott had "done for his native Scotland: —he has called up from its grave the dead past and made it live

again by a strange spell, scarce inferior, if inferior at all, to that of the great
Wizard of the North." Noting that Kirby's work gave "evidence of an amount
of research and careful study and conscientious labour not often bestowed
on a work of this character," he pointed particularly to "the chapter entitled
'Olympic Chariots and much learned Dust'" that delighted the reader,
although it did not advance the plot. He also found "few things in literature
more beautiful than the lovely character of Amelie de Repentigny." To
conclude, he quoted the statement of Francis Parkman, who was "more
familiar with the details of our Canadian past" than any other "man living,"
that he expected the novel to receive "'a good deal of attention.'"[189]

Le Moine's first contact with Kirby on the subject of "'le Chien D'Or'"
came in his letter of 10 March 1877. The Quebecker had noticed "in the
Montreal papers, mention of a new Canadian Book." He wished to secure
a copy for the Quebec Literary and Historical Society, which, founded in
1824, bought "all Canadian books." In the meantime, he would do all he
could "to favor its introduction amongst Quebec Readers."[190] By 22 March
Le Moine had received Kirby's "elegant & interesting Volume." He had
read only "the first few chapters," but he was impressed by the enormous
amount of work that Kirby must have done "to produce such a resumé" of
Canadian history and such "splendidly drawn" characters as "Angelique
des Meloises—Bigot," and "the travelling notary." He would, thus, be
pleased to review the novel in the "Chronicle & Journal de Quebec."[191]
Kirby gratefully accepted Le Moine's offer. On 27 March 1877 he wrote
that he would be "proud" to have Le Moine assess his work because it
would "not only be fairly done, but done by one the most competent to
judge any work illustrative of any period of Canadian history."[192] Reiterating
these sentiments in his next letter to Le Moine, Kirby added his hope
that Georges-Louis Lemoine, "the Chaplain of the Ursulines" and James'
"worthy brother," would approve of the "references to the Religieuses of
130 years ago." "The romance of New France," Kirby explained, permeated
"the old Convent through and through," and its "traditions" were "so
intermingled with the early history of the Colony that a work like" his
"would be sadly incomplete as a picture of the times, without reference
to them."[193] On 2 April Le Moine wrote to Kirby that he had completed
both reviews and trusted that they would "soon appear." In the meantime,
he concluded, "I have no hesitation in predicting to your book—a great—a
very great success, and I would feel very proud of it, had I written it."[194]

The review that Le Moine prepared for the *Journal De Québec* was published on 4 April 1877. Three days later its longer English version appeared in the Quebec *Morning Chronicle*. Kirby had "given the fruit ... of many years labor, in a historical novel of rare merit" that "dove-tailed, in one narrative, two of the most dramatic and thrilling incidents of Quebec history under the *ancien regime*: the hapless love of Caroline de St. Castin ... for the gay, reckless, brave and dissipated Francois Bigot ... and the mysterious tale of revenge connected through received traditions with the 'Golden Dog, gnawing his bone.'" Although there were anachronisms, Kirby's "magic touch" made "the chords of love, of hatred, of revenge, of manhood, of lust, of jealousy, to vibrate strongly." As a result, Quebec owed him "a debt of gratitude," for there would be a "flood of tourists" coming to the city and spending money there.[195] In his letter of 29 April 1877, Le Moine informed Kirby that he had "revised" the review that had appeared in the *Morning Chronicle* and sent it "duly signed & enlarged" to the *Canadian Antiquarian and Numismatic Journal.* If *The Chien D'Or* did not yet have all the "encouragement" that "it so richly" deserved, it would not be his "fault," Le Moine announced.[196] The third version of Le Moine's review, included in the July 1877 issue of this Toronto publication, had, among its relatively little new material, a comment on "some crude expressions, and cruder details about Bigot's orgies, calculated to offend the purity of the female reader, which might be dropped with advantage, in a second edition."[197]

On 10 March 1877 Sulte informed Kirby that he had received his copy of the novel, and that he intended to review it "dans l'une de nos bonnes revues."[198] On 9 April, having prepared his article, Sulte was sure that it was "le meilleur roman canadien" in the English language, although he would leave it to Anglophones to make the final decision on that subject. In the meantime, he wrote, "vous avez saisi avec un grand bonheur la vérité historique. Ceci est un mérite considérable et il est encore relevé aux yeux des Canadiens-français par la manière sympathique avec laquelle vous traitez ce qui les concerne."[199]

In a letter written the next day, Sulte congratulated Kirby again on following "la donnée historique" in his novel. He did, however, make some "observations" on faults that were "de bien petite importance." These included some anachronisms—the so-called Friponne, for example, did not exist until the mid 1750s in Quebec; some mistakes in French expressions— "'chevalier preux'" should have been "'preux chevalier,'" and "'C'est la faute à lui,'" "'C'est sa faute'"; and at least one misreading of Kirby's French, apparently by the compositors—"'conseillez'" should have been

" 'consultez' " in the phrase " 'Si vous conseillez nos auteurs.' " As well, it was Samuel de Champlain, not Jacques Cartier, who brought French songs to Quebec. "La première colonisation date à peine de 1608," Sulte explained, "Toute chose date des jours de Champlain: Nos familles, nos habitations et nos traditions purement canadiennes."[200]

Sulte ignored these problems in his review, which appeared in the *Opinion Publique* on 3 May 1877. It began by saluting both *The Chien D'Or* and its author, "Saluons un Anglais qui a étudié l'histoire de la Nouvelle-France. Saluons l'un des meilleurs romans canadiens qui aient été écrits en langue anglaise." The spirit of the book, he continued, was "éminemment sympathique aux Canadiens-français," about whose history Kirby must have read "deux cents volumes." Sulte was especially impressed with the Englishman's knowledge of the popular songs of French Canada, "M. Kirby les fait valoir partout. Ses commentaires là dessus sont excellents et justes. Elles sont à nous, nos chansons, et c'est déjà beaucoup en faveur d'un petit peuple. Qui sait chanter sait se battre, et qui sait se battre ira loin." Emphasizing again the importance of its history for the "race canadienne-française," he concluded, "Tant que nous resterons ce que nous avons été, tout ira bien, en notre honneur."[201]

In a review published in January 1878 in the *Foyer Domestique*, the Ottawa serial to which he contributed, Sulte repeated his views about the importance of Kirby's novel in making French Canadians better known and understood. Commenting on three recent books "écrits en anglais mais consacrés à l'histoire du Canada français," *The Bastonnais: Tale Of The American Invasion Of Canada In 1775–76* (1877) by John Lesperance, the American-born author and journalist who had become very much involved in creating a national identity for his adopted Canadian homeland, *Count Frontenac And New France Under Louis XIV* (1877) by Francis Parkman, and *The Chien D'Or*, Sulte stated that it would be impossible for their readers not to change their prejudiced—and negative—views of French Canadians. "Ce sera une conquête," he added, "que nous leur devrons."[202] In a letter written the same month, Sulte had already commented that Kirby and Parkman had opened a way that would go far to educating English readers in both Canada and the United States "—et en Angleterre"—about French Canada.[203]

Benjamin Sulte was not the only person who hoped that there would be readers in Great Britain for *The Chien D'Or*. In his letter of 29 January 1877, Graeme Mercer Adam told Kirby that he was "waiting for copies to send to various English Publishers ... with the view of placing the work there—

say bound in two volumes for Library use."[204] In his letter of 20 February, Adam asked the author to let him know what Maria Susan Rye had done, or intended to do, about "getting the book brought out in England."[205] Adam had previously suggested that instead of dedicating his book to her, Kirby should have dedicated it to Frederick Temple Blackwood, Lord Dufferin. The governor general of Canada from 1872 to 1878, he made many "personal efforts to save and beautify the fortifications at Quebec City and to have Queen Victoria stamp them with her imprimatur as the sponsor of a new gateway (the Kent Gate)."[206] Kirby probably did not have a formal arrangement with Rye, as Adam apparently suspected, but, when she was visiting England, Kirby sent her a copy for herself and arranged with the publisher to send her "three copies for Pall Mall, Times & Daily News." "I will give them to the several editors," she wrote on 13 March 1877, "though I cannot promise that they will be noticed ever!"[207] One, perhaps the only, result of Adam's efforts was an entry in the *Bookseller* on 2 April 1877 that announced that "Le Chien d'Or (The Golden Dog): A Story founded on the Legend of Quebec" was available for ten shillings.[208] As late as June 1877, nevertheless, Adam was still looking "for word from England soon."[209] As for Rye's attempts to have the book reviewed, they apparently came to naught.

Reception

Without the relevant records of the Lovell Printing and Publishing Company, it is impossible to ascertain how many copies of *The Chien D'Or* were actually produced. That the publisher expected the novel to be successful is perhaps indicated by John Wurtele Lovell's comment on 12 January 1877 that if Kirby noticed "any errors," he should mark them on the "advance copy in sheets" that he was being sent so that the company could "correct plates before printing" another impression.[210] Whatever the size of the first impression, William Henry Withrow had heard by early February 1878 that "a second" was "called for."[211]

Of the copies printed in 1877, at least twenty-five were distributed to newspapers and periodicals in the United States, Canada, and Great Britain for notice and review. Dawson Brothers took "50 copies" to "supply the trade in Quebec and the Lower Provinces."[212] By 24 March 1877, according to James MacPherson Le Moine, "Dawson ... of Quebec" had "sold all the copies their Montreal house sent them."[213] According to Adam, the sales "in Quebec city" continued to go "on well" throughout the spring.[214]

Some of the copies were sold to libraries. The Quebec Literary and Historical Society bought one in March 1877, an acquisition that was announced at its "regular monthly meeting" in April 1877.[215] The next month Kirby, one "of the few elected" for this recognition, was made an honorary member of this institution.[216] "The Golden Dog, by William Kirby" was one "of the new books ... added" in April "for the use of subscribers" at Lancefield's Circulating Library in Hamilton.[217] Shortly after its publication the Niagara Mechanics' Institute, the Mechanics' Institute of Montreal, and the Toronto Public Library each acquired a copy of *The Chien D'Or*.

Kirby himself ordered and distributed at least twenty-four copies; in June 1877, for example, he paid for twenty at the author's reduced price of "$2.00 less 1/3rd" each.[218] As well as Rye, the recipients of these copies included his sisters, Hannah and Josephine Lowe, and Lord Dufferin. His copy, sent on 15 March 1877, was accompanied by a letter stating that *Le Chien d'or* had "the advantage, and disadvantage, of being the first attempt in English to draw from the romantic history of New France, the materials for a work of Fiction," and that like "all first attempts" only time would tell if "a work of this genre" would succeed in the "hard practical country" that was Canada.[219]

Kirby, of course, was anxious to hear how readers reacted to his work. He wished particularly to discover Lord Dufferin's response. On 8 November 1877 Sulte reported that the governor general was reading *The Chien D'Or*. By January 1878, however, Sulte still did not know "son opinion."[220] There were, nevertheless, other assessments. Sulte himself transmitted to Kirby a letter that he had received from a friend. A "juge du mérite littéraire," he wrote that he had bought "the 'Golden Dog'" as a Christmas present, and that he had "read it aloud to the folks at home of evenings." It was, he added, "remarkably well written, and much superior to most Canadian romances."[221] Kirby included among the reviews of the novel that he collected a quotation from another letter written in 1878, this one by the daughter of a friend in Niagara. Words failed her in describing "the pleasure" that the work gave her, "I have gone as far as the death of poor Caroline and inwardly shed tears at her sad fate. What a grand chapter that is of the Governor & his friends it makes me feel proud of Mr. Kirby—proud of him as a Niagarian, still prouder of his being an Englishman."[222]

Compliments about the novel came from more exalted sources as well. In the fall of 1879 John George Edward Henry Douglas Sutherland

Campbell, Marquess of Lorne and 9th Duke of Argyll, who had succeeded Lord Dufferin as governor general of Canada, told Josiah Burr Plumb how much he admired Kirby's book. Chuffed with this comment, Kirby recorded in his diary for 22 October 1879, "M. Plumb [m'a] raconté ce que lui dit Le M[arquis] de Lorne à propos du Chien d'Or."[223] In May 1883, when Kirby visited Ottawa to attend a meeting of the Royal Society of Canada, of which he had become a Fellow shortly after its foundation by the governor general in 1882, he met, "in the grounds" of "Gov[ernmen]t House," Lorne's wife, Princess Louise, "the most beautiful of Queen Victoria's daughters."[224] During their conversation she told him "how much pleasure" she, her brother Prince Leopold, and her mother had when each read "the Chien d'or." The Queen in particular had been "charmed."[225] Another compliment came in a letter that Kirby received from Hallam Tennyson in 1886. Writing on behalf of his father, Alfred, now Lord, Tennyson, he reported, "*We all read your powerful novel ... last winter.*"[226]

Bankruptcy of Lovell, Adam, Wesson and Company

Kirby, unfortunately, did not have long to enjoy the early praise of his novel, for there soon occurred another in what William Henry Withrow called the "perfect Iliad of disasters" that befell *Le Chien d'or.*[227] This one came in the form "of the failure of Lovell, Adam, Wesson & Co. in New York."[228] The partnership had not worked. John Wurtele Lovell left in 1877, and the firm went into receivership shortly after. The "assignee" was "Wesson"; that is, either Frank L. Wesson himself, who went back to work at Smith and Wesson, or, more likely, his wealthy father.[229] The "project in New York not having answered," Graeme Mercer Adam returned to Toronto where he opened the "English and American Book Agency" to represent "Publishing Houses" from Great Britain and the United States.[230] And the plates of *The Chien D'Or* were bought by Richard Worthington. An Englishman who had "established a small book-publishing firm in Montreal" in the 1850s,[231] he had transferred his business to Boston and then to New York.

Kirby most likely heard about the bankruptcy soon after it occurred, for early in the winter of 1878 he consulted Withrow about the fate of *The Chien D'Or.* In his letter of 7 February, the latter not only referred to the demise of Lovell, Adam, Wesson when he used the phrase about the "Iliad of disasters" suffered by the novel, but he also expressed the hope that "the parties who" then had "the plates would issue a new edition subject to" Kirby's "copyright."[232] It was not until 2 April 1878, however, that John

Lovell informed Kirby that Lovell, Adam, Wesson had collapsed. In his letter Lovell urged Kirby to buy the plates, which were being "offered for sale" by "the creditors" and might be bought for "$100. cash"; certainly they should cost no more than "$200." "Should they fall into the hands of a Canadian," Lovell added, "you will, I believe, lose all right of royalty." In order to expedite matters, the Montreal publisher also suggested that Kirby write directly to John Wurtele Lovell, who was "in New York" and could be reached through "Worthington / Publisher / 750 Broad Way / New York."[233]

Kirby immediately asked Withrow for advice. On 9 April 1878 the latter urged his friend to "secure the plates even at a cost of $200," as they were "very cheap," and then to ask the Rose-Belford Publishing Company, which had been incorporated by George Maclean and Robert James Belford that same month, to publish a Canadian edition. Withrow also thought that Kirby should "file a claim if not too late, as a creditor of the Lovell Adam & Wesson Estate for a pro rated dividend." "Your book is sure to be heard of," he comforted Kirby, "hold on to it." Assuming that Kirby did have copyright, Withrow queried finally, "Does your copy right or did it protect you from infringement by surreptitious publishers in Canada, <u>as</u> it was manufactured in the US?"[234]

Kirby also wrote to John Wurtele Lovell, who answered on 11 April 1878. Acknowledging Kirby's letter "of the 6th in regard to plates Le Chien d'or," he explained that they had been "sold ... with a number of others to a publisher here." "This publisher," he continued, "speaks of selling them to some one in Canada and of course if he does so or if he publishes the book himself he will not pay any royalty nor will the parties he sells to." Because the plates could be purchased "for about $200 or thereabouts," Lovell had the idea that Kirby, "to protect" his novel, should buy them himself. He could then "place them in the hands of some publisher in Canada ... who would publish the book" on Kirby's "account, charging for a commission for selling the books and paying for balance of proceeds." Before he did this, however, Lovell, who still believed that the book would have "a good sale," advised the author to have "500 copies" printed from the plates in the United States. If, Lovell added, he had "the amount to spare," he "would like to buy" the plates himself. Since he did not, he could at least "publish" a new impression.[235] Presumably he would have had it issued by John W. Lovell, the new company he formed in 1878 in New York to sell "pirated reprints at the lowest possible cost" and, thus, to open "up a completely new market among the masses."[236]

In his 1925 "Brief" about the publication of *Le Chien d'or*, William Kirby stated that his grandfather had "tried" to buy the plates, "but then the trickery became more plain, for as Kirby bid so rose the price until he had to stop at an impossible situation."[237] There is no evidence in the Kirby papers to support this statement. Since Lovell was using Worthington's address on Broadway, and since it was this publisher who had bought the plates of the novel by early July 1878, it is possible, nevertheless, that these two entrepreneurs did connive to keep them from Kirby and in the United States.

An Alleged Plagiarism of The Chien D'Or

In 1878 Kirby faced yet another challenge, one, furthermore, that demonstrated not only the vexed question of literary plagiarism but also the appeal of the Golden Dog as a source of inspiration for writers as well as the maze of British, Canadian, imperial, and international copyright in which *Le Chien d'or* had to wander. In the early summer Kirby's attention was drawn to "Le Chien d'Or," a short story written by Walter Besant and James Rice, the two Englishmen whose "remarkable literary partnership" produced nine novels and many shorter works of fiction between 1872 and 1882.[238] Set in "the city of Quebec" between 1697 and 1727, "Le Chien d'Or" told the tale of "Philippe d'Estrée, the young Seigneur of St. André de Tilly" and his schoolmate the Chevalier de la Perade; their love for Clairette de Montmagny; their duel in which Philippe was killed and after which the Chevalier, married to Clairette, lived abroad in, among other places, India and France; and, many years later, the murder in Quebec of the Chevalier, then a widower, by Philippe's brother Jean. He had discovered the circumstances of Philippe's death and the name of his killer through "an old Red Indian" and, thus, had erected on his family's townhouse in the main square of the city the tablet of "the golden dog." After plunging his "weapon straight into" the Count's heart, Jean whispered to the dying man, " 'In the midst of life we are in death. You are going to your long rest, after which you will remember this moment. Un temps viendra qui n'est pas venu / Que je mordrai qui m'aura mordu.' "[239] This work of fiction was published in the London *Graphic* in its summer number for 1878 and in the Supplement to *Harper's Weekly* on each of 13 and 20 July the same year. It was also serialized in the *Australasian*, the weekly newspaper published in Melbourne, on 17, 24, and 31 August 1878.

Kirby wrote on his copy of the issue of the *Graphic* that contained the story, "a piece of piracy badly performed from my book."[240] He first became aware of it, however, through its appearance in *Harper's Weekly*, issues of which regularly arrived in Canada well before the date printed on them. As a consequence, on 5 July 1878 he composed a letter to the periodical in which he questioned the source of the "novel" by the Englishmen. Stillman S. Conant, the editor of the *Weekly*, replied on 12 July. "Messrs. Harper & Brothers would very much regret to be made even inadvertently the medium of any injustice towards" Kirby, Conant began, but he hoped that the author would see that his "apprehensions in regard to the story were unfounded." "Le Chien d'Or" was a short story, not a novel, and was "concluded in the second number." On "a careful comparison" of it with Kirby's work, the editor continued, "I do not find that Messrs. Rice & Besant have in any manner followed the course of your plot. Am I mistaken in supposing the 'Chien d'Or', on which both stories are founded, is historical, and therefore public property?"[241]

On 8 July 1878 Kirby had already informed Benjamin Sulte that the novel had been plagiarized. In his reply of 18 July the latter thought this act "bon signe" because robbers prefer "les pièces d'or." Still, he advised, "Réclamez! protestez!" And he promised to put a note about the affair in the *Opinion Publique*.[242] Sulte's notice, which appeared anonymously in the newspaper on 1 August 1878, announced that Kirby's "roman canadien" had become as popular as had been predicted. What had not been foreseen was its theft in England and in the United States "avec une effronterie sans pareille." The height of this robbery was, Sulte concluded, "un 'auteur' américain," who had published in *Harper's Weekly*, under the title of "*Chien d'Or*, le roman de M. Kirby," to which he had made hardly any changes.[243]

The similarity between the two stories was also commented upon in the Ontario press. An editorial note in the Toronto *Mail* on 15 July announced, "There has just appeared in *Harper's Weekly* a short story called *Le Chien d'or*— a name which, by the way, would seem to have been appropriated from the admirable novel of Mr. William Kirby, of Niagara, which was published a year or so ago."[244] On 26 July 1878 the *Orillia Packet* also remarked upon the "new story" in *Harper's Weekly* "bearing the title of 'Le Chien D'Or.'" Although it allowed that there was "something singular about the appearance of the latter" so soon after the publication of *The Chien D'Or*, it hoped that it might "have the effect of directing attention to the merits of" Kirby's "admirable" novel, which was, "perhaps, the best work ever written on a

Canadian subject."[245]

After Kirby, the person who took the most interest in "Le Chien d'Or" was Graeme Mercer Adam. In his letter of 11 July 1878, he not only informed Kirby that he had arrived back in Toronto and that the owner of *The Chien D'Or* was Richard Worthington, "who acquired most of the plates and stock of" Lovell, Adam, Wesson and Company's books when the partners "declined further business" in New York. He also called Kirby's attention to the Besant and Rice story. Although he had "not read any portion of their novel," Adam was concerned that they might have plagiarized Kirby's work. Perhaps either he or Kirby should write to the London *Athenæum* to complain.[246] Adam had recently corresponded with this weekly newspaper on copyright for British authors in Canada, on which there had been a report by "the Royal Commission on Copyright."[247] In an undated letter, possibly written on 12 July, Adam further informed his friend that he had seen "the first part" of the Besant and Rice story in "the gorgeous midsummer" number of the *Graphic.* It was "illustrated," looked "attractive," and bore no evidence of "the 'scarlet sin' of the literary theft." Nevertheless, he wondered what should be done. Should Worthington, for example, "bring an action ag[ains]t Harpers to restrain the use of the title," or should there be that "quietly written letter to 'The Athenaeum?'"[248]

As it happened, neither suggestion was followed. Rather, on 26 July 1878 Adam wrote a letter on "Copyright And Authors' Rights And Wrongs" and sent it, with his letter on copyright that the *Athenæum* had published earlier in the month, to the Toronto *Mail.* Both appeared the next day. In the letter to the *Mail* Adam used what he called the "unblushing plagiarism" by Besant and Rice of Kirby's "notable historical novel" both to illustrate "the necessity for copyright protection, in England, for works originally published in the colonies" and to attack the English authors. The "misdemeanour of literary larceny" did "not look well in writers of" their standing, and he regretted, therefore, "that they should injure their otherwise creditable reputation by so grave an infringement of morals as their act" disclosed.[249]

On 3 September 1878 Besant and Rice responded by sending a telegram from London to the editor of the *Mail.* In it they announced that their "attention" having been called to Adam's "mischievous and malicious lie" about their "*Graphic* story," they were preparing a statement of facts. In the meantime, they had placed the matter in the hands of their solicitors. The next day the telegram, published at their request, appeared in the *Mail* under the heading "An Alleged Plagiarism Denied."[250]

The *Mail* printed Adam's reply on 5 September. Written the previous "evening," Adam accepted "the responsibility of the charge" that he had made against Besant and Rice, although he deferred "any necessary substantiation of it until the appearance" of their " 'statement of facts.' " He asked, therefore, that readers "suspend their judgment upon the matter." He concluded, however, "I am sure ... that the strong phrase by which the twin-authors express their opinion of my criticism of their work will be regarded as a manifestly intemperate one, which I feel sure it will be difficult to justify. If otherwise, then we may add to the 'curiosities of literature' another extraordinary instance of unconscious mental assimilation, or a remarkable case of literary coincidence."[251]

On 4 September 1878 Adam also wrote to Kirby to inform him about the Besant and Rice item in the *Mail*. Adam did not fear the authors' "wrath," but, nevertheless, he asked that Kirby either send a letter to the newspaper to corroborate what the former "had to say," or that he supply "detail of evidence of similarity of the two stories." He also requested a "copy of Harper's letter." "The only mistake," Adam commented, that he and Kirby seemed "to have made was in supposing that Besant & Rice intended to write a continuous story & further to filch from" Kirby's book, "instead of writing merely a novelette upon the historic facts."[252] Kirby replied to this letter, but he did not correspond with the newspaper, and, at this point, he did not send any precise evidence. Adam, therefore, wrote again on 9 September. In wishing to collect information, he was anticipating that the letter of Besant and Rice would "be a strong & violent one." He, thus, needed Kirby, who had "intimate familiarity" with his novel, to prepare a list "in parallel columns" of similarities between the two works. "I should like to reply to their letter in the following day's Mail, & would like to have all the powder & shot ready for them," he concluded.[253]

Dated 5 September 1878, the letter of Besant and Rice appeared in the Toronto *Mail* and the Toronto *Evening Telegram* on 17 September and in the Toronto *Globe* the next day. In it, after stating that their lawyers would "communicate" privately with Adam, they affirmed categorically that they did not steal from Kirby's novel. "*We have neither of us ever seen or even heard of his novel*," they stated. Rather, in "1876, being together in Canada," they had collected "books illustrating points in Canadian history." One of these, "called 'Maple Leaves,' a work well known to most Canadians, especially of Quebec, by M. Le Moine, ... contained a collection of legends which had gathered round a very remarkable old house pulled down only seven years ago, and ... well remembered in Quebec." The "most striking of the stories" was that concerning the murder of Nicolas Jacquin *dit* Philibert "by one Repentigny in a quarrel." It was this legend that had inspired Besant and Rice, although their "Le Chien d'or" differed from the former in time, characters, and plot. Thanking the newspaper for giving them "the opportunity of denying a falsehood" and of defending themselves "after the mud throwing," they reiterated, "The mud thrower will understand that we make no further reply to him save by the intermediacy of our legal adviser."[254]

Kirby, who probably read Besant and Rice's letter in the Toronto *Evening Telegram*, wrote to Adam about it on 18 September. The latter replied the same day. Despite the "hornets' nest" that he had brought upon himself,[255] he remained defiant. The editorial in that day's *Evening Telegram*, which declared that there was no plagiarism, and that Adam should apologize and, thus, do "full justice" to the English authors,[256] was "evidently inspired by B & R's legal advisors with the object of soothing" him "into silence." Although Adam supposed that he would have "to retract," he wished still "to make a strong case before the public to justify the charge" against Besant and Rice and "to make their theft ... as palpable as possible." Adam now requested that Kirby send him a record of anything in their story that came not from "history," but from the Canadian author's "pure creations" in the novel. Adam needed information of this type "at once."[257]

Kirby answered this letter on 20 September. It arrived, therefore, too late to be of use to Adam, who had composed his response to Besant and Rice the day before. In his reply to the English authors, however, Adam did incorporate an earlier report by Kirby on the similarities between his novel and their short story. The first likeness was the title. Perhaps misremembering what had actually occurred with regard to it when the Lake Shore Press was typesetting *The Chien D'Or*, and apparently confused about his novel's actual title, at least on the title-page and in the running heads, Kirby stated that the English authors "would seem to have taken the title of their story from" him. Although he had written "The Chien d'or" and, thus, followed the "common usage" of "the English of Quebec," the "The" in his title had been "changed" to "Le" "by the publisher." The other similarities included the opening scene where "a group of French Gentlemen & Colonists" met "near the spot" indicated in the 1870s "by the Grand Battery"; the "description of the Landscape & buildings seen from that point"—that of "the less accurate authors of Chien d'or the second" differed only from Kirby's when it was "wrong"; the choice of a mature woman and a young girl as principal characters; the introduction of the seigneury of Tilly with its manor outside the city and its "mansion" on the main square; the account of the education "of two of the leading" male characters at the Seminary of Quebec and the "principal female characters" at the Ursuline Convent there; and the "description of the act of homage." These likenesses, Kirby concluded, would "suffice to show that if" Besant and Rice's story were "not a plagiarism," then it was "to say the least one of those unconscious assimilations that require greater psychological science to account for them than the world yet possesses."[258]

Adam's long letter on "The 'Chien D'Or' Alleged Plagiarism" appeared in the Toronto *Mail* on 20 September 1878 and in the Toronto *Globe* the next day. He began by reiterating much of what he had said about copyright in his July letter to the *Mail.* Then, often repeating Kirby's exact words, he explained in detail the similarities between *The Chien D'Or* and "Le Chien d'Or" that the author's report had listed. Nevertheless, Adam withdrew the "charge of plagiarism."[259] As he wrote to Kirby on 21 September, although he had "frankly retracted," he had given Besant and Rice "whatever sting" he could, "in a gentlemanly way, in return for their vulgar letter." Judging "from the talk in the town," furthermore, he had "by far the best" of the controversy.[260] Still, Adam expected to hear from the English authors' solicitors. When by 13 November 1878 he had not, with evident relief he reported to Kirby, "No word further re Besant & Rice."[261]

Throughout his correspondence on the Besant and Rice story, Adam's primary concern was the possible plagiarism of Kirby's novel, although he also clearly intended to keep the issue of copyright, especially as it was illustrated by *The Chien D'Or,* before the British and Canadian public. In addition to these important motives, however, Adam's interest in the success of the novel and its publication in both Canada and Great Britain continued. In his undated July 1878 letter, for example, he expressed regret that Kirby had not "purchased" the plates of the novel "for the Canada field at any rate," especially since this might have opened a way to achieve copyright for the book in Great Britain.[262]

Adam was triumphant, however, when, on 21 September 1878, Willing and Williamson announced in both the Toronto *Globe* and the Toronto *Mail* that the Lovell, Adam, Wesson and Company edition was for sale for "$1."[263] Their advertisement, placed by "their own volition," showed "the effect of the controversial passage at arms." He only wished that "one could send the whole controversy home to England ... & have B & R shown up." If this happened, "Doubtless some publisher would take up the book & bring out an Edition of it." "I will see to this," he promised.[264] But if he tried, he was not successful.

Trying for a Canadian Edition

In the late 1870s and in the 1880s, Kirby continued his professional and public life. He also wrote a series of poems called "Canadian Idylls" that were first published in the *Canadian Methodist Magazine* and in *Rose-Belford's Canadian Monthly and National Review*, which Graeme Mercer Adam edited from July 1879 until its demise with the June 1882 issue. In 1888 Kirby bound some of these previously printed poems in a volume that he copyrighted as *Canadian Idylls*; a second, enlarged edition was published in 1894. In addition to these activities, he attempted to have published both a Canadian and an English edition of *Le Chien d'or*.

Probably in May 1882 Kirby approached Dawson Brothers, "Booksellers, Stationers, & Bookbinders," of Montreal; run by Samuel Edward Dawson and his brother William Valentine Dawson, it operated from 1860 to 1889. The firm replied on 2 June 1882 that it knew that Richard Worthington had "bought the balance of the" Lovell, Adam, Wesson edition, although it thought that "the book" was "nearly out of print"— "Very few copies were left last year." If "the plates" still existed, and if "a cheap edition" were issued in the United States, it "would be difficult to shut out." "A second edition of a book," furthermore, was "always risky." Still, it would "find out the precise state" of *The Chien D'Or*.[265]

While Kirby was awaiting the publisher's response, the Marquess of Lorne sent him a note in which he "enclosed a letter he had received from a Bookseller in Quebec informing him that no copies of the Chien d'or were to be had." They were, in fact, "all sold," and the book was "out of print." The governor general, unable, therefore, to purchase the "nine copies" that he needed, suggested "that there ought to be a new edition published." Kirby, who reported this news in a letter that he wrote to his son John Colborne Kirby on 21 June 1882, concluded:

> I think so too—but I have not heard from Dawson of Montreal yet on the subject, since the first letter he sent me.
>
> If I can get it published in Canada we will prevent the Yankee book pirates from interfering here with its sale.[266]

In view of Lorne's endorsement, Kirby must have been particularly disappointed when the reply of Dawson Brothers dated 24 June 1882 arrived. The firm had "all the facts relating to" Kirby's novel. It was sorry, but "through the way it was published," the author had "not only ... lost the profit of the first edition"; he had also "absolutely lost the copyright." "We have before us," the letter continued, "a copy of Le Chien d'Or. It was printed in the United States not in Canada as it ought to have been and it contains no certificate of registration at Ottawa which it ought to contain." Because of this mismanagement, Kirby had "no valid copyright in the book." The plates existed, however, and Worthington, who was still their owner, had offered them to Dawson for "$200." For various reasons the Montreal firm would not buy them. "Our experience with Canadian books is not satisfactory," it explained, "but unfortunately for us we are the people who have lost money, not the author. We are not at present disposed to buy the plates because we do not wish just now to lock up any more in plates—and the freshness of the date of this book has been taken off so the returns would be slow." It was very regrettable, nevertheless, "that so good a book should have been spoiled in publishing."[267]

Kirby communicated at least twice more with Dawson Brothers on what Samuel Edward Dawson, who was by then signing the letters with his name, called "a most unusual" case. On 28 July 1882 he advised Kirby that "the right way" to obtain copyright was "to buy the plates." He "would do it but for a few months" he could "not entertain any new literary business."[268] Two years later, on 2 September 1884, Dawson "with great reluctance" declined again to publish a new edition of the novel. His reasons, he reminded Kirby, were the same as in 1882. The owner of the plates was still "the master of the position because there being no copyright," he could "at any moment kill a second edition by printing at a low price a few copies of his plates" that would certainly "come into Canada." It was "very unsafe," therefore, "to go to the expense of resetting a book" that Dawson "would hold on the sufferance of another." He thanked Kirby, nevertheless, for giving his firm "the preference" over another proposal to publish the novel in Canada.[269]

This proposition had come from Adam. On 27 August 1884 he had written to Kirby to tell him about his idea of issuing "a Canadian Library." According to the "brief draft of a Prospectus" that he enclosed, Adam, "assisted by a staff of writers & translators," would edit "Selections, chiefly from native writers, in the Departments of Canadian History, Biography, Travel, Poetry, Fiction & Adventure together with new editions of Works of Permanent interest to the Canadian People," including "Reprints of Historical works" and "translations of books relating to <u>France</u> in the <u>New World</u>." Twenty-four crown octavo volumes were planned; eight would be issued a year; each would be priced at $1.50. The publisher would be John Lovell of Montreal. One of "the early reprints" that Adam hoped to include was "The Chien D'Or." Adam proposed to bring it out "in 2 vols," either "by printing a special edition, by arrangement with the N[ew] Y[ork] owners of the plates," or of resetting the novel "uniform with the series." A new typesetting would probably not be justified owing to the expense involved. If a new edition were to be made, however, Adam asked, would Kirby "think of revising it, & cutting it down in any degree, also of changing its title?" The author might consider, for example, renaming his novel " 'Angelina de Repentigny, A Tale of the Courtly Days of Louis Quinze in New France.' "[270] It was the receipt of this letter that had prompted Kirby to turn to Dawson Brothers.

This publisher having declined to set a new edition, Kirby pursued Adam's proposal. Acknowledging a letter from Kirby, Adam replied on 21 October 1884 on the stationery of Williamson and Company, the successor to "Willing & Williamson, Publishers, Booksellers, And Stationers," and the firm that he was to manage the next year. In his letter Adam told Kirby that a two-volume edition "would not be possible"; he was, therefore, "in treaty for a single vol . . . to sell at $1.25 or $1.50." He would let Kirby know when this was arranged.[271] A month later, the latter, having heard nothing, inquired again about this reprint. On 21 November, thus, Adam responded with the news that he had been to New York and had discussed with John Wurtele Lovell, who had bought the plates, "a special edition, on better paper & more carefully Printed & to be bound in cloth to sell . . . at $1 or [$1].20." The New York publisher was ready to produce this edition for the Canadian market. Adam had not arranged for its distribution through "a house" in Canada, however, so it "for the time was postponed." But, he continued, "Since then I have been speaking with Williamson ab[ou]t bringing out an edition for this market from the NY plates & he seems inclined to do it. I will tell you later of the result." In the meantime, Williamson and Company had "imported 50" copies of the impression of the first edition of *The Chien D'Or* that Lovell had recently issued.[272]

Trying for an English Edition

When William Henry Withrow learned from Kirby about the Marquess of

Lorne's praise of *The Chien D'Or* that Josiah Burr Plumb had passed on to the author in October 1879, he responded in a letter dated 19 January 1880 by wishing that the governor general would "say as much to some English house about the" novel. It was "too bad," he added, that the work could not "get well before the world."[273] Such comments undoubtedly encouraged Kirby to continue his quest to have an edition published in England and, thus, to obtain an English copyright for his work. It was not until 1884, however, when the prospect of a Canadian edition had not materialized, that he took the matter in hand. Over a period of several months in 1884–85, he contacted three institutions in London. One was the Stationers' Company. Responding on 25 March 1885 to the author's letter of 9 March, it thanked him "for the offer" of publishing "Le Chien D'Or," but it had to refuse because it did "not publish works" on its "own account."[274] The other two, Richard Bentley and Son and Macmillan and Company, were, however, well-established London publishers.

Bentley seemed a particularly suitable choice. The firm was one of the leading publishers of fiction, particularly in the form of three-volume novels that were specifically designed for circulating libraries. From 1864 until 1894, in fact, Bentley, which "could be called (in language of a later date) the 'king of the three-decker,'" was a part-owner of Mudie's Circulating Library, the "most powerful" of these establishments.[275] Bentley, furthermore, had not only published works of fiction, often in three volumes, by American writers like James Fenimore Cooper and Herman Melville, but in the 1850s and 1860s it had also issued several novels by the Canadian author Susanna Strickland Moodie, including in 1868 the three-decker *The World Before Them.* As well as its length, Kirby's novel shared several characteristics of these "prose epics," among them, "the use of incident, the tendency to extended description, multiple plots, encouragement of character portrayal, lavish details, and the author's digressions, reflections, or chats with the reader."[276] Still, when Bentley responded on 19 December 1884 to Kirby's approach, which had been made sometime that fall, the firm thanked the author "for the opportunity ... of perusing 'The Chien D'Or,'" which had been "done with some interest." It regretted, however, that it did not find itself "in a position to make" Kirby "an offer for the publication of the work." Its reason was that the "interest of the story" was "peculiar to Canada." "We fear," the letter continued, "that but few readers in England would be attracted by an almost historical treatment of Quebec so far ago as the middle of last century." Bentley would keep what it called "the M.S.," but what was really a copy of the first edition, until it received Kirby's "instructions as to its disposal."[277]

Undeterred, on 5 January 1885 Kirby approached Macmillan about "the publication of an English Edition" of *The Chien D'Or*, but his offer was quickly rejected when in a letter dated 20 January the firm announced that it was "not inclined to undertake" the project.[278] Sometime later "a distinguished friend" gave Alexander Macmillan, one of the two brothers who had founded the company in the 1840s, a copy of the novel, which he "read ... carefully through with much interest & admiration." As a result, when the copy that Bentley had kept was delivered to Macmillan, Alexander arranged to have it assessed by "the best literary critic" whom he knew.[279] This critic may have been John Morley. A writer as well as a politician, he regularly assessed fiction manuscripts for the publisher.

In the same letter of 16 April 1885, Alexander Macmillan, who "built Macmillan into one of London's leading publishing houses" partly through the publication of three-volume novels for subscription libraries like Mudie's,[280] delineated his reasons for not agreeing to issue an English edition. Although he had "no sort of prejudice against Canadian, or in favour of American authors," one problem with *The Chien D'Or* was that it introduced at "too great" a length "names & families" that were "quite unfamiliar to British people." Another was that "the book" was "too long altogether." If it "had come to us first in MS.," he added, "I think we would have asked you to consider these points & see if you could not shorten these parts." Still another problem was its "publication in Canada & in the States," which "blurred these markets" for the English publisher. Despite these negatives, Macmillan urged Kirby to submit another work "before publication."[281]

With this letter Macmillan sent the reader's report, which he deemed less favourable than his, but which repeated some of his objections. Called "Chien d'Or," the report began by identifying the work as "A Canadian novel of the date when Canada was still a French province." "Some of the principal characters—Bigot, Cadet etc. and their villainies," it continued, "are well described in Parkmans last volume. The author has worked them in with a highly melodramatic story—poisoning, assassination, intrigues,— of the most sensational kind." He had, furthermore, told "his story in good English and straightforwardly; and one or two of the situations" were "vigorous and striking: viz. the murder of the unfortunate young lady by the poisoned bouquet." Still, the assessor concluded, "I doubt whether the times are of much interest to many of our public. They are unfamiliar, and we have no tradition of them living at the back of our minds. As a historic romance it is not bad, but I do not expect that it would make a mark." Much later, when William Kirby was going through his grandfather's papers, he wrote on this report, "What a mark it has made—for the publishers—& name for the Author."[282]

Kirby, obviously disappointed, replied to Macmillan's letter shortly after he received it. Although this response, which included a reference to Trübner and Company's rejection many years before, has apparently not survived, Macmillan's answer has. Ever polite as was his wont with authors, he defended his decision not to accept *The Chien D'Or*, "I am sure that my old friend, the late Mr Nicholas Trübner was wrong in saying that a book dealing with Canadian subject would on that ground be tabooed in England. If you ever write another story we shall be glad to look at it—but not after it has been published in the States as well as in Canada. Believe me we have no prejudice against our Canadian Fellow Subjects." To reinforce his point, Macmillan added in a postscript, "Mr Parkmans criticism seems to me wholly right."[283]

Its Canadian subject matter and its previous publication were good reasons for both Bentley and Macmillan to turn down Kirby's work. In the mid 1880s there were others, however. These included the growing dissatisfaction with both the form and the content of the three-volume novel, its expense, and its distribution, at least initially, chiefly through the subscription libraries. Kirby's historical fiction, therefore, had not only the wrong times for its subject matter to be of much interest to British readers; it was also wrong for the publishing times.

Nevertheless, during the 1880s and 1890s there were two further attempts to have *The Chien D'Or* published in England. One was made by the ever-obliging Maria Susan Rye, who returned to London from Niagara-on-the-Lake in the spring of 1886 with instructions from Kirby to locate the copy of *The Chien D'Or* that Bentley and Macmillan had considered and to try again to find a publisher for it in London. On 27 May, therefore, Rye reported from her "Emigration Home for destitute little girls" that she had called at both publishers. The first informed her that it had "sent the book on to McMillans"; the second, that it had "sent the book back direct to" Kirby. One "of the heads of the firm" had also told her that Alexander Macmillan himself had written to Kirby on the matter—"a thing he rarely can do now." Not having found the English copy, Rye then urged Kirby to send another to "Professor Morely," or "Morley," "care of Will[ia]m Cassell, & ask him, if he would treat with you for the re-print in either Cassells or Routledges re-print of popular books."[284] Morley, who seems to have been Henry Morley, "professor of English language and literature at University College, London," and the editor of "some 300 volumes of English and foreign classics, which constituted Morley's Universal Library, Cassell's National Library, and other series,"[285] would, she thought, "jump at the chance." Books like Kirby's, she explained, were being reprinted and sold "at 6d each simultaneously <u>almost</u>" with their considerably more expensive first edition, "so make the offer."[286] Just over a month later, on 30 June 1886, in reply to Kirby's letter of 9 June, Rye explained that "Professor Morley" was "electioneering" as a result of the dissolution of Parliament on 8 June. Since he was the Prime Minister's "right hand man," she "had better write the man in the moon than Mr. M__ just now!"[287] Apparently this time she was referring to John Morley, who in 1886 held "the post of Irish secretary" in the cabinet of William Ewart Gladstone.[288]

Neither Henry nor John Morley, however, received this copy of the novel, for the one sent by Kirby for this purpose had gone to Henry Irving, the actor-manager of the Lyceum Theatre in London and "one of the icons of Britain at the proudest reach of her history."[289] Rye had taken with her to England the manuscript of a play based on *Le Chien d'or* that Kirby had written and that he had asked her to help get produced. Although it is unidentified in the correspondence, it may have been a version of a tragedy named "Beaumanoir," of which a much revised remnant in Kirby's hand still exists.[290] Rye discussed this "drama" in both her May and June 1886 letters. On 30 June she announced that the Marquess of Lorne, who had completed his term as governor general of Canada in 1883, had provided her with an introduction to the famous actor-manager. She had, thus, submitted to him both the manuscript and the copy of *The Chien D'Or*. Rye "thought the novel being in <u>print</u>, he might be tempted."[291] Responding to her letter on 13 July 1886, however, Irving regretted that he was "unable to give a practical consideration to any new work." He "sincerely" hoped, nevertheless, that Rye could "find another manager to whom Mr Kirby's play" would "be acceptable."[292] As she anticipated in her June letter to Kirby, Irving probably kept the copy of the novel.

The second attempt to have *The Chien D'Or* reprinted in Great Britain came via Sarah Anne Vincent Curzon, a "journalist, poet, and feminist,"[293] who in 1894 wrote the biography of Kirby that appeared in the "Prominent Canadians" series in the Toronto *Week*. In her article she began her comments on " 'Le Chien d'Or' " by noting that this "romance ... must ever impress the reader with the genius that produced it."[294] Curzon, who had immigrated to Canada from her native England in 1862, was particularly interested in the events that had occurred on the Niagara frontier in the eighteenth- and early nineteenth-centuries. She and Kirby first corresponded, in fact, about the time that her *Laura Secord, The Heroine of 1812: A Drama. And Other Poems* was published in 1887.

On 14 October 1892 Curzon informed Kirby that she had sent a copy of *The Chien D'Or* to Charles Mason, a native of Kingston Upon Hull, who still resided there, and who in the 1891 census was described as "Living on his own means" and being "Deaf."[295] Curzon knew him at least partly because both wrote columns for the *Preston Herald*. Mason was also "a learned French Scholar" who had told her that "he had never read a French novel nor ever would." Curzon had challenged him to change his mind by mailing him Kirby's book, which she described "as 'a French-Canadian novel which he would read.' " And indeed he had. Curzon had just received a letter from Mason in which he called the work "magnificent." He also asked if, there being no "legal objection," he could sell it as a serial to the *Preston Herald* "at a fair price," and if, this becoming a necessity, it could be "slightly condensed." Curzon suspected that Kirby would not be enthusiastic about "the publication of The Golden Dog in an English Provincial newspaper." Nevertheless, she pleaded, "to give such a story to a new set of readers would be of service to humanity."[296]

As it turned out, Kirby was interested. By 8 November 1892 the author had sent a reply to Mason's proposal to Curzon, she had mailed "a part" of it to him, and he had had time to respond. Mason had also written to James MacPherson Le Moine, with whom he may have been acquainted, to ask him to transmit his plan for *The Chien D'Or* to Kirby. Both letters contained much the same details. Since the novel had been neither copyrighted nor published in England, Mason proposed to have it serialized in one or more British newspapers; he would start by having it printed in, and stereotyped by, the *Preston Herald*. He would then arrange to use the plates to have it published in such newspapers as the *Glasgow Herald*, the *Newcastle Chronicle*, which was issued both daily and weekly, the Sheffield *Weekly Telegraph*, the *Yorkshire Post* (Leeds), and the *Dundee Advertiser*. He also thought that *The Chien D'Or* "would sell well as a stereotyped novel" in volume form, and that, although there would be expenses, he and Kirby could share the expected profits. "Le Chien d'Or," he insisted, was "one of the most beautiful books in the English language." It rivaled *The Last Of The Barons* (1843) and *Harold, The Last Of The Saxon Kings* (1848), both by Edward Bulwer Lytton, and *Hereward The Wake, "Last Of The English"* (1866) by Charles Kingsley. "It is utterly impossible to find a better book of its class," he continued, "I have read it with the extremest pleasure."[297]

Kirby received this letter, which Mason had sent to the *Orillia Packet*, sometime after 25 November 1892. His answer, dated 30 November, arrived in Kingston Upon Hull on 12 December, and Mason began immediately "making efforts to construct a Kennel for the Golden Dog." By 23 January 1893 he reported to Kirby that he was negotiating with a "friend" and fellow journalist on the *Preston Herald* named A. Allen Hurst, who might agree to the following terms:

> 1.—The 1st paper that prints The Golden Dog completely is to have the copy for nothing.
> 2.—The 1st paper that prints it is to provide 150 circulars and ... 2 or 3 chapters as specimens of the style & indication of nature of the work.
> 3.—They are to print 80 proofs, for use in other newspapers, gratis, as it appears.
> 4.—In addition [Mason had] told Hurst to get £4. more if he can.

Finally, Mason and Hurst calculated that even if twenty of the "150 newspapers in Eng[lan]d which 'run' such stories" took "the tale," they would receive payments totaling "£150." Mason would not leave "a stone unturned," he reassured Kirby, "to carry out" their "objects" for the novel "in all forms."[298] Despite, perhaps because of, these ambitious plans, nothing came of Mason's project. For twenty years, in fact, the only available edition of Kirby's work was that first published in 1877 by Lovell, Adam, Wesson and Company of New York and Montreal.

Post 1877 Issues and Impressions of Lovell, Adam, Wesson and Company Edition

In the summer of 1878, while Kirby and his associates were fussing about "Le Chien d'Or" by Walter Besant and James Rice, Richard Worthington produced an impression of Kirby's novel from the plates that he had acquired as a result of the failure of Lovell, Adam, Wesson and Company. Printed in New York by J. J. Little, Printers, of 10 to 20 Astor Place and advertised as selling for "$2.00,"[299] this impression was issued in the fall of 1878. Its publisher's imprint on the title-page, dated 1878, was "NEW YORK: / R. WORTHINGTON, 750 BROADWAY." Its contents were identical to the Lovell, Adam, Wesson impression.

Kirby, who purchased his copy for "$1.50" from Graeme Mercer Adam's English and American Book Agency,[300] received it before 23 October 1878. On 12 November he wrote to Adam to complain about the flaws in this publication. Adam responded the next day. "You had better," he advised, "drop a note to Mr Worthington telling him that you w[oul]d give him a new preface should he go to press soon again with the work." Adam continued, "The book being stereotyped, he could not now alter the errors in the plates very well. But write to him. Some day he may be inking a new ed[itio]n."[301]

For the next eighteen months Kirby worried about this impression. In his letter to the author of 14 February 1879, William Henry Withrow enthused again about *The Chien D'Or*. It grew upon him "every time" that he took it up; he wondered where Kirby got his elevated and dignified style. Then, in an obvious reference to his friend's concern about the Worthington impression, Withrow advised, "I would write to the papers or get Mercer Adam to do so about the American piracy." Concentrating on its distribution, however, he added, "I see Adam has some copies. I will urge him to send a circular to every Mech[anics] Ins[titute] & YMCA Library in the country."[302] On 22 March 1880 Russell Wilkinson, the Toronto bookseller, writing to Kirby about some books that he had ordered for the Niagara Mechanics' Institute, sympathized with the author about "the position" in which he had been "placed as regards" his "book." "I am much afraid," he continued, "that in this case fame will form the greater part of your reward. The 'name,' to some might be a sufficient return, but when others … reap the pecuniary benefit accruing from ones own labour, I think the feeling of annoyance & agony could hardly be considered reprehensible." Kirby "should go in, for a wholesale denunciation of such practices." And Wilkinson, therefore, both wondered at and admired "the coolness" with which his customer treated "the matter."[303]

Kirby received this letter shortly before he tackled Worthington. Although he may have done it later, it seems likely that he had already marked his copy to show its faults and to prepare it to be used as a copy-text in case the publisher wished to print a new edition. On the recto of its white front free endpaper he had written, "This is a pirated edition published in New York"; on its verso he had copied the passage from Alessandro

Manzoni's *I Promessi Sposi* and its English translation that he intended to be the preface to his novel. Throughout he had added corrections. Thus prepared, on 12 April 1880 Kirby contacted Worthington. "The copies of the Chien d'or issued by you seem to be the only ones in the market at present," the letter began. "It is useless," Kirby continued, "for me to find fault with you for publishing my book nor can I prevent it, seeing that my original publishers failed to register copyright for me as they should have done." What the author wished to say, nevertheless, was that if Worthington were "going to continue the issue of it," the novel should "be corrected." "The work," Kirby explained, "was got out by Messrs Lovell Wesson & Co in a hurry and was stereotyped without being revised, and contains many typographical errors, which I would willingly correct, merely for the sake of seeing the work made as creditable & free from error as I wrote it." If the publisher would send him a copy, Kirby offered to "correct it … and add the short preface which Lovell by oversight left out."[304]

Three days later, on 15 April 1880, Worthington replied that he would "bear in mind" Kirby's proposal when the novel was reprinted. But it would "be much better" if the author would "buy the plates" for a Canadian edition, which should sell "very well." The lead in the plates was worth $75.00. Worthington would let Kirby have them "for 125.00." They "would cost over 1000.00 to recast."[305] Needless to say, Kirby does not seem to have received a copy of the 1878 impression from the publisher. He certainly did not buy the plates, and Worthington neither reused them nor reset the novel. It was John Wurtele Lovell who produced the next impression of *The Chien D'Or*.

Lovell operated the firm of John W. Lovell that he had established in New York in 1878 until it failed in 1881. The next year he "reorganized" and reopened in the same city as John W. Lovell Company, a business that "soon emerged as one of the largest publishers of inexpensive popular and literary books in America." "Lovell's Library—a series of paperbacks" that included "such literary reprints as Bunyan's *The Pilgrim's Progress* (1883), Thackeray's *Vanity Fair* (1883), and Longfellow's *Voices of the Night* (1885)"—was one of his most important endeavours. With at least one title being issued a week, the series sold over "seven million volumes a year" and held "over four million" volumes "in stock. By 1890 the firm had published nearly 1,500 titles," and Lovell had earned "the nickname of 'Book-a-Day Lovell.' "[306] It was into this series in 1884 that Lovell introduced *The Chien D'Or* as Volume 9, Number 454.

Lovell may have acquired the plates of Kirby's novel at the time that Worthington's publishing firm failed yet again early in 1884. Certainly Lovell owned them when Adam visited New York that fall. On 21 November, when Adam replied to Kirby's letter of 20 November, he reported that on his recent visit there he had asked Lovell "if he wouldn't put" Kirby's "book on the Press & bring out a cheap edition." The publisher, having agreed, was issuing "it in the Lovell Library at 40¢."[307] A paperback printed on newsprint by Trow's Printing and Bookbinding Company, New York, its contents were identical to Worthington's impression. Page 212, which had been wrongly numbered 112 in the first two impressions, however, was corrected; *A Legend Of Quebec* was dropped from its title; and *The Golden Dog* preceded *Le Chien D'Or.* On the title-page, thus, Kirby's work was called "THE GOLDEN DOG / (LE CHIEN D'OR)." The publisher's imprint on the same page was "NEW YORK / JOHN W. LOVELL COMPANY / 14 AND 16 VESEY STREET."

The day before he wrote to Adam, Kirby had sent a letter to Lovell requesting "a payment for Le Chien d'or." In his reply of 22 November 1884, Lovell confirmed that he had "printed 5000 copies" of the novel for "the Lovell Library." If all these copies sold, there would be "a gross profit of about 500.00." This, however, would be used to offset the cost of "the plates" and to recoup losses on the book dating from 1877. The "publication of the work," Lovell alleged, had "been a great loss" to him "personally," "I made the plates at Rouses Point at a cost of over $1000.00 with the understanding that half of the cost was to be paid by you, but I failed to get anything from you, and through the failure of the sale of the book, and also from the failure of Lovell, Adam Wesson & Co I did not even get anything for the copies printed an additional loss of some $400 or $500."[308]

This impression was popular in Quebec. In December 1885 James MacPherson Le Moine informed Kirby that the "Yankee pirated edition" was "selling off rapidly at 40 cents." One city bookseller had sold, in fact, "more than 200 copies." It was "a shame," he added, that Kirby "should thus be defrauded of" his "hard earned laurels & gains."[309] Almost three years later, on 27 October 1888, Le Moine reported that "the 40 cent edition" of *Le Chien d'or* was still "selling rapidly" in Quebec. It was especially being "bought by all the tourists."[310]

In September 1889 Le Moine asked Kirby if he were "aware of a new edition (1889)" of *Le Chien d'or,* which the Quebecker described as "by J. Lovell—New York—large print—good paper—price 50 cents a very nice edition, it looks."[311] This paperback, which was another impression, appeared as Number 2 in Lovell's American Novelists' Series, "one of a number of series added to 'Lovell's Library' after" the firm's "purchase of the famous Munro Library in 1888."[312] Since the company was soon absorbed into the United States Book Company, the "new firm" that Lovell "incorporated under New Jersey law in July 1890,"[313] there may not have been many copies of the novel produced for this series.

One of the subsidiaries of the United States Book Company was Lovell, Coryell and Company founded in New York by Lovell and Vincent M. Coryell as a response to "the passage of the International Copyright Act of 1891" that threatened to ruin Lovell's "cheap book conglomerate." The aim of Lovell, Coryell and Company was to produce "reprints of better quality."[314] One of these was a new impression of Kirby's novel made from the plates that the company had acquired from the John W. Lovell Company by way of the United States Book Company. Priced at fifty cents, and issued as Number 3 in Lovell, Coryell's "Series of American Novels," this impression was available in December 1891. On the title-page it was named "THE GOLDEN DOG / (LE CHIEN D'OR) / A ROMANCE OF THE DAYS OF LOUIS QUINZE IN QUEBEC," and its author was identified as "WILLIAM KIRBY, F. R. S. C.," that is, Fellow of the Royal Society of Canada. Both additions, the first broadening the historical interest of the novel and the second enhancing the prestige of its creator, perhaps reflected Lovell's wish to improve the quality of his reprints. Its publisher's imprint was "NEW YORK / LOVELL, CORYELL & COMPANY / 310–318 SIXTH AVENUE." The contents of this impression were identical to the earlier ones.

Despite Lovell's efforts to adjust to the new circumstances due to the United States' having accepted international copyright, by early 1894 the United States Book Company was in "receivership, and Lovell was forced to resign from the business he had originated."[315] Probably to help recoup losses, during this troubled year Lovell, Coryell put out what was most likely a second issue of the 1891 impression of *The Golden Dog (Le Chien D'Or) A Romance Of The Days Of Louis Quinze In Quebec*. By 1 October 1894 A. M. Campbell, a reader in Ottawa, had acquired a copy.[316] The next month Kirby himself ordered one from A. P. Watts and Company, "Booksellers And Publishers' Agents" of Toronto. In its letter of 20 November, it informed the author that it expected "a copy of the new Edition of 'The Golden Dog' in a day or so" and would mail it to him immediately. It was "shameful," it added, that "so many pirated editions" had "been printed which" Kirby had "not benefited by." It further advised, "We think you should write to Chas. W. Gould, Receiver, International Book Co. 310 Sixth Avenue New York and ask for Royalty on the Edition just printed, & tell them the circumstances—it might do good."[317] The International Book Company was another subsidiary created by the United States Book Company.

It seems to have been a copy of this 1894 issue that prompted a commentary on Kirby's novel in the December 1897 issue of *New Church Life*, the monthly magazine devoted to the teachings revealed through Emanuel Swedenborg. Written by Carl Theophilus Odhner, a Swedenborgian minister who was a frequent contributor to the periodical, the article began by stating that although favourable notices of Swedenborg were "by no means unusual," there had apparently been no "mention of William Kirby's masterful novel, *The Golden Dog—Le Chien D'Or—A Legend of Quebec*. (New York, Lovell, 1877 and 1894)." "In the course of a somewhat extensive reading of novels (historical and otherwise)," Odhner continued, "we have never come across a more affirmative notice of Swedenborg and his mission, nor one introduced with more accuracy and artistic skill." After a brief account of the subject of the novel, which he strongly recommended for "its own intrinsic worth," the minister focused on the conversation about Swedenborg that occurred "in the then wilds of Canada, in the year 1748." After quoting from this discussion in Chapter 39 of the first edition, he added, "It is quite evident that the author is more than a mere admirer of Swedenborg .... he is an affirmative and profound student of the Writings" and "their application to the things of Science, Philosophy, and Life."[318]

After prolonged negotiations during 1894, the creditors of the United States Book Company "organized the American Publishers Corporation, which subsumed Lovell, Coryell and Company and the firm's other subsidiaries."[319] In 1896, thus, it was this firm that issued the fifth impression of the first edition of Kirby's novel. A volume in the Fortnightly Series, it sold for fifty cents. Except for the substitution of "AMERICAN PUBLISHERS CORPORATION" for "LOVELL, CORYELL & COMPANY" on the title-page, its contents were identical to the 1891 impression.

The next year either another issue of the fifth impression or a sixth impression was marketed by the American Publishers Corporation, the address of which was 310–318 Sixth Avenue, New York. Advertised in the New York *Sun* on 25 September 1897, it was available in "Paper" for fifty cents and in "Cloth" for a dollar. After quoting the opening lines of the novel, the notice continued:

"The Golden Dog" takes its name from an old tablet still to be seen in Quebec, in the front of a historic building, once the establishment of the great citizen-merchant Philibert. The author chooses for his time the exciting years following 1748, when the great empire of New France was tottering to its fall, when wars without and fighting corruption within, and the cruel indifference of the French court to the needs of its transatlantic empire, gave this priceless possession to England, and changed the destiny of America. Mr. Kirby introduces several historical personages— Louis XV., Mme. de Pompadour, Gen. Montcalm, Pierre Philibert, Kalm, diplomatists and statesmen forgotten of men.[320]

During this period the American Publishers Corporation also sold the book stock and plates that had belonged to the United States Book Company and its subsidiaries. Two items put on the market were the remaining sheets and the plates of the first edition of Kirby's work. One purchaser of the sheets was the Joseph Knight Company, the firm formed in 1892 when Joseph Knight, a partner in Nims and Knight of Troy, New York, hived off its "publishing business" and established "a permanent publishing concern in Boston"[321] as a subsidiary of the "bookselling and publishing" partnership formed in Boston in 1872 as "Estes & Lauriat."[322] Knight issued the novel in 1896 in its "Classics of Fiction," which it described as a series "of Masterpieces of Modern Literature, printed on a high grade of paper and bound in cloth, with rich and handsome designs." Each volume, "illustrated with a series of 12 half-tones from original drawings," sold for $1.25. Among the novels advertised in this series in the list inserted in at least some copies of the Knight issue of *The Golden Dog* were Edward Bulwer Lytton's *The Last Days Of Pompeii* (1834) and Charles Kingsley's *Hypatia* (1853).

In this advertisement Kirby's classic was epitomized as "A Romance of Quebec. A powerful story of love, intrigue and adventure in the times of Louis XV. and Madam de Pompadour, when the French Colonies were making their great struggle to retain for an ungrateful court the fairest jewels in the Colonial diadem of France." The title-page named the volume as "THE GOLDEN DOG / (LE CHIEN D'OR) / A ROMANCE OF THE DAYS OF LOUIS QUINZE IN QUEBEC / BY / WILLIAM KIRBY, F. R. S. C." It omitted the usual illustration of the tablet of the Golden Dog, but it announced that the novel was "*ILLUSTRATED.*" The volume included ten illustrations, five of them by J. W. Kennedy, whose work was popular in the late nineteenth century. The publisher's imprint was "BOSTON / JOSEPH KNIGHT COMPANY / 1896." The verso of the title-page read, "COPYRIGHT, 1896, BY / JOSEPH KNIGHT COMPANY." In fact, two copies of this issue were deposited in the United States Copyright Office in the Library of Congress on 11 July 1896.

A review of the Joseph Knight Company's issue of *The Golden Dog* appeared in the *Canada Bookseller And Stationer* in December. Welcomed as "really a beautiful edition," the "famous book" was highly recommended, especially to those who had read Gilbert Parker's *The Seats Of the Mighty Being The Memoirs Of Captain Robert Moray, Sometime An Officer In The Virginia Regiment, And Afterwards Of Amherst's Regiment* (1896). The notice concluded, "no Canadian who professes to keep abreast of the best native writing should be without the book."[323] It was probably this notice in the Toronto periodical that prompted Kirby to complain to the publisher on 3 December 1896 about what he apparently called the theft of his novel.

L. C. (Lewis Coues) Page replied to the author two days later. This "colorful Boston publisher,"[324] who had joined Estes and Lauriat—Dana Estes was his stepfather—immediately after his graduation from Harvard University in 1891, had moved to the Joseph Knight Company at its inception and was then its president. In his response Page thanked Kirby for his letter "in regard to 'The Golden Dog' " and assured him that he appreciated his "position keenly," "It is indeed a great hardship for an author to have his book stolen and to obtain no results from the product of his work and imagination, while the publisher is comparatively making a good thing out of his book." He pointed out, however, that Kirby had "no legal redress in any way, as before the International copyright law was passed the American publisher ... could make any book by a foreign author that he thought would be a profitable undertaking." Page further explained how Knight had got the book and what it was:

We are not publishers of the book in the sense that the term is ordinarily meant, although we have it on our list. The writer was in Quebec a season or two ago and like all other tourists was interested in the romance of "Le Chien d'or" and procured a copy of your capital novel.

On looking into the matter we found out that there had been one edition made as far as we knew, which was not copyrighted, viz., by the Lovell Bro's. This Concern has failed two or three times, but their interests, plant, plates etc, are all at present included in the American Publishers' Corporation, successors to the U. S. Book Co., who were successors to the Lovell's. Consequently, as is often the case, knowing that their cheap edition, 50ct. book of paper, was well established and having a good sale, we decided not to make a new set of plates, but merely to buy sheets from the American Publisher's Corporation. This we did, adding twelve full page illustrations and binding the book in a handsome cloth style. We thus took no risk for plant and do not own any plates, and so are not publishers of the book in the regular sense of the term.

Page concluded by taking "pleasure in sending" Kirby "a copy" of the Knight edition.[325]

In a letter dated 22 September 1897 from what had become "L. C. Page & Company, (Incorporated,) Successors To Joseph Knight Company," George Page, L. C.'s brother and the firm's treasurer, mentioned "unauthorized American Editions" that were still circulating in the United States and "some cheap paper editions" that had "a wide sale in Canada."[326] One of these was put out by the Montreal News Company in 1897. Apparently issued twice that year, it was advertised in the August 1897 *Bookseller And Stationer* as one of the Montreal News Company's "Special Editions Of Latest Novels Published Exclusively For Canada." Available in "Paper" for "50¢,"[327] a note in the same issue of the periodical further explained that its "first edition" was "already exhausted, and the second edition" would "be on the market in a day or two."[328] Probably printed from "the J. W. Lovell set of plates of The Golden Dog" that the Montreal News Company had "had for some years" in 1906,[329] the title-page of what was technically the first Canadian edition of Kirby's novel read, "THE GOLDEN DOG / (LE CHIEN D'OR) / A ROMANCE OF THE DAYS OF LOUIS QUINZE IN QUEBEC / BY / WILLIAM KIRBY, F. R. S. C. / [Illustration of tablet of the Golden Dog] / MONTREAL NEWS COMPANY, LIMITED / MONTREAL."

Some time, possibly in the fall of 1897, the Montreal News Company sent the Lovell plates to Toronto where a new impression was printed by the Hunter, Rose Company. Some copies of this impression were issued in Toronto by "THE MUSSON BOOK COMPANY, / LIMITED"; others, with no place of publication provided, by "THE AMERICAN NEWS COMPANY / LIMITED." For "almost a century" this company, which had bought out the Toronto News Company and had links with both the Montreal News Company and the Musson Book Company, was North "America's leading distributor of periodicals, newspapers, and books."[330] Except for the imprint, the title-page of both issues was identical. Each had a half-title page marked "THE GOLDEN DOG / (LE CHIEN D'OR)," a frontispiece tipped-in opposite the title-page, and the printer's imprint, "Press of The Hunter-Rose Co., Limited, Toronto," on the verso of this page. Although the frontispiece was "Angélique And Bigot In The Garden" by J. W. Kennedy and, thus, one of the illustrations first used in the Joseph Knight Company issue, there appears to be no other relationship between this issue and the Hunter, Rose impression.

Negotiating with L. C. Page

In his letter to Kirby of 5 December 1896, L. C. Page had introduced the idea of publishing "an authorized edition" that "would prevent the original pirates from having a sale from their book and give" the Joseph Knight Company "a good sale." At that point, however, he had dismissed the notion as "impossible," unless there were "some way of adding a chapter or incorporating some other matter in a new edition." Even this strategy, he concluded, "would probably not have the desired results because the pirate publisher could still go on and publish the book as originally written and as they pay no royalty and the book originally cost them nothing they could sell it much cheaper than the protected edition could be sold."[331] Nevertheless, just over three months later, on 25 March 1897, Page, at that point the treasurer of L. C. Page and Company, dictated a letter to Kirby to propose the publication of a new edition.

His "plan" included the following components:

1. the novel would have to be re-written "quite extensively, perhaps adding a little new matter," in order for it to be copyrighted;

2. it would also have to be shortened from its current "700 pages" to "500 pages," a volume that "would be, all things considered, a much better length"; and

3. Kirby would have to "add an explanatory preface authorizing" the firm "to undertake the publication and explaining briefly that this" was "the only proper edition."

In return for Kirby's agreement with these terms, the publisher would pay a royalty "on all copies of the book sold." "It will be a considerable expence to us, to make a new set of plates," the letter concluded, "but we have faith in the book, and believe that in time we will recover ourselves for our outlay, particularly if we have any way of heading off the Pirate Publishers."[332]

Kirby's response was immediate—and negative. On 30 March 1897 he informed the Boston publisher that it could "make the new plates of 'The Golden Dog' " provided they were made "without the modifications" that Page had requested.[333] The next day, writing to James MacPherson Le Moine, Kirby declared:

> A firm in Boston L C Page & Co. want to print a new edition of The Golden Dog, offering me compensation, for an authority of my name, but ask me to cut the book down to 500 pages. I refuse to [mutilate] the work. I will not consent to an abridged—"cheap & nasty" edition—just for publishers profit. The Golden Dog is too good, too complete a work for vivisection. So as far as I am concerned it will not be altered.

He still hoped, however, that a Quebec publisher would "issue an edition . . .—complete and with" his "authorization—and not let the Yankee pirates hold their home market." Such an "edition, with new type, & well corrected, would drive out the copies printed on the old worn out plates, of the Boston publishers."[334]

When Page received Kirby's refusal, it took a few days "to thoroughly consider" what to do before it replied on 9 April 1897. We "regret to tell you," its letter read, "that we do not see our way clear to going to the expense of a new set of plates, unless you care to re-write and condense the book and accept the terms we quoted you in our letter of March 25th."[335] Kirby did not respond. He was most likely surprised, therefore, to receive another letter dated 17 April 1897 that demanded, "Kindly reply definitely to our letter of April 9th., as the season is advancing and we wish to know promptly whether or no we are to make any plans to have the authorized edition of 'The Golden Dog' on the terms we outlined to you."[336] On 23 April, shortly after he had received this missive, Kirby finally replied. Once again he refused to agree to the publisher's issuing an abridged edition. By then, however, Page seems to have been determined to publish a new edition of *Le Chien d'or*; perhaps, in fact, it was already being prepared.

In its answer of 26 April 1897, the Boston firm recorded that it was "disappointed" that Kirby did "not feel disposed to agree . . . in the advisability of making a condensed edition of 'The Golden Dog.' " It was "a considerable expense to make the new set of plates containing so great a number of words as ... the present book," and it was "a great problem whether the sale" would "continue to be sufficiently popular to warrant the undertaking from a business point of view." Nevertheless, Page had "decided" to "make a new set of plates of the complete book, with the proviso that as offered" before, Kirby would provide "an authorized edition and accept a royalty of 2 $^1/_2$ %." This deal, the letter affirmed, was "a very fair one," especially since "legally" Kirby had "no rights at all" in the book, which was "public property." "If you agree with us," it concluded, "kindly advise us promptly and send on copy for such preliminary matter, including the authorization as you wish included in the book, as we wish to start setting at once."[337]

This time Kirby replied immediately. On 29 April he wrote that "the type setting" could begin even without his agreement on specific terms with Page. "If I accept 2 $^1/_2$ % royalty," he continued, "I should wish it settled <u>or</u> compounded & paid me & have done with it." The royalty received in this manner, he "would authorize" the Page edition. "I do not need reminding," Kirby concluded, "that I have been shamefully cheated out of my right in the Golden Dog and any body is at liberty to make prize of it. The law is scandalous as regards literary property. If a thief had run off with my horse or purse I could retake it whenever found but the product of my pen made with immense work & cost I cannot recover."[338]

Two days later the publisher responded by sending Kirby two copies of a contract. According to this "MEMORANDUM OF AGREEMENT," dated 1 May 1897, Kirby, "being author of ... 'The Golden Dog' ... and said book having been issued without being copyrighted so that said ... Kirby consequently" derived "no benefit from royalty or otherwise from it," agreed that Page should "publish the only duly authorized edition of said book, and that he as author" would "authorize and hereby" authorized this firm "to publish such an edition with his complete sanction and endorsement." The author, it continued, should "send such sanction and endorsement in writing" to the publisher "on or before June 1st., 1897." This "sanction and endorsement" would then be "incorporated in said authorized edition of the book as preliminary matter or otherwise." Kirby having agreed to these "covenants," Page would pay "a royalty of 2 $^1/_2$ % on the retail price of all copies ... sold ... on or about Feb. 1st., of each year beginning with Feb. 1st. 1898." Free "and editorial copies" were "exempt from said royalty."[339]

In the letter in which the memorandum was enclosed, Page explained that this contract was "drawn up on the ... lines" that the firm had "previously" offered. It, therefore, would not pay "a lump sum ... to take the place of the proposed royalty." Kirby should "sign both" copies and "return one." "If you do not care to accept our offer," the letter concluded, "we shall very likely have the book re-written in condensed form, and make a new set of plates on that basis. Of course if you accept our offer and authorize our edition, we will set the book in its present exact form, except for the preliminary matter of your authorization."[340] Thus reassured—and cornered, Kirby signed the memorandum of agreement and returned it in a letter dated 7 May 1897.

Three days later Page acknowledged its receipt of the contract. In return it was enclosing "a rough draft" of its "idea of an authors prefatory note for the new edition" that Kirby should "edit" as he thought best. It was mailing "under another cover two copies of the 'Golden Dog', one for the corrections and revisions" as the author suggested, "and the other for" his "personal use." It would also provide him with "the usual author's copies (10) of the new edition as soon as it" was published. Since it intended "to copyright the new edition in England as well as" in the United States, it needed "to know whether the old edition was copyrighted ... in Canada or England." "How did you first bring out your own edition or how did it get on the market?" it inquired. Then it advised, "We suggest that for the advantage of obtaining as much copyright matter as possible for the new edition, you revise, eliminate and add to the new edition as you think best."[341] Three days later, on 13 May, Kirby informed the firm about "the unfortunate way in which" he lost his "copyright of the book." He also enclosed "the revised copy of 'The Golden Dog' "[342] and his presumably edited version of the author's preface.

Kirby kept a holograph copy of this document signed "William Kirby" and dated "Niagara Canada May 1897." "In 1877," he untruthfully began, "an edition of The Golden Dog—(Le Chien d'or) was brought out for the American market entirely without my knowledge or sanction." "Owing to the inadequacy of the existing copyright laws at that time and afterwards," he continued, "I have been powerless to prevent the publication, which I understand has been a successful and profitable undertaking for all concerned except the author, the book having gone through many editions." Finally, beginning a new paragraph, he concluded:

It was consequently a source of gratification to me when I was approached by Messrs L C Page & Co of Boston with a request to revise the Golden Dog & republish it through them. The result is the present edition which I have corrected and revised in the light of the latest developments in the history of Quebec and which is the only edition offered to my readers with the sanction & approval of its author.[343]

Page responded to Kirby's letter on 19 May 1897. It did not comment on the prefatory note. It did, however, express disappointment that Kirby "did not feel like putting in much new matter or condensing the book appreciably," but it thought "that the few corrections" would "very materially improve the book." Then, writing in the first person, L. C. Page announced:

In order to prevent the matter in the chapters from running over into additional pages in our new set of plates, which we will set, starting each new chapter on a new page instead of running the chapters all together, I have taken the liberty of cutting out occasional sentences or parts of paragraphs which will not effect the contents materially, and trust that you will not object to this.

It is really a necessity to have done so i. e. cut out some matter, as the old plates were set in an old fashioned style and making new plates will cause the book to be even larger (more pages) than the old one.

Page continued his letter by informing Kirby of "a pleasant interview" with one of his "compatriots," Margaret Marshall Saunders, the author of *Beautiful Joe An Autobiography* (1894). She had expressed her "appreciation" for the *Le Chien d'or* and "asked 'Why does not Mr. Kirby continue writing fiction?'" Page concluded, "Can you not give us a similar book to 'The Golden Dog' for publication next year?"[344]

The L. C. Page and Company Edition

The first impression of the L. C. Page and Company edition appeared sometime in the late summer of 1897. A volume in the "Red Letter Fiction Series," which also included *The Shadow Of A Crime* (1885), the "first novel" by Thomas Henry Hall Caine, the English writer who "became astonishingly popular and famous,"[345] it sold for $1.25. With the exception of the publisher's imprint, which now read "BOSTON / L. C. PAGE

AND COMPANY / (INCORPORATED) / 1897," its title-page repeated the information that had appeared on that of the Joseph Knight issue of the first edition. Thus, its title was "THE GOLDEN DOG / (LE CHIEN D'OR) / A Romance of the Days of Louis Quinze in Quebec" [in Gothic script]; its author was "WILLIAM KIRBY, F. R. S. C."; and it was "*ILLUSTRATED*" with the same ten illustrations that had been tipped into the Knight issue. The one addition on the title-page was the monogram of Page with the Latin motto of the Page family, "SPE LABOR LEVIS" ("Make Light Work" or "Hope Lightens Labour"). The verso of the title-page carried the 1896 Joseph Knight copyright notice as well as "*Copyright, 1897* / BY L. C. PAGE AND COMPANY / (INCORPORATED)" and the printer's imprint, "Colonial Press [in Gothic script] / C. H. Simonds & Co., Boston, Mass., U. S. A." The publisher had copyrighted this second edition by depositing two copies at the United States Copyright Office, Library of Congress, on 11 August 1897.

Among its preliminaries, which ran to ten pages, was the "AUTHOR'S PREFATORY NOTE." Signed "WILLIAM KIRBY" and dated "*Niagara, Canada, May, 1897,*" its contents, including the statement that the novel had been "corrected and revised in the light of the latest developments in the history of Quebec," were virtually identical to the copy that Kirby had returned to the publisher.[346] The text itself, on pages 11 to 624, was 613 pages long. Each chapter, as L. C. Page had promised, began on a new page.[347]

Page announced its edition in September 1897. In a notice circulated to North American serials, it emphasized, furthermore, that this *Golden Dog* was an authorized version of Kirby's popular and well-known work. Several American and Canadian newspapers and periodicals repeated this information. In its September 1897 issue the *Bookseller And Stationer* stated that Kirby's "splendid romance" having "been out of print for a good many years," the new "authorized edition" was "undoubtedly rendering a service" to the book's "many admirers."[348] On 16 September the Chicago *Dial* reported that this "new edition" of *The Golden Dog* was "authorized by Mr. Kirby." It commented further that "the fact that the author" was "still living" would "come as a surprise to many readers, for his book" seemed "to belong to a very remote past." It was "still very popular in Canada," however.[349] In a similarly brief entry in its "New Literature" section on 18 September, the *Boston Daily Globe* welcomed the "new edition" of Kirby's "splendid romance of Quebec, which" had "been out of print for years." "It is stated," it continued, "that one entirely unauthorized American edition of this celebrated work was once published from the very large sale of which the author reaped absolutely no benefit. This Page edition is from a fine set of new plates, printed on fine paper, and is illustrated from original drawings and scenes in and about Quebec."[350] On 29 September the *Boston Evening Transcript* printed an almost identical note in its "Books Of The Day."

A review of the new edition that appeared in the *New York Herald* on 4 September 1897 repeated this information. Its author, who had read the novel in its entirety, explained that it was strictly "speaking ... not a new book." Since the first edition had "long since disappeared," however, "so far as the great army of readers" was "concerned, the book" was "really new." Praising the "rare vigor and grace" with which Kirby had described eighteenth-century Quebec, he noted that from "a historical point of view," the novel was "singularly instructive." "Too little is known about the early days of Canada, and it is well for us to turn for instruction on this subject to a man like Mr. Kirby, who is not only an interesting writer, but also a thorough scholar. He seems to be entirely at home in old Canada, and his descriptions of life therein may ... be regarded as correct," he continued. After quoting a passage from the scene of Caroline de St Castin's death and commending highly the section about La Corriveau, the reviewer compared Kirby to Alexandre Dumas père. Like this "gifted Frenchman," the Canadian author possessed "the rare art of giving new life to the dead past" and, thus, was "entitled to high rank" as a writer of historical novels.[351]

Sales and Distribution of L. C. Page and Company Edition

According to his grandson, Kirby heard sometime in mid September 1897 that "the Page edition was 'on the market.' "[352] As a result, on 19 September he wrote to L. C. Page and Company to inquire about its progress. In his reply on 22 September, George Page apologized for the company's "carelessness in not notifying" Kirby "of the publication of the new edition of 'Golden Dog' which came out some little time ago." In his brother's absence, he was uncertain about "the number of copies" that he should send. "Five copies," however, would be expressed to Kirby that day. "If this is not the number that was promised you," he continued, "kindly let us know." Finally, he reported, "The new edition is meeting with a very favorable reception as it was bound to, and although of course we do not expect any large sale on the book this year, we feel confident that it will sell steadily for many years to come."[353] By early December, however, the American publisher was not only asking Kirby for "a new volume of historical romantic fiction on the same general lines as 'The Golden Dog,' " a request that was repeated at least twice in the coming years, but it was also announcing that his novel had "sold in the neighborhood of a thousand copies so far."[354]

In early February 1898 Kirby received his first formal report on the sales of *The Golden Dog* and his first royalty cheque from Page. Dated 1 February, this record of the "Copyright Account" revealed that 1,290 copies of the novel had been bound. Of these, 207 remained "*on hand*," 98 had been used for "*Editorials & Gratuities*," and 985 had been sold. Kirby received $30.83 as his royalty.[355] Responding to his letter of 14 February, in which he must have expressed his delight at this payment, the publisher replied that it was "very glad to have been the means" of the author's "having realized a trifle at least from the 'Golden Dog.' " "We will continue to push the book to the best of our ability," it assured Kirby, "and trust to be able to favor you with a small check, at least, the first of each year for several years to come." Then, replying to his "point as to the sale of the book in Ontario," the publisher explained that it had "considerable Canadian trade" and had "placed" the novel "in all the large Canadian cities in about the same proportion as" it had "in American cities."[356]

Kirby received an annual report in the form of a "Royalty Statement" and a "Remittance Statement" every year from 1898 to 1906. According to these records, 7,269 copies of the second edition were sold from its first appearance in 1897 until the end of 1905, and Kirby was paid $200.22 in royalties. Among these issues and impressions were what was recorded as a "regular edition," a "special cheap edition" noted in the 1903 report, and a "special Canadian edition," also described as "cheap," noted in the reports from 1902 to 1906.[357]

In November 1897 a second impression of the Page edition was issued in the United States. That same month the Montreal News Company announced in *Bookseller And Stationer* that the "two editions" of *The Golden Dog* that it had "got out in the summer" were "exhausted," but that "another" would "be ready immediately."[358] This one was most likely the Page edition issued with the tipped-in title-page that had as its publisher's imprint "THE MONTREAL NEWS / CO., LIMITED PUBLISHERS." About this time the American firm apparently arranged with the Canadian company for it to take "the J. W. Lovell set of plates ... out of the market" and to become the Boston publisher's "exclusive agent" for the book "in Canada."[359] From the evidence provided by the advertisements for Page publications bound in with some volumes, it is clear that copies of Kirby's novel were being sold with the 1897 title-page as late as 1900 and possibly beyond. In 1900 as well, some copies of *The Golden Dog* with the Page imprint were included as Number 2 in its Fleur de Lis Library.

During these years the American publisher also continued to provide copies of its edition for the Montreal News Company, a firm that controlled "almost all the periodical and novel trade of Eastern Canada."[360] In the July 1898 issue of *Bookseller And Stationer*, for example, the Montreal News Company advertised *The Golden Dog* as one of "Three Great Canadian Books" that were particularly suitable for "the season of summer travel" when "tourists" were "on the lookout for interesting books"; the other two were Gilbert Parker's *The Seats Of The Mighty* and William Henry Drummond's *The Habitant And Other French-Canadian Poems* (1897). Kirby's novel was available in an "Author's Edition, with 10 full-page illustrations, Cloth, gilt" for "$1.25" and in a "Popular Edition, Paper cover" for "50 cents."[361] An item on "Summer Editions" in the same issue explained, "A 50c. paper edition of Kirby's 'Golden Dog' is another summer specialty." "The demand for it," it added, was "really amazing. Although it is 21 years since it first appeared[,] there are more copies being sold now than ever, and recently the publishers disposed of 500 copies in the city of Quebec alone."[362]

The work's popularity was underlined again in the same issue of *Bookseller And Stationer* in an advertisement announcing the publication of *The False Chevalier Or The Lifeguard of Marie Antoinette* (1898) by William Douw Lighthall. A Montreal lawyer, he had already made a major contribution to Canadian literature in the form of the anthology *Songs Of The Great Dominion: Voices From The Forests And Waters, The Settlements And Cities Of Canada* (1889), in which he included two poems by Kirby. The notice about his novel described it as "the sequel to the well known Quebec Legend of THE GOLDEN DOG (Le Chien D'Or)" and alleged that everyone who had read Kirby's work would "want a copy of 'The False Chevalier.' "[363]

Kirby's novel continued to be mentioned in *Bookseller And Stationer* in 1899 and 1900. In April 1899 it was included in the Montreal News Company's full-page advertisement of "New Fiction." The issue of January 1900 announced that this company had "arranged for an authorized edition of 'Le Chien d'Or,' " although the "contract" would "not come into effect for some months."[364] The words "AUTHORISED EDITION" were added to the title-page of the Canadian company's impressions sometime that year.

In an article on "Montreal Trade News" in the August 1900 issue, Ernest H. Cooper, who contributed several items from the city in 1900 and 1901, commented that there was "no new book in the Montreal market" that was "creating anything like a stir." Kirby's *The Golden Dog*, however, continued to be one of the "tourists' chief favorites."[365]

The special cheap edition mentioned in Page's annual report to Kirby for 1903 may have been the impression that had as the publisher's imprint on the title-page "*Boston* [emblem] L. C. PAGE / & COMPANY [emblem] *Mcmiii.*" It was printed on poorer quality paper, and it contained only eight of the original ten illustrations. "A Group of Habitans" and "Quebec from Point Levis," both taken from nineteenth-century photographs, were omitted in this and the other Page impressions issued in the years before Kirby's death.

According to the annual reports that Kirby received from 1902 to 1906, 2,318 copies of the special Canadian edition were sold between 1901 and 1905. Most, if not all, of these copies carried the imprint of the Montreal News Company Limited on the title-page. Some were dated on this page "*Mcmiii.*" Some, undated, were being sold well into 1906. Printed on the same quality paper as the special cheap edition, they also omitted as illustrations the two late nineteenth-century photographs.

The "Poor Mutilated" L. C. Page and Company Edition

By the time of Kirby's death, L. C. Page and Company had not only succeeded in knocking off the market what it called the "unauthorized American Editions" made from the Lovell, Adam, Wesson plates,[366] but it had also established its edition as the one that carried the author's final intentions with regard to his text. In fact, however, the second edition was not set in the "exact form" of the Lovell, Adam, Wesson edition as Kirby had demanded, and as Page had promised when it sent the contract for the author to sign.[367] Its text did not follow the copy of the first edition that Kirby had corrected for the publisher. It was not even that of this edition minus "occasional sentences" and "parts of paragraphs" as L. C. Page had explained in his letter to Kirby of 19 May 1897.[368] This 1897 edition was, rather, "some 96 pages (or 14 %)" shorter than that of 1877. Its excisions involved "hundreds of significant deletions ..., the majority being large blocks of narrative ranging from single paragraphs to an entire chapter."[369] This omitted chapter, numbered XXXIX and entitled "Olympic Chariots And Much Learned Dust" in the Lovell, Adam, Wesson edition, described the dinner party at which famous Swedes, including Emanuel Swedenborg, were discussed, and topics integral to Kirby's Canadian national themes were introduced. This was the chapter, furthermore, that several reviewers had singled out for its interest, and that Carl Theophilus Odhner had commended in *New Church Life* for its treatment of the Swedish philosopher. It was the absence of these passages that led Kirby to make a formal complaint about the second edition.

It is not clear when Kirby discovered that his novel had become, thanks to Page's editing, " 'not his book but the publisher's, a poor mutilated thing,' " variations of which phrase he repeated over the years.[370] His grandson claimed that Kirby "read the book over at his leisure" and was greatly surprised to find "not his book as authorized at all." He "took legal counsel on the matter, but owing to his advanced age," his physical disabilities, "and the fact that should he win against Page the proceeds of royalty would fall far below the cost of action, he could do nothing to prevent Page & Co. from continuing their fraud on the public."[371] Kirby may also have realized that since his novel had not been copyrighted in his name in either the United States or Canada in 1877, he probably could not win the case. He did, however, take the quality of its edition up with L. C. Page in early 1903.

It was then that he received a letter from Frank Sewall, the "writer and educator" who had been president of Urbana University in Ohio from 1870 to 1886, and who in 1903 was pastor of the Swedenborgian "Church of the New Jerusalem" in Washington, D. C.[372] In his letter dated 11 February 1903, Sewall, who had apparently read a copy of the first edition of Kirby's novel, informed the author that he had acquired a copy of the Page edition only to discover the omission of "chapters, and especially of those interviews where mention is made of Swedenborg and his early philosophical studies at Upsala and Stockholm." Since this material "lent a rare and great attraction to the book," he wished to know why these passages "were omitted," and where he could find a copy of an edition "containing those portions" about "that wonderful 'Prophat du Nord.' "[373]

When he received this letter, Kirby immediately enclosed it in one of his own to L. C. Page. Writing on 23 February 1903, the author remarked on the "small" royalty that he had just received, especially since *The Golden Dog* was "gaining in popularity every year." Then he continued, "One thing however I must complain of—that is the excision of chapter 39, as in Knights & all other editions—one of the very best in the book." He concluded,

"If I get no profit out of the book, I ought to preserve the credit as an author of what I really have written."[374] By the time Page received Kirby's letter, however, his company had already replied to the one that Sewall had written on 7 February. Page, its response affirmed, took "pleasure in stating that the reason the chapters you mention, together with a large amount of other matter, were omitted from the revised edition, was because our editor considered such omissions were extraneous matter, and that the romance was, consequently, improved."[375] To Kirby the publisher opined, "It is, of course, merely a question of judgment as to whether a book is benefited by revision, but naturally we do not agree with Mr. Sewall."[376]

Sewall's response came in May 1903 in the form of a review of an issue of the first edition put out by the Montreal News Company in 1897. Published in the *New Church Messenger*, the item emphasized the "peculiar interest" that *Le Chien d'or* held for "New-Churchmen," particularly in Chapter 39 when the diners discussed "the origin of the Indians" and their connection to "the Ancient Church of which they may be the relics." This conversation showed, Sewall stated, "a profound understanding of Swedenborg's teaching on the subject of those past and natural religions." Sewall warned, however, "New-Churchmen desirous of reading these interesting allusions to Swedenborg ... must be careful to inquire for one of the earlier editions of the Montreal Company, or other publishers, and not buy that of L. C. Page & Company, of Boston, who issue an edition with the chapters relating to Swedenborg carefully eliminated as 'extraneous matter' " as, he announced, "they have explained to the present writer."[377]

Kirby's response was more diffuse. On 22 October 1903, for example, the Marquess of Lorne informed the author that one of the books that he was "marking for Purchase ... from a catalogue sent" to him from Mudie's Circulating Library was " 'The Golden Dog.' "[378] On receiving this letter, Kirby immediately warned Lorne against the Page edition. He was "flattered," he told the former governor general, by his "mention of buying a copy" of what he called "my Chien d'or." He hoped, however, that "it was not the latest edition." He continued, "I must tell you that Page & Co's edition of Boston—has been—without my consent or knowledge—abridged & cut up—so that it is not my work at all as in all earlier editions. If the copy you bought is Pages edition pray do not read it as my Golden Dog." "I am vexed," he concluded, "over such a mutilated book as it now is."[379] Two years later, in the same letter to Hannah Lowe Servos in which he reported on his "long and severe illness" and reminisced about her and her sister's copying his manuscript thirty years before, he commented, "I was able to write ... then! but some of the printers botched my work." Then he added, "As it is now published the whole 39th Chapter is without my consent left out—The longest chapter & some think the best in the book."[380]

The "Author's Prefatory Note" to the 1897 edition caused another exchange of letters, this time in 1904. The previous year Narcisse-Eutrope Dionne, the physician who had been "librarian of the Legislative Assembly" of Quebec since 1892,[381] and Arthur George Doughty, who had been appointed "joint Legislative Librarian of Quebec" in 1901,[382] had published *Quebec Under Two Flags: A Brief history of the City* that included a chapter on the tablet of the Golden Dog in which they criticized the story told about it by Kirby. His novel was "a very interesting romance, and if Mr. Kirby had presented it to his readers simply as a work of fiction," they should not have felt "called upon to pass any remarks upon it." In the preface to the 1897 edition, however, the author claimed to " 'have corrected and revised' " *The Golden Dog* " 'in the light of the latest developments in the history of Quebec.' " They, thus, were forced to insist "that the romance woven around the names of Bigot, Repentigny and Philibert" by Kirby was entirely untrue. They then provided documents about Pierre-Jean-Baptiste-François-Xavier Legardeur de Repentigny that dealt with his court martial for the murder of Nicolas Jacquin *dit* Philibert, his pardon, and subsequent events in his life that partly contradicted the novel's plot.[383]

It was these comments that John Alexander Cooper, the editor of the *Canadian Magazine* from 1896 to 1906, not only brought to Kirby's attention in January 1904 but also offered to answer. On 20 January the author responded to Cooper's first letter on the subject written two days before. Kirby had "not seen the book" in question and had "no opinion to give on criticism of any kind." His "story of the Chien d'or" was "not a history, but a romance," and, therefore, "must be judged by the higher laws of poetic & dramatic fiction than by the dry rule & figures work of history." There were, he continued, "many current versions of the legend of the Golden Dog, not one a certainty"; his was "as good as any." He had, in fact, "no explanation, excuses or rectification to offer on behalf of the Golden Dog." "It has," he asserted, "stood for thirty years on its own feet, and I think needs no propping up. It will never get any from me." Then he added, "By the way, if you have to look into the Golden Dog, get one of the early editions. They are correct as to text, the latest—not so—much to my disgust."[384]

In his response to Kirby on 25 January, Cooper further explained that the "Doughty & Dionne book" based "its criticism on the fact that in an introduction to an edition of 1897," Kirby had claimed that his story was "historically true." "You are wise," Cooper advised, "to avoid a controversy, but you cannot avoid this one. It is here. You may refuse to answer, but your refusal is your condemnation. Not that it matters a whit except as a bit of our literary history."[385] Although in his earlier letter Kirby had told the editor that at his "time of life"—he was eighty-six—he would "not let criticism bore" him,[386] he nevertheless responded immediately. Neither he nor anyone else, as far as he knew, had ever written "an introduction of any kind to the Golden Dog." "The book," however, had "been pirated and mutilated by American publishers and some of them" might "have added an introduction to it." "It had no copy right in the States, because when it came out, a British subject was debarred from copy right in that country— so as a possession" he had "lost" his work.[387] In 1899, when Page's edition was published in England, Kirby also lost the possibility of copyrighting his novel there.

The English Edition

In April 1899 Jarrold and Sons of London and Norwich received for sale in its bookstore three copies of *The Golden Dog* from L. C. Page and Company, with which it had various business dealings. The publisher of the first edition of Anna Sewell's *Black Beauty: His Grooms And Companions. The Autobiography Of A Horse* in 1877 and the English edition of Margaret Marshall Saunders' *Beautiful Joe* in 1895, Jarrold may have been drawn to Kirby's novel because its title suggested that it was also an animal story. Whatever its surprise when it discovered the actual subject of this work, the English publisher decided to produce its own edition. It, therefore, purchased "a duplicate set of plates" from Page through a contract that gave the English firm "the rights of publication for England and the colonies, except Canada," this market "being definitely and clearly withheld."[388] That same year Jarrold entered "Golden Dog" by "Wm. Kirby F. R. C. S." in its List of Copyrights; it had "British Rights, not Canada."[389] "THE GOLDEN DOG: a Romance of the Days of Louis Quinze"[390] was included in the publisher's announcement of forthcoming fiction priced at six shillings that appeared in late September and early October in several London periodicals, among them the *Publishers' Circular*, the *Academy*, the *World*, and the *Bookseller*. In its notice of 11 October 1899, the *World* stated that "Mr. William Kirby's romance of the days of Louis XV. in Quebec, entitled *The Golden Dog*," was "to be ready next week."[391]

In the second half of October 1899, Jarrold printed its impression from the American plates and began distributing advance copies of what was technically the first English edition of Kirby's novel. The accompanying letter explained that the "first edition" had "appeared in the United States, entirely without the knowledge or sanction of the author but, owing to the inadequacy of the then existing copyright laws, he was powerless to prevent its continued publication." The "present edition," however, had "been corrected, and revised in the light of the latest developments in the history of Quebec" and was "published with the sanction of the author" by Jarrold "in this country" and by Page "in the United States." "We believe," the letter concluded, "it covers a period of history which will be interesting to a large section of the British public, and shall greatly value your kindly notice."[392]

The novel, a crown octavo volume, was issued shortly after. Bound in boards covered in blue art linen with gold lettering, a list of "Jarrold & Sons' Six Shilling Novels" was printed on the verso of its half title-page. On its title-page the novel was announced as "THE GOLDEN DOG / (LE CHIEN D'OR) / *A ROMANCE OF THE DAYS OF LOUIS QUINZE IN QUEBEC* / BY / WILLIAM KIRBY, F. R. S. C." This page also carried the publisher's device, in this case the motto "SANS PEUR ET SANS REPROCHE," and a design incorporating the initials J, S, L, and N; the publisher's imprint, "LONDON: JARROLD & SONS / 10 AND 11 WARWICK LANE, E. C."; and the phrase "ALL RIGHTS RESERVED." The copy that Jarrold deposited in the British Museum for purposes of copyright was officially received on 25 November 1899.[393]

By then several British newspapers had noticed the novel. One of the earliest reviews appeared in the *Scotsman*, the Edinburgh newspaper that had listed *The Golden Dog* in its "NEW BOOKS" column on 2 November. Four days later its analysis in its "*FICTION*" column began, "This is an excellent historical romance." Although it was too long, and "condensation, alike in dialogue and description, would have improved the book both as an artistic work and as a popular romance," it deserved "more than passing popularity." Kirby, it concluded, had "made careful study, not merely of the historical events and personages of the time, but of the undercurrent of tendencies and the manners and customs, the home life, superstitions, and folk songs of the French colonists on the St. Lawrence."[394]

Such notices continued to appear for several weeks. On 14 November 1899 the *Manchester Guardian* welcomed this "really scholarly historical novel" and hoped that it would "reap that harvest of appreciation" that it deserved. Its being "repeatedly pirated in the United States" must have annoyed "Mr. Kirby, but it was flattering testimony to the merits of his book."[395] On 23 November the *Dundee Advertiser* began its comments on *The Golden Dog* by describing it as "a powerfully written historical romance."[396] On 29 November the *Sheffield And Rotherham Independent* praised it as "a really capital historical novel made up of a strong mixture of love, and romance, and crime." "Brimful of interest and excitement," it was a novel that might be "read with pleasure and finished with regret."[397] On 11 December the *Glasgow Herald* called Kirby's work "able but prolix." Nevertheless, it concluded, "Mr. Kirby ... is so zealous, so painstaking, and, with all his prolixity, so good a story-teller that the reader who has time to devote to taking it all in will find 'The Golden Dog' a novel of many solid attractions."[398]

"SOME PRESS OPINIONS," including a selection from the review in each of the Glasgow, Manchester, and Sheffield newspapers, appeared in the full-page advertisement for *The Golden Dog* that Jarrold bound into copies of other novels that it issued in the next two years. This notice also stated that the publisher had "the British and Colonial rights in this celebrated Historical Romance," which gave "a faithful and vivid portrayal of an intensely dramatic and interesting epoch of eighteenth century history," and which had "attained immense popularity in Canada and the United States of America."[399] In a catalogue of its imprints published in late 1900, Jarrold announced a second issue or impression of *The Golden Dog* as a "SECOND EDITION"; the story was described as one of "The Early Days of Canada" and "Of Special Interest."[400] By 1901 Jarrold was advertising a "*Third Edition*" of the novel, which had sold "Over One Hundred Thousand Copies ... in America."[401]

In November 1899 *Bookseller And Stationer* published an article called "The New English Fiction" that included the announcement that "Jarrold & Co." was "issuing an English edition of 'The Golden Dog,' by William Kirby, of Canada."[402] It is unlikely, however, that copies were imported into Canada, especially since this was forbidden under the terms of the arrangement that Jarrold had made with Page. It also seems unlikely that Kirby ever knew of this edition. In his November 1903 letter to the Marquess of Lorne, for example, the author finished his warning about the "mutilated" Page edition with the comment, "How glad I would be if some London Publisher would undertake a correct edition, which I could furnish."[403]

The next year Gilbert Parker, who had become a Member of Parliament in the House of Commons in London, agreed to "try and place ... with a London publisher"[404] both *Canadian Idylls* and *The Golden Dog*, which he had "read and admired ... so many years ago."[405] When neither project succeeded, Kirby penned a letter to this other well-known Canadian novelist in which he repeated what had happened "some thirty years ago" when he had sent the manuscript of *Le Chien d'or* to Trübner and Company. This "prominent London publisher ... took all the conceit of expectation out of" the author when he was informed " 'that no Canadian book, whatever might be its merits, could find sale for a single copy in England!' " "I drew in my horns at once and never tried again in London until now tempted by your kindness for which accept my most hearty thanks," he continued.[406] In 1905, writing to the Marquess of Lorne, Kirby repeated yet once more the story of Trübner's return of the manuscript. He prefaced his remarks about this "curt" rejection with a general criticism of the attitudes of "English publishers, writers and critics" towards what he called "Colonial productions," which received "barely ... fair play in the literary arena."[407]

Some data indicate how many copies of Jarrold's edition were bound and sold, and where they were distributed. In early January 1900 subscribers to Mullen's Library in Melbourne, Australia, could borrow copies; they were also available for purchase for "3/6, by post 6/" each.[408] *The Golden Dog* that the Marquess of Lorne was proposing to order from the Mudie catalogue in 1903 was most likely a copy of the English edition. "*The Times /* (Book Club)"at "376–384 Oxford Street / London"[409] also owned a copy of this edition, which was listed as "Golden Dog. *William Kirby*" in the fiction section of *A Catalogue Of The Library Of* The Times Book Club published in 1908.[410] Established in 1905, this club functioned not only as a lending library for the newspaper's subscribers, but also as a seller, at discounted prices, of slightly used books. The copy of the third issue or impression held at Rhodes University Library in Grahamstown, South Africa, that contains the sticker of the Times Book Club was, presumably, one of those discounted books. Despite its wide geographical distribution, however, in 1906 Jarrold still had in stock at least 450 copies of Kirby's novel in sheets as well as the plates that it had bought from Page.

The Briggs, Jarrold, Page Controversy

On 2 March 1906 William Briggs, the Methodist minister who from 1879 to 1918 was the "book steward, or business manager" of the Methodist

Book and Publishing House in Toronto, a firm that had become by the first decade of the twentieth century an important Canadian publisher, particularly of works on Canadian subjects,[411] wrote to Jarrold and Sons to ask for a quotation "on 'The Golden Dog' by Kirby in sheets." There was, he warned, "a cheap American edition of this book," so "the price" of the sheets would "have to be very low in order to compete."[412] The same month Jarrold offered to sell Briggs 450 copies of the novel in sheets for 1s2d per copy, an amount that the Canadian publisher refused. There was, Briggs explained, "a 2/– Edn in Canada in <u>paper</u> or rather 50¢ Edn." He would, thus, purchase "the 450 copies" for <u>one</u> shilling each.[413] When Jarrold received this reply, employees of this English publisher discussed whether the offer of the Methodist Publishing House should be accepted, and whether it should be sold the plates either instead of, or as well as, the sheets. Although it was finally decided that the Canadians would not pay "a fair price" for the plates, their offer for the 450 copies of *The Golden Dog* in sheets was taken.[414]

When the Methodist Publishing House received these copies, which had been shipped in mid April 1906, it prepared to bind them. On 4 July it requested L. C. Page and Company "to supply ... the cover dies of THE GOLDEN DOG" for its " 'English edition.' " The American publisher's response was polite but stern. It published "the authorized edition, (the only edition in print of the work)" of *The Golden Dog*. Its "exclusive and authorized" agent for the book in Canada was the Montreal News Company. It had sold "a duplicate set of plates" to Jarrold, but this publisher only had "the rights of publication for England and the colonies, except Canada." Page would, therefore, "be glad to hear by return" mail that the Toronto firm had "given up any plans to publish, issue, or offer for sale" *The Golden Dog*. "Otherwise," it continued, "we shall be obliged, in order to protect our interests, and those of the Montreal News Co., to bring suit for an injunction to restrain your publishing an edition, or offering the book for sale. We presume that this will not be necessary, and that you will cancel your arrangements for the edition."[415]

In his reply of 10 July 1906 to Page, Briggs regretted that his firm's "purchase of sheets" of the English edition disturbed what the American publisher regarded as its "rights to the book in the Canadian market." The Methodist Publishing House had not known of Page's "arrangement with the Montreal News Co." when it acquired the sheets. These, however, "were bought from the publisher of the English copyright edition," which could "be imported into any of the British colonies." *The Golden Dog*, furthermore, was "not copyrighted" in Canada. "If there has been infringement of your rights," Briggs argued, "it will be clear to you this has not been on ou[r] part—it is a matter between you and the English publisher with whom your Agreement as to the marketing of the book in Canada was made." Briggs, however, "would be very sorry to have any disturbed feeling between" his publishing house and Page "over this matter." He suggested, therefore, that the American publisher purchase the "sheets in behalf of your Canadian Agent" for "35¢" per copy, an amount that "would cover the cost" of their being imported into Canada.[416]

Page's response on 13 July was as polite, and as tough, as its first complaint. It would not purchase the sheets of the English edition for the following reasons: "In the first place, it costs us a much smaller sum to produce the sheets from our own plates. In the second place, if we purchased these sheets, and you accordingly settled with the London publishers, there would be nothing to prevent them from later selling another edition to some unscrupulous Canadian publisher or jobber, as they would naturally feel that we had overlooked their breach of contract." The American publisher would not admit that it did not hold a Canadian copyright of the novel "until the matter" had "been settled by the courts, since" it "arranged for the present authorized edition." Because "the London publisher" had "broken his contract ... in supplying sheets for Canada," Page deemed that the Methodist Publishing House was acting "as his agents by aiding and abetting him by purchasing the sheets for publication in Canada." The American publisher thus warned, "we can secure the same legal redress against you as against him." Quoting the letter from the Montreal News Company of 9 July that affirmed its ownership of "the J. W. Lovell set of plates of THE GOLDEN DOG," Page further threatened to issue "cheap editions from either their plates or ours," a step that would "destroy the value" of the Briggs' publication, even if the Toronto firm succeeded "in publishing it." Urging the Methodist Publishing House, which it deemed "a house of ... recognized importance, both in the publishing and denominational world," to "return the shipment to the London house" from which it had been sent, it gave Briggs five days to respond. "If by that time we have not heard from you further," it concluded, "we will presume that you prefer litigation, and will give the matter to our Toronto attorneys to proceed with."[417] Briggs' response came three days later.

In his letter of 16 July, Briggs denied that the Methodist Publishing House was "in any legal sense" an agent of Jarrold. He equally denied that there was a "Canadian copyright covering" *The Golden Dog*. If "we wish to bind up the English edition of this book, and sell it in Canada, we cannot be prevented," he insisted. "But rather than cause any ill-feeling between you or the Montreal News Co. and ourselves," Briggs continued, "and as we bought the books in good faith from the English publishers, knowing them to be an honorable firm, who would not willingly or knowingly break any contract which they had made, we are writing them fully in regard to the matter, and will not proceed with the book until we hear from them."[418] The same day Briggs, "enclosing all the correspondence" between the Methodist Publishing House and Page, wrote to Jarrold to inquire "if through some error or misunderstanding" it had sold the sheets of *The Golden Dog* even though it "had a contract with Page & Co. not to do so." If this was the case, despite the book's not being "copyrighted in Canada," the Canadian firm would not "go ahead with the matter."[419]

There was consternation at Jarrold when it received this letter with its enclosures from Briggs. William Tillyer, who had been working for Jarrold since 1867 and was one of its most trusted employees in its London office, noted in chagrin that the company "had quite overlooked" its agreement with Page with regard to *The Golden Dog*. "I am quite certain I should not have sent them had I known," he underlined in a letter about the sheets probably written to the branch of Jarrold in Norwich.[420] For the next several months the English publisher discussed what to do about these sheets with the Methodist Publishing House. By 17 October 1906, however, Briggs had given up on making "satisfactory arrangements" as to their disposal. He was, thus, returning them to Jarrold and invoicing it "for the amount" that the English publisher had charged the Toronto firm, "namely £22:10," as well as for £5.6.9 for "Folding etc." Jarrold could deduct from this account the royalty that the Methodist Publishing House owed for its recent impression of Anna Sewell's *Black Beauty*.[421]

One remarkable characteristic of this eight-month correspondence among the three publishers was that the author of *Le Chien d'or* was barely mentioned. Another was that his rights were ignored. Yet Kirby was alive when the arrangements for what would have been technically the third Canadian edition were initiated. Only once, in fact, did Kirby manage to obtain a copyright for his novel. That was for its translation into French.

The French Translation

Even before the appearance of his review in the *Opinion Publique* on 3 May 1877, Benjamin Sulte had wondered if Kirby's novel "ne devrait pas être traduit en français."[422] In his letter of 17 May 1877, however, Sulte explained, in reply to Kirby's positive response, that bringing a French translation to pass would not be easy. One reason was that the publishing conditions in Quebec were not yet in place, and, therefore, it was difficult "pour nous créer tous les éléments qui composent une littérature nationale." Another was the problem of finding a suitable translator. "Comme c'est moi qui ai parlé de l'entreprise le premier, je ne cesserai pas d'y penser, et s'il se présente une occasion je vous la signalerai avec empressement," he continued. It was even possible, he added, that "quelque écrivain Canadien-français" might offer to do the job, but for the moment Sulte did not see anyone whom he could recommend.[423]

Over the next seven years there were at least three projects to translate the novel and four possible translators. In 1880 Sulte himself was approached about taking on the task by George Bull Burland, one of the owners of the *Opinion Publique*. "The proposal bore no fruit" because the newspaper "was already in financial difficulty."[424] Kirby, however, was prompted to contemplate the possibility, suggested by Sulte in the letter in which he discussed terms for the translation, of selling a "texte français ... à Paris."[425] This was especially important because, as the author heard from the federal Department of Agriculture, if he could "copyright a French translation in France," he could "by a deposit, made at the Stationers' Hall, in London, of the French book, acquire the privilege of a British copyright, in accordance with the International Treaty on copyright, between France and the United Kingdom."[426]

In 1884 Kirby pursued the idea of a French version of *The Chien D'Or* published in Paris in the letters that he exchanged with Louis Fréchette, the "journalist, writer, lawyer, politician, and office holder" who became "an important figure in the history of letters and thought in Quebec."[427] In a letter dated 17 January, Fréchette reminded Kirby that they had already discussed the possibility of his translating the "interesting novel The Chien d'Or." He had now been "offered so much a page by one of our literary journals here," and he "would like to know on what condition or terms" Kirby "would allow" him "to accept." The amount that he would be paid for the translation, he added, was "only a trifle and not perfectly determined yet," but he was "anxious, in the interest of our literature that" the "book should be published in both languages."[428] In his reply of 21 January, Kirby stated that his novel was "essentially a French book and ought to have been translated long ago," but he mentioned his concern about "its publication in Paris," his need to have "interim copy right," and his wish to "share equitably" in any profits. He concluded, however, that Fréchette should make him an offer.[429] The pair exchanged another set of letters in the same month, in which both continued to discuss the terms of the translation, but a deal was not reached.

It was F-X-A (François-Xavier-Anselme) Trudel who finally succeeded in getting Kirby's work translated, serialized in the *Etendard*, his Montreal newspaper, in 1884–85, and then published in a two-volume edition in 1885. Trudel, a lawyer, journalist, and politician, who also wrote essays and pamphlets to support his views, was known throughout his life for "his unshakeable attachment to the Roman Catholic Church and its clergy" and his unswerving commitment "to militant Catholic action." A follower of "ultramontanism," especially as it was conceived in France in the nineteenth century, he believed in the supremacy of the Roman Catholic church in every sphere of human life and, therefore, of the subordination of the state to the church.[430] His main reason, in fact, for establishing the *Etendard* in 1883 was to provide a venue for publishing ultramontane views. And, although it was certainly not supported by all the clergy, the *Etendard* was reasonably successful during the 1880s. The newspaper issued a morning, noon, and evening edition each day, as well as publishing a weekly. Already in 1883 it had a total circulation of over nine thousand among its "preferred public" of "clergymen, politicians, professionals, 'citoyens éminents,' and teaching and religious institutions," and it had become "the ... ultramontane flagship in Montreal."[431] One of the items it regularly provided for this readership was a serialized novel.

Trudel, who had been a member of the Senate of Canada since 1873, probably heard of *The Chien D'Or* through his federal connections. At any rate, on 24 April 1884 he wrote to Kirby that he had just finished reading "cette belle oeuvre littéraire," and that a fellow senator and a minister in Sir John A. Macdonald's cabinet as well as Sulte had recommended that he approach the author about a project that he was meditating. This was "celui de publier en feuilleton, dans mon journal 'L'Etendard,' puis mettre en volume votre admirable roman Canadien: 'Le Chien d'or.' " He was particularly interested in publishing a translation of Kirby's work because it

offered "un enseignement chrétien & moral très précieux." As the translator
he suggested Félicité Angers, who, as Laure Conan, was the author of
Angélique de Montbrun, the psychological novel set in nineteenth-century
Quebec that had been serialized in the *Revue Canadienne* in 1881–82, and
that was published in volume form in 1884.

The publisher wanted, however, "quelques modifications de détails,"
including the shortening of overlong passages, the deletions of repetitions,
the corrections of minor errors in history, and the omission of "certaines
allusions a des divisions religieuses qui ont été dénaturées & qui
froisseraient inutilement grand nombre de lecteurs." His specific example
of the last was "The Market Place on St. Martin's Day," the chapter that
described the scene in the market place of Quebec just before the murder
of the Bourgeois Philibert. Trudel also cited the scene in the convent where
Amelie dies in the arms of Pierre, which was "une pièce d'invraisemblance,"
and some love scenes between the various couples, which were "un peu
trop libres." There were, he added, "quelques libertés que la sévérité de
nos moeurs n'admettent pas, <u>même entre fiancés.</u>" But, Trudel reassured
Kirby, apart from the overlong passages and the "St. Martin" chapter, "tout
le reste des modifications ne comprendraient peut être pas plus d'une
vingtaine de lignes en tout."[432]

Over the next month Trudel and Kirby continued to discuss the
translation. In his letter of 3 May 1884, the former reported that Conan had
refused to translate the novel. Sulte, whom he had also asked, did not have
time to do it. He proposed, therefore, that Pamphile Le May, the librarian
at the Quebec Legislative Assembly, the translator of Henry Wadsworth
Longfellow's *Evangeline A Tale of Acadia* (1847), and a poet and novelist in
his own right, should undertake the job. On 16 May Trudel wrote to Kirby
that he was in the process of making the necessary arrangements with Le
May, even though he would have preferred Sulte. He hoped, however, that
the latter would have time to review Le May's version "de sorte que nous
pouvons toujours bénéficier de son bon gout."[433]

Kirby's responses to Trudel's letters are apparently not extant, so it
is difficult to know how he reacted to Le May as the translator. In 1866,
however, Sulte had sent Kirby a copy of Le May's *Essais poétiques* (1865),
which included his translation of *Evangeline*, and which Kirby had found
"tres bien faite."[434] By June 1884 Le May himself was communicating directly
with the author. The librarian wished to know, among other matters, who
had the rights to translate *The Chien D'Or*. Was it Fréchette or Trudel? If it

were the former, he would cede "ses droits" to Le May. Trudel, he added, was prepared to pay him "quelque peu pour faire cette traduction."[435]

In the meantime, Trudel and Kirby successfully concluded their negotiations in regard to the terms of the translation. They agreed that Kirby would copyright the translation in Canada in his name, but that he would give the rights to it to the *Etendard* for five years. Kirby also promised not to approve another translation during this time. Trudel would pay Kirby nothing for the serial itself but a royalty of 10% when it was published in volume form. The serial would begin to appear "some time between June and September 1884."[436] Trudel had originally hoped that the first parts of the serial would be ready for "notre grande fête nationale de la St. Jean Baptiste, le 24 juin."[437] In the letter of 31 May 1884, in which Trudel enclosed a copy of the formal agreement with Kirby, he explained, however, that the pressure of Le May's work at the Parliamentary Library coupled with "the special care" he intended "to give to the translation" meant that it would not be ready for "the 24 june" commencement.[438] This proposed date prompted Kirby, nevertheless, to have a notice inserted in the *Toronto Daily Mail* on 28 June. "The publishers of *L'Etendard,* Montreal, intend issuing shortly a French edition of 'Le Chien d'or,' by Mr. William Kirby, of Niagara," it read in part. "This beautiful romance," it continued, "has won the unbounded admiration of the literary world .... There is no doubt that its publication in French will be hailed with delight by the people of Quebec, for whom it possesses a special interest."[439] In the end "Le Chien d'Or! Légende Canadienne" appeared in one or two columns on the front page of each of 138 issues of the *Etendard* from 30 August 1884 to 16 February 1885.

In the months following their agreement, various letters were exchanged among Kirby, the librarian, and the newspaper owner. On 5 August 1884, for example, Kirby informed Trudel that the part of the translation sent to him was "tres bonne, à l'exception toujours de ces adoucissemens" that the publisher was permitting. He would not create a fuss, "mais toujours il faudra bien ne pas trop adoucir." It was in this letter as well that Kirby denied that Sulte "avait fourni 'd'amples notes, et d'un plan de l'ouvrage.'" Certainly, he added, "personne ne m'a donné ni notes ni plan quelconque—en effet le livre, à mon guise, n'avait pas de plan. Il emit comme un arbre—son germe se trouvait dans le 'Maple Leaf' de M. J. M. Lemoine .... Apres cela j'ai fais mon butin littéraire partout où j'ai pu le trouver."[440] On 30 November Le May reported to Kirby that he had just finished his translation of the novel, which he praised highly for the knowledge that it showed of French Canada and Roman Catholicism. He concluded, "Vous possédez notre histoire et vous avez pénétré dans l'intimité de nos usages. Merci! au nom de mes compatriotes. Mille fois—Merci!"[441]

During this time Trudel puffed his serial in various ways, particularly in the pages of the *Etendard*. On 1 August he announced that the translation of "Le Chien D'Or," this "admirable" novel, was coming along quickly and promised to be a great success. In fact, "les richesses de la langue française permettent au traducteur de rendre souvent d'une manière plus poétique encore la pensée de l'auteur." The work, he concluded, was in every way "la glorification de nos ancêtres . . . une apothéose de notre jeune patrie."[442] Six days later, on 7 August, Trudel reported that this "Roman Historique des plus Emouvants" would begin running in the newspaper "vers le 25 Aout courant." He also provided more practical information for his subscribers. The translation was being printed in the newspaper in a way that would make it available in book form without its having to be typeset again. Subscribers to the weekly *Etendard* would receive the serial in separate parts with their newspaper. Subscribers to the daily who had paid for a year's subscription in advance would be entitled to two paperback volumes of "500 pages" each as soon as the serial finished running. They had only to request a copy from the office of the *Etendard*. Other subscribers to the daily could have the two volumes at half price provided they paid for a year in advance.[443] On Wednesday, 27 August, a notice appeared in the newspaper announcing that this "admirable ouvrage canadien" would begin on Saturday. It particularly recommended the serial even to those who did not usually read novels, including "hommes instruits," members of the clergy, and all those "qui s'occupent de nos intérêts nationaux." In fact, the notice concluded, "*Que tous les Canadiens-Français lisent donc Le Chien d'Or!*"[444] On 15 October, under the title "Une oeuvre nationale," the newspaper included a letter dated "Québec, 10 octobre 1884," from a man who signed himself "Patriote." He never read novels of any kind, but he had been convinced by his wife to peruse this "chef-d'oeuvre" that rendered such a great homage "à notre religion et à notre nationalité." Now he was recommending it wholeheartedly to his children, his friends, and, most importantly, to those who gloried in the name of "patriote" itself.[445] The final notice in the *Etendard*, which began to appear in March 1885, announced the publication of the novel in two "beaux volumes." They cost one dollar for a deluxe set, and seventy-five cents "Sur papier ordinaire."[446]

On 6 March 1885, before the novel appeared in volume form as *Le Chien D'Or Légende Canadienne,* Trudel related to Kirby that he had had difficulty persuading the administrators of his newspaper to publish it as a book. The novel had not been a popular serial, and it had been criticized for its morality. He had, therefore, to retouch "certaines expressions" to make them more acceptable, particularly to his Roman Catholic readers. For this reason too, to protect himself from criticism about Kirby's portrait of Catholicism, Trudel had emphasized in the introduction that Kirby was "anglais protestant."[447] The additional material, however, was mainly aimed to remind readers that "*Le Chien d'Or*" was "un superbe hommage rendu aux ancêtres des Canadiens-Français."[448] This message was repeated in "La Légende Du Chien D'Or," an article that preceded the main text, and in notes on the text. Trudel began "La Légende Du Chien D'Or" with the epigraph from Alessandro Manzoni's *I Promessi Sposi* that Kirby had intended to include in *The Chien D'Or* when it was published in 1877. He concluded the article by reprinting the prospectus that ended by urging "tous les Canadiens-Français" to read the novel.[449]

Despite Trudel's hopes, *Le Chien D'Or* apparently had a limited success, at least when it was first published. A review of the French version of Kirby's work that appeared in the *Montreal Daily Star* on 4 April 1885 called the translation, which would "repay perusal," "remarkable for its ease and purity of language." Kirby has marked on his copy, however, "The writer certainly never read the book."[450] In May 1885, answering an inquiry from Kirby about reviews in the French newspapers in Quebec, James MacPherson Le Moine explained, "I see few of the French papers of Montreal & cannot say what opinion they expressed of the French 'Chien d or.' What I heard was favorable."[451] The next month William Henry Withrow, attending a meeting of the Royal Society of Canada in Ottawa, reported to Kirby, who was absent, "Much interest was expressed by some of the French members in the translation of the Chien d'or."[452] Still, as Trudel wrote to Le Moine on 13 February 1886, the costs of the publication, including its translation—Le Moine had previously written to Kirby that Le May had received "$400 to translate it"[453]—were not recovered by the newspaper. In Trudel's words, "le succès n'a pas couronné cette tentative de faire lire & apprécier un livre si éminemment Canadien." Nevertheless, he did not regret the money that was lost, and he would do his best to pay Kirby according to their contract.[454] Le May's last letter to Kirby on the subject recorded once again the great interest that he had taken in the novel and the "vif plaisir" that he had in translating it.[455]

But even if there was no immediate profit for either the *Etendard* or Kirby, the translation, which differed from its original not only in the changes demanded by Trudel but also in its vision of the nation as essentially French-Canadian, did make its way. On 12 November 1887 Valentin Augustus Landry wrote to Kirby to ask his permission to serialize "the French translation" of *The Chien D'Or* in *Evangeline*, the newspaper that he was establishing in Digby, Nova Scotia, "in the interest of the French Acadians of the Maritime Provinces." He wished "to commence" the novel "with the first issue; as it is very interesting and quite unfamiliar to our Acadians, we should consider it a great acquisition to our journal." Trudel, he reported, had agreed to the proposition; he now needed Kirby's permission. He promised, moreover, not to issue his serial "in pamphlet form," but to "advertise" the Montreal edition and to sell copies of it "without commission."[456] In the end, however, Landry chose Longfellow's *Evangeline* as his literary selection in the first issue of the newspaper published on 23 November 1887 and, thus, emphasized Acadian subject matter.

In 1898 Kirby discussed with L. C. Page and Company the possibility of having Le May's translation published in France. On 16 February, replying to the author about his inquiry on this "French edition," the publisher stated that its "representative," who would "shortly be in Europe," would "if circumstances make it advisable ... try and place a French edition."[457] On 25 February, answering Kirby's letter of 19 February on this subject, Page reiterated that its "representative" would do what he could "to make arrangements" for the French publication, but, it warned, "it is very unlikely that he will be able to make such arrangements unless a set of plates is already in existence of which you are the owner, or of which you can procure the use. Let us know ... also whether you know of any copyright for the French market or if you can procure the assignment to you, or to us, of such a copyright if any exists."[458] Negotiations continued over the next year during which Kirby inquired about plates of the *Etendard* edition—apparently none had been made. In the end, on 21 February 1899, the Boston publisher reported to Kirby that it had been "unable to make arrangements to place ... a French edition."[459]

Kirby's Death

On 25 February 1905 the Toronto *Globe* published an article on "Canada's Oldest Living Novelist." Its author, Frank Yeigh, an Ontario civil servant who took an avid interest in Canadian history, had interviewed Kirby at his house in "quiet old Niagara, the mother town of Ontario." He had found the author in what the latter described as " 'good old age ... amid old scenes, old books, old friends, and looking not without hope more to the future than to the past and waiting like Simeon of old for the consolation of Israel.' " For Kirby, as he further explained, this meant both " 'the federation of the British Empire, the mightiest instrument for good, after God's word and ordinances, that has ever been given to mankind' "—and a peaceful departure from this world.[460] Kirby died on 23 June 1906.

His death, followed by his "Funeral from his late residence to St. Mark's Cemetery, Niagara-on-the-Lake, on Tuesday, the 26th" June,[461] was noticed by many Canadian newspapers, especially in Ontario and Quebec. Several commented that, at nearly ninety, Kirby was "Canada's oldest litterateur";[462] that he had "always been known as a strong advocate" for a "British connection";[463] and that his last work was *Annals Of Niagara* (1896), which related "many almost forgotten stories of early days in the old capital."[464] All acknowledged that he was most "famous" as the author of *Le Chien d'or.*[465] In the words of the Montreal newspaper, the *Patrie,* for example, it was this "roman historique canadien qui lui valut une grande renommée."[466] Some added that this novel, which still enjoyed good sales, was "perhaps the best Canadian historical romance ever written."[467] In his presidential address on 14 May 1907 to the "English History, Literature, Archeology, Etc." section of the Royal Society of Canada, Nathanael Burwash, the Methodist minister who was "chancellor and president of Victoria University," Toronto, from 1887 to 1913,[468] described Kirby as the first English-Canadian man of letters who "won the attention of the outside world to Canadian themes and directed the feet of sentimental pilgrims to the holy places" of Canadian history.[469] Over the next hundred years the fame of Kirby and his novel waxed and waned, but both kept their stature as icons of Canadian literature.

Later Impressions of L. C. Page and Company Edition

After Kirby's death L. C. Page and Company continued to issue impressions of the 1897 edition of *Le Chien d'or.* All contained the same eight illustrations, although they were sometimes tipped in in a different order. Each impression also had the phrase "AUTHORISED EDITION" on its title-page, which was not dated. From 1911 on, however, the verso of the title-page carried not only the statement of copyright but also the number and date of the impression. Page, for example, issued what it called the twenty-second impression in October 1911 and the twenty-third in March 1913. Others, the twenty-fourth, the twenty-fifth, and the twenty-sixth, came out in March 1914, January 1916, and January 1917 respectively. In 1926, possibly to compete with the two editions that had recently been published in Toronto, Page issued the twenty-ninth impression in January and the thirtieth in September. The thirty-first appeared in May 1927. The thirty-second, and likely the last, was dated February 1936. Some of these impressions were distributed in Canada.

For many years Page also supplied the Montreal News Company with copies that carried its name on the title-page. This firm, for example, inserted in the July 1906 issue of *Bookseller And Stationer* an advertisement that listed "Important Books for Your Summer Trade." One of them was *The Golden Dog*, which was available in "Paper" for "50¢," in "Cloth" for "$1.25," and in "Leather" for "$2.00."[470] Some of these copies were sold by J. A. Kirouac, "booksellers and dealers in church ornaments" in de la Fabrique Street in Quebec.[471] Others were available from Morris Michaels, whose store in the rotunda of the Windsor Hotel in Montreal stocked, among other items, "Enamelled Souvenirs, Books, Pamphlets and Magazines."[472] A copy purchased in that shop was read in 1910 by Gertrude B. Goldsmith of Manchester, New Hampshire, who had borrowed it from a friend. After describing "The Golden Dog" as a "Story of old Quebec in time of Bigot. Bourgeoise Phillibert and his son the two heroes," she commented, "Interesting as a bit of history and gives fine atmosphere but rather long and slow as a story."[473]

The Canadian firm issued several other impressions. In 1908 it brought out a "Limited Tercentenary Edition" of five hundred copies to celebrate the three-hundredth anniversary of the founding of Quebec. Its title-page read *Limited Tercentenary Edition* / *The Golden Dog* / *(Le Chien d'Or)* / A Romance of the Days of Louis Quinze in Quebec / By William Kirby, F. R. S. C. / *Illustrated* / The Montreal News Company / Limited [four stylized acorns] MDCCCCVIII. This impression's origin with Page was signaled by the presence of this firm's monogram on the title-page. Possibly in 1908 as well, one hundred copies of a Page impression were produced with a title-page that carried the name of both the Montreal News Company Limited and the Musson Book Company Limited of Toronto. Some of these included "Limited Edition" on the title-page. The Montreal News Company also had its name on the title-page of impressions of the Page edition issued in 1913 and 1914. The Librairie Du Clergé at 47 Buade Street, Quebec, sold copies of the 1913 impression.

The 1921 Musson Edition

From the early 1920s until the early 1930s, there were six projects to republish *Le Chien d'or*. Some of this activity was due to the renewed interest in early Canadian literature inspired by the nationalistic feelings that resulted from Canada's achievements in World War One; some, from the mid 1920s on, to the efforts of Kirby's grandson to profit from his grandfather's name. The earliest of these projects was that of the Musson Book Company of Toronto. In its issue of August 1921 the *Canadian Magazine* announced in its "Book Reviews" that Musson was distributing "A NEW edition of the famous old book 'The Golden Dog.'" One of "a number of new editions" that this company had put out since its premises were destroyed by fire on 24 December 1920, it was "gratifying to know that this classic" would "again be on the Canadian market." "It is," the notice continued, "the most widely-read book on Canada [ever] published, and has held its place for many years in all parts of the Dominion." The edition was appearing "in sepia jacket, with a scene full of movement from the book, portrayed."[474]

This Musson edition was "an unabridged reprinting (from a new typesetting) of the first which, although much closer to it in substantive readings," introduced "a score of accidental alterations deriving largely from the publisher's house style."[475] The text, which consisted of 528 pages, was printed, according to the entry on the verso of its title-page, by the "Press of T. H. Best Printing Co., Limited, Toronto," and it had as its tipped-in frontispiece an unsigned "photolithograph from a watercolor painting"[476] by Charles William Jefferys, the artist who became well known for his illustrations of Canadian historical subjects. Inscribed at the bottom of this illustration of a troop of soldiers on horseback dispersing a crowd of habitants were the lines "The whole troop plunged madly at the crowd. A violent scuffle ensued; many *habitans* were ridden down."

The first impression of this publication was issued with five different title-pages. All read, "THE GOLDEN DOG / (LE CHIEN D'OR) / A

ROMANCE OF THE DAYS OF LOUIS QUINZE IN QUEBEC / BY / WILLIAM KIRBY, F. R. S. C.," and all reproduced the tablet of the Golden Dog. The publisher's imprint varied, however. One was "TORONTO: / MUSSON BOOK COMPANY, LIMITED / DISTRIBUTORS." A second was "QUEBEC: CHATEAU CIGAR AND NEWS STAND / CHATEAU FRONTENAC / QUEBEC / TORONTO: / MUSSON BOOK COMPANY, LIMITED / DISTRIBUTORS"; a third, "QUEBEC: / CHATEAU CIGAR & NEWS STAND / CHATEAU FRONTENAC"; and a fourth, "CAMBRIDGE BOOK STORE / HEADQUARTERS FOR SOUVENIRS / QUEBEC / TORONTO: / MUSSON BOOK COMPANY, LIMITED / DISTRIBUTORS." A fifth was "MONTREAL, QUE.: / F. E. PHELAN, LIMITED." Located on St. Catherine Street West in Montreal, in 1920–21 Phelan advertised itself as "The Largest Book Store in Canada."[477] A copy with this firm's title-page owned by the Royal Military College of Canada is inscribed, "Bought on the boat from Quebec to Montreal on our way home from Sydney Nova Scotia. August 7, 1923."

What was most likely a second impression of the 1921 Musson edition of *Le Chien d'or* was listed in *The Canadian Catalogue of Books* for 1921 and 1922 as having been published in 1922. This impression had the same unsigned illustration by Jefferys, although it was smaller, and carried the same information as the first, except that on the verso of the title-page "PRINTED IN CANADA" was added. The title, the author, and the reproduction of the tablet of the Golden Dog were also identical to the title-page of the first impression. The second impression had three variations in the publisher's imprint. One read "TORONTO: / MUSSON BOOK COMPANY, LIMITED / DISTRIBUTORS"; another, "CHATEAU CIGAR AND NEWS STAND / CHATEAU FRONTENAC / QUEBEC"; and still another, "QUEBEC / CAMBRIDGE BOOK STORE / HEADQUARTERS FOR SOUVENIRS."

The 1925 Musson Edition

In 1925 the Musson Book Company, Limited, of Toronto published an edition of *Le Chien d'or* that would dominate the market for the next four decades. Based on its 1921 typesetting, this new version had been abridged by Thomas Guthrie Marquis, a teacher who had retired early in order to immerse himself in Canadian culture. In his "Introduction," which appeared in all but one of the 1925 issues, Marquis explained that Kirby's text had undergone a "thorough revision." The author, he continued, "gathered together a vast amount of information bearing on the period of his story and of his characters . . . . As a result, *The Golden Dog*, as originally published," contained "patches of general and scientific information that" marred "the flow of the story and" wearied "the reader." The editor had, thus, "judiciously cut out" much of this material, although he had omitted nothing that was "essential to the narrative."[478]

Set in larger type than the 1921 edition, the new Musson version of Kirby's work ran to 580 pages of text. It was issued in a variety of casings, with different publishing information on the title-page, and with varying data. The most stripped-down issue was one prepared for use in Alberta schools. It, like all the other issues that appeared in 1925, contained the frontispiece by Jefferys that had already been used in the 1921 edition; in the lower left-hand corner, however, it was now signed "C. W. Jefferys." Like all these issues as well, it had five other illustrations tipped in throughout the text and "PRINTED IN CANADA / T. H. BEST PRINTING CO., LIMITED / TORONTO, ONT." on the verso of the title-page. Like two other early issues, Louis XIV was referred to as "Louis IV" in the "LIST OF ILLUSTRATIONS" and as "LOUIS IV." in the caption for the same illustration facing page 128. This issue, however, omitted Marquis' introduction, and it carried on its title-page, which had the same design as that of the 1921 edition, the title of this edition. The title-page read, thus, "THE GOLDEN DOG / (LE CHIEN D'OR) / A ROMANCE OF THE DAYS OF LOUIS QUINZE IN QUEBEC / BY / WILLIAM KIRBY, F. R. S. C. / [tablet of the Golden Dog] / *Authorised Edition for School / use in the Province of Alberta.* / TORONTO: / THE MUSSON BOOK COMPANY, / LIMITED."

Three other early issues had the Louis XIV errors, but they contained Marquis' introduction, although it was unsigned. They had as end-papers a map of the city of Quebec and of the environs of Quebec signed by Jefferys and a title-page that he had also designed. Signed and dated "1925," and enclosed in a fancy frame that had an open shell at the top, it carried the title "*The / Golden Dog / {Le Chien d'Or }/ A Romance / of / Old Quebec,*" a sketch of the tablet of the Golden Dog followed by the date "1736" in square brackets, and "*By / William Kirby, F. R. S. C.*" highlighted by three fleur-de-lis. The publisher's imprint on one of these issues was "*TORONTO /* The Musson Book Company / Limited." On another it was "Canada Railway News Co. / (Limited) / Montreal," a store in that city's Bonaventure Station. On still another, the publisher's imprint read, "*The American News Company, Ltd. / & Branches / Toronto Vancouver Halifax Ottawa / Montreal Winnipeg St.*

John / Hamilton." A copy of this issue owned by the University of Michigan was signed by the donor, who had apparently acquired it in Quebec in September 1927.

By then three more issues of the 1925 Musson edition had appeared. All three contained minor changes that included the correction of the "Louis IV" mistake to "Louis XIV" in the list of illustrations and to "LOUIS XIV." in the caption to the illustration facing page 128. The introduction in these issues was signed "T. G. Marquis." One had "*TORONTO / The Musson Book Company / Limited*" as the publisher's imprint on the title-page. Another had as this imprint "*Montreal: / Gordon & Gotch (Canada) Ltd.*" Gordon and Gotch were "wholesale newsdealers & booksellers" whose business was located on Craig Street West in Montreal.[479] The end-papers, title-page, and other preliminaries of these two issues were identical to the other 1925 ones, except for that for the Alberta schools. The third issue, a second for the Alberta schools, had the same title-page as the earlier issue "*for School use in the Province.*" The corrections made in these three issues appeared in all subsequent printings of the 1925 edition.

In 1929 Musson prepared a new impression of Kirby's novel that differed from the earlier issues only in the placing of its illustrations. "LOUIS XIV.," for example, now faced page 134 instead of page 128. This new, so-called "LARGE TYPE EDITION WITH ILLUSTRATION" was available in "Cloth" for $2.00, in "Antique Leather Craft" for $2.50, in "Full Crushed Levant" for $3.50, in "Half Crushed Levant" for $3.00, and in "Full Fine Grain Morocco" for $3.50. "THIN PAPER" was used in the last three bindings.[480] Some copies of this impression were issued with "*TORONTO / THE MUSSON BOOK COMPANY / LIMITED*" as the publisher's imprint on the title-page. Others recorded the publisher as "*The Cambridge Book Store / Leading Booksellers / Quebec, P. Q.*" Still others had on the title-page "TORONTO: / THE MUSSON BOOK COMPANY, / LIMITED" as the publisher's imprint and "*Authorized Edition for School / use in the Province of Alberta.*" The design of the title-page of this "School Edition" was the same as those in the earlier impression prepared for students.

Musson issued a new impression of the 1925 edition of *The Golden Dog* in 1941. "ALL RIGHTS RESERVED"; the MUSSON emblem, a maple leaf with the words "MADE IN CANADA"; "*Printed in Canada*"; and "PRESS OF THE HUNTER-ROSE CO., LIMITED, TORONTO" appeared in descending order on the verso of the title-page. The publisher's imprint on the title-page was "*TORONTO / The Musson Book Company / Limited.*" Forty-one copies of this impression were supplied in 1943 to the Canadian Committee, a "non-government organization . . . created in 1942 to provide information about Canada to British and American servicemen stationed in this country" during World War Two. When this committee, based in Ottawa, requested another five copies in 1944, however, the "GOLDEN DOG" was "out of print."[481]

A new impression was issued in 1946. It had the same publisher's imprint on the title-page as in 1941. On the verso of this page, however, only "ALL RIGHTS RESERVED" and the Musson emblem appeared. The printer's record in the form of the Hunter, Rose circular colophon was placed on the verso of the blank leaf that followed page 580. This impression was advertised in *The Canadian Catalogue of Books* for 1946 as a "New edition" that sold for "$2.50."[482] One bookstore whose stamp was entered on several extant copies was the Librairie Garneau of Quebec. It was probably a copy of this impression that was chosen as one of the "Canadian Books for Display" at the "National Book League's Exhibition of Book Design" held in London, England, in June 1947.[483]

Musson prepared yet another impression in 1949. This one replaced the illustrations in the earlier impressions with a new frontispiece, "The house of the Golden Dog," and four tipped-in illustrations by Estelle Muriel Kerr, an Ontario artist and author. It also had a new title-page that carried the same information as the earlier ones, but that had a square frame of two lines instead of the elaborate scrolls and curlicues and plain type instead of the italics and other fancy typefaces. "TORONTO / THE MUSSON BOOK COMPANY / LIMITED" was apparently the only publisher's imprint on the title-page. "ALL RIGHTS RESERVED" and the Musson emblem continued to appear on the verso of the title-page, but the printer's imprint was placed on page 580 in the form of the Hunter, Rose colophon. This version of the 1925 edition, which originally sold for $2.50, was available for "$4.50" in 1968.[484]

Two Projected Editions

While the Musson Book Company of Toronto was issuing its *Golden Dogs*, three other editions were also planned. In the early 1920s John William Garvin, who had already edited *The Collected Poems of Isabella Valancy Crawford* (1905), planned to prepare twenty-five volumes in a series called "MASTER-WORKS of CANADIAN LITERATURE." Volume "XV" was to be " 'The Golden Dog' (Le Chien d'Or), by William Kirby." Garvin's note to this projected volume explained, "One of the legends of 'Le Chien D'Or' suggested to Kirby the theme and plot of this remarkable historic romance. It was first published in 1877, but at that time brought no monetary profit to the author. It was subsequently pirated in several editions. But in 1897 L. C. Page and Company of Boston issued a revised and authorized edition with an Introduction by the author. This edition is reproduced in this Series."[485] William Douw Lighthall submitted a draft introduction for it to Garvin on 5 March 1923. Dated 27 February the same year, it praised Kirby as the pioneer who "revealed the possibilities of French-Canada's romantic past" and his novel as one that would "continue to delight an ever-increasing circle of lovers of historical romance."[486] *The Golden Dog*, however, was not one of the four volumes that appeared before the series was suspended due to Garvin's death in 1935.

On 25 October 1930 the *Toronto Daily Star* reported another scheme to publish an edition of *Le Chien d'or*. Felix Paul Greve, the German author known in Canada as Frederick Philip Grove, had become the "general manager and editor" of Graphic Publishers in Ottawa. Among his "ambitious plans" for the recently-established company was "the launching of a series of Canadian classics, historical and literary," that would "ultimately" include "all the worthwhile books of older Canadian life, from the Letters of Montcalm to Kirby's Golden Dog." Probably "50 to 60" in all, they would be "uniformly bound and edited by authorities"; they would sell "from $2 to $2.50."[487] Only two works were issued in "The Canada Series," however, one of them Frances Brooke's *The History of Emily Montague* (1769), which appeared in 1931.

Macmillan's Projected "Definitive" Edition

In his will, which was probated in August 1906, Kirby requested that John Colborne Kirby should "carefully preserve" his books, manuscripts, and papers, which included the manuscript of *Le Chien d'or* that Lovell, Adam, Wesson and Company had used as copy for its edition.[488] Much of this material, in fact, had been left intact and in situ in "the old Kirby homestead" in Niagara-on-the-Lake even after the death of this son in 1918. It was in the fall of 1924 that Lorne Pierce, the editor of the Ryerson Press from 1922 to 1960, heard on a visit to the town that John Colborne's son was occupying the house. Pierce knocked on its door, and when the younger William Kirby answered, the avid promoter of Canadian literature informed him that he was "writing a life of his grandfather" and wondered if he had any material.

"Boxes and Boxes" was the reply.[489] Thus began a relationship between Pierce and Kirby's grandson and then among Pierce, Kirby's grandson, and the Macmillan Company of Canada.

These connections, which lasted almost nine years, were sometimes difficult, but they had many results. By the time the article announcing "the discovery" of the Kirby "treasure trove" was published in the *Toronto Daily Star* on 17 March 1925,[490] Pierce and William Kirby were already "engaged in the sorting & classifying" of the "voluminous letters & documents" that had not "hitherto been public property."[491] Pierce, for example, made lists of books in Kirby's library and "arranged a sale in Toronto" of their "odds and ends."[492] Percy Parker Ghent, a local collector, "purchased a number of books" at this "auction."[493] Pierce also "arranged a sale of important documents in New York."[494] Among those auctioned at the Anderson Galleries in that city on 30 November 1925 were "papers and books"[495] that had once belonged to Christian Daniel Claus, the German-born "Indian department official" who in the 1780s "supervised ... the establishment of various groups of Six Nations Indians on British soil, particularly at the Bay of Quinte and the Grand River" in Ontario.[496] In addition, Pierce, having "made a contract" with the Kirby estate that gave him "sole rights as Editor, to publish all and sundry, as" he "saw fit,"[497] produced a new edition of *Annals of Niagara* (1927), edited *Alfred, Lord Tennyson and William Kirby: Unpublished correspondence to which are added some letters from Hallam, Lord Tennyson* (1929), and wrote *William Kirby The Portrait of a Tory Loyalist* (1929). All three were published by Macmillan which, under Hugh Eayrs, had set out to help build " 'a distinctively national Canadian literature' " by issuing works by Canadian authors.[498]

In May 1927 Macmillan signed one contract with Mary Susannah Blake Kirby, John Colborne Kirby's widow and the younger William Kirby's mother, to publish an edition of "THE GOLDEN DOG (LE CHIEN D'OR)"[499] and another with Pierce, "who was to edit and annotate the work."[500] The book was to sell for "not less than $2.00 ... cloth style, and not more than $3.50 ... cloth style." Kirby's daughter-in-law was to receive a "seven per cent" royalty on the first "two thousand five hundred copies" bought at the "trade list (retail) price"; after this number the royalty was to increase incrementally until it reached "15%" when "10000" copies had been purchased.[501] Pierce was to get a "three per cent" royalty on the trade list price on each of the first "ten thousand ... copies" sold, after which his payments would "cease."[502] This "definitive edition" was formally announced in the note on "The Famous William Kirby Material" that appeared in Macmillan's catalogue of new books for the fall and winter of 1927–28.[503]

By then Pierce had begun to prepare what he later called "a critical introduction, a definitive text, and notes, with a few illustrations." The only possible choice for a copy-text, he decided, was the Lovell edition. Kirby's grandson, thus, lent him a copy of this edition corrected by his grandfather. When the younger Kirby became "anxious to have" it "returned," however, Pierce gave it back and used as his "working copy" the 1921 Musson edition. It "perpetuated all the errors of the first Lovell edition. But this book was the full story as Kirby first wrote it, and as he wanted it." From this version of the first edition Pierce set out to create "an impeccable text."

This "editorial work," as he further explained, "was not exactly that of a hack." To perfect the text and to prepare the introduction and the notes required much effort. There were "literally thousands of blunders" in "Names, dates, quotations etc." Pamphile Le May's translation helped him "to correct certain French songs etc in the original," but there were "endless searches" for other data. The job itself took much longer, therefore, than Pierce had calculated. Still, by the fall of 1932 he had "completed one third of the MS." He had also "assisted Mr. Eayrs in getting possession of the plates" that Jarrold and Sons had acquired from L. C. Page and Company to produce its English edition, and he had "made arrangements" to use Charles William "Jefferys' drawings."[504] He intended, furthermore, to finish "this work ... for publication in the autumn of 1933."[505]

This event might well have happened had there not been other problems. One was the economic downturn in the 1930s that meant that for many years the publication of new books had to be seriously curtailed. Another was the difficulty experienced by Pierce and Macmillan in dealing with Kirby's grandson. What Eayrs later described as his "badgering"[506] probably began in the fall of 1927 shortly after Kirby heard from the "Treasury Department, Province of Ontario Pictures," that it was interested in producing a film of "The Golden Dog ... within the near future."[507] Kirby's pressuring really got underway in the following spring. On 7 April 1928 he reported to Eayrs that he was expecting to have to "transmit" a copy of "the G. D." to "the picture people inside of the next couple of weeks." It was "deplorable," therefore, that, since Pierce apparently planned to "hold over" his edition "for a season," he would have to give them a copy of "the old Musson Edition."[508] On 16 April, having spoken to Pierce and realized "his present ill health & strain generally," Kirby, nevertheless, suggested to Eayrs that it would be desirable if "the Dr." could finish both the life of his grandfather and the edition of "G. D." for "1929 instead of spreading them over for 2 years more."[509] Despite Eayrs' equivocal reply to this letter, Kirby still discussed with Pierce the possibility of publishing his edition in 1928. When in June 1928 the latter assured him that "the MSS" of the novel would not be "ready by 15th July," Kirby persuaded him to try to "have it ready by the 1st of Oct.," a date that would guarantee a 1929 publication.[510]

Kirby discussed the date of publication of "The Golden Dog" again with Pierce in August 1928. This time the latter promised to have the novel "groomed" for 1930.[511] By November, however, Kirby was writing again about the need to have the publication date of "the Definitive Ed." of *Le Chien d'or* confirmed as 1930[512] and the desirability of bringing it out in conjunction with the two films of the work that he was negotiating. The most recent possibility was that the Quebec government would make "a great propaganda film of the story."[513] On 28 November 1928 Eayrs tried to reassure Kirby "that THE GOLDEN DOG, Definitive Edition," would "normally" appear "in the Autumn of 1930." "If by any chance it could be done before the Fall of 1930 so much the better," he added.[514] Pierce's edition, however, did not appear that year.

On 19 January 1931 Kirby wrote again about "the definitive Ed. of the Golden Dog." "Things," he informed the publisher, were finally "shaping towards a possible motion picture production of it." It seemed "a crime," therefore, "that the present (pirates) … should reap the benefit of any advertising, which would be tremendous in this case, from such proceedings." He was proposing, thus, that "a cheap definitive Ed. be undertaken at an early date, which could be put into a more elaborate form, at a later time, as the demand should warrant." "I realize," he continued, "what you say respecting the general publishing business, but I do feel that when I am called upon to enter into negotiations such as the above, that we ought to be able to put into the producers hands, our edition, and make it the basis for all advertising etc. which goes with the proposition."[515] When Eayrs replied three days later, he agreed with Kirby "as to the wisdom of synchronizing the definitive edition in book form with the motion picture when it" was produced. But he did not think that it was possible, given the economic conditions, "to issue the definitive edition this year."[516]

In June 1931 Kirby wondered if a proposal by the Federal Government in Ottawa "to provide adequate protection in order to stimulate Canadian publishing Houses" might "not assist in the Definitive Edition of the Golden Dog being undertaken at some reasonable early date."[517] The position of Macmillan had not changed, however. "We still feel," Eayrs replied, "we cannot, in view of conditions obtaining in the publishing business, not merely here but in the States and in London, go further in the matter of the Definitive Edition of 'The Golden Dog'. We are bound because of conditions obtaining now, and prospects as we can see them for the fall and winter, to keep our lists of new books at a very low level indeed, it is not a matter of choice: it is rather one of necessity."[518] Despite this refusal to publish a new edition of *Le Chien d'or*, it was this year that the publisher acquired "the plates" of what he called "the old English edition"; that is, the edition of *Le Chien d'or* first published by Jarrold in 1899.[519]

Macmillan's St. Martin's Classics Edition

Ironically, during the months of 1931 when Hugh Eayrs was assuring William Kirby that it was not possible to bring out Lorne Pierce's edition of *Le Chien d'or*, he was negotiating an edition of Kirby's novel that was to be part of the St. Martin's Classics that the Macmillan Company of Canada published for the use of schools. E. C. (Edward Carruthers) Woodley, a Quebec author and educator who "from 1930 to his retirement in 1945 was a special officer of the department of education for the province of Quebec,"[520] had apparently agreed to prepare this edition well before Eayrs wired him on 9 February 1931 to ask if he could submit his manuscript by 1 April. The reason for the request was that "twenty-five hundred copies of the GOLDEN DOG" were "required for use in Alberta this approaching school year." Eayrs thought that if Macmillan "could rush the book through" the press, it would be both "a nice start" for the editor and good business for the publisher.[521] Woodley, who was to receive a royalty of "6%, on the list price of the book,"[522] agreed to the proposal the same day.

Throughout February 1931 the editor and the publisher exchanged letters about the length and the nature of the St. Martin's text. On 10 February Woodley explained to Eayrs that he would use as his base text the 1925 Musson edition; he called it "the ordinary edition which" had "been compressed a little by Marquis." Still, this "book of 580 pages" was "about twice the length it should be" for the Macmillan series. Woodley proposed, thus, to "abridge" the novel. "Kirby's Golden Dog," he told Eayrs, contained "two complete stories," that of "the Golden Dog" and that of "the tragic Romance of Caroline of Beaumanoir." Woodley would concentrate on "the story of the Golden Dog proper, the tale of the antagonism of Philibert and Bigot, and the loves of the de Repentigny and Philibert families. Caroline of Beaumanoir" would "hardly enter into the tale at all," although "an occasional note" in the text might be necessary "to explain an allusion in the Golden Dog which" was "due to the blending of the two tales." To this shortened text Woodley would add an "introduction" with "sections dealing with the life of Kirby; the historic background of the incidents; Kirby's treatment of his theme and the circumstances of his writing; also a bibliography of the subject and the closing years of the French Régime."[523] Three days later, on 13 February, Woodley informed Eayrs that he "should plan for 250–300 pages," thirty of which would be for the "necessary introduction and notes." He did not, he affirmed, wish "to spoil the story by too great abridgment."[524] The next day Eayrs approved Woodley's plan. He had concerns, however. A "book in the St. Martin's Classics Series" retailed "for 50 cents." "Therefore," he continued, "I think all possible compression of the story proper should be used, and that applies with just as much, or perhaps even more force, to both front and back matter."[525] On 20 February Woodley wrote to tell Eayrs that his "work on the GOLDEN DOG" was "progressing very well." He had "succeeded in completely separating the two stories" so that the "book" read "as a continuous narrative, without any appearance of the very large excisions" that he had made. Because he had reduced "a volume of 230,000 words to 92,000," with the added "5000" for the introduction and notes, the edition would be "a total of 97,000 words."[526] When Eayrs replied on 24 February, he expressed again his preference for "a still shorter book," but he did not wish "to abbreviate the story so much" that "its quality" would be hurt. "We are not a House to spoil a ship for a ha'porth of tar," he advised, "and if you feel that any further abridgment is positively not practical, then we must leave it with you."[527]

When the edition was printed, its text was 223 pages or just over 80,000 words. Its chapters had no titles. All but two references to Caroline de St Castin had been omitted. Four passages that Woodley wrote as links to Kirby's text appeared in italics. It also had a four-page "Introduction," a three-page "Biographical Note On William Kirby," and a four-page "Glossary" that provided "Notes On Persons," "Notes On Places," and "Miscellaneous Notes." The opening paragraph of the introduction explained that "Kirby's great story" was "a very long historical romance" with "many bypaths" and "two complete tales," that "of the Golden Dog" and that of "the dark tragedy of Caroline of Beaumanoir." In his edition Woodley had told "only the story of the Golden Dog, the tale of the mutual hatred of Bigot and Philibert, and of the young lives broken by that hatred."[528]

It is not clear when Woodley submitted his manuscript, but it was being printed in May 1931. On 29 May he was sent "galleys 1–27."[529] By 4 June Macmillan planned to mail "galleys 36–48," "proof of the introduction," and, if they were ready, "galleys 49–55."[530] Although Woodley and the publisher exchanged letters about the proofs for the next month, by late July the St. Martin's Classics edition of "THE GOLDEN DOG / (LE CHIEN D'OR) / A ROMANCE OF OLD QUEBEC / BY / WILLIAM KIRBY, F. R. S. C. / SHORTENED, WITH INTRODUCTION AND GLOSSARY / BY / E. C. WOODLEY, M. A." had been issued in Toronto by "THE MACMILLAN COMPANY OF CANADA LIMITED, AT ST. MARTIN'S HOUSE." It was registered at the copyright office in Ottawa on 3 August 1931. By the end of the year the standing type of the Macmillan edition had been further corrected, and plates had been made.

This shortened version of *Le Chien d'or*, based on the already abbreviated 1925 Musson edition, thus began its life of more than forty-five years. It arrived "too late to secure use in Alberta" for the school year 1931–32;[531] still, by 12 November 1931 it had sold about "750" copies, "almost wholly" in Ontario. The publisher, however, was canvassing the edition in the "West," and despite the economy's being "dull as ditch water" there, it was hoping "to get a substantial order."[532] Sales of the book in Quebec were slow because it was "not on the general market." Nevertheless, on 25 November 1931 Woodley was looking "forward with assured hope" that his edition would soon be adopted for use in the English-speaking schools of the province.[533] In fact, according to the changes to its title-page over the years, by 1932 this version of Kirby's novel had been "*Authorized by the Ministers of Education for British Columbia and Quebec*"; by 1936 it had been "*Authorized by the Ministers of Education for British Columbia, Quebec and Nova Scotia.*" It also formed part of the high school curriculum in Ontario. In an advertisement in the *Toronto Daily Star* on 30 August 1941, for example, Simpson's, one of the major department stores in Toronto, listed the "St. Martin's Edition" of "The Golden Dog," for sale at fifty cents, as one of the books for Grade Ten English.[534] Altogether there were at least fifteen impressions of this version of Kirby's novel from the time that the plates were made in late 1931 to sometime in the 1950s; these included the ones dated 1932, 1935, 1936, 1937, 1938, 1939, 1940, in which year there were two, 1942, 1943, 1944, 1945, and 1948, and two undated impressions that appeared later. Copies of the book were still available in 1977. By then its price had risen to "$1.50."[535] It had also survived a near lawsuit that, had it continued, might have killed it just as it had ended any hope of Pierce ever finishing his edition of *Le Chien d'or.*

Kirby's Grandson versus the Macmillan Company of Canada and Lorne Pierce

William Kirby's frustration at the non-appearance of Lorne Pierce's edition of his grandfather's novel was further exacerbated when he learned of the publication of the "condensed version" of this work in the St. Martin's Classics. He, thus, hired a law firm in St. Catharines, Ontario, to launch an action against the Macmillan Company of Canada. This suit, outlined in a letter dated 23 March 1932, alleged that Macmillan's "mongrel edition" used material in its introduction that was owned by the younger Kirby, and that it breached the contract between the author's daughter-in-law and the publisher to issue a " 'definitive edition.' " It further argued that the appearance of "the dwarfed edition," which was one-quarter the size of the original novel, "practically shut off completely the market for a definitive and authorized edition of Le Chien D'Or." [536]

In its reply of 2 April 1932, the law firm hired by Macmillan explained "very fully ... the position" of the case "as viewed by" its client. The Kirbys were "in error in claiming to have a copyright in 'The Golden Dog,' " for it had "been in the public domain for a number of years." There had been no breach of the contract between Kirby's daughter-in-law and the publisher. The firm still intended to publish Pierce's edition, but it was "not ready" and could not "be ready for at least six months." Besides, it was "well recognized that" it was "not a good time to put a book on the market," especially when "both the Company and Mrs. Kirby might lose a considerable amount of money by a precipitate publication." The St. Martin's Classics edition "was undertaken for an entirely different purpose. This edition was prepared so that the school children of the Dominion could have an opportunity of reading one of the foremost Canadian Novels in an abridged form." The letter further explained, "The original book is entirely too long for this purpose. This book is sold almost entirely to Provincial Departments of Education and Boards of Education and appeals only to younger students. Our client is fully satisfied that, rather than detrimentally affecting the market for the definitive edition, it enlarges the market by creating a greater demand for the full size book." It concluded that Macmillan hoped that "the matter" could be arranged "on an amicable basis without the necessity of suit."[537]

Negotiations to settle the case dragged on, nevertheless. In a letter that Hugh Eayrs wrote to Pierce on 28 May 1932, he explained that Kirby was "impossible." The only way out of a suit seemed to be a "new contract for the definitive edition" and "a guarantee of publication date" from the editor. It was at that point that the publisher suggested that it print an impression "of the old English edition" and add Pierce's "annotations and so on."[538] Pierce's response was his "Memorandum Re Kirby." After a long description of his dealings with Kirby, his accomplishments with the Kirby material, and his determination to finish the edition, Pierce terminated this document by offering to "drop out" and let "the Estate ... find a competent man to complete the work."[539] Probably on 24 October 1932 he also wrote a letter to Kirby in which he repeated the points that he had made in his memorandum. This letter, however, was answered by Kirby's lawyer, who announced that Pierce's correspondence with Kirby could be used in the case against Macmillan. Pierce, furious, toyed with launching his own action.

Despite these events, by December 1932 Kirby and his mother had "consented to settle." The agreement, which was signed by the various parties in January 1933, involved several terms. Macmillan was to pay Kirby's daughter-in-law and grandson "the sum of $500.00 cash." It was also to pay "the plaintiffs' costs on the basis of solicitor and client in the sum of $300.00." All claims among the parties "in respect of The Golden Dog" were to be cancelled. The publisher was "to turn over to the Plaintiffs ... all material in respect of The Golden Dog" that it had, "including the revision of Dr. Pierce in so far as" it had "been completed" and "the original plates of the book purchased by" Macmillan "in England."[540] These terms being fulfilled, the case closed in February 1933 when Kirby and his lawyer reimbursed Macmillan the sum of $3.43 for shipping "2 cases" that contained the plates of "Kirby The Golden Dog" to Niagara-on-the-Lake.[541]

McClelland and Stewart's New Canadian Library Edition

The last edition of *Le Chien d'or* published in the twentieth century was the second abridgment of the 1925 Musson edition. Produced by McClelland and Stewart Limited as one "of the seventeen pre-1900 prose works issued in the Main series of the" New Canadian Library (NCL),[542] like seven others in this category, it was shortened for reasons of cost, and for what

Jack McClelland, the president of the publishing firm, considered the needs of the contemporary reader. Derek Crawley, the professor of English who prepared Kirby's work, was "told how much of the text to cut," but was "otherwise given a free editorial hand in choosing" a "base text and determining" how much of it to excise.[543]

Thus instructed, Crawley "substantially" reduced the text of the 1925 edition to 307 pages or about 110,000 words. His introduction reveals what he considered to be "the tastes of the modern reader." Beginning with the statement that while most Canadians had "heard of William Kirby's *The Golden Dog*," "too few" had actually "read it," he suggested that "the 678 pages of the first edition" were "a discouraging length for the average reader." With this new edition, however, there was "little excuse for leaving this famous Canadian story unread!" The novel, moreover, lent "itself to cutting." Crawley, for example, had eliminated "details of feasts, social entertainments and the niceties of decorous conversation"; characters like "the brother of Angélique" des Meloises and "the itinerant notary, Master Pothier"; and passages "devoted to sticky love scenes between Amélie and Pierre and ... Angélique's flirtations." He had also reduced wherever "possible the historical details not directly related to characters and events in the story."[544] When W. H. (William Herbert) New reviewed Crawley's version in *Canadian Literature*, he commented that while the "Gothic atmosphere" of Kirby's "romance" had been maintained, its function "as a political exemplum ... to show that corruption weakens from within" had been lost. The novel, in fact, had become "primarily ... an exotic entertainment."[545]

Although Crawley signed his introduction "Queen's University, Spring, 1967,"[546] his edition was not issued until the spring of 1969. Its title-page read "THE / GOLDEN DOG / [LE CHIEN D'OR] / *A Romance of Old Quebec* / by William Kirby FRSC / [ornament] / Introduction *Derek Crawley* / [small ornament] General Editor *Malcolm Ross* [same small ornament] / New Canadian Library No 65 / [publisher's insignia] / McCLELLAND AND STEWART LIMITED / TORONTO/MONTREAL." A paperback like the other NCLs, it had a predominantly white and gold cover designed by Robert Daigneault; a sketch of Kirby appeared on its front.

Reprints of this McClelland and Stewart edition were issued in 1973, 1976, 1977, 1984, 1989, and 1993. The first three had a cover that was mainly red and gold with one of the abstract designs on the front that had been introduced in the New Canadian Library in 1970. The last three had a cover that reflected the designs used in the series in the 1980s; this one was largely black and white with, on its front, a sketch of a woman mourning beside a tomb. The price of this edition rose from $2.95 in 1969 to $3.95 in 1979 and to $4.95 in 1981. In 1984 it cost $5.95, in 1987 $6.95, and in 1994 $8.95. It was still listed at that price when *Canadian Books In Print*, from which these data were taken, ceased publishing its annual volume in 2006. In February 2009 it was listed in *Bowker's Global Books In Print* as "Out of Print" and "Hard to Find."[547] *The Golden Dog* sold 10,468 copies between 1969 and 1979. These included 989 in 1974, 1,506 in 1975, and 1,767 in 1976, the three years when the sale of books in the NCL series peaked.[548]

Electronic Versions

Since the early twenty-first century suppliers have provided what at least two scholarly editors have called "print-on-demand artifacts" of scarce texts, including *Le Chien d'or*.[549] Reprinted from electronic databases like Early Canadiana Online, these one-offs of Kirby's novel were listed in 2009 for as much as $64.95 (US) and £35.99.[550] A copy purchased in 2007 for $38.88 (US) from Dodo Press, a specialist "in the publication and distribution of rare and out-of-print books," reproduced the 1897 L. C. Page and Company edition. It provided no information about the source of the text, however, and its back cover contained several incorrect statements about both Kirby and his novel. Other print-on-demand versions are equally unreliable.

Twentieth-Century Reprints of the French Translation

As well as the impressions of the L. C. Page and Company edition and the four new editions published in English after Kirby's death, there were reprintings of Pamphile Le May's translation of *Le Chien d'or*. In 1926 a second edition was published in Quebec by Librairie Garneau. A two-volume paperback, its title-pages read, "WILLIAM KIRBY / [line] / LE CHIEN D'OR / [smaller line] / Traduit de l'anglais par / PAMPHILE LE MAY / [same smaller line] / SECONDE ÉDITION / TOME I [II] / [same smaller line] / QUÉBEC / LIBRAIRIE GARNEAU, LIMITÉE / 47, rue Buade, 47 / 1926." Opposite the title-page in Volume One was a tipped-in photograph of Kirby that, according to Benjamin Sulte, was taken when the author visited Quebec in 1865. This volume also contained "Un Mot Au Lecteur" and a preface written by Sulte.

In the note for the reader, the publisher expressed pride in being able to bring out a work "qui fit les délices de la génération d'il y a quarante ans, et dont le texte français n'apparaît que peu souvent chez les bouquinistes, et s'y vend fort cher."[551] In the preface Sulte praised Kirby's novel for, among other reasons, showing that French Canadians had "une âme collective." He listed several French-Canadian authors, including Narcisse-Henri-Édouard Faucher de Saint-Maurice, Louis Fréchette, Pamphile Le May, and Joseph Marmette, whose works Kirby was supposed to have read in the Legislative Library during his stay in Quebec in 1865. Sulte also related what was almost certainly an exaggerated account of his own role in the creation of the novel.[552] At the end of the text, which had been revised and polished by Le May, there were several "Notes Historiques" prepared by Sulte. This new edition received at least two enthusiastic reviews. One, by Damase Potvin, was published in the *Terroir* in June 1926; the other, by Gérard Malchelosse, appeared the following June in the *Revue Nationale*. Potvin particularly admired the novel because it allowed French Canadians to see that they had "une héroïque histoire."[553]

One further comment on this edition was made in a letter that Kirby's grandson wrote on behalf of his mother. Dated 24 January 1928, in it he asked the Librairie Garneau "to withdraw" the edition, "to undertake to destroy all unsold copies, together with all plates, matrixes, standing type, and all forms in which the book" might exist, and to pay "a minimum of 10% royalty" to Mary Susannah Blake Kirby.[554] There is no evidence, however, that the Kirbys had renewed the author's copyright on the French translation within the year of its expiration in 1913. It is unlikely, therefore, that they had a case against the publisher. Certainly the plates of this corrected edition were not destroyed.

Using these plates, in fact, Éditions Garneau published a new impression in 1971. Issued in two volumes bound in one, its title-page, which had a sketch of the tablet of the Golden Dog at its top, read "William Kirby / LE CHIEN D'OR / Traduit de l'anglais par / PAMPHILE LE MAY / Troisième édition / [star] / Première [Deuxième] partie / [publisher's insignia] / Éditions Garneau, / 47 rue Buade, / Québec." This impression reproduced the photograph of Kirby, Sulte's preface, and his notes. It had a new introduction, however, in which the publisher called Kirby's novel a "grand classique canadien" and Le May's translation "une oeuvre de création bien que son honnêteté de traducteur ne pourra jamais être mise en doute."[555] Briefly noticed in the Montreal *Devoir* on 28 July 1971 as a novel "écrit au siècle dernier par un anglophone québécois,"[556] its availability for $4.95 had been announced in the same newspaper on 24 July. "Dans ce livre," this advertisement proclaimed, "l'auteur fait une évocation colorée des évènements qui constituent la trame de l'histoire de la Nouvelle-France au cours de la première partie du XVIII siècle."[557]

The third impression of the 1926 edition was published in two volumes by Stanké of Montreal in 1989 as part of the Québec 10/10 series. Its title-page read simply "William Kirby / Le Chien d'Or / Stanké roman [insignia of 10/10 series]." This reprint kept Sulte's notes, but it had a new preface by Roger Lemelin, and it added a "Dossier" of extracts of comments made by various critics on Kirby's novel. In his preface the author of *Les Plouffes* (1948), the well-loved work about life in Quebec, called *Le Chien d'Or* a "grand roman." It so enriched the reader's knowledge of the history of Quebec that he wondered why it had not yet inspired "chez nos créateurs le livret d'un opéra ou un film historique."[558]

Le Chien d'or *in Other Media*

In fact, there had been various attempts to transform *Le Chien d'or* into other media. Two were successful. In the year after the publication of the novel, Kirby himself produced "Caroline and La Corriveau," a "TABLEAU" in four parts "From the 'Chien d'or.'" It was presented on 16 January 1878 at an entertainment for the benefit of the Niagara Mechanics' Institute at the Court House in Niagara-on-the-Lake.[559] In 1951 Radio-Canada broadcast in its series "*Les Grands Romans Canadiens*" a dramatization of "'Le Chien d'or,'" which it described as "un des plus célèbres romans historiques canadiens." Based on Pamphile Le May's translation, the first of its two parts was aired on 2 September 1951.[560]

Maria Susan Rye's attempt to have Kirby's play based on an episode in his novel produced in England and William Kirby's various efforts to have a film made from his grandfather's work were two of several unsuccessful projects to present the novel in other forms. In August 1892 Kirby exchanged letters with Louis A. Tonchet, who wrote from Cambridge, Massachusetts, to ask permission to dramatize the "story" for "a stock company" that would perform it "in Large cities."[561] When Kirby responded favourably, Tonchet agreed to pay the author "one quarter (1/4) of the first payment and Royalties." The dramatist thought that his play "could be staged, May be in six months. Perhaps in two years."[562] There is no evidence that Tonchet's adaptation was ever performed, however.

In October 1906 Rodolphe Girard, the French-Canadian dramatist and novelist who was working as a civil servant in Ottawa, informed his friend and fellow journalist Albert Laberge, whose *La Scouine* (1918) has been described as "le premier roman naturaliste des lettres québécoises,"[563] that he was preparing Kirby's "roman célèbre"[564] for "le Théâtre National. Affaire d'argent, voilà tout."[565] Four months later, in February 1907, Girard, having submitted his dramatization to the Montreal company, told Laberge that he was awaiting its response. "On me promet beaucoup de succès avec cette pièce," he stated, "Je le souhaite."[566] The same year Girard obtained a copyright for his play, but it was apparently never produced.

For several years, from 1919 to 1924, Launcelot Cressy Servos, claiming at one point to be functioning "as a co-author" with Kirby's grandson, prepared "dramatic and liter[ar]y works" based on *Le Chien d'or*.[567] One of these was "La Corriveau," a script adapted in part from the passages in Kirby's novel having to do with the so-called "Affair of the Poisons" in seventeenth-century France. An "Aierial Drama" featuring Louis XIV as a tenor and Louise de la Vallière, the "King's Mistress," as a contralto, it was the ninth episode of what Servos described as "this great Canadian drama" that was intended to be broadcast as a radio serial.[568] Another was "THE GOLDEN DOG or Le Chien d'Or an Operatic Drama" in four acts. Servos copyrighted these adaptations in Canada and in the United States.

Popular Reception of Kirby's Novel

In addition to the efforts to present *Le Chien d'or* in other media, there is more evidence of its popularity. In advertisements, columns, and letters that appeared in such newspapers as the Toronto *Globe* and the *Toronto Daily Star*, it was often described as a "favorite" book,[569] or as one of the "best" novels to "represent the works of Canadian authors to readers who" wished "to know something of Canadian life."[570] In this capacity it was sometimes offered as a gift to foreigners or to such distinguished visitors to Canada as Prince George, the future Duke of Kent. " 'The Golden Dog,' by William Kirby," for instance, was one of the twenty books presented to him when he came to Quebec in 1928.[571] By this time "a blind girl living in Lunenburg, Nova Scotia," had laboriously made a copy of the novel "in braille by hand"; in 1927 its "13 volumes" were held in the library of the Canadian National Institute for the Blind in Toronto.[572] On 14 May 1988 it was the subject of Donald Jones' column on "Historical Toronto" in the *Toronto Star*; the article described "*The Golden Dog*" as "one of the most famous Canadian novels of all time."[573] The next year "*The Golden Dog*" was reported as being read and discussed at book clubs.[574]

Le Chien d'or permeated popular Canadian culture in other ways. At their annual at-homes held in the early 1930s at the Art Gallery of Ontario, members of the Canadian Literature Club of Toronto dressed as characters from Canadian books. In 1932 "an onlooker recognized Amelie from Kirby's Golden Dog";[575] the next year the winner of the first prize in "the costume contest" was a woman "representing Angelique de Meloise from Kirby's 'Golden Dog.' "[576] In 1947 this character, described as a "proud, pompadoured daughter of New France," took part in a "Cavalcade of Canadiana" pageant at the Canadian National Exhibition.[577] The same year one of the objects on display at the Exhibition was the incomplete early holograph manuscript of "William Kirby's 'The Golden Dog,' " which was then owned by Launcelot Cressy Servos.[578]

Especially in Quebec, where souvenirs like brooches, mugs, plates, and postcards featuring images of the Golden Dog could be purchased, some of the interest in its story arose from the tablet over the front door of the city's main post office. It was, however, often an edition of Kirby's "splendid work of fiction," either in English or in French, that was "doubtless responsible for bringing many tourists to Quebec" in the first place.[579] It was also Kirby's version of the legend of the Golden Dog that lodged itself in literary criticism as a major work of early Canadian prose.

Critical Reception of Kirby's Novel

Since almost its first publication, Kirby's name and that of his most famous creation have regularly appeared in critical sources in Canada, Great Britain, and the United States. They have been treated in such standard Canadian biographical dictionaries as *A Cyclopaedia Of Canadian Biography: Being Chiefly Men Of The Time* (1886) edited by George Maclean Rose; the various editions of *The Macmillan Dictionary of Canadian Biography* (1926 ff.); and the *Dictionary of Canadian Biography* (Volume 13, 1994). They have been dealt with in such encyclopedias as Grolier's *Encyclopedia Canadiana* (1957 ff.) and *The Canadian Encyclopedia* (1985 ff.). They have had entries in literary dictionaries, including *Biographical Dictionary And Synopsis of Books* (1896) edited by Charles Dudley Warner; *The Oxford Companion to Canadian History and Literature* (1967) by Norah Story and its successors; *A Dictionary of Literature in the English Language From Chaucer to 1940* (1970) compiled and edited by Robin Myers; *Dictionnaire Des Oeuvres Littéraires Du Québec ... Des Origines À 1900* (1978) edited by Maurice Lemire; and *Dictionary of*

Literary Biography: ... *Canadian Writers Before 1890* (1990) and *Encyclopedia of Literature in Canada* (2002), both edited by W. H. New.

They have been discussed in histories of Canadian literature. John George Bourinot's *Our Intellectual Strength And Weakness: A Short Historical And Critical Review Of Literature, Art And Education In Canada* (1898), published in both Canada and England under the auspices of the Royal Society of Canada, is an early example. Others include Thomas Guthrie Marquis' chapter on "English-Canadian Literature" in *Canada And Its Provinces: A History Of The Canadian People And Their Institutions* (Volume 12: *The Dominion Missions; Arts And Letters,* 1914) edited by Adam Shortt and Arthur George Doughty; *The Cambridge History of English Literature* (Volume 14, 1917) edited by A. W. Ward and A. R. Waller; Camille Roy's *Histoire De La Littérature Canadienne* (1930); and *Literary History Of Canada: Canadian Literature in English* (1965 and 1976) edited by Carl F. Klinck and others.

Studies on specific aspects of Canadian literature also consider Kirby and *Le Chien d'or.* Although they concentrated on *The U. E.,* both Leslie Monkman in *A Native Heritage: Images Of The Indian In English-Canadian Literature* (1981) and Daniel Coleman in *White Civility: The Literary Project of English Canada* (2006) dealt briefly with Kirby's novel. Carole Gerson discussed it from several angles in *A Purer Taste: The Writing And Reading Of Fiction In English In Nineteenth-Century Canada* (1989). Dennis Duffy devoted a chapter to "William Kirby and the Garden" in *Gardens, Covenants, Exiles: Loyalism in the Literature of Upper Canada / Ontario* (1982), as did Margot Northey in *The Haunted Wilderness: The Gothic and Grotesque in Canadian Fiction* (1976). Its publishing history has been explored in such works as H. Pearson Gundy's *Book Publishing And Publishers In Canada Before 1900* (1965); George L. Parker's *The Beginnings of the Book Trade in Canada* (1985); and *History Of The Book In Canada,* Volume 2: *1840–1918* (2005) edited by Yvan Lamonde, Patricia Lockhart Fleming, and Fiona A. Black.

William Renwick Riddell's *William Kirby,* the first book on the author, appeared in 1923 in the Makers of Canadian Literature series edited by Lorne Pierce. Its chapter on Kirby's "Prose Works" was devoted to the " 'Golden Dog.' "[580] Pierce's *William Kirby The Portrait of a Tory Loyalist* (1929), based on "the bewildering mass of material" that he had helped Kirby's grandson organize in the 1920s,[581] provided a comprehensive survey of Kirby and his works, including a long chapter on his only novel. Much of this information was repeated in Ken McLean's "William Kirby" (1986), an entry that appeared in the "Profiles in Canadian Literature" series edited by Jeffrey M. Heath, and in Northey's "William Kirby and His Works" (1989), issued in Volume Two of the Fiction Series of *Canadian Writers And Their Works* edited by Robert Lecker, Jack David, and Ellen Quigley. In "Abridgment As Criticism: A Textual Study Of William Kirby's *The Golden Dog*," an MA thesis submitted to the University of Alberta in 1980, Leonard Vandervaart, concentrating on the differences between the text of the first edition and that of the New Canadian Library version, argued that the novel's abbreviations "seriously distorted" its content, its criticism, and, therefore, its significance in Canadian culture.[582] In addition to the pioneering work done by Elizabeth Brady, bibliographical work on the novel is available on Thomas B. Vincent's *Bibliofiles: A bibliographical database of Canadian authors, their publications and editions*, http://www.bibliofiles.ca/. The novel has also been the principal subject of several critical articles.

Without exception this material agreed that Kirby's "chief work" was, "undoubtedly, the novel, 'Le Chien d'Or.' "[583] Its length and other characteristics were criticized, however. Edward A. McCourt, writing about "The Canadian Historical Novel" in the *Dalhousie Review* in 1946, called *"The Golden Dog"* a "ponderous account of corruption in high places."[584] Still, most critics considered it both an important work of nineteenth-century Canadian fiction and an artistic success. In *Creative Writing in Canada* (1952), Desmond Pacey described the novel, despite its "faults," as "a great achievement."[585] In his expanded and revised edition of *Canadian Literature in English* (2006), W. J. Keith reminded readers that these "faults" became "especially conspicuous" only when one evoked "the hardly relevant criteria of realistic fiction," and that Kirby's work was "perhaps the most substantial narrative written in Canada in the nineteenth century."[586]

The story has been studied in a variety of international contexts. In "George Eliot in Canada: *Romola* and *The Golden Dog*" (1984), Eva-Marie Kröller argued that "*The Golden Dog*," which she dubbed "the most successful Canadian historical novel of the nineteenth century," had "absorbed not only much of Canada's fascination with Italy, but also the ambiguities attached to that fascination." It, moreover, "resembled *Romola*," George Eliot's novel set in the Italian Renaissance and published "in 1862/63."[587] In "Myth And Prejudice In Kirby, Richardson, And Parker" (1979), L. R. Early made the point that it "was likely quite consciously that" Kirby "adopted the elemental plot of many Jacobean tragedies." He explained, "Plays by Shakespeare, Tourneur, Webster, and Ford portray the dissolution of an all-but harmonious order into chaos masked by a false regime; genuine order is usually restored, but at tragic cost, and on a level inferior to the original order."[588] In "English Social Patterns in Early Australian and Canadian Fiction" (1970), Reginald Eyre Watters compared such classic Australian works as "Marcus Clarke's *For the Term of his Natural Life* (1870–72)" and "Rolf Boldrewood's *Robbery Under Arms* (1881)" with "Rosanna Leprohon's *Antoinette de Mirecourt,* William Kirby's *The Golden Dog,* and Gilbert Parker's *Seats of the Mighty.*"[589]

Early and Watters were only two of many critics who placed *Le Chien d'or* in contexts of both English- and French-Canadian literature. In her MA thesis accepted at Simon Fraser University in 1993, Deborah Blacklock wrote about "Constancy In The Canadian Canon: The Reception History Of Rosanna Leprohon's Antoinette De Mirecourt and William Kirby's The Golden Dog." In "The *Lumpenproletariat* in *The Golden Dog* and *Roger Sudden*" (1989), E. J. Wiens "attempted a somewhat oblique reading of the two novels," the second by Thomas Raddall, by focusing on "the lowest portion of the urban poor" in each.[590] The novel also elicited comparisons with Philippe-Joseph Aubert de Gaspé's *Les Anciens Canadiens.* Marie Lessard's "Narration et écriture de l'Histoire: Paradigme narrative de la chute et du salut et récits de conquête" in *Textual Studies in Canada,* 5 (1994) and Robert David Stacey's "Romance, Pastoral Romance, and the Nation in History: William Kirby's *The Golden Dog* and Philippe-Joseph Aubert de Gaspé's *Les Anciens Canadiens*" in *Recalling Early Canada: Reading the Political in Literary and Cultural Production* (2005) are examples.

Two characteristics of *Le Chien d'or* have been sites of particular critical interest. One is its historical authenticity. In "Historical Accuracy And Inaccuracy Found In The Golden Dog," an MA thesis submitted to Laval University in 1963, Raymond G. Richard dealt with this subject from the point of view of government and feudalism as described in the novel, its setting, and its principal characters. Most commentators, however, intrigued by what Kirby had done with eighteenth-century New France, concentrated on such topics as the origin of the tablet of the Golden Dog in Quebec, the murder of Nicolas Jacquin *dit* Philibert by Pierre-Jean-Baptiste-François-Xavier Legardeur de Repentigny and its aftermath, and Kirby's representation of such historical characters as Angélique Renaud d'Avène des Méloizes and François Bigot.

Two years after the publication of the chapter on the tablet of the Golden Dog in *Quebec Under Two Flags: A Brief history of the City,* the quest after the facts about its origin was given an important boost by Philippe-Baby

Casgrain, a Quebec lawyer, author, and political figure, and a president of the Quebec Literary and Historical Society. In his pamphlet on *La Maison Du Chien-D'Or* (1905), he repeated what nineteenth-century writers, including Kirby, whose "beau roman" continued "d'avoir une vogue bien méritée,"[591] had reported. He concluded, however, that he believed that the inscription on the tablet originated in France. Using the pseudonym "Québec," he had, therefore, posed this question in "Enseigne: 'Le Chien d'or.'" Published in *L'Intermédiaire Des Chercheurs Et Curieux*, the French journal dedicated to "Questions Et Réponses Littéraires, Historiques, Scientifiques Et Artistiques Trouvailles Et Curiosités," the item mentioned that the tablet had given rise to "plusieurs légendes romanesques et diverses, entre autres le beau roman de Kirby, *The Golden Dog*."[592] The answer to Casgrain's question, that there was a similar inscription on a stone near Pézenas in France and that Timothée Roussel, a native of the region, had probably installed a replica on his house in Quebec, was reported by various critics, including Benjamin Sulte and Pierre-Georges Roy.

The latter's long article on "L'Histoire vraie du Chien d'Or" published in the *Cahiers Des Dix* in 1945 presented a good deal of information about "La famille Le Gardeur"; "L'officier Le Gardeur de Repentigny"; "Nicolas Jacquin *dit* Philibert"; the events that followed his murder, including the trial, pardon, later life, and death in India of "M. Le Gardeur de Repentigny"; the authors who wrote about the Golden Dog; its connection with Pézenas and Timothée Roussel; and the various people and groups that had occupied the Philibert house. Roy concluded, however, by telling the story of Kirby and his novel, "qui a réveillé les Québécois de leur somnolence et contribué à répandre la belle légende au Canada et aux Etats-Unis."[593] Five years later, in *Bigot Et Sa Bande Et L'Affaire Du Canada*, Roy returned to "*Le Golden Dog* de William Kirby." This time he concentrated on "quelques honnêtes gens" whom Kirby, "mal informé par ceux qui le documentèrent," had mistakenly placed among "les amis et les créateurs de l'infâme Bigot."[594] The project of sorting fact from fiction in *Le Chien d'or* was continued in two articles published in *Revue D'Histoire De L'Amérique Française*, Juliette Lalonde-Rémillard's "Angélique Des Méloizes" (1966) and Lemire's "La Trahison De Bigot Dans Le Roman Historique Canadien" (1968).

Lemire's article, which also appeared as a chapter in his book *Les Grands Thèmes nationalistes du roman historique canadien-français* (1970), argued that Kirby, like several French-Canadian authors, including Joseph Marmette in *L'Intendant Bigot*, deliberately gave the last Intendant of

New France the "traits de monstre." Their reasons were two: they wished to exonerate the French Canadians from blame in the loss of Quebec; in order to accomplish this goal, they had to lay "une charge contre Bigot et l'administration métropolitaine." Kirby's purpose in developing these points, however, was to serve not French-Canadian nationalism, but a "nationalisme pancanadien." On the one hand, then, Kirby was the only English-Canadian novelist who penetrated "la mentalité canadienne-française" deeply enough to discover its "complexe d'infériorité." On the other, in shaping his novel to help cure "ce traumatisme," he aimed to portray "une seule grande nation" in which French Canadians could only accomplish "leur destinée qu'en associant aux Canadiens anglais."[595]

The second much-debated characteristic of Kirby's novel concerned its nature as a work of historical fiction. Was "*The Golden Dog* ... a pot-boiler," albeit "of high order," as John Moss suggested in *A Reader's Guide to the Canadian Novel* (1981)?[596] Was it "a costume gothic" that drew readers for its "melodrama," as New claimed in *A History Of Canadian Literature* (1989)?[597] Did it "hardly" qualify "as serious historical fictional explanation" because Kirby exaggerated "his characterization" and incorporated "eccentric moralistic explanations in place of genuine historical determinants," as Ronald Hatch argued in "Narrative Development In The Canadian Historical Novel" (1986)?[598] Was it "English-Canadian historical fiction at its high, romantic fullest" that sprang "from an imperialist nationalism that once flourished in English Canada," as Duffy contended in *Sounding The Iceberg: An Essay on Canadian Historical Novels* (1986)?[599] Was it an historical novel that had been transformed into "an epic narrative that imaginatively occupied the ... space" of the Dominion of Canada created in 1867, and that "suggested characteristics of its identity," as Mary Jane Edwards maintained in "Occupying Space: William Kirby's Imagination of Canadian Identity in *Le chien d'or / The Golden Dog*" (1998)?[600] Was it, despite its historical setting and its "romantic aspects," an exploration of "a morally complex universe" where "divine," rather than "profane," justice is celebrated, as Joy Kuropatwa posited in "Dante & 'The Golden Dog'" (1980),[601] and as the numerous Christian references in the text itself suggest?

These varying views depended on such matters as the critical stance of each analyst as well as his or her definition of literary terms like melodrama and romance. They depended, perhaps most of all, however, on the version of the novel that each commentator used. Since only the first edition and the 1921 Musson edition came close to representing what Kirby intended to write about eighteenth-century Quebec, those who studied another edition were both interpreting a flawed text and contributing, albeit often unknowingly, to an incomplete and distorted reading of this important artifact of nineteenth-century Canadian culture.

THE TEXT

The principal purpose of this edition of William Kirby's *Le Chien d'or* is to provide the reader with a reliable text of what is one of the most popular, and most important, historical novels ever written in Canada. From among the material artifacts of this work, therefore, the editor has to select not only a copy-text that represents a complete version, but also one that best reveals what is known about the author's intentions in its regard.

Its French translation by Pamphile Le May was published during Kirby's lifetime and made with his knowledge. He read some of it as it was being prepared. Although he noted its "adoucissemens," he accepted it, nevertheless, as "tres bonne."[602] This translation was, moreover, the only version of the novel for which its author held a copyright. Still, Le May's rendition of the English text was both "a very free one," as David M. Hayne has explained,[603] and one that changed Kirby's vision of the new Dominion in various ways, most notably in its "transformation" of the Canadian nation into that of French Canada, as Mary Jane Edwards has observed.[604] The revised edition that appeared in 1926 and its subsequent impressions improved the quality of Le May's original translation, but, by embedding it more fully in French-Canadian culture, these issues also moved it further away from Kirby's version. Thus, while the printings in French sometimes provide information, especially in regard to explanations about customs in Quebec, the French text itself is not a suitable choice as a copy-text or as a source of emendation.

None of the editions in English published after Kirby's death is appropriate for these purposes either. *The Golden Dog (Le Chien D'Or) A Romance Of The Days of Louis Quinze In Quebec*, first issued by the Musson Book Company in 1921, was printed from a copy of the Lovell, Adam, Wesson and Company edition that first appeared in 1877. As a new typesetting, this Musson version differed from the earlier one in substantives and accidentals. Nevertheless, it might have been a candidate for copy-text had no copy of the first edition existed. Since there are copies of this edition, however, the first Musson edition has no role to play in creating an authoritative text of Kirby's novel. The abridgment of this edition issued by the same publisher in 1925 is likewise irrelevant to the choice of copy-text as are the other two editions produced in the twentieth century. *The Golden Dog (Le Chien D'Or) A Romance Of Old Quebec* in the St. Martin's Classics, first issued by the Macmillan Company of Canada in 1931, and *The Golden Dog [Le Chien D'Or] A Romance of Old Quebec* in the New Canadian Library, first issued by McClelland and Stewart in 1969, were not only set from the abridged 1925 Musson edition, but each was also a shortened version of it. None of the twenty-first century print-on-demand reproductions of the novel constitutes a reliable choice for copy-text.

The earliest of the four abridgments of *Le Chien d'or* was that first published by L. C. Page and Company in 1897. This was the so-called "authorized edition" for which Kirby signed the "Memorandum Of Agreement" in May 1897. For this typesetting Kirby entered his changes into the copy of the Lovell, Adam, Wesson edition, now apparently lost, sent to him by Page "for the corrections and revisions" that it expected him to make.[605] He consented to the text of the "Author's Prefatory Note," in which he assured his readers that this was the sole version of his novel that had his "sanction and approval."[606] And he received the only royalties that he was ever paid for what he called this "product of my pen made with immense work & cost."[607] Nevertheless, neither the 1897 impression nor the later ones, including the first English edition issued in 1899 that Jarrold and Sons made from the plates that it had purchased from Page, represented what Kirby thought he was getting when he made his arrangements with the American publisher. Thus, although it was set from the first edition, because it was shortened in ways that its author never intended, the Page version is not a suitable choice for copy-text.

Among the printed versions of *Le Chien d'or*, thus, only the Lovell, Adam, Wesson edition remains as a possible copy-text. Kirby never held its copyright. Although he did correct and revise a first set of galley proofs, he did not read a second, and, therefore, he did not have the opportunity to verify that his requested changes had been made or to make additional ones. As a result, there were "errors."[608] The compositors who set the first edition also altered both its substantives and accidentals. The adoption of American usages was especially pronounced. Words like "colour," "favour," and "honour," for example, that Kirby habitually spelled with a "u" were routinely rendered as "color," "favor," and "honor," and a word like "king," particularly when it referred to the British monarch, was not capitalized.

As well, the preface that Kirby intended to include was omitted.

Nevertheless, *The Chien D'Or / The Golden Dog / A Legend of Quebec* issued in 1877 appeared with Kirby's knowledge and permission. While his manuscript was being typeset, he was in constant contact with the publisher, and he did correct the first set of galleys. He continued to perfect this text by entering emendations in the copy of the first impression that once belonged to Maria Susan Rye, now held at the Archives of Ontario (Kirby, F-1076, Kirby Library, MU1675, L-65, Box 41), and in his copy of the impression issued by Richard Worthington, now owned by the Royal Military College of Canada, as well as in the copy of the first edition that he returned to Page. He sought to have the Lovell, Adam, Wesson edition reprinted in Canada, Great Britain, and the United States. And, especially after the appearance of Page's "mutilated" version,[609] he repeatedly recommended the first edition to his correspondents. A printing based on the first impression of this edition, emended by Kirby's corrections in the Rye copy and in the copy of the Worthington impression that he prepared in case this publisher was willing to issue a new edition, and further supplemented, albeit sparingly, by changes in the Page edition that were most likely taken from the copy corrected for the publisher by the author, would produce, therefore, an edition of the novel that carried more authority than any other printed version. Such a choice is complicated, however, by the existence of the two manuscript versions of this iconic Canadian work.

The first is the holograph manuscript of the two fragments of "The / Golden Dog / A Legend of Quebec" presented by Lorne Pierce to Queen's University in 1956. These were the fragments composed between 1869 and 1872 that survived from the manuscript copied by Hannah and Josephine Lowe, their mother, and, possibly, Mary Torrance and Mrs. Kirby. They reveal a good deal about the author's methods of composition, including his entry of text on the verso of leaves in notebooks and his corrections and revisions on the verso and on the recto opposite each verso. They demonstrate his habitual English, as opposed to American, spelling, his transcription—often without accents—of French words, and his sometimes inconsistent capitalization. They also indicate his intention to follow a system of punctuation that pointed to how to read his prose aloud as well as silently.

These fragments cannot serve as copy-text, however. They represent a part of a version that was recopied and revised at least twice and then either completely rewritten by Kirby on fresh leaves or substantially emended by him on the latest recopied leaves. Thus, the text in these fragments differs greatly from that of *Le Chien d'or* submitted to John Lovell in 1876. According to his grandson, moreover, Kirby thought that these fragments, like the rest of the early draft to which they belonged, "had been burned, & destroyed."[610]

The second manuscript, held in the Kirby Collection at the Archives of Ontario, was the one included among the papers that Kirby left to his son John Colborne Kirby, and that remained in the possession of the family until they were sold to the Niagara Parks Commission in 1944.[611] There are marks on this manuscript that are difficult to interpret because of the way it was conserved by the Archives. It was damaged before it came to this repository. There are, therefore, missing leaves and parts of leaves, and there are passages that are unreadable.[612] Approximately 600 of the 1035 numbered leaves were transcribed by the Lowe sisters, their mother, Mary Torrance, and Mrs. Kirby from a revised copy of the earlier manuscript. Due to mistakes made by these copyists both in reading and transcribing Kirby's writing, some accidentals and substantives are undoubtedly not the author's. Since it served as the copy for the Lovell, Adam, Wesson edition, it also incorporated data relevant to its printing, including stint marks that correspond with line breaks in the first edition.

Still, this manuscript is the best extant material witness to *Le Chien d'or*. More than 400 of its leaves are written in Kirby's hand and represent the revisions that he made to his text between 1873 and 1875. Kirby has incorporated many changes into the leaves copied by the five women. All the leaves carry the alterations in pointing, the addition of quotation marks around "the conversational parts," and the identification of each speaker that John Lovell requested when he accepted the novel for publication in July 1876.[613] The last 137 leaves contain the "subject heading for each chapter" that John Wurtele Lovell required the next month.[614]

Despite its physical deficiencies and its varying authority, then, this manuscript represents not only the text that Kirby corrected and revised most carefully over several years but also the one in which his capitalization, his spelling of both English and French words, and his punctuation are most evident. Given his intention to write a Canadian novel for the new constitutional monarchy in the northern half of North America and to distinguish it from the United States by providing the Dominion with an epic past that combined the heroic histories of Great Britain and France, these features are especially important. The manuscript held by the Archives of

Ontario, therefore, is the principal copy-text for the CEECT edition. When its leaves are missing or unreadable, the Lovell, Adam, Wesson edition, printed from this manuscript, is the copy-text.

In the preparation of this scholarly edition, one of the many challenges was the achievement of an electronic transcription of the manuscript copy-text that interpreted as accurately as possible what its leaves contained. The typists who entered these data into the computer worked from a photocopy made from a microfilm of the manuscript that CEECT acquired from the Archives of Ontario. None had read *Le Chien d'or*, and none had much knowledge about it. Each was asked, furthermore, not to consult the first edition or any other version of the novel for help in interpreting what was written on the leaves, but to type what she saw. Each was told, however, that every mark had to be accounted for. And each was provided with a list of codes to help identify the nature of each mark. The mark "/ow" ("other writing"), for example, introduced words and passages that Kirby apparently intended to incorporate into his text as additions to, or replacements for, what was originally on the leaf. This new material was enclosed within parentheses.

When the electronic transcription of the manuscript copy-text was generated, it was proofread twice in its entirety against the photocopy, each time by one member of the CEECT team reading aloud from the photocopy and a second checking the computer transcription. Parts of it were also proofread many more times by different people at CEECT. Some of these verifications involved studying the photocopy on a light-table in an attempt to decipher sections of the text that the typists were unable to read and to identify the passages that Kirby intended to eliminate and those he intended to keep. This was particularly important because the processes of microfilming and photocopying sometimes highlighted the text that he had rejected rather than that he had finally accepted.

These in-house proofreadings allowed the computer-generated text to be altered in various ways. Since they had nothing to do with establishing the text of the novel, all the codes that indicated marks added in the course of printing the first edition were deleted. Such compositorial errors as eye skips, reversed letters, and misreadings, sometimes caused by the CEECT typists' anticipation of a certain word or phrase, were corrected. Other transcriptions, however, were more problematic. Neither Kirby's handwriting nor that of each amanuensis was always easy to decipher. The capitalization of words that were not proper nouns; the spelling of both

English and French words; the incorporation of accents on the latter; the choice of punctuation marks, including dashes, exclamations, periods, and questions; and the placement of quotation marks: all provided topics of debate for the CEECT staff and moments of indecision for the editor. On three different occasions, therefore, the corrected version of the computer-generated text was taken to the Archives of Ontario and read orally against the text on the leaves of the actual manuscript, each time by the editor and another, different member of the CEECT team. Through these proof-readings the problems with the passages highlighted in error by the filming processes were resolved and the questions regarding Kirby's accidentals were answered. As accurately as possible, thus, Kirby's intentions for the text of *Le Chien d'or* contained in the manuscript copy-text were deduced, and a viable transcription established. The result is a text that is inconsistent, and that may appear in instances, for example, where the apostrophe is missing in an elided word like "don't" or in possessives even incorrect to the contemporary reader. Nevertheless, the CEECT text captures, especially in its punctuation, the rhetorical nature of Kirby's language and the grandeur of his epic style.

The preparation of the Lovell, Adam, Wesson edition of Kirby's novel was equally careful. Six copies of this edition were microfilmed and photocopied for CEECT according to its specifications. These comprised three different copies of the first impression issued in 1877, two copies of the Lovell, Coryell and Company impression issued respectively in 1891 and in 1894, and one copy of the impression printed in Toronto by the Hunter, Rose Company and issued by the American News Company Limited in 1897 or 1898. To establish states within the first printing, changes to the 1877 plates, and the relationship among the various impressions made from them, these photocopies and other actual copies of the first edition were then compared to one another through a series of light-table and other forms of ocular collations, oral collations, and computer collations. Results from these bibliographical analyses are reported at various points in this introduction and in "Bibliographical Description of Published Copy-text" (893). Two copies of the first edition, one, privately owned, from the 1877 impression, and one, owned by Library and Archives Canada (PS8471 I73G6 1877a), from the Lovell, Coryell impression, were entered on the computer. The two copies were then proofread and corrected by means of a computer program especially prepared for CEECT. This perfected text of the first edition was used as the published copy-text. Readings from this perfected text of the first edition that replace material that is either missing or unrecoverable in the manuscript copy-text are listed in "Unrecoverable Manuscript Readings: Readings from Published Copy-text" (903).

Detailed bibliographical analyses were carried out on copies that formed part of each of the other editions of *Le Chien d'or*. Because it carried Kirby's statement that it was "the only edition offered" to readers "with the sanction and approval of its author,"[615] and because, therefore, it has frequently been accepted by critics as the only authorized version of his novel, particular attention was paid to the Page edition. Four copies were microfilmed and photocopied for CEECT according to its specifications. These comprised two that carried the Boston: L. C. Page and Company, 1897 imprint and two that carried the Montreal News Company Limited imprint. The Canadian copies were undated, but, because they had the words "Authorised Edition" on the title-page, they had to have been issued in 1899 or later. All four copies were used in a series of collations to establish states within the Page edition and the relationship among its impressions. The two Montreal News Company copies, both owned by Library and Archives Canada (PS8471 I73G6 1897, and PS8471 I73G6 1897, copy 3), were entered on the computer and then proofread and corrected by means of the computer program especially prepared for CEECT for that purpose.

Several collations were performed in order to establish both the genealogy of Kirby's novel in its English and its French versions and the relationship of Kirby's English text to Le May's translation. An oral collation, for example, was done to compare the two fragments of the early manuscript held at Queen's with the relevant parts of the manuscript owned by the Archives of Ontario. One computer collation compared the manuscript copy-text with the 1877 edition. Another compared the manuscript copy-text with the 1877 and 1897 editions. These two versions were collated orally with all the editions published after Kirby's death. The translation of *Le Chien d'or* as it appeared in the *Etendard* was compared visually with the text in the two-volume edition issued by this newspaper. An oral collation, using this 1884 French edition as the standard of comparison and the Lovell, Adam, Wesson edition as the other copy, was carried out. The results of these procedures are summarized in the "Editor's Introduction" and in other parts of this edition. Complete records of the findings are included in the papers from the CEECT project held by the Carleton University Archives.

These various activities provided the information that allowed the CEECT text of *Le Chien d'or* to be created. Silent emendations were made to both copy-texts. Throughout the manuscript copy-text, for example, "and" was indicated both by the word itself and by the ampersand. All the latter were emended so that they read "and." In each copy-text quotation marks were regularized, and they were made to appear after marks of punctuation. A single punctuation mark was enclosed in a double one when there was a quotation within a quotation. Kirby's predominant practice of not putting a period after "St," the shortened form of "Saint," was followed. During the typesetting of the novel Kirby asked John Wurtele Lovell about the printer's supply of "accented letters."[616] In the parts of the manuscript copy-text in the author's hand, however, he did not always put accents on French words, and he usually wrote "Amelie" and "Angelique" when he transcribed the names of the novel's two main female characters. When the Lovell, Adam, Wesson edition, therefore, is the copy-text, it has been silently emended to reflect Kirby's habitual French spellings. Chapter numbers have been rendered in their Arabic form, and the first word of each chapter has been capitalized. Each chapter begins on a new page.

All the other emendations made to both copy-texts are listed in "Emendations in Copy-texts" (919). They fall into several categories. New material has been incorporated. One substantive addition is the preface in the form of the passage from Alessandro Manzoni's *I Promessi Sposi* and its English translation that Kirby transcribed in his copy of the Worthington impression of the first edition. Another is the title for each chapter that Kirby had not already supplied in the manuscript; that is, the title for each of the first fifty-two chapters of the novel. The author almost certainly added these headings to the first set of proofs, but, these galleys not having survived, their source for the CEECT text is the Lovell, Adam, Wesson edition.

Another category of emendation is that of the passages in the first edition that differ from those in the manuscript copy-text. Some of these, like the one that describes the "sunset ... on the shores of the Bay of Minas" when François Bigot and Caroline de St Castin exchange their vows of love (170), may well have been revised by Kirby when he was proofreading the galleys. In the CEECT text these probable authorial changes have replaced readings in the manuscript copy-text. The source of most of the variants that affect meaning, however, appears to be due, rather than to the author, to such causes as the compositors' misreading the manuscript or anticipating certain words in a passage. These readings, which have not been incorporated into the CEECT text, are recorded in the "Historical

Collation" (943).

Most of the emendations derive from the need to correct substantives and to add accidentals in the copy-texts. The compositors of the first edition routinely omitted the repetition of words like "of the," especially as Kirby and his copyists tended to use them as catchwords at the bottom of one leaf to indicate the first words at the top of the next. The compositors also added marks of punctuation when Kirby and his copyists forgot them.

From the time Kirby saw his text in galleys until his preparation of the Page copy of the first edition for its 1897 printing, he also continued to perfect his novel. In his manuscript copy-text, for example, he had written "Beaucé" instead of "Beauce" for the name of the region of Quebec (67) and "Dechenaux" instead of "Deschenaux" for the name of Joseph Brassard Deschenaux (69–70). These misspellings were all corrected, most probably by the author as he read the first set of proofs. Kirby recorded further emendations in the three copies that he is known to have had in his possession at one time or another. Responding to Benjamin Sulte's comments on his French in his letter of 10 April 1877, Kirby changed "*Chevalier preux*" to "*preux Chevalier*" (181) and "*la faute à lui*" to "*sa faute*" (403) in Rye's copy. In his copy of the Worthington impression he altered "tulips" to "sunflowers" (333) and, thus, made the flower more consistent with the autumnal setting of his novel. It was most likely Kirby as well who emended "Goupion" to "Glapion" (665) in the copy that he corrected for Page and, thus, righted in the chapter entitled "The Market Place On St Martin's Day" in the second edition the name of Augustin-Louis de Glapion, the superior of the Jesuits in New France. Like the other emendations, the corrections incorporated into the CEECT edition from Rye's copy, Kirby's copy of the Worthington impression, and the Page edition are listed in "Emendations in Copy-texts" (919).

The editor has made a few emendations. Most of these have to do with restoring Kirby's habitual spelling of words like "colour," "favour," and "honour" in the parts of the manuscript copied by his amanuenses and in the 1877 edition when it serves as copy-text. The editor has also decided to use as the title of the CEECT edition *Le Chien d'or / The Golden Dog: A Legend of Quebec*. This title reflects the name that Kirby gave to each of the two extant manuscripts of his work and the title of the Lovell, Adam, Wesson impression of the first edition. It also contextualizes his heroic narrative not only in the literature of legend and myth but also in the city, and in the province, of Quebec—the French settlement that was founded by Samuel de Champlain in 1608; the scene of the battle of the Plains of Abraham in 1759; the place where the idea of the Canadian confederation of 1867 was first discussed in 1864; and the former colony on the St. Lawrence River where the two peoples that formed Kirby's bicultural and bilingual Canada could—and did—most readily interact.

In creating the text for the CEECT edition of *Le Chien d'or*, the editor has used as much data as can be ascertained from the material artifacts of this work to present a version of Kirby's historical novel that reflects his intentions to develop a fiction that provided an epic past for the Dominion of Canada, and that suggested a model of nationhood for this union of the former British and French colonies. That this narrative resonated with Canadians, both English-speaking and French-speaking, is witnessed by its popularity since its first publication, despite the changes made to its text in its abridgments and translation. The CEECT edition of this iconic literary achievement should help twenty-first century Canadians understand whence their country came, how the new nation was envisaged by many of its inhabitants at the time of Confederation, and maybe even why it has evolved into a similar, but different, multicultural and multilingual society.

ENDNOTES TO INTRODUCTION

[1] Illustration: "L'Inscription Du Chien D'Or," in Pierre-Georges Roy, *La Ville De Québec Sous Le Régime Français* (Québec: Rédempti Paradis, 1930), Vol. 2, between pp. 154 and 155. In this, and in all other quotations included in the introduction, the grammar, the punctuation, and the spelling of the original have been retained except in a few cases where the style of the passage makes its meaning unclear. In these instances the editorial changes are indicated in square brackets. When the first letter of a word in the title of a work cited is capitalized, this initial capitalization has also been kept. The tablet of the Golden Dog decorates the façade of the main post office built in Quebec in the 1870s.

[2] William Kirby, *Le Chien d'or / The Golden Dog: A Legend of Quebec*, ed. Mary Jane Edwards (Montreal and Kingston: McGill-Queen's University Press, 2012), p. 132. All subsequent references to this edition are included in the text as (x) or (x.y), where "x" is the page number or numbers and "y" the relevant line or lines on the page.

[3] *Le Chien d'or* is the title used in this introduction to refer to Kirby's text generically. The title of each issue, impression, or edition, which may vary even in its capitalization, is recorded as it appears on its title-page.

[4] "Kirby, William," *DCB*, Vol. 13, pp. 551–54.

[5] OTAR, Kirby, F-1076, Photographs, MU1664, K-120, Large photo of one

class of the Public School, Newby Wiske, parish of Kirby Wiske, Yorkshire, England. 1902. Kirby wrote the notation on the back of this picture. Kirby is used throughout these notes to refer to the author. His grandson is referred to as William Kirby when documents written by him are cited.

[6]Kirby, "A Reminiscence Of Two Days In Quebec, July, 1839," *Quebec Chronicle*, 26 January 1903, p. [4].

[7]Edwin C. Guillet, *The Great Migration: The Atlantic Crossing by Sailing-ship Since 1770* (1937, rpt. Toronto: University of Toronto Press, 1963), p. vii.

[8]Steven J. Ross, *Workers On the Edge: Work, Leisure, And Politics In Industrializing Cincinnati, 1788–1890* (New York: Columbia University Press, 1985), p. 25.

[9]Albert M. Fletcher, "Sketch Of The Author's Life," in Alexander Kinmont, *Twelve Lectures On The Natural History Of Man, And The Rise And Progress Of Philosophy* (Cincinnati: U. P. James, 1839), pp. 9 and 12.

[10]OTAR, Kirby, F-1076, Scrapbook, MU1653, H-3, Clipping from *Cincinnati Gazette*, 16 December 1879. This clipping contains a letter that Kirby wrote earlier in the month to William Cooper Howells. The latter, then the United States Consul in Toronto, sent it to the *Gazette* as a further tribute to Kinmont. On 2 December 1879 this newspaper had printed an article on this "Scholar, Orator, Philosopher, Educator, Author, Christian, and Honest Man" in its series on "Eminent Cincinnatians"; a clipping of this article is included in the same scrapbook. William Cooper Howells, the father of William Dean Howells, was, like Kinmont, a follower of Emanuel Swedenborg.

[11]Steven J. Ross, *Workers On the Edge: Work, Leisure, And Politics In Industrializing Cincinnati, 1788–1890* (New York: Columbia University Press, 1985), p. 26.

[12]Kirby's papers include a prose epilogue about Emanuel Swedenborg's theories; dated 1838, it is described as "A treatise written in Latin while Kirby was a Master of Languages at Kinmount College." See OTAR, Kirby, F-1076, Miscellaneous Manuscripts, MU1647, D-33, Epilogos e regno animali emanuilis swedenborgii, 1838.

[13]Kirby, "A Reminiscence Of Two Days In Quebec, July, 1839," *Quebec Chronicle*, 26 January 1903, p. [4]. The quotations about Kirby's entry into Canada and visit to Quebec are all taken from this source.

[14]George Bourne, *Picture Of Quebec* (Quebec: D. and J. Smillie, 1829), p. [121].

[15]"Cockburn, James Pattison," *DCB*, Vol. 7, pp. 193–96.

[16]"Hawkins, Alfred," *DCB*, Vol. 8, pp. 384–86. This article describes Hawkins and Maquay's store "in Upper Town" as in "the Quebec Freemason's Hall," a common name for the Roussel house in the nineteenth century. Bourne and Cockburn both say that the instigator of the attack on Philibert was François Bigot, the intendant of New France from 1748 to 1760; Hawkins attributes its source to Michel Bégon de la

Picardière, the intendant of New France from 1710 to 1726.

[17]Fred Habermehl and Donald L. Combe, *St. Mark's: Persons of Hopeful Piety* (Niagara-on-the-Lake: Archives Committee, St. Mark's Anglican Church, 2000), p. 65.

[18]"Metcalfe, Charles Theophilus, 1st Baron Metcalfe," *DCB*, Vol. 7, pp. 603–08.

[19]Kirby, *The U. E. A Tale Of Upper Canada* (Niagara, 1859), p. 178.

[20]Ibid., p. [5].

[21]Kirby to John Reade, 13 April 1903, "Old and New," *Gazette* (Montreal), 25 April 1903, p. 11.

[22]OTAR, Kirby, F-1076, Diaries, MU1640, Series B, William Kirby, Entries for 25 July 1865.

[23]Ibid., The LeMoine Papers, MU1634, A-1, ALS, Kirby to James MacPherson Le Moine, 7 April 1877.

[24]"Sulte, Benjamin," *DCB*, Vol. 15, pp. 985–87.

[25]OTAR, Kirby, F-1076, The Sulte Correspondence, MU1634, A-2, Kirby's holograph copy of letter to Benjamin Sulte, 24 July 1865.

[26]"Le Moine, Sir James MacPherson," *DCB*, Vol. 14, pp. 646–48.

[27]*Maple Leaves*, p. 8.

[28]Ibid., pp. 31–32.

[29]OTAR, Kirby, F-1076, The LeMoine Papers, MU1634, A-1, ALS, Kirby to James MacPherson Le Moine, 7 April 1877.

[30]Ibid., Miscellaneous Manuscripts, MU1648, E-17, Appointment of Kirby as Collector of Customs, 1 July 1871.

[31]"Carnochan, Janet," *DCB*, Vol. 15, pp. 183–85.

[32]Janet Carnochan, "Reminiscences Of William Kirby, F. R. S. C.," *The United Empire Loyalists' Association of Canada Annual Transactions 1904 to 1913* (Brampton: The Conservator Book Department, 1914), pp. 49–56.

[33]OTAR, Kirby, F-1076, Broadsheets, Circulars, Posters, Programmes Etc., MU1651, G-6, "Canadians Forever: A National Song."

[34]Kirby to Alfred Tennyson, 26 March 1870, *Alfred, Lord Tennyson and William Kirby: Unpublished correspondence to which are added some letters from Hallam, Lord Tennyson,* ed. Lorne Pierce (Toronto: The Macmillan Company of Canada, 1929), p. 42. "Opinion In Canada," a passage from this letter first printed in the London *Spectator* on 23 April 1870, p. 523, appeared in the Toronto *Globe* on 6 May 1870, p. 3.

[35]Benjamin Sulte, *Les Laurentiennes* (Montreal: Eusèbe Senécal, 1870), p. [125].

[36]Ibid., p. 128.

[37]Kirby to Benjamin Sulte, 18 November 1867, *Ordre* (Montreal), 27 November 1867, p. [1]. The letter was published as part of an article on the growing interest that French-Canadian and English-Canadian writers were taking in each other, a rapprochement that would lead to "honneur au pays," for the new "Canadiens, fils de deux races autrefois rivales, peuvent

et doivent vivre fraternellement ensemble."

[38] See, for example, Kirby, "A Biographical Sketch of the Author of 'Maple Leaves,' " *Maple Leaves 1894*, by James MacPherson Le Moine (Quebec: L. H. Demers, 1894), pp. [7]–11.

[39] Auguste Soulard, "Chronique Canadienne. Le Chien D'Or, A Québec," *Canadien* (Quebec), 20 November 1839, p. [1].

[40] Joseph Marmette, *L'Intendant Bigot* (Montreal: George E. Desbarats, 1872), title-page et passim.

[41] Mouffle d'Angerville, *Vie Privée De Louis XV* (London, 1788), Vol. 4, p. 59. The pages copied from this edition (Vol. 4, pp. 58–64) are included in Kirby's papers. See OTAR, Kirby, F-1076, Miscellaneous Manuscripts, MU1646, D-19, Twenty-four small note-books filled with miscellaneous notations by Kirby.

[42] OTAR, Kirby, F-1076, The Josephine Lowe Correspondence, MU1638, A-17, ALS, Josephine Lowe to Kirby, 17 March 1869.

[43] Ibid., Josephine Lowe, "Paintings In the Church of the Ursuline Convent," 22 April 1869.

[44] OONA, MG29, D91, Letters from William Kirby to Hannah Catharine Lowe Servos, ALS, Kirby to Hannah Lowe, 19 July 1872.

[45] OTAR, Kirby, F-1076, Miscellaneous Manuscripts, MU1648, E-32, A sketch of the ruins of Chateau Bigot with descriptive notes, 7 August 1872.

[46] Ibid., The Sulte Correspondence, MU1634, A-2, Kirby's holograph copy of Marmette's letter to Sulte, 12 August 1872.

[47] "Faucher De Saint-Maurice, Narcisse-Henri-Édouard," *DCB*, Vol. 12, pp. 308–09.

[48] OTAR, Kirby, F-1076, The Sulte Correspondence, MU1634, A-2, ALS, Benjamin Sulte to Kirby, 6 May 1869.

[49] John Symons, *High-Street, Hull, Some Years Since, And Biographical Sketches* (Kingston-Upon-Hull: J. W. Leng, 1862), pp. 119 and 121.

[50] T. Windall Wildridge, *Old And New Hull: A series of Drawings of the Town of Kingston-upon-Hull, With Descriptive And Historical Notices; Also, Portraits Of Local Worthies, With Biographical And Genealogical Notes* (Hull: M. C. Peck & Son, 1884), p. 126.

[51] James MacPherson Le Moine, "Le Chien D'Or Son Origine—Son Histoire," *Canadien* (Quebec), 9 January 1886, p. [2].

[52] OKQ, Archives, William Kirby Fonds, 2055.8, Photocopies of Letters etc. re provenance of Manuscript of Golden Dog, TLS, Launcelot Cressy Servos to Lorne Pierce, 7 April 1956.

[53] OTAR, Kirby, F-1076, Photographs, MU1665, K-152, Photograph of Hope Sewell.

[54] Ibid., The LeMoine Papers, MU1634, A-1, ALS, Kirby to James MacPherson Le Moine, 23 January 1879.

[55] Ibid., ALS, Kirby to James MacPherson Le Moine, 13 April 1877.

[56] OKQ, Archives, William Kirby Fonds, 2055.8 and 2055.9, Manuscript

of Golden Dog, Notebook 1, leaf 1, recto.

[57] Ibid., Notebook 19, leaf 433, recto.

[58] Ibid., Notebook 23, leaf 576, verso.

[59] OTAR, Kirby, F-1076, Scrapbooks, MU1653, H-3, Note on "Chapter XXVIII."

[60] Ibid., The Sulte Correspondence, MU1634, A-2, ALS, Benjamin Sulte to Kirby, 6 May 1869.

[61] Ibid., ALS, Kirby to Benjamin Sulte, 1 November 1870.

[62] OONA, MG29, D91, Letters from William Kirby to Hannah Catharine Lowe Servos, ALS, Kirby to Hannah Lowe, 2 June 1872.

[63] OKQ, Archives, William Kirby Fonds, 2055.8, Photocopies of Letters etc. re provenance of Manuscript of Golden Dog, TLS, Launcelot Cressy Servos to Lorne Pierce, 7 April 1956.

[64] Ibid., William Kirby Fonds, 2055.8 and 2055.9, Manuscript of Golden Dog, Notebook 22, leaf 546, recto.

[65] Ibid., Notebook 17, leaf 373, recto.

[66] Ibid., William Kirby Fonds, 2055.8, Photocopies of Letters etc. re provenance of Manuscript of Golden Dog, TLS, Launcelot Cressy Servos to Lorne Pierce, 7 April 1956.

[67] Janet Carnochan, "More About William Kirby," *Globe* (Toronto), 4 April 1925, p. 4.

[68] OONA, MG29, D91, Letters from William Kirby to Hannah Catharine Lowe Servos, ALS, Kirby to Hannah Lowe Servos, 1 November 1905.

[69] "Withrow, William Henry," *DCB*, Vol. 13, pp. 1103–05.

[70] OTAR, Kirby, F-1076, Correspondence With Publishers, MU1635, A-6, Kirby's holograph copy, William Henry Withrow to Harper and Brothers, 2 January 1873. Withrow's *The Catacombs Of Rome, And Their Testimony Relative To Primitive Christianity* was published by Nelson and Phillips of New York and Hitchcock and Walden of Cincinnati in 1874.

[71] Ibid., ALS, William Henry Withrow to Kirby, 22 December 1873.

[72] Ibid., Kirby's holograph copy, William Henry Withrow to Harper and Brothers, 2 January 1873.

[73] Ibid., ALS, Harper and Brothers, to Kirby, 14 March 1873.

[74] Ibid., ALS, James R. Osgood and Company to Kirby, 31 March 1873.

[75] Ibid., ALS, James R. Osgood and Company to Kirby, 12 June 1873.

[76] Ibid., Kirby's holograph copy of letter to Trübner and Company, 31 March 1873.

[77] Ibid., ALS, Trübner and Company to Kirby, 5 May 1873.

[78] Ibid., ALS, John Webb to Kirby, 3 December 1874.

[79] Ibid., ALS, James Campbell and Son to Kirby, 8 October 1875.

[80] Ibid., ALS, William Henry Withrow to Kirby, 9 December 1875.

[81] Ibid., ALS, Belford Brothers to Kirby, 27 December 1875.

[82] "Rye, Maria Susan," *DCB*, Vol. 13, pp. 916–17.

[83] OTAR, Kirby, F-1076, Correspondence With Publishers, MU1635, A-6,

ALS, Daldy, Isbister and Company to Maria Susan Rye, 29 May 1876.

[84]Ibid., ALS, Maria Susan Rye to Kirby, undated.

[85]Ibid., ALS, Adam, Stevenson and Company to Kirby, 19 May 1873. Although the signature on the letter is that of the company, it was Graeme Mercer Adam who actually wrote it.

[86]"Adam, Graeme Mercer," *DCB*, Vol. 14, pp. 5–7.

[87]"Smith, Goldwin," *DCB*, Vol. 13, pp. 968–74.

[88]OTAR, Kirby, F-1076, Correspondence With Publishers, MU1635, A-6, ALS, William Whitelaw to Kirby, 8 July 1873.

[89]Ibid., ALS, William Henry Withrow to Kirby, 22 December 1873.

[90]Ibid., ALS, Graeme Mercer Adam to Kirby, 14 February 1874.

[91]Ibid., ALS, Henry S. King and Company to Adam, Stevenson and Company, 10 June 1874.

[92]Ibid., ALS, Adam, Stevenson and Company to Kirby, 22 June 1874.

[93]Ibid., ALS, Graeme Mercer Adam to Kirby, 20 January 1876.

[94]Ibid., ALS, Graeme Mercer Adam to Kirby, 25 May 1875.

[95]"Rose, George Maclean," *DCB*, Vol. 12, pp. 921–24.

[96]OTAR, Kirby, F-1076, Correspondence With Publishers, MU1635, A-6, Kirby's holograph copy of letter to Graeme Mercer Adam, June [1875].

[97]Ibid., ALS, Graeme Mercer Adam to Kirby, 12 July 1875.

[98]Ibid., ALS, William Henry Withrow to Kirby, 8 April 1876.

[99]"Lovell, John," *DCB*, Vol. 12, pp. 569–74.

[100]"Miscellany. Lake Shore Press. The Monster Printing House at Rouses Point," *Plattsburgh Sentinel*, 3 September 1875, p. [1].

[101]OTAR, Kirby, F-1076, Correspondence With Publishers, MU1635, A-6, ALS, Graeme Mercer Adam to Kirby, 5 October 1875.

[102]Ibid., ALS, Graeme Mercer Adam to Kirby, 20 January 1876.

[103]Ibid., ALS, Graeme Mercer Adam to Kirby, 24 May 1876.

[104]Ibid., ALS, John Lovell to Graeme Mercer Adam, 12 July 1876.

[105]Ibid., Diaries, MU1640, Series B, William Kirby, Entry for 14 July 1876.

[106]Ibid., Correspondence With Publishers, MU1635, A-6, Kirby's holograph copy of letter to Trübner and Company, 31 March 1873.

[107]Ibid., Kirby's holograph copy of letter to Graeme Mercer Adam, June 1875.

[108]Ibid., ALS, Graeme Mercer Adam to Kirby, 12 July 1875.

[109]See "Description of Manuscript Copy-text" for a fuller explanation of its leaf and page count (887).

[110]OTAR, Kirby, F-1076, Correspondence With Publishers, MU1635, A-6, ALS, John Lovell to Kirby, 27 July 1876.

[111]Ibid., ALS, John Wurtele Lovell to Kirby, 17 August 1876.

[112]Ibid., Diaries, MU1640, Series B, William Kirby, Entry for 17 August 1876.

[113]Ibid., Correspondence With Publishers, MU1635, A-6, ALS, John Wurtele Lovell to Kirby, 7 December 1876.

[114] Ibid., ALS, John Wurtele Lovell to Kirby, 12 January 1877.

[115] Ibid., ALS, John Wurtele Lovell to Kirby, 18 September 1876.

[116] Ibid., ALS, John Wurtele Lovell to Kirby, 7 December 1876.

[117] Ibid., ALS, John Wurtele Lovell to Kirby, 17 August 1876.

[118] Ibid., The John C. Kirby Correspondence, MU1636, A-7, ALS, Kirby to John Colborne Kirby, 9 March 1877.

[119] Ibid., Correspondence With Publishers, MU1635, A-6, ALS, John Lovell to Kirby, 27 July 1876.

[120] Ibid., ALS, John Wurtele Lovell to Kirby, 17 August 1876.

[121] Ibid., ALS, John Wurtele Lovell to Kirby, 18 September 1876.

[122] "Miscellany. Lake Shore Press. The Montreal Printing House at Rouses Point," *Plattsburgh Sentinel*, 3 September 1875, p. [1].

[123] OTAR, Kirby, F-1076, Correspondence With Publishers, MU1635, A-6, ALS, John Wurtele Lovell to Kirby, 17 August 1876.

[124] Ibid., ALS, John Wurtele Lovell to Kirby, 18 September 1876.

[125] "Miscellany. Lake Shore Press. The Montreal Printing House at Rouses Point," *Plattsburgh Sentinel*, 3 September 1875, p. [1].

[126] OTAR, Kirby, F-1076, Correspondence With Publishers, MU1635, A-6, ALS, John Wurtele Lovell to Kirby, 18 September 1876.

[127] Ibid., ALS, John Wurtele Lovell to Kirby, 7 December 1876.

[128] Ibid., ALS, John Wurtele Lovell to Kirby, 12 January 1877.

[129] Ibid., ALS, Robert Kurczyn Lovell to Kirby, 16 January 1877.

[130] Ibid., ALS, Graeme Mercer Adam to Kirby, 29 January 1877.

[131] Ibid., ALS, John Wurtele Lovell to Kirby, 17 August 1876.

[132] Ibid., Memorandum, Robert Kurczyn Lovell to Kirby, 21 February 1877.

[133] Ibid., The LeMoine Papers, MU1634, A-1, ALS, James MacPherson Le Moine to Kirby, 22 March 1877.

[134] Ibid., ALS, Kirby to James MacPherson Le Moine, 27 March 1877.

[135] Ibid., Correspondence With Publishers, MU1635, A-6, ALS, Graeme Mercer Adam to Kirby, 29 January 1877.

[136] OTMCL, Typescript, William Kirby, Junior, "Brief Of The Publications Of William Kirby's Novel 'Le Chien D'Or' (The Golden Dog) To Dr. Lorne Pierce," 1925.

[137] OTAR, Kirby, F-1076, Correspondence With Publishers, MU1635, A-6, ALS, Graeme Mercer Adam to Kirby, 17 March 1880.

[138] George L. Parker, *The Beginnings of the Book Trade in Canada* (Toronto, Buffalo, and London: University of Toronto Press, 1985), p. 191.

[139] See "Bibliographical Description of Published Copy-text" (893) for more details about this copy, which belongs to BVAU.

[140] OTAR, Kirby, F-1076, Correspondence With Publishers, MU1635, A-6, ALS, Graeme Mercer Adam to Kirby, [12?] July 1878.

[141] Ibid., ALS, Graeme Mercer Adam to Kirby, 17 March 1880.

[142] Canada, An Act respecting Copyrights, 38 Victoria (1875).

[143] OTAR, Kirby, F-1076, Correspondence With Publishers, MU1635, A-6,

ALS, John Wurtele Lovell to Kirby, 11 April 1878.

[144]"Plumb, Josiah Burr," *DCB*, Vol. 11, pp. 697–98.

[145]OTAR, Kirby, F-1076, Correspondence With Publishers, MU1635, A-6, ALS, Joseph-Charles Taché to Josiah Burr Plumb, 10 March 1880.

[146]George L. Parker, "English-Canadian Publishers and the Struggle for Copyright," in *History Of The Book In Canada*, Vol. 2: *1840–1918*, ed. Yvan Lamonde, Patricia Lockhart Fleming, and Fiona A. Black (Toronto, Buffalo, and London: University of Toronto Press, 2005), p. 152.

[147]Ibid., *The Beginnings of the Book Trade in Canada* (Toronto, Buffalo, and London: University of Toronto Press, 1985), p. 191.

[148]OTAR, Kirby, F-1076, Correspondence With Publishers, MU1635, A-6, ALS, Graeme Mercer Adam to Kirby, 29 January 1877.

[149]"Parkman, Francis," *DCB*, Vol. 12, pp. 823–27.

[150]OTAR, Kirby, F-1076, Correspondence With Publishers, MU1635, A-6, ALS, Graeme Mercer Adam to Kirby, 29 January 1877.

[151]Ibid., Copy of letter, Francis Parkman to Graeme Mercer Adam, 19 February 1877.

[152]"New Advertisements," *Quebec Daily Evening Mercury*, 12 March 1877, p. [3].

[153]OTAR, Kirby, F-1076, Correspondence With Publishers, MU1635, A-6, ALS, Graeme Mercer Adam to Kirby, 29 January 1877.

[154]Ibid., ALS, Graeme Mercer Adam to Kirby, 1 June 1877. No copy of this circular has been found.

[155]Elizabeth Hulse, *A Dictionary Of Toronto Printers, Publishers, Booksellers And The Allied Trades 1798–1900* (Toronto: Anson-Cartwright Editions, 1982), p. 40.

[156]OTAR, Kirby, F-1076, Correspondence With Publishers, MU1635, A-6, ALS, Graeme Mercer Adam to Kirby, 29 January 1877.

[157]Ibid., ALS, Graeme Mercer Adam to Kirby, 20 February 1877.

[158]Ibid., ALS, Graeme Mercer Adam to Kirby, 1 June 1877.

[159]"New Advertisements," *Quebec Daily Evening Mercury*, 12 March 1877, p. [3].

[160]OTAR, Kirby, F-1076, Correspondence With Publishers, MU1635, A-6, ALS, Robert Kurczyn Lovell to Kirby, 12 March 1877.

[161]Ibid., ALS, Robert Kurczyn Lovell to Kirby, 14 April 1877.

[162]"LE CHIEN D'OR," *Quebec Daily Evening Mercury*, 11 May 1877, p. [2].

[163]"NEW BOOKS," *Gazette* (Montreal), 2 April 1877, p. [2].

[164]"LE CHIEN D'OR!," *Quebec Daily Evening Mercury*, 4 April 1877, p. [3], and *Morning Chronicle* (Quebec), 4 April 1877, p. [2].

[165]"BOOK REVIEWS," *Morning Chronicle* (Halifax), 5 April 1877, p. [2].

[166]"NEW BOOKS," *Saint John Daily News*, 11 April 1877, p. [4].

[167]"J. & A. McMILLAN'S List of New Books," *Evening Telegraph* (Saint John), 31 May 1877, p. [3].

[168]"THE LATEST BOOKS," *Mail* (Toronto), 28 April 1877, p. [2].

[169] George L. Parker, *The Beginnings of the Book Trade in Canada* (Toronto, Buffalo, and London: University of Toronto Press, 1985), p. 177.

[170] "Books and Stationery," *Globe* (Toronto), 7 May 1877, p. 2.

[171] "Jas. Campbell & Son's BOOK LIST," *Globe* (Toronto), 9 May 1877, p. 2.

[172] "NEW BOOKS," *Free Press* (Ottawa), 14 April 1877, p. [3].

[173] "BOOKS," *Free Press* (London), 18 May 1877, p. [2].

[174] "THE NEW BOOK STORE," *British Whig* (Kingston), 17 May 1877, p. [2].

[175] OTAR, Kirby, F-1076, Correspondence With Publishers, MU1635, A-6, ALS, Robert Kurczyn Lovell to Kirby, 12 March 1877.

[176] Ibid., ALS, Robert Kurczyn Lovell to Kirby, 14 April 1877.

[177] "Publications Received," *North American Review*, 124 (1877), 515.

[178] "New Books," *New York Evening Mail*, 4 May 1877, p. [1].

[179] "LE CHIEN D'OR—THE GOLDEN DOG," *Gazette* (Montreal), 21 February 1877, p. [2].

[180] "LE CHIEN D'OR," *Daily Witness* (Montreal), 9 March 1877, p. [4].

[181] "LITERATURE," *Montreal Herald*, 21 March 1877, p. [4].

[182] "Books Received," *Canadian Monthly and National Review*, 2 (1877), 456.

[183] "BOOK REVIEWS: LE CHIEN D'OR," *Canadian Monthly and National Review*, 2 (1877), 564–65.

[184] "LE CHIEN D'OR," *Daily News* (St. Catharines), 5 July 1877, p. [2].

[185] Pantaléon Hudon, "BIBLIOGRAPHIE," *Revue Canadienne*, 4 (1877), [227].

[186] "BOOK REVIEWS," *Morning Chronicle* (Halifax), 5 April 1877, p. [2].

[187] OTAR, Kirby, F-1076, Correspondence With Publishers, MU1635, A-6, ALS, William Henry Withrow to Kirby, 24 February 1877.

[188] Ibid., ALS, William Henry Withrow to Kirby, 8 March 1877.

[189] "Book Notices," *Canadian Methodist Magazine*, 5 (1877), 378–80.

[190] OTAR, Kirby, F-1076, The LeMoine Papers, MU1634, A-1, ALS, James MacPherson Le Moine to Kirby, 10 March 1877.

[191] Ibid., ALS, James MacPherson Le Moine to Kirby, 22 March 1877.

[192] Ibid., ALS, Kirby to James MacPherson Le Moine, 27 March 1877.

[193] Ibid., ALS, Kirby to James MacPherson Le Moine, 28 March 1877.

[194] Ibid., ALS, James MacPherson Le Moine to Kirby, 2 April 1877.

[195] James MacPherson Le Moine, "The Chien d'Or—The Golden Dog," *Morning Chronicle* (Quebec), 7 April 1877, p. [1].

[196] OTAR, Kirby, F-1076, The LeMoine Papers, MU1634, A-1, ALS, James MacPherson Le Moine to Kirby, 29 April 1877.

[197] James MacPherson Le Moine, "THE CHIEN D'OR—THE GOLDEN DOG," *Canadian Antiquarian and Numismatic Journal*, 6 (1877), 10–14.

[198] OTAR, Kirby, F-1076, The Sulte Correspondence, MU1634, A-2, ALS, Benjamin Sulte to Kirby, 10 March 1877.

[199] Ibid., ALS, Benjamin Sulte to Kirby, 9 April 1877.

[200] Ibid., ALS, Benjamin Sulte to Kirby, 10 April 1877.

[201] Benjamin Sulte, " 'Le Chien D'Or,' " *Opinion Publique* (Montreal), 3 May 1877, p. 208.

[202] Benjamin Sulte, "Revue des Livres nouveaux," *Foyer Domestique* (Ottawa), 17 January 1878, p. 35.

[203] OTAR, Kirby, F-1076, The Sulte Correspondence, MU1634, A-2, ALS, Benjamin Sulte to Kirby, 7 January 1878.

[204] Ibid., Correspondence With Publishers, MU1635, A-6, ALS, Graeme Mercer Adam to Kirby, 29 January 1877.

[205] Ibid., ALS, Graeme Mercer Adam to Kirby, 20 February 1877.

[206] "Blackwood . . . , Frederick Temple," *DCB*, Vol. 13, pp. 72–76.

[207] OTAR, Kirby, F-1076, The Rye Correspondence, MU1637, A-16, ALS, Maria Susan Rye to Kirby, 13 March 1877.

[208] "Publications Of The Month: Fiction," *Bookseller* (London), 2 April 1877, p. 330.

[209] OTAR, Kirby, F-1076, Correspondence With Publishers, MU1635, A-6, ALS, Graeme Mercer Adam to Kirby, 1 June 1877.

[210] Ibid., ALS, John Wurtele Lovell to Kirby, 12 January 1877.

[211] Ibid., ALS, William Henry Withrow to Kirby, 7 February 1878.

[212] Ibid., ALS, Robert Kurczyn Lovell to Kirby, 14 April 1877.

[213] Ibid., The LeMoine Papers, MU1634, A-1, ALS, James MacPherson Le Moine to Kirby, 24 March 1877.

[214] Ibid., Correspondence With Publishers, MU1635, A-6, ALS, Graeme Mercer Adam to Kirby, 1 June 1877.

[215] "Literary and Historical Society," *Morning Chronicle* (Quebec), 17 April 1877, p. [1].

[216] OTAR, Kirby, F-1076, The LeMoine Papers, MU1634, A-1, ALS, James MacPherson Le Moine to Kirby, 10 May 1877.

[217] "LANCEFIELD'S CIRCULATING LIBRARY," *Spectator* (Hamilton), 16 April 1877, p. [1].

[218] OTAR, Kirby, F-1076, Correspondence With Publishers, MU1635, A-6, Statement of account, Lovell, Adam, Wesson and Company to Kirby, 1 June 1877.

[219] Ibid., Correspondence With Famous Persons, MU1638, A-22, Kirby's holograph copy of letter to Lord Dufferin, 15 March 1877. See also *Canadian Novelists and the Novel*, ed. Douglas Daymond and Leslie Monkman (Ottawa: Borealis Press, 1981), pp. 60–61.

[220] OTAR, Kirby, F-1076, The Sulte Correspondence, MU1634, A-2, ALS, Benjamin Sulte to Kirby, 8 November 1877.

[221] Ibid., ALS, Benjamin Sulte to Kirby, 7 January 1878.

[222] Ibid., Scrapbook, MU1655, H-8, 1st Items re Printing Chien D'Or.

[223] Ibid., Diaries, MU1640, Series B, William Kirby, Entry for 22 October 1879.

[224] "Campbell, John George Edward Henry Douglas Sutherland," *DCB*, Vol. 14, pp. 177–80.

[225] OTAR, Kirby, F-1076, Scrapbook, MU1655, H-8, Kirby, Holograph note re meeting Princess Louise on 24 May 1883.

[226] Hallam Tennyson to Kirby, 4 August 1886, *Alfred, Lord Tennyson and William Kirby: Unpublished correspondence to which are added some letters from Hallam, Lord Tennyson*, ed. Lorne Pierce (Toronto: The Macmillan Company of Canada, 1929), p. 60.

[227] OTAR, Kirby, F-1076, Correspondence With Publishers, MU1635, A-6, ALS, William Henry Withrow to Kirby, 7 February 1878.

[228] Ibid., ALS, John Lovell to Kirby, 2 April 1878.

[229] Ibid., ALS, John Wurtele Lovell to Kirby, 11 April 1878.

[230] Ibid., ALS, Graeme Mercer Adam to Kirby, 11 July 1878.

[231] "The Obituary Record: Richard Worthington," *New York Times*, 9 October 1894, p. 3.

[232] OTAR, Kirby, F-1076, Correspondence With Publishers, MU1635, A-6, ALS, William Henry Withrow to Kirby, 7 February 1878.

[233] Ibid., ALS, John Lovell to Kirby, 2 April 1878.

[234] Ibid., ALS, William Henry Withrow to Kirby, 9 April 1878.

[235] Ibid., ALS, John Wurtele Lovell to Kirby, 11 April 1878.

[236] David Dzwonkoski, "John W. Lovell Company," *DLB*, Vol. 49: *American Literary Publishing Houses, 1638–1899 Part 1: A-M*, pp. 282–86.

[237] OTMCL, Typescript, William Kirby, Junior, "Brief Of The Publications Of William Kirby's 'Le Chien D'Or' (The Golden Dog) To Dr. Lorne Pierce," 1925.

[238] Richard Garnett, rev. Megan A. Stephan, "Rice, (Samuel) James (1844–1882)," *ODNB* [http://www.oxforddnb.com.proxy.library.carleton. ca/view/article/23478, accessed 9 August 2008]. See also Simon Eliot, "Besant, Sir Walter (1836–1901)," *ODNB* [http://www.oxforddnb.com. proxy.library.carleton.ca/view/article/30736, accessed 9 August 2008].

[239] Walter Besant, and James Rice, "Le Chien d'Or," *Graphic* (Summer 1878), 12–13, 16, and 19–20. Illustrations of the story appear on pp. 19 and 22.

[240] OTAR, Kirby, F-1076, Newspapers and Periodicals, MU1660, I-52, *Graphic* (Summer 1878), 12.

[241] Ibid., Correspondence with Publishers, MU1635, A-6, ALS, Stillman S. Conant to Kirby, 12 July 1878.

[242] Ibid., The Sulte Correspondence, MU1634, A-2, ALS, Benjamin Sulte to Kirby, 18 July 1878.

[243] Benjamin Sulte, "Le *Chien d'Or*," *Opinion Publique* (Montreal), 1 August 1878, p. 365.

[244] "Editorial Notes," *Mail* (Toronto), 15 July 1878, p. [2].

[245] *Orillia Packet*, 26 July 1878, p. [1].

[246] OTAR, Kirby, F-1076, Correspondence With Publishers, MU1635, A-6, ALS, Graeme Mercer Adam to Kirby, 11 July 1878.

[247] Graeme Mercer Adam, "Copyright In Canada," *Athenæum* (London),

13 July 1878, pp. 47–48.

[248] OTAR, Kirby, F-1076, Correspondence With Publishers, MU1635, A-6, ALS, Graeme Mercer Adam to Kirby, [12?] July 1878.

[249] Graeme Mercer Adam, "Communications. Copyright And Authors' Rights And Wrongs," *Mail* (Toronto), 27 July 1878, p. [4].

[250] "An Alleged Plagiarism Denied," *Mail* (Toronto), 4 September 1878, p. [2].

[251] Graeme Mercer Adam, "Communications. The 'Chien D'Or' Alleged Plagiarism," *Mail* (Toronto), 5 September 1878, p. [4].

[252] OTAR, Kirby, F-1076, Correspondence With Publishers, MU1635, A-6, ALS, Graeme Mercer Adam to Kirby, 4 September 1878.

[253] Ibid., ALS, Graeme Mercer Adam to Kirby, 9 September 1878.

[254] Walter Besant, and James Rice, "AUTHORSHIP OF 'LE CHIEN D'OR," *Evening Telegram* (Toronto), 17 September 1878, p. [4].

[255] OTAR, Kirby, F-1076, Correspondence With Publishers, MU1635, A-6, ALS, Graeme Mercer Adam to Kirby, 18 September 1878.

[256] "A Literary Matter," *Evening Telegram* (Toronto), 18 September 1878, p. [2].

[257] OTAR, Kirby, F-1076, Correspondence With Publishers, MU1635, A-6, ALS, Graeme Mercer Adam to Kirby, 18 September 1878.

[258] Ibid., Miscellaneous Manuscripts Compiled or Copied by Kirby, MU1646, D-21, A draft by Kirby of a report made to G. Mercer Adams re the "Besant-Rice" piracy of the Chien d'Or, which appeared in the London *Graphic* in 1878.

[259] Graeme Mercer Adam, "Communications. The 'Chien D'Or' Alleged Plagiarism," *Mail* (Toronto), 20 September 1878, p. [4].

[260] OTAR, Kirby, F-1076, Correspondence With Publishers, MU1635, A-6, ALS, Graeme Mercer Adam to Kirby, 21 September 1878.

[261] Ibid., ALS, Graeme Mercer Adam to Kirby, 13 November 1878.

[262] Ibid., ALS, Graeme Mercer Adam to Kirby, [12?] July 1878.

[263] *Globe* (Toronto), 21 September 1878, p. 4, and *Mail* (Toronto), 21 September 1878, p. [4].

[264] OTAR, Kirby, F-1076, Correspondence With Publishers, MU1635, A-6, ALS, Graeme Mercer Adam to Kirby, 21 September 1878.

[265] Ibid., ALS, Dawson Brothers to Kirby, 2 June 1882.

[266] Ibid., The John C. Kirby Correspondence, MU1636, A-7, ALS, Kirby to John Colborne Kirby, 21 June 1882.

[267] Ibid., Correspondence With Publishers, MU1635, A-6, ALS, Dawson Brothers to Kirby, 24 June 1882.

[268] Ibid., ALS, Samuel Edward Dawson to Kirby, 28 July 1882.

[269] Ibid., ALS, Samuel Edward Dawson to Kirby, 2 September 1884.

[270] Ibid., ALS, Graeme Mercer Adam to Kirby, 27 August 1884.

[271] Ibid., ALS, Graeme Mercer Adam to Kirby, 21 October 1884.

[272] Ibid., ALS, Graeme Mercer Adam to Kirby, 21 November 1884.

The Williamson mentioned in this letter was probably Thomas Gibbs Williamson; he established Williamson and Company in 1884.

[273]Ibid., ALS, William Henry Withrow to Kirby, 19 January 1880.

[274]Ibid., ALS, W. F. Graham to Kirby, 25 March 1885.

[275]Guinevere L. Griest, *Mudie's Circulating Library and the Victorian Novel* (Bloomington and London: Indiana University Press, 1970), p. 24.

[276]Ibid., p. 101.

[277]OTAR, Kirby, F-1076, Correspondence With Publishers, MU1635, A-6, ALS, Richard Bentley and Son to Kirby, 19 December 1884.

[278]British Library, Add. Ms. 55419, Macmillan Archives, Letter Books, 24 December 1884–23 June 1885, folio 205, Macmillan and Company to Kirby, 20 January 1885.

[279]OTAR, Kirby, F-1076, Correspondence With Publishers, MU1635, A-6, ALS, Alexander Macmillan to Kirby, 16 April 1885. See also British Library, Add. Ms. 55419, Macmillan Archives, Letter Books, 24 December 1884–23 June 1885, folio 979.

[280]Rosemary T. Van Arsdel, "Macmillan family (*per. c. 1840–1986*)," *ODNB* [http://www.oxforddnb.com.proxy.library.carleton.ca/view/article/63220, accessed 1 September 2008].

[281]OTAR, Kirby, F-1076, Correspondence With Publishers, MU1635, A-6, ALS, Alexander Macmillan to Kirby, 16 April 1885. See also British Library, Add. Ms. 55419, Macmillan Archives, Letter Books, 24 December 1884–23 June 1885, folio 979.

[282]Ibid., "Chien d'Or." See also British Library, Add. Ms. 55937, Macmillan Archives, Readers' Reports, Vol. MCLII, 1883–1885, p. 67. This, the original report, contains the following sentences that were omitted in the version sent to Kirby, "In its kind it is not bad. But I have a strongish impression that a taste for the romance of the G. P. R. James school has gone out altogether. It would require a writer of great power to revive it, and the present writer is not in any way powerful." In the 1830s, 1840s, and 1850s George Payne Rainsford James was a prolific writer of "fast-paced historical romances set in a wide variety of places and periods" in the tradition of Sir Walter Scott. See Stephanie L. Barczewski, "James, George Payne Rainsford (1801–1860)," *ODNB* [http://www.oxforddnb.com.proxy.library.carleton.ca/view/article/14605, accessed 3 September 2008].

[283]Ibid., ALS, Alexander Macmillan to Kirby, 19 May 1885. See also British Library, Add. Ms. 55424, Macmillan Archives, Letter Books, 24 December 1884–23 June 1885, folio 1187.

[284]Ibid., ALS, Maria Susan Rye to Kirby, 27 May 1886.

[285]Fred Hunter, "Morley, Henry (1822–1894)," *ODNB* [http://www.oxforddnb.com.proxy.library.carleton.ca/view/article/19286, accessed 18 August 2008].

[286]OTAR, Kirby, F-1076, Correspondence With Publishers, MU1635, A-6, ALS, Maria Susan Rye to Kirby, 27 May 1886.

[287] Ibid., The Rye Correspondence, MU1637, A-16, ALS, Maria Susan Rye to Kirby, 30 June 1886.

[288] David Hamer, "Morley, John, Viscount Morley of Blackburn (1838–1923)," *ODNB* [http://www.oxforddnb.com.proxy.library.carleton. ca/view/article/35110, accessed 2 September 2008].

[289] Robertson Davies, "Irving, Sir Henry (1838–1905)," *ODNB* [http://www.oxforddnb.com.proxy.library.carleton.ca/view/article/34116, accessed 4 September 2008].

[290] OTAR, Kirby, F-1076, Miscellaneous Manuscripts Compiled or Copied by Kirby, MU1646, D-13, A manuscript copy of a tragedy dramatization of the Chien d'Or entitled "Beaumanoir." The fragment consists of parts of Act Five.

[291] Ibid., The Rye Correspondence, MU1637, A-16, ALS, Maria Susan Rye to Kirby, 30 June 1886.

[292] Ibid., Correspondence With Publishers, MU1635, A-6, ALS, Henry Irving to Maria Susan Rye, 13 July 1886.

[293] "Vincent, Sarah Anne (Curzon)," *DCB*, Vol. 12, pp. 1075–76.

[294] Sarah Anne Vincent Curzon, "Prominent Canadians.—No. XLVII. William Kirby, F. R. S. C.," *Week* (Toronto), 19 January 1894, pp. 176–79.

[295] Public Record Office, London, RG12/3928, folio 36, p. 24, Census for 1891, Kingston Upon Hull, Yorkshire, England.

[296] OTAR, Kirby, F-1076, The Curzon-Currie Correspondence, MU1634, A-5, ALS, Sarah Anne Vincent Curzon to Kirby, 14 October 1892.

[297] Ibid., Correspondence With Publishers, MU1635, A-6, ALS, Charles Mason to Kirby, 8 November 1892.

[298] Ibid., ALS, Charles Mason to Kirby, 23 January 1893.

[299] Elizabeth Brady, "A Bibliographical Essay On William Kirby's *The Golden Dog* 1877–1977," *Papers of the Bibliographical Society of Canada*, 15 (1976), 24–48.

[300] OTAR, Kirby, F-1076, Correspondence With Publishers, MU1635, A-6, ALS, Graeme Mercer Adam to Kirby, 23 October 1878.

[301] Ibid., ALS, Graeme Mercer Adam to Kirby, 13 November 1878.

[302] Ibid., ALS, William Henry Withrow to Kirby, 14 February 1879.

[303] Ibid., ALS, Russell Wilkinson to Kirby, 22 March 1880. Kirby's grandson, probably confusing R. Wilkinson with R. Worthington, added the following note to this letter in 1924, "This is one of the (Skunks) who was supposed to be implicated in the theft of the original ms."

[304] Ibid., Kirby's holograph copy of letter to Richard Worthington, 12 April 1880.

[305] Ibid., ALS, Richard Worthington to Kirby, 15 April 1880.

[306] David Dzwonkoski, "John W. Lovell," *DLB*, Vol. 49: *American Literary Publishing Houses, 1638–1899 Part 1: A-M*, pp. 282–86.

[307] OTAR, Kirby, F-1076, Correspondence With Publishers, MU1635, A-6, ALS, Graeme Mercer Adam to Kirby, 21 November 1884.

[308] Ibid., ALS, John Wurtele Lovell to Kirby, 22 November 1884.

[309] Ibid., The LeMoine Papers, MU1634, A-1, ALS, James MacPherson Le Moine to Kirby, 25 December 1885.

[310] Ibid., ALS, James MacPherson Le Moine to Kirby, 27 October 1888.

[311] Ibid., ALS, James MacPherson Le Moine to Kirby, 25 September 1889.

[312] Elizabeth Brady, "A Bibliographical Essay On William Kirby's *The Golden Dog* 1877–1977," *Papers of the Bibliographical Society of Canada*, 15 (1976), 24–48.

[313] David Dzwonkoski, "John W. Lovell," *DLB*, Vol. 49: *American Literary Publishing Houses, 1638–1899 Part 1: A-M*, pp. 282–86.

[314] Ibid., "Lovell, Coryell and Company," *DLB*, Vol. 49: *American Literary Publishing Houses, 1638–1899 Part 1: A-M*, pp. 286–87.

[315] Ibid., "United States Book Company ... American Publishers Corporation," *DLB*, Vol. 49: *American Literary Publishing Houses, 1638–1899 Part 2: N-Z*, pp. 472–73.

[316] This copy is now owned by Library and Archives Canada; its call number is PS8471 I73G6 1877a.

[317] OTAR, Kirby, F-1076, Correspondence With Publishers, MU1635, A-6, ALS, A. P. Watts and Company to Kirby, 20 November 1894.

[318] Carl Theophilus Odhner, "*The Golden Dog*," *New Church Life*, 17 (1897), 189–90.

[319] David Dzwonkoski, "United States Book Company ... American Publishers Corporation," *DLB*, Vol. 49: *American Literary Publishing Houses, 1638–1899 Part 2: N-Z*, pp. 472–73.

[320] "The Golden Dog (Le Chien d'Or.)," *Sun* (New York), 25 September 1897, p. 7.

[321] "H. B. NIMS & CO.—JOSEPH KNIGHT CO.," *Publishers' Weekly*, 23 April 1892, p. 642.

[322] "Page Company Absorbs Dana Estes & Co.," *Publishers' Weekly*, 28 March 1914, pp. 1098–1100.

[323] "New Books Reviewed," *Canada Bookseller And Stationer*, 12 (December 1896), 2.

[324] "Obituary Notes. Lewis Coues Page," *Publishers' Weekly*, 28 May 1956, p. 2257.

[325] OTAR, Kirby, F-1076, Correspondence With Publishers, MU1635, A-6, TLS, L. C. Page to Kirby, 5 December 1896. Kirby's grandson wrote on this letter, "A pretty Yankee trick."

[326] Ibid., TLS, George Page to Kirby, 22 September 1897.

[327] "Special Editions Of Latest Novels," *Bookseller And Stationer*, 13 (August 1897), 19.

[328] "The Montreal News Co.," *Bookseller And Stationer*, 13 (August 1897), 5.

[329] Norwich, England, Jarrold and Sons, Archives, Copyright Agreements and Agreements with Other Publishers, Methodist Publishing Company, Letters re *The Golden Dog*, Typed Copy, TLS, L. C. Page and Company to

Methodist Book and Publishing House, 13 July 1906.

[330]Donna Nance, "American News Company," *DLB*, Vol. 49: *American Literary Publishing Houses, 1638–1899 Part 1: A-M*, pp. 10–11.

[331]OTAR, Kirby, F-1076, Correspondence With Publishers, MU1635, A-6, TLS, L. C. Page to Kirby, 5 December 1896.

[332]Ibid., TLS, L. C. Page and Company to Kirby, 25 March 1897.

[333]Ibid., TLS, L. C. Page and Company to Kirby, 9 April 1897.

[334]OONA, MG29, D72, Vol. 7, Correspondence, James MacPherson Le Moine, ALS, Kirby to James MacPherson Le Moine, 31 March 1897.

[335]OTAR, Kirby, F-1076, Correspondence With Publishers, MU1635, A-6, TLS, L. C. Page and Company to Kirby, 9 April 1897.

[336]Ibid., TLS, L. C. Page and Company to Kirby, 17 April 1897.

[337]Ibid., TLS, L. C. Page and Company to Kirby, 26 April 1897.

[338]Ibid., Kirby's holograph copy of letter to L. C. Page and Company, 29 April 1897.

[339]Ibid., Miscellaneous Manuscripts (Other Than Kirby's), MU1648, E-6, Contract with L. C. Page and Company, Boston, to print an authorized version of The Golden Dog. 1 May 1897.

[340]Ibid., TLS, L. C. Page and Company to Kirby, 1 May 1897.

[341]Ibid., TLS, L. C. Page and Company to Kirby, 10 May 1897.

[342]Ibid., TLS, L. C. Page and Company to Kirby, 19 May 1897.

[343]Ibid., Miscellaneous Manuscripts Compiled or Copied by Kirby, MU1646, D-22, A draft of the proposed author's prefatory note by Kirby to be inserted in an edition of the Chien d'Or which L. C. Page and Company intended to publish. May 1897.

[344]Ibid., Correspondence With Publishers, MU1635, A-6, TLS, L. C. Page to Kirby, 19 May 1897. Despite what might be considered his shady dealings with Kirby, in addition to issuing works by Margaret Marshall Saunders, Page and his company were also the publishers of such other Canadian authors as Lucy Maud Montgomery and Charles G. D. Roberts.

[345]Vivien Allen, "Caine, Sir (Thomas Henry) Hall (1853–1931)," *ODNB* [http://www.oxforddnb.com.proxy.carleton.ca/view/article/32237, accessed 13 October 2008].

[346]Kirby, "Author's Prefatory Note," *The Golden Dog (Le Chien D'Or) A Romance of the Days of Louis Quinze in Quebec* (Boston: L. C. Page and Company, 1897), p. [iii].

[347]For further descriptions of this edition, see Elizabeth Brady, "A Bibliographical Essay On William Kirby's *The Golden Dog* (1877–1977)," *Papers of the Bibliographical Society of Canada*, 15 (1976), 24–48.

[348]"Canadian Books And Writers," *Bookseller And Stationer*, 13 (September 1897), 3.

[349]"Literary Notes," *Dial* (Chicago), 16 September 1897, p. 161.

[350]"New Literature," *Boston Daily Globe*, 18 September 1897, p. 2.

[351]"STIRRING ROMANCE OF CANADIAN LIFE. Strange Adventures in

Quebec During the Time of Louis Quinze," *New York Herald,* 4 September 1897, p. 13.

[352]OTMCL, Typescript, William Kirby, Junior, "Brief Of The Publications Of William Kirby's 'Le Chien D'Or' (The Golden Dog) To Dr. Lorne Pierce," 1925.

[353]OTAR, Kirby, F-1076, Correspondence With Publishers, MU1635, A-6, TLS, L. C. Page and Company to Kirby, 22 September 1897.

[354]Ibid., TLS, L. C. Page and Company to Kirby, 8 December 1897.

[355]Ibid., Copyright Account, L. C. Page and Company for Kirby, 1 February 1898.

[356]Ibid., TLS, L. C. Page and Company to Kirby, 16 February 1898.

[357]Ibid., L. C. Page and Company to Kirby, 7 November 1897 to 9 February 1906.

[358]"Montreal Book Notes," *Bookseller And Stationer,* 13 (November 1897), 6.

[359]Norwich, England, Jarrold and Sons, Archives, Copyright Agreements and Agreements with Other Publishers, Methodist Publishing Company, Letters re *The Golden Dog,* Typed Copy, TLS, L. C. Page and Company to Methodist Book and Publishing House, 13 July 1906.

[360]"Mr. Henry Brophy. Manager Montreal News Co.," *Bookseller And Stationer,* 15 (July 1899), 23.

[361]"THREE GREAT CANADIAN BOOKS," *Ibid.,* 14 (July 1898), 7.

[362]"SUMMER EDITIONS," *Ibid.,* 14 (July 1898), 3.

[363]Advertisement of F. E. Grafton and Sons, Montreal, *Ibid.,* 14 (July 1898), 6.

[364]"Notes," *Ibid.,* 16 (January 1900), 2.

[365]Ernest H. Cooper, "Montreal Trade News," *Ibid.,* 16 (August 1900), 8.

[366]OTAR, Kirby, F-1076, Correspondence With Publishers, MU1635, A-6, TLS, L. C. Page and Company to Kirby, 22 September 1897.

[367]Ibid., TLS, L. C. Page and Company to Kirby, 1 May 1897.

[368]Ibid., TLS, L. C. Page and Company to Kirby, 19 May 1897.

[369]Elizabeth Brady, "A Bibliographical Essay On William Kirby's *The Golden Dog* 1877–1977," *Papers of the Bibliographical Society of Canada,* 15 (1976), 24–48.

[370]Lorne Pierce, *William Kirby The Portrait of a Tory Loyalist* (Toronto: The Macmillan Company of Canada, 1929), p. 255.

[371]OTMCL, Typescript, William Kirby, Junior, "Brief Of The Publications Of William Kirby's 'Le Chien D'Or' (The Golden Dog) To Dr. Lorne Pierce," 1925.

[372]"The Rev. Dr. Frank Sewall," *New York Times,* 8 December 1915, p. 16.

[373]OTAR, Kirby, F-1076, Correspondence With Publishers, MU1635, A-6, ALS, Frank Sewall to Kirby, 11 February 1903.

[374]Ibid., Kirby's holograph copy of letter to L. C. Page, 23 February 1903.

[375]Ibid., TL-C, L. C. Page and Company to Frank Sewall, 9 February 1903.

[376]Ibid., TLS, L. C. Page and Company to Kirby, 25 February 1903.

[377] Frank Sewall, "A Canadian Retrospect," *New Church Messenger*, 6 May 1903, p. 282. A copy of this review was pasted into the copy of the Joseph Knight impression of the first edition held at OTAR. See Kirby, F-1076, Kirby Library, MU1675, L-68, Box 41.

[378] OTAR, Kirby, F-1076, The Marquis of Lorne Correspondence, MU1637, A-12, ALS, Marquess of Lorne to Kirby, 22 October 1903.

[379] Ibid., ALS, Kirby to Marquess of Lorne, 9 November 1903.

[380] OONA, MG29, D91, Letters from William Kirby to Hannah Catharine Lowe Servos, ALS, Kirby to Hannah Lowe Servos, 1 November 1905.

[381] "Dionne, Narcisse-Eutrope," *DCB*, Vol. 14, pp. 300–02.

[382] "Sir Arthur George Doughty (1860–1935)," *Behind the Diary*, http: //www.collectionscanada.gc.ca/king/05320113/053201130416_e.html.

[383] Arthur George Doughty and Narcisse-Eutrope Dionne, *Quebec Under Two Flags: A Brief history of the City* (Quebec: The Quebec News Company, 1903), pp. 147–65.

[384] OONA, MG30, D47, John Alexander Cooper Fonds, ALS, Kirby to John Alexander Cooper, 20 January 1904.

[385] OKQ, Archives, Lorne and Edith Pierce Collection, 2001.1, Box 42, File 6, ALS, John Alexander Cooper to Kirby, 25 January 1904.

[386] OONA, MG30, D47, John Alexander Cooper Fonds, ALS, Kirby to John Alexander Cooper, 20 January 1904.

[387] Ibid., ALS, Kirby to John Alexander Cooper, 27 January 1904.

[388] Norwich, England, Jarrold and Sons, Archives, Copy, TLS, L. C. Page and Company to William Briggs, Methodist Book and Publishing House, 6 July 1906.

[389] Ibid., List of Copyrights, Vol. 1.

[390] Advertisement: Jarrold and Sons, *Publishers' Circular* (London), 30 September 1899, p. 367.

[391] "Forthcoming Publications," *World* (London), 11 October 1899, p. 29.

[392] Norwich, England, Jarrold and Sons, Archives, Scrapbook of book announcements [1896–1900], "The Golden Dog," p. 179.

[393] The description of the Jarrold edition of 1899 is based on this copy, now registered as call number 012703.ee.39 in the British Library.

[394] "*FICTION*," *Scotsman* (Edinburgh), 6 November 1899, p. 3.

[395] Review of *The Golden Dog*, *Manchester Guardian*, 14 November 1899, p. 4.

[396] "FICTION—OLD AND NEW," *Dundee Advertiser*, 23 November 1899, p. 2.

[397] "LITERARY NOTICES," *Sheffield And Rotherham Independent*, 29 November 1899, p. 2.

[398] "LITERATURE: *NOVELS AND STORIES*," *Glasgow Herald*, 11 December 1899, p. 11.

[399] This advertisement can be seen, for example, in at least some copies of *In The Promised Land A Novel*, a translation of *Za Chleben* by Henryk Sienkiewicz, the Polish author who won the Nobel Prize for Literature in

1905.

[400] *Catalogue Of Messrs. Jarrold & Sons' Publications* (London: Jarrold & Sons, [1900]), p. 13.

[401] See, for example, *Selections from Jarrold & Sons' List of Fiction*, 1901, a copy of which is bound into at least some copies of *Autumn Glory Or The Toilers of the Field*, a translation of *La Terre Qui Meurt* by the French author René Bazin that Jarrold published in 1901.

[402] "The New English Fiction," *Bookseller And Stationer*, 15 (November 1899), 19.

[403] OTAR, Kirby, F-1076, The Marquis of Lorne Correspondence, MU1637, A-12, ALS, Kirby to Marquess of Lorne, 9 November 1903.

[404] Ibid., The Sir Gilbert Parker Correspondence, MU1634, A-3, TLS, Gilbert Parker to Kirby, 18 February 1904.

[405] Ibid., ALS, Gilbert Parker to Kirby, 29 October 1900.

[406] Ibid., ALS, Kirby to Gilbert Parker, 27 April 1904.

[407] Ibid., The Marquis of Lorne Correspondence, MU1637, A-12, ALS, Kirby to Marquess of Lorne, 31 July 1905.

[408] "NEW BOOKS AND PUBLICATIONS," *Argus* (Melbourne), 13 January 1900, p. 4.

[409] This information is contained on a sticker on the inside back cover of the copy in the Rhodes University Library.

[410] "Fiction Section," *A Catalogue Of The Library Of* The Times Book Club (London: *The Times*, 1908), p. 599.

[411] "Briggs, William," *DCB*, Vol. 15, pp. 147–49.

[412] Norwich, England, Jarrold and Sons, Archives, Copyright Agreements and Agreements with Other Publishers, Methodist Publishing Company, Letters re *The Golden Dog*, 1906, TLS, William Briggs to Jarrold and Sons, 2 March 1906.

[413] Ibid., ALS, William Briggs to Jarrold and Sons, 27 March 1906.

[414] Ibid., ALS, William Tillyer to Jarrold and Sons, 30 July 1906.

[415] Ibid., Typed Copy, TLS, L. C. Page and Company to Methodist Book and Publishing House, 6 July 1906.

[416] Ibid., Typed Copy, TLS, William Briggs to L. C. Page and Company, 10 July 1906.

[417] Ibid., Typed Copy, TLS, L. C. Page and Company to Methodist Book and Publishing House, 13 July 1906.

[418] Ibid., Typed Copy, TLS, William Briggs to L. C. Page and Company, 16 July 1906.

[419] Ibid., TLS, William Briggs to Jarrold and Sons, 16 July 1906.

[420] Ibid., ALS, William Tillyer to Jarrold and Sons, 30 July 1906.

[421] Ibid., TLS, William Briggs to Jarrold and Sons, 17 October 1906.

[422] OTAR, Kirby, F-1076, The Sulte Correspondence, MU1634, A-2, ALS, Benjamin Sulte to Kirby, 9 April 1877.

[423] Ibid., ALS, Benjamin Sulte to Kirby, 17 May 1877.

[424]David M. Hayne, "*The Golden Dog* and *Le Chien d'or*: Le May's French Translation of Kirby's Novel," *Publications of the Bibliographical Society of Canada*, 20 (1981), 50–62.

[425]OTAR, Kirby, F-1076, The Sulte Correspondence, MU1634, A-2, ALS, Benjamin Sulte to Kirby, 28 February 1880.

[426]Ibid., Correspondence With Publishers, MU1635, A-6, ALS, Joseph-Charles Taché, Department of Agriculture, Ottawa, to Josiah Burr Plumb, 10 March 1880.

[427]"Fréchette, Louis," *DCB*, Vol. 13, pp. 358–62.

[428]OTAR, Kirby, F-1076, Correspondence With Publishers, MU1635, A-6, ALS, Louis Fréchette to Kirby, 17 January 1884.

[429]Ibid., Kirby's holograph copy of letter to Louis Fréchette, 21 January 1884.

[430]"Trudel, François-Xavier-Anselme," *DCB*, Vol. 11, pp. 891–95.

[431]Paul Rutherford, *A Victorian Authority: the daily press in late nineteenth-century Canada* (Toronto: University of Toronto Press, 1982), p. 63.

[432]OTAR, Kirby, F-1076, Correspondence With Publishers, MU1635, A-6, ALS, F-X-A Trudel to Kirby, 24 April 1884.

[433]Ibid., ALS, F-X-A Trudel to Kirby, 16 May 1884.

[434]Ibid., The Sulte Correspondence, MU1634, A-2, ALS, Kirby to Benjamin Sulte, 18 March 1866.

[435]Ibid., Correspondence With Publishers, MU1635, A-6, ALS, Pamphile Le May to Kirby, 2 June 1884.

[436]Ibid., Miscellaneous Manuscripts, MU1648, E-9, Agreement between the Etendard Publishing Company of Montreal and Kirby, 26 May 1884.

[437]Ibid., Correspondence With Publishers, MU1635, A-6, ALS, F-X-A Trudel to Kirby, 16 May 1884.

[438]Ibid., Miscellaneous Manuscripts, MU1648, E-9, ALS, F-X-A Trudel to Kirby, 31 May 1884.

[439]"Current Literary Topics," *Toronto Daily Mail*, 28 June 1884, p. 6.

[440]OTAR, Kirby, F-1076, Correspondence With Publishers, MU1635, A-6, ALS, Kirby to F-X-A Trudel, 5 [August] 1884.

[441]Ibid., ALS, Pamphile Le May to Kirby, 30 November 1884.

[442]"Le Chien D'Or. *Prochain feuilleton de 'L'Etendard,'*" *Etendard* (Montreal), 1 August 1884, p. [2].

[443]"Le Chien d'Or," *Etendard* (Montreal), 7 August 1884, p. [2].

[444]"Littérature Canadienne. Le Chien D'Or," *Etendard* (Montreal), 27 August 1884, p. [2].

[445]Patriote, "Une oeuvre nationale," *Etendard* (Montreal), 15 October 1884, p. [2].

[446]"Le Chien D'Or," *Etendard* (Montreal), 30 March 1885, p. [2].

[447]OTAR, Kirby, F-1076, Correspondence With Publishers, MU1635, A-6, ALS, F-X-A Trudel to Kirby, 6 March 1885.

[448]Les Editeurs, "Pourquoi *Le Chien D'Or* Traduit En Français," *Le Chien*

D'Or: Légende Canadienne, by William Kirby (Montréal: Imprimerie De 'L'Etendard', 1884), Vol. 1, p. v. Both volumes are dated 1884, but they appeared in 1885.

[449]"La Légende Du Chien D'Or," *Le Chien D'Or*, 1884, Vol. 1, p. 6.

[450]"NEW BOOKS," *Montreal Daily Star*, 4 April 1885, p. 3. For Kirby's comment, see OTAR, Kirby, F-1076, Scrapbooks, MU1653, H-3.

[451]OTAR, Kirby, F-1076, The LeMoine Papers, MU1634, A-1, ALS, James MacPherson Le Moine to Kirby, 11 May 1885.

[452]Ibid., Correspondence With Publishers, MU1635, A-6, ALS, William Henry Withrow to Kirby, 8 June 1885.

[453]Ibid., The LeMoine Papers, MU1634, A-1, ALS, James MacPherson Le Moine to Kirby, 20 February 1885.

[454]Ibid., Correspondence With Publishers, MU1635, A-6, ALS, F-X-A Trudel to Kirby, 13 February 1886.

[455]Ibid., ALS, Pamphile Le May to Kirby, 20 April 1886. Le May added in the same letter the rather odd comment that the task of translating the novel was arduous "pour un traducteur qui ne sait pas l'anglais."

[456]Ibid., ALS, Valentin Augustus Landry to Kirby, 12 November 1887.

[457]Ibid., TLS, L. C. Page and Company to Kirby, 16 February 1898.

[458]Ibid., TLS, L. C. Page and Company to Kirby, 25 February 1898.

[459]Ibid., TLS, L. C. Page and Company to Kirby, 21 February 1899.

[460]Frank Yeigh, "Canada's Oldest Living Novelist," *Globe* (Toronto), 25 February 1905, p. M3.

[461]"Deaths," *Daily Mail and Empire* (Toronto), 25 June 1906, p. 5.

[462]"Death of W. Kirby," *Quebec Chronicle*, 25 June 1906, p. [1].

[463]"The Death Of William Kirby," *Daily Standard* (St. Catharines), 25 June 1906, p. [1].

[464]"Canadian Author Dead In Niagara," *Montreal Daily Star*, 25 June 1906, p. 13.

[465]"Poet And Novelist Dead. William Kirby, Author Of 'Le Chien D'Or' Passes Away," *Globe* (Toronto), 25 June 1906, p. 4.

[466]"William Kirby. Le plus vieux littérateur anglais décédé," *Patrie* (Montreal), p. 3.

[467]"William Kirby Dead," *Gazette* (Montreal), 25 June 1906, p. 7.

[468]"Burwash, Nathanael," *DCB*, Vol. 14, pp. 161–64.

[469]Nathanael Burwash, "Inaugural Introduction to Section II, Royal Society of Canada, 1907," *Transactions Of The Royal Society Of Canada*, Series 3, Vol. 1 (1907), 3–13.

[470]The Montreal News Company Limited, "Important Books for Your Summer Trade," *Bookseller And Stationer* 22 (July 1906), 18.

[471]*L'Annuaire Des Adresses De Québec Et Lévis* (Québec: L'Imprimerie "L'Action Sociale," 1908), p. 539.

[472]*Lovell's Montreal Directory for 1902–1903* (Montreal: John Lovell and Son, 1902), p. 1176.

[473] *Books I Have Read* (New York: Dodd, Mead, 1906), pp. 122–23.

[474] "New Edition Of Kirby's Golden Dog," *Canadian Magazine*, 57 (1921), 350.

[475] Elizabeth Brady, "A Bibliographical Essay On William Kirby's *The Golden Dog* 1877–1977," *Papers of the Bibliographical Society of Canada*, 15 (1976), 24–48.

[476] Ibid.

[477] *Lovell's Montreal Directory 1920–1921* (Montreal: John Lovell and Son, 1920), p. 1629.

[478] Thomas Guthrie Marquis, "Introduction," *The Golden Dog (Le Chien d'Or) A Romance of Old Quebec*, by Kirby (Toronto: The Musson Book Company Limited, [1925]), p. [v].

[479] *Lovell's Montreal Directory 1924–1925* (Montreal: John Lovell and Son, 1924), p. 883.

[480] Elizabeth Brady, "A Bibliographical Essay On William Kirby's *The Golden Dog* 1877–1977," *Papers of the Bibliographical Society of Canada*, 15 (1976), 24–48.

[481] OONA, MG28, I179, Canada Foundation (1942–1971). Ottawa, Vol. 44, File 2, Publishers. The Musson Book Company Ltd. 1943–1945.

[482] *The Canadian Catalogue of Books published in Canada, about Canada, as well as those written by Canadians, with imprint 1921–1949 (Consolidated English Language Reprint Edition) with Cumulated Author Index* (Toronto: Toronto Public Libraries, 1967), p. ZA12.

[483] "Canadian Books for Display at National Book League's Exhibition of Book Design, London, England, June 1947," *Globe and Mail* (Toronto), 7 June 1947, p. 12.

[484] *Canadian Books in Print. Catalogue des livres canadiens en librairie 1968*, ed. Gérard Simoneau (Toronto: Canadian Books in Print Committee, 1969), p. 244.

[485] McGill University, Montreal, Quebec, Osler Library, William Henry Drummond Papers, 439.10.37/7, Prospectus for "MASTER-WORKS of CANADIAN AUTHORS" Series, 1923.

[486] OKQ, Archives, Lorne and Edith Pierce Collection, 2001.1, Box 49, File 11, William Douw Lighthall, Typed draft of proposed introduction to edition of *The Golden Dog*: "The Golden Dog. (Le Chien D'Or," 27 February 1923.

[487] "Frederick P. Grove Now Heads Publishing Firm," *Toronto Daily Star*, 25 October 1930, p. 4.

[488] OTAR, Register of Wills, Lincoln County, MS887, Reel 1254, Number 2770, Kirby's Will, 15 June 1905.

[489] "Kirby Letters Big Find For Canadian Letters," *Toronto Daily Star*, 17 March 1925, pp. 1–2.

[490] Ibid.

[491] OKQ, Archives, Lorne and Edith Pierce Collection, 2001.1, Box 42,

File 16, Autograph Manuscript Signed, William Kirby, "A Reminiscence," 25 March 1925.

[492] OHM, Ready, Macmillan Canada fonds, Box 111, File 6, Kirby, William. The Golden Dog, 1927–33, Lorne Pierce, Memorandum Re Kirby, 1932.

[493] Percy Parker Ghent, *Literary and Historic Fragments Of Canadian Interest* (Toronto: Belcher Print Company, [1927]), p. 41.

[494] OHM, Ready, Macmillan Canada fonds, Box 111, File 6, Kirby, William. The Golden Dog, 1927–33, Lorne Pierce, Memorandum Re Kirby, 1932.

[495] The Anderson Galleries, Sale No. 2002 Catalogue, 1925, p. 16.

[496] "Claus, Christian Daniel," *DCB*, Vol. 4, pp. 154–55.

[497] OHM, Ready, Macmillan Canada fonds, Box 111, File 6, Kirby, William. The Golden Dog, 1927–33, Lorne Pierce, Memorandum Re Kirby, 1932.

[498] Ruth Panofsky, "Barometers of Change, Presidents Hugh Eayrs and John Gray of the Macmillan Company of Canada," *Journal of Canadian Studies/ Revue d'études canadiennes*, 37 (Hiver 2002 / Winter 2003), 92–111. Panofsky is quoting from Hugh Eayrs, *A Canadian Publishing House* (Toronto: Macmillan, 1923), p. 19.

[499] OHM, Ready, Macmillan Canada fonds, Box 297, Contracts, TLS, Hugh Eayrs to Lorne Pierce, 20 May 1927.

[500] Ibid., Box 111, File 6, Kirby, William. The Golden Dog, 1927–33, TL, McLaughlin, Johnston, Moorhead, and Macaulay to Collier, Schiller, and Bench, 2 April 1932.

[501] Ibid., Box 297, Contracts, Memorandum of Agreement between Mary Susannah Blake Kirby and the Macmillan Company of Canada, 20 May 1927.

[502] Ibid., TLS, Hugh Eayrs to Lorne Pierce, 20 May 1927.

[503] *The Macmillans In Canada present the new Macmillan Books for Autumn and Winter 1927* (Toronto: The Macmillan Company Of Canada Limited, 1927), p. 7.

[504] OHM, Ready, Macmillan Canada fonds, Box 111, File 6, Kirby, William. The Golden Dog, 1927–33, Lorne Pierce, Memorandum Re Kirby, 1932.

[505] Ibid., TL-C, Lorne Pierce to W. W. McLaughlin, 9 November 1932.

[506] Ibid., TL-C, Hugh Eayrs to Lorne Pierce, 28 May 1932.

[507] Ibid., Box 111, File 7, Kirby, William. Annals of Niagara, 1926–31, TL-C, Province of Ontario Pictures to William Kirby, 11 August 1927.

[508] Ibid., ALS, William Kirby to Hugh Eayrs, 7 April 1928.

[509] Ibid., ALS, William Kirby to Hugh Eayrs, 16 April 1928.

[510] Ibid, ALS, William Kirby to Hugh Eayrs, 22 June 1928.

[511] Ibid., Box 111, File 6, Kirby, William. The Golden Dog, 1927–33, TLS, Lorne Pierce to Hugh Eayrs, 14 August 1928.

[512] Ibid., Box 111, File 7, Kirby, William. Annals of Niagara, 1926–31, ALS, William Kirby to Hugh Eayrs, 20 November 1928.

[513] Ibid., ALS, William Kirby to Hugh Eayrs, 30 November 1928.

[514]Ibid., TL-C, Hugh Eayrs to William Kirby, 28 November 1928.

[515]Ibid., Box 111, File 6, Kirby, William. The Golden Dog, 1927–33, ALS, William Kirby to Hugh Eayrs, 19 January 1931.

[516]Ibid., TL-C, Hugh Eayrs to William Kirby, 22 January 1931.

[517]Ibid., Box 111, File 7, Kirby, William. Annals of Niagara, 1926–31, TLS, William Kirby to Hugh Eayrs, 30 June 1931.

[518]Ibid., TL-C, Hugh Eayrs to William Kirby, 4 July 1931.

[519]Ibid., Box 111, File 6, Kirby, William. The Golden Dog, 1927–33, TL-C, Hugh Eayrs to Lorne Pierce, 28 May 1932.

[520]"Woodley, Edward Carruthers," *The Macmillan Dictionary Of Canadian Biography*, by W. Stewart Wallace (London and Toronto: Macmillan, 1963), p. 812.

[521]OHM, Ready, Macmillan Canada fonds, Box 111, File 6, Kirby, William. The Golden Dog, 1927–33, TL-C, Hugh Eayrs to E. C. Woodley, 9 February 1931.

[522]Ibid., TL-C, Hugh Eayrs to E. C. Woodley, 14 February 1931.

[523]Ibid., TLS, E. C. Woodley to Hugh Eayrs, 10 February 1931.

[524]Ibid., TLS, E. C. Woodley to Hugh Eayrs, 13 February 1931.

[525]Ibid., TL-C, Hugh Eayrs to E. C. Woodley, 14 February 1931.

[526]Ibid., TLS, E. C. Woodley to Hugh Eayrs, 20 February 1931.

[527]Ibid., TL-C, Hugh Eayrs to E. C. Woodley, 24 February 1931.

[528]Kirby, *The Golden Dog (Le Chien D'Or) A Romance Of Old Quebec*, ed. E. C. Woodley (Toronto: The Macmillan Company Of Canada Limited, At St. Martin's House, 1932), p. [v].

[529]OHM, Ready, Macmillan Canada fonds, Box 111, File 6, Kirby, William. The Golden Dog, 1927–33, TL-C, The Macmillan Company of Canada Limited to E. C. Woodley, 29 May 1931.

[530]Ibid., TL-C, The Macmillan Company of Canada Limited to E. C. Woodley, 4 June 1931.

[531]Ibid., TL-C, Hugh Eayrs to E. C. Woodley, 1 September 1931.

[532]Ibid., TL-C, Hugh Eayrs to E. C. Woodley, 12 November 1931.

[533]Ibid., TLS, E. C. Woodley to Hugh Eayrs, 25 November 1931.

[534]"Tuesday! Young Toronto Comes To Simpson's For Books and Supplies," *Toronto Daily Star*, 30 August 1941, p. 20.

[535]*Canadian Books in Print Author And Title Index 1977*, ed. Martha Pluscauksas (Buffalo and Toronto: University of Toronto Press, 1978), p. 258.

[536]OHM, Ready, Macmillan Canada fonds, Box 111, File 6, Kirby, William. The Golden Dog, 1927–33, TL-C, Collier, Schiller, and Bench to McLaughlin, Johnston, Moorhead, and Macaulay, 23 March 1932.

[537]Ibid., TL-C, McLaughlin, Johnston, Moorhead, and Macaulay to Collier, Schiller, and Bench, 2 April 1932.

[538]Ibid., TL-C, Hugh Eayrs to Lorne Pierce, 28 May 1932.

[539]Ibid., Lorne Pierce, Memorandum Re Kirby, 1932.

[540] Ibid., TLS, McLaughlin, Johnston, Moorhead, and Macaulay to Hugh Eayrs, 28 December 1932.

[541] Ibid., Order, 3 February 1933.

[542] Janet B. Friskney, *New Canadian Library: The Ross-McClelland Years, 1952–1978* (Toronto, Buffalo, and London: University of Toronto Press, 2007), p. 137.

[543] Ibid., pp. 141–42. Friskney cites a letter written to her by Derek Crawley on 2 July 1997.

[544] Derek Crawley, "Introduction," *The Golden Dog [Le Chien D'Or] A Romance of Old Quebec*, by Kirby (Toronto and Montreal: McClelland and Stewart, 1969), p. vii.

[545] W. H. New, Review of *The Golden Dog*, by Kirby, "Books In Review," *Canadian Literature*, 41 (Summer 1969), 142.

[546] Derek Crawley, "Introduction," *The Golden Dog [Le Chien D'Or] A Romance of Old Quebec*, by Kirby (Toronto and Montreal: McClelland and Stewart, 1969), p. xi.

[547] http://www.globalbooksinprint.com/ (consulted 10 February 2009).

[548] Janet B. Friskney, *New Canadian Library: The Ross-McClelland Years, 1952–1978* (Toronto, Buffalo, and London: University of Toronto Press, 2007), p. 199.

[549] Rolf Boldrewood, *Robbery Under Arms*, ed. Paul Eggert and Elizabeth Webby (St. Lucia, Queensland: University of Queensland Press, 2006), p. lxxxviii.

[550] http://www.globalbooksinprint.com/ (consulted 10 February 2009).

[551] Les Éditeurs, "Un Mot Au Lecteur," *Le Chien D'Or*, by Kirby, trans. Pamphile Le May (Québec: Librairie Garneau, 1926), Vol. 1, p. [7].

[552] Benjamin Sulte, "Préface," *Ibid.*, Vol. 1, pp. [9]–20.

[553] Damase Potvin, "A propos du 'Chien d'or,'" *Terroir*, 7 (1926), 264.

[554] OHM, Ready, Macmillan Canada fonds, Box 111, File 7, Kirby, William. *Annals of Niagara*, 1926–31, TL-C, William Kirby to Librairie Garneau, 24 January 1928.

[555] Les Éditeurs, "Introduction," *Le Chien D'Or*, by Kirby, trans. Pamphile Le May (Québec: Éditions Garneau, 1971), pp. [7–8].

[556] Robert Guy Scully, "Lectures," *Devoir* (Montreal), 28 July 1971, p. 8.

[557] Advertisement, *Devoir* (Montreal), 24 July 1971, p. [9].

[558] Roger Lemelin, "Préface: Roger Lemelin Relit *Le Chien D'Or*," *Le Chien d'Or*, by Kirby (Montreal: Stanké, 1989), pp. [5]–10.

[559] OTAR, Kirby, F-1076, Scrapbooks, MU1653, H-3, Playbill.

[560] "'Le Chien d'or' de Kirby à l'émission des 'Grands Romans,'" *La semaine À Radio-Canada*," 2 August–8 September 1951, p. 3.

[561] OTAR, Kirby, F-1076, Correspondence With Publishers, MU1635, A-6, ALS, Louis A. Tonchet to Kirby, 13 August 1892.

[562] Ibid., ALS, Louis A. Tonchet to Kirby, 20 August 1892.

[563] Albert Laberge, *La Scouine*, ed. Paul Wyczynski (Montréal: Les Presses

de l'Université de Montréal, 1986), p. 50.

[564]Madeleine Charlebois-Dirschauer, *Rodolphe Girard (1879–1956) sa vie, son oeuvre* (Montréal: Fides, 1986), p. 37.

[565]Laval University, Quebec, Quebec, Archives, Fonds Albert Laberge, 241-1/3/8/32, ALS, Rodolphe Girard to Albert Laberge, 1 October 1906.

[566]Ibid., 241-1/3/8/33, ALS, Rodolphe Girard to Albert Laberge, 7 February 1907. Girard's much worked-over typescript of "Le Chien D'Or," a drama with a prologue and five acts that closely follows the plot of Kirby's novel, is held in Montreal at the National Library and Archives of Quebec.

[567]OONA, MG30, D247, Launcelot Cressy Servos Papers, Volume 5, Correspondence 1919, TL-C, Launcelot Cressy Servos to Thomas Mulvey, 15 April 1919.

[568]Ibid., Volume 2, Launcelot Cressy Servos, Script No. 9, The Golden Dog.

[569]"The Homemaker," *Globe* (Toronto), 19 March 1927, p. 19.

[570]Advertisement, T. Eaton Company Limited, *Globe* (Toronto), 2 April 1923, p. 16.

[571]"Prince George Arrives With Little Ceremony As Old Quebec Sleeps," *Toronto Daily Star*, 18 August 1928, pp. [1]–2.

[572]"Gift Made Institute for Blind For Up-to-Date Printing Plant," *Globe* (Toronto), 7 July 1927, p. [9].

[573]Donald Jones, "First novel dedicated to 'Canadian subject matter,' " *Toronto Star*, 14 May 1988, p. M3.

[574]Cathy Dunphy, "Book clubs breed bonds that run deep," *Toronto Star*, 19 August 1989, p. M3.

[575]"Books' Characters Are Seen In 'Life,' " *Globe* (Toronto), 20 January 1932, p. 12.

[576]"Costumes Represent Fiction Characters," *Toronto Daily Star*, 20 January 1933, p. 3.

[577]"Toronto Girls Appear at C. N. E. In 'Cavalcade of Canadiana,' " *Toronto Daily Star*, 27 August 1947, p. 21.

[578]"Author, Golf-Player To See 'Ex' Pageant," *Ibid.*

[579]"Old Quebec, The Background Of Canadian Fiction," *Saturday Night* (Toronto), 4 January 1919, pp. [17] and 24.

[580]William Renwick Riddell, *William Kirby* (Toronto: The Ryerson Press, 1923), p. 129.

[581]Lorne Pierce, *William Kirby The Portrait of a Tory Loyalist* (Toronto: The Macmillan Company of Canada, 1929), p. xiii.

[582]Leonard Vandervaart, "Abridgment As Criticism: A Textual Study Of William Kirby's *The Golden Dog*" (University of Alberta: MA Thesis, 1980), p. v.

[583]Henry James Morgan, *The Canadian Men And Women Of The Time: A Hand-book of Canadian Biography* (Toronto: William Briggs, 1898), p. 541.

[584]Edward A. McCourt, "The Canadian Historical Novel," *Dalhousie Review*,

26 (1946–47), [30]–36.

[585]Desmond Pacey, *Creative Writing in Canada: A Short History of English-Canadian Literature* (Toronto: The Ryerson Press, 1952), p. 71.

[586]W. J. Keith, *Canadian Literature in English* (Erin, Ontario: The Porcupine's Quill, 2006), Vol. 1, p. 72.

[587]Eva-Marie Kröller, "George Eliot in Canada: *Romola* and *The Golden Dog*," *American Review of Canadian Studies*, 14 (1984), 312–21.

[588]L. R. Early, "Myth And Prejudice In Kirby, Richardson, And Parker," *Canadian Literature*, 81 (Summer 1979), 24–36.

[589]Reginald Eyre Watters, "English Social Patterns in Early Australian and Canadian Fiction," *National Identity: Papers delivered at the Commonwealth Literature Conference, University of Queensland, Brisbane, 9th–15th August, 1968*, ed. K. L. Goodwin (London and Melbourne: Heinemann Educational Books, 1970), pp. 66–75.

[590]E. J. Wiens, "The *Lumpenproletariat* in *The Golden Dog* and *Roger Sudden*," *SCL: Studies in Canadian Literature*, 14:2 (1989), 63–83.

[591]Philippe-Baby Casgrain, *La Maison Du Chien-D'Or: Données Authentiques Sur Son Origine Et Sa Construction* (1905), p. 3. http://www.ourroots.ca/. 11 June 2007.

[592]Québec, "Enseigne: 'Le Chien d'or,'" *L'Intermédiaire Des Chercheurs Et Curieux*, 10 May 1904, Col. 730.

[593]Pierre-Georges Roy, "L'Histoire vraie du Chien d'Or," *Cahiers Des Dix*, 10 (1945), [103]–168.

[594]Ibid., *Bigot Et Sa Bande Et L'Affaire Du Canada* (Lévis, Québec, 1950), p. 235.

[595]Maurice Lemire, "La Trahison De Bigot Dans Le Roman Historique Canadien," *Revue D'Histoire De L'Amérique Française*, 22 (1968), 65–88.

[596]John Moss, *A Reader's Guide to the Canadian Novel* (Toronto: McClelland and Stewart, 1981), p. 141.

[597]W. H. New, *A History Of Canadian Literature* (Basingstoke and London: Macmillan Education, 1989), pp. 93–94.

[598]Ronald Hatch, "Narrative Development In The Canadian Historical Novel," *Canadian Literature*, 110 (Fall 1986), 79–96.

[599]Dennis Duffy, *Sounding The Iceberg: An Essay on Canadian Historical Novels* (Toronto: ECW Press, 1986), p. 11.

[600]Mary Jane Edwards, "Occupying Space: William Kirby's Imagination of Canadian Identity in *Le chien d'or/The Golden Dog*," *new literatures review*, 35 (Summer 1998), 15–31.

[601]Joy Kuropatwa, "Dante & 'The Golden Dog,'" *Canadian Literature*, 86 (Autumn 1980), 49–58.

[602]OTAR, Kirby, F-1076, Correspondence With Publishers, MU1635, A-6, ALS, Kirby to F-X-A Trudel, 5 [August] 1884.

[603]David M. Hayne, "*The Golden Dog* and *Le Chien d'or*: Le May's French Translation of Kirby's Novel," *Publications of the Bibliographical Society of*

Canada, 20 (1981), 50–62.

[604] Mary Jane Edwards, "William Kirby's *The Chien D'Or / The Golden Dog / A Legend Of Quebec*: Translation and Transformation," *Script & Print* Special Issue: *Superior in His Profession: Essays in Memory of Harold Love*, ed. Meredith Sherlock, Brian McMullen, and Wallace Kirsop, 33 (2009), 234–50.

[605] OTAR, Kirby, F-1076, Correspondence With Publishers, MU1635, A-6, TLS, L. C. Page and Company to Kirby, 10 May 1897.

[606] Kirby, "Author's Prefatory Note," *The Golden Dog (Le Chien D'Or) A Romance of the Days of Louis Quinze in Quebec* (Boston: L. C. Page and Company, 1897), p. [iii].

[607] OTAR, Kirby, F-1076, Correspondence With Publishers, MU1635, A-6, Kirby's holograph copy of letter to L. C. Page and Company, 29 April 1897.

[608] Ibid., The John C. Kirby Correspondence, MU1636, A-7, ALS, Kirby to John Colborne Kirby, 9 March 1877.

[609] Ibid., The Marquis of Lorne Correspondence, MU1637, A-12, ALS, Kirby to Marquess of Lorne, 9 November 1903. Kirby also inscribed the words "Mutilated Copy" on the title-page of a copy of the 1897 impression of the L. C. Page edition now held at OTAR. See Kirby, F-1076, Kirby Library, MU1675, L-69, Box 41.

[610] OKQ, Archives, William Kirby Fonds, 2005.8, Photocopies of Letters etc. re provenance of Manuscript of Golden Dog, TLS, William Kirby to Lorne Pierce, 22 April 1956.

[611] See "Description of Manuscript Copy-text" (887) for a complete description of this document.

[612] See "Unrecoverable Manuscript Readings: Readings from Published Copy-text" (903) for a listing of these lacunae.

[613] OTAR, Kirby, F-1076, Correspondence With Publishers, MU1635, A-6, ALS, John Lovell to Kirby, 12 July 1876.

[614] Ibid., ALS, John Wurtele Lovell to Kirby, 17 August 1876.

[615] Kirby, "Author's Prefatory Note," *The Golden Dog (Le Chien D'Or) A Romance of the Days of Louis Quinze in Quebec* (Boston: L. C. Page and Company, 1897), p. [iii].

[616] OTAR, Kirby, F-1076, Correspondence With Publishers, MU1635, A-6, ALS, John Wurtele Lovell to Kirby, 29 September 1876.

Constable

was the extent of her repentance — The ~~secret~~
~~secret~~ of ~~Beaumanoir~~ was never revealed —
He awaited, and ~~awaited~~ awaits still, the
judgment of the final day of accompt —

Bigot in his heart suspected her of ~~the~~ bloody
deed — but proofs failed — nor could he ever detect
~~when~~ her countenance off-guard, ~~or any~~
~~any~~ ~~one~~ sign of the guilt she kept so well
concealed from ~~his eye~~ — He was never quite satisfied
~~however~~ with her innocence ~~and~~ although ~~he was~~
deeply smitten by her beauty & fascinations, he would not
marry her —

Angelique had intrigued and sinned in vain —
She feared Bigot knew more than he really did
in reference to the death of Caroline — and oft
while laughing in his face — she trembled in
her heart when he played and equivocated
with her earnest appeals to marry her — !
Wearied out at length with waiting for his
decisive ~~answer~~ Angelique mortified by
wounded pride and stung by the scorn of
the gardens, on his return to the Colony —
suddenly accepted ~~the hand~~ of the Chevalier de
Pean — ~~as reputed~~ became the recognized Mistress
of the Intendant — imitating as far as she was able
the splendour and ~~magnificence~~ of La Pompadour
~~and making the palace of Bigot~~
~~brilliant as that of~~
Versailles —

Angelique lived thenceforth a life of splendid sin — She
clothed herself in purple and fine linen — while the
noblest ladies of the land were reduced by the war, to
rags and beggary, She fared sumptuously still ~~every~~ ~~day~~

THE

CHIEN D'OR

THE GOLDEN DOG

A LEGEND OF QUEBEC

BY

WILLIAM KIRBY

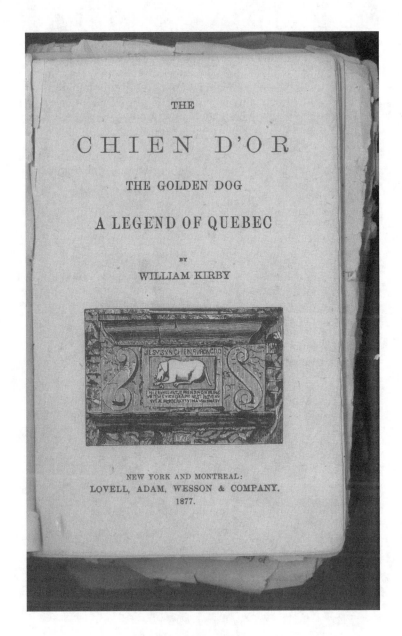

NEW YORK AND MONTREAL:
LOVELL, ADAM, WESSON & COMPANY.
1877.

Title-page of First Edition,
Lovell, Adam, Wesson Impression, 1877,
of *Le Chien d'or*

PREFACE

"In questo racconto il nostro fine non è, per dir la verita, soltanto di rappresentar lo stato delle cose nel qualé verranno à trovarsi i nostri personaggi, ma di far conoscere insieme, per quanto si puo in ristretto, e per quanto si puo da noi, un tratto di storia patria piu famoso che conoscinto."

Manzoni

We confess that our intention in writing this book, is not merely to give a picture of the times in which our characters lived, but also to make known briefly, and as well as we are able, a fragment of our country's history, that is more talked about than understood.

1

CHAPTER 1

MEN OF THE OLD REGIME

"'See Naples and then die!' That was a proud saying, Count, which we used to hear as we cruised under lateen sails about the glorious bay that reflects from its waters the fires of Vesuvius.

We believed the boast then Count. But I say now see Quebec and live for ever. Eternity would be too short to weary me of this lovely scene. This bright Canadian morning is worthy of Eden, and the glorious landscape worthy of such a sun rising!—"

Thus exclaimed a tall fair Swedish gentleman his blue eyes sparkling and every feature glowing with enthusiasm, Herr Peter Kalm, to his Excellency Count de la Galissoniere Governor of New France as they stood together on a bastion of the Ramparts of Quebec in the year of grace 1748.

A group of French and Canadian officers in the military uniforms of Louis XV. stood leaning on their swords as they conversed gaily together on the broad gravelled walk at the foot of the rampart. They formed the suite in attendance upon the Governor who was out by sun rise this morning to inspect the work done during the night by the citizens of Quebec and the Habitans of the surrounding country who had been hastily summoned to labour on the defences of the city.

A few Ecclesiastics, in black cassocks, dignitaries of the church, mingled cheerfully in the conversation of the officers. They had accompanied the Governor, both to show their respect and to encourage by their presence and exhortations, the zeal of the colonists in the work of fortifying the capital.

War was then raging between old England and old France, and between New England and New France. The vast region of

3

North America stretching far into the interior and south west from Canada to Louisiana had for three years past been the scene of fierce hostilities between the rival nations. While the savage Indian tribes ranged on the one side and on the other, steeped their mocassins in the blood of French and English colonists, who in their turn became as fierce and carried on the war as relentlessly as the Savages themselves.

Louisbourg the bulwark of New France, projecting its mailed arm boldly into the Atlantic, had been cut off by the English, who now overran Acadia and began to threaten Quebec with invasion by sea and land. Busy rumours of approaching dangers were rife in the Colony, and the gallant Governor issued orders, which were enthusiastically obeyed, for the people to proceed to the walls and place the city in a state of defence to bid defiance to the enemy.

Rolland Michel Barrin, Count de la Galissoniere was remarkable no less for his philosophical attainments, that ranked him high among the Savans of the French Academy, than for his political abilities, and foresight as a statesman. He felt strongly the vital interests involved in the present war, and saw clearly what was the sole policy necessary for France to adopt in order to preserve her magnificent dominion in North America. His counsels were neither liked nor followed by the Court of Versailles, then sinking fast into the slough of corruption that marked the closing years of the reign of Louis XV.

Among the people who admired deeds more than words, the Count was honoured as a brave and skilful Admiral, who had borne the flag of France triumphantly over the seas and in the face of her most powerful enemies, the English and Dutch. His memorable repulse of Admiral Byng eight years after the events here recorded, which led to the death of that brave and unfortunate officer who was shot by sentence of Court Martial to atone for that repulse, was a glory to France, but to the Count brought after it a manly sorrow, for the fate of his opponent, whose death he regarded as a cruel and unjust act, unworthy of the English nation, usually generous and merciful as it is brave and considerate.

The Governor was already well advanced in years. He had entered upon the winter of life that sprinkles the head with snow that never melts, but he was still hale, ruddy and active. Nature had indeed moulded him in an unpropitious hour for personal comeliness, but in compensation had seated a great heart and a graceful mind in a body low of stature and marked by a slight deformity. His piercing eyes, luminous with intelligence and full of sympathy for every thing noble and elevated, overpowered with their fascination the blemishes that a too curious scrutiny might discover upon his figure, while his mobile handsome lips poured out the natural eloquence of clear thoughts and noble sentiments. The Count grew great while speaking. His listeners were carried away by the magic of his voice and the clearness of his intellect.

He was very happy this morning by the side of his old friend Peter Kalm, who was paying him a most welcome visit in New France. They had been fellow students both at Upsal and at Paris, and loved each other with a cordiality that like good wine grew richer and more generous with age.

Herr Kalm stretching out his arms as if to embrace the lovely landscape, and clasp it to his bosom, exclaimed with fresh enthusiasm, "See Quebec and live for ever!—"

"Dear Kalm!" said the Governor catching the fervor of his friend as he rested his hand affectionately on his shoulder, "you are as true a lover of nature as when we sat together at the feet of Linneus our glorious young master and heard him open up for us the arcana of Gods works, and we used to feel like him too, when he thanked God for permitting him to look into his treasure house, and see the precious things of creation which he had made."

"Till men see Quebec," replied Kalm, "they will not fully realize the meaning of the term 'Gods footstool.' It is a land worth living for—."

"Not only a land to live for, but a land to die for—And happy the man who dies for it!—Confess Kalm, thou who hast travelled in all lands thinkst thou not, it is indeed worthy of its proud title of New France?"

"It is indeed worthy," replied Kalm, "I see here a scion

of the old oak of the Gauls, which if let grow, will shelter the
throne of France itself in an empire wider than Caesar wrested
from Ambiotrix."

"Yes," replied the Count, kindling at the words of his
friend. "It is old France transplanted transfigured and
glorified! where her language religion and laws shall be
handed down to her posterity, the glory of North America
as the Mother land is the glory of Europe."

The enthusiastic Galissoniere stretched out his hands and
implored a blessing upon the land entrusted to his keeping.

It was a glorious morning. The sun had just risen over
the hill tops of Lauzon, throwing aside his drapery of gold
purple and crimson. The soft haze of the summer morning
was floating away into nothingness leaving every object fresh
with dew and magnified in the limpid purity of the air.

The broad St Lawrence far beneath their feet, was still
partially veiled in a thin blue mist, pierced here and there by
the tall masts of a King's ship or merchantman lying unseen
at anchor, or as the fog rolled slowly off, a swift canoe might
be seen shooting out into a streak of sunshine with the first
news of the morning from the South Shore.

Behind the Count and his companion rose the white
glistening walls of the Hotel Dieu, and farther off the tall tower
of the newly restored Cathedral, the Belfry of the Recollets,
and the roofs of the ancient college of the Jesuits. An avenue
of old oaks and maples shaded the walk and in the branches
of the trees a swarm of birds fluttered and sang, as if in rivalry
with the gay French talk and laughter of the group of officers
who waited the return of the Governor from the Bastion where
he stood showing the glories of Quebec to his friend.

The walls of the city ran along the edge of the cliff upwards
as they approached the broad gallery and massive front of the
Castle of St Louis, and ascending the green slope of the broad
glacis culminated in the lofty citadel where streaming in the
morning breeze and radiant in the sunshine, alone in the blue
sky, waved the white banner of France, the sight of which sent
a thrill of joy and pride into the hearts of her faithful subjects
in the New World.

The broad Bay lay before them round as a shield and glittering like a mirror as the mist blew off its surface. Behind the sunny slopes of Orleans which the river encircled in its arms like a giant lover his fair mistress, rose the bold dark crests of the Laurentides, lifting their bare summits far away along the course of the ancient river, leaving imagination to wonder over the wild scenery in their midst, the woods, glens and unknown lakes and rivers that lay hid far from human ken, or known only to rude savages wild as the beasts of chase they hunted in those strange regions.

Across the broad valley of the St Charles, covered with green fields and ripening harvests, and populous with quaint old homesteads redolent with memories of Normandy and Britany, rose a long mountain ridge covered with primeval woods, on the slope of which rose the glittering spire of Charlebourg, once a dangerous outpost of civilization. The pastoral Lairet was seen mingling its waters with the St Charles in a little Bay that preserves the name of Jacques Cartier, who with his hardy companions spent their first winter in Canada on this spot, the guests of the hospitable Donacana, Lord of Quebec and of all the lands seen from its lofty Cape.

Directly beneath the feet of the Governor on a broad strip of land that lay between the beach and the precipice stood the many gabled Palace of the Intendant, the most magnificent structure in New France. Its long front of eight hundred feet overlooked its royal terraces and gardens, and beyond these the quays and magazines where lay the ships of Bordeaux St Malo and Havre unloading the merchandise and luxuries of France in exchange for the more rude but not less valuable products of the Colony.

Between the Palace and the Basseville, the waves at high tide washed over a shingly beach where there were already the beginnings of a street. A few rude inns desplayed the sign of the Fleur de Lys, or the imposing head of Louis XV. Round the doors of these inns in summer time might always be found groups of loquacious Breton and Norman sailors, in red caps, and sashes, voyageurs and canoemen from the far west, in half Indian costume drinking Gascon wine and norman cider or the still more potent liquors filled with the fires of the Antilles. The Batture kindled into life on the arrival of the fleet from Home, and in the evenings of summer as the sun set behind the Cote à Bonhomme. The natural magnetism of companionship, drew the lasses of Quebec down to the beach where amid old refrains of French ditties and the music of violins and tambours de Basque, they danced on the green, with the jovial sailors who brought news from the old land beyond the Atlantic.

"Pardon me Gentlemen for keeping you waiting," said the Governor as he descended from the Bastion and rejoined his suite. "I am so proud of our beautiful Quebec, that I can scarcely stop showing off its charms to my friend Herr Kalm, who knows so well how to appreciate them. But," continued he looking round admiringly on the bands of citizens and Habitans, who were at work strengthening every weak point in the fortifications "My brave Canadians are busy as beavers on their dam. They are determined to keep the saucy English out of Quebec. They deserve to have the Beaver for their crest, industrious fellows that they are!—I am sorry I kept you waiting however."—

"We can never count the moments lost, which your Excellency gives to the survey of our fair land," replied the Bishop, a grave earnest looking man. "Would that His Majesty himself, could stand on these walls and see with his own eyes, as you do, this splendid patrimony of the crown of France. He would not dream of bartering it away in exchange for petty ends and corners of Germany and Flanders, as is rumoured My Lord."

"True words and good my Lord Bishop!" replied the Governor. "The retention of all Flanders, now in the strong hands of the Marshal de Saxe, would be a poor compensation for the surrender of a glorious land like this to the English."

Flying rumours of some such proposal on the part of France had reached the colony, with wild reports arising out of the endless chaffering between the negociators for a peace who had already assembled at Aix La Chapelle. "The fate of America will one day be decided here," continued the

Governor. "I see it written on this rock: Whoever rules Quebec will sway the destinies of the continent. May our noble France be wise and understand in time the signs of Empire and of destiny!—"

The Bishop looked upwards with a sigh:—"Our noble France has not yet read those tokens or she misunderstands them!—O these faithful subjects of hers! Look at them, your Excellency!—" The Bishop pointed towards the crowd of citizens hard at work on the walls. "There is not a man of them, but is ready to risk life and fortune for the honour and dominion of France. And yet they are treated by the Court with cruel neglect and burthened with exactions that take from life the sweet reward of labour. They cannot do the impossible, that France requires of them—Fight her battles, till their fields and see their bread taken from them, by these new ordinances of the Intendant—."

"Well, my Lord," replied the Governor affecting a jocularity he did not feel. For he knew how true were the words of the Bishop. " We must all do our duty nevertheless!— If France requires impossibilities of us, we must perform them!—That is the old spirit! If the skies fall upon our heads, we must, like true Gauls, hold them up on the points of our lances!—What say you, Rigaud de Vaudreuil!—cannot one Canadian surround ten New Englanders?"—The Governor alluded to an exploit of the gallant officer whom he turned to address.

"*Probatum est*, your Excellency—! I once with six hundred Canadians surrounded all New England. Prayers were put up in all the churches of Boston for deliverance, when we swept the Connecticut from end to end with a broom of fire."

"Brave Rigaud! France has too few like you!" remarked the Governor with a look of admiration.

Rigaud bowed and shook his head modestly. "I trust she has ten thousand better." But added looking at his fellow officers who stood conversing at a short distance, "Marshal Saxe has few the equals of those in his Camp My Lord Count!"—And well was the compliment deserved.

They were gallant men, intelligent in looks, polished in

manners and brave to a fault, and all full of that natural gaiety that sits so gracefully on a French soldier.

Most of them wore the laced coat and waistcoat, chapeau, boots, lace ruffles, sash and rapier of the period, a martial costume befitting brave and handsome men. Their names were household words in every cottage in New France and many of them as frequently spoken of in the English Colonies, as in the streets of Quebec.

There stood the Chevalier de Beaujeu, a gentleman of Norman family, who was already famed upon the Frontier, and who seven years later in the forests of the Mononghala crowned a life of honour by a soldier's death on the bloody field won from the unfortunate Braddock, defeating an army ten times more numerous than his own.

Talking gaily with De Beaujeu were two gallant looking young men, of a Canadian family which out of seven brothers lost six slain in the service of their King—Jumonville de Villiers who was afterwards in defiance of a flag of truce, shot down by order of Colonel Washington, in the far off forests of the Alleghanies, and his brother Coulon De Villiers who received the sword of Washington when he surrendered himself and garrison prisoners of war, at Fort Necessity, in 1754.

Coulon de Villiers imposed ignominious conditions of surrender upon Washington, but scorned to take other revenge for the death of his brother. He spared the life of Washington who lived to become the leader and idol of his nation, which but for the magnanimity of the noble Canadian might have never struggled into independance.

There stood also the Sieur De Lery, the Kings Engineer, charged with the fortifications of the Colony, a man of Vauban's genius in the art of defence. Had the schemes which he projected and vainly urged upon the heedless Court of Versailles, been carried into effect, the Conquest of New France would have been an impossibility.

Arm in arm with De Lery in earnest conversation, walked the handsome Claude de Beauharnois, brother of a former Governor of the Colony, a graceful gallant looking soldier. De Beauharnois was the ancestor of a vigorous and beautiful race, among whose posterity was the fair Hortense de Beauharnois, who in her son Napoleon III. seated an offshoot of Canada upon the Imperial throne of France long after the abandonment of the ancient Colony by the corrupt House of Bourbon.

Conspicuous among the distinguished officers by his tall straight figure and quick movements was the Chevalier La Corne St Luc, supple as an Indian and almost as dark from exposure to the weather, and incessant campaigning. He was fresh from the blood and desolation of Acadia where France indeed lost her ancient colony, but St Luc had reaped a full sheaf of glory at Grand Pré in the Bay of Minas, by the capture of an army of New Englanders. The rough old soldier was just now all smiles and gaiety as he conversed with Monseigneur De Pontbriant the venerable Bishop of Quebec and Father De Berey the Superior of the Recollets.

The Bishop a wise ruler of his Church, was also a passionate lover of his country. The surrender of Quebec to the English broke his heart, and he died a few months after the announcement of the final cession of the Colony. Father De Berey, a jovial monk wearing the grey gown and sandals of the Recollets, was renowned throughout New France for his wit more than for his piety. He had once been a soldier and he wore his gown as he had worn his uniform with the gallant bearing of a Kings guardsman. But the people loved him all the more for his jests, which never lacked the accompaniment of genuine charity. His sayings furnished all New France with daily food for mirth and laughter without detracting an iota of the respect in which the Recollets were held throughout the Colony.

Father Glapion the Superior of the Jesuits also accompanied the Bishop. His close black soutane contrasted oddly with the grey loose gown of the Recollet. He was a meditative taciturn man, seeming rather to watch the others than to join in the lively conversation that went on around him. Any thing but cordiality and brotherly love reigned between the Jesuits and the order of St Francis but the superiors were too wary to manifest towards each other the mutual jealousies of their subordinates.

The long line of fortifications presented a stirring appearance that morning. The watch fires that had illuminated the scene during the night, were dying out, the red embers paling under the rays of the rising sun. From a wide circle surrounding the city the people had come in— many were accompanied by their wives and daughters to assist in making the bulwark of the Colony impregnable against the rumoured attack of the English.

The people of New France taught by a hundred years of almost constant warfare, with the English and with the Savage nations on their frontiers, saw as clearly as the Governor that the key of French Dominion hung inside the walls of Quebec, and that for an enemy to grasp it, was to lose all they valued as subjects of the crown of France.

CHAPTER 2

THE WALLS OF QUEBEC

Count de La Galissoniere accompanied by his distinguished attendants proceeded again on their round of inspection. They were everywhere saluted with heads uncovered and welcomed by hearty greetings. The people of New France had lost none of the natural politeness and ease of their ancestors, and as every gentleman of the Governor's suite was at once recognized a conversation friendly even to familiarity ensued between them and the citizens and Habitans who worked as if they were building their very souls into the walls of the old city.

"Good morning, Sieur De St Denis!" gaily exclaimed the governor to a tall courtly gentleman who was superintending the labour of a body of his censitaires from Beauport. "'Many hands make light work,' says the proverb. That splendid battery you are just finishing deserves to be called Beauport. What say you my Lord Bishop?" turning to the smiling ecclesiastic. "Is it not worthy of baptism."

"Yes, and blessing both. I give it my episcopal benediction," replied the Bishop, "and truly I think most of the earth of it is taken from the consecrated ground of the Hotel Dieu. It will stand fire!—"

"Many thanks my Lord!" The Sieur de St Denis, bowed very low. "Where the Church bars the door, Satan will never enter nor the English either! Do you hear men," continued he, turning to his censitaires, "my Lord Bishop christens our battery: Beauport, and says it will stand fire."

"Vive le Roi!—" was the response, an exclamation that came spontaneously to the lips of all Frenchmen on every emergency of danger or emotion of joy.

13

A sturdy Habitant came forward, and doffing his red tuque or cap, addressed the Governor. "This is a good battery my Lord-Governor, but there ought to be one as good in our village. Permit us to build one and man it, and we promise your excellency that no Englishman shall ever get into the back door of Quebec while we have lives to defend it." The old Habitant had the eye of a soldier. He had been one. The governor knew the value of the suggestion, and at once assented to it, adding: "no better defenders of the city, could be found anywhere than the brave habitans of Beauport."

The compliment was never forgotten, and years afterwards when Wolfe beseiged the city, the batteries of Beauport repelled the assault of his bravest troops, and well nigh broke the heart of the young hero over the threatened defeat of his great undertaking, as his brave Highlanders and Grenadiers lay slain by hundreds on the beach of Beauport.

The countenances of the hardy workers were suddenly covered with smiles of welcome recognition, at sight of the well known, Superior of the Recollets.

"Good morning!" cried out a score of voices. "Good morning, Father De Berey! The good wives of Beauport send you a thousand compliments. They are dying to see the good Recollets down our way again. The grey brothers have forsaken our parish!—"

"Ah!" replied the Superior in a tone of mock severity, while his eyes overran with mirthfulness, "you are a crowd of miserable sinners, who will die without benefit of Clergy, only you dont know it! Who was it boiled the Easter eggs hard as agates which you gave to my poor brother Recollets, for the use of our Convent? Tell me that, pray!—All the salts and senna in Quebec have not sufficed to restore the digestion of my poor monks since you played that trick upon them, down at your misnamed village of Beauport—!—"

"Pardon! Reverend Father De Berey!" replied a smiling Habitant. "It was not we, but the sacreligious canaille of St Anne's who boiled the Easter eggs! If you dont believe us send some of the good grey Friars down to try our love. See if they do not find every thing soft for them in Beauport, from our hearts to our feather beds! to say nothing of our eggs and bacon. Our good wives are fairly melting with longing for a sight of the grey gowns of St Francis once more in our village."

"O! I dare be bound, the Canaille of St Anne are lost dogs like yourselves! *Catuli Catulorum!*"

The habitans thought this sounded like a doxology, and some crossed themselves amid the dubious laughter of others, who suspected Father De Berey of a clerical jest.

"O!" continued he, "if fat father Ambrose the Cook of the Convent only had you, one at a time, to turn the spit for him in place of the poor dogs of Quebec which he has to catch as best he can, and set to work in his kitchen! but vagabonds that you are! you are rarely set to work now on the Kings corvée! all work, little play and no pay!"

The men took his raillery in excellent part, and one their spokesman, bowing low to the Superior, said, "Forgive us all the same good Father. The hard eggs of Beauport will be soft as lard compared with the iron shells we are preparing for the English breakfast when they appear some fine morning before Quebec."

"Ah well. In that case I must pardon the trick you played upon Brothers Mark and Alexis, and I give you my blessing too on condition you send some salt to our convent to cure our fish, and save your reputations which are very stale just now among my good Recollets."

A general laugh followed this sally and the Reverend Superior went off, laughing as he hastened to catch up with the Governor, who had moved on to another point in the line of fortifications.

Near the Gate of St John, they found a couple of ladies, encouraging by their presence and kind words a numerous party of Habitans, one an elderly lady of noble bearing and still beautiful, the rich and powerful feudal mistress of the Lordship or Seigneurie of Tilly, the other, her orphan niece in the bloom of youth and of surpassing loveliness, the fair Amelie De Repentigny who had loyally accompanied her aunt to the Capital, with all the men of the Seigneurie of Tilly, to assist in the completion of its defences.

To features which looked to be chiselled out of the purest Parian marble just flushed with the glow of morn, and cut in those perfect lines of proportion which nature only bestows on a few chosen favorites at intervals, to show the possibilities of feminine beauty, Amelie de Repentigny added a figure which in its perfect symmetry looked smaller than it really was, for she was a tall girl. It filled the eye and held fast the fancy with the charms of a thousand graces as she moved or stood, suggestive of the beauty of a tamed fawn that in all its movements preserves somewhat of the coyness and easy grace of its free life.

Her hair was very dark and thick matching her deep liquid eyes, that lay for the most part so quietly and restfully beneath their long shading lashes. Eyes gentle frank and modest looking tenderly on all things innocent, fearlessly on all things harmful. Eyes that nevertheless noted every change of your countenance and read unerringly your meaning more from your looks than from your words. Nothing seemed to hide itself from that pure searching glance, when she chose to look at you.

In their depths you might read the tokens of a rare and noble character—a capability of loving which once enkindled by a worthy object might make all things that are possible to devoted womanhood, possible to this woman, who would not count her life any thing either for the man she loved or the cause she espoused. Amelie de Repentigny will not yield her heart without her judgment, but when she does, it will be a royal gift never to be recalled, never to be repented of, to the end of her life. Happy the man upon whom she shall bestow her affection!—It will be his forever—unhappy all others who may love her! She may pity, but she will listen to no voice but the one that rules her heart, to her lifes end.

Both ladies were in mourning, yet dressed with elegant simplicity befitting their rank and position in society. The Chevalier Le Gardeur De Tilly had fallen two years ago fighting gallantly for his king and country, leaving a childless widow to manage his vast domain and succeed as sole guardian of their orphan niece Amelie de Repentigny and her only brother Le Gardeur, left in infancy to the care of their noble relatives who in every respect treated them as their own, and who indeed were the legal inheritors of the Lordship of Tilly.

Only a year ago, Amelie had left the ancient Convent of the Ursulines perfected in all the graces and accomplishments, taught in the famous cloister founded by Mere Marie de l'Incarnation, for the education of the daughters of New France,—generation after generation of whom were trained according to her precepts, in graces of manner as well as in the learning of the age. The latter might be forgotten, the former never. As they became the wives and mothers of succeeding times they have left upon their decendants an impress of politeness and urbanity that distinguishes the people of Canada to this day.

Of all the crowd of fair eager aspirants contending for honours on the day of examination in the great school, crowns had only been awarded to Amelie and Angelique des Meloises, two the equal, in beauty, grace and accomplishments, but unlike in character and in destiny. The currents of their lives ran smoothly together at the beginning. How widely different was to be the ending of them!—

The brother of Amelie, Le Gardeur de Repentigny was her elder by a year. An officer in the Kings service handsome brave, generous devoted to his sister and aunt but not free from some of the vices of the times prevalent among the young men of rank and fortune in the colony who in dress luxury and immorality strove to imitate the brilliant dissolute court of Louis XV.

Amelie passionately loved her brother and endeavoured, not without success, as is the way with women, to blind herself to his faults. She saw him seldom however, and in her solitary musings in the far off Manor House of Tilly, she invested him with all the perfections he did and did not possess, and turned a deaf almost an angry ear to tales whispered in his disparagement.

CHAPTER 3

A CHATELAINE OF NEW FRANCE

The Governor was surprised and delighted to encounter Lady De Tilly and her fair neice both of whom were well known to and highly esteemed by him. He and the Gentlemen of his suite saluted them with profound respect not unmingled with chivalrous admiration for noble high spirited women.

"My honoured Lady De Tilly and Mademoiselle De Repentigny!" said the Governor hat in hand, "welcome to Quebec!—It does not surprize but it does delight me beyond measure to meet you here at the head of your loyal censitaires. But it is not the first time the Ladies of the House of Tilly have turned out to defend the Kings forts against his enemies."

This he said in allusion to the gallant defence of a fort on the wild Iroquois frontier by a former lady of her house, who while her husband lay wounded within the walls, assumed the command of the garrison, repulsed the savage enemy, and saved the lives of all from the fire and scalping knife.

"My Lord Count!" replied the Lady with quiet dignity. "Tis no special merit of the house of Tilly to be true to its ancient fame. It could not be otherwise. But your thanks are at this time more due to these loyal Habitans, who have so promptly obeyed your proclamation. It is the Kings Corvée to restore the walls of Quebec, and no Canadian may withhold his hand from it without disgrace."

"The Chevalier La Corne St Luc will think us two poor women a weak accession to the garrison," added she, turning to the Chevalier and cordially offering her hand to the brave old officer, who had been the comrade in arms of her husband and the dearest friend of her family.

"Good blood never fails! My Lady!" returned the Chevalier

18

warmly grasping her hand, "you out of place here?—no! no! you are at home on the ramparts of Quebec, quite as much as in your own drawing room at Tilly. The gallant King Francis used to say, that a court without ladies, was a year without a spring or a summer without roses. The walls of Quebec without a Tilly and a Repentigny would be a bad omen indeed! worse than a year without a spring or a summer without roses. But where is my dear Goddaughter Amelie?"

As he spoke, the old soldier embraced Amelie and kissed her cheek with fatherly effusion. She was a prodigious favorite. "Welcome Amelie!" said he "The sight of you is like flowers in June. What a glorious time you have had growing taller and prettier every day, all the time I have been sleeping by camp fires in the forests of Acadia! But you girls are all alike. Why I hardly knew my own pretty Agathe when I came home. The saucy minx almost kissed my eyes out to dry the tears of joy in them, she said—!"

Amelie blushed deeply at the praises bestowed upon her, yet felt glad to know that her Godfather retained all his old affection. "Where is Le Gardeur?" asked he, as she took his arm and walked a few paces apart from the throng.

Amelie coloured afresh and hesitated a moment. "I do not know, Godfather! We have not seen Le Gardeur since our arrival." Then after a nervous silence she added "I have been told that he is at Beaumanoir, hunting with His Excellency the Intendant."

La Corne seeing her embarrassment, understood the reluctance of her avowal and sympathized with it. An angry light flashed beneath his shaggy eyelashes, but he suppressed his thoughts. He could not help remarking however, "With the Intendant at Beaumanoir! I could have wished Le Gardeur in better company!—No good can come of his intimacy with Bigot, Amelie, you must wean him from it. He should have been in the city to receive you and the Lady De Tilly."

"So he doubtless would have been, had he known of our coming—We sent word—but he was away when our messenger reached the city."

Amelie felt half ashamed, for she was conscious that she

was offering something unreal to extenuate the fault of her brother—Her hopes rather than her convictions.

"Well, well! Goddaughter! we shall at any rate soon have the pleasure of seeing Le Gardeur. The Intendant himself has been summoned to attend a council of war to day. Colonel Philibert left an hour ago for Beaumanoir."

Amelie gave a slight start at the name. She looked inquiringly, but did not yet ask the question that trembled on her lips.

"Thanks, Godfather, for the good news of Le Gardeurs speedy return." Amelie talked on, her thoughts but little accompanying her words, as she repeated to herself the name of Philibert. "Have you heard that the Intendant wishes to bestow an important and honorable post in the Palace upon Le Gardeur. My brother wrote to that effect—?"

"An important and honorable post in the Palace?" the old soldier emphasized the word *honorable*, "no! I had not heard of it! never expect to hear of an honorable post in the company of Bigot, Cadet, Varin, De Pean and the rest of the scoundrels of the Friponne!—Pardon me dear. I do not class Le Gardeur among them, far from it, dear deluded boy! My best hope is that Colonel Philibert will find him and bring him clean and clear out of their clutches."—

The question that had trembled on her lips came out now. For her life she could not have retained it longer.

"Who is Colonel Philibert? Godfather," asked she, surprize, curiosity and a still deeper interest marking her voice, in spite of all she could do to appear indifferent.

"Colonel Philibert?" repeated La Corne. "Why, do not you know—? Who but our young Pierre Philibert, you have not forgotten him surely, Amelie? At any rate he has not forgotten you. In many a long night by our watch fires in the forest, has Colonel Philibert passed the hours talking of Tilly and the dear friends he left there. Your brother at any rate will gratefully remember Philibert when he sees him!"

Amelie blushed a little as she replied somewhat shyly, "yes, Godfather, I remember Pierre Philibert very well, with gratitude I remember him, but I never heard him called

Colonel Philibert before."

"O True! He has been so long absent. He left a simple Ensign *en second* and returns a Colonel and has the stuff in him to make a Field Marshal! He gained his rank where he won his glory, in Acadia. A noble fellow Amelie, loving as a woman to his friends but to his foes stern as the old Bourgeois his father who placed that tablet of the Golden Dog upon the front of his house to spite the Cardinal they say. The act of a bold man, let what will be the true interpretation of it."

"I hear every one speak well of the Bourgeois Philibert," remarked Amelie. "Aunt de Tilly is ever enthusiastic in his commendation. She says he is a true gentleman, although a trader."

"Why, he is noble by birth, if that be needed and has got the Kings licence to trade in the colony like some other Gentlemen I wot of. He was Count Philibert in Normandy, although he is plain Bourgeois Philibert in Quebec!—And a wise man he is too, for with his ships and his comptoirs and his ledgers he has traded himself into the richest man in New France, while we with our Nobility and our swords have fought ourselves poor, and receive nothing but contempt from the ungrateful courtiers of Versailles."

Their conversation was interrupted by a sudden rush of people, making room for the passage of the Regiment of Bearn, which composed part of the garrison of Quebec, on their march to their morning drill, and guardmounting— Bold dashing Gascons in blue and white uniforms, tall caps and long queues rollicking down their supple backs seldom seen by an enemy.

Mounted officers laced and ruffled gaily rode in front. Subalterns with spontoons and Sergeants with halberts dressed the long line of glistening bayonets. The drums and fifes made the streets ring again, while the men in full chorus, *à gorge deployée*, chanted the gay refrain of *La Belle Canadienne*, in honour of the lasses of Quebec, whose bright eyes ever looked kindly on the royal uniform and whose sweet smiles were never withheld from the gallant soldiers wearing it, whether Gaul or Briton.

The Governor and his suite had already mounted their horses which were waiting for them at the City Gate, and cantered off to the Esplanade to witness the review.

"Come and dine with us to day!" said the Lady de Tilly to La Corne St Luc, as he too bade the ladies a courteous adieu, and got on horseback to ride after the Governor.

"Many thanks! but I fear it will be impossible my lady. The Council of war meets at the Castle this afternoon. The hour may be deferred however should Colonel Philibert not chance to find the Intendant at Beaumanoir and then I might come. But best not expect me."

A slight conscious flush just touched the cheek of Amelie at the mention of Colonel Philibert.

"But come if possible godfather," added she "We hope to have Le Gardeur home this afternoon. He loves you so much, and I know you have countless things to say to him."

Amelie's trembling anxiety about her brother, made her most desirious to bring the powerful influence of La Corne St Luc to bear upon him.

Their kind old godfather was regarded with filial reverence by both. Amelie's father dying on the battle field, had with his latest breath commended the care of his children to the love and friendship of La Corne St Luc.

"Well Amelie, blessed are they who do not promise and still perform. I must try and meet my dear boy. So do not quite place me among the impossibles. Goodby, My Lady. Goodby Amelie."—The old soldier gaily kissed his hand and rode away.

Amelie was thoroughly surprised, and agitated out of all composure by the news of the return of Pierre Philibert. She turned aside from the busy throng that surrounded her, leaving her Aunt engaged in eager conversation with the Bishop and Father De Berey. She sat down in a quiet embrasure of the walls, and with one hand resting her drooping cheek, a train of reminiscences flew across her mind like a flight of pure doves suddenly startled out of a thicket.

She remembered vividly Pierre Philibert the friend and fellow student of her brother. He spent so many of his holidays at the old Manor house of Tilly, when she a still younger girl shared their sports, wove chaplets of flowers for them, or on her shaggy pony rode with them on many a scamper through the wild woods of the Seigneurie. Those summer and winter vacations of the old Seminary of Quebec, used to be looked forward to by the young lively girl as the brightest spots in the whole year, and she grew hardly to distinguish the affection she bore her brother from the regard in which she held Pierre Philibert.

A startling incident happened one day that filled the inmates of the Manor House with terror followed by a great joy, and which raised Pierre Philibert to the rank of an unparalleled hero in the imagination of the young girl.

Her brother was gambolling carelessly in a canoe while she and Pierre sat on the bank watching him. The light craft suddenly upset. Le Gardeur struggled for a few moments and sank under the blue waves that look so beautiful and are so cruel.

Amelie shrieked in the wildest terror and in helpless agony, while Philibert rushed without hesitation into the water, swam out to the spot and dived with the agility of a beaver. He presently reappeared bearing the inanimate body of her brother to the shore. Help was soon obtained and after long efforts to restore Le Gardeur to consciousness, efforts which seemed to last an age to the despairing girl, they at last succeded—and Le Gardeur was restored to the arms of his family. Amelie in a delirium of joy and gratitude ran to Philibert, threw her arms round him and kissed him again and again pledging her eternal gratitude, to the preserver of her brother, and vowing that she would pray for him to her life's end.

Soon after that memorable event in her young life, Pierre Philibert was sent to the great military schools in France to study the art of war with a view to entering the Kings service, while Amelie was placed in the Convent of the Ursulines to be perfected in all the knowledge and accomplishments of a lady of highest rank in the Colony.

Despite the cold shade of a Cloister where the idea of a lover is forbidden to enter, the image of Pierre Philibert did intrude and became inseparable from the recollection of her brother in the mind of Amelie. He mingled as the fairy prince in the day dreams and bright imaginings of the young poetic girl. She had vowed to pray for him to her life's end and in pursuance of her vow added a golden bead to her chaplet to remind of her duty in praying for the safety and happiness of Pierre Philibert.

But in the quiet life of the Cloister, Amelie heard little of the storms of war upon the frontiers and down in the far vallies of Acadia. She had not followed the career of Pierre from the military school to the camp and the battle field nor knew of his rapid promotion as one of the ablest officers in the Kings service to a high command in his native Colony.

Her surprise therefore was extreme when she learned that the boy companion of her brother and herself was no other than the renowned Colonel Philibert, Aide de Camp of his Excellency the Governor General.

There was no cause for shame in it, but her heart was suddenly illumined by a flash of introspection. She became painfully conscious how much Pierre Philibert had occupied her thoughts for years, and now all at once she knew he was a man, and a great and noble one. She was thoroughly perplexed and half angry. She questioned herself sharply as if running thorns into her flesh, to inquire whether she had failed in the least point of maidenly modesty and reserve, in thinking so much of him, and the more she questioned herself, the more agitated she grew under her self accusation. Her temples throbbed violently, she hardly dared lift her eyes from the ground lest some one, even a stranger she thought might see her confusion and read its cause. "Sancta Maria," she murmured pressing her bosom with both hands: "calm my soul with thy divine peace, for I know not what to do!—"

So she sat alone in the embrasure, living a life of emotion in a few minutes, nor did she find any calm for her agitated spirits until the thought flashed upon her that she was distressing herself needlessly. It was most improbable that Colonel Philibert after years of absence and active life in the worlds great affairs could retain any recollection of the school girl of the Manor House of Tilly. She might meet him, nay was certain to do so in the society in which both moved, but it would surely be as a stranger on his part, and she must make it so on her own.

With this empty piece of casuistry, Amelie like others of her sex, placed a hand of steel encased in a silken glove, upon her heart, and tyrannically suppressed its yearnings. She was victrix with the outward show of conquest over her feelings. In the consciousness of Philiberts imagined indifference, and utter forgetfulness, she could meet him now she thought with equanimity, nay rather wished to do so, to make sure that she had not been guilty of weakness in regard to him. She looked up, but was glad to see her aunt still engaged in conversation with the Bishop, and on a topic which Amelie knew was dear to them both—the care of the souls and bodies of the poor and in particular those for whom the Lady de Tilly felt herself responsible to God and the King.

While Amelie sat thinking over the strange chances of the morning, a sudden whirl of wheels drew her attention. A gay caleche drawn by two spirited horses *en fleche*, dashed through the gate way of St John, and wheeling swiftly towards Amelie suddenly halted. A young lady attired in the rich gay fashion of the period throwing the reins to a groom, sprang out of the caleche with the ease and elasticity of an antelope. She ran up the rampart to Amelie with a glad cry of recognition, repeating her name in a clear musical voice which Amelie at once knew belonged to no other than the gay beautiful Angelique des Meloises. The new comer embraced Amelie and kissed her with warmest expressions of joy at meeting her thus unexpectedly in the city. She had learned the Lady de Tilly had returned to Quebec she said, and she had therefore taken the earliest opportunity to find out her dear friend and school fellow to tell her all the doings in the city.

"It is kind of you Angelique!" replied Amelie returning her caress, warmly but without effusion. "We have simply come with our people to assist in the Kings *corvée*. When that is done we shall return to Tilly. I felt sure I should meet you and thought I should know you again easily, which I hardly do. How you are changed—for the better I should say—since we left off conventual cap and costume!—" Amelie could not but look admiringly on the beauty of the radiant girl. "How handsome you have grown! but you were always that!—We both took the crown of honour together, but you would alone take the crown of beauty Angelique." Amelie stood off a pace or two and looked at her friend from head to foot with honest admiration, "and you would deserve to wear it too!" added she.

"I like to hear you say that, Amelie, and I would prefer the crown of beauty to all other crowns! You half frown at that, but I must tell the truth, if you do. But you were always a truth teller you know in the convent, and I was not so! Let us cease flatteries!"

Angelique felt highly flattered by the praise of Amelie whom she had sometimes condescended to envy for her graceful figure and lovely expressive features. "Gentlemen often say as you do Amelie," continued she "but pshaw! they cannot judge as girls do, you know. But do you really think me beautiful? and how beautiful, compare me to some one we know."—

"I can only compare you to yourself Angelique you are more beautiful than any one I know." Amelie burst out in frank enthusiasm.

"But really and truly do you think me beautiful not only in your eyes but in the judgment of the world?" Angelique brushed back her glorious hair and stared fixedly in the face of her friend, as if seeking confirmation of something in her own thoughts.

"What a strange question Angelique. Why do you ask me in that way?"—

"Because," replied she with bitterness, "I begin to doubt it. I have been praised for my good looks until I grow weary of the iteration, but I believed the lying flattery once as what woman would not, when it is repeated every day of her life."

Amelie looked sufficiently puzzled. "What has come over you Angelique? Why should you doubt your own charms—? or really, have you at last found a case in which they fail you?—"

Very unlikely! a man would say, at first second and third sight of Angelique des Meloises. She was indeed a fair girl to look upon, tall and fashioned in natures most voluptuous mould, perfect in the symmetry of every part, with an ease and beauty of movement, not suggestive of spiritual graces like Amelies, but of terrestrial witcheries like those great women of old who drew down the very Gods from Olympus, and who in all ages have incited men to the noblest deeds or tempted them to the greatest crimes.

She was beautiful of that rare type of beauty which is only reproduced once or twice in a century to show mankind the possibilities of feminine perfection. Her complexion was clear and radiant as of a descendant of the Sun God. Her bright hair, if its golden ripples were shaken out would reach to her knees. Her face was worthy of immortality by the pencil of a Titian. Her dark eyes drew with a magnetism which attracted men in spite of themselves, withersoever she would lead them. They were never so dangerous as when in apparent repose. They sheathed their fascination for a moment, and suddenly shot a backward glance like a Parthian arrow from under their long eyelashes, that left a wound to be sighed over over many a day.

The spoiled and petted child of the brave careless Renaud d'Avesne des Meloises, of an ancient family in the Nivernois, Angelique grew up a motherless girl, clever above most of her companions, conscious of superior charms,—always admired and flattered, and since she left the Convent worshipped as the idol of the gay gallants of the city and the despair and envy of her own sex. She was a born sovereign of men, and she felt it. It was her divine right to be preferred. She trod the earth with dainty feet and a step aspiring as that of the fair Louise de La Valiere when she danced in the Royal Ballet in the forest of Fontainebleau, and stole a kings heart by the flashes of her pretty feet. Angelique had been indulged by her father in every caprice and in the gay world inhaled the incense of adulation until she regarded it as her right and resented passionately when it was withheld.

She was not by nature bad, although vain, selfish and

aspiring. Her footstool was the hearts of men and upon it she set hard her beautiful feet indifferent to the anguish caused by her capricious tyranny. She was cold and calculating under the warm passions of a voluptuous nature. Although many might believe they had won the favour none felt sure they had gained the love of this fair capricious girl.

CHAPTER 4

CONFIDENCES

ANGELIQUE took the arm of Amelie in her old familiar school girl way, and led her to the sunny corner of a bastion where lay a dismounted cannon. The green slope of the long hill side of Charlebourg was visible through an embrasure, like a Landscape framed in massive stone.

The girls sat down on the old gun. Angelique held Amelie by both hands as if hesitating how to express something she wished to say. Still when Angelique did speak, it was plain to Amelie that she had other things on her mind, than what her tongue gave loose to.

"Now we are quite alone, Amelie" said she. "We can talk as we used to do in our school days. You have not been in the city during the whole summer, and have missed all its gaieties—?"

"I was well content! how beautiful the country looks from here—!" replied Amelie glancing out of the embrasure, at the green fields and gorgeous summer woods that lay across the valley of the St Charles. "How much pleasanter to be in it, revelling among the flowers and under the trees. I like to touch the country as well as look at it from a distance as you do in Quebec."—

"Well I never care for the Country, if I can only get enough of the City. Quebec was never so gay as it has been this year. The Royal Roussillon and the freshly arrived regiments of Bearn and Ponthieu have turned the heads of all Quebec of the girls that is. Gallants have been plenty as bilberries in August, and you may be sure I got my share Amelie!"— Angelique laughed aloud at some secret reminiscences of her summer campaign.

"It is well I did not come to the city Angelique to get my

29

head turned like the rest! but now that I am here, suppose I should mercifully try to heal some of the hearts you have broken?"

"I hope you wont try, those bright eyes of yours would heal too effectually the wounds made by mine, and that is not what I desire." replied Angelique, laughing.

"No? then, your heart is more cruel than your eyes. But tell me, who have been your victims this year, Angelique—?"

"Well to be frank, Amelie, I have tried my fascinations on the Kings officers very impartially, and with fair success. There have been three duels, two deaths, and one Captain of the Royal Roussillon turned Cordelier for my sake. Is that not a fair return for my labour—?"

"You are shocking as ever Angelique! I do not believe you feel proud of such triumphs!" exclaimed Amelie.

"Proud no!—I am not proud of conquering men. That is easy—! my triumphs are over the women! and the way to triumph over them is to subdue the men. You know my old rival at school, the haughty Francoise de Lantagnac. I owed her a grudge, and she has put on the black veil for life instead of the white one and orange blossoms for a day—! I only meant to frighten her however, when I stole her lover, but she took it to heart and went into the Convent. It was dangerous for her to challenge Angelique des Meloises to test the fidelity of her affianced, Julien de St Croix."

Amelie rose up in honest indignation, Her cheek burning like a coal of fire. "I know your wild talk of old Angelique, but I will not believe you are so wicked as to make deadly sport of our holiest affections."

"Ah, if you knew men as I do, Amelie! you would think it no sin to punish them for their perjuries. But you are a Nun in experience, and never woke out of a girls dream of love, as I have done."—Angelique seemed to make this remark in a hard monotone as much to herself as to her companion.

"No, I dont know men" replied Amelie, "but I think a good noble man is after God the worthiest object of a woman's devotion. We were better dead than finding amusement in the pain of those who love us—pray, what became of Julien de

St Croix after you broke up his intended marriage with poor Francoise—!"

"O! him I threw to the fishes! What did I care for him? It was mainly to punish Francoise' presumption that I showed my power and made him fight that desperate duel with Captain Le Franc."

"O, Angelique, how could you be so unutterably wicked?"

"Wicked? It was not my fault you know, that he was killed. He was my champion and ought to have come off victor. I wore a black ribbon for him a full half year, and had the credit of being devoted to his memory. I had my triumphs in that if in nothing else."

"Your triumphs! for shame Angelique. I will not listen to you. You profane the very name of love by uttering such sentiments. The gift of so much beauty was for blessing, not for pain. St Mary pray for you Angelique you need her prayers!" Amelie rose up suddenly.

"Nay do not get angry, and go off that way, Amelie," ejaculated Angelique. "I will do penance for my triumphs by relating my defeats, and my special failure of all, which I know you will rejoice to hear."

"I? Angelique! What have your triumphs or failures to do with me? No, I care not to hear." Angelique held her half forcibly by the scarf.

"But you will care when I tell you, that I met an old and valued friend of yours last night at the Castle. The new Aide de Camp of the Governor, Colonel Philibert. I *think* I have heard you speak of Pierre Philibert, in the Convent Amelie—?—"

Amelie felt the net thrown over her by the skilful Retiaria. She stood stock still in mute surprise, with averted eye and deeply blushing cheek, fighting desperately with the confusion she feared to let Angelique detect. But that keen sighted girl saw too clearly—she had caught her fast as a bird is caught by the fowler.

"Yes, I met with a double defeat last night" continued Angelique.

"Indeed! pray from whom?" Amelie's curiosity though not usually a troublesome quality was by this time fairly roused.

Angelique saw her drift, and played with her anxiety, for a few moments.

"My first rebuff, was from that gentlemanly Philosoph from Sweden, a great friend of the Governor, you know. But alas I might as well have tried to fascinate an iceberg! His talk was all of the flowers of the field. He has not gallantry to give you a rose before he has dissected it to the very calyx. I do not believe that he knew after half an hour's conversation with me, whether I was man or woman. That was defeat number one."

"And what was number two?" Amelie was now thoroughly interested in Angelique's gossip.

"I left the dry unappreciative Philosopher, and devoted myself to charm the handsome Colonel Philibert. He was all wit and courtesy. But my failure was even more signal with him than with the cold Swede."

Amelie's eyes gave a sparkle of joy, which did not escape Angelique, but she pretended not to see it. "How was that? tell me pray, how you failed with Colonel Philibert?"

"My cause of failure would not be a lesson for you, Amelie. Listen, I got a speedy introduction to Colonel Philibert, who I confess is one of the handsomest men I ever saw. I was bent on attracting him."

"For shame Angelique! How could you confess to ought so unwomanly?—" There was a warmth in Amelie's tone, that was less noticed by herself than by her companion.

"Well, It is my way of conquering the Kings army. I shot my whole quiver of arrows at Colonel Philibert, but to my chagrin hit not a vital part!—he parried every one and returned them broken at my feet. His persistent questioning about yourself, as soon he discovered we had been school companions in the Convent, quite foiled me. He was full of interest about you, and all that concerned you, but cared not a fig about me!"

"What could Colonel Philibert have to ask you about me?" Amelie unconsciously drew closer to her companion and even clasped her arm by an involuntary movement—which did not escape her friend.

"Why he asked every thing a gentleman could with proper

respect ask about a lady."—

"And what did you say?"

"O not half enough to content him. I confess I felt piqued that he only looked on me as a sort of Pythoness to solve enigmas about you. I had a grim satisfaction, in leaving his curiosity irritated but not satisfied. I praised your beauty, goodness and cleverness up to the skies however. I was not untrue to old friendship, Amelie—!" Angelique kissed her friend on the cheek, who silently allowed what in her indignation a few moments ago she would have refused.

"But what said Colonel Philibert of himself?—never mind about me."—

"O impatient that you are! He said nothing of himself. He was absorbed in my stories concerning you, and I told him as pretty a fable as La Fontaine related of the, *Avare qui avait perdu son tresor!*—I said, you were a beautiful Chatelaine beseiged by an army of lovers, but the knight errant Fortunatus had alone won your favour and would receive your hand—!—The brave Colonel! I could see he winced at this. His steel cuirass was not invulnerable! I drew blood which is more than you would have dared to do Amelie! But I discovered the truth, hidden in his heart. He is in love with you, Amelie De Repentigny!"

"Mad girl! How could you? How dared you speak so of me? What must Colonel Philibert think?—"

"Think?—He thinks you must be the most perfect of your sex! Why, his mind was made up about you, Amelie before he said a word to me. Indeed, he only just wanted to enjoy the supernal pleasure of hearing *me* sing the praizes of Amelie De Repentigny, to the tune composed by himself."

"Which you seem to have done, Angelique!"

"As musically as Aunt Mere St Borgia, when singing vespers in the Ursulines." was Angelique's flippant reply.

Amelie knew how useless it was to expostulate. She swallowed her mingled pleasure and vexation, salt with tears she could not help, and she changed the subject by a violent wrench, and asked Angelique, when she had last seen Le Gardeur?

"At the Intendant's Levee the other day. How like you he

is too, only less amiable!" Angelique did not respond readily to her friends question about her brother.

"Less amiable? That is not like my brother. Why do you think him less amiable than me?"

"Because he got angry with me at the Ball given in honour of the arrival of the Intendant, and I have not been able yet to restore him to perfect good humour with me since."

"O, then Le Gardeur completes the trio of those who are proof against your fascinations—?"—Amelie was secretly glad to hear of the displeasure of Le Gardeur with Angelique.

"Not at all, I hope Amelie. I dont place Le Gardeur in the same category with my other admirers. But he got offended because I seemed, to neglect him a little, to cultivate this gay new Intendant. Do you know him?"

"No! nor wish to! I have heard much said to his disadvantage. The Chevalier La Corne St Luc has openly expressed his dislike of the Intendant, for something that happened in Acadia."—

"O, the Chevalier La Corne is always so decided in his likes and dislikes—one must either be very good or very bad to satisfy him," replied Angelique with a scornful pout on her lips.

"Dont speak ill of my Godfather, Angelique, better be profane on any other topic. You know my idol of manly virtues is the Chevalier La Corne." replied Amelie.

"Well I wont pull down your idol then! I respect the brave old soldier too! but could wish him with the army in Flanders—!—"—

"Thousands of estimable people augur ill from the accession of the Intendant Bigot in New France, besides the Chevalier La Corne," Amelie said after a pause. She disliked censuring even the Intendant.

"Yes," replied Angelique, "the *Honnetes Gens* do, who think themselves bound to oppose the Intendant, because he uses the royal authority in a regal way, and makes everyone high and low do their devoir, to Church and State."

"While he does his devoir to none! But I am no politician Angelique. But when so many good people call the Intendant a bad man, It behoves one to be circumspect in 'cultivating him,' as you call it—."

"Well, he is rich enough to pay for all the broken pots! They say he amassed untold wealth in Acadia, Amelie—!"

"And lost the Province for the King!" retorted Amelie, with all the asperity her gentle but patriotic spirit was capable of—"some say he sold the country."

"I dont care!" replied the reckless beauty. "He is like Joseph in Egypt, next to Pharoah in authority. He can shoe his horses with gold! I wish he would shoe me with golden slippers. I would wear them, Amelie—!"—Angelique stamped her dainty foot on the ground as if in fancy she already had them on.

"It is shocking, if you mean it!" remarked Amelie pityingly, for she felt Angelique was speaking her genuine thoughts. "But is it true that the Intendant is really so dissolute, as rumour says."

"I dont care if it be true! He is noble gallant, polite, rich and all powerful at Court. He is reported too to be a prime favorite of the Marquise De Pompadour. What more do I want Amelie?" replied Angelique warmly.

Amelie knew enough by report of the French Court to cause her to shrink instinctively as from a repulsive insect, at the name of the mistress of Louis XV. She trembled at the thought of Angelique's infatuation, or perversity in suffering herself to be attracted by the glitter of the vices of the Royal Intendant.

"Angelique!" exclaimed she, "I have heard things of the Intendant that would make me tremble for you, were you in earnest."

"But I am in earnest. I mean to win and wear the Intendant of New France, to show my superiority over the whole bevy of beauties competing for his hand. There is not a girl in Quebec but would run away with him tomorrow."—

"Fie, Angelique! such a libel on our sex!—you know better. But you cannot love him?"

"Love him? No!" Angelique repeated the denial bitterly. "Love him? I never thought of love and him together—! He is not handsome like your brother Le Gardeur who is my beau ideal of a man I could love, nor has he the intellect and nobility of Colonel Philibert, who is my model of a heroic man. I could love such men as these. But my ambition would not be content with less than a Governor or Royal Intendant in New France—! In old France I would not put up with less than the King himself—!—"

Angelique laughed at her own extravagance, but she believed in it all the same. Amelie though shocked at her wildness could not help smiling at her folly.

"Have you done raving?" said she. "I have no right to question your selection of a lover or doubt your power, Angelique—! But are you sure there exists no insurmountable obstacle to oppose these high aspirations—? It is whispered that the Intendant has a wife whom he keeps in the seclusion of Beaumanoir. Is that true?"

The words burnt like fire. Angeliques eyes flashed out daggers. She clenched her delicate hands until her nails drew blood from her velvet palms. Her frame quivered with suppressed passion. She grasped her companion fiercely by the arm, exclaiming "You have hit the secret now, Amelie. It was to speak of that, I sought you out this morning, for I know you are wise, discreet and every way better than I. It is all true what I have said and more too, Amelie. Listen! The Intendant has made love to me, with pointed gallantry, that could have no other meaning but that he honorably sought my hand. He has made me talked of, and hated by my own sex, who envied his preference of me. I was living in the most gorgeous of fool's paradises, when a bird brought to my ear the astounding news that a woman beautiful as Diana, had been found in the forest of Beaumanoir, by some Hurons of Lorette, who were out hunting with the Intendant. She was accompanied by a few Indians of a strange tribe, the Abenaquais of Acadia. The woman was utterly exhausted by fatigue, and lay asleep on a couch of dry leaves under a tree, when the astonished Hurons led the Intendant to the spot where she lay."

"Dont interrupt me, Amelie! I see you are amazed but let me go on!—" She held the hands of her companion firmly down in her lap as she proceeded—:

"The Intendant was startled out of all composure at the apparition of the sleeping lady. He spoke eagerly to the Abenaquais in their own tongue which was unintelligible to the Hurons. When he had listened to a few words of their explanation, He ran hastily to the lady, kissed her, called her by name, Caroline! She woke up suddenly. She started up and recognizing the Intendant, embraced him, crying Francois! Francois! and fainted in his arms.

"The Chevalier was profoundly agitated, blessing and banning in the same breath, the fortune that had led her to him. He gave her wine, restored her to consciousness, talked with her long and sometimes angrily. But to no avail, for the woman in accents of despair exclaimed in French which the Hurons understood, that the Intendant might kill and bury her there, but she would never, never, return home anymore."

Angelique took not breath as she continued her eager recital, "The Intendant overpowered either by love of her or fear of her, ceased his remonstrances. He gave some pieces of gold to the Abenaquis and dismissed them. The strange Indians kissed her on both hands as they would a queen, and with many adieus vanished into the forest. The lady attended by Bigot remained seated under the tree till nightfall when he conducted her secretly to the Chateau, where she still remains in perfect seclusion, in a secret chamber they say, and has been seen by none save one or two of the Intendants most intimate companions."

"Heavens! what a tale of romance! How learned you all this, Angelique?" exclaimed Amelie who had listened with breathless attention to the narrative.

"O, partly a hint from a Huron girl, and the rest from the Intendants secretary. Men cannot keep secrets that women are interested in knowing—! I could make De Pean talk the Intendants head off his shoulders if I had him an hour in my confessional. But all my ingenuity could not extract from him what he did not know, who that mysterious lady is, her name and family—?"

"Could the Huron hunters give no guess?—" asked Amelie thoroughly interested in Angeliques story.

"No. They learned by signs however from the Abenaquis that she was a lady of noble family in Acadia, which had mingled its Patrician blood with that of the native Chiefs and possessors of the soil. The Abenaquis were chary of their information however. They would only say she was a great white lady, and as good as any saint in the calendar."

"I would give five years of my life to know who and what that woman is!" Angelique added as she leaned over the parapet gazing intently at the great forest that lay beyond Charlebourg, in which was concealed the Chateau of Beaumanoir.

"It is a strange mystery. But I would not seek to unravel it Angelique," remarked Amelie "I feel there is sin in it. Do not touch it! It will only bring mischief upon you if you do!—"

"Mischief! so be it! but I will know the worst! The Intendant is deceiving me! woe be to him and her if I am to be their intended victim!! Will you not assist me Amelie to discover the truth of this secret?—"

"I? how can I? I pity you Angelique but it were better to leave this Intendant to his own devices."

"You can very easily help me if you will. Le Gardeur must know this secret. He has seen the woman, but he is angry with me, for—for—slighting him, as he thinks, but he was wrong. I could not avow to him my jealousy in this matter. He told me just enough to madden me, and angrily refused to tell the rest when he saw me so—infatuated—he called it, over other people's love affairs. O Amelie, Le Gardeur will tell you all if you ask him—!—"

"And I repeat it to you, Angelique, I cannot question Le Gardeur on such a hateful topic. At any rate I need time to reflect and will pray to be guided right."

"O pray not at all! If you pray you will never aid me! I know you will say the end is wicked and the means dishonorable. But find out I will—and speedily—!—It will only be the price of another dance with the Chevalier de Pean, to discover all I want. What fools men are when they believe we love them for their sakes and not for our own!—"

Amelie pitying the wild humours as she regarded them of

her old school companion, took her arm to walk to and fro in the Bastion, but was not sorry to see her Aunt and the Bishop and Father De Berey approaching.

"Quick," said she to Angelique, "smooth your hair and compose your looks. Here come my Aunt and the Bishop, Father De Berey too—! Sad thoughts are ever banished where he comes, although I dont admire quite so much gaiety in a priest!"

Angelique prepared at once to meet them, and with that wonderful power of adaptation transformed herself in a moment into a merry creature all light and gaiety. She saluted the Lady de Tilly and the Reverend Bishop in the frankest manner, and at once accepted an interchange of wit and laughter with Father De Berey. Her voice so clear and silvery would have put the wisdom of Solomon at fault to discover one trace of care in the mind of this beautiful girl.

She could not remain long however in the Church's company, she said. She had her morning calls to finish. She kissed the cheek of Amelie and the hand of the Lady De Tilly and with a coquettish courtsey to the Gentlemen, leaped nimbly into her Calesche, whirled round her spirited horses like a practiced charioteer and drove with rapid pace down the crowded street of St John, the observed of all observers, the admiration of the men, and the envy of the women as she flashed by.

Amelie and the Lady De Tilly having seen a plenteous meal distributed among their people proceeded to their City Home, their Seigneurial residence when they chose to live in the capital.

CHAPTER 5

THE ITINERANT NOTARY

MASTER Jean Le Nocher, the sturdy ferryman's patience had been severly tried for a few days back, passing the troops of Habitans over the St Charles to the city of Quebec. Being on the King's corvée they claimed the privilege of all persons in the Royal service. They travelled toll-free, and paid Jean with a nod or a jest in place of the small coin that worthy used to exact on ordinary occasions.

This morning had begun auspiciously for Jean's temper however. A Kings officer on a grey charger, had just crossed the Ferry and without claiming the exemption from toll which was the right of all wearing the Kings uniform, the officer had paid Jean more than his fee in solid coin, and rode on his way after a few kind words to the Ferryman and a polite salute to his wife Babet who stood courtseying at the door of their cottage.

"A noble gentleman that, and a real one!" exclaimed Jean to his buxom pretty wife, "and as generous as a prince—! See! what he has given me." Jean flipped up a piece of silver admiringly and then threw it into the apron of Babet which she spread out to catch it.

Babet rubbed the silver piece caressingly between her fingers and on her cheek. "It is easy to see that handsome officer is from the Castle," said Babet, "and not from the Palace, and so nice looking he is too, with such a sparkle in his eye and a pleasant smile on his mouth. He is as good as he looks or I am no judge of men."

"And you are an excellent judge of men I know Babet," he replied "or you would never have taken me!"—Jean chuckled richly over his own wit, which Babet nodded lively approval to. "Yes, I know a hawk from a handsaw," replied Babet, "and a woman who is as wise as that will never mistake a gentleman, Jean!—I have not seen a handsomer officer than that in seven years!"

"He is a pretty fellow enough I dare say, Babet. Who can he be? He rides like a Field Marshal, too, and that grey horse has ginger in his heels!" remarked Jean, as the officer was riding at a rapid galop up the long white road to Charlebourg. "He is going to Beaumanoir belike to see the Royal Intendant, who has not returned yet from his hunting party."

"Whither they went three days ago, to enjoy themselves in the chace and drink themselves blind in the chateau, while every body else is summoned to the city to work on the walls!" replied Babet, scornfully. "I'll be bound that officer has gone to order the gay gallants of the Friponne back to the city to take their share of work with honest people."—

"Ah! the Friponne! The Friponne!" ejaculated Jean "The foul fiend fly away with the Friponne! My ferry boat is laden every day with the curses of the Habitans returning from the Friponne, where they cheat worse than a Basque Pedler, and without a grain of his politeness!"—

The Friponne, as it was styled in popular parlance was the immense Magazine established by the Grand Company of Traders in New France. It claimed a monopoly in the purchase and sale of all imports and exports in the Colony. Its privileges were based upon royal ordinances and decrees of the Intendant and its rights enforced in the most arbitrary manner, and to the prejudice of every other mercantile interest in the Colony. As a natural consequence it was cordially hated and richly deserved the maledictions which generally accompanied the mention of the Friponne— the swindle—a rough and ready epithet which sufficiently indicated the feeling of the people whom it at once cheated and oppressed.

"They say Jean," continued Babet, her mind running in a very practical and womanly way upon the price of commodities, and good bargains. "They say Jean, that the Bourgeois Philibert will not give in like the other merchants.

He sets the Intendant at defiance and will continue to buy and sell in his own Comptoir as he has always done—in spite of the Friponne."

"Yes, Babet! that is what they say. But I would rather he stood in his own shoes, than I in them if he is to fight this Intendant, who is a Tartar they say."—

"Pshaw Jean! you have less courage than a woman—all the women are on the side of the good Bourgeois! He is a honest merchant, sells cheap and cheats nobody." Babet looked down very complacently upon her new gown, which had been purchased at a great bargain at the magazin of the Bourgeois. She felt rather the more inclined to take this view of the question inasmuch as Jean had grumbled, just a little, he would not do more, at his wife's vanity in buying a gay dress of French fabric, like a City Dame, while all the women of the Parish were wearing home spun, grogram or linsy woolsey, whether at church or market.

Jean had not the heart to say another word to Babet about the French gown. In truth he thought she looked very pretty in it. Better than in grogram or in linsy woolsey although at double the cost. He only winked knowingly at Babet and went on speaking of the Bourgeois.

"They say the King has long hands, but this Intendant has claws longer than Satans. There will be trouble by and by at the Golden Dog—mark that, Babet! It was only the other day the Intendant was conversing with the Sieur Cadet as they crossed the ferry. They forgot me, or thought I did not hear them, but I had my ears open as I always have. I heard something said, and I hope no harm will come to the good Bourgeois, that is all!—"

"I dont know where Christian folk would deal if any thing happened him," said Babet reflectively. "We always get civility and good pennyworths at the Golden Dog. Some of the lying cheats at the Friponne talked in my hearing one day about his being a Huguenot. But how can that be Jean? When he gives the best weight and longest measure of any merchant in Quebec. Religion is a just yard wand—that is my belief Jean—!"

Jean rubbed his head with a perplexed air. "I do not know whether he be a Huguenot, nor what a Huguenot is. The Curé one day said, he was a Jansenist on all fours, which I suppose is the same thing Babet, and it does not concern either you or me. But a merchant who is a gentleman, and kind to poor folk, and gives just measure and honest weight speaks truth and harms nobody, is christian enough for me. A Bishop could not trade more honestly and the word of the Bourgeois is as reliable as a Kings."

"The Curé may call the Bourgeois what he likes," replied Babet. "But there is not another Christian in the city if the good Bourgeois be not one, and next the church, there is not a house in Quebec better known or better liked by all the Habitans, than the Golden Dog, and such bargains too as one gets there!—"

"Aye, Babet! a good bargain settles many a knotty point with a woman."—

"And with a man too if he is wise enough to let his wife do his marketing as you do Jean. But who have we here—?" Babet set her arms a kimbo and gazed.

A number of hardy fellows came down towards the Ferry to seek a passage.

"They are honest habitans of St Anne," replied Jean. "I know them. They too are on the Kings Corvée and travel free every man of them! So I must cry *vive le Roi*! and pass them over to the city. It is like a holiday when one works for nothing."

Jean stepped nimbly into his boat followed by the rough country fellows, who amused themselves by joking at Jean Le Nocher's increasing trade, and the need of putting on an extra boat these stirring times. Jean put a good face on it, laughed and retorted their quips, and plying his oars stoutly, perfomed his part in the King's Corvée by safely landing them on the other shore.

Meantime the officer who had lately crossed the ferry rode rapidly up the long straight highway, that led up the side of the mountain to a cluster of white cottages, and a tall church surmounted by a belfry whose sweet bells were ringing melodiously in the fresh air of the morning.

The sun was pouring a flood of golden light over the Landscape. The still glittering dew drops hung on the trees, shrubs and long points of the grass by the way side—all were tipped with jewels to greet the rising King of day.

The wide open fields, of meadow and corn fields, ripening for harvest stretched far away, unbroken by hedge or fence. Slight ditches or banks of turf covered with nests of violets, ferns and wild flowers of every hue, separated contiguous fields. No other division seemed necessary in the mutual good neighbourhood that prevailed among the colonists, whose fashion of agriculture had been brought with many hardy virtues from the old plains of Normandy.

White walled red roofed cottages, or more substantial farm houses, stood conspicuously in the green fields or peered out of embowering orchards, their casements all open to catch the balmy airs, while in not a few the sound of clattering hoofs on the hard road drew fair faces to the window or door to look inquisitively, after the officer wearing the white plume in his military chapeau, as he dashed by on the gallant grey.

Those who caught sight of him, saw a man worth seeing— tall, deep chested, and erect. His Norman features without being perfect were handsome and manly. Steel blue eyes solidly set under a broad forehead looked out searchingly yet kindly, while his well formed chin and firm lips gave an air of resolution to his whole look, that accorded perfectly with the brave loyal character of Colonel Philibert. He wore the royal uniform. His auburn hair he wore tied with a black ribbon. His good taste discarded perukes and powder although very much in fashion in those days.

It was long since he had travelled on the highway of Charlebourg, and thoroughly enjoyed the beauty of the road he traversed. But behind him as he knew, lay a magnificent spectacle—the sight of the great promontory of Quebec crowned with its glorious fortifications and replete with the richest memories of North America. More than once the young soldier turned his steed and halted a moment or two to survey the scene with enthusiastic admiration. It was his native city, and the thought that it was threatened by the national enemy roused like an insult offered to the mother that bore him. He rode onward more than ever impatient of delay, and not till he passed a cluster of elm trees which reminded him of an adventure of his youth did the sudden heat pass away, caused by thought of the threatened invasion.

Under these trees, he remembered that he and his school companion Le Gardeur de Repentigny had once taken refuge during a violent storm. The tree they stood under was shattered by a thunderbolt. They were both stunned for a few minutes and knew they had had a narrow escape from death—neither of them ever forgot it.

A train of thoughts, never long absent from the mind of Philibert, started up vividly at the sight of these trees. His memory flew back to Le Gardeur and the Manor House of Tilly, and the fair young girl who captivated his boyish fancy, and filled his youth with dreams of glorious achievements to win her smiles and do her honour. Among a thousand pictures of her hung up in his mind and secretly worshipped, he loved that which presented her likeness on that day when he saved her brother's life and she kissed him in a passion of joy and gratitude vowing she would pray for him to the end of her life.

The Imagination of Pierre Philibert had revelled in the romantic visions that haunt every boy destined to preeminence, visions kindled by the eye of woman and the hope of love.

The world is ruled by such dreams—dreams of impassioned hearts and improvisations of warm lips, not by cold words linked in chains of iron sequence—by love, not logic.

The heart with its passions not the understanding with its reasonings sways in the long run the actions of mankind.

Pierre Philibert possessed that rich gift of nature a creative imagination in addition to the solid judgment of a man of sense, schooled by experience and used to the consideration and responsibilities of weighty affairs.

His love for Amelie de Repentigny had grown in secret. Its roots reached down to the very depths of his soul. It mingled consciously or unconsciously with all his motives and plans of life, and yet his hopes were not sanguine. Years of absence, He remembered, work forgetfulness. New ties and associations might have wiped out the memory of him in the mind of a young girl, fresh to society and its delights. He experienced a disappointment in not finding her in the city on his return a few days ago, and the state of the Colony and the stress of military duty, had so far prevented his renewing his acquaintance with the Manor House of Tilly.

The old fashioned hostelry of the *Couronne de France* with its high pitched roof, pointed gables and broad gallery stood directly opposite the rustic church and tall belfry of Charlebourg—not as a rival, but as a sort of adjunct to the sacred edifice. The sign of the Crown, bright with gilding swung from the low projecting arm of a maple tree, thick with shade and rustling with the beautiful leaves of the emblem of Canada. A few rustic seats, under the cool maple were usually occupied towards the close of the day, or about the ringing of the Angelus by a little gathering of parishioners from the village, talking over the news of the day, the progress of the war, the ordinances of the Intendant or the exactions of the Friponne.

On Sundays, after Mass and Vespers, the habitans of all parts of the extended parish, naturally met and talked over the affairs of the Fabrique—the value of tithes for the year, the abundance of Easter eggs and the weight of the first salmon of the season which was always presented to the Curé, with the first fruits of the field to ensure the blessing of plenty for the rest of the year.

The Reverend Curé frequently mingled in these discussions. Seated in his accustomed arm chair, under the shade of the maple in summer and in winter by the warm fire side he defended *ex cathedra*, the rights of the Church, and good humouredly decided all controversies. He found his parishioners more amenable to good advice over a mug of Norman cider and a pipe of native tobacco, under the sign of the Crown of France, than when he lectured them in his best and most learned style from the pulpit.

This morning however all was very quiet round the old Inn. The birds were singing and the bees humming in the pleasant sun shine. The house looked clean and tidy, and no one was to be seen except three persons bending over a table— With their heads close together deeply absorbed in whatever business they were engaged in. Two of these persons were Dame Bedard the sharp landlady of the Crown of France and her no less sharp and pretty daughter Zoe. The third person of the trio was an old alert looking little man writing at the table as if for very life. He wore a tattered black robe shortened at the knee to facilitate walking, a frizzled wig looking as if it had been dressed with a curry comb. A pair of black breeches well patched with various colours and gamashes of brown leather such as the habitans wore, completed his odd attire and formed the professional costume of Master Pothier *dit* Robin the travelling Notary, one of that not unuseful order of itinerants of the law, which flourished under the old regime in New France.

Upon the table near him stood a black bottle, an empty trencher and a thick scatter of crumbs, showing that the old Notary had dispatched a hearty breakfast before commencing his present work of the pen.

A hairy knapsack lay open upon the table near his elbow, disclosing some bundles of dirty papers tied up with red tape, a tattered volume or two of the *Coutume de Paris* and little more than the covers of an odd tome of Pothier, his great namesake and prime authority in the law. Some linen, dirty and ragged as his law papers was crammed into his knapsack with them. But that was neither here nor there in the estimation of the Habitans. So long as his law smelt strong in the nostrils of their opponents in litigation, they rather prided themselves on the roughness of their travelling notary.

The reputation of Master Pothier *dit* Robin was of course very great among the Habitans, as he travelled from parish to parish and from Seigneurie to Seigneurie drawing bills and hypothecations, marriage contracts and last wills and testaments, for the peasantry, who had a genuine Norman predilection for law and chicanry, and a respect amounting to veneration for written documents, red tape and sealing wax. Master Pothier's acuteness in picking holes in the *actes* of a rival notary was only surpassed by the elaborate intricacy of his own, which he boasted, not without reason, would puzzle the parliament of Paris and confound the ingenuity of the sharpest advocate of Rouen. Master Pothier's *actes* were as full of embryo disputes as a fig is full of seeds, and usually kept all parties in hot water and litigation for the rest of their days. If he did happen now and then to settle a dispute between neighbours, he made ample amends for it by setting half the rest of the parish by the ears.

Master Pothier's nose sharp and fiery as if dipped in red ink almost touched the sheet of paper on the table before him, as he wrote down from the dictation of Dame Bedard, the articles of a marriage contract between her pretty daughter Zoe and Antoine La Chance, the son of a comfortable but keen widow of Beauport.

Dame Bedard had shrewdly availed herself of the presence of Master Pothier, and in payment of a nights lodging, at the Crown of France, to have him write out the contract of marriage in the absence of Dame La Chance the mother of Antoine who would of course object to the insertion of certain conditions in the contract which Dame Bedard was quite determined upon as the price of Zoe's hand and fortune.

"There! Dame Bedard!" cried Master Pothier sticking his pen behind his ear, after a magnificent flourish at the last word. "There is a marriage contract fit to espouse King Solomon to the Queen of Sheba! A dowry of a hundred livres Tournoises, two cows, and a feather bed, bedstead and chest of linen! A *donation entre vifs*!"

"A what? Master Pothier! now mind! are you sure that is the right word of the grimoire!" cried Dame Bedard, instinctively perceiving that here lay the very point of the contract. "You know I only give on condition! Master Pothier."

"O yes! trust me Dame Bedard, I have made it, a *donation entre vifs, revocable pour cause d'ingratitude*, if your future son in law Antoine La Chance should fail in his duty to you and to Zoe."

"And he wont do his duty to Zoe unless he does it to me, Master Pothier. But are you sure it is strong enough. Will it hold Dame La Chance by the foot so that she cannot revoke her gifts although I may revoke mine?"

"Hold Dame La Chance by the foot? It will hold her fast as a snapping turtle does a frog. In proof of it see what Ricard says: page 970. Here is the book!" Master Pothier opened his tattered volume, and held it up to the Dame. She shook her head.

"Thanks, I have mislaid my glasses. Do you please."

"Most cheerfully good Dame. A notary must have eyes for everybody—eyes like a cats to see in the dark, and power to draw them in like a turtle so that he may see nothing that he does not want to see."

"O bless the eyes of the Notary!"—Dame Bedard grew impatient. "Tell me what the book says about gifts revocable. That is what concerns me, and Zoe."

"Well here it is Dame, 'Donations stipulated revocable at the pleasure of the donor are nul. But this condition does not apply to donations by contract of marriage.' Bourdon also says— —"

"A fig for Bourdon, and all such drones—! I want my gift made revocable and Dame La Chance's not. I know by long experience with my dear *feu* Bedard how necessary it is to hold the reins tight over the men. Antoine is a good boy, but he will be all the better for a careful mother in law's supervision!—"

Master Pothier rubbed the top of his wig with his forefinger. "Are you sure Dame that Antoine La Chance will wear the bridle easily?"

"Assuredly! I should like to see son in law of mine who would not! Besides Antoine is in the humour just now to refuse nothing for sake of Zoe. Have you mentioned the children, Master Pothier? I do not intend to let Dame La Chance control the children any more than Zoe and Antoine."

"I have made you *tutrice perpetuelle*, as we say in the Court, and here it is," said he placing the tip of his finger on a certain line in the document.

Zoe looked down and blushed to her finger ends. She

presently rallied and said with some spirit, "Never mind *them*, Master Pothier! Dont put *them* in the contract! Let Antoine have something to say about them. He would take me without a dower I know, and time enough to remind him about children when they come."

"Take you without dower! Zoe Bedard! you must be mad!" exclaimed the Dame in great heat. "No girl in New France can marry without a dower, if it be only a pot and a bedstead—! You forget too that the dower is given not so much for you as to keep up the credit of the family. As well be married without a ring—! without a dower indeed!"

"Or without a contract written by a Notary and signed sealed and delivered!" chimed in Master Pothier.

"Yes Master Pothier! and I have promised Zoe a three days wedding, which will make her the envy of all the parish of Charlebourg. The Seigneur has consented to give her away in place of her poor defunct father, and when he does that, he is sure to stand Godfather for all the children, with a present for every one of them—! I shall invite you too Master Pothier!"

Zoe affected not to hear her mothers remark, although she knew it all by heart, for it had been dinned into her ears twenty times a day for weeks, and sooth to say, she liked to hear it, and fully appreciated the honours to come from the patronage of the Seigneur.

Master Pothier pricked up his ears, till they fairly raised his wig, at the prospect of a three days wedding at the Crown of France. He began an elaborate reply, when a horse's tramp broke in upon them, and Colonel Philibert wheeled up to the door of the Hostelry.

Master Pothier seeing an officer in the Kings uniform rose on the instant, and saluted him with a profound bow, While Dame Bedard and Zoe standing side by side dropped their lowest courtsey, to the handsome gentleman as with woman's glance they saw in a moment he was.

Philibert returned their salute courteously, as he halted his horse in front of Dame Bedard. "Madame!" said he, "I thought I knew all roads about Charlebourg, but I have either forgotten or they have changed the road through the forest to Beaumanoir. It is surely altered from what it was."

"Your honour is right," answered Dame Bedard. "The Intendant has opened a new road through the forest." Zoe took the opportunity while the officer looked at her mother, to examine his features, dress and equipments, from head to foot, and thought him the handsomest officer she had ever seen.

"I thought it must be so," replied Philibert "You are the landlady of the Crown of France I presume—?" Dame Bedard carried it on her face as plainly marked as the royal emblem on the sign over her head.

"Yes, your honour, I am Widow Bedard, at your service, and I hope keep as good a hostelry as your honour will find in the Colony. Will your honour alight and take a cup of wine such as I keep for guests of quality?"

"Thanks Madame Bedard. I am in haste. I must find the way to Beaumanoir. Can you not furnish me a guide, for I like not to lose time by missing my way—?"

"A guide Sir! The men are all in the city on the Kings Corvée. Zoe could show you the way easily enough." Zoe twitched her mother's arm nervously as a hint not to say too much she felt flattered and fluttered too, at the thought of guiding the strange handsome gentleman through the forest, and already the question shot through her fancy, "What might come of it? Such things have happened in stories!"—Poor Zoe! She was for a few seconds unfaithful to the memory of Antoine La Chance. But Dame Bedard settled all surmises, by turning to Master Pothier who stood stiff and upright as became a limb of the law. "Here is Master Pothier, your honour, who knows every highway and byway in ten seigneuries. He will guide your honour to Beaumanoir."

"As easy as take a fee, or enter a process, your honour," remarked Master Pothier, whose odd figure had several times drawn the criticising eye of Colonel Philibert.

"A fee! ah! you belong to the law then, my good friend? I have known many advocates, but—" Philibert stopped—he was too good natured to finish his sentence.

"You never saw one like me! Your honour was going to say.

True, you never did. I am Master Pothier *dit* Robin, the poor travelling Notary at your honour's service ready to draw you a bond, frame an *acte* of *convention matrimoniale* or write your last will and testament with any notary in New France. I can moreover guide your honour to Beaumanoir, easy as drink your health in a cup of cogniac."

Philibert could not but smile at the travelling notary, and thinking to himself, "Too much cogniac at the end of that nose of yours my friend!"—and which indeed looked fiery as Bardolphs, with hardly a cool spot for a fly to rest his foot upon without burning.

"But how will you go friend?" asked Philibert looking down at Master Pothiers gamaches. "You dont look like a fast walker—?"

"O your honour!" interrupted Dame Bedard, impatiently for Zoe had been twitching her hard to let her go. "Master Pothier can ride the old sorrel nag that stands in the stable eating its head off, for want of hire. Of course your honour will pay livery?—"

"Why certainly Madame, and glad to do so. So Master Pothier make haste—get the sorrel nag and let us be off."

"I will be back in the snap of a pen, or in the time Dame Bedard can draw that cup of Cogniac your Honour."

"Master Pothier is quite a personnage I see" remarked Philibert as the old notary shuffled off, to saddle the nag.

"O quite Your Honour. He is the sharpest notary they say, that travels the road. When he gets people into law, they never can leave off. He is so clever every body says! Why he assures me that even the Intendant consults him sometimes as they sit eating and drinking half the night together in the buttery at the Chateau!—"

"Really! I must be careful what I say," replied Philibert laughing, "or I shall get into hot water! But here he comes."

As he spoke Master Pothier came up mounted on a raw boned nag lank as the remains of a twenty years law suit. Zoe at a hint from the Colonel handed him a cup of cogniac which he quaffed without breathing, smacking his lips emphatically after it and he called out to the Landlady, "Take care of my knapsack, Dame! You had better burn the church than lose my papers—! Adieu Zoe! study over the marriage contract till I return, and I shall be sure of a good dinner from your pretty hands."

They set off at a round trot. Colonel Philibert impatient to reach Beaumanoir spurred on for a while, hardly noticing the absurd figure of his guide, whose legs stuck out like a pair of compasses beneath his tattered gown His shaking head threatening dislodgment to hat and wig, while his elbows churned at every jolt making play with the shuffling gait of his spavined and wall eyed nag.

CHAPTER 6

BEAUMANOIR

THEY rode on in silence. A little beyond the village of Charlebourg they suddenly turned into the forest of Beaumanoir, where a well beaten track practicable both for carriages and horses, gave indications that the resort of visitors to the Chateau, was neither small nor seldom.

The sun's rays scarcely penetrated the sea of verdure overhead. The ground was thickly strown with leaves, the memorials of past summers, delicate ferns clustered round upturned roots of trees. The pretty star flowers, dark purple trilliums and St Johns wort nestled in sunny spots, and the dark green pines breathed out a resinous odour fresh and invigorating to the passing rider.

A little brook peeped here and there shyly in the forest as it wound through swales clothed in spiry grass. Its tiny banks spotted with silvery anemones or tufts of ladies slippers mingled with rosy bells of the Linneus Borealis.

Colonel Philibert, while his thoughts were for the most part fixed on the public dangers which led to this hasty visit of his to the Chateau of Beaumanoir had still an eye for the beauty of the forest, and not a squirrel leaping, nor a bird fluttering among the branches escaped his notice as he passed by. Still he rode on rapidly and having got fairly into the road, soon outstripped his guide.

"A crooked road this to Beaumanoir!" remarked he at length, drawing bridle to allow Master Pothier to rejoin him. "It is as mazy as the law. I am fortunate I am sure, in having a sharp Notary like you to conduct me through it."

"Conduct you! Your Honour is leading me! But the road to Beaumanoir is intricate as the best case ever drawn up by

54

an itinerant notary."

"You seldom ride Master Pothier?" said Philibert, observing his guide jolting with an audible grunt at every step of his awkward nag.

"Ride your Honour! N—no! Dame Bedard shall call me *plaisant Robin*, if she ever tempts me again to mount her livery horse. If fools only carried cruppers! as Panurge says!—"

"Why Master Pothier!" Colonel Philibert began to be amused at his odd guide.

"Why then, I should be able to walk tomorrow. That is all! This nag will finish me, hunc!, hanc! hoc! He is fit to be Latin Tutor at the Seminary—! *hoc! hanc! hunc!*—I have not declined my pronouns since I left my accidence at the High School of Tours—not till to day—*hunc! hanc, hoc!*—I shall be jolted to jelly! *Hunc! hanc! hoc!*"

Philibert laughed at the classical reminiscences of his guide, but fearing that Master Pothier might fall off his horse which he straddled like a hay fork, He stopped to allow the worthy notary to recover his breath and temper.

"I hope the world appreciates your learning and talent and that it uses you more gently than that horse of yours" remarked he.

"O your honour! It is kind of you to rein up by the way. I find no fault with the world if it finds none with me. My philosophy is this, that the world is as men make it—!"

"As the old saying is:

To lend or to spend or to give in
Tis a very good world that we live in.
But to borrow or beg or to get a man's own
Tis the very worst world that ever was known."

"And you consider yourself in the latter category Master Pothier—?" Philibert spoke doubtingly for more self complacent face than his companion's he never saw—every wrinkle twinkled with mirth. Eyes, cheeks chin and brow, surrounded that jolly red nose of his, like a group of gay boys round a bonfire.

"O I am content your honour! We notaries are privileged

to wear furred cloaks in the Palais de Justice, and black gowns in the Country when we can get them!—look here at my robe of dignity—!" He held up the tattered tail of his gown with a ludicrous air. "The profession of notary is meat drink and lodging. Every man's house is free to me, his bed and board I share—there is neither wedding, christening nor funeral in ten parishes that can go on without me; Governors and Intendants flourish and fall, but Jean Pothier *dit* Robin the itinerant notary lives merrily. Men may do without bread but they will not live without law, at least in this noble litigious New France of ours—!"

"Your profession seems quite indispensible then!" remarked Philibert.

"Indispensible! I should think so! without proper *actes*, the world would soon come to an end, as did Adam's happiness in Eden, for want of a notary."

"A notary, Master Pothier?"

"Yes, your honour. It is clear that Adam lost his first estate *de usis et fructibus*, in the Garden of Eden, simply because there was no notary to draw up for him an indefeasible lease. Why he had not even *à bail à chaptal* a chattel mortgage over the beasts he had himself named!—"

"Ah," replied Philibert smiling, "I thought Adam lost his estate through a cunning notary who persuaded his wife to break the lease he held, and poor Adam lost possession because he could not find a second notary to defend his title."

"Hum! that might be, but judgment went by default as I have read. It would be different now. There are notaries in New France and old capable of beating Lucifer himself in a process for either soul body or estate—!—But thank fortune we are out of this thick forest now!"

The travellers had reached the other verge of the forest of Beaumanoir. A broad plain dotted with clumps of fair trees spread out in a royal domain, overlooked by a steep wooded mountain. A silvery brook crossed by a rustic bridge ran through the park. In the center was a huge cluster of gardens and patriarchal trees, out of the midst of which rose the steep roofs chimnies and gilded vanes flashing in the sun of the Chateau of Beaumanoir.

The Chateau was a long heavy structure of stone, gabled and pointed in the style of the preceding century, strong enough for defence and elegant enough for the abode of the Royal Intendant of New France. It had been built some four score years previously, by the Intendant Jean Talon, as a quiet retreat when tired with the importunities of friends or the persecution of enemies, or disgusted with the cold indifference of the Court to his statesmanlike plans for the colonization of New France. Here he loved to retire from the city and in the companionship of a few chosen friends talk of the splendid literature of the age of Louis XIV. or discuss the new philosophy that was everywhere springing up in Europe.

Within the walls of the Chateau of Beaumanoir had the Sieur Joliet recounted the story of his adventurous travels, and Father Marquette confirmed the vague rumours that had long circulated in the Colony, of a wonderful river called the Father of Waters, that flowed southwards into the Gulf of Mexico. Here too, had the gallant La Salle taken counsel of his friend and patron Talon, when he set off to explore the great river Mississippi seen by Joliet and Marquette, and claim it by right of discovery as the possession of France.

A short distance from the Chateau rose a tower of rough masonry *crenellated* on top and loop holed on the sides, which had been built as a place of defence and refuge during the Indian wars of the preceding century.

Often had the prowling bands of Iroquois turned away baffled and dismayed at the sight of the little fortalice surmounted by a culverin or two, which used to give the alarm of invasion to the colonists on the slopes of Bourg Royal, and to the dwellers along the wild banks of the Montmorency.

The tower was now disused and partly dilapidated. But many wonderful tales existed among the neighbouring habitans of a secret passage that communicated with the vaults of the Chateau. But no one had ever seen the passage, still less been bold enough to explore it had they found it, for it was guarded by a *Loup Garou*, that was the terror of children old and young, as they crowded close together round the blazing fire on winter nights, and repeated old legends of Britanny and Normandy, altered to fit the wild scenes of the New World.

Colonel Philibert and Master Pothier rode up the broad avenue that led to the Chateau, and halted at the main gate, set in a lofty hedge of evergreens, cut into fantastic shapes after the fashion of the Luxembourg. Within the gate a vast and glowing garden was seen, all squares circles and polygons. Its beds were laden with flowers, shedding delicious odours on the morning air, as it floated by, while the ear was soothed by the hum of bees and the song of birds, revelling in the bright sunshine.

Above the hedge peered the tops of heavily laden fruit trees, brought from France and planted by Talon—Cherries red as the lips of Breton maidens, plums of Gascony, Norman apples and pears from the glorious vallies of the Rhone. The bending branches were just transmuting their green unripeness into scarlet gold and purple the imperial colours of nature when crowned for the festival of autumn.

A lofty dove-cote surmounted by a glittering vane turning and flashing with every shift of the air stood near the chateau. It was the home of a whole colony of snow white pigeons, which fluttered in and out of it, wheeled in circles round the tall chimney stacks or strutted cooing and bowing together on the high roof of the Chateau, a picture of innocence and happiness.

But neither happiness nor innocence was suggested by the look of the Chateau itself, as it stood bathed in bright sunshine. Its great doors were close shut in the face of all the beauty of the world without. Its mullioned windows that should have stood wide open to let in the radiance and freshness of morning were closely blinded like eyes wickedly shut against Gods light that beat upon them vainly seeking entrance.

Outside all was still. The song of birds and the rustle of leaves alone met the ear. Neither man nor beast was stirring to challenge Colonel Philibert's approach, but long ere he reached the door of the Chateau, a din of voices within, a wild medley of shouts song, and laughter, a clatter of wine cups, and pealing notes of violins struck him with amazement and disgust. He distinguished drunken voices singing snatches of Bacchanalian songs, while now and then stentorian mouths called for fresh brimmers and new toasts were drunk with uproarious applause.

The Chateau seemed a very Pandemonium of riot and revelry, that prolonged the night into the day, and defied the very order of nature by its audacious disregard of all decency of time place and circumstance.

"In God's name what means all this, Master Pothier?" exclaimed Philibert as they hastily dismounted and tying their horses to a tree, entered the broad walk that led to the terrace.

"That concert going on, your honour?—" Master Pothier shook his head to express disapproval and smiled to express his inborn sympathy with feasting and good fellowship. "That your Honour, is the heel of the hunt, the hanging up of the antlers of the stag by the gay chasseurs who are visiting the Intendant."

"A hunting party you mean—? To think that men could stand such brutishness even to please the Intendant!—"

"Stand! your Honour! I wager my gown that most of the chasseurs are underlying the table by this time, although by the noise they make it must be allowed there are some burly fellows upon their legs yet, who keep the wine flowing like the cow of Montmorency."

"Tis horrible! Tis damnable!" Philibert grew pale with passion and struck his thigh with his palm as was his wont when very angry. "Rioting in drunkness when the Colony demands the cool head, the strong arm, and the true heart of every man among us—! O my Country! my dear Country! What fate is thine to expect when men like these are thy rulers?—"

"Your Honour must be a stranger in New France or you would not express such hasty honest sentiments, upon the Intendants hospitality! It is not the fashion except among plain spoken habitans who always talk downright Norman—!" Master Pothier looked approvingly at Colonel Philibert, who listening with indignant ears scarcely heeded his guide.

"That is a jolly song your Honour!" continued Pothier

waving one hand in cadence to a ditty in praise of wine which a loud voice was heard singing in the Chateau, accompanied by a rousing chorus which startled the very pigeons on the roof and chimney stacks. Colonel Philibert recognized the song as one he had heard in the *Quartier Latin*, during his student life in Paris. He fancied he recognized the voice also—

"Pour des vins de prix
Vendons tous nos livres!—
C'est peu d'etre gris
Amis soyons ivres!

    Bon—
La Faridondaine!—

    Gai—
La Faridondé!—"

A roar of voices and a clash of glasses followed the refrain. Master Pothier's eyes winked and blinked in sympathy. The old Notary stood on tiptoe, with outspread palms, as with *ore rotundo* he threw in a few notes of his own, to fill up the Chorus.

Philibert cast on his guide a look of scorn biting his lip angrily. "Go," said he, "knock at the door. It needs God's thunder to break in upon that infamous orgie! say that Colonel Philibert brings orders from His Excellency the Governor to the Chevalier Intendant."—

"And be served with a writ of ejectment! Pardon me! Be not angry! Sir," pleaded Pothier supplicatingly, "I dare not knock at the door when they are at the Devils mass inside! The Valets! I know them all. They would duck me in the brook, or drag me into the Hall, to make sport for the Philistines, and I am not much of a Samson your honour! I could not pull the Chateau down upon their heads! I wish I could!"

Master Pothier's fears did not appear ill-grounded to Philibert as a fresh burst of drunken uproar assailed his ears. "Wait my return" said he, "I will knock on the door myself." He left his guide ran up the broad stone steps knocked loudly upon the door again and again! he tried it at last, and to his surprize found the door unlatched, he pushed it open. No servitor appearing to admit him Colonel Philibert went boldly in. A blaze of light almost dazzled his eyes. The Chateau was lit up with lamps and candelabra in every part. The bright rays of the sun beat in vain for admittance upon the closed doors and blinded windows, but the splendour of midnight oil pervaded the interior of the stately mansion, making an artificial night that prolonged the wild orgie of the Intendant into the hours of day.

CHAPTER 7

THE INTENDANT BIGOT

THE Chateau of Beaumanoir had since the advent of the Intendant Bigot been the scene of many a festive revelry that matched in Bachanalian frenzy, the past orgies of the Regency, and the present debaucheries of Croissy and the *petits appartemens* of Versailles. Its splendour, its luxury, its riotous feasts lasting without intermission sometimes for days were the themes of wonder and disgust to the unsophisticated people of New France, and of endless comparison between the extravagance of the royal Intendant, and the simple manners and inflexible morals of the Governor General.

The great hall of the chateau, the scene of the gorgeous feasts of the Intendant, was brilliantly illuminated with silver lamps glowing like globes of sun light as they hung from the lofty ceiling, upon which was painted a frescoe of the apotheosis of Louis XIV. where the grand Monarque was surrounded by a cloud of Condés, Orleanois and Bourbons of near and more remote consanguinity. At the head of the room hung a full length portrait of the Marquise de Pompadour, the mistress of Louis XV. and the friend and patroness of the Intendant Bigot—her bold voluptuous beauty seemed well fitted to be the presiding genius of his house. The walls bore many other paintings of artistic and historic value— the King and Queen, the dark eyed Montespan, the crafty Maintenon, and the pensive beauty of Louise de la Valiere, the only mistress of Louis XIV who loved him for his own sake, and whose portrait copied from this picture may still be seen in the Chapel of the Ursulines of Quebec where the fair Louise is represented as St Thaïs, kneeling at prayer among the Nuns.

The table in the great hall, a masterpiece of workmanship was made of a dark Canadian wood then newly introduced and stretched the length of the Hall. A massive gold epergne of choicest Italian art, the gift of La Pompadour stood on the center of the table. It represented Bacchus enthroned on a tun of wine, presenting flowing cups to a dance of fauns and satyrs.

Silver cups of Venetian sculpture, and goblets of Bohemian manufacture, sparkled like stars on the brilliant table, brimming over with the gold and ruby vintages of France and Spain, or lay overturned amid pools of wine that ran down upon the velvet carpet. Dishes of Parmesan cheese, caviare and other provocatives to thirst stood upon the table amid vases of flowers, and baskets of the choicest fruits of the Antilles.

Round this magnificent table sat a score or more of revellers, in the garb of gentlemen, but all in disorder and soiled with wine. Their countenances were enflamed, their eyes red and fiery, their tongues loose and loquacious. Here and there a vacant or overturned chair showed where a guest had fallen in the debauch and been carried off by the valets who in gorgeous liveries waited on the table. A band of musicians sat up in a gallery at the end of the Hall and filled the pauses of the riotous feast with the ravishing strains of Lulli and Destouches.

At the head of the table first in place as in rank sat Francois Bigot, Intendant of New France. His low well set figure, dark hair, small keen black eyes and swarthy features full of fire and animation bespoke his Gascon blood. His countenance was far from comely—nay when in repose, even ugly and repulsive—but his eyes were magnets that drew men's looks towards him, for in them lay the force of a powerful will and a depth and subtlety of intellect that made men fear, if they could not love him. Yet when he chose, and it was his usual mood, to exercise his blandishments on men, he rarely failed to captivate them, while his pleasant wit, courtly ways and natural gallantry towards women exercised with the polished seductiveness he had learned in the Court of Louis XV. made

Francois Bigot the most plausible and dangerous man in New
France.

He was fond of wine and music, passionately addicted
to gambling, and devoted to the pleasant vices that were
rampant in the Court of France. Finely educated, able in the
conduct of affairs and fertile in expedients to accomplish his
ends, Francois Bigot might have saved New France had he
been honest as he was clever, but he was unprincipled and
corrupt. No conscience checked his ambition or his love of
pleasure. He ruined New France for the sake of himself and
his patroness, and the crowd of courtiers and frail beauties
who surrounded the King, and whose arts and influence kept
him in his high office despite all the efforts of the *Honnetes
gens*, the good men and true of the colony to remove him.

He had already ruined and lost the ancient colony of
Acadia, through his defrauds and malversations as chief
commissary of the army, and instead of trial and punishment,
had lately been exalted to the higher and still more important
office of Royal Intendant of New France.

On the right of the Intendant sat his bosom friend the
Sieur Cadet, a large sensual man with twinkling grey eyes,
thick nose and full red lips. His broad face flushed with wine
glowed like the harvest moon rising above the horizon. Cadet
had it was said been a butcher in Quebec. He was now for the
misfortune of his country chief commissary of the army, and
a close confederate of the Intendant.

On the left of the Intendant sat his secretary De Pean,
crafty and unscrupulous. A Parasite too who flattered his
master and ministered to his pleasures, De Pean was a military
man and not a bad soldier in the field, but he loved gain
better than glory, and amassed an enormous fortune out of
the impoverishment of his country.

Le Mercier too was there, commandant of artillery a brave
officer but a bad man—Varin a proud arrogant libertine,
commissary of Montreal who outdid Bigot in rapine and
Cadet in coarseness—De Breard comptroller of the Marine,
a worthy associate of Penisault, whose pinched features and
cunning leer were in keeping with his important office of

chief manager of the Friponne—Perrault, D'Estebe Morin and Vergor, all creatures of the Intendant swelled the roll of infamy, as partners of the "Grand Company of associates trading in New France," as their charter named them, the "grand company of thieves," as the people in their plain Norman called them, who robbed them in the Kings name, and under pretence of maintaining the war, passed the most arbitrary decrees, the only object of which was to enrich themselves and their higher patrons at the Court of Versailles.

The rest of the company seated round the table comprized a number of dissolute Seigneurs, and gallants of fashion about town—men of great wants and great extravagance, just the class so quaintly described by Charlevoix a quarter of a century previous, as "Gentlemen thoroughly versed in the most elegant and agreable modes of spending money, but greatly at a loss how to obtain it."

Among the gay young Seigneurs who had been drawn into the vortex of Bigots splendid dissipation was the brave handsome Le Gardeur de Repentigny, a captain of the Royal Marine, a colonial corps, recently embodied at Quebec. In general form and feature Le Gardeur was a manly reflex of his beautiful sister Amelie, but his countenance was marred with traces of debauchery. His face was enflamed, and his dark eyes so like his sisters, by nature tender and true, were now glittering with the adder tongues of the cursed wine serpent.

Taking the cue from Bigot, Le Gardeur responded madly to the challenges to drink from all around him. Wine was now flooding every brain, and the table was one scene of riotous debauch.

"Fill up again Le Gardeur!" exclaimed the Intendant with a loud and still clear voice. "The lying horloge says it is day, broad day, but neither cock crows nor day dawns in the Chateau of Beaumanoir save at the will of its master and his merry guests!—Fill up companions all. The lamp light in the wine cup is brighter than the clearest sun that ever shone."

"Bravo Bigot! name your toast, and we will pledge it till the seven stars count fourteen," replied Le Gardeur, looking hazily at the great clock in the hall. "I see four clocks in the room and every one of them lies, if it says it is day."

"You are mending Le Gardeur de Repentigny! You are worthy to belong to the Grand Company! But you shall have my toast. We have drank it twenty times already, but it will stand drinking twenty times more. It is the best prologue to wine ever devised by wit of man—a woman."

"And the best epilogue too, Bigot!" interjected Varin, visibly drunk, "but let us have the toast—my cup is waiting—!"

"Well, fill up all, then, and we will drink the health, wealth and love by stealth, of the jolliest Dame in sunny France, the Marquise de Pompadour!—"

"La Pompadour! La Pompadour!" Every tongue repeated the name. The goblets were drained to the bottom, and a thunder of applause and clattering of glass followed the toast of the Mistress of Louis XV. who was the special protectress of the Grand Company, a goodly share of whose profits in the monopoly of trade in New France was thrown into the lap of the powerful favorite.

"Come Varin! your turn now!" cried Bigot turning to the Commissary. "A toast for Ville Marie! merry Montreal! where they eat like rats of Poitou and drink till they ring the fire bells, as the Bordelais did to welcome the collectors of the Gabelle. The Montrealers have not rung the fire bells yet against you, Varin! but they will by and by—!"

Varin filled his cup with an unsteady hand till it ran over, and propping his body against the table as he stood up, replied, "A toast for Ville Marie! and our friends in need, the blue caps of the Richelieu—!"—This was in allusion to a recent ordinance of the Intendant authorizing him to seize all the corn in store at Montreal and in the surrounding country under pretence of supplying the army, really to secure the monopoly of it for the Grand Company.

The toast was drank amid rapturous applause. "Well said Varin," exclaimed Bigot, "that toast implied both business and pleasure. The business was to sweep out the granges of the farmers, the pleasure is to drink in honour of your success."—

"My forragers sweep clean!" said Varin, resuming his seat and looking under his hand to steady his gaze. "Better brooms were never made in Besancon. The country is swept clean as a ball room. Your Excellency and the Marquise might lead the dance over it, and not a straw lie in your way."—

"And did you manage it without a fight, Varin?" asked the Sieur d'Estebe with a half sneer.

"Fight! Why fight? The habitans will never resist the Kings name. We conjure the devil down with that. When we skin our eels we dont begin at the tail! If we did, the habitans would be like the eels of Melun cry out before they were hurt. No! No! D Estebe! We are more politic in Ville Marie. We tell them the Kings troops need the corn. They doff their caps and with tears in their eyes, say: Monsieur Le Commissaire! the King can have all we possess, and ourselves too—if he will only save Canada from the Bostonais. This is better than stealing the honey and killing the *bees that made it*, D Estebe!"

"But what became of the families of the Habitans, after this swoop of your forragers?" asked the Seigneur de Beauce, a country gentleman who retained a few honorable ideas floating on top of the wine he had swallowed.

"O, the families, that is the women and children! for we took the men for the army—! You see De Beauce!" replied Varin with a mocking air as he crossed his thumbs like a peasant of Languedoc, when he wishes to inspire belief in his words. "The families have to do what the gentlemen of Beauce practise in times of scarcity, breakfast by gaping! or they can eat wind like the people of Poitou. It will make them spit clean!"

De Beauce was irritated at the mocking sign and the proverbial allusion to the gaping of the people of Beauce. He started up in wrath, and striking his fist on the table:—

"Monsieur Varin!" cried he, "do not cross your thumbs at me, or I will cut them off! Let me tell you the gentlemen of Beauce do not breakfast on gaping, but have plenty, to stuff even a commissary of Montreal."

The Sieur Le Mercier at a sign from Bigot interposed to stop the rising quarrel. "Dont mind Varin," said he whispering to De Beauce, "he is drunk and a row will anger the Intendant. Wait, and by and by you shall toast Varin as the chief Baker of

Pharoah, who got hanged because he stole the King's corn!"

"As he deserves to be for his insult to the gentlemen of Beauce—!" insinuated Bigot leaning over, to his angry guest, at the same time winking good humouredly at Varin. "Come now, De Beauce friends all. *Amantium irae*, you know, which is Latin for love; and I will sing you a stave in praise of this good wine, which is better than Bacchus ever drank." The Intendant rose up and holding a brimming glass in his hand chanted in full musical voice, a favorite ditty of the day, as a ready mode of restoring harmony among the Company—

> Amis! dans ma bouteille,
> Voila le vin de France!—
> C'est le bon vin qui danse ici,
> C'est le bon vin qui danse!
> Gai lon la!
> Tire la lirette
> Des Fillettes
> Il y en aura!

"*Vivent les Fillettes!* The Girls of Quebec! first in beauty last in love and nowhere in scorn of a gallant worthy of them!" continued Bigot. "What say you De Pean? are you not prepared to toast the Belle of Quebec?—"

"That I am your Excellency!" De Pean was unsteady on his feet as he rose to respond to the Intendants challenge. He potvaliantly drew his sword and laid it on the table. "I will call on the honorable company to drink this toast on their knees—! and there is my sword to cut the legs off any gentleman who will not kneel down and drink a full cup to the bright eyes of the Belle of Quebec, the incomparable Angelique des Meloises!"

The toast suited their mood. Every one filled up his cup in honour of a beauty so universally admired.

"Kneel down all!" cried the Intendant, "or De Pean will hamstring us!" All knelt down with a clash, some of them unable to rise again. "We will drink to the Angelique charms of the fair Des Meloises. Come now all together! as the jolly Dutchmen of Albany say, '*Upp seys over!*'"

Such of the company as were able resumed their seats amid great laughter and confusion. When the Sieur Deschenaux a reckless young gallant, ablaze with wine and excitement stood up leaning against the table his fingers dabbled in his wine cup, as he addressed them, but he did not notice it.

"We have drank with all the honours" said he, "to the bright eyes of the Belle of Quebec. I call on every gentleman now, to drink to the still brighter eyes of the Belle of New France."

"Who is she? Name! name!" shouted a dozen voices, "who is the Belle of New France?"

"Who is she? why who can she be, but the fair Angelique whom we have just honoured!" replied De Pean hotly, jealous of any precedence in that quarter.

"Tut!" cried Deschenaux, "you compare glow worms with evening stars, when you pretend to match Angelique Des Meloises with the lady I propose to honour! I call for full brimmers, Cardinals hats! in honour of the Belle of New France, the fair Amelie de Repentigny!"

Le Gardeur de Repentigny was sitting leaning on his elbow, his face beaming with jollity as he waited with a full cup for Deschenaux' toast. But no sooner did he hear the name of his sister from those lips, than he sprang up as if a serpent had bit him. He hurled his goblet at the head of Deschenaux, with fierce imprecation and drew his sword as he rushed towards him.

"A thousand lightenings strike you! how dare you pollute that holy name Deschenaux—? Retract that toast, instantly, or you shall drink it in blood—retract I say—!" The guests rose to their feet in terrible uproar. Le Gardeur struggled violently to break through a number of them who interposed between him and Deschenaux, who roused to fury by the insult from Le Gardeur had also drawn his sword and stood ready to receive the assault of his antagonist.

The Intendant whose courage and presence of mind never forsook him, pulled Deschenaux down upon his seat and held fast his sword arm, shouting in his ear

"Are you mad Deschenaux? You knew she was his

sister, and how he worships her! retract the toast—it was inopportune! Besides recollect! We want to win over De Repentigny to the Grand Company."

Deschenaux struggled for a minute, but the influence of the Intendant was all powerful over him. He gave way. "Damn De Repentigny!" said he, "I only meant to do honour to the pretty witch. Who would have expected him to take it up in that manner?"

"Any one who knows him! Besides," continued the Intendant, "If you must toast his sister, wait till we get him body and soul made over to the Grand Company, and then he will care no more for his sister's fame than you do for yours."

"But the insult! He has drawn blood with the goblet!" said Deschenaux wiping his forehead with his finger. "I cannot pardon that—!"

"Tut, tut, fight him another day. But you shall not fight here! Cadet and Le Mercier have pinned the young Bayard I see, so you have a chance to do the honorable, Deschenaux. Go to him, retract the toast and say you had forgotten the fair lady was his sister!"

Deschenaux swallowed his wrath, rose up and sheathed his sword. Taking the Intendant by the arm he went up to Le Gardeur, who was still trying to advance. Deschenaux held up his hand deprecatingly, "Le Gardeur!" said he with an air of apparent contrition, "I was wrong to offer that toast. I had forgotten the fair lady was your sister. I retract the toast, since it is disagreable to you, although all would have been proud to drink it."

Le Gardeur was as hard to appease as he was easy to excite to anger. He still held his drawn sword in his hand.

"Come!" cried Bigot, "you are hard to please as Villiers Vendome whom the King himself could not satisfy. Deschenaux says he is sorry. A gentleman can not say more. So shake hands and be friends, De Repentigny!"

Impervious to threats and often to reason, Le Gardeur could not resist an appeal to his generosity.

He sheathed his sword and held out his hand with frank

forgiveness. "Your apology is ample Sieur Deschenaux! I am satisfied, you meant no affront to my sister!! It is my weak point Messieurs!" continued he, looking firmly at the Company, ready to break out had he detected the shadow of a sneer on any one's countenance. "I honour her as I do the Queen of Heaven. Neither of their names ought to be spoken here."—

"Well said! Le Gardeur!" exclaimed the Intendant. "That's right, shake hands and be friends again. Blessed are quarrels that lead to reconciliation! and the washing out of feuds in wine. Take your seats gentlemen!"

There was a general scramble back to the table. Bigot stood up in renewed force. "Valets!" cried he, "bring in now the largest cups! We will drink a toast five fathoms deep, in water of life strong enough to melt Cleopatra's pearls and to a jollier Dame than Egypts Queen—! But first we will make Le Gardeur de Repentigny free of the guild of noble partners of the Company of Adventurers trading in New France!—"

The valets flew in and out. In a few minutes the table was replenished with huge drinking cups, silver flagons, and all the heavy impedimenta of the army of Bacchus.

"You are willing to become one of us, and enter the jolly guild of the Grand Company?" exclaimed the Intendant, taking Le Gardeur by the hand.

"Yes, I am a stranger and you may take me in. I claim admission," replied Le Gardeur with drunken gravity, "and by St Picot! I will be true to the guild!"

Bigot kissed him on both cheeks. "By the boot of St Benoit you speak like the King of Yvetot, Le Gardeur de Repentigny! You are fit to wear fur in the court of Burgundy."—

"You can measure my foot, Bigot!" replied Le Gardeur, "and satisfy the company that I am able to wear the boot of St Benoit."—

"By jolly St Chinon, and you shall wear it, Le Gardeur!" exclaimed Bigot handing him a quart flagon of wine, which Le Gardeur drank without drawing breath. "That boot fits!" shouted the Intendant exultingly "now for the chant! I will lead! Stop the breath of any one will not join in the chorus!—"

The Intendant in great voice led off a macaronic verse of

Moliere, that had often made merry the orgies of Versailles:

"Bene, Bene, Bene, respondere,
Dignus Dignus es entrare
In nostro laeto corpore!"

A tintamarre of voices and a jingle of glasses accompanied the violins and tambours de Basque, as the company stood up and sang the song, winding up with a grand burst at the Chorus:—

"Vivat! vivat! vivat! cent fois vivat!
Novus socius qui tam bene parlat!
Mille, mille, annis et manget et bibat
Fripet et friponnat!"—

Hands were shaken all round, congratulations embracings and filthy kisses showered upon Le Gardeur to honour his admission as a partner of the Grand Company.

"And now," continued Bigot, "we will drink a draught long as the bell rope of Notre Dame, fill up brimmers of the quintessence of the grape, and drain them dry in honour of the Friponne!—"

The name was electric. It was in the Country a word of opprobrium, but at Beaumanoir, it was laughed at with true Gallic nonchalance. Indeed to show their scorn of public opinion, the Grand Company had lately launched a new ship on the Great lakes to carry on the fur trade, and had appropriately and mockingly named her, "*La Friponne.*"

"Let them laugh that win!" said Bigot one day to D'Estebe, who was in a rage at having heard the hateful epithet used by a plain spoken Habitan. "We accept the name and can withstand the blame! If they say more I will paint it in letters a yard long upon the Front of the Palais and make it the horn book from which the rustics shall take their first lesson in reading and spelling."

The toast of La Friponne! was drunk with applause, followed by a wild Bachanalian song—La Friponne is a jolly dame, From France she came.

The Sieur Morin had been a merchant in Bordeaux

whose bond was held in as little value as his word. He had lately removed to New France transferred the bulk of his merchandise, to the Friponne and become an active agent of the Grand Company.

"La Friponne!" cried he. "I have drunk success to her with all my heart and throat. But I say, she will never wear a night cap and sleep quietly in our arms, until we muzzle the Golden Dog that barks at us night and day in the Rue Buade."

"That is true, Morin!" interrupted Varin, roused to wrath at the mention of the Golden Dog. "The Grand Company will never know peace until we send the Bourgeois his master back to the Bastille. The Golden Dog is— —"

"Damn the Golden Dog!" exclaimed Bigot passionately, "Why do you utter his name, Varin! to sour our wine?—I hope one day to pull down the Dog, as well as the whole kennel of the insolent Bourgeois." Then as was his wont, concealing his feelings under a mocking gibe, "Varin!" said he, "they say, that is your marrow bone, the Golden Dog is gnawing—ha! ha! ha!"—

"More people believe it is your Excellency's!" Varin knew he was right, but aware of Bigots touchiness on that point, added as is the wont of panders to great men, "It is either yours or the Cardinals."

"Let it be the Cardinals then!—He is still in purgatory and will wait there the arrival of the Bourgeois! to balance accounts with him."—

Bigot hated the Bourgeois Philibert as one hates the man he has injured. Bigot had been instrumental in his banishment years ago from France, when the bold Norman Count defended the persecuted Jansenists in the Parliament of Rouen. The Intendant hated him now for his wealth and prosperity in New France. But his wrath turned to fury, when he saw the tablet of the Golden Dog, with its taunting inscription, glaring upon the front of the Magazin in the Rue Buade. Bigot felt the full meaning and significance of the words, that burned into his soul, and for which he hoped one day to be revenged.

"Confusion to the whole litter of the Golden Dog, and that

is the party of the *Honnetes Gens*—!" cried he. "But for that canting Savant, who plays the Governor here, I would pull down the sign and hang its master up in its stead tomorrow!"

The company now grew still more hilarious and noisy in their cups. Few paid attention to what the Intendant was saying. But De Repentigny heard him utter the words—"O for men who dare do men's deeds!"—He caught the eye of De Repentigny and added, "But we are all cowards in the Grand Company, and are afraid of the Bourgeois!—"

The wine was bubbling in the brain of Le Gardeur. He scarcely knew what the Intendant said, but he caught the last words. "Whom do you call cowards Chevalier? I have joined the Grand Company. If the rest are cowards I am not. I stand ready to pluck the perruque off the head of any man in New France and carry it on my sword to the Place D'Armes where I will challenge all the world to come and take it."

"Pish! That is nothing! Give me man's work. I want to see the partner in the Grand Company who dare pull down the Golden Dog."

"I dare, and I dare!" exclaimed a dozen voices at once in response to the appeal of the Intendant, who craftily meant his challenge to ensnare only Le Gardeur.

"And I dare and I will too! if you wish it Chevalier—!" shouted Le Gardeur, mad with wine and quite oblivious of the thousand claims of the father of his friend Pierre Philibert upon him.

"I take you at your word Le Gardeur! and bind your honour to it in the presence of all these gentlemen," said Bigot with a look of intense satisfaction.

"When shall it be done? to day?"—Le Gardeur seemed ready to pluck the moon from the sky in his present state of exstacy.

"Why no, not to day! Not before the pear is ripe will we pluck it. Your word of honour will keep till then?"

Bigot was in great glee over the success of his stratagem to entrap De Repentigny.

"It will keep a thousand years!" replied Le Gardeur, amid a fresh outburst of merriment round the board which culminated in a shameless song fit only for a revel of satyrs.

The Sieur Cadet lolled lazily in his chair, his eyes blinking with a sleepy leer. "We are getting stupidly drunk Bigot!" said he. "We want something new to rouse us all to fresh life. Will you let me offer a toast."

"Go on Cadet, offer what you please. There is nothing in heaven, hell or upon earth, that I wont drink to, for your sake."

"I want you to drink it on your knees, Bigot! Pledge me that and fill your biggest cups!—"

"We will drink it on all fours if you like!—come out with your toast Cadet! you are as long over it as Father Glapion's sermon in Lent! and it will be as interesting I dare say!"

"Well Chevalier! The Grand Company after toasting all the beauties of Quebec desires to drink the health of the fair mistress of Beaumanoir and in her presence too!—" said Cadet with owlish gravity.

Bigot started—drunk and reckless as he was he did not like his secret to be divulged. He was angry with Cadet for referring to it in the presence of so many who knew not that a strange lady was residing at Beaumanoir. He was too thoroughly a libertine of the period to feel any moral compunction for any excess he committed. He was habitually more ready to glory over his conquests, than to deny or extenuate them. But in this case he had to the surprize of Cadet, been very reticent and shy of speaking of this lady even to him.

"They say she is a miracle of beauty, Bigot!" continued Cadet "and that you are so jealous of the charms of your belle Gabrielle, you are afraid to show her to your best friends."

"My belle Gabrielle is at liberty to go where she pleases, Cadet!" Bigot saw the absurdity of anger, but he felt it nevertheless. "She chooses not to leave her bower, to look even on you, Cadet! I warrant you she has not slept all night listening to your infernal din."

"Then I hope you will allow us to go and beg pardon on our knees for disturbing her rest. What says the good Company?—"

"Agreed! agreed!" was the general response and all

pressed the Intendant vociferously to allow them to see the fair mistress of Beaumanoir, about whose beauty so much had been privately talked among Bigots intimate associates.

Varin however, proposed that she should be brought into the hall. "Send her to us O King," cried he. "We are nobles of Persia and this is Shushan the palace, where we carouse according to the law of the Medes, seven days at a stretch. Let the King bring in Queen Vashti, to show her beauty to the princes and nobles of his court!—"

Bigot too full of wine to weigh scruples, yielded to the wish of his boon companions. He rose from his chair which in his absence was taken by Cadet. "Mind," said he, "if I bring her in, you shall show her every respect!"

"We will kiss the dust of her feet," answered Cadet, "and consider you the greatest king of a feast in New France or old!"—

Bigot without further parley passed out of the hall, traversed a long corridor and entered an anteroom where he found Dame Tremblay the old houskeeper dozing on her chair. He roused her up and bade her go to the inner chamber to summon her mistress.

The housekeeper rose in a moment at the voice of the Intendant. She was a comely Dame, with ruddy cheek and an eye in her head, that looked inquisitively at her master as she arranged her cap, and threw back her rather gay ribbons.

"I want your mistress up in the great Hall! go summon her at once." repeated the Intendant.

The Housekeeper curtseyed, but pursed her lips together, as if to prevent them from speaking in remonstrance. She went at once on her ungracious errand.

CHAPTER 8

CAROLINE DE ST CASTIN

Dame Tremblay entered the suite of appartments and returned in a few moments, saying "that her lady was not there but had gone down to the secret chamber to be, she supposed, more out of hearing of the noise which had distressed her so much."

"I will go find her then," replied the Intendant, "you may return to your own room Dame—!" He walked across the drawing room to one of the gorgeous panels that decorated the wall, touched a hidden spring.—A door flew open disclosing a stair heavily carpeted that led down to the huge vaulted foundations of the Chateau.

He descended the stair with hasty though unsteady steps. It led to a spacious room, lighted with a gorgeous lamp that hung pendant in silver chains from the frescoed ceiling. The walls were richly tapestried with products of the looms of the Gobelins representing the plains of Italy filled with sunshine where groves temples and colonnades were pictured in endless vistas of beauty. The furniture of the chamber was of regal magnificence. Nothing that luxury could desire or art furnish had been spared in its adornment. On a sofa lay a guitar and beside it a scarf, and a dainty glove fit for the hand of the faery queen.

The Intendant looked eagerly round, as he entered this bright chamber of his fancy, but saw not its expected occupant. A recess in the deep wall at the farther side of the room contained an oratory, with an altar and a crucifix upon it. The recess was partly in the shade. But the eyes of the Intendant discerned clearly enough, the kneeling or rather the prostrate figure, of Caroline de St Castin. Her hands were clasped beneath her head, which was bowed to the ground. Her long black hair lay dischevelled over her back, as she lay in her white robe like the angel of Sorrow, weeping and crying from the depths of her broken heart—: "Lamb of God that takest away the sins of the world, have mercy upon me!—" She was so absorbed in her grief that she did not notice the entrance of the Intendant.—

Bigot stood still for a moment, stricken with awe at the spectacle of this lovely woman weeping by herself in the secret Chamber. A look of something like pity stole into his eyes. He called her by name, ran to her, assisted her to rise, which she did slowly turning towards him that weeping Madonna like face, which haunts the ruins of Beaumanoir to this day.—

She was of medium stature, slender and lissom looking taller than she really was. Her features were chiselled with exquisite delicacy, Her hair of a raven blackness and eyes of that dark luster which reappears for generations in the descendants of Europeans who have mingled their blood with that of the Aborigines of the forest. The Indian eye, is preserved as an heir loom, long after all memory of the Red strain has vanished from the traditions of the family. Her complexion was pale, naturally of a rich olive, but now through sorrow of a wan and bloodless hue—still very beautiful and more appealing than the rosiest complexion.

Caroline de St Castin was an Acadienne of ancient and noble family, whose head and founder the Baron de St Castin had married the beautiful daughter of the high chief of the Abenaquis.

Her father's house, one of the most considerable in the Colony, had been the resort of the royal officers, civil and military serving in Acadia. Caroline the only daughter of the noble house, had been reared in all the refinements and luxuries of the period, as became her rank and position both in France and her native Province.

In an evil hour for her happiness this beautiful and accomplished girl, met the Chevalier Bigot who as chief commissary of the army was one of the foremost of the royal officers in Acadia. His ready wit and graceful manners pleased and flattered the susceptible girl, not used to the seductions of the polished courtiers of the Mother land of France. She was of a joyous temper gay, frank and confiding. Her father, immersed in public affairs left her much to herself, nor, had he known it, would he have disapproved of the gallant courtesies of the Chevalier Bigot for the Baron was the soul of honour and dreamt every gentleman as well as himself possessed it.

Bigot, to do him justice, felt as sincere a regard for this beautiful amiable girl as his nature was capable of entertaining. In rank and fortune she was more than his equal and left to himself, he would willingly have married her, before he learned that his project of a marriage in the Colony, was scouted at Court. He had already offered his love to Caroline de St Castin and won easily the gentle heart that was but too well disposed to receive his homage.

Her trust went with her love. Earth was never so green, no air so sweet, no skies so bright and azure as those of Caroline's wooing, on the shores of the beautiful bay of Minas. She loved this man with a passion that filled with exstacy her whole being. She trusted his promises as she would have trusted God's. She loved him better than she loved herself, better than she loved God or God's law, and counted as a gain, every loss she suffered for his sake and for the affection she bore him.

After some months spent in her charming society, a change came over Bigot. He received formidable missives from his great patroness at Versailles, the Marquise de Pompadour, who had other matrimonial designs for him. Bigot was too slavish a courtier to resent her interference, nor was he honest enough to explain his position to his betrothed. He deferred his marriage. The exigences of the war called him away. He had triumphed over a fond confiding woman, but he had been trained among the dissolute spirits of the Regency too thoroughly, to feel more than a passing regret for a woman whom probably he loved better than any other of the victims of his licentious life.

When he finally left Acadia a conquered Province in the hands of the English he also left behind him, the one true loving heart that believed in his honour, and still prayed for his happiness.

The days of Caroline's disillusion soon came. She could not conceal from herself that she had been basely deceived and abandoned by the man she loved so ardently. She learned that Bigot had been elevated to the high office of Intendant of New France. But felt herself as utterly forgotten by him as the rose that had bloomed and withered in her garden, two summers ago.

Her father had been summoned to France on the loss of the Colony, and fearing to face him on his return, Caroline suddenly left her home and sought refuge in the forest among her far off kindred the red Abenaquis.

The Indians welcomed her with joy and unbounded respect, recognizing her right to their devotion and obedience. They put upon her feet the mocassins of their tribe and sent her with a trusty escort through the wilderness, to Quebec, where she hoped to find the Intendant, not to reproach him for his perfidy—Her gentle heart was too much subdued for that—but to claim his protection and if refused, to die at his door.

It was under such circumstances that the beautiful high born Caroline de St Castin became an inmate of Beaumanoir. She had passed the night of this wild debauch in a vigil of prayers tears and lamentations over her sad lot and the degradation of Bigot by the life which she now knew he led. Sometimes her maddened fancy was ready to accuse Providence itself of cruelty and injustice. Sometimes, magnifying her own sin she was ready to think all earthly punishment upon herself as too light, and invoked death and judgment as alone adequate to her fault. All night long she had knelt before the altar, asking for mercy and forgiveness. Sometimes starting to her feet in terror as a fresh burst of revelry, came rushing from the great Hall above, and shook the door of her secret chamber. But no one came to her help. No one looked in upon her desolation. She deemed herself utterly forgotten and forsaken of God and man.

Occasionally she fancied she could distinguish the voice of

the Intendant amid the drunken uproar, and she shuddered at the infatuation which bound her very soul to this man, and yet when she questioned her heart, she knew that base as he was, all she had done and suffered for him she would infallibly do again. Were her life to live over, she would repeat the fault of loving this false ungrateful man—!—The promise of marriage had been equivalent to marriage in her trust of him, and nothing but death could now divorce her from him.

Hour after hour passed by, each seeming an age of suffering. Her feelings were worked up to frenzy. She fancied she heard her father's angry voice calling her by name, or she heard accusing angels jeering at her fall. She sank prostrate at last, in the abandonment of despair calling on God to put an end to her miserable life.—

Bigot raised her from the floor with words of pity and sympathy. She turned on him a look of gratitude which had he been of stone he must have felt it. But Bigots words meant less than she fancied. He was still too intoxicated to reflect or feel the shame of his present errand.

"Caroline!" said he, "what do you here? This is the time to make merry not to pray! The honorable company in the Great Hall desire to pay their respects to the lady of Beaumanoir—come with me!"—

He drew her hand through his arm with a courtly grace that seldom forsook him even in worst moments. Caroline looked at him in a dazed manner not comprehending his request. "Go with you Francois? you know I will, but where?—"

"To the great Hall" repeated he "my worthy guests desire to see you and to pay their respects to the fair lady of Beaumanoir."—

It flashed on her mind what he wanted. Her womanly pride was outraged as it had never been before—she withdrew her hand from his arm with shame and terror stamped on every feature.

"Go up there!—Go to show myself to your guests?" exclaimed she, with choking accents as she stepped back a pace from him. "O, Francois Bigot Spare me that shame and humiliation. I am I know contemptible beyond human respect, but still, still—God help me! I am not so vile as to be made a spectacle of infamy to those drunken men, whom I hear clamouring for me even now."

"Pshaw! you think too much of the proprieties Caroline!" Bigot felt sensibly perplexed at the attitude she assumed. "Pshaw! The fairest Dames of Paris, dressed as Hebes and Ganymedes thought it a fine jest to wait on the Regent Duke of Orleans and Cardinal du Bois, in the gay days of the Kings bachelorhood and they do the same now when the King gets up one of his grand fetes at Choissy—so come sweetheart—come!" He drew her towards the door.

"Spare me, Francois!" Caroline knelt at his feet clasping his hand and bathing it in tears. "Spare me!" cried she. "O, would to God, I had died, ere you came to command me to do, what I cannot and will not do—! Francois," added she, clasping hard the hand of the Intendant, which she fancied relaxed somewhat of its iron hardness.

"I did not come to command you, Caroline! but to bear the request of my guests. No, I do not even ask you, on my account to go up to the Great Hall. It is to please my guests only." Her tears and heart-rending appeal, began to sober him. Bigot had not counted on such a scene as this.

"O thanks Francois! for that word—! you did not come to command my obedience in such a shameful thing?—You had some small regard left for the unfortunate Caroline? Say you will not command me to go up there," added she, looking at him with eyes of pitiful pleading, such as no Italian art ever portrayed in the face of the sorrowing Madonna.

"No," he replied, impatiently. "It was not I proposed it. It was Cadet. He is always a fool when the wine overflows, as I am too, or I would not have hearkened to him! Still Caroline, I have promised and my guests will jeer me finely if I return without you." He thought she hesitated a moment in her resolve at this suggestion. "Come for my sake, Caroline. Do up that disordered hair. I shall be proud of you my Caroline. There is not a lady in New France can match you when you look yourself, my pretty Caroline!—"

"Francois!" said she with a sad smile, "it is long since you flattered me thus!—But I will arrange my hair, for you alone," added she blushing as with deft fingers she twisted her raven locks in a coronal about her head. "I would once have gone with you to the end of the world to hear you say you were proud of me. Alas! you can never be proud of me any more, as in the old happy days at Grand Pré. Those few brief days of love and joy can never return never—never—!"

Bigot stood silent, not knowing what to say or do. The change from the Bachannalian riot in the Great Hall to the solemn pathos and woe of the secret chamber sobered him rapidly. Even his obduracy gave way at last. "Caroline," said he, taking both her hands in his, "I will not urge you longer. I am called bad and you think me so, but I am not brutal. It was a promise made over the wine. Varin the drunken lout called you Queen Vashti, and challenged me to show your beauty to them, and I swore not one of their toasted beauties could match my fair Acadienne."

"Did the Sieur Varin call me Queen Vashti? Alas! he was a truer prophet than he knew," replied she with ineffable sadness. "Queen Vashti refused to obey even her king, when commanded to unveil her face to the drunken nobles. She was deposed, and another raised to her place. Such may be my fate, Francois."

"Then you will not go, Caroline?"

"No—kill me if you like, and bear my dead body into the Hall—but living, I can never show my face again before men— hardly before you, Francois," added she, blushing, as she hid her tearful eyes on his shoulder.

"Well then, Caroline," replied he, really admiring her spirit and resolution. "They shall finish their carouse without seeing you. The wine has flowed to night in rivers, but they shall swim in it without you."

"And tears have flowed down here," said she sadly "O, so bitter! may you never taste their bitterness, Francois!"

Bigot paced the chamber with steadier steps than he had entered it. The fumes were clearing from his brain. The song that had caught the ear of Colonel Philibert as he approached the Chateau, was resounding at this moment. As it ceased

Bigot heard the loud impatient knocking of Philibert at the outer door.

"Darling!" said he, "lie down now, and compose yourself. Francois Bigot is not unmindful of your sacrifices for his sake. I must return to my guests who are clamouring for me, or rather for you, Caroline!—"

He kissed her cheek and turned to leave her, but she clung to his hand as if wanting to say something more ere he went. She trembled visibly as her low plaintive tones struck his ear.

"Francois! if you would forsake the companionship of those men and purify your table of such excess Gods blessing would yet descend upon you and the people's love follow you—! It is in your power to be as good as you are great—! I have many days wished to say this to you, but alas I feared you too much. I do not fear you to day, Francois, after your kind words to me."—

Bigot was not impenetrable to that low voice so full of pathos and love. But he was at a loss what to reply. Strange influences were flowing round him carrying him out of himself. He kissed the gentle head that reclined on his bosom. "Caroline," said he, "your advice is wise and good as yourself. I will think of it, for your sake if not for my own. Adieu, darling! go and take rest. These cruel vigils are killing you and I want you to live in hope of brighter days."—

"I will," replied she looking up with ineffable tenderness. "I am sure I shall rest after your kind words Francois!—No dew of Heaven was ever more refreshing, than the balm they bring to my weary soul. Thanks, O my Francois for them!—" She kissed his lips and Bigot left the secret Chamber a sadder and for the moment a better man than he had ever been before.

Caroline overcome by her emotions threw herself on a couch invoking blessings upon the head of the man by whom she had been so cruelly betrayed. But such is woman's heart, full of mercy compassion and pardon for every wrong when Love pleads for forgiveness.

"Ha! Ha!" cried Cadet as the Intendant reentered the Great Hall, which was filled with Bacchanalian frenzy. "Ha!

Ha!—His Excellency has proposed and been rejected—! The fair lady has a will of her own and wont obey—! Why the Intendant, looks as if he had come from Quintin Corentin, where nobody gets anything they want!—"

"Silence Cadet! Dont be a fool!—" replied Bigot impatiently, although in the Intendant's usual mood nothing too gross or too bad could be said in his presence, but he could cap it with something worse.

"Fool, Bigot? It is you who have been the fool of a woman!" Cadet was privileged to say any thing and he never stinted his speech. "Confess your Excellency! She is splay footed as St Pedauque of Dijon! She dare not trip over our carpet for fear of showing her big feet!"

Cadets coarse remark excited the mirth of the Intendant. The influences of the great Hall were more powerful than those of the secret Chamber. He replied curtly however, "I have excused the lady from coming, Cadet. She is ill, or she does not please to come, or she has a private fancy of her own to nurse. Any reason is enough to excuse a lady, or for a gentleman to cease pressing her."

"Dear me!" muttered Cadet. "The wind blows fresh from a new quarter!—It is Easterly and betokens a storm—!" and with drunken gravity Cadet commenced singing, a hunting refrain of Louis XIV.

"Sitot qu'il voit sa chienne
Il quitte tout pour elle!—"

Bigot burst out into immoderate laughter. "Cadet!" said he, "you are when drunk the greatest ruffian in Christendom, and the biggest knave when sober. Let the lady sleep in peace, while we drink ourselves blind in her honour. Bring in Brandy, Valets! and we will not look for day until midnight booms on the old clock of the Chateau."

The loud knocking of Philibert in the great Hall reverberated again and again through the house. Bigot bade the valets go see who disturbed the Chateau in that bold style.

"Let no one in!—" added he. "Tis against the rule, to open the doors when the Grand Company are met for business!

Take whips Valets! and scourge the insolent beggars away. Some miserable habitans I warrant whining for the loss of their eggs and bacon taken by the Kings purveyors!"

A servant returned with a card on a silver salver. "An officer in uniform waits to see your Excellency. He brings orders from the Governor" said he to the Intendant.

Bigot looked at the card with knitted brows. Fire sparkled in his eyes as he read the name.

"Colonel Philibert!" exclaimed he, "Aide de Camp of the Governor! What the fiend brings *him* at such a time? Do you hear!" continued he turning to Varin. "It is your friend from Louisbourg, who was going to put you in irons and send you to France for trial, when the mutinous garrison threatened to surrender the place if we did not pay them."—

Varin was not so intoxicated but the name of Philibert roused his anger. He set his cup down with a bang on the table. "I will not taste a drop more till he is gone" said he, "curse Galissoniere's crooked neck. Could he not have selected a more welcome messenger to send to Beaumanoir? But I have got his name in my list of debtors and he shall pay up one day for his insolence at Louisbourg."

"Tut! shut up your books. You are too mercantile for gentlemen," replied Bigot. "The question is, shall we allow Colonel Philibert to bring his orders into the Hall—? Par Dieu! we are scarcely presentable!"

But whether presentable or no, the words were scarcely spoken, when impatient of the delay, Philibert took advantage of the open door and entered the Great Hall. He stood in utter amazement for a moment at the scene of drunken riot which he beheld. The enflamed faces, the confusion of tongues, the disorder filth and stench of the prolonged debauch sickened him, while the sight of so many men of rank and high office revelling at such an hour, raised a feeling of indignation which he had difficulty in keeping down while he delivered his message to the Intendant.

Bigot however, was too shrewd to be wanting in politeness. "Welcome Colonel Philibert!" said he "you are an unexpected guest, but a welcome one. Come and taste the hospitality of

Beaumanoir before you deliver your message. Bustle Valets, bring fresh cups and the fullest carafs for Colonel Philibert."

"Thanks for your politeness Chevalier!—your Excellency will please excuse me, if I deliver my message at once. My time is not my own to day, so I will not sit down. His Excellency the Governor desires your presence and that of the royal commissaries at the Council of war this afternoon. Despatches have just arrived by the Fleur de Lys from home, and the Council must assemble at once."

A red flush rested on the brow of Philibert as in his thoughts, he measured the important business of the Council, with the fitness of the men whom he summoned to attend it. He declined the offer of wine and stepped backward from the table, with a bow to the Intendant and the Company and was about to depart when a loud voice on the further side of the table, cried out—

"It is he, by all that is sacred!—Pierre Philibert! wait!—" Le Gardeur de Repentigny rushed like a storm through the hall, upsetting chairs and guests in his advance. He ran towards Colonel Philibert who not recognizing the flushed face and disordered figure that greeted him, shrank back from his embrace.

"My God! do you not know me Pierre?" exclaimed Le Gardeur, wounded to the quick by the astonished look of his friend. "I am Le Gardeur de Repentigny! O dear friend, look and recognize me—!"

Philibert stood transfixed with surprize and pain as if an arrow had stricken his eyes. "You—? You? Le Gardeur de Repentigny? It is impossible! Le Gardeur never looked like you, much less was ever found among people like these—!"— The last words were rashly spoken. But fortunately not heard amid the hubbub in the Hall or Philiberts life might have paid the penalty from the excited guests.

"And yet it is true, Pierre!—Look at me again. I am no other than he whom you drew out of the St Lawrence—the only brother of Amelie!—"—

Philibert looked hard in the eyes of Le Gardeur, and doubted no longer. He pressed his old friend to his heart, saying in a voice full of pathos—:—

"O, Le Gardeur! I do recognize you now, but under what change of look and place—? Often have I forecast our meeting again, but it was in your pure virtuous home of Tilly, not in this place—! What do you here Le Gardeur?"

"Forgive me Pierre, for the shame of meeting me here!" Le Gardeur stood up like a new man, in the glance of his friend. The shock seemed to have sobered him at once. "What do I here—? say you, O dear friend?" said he glancing round the Hall. "It is easier seen than told what I do here. But by all the Saints! I have finished here for to day!—You return to the city at once Pierre?"

"At once Le Gardeur. The Governor awaits my return."

"Then I will return with you. My dear Aunt and Sister are in the city. News of their arrival reached me here—my duty was to return at once—but the Intendants wine cups were too potent for me—curse them for they have disgraded me in your eyes, Pierre, as well as my own—!"

Philibert started at the information that Amelie was in the city. "Amelie in the city!" repeated he with glad surprize. "I did not expect to be able to salute her and the noble lady de Tilly so soon—!" His heart bounded in secret at the prospect of again seeing the fair girl who had filled his thoughts for so many years, and been the secret spring of so much that was noble and manly in his character.

"Come Le Gardeur, let us take leave of the Intendant and return at once to the city.—But not in that plight!" added he smiling, as Le Gardeur oblivious of all but the pleasure of accompanying him, grasped his arm to leave the great Hall. "Not in that garb, Le Gardeur! Bathe, purify and dress yourself. I will wait outside in the fresh air. The odour of this room stifles me!"—

"You are not going to leave us, Le Gardeur!" Varin called across the table, "and break up good company—? Wait till we finish a few more rounds, and we will all go together."

"I have finished all the rounds for to day, Varin, may be for ever—! Colonel Philibert is my dearest friend in life. I must leave even you, to go with him, so pray excuse me—!"—

"You are excused Le Gardeur." Bigot spoke very courteously to him, much as he disliked the idea of his companionship with Philibert. "We must all return by the time the Cathedral bells chime noon. Take one parting cup before you go Le Gardeur, and prevail on Colonel Philibert to do the same, or he will not praise our hospitality I fear."—

"Not one drop more this day, were it from Jove's own poculum!" Le Gardeur repelled the temptation the more readily, as he felt a twitch on his sleeve from the hand of Philibert.

"Well as you will, Le Gardeur. We have all had enough and over, I dare say—ha! ha!—Colonel Philibert rather puts us to the blush or would do were our cheeks not so well painted in the hues of rosy Bacchus."

Philibert with official courtesy bade adieu to the Intendant and the company. A couple of Valets waited upon Le Gardeur, whom they assisted to bathe and dress. In a short time he left the Chateau almost sobered, and wholly metamorphosed into a handsome fresh Cavalier. A perverse redness about the eyes alone remained to tell the tale of the last nights debauch.

Master Pothier sat on a horse-block at the door, with all the gravity of a judge, while he waited for the return of Colonel Philibert and listened to the lively noise in the Chateau, the music, song and the jingle of glass forming a sweet concert in the ears of the jolly old notary.

"I shall not need you to guide me back, Master Pothier!" said Philibert, as he put some silver pieces into his hollow palm. "Take your fee. The cause is gained! is it not Le Gardeur?" He glanced triumphantly at his friend.

"Goodby Master Pothier!—" said he, as he rode off with Le Gardeur. The old notary could not keep up with them, but came jolting on behind, well pleased to have leisure to count and jingle his coins. Master Pothier was in that state of joyful anticipation, when hope outruns realization. He already saw himself seated in the old arm chair in the snug parlour of Dame Bedard's Inn—his back to the fire, his belly to the table, a smoking dish of roast in the middle, an ample trencher before him, with a bottle of cogniac on one flank and a jug of Norman cider on the other, an old crony or two to eat and drink with him and the light foot and deft hand of pretty Zoe Bedard to wait upon them.

This picture of perfect bliss floated before the winking eyes of Master Pothier, and his mouth watered in anticipation of his Eden—not of flowers and trees but of tables cups and platters and plenty to fill them, and empty them as well.

"A worthy gentleman and a brave officer I warrant!" said Pothier as he jogged on alone. "He is generous as a prince and considerate as a bishop, and fit for a judge nay a chief justice—!—What would you do for him Master Pothier?—" the old notary asked himself. "I answer the interrogatory of the Court! I would draw up his contract of marriage, or write his will and testament with the greatest pleasure and without a fee—!—And no Notary in New France could do more for him!—" Pothier's imagination fell into a vision over a consideration of his favorite text—that of the great sheet wherein was all manner of flesh and fowl good for food, but the tongue of the old notary would trip at the name of Peter, and perversly say, "rise Pothier! kill and eat!—"

CHAPTER 9

PIERRE PHILIBERT

Colonel Philibert and Le Gardeur rode rapidly through the forest of Beaumanoir, pulling up occasionally in an eager and sympathetic exchange of questions and replies as they recounted the events of their lives since their separation, or recalled their schooldays and glorious holidays and rambles in the woods of Tilly, with frequent mention of their gentle fair companion Amelie de Repentigny, whose name on the lips of her brother sounded sweeter than the chime of the bells of Charlebourg, to the ear of Pierre Philibert.

The bravest man in New France felt a tremour in his breast as he asked Le Gardeur, a seemingly careless question—seemingly—for in truth it was vital in the last degree to his happiness and he knew it. He expressed a fear that Amelie would have wholly forgotten him after so long an absence from New France.

His heart almost ceased beating as he waited the reply of Le Gardeur, which came impetuously. "Forgotten you Pierre Philibert?—she would forget me as soon—! but for you she would have had no brother to day! and in her prayers she ever remembers both of us, you by right of a sisters gratitude, me, because I am unworthy of her saintly prayers, and need them all the more! O, Pierre Philibert, you do not know Amelie, if you think she is one ever to forget a friend like you."

The heart of Philibert gave a great leap for joy. Too happy for speech, he rode on a while, in silence.

"Amelie will have changed much in appearance?" he asked at last. A thousand questions were crowding upon his lips.

"Changed? O yes," replied Le Gardeur gaily, "I scarcely recognize my little bright eyed sister in the tall perfect young lady that has taken her place. But the loving heart the pure mind, the gentle ways and winning smiles are the same as ever. She is somewhat more still and thoughtful perhaps, more strict in the observances of religion, and you will remember, I used to call her in jest our St Amelie! I might call her that in earnest now, Pierre, and she would be worthy of the name."—

"God bless you Le Gardeur!" burst out Colonel Philibert —his voice could not repress the emotion he felt. "And God bless Amelie! Think you she would care to see me to day, Le Gardeur—?" Philiberts thoughts flew far and fast; and his desire to know more of Amelie was a rack of suspense to him. She might indeed recollect the youth Pierre Philibert, thought he as she did a sunbeam that gladdened long past summers—but how could he expect her to regard him, the full grown man as the same—? Nay, was he not nursing a fatal fancy in his breast that would sting him to death? for among the gay and gallant throng about the capital was it not more than possible that so lovely and amiable a woman had already been wooed and given the priceless treasure of her love to another—? It was therefore with no common feeling that Philibert said, "Think you she will care to see me to day, Le Gardeur?"—

"Care to see you Pierre Philibert?—What a question! She and Aunt de Tilly take every occasion to remind me of you, by way of example to shame me of my faults, and they succeed too—! I could cut off my right hand this moment, Pierre! that it should never lift wine again to my lips! and to have been seen by you in such company—!—what must you think of me?—"

"I think your regret could not surpass mine! But tell me how you have been drawn into these rapids and taken the wrong turn, Le Gardeur?"

Le Gardeur winced as he replied: "O, I do not know. I found myself there before I thought. It was the wit, wine and enchantments of Bigot, I suppose, and the greatest temptation of all, a woman's smiles that led me to take the wrong turn as you call it. There, you have my confession!—and I would put my sword through any man but you, Pierre, who dared ask me to give such an account of myself. I am ashamed of it all Pierre Philibert."

"Thanks Le Gardeur, for your confidence, I hope you will outride this storm!" He held out his hand nervous and sinewy as that of Mars. Le Gardeur seized it and pressed it hard in his. "Dont you think it is still able to rescue a friend from peril?" added Philibert smiling.

Le Gardeur caught his meaning, and gave him a look of unutterable gratitude. "Besides this hand of mine are there not the gentler hands of Amelie to intercede for you, with your better self," said Philibert.

"My dear Sister!" interjected Le Gardeur, "I am a coward when I think of her, and I shame to come into her pure presence."

"Take courage Le Gardeur! There is hope where there is shame of our faults. Be equally frank with your sister as with me, and she will win you in spite of yourself from the enchantments of Bigot Cadet and the still more potent smiles you speak of that led you to take the wrong turn in life."

"I doubt it is too late, Pierre! Although I know that were every other friend in the world to forsake me, Amelie would not! She would not even reproach me except by excess of affection."

Philibert looked on his friend admiringly, at this panegyric of the woman he loved. Le Gardeur was in feature so like his sister that Philibert at the moment caught the very face of Amelie as it were looking at him through the face of her brother.—"You will not resist her pleadings Le Gardeur?"— Philibert thought it an impossible thing. "No guardian angel ever clung to the skirts of a sinner, as Amelie will cling to you!" said he. "Therefore I have every hope of my dear friend Le Gardeur de Repentigny."

The two riders emerged from the forest and drew up for a minute in front of the hostelry of the Crown of France, to water their horses at the long trough, before the door, and inform Dame Bedard who ran out to greet them, that Master Pothier was following with his ambling nag, at a gentle pace as befitted the gravity of his profession.

"O, Master Pothier never fails to find his way to the Crown of France, but wont your honours take a cup of wine? The day is hot, and the road dusty. 'A dry rider makes a wet nag,'" added the Dame with a smile, as she repeated an old saying, brought over with the rest of the *butin*, in the ships of Cartier and Champlain.

The Gentlemen bowed their thanks, and as Philibert looked up he saw pretty Zoe Bedard poring over a sheet of paper bearing a red seal, and spelling out the crabbed law text of Master Pothier. Zoe like other girls of her class had received a tincture of learning in the day schools of the Nuns, but although the paper was her marriage contract it puzzled her greatly to pick out the few chips of plain sense that floated in the sea of legal verbiage it contained. Zoe with a perfect comprehension of the claims of *meum* and *tuum*, was at no loss however, in arriving at a satisfactory solution of the true merits of her matrimonial contract with honest Antoine La Chance.

She caught the eye of Philibert, and blushed to the very chin, as she huddled away the paper, and returned the salute of the two handsome gentlemen, who having refreshed their horses rode off at a rapid trot down the great highway that led to the city.

Babet Le Nocher in a new gown, short enough to reveal a pair of shapely ankles in clocked stockings and well shod feet that would have been the envy of many a duchesse sat on the thwart of the boat knitting. Her black hair was in the fashion recorded by the grave Peter Kalm who in his account of New France says: "The peasant women all wear their hair in ringlets, and nice they look!"

"As I live!" exclaimed she to Jean who was enjoying a pipe of native tobacco, "here comes that handsome officer back again! and in as great a hurry to return as he was to go up the highway!—"

"Aye, Aye, Babet. It is plain to see he is either on the Kings errand or his own. A fair lady awaits his return in the City or one has just dismissed him where he has been! Nothing like a woman to put quicksilver in a man's shoes, eh! Babet?—"

"Or foolish thoughts into their hearts! Jean!" replied she, laughing.

"And nothing more natural, Babet, if women's hearts are wise enough in their folly to like our foolish thoughts of them. But there are two! Who is that riding with the gentleman—your eyes are better than mine Babet—!"—

"Of course Jean! that is what I always tell you, but you wont believe me—trust my eyes and doubt your own!—The other gentleman," said she looking fixedly while her knitting lay still in her lap, "The other is the young Chevalier De Repentigny. What brings him back before the rest of the hunting party I wonder?"

"That officer must have been to Beaumanoir and is bringing the young Seigneur back to town," remarked Jean, puffing out a long thread of smoke from his lips.

"Well it must be something better than smoke, Jean!" Babet coughed—she never liked the pipe—"the young Chevalier is always one of the last to give up when they have one of their three days drinking bouts at the Chateau. He is going to the bad, I fear, more the pity—such a nice handsome fellow too!—"

"All lies and calumny!" replied Jean in a heat. "Le Gardeur de Repentigny is the son of my dear old Seigneur. He may get drunk but it will be like a gentleman if he does and not like a carter, Babet! or like a—"

"Boatman! Jean! but I dont include *you*—you have never been the worse for drinking-water since I took care of your liquour, Jean—!"

"Aye, you are intoxication enough of yourself for me Babet. Two bright eyes like yours, a pipe, and bitters with grace before meat, would save any Christian man in this world."— Jean stood up politely doffing his red tuque to the Gentlemen. Le Gardeur stooped from his horse to grasp his hand for Jean had been an old servitor at Tilly and the young Seigneur was too noble minded and polite to omit a kindly notice of even the humblest of his acquaintance.

"Had a busy day Jean, with the old ferry?" asked Le Gardeur cheerily.

"No, your honour, but yesterday I think half the country side crossed over to the city on the Kings Corvée. The men went to work and the women followed to look after them—ha! ha!—" Jean winked provokingly at Babet, who took him up sharply.

"And why should not the women go after the men? I trow men are not so plentiful in New France, as they used to be before this weary war began. It well behoves the women to take good care of all that are left."

"That is true as the Sunday sermon," remarked Jean "Why it was only the other day I heard that great foreign gentleman who is the guest of his Excellency the Governor say, sitting in this very boat, that there are at this time four women to every man in New France! If that is true, Babet—and you know he said it, for you were angry enough—A man is a prize indeed in New France and women are plenty as eggs at Easter—!"

"The foreign gentleman had much assurance to say it even if it were true. He were much better employed picking up weeds and putting them in his book!" exclaimed Babet hotly.

"Come! Come!" cried Le Gardeur, interrupting this debate on the population, "Providence knows the worth of Canadian women and cannot give us too many of them—! We are in a hurry to get to the city Jean, so let us embark. My Aunt and Amelie are in the old home in the city. They will be glad to see you and Babet," added he kindly, as he got into the boat.

Babet dropped her neatest curtsey, and Jean, all alive to his duty, pushed off his boat bearing the two gentlemen and their horses, across the broad St Charles, to the King's Quay, where they remounted and riding past the huge palace of the Intendant, dashed up the steep *Cote au Chien* and through the city gate, disappearing from the eyes of Babet, who looked very admiringly after them. Her thoughts were especially commendatory of the handsome officer in full uniform, who had been so polite and generous in the morning.

"I was afraid Jean you were going to blurt out about Mademoiselle des Meloises!" remarked Babet to Jean on his return, "men are so indiscreet always."

"Leaky boats! Leaky boats! Babet! no rowing them, with

a woman aboard! Sure to run on the bank but what about Mademoiselle des Meloises?—" Honest Jean had passed her over the ferry an hour ago, and been sorely tempted to inform Le Gardeur of the interesting fact.

"What about Mademoiselle des Meloises?" Babet spoke rather sharply. "Why all Quebec knows that the Seigneur de Repentigny is mad in love with her."—

"And why should he not be mad in love with her if he likes?" replied Jean. "She is a morsel fit for a king, and if Le Gardeur should lose both his heart and his wits on her account it is only what half the gallants of Quebec have done."

"O Jean! Jean! It is plain to see you have an eye in your head, as well as a soft place!—" ejaculated Babet recommencing her knitting with fresh vigor, and working off the electricity that was stirring in her.

"I had two eyes in my head when I chose you, Babet, and the soft place was in my heart!" replied Jean, heartily. The compliment was taken with a smile, as it deserved to be. "Look you Babet, I would not give this pinch of snuff," said Jean raising his thumb and two fingers holding a good dose of the pungent dust, "I would not give this pinch of snuff for any young fellow, who could be indifferent to the charms of such a pretty lass as Angelique des Meloises—!"

"Well I am glad you did not tell the Seigneur de Repentigny, that she had crossed the ferry and gone—not to look for him, Ill be bound—! I will tell you something by and by Jean! if you will come in and eat your dinner, I have something you like."

"What is it Babet?"—Jean was after all more curious about his dinner than about the fair lady.

"Ah, something you like—that is a wife's secret. Keep the stomach of a man warm and his heart will never grow cold. What say you to fried eels?"

"Bravo!" cried the gay old boatman, as he sang:

"Ah! ah, ah! frit à l'huile,
Frit au beurre et à l'ognon!—"

and the jolly couple danced into their little cottage, no King and Queen in Christendom half so happy as they.

CHAPTER 10

AMELIE DE REPENTIGNY

THE town house of the Lady de Tilly stood on the upper part of the Place d'Armes, a broad roughly paved square. The Chateau of St Louis, with its massive buildings, and high peaked roofs filled one side of the square—on the other side, embowered in ancient trees that had escaped the axe of Champlain's hardy followers stood the old fashioned Monastry of the Recollets with its high belfry, and broad shady porch where the monks in gray gowns and sandals sat in summer reading their breviaries or exchanging salutations with the passers by, who always had a kind greeting for the brothers of St Francis.

The mansion of the Lady de Tilly was of stone, spacious and ornate as became the rank and wealth of the Seigneurs de Tilly. It overlooked the Place d'Armes, and the noble gardens of the Chateau of St Louis, with a magnificent sweep of the St Lawrence, flowing majestically under the fortress crowned cape, and the high wooded hills of Lauzon closing the view on the farther side of the river.

In the recess of an ornate mullioned window, half concealed by the rich heavy curtains of a noble room, Amelie de Repentigny sat alone, very quiet in look and demeanour, but no little agitated in mind, as might be noticed in the nervous contact of her hands, which lay in her lap clasping each other very hard as if trying to steady her thoughts.

Her Aunt was receiving some lady visitors in the great drawing room. The hum of loud feminine voices, reached the ear of Amelie, but she paid no attention, so absorbed was she in the new and strange thoughts that had stirred in her mind since morning, when she had learned from the Chevalier La

98

Corne of the return to New France of Pierre Philibert. The news had surprized her to a degree she could not account for. Her first thought was how fortunate for her brother that Pierre had returned! her second, how agreable to herself—! why? she could not think why. She wilfully drew an inference away from the truth that lay in her heart. It was wholly for sake of her brother she rejoiced in the return of his friend and preserver. Her heart beat a little faster than usual, that was the result of her long walk and disappointment at not meeting Le Gardeur on her arrival yesterday—! But she feared to explore her thoughts—a rigid self examination might discover what she instinctively felt was deeply concealed there.

A subtle indefinable prevision had suggested to her that Colonel Philibert would not have failed to meet Le Gardeur at Beaumanoir, and that he would undoubtedly accompany her brother on his return, and call to pay his respects to the Lady de Tilly, and, to herself. She felt her cheek glow at the thought, yet was half vexed at her own foolish fancy, as she called it. She tried to call up her pride but that came very laggardly to the relief of her discomposure.

Her interview too with Angelique des Meloises had caused her no little disquiet. The bold avowals of Angelique with reference to the Intendant had shocked Amelie. She knew that her brother had given more of his thoughts to this beautiful reckless girl than was good for his peace, should her ambition ever run counter to his love.

The fond sister sighed deeply when she reflected that the woman who had power to make prize of Le Gardeur's love was not worthy of him. It is no rare thing for loving sisters who have to resign their brothers to other's keeping, to think so. But Amelie knew that Angelique des Meloises was incapable of that true love which only finds its own in the happiness of another. She was vain selfish ambitious and what Amelie did not yet know, possessed of neither scruple nor delicacy in attaining her objects.

It had chimed the hour of noon on the old clock of the Recollets, and Amelie still sat looking wistfully over the great square of the Place d'Armes, and curiously scanning every horseman that rode across it. A throng of people moved about the square, or passed in and out of the great arched gate-way of the Castle of St Louis. A bright shield bearing the crown and *fleur de lys* surmounted the gate, and under it walked with military pace a couple of sentries their muskets and bayonets flashing out in the sun every time they wheeled to return on their beat. Occasionally there was a ruffle of drums, the whole guard turned out and presented arms as some officer of high rank or Ecclesiastical dignitary passed through to pay their respects to the Governor, or transact business at the vice regal court. Gentlemen on foot with chapeaux and swords, carrying a cloak on their shoulders, ladies in visiting dress, habitans and their wives in unchanging costume, soldiers in uniform and black gowned Clergy mingled in a moving picture of city life which, had not Amelie's thoughts been so preoccupied to day, would have afforded her great delight to look out upon.

The Lady de Tilly had rather wearied of the visit of the two ladies of the city, Madame de Grandmaison and Madame Couillard who had bored her with all the current gossip of the day. They were rich and fashionable, perfect in etiquette, and costume, and most particular in their society, but the rank and position of the noble Lady de Tilly made her friendship most desirable, as it conferred in the eyes of the world, a patent of gentility which held good against every pretention to overtop it.

The stream of city talk from the lips of the two ladies had the merit of being perfect of its kind, softly insinuating and sweetly censorious, superlative in eulogy and infallible in opinion. The good visitors most conscientiously discharged what they deemed a great moral and social duty by enlightening the Lady de Tilly on all the recent lapses and secrets of the capital. They slid over slippery topics like skaters upon thin ice, filling their listener with anxiety lest they should break through. But Madame De Grandmaison and her companion were too well exercised in the gymnastics of gossip to overbalance themselves—half Quebec was run over and run down in the course of an hour.

Lady de Tilly listened with growing impatience to their

frivolities but she knew society too well to quarrel with its follies, when it was of no service to do so. She contented herself with hoping it was not so bad. The Pope was not Catholic enough to suit some people but for her part she had generally found people better than they were called.

A rather loud but well bred exclamation of Madame de Grandmaison, roused Amelie from her day dream.

"Not going to the Intendants ball at the Palace! my Lady de Tilly! neither you nor Mademoiselle de Repentigny, whom we are so sorry not to have seen to day—? Why it is to be the most magnificent affair ever got up in New France. All Quebec has rung with nothing else for a fortnight, and every Milliner and Modiste in the city has gone almost insane over the superlative costumes to be worn there.—"

"And it is to be the most select in its character," chimed in Madame Couillard, "all gentry and noblesse, not one of the Bourgeois to be invited. That class, especially the female portion of them, give themselves such airs now a days! As if their money made them company for people of Quality. They must be kept down I say."

"And the Royal Intendant quite agrees with the general sentiment of the higher circles," responded Madame de Grandmaison. "He is for keeping them down.—"

"Noblesse! Noblesse!" The Lady de Tilly spoke with visible impatience, "who is this Royal Intendant who dares cast a slight on the worthy honest Bourgeoisie of this city? Is he noble himself? not that I would think worse of him were he not, but I have heard it disputed! He is the last one who should venture to scorn the Bourgoisie."

Madame de Grandmaison fanned herself in a very stately manner. "O my Lady, you surely forget—!—The Chevalier Bigot is a not distant relative of the Count de Marville! and the Chevalier de Grandmaison is a constant visitor at the Intendants! but he would not have sat at his table an hour had he not known that he was connected with the Nobility. The Count de Marville—"

"The Count de Marville!" interrupted the Lady de Tilly, whose politeness almost gave way. "Truly a man is known by the company he keeps—no credit to any one to be connected with the Count de Marville."

Madame de Grandmaison felt rather subdued. She perceived that the Lady de Tilly was not favorably impressed towards the Intendant, but she tried again: "And then My Lady, the Intendant is so powerful at Court. He was a particular friend of Madame D'Etioles, before she was known at Court, and they say he managed her introduction to the King at the famous masked ball at the Hotel de Ville, when His Majesty threw his handkerchief at her, and she became first *dame du palais*, and the Marquise de Pompadour—! She has ever remained his firm friend, and in spite of all his enemies could do to prevent it, His Majesty made him Intendant of New France."

"In spite of all the Kings friends could do, you mean!" replied the Lady de Tilly in a tone, the accent of which caught the ear of Amelie and she knew her Aunt was losing patience with her visitors. Lady de Tilly heard the name of the royal mistress with intense disgust, but her innate loyalty prevented her speaking disparagingly of the King. "We will not discuss the court," said she, "nor the friendships of this Intendant. I can only pray that his future may make amends for his past. I trust New France may not have as much reason as poor lost Acadia to lament the day of his coming to the Colonies."

The two lady visitors were not obtuse. They saw they had roused the susceptibilities (prejudices they called them,) of the Lady de Tilly. They rose and smothering with well bred phrases their disappointment, took a most polite leave, of the dignified old lady who was heartily glad to be rid of them.

"The disagreable old thing! to talk so of the Intendant!—" exclaimed Madame Couillard, spitefully. "When her own nephew and heir in the Seigneury of Tilly is the Intendant's firmest friend and closest companion."

"Yes she forgot about her own house—people always forget to look at home, when they pass judgment upon their neighbours," replied Madame de Grandmaison "But I am mistaken if she will be able to impress Le Gardeur de Repentigny with her uncharitable and unfashionable opinions of the Intendant. I hope the ball will be the greatest social success ever seen in the city, just to vex her and her neice, who is as proud and particular as she is herself."

Amelie de Repentigny had dressed herself to day in a robe of soft muslin of Deccan, the gift of a relative in Pondichery. It envelloped her exquisite form without concealing the grace and lissomeness of her movements. A broad blue ribbon round her waist, and in her dark hair, a blue flower, were all her adornments except a chain and cross of gold which lay upon her bosom, the rich gift of her brother, and often kissed with a silent prayer for his welfare and happiness.

More than once under the influence of some indefinable impulse, she rose and went to the mirror, comparing her features now with a portrait of herself taken as a young girl in the garb of a shepherdess of Provence. Her father used to like that picture of her and to please him she often wore her hair in the fashion of Provence. She did so to day. Why? The subtle thought in many Protean shapes played before her fancy, but she would not try to catch it—no! rather shyly avoided its examination.

She was quite restless, and sat down again in the deep recess of the window watching the Place d'Armes for the appearance of her brother.

She gave a sudden start at last as a couple of officers galloped into the square and rode towards the great gate of the Chateau. One of them she instantly recognized as her brother, the other, a tall martial figure in full uniform upon a fiery grey, she did not recognize, but she knew in her heart it could be no other than Colonel Philibert.

Amelie felt a thrill almost painful in its pleasure agitating her bosom, as she sat watching the gate way they had entered. It was even a momentary relief to her, that they had turned in there instead of riding directly to the house. It gave her time to collect her thoughts and summon up all her fortitude for the coming interview. Her fingers wandered down to the rosary in the folds of her dress and the golden bead which had so often prompted her prayer for the happiness of Pierre Philibert seemed to burn to the touch. Her cheek crimsoned for a strange thought suddenly intruded itself. The boy Pierre Philibert whose image and memory she had so long and innocently cherished, was now a man—a soldier—a councillor trained in courts and camps—! how unmaidenly she had acted, forgetting all that, in her childish prayers until this moment—! "I meant no harm!" was all the defence she could think of. Nor had she time to think more of herself, for after remaining ten minutes in the Chateau just long enough to see the Governor and deliver the answer of the Intendant to his message, the grey charger emerged from the Gate. His rider was accompanied by her brother and the well known figure of her God Father La Corne St Luc, who rode up the hill, and in a minute or two dismounted at the door of the mansion of the Lady de Tilly.

The fabled Lynx whose eye penetrates the very earth to discover hidden treasure, did not cast keener and more inquisitive glance, than that which Amelie, shrouded behind the thick curtains, directed from the window at the tall manly figure and handsome countenance of him whom she knew to be Pierre Philibert. Let it not detract from her that she gave way to an irresistible impulse of womanly curiosity. The Queen of France would under the same temptation have done the same thing, and perhaps without feeling half the modest shame of it that Amelie did. A glance sufficed, but a glance that impressed upon her memory for ever the ineffaceable and perfect image of Pierre Philibert, the man, who came in place of Pierre Philibert the boy friend of Le Gardeur and of herself.

CHAPTER 11

THE SOLDIER'S WELCOME

THE voices of the Gentlemen mingled with her aunts in eager greetings. She well knew which must be the voice of Colonel Philibert, the rest were all so familiar to her ear. Suddenly footsteps ran up the grand stair, clearing three at a time. She waited trembling with anticipation. Le Gardeur rushed into the room with outstretched arms and embraced her and kissed her in a transport of brotherly affection.

"O, Le Gardeur!" cried she, returning his kiss with fond affection and looked in his face with tenderness and joy. "O, my brother how I have prayed and longed for your coming. Thank God! you are here at last. You are well brother are you not?" said she, looking up with a glance that seemed to betray some anxiety.

"Never better Amelie," replied he in a gayer tone than was quite natural to him, and shyly averting his eyes from her tender scrutiny. "Never better. Why if I had been in my grave I should have risen up to welcome a friend whom I have met to day after years of separation. O Amelie I have such news for you!"—

"News for me Le Gardeur! What can it be?" A blush stole over her countenance, and her bosom heaved for she was very conscious of the nature of the news her brother was about to impart.

"Guess! you unsuspecting Queen of Shepherdesses" cried he, archly twitching a lock of her hair that hung over her shoulder. "Guess, you pretty Gypsy, you!—"

"Guess? how can I guess, Le Gardeur? Can there be any news left in the city of Quebec after an hours visit from Madame de Grandmaison and Madame Couillard. I did not go down, but I know they inquired much after you by the way!"—Amelie with a little touch of feminine perversity, shyly put off the grand burst of Le Gardeur's intelligence knowing it was sure to come.

"Pshaw! who cares for those old scandal mongers!—But you can never guess my news, Amelie, so I may as well tell you." Le Gardeur fairly swelled with the announcement he was about to make.

"Have mercy then Brother! and tell me at once, for you do now set my curiosity on tip-toe." She was a true woman and would not for any thing have admitted her knowledge of the presence of Colonel Philibert in the house.

"Amelie," said he, taking her by both hands, as if to prevent her escape, "I was at Beaumanoir you know. The Intendant gave a grand hunting party," added he, noticing the quick glance she gave him, "and who do you think came to the Chateau and recognized me or rather I recognized him? A stranger and not such a stranger either! Amelie—!"

"Nay, go on brother! Who could this mysterious stranger and no stranger have been?—"

"Pierre Philibert! Amelie! Pierre, our Pierre! You know! you recollect him Sister."

"Recollect Pierre Philibert? Why how could I ever forget him, while you are living? since to him we are all endebted for your dear life, Brother!"

"I knew that! Are you not glad as I am, at his return," asked Le Gardeur, with a penetrating look.

She threw her arms round him involuntarily, for she was much agitated. "Glad brother? yes I am glad, because you are glad."—

"No more than that Amelie? That is a small thing to be glad for."

"O, brother! I am glad for gladness sake!—We can never overpay the debt of gratitude we owe Pierre Philibert."

"O my sweet Sister!—" replied he, kissing her, "I knew my news would please you. Come! we will go down and see him! at once. For Pierre is in the house."—

"But Le Gardeur!" she blushed and hesitated, "Pierre

Philibert I knew, I could speak to him but I shall hardly dare recognize him in the stately soldier of to day—voila la difference!" added she repeating the refrain of a song very popular both in New France and in old, at that period.

Le Gardeur did not comprehend her hesitation "True," said he, "Pierre is wonderfully changed since he and I wore the green sash of the seminary. He is taller than I, wiser and better, he was always that! but in heart the same generous noble Pierre Philibert he was when a boy—voila la ressemblance!" added he, pulling her hair archly as he repeated the antistrophe of the same ditty.

Amelie gave her brother a fond look, but she did not reply except by a tight pressure of the hand. The voices of the Chevalier La Corne and the Lady de Tilly and Colonel Philibert were again heard, in animated conversation. "Come brother we will go now," said she, and quick in executing any resolution she had formed, she took the arm of her brother, swept with him down the broad stair and entered the drawing room.

Philibert rose to his feet in admiration of the vision of loveliness that suddenly beamed on his eyes. It was the incarnation of all the shapes of grace and beauty that had passed through his fervid fancy during so many years of absence from his native land. Something there was of the features of the young girl who had ridden with flying locks like a sprite through the woods of Tilly. But comparing his recollection of that slight girl with the tall lithe perfect womanhood of the half blushing girl before him, he hesitated although intuitively aware it could be no other than the idol of his life, Amelie de Repentigny.

Le Gardeur solved the doubt in a moment by exclaiming in a tone of exultation, "Pierre Philibert, I bring an old young friend to greet you, my sister Amelie!—"

Philibert advanced as Amelie raised her dark eyes with a momentary glance, that drew into her heart the memory of his face for ever. She held out her hand frankly and courteously. Philibert bent over it as reverently as he would over the hand of the Madonna.

The greeting of the Lady de Tilly and La Corne St Luc had been cordial, nay affectionate, in its kindness. The good Lady kissed Pierre as a mother might have done a long absent son.

"Colonel Philibert," said Amelie straining her nerves to the tension of steel to preserve her composure, "Colonel Philibert is most welcome. He has never been forgotten in this house." She glanced at her aunt, who smiled approvingly at Amelie's remark.

"Thanks Mademoiselle de Repentigny. I am indeed happy to find myself remembered here. It fulfils one of my most cherished hopes in returning to my native land."

"Aye, Aye, Pierre!" interrupted La Corne St Luc who looked on this little scene very admiringly. "Good blood never lies.—Look at Colonel Philibert there, with the Kings epaulets on his shoulders. I have a sharp eye, as you know Amelie, when I look after my pretty God daughter, but I should not have recognized our lively Pierre in him had Le Gardeur not introduced him to me, and I think you would not have known him either!"—

"Thanks for your looking after me Godfather!" replied Amelie, merrily, thanking him in her heart for his appreciation of Pierre, "but I think neither Aunt nor I would have failed to recognize him."

"Right my Amelie!" said the Lady de Tilly "We would not! And we shall not be afraid, Pierre. I must call you Pierre or nothing. We shall not be afraid although you do lay in a new stock of acquaintance in the Capital, that old friends will be put aside as unfashionable remnants."

"My whole stock of friendship consists of those remnants, my Lady, memories of dear friends I love and honour. They will never be unfashionable with me. I should be bankrupt indeed were I to part with one of them."

"Then they are of a truer fabric than Penelope's web, for she, I read, pulled in pieces at night all she had woven through the day," replied Lady de Tilly. "Give me the friendship that wont unravel."

"But not a thread of my recollections has ever unravelled

or ever will," replied Pierre looking at Amelie as she clasped the arm of her Aunt, feeling stronger as is woman's way by the contact with another.

"Zounds! What is all this merchants talk about webs and threads and thrums?" exclaimed La Corne. "There is no memory so good as a soldiers, Amelie! and reason good. A soldier on our wild frontiers is compelled to be faithful to old friends and old flannels. He cannot help himself to new ones if he would. I was five years and never saw a woman's face except red ones—some of them were very comely by the way!" added the old warrior with a smile.

"The gallantry of the Chevalier La Corne is incontestable," remarked Pierre, "for once when we captured a convoy of soldiers wives from New England, he escorted them with drums beating to Grand Pré, and sent a cask of Gascon wine for them to celebrate their reunion with their husbands."

"Frowzy huzzies! not worth the keeping, or I would not have sent them! fit only for the bob-tail militia of New England!—" exclaimed La Corne.

"Not so thought the New Englanders, who had a three days feast when they remarried their wives, and handsome they were too," said Philibert. "The healths they drank to the Chevalier were enough to make him immortal!"

La Corne always brushed aside compliments to himself. "Tut! my lady! It was more Pierre's good nature than mine. He out of kindness let the women rejoin their husbands. On my part it was policy and strategem of war. Hear the sequel! The wives spoiled the husbands, as I guessed they would do, taught them to be too late at reveillée, too early at tatoo. They neglected guards and pickets, and when the long nights of winter set in, the men hugged their wives by the fire side instead of their muskets by their watch fires. Then came destruction upon them! In a blinding storm, amid snow drifts and darkness, Coulon de Villiers with his troops on snow shoes marched into the New England camp, and made widows of most of the poor wives who fell into our hands a second time—! Poor creatures! I saw that day how hard it is to be a soldiers wife!" La Corne's shaggy eye lash twinkled with moisture. "But it was the fortune of war—! the fortune of war and a cruel fortune it is at best!—"

The Lady de Tilly pressed her hand to her bosom to suppress the rising emotion. "Alas! Chevalier! poor widows! I feel all they suffered. War is indeed a cruel fortune as I too have had reason to learn."

"And what became of the poor women God father?" Amelie's eyes were suffused with tears. It was in her heart, if ever in any mortal, to love her enemies.—

"Oh, we cared for them the best we could. The Baron de St Castin sheltered them in his Chateau for the winter, and his daughter devoted herself to them with the zeal and tenderness of a Saint from heaven. A noble lovely girl, Amelie!" added La Corne impressively. "The fairest flower in all Acadia and the most unfortunate! poor girl! Gods blessing rest on her wherever she may be!" La Corne St Luc spoke with a depth of emotion he rarely manifested.

"How was she unfortunate? God Father?" Philibert watched the cheek flush and the eye lid quiver of the fair girl, as she spoke carried away by her sympathy. His heart went with his looks.

"Alas!" replied La Corne, "I would fain not answer, lest I distrust the moral government of the universe. But we are blind creatures, and Gods ways are not fashioned in our ways. Let no one boast that he stands lest he fall! We need the help of the host of heaven to keep us upright, and maintain our integrity. I can scarcely think of that noble girl without tears. O the pity of it! The pity of it!—"

Lady de Tilly looked at him wonderingly. "I knew the Baron de St Castin," said she. "When he came to perform homage at the Castle of St Louis for the grant of some lands in Acadia he was accompanied by his only daughter a child perfect in goodness grace and loveliness. She was just the age of Amelie. The ladies of the city were in raptures over 'the pretty May flower,' as they called her. What in heaven's name has happened to that dear child—? Chevalier La Corne!—"

La Corne St Luc half angry with himself for having broached the painful topic, and not used to pick his words replied bluntly, "Happened? my Lady. What is it happens worst to a woman—? She loved a man unworthy of her love. A villain in spite of high rank and Kings favour, who deceived this fond confiding girl, and abandoned her to shame—! Faugh! It is the way of the Court, they say, and the King has not withdrawn his favour but heaped fresh honours upon him—!" La Corne put a severe curb upon his utterance and turned impatiently away—lest he might curse the King as well as the favorite.

"But what became of the poor deceived girl?" asked the Lady de Tilly, after hastily clearing her eyes with her handkerchief.

"O, the old old story followed. She ran away from home in an agony of shame and fear, to avoid the return of her father from France. She went among the Indians of the St Croix they say and has not been heard of since. Poor dear girl! her very trust in virtue was the cause of her fall—!"

Amelie turned alternately pale and red at the recital of her Godfather. She riveted her eyes upon the ground as she pressed close to her Aunt, clasping her arm, as if seeking strength and support.

Lady de Tilly was greatly shocked at the sad recital. She inquired the name of the man of rank who had acted so treacherously to the hapless girl—.

"I will not utter the name to day, My Lady! It has been revealed to me as a great secret. It is a name too high for the stroke of the law if there be any law left us but the will of a Kings mistress—! God however has left us the law of a gentleman's sword to avenge its master's wrong. The Baron de St Castin will soon return to vindicate his own honour and whether or no, I vow to heaven My Lady! that the traitor who has wronged that sweet girl will, one day, have to try whether his sword be sharper than that of La Corne St Luc!—But Pshaw!—I am talking bravado like an Indian at the war post. The story of those luckless New England wives has carried us beyond all bounds—."

Lady de Tilly looked admiringly, without a sign of reproof at the old soldier, sympathizing with his honest indignation at so foul a wrong to her sex. "Were that dear child mine, woman as I am, I would do the same thing!—" said she with a burst of feeling. She felt Amelie press her arm as if she too, shared the spirit of her bolder Aunt.

"But here comes Felix Baudoin to summon us to dinner!" exclaimed Lady de Tilly. An old white headed servitor in livery, appeared at the door with a low bow, announcing that dinner was served.

Le Gardeur and La Corne St Luc greeted the old servitor with the utmost kindness, inquiring after his health, and begging a pinch from his well worn snuff box. Such familiarities were not rare in that day, between the gentlemen of New France and their old servants, who usually passed their life time in one household. Felix was the Major domo of the Manor House of Tilly, trusty, punctilious and polite, and honoured by his Mistress more as a humble friend than as a servant of her house.

"Dinner is served My Lady!" repeated Felix with a bow. "But my Lady must excuse! The kitchen has been full of habitans all day. The Trifourchettes, the Doubledens and all the best eaters in Tilly have been here. After obeying my lady's commands to give them all they could eat, we have had difficulty in saving anything for my lady's own table."—

"No matter Felix! we shall say grace all the same! I could content myself with bread and water, to give fish and flesh to my censitaires who are working so willingly on the Kings Corvée—! But that must be my apology to you Pierre Philibert, and the Chevalier La Corne for a poorer dinner than I could wish."—

"O, I feel no misgivings my Lady!" remarked La Corne St Luc laughing. "Felix Baudoin is too faithful a servitor, to starve his mistress for the sake of the Trifourchettes the Doubledens and all the best eaters in the Seigneurie!—! no—no I will be bound your ladyship will find Felix has tolled and tithed from them enough to secure a dinner for us all. Come Amelie with me."

Lady de Tilly took the arm of Colonel Philibert followed by Le Gardeur, La Corne and Amelie, and marshalled by the Major Domo, proceeded to the dining room, a large lofty room wainscotted with black walnut, a fine wood lately introduced. The ceiling was coved, surrounded by a rich frieze of carving. A large table suggestive of hospitality was covered with drapery of the snowiest linen, the product of the spinning wheels and busy looms of the women of the Seigneurie of Tilly. Vases of China filled with freshly gathered flowers, shed sweet perfumes while they delighted the eye with their beauty, etherializing the elements of bread and meat by suggestions of the poetry and ideals of life. A grand old Buffet, a prodigy of cabinet makers art, displayed a mass of family plate. A silver shield embossed with the arms of Tilly, a gift of Henry of Navarre to their ancient and loyal house hung on the wall over the Buffet.

In spite of the Trifourchettes and the Double Dens, Felix Baudoin had managed to set an excellent dinner upon the table of his Lady, who looked archly at the Chevalier La Corne as if assenting to his remark on her old servitor.

The Lady remained standing at the head of her table until they all sat down when clasping her hands, she recited with feeling and clearness the old latin grace: "*Benedic Domine nos et haec tua dona,*" sanctifying her table by the invocation of the blessing of God upon it, and upon all who sat round it.

A soup rich and savory was the prelude to all dinners in New France. A salmon speared in the shallows of the Chaudiere, and a dish of blood speckled trout from the mountain streams of St Joachim, smoked upon the board. Little oval loaves of wheaten bread were piled up in baskets of silver filigree. For in those days the fields of New France produced crops of finest wheat a gift which Providence has since withheld. "The wheat went away with the Bourbon lillies and never grew afterwards," said the old habitans. The meat in the larder had all really been given to the hungry censitaires in the kitchen, except a capon from the *Basse cour* of Tilly and a standing pie, the contents of which came from the manorial dove cote. A reef of Raspberries red as coral, gathered on the tangled slopes of Cote à Bonhomme, formed the desert with Blue whortleberries from Cape Tourment, Plums sweet as honey drops, and small grey coated apples from Beaupré delicious as those that comforted the Rose of Sharon. A few carafes of choice wine from the old manorial cellar completed the entertainment.

The meal was not a protracted one, but to Pierre Philibert the most blissful hour of his life. He sat by the side of Amelie, enjoying every moment as if it were a pearl dropped into his bosom, by word, look or gesture of the radiant girl who sat beside him.

He found Amelie, although somewhat timid at first, to converse, a willing nay an eager listener. She was attracted by the magnetism of a noble sympathetic nature, and by degrees ventured to cast a glance at the handsome manly countenance where feature after feature revealed itself, like a landscape at dawn of day, and in Colonel Philibert she recognized the very looks speech and manner of Pierre Philibert of old.

Her questioning eyes hardly needed the interpretation of her tongue, to draw him out to impart the story of his life, during his long absence from New France, and it was with secret delight, she found in him a powerful cultivated intellect and nobility of sentiment such as she rightly supposed belonged only to a great man, while his visible pleasure at meeting her again, filled her with a secret joy, that unnoticed by herself suffused her whole countenance with radiance, and incited her to converse with him more freely than she had thought it possible, when she sat down at table.

"It is long since we all sat together, Mademoiselle at the table of your noble Aunt," remarked Philibert. "It fulfills an often and often repeated day dream of mine, that I should one day find you just the same."—

"And do you find me just the same?" answered she archly. "You take down the pride of ladyhood immensely, Colonel! I had imagined I was something quite other than the wild child of Tilly!—"

"I hardly like to consider you as in the pride of ladyhood, Mademoiselle, for fear I should lose the wild child of Tilly, whom I should be so glad to find again."

"And whom you do find, just the same in heart mind and regard too—!" thought she, to herself but her words were, "My school mistresses would be ashamed of their work, Colonel, if they had not improved on the very rude material my aunt sent them up from Tilly to manufacture into a fine lady! I was the crowned queen of the year, when I left the Ursulines! so beware of considering me 'the child of Tilly' any longer."

Her silvery laugh caught his heart, for in that he recognized vividly, the gay young girl whose image he was every instant develloping out of the tall lovely woman beside him.

La Corne St Luc and the Lady de Tilly found a thousand delights in mutual reminiscences of the past. Le Gardeur somewhat heavy, joined in conversation with Philibert and his sister. Amelie guessed and Philibert knew the secret of Le Gardeur's dullness. Both strove to enliven and rouse him. His Aunt guessed too that Le Gardeur had passed the night as the guests of the Intendant always passed it, and knowing his temper and the regard he had for her good opinion, she brought the subject of the Intendant in to conversation, in order casually as it were to impress Le Gardeur with her opinion of him. Pierre Philibert, too, thought she shall be put on his guard against the crafty Bigot.

"Pierre," said she, "you are happy in a father who is a brave honorable man, of whom any son in the world might be proud. The country holds by him immensely, and he deserves their regard. Watch over him now you are at home, Pierre. He has some relentless and powerful enemies, who would injure him if they could."

"That has he!" remarked La Corne St Luc. "I have spoken to the Sieur Philibert and cautioned him, but he is not impressible on the subject of his own safety. The Intendant spoke savagely of him in public the other day."

"Did he? Chevalier?" replied Philibert his eyes flashing with another fire than that which had filled them looking at Amelie.

"He shall account to me for his words, were he Regent instead of Intendant."

La Corne St Luc looked half approvingly at Philibert. "Dont quarrel with him—yet, Pierre! You cannot make a quarrel of of what he said—yet."

Lady de Tilly listened uneasily and said—"Dont quarrel with him at all, Pierre Philibert!—Judge him, and avoid him as a Christian man would do. God will deal with Bigot as he deserves. The crafty man will be caught in his own devices some day."—

"O, Bigot is a gentleman, Aunt, too polite to insult any one," remarked Le Gardeur, impatient to defend one whom he regarded as a friend. "He is the prince of good fellows, and not crafty I think, but all surface and sunshine."—

"You never explored the depths of him Le Gardeur!" remarked La Corne. "I grant he is a gay jesting, drinking and gambling fellow in company, but trust me, he is deep and dark as the Devils cave that I have seen in the Ottawa Country. It goes story under story, deeper and deeper, until the imagination loses itself in contemplating the bottomless pit of it. That is Bigot, Le Gardeur."

"My censitaires report to me," remarked the Lady de Tilly, "that his commissaries are seizing the very seed corn of the country. Heaven knows what will become of my poor people next year if the war continue."

"What will become of the Province in the hands of Francois Bigot," replied La Corne St Luc. "They say, Philibert, a certain great lady at Court, who is his partner or patroness or both, has obtained a grant of your father's sequestrated estate in Normandy, for her relative the Count de Marville. Had you heard of that Philibert? It is the latest news from France."

"O yes Chevalier! Ill news like that never misses the mark it is aimed at. The news soon reached my father!"

"And how does your father take it?"

"My father is a true philosopher. He takes it as Socrates might have taken it. He laughs at the Count de Marville, who will he says want to sell the estate to him before the year is out, to pay his debts of honour the only debts he ever does pay."

"If Bigot had anything to do with such an outrage," exclaimed Le Gardeur warmly, "I would renounce him on the spot. I have heard Bigot speak of this gift to De Marville, whom he hates. He says it was all La Pompadour's doing from first to last, and I believe it—."

"Well," remarked La Corne, "Bigot has plenty of sins of his own, to answer for to the Sieur Philibert, on the day of accompt, without reckoning this among them."

The loud report of a cannon shook the windows of the room and died away in long repeated echoes among the distant hills.

"That is the signal for the Council of War, my Lady," said La Corne. "A soldiers luck! Just as we were going to have music and heaven we are summoned to field camp or Council!"

The gentlemen rose and accompanied the ladies to the drawing room, and prepared to depart. Colonel Philibert took a courteous leave of the ladies of Tilly, looking in the eyes of Amelie for something, which had she not turned them quickly upon a vase of flowers, he might have found there. She plucked a few sprays from the bouquet and handed them to him as a token of pleasure at meeting him again in his own land.

"Recollect! Pierre Philibert!" said the Lady de Tilly, holding him cordially by the hand. "The Manor House of Tilly is your second home, where you are ever welcome."

Philibert was deeply touched by the genuine if stately courtesy of the lady. He kissed her hand with grateful reverence and bowing to both the ladies, accompanied La Corne St Luc and Le Gardeur to the Castle of St Louis.

Amelie sat in the recess of the window, resting her cheek on her tremulous hand, as she watched the gentlemen proceed on their way to the Castle. Her mind was overflowing with thoughts and fancies, new, enigmatical, yet delightful. Her nervous manner did not escape the loving eye of her aunt, but she spoke not. She was silent under the burthen of a secret joy, that found not vent in words.

Suddenly Amelie rose from the window and seated herself in her impulsive way at the organ. Her fingers touched the keys timidly at first, as she began a trembling prelude of her own fantasy. In music her pent up feelings found congenial expression! The fire kindled and she presently burst out with the voice of a Seraph, into that glorious Psalm: the 116th.

Toto pectore diligam
Unice et Dominum colam,
Qui lenis mihi supplici
Non duram appulit aurem.

Aurem qui mihi supplici,
Non duram dedit; hunc ego
Donec pectora spiritus
Pulset semper, Amabo.—

The Lady de Tilly half guessing the truth would not wound the susceptibilities of her neice, by appearing to do so, rose quietly from her seat, and placed her arms gently round Amelie when she finished the Psalm. She pressed her to her bosom, kissed her fondly, and without a word left her to find in music relief from her high wrought feelings. Her voice rose in sweeter and loftier harmonies to the pealing of the organ as she sang to the end, the joyful yet solemn psalm in a version made for Queen Mary of France and Scotland when life was good and hope all brightness, and dark days as if they would never come.

CHAPTER 12

THE CASTLE OF ST LOUIS

THE Count de la Galisonniere with a number of officers of rank in full uniform were slowly pacing up and down the long gallery that fronted the Castle of St Louis, waiting for the Council of war to open, for although the hour had struck, the Intendant and many other high officials of the Colony had not yet arrived from Beaumanoir.

The Castle of St Louis, a massive structure of stone, with square flanking towers, rose loftily from the brink of the precipice, overlooking the narrow tortuous streets of the Lower Town. The steeple of the old church of Notre Dame des Victoires with its gilded vane lay far beneath the feet of the observer as he leaned over the balustrade of iron that guarded the gallery of the Chateau.

A hum of voices and dense sounds rose up from the market of Notre Dame, and from the quay where ships and bateaux were moored. The cries of sailors, carters and habitans in thick medley, floated up the steep cliffs, pleasant sounds to the ear of the worthy Governor, who liked the honest noises of industry and labour better than all the music of the academy.

A few merchantmen which had run the blockade of the English cruisers lay at anchor in the stream where the broad river swept majestically round the lofty cape. In the midst of them, a newly arrived Kings ship, the *Fleur de Lys* decorated with streamers floated proudly like a swan among a flock of teal.

Le Gardeur as an officer of the Garrison went to report himself to the military commandant while La Corne St Luc and Colonel Philibert proceeded to the Gallery where a crowd of officers were now assembled waiting for the Council.

119

The Governor called Philibert at once aside and took his arm. "Philibert," said he, "I trust you had no difficulty in finding the Intendant?"

"No difficulty whatever your Excellency. I discovered the Intendant and his friends by ear long before I got sight of them." An equivocal smile accompanied Philiberts words, which the Governor rightly interpreted.

"Ah! I understand, Philibert! They were carousing at that hour of daylight? Were they all ——?? Faugh! I shame to speak the word. Was the Intendant in a condition to comprehend my summons—?" The Governor looked sad rather than surprized or angry, for he had expected no less than Philibert had reported to him.

"I found him less intoxicated I think than many of his guests. He received your message with more politeness than I expected and promised to be here punctually at the hour for opening the Council."

"O Bigot never lacks politeness drunk or sober. That strong intellect of his seems to defy the power of wine as his heart is proof against moral feeling. You did not prolong your stay in Beaumanoir, I fancy!" remarked the Governor, dinting the point of his cane into the floor.

"I hastened out of it as I would out of hell itself! After making prize of my friend De Repentigny, and bringing him off with me, as I mentioned to you, I got quickly out of the Chateau."

"You did rightly Philibert! The Intendant is ruining half the young men of birth in the Colony—."

"He shall not ruin Le Gardeur, if I can save him," said Philibert resolutely. "May I count upon your Excellency's cooperation?" added he.

"Assuredly Philibert! command me in any thing you can devise to rescue that noble young fellow from the fatal companionship of Bigot. But I know not how long I shall be permitted to remain in New France. Powerful intrigues are at work for my removal!" added the Governor. "I care not for the removal, so that it be not accompanied with insult."

"Ah! You have received news to day by the Frigate?" said

Philibert looking down at the Kings ship at anchor in the stream.

"News! yes, and such news, Philibert!" replied the Governor in a tone of despondency. "It needs the wisdom of Solon to legislate for this land, and a Hercules to cleanse its augean stables of official corruption. But my influence at court is nil—you know that, Philibert!—"

"But while you are Governor, your advice ought to prevail with the King," replied Philibert.

"My advice prevail! listen Philibert my letters to the King and the Minister of Marine and Colonies have been answered—by whom think you?—"

"Nay I cannot conceive, who out of the legal channel would dare reply to them."

"No! no man could guess that my official despatches have been answered by the Marquise de Pompadour! She replies to my despatches to my sovereign!"

"La Pompadour!" exclaimed Philibert in a burst of indignation "She! The King's mistress!—reply to your despatches—! Has France come to be governed by courtesans like Imperial Rome?"

"Yes! and you know the meaning of that insult, Philibert! They desire to force me to resign, and I shall resign as soon as I see my friends safe. I will serve the King in his fleet, but never more in a Colony. This poor land is doomed to fall into the hands of its enemies, unless we get a speedy peace. France will help us no more!—"

"Dont say that your Excellency! France will surely never be untrue to her children in the New World—! But our resources are not yet all exhausted—we are not driven to the wall yet, your Excellency!—"

"Almost I assure you, Philibert! but we shall understand that better after the Council."

"What say the despatches touching the negociations going on for peace—?" asked Philibert who knew how true were the Governor's vaticinations.

"They speak favorably of peace, and I think correctly, Philibert! and you know the Kings armies and the Kings

mistresses cannot all be maintained, at the same time—
women or war one or other must give way—and one need
not doubt which it will be when the women rule court and
camp in France at the present time!—"

"To think that a woman picked out of the gutters of
Paris, should rule France and answer your despatches!" said
Philibert angrily. "It is enough to drive honorable Frenchmen
mad. But what says the Marquise de Pompadour?"

"She is specially severe upon my opposing the fiscal
measures and commercial policy as she calls it, of her friend,
the Intendant—!—She approves of his grant of a monopoly
in trade to the Grand Company, and disputes my right as
Governor to interfere with the Intendant in the finances of
the Colony."

Philibert felt deeply this wound to the honour and dignity
of his chief. He pressed his hand in warmest sympathy.

The Governor understood his feelings. "You are a true
friend Philibert" said he. "Ten men like you might still save
this Colony!—But it is past the hour for the Council and still
Bigot delays! he must have forgotten my summons."

"I think not, but he might have to wait until Cadet, Varin,
Deschenaux and the rest of them were in a condition fit to
travel," answered Philibert, with an air of disgust.

"O, Philibert! the shame of it! The shame of it—! for such
thieves to have the right to sit among loyal honorable men!"
exclaimed or rather groaned the Governor. "They have the
real power in New France, and we the empty title and the
killing responsibility! Dine with me to night after the Council
Philibert! I have much to say to you."

"Not to night your Excellency! My father has killed the
fatted calf for his returned prodigal. I must dine with him to
night," answered Philibert.

"Right! be it next day then! come on Wednesday," replied
the Governor. "Your father is a gentleman who carries the
principles of true nobility into the walks of trade. You are
happy in such a father Philibert, as he is fortunate in such
a son." The Governor bowed to his friend, and rejoined the
groups of officers on the Terrace.

A flash and a column of smoke white and sudden rose from the great battery that flanked the Chateau. It was the second signal for the Council to commence. The Count de la Galissoniere taking the arm of La Corne St Luc entered the Castle, and followed by the crowd of officers proceeded to the great Hall of Council and audience. The Governor followed by his secretaries, walked forward to the vice regal chair which stood on a daïs, at the head of a long table covered with crimson drapery—on each side of the table the members of the Council took the places assigned to them in the order of their rank and precedence. But a long array of chairs, remained unoccupied. The seats belonging to the Royal Intendant and the other high officers of the Colony who had not yet arrived to take their places in the Council stood empty.

The great Hall of the Castle of St Louis was palatial in its dimensions and adornments. Its lofty coved ceiling rested on a cornice of rich frieze of carved work, supported on polished pilasters of oak. The panels of wainscotting upon the walls were surrounded by delicate arabesques, and hung with paintings of historic interest—portraits of the Kings, Governors, Intendants and Ministers of State who had been instrumental in the colonization of New France.

Over the Governor's seat, hung a gorgeous escutcheon of the Royal arms, draped with a cluster of white flags sprinkled with golden lillies, the emblems of French sovereignty in the colony.

Among the portraits on the walls besides those of the late and present King, which hung on each side of the escutcheon, might be seen the features of Richelieu, who first organized the rude settlements on the St Lawrence into a body politic, a reflex of feudal France, and of Colbert who made available its natural wealth and resources by peopling it with the best scions of the mother land, the Noblesse and peasantry of Normandy Britany and Aquitaine. There too might be seen the keen bold features of Cartier the first discoverer and of Champlain the first explorer of the new land and the founder of Quebec. The gallant restless Louis Buade de Frontenac was pictured there side by side with his fair Countess, called by reason of her surpassing loveliness "The Divine"—Vaudreuil too who spent a long life of devotion to his country and Beauharnois who nourished its young strength until it was able to resist not only the powerful confederacy of the Five Nations but the still more powerful League of New England and the other English Colonies. There also were seen the sharp intellectual face of Laval its first bishop who organized the Church and education in the Colony, and of Talon, wisest of Intendants who devoted himself to the improvement of agriculture the increase of trade and the well being of all the Kings subjects in New France. And one striking portrait was there, worthy to rank among the statesmen and rulers of New France—the pale calm intellectual features of Mere Marie de l'Incarnation, the first superior of the Ursulines, of Quebec, who in obedience to heavenly visions as she believed, left France to found schools for the children of the new colonists, and who taught her own womanly graces to her own sex, who were destined to become the future mothers of New France.

In marked contrast with the military uniforms of the officers surrounding the Council table, were the black robes and tonsured heads of two or three Ecclesiastics, who had been called in by the Governor to aid the Council with their knowledge and advice. These were the Abbé Metavet of the Algonquins of the North, Pere Oubal the Jesuit missionary of the Abenaquis of the East and his confrere La Richardie from the wild tribes of the far west, but conspicuous among these able and influential missionaries, who were the real rulers of the Indian Nations allied with France was the famous Sulpicien, Abbé Piquet "The King's Missionary," as he was styled in Royal ordinances, and the Apostle to the Iroquois, whom he was labouring to convert and bring over to the side of France, in the great disputes raised between France and England for supremacy in North America.

On the wall behind the vice regal chair hung a great map, drawn by the bold hand of Abbé Piquet, representing the claims as well as actual possessions of France in America. A broad red line beginning in Acadia, traversed the map westerly, taking in Lake Ontario and running southerly along the crests and ridges of the Appalachian mountains. It was traced with a firm hand down to far off Louisiana, claiming for France the great vallies of the Ohio, the Mississippi, and the vast territories watered by the Missouri and the Colorado—thus hemming the English in between the walls of the Appalachian range on the West, and the sea coast on the East.

The Abbé Piquet had lately in a canoe descended the *Belle Riviere*, as the voyageurs called the noble Ohio. From its source to its junction with the solitary Mississippi the Abbé had planted upon its conspicuous bluffs the ensigns of France, with tablets of lead bearing the Fleur de Lys, and the proud inscription: "*Manibus date lilia plenis*" Lillies destined after a fierce struggle for empire to be trampled in to the earth by the feet of the victorious English.

The Abbé deeply impressed with the dangers that impended over the Colony, laboured zealously to unite the Indian nations in a general alliance with France. He had already brought the powerful Algonquins and Nipissings into his scheme, and planted them at Two Mountains as a bulwark to protect the city of Ville Marie. He had caused a great schism in the powerful Confederacy of the Five Nations, by adroitly fanning into a flame their jealousy of English encroachments on their ancient territory on Lake Ontario, and bands of Iroquois had not long since held conference with the Governor of New France, denouncing the English for disregarding their exclusive right to their own country. "The lands we possess" said they at a great Council in Ville Marie, "the lands we possess were given to us by the Master of Life, and we acknowledge to hold of no other!—"—

The Abbé had now strong hopes of perfecting a scheme, which he afterwards accomplished. A powerful body of the Iroquois left their villages and castles on the Mohawk and Gennessee rivers, and under the guidance of the Abbé, settled round the new Fort of La Presentation on the St Lawrence, and thus barred the way for the future, against the destructive inroads of their countrymen who remained faithful to the

English alliance.

Pending the arrival of the Royal Intendant the members of the Council indulged freely in conversation, more or less bearing on the important matters to be discussed, the state of the country, the movements of the enemy and not seldom, intermingled remarks of dissatisfaction and impatience, at the absence of the Intendant.

The late revel at Beaumanoir was well known to them and eyes flashed and lips curled in open scorn at the well understood reason of the Intendants delay.

"My private letters by the *Fleur de Lys*," remarked Beauharnois, "relate among other Court Gossip, that orders would be sent out to stop the defensive works at Quebec, and pull down what is built—! They think the cost of walls round our city can be better bestowed on political favorites, and certain high personnages at Court." De Beauharnois turned towards the Governor, "Has your Excellency heard ought of this?" asked he.

"Yes! It is true enough! Beauharnois! I have also received communications to that effect!" replied the Governor, with an effort at calmness, which ill concealed the shame and disgust that filled his soul.

There was an indignant stir among the officers, and many lips seemed trembling with speech. The impetuous Rigaud de Vaudreuil broke the fierce silence. He struck his fist heavily on the table.

"Ordered us to stop the building of the walls of Quebec? and to pull down what we have done by virtue of the Kings Corvée?—Did I hear your Excellency aright?" repeated he in a tone almost of incredulity. "The King is surely mad to think of such a thing!"

"Yes, Rigaud. It is as I tell you. But we must respect the royal command, and treat his Majestys name as becomes loyal servants."

"*Ventre saint bleu*! heard ever Canadian or Frenchman such moonshine madness! I repeat it your Excellency—! Dismantle Quebec! How in Gods name are the Kings dominions and the Kings subjects to be protected?" Rigaud got warmer. He was fearless, and would as every one knew have out his say, had the King been present in person. "Be assured your Excellency it is not the King who orders that affront to his faithful Colony. It is the Kings ministers, the Kings mistresses, the snuff box tapping courtiers at Versailles! who can spend the public money in more elegant ways, than in raising up walls round our brave old city—! Ancient honour and chivalry of France what has become of you?"—

Rigaud sat down, angrily. The emotion he displayed was too much in accord with the feelings of the gallant officers present to excite other than marks of approbation, except among a few personal friends of the Intendant, who took their cue from the avowed wishes of the Court.

"What reason does his Majesty give?" asked La Corne St Luc, "for this singular communication."

"The only reason given is found in the concluding paragraph of the despatch. I will allow the Secretary to read so much of it, and no more, before the Intendant arrives." The Governor looked up at the great clock in the Hall with a grim glance of impatience—as if mentally calling down any thing but a blessing upon the head of the loitering Intendant.

The Secretary a lean, spectacled man, in black gown and bands, turned over the pages of stiff paper on which was written the Royal despatch. He read the concluding paragraph in a dry official tone but every word seemed weighted like a stone that dropped heavily into the hearts of the loyal gentlemen around the Council table.

"The Count de la Galissoniere, ought to know," said the despatch, sneeringly, "that works like those of Quebec are not to be undertaken by the Governors of Colonies except under express orders from the King! Therefore it is His Majesty's desire that upon the reception of this despatch, your Excellency will discontinue the works that have been begun upon Quebec. Extensive fortifications require strong garrisons for their defence, and the Kings treasury is already exhausted by the extraordinary expenses of the war in Europe. It cannot at the same time carry on the war in Europe and meet the heavy draughts made upon it, from North America."

The Secretary folded the despatch, and sat down without altering a line of his impassive face—not so the majority of the officers round the table. They were excited and ready to spring up in their indignation. The Kings name restrained them all, but Rigaud de Vaudreuil, who impetuously burst out with an oath:—exclaiming, "They may as well sell New France at once to the enemy, if we are not to defend Quebec—! The treasury wants money for the war in Europe forsooth! No doubt it wants money for the war, when so much is lavished upon the pimps, panders and harlots of the Court!"

The Governor rose suddenly, striking the table with his scabbard to stop Rigaud in his rash and dangerous speech. "Not a word more of comment! Chevalier Rigaud!" said he, with a sharp imperative tone that cut short debate, "not another word! His Majesty's name and those of his Ministers must be spoken here respectfully, or not at all—! Sit down Chevalier de Vaudreuil! You are inconsiderate."

"I obey your Excellency! I am I dare say inconsiderate! but I am right!" Rigaud's passion was subsiding, but not spent. He obeyed the order however. He had had his say, and flung himself heavily on his chair.

"The Kings despatch demands respectful and loyal consideration," remarked De Lery, a solid grave officer of Engineers, "and I doubt not that upon a proper remonstrance from this Council, His Majesty will graciously reconsider his order. The fall of Louisbourg is ominous of the fall of Quebec. It is imperative to fortify the city in time to meet the threatened invasion. The loss of Quebec would be the loss of the Colony— and the loss of the Colony the disgrace of France and the ruin of our Country."—

"I cordially agree with the Chevalier de Lery," said La Corne St Luc. "He has spoken more sense than would be found in a ship load of such despatches as that just read—! Nay, your Excellency," continued the old officer smiling, "I shall not affront my sovereign by believing that so, ill-timed a missive came from *him*—! Depend upon it, His Majesty has neither seen nor sanctioned it. It is the work of the minister and his mistresses not the Kings!—"

"La Corne! La Corne!" The Governor raised his finger with a warning look. "We will not discuss the point farther, until we are favoured with the presence and opinion of the Intendant. He will surely be here shortly!" At this moment a distant noise of shouting was heard in some part of the city.

An officer of the day, entered the Hall in great haste, and whispered in the Governor's ear.

"A riot in the streets!" exclaimed the Governor. "The mob attacking the Intendant! you do not say so! Captain Duval, turn out the whole guard at once and let Colonel St Remi take the command and clear the way for the Intendant, and also clear the streets of all disturbers."—

A number of officers sprang to their feet. "Keep seated gentlemen!—we must not break up the Council," said the Governor. "We are sure to have the Intendant here in a few minutes, and learn the cause of this uproar. It is some trifling affair of noisy habitans I have no doubt."

Another loud shout, or rather yell made itself distinctly heard in the Council Chamber. "It is the people cheering the Intendant on his way through the city!" remarked La Corne St Luc ironically. "Zounds! what a vacarme they make—! See what it is to be popular with the citizens of Quebec!"

There was a smile all round the table at La Corne's sarcasm. It offended a few friends of the Intendant however.

"The Chevalier La Corne speaks boldly in the absence of the Intendant," said Colonel Leboeuf. "A gentleman would give a Louis d'or any day to buy a whip to lash the rabble, sooner than a sou to win their applause—! I would not give a red herring for the good opinion of all Quebec!—"

"They say in France, Colonel" replied La Corne St Luc scornfully, "that Kings chaff is better than other peoples corn, and that fish in the market is cheaper than fish in the sea!—I believe it, and can prove it to any gentleman who maintains the contrary—!"

There was a laugh at La Corne's allusion to the Marquise de Pompadour, whose original name of Jeanne Poisson, gave rise to infinite jests and sarcasms among the people of low and high degree.

Colonel Le Boeuf choleric as he was, refrained from pressing the quarrel with La Corne St Luc. He sat sulkily smothering his wrath, longing to leave the Hall and go to the relief of the Intendant, but kept against his will by the command of the Governor.

The drums of the Main Guard beat the assembly. The clash of arms and the tramp of many feet resounded from the court yard of the Chateau. The members of the Council looked out of the windows as the troops formed in column, and headed by Colonel St Remi, defiled out of the Castle Gate, the thunder of their drums drowning every other sound and making the windows shake as they marched through the narrow streets to the scene of disturbance.

CHAPTER 13

THE CHIEN D'OR

On the Rue Buade, a street commemorative of the gallant Frontenac, stood the large imposing edifice newly built by the Bourgeois Philibert as the people of the Colony fondly called Nicholas Jaquin Philibert, the great and wealthy merchant of Quebec, and their champion against the odious monopolies of the Grand Company favored by the Intendant.

The edifice was of stone, spacious and lofty, but in style solid plain and severe. It was a wonder of architecture in New France, and the talk and admiration of the Colony from Tadousac to Ville Marie. It comprised the city residence of the Bourgeois as well as suites of offices and warerooms connected with his immense business.

The house was bare of architectural adornments but on its facade, blazing in the sun was the gilded sculpture that so much piqued the curiosity of both citizens and strangers, and was the talk of every seigneurie in the land—the tablet of the *Chien d'or*. The Golden dog with its enigmatical inscription, looked down defiantly upon the busy street beneath, where it is still to be seen, perplexing the beholder to guess its meaning and exciting our deepest sympathies over the tragedy of which it remains the sole sad memorial.

Above and beneath the figure of a couchant dog, gnawing the thigh bone of a man, is graven the weird inscription cut deeply in the stone, as if for all future generations to read, and ponder over its meaning—:

Je suis un chien qui ronge l'os,
En le rongeant je prends mon repos.
Un tems viendra qui n'est pas venu
Que je mordrai qui m'aura mordu.

1736

131

or in English:—

> "I am a dog that gnaws his bone,
> I couch and gnaw it all alone.
> A time will come which is not yet,
> When I'll bite him, by whom I'm bit."

The magazines of the Bourgeois Philibert presented not only an epitome, but a substantial portion of the commerce of New France. Bales of furs which had been brought down in fleets of canoes from the wild, almost unknown regions of the North west lay in piles to the beams—Skins of the smooth beaver, the delicate otter, Black and silver fox so rich to the eye and silky to the touch, that the proudest beauties longed for their possession, Seal skins to trim the gowns of portly Burgomasters and Ermine to adorn the robes of nobles and kings. The spoils of the wolf, bear and buffalo, worked to the softness of cloth by the hands of Indian women, were stored, for winter wear, and to fill the sledges with warmth and comfort when the North west wind freezes the snow to fine dust and the aurora borealis moves in stately procession like an army of spearmen across the northern sky. The harvests of the colonists, the corn the wool, the flax, the timber, enough to build whole navies and mighty pines fit to mast the tallest admiral were stored upon the wharves and in the warehouses of the Bourgeois upon the banks of the St Lawrence, with iron from the royal forges of the Three Rivers, and heaps of Ginseng from the forests a product worth its weight in gold, and eagerly exchanged by the Chinese for their teas silks and syce silver.

The stately mansion of Belmont overlooking the picturesque valley of the St Charles, was the residence proper of the Bourgeois Philibert, but the shadow that in time falls over every hearth, had fallen upon his, when the last of his children, his beloved son Pierre left home to pursue his military studies in France. During Pierre's absence the home at Belmont although kept up with the same strict attention which the Bourgeois paid to everything under his rule, was not occupied by him. He preferred his city mansion as more convenient for his affairs and resided therein. His partner of many years of happy wedded life, had been long dead. She left no void in his heart that another could fill. But he kept up a large household for friendship sake and was lavish in his hospitality. In secret, he was a grave solitary man, caring for the present only for the sake of the thousands depending on him, living much with the memory of the dear dead, and much with the hope of the future in his son Pierre.

The Bourgeois was a man worth looking at, and at a glance one to trust to, whether you sought the strong hand to help, the wise head to counsel or the feeling heart to sympathize with you. He was tall, strongly knit with features of a high patrician cast, a noble head covered thick with grizly hair, one of those heads so tenacious of life that they never grow bald, but carry to the grave the snows of a hundred years. His quick grey eyes caught your meaning ere it was half spoken. A nose and chin moulded with beauty and precision accentuated his handsome face. His lips were grave even in their smile, for gaiety was rarely a guest in the heart of the Bourgeois. A man keenly susceptible to kindness, but strong in resentments and not to be placated without the fullest atonement.

The Bourgeois sat by the table in his spacious well furnished drawing room which overlooked the Rue Buade, and gave him a glimpse of the tall new Cathedral, and the trees and gardens of the Seminary. He was engaged in reading letters and papers just arrived from France by the Frigate, quickly extracting their contents, and pencilling on their margins memos for further reference to his clerks.

The only other occupant of the room was a very elderly lady in a black gown of rigid Huguenot fashion. A close white cap tied under her chin set off to the worst advantage her sharp yet kindly features—not an end of ribbon or edge of lace could be seen to point to one hairbreadth of indulgence in the vanities of the world, by this strict old Puritan, who under this unpromising appearance possessed the kindest heart in Christendom. Her dress, if of rigid severity was of Saintly purity, and almost pained the eye with its precision and neatness. So fond are we of some freedom from overmuch care as from overmuch righteousness, that a stray tress, a loose ribbon, a little rent even will relieve the eye, and hold it with a subtle charm. Under the snow white hair of Dame Rochelle, for she it was, the worthy old housekeeper and ancient Governess of the House of Philibert, you saw a kind intelligent face. Her dark eyes bespoke her Southern origin, confirmed by her speech which although refined by culture retained the soft intonations and melody of her native Langue d'oc.

Dame Rochelle, the daughter of an ardent Calvinist minister, was born in the fatal year of the revocation of the Edict of Nantes, when Louis XIV. undid the glorious work of Henry Quatre and covered France with persecution and civil war, filling foreign countries with the elect of her population, her industry and her wealth, exiled in the name of religion.

Dame Rochelle's childhood had passed in the trying scenes of the great persecution, and in the succeding civil war of the Cevennes, she lost all that was nearest and dearest to her—her father, her brothers, her kindred nearly all, and lastly a gallant gentleman of Dauphiny to whom she was betrothed. She knelt beside him at the place of execution, or martyrdom for he died for his faith, and holding his hands in hers pledged her eternal fidelity to his memory and faithfully kept it all her life.

The Count de Philibert, elder brother of the Bourgeois was an officer of the King. He witnessed this sad scene took pity on the hapless girl, and gave her a home and protection with his family in the Chateau of Philibert, where she spent the rest of her life until the Bourgeois succeded to his childless brother. On the ruin of his house she would not consent to leave them but followed their fortunes to New France. She had been the faithful friend and companion of the wife of the Bourgeois and the educator of his children, and was now in her old age, the trusted friend and manager of his household. Her days were divided between the exercises of religion and the practical duties of life. The light that illumined her though flowing through the narrow window of a narrow creed, was still light of Divine origin. It satisfied her faith and filled her with resignation hope and comfort.

Her three studies were the Bible, the Hymns of Marot and the sermons of the famous Jurieu. She had listened to the prophecies of Grande Marie, and had even herself been breathed upon, on the top of Mount Peira by the Huguenot Prophet De Serre.

Good Dame Rochelle was not without a feeling that at times the spiritual gift she had received when a child made itself manifest by intuitions of the future, which were after all perhaps only emanations of her natural good sence and clear intellect—the foresight of a pure mind.

The wasting persecutions of the Calvinists in the mountains of the Cevennes, drove men and women wild with desperate fanaticism. De Serre had an immense following. He assumed to impart the holy spirit and the gift of tongues by breathing upon the believers. The refugees carried his doctrines abroad to England and finally handed down their singular ideas to modern times, and a sect may still be found which believes in the gift of tongues and practices the power of prophesying as taught originally in the Cevennes.

The good Dame was not reading this morning although the volume before her lay open. Her glasses lay upon the page. She sat musing by the open window, seldom looking out however, for her thoughts were chiefly inward. The return of Pierre Philibert, her foster child, had filled her with joy and thankfulness and she was pondering in her mind the details of a festival which the Bourgeois intended to give in honour of the return of his only son.

The Bourgeois had finished the reading of his packet of letters, and sat musing in silence. He too was intently thinking of his son. His face was filled with the satisfaction of old Simeon when he cried out of the fulness of his heart, "*Domine! nunc dimittis.*"

"Dame Rochelle," said he. She turned promptly to the voice of her master, as she ever insisted on calling him. "Were I superstitious I should fear that my great joy at Pierre's return might be the prelude to some great sorrow."—

"God's blessing on Pierre!" said she. "He can only bring

joy to this house. Thank the Lord, for what he gives and what he takes! He took Pierre a stripling from his home and returns him a great man fit to ride at the Kings right hand, and to be over his host like Beniah the son of Jehoiada, over the host of Solomon."

"Grand merci for the comparison Dame!" said the Bourgeois smiling as he leaned back in his chair.

"But Pierre is a Frenchman and would prefer commanding a brigade in the army of the Marshal de Saxe to serving in the host of King Solomon. But," continued he gravely, "I am strangely happy to day, Deborah!" He was wont to call her Deborah when very earnest—"and I will not anticipate any mischief to mar my happiness! Pshaw! It is only the reaction of overexcited feelings. I am weak in the strength of my joy."

"The still small voice speaks to us in that way Master! to remind us to place our trust in heaven, and not on earth, where all is transitory and uncertain, for if a man live many years, and rejoice in them all, let him remember the days of darkness for they are many—! We are no strangers to the vanity and sadness of human life, Master! but Pierre's return is like sunshine breaking through the clouds. God is pleased if we bask in the sunshine, when he sends it."

"Right Dame! so we will, and the old walls of Belmont shall ring with pleasure over the return of their heir and future owner."

The Dame looked up delightedly at the remark of the Bourgeois. She knew he had destined Belmont as a residence for Pierre. But the thought suggested in her mind, was perhaps the same which the Bourgeois had mused upon, when he gave expression to a certain anxiety.

"Master," said she. "Does Pierre know that the Chevalier Bigot was concerned in the false accusations against you, and that it was he prompted by the Cardinal, and the Princess de Carignan who enforced the unjust decree of the Court?"

"I think not, Deborah. I never told Pierre that Bigot was ever more than the *avocat du Roi* in my persecution."

"It is what troubles me amidst my joy—! If Pierre knew that the Intendant had been my false accuser on the part of the Cardinal, his sword would not rest a day in its scabbard without calling Bigot to a bloody account. Indeed it is all I myself can do, to refrain! I met him for the first time here, in the Palace Gate. I knew him again, and looked him full in the eyes—and he knew me. He is a bold hound, and glared back at me, without shrinking! Had he smiled I should have struck him. But we passed in silence with a salute as mortal enemies ever gave each other—! It is well perhaps I wore not my sword that day, for I felt my passion rising, a thing I abhor. Pierre's young blood would not remain still, if he knew the Intendant as I know him. But I dare not tell him. There would be blood shed at once, Deborah!"—

"I fear so, Master! I trembled at Bigot in the old land. I tremble at him here, where he is more powerful than before. I saw him passing one day. He stopped to read the inscription of the Golden Dog. His face was the face of a fiend as he turned and rode hastily away. He knew well how to interpret it."

"Ha! you did not tell me that before, Deborah!" The Bourgeois rose excitedly. "Bigot read it all, did he?—I hope every letter of it was branded on his soul as with red hot iron—!"

"Dear Master that is an unchristian saying, and nothing good can come of it. Vengeance is mine saith the Lord—! our worst enemies are best left in his hands."

The Dame was proceeding in a still more moralizing strain, when a noise arose in the street from a crowd of persons, habitans for the most part congregated round the house. The noise increased to a degree that they stopped their conversation and both the Dame and the Bourgeois looked out of the window at the increasing multitude that was gathered in the street.

The crowd had come to the Rue Buade, to see the famous tablet of the Golden Dog, which was talked of in every Seigneurie in New France. Still more perhaps to see the Bourgeois Philibert himself—the great merchant who contended for the rights of the habitans, and who would not yield an inch to the Friponne.

The Bourgeois looked down at the ever increasing throng—country people for the most part with their wives, with not a few citizens whom he could easily distinguish, by their dress and manner. The Bourgeois stood rather withdrawn from the front, so as not to be recognized for he hated intensely anything like a demonstration still less an ovation. He could hear many loud voices however in the crowd, and caught up the chief topics they discussed with each other.

His eyes rested several times on a wiry jerking little fellow, whom he recognized as Jean La Marche the fiddler, a censitaire of the Manor of Tilly. He was a well known character and had drawn a large circle of the crowd around himself.

"I want to see the Bourgeois Philibert!" exclaimed Jean La Marche. "He is the bravest merchant in New France— the people's friend. Bless the Golden dog, and curse the Friponne!"

"Hurrah for the Golden Dog, and curse the Friponne!" exclaimed a score of voices. "Wont you sing, Jean?"

"Not now. I have a new ballad ready on the Golden Dog, which I will sing to night, that is if you will care to listen to me." Jean said this with a very demure air of mock modesty knowing well that the announcement of a new ballad from him, would equal the furor for a new *aria* from the prima donna of the opera at Paris.

"We will all come and hear it Jean!" cried they. "But take care of your fiddle or you will get it crushed in this crowd."

"As if I did not know how to take care of my darling baby!" said Jean holding his violin high above his head. "It is my only child. It will laugh and cry, and love and scold as I bid it, and make every body else do the same when I touch its heart strings." Jean had brought his violin under his arm in place of a spade, to help build up the walls of the city. He had never heard of Amphion, with his lyre building up the walls of Thebes, but Jean knew that in his violin lay a power of work—by others hands—if he played while they laboured. It lightened toil and made work go merrily as the Bells of Tilly at a wedding said he.

There was immense talk with plenty of laughter and no thought of mischief among the crowd. The habitans of *en haut* and the habitans of *en bas*, commingled as they rarely did in a friendly way. Nor was any thing to provoke a quarrel said even to the Acadians, whose rude patois, was a source of merry jest to the better speaking Canadians.

The Acadians had flocked in great numbers into Quebec on the seizure of their Province by the English—hardy robust quarellsome fellows, who went about challenging people in their reckless way, *Etions pas mon maitre monsieur!* But all were civil to day, and tuques were pulled off, and bows exchanged in a style of easy politeness that would not have shamed the streets of Paris.

The crowd kept increasing in the Rue Buade. The two sturdy beggars who vigorously kept their places on the stone steps of the Barrier or Gate way of the Basse Ville reaped an unusual harvest of the smallest coin—Max Grimau an old disabled soldier in ragged uniform which he had worn at the defence of Prague under the Marshal de Belleisle, and blind Barthemy a mendicant born—the former loud tongued and importunate, the latter silent and only holding out a shaking hand for charity. No finance minister or Royal Intendant studied more earnestly the problem how to tax the Kingdom than Max and Blind Barthemy how to toll the passers by—and with less success perhaps.

To day was a red letter day for the sturdy beggars, for the news flew fast that an ovation of some popular kind was to be given to the Bourgeois Philibert. The Habitans came trooping up the rough mountain road that led from the Basse Ville to the Upper Town, and up the long stairs, lined with the stalls of Basque pedlars—cheating loquacious varlets!— which formed a By-way from the lower regions of the Rue de Champlain, a break neck thoroughfare little liked by the old and asthmatical, but nothing to the sturdy "climbers" as the Habitans called the lads of Quebec, or the light footed lasses, who displayed their trim ankles as they flew up the breezy steps to church or market.

Max Grimau and Blind Barthemy had ceased counting

their coins. The passers by came up in still increasing numbers until the street from the Barrier of the Basse Ville to the Cathedral was filled with a noisy good humoured crowd, without an object, except to stare at the Golden Dog, and a desire to catch a glimpse of the Bourgeois Philibert.

The crowd had become very dense when a troop of gentlemen rode at full speed into the Rue Buade, and after trying recklessly to force their way through came to a sudden halt, in the midst of the surging mass.

The Intendant, Cadet and Varin, had ridden from Beaumanoir followed by a train of still flushed guests who after a hasty purification had returned with their host to the city—a noisy troop, loquacious, laughing, shouting, as is the wont of men, reckless at all times, and still more defiant when under the influence of wine.

"What is the meaning of this Rabble, Cadet—?" asked Bigot. "They seem to be no friends of yours! That fellow is wishing you in a hot place!" added Bigot laughing, as he pointed out a Habitan who was shouting, "À bas Cadet!—"—

"Nor friends of yours either," replied Cadet. "They have not recognized you yet, Bigot. When they do, they will wish you in the hottest place of all—!"

The Intendant was not known personally to the Habitans, as were Cadet Varin and the rest. Loud shouts of execration were freely vented against these as soon as they were recognized.

"Has this rabble way laid us to insult us?" asked Bigot. "But it can hardly be that they knew of our return to the city to day!" The Intendant began to jerk his horse round impatiently, but without avail.

"Oh no, Your Excellency. It is the rabble which the Governor has summoned to the Kings Corvée! They are paying their respects to the Golden Dog, which is the image the mob worships just now. They did not expect us to interrupt their devotions I fancy."

"The vile moutons! their fleece is not worth the shearing!" exclaimed Bigot angrily at the mention of the Golden Dog, which as he glanced upwards seemed to glare defiantly upon him.

"Clear the way! Villains!" cried Bigot loudly, while dashing his horse into the crowd, "plunge that Flanders cart horse of yours into them, Cadet!—and do not spare their toes!—"

Cadet's rough disposition chimed well with the Intendants wish. "Come on Varin and the rest of you," cried he "give spur and fight your way through the rabble."

The whole troop plunged madly at the crowd striking right and left with their heavy hunting whips. A violent scuffle ensued. Many Habitans were ridden down and some of the horsemen dismounted. The Intendants Gascon blood got furious. He struck heavily, right and left and many a bleeding tuque marked his track in the crowd.

The Habitans recognized him at last, and a tremendous yell burst out—"Long live the Golden Dog—! Down with the Friponne!—"—while the more bold ventured on the cry— "Down with the Intendant and the thieves of the Grand Company—!"

Fortunately for the troop of horsemen, the habitans were utterly unarmed. But stones began to be thrown, and efforts were made by them not always unsuccessfully to pull the riders off their horses. Poor Jean La Marche's darling child, his favorite violin, was crushed at the first charge. Jean rushed at the Intendants bridle, and received a blow which levelled him.

The Intendant and all the troop now drew their swords. A bloody catastrophe seemed impending, when the Bourgeois Philibert, seeing the state of affairs despatched a messenger with tidings to the Castle of St Louis, and rushed himself into the street, amidst the surging crowd, imploring, threatening and compelling them to give way.

He was soon recognized, and cheered by the people but even his influence might have failed to calm the fiery passions excited by the Intendants violence, had not the drums of the approaching soldiery suddenly resounded above the noise of the riot. In a few minutes long files of glittering bayonets were seen streaming down the Rue du Fort. Colonel St Remi rode at their head, forming his troops in position to charge the crowd.

The Colonel saw at once the state of affairs, and being a man of judgment commanded peace before resorting to force. He was at once obeyed. The people stood still and in silence. They fell back quietly before the troops. They had no purpose to resist the authorities—Indeed had no purpose whatever. A way was made clear by the soldiers, and the Intendant and his friends were extricated from their danger.

They rode at once out of the mob, amid a volley of execrations, which were replied to by angry oaths and threats of the cavaliers as they gallopped across the Place D'Armes, and rode pele mele into the Gate way of the Chateau of St Louis.

The crowd relieved of their presence, grew calm and some of the more timid of them got apprehensive of the consequences of this outrage upon the Royal Intendant. They dispersed quietly, singly or in groups, each one hoping that he might not be called on to account for the days proceedings.

CHAPTER 14

THE COUNCIL OF WAR

THE Intendant and his cortege of friends rode furiously into the Court yard of the Chateau of St Louis, decheveled, bespattered and some of them hatless. They dismounted and foaming with rage rushed through the lobbies and with heavy tramping of feet, clattering of scabbards and a bedlam of angry tongues, burst into the Council Chamber.

The Intendants eyes shot fire. His Gascon blood was at fever heat flushing his swarthy cheek like the purple hue of a hurricane. He rushed at once to the Council table, and seeing the Governor, saluted him but spoke in tones forcibly kept under by a violent effort.

"Your Excellency and Gentlemen of the Council will excuse our delay" shouted Bigot: "when I inform you that I, the Royal Intendant of New France have been insulted pelted and my very life threatened by a seditious mob congregated in the Streets of Quebec."

"I grieve much, and sympathize with your Excellency's indignation," replied the Governor warmly. "I rejoice you have escaped unhurt. I despatched the troops to your assistance but have not yet learned the cause of the riot."

"The cause of the riot was the popular hatred of myself, for enforcing the royal ordinances and the seditious example set the rabble by the notorious merchant, Philibert, who is at the bottom of all mischief in New France."

The Governor looked fixedly at the Intendant, as he replied quietly: "The Sieur Philibert, although a merchant, is a gentleman of birth and loyal principles and would be the last man alive I think to excite a riot. Did you see the Bourgeois? Chevalier."

143

"The crowd filled the street near his magazines cheering for the Bourgeois and the Golden Dog. We rode up, and endeavoured to force our way through. But I did not see the Bourgeois himself until the disturbance had attained its full proportions."

"And then, your Excellency—? surely the Bourgeois was not encouraging the mob,—or participating in the riot?—"

"No, I, do not charge him with participating in the riot, although the mob were all his friends and partizans. Moreover," said Bigot frankly, for he felt he owed his safety to the interference of the Bourgeois, "it would be unfair not to acknowledge that he did what he could to protect us from the rabble. I charge Philibert with sowing the sedition that caused the riot, not with rioting himself."

"But I accuse him of both, and of all the mob has done!" thundered Varin enraged to hear the Intendant speak with moderation and justice. "The House of the Golden Dog is a den of traitors. It ought to be pulled down and its stones built into a monument of infamy, over its owner hung like a dog in the market place."

"Silence Varin!" exclaimed the Governor sternly "I will not hear the Sieur Philibert spoken of in these injurious terms. The Intendant does not charge him with this disturbance— neither shall you."

"*Par Dieu*! you shall not! Varin!" burst in La Corne St Luc, roused to unusual wrath by the opprobrium heaped upon his friend the Bourgeois, "and you shall answer to me for that you have said!"

"La Corne! La Corne!" The Governor saw a challenge impending, and interposed with vehemence. "This is a Council of war, and not a place for recriminations. Sit down, dear old friend, and aid me to get on with the business of the King and his Colony which we are here met to consider."

The appeal went to the heart of La Corne. He sat down. "You have spoken generously, Chevalier Bigot, respecting the Bourgeois Philibert," continued the Governor. "I am pleased that you have done so. My Aide de camp Colonel Philibert who is just entering the Council will be glad to hear that your

Excellency does justice to his father in this matter."

"The blessing of St Bennets boots upon such justice!" muttered Cadet to himself. "I was a fool not to run my sword through Philibert when I had the chance!"

The Governor repeated to Colonel Philibert what had been said by Bigot.

Colonel Philibert bowed to the Intendant. "I am under obligation to the Chevalier Bigot," said he. "But it astonishes me much that any one should dare implicate my father in such a disturbance. Certainly the Intendant does him but justice."

This remark was not pleasing to Bigot, who hated Colonel Philibert equally with his father. "I merely said, he had not participated in the riot, Colonel Philibert! which was true. I did not defend your father for being at the head of the party among whom these outrages arise. I simply spoke truth, Colonel Philibert. I do not eke out by the inch my opinion of any man. I care not for the Bourgeois Philibert more than for the meanest blue cap in his following."

This was an ungracious speech. Bigot meant it to be such. He repented almost of the witness he had borne to the Bourgeois' endeavours to quell the mob. But he was too profoundly indifferent to men's opinions respecting himself, to care to lie. Truth was easier than lying, and suited better his moral hardihood. Not that he loved truth for its own sake— far from it—but lying is born of cowardice, and Bigot was no coward, he feared no one, respected no one. When he did lie it was with deliberate purpose and without scruple, but he only did it when the object in his judgment was worth lying for, and even then, he felt self accused of unmanly conduct.

Colonel Philibert resented the Intendants sneer at his father. He faced Bigot saying to him: "The Chevalier Bigot has done but simple justice to my father with reference to his conduct in regard to the riot. But let the Intendant recollect that although a merchant, my father is above all things a Norman gentleman, who never swerved a hair breadth from the path of honour, a gentleman whose ancient nobility would dignify even the Royal Intendant." Bigot looked daggers at this thrust at his own comparatively humble origin. "And this

I have further to say," continued Philibert looking straight in the eyes of Bigot Varin and Cadet. "Whoever impugns my father's honour impugns mine, and no man high or low shall do that and escape chastisement."

The greater part of the officers seated round the Council Board listened with marks of approval to Philibert's vindication of his father. But no one challenged his words, although dark ominous looks glanced from one to another among the friends of the Intendant. Bigot smothered his anger for the present however, and to prevent further reply from his followers he rose and bowing to the Governor, begged His Excellency to open the Council.

"We have delayed the business of the King too long, with these personal recriminations" said he. "I shall leave this riot to be dealt with by the Kings courts who will sharply punish both instigators and actors in this outrage on the royal authority." That seemed to end the matter for the present:—

The Council now opened in due form. The Secretary read the royal despatches, which were listened to with attention, and respect although with marks of dissent on the countenances of many of the officers.

The Governor rose and in a quiet almost a solemn strain, addressed the Council. "Gentlemen," said he, "from the tenor of the royal despatches just read by the Secretary, it is clear that our beloved New France is in great danger. The King overwhelmed by the powers in alliance against him, can no longer reinforce our army here. The English fleet is supreme—for the moment only, I hope," added the Governor, as if with a prevision of his own future triumphs on the ocean. "Their troops are pouring into New York and Boston to combine with the Militia of New England and the middle colonies in a grand attack upon New France. They have commenced to erect a great Fort at Chouagen on Lake Ontario to dispute supremacy with our stronghold at Niagara, and the gates of Carillon may ere long have to prove their strength in keeping the enemy out of the valley of the Richelieu. I fear not for Carillon, Gentlemen in the ward of the gallant Count de Lusignan, whom I am glad to see at our

Council, I think Carillon is safe."

The Count de Lusignan a grey headed officer, of soldierly bearing, bowed low to this compliment from the Governor. "I ask the Count de Lusignan," continued the Governor, "what he thinks would result from our withdrawing the garrison from Carillon, as is suggested in the despatches—?"

"The Five Nations would be on the Richelieu in a week, and the English in Montreal within a month after such a piece of folly on our part," exclaimed the Count de Lusignan.

"You cannot counsel the abandonment of Carillon, then, Count?" A smile played over the face of the Governor, as if he too felt the absurdity of his question.

"Not till Quebec itself falls into the enemies hands. When that happens His Majesty will need another adviser, in the place of the old Count de Lusignan."

"Well spoken Count! In your hands Carillon is safe, and will one day, should the enemy assail it, be covered with wreaths of victory and its flag the glory of New France."

"So be it Governor. Give me but the Royal Roussillon, and I pledge you neither English Dutch nor Iroquois shall ever cross the waters of St Sacrament."—

"You speak like your ancestor the crusader, Count. But I cannot spare the Royal Roussillon. Think you you can hold Carillon with your present garrison."

"Against all the force of New England. But I cannot promise the same against the English regulars now landing at New York."

"They are the same whom the King defeated at Fontenoy, are they not?"—interrupted the Intendant who courtier as he was, disliked the tenor of the royal despatches as much as any officer present—all the more as he knew that La Pompadour was advising peace out of a woman's considerations, rather than upholding the glory of France.

"Among them are many troops who fought us at Fontenoy. I learned the fact from an English prisoner whom our Indians brought in from Fort Lydius," replied the Count de Lusignan.

"Well the more of them the merrier," laughed La Corne St Luc. "The bigger the prize the richer they who take it—! The treasure chests of the English, will make up for the beggarly packs of the New Englanders. Dried stock fish and eel skin garters to drive away the Rhumatism were the usual prize we got from them down in Acadia—!"

"The English of Fontenoy are not such despicable foes," remarked the Chevalier de Lery. "They sufficed to take Louisbourg, and if we discontinue our walls, will suffice to take Quebec."—

"Louisbourg was not taken by *them*, but fell through the mutiny of the base Swiss!—" replied Bigot touched sharply by any allusion to that Fortress where he had figured so discreditably. "The vile hirelings demanded money of their commander, when they should have drawn the blood of the enemy—" added he angrily.

"Satan is bold! but he would blush in the presence of Bigot!—" remarked La Corne St Luc to an Acadian officer seated next him. "Bigot kept the Kings treasure, and defrauded the soldiers of their pay—hence the mutiny—and the fall of Louisbourg."—

"It is what the whole army knows!" replied the officer, "but hark! the Abbé Piquet is going to speak! It is a new thing to see Clergy in a Council of war!—"

"No one has a better right to speak here than the Abbé Piquet," replied La Corne. "No one has sent more Indian allies into the field to fight for New France, than the patriotic Abbé."

Other officers did not share the generous sentiments of La Corne St Luc. They thought it derogatory to pure military men to listen to a priest on the affairs of the war.

"The Marshal de Belleisle would not permit even Cardinal de Fleury to put his red stockings beneath *his* council table," remarked a strict martinet of La Serre. "And here we have a whole flock of black gowns darkening our regimentals—! What would Voltaire say?"

"He would say that when Priests turn soldiers it is time for soldiers to turn tinkers and mend holes in pots instead of making holes in our enemies—!" replied his companion a fashionable freethinker of the day.

"Well, I am ready to turn pedlar any day. The Kings army will go to the dogs fast enough since the Governor commissions Recollets and Jesuits to act as royal officers," was the petulant remark of another officer of La Serre.

A strong prejudice existed in the army against the Abbé Piquet for his opposition to the presence of French troops in his Indian missionary villages. They demoralized his neophytes, and many of the officers shared in the lucrative traffic of fire water to the Indians. The Abbé was zealous in stopping those abuses, and the officers complained bitterly of his over protection of the Indians.

The famous "Kings Missionary" as he was called, stood up with an air of dignity and authority that seemed to assert his right to be present in the Council of war, for the scornful looks of many of the officers had not escaped his quick glance.

The keen black eye, thin resolute lips, and high swarthy forehead of the Abbé, would have well become the plumed hat of a Marshal of France. His loose black robe looped up for freedom, reminded one of a grave Senator of Venice whose eye never quailed at any policy however severe, if required for the safety of the state.

The Abbé held in his hand a large roll of wampum, the tokens of treaties made by him with the Indian nations of the West, pledging their alliance and aid to the Great Onontio, as they called the Governor of New France.

"My Lord Governor!" said the Abbé, placing his great roll on the table, "I thank you for admitting the missionaries to the Council. We appear less as churchmen on this occasion than as the King's ambassadors, although I trust that all we have done will redound to Gods glory, and the spread of religion among the heathen. These belts of wampum are tokens of the treaties we have made with the numerous and warlike tribes of the Great West. I bear to the Governor pledges of alliance from the Miamis and Shawnese of the great valley of the Belle Riviere, which they call the Ohio. I am commissioned to tell Onontio, that they are at peace with the King and at war with his enemies from this time forth for ever. I have set up the arms of France on the banks of the Belle Riviere, and claimed all its lands and waters as the just appanage of our sovereign from the Alleghanies to the plantations of Louisiana. The Sacs and Foxes, of the Mississippi, the Pottawatomies Winnebagoes and Chippewas of a hundred bands who fish in the great rivers and lakes of the west, the warlike Ottawas who have carried the Algonquin tongue to the banks of Lake Erie, In short every enemy of the Iroquois have pledged themselves to take the field whenever the Governor shall require the axe to be dug up and lifted against the English and the Five Nations. Next summer the chiefs of all these tribes will come to Quebec and ratify in a solemn general council the wampums they now send by me and the other missionaries, my brothers in the Lord—!"

The Abbé with the slow formal manner of one long accustomed to the speech and usages of the Indians unrolled the belts of wampum many fathoms in length fastened end to end to indicate the length of the alliance of the various tribes with France. The Abbé interpreted their meaning, and with his finger pointed out the totems or signs manual, usually a bird beast or fish, of the chiefs who had signed the roll.

The Council looked at the wampums with intense interest, well knowing the important part these Indians were capable of assuming in the war with England.

"These are great and welcome pledges you bring us Abbé," said the Governor. "They are proofs at once of your ability and of your zealous labours for the King. A great public duty has been ably discharged, by you and your fellow missionaries, whose loyalty and devotion to France it shall be my pleasure to lay before his Majesty. The star of hope glitters on the Western horizon, to encourage us under the clouds of the Eastern. Even the loss of Acadia, should it be final, will be compensated by the acquisition of the boundless fertile territories of the Belle Riviere, and of the Illinois. The Abbé Piquet and his fellow missionaries have won the hearts of the native tribes of the West. There is hope now at last of uniting New France with Louisiana in one unbroken chain of French territory."

"It has been my ambition since His Majesty honoured me with the Government of New France to acquire possession of those vast territories covered with forests old as time and in soil rich and fertile as Provence and Normandy."

"I have served the King all my life," continued the Governor "served him with honour and even distinction— permit me to say thus much of myself."

He spoke in a frank manly way, for vanity prompted no part of his speech. "Many great services have I rendered my Country, but I feel that the greatest service I could yet do old France or New, would be the planting of ten thousand sturdy peasants and artizans of France in the valley of the far West to make its forests vocal with the speech of our native land."

"This present war may suddenly end—! I think it will. The late victory at Lawfelt has stricken the allies under the Duke of Cumberland a blow, hard as Fontenoy. Rumours of renewed negociations for peace, are flying thick through Europe. God speed the peace makers and bless them, I say! With peace comes opportunity. Then if ever, if France be true to herself and to her heritage in the New World, she will people the valley of the Ohio and secure for ever her supremacy in America."

"But our forts far and near must be preserved in the meantime. We must not withdraw from one foot of French territory. Quebec must be walled and made safe against all attack by land or water—! I therefore will join the Council in a respectful remonstrance to the Count de Maurepas, against the inopportune despatches just received from His Majesty. I trust the Royal Intendant will favour the Council now with his opinion on this important matter, and I shall be happy to have the cooperation of his Excellency in measures of such vital consequence to the Colony and to France."

The Governor sat down after courteously motioning to the Intendant to rise and address the Council.

The Intendant hated the mention of peace. His interests and the interests of his associates of the Grand Company were all in the prolongation of the war.

War enabled the Grand Company to monopolize the trade and military expenditure of New France. The enormous fortunes its members made and spent with such reckless prodigality would by peace be dried up in their source. The yoke would be thrown off the people's neck. Trade would be again free. Bigot was far sighted enough to see that clamours would be raised and listened to in the leisure of peace. Prosecutions for illegal exactions might follow, and all the support of his friends at Court might not be able to save him and his associates from ruin, perhaps punishment.

The Parliaments of Paris Rouen and Britany still retained a shadow of independance. It was only a shadow, but the fury of Jansenism supplied the lack of political courage, and men opposed the court and its policy under pretence of defending the rights of the Gallican Church and the old religion of the nation.

Bigot knew he was safe so long as the Marquise de Pompadour governed the King and the Kingdom. But Louis XV was capricious and unfaithful in his fancies. He had changed his mistresses and his policy with them many times, and might change once more to the ruin of Bigot, and all the dependants of La Pompadour.

Bigot's letters by the Fleur de Lys were calculated to alarm him. A rival was springing up at Court, to challenge La Pompadour's supremacy. The fair and fragile Lange Vaubernier had already attracted the King's eye and the Courtiers versed in his ways, read the incipient signs of a future favorite.

Little did the laughing Vaubernier foresee the day, when as Madame du Barri she would reign as *Dame du Palais*, after the death of La Pompadour. Still less could she imagine, that in her old age in the next reign, she would be dragged to the guillotine, filling the streets of Paris with her shrieks heard above the howlings of the mob of the revolution—: "Give me life!—Life! for my repentance!—Life! to devote it to the republic. Life! for the surrender of all my wealth to the nation!—"—and death, not life, was given in answer to her passionate pleadings.

These dark days were yet in the womb of the future, however. The giddy Vaubernier was at this time gaily catching at the heart of the King. But her procedure filled the mind of Bigot with anxiety. The fall of La Pompadour would entail swift ruin upon himself and associates. He knew that it was the intrigues of this girl which caused La Pompadour suddenly to declare for peace in order to watch the King more surely in his palace. Still the word peace and the name of Vaubernier, were equally odious to Bigot and he was perplexed in no small degree how to act.

Moreover be it confessed that although a bad man and corrupt statesman, Bigot was a Frenchman proud of the national success and glory. While robbing her treasures with one hand, the other was ever ready with his sword to risk life and all in her defence. Bigot was bitterly opposed to English supremacy in North America. The loss of Louisbourg though much his fault, stung him to the quick, as a triumph of the national enemy, and in those last days of New France, after the fall of Montcalm, Bigot was the last man to yield, when all others counselled retreat and he would not consent to the surrender of Quebec to the English.

To day in the Council of War, Bigot stood up to respond to the appeal of the Governor. He glanced his eyes coolly yet respectfully over the Council. His raised hand sparkled with gems the gifts of Courtiers and favorites of the King. "Gentlemen of the Council of war!" said he, "I approve with all my heart of the words of His Excellency the Governor with reference to our fortifications and the maintainance of our Frontiers. It is our duty to remonstrate as councillors of the King in the Colony, against the tenor of the despatches of the Count de Maurepas. The city of Quebec properly fortified will be equivalent to an army of men in the field, and the security and defence of the whole Colony depend on its walls. There can be but one intelligent opinion in the Council on that point, and that opinion should be laid before His Majesty before this despatch be acted on."

"The pressure of the war is great upon us just now. The loss of the fleet of the Marquis de Jonquiere, has much interrupted our communications with France, and Canada is left much to its own resources. But Frenchmen! The greater our peril, the greater the glory of our defence—! And I feel a lively confidence." Bigot glanced proudly round the table at the brave animated faces that turned towards him. "I feel a lively confidence that in the skill, devotion and gallantry of the officers I see around this Council table we shall be able to repel all our enemies and bear the royal flag to fresh triumphs in North America."

This timely flattery was not lost upon the susceptible minds of the officers present, who testified their approval by vigorous tapping upon the table and cries of, "Well said! Chevalier Intendant!"

"I thank heartily the venerable Abbé Piquet" continued he, "for his glorious success in converting the warlike savages of the West, from foes to fast friends of the King, and as Royal Intendant, I pledge the Abbé all my help in the establishment of his proposed Fort and Mission at La Presentation, for the purpose of dividing the power of the Iroquois."

"That is right well said, if the Devil said it," remarked La Corne St Luc, to the Acadian sitting next him. "There is bell metal in Bigot, and he rings well, if properly struck. Pity so clever a fellow should be a knave!—"—

"Fine words butter no parsnips, Chevalier La Corne!" replied the Acadian, whom no eloquence could soften. "Bigot sold Louisbourg." This was a common but erroneous opinion in Acadia.

"Bigot butters his own parsnips well! Colonel," replied La Corne St Luc. "But I did not think he would have gone against the despatches! It is the first time he ever opposed Versailles! There must be something in the wind!—a screw loose somewhere, another woman in the case!—But hark he is going on again!—"

The Intendant after examining some papers entered into a detail of the resources of the Colony, the number of men capable of bearing arms, the munitions and material of war in the Magazins, and relative strength of each district of the Province. He manipulated his figures with the dexterity of an Indian juggler throwing balls, and at the end brought out a totality of force in the Colony capable unaided of prolonging the war for two years against all the powers of the English.

At the conclusion of his speech Bigot took his seat. He had made a favorable impression upon the Council, and even his most strenuous opponents admitted that on the whole the Intendant had spoken like an able administrator and a true Frenchman.

Cadet and Varin supported their chief warmly. Bad as they were, both in private life and public conduct, they lacked neither shrewdness nor courage. They plundered their country, but were ready to fight for it against the national enemy.

Other officers followed in succession—men whose names were already familiar, or destined to become glorious in New France, La Corne St Luc, Celeron de Bienville, Colonel Philibert, the Chevalier de Beaujeu, the De Villiers, Le Gardeur de St Pierre and De Lery. One and all supported that view of the despatches taken by the Governor and the Intendant. All agreed upon the necessity of completing the walls of Quebec, and of making a determined stand at every point of the Frontier against the threatened invasion. In case of the sudden patching up of a peace by the negociators at Aix La Chapelle, as really happened, on the terms of *uti possidetis*, it was of vital importance that New France held fast to every shred of her territory both East and West.

Long and earnest were the deliberations of the Council of War. The reports of the commanding officers from all points of the frontier were carefully studied. Plans of present defence and future conquest were discussed with reference to the strength and weakness of the Colony, and an accurate knowledge of the forces and designs of the English, obtained from the disaffected remnant of Cromwellian Republicans in New England, whose hatred to the Crown ever outweighed their loyalty, and who kept up a traitorous correspondance for purposes of their own, with the Governors of New France.

The lamps were lit and burned far into the night when the Council broke up. The most part of the officers partook of a cheerful refreshment with the Governor before they retired to their several quarters. Only Bigot and his friends declined to sup with the Governor.—They took a polite leave, and rode away from the Chateau, to the Palais of the Intendant where a more gorgeous repast and more congenial company awaited them.

The wine flowed freely, at the Intendants table, and as the irritating events of the day were recalled to memory, the pent up wrath of the Intendant broke forth. "Damn the Golden Dog! and his master both!" exclaimed he. "Philibert shall pay with his life for the outrage of to day, or I will lose mine! The dirt is not off my coat yet, Cadet!" said he as he pointed to a spatter of mud upon his breast. "A pretty medal that for the Intendant to wear in a Council of war!—"—

"Council of war!" replied Cadet, setting his goblet down with a bang upon the polished table, after draining it to the bottom. "I would as lief go through that mob again! I would pull an oar in the galleys of Marseilles, rather than be questioned with that air of authority, by a botanizing Quack like La Galissoniere! Such villainous questions as he asked me, about the state of the royal magazines! La Galissoniere had more the air of a judge cross-examining a culprit, than of a governor asking information of a Kings officer—!"

"True Cadet!" replied Varin, who was always a flatterer and who at last saved his illgotten wealth by the surrender of his wife as a love gift to the Duc de Choiseul. "We all have our own injuries, to bear. The Intendant was just showing us the spot of dirt cast upon him by the mob. And I ask what satisfaction he has got in the Council for the insult?"

"Get Satisfaction!" replied Cadet with a laugh!—"Let him take it. Satisfaction! We will all help him!—But I say that the hair of the dog that bit him will alone cure the bite! What I laughed at the most, was, this morning at Beaumanoir to see how coolly that whelp of the Golden Dog young Philibert, walked off with De Repentigny from the very midst of all the Grand Company!—"

"We shall lose our young neophyte, I doubt Cadet! I was a fool to let him go with Philibert—!" remarked Bigot.

"O, I am not afraid of losing him. We hold him by a strong triple cord, spun by the Devil. No fear of losing him!—" answered Cadet grinning good humouredly.

"What do you mean, Cadet?" The Intendant took up his cup and drank very nonchalantly as if he thought little of Cadets view of the matter. "What triple cord holds de Repentigny to us?"

"His love of wine, his love of gaming and his love of women! or rather his love of a woman, which is the strongest strand in the string for a young fool, like him, who is always chasing virtue and hugging vice—!"

"O! A woman has got him! eh Cadet? pray who is she—? When once a woman catches a fellow by the gills, he is a dead mackerel. His fate is fixed for good or ill, in this world, but who is she, Cadet? she must be a clever one!" said Bigot, sententiously!

"So she is! and she is too clever for young De Repentigny! She has got *her* pretty fingers in his gills and can carry her fish to whatever market she chooses!"

"Cadet! Cadet! out with it!—" repeated a dozen voices. "Yes, out with it!" repeated Bigot, "we are all companions under the rose and there are no secrets here about wine or women—!"

"Well I would not give a filbert for all the women born since Mother Eve," said Cadet flinging a nut shell at the ceiling. "But this is a rare one, I must confess. Now stop! dont cry out again, Cadet! out with it!—and I will tell you—! What think you of the fair jolly Mademoiselle des Meloises—?"

"Angelique?—Is De Repentigny in love with her?" Bigot looked quite interested now.

"In love with her? He would go on all fours after her, if she wanted him—! He does almost, as it is."—

Bigot placed a finger on his brow and pondered for a moment. "You say well Cadet. If De Repentigny has fallen in love with that girl, he is ours for ever! Angelique des Meloises never lets go her ox until she offers him up as a burnt offering!! The *Honnetes Gens* will lose one of the best trouts in their stream, if Angelique has the tickling of him!"

Bigot did not seem to be quite pleased with Cadets information. He rose from his seat somewhat flushed and excited by this talk respecting Angelique des Meloises. He walked up and down the room a few turns, recovered his composure, and sat down again.

"Come gentlemen!" said he. "Too much care will kill a cat! let us change our talk to a merrier tune—fill up and we will drink to the loves of De Repentigny and the fair Angelique! I am much mistaken if we do not find in her the *Dea ex machina*, to help us out of our trouble with the *honnetes gens*."—

The glasses were filled and emptied. Cards and dice were then called for. The Company drew their chairs into a closer circle round the table. Deep play and deeper drinking set in. The Palais resounded with revelry until the morning sun looked into the great window blushing red at the scene, of drunken riot, that had become habitual in the Palace of the Intendant.

CHAPTER 15

THE CHARMING JOSEPHINE

The few words of sympathy dropped by Bigot in the secret chamber had fallen like manna on the famine of Caroline's starving affections. She remained on the sofa where she had half fallen, pressing her bosom with her hands as if a newborn thought lay there—! "I am sure he meant it!" repeated she to herself. "I feel that his words were true, and for the moment his look and tone were those of my happy maiden days in Acadia! I was too proud then of my fancied power, and thought Bigots love deserved the surrender of my very conscience to his keeping. I forgot God in my love for him, and alas, for me—! that now is part of my punishment! I feel not the sin of loving him. My penitence is not sincere when I can still rejoice in his smile! Wo is me—! Bigot! Bigot! unworthy as thou art, I cannot forsake thee! I would willingly die at thy feet. Spurn me not away, nor give to another the love that belongs to me and for which I have paid the price of my immortal soul—!"

She relapsed into a train of bitter reflections as her thoughts reverted to herself. Silence had been gradually creeping through the house. The noisy debauch was at an end. There were trampings, voices and footfalls for a while longer, and then they died away, and the whole was still and silent as the grave. She knew the feast was over and the guests departed, but not whether Bigot had accompanied them.

She sprang up as a low knock came to her door, thinking it was he come to bid her, adieu. It was with a feeling of disappointment she heard the voice of Dame Tremblay saying "My Lady, may I enter?"

Caroline ran her fingers through her disordered hair, pressed her handkerchief into her eyes and hastily tried to obliterate every trace of her recent agony. She bade her enter.

Dame Tremblay, shrewd as became the whilome Charming Josephine of Lake Beauport, had a kind heart nevertheless under her old fashioned boddice. She sincerely pitied this young creature who was passing her days in prayers and her nights in weeping, although she might rather blame her in secret for not appreciating better the honour of a residence at Beaumanoir and the friendship of the Intendant.

"I do not think she is prettier than I, when I was the charming Josephine!—" thought the old Dame. "I did not despise Beaumanoir, in those days, and why should she now? But she will be neither maid nor mistress here long I am thinking—!" The Dame saluted the young lady with great deference and quietly asked if she needed her service.

"O, it is you good Dame!" Caroline answered her own thoughts rather than the question. "Tell me what makes this unusual silence in the Chateau?"

"The Intendant and all the guests have gone to the city, My Lady. A great officer of the Governor came to summon them. To be sure, not many of them were fit to go, but after a deal of bathing and dressing the gentlemen got off! Such a clatter of horsemen as they rode out, I never heard before my Lady. You must have heard them even here!"

"Yes Dame!—" replied Caroline, "I heard it. And the Intendant, has he accompanied them?"

"Yes my Lady, the freshest and formost cavalier of them all. Wine and late hours never hurt the Intendant. It is for that I praise him, for he is a gallant gentleman who knows what politeness is to men and women—."

Caroline shrank a little at the thought expressed by the Dame. "What causes you to say that—?" asked she.

"I will tell my Lady—! 'Dame Tremblay!' said he just before he left the Chateau, 'Dame Tremblay' He always calls me that when he is formal but sometimes when he is merry, he calles me 'Charming Josephine' in remembrance of my young days, concerning which he has heard flattering stories I dare say."—

"In Heaven's name! Go on Dame!" Caroline depressed as she was, felt the Dame's garrulity like a pinch on her impatience. "What said the Intendant to you on leaving the Chateau?"

"O, he spoke to me quite feelingly—of you that is—bade me take the utmost care of the poor lady in the secret chamber. I was to give you everything you wished, and keep off all visitors if such was your own desire."—

A train of powder does not catch fire from a spark more quickly than Caroline's imagination from these few words of the old housekeeper. "Did he say that, good Dame? God bless you and bless him for those words!" Her eyes filled with tears at the thought of his tenderness which although half fictitious, she wholly believed.

"Yes Dame!" replied she. "It is my most earnest desire to be secluded from all visitors. I wish to see no one but yourself. Have you many visitors, ladies, I mean at the Chateau?"

"O yes. The ladies of the City are not likely to forget the invitations to the balls and dinners of the bachelor Intendant of New France. It is the most fashionable thing in the City and every body is wild to attend them. There is one, the handsomest and gayest of them all, who they say, would not object even to become the bride of the Intendant."

It was a careless shaft of the old Dame's but it went to the heart of Caroline. "Who is she good Dame? pray tell me—!"—

"O my Lady I should fear her anger if she knew what I say. She is the most terrible coquette in the city—worshipped by the men and hated of course by the women, who all imitate her in dress and style as much as they possibly can because they see it takes—! But every woman fears for either husband or lover when Angelique des Meloises, is her rival."

"Is that her name. I never heard it before Dame," remarked Caroline with a shudder. She felt instinctively that the name was one of direful omen to herself.

"Pray God, you may never have reason to hear it again," replied Dame Tremblay "She it was who went to the mansion of the Sieur Tourangeau and with her riding whip lashed the mark of a red cross upon the forehead of his daughter Cecile, scarring her forever, because she had presumed to smile kindly on a young officer, a handsome fellow; Le Gardeur de Repentigny, whom any woman might be pardoned for admiring!" added the old Dame, with a natural touch of the candour of her youth. "If Angelique takes a fancy to the Intendant it will be dangerous for any other woman to stand in her way—."

Caroline gave a frightened look at the Dame's description of a possible rival in the Intendants love. "You know more of her Dame! Tell me all! Tell me the worst I have to learn," pleaded the poor girl.

"The worst my lady? I fear no one can tell the worst of Angelique des Meloises—at least would not dare to—although I know nothing very bad of her, except that she would like to have all the men to herself, and so spite all the women!"

"But she must regard that young officer with more than common affection, to have acted so savagely to Mademoiselle Tourangeau?"—Caroline with a woman's quickness had caught at that gleam of hope through the darkness.

"O yes, my Lady. All Quebec knows that Angelique loves the Seigneur de Repentigny, for nothing is a secret in Quebec if more than one person knows it, as I myself well recollect, for, when I was the Charming Josephine, my very whispers were all over Quebec by the next dinner hour, and repeated at every table, as gentlemen cracked their almonds and drank their wine in toasts to the Charming Josephine."

"Pshaw! Dame! Tell me about the Seigneur de Repentigny! Does Angelique des Meloises love him think you—?" Caroline's eyes were fixed like stars upon the Dame awaiting her reply.

"It takes women to read women they say," replied the Dame, "and every lady in Quebec would swear that Angelique loves the Seigneur de Repentigny, but I know that, if she can, she will marry the Intendant, whom she has fairly bewitched with her wit and beauty! and you know a clever woman can marry any man she pleases if she only goes the right way about it! Men are such fools."

Caroline grew faint. Cold drops gathered on her icy brow. A veil of mist floated before her eyes.—"Water! Good Dame! water!" she articulated after several efforts.

Dame Tremblay, ran and got her a drink of water and such restoratives as were at hand. The Dame was profuse in words of sympathy. She had gone through life with a light lively spirit as became the charming Josephine, but never lost the kindly heart that was natural to her.

Caroline rallied from her faintness. "Have you seen what you tell me Dame? or is it but the idle gossip of the City. No truth in it?—O, say it is the idle gossip of the City—! Francois Bigot is not going to marry this lady. He is not so faithless—to me," she was about to add but did not.

"So faithless—to her, she means! Poor Soul!" soliloquized the Dame. "It is but little you know my gay master, if you think he values a promise made to any woman except to deceive her! I have seen too many birds of that feather not to know a hawk, from beak to claw. When I was the Charming Josephine, I took the measure of men's professions, and never was deceived but once. Their promises are big as clouds and as empty and as unstable—!"

"My good Dame, I am sure you have a kind heart!" said Caroline in reply to a sympathizing pressure of the hand. "But you do not know, you cannot imagine, what injustice you do the Intendant!" Caroline hesitated and blushed, "by mentioning the report of his marriage with—that Lady—men speak untruly of him—!"

"My dear Lady. It is what the women say, that frightens one. The men are angry and wont believe it. The women are jealous and will believe it even if there be nothing in it—! As a faithful servant I ought to have no eyes to watch my master, but I have not failed to observe that the Chevalier Bigot is caught—man fashion, if not husband fashion—in the snares of the artful Angelique. But may I speak my real opinions to you my Lady?"

Caroline was eagerly watching the lips of the garrulous Dame. She started, brushed back with a stroke of her hand, the thick hair that had fallen over her ear. "O, speak all your thoughts, good Dame! If your next words were to kill me,— speak them!—"—

"My next words will not harm you my Lady!" said she

with a meaning smile. "If you will accept the opinion of an old woman, who learned the ways of men when she was the Charming Josephine—!—You must not conclude that because the Chevalier Intendant admires or even loves Angelique des Meloises, he is going to marry her. That is not the fashion of these times. Men love beauty and marry money. Love is more plenty than matrimony both at Paris and at Quebec, at Versailles as well as at Beaumanoir, or even at Lake Beauport, as I learned to my cost when I was the Charming Josephine—!"

Caroline blushed crimson, at the remark of Dame Tremblay. Her voice quivered with emotion. "It is sin to cheapen love like that, Dame!—and yet I know we have sometimes to bury our love in our heart with no hope of resurrection."—

"Sometimes? Almost always, my Lady! When I was the Charming Josephine—nay listen lady my story is instructive." Caroline composed herself to hear the Dame's recital. "When I was the Charming Josephine of Lake Beauport, I began by believing that men were angels sent for the salvation of women. I thought that love was a better passport than money to lead to matrimony. But I was a fool for my fancy! I had a good score of lovers any day. The gallants praised my beauty, and it was the envy of the city. They flattered me for my wit, nay even fought duels for my favour, and called me the Charming Josephine, but not one offered to marry me—! At twenty I ran away for love, and was forsaken. At thirty I married for money and was rid of all my illusions. At forty I came as Housekeeper to Beaumanoir and have lived here comfortably ever since. I know what Royal Intendants are—! Old Hocquart wore nightcaps in the day time, took snuff, every minute and jilted a lady in France, because she had not the dower of a Duchesse, to match his hoards of wealth—!—The Chevalier Bigots black eye and jolly laugh draw after him all the girls of the city, but not one will catch him! Angelique des Meloises is first in his favour. But I see it as clear as print, in the eye of the Intendant, that he will never marry her, and you will prevent him my Lady!—"—

"I! I! prevent him?" exclaimed Caroline in amaze. "Alas! good Dame, you little know how lighter than thistle down floating on the wind is my influence with the Intendant."—

"You do yourself injustice my Lady. Listen—I never saw a more pitying glance fall from the eye of man than the Intendant cast upon you one day when he saw you kneeling in your oratory unconscious of his presence. His lips quivered and a tear gathered under his thick eye lashes. As he silently withdrew, I heard him mutter a blessing upon you, and curses upon La Pompadour for coming between him and his hearts desire! I am a faithful servant and kept my counsel. I could see however that the Intendant thought more of the lovely Lady of Beaumanoir than of all the ambitious demoiselles of Quebec."

Caroline sprang up, and casting off the deep reserve she had maintained, threw her arms round the neck of Dame Tremblay, and half choked with her emotion, exclaimed:

"Is that true? Good dear friend of friends! Did the Chevalier Bigot bless me and curse La Pompadour for coming between him and his heart's desire? His heart's desire? but you do not know, you cannot guess what that means, Dame!—"

"If I do not know a man's hearts desire, I am a woman and can guess—! I was not the Charming Josephine for nothing good Lady—!" replied the Dame smiling as the enraptured girl laid her fair smooth cheek upon that of the old Housekeeper.

"And did he look so pityingly as you describe? and bless me as I was praying unwitting of his presence?" repeated she with a look that searched the Dame, through and through.

"He did my Lady. He looked just then, as a man looks upon a woman whom he really loves. I know how men look when they really love us, and when they only pretend to! No deceiving me!" added she. "When I was the charming Josephine— —"

"*Ave Marie!*" said Caroline crossing herself with deep devotion, not heeding the Dames reminiscences of Lake Beauport. "Heaven has heard my prayers. I can die happy!—"

"Heaven forbid, you should die at all my Lady! you die?

The Intendant loves you. I see it in his face that he will never marry Angelique des Meloises. He may indeed marry a great Marchionesse with her lap full of gold and chateaux, that is if the King commands him. That is how the grand gentlemen of the Court marry. They wed rank and love beauty. The heart to one the hand to another. It would be my way too were I a man and women so simple as we all are. If a girl cannot marry for love, she will marry for money, and if not for money she can always marry for spite.—I did when I was the Charming Josephine."

"It is a shocking and a sinful way to marry without love!" said Caroline warmly.

"It is better than no way at all!" replied the Dame, regretting her remark when she saw her lady's face flush like crimson. The Dames opinions were rather the worse for wear in her long journey through life, and would not be adopted by a jury of prudes. "When I was the Charming Josephine" continued she "I had the love of half the gallants of Quebec, but not one offered his hand. What was I to do? Crook a finger or love and linger; as they say in Alencon, where I was born?"

"Fie Dame! Dont say such things!" said Caroline with a shamed reproving look. "I would think better of the Intendant!"—Her gratitude led her to imagine excuses for him. The few words reported to her by Dame Tremblay she repeated with silently moving lips and tender reiteration. They lingered in her ear like the fugue of a strain of music sung by a choir of angelic spirits. "Those were his very words Dame?" asked she again, repeating them, not for inquiry but for secret joy.

"His very words my Lady! But why should the Royal Intendant not have his hearts desire, as well as that great Lady in France. If any one had forbidden my marrying the poor Sieur Tremblay, for whom I did not care two pins, I would have had him for spite—yes if I had to marry him as the crows do, on a tree top!—"

"But no one bade you or forbade you Dame! You were happy, that no one came between you and your hearts desire!—" replied Caroline.

Dame Tremblay laughed out merrily at the idea. "Poor Giles Tremblay *my* hearts desire!—Listen Lady, I could no more get that than you could. When I was the charming Josephine there was but one out of all my admirers, whom I really cared for—and he poor fellow had a wife already—! So what was I to do—! I threw my line at last in utter dispair, and out of the troubled sea I drew the Sieur Tremblay, whom I married and soon put cosily under ground with a heavy tomb-stone on top of him to keep him down, with this inscription, which you may see for yourself my lady, if you will in the church yard at Beauport,

"Ci git mon Giles,
Ah! qu'il est bien,
Pour son repos,
Et pour le mien!—"—

"Men are like my Angola tabby. Stroke them smoothly they will purr and rub noses with you, but stroke them the wrong way, and whirr! They scratch your hands and out of the window they fly!—When I was the Charming — —"

"O, good Dame, thanks! thanks! for the comfort you have given me!" interrupted Caroline, not caring for a fresh reminiscence of the Charming Josephine. "Leave me, I pray. My mind is in a sad tumult. I would fain rest. I have much to fear, but something also to hope for, now," she said leaning back in her chair, as if in deep and quiet thought.

"The Chateau is very still now, my Lady," replied the Dame. "The servants are all worn out with long attendance and are asleep. Let my Lady go to her own appartments, where it is bright and airy. It will be better for her than this secret chamber."

"True Dame!" Caroline rose at the suggestion. "I like not this secret chamber. It suited my sad mood, but now I seem to long for air and sunshine. I will go with you to my own room."

They ascended the winding stair, and Caroline seated herself by the window of her own chamber, overlooking, the park and gardens of the Chateau. The huge sloping forests upon the mountain side, formed in the distance with the blue sky above it, a landscape of beauty upon which her eyes lingered with a sense of freshness and delight.

Dame Tremblay, left her to her musings to go she said, to rouse up the lazy maids and menservants to straighten up the confusion of every thing in the Chateau, after the late long feast.

On the great stair she encountered Mons Froumois the Intendants Valet, a favorite gossip of the Dames who used to invite him into her snug parlour where she regaled him with tea and cake, or if late in the evening with, wine and nipperkins of Cognac, while he poured into her ear stories of the gay life of Paris, and the *bonnes fortunes* of himself and master. For the Valet in plush would have disdained being less successful among the maids in the servants hall, than his master in velvet in the boudoirs of their mistresses.

Mons Froumois accepted the Dame's invitation, and the two were presently engaged in a melée of gossip over the sayings and doings of fashionable society in Quebec.

The Dame holding between her thumb and finger a little China cup of tea, well laced, she called it, with Cognac, remarked—:"They fairly run the Intendant down, Froumois! There is not a girl in the city but laces her boots to distraction since it came out that the Intendant admires a neat trim ankle. I had a trim ankle myself when I was the Charming Josephine, Mons Froumois!"

"And you have yet Dame—If I am a judge," replied Froumois, glancing down with an air of gallantry.

"And you are accounted a judge, and ought to be a good one Froumois!—A gentleman cant live at court as you have done and learn nothing of the points of a fine woman." The good Dame liked a compliment as well as ever she had done at Lake Beauport in her hey day of youth and beauty.

"Why no, Dame," replied he, "one cant live at Court and learn nothing! We study the points of fine women as we do fine statuary in the gallery of the Louvre. Only the living beauties will compel us to see their good points, if they have them." Mons Froumois looked very critical, as he took a pinch from the Dames box, which she held out to him. Her hand and wrist were yet unexceptionable, as he could not help remarking.

"But what think you really, of our Quebec beauties? Are they not a good imitation of Versailles?" asked the Dame.

"Good imitation! They are the real porcelain! For beauty and affability, Versailles cannot exceed them. So says the Intendant and so say I," replied the gay Valet.

"Why look you Dame Tremblay!" continued he extending his well ringed fingers. "They do give gentlemen no end of hopes here! we have only to stretch out our ten digits and a lady bird will light on every one of them. It was so at Versailles, it is just so here. The ladies in Quebec do know how to appreciate a real Gentleman!—"—

"Yes. That is what makes the ladies of Ville Marie so jealous and angry" replied the Dame, "the Kings officers and all the great catches, land at Quebec first, when they come out from France, and we take toll of them—! We dont let a gentleman of them get up to Ville Marie without a Quebec engagement tacked to his back, so that all Ville Marie can read it and die of pure spite!—I say we, Froumois! but you understand I speak of myself only as the Charming Josephine of Lake Beauport. I must content myself now with talking over past glories."—

"Well Dame I dont know. But you are glorious yet! But tell me, what got over my master to day? was the unknown lady unkind? Something angered him I am sure!—"

"I cannot tell you Froumois! women's moods are not to be explained even by themselves." The Dame had been sensibly touched by Carolines confidence in her and she was too loyal to her sex to repeat even to Froumois her recent conversation with Caroline. They found plenty of other topics however, and over the tea and cogniac, the Dame and Valet passed an hour of delightful gossip.

Caroline left to the solitude of her chamber sat silently with her hands clasped on her lap. Her thoughts pressed inwards upon her. She looked at without seeing the fair landscape before her eyes.

Tears and sorrow she had welcomed in a spirit of bitter penitence for her fault in loving one who no longer regarded her. "I do not deserve any man's regard," murmured she as she laid her soul on the rack of self-accusation and wrung its tenderest fibres with the pitiless rigour of a secret Inquisitor. She utterly condemned herself, while still trying to find some excuse for her unworthy lover. At times a cold half persuasion fluttering like a bird in the snow, came over her that, Bigot could not be utterly base. He could not thus forsake one who had lost all—name, fame, home and kindred for his sake! She clung to the few pitying words spoken by him as a ship wrecked sailor to the plank which chance has thrown in his way. It might float her for a few hours, and she was grateful.

Immersed in these reflections Caroline sat gazing at the clouds, now transformed into royal robes of crimson and gold, the gorgeous train of the sun that filled the Western horizon. She raised her pale hands to her head lifting the mass of dark hair from her temples. The fevered blood madly coursing, pulsed in her ear like the stroke of a bell. She remembered a sunset like this on the shores of the Bay of Minas, where the thrush and oriole twittered their even-song before seeking their nests, where the foliage of the trees was all ablaze with golden fire, and a shimmering path of sunlight lay upon the still waters like a glorious bridge leading from themselves to the bright beyond.

On that well remembered night, her heart had yielded to Bigots pleadings. She had leaned her head upon his bosom and received the kiss and gave the pledge that bound her to him for ever.

The sun kept sinking. The forests on the mountain tops burst into a bonfire of glory. Shadows went creeping up the hill sides until the highest crest alone flamed out a beacon of hope to her troubled soul.

Suddenly like a voice from the spirit world the faint chime of the bells of Charlebourg floated on the evening breeze. It was the Angelus, calling men to prayer, and rest from their daily labour. Sweetly the soft reverberation floated through the forests, up the hill sides, by plain and river, entering the open lattices of Chateau and Cottage summoning rich and poor alike to their duty of prayer and praise. It reminded men of the redemption of the world by the divine miracle of the incarnation, announced by Gabriel the Angel of God, to the ear of Mary blessed among women.

The soft bells rang on. Men blessed them and ceased from their toils in field and forest. Mothers knelt by the cradle and uttered the sacred words with emotions such as only mothers feel. Children knelt by their mothers and learned the story of Gods pity in appearing upon earth as a little child, to save mankind from their sins. The dark Huron setting his snares in the forest and the fisher on the shady stream stood still. The voyageur sweeping his canoe over the broad river suspended the oar as the solemn sounds reached him and he repeated the angel's words and went on his way, with renewed strength.

The sweet bells came like a voice of pity and consolation to the ear of Caroline. She knelt down and clasping her hands repeated the prayer of millions—

"Ave Maria gratia plena."

She continued kneeling offering up prayer after prayer for Gods forgiveness both for herself and for him who had brought her to this pass of sin and misery. "*Mea culpa! Mea maxima culpa!*" repeated she, bowing herself to the ground. "I am the chief of Sinners; who shall deliver me from this body of sin and affliction?"—

The sweet bells kept ringing. They woke reminiscences of voices of bygone days. She heard her Father's tones, not in anger as he would speak now, but kind and loving as in her days of innocence. She heard her mother long dead. O how happily dead for she could not die of sorrow now, over her dear childs fall. She heard the voices of the fair companions of her youth, who would think shame of her now, and amidst them all the tones of the persuasive tongue that wooed her maiden love. How changed it all seemed! Yet as the repetition of two or three notes of a bar of music brings to recollection the whole air and harmony to which it belongs, the few kind words of Bigot spoken that morning swept all before them in a drift of hope, like a star struggling in the mist. The faint voices of angels were heard afar off in the darkness.

The ringing of the Angelus went on. Her heart was utterly

melted. Her eyes long parched as a spent fountain in the burning desert were suddenly filled with tears. She felt no longer the agony of the eyes that cannot weep. The blessed tears flowed quietly as the waters of Shiloh, bringing relief, to her poor soul famishing for one true word of affection. Long after the sweet bells ceased their chime, Caroline kept on praying, for him, and long after the shades of night had fallen over the Chateau of Beaumanoir.

CHAPTER 16

ANGELIQUE DES MELOISES

"COME and see me to night Le Gardeur!—" Angelique des Meloises drew the bridle sharply, as she halted her spirited horse in front of the officer of the Guard, at the St Louis Gate. "Come and see me to night, and I shall be at home to no one but you. Will you come?" Had Le Gardeur de Repentigny been ever so laggard and indifferent a lover, the touch of that pretty hand and the glance from the dark eye that shot fire down into his very heart would have decided him, to obey this seductive invitation.

He held her hand as he looked up with a face radiant with joy. "I will surely come Angelique. But tell me— —" She interrupted him laughingly.

"No, I will tell you nothing until you come. So goodby till then!"—He would fain have prolonged the interview, but she capriciously shook the reins and with a silvery laugh rode through the Gate way and into the city.—In a few minutes she dismounted at her own home, and giving her horse in charge of a groom ran lightly up the broad steps into the house.

The family mansion of the Des Meloises was a tall and rather pretentious edifice overlooking the fashionable Rue St Louis, where it still stands, old and melancholy now as if mourning over its departed splendours. Few eyes look up nowadays to its broad facade. It was otherwise when the beautiful Angelique des Meloises sat of summer evenings on the balcony, surrounded by a bevy of Quebec's fairest daughters who loved to haunt her windows, where they could see and be seen to the best advantage, exchanging salutations smiles and repartees with the gay young officers and gallants who rode or walked along the lively thoroughfare.

The house was by a little artifice on the part of Angelique, empty of visitors this evening. Even her brother the Chevalier des Meloises with whom she lived, a man of high life and extreme fashion was to night enjoying the more congenial society of the officers of the Regiment de Bearn. At this moment amid the clash of glasses and the bubbling of wine, the excited and voluble Gascons were discussing in one breath, the war, the Council, the Court, the ladies, and whatever gay topic was tossed from end to end of the crowded mess table.

"Mademoiselle's hair has got loose and looks like a Huron's!" said her maid Lizette as her nimble fingers rearranged the rich dark-golden locks of Angelique, which reached to the floor as she sat upon her fauteuil.

"No matter Lizette! Do it up *à la Pompadour*, and make haste! My brain is in as great confusion as my hair. I need repose for an hour. Remember, Lizette! I am at home to no one, to night, except the Chevalier De Repentigny!"

"The Chevalier called this afternoon Mademoiselle, and was sorry he did not find you at home!" replied Lizette who saw the eye lashes of her mistress quiver and droop while a flush deepened for an instant the roseate hue of her cheek.

"I was in the Country—that accounts for it! There! my hair will do!" said Angelique giving a glance in the great Venetian mirror before her. Her freshly donned robe of blue silk edged with a foam of snowy laces and falbelas, set off her tall lithe figure. Her arms bare to the elbows would have excited Juno's jealousy, and Homer's verse to greater efforts in praise of them. Her dainty feet shapely, aspiring and full of Character, as her face, were carelessly thrust forward, and upon one of them lay a flossy spaniel, a privileged pet of his fair mistress.

The Boudoir of Angelique was a nest of luxury and elegance. Its furnishings and adornings were of the newest Parisian style. A rich carpet woven in the pattern of a bed of flowers, covered the floor. Vases of Sevre and Porcelain filled with roses and jonquils stood on marble tables. Grand Venetian mirrors reflected the fair form of their mistress, from every point of view, who contemplated herself before and behind with a feeling of perfect satisfaction and a sense of triumph over every rival.

A harpsichord occupied one corner of the room and an elaborate book case well filled, with splendidly bound volumes, another.

Angelique had small taste for reading yet had made some acquaintance with the literature of the day. Her natural quick parts and good taste enabled her to shine even in literary conversation. Her bright eyes looked volumes. Her silvery laugh was wiser than the wisdom of a *Precieuse*. Her witty repartees covered acres of deficiencies with so much grace and tact that men were tempted to praise her knowledge no less than her beauty.

She had a keen eye for artistic effects. She loved paintings, although her taste was sensuous and voluptuous. Character is shown in the choice of pictures as much as in that of books or of companions.

There was a painting of Vanloo, a lot of full blooded horses in a field of clover. They had broken fence and were luxuriating in the rich forbidden pasture. The triumph of Cleopatra over Antony, by Le Brun, was a great favorite with Angelique, because of a fancied if not a real ressemblance between her own features and those of the famous Queen of Egypt. Portraits of favorite friends, one of them Le Gardeur de Repentigny, and a still more recent acquisition, that of the Intendant Bigot adorned the walls. And among them one was distinguished for its contrast to all the rest, the likeness in the garb of an Ursuline of her beautiful Aunt, Marie des Meloises, who in a fit of caprice, some years before had suddenly forsaken the world of fashion and retired to the convent. Her sweet soprano voice as it led the choirs in the old chapel was the talk and the admiration of the city, and men stood in the street to listen to the angelic voice of the unseen Nun, whose hidden beauty was said to be reflected in the matchless charms of Angelique, but her singing no one in New France, could equal.

The proud beauty threw back her thick golden tresses as she scanned her fair face and magnificent figure in the tall Venetian mirror. She drank the intoxicating cup of self flattery to the bottom, as she compared herself feature by feature with every beautiful woman she knew in New France. The longer she looked the more she felt the superiority of her own charms over them all. Even the portrait of her aunt, so like her in feature so different in expression, was glanced at with something like triumph spiced with contempt.

"She was handsome as I," cried Angelique. "She was fit to be a queen and made herself a nun, and all for sake of a man!—I am fit to be a queen too, and the man who raises me nighest to a queen's estate, gets my hand—! My heart?"—she paused a few moments. "Pshaw!" A slight quiver passed over her lips. "My heart must do penance for the fault of my hand—!—"

Petrified by vanity and devoured by ambition Angelique retained under the hard crust of selfishness, a solitary spark of womanly feeling. The handsome face and figure of Le Gardeur de Repentigny was her beau ideal of manly perfection. His admiration flattered her pride. His love, for she knew infallibly with a woman's instinct, that he loved her touched her into a tenderness such as she felt for no man beside. It was the nearest approach to love her nature was capable of, and she used to listen to him with more than complacency while she let her hand linger in his warm clasp while the electric fire passed from one to another and she looked in his eyes, and spoke to him in those sweet undertones that win men's hearts to woman's purposes.

She believed she loved Le Gardeur, but there was no depth in the soil where a devoted passion could take firm root. Still she was a woman keenly alive to admiration, jealous and exacting of her suitors, never wittingly letting one loose from her bonds, and with warm passions and a cold heart was eager for the semblance of love although never feeling its divine reality.

The idea of a union with Le Gardeur some day when she should tire of the whirl of fashion, had been a pleasant fancy of Angelique. She had no fear of losing her power over him. She held him by the very heart strings and she knew it. She might procrastinate, play fast and loose, drive him to the very verge of madness by her coquettries, but she knew she could draw him back like a bird held by a silken string. She could excite, if she could not feel the fire of a passionate love. In her heart she regarded men as beings created for her service, amusement and sport, to worship her beauty, and adorn it with gifts. She took everything as her due giving nothing in return. Her love was an empty shell that never held a kernel of real womanly care for any man.

Amid the sunshine of her fancied love for Le Gardeur, had come a day of eclipse, for him, of fresh glory for her. The arrival of the new Intendant Bigot changed the current of Angelique's ambition. His high rank, his fabulous wealth, his connections with the court, and his unmarried state, fanned into a flame the secret aspirations of the proud ambitious girl. His wit and gallantry, captivated her fancy and her vanity was full fed by being singled out as a special object of the Intendants admiration.

She already indulged in dreams which regarded the Intendant himself as but a stepping stone to further greatness. Her vivid fancy, conjured up scenes of royal splendour, where introduced by the courtly Bigot Princes and nobles would follow in her train, and the smiles of Majesty itself would distinguish her in the royal halls of Versailles.

Angelique felt she had power to accomplish all this, could she but open the way.—The name of Bigot she regarded as the open sesame to all greatness. "If women rule France by a right more divine than that of Kings, no woman has a better right than I!" said she, gazing into the mirror before her. "The Kingdom should be mine, and death to all other pretenders!—And what is needed after all?" thought she, as she brushed her golden hair from her temples with a hand firm as it was beautiful. "It is but to pull down the heart of a man! I have done that, many a time for my pleasure. I will now do it for my profit, for supremacy over my jealous and envious sex—!—"

Angelique was not one to quail, when she entered the battle in pursuit of any object of ambition or fancy. "I never saw the man yet," said she, "whom I could not bring to my feet if I willed it—! The Chevalier Bigot would be no exception,—that is, he would be no exception— —" The voice of Angelique fell into a low hard monotone as she finished the sentence— "were he free from the influence of that mysterious woman at Beaumanoir, who they say claims the title of wife by a token which even Bigot may not disregard—! Her pleading eyes, may draw his compassion, where they ought to excite his scorn. But men are fools to woman's faults and are often held by the very thing women never forgive. While she crouches there like a lioness in my path, the chances are I shall never be Chatelaine of Beaumanoir—never until she is gone—!—"

Angelique fell into a deep fit of musing and murmured to herself, "I shall never reach Bigot unless she be removed. But how to remove her?"

Aye! that was the riddle of the Sphinx. Angelique's whole life as she had projected it, depended upon the answer to that question.

She trembled with a new feeling. A shiver ran through her veins, as if the cold breath of a spirit of evil had passed over her. A miner boring down into the earth strikes a hidden stone that brings him to a dead stand. So Angelique struck a hard dark thought far down in the depths of her secret soul. She drew it to the light and gazed on it shocked and frightened.

"I did not mean that!" cried the startled girl crossing herself. "Mere de Dieu! I did not conceive a wicked thought like that!—I will not! I cannot contemplate that!"—She shut her eyes, pressing both hands over them, as if resolved not to look at the evil thought that like a spirit of darkness came when evoked and would not depart when bidden.

The first suggestion of sin comes creeping in our hour of moral darkness, like a feeble mendicant who craves admission to a corner of our fireside. We let him in, warm and nourish him. We talk and trifle with him from our high seat thinking no harm or danger. But woe to us! if we let the secret assassin lodge under our roof—! He will rise up stealthily at midnight, and strangle conscience in her bed, murder the sleeping watchman of our uprightness, lulled to rest by the opiate of strong desire.

Angelique sat as in an enchanted circle round which fluttered shapes unknown to her before, and the face of Caroline de St Castin went and came now approaching now receding like the phantom of a phantasmagoria. She fancied she heard a rustle as of wings, a sharp cry out of the darkness and all was still! She sprang up trembling in every limb, and supporting herself against a table seized a gilded carafe and poured out a full goblet of wine, which she drank. It revived her fainting spirit. She drank another, and stood up herself again laughing at her own weakness.

She ran to the window and looked out into the night. The bright stars shone overhead. The lights in the street reassured her. The people passing by, and the sound of voices brought back her familiar mood. She thought no more of the temptation from which she had not prayed to be delivered, just as the daring skater forgets the depths that underlie the thin ice over which he skims careless as a bird in the sun shine.

An hour more was struck by the loud bell of the Recollets. The drums and bugles of the garrison sounded the signal for the closing of the Gates of the City and the setting of the watch for the night. Presently the heavy tramp of the Piquet was heard in the street. Sober Bourgeois walked briskly home while belated soldiers ran hastily to get into their quarters ere the drums ceased beating the tattoo.

The sharp galop of a horse rang on the stony pavement, and stopped suddenly at the door. A light step and the clink of a scabbard rang on the portico. A familiar rap followed. Angelique with the infallible intuition of a woman who recognizes the knock and footstep of her lover from ten thousand others, sprang up, and met Le Gardeur de Repentigny as he entered the Boudoir. She received him with warmth, even fondness, for she was proud of Le Gardeur and loved him in her secret heart beyond all the rest of her admirers.

"Welcome Le Gardeur!" exclaimed she giving both hands in his. "I knew you would come—you are welcome as the returned prodigal—!—"

"Dear Angelique!" replied he after kissing her hands with fervour. "The prodigal was sure to return. He could not live longer on the dry husks of mere recollections."

"So he rose and came to the house that is full and overflowing with welcome for him! It is good of you to come Le Gardeur! Why have you staid so long away—?" Angelique in the joy of his presence, forgot for the moment her meditated infidelity.

A swift stroke of her hand swept aside her flowing skirts to clear a place for him upon the sofa, where he sat down beside her.

"This is kind of you Angelique," said he. "I did not expect so much condescention after my petulance at the Governors ball. I was wicked that night—forgive me."

"The fault was more mine, I doubt, Le Gardeur." Angelique recollected how she had tormented him on that occasion by capricious slights while bounteous of her smiles to others. "I was angry with you because of your too great devotion to Cecile Tourangeau."

This was not true, but Angelique had no scruple to lie to a lover. She knew well that it was only in his vexation at her conduct, that Le Gardeur had pretended to renew some long intermitted coquettries with the fair Cecile. "But why were you wicked at all that night?" inquired she with a look of sudden interest, as she caught a red cast in his eye, that spoke of much dissipation. "You have been ill, Le Gardeur—!" But she knew he had been drinking deep and long to drown vexation perhaps, over her conduct.

"I have not been ill," replied he. "Shall I tell you the truth Angelique?"

"Always and all of it! The whole truth and nothing but the truth!" Her hand rested lightly on his. No word of equivocation was possible under that mode of putting her lover to the question. "Tell me why you were wicked that night!—"

"Because I loved you to madness Angelique, and I saw myself thrust from the first place in your heart, and a new idol set up in my stead. That is the truth."

"That is not the truth!" exclaimed she vehemently. "And never will be the truth, if I know myself and you. But you dont know women Le Gardeur," added she with a smile. "You dont know me, the one woman you ought to know, better than that!—"

It is easy to recover affection that is not lost. Angelique knew her power, and was not indisposed to excess in the exercise of it. "Will you do something for me Le Gardeur?" asked she tapping his fingers coquettishly with her fan.

"Will I not? Is there any thing in earth, heaven or hell, Angelique I would not do for you, if I only could win what I covet more than life—?"

"What is that—?" Angelique knew full well, what he coveted more than life—her own heart began to beat responsively to the passion she had kindled in his. She nestled up closer to his side.—"What is that Le Gardeur?—"

"Your love, Angelique! I have no other hope in life if I miss that! Give me your love and I will serve you with such loyalty as never man served woman with since Adam and Eve were created."

It was a rash saying, but Le Gardeur believed it, and Angelique too. Still she kept her aim before her. "If I gave you my love," said she passing her hand through his thick locks, sending from her fingers a thousand electric fires, "will you really be my knight, my *preux Chevalier*, to wear my colours and fight my battles with all the world—?"

"I will by all that is sacred in man or woman! Your will shall be my law Angelique! Your pleasure my conscience. You shall be to me all reason and motive for my acts, if you will but love me."

"I do love you Le Gardeur!" replied she impetuously. She felt the vital soul of this man breathing on her cheek. She knew he spoke true, but she was incapable of measuring the height and immensity of such a passion. She accepted his love, but she could no more contain the fullness of his overflowing affection than the pitcher that is held to the Fountain can contain the stream that gushes forth perpetually.

Angelique was *almost* carried away from her purpose,

however. Had her heart asserted its rightful supremacy, or that is, had nature fashioned it larger and warmer, she had there and then thrown herself into his arms and blessed him by the consent he sought. She felt assured that here was the one man God had made for her, and she was cruelly sacrificing him to a false idol of ambition and vanity. The word he pleaded for hovered on her tongue, ready like a bird to leap down into his bosom, but she resolutely beat it back into its iron cage.

The struggle was the old one, old as the race of man. In the losing battle between the false and true, love rarely comes out of that conflict unshorn of life or limb. Untrue to him, she was true to her selfish self. She thought of the Intendant and the glories of life opening to her, and closed her heart not to the pleadings of Le Gardeur—them she loved—but to the granting of his prayer.

The die was cast, but she still clasped hard his hand in hers, as if she could not let him go. "And will you do all you say Le Gardeur—make my will your law, my pleasure your conscience and let me be to you all reason and motive? Such devotion terrifies me Le Gardeur?"

"Try me! Ask of me the hardest thing, nay the wickedest, that imagination can conceive or hands do, and I would perform it for your sake." Le Gardeur was getting beside himself. The magic power of those dark flashing eyes of hers were melting all the fine gold of his nature to folly.

"Fie!" replied she. "I do not ask you to drink the sea. A smaller thing would content me. My love is not so exacting as that Le Gardeur."

"Does your brother need my aid?" asked he. "If he does he shall have it to half my fortune for your sake!" Le Gardeur was well aware that the prodigal brother of Angelique was in a strait for money as was usual with him. He had lately importuned Le Gardeur and obtained a large sum from him.

She looked up with well affected indignation. "How can you think such a thing Le Gardeur. My brother was not in my thought. It was the Intendant I wished to ask you about. You know him better than I."

This was not true. Angelique had studied the Intendant

in mind person and estate weighing him scruple by scruple to the last attainable atom of information. Not that she had sounded the depths of Bigot's soul. There were regions of darkness in his character, which no eye but Gods ever penetrated. Angelique felt that with all her acuteness she did not comprehend the Intendant.

"You ask what I think of the Intendant?" asked he, surprized somewhat at the question.

"Yes! an odd question is it not, Le Gardeur?" and she smiled away any surprize, he experienced.

"Truly, I think him the most jovial gentleman ever was in New France" was the reply, "frank and open handed to his friends, laughing and dangerous to his foes. His wit is like his wine, Angelique; one never tires of either, and no lavishness exhausts it. In a word I like the Intendant. I like his wit, his wine, his friends—some of them that is—! but above all I like you Angelique and will be more his friend than ever for your sake, since I have learned his generosity towards the Chevalier des Meloises."—

The Intendant had recently bestowed a number of valuable shares in the Grand Company upon the brother of Angelique, making the fortune of that extravagant young nobleman.

"I am glad you will be his friend, if only for my sake," added she coquettishly. "But some great friends of yours like him not. Your sweet sister Amelie shrank like a sensitive plant at the mention of his name, and the Lady de Tilly put on her gravest look to day, when I spoke of the Chevalier Bigot."

Le Gardeur gave Angelique an equivocal look at mention of his sister. "My sister Amelie is an angel in the flesh," said he. "A man need be little less than divine to meet her full approval. And my good aunt has heard something of the genial life of the Intendant, one may excuse a reproving shake of her noble head."—

"Colonel Philibert too! he shares in the sentiments of your aunt and sister, to say nothing of the standing hostility of his father the Bourgeois," continued Angelique provoked at Le Gardeur's apparent want of adhesion!—

"Pierre Philibert! He may not like the Intendant. He has reason for not doing so, but I stake my life on his honour. He will never be unjust towards the Intendant or any man." Le Gardeur could not be drawn into a censure of his friend.

Angelique sheathed adroitly the stiletto of innuendo she had drawn. "You say right" said she craftily. "Pierre Philibert is a gentleman worthy of every regard. I confess I have seen no handsomer man in New France. I have been dreaming of one like him all my life—!—What a pity I saw you first Le Gardeur?" added she pulling him by the hair.

"I doubt you would throw me to the fishes were Pierre my rival, Angelique!" replied he merrily, "but I am in no danger. Pierre's affections are I fancy forestalled in a quarter where I need not be jealous of his success."

"I shall, at any rate, not be jealous of your sister, Le Gardeur," said Angelique, raising her face to his, suffused with a blush.—"If I do not give you the love you ask for, it is because you have it already, but ask no more at present from me.—That at least is yours." She kissed him twice, without prudery or hesitation. That kiss from those adored lips sealed his fate. It was the first—better it had been the last—better he had never been born than drank the poison of her lips. "Now answer me my question Le Gardeur" added she, after a pause of fond blandishments.

Le Gardeur felt her fingers playing with his hair, as like Delilah, she cut off the seven locks of his strength.

"There is a lady at Beaumanoir. Tell me who and what she is Le Gardeur—!" said she.

He would not have hesitated to betray the gate of heaven, at her prayer, but as it happened, Le Gardeur could not give her the special information she wanted, as to the particular relation in which that lady stood to the Intendant.

Angelique with wonderful coolness, talked away and laughed at the idea of the Intendants gallantry. But she could get no confirmation of her suspicions from Le Gardeur. Her inquiry was for the present a failure, but she made Le Gardeur promise to learn what he could, and tell her the result of his inquiries.

They sat long conversing together until the bell of the Recollets sounded the hour of midnight. Angelique looked in the face of Le Gardeur with a meaning smile, as she counted each stroke with her dainty finger upon his cheek. When finished she sprang up and looked out of the lattice at the summer night.

The stars were twinkling like living things. Charles wain lay inverted on the northern horizon; Bootes was driving his sparkling herd down the slope of the Western sky.

A few thick tresses of her golden hair hung negligently over her bosom and shoulders. She placed her arm in Le Gardeur's, hanging heavily upon him as she directed his eyes to the starry heavens.

The selfish schemes she carried in her bosom dropped for a moment to the ground. Her feet seemed to trample them into the dust while she half resolved to be to this man all that he believed her to be, a true and devoted woman. "Read my destiny Le Gardeur!" said she, earnestly. "You are a Seminarist. They say the wise fathers in the Seminary study deeply the science of the stars, and the students all become adepts in it."

"Would that my starry heaven were more propitious! Angelique," replied he gaily kissing her eyes. "I care not for other skies than these. My Fate and fortune are here."

Her bosom heaved with mingled passions. The word of hope and the word of denial struggled on her lips for mastery. Her blood throbbed quicker than the beat of the golden pendule on the marble table. But like a bird, the good impulse again escaped her grasp.

"Look Le Gardeur!" said she, her delicate finger pointed at Perseus who was ascending the Eastern heavens. "There is my star!—Mere Malheur, you know her—! She once said to me, that one was my natal star, which would rule my life—!" Like all whose passions pilot them, Angelique believed in destiny.

Le Gardeur had sipped a few drops of the cup of astrology from the venerable Professor Vallier. Angelique's finger pointed to the star Algol, that strange mutable star that changes from bright to dark with the hours, and some believe, turns mens hearts to stone.

"Mere Malheur lied!" exclaimed he, placing his arm round her as if to protect her from the baleful influence. "That cursed star never presided over your birth, Angelique! That is the Demon star, Algol—!"

Angelique shuddered and drew still closer to him as if in fear. "Mere Malheur would not tell me the meaning of that star, but bade me, if a Saint, to watch and wait, if a sinner to watch and pray! What means Algol, Le Gardeur?" she half faltered.

"Nothing for you love. A fig for all the stars in the sky. Your bright eyes outshine them all in radiance and overpower them in influence, and all the music of the spheres is to me discord, compared with the voice of Angelique des Meloises whom alone I love."

As he spoke a strain of heavenly harmony rose from the Chapel of the Convent of the Ursulines where they were celebrating midnight service for the safety of New France. Amid the sweet voices that floated up on the notes of the pealing organ, was clearly distinguished that of Mere de St Borgia, the aunt of Angelique, who led the choir of nuns. In trills and cadences of divine melody the voice of Mere St Borgia rose higher and higher like a spirit mounting the skies. The words were indistinct but Angelique knew them by heart. She had visited her aunt in the Convent, and had learned the new Hymn composed by her for this solemn service:—

As they listened with quiet awe to the supplicating strain, Angelique repeated for Le Gardeur the words of the hymn, as it was sung by the Choir of Nuns,

"Soutenez, grande Reine,
Notre pauvre pays!
Il est votre domaine
Faites fleurir nos lis!—
L'Anglais sur nos frontieres
Porte ses etendards.
Exaucez nos prieres
Protegez nos remparts!—"

The hymn ceased. Both stood mute, until the Watchman cried the hour in the silent street.

"God bless their holy prayers and good night and God bless you! Angelique," said Le Gardeur kissing her. He departed suddenly leaving a gift in the hand of Lizette, who curtseyed low to him with a smile of pleasure as he passed out, while Angelique leaned out of the window listening to the horses hoofs until the last tap of them died away on the stony pavement.

She threw herself upon her couch and wept silently. The soft music had touched her feelings. Le Gardeur's love, was like a load of gold crushing her with its weight. She could neither carry it onward, nor throw it off. She fell at length into a slumber filled with troubled dreams. She was in a sandy wilderness carrying a pitcher of clear cold water, but though dying of thirst she would not drink, but perversely poured it upon the ground:—She was falling down into unfathomable abysses and pushed aside the only hand stretched out to save her. She was drowning in deep waters and she saw Le Gardeur buffetting the waves to save her; but she wrenched herself out of his grasp. She would not be saved and was lost. Her couch was surrounded with indefinite shapes of embryo evil. She fell asleep at last.

When she woke the sun was pouring in her windows. A fresh breeze shook the trees. The birds sang gaily in the garden. The street was alive and stirring with people. It was broad day. Angelique des Meloises was herself again. Her day dream of ambition resumed its power. Her night dream of love was over. Her fears vanished, her hopes were all alive, and she began to prepare for a possible morning call from the Chevalier Bigot.

CHAPTER 17

"SPLENDIDE MENDAX"

AMID the ruins of the once magnificent palace of the Intendant, massive fragments of which still remain to attest its former greatness, there may still be traced the outline of the room where Bigot walked restlessly up and down the morning after the Council of war. The disturbing letters he had received from France, on both public and private affairs irritated him, while it set his fertile brain at work to devise means, at once to satisfy the Marquise de Pompadour and have his own way still.

The walls of his cabinet now bare, shattered and roofless with the blasts of six score winters were hung with portraits of ladies and statesmen of the day, conspicuous among which was a fine picture from the pencil of Vanloo of the handsome voluptuous Marquise de Pompadour.

With a world of faults, that celebrated Dame who ruled France in the name of Louis XV. made some amends by her persistent good nature and her love for art. The painter, the architect, the sculptor and above all the men of literature in France were objects of her sincere admiration, and her patronage of them was generous to profusion. The picture of her in the Cabinet of the Intendant had been a work of gratitude by the great artist who painted it, and was presented by her, to Bigot as a mark of her friendship and demi royal favour. The Cabinet itself was furnished in a style of regal magnificence which the Intendant carried into all details of his living.

The Chevalier de Pean the secretary and confidential friend of the Intendant was writing at a table. He looked up now and then with a curious glance as the figure of his

Chief moved to and fro with quick turns across the room. But neither of them spoke.

Bigot would have been quite content with enriching himself and his patroness, and turning out of doors, the crowd of courtly sycophants who clamoured for the plunder of the Colony. He had sense to see that the course of policy in which he was embarked would eventually ruin New France. Nay having its origin in the Court would undermine the whole fabric of the monarchy. He consoled himself however with the reflection, that it could not be helped. He formed but one link in the great chain of corruption, and one link could not stand alone. It could only move by following those which went before and dragging after it all that came behind. Without debating a useless point of morals, Bigot quietly resigned himself to the service of his masters or rather mistresses after he had first served himself.

If the enormous plunder made out of the administration of the war and by the great monopoly he had established were suddenly to cease, Bigot felt that his genius would be put to a severe test. But he had no misgivings because he had no scruples. He was not the man to go under, in any storm. He would light upon his feet, as he expressed it, if the world turned upside down.

Bigot suddenly stopped in his walk. His mind had been dwelling on the great affairs of his Intendancy and the mad policy of the Court of Versailles. A new thought struck him. He turned and looked fixedly at his Secretary.

"De Pean!" said he. "We have not a sure hold of the Chevalier de Repentigny! That young fellow plays fast and loose with us. One who dines with me at the palace and sups with the Philiberts at the Chien d'Or, cannot be a safe partner in the Grand Company!—"

"I have small confidence in him either!" replied De Pean. "Le Gardeur has too many loose ends of respectability hanging about him to make him a sure card for our game."

"Just so! Cadet, Varin and the rest of you have only half haltered the young colt. His training so far is no credit to you!—The way that cool bully Colonel Philibert walked off with him out of Beaumanoir, was a sublime specimen of impudence. Ha! Ha! The recollection of it has salted my meat ever since—! It was admirably performed! although egad! I should have liked to run my sword through Philiberts ribs. And not one of you all was man enough to do it for me!—"

"But your Excellency gave no hint. You seemed full of politeness towards Philibert," replied De Pean, with a tone that implied he would have done it, had Bigot given the hint.

"Zounds! as if I do not know it! But it was provoking to be flouted so politely too by that whelp of the Golden Dog. The influence of that Philibert is immense over young De Repentigny. They say he once pulled him out of the water, and is moreover a suitor of the sister. A charming girl De Pean—! with no end of money lands and family power. She ought to be secured as well as her brother in the interests of the Grand Company. A good marriage with one of our party, would secure her, and none of you dare propose, by God!"

"It is useless to think of proposing to her," replied De Pean. "I know the proud minx. She is one of the angelic ones, who regard marriage as a thing of heaven's arrangement. She believes God never makes but one man for one woman and it is her duty to marry him or nobody. It is whispered among the knowing girls who went to school with her at the Convent— (and the Convent girls do know everything and something more!) that she always cherished a secret affection for this Philibert, and that she will marry him some day."

Marry Satan! Such a girl as that to marry a cursed Philibert! Bigot was really irritated at the information. "I think" said he, "women are ever ready to sail in the Ships of Tarshish, so long as the cargo is, gold, silver, ivory, apes and peacocks! It speaks ill for the boasted gallantry of the Grand Company if not one of them can win this girl. If we could gain her over, we should have no difficulty with the brother, and the point is to secure him."

"There is but one way I can see, your Excellency." De Pean did not appear to make his suggestion very cheerfully, but he was anxious to please the Intendant.

"How is that?" the Intendant asked sharply. He had not

the deepest sense of De Pean's wisdom.

"We must call in woman to fight woman in the interests of the Company," replied the Secretary.

"A good scheme if one could be got to draw the herring but do you know any woman who can lay her fingers on Le Gardeur de Repentigny, and pull him out from among the *Honnetes Gens*?"

"I do, your Excellency. I know the very one who can do it," replied De Pean, confidently.

"You do! Why do you hesitate then? Have you any *arriere pensée* that keeps you from telling her name at once—?" asked the Intendant impatiently.

"It is Mademoiselle des Meloises. She can do it and no other woman in New France need try," replied De Pean.

"Why she is a clipper certainly! Bright eyes like hers rule the world of fools, (and of wise men too,)" added Bigot, in a parenthesis. "However, all the world is caught by that bird-lime. I confess I never made a fool of myself but a woman was at the bottom of it. But for one who has tripped me up I have taken sweet revenge on a thousand. If Le Gardeur be entangled in Neræa's hair, he is safe in our toils. Do you think Angelique is home, De Pean?—"

The Intendant looked up at the clock. It was the usual hour for morning calls in Quebec.

"Doubtless she is at home at this hour, your Excellency," replied De Pean. "But she likes her bed like other pretty women, and is practicing for the *petite levée*, like a Duchesse. I dont suppose she is up!"

"I dont know that," replied Bigot. "A greater run a gate in petticoats there is not in the whole city. I never pass through the streets, but I see her."

"Aye, that is because she intends to meet your Excellency!"—Bigot looked sharply at De Pean. A new thought flashed in his eyes.

"What! Think you she makes a point of it? De Pean!"

"I think she would not go out of the way of your Excellency." De Pean shuffled among his papers. But his slight agitation was noticed by the Intendant.

"Hum! is that your thought De Pean? Looks she in this quarter?" Bigot meditated with his hand on his chin for a moment or two. "You think she is doubtless at home this morning?" added he.

"It was late when De Repentigny left her last night, and she would have long and pleasant dreams after that visit I warrant," replied the Secretary.

"How do you know—? By St Picot! you watch her closely De Pean—!"

"I do your Excellency. I have reason," was the reply.

De Pean did not say what his reason for watching Angelique, was. Neither did Bigot ask. The Intendant cared not to pry into the personal matters of his friends. He had himself too much to conceal not to respect the secrets of his associates.

"Well De Pean! I will wait on Mademoiselle des Meloises this morning. I will act on your suggestion, and trust I shall not find her unreasonable."

"I hope your Excellency will not find her unreasonable, but I know you will, for if ever the devil of contradiction was in a woman, he is in Angelique des Meloises," replied De Pean savagely as if he spoke from some experience of his own.

"Well I will try to cast out that devil by the power of a still stronger one. Ring for my horse De Pean—!"

The Secretary obeyed and ordered the horse. "Mind De Pean!" continued the Intendant. "The Board of the Grand Company meet at three, for business! actual business! not a drop of wine upon the table, and all sober—! not even Cadet shall come in if he show one streak of the grape on his broad face. There is a storm of peace coming over us and it is necessary to shorten sail, take soundings, and see where we are, or we may strike on a rock."

The Intendant left the palace attended by a couple of Equerries. He rode through the Palace Gate and into the City. Habitans and citizens bowed to him, out of habitual respect for their superiors. Bigot returned their salutations with official brevity, but his dark face broke into sunshine as he passed ladies and citizens whom he knew, as partners of the Grand Company or partizans of his own faction.

As he rode rapidly through the streets many an ill wish followed him, until he suddenly dismounted before the mansion of the Des Meloises.

"As I live it is the Royal Intendant himself," screamed Lizette as she ran out of breath to inform her mistress, who was alone sitting in the summer house in the garden, behind the mansion a pretty spot tastefully laid out with flower beds and statuary. A thick hedge of privet cut into fantastic shapes by some disciple of the school of Le Nostre, screened it from the slopes that ran up towards the green glacis of Cape Diamond.

Angelique looked beautiful as Hebe the golden haired, as she sat in the arbour this morning. Her light morning dress of softest texture fell in graceful folds about her exquisite form. She held a book of Hours in her hand, but had not once opened it since she sat down. Her dark eyes looked not soft, not kindly, but bright, defiant, wanton and even wicked in their expression, like the eyes of an Arab steed whipped, spurred and brought to a desperate leap. It may clear the wall before it or may dash itself dead against the stones. Such was the temper of Angelique this morning.

Hard thoughts and many respecting the lady of Beaumanoir, fond almost savage regret at her meditated rejection of De Repentigny, glittering fancies of the Royal Intendant and of the splendours of Versailles, passed in rapid succession through her brain, forming a phantasmagoria in which she coloured everything according to her own fancy. The words of her maid roused her in an instant.

"Admit the Intendant and show him into the garden Lizette—! Now!" said she "I will end my doubts about that lady! I will test the Intendants sincerity! Cold calculating woman slayer that he is—! It shames me to contrast his half heartedness with the perfect adoration of my handsome Le Gardeur de Repentigny!"

The Intendant entered the garden. Angelique with that complete self control which distinguishes a woman of half a heart or no heart at all, changed her whole demeanour in a moment from gravity to gaiety—her eyes flashed out pleasure and her dimples went and came, as she welcomed the Intendant to her arbour.

"A friend is never so welcome as when he comes of his own accord!" said she, presenting her hand to the Intendant, who took it with empressement. She made room for him on the seat beside her, dashing her skirts aside somewhat ostentatiously.

Bigot looked at her admiringly. He thought he had never seen in painting statuary or living form, a more beautiful and fascinating woman.

Angelique accepted his admiration as her due, feeling no thanks, but looking many.

"The Chevalier Bigot does not lose his politeness however long he absents himself!" said she, with a glance like a Parthian arrow well aimed to strike home.

"I have been hunting at Beaumanoir," replied he, extenuatingly. "That must explain, not excuse, my apparent neglect." replied Bigot, feeling that he had really been a loser by his absence.

"Hunting! indeed!" Angelique affected a touch of surprize as if she had not known every tittle of gossip about the gay party and all of their doings at the Chateau. "They say game is growing scarce near the city Chevalier," continued she, nonchalantly, "and that a hunting party at Beaumanoir is but a pretty metonymy for a party of pleasure—is that true?"—

"Quite true! Mademoiselle," replied he laughing. "The two things are perfectly compatible like a brace of lovers all the better for being made one."

"Very gallantly said!—" retorted she with a ripple of dangerous laughter. "I will carry the comparison no further. Still I wager Chevalier, that the game is not worth the hunt."

"The play is always worth the candle in my fancy," said he, with a glance of meaning. "But there is really good game yet in Beaumanoir, as you will confess Mademoiselle if you will honour our party some day with your presence."

"Come now Chevalier!" replied she fixing him mischievously with her eye, "Tell me what game do you find in the forest of Beaumanoir?"

"O, rabbits, hares and deer, with now and then a rough bear to try the mettle of our chasseurs."

"What! no foxes to cheat foolish crows? no wolves to devour pretty Red Riding Hoods straying in the forest? Come Chevalier! There is better game than all that," said she.

"O, yes!" He half surmised she was rallying him now, "plenty! but we dont wind horns after them."

"They say," continued she "there is much fairer game than bird or beast in the forest of Beaumanoir Chevalier." She went on recklessly—"stray lambs are picked up by Intendants, sometimes, and carried tenderly to the Chateau!—The Intendant comprehends a gentleman's devoirs to our sex I am sure."

Bigot understood her now, and gave an angry start. Angelique did not shrink from the temper she had evoked.

"Heavens how you look, Chevalier!" said she in a tone of half banter. "One would think I had accused you of murder, instead of saving a fair ladys life in the forest! although woman killing is no murder I believe by the laws of gallantry, as read by gentlemen—of fashion."

Bigot rose up with a hasty gesture of impatience and sat down again. "After all," he thought "what could this girl know about Caroline de St Castin?" He answered her with an appearance of frankness, deeming that to be the best policy.

"Yes Mademoiselle! I one day found a poor suffering woman in the forest. I took her to the Chateau where she now is.—Many ladies beside her have been to Beaumanoir! Many more will yet come and go, until I end my bachelordom, and place one there in perpetuity as mistress of my heart, and home as the song says."—

Angelique could coquette in half meanings with any lady of honour at Court. "Well Chevalier! It will be your fault not to find one fit to place there. They walk every street of the City. But they say this lost and found lady is a stranger."

"To me she is—not to you, perhaps, Mademoiselle?"—The fine ear of Angelique detected the strain of hypocricy in his speech. It touched a sensitive nerve. She spoke boldly now.

"Some say she is your wife, Chevalier Bigot!" Angelique

gave vent to a feeling long pent up. She who trifled with men's hearts every day, was indignant at the least symptom of repayment in kind. "They say she is your wife, or if not your wife she ought to be Chevalier!—and will be perhaps, one of these fine days when you have wearied of the distressed damsels of the city."

It had been better for Bigot, better for Angelique, that these two could have frankly understood each other. Bigot in his sudden admiration of the beauty of this girl, forgot that his object in coming to see her, had really been to promote a marriage in the interests of the Grand Company between her and Le Gardeur. Her witcheries had been too potent for the man of pleasure. He was himself caught in the net he spread for another. The adroit bird catching of Angelique, was too much for him in the beginning. Bigot's tact and consummate heartlessness with women might be too much for her in the end!—At the present moment he was fairly dazzled with her beauty spirit and seductiveness.

"I am a simple quail!" thought he, "to be caught by her piping. Par Dieu! I am going to make a fool of myself, if I do not take care! Such a woman as this I have not found between Paris and Naples. The man who gets her and knows how to use her might be prime minister of France—! And to fancy it!—I came here to pick this sweet chesnut out of the fire for Le Gardeur de Repentigny!—Francois Bigot! as a man of gallantry and fashion I am ashamed of you—!"—

These were his thoughts, but in words he replied: "The Lady of Beaumanoir is not my wife,—perhaps never will be!": Angelique's eager question fell on very unproductive ground.

Angelique repeated the word superciliously— "perhaps!"—"'perhaps,' in the mouth of a woman is consent half won! In the mouth of a man, I know it has a laxer meaning. Love has nothing to say to 'perhaps.' It is will or shall and takes no perhaps though a thousand times repeated!"

"And you intend to marry this treasure trove of the forest— perhaps?" continued Angelique tapping the ground with a daintier foot than the Intendant had ever scanned before.

"It depends much on you, Mademoiselle des Meloises!"

said he. "Had you been my treasure trove there had been no 'perhaps,' about it."—Bigot spoke bluntly, and to Angelique it sounded like sincerity. Her dreams were accomplishing. She trembled with the intensity of her gratification, and felt no repugnance at his familiar address.

The Intendant held out his hand as he uttered the dulcet flattery and she placed her hand in his, but it was cold and passionless. Her heart did not send the blood leaping into her finger ends, as when they were held in the loving grasp of Le Gardeur.

"Angelique!" said he. It was the first time the Intendant called her by her name. She started! It was the unlocking of his heart she thought, and she looked at him with a smile which she had practiced with infallible effect upon many a foolish admirer.

"Angelique! I have seen no woman like you in New France or in old. You are fit to adorn a court, and I predict you will—if—if—"

"If what? Chevalier!" Her eyes fairly blazed with vanity and pleasure. "Cannot one adorn courts, at least French Courts without ifs?"

"You can, if you choose to do so!" replied he looking at her admiringly, for her whole countenance flashed intense pleasure at his remark.

"If I choose to do so! I do choose to do so! But who is to show me the way to the Court, Chevalier? It is a long and weary distance from New France."

"I will show you the way if you will permit me, Angelique. Versailles is the only fitting theater for the display of beauty and spirit like yours."

Angelique thoroughly believed this and for a few moments was dazed and overpowered, by the thought of the golden doors of her ambition opened by the hand of the Intendant. A train of images full winged and gorgeous as birds of paradise flashed across her vision. "La Pompadour was getting old men said, and the King was already casting his eyes round the circle of more youthful beauties in his Court for a successor. And what woman in the world" thought she, "could vie with

Angelique des Meloises, if she chose to enter the arena, to supplant La Pompadour? Nay more—! If the prize of the King was her lot, she would outdo La Maintenon herself, and end by sitting on the throne."

Angelique was not however, a milk maid to say yes! before she was asked. She knew her value, and had a natural distrust of the Intendants gallant speeches. Moreover the shadow of the lady of Beaumanoir would not wholly disappear.

"Why do you say such flattering things to me Chevalier?" asked she. "One takes them for earnest, coming from the Royal Intendant. You should leave trifling to the idle young men of the City, who have no business to employ them but gallanting us women."

"Trifling! By St Jeanne de Choisy!—I was never more in earnest, Mademoiselle," exclaimed Bigot. "I offer you the entire devotion of my heart."—St Jeanne de Choisy was the subriquet in the *petits appartemens* of Choisy, for La Pompadour. Angelique knew it very well, although Bigot thought she did not.

"Fair words are like flowers Chevalier," replied she, "sweet to smell and pretty to look at, but love feeds on ripe fruit. Will you prove your devotion to me if I put it to the test?"

"Most willingly, Angelique!" Bigot thought she contemplated some idle freak that might try his gallantry, perhaps his purse; but she was in earnest, if he was not.

"I ask then Chevalier Bigot, that before he speaks to me again of love and devotion, he shall remove that lady whoever she may be, from Beaumanoir!—" Angelique sat erect and looked at him with a long fixed look, as she said this.

"Remove that lady from Beaumanoir!" exclaimed he in complete surprize. "Surely that poor shadow does not prevent your accepting my devotion, Angelique?"

"Yes, but it does, Chevalier! I like bold men—most women do—but I did not think that even the Intendant of New France, was bold enough to make love to Angelique des Meloises while he kept a wife or mistress in stately seclusion at Beaumanoir!—"—

Bigot cursed the shrewishness and innate jealousy of the

sex which would not content itself with just so much of a man's favour as he choose to bestow, but must ever want to rule single and alone. "Every woman is a despot" thought he "and has no mercy upon pretenders to her throne."

"That lady" replied he, "is neither wife nor mistress, Mademoiselle. She sought the shelter of my roof with a claim upon the hospitality of Beaumanoir."

"No doubt!" Angelique's nostril quivered with a fine disdain. "The hospitality of Beaumanoir is as broad and comprehensive as its masters admiration for our sex!—" said she.

Bigot was not angry. He gave a loud laugh. "You women are merciless upon each other, Mademoiselle—!" said he.

"Men are more merciless to women, when they beguile us with insincere professions," replied she rising up in well affected indignation.

"Not so, Mademoiselle—!" Bigot began to feel annoyed. "That lady is nothing to me," said he, without rising as she had done. He kept his seat.

"But she has been! you have loved her at some time, or other! and she is now living on the scraps and leavings of former affection. I am never deceived, Chevalier!" continued she, glancing down at him, a wild light playing under her long eye-lashes, like the illumined under edge of a thunder cloud.

"But how in St Picot's name did you arrive at all this knowledge, Mademoiselle?" Bigot began to see that there was nothing for it but to comply with every caprice of this incomprehensible girl, if he would carry his point.

"O nothing is easier than for a woman to divine the truth in such matters Chevalier," said she. "It is a sixth sense given to our sex, to protect our weakness. No man can make love to two women, but each of them knows instinctively to her finger tips, that he is doing it."

"Surely woman is a beautiful book written in golden letters, but in a tongue hard to understand as the Hieroglyphics of Egypt," said Bigot rather puzzled how to proceed with this incomprehensible girl.

"Thanks for the comparison Chevalier," replied she with

a laugh. "It would not do for men to scrutinize us too closely, yet one woman reads another easily as a horn book of Troyes, which they say is so easy that the children read it without learning."

To boldly set at defiance a man who had boasted a long career of success was the way to rouse his pride, and determine him to overcome her resistance. Angelique was not mistaken. Bigot saw her resolution and although it was with a mental reservation to deceive her, he promised to banish Caroline from his Chateau.

"It was always my good fortune to be conquered in every passage of arms with your sex Angelique," said he, at once radiant and submissive. "Sit down by me in token of amity."

She complied without hesitation, and sat down by him, gave him her hand again, and replied with an arch smile, while a thousand inimitable coquetteries played about her eyes and lips. "You speak now like an *Amant Magnifique*, Chevalier!

'Quelque fort qu'on s'en defende,
Il y faut venir un jour!—'"

"It is a bargain henceforth and for ever! Angelique!" said he, "but I am a harder man than you imagine. I give nothing for nothing, and all for every thing. Will you consent to aid me and the Grand Company in a matter of importance?"

"Will I not? What a question Chevalier! Most willingly I will aid you, in anything proper for a lady to do!—" added she with a touch of irony.

"I wish you to do it right or wrong, proper or improper, and although there is no impropriety in it, *im*proper becomes proper if you do it, Mademoiselle."

"Well, what is it, Chevalier? This fearful test to prove my loyalty to the Grand Company—? and which makes you such a matchless flatterer?"—

"Just this Angelique!" replied he. "You have much influence with the Seigneur de Repentigny—?"

Angelique coloured up to the eyes. "With Le Gardeur! What of him—? I can take no part against the Seigneur de Repentigny!" said she hastily.

"Against him? No! for him! We fear much that he is about to fall into the hands of the *Honnetes Gens*. You can prevent that if you will Angelique?"

"I have an honest regard for the Seigneur de Repentigny!" said she, more in answer to her own feelings than to the Intendants remark—her cheek flushed, her fingers twitched nervously at her fan, which she broke in her agitation and threw the pieces vehemently upon the ground.—"I have done harm enough to Le Gardeur, I fear," continued she. "I had better not interfere with him any more!—who knows what might result?" She looked up almost warningly at the Intendant.

"I am glad to find you so sincere a friend to Le Gardeur," remarked Bigot craftily. "You will be glad to learn that our intention is to elevate him to a high and lucrative office in the administration of the Company unless the *Honnetes Gens* are before us in gaining full possession of him."

"They shall not be before us, if I can prevent it! Chevalier," replied she warmly. She was indeed grateful for the implied compliment to Le Gardeur. "No one will be better pleased at his good fortune than myself."—

"I thought so. It was partly my business to tell you, of our intentions towards Le Gardeur."

"Indeed!" replied she in a tone of pique. "I flattered myself your visit was all on my own account Chevalier!—"

"So it was!" Bigot felt himself on rather soft ground. "Your brother the Chevalier des Meloises has doubtless consulted you upon the plan of life he has sketched out for both of you—?"

"My good brother sketches so many plans of life that I really am not certain, I know the one you refer to." She guessed what was coming and held her breath hard, until she heard the reply.

"Well, you of course know that his plan of life depends mainly upon an alliance between you and the Chevalier de Repentigny!"

She gave vent to her anger and disappointment. She rose up suddenly and grasping the Intendants arm fiercely turned him half round in her vehemence: "Chevalier Bigot! did you come here to propose for me on behalf of Le Gardeur de Repentigny?"

"Pardon me, Mademoiselle. It is no proposal of mine, on behalf of Le Gardeur! I sanctioned his promotion. Your brother and the Grand Company generally would prefer the Alliance. I dont!"—He said this with a tone of meaning, which Angelique was acute enough to see implied Bigot's unwillingness to her marrying any man—but himself, was the *addendum* she at once placed to his credit. "I regret I mentioned it," continued he, blandly "if it be contrary to your wishes—!"

"It is contrary to my wishes—!" replied she relaxing her clutch of his arm. "Le Gardeur de Repentigny can speak for himself. I will not allow even my brother to suggest it. Still less will I discuss such a subject with the Chevalier Bigot."

"I hope you will pardon me Mademoiselle. I will not call you Angelique, until you are pleased with me again. To be sure I should never have forgiven you had you conformed to your brother's wishes. It was what I feared might happen, and I—I wished to try you—that was all—!"—

"It is dangerous trying me Chevalier," replied she resuming her seat with some heat.

"Dont try me again, or I shall take Le Gardeur out of pure *spite!*" she said—pure love was in her mind, but the other word came from her lips. "I will do all I can to rescue him from the *Honnetes Gens*, but not by marrying him, Chevalier— at present!"

They seemed to understand each other now. "It is over with now," said Bigot. "I swear to you Angelique I did not mean to offend you. You cut deep."

"Pshaw!" retorted she smiling, "wounds by a lady are easily cured. They seldom leave a mark behind, a year after!"

"I dont know that! The slight repulse of a lady's finger, a touch that would not crush a gnat, will sometimes kill a strong man, like a sword stroke! I have known such things to happen," said Bigot.

"Well, happily my touch did not hurt you, Chevalier. But

having vindicated myself, I feel I owe you a reparation. You speak of rescuing Le Gardeur from the Honnetes Gens—in what way can I aid you?"

"In many ways and all ways. Withdraw him from them.— The great festival, at the Philiberts, when is it to be?"

"Tomorrow. See they have honoured me with a special invitation." She drew a note from her pocket. "This is very polite of Colonel Philibert, is it not?" said she.

Bigot glanced superciliously at the note. "Do you mean to go, Angelique," asked he.

"No, although, had I no feelings but my own to consult, I would certainly go."

"Whose feelings do you consult, Angelique," asked the Intendant, "if not your own?"

"O dont be flattered! The Grand Companys! I am loyal to the association without respect to persons."

"So much better," said he. "By the way, it would not be amiss to keep Le Gardeur away from the festival. These Philiberts and the Heads of the *Honnetes Gens* have great sway over him."—

"Naturally, they are all his own kith and kin, but I will draw him away, if you desire it. I cannot prevent his going, but I can find means to prevent his staying," added she with a smile of confidence in her power.

"That will do Angelique! any thing to make a breach with them!—"

While there were abysses in Bigots mind which Angelique could not fathom, as little did Bigot suspect that when Angelique seemed to flatter him by yielding to his suggestions, she was following out a course she had already decided upon in her own mind from the moment she had learned that Cecile Tourangeau, was to be at the festival of Belmont, with unlimited opportunities of explanation with Le Gardeur as to her treatment by Angelique.

The Intendant after some pleasant badinage rose and took his departure, leaving Angelique agitated puzzled and dissatisfied on the whole with his visit. She reclined on the seat resting her head on her hand for a long time, in appearance the idlest, in reality the busiest brain of any girl in the City of Quebec. She felt she had much to do, and great sacrifice to make, but firmly resolved at whatever cost to go through with it, for after all the sacrifice was for herself and not for others!

CHAPTER 18

THE MEROVINGIAN PRINCESS

THE interior of the Cathedral of St Marie, seemed like another world compared with the noisy bustling market place in front of it.

The garish sunshine poured hot and oppressive in the square outside, but was shorn of its strength as it passed through the painted windows of the cathedral, filling the vast interior with a cool, dim religious light, broken by tall shafts of columns, swelling out into ornate capitals and supporting a lofty ceiling on which was painted the open heavens with Saints and angels adoring the Lord.

A lofty arch of cunning work, overlaid with gold, the masterpiece of Le Vasseur, spanned the chancel, like the rainbow round the throne. Lights were burning on the altar. Incense went up in spirals to the roof, and through the wavering cloud the saints and angels seemed to look down with living faces upon the crowd of worshippers who knelt upon the broad floor of the church.

It was the hour of Vespers. The voice of the priest was answered by the deep peal of the organ and the chanting of the Choir. The vast edifice was filled with harmony, in the pauses of which the ear seemed to catch the sound of the river of life as it flows out of the throne of God and the lamb.

The demeanour of the crowd of worshippers was quiet and reverential. A few gay groups however whose occupation was mainly to see and be seen exchanged the idle gossip of the day with such of their friends as they met there. The fee of a prayer or two did not seem excessive for the pleasure, and it was soon paid.

The Perron outside was a favorite resort of the gallants of

fashion at the hour of Vespers, whose practice it was to salute the ladies of their acquaintance at the door by sprinkling their dainty fingers with holy water. Religion combined with gallantry is a form of devotion not quite obsolete at the present day, and at the same place.

The Church door was the recognized spot for meeting, gossip, business, love making and announcements. Old friends stopped to talk over the news, merchants their commercial prospects. It was at once the Bourse and the Royal Exchange of Quebec. There were promulgated by the brazen lungs of the city crier, royal proclamations, of the Governor, Edicts of the Intendant, orders of the Court of Justice, vendues public and private. In short the life and stir of the city of Quebec seemed to flow about the door of St Marie, as the blood through the heart of a healthy man.

A few old trees, relics of the primeval forest had been left for shade and ornament in the great market place. A little rivulet of clear water ran sparkling down the slope of the square where every day the shadow of the cross upon the tall steeple lay over it like a benediction.

A couple of young men fashionably dressed loitered this afternoon near the great door of the Convent in the narrow street that runs into the great square of the market. They walked about with short impatient turns, occasionally glancing at the clock of the Recollets, visible through the tall elms that bounded the garden of the Grey Friars. Presently the door of the Convent opened. Half a dozen gaily attired young ladies, *Internes* or pupils of the Convent sallied out. They had exchanged their conventual dress for their usual attire outside and got leave to go out "into the world," on some errand real or pretended, for one hour and no more.

They tripped lightly down the broad steps and were instantly joined by the young men who had been waiting for them. After a hasty merry hand shaking the whole party proceeded in great glee towards the market place where the shops of the mercers and confectioners offered the attractions they sought. They went on purchasing bonbons and ribbons, from one shop to another until they reached the Cathedral, when a common impulse seized them to see who was there. They flew up the steps and disappeared in the church.

In the midst of their devotions as they knelt on the floor, the sharp eyes of the young ladies were caught by the gesticulations of the well gloved hand of the Chevalier des Meloises, as he saluted them across the aisle.

The hurried recitation of an Ave or two had quite satisfied the devotion of the Chevalier, and he looked round the church with an air of condescension, criticizing the music, and peering into the faces of such of the ladies as looked up, and many did so, to return his scrutiny.

The young ladies encountered him in the aisle as they left the Church before the service was finished. It had long since been finished for him, and was finished for the young ladies also, when they had satisfied their curiosity to see who was there and who with whom.

"We cannot pray for you any longer, Chevalier des Meloises!" said one of the gayest of the group "The Lady Superior has economically granted us but one hour in the city, to make our purchases, and attend vespers. Out of that hour we can only steal forty minutes for a promenade through the city. So goodby, if you prefer the church to our company, or come with us and you shall escort two of us. You see we have only a couple of gentlemen to six ladies!"—

"I much prefer your company, Mademoiselle de Brouague!" replied he gallantly, forgetting the important meeting of the managers of the Grand Company at the Palace which however was being cleverly transacted without his help.

Louise de Brouague had no great esteem for the Chevalier des Meloises, but as she remarked to a companion, he made rather a neat walking stick if a young lady could procure no better, to promenade with. "We come out in full force to day, Chevalier," said she, with a merry glance round the group of lively girls. "A glorious sample of the famous class of 'the Louises,' are we not?"

"Glorious! Superbe! incomparable!!" The Chevalier replied as he inspected them archly through his glass. "But how did you manage to get out? One Louise at a time is

enough to storm the city—! but six of them at once!—The
Lady Superior is full of mercy! to day!"

"O, is she!—listen! We should not have got permission to
come out to day, had we not first laid seige to the soft heart
of Mere des Seraphins! She it was interceded for us; and Lo!
here we are, ready for any adventure that may befall errant
demoiselles in the streets of Quebec!"

Well might the fair Louise de Brouague boast of the
famous class of "the Louises," all composed of young ladies of
that name, distinguished for beauty, rank and fashion in the
world of New France.

Prominent among them at that period, was the beautiful,
gay, Louise de Brouague. In the full maturity of her charms
as the wife of the Chevalier de Lery, she accompanied
her husband to England after the cession of Canada, and
went to Court to pay homage to their new Sovereign,
George III., when the young King struck with her grace and
beauty, gallantly exclaimed—: "If the ladies of Canada are as
handsome as you, I have indeed made a conquest!—"—

To escort young ladies, *Internes* of the Convent, when
granted permission to go out into the city, was a favorite
pastime, truly a labour of love, of the young gallants of that
day. An occupation if very idle, was at least very agreable to
those participating in these stolen promenades, and which
have not perhaps, been altogether discontinued in Quebec
even to the present day!—

The pious nuns were of course intirely ignorant of the
contrivances of their fair pupils to amuse themselves in
the city. At any rate they good naturedly overlooked things
they could not quite prevent. They had human hearts still
under their snowy wymples, and perhaps did not wholly lack
womanly sympathy with the dear girls in their charge.

"Why are you not at Belmont to day, Chevalier des
Meloises—?" boldly asked Louise Roy, a fearless little
questioner, in a gay summer robe. She was light and sprightly
as Titania. Her long chesnut hair was the marvel and boast
of the Convent, and what she prized more, the admiration
of the city. It covered her like a veil down to her knees when

she chose to let it down in a flood of splendour. Her deep grey eyes contained wells of womanly wisdom. Her skin fair as a lilly of Artois had borrowed from the sun, five or six faint freckles just to prove the purity of her blood and distract the eye with a variety of charms. The Merovingian Princess, the long haired daughter of kings, as she was fondly styled by the nuns, queened it wherever she went, by right divine of youth wit and beauty.

"I should not have had the felicity of meeting you, Mademoiselle Roy, had I gone to Belmont," replied the Chevalier, not liking the question, at all. "I preferred not to go."

"You are always so polite and complimentary," replied she, a little trace of pout visible on her lips. "I do not see how any one could stay away who was at liberty to go to Belmont! And the whole city has gone I am sure! for I see nobody in the street!" She held an eye glass coquettishly to her eye. "Nobody at all!" repeated she. Her companions accused her afterwards of glancing equivocally at the Chevalier as she made this remark, and she answered with a merry laugh, that might imply either assent or denial.

"Had you heard in the Convent of the festival at Belmont, Mademoiselle Roy?" asked he, twirling his cane rather majestically.

"We have heard of nothing else, and talked of nothing else, for a whole week!" replied she. "Our mistresses have been in a state of distraction trying to stop our incessant whispering in the school, instead of minding our lessons, like good girls, trying to earn good conduct marks. The feast, the ball, the dresses, the company, beat learning out of our heads—and hearts—! Only fancy! Chevalier!" she went on in her voluble manner, "Louise de Beaujeu here was asked to give the Latin name for heaven, and she at once translated it Belmont!—"

"Tell no school tales, Mademoiselle Roy!" retorted Louise de Beaujeu, her black eyes flashing with merriment. "It was a good translation!—but who was it stumbled in the Greek Class, when asked for the proper name of the Anax Andron the king of men in the Iliad—?"—Louise Roy looked archly and said defiantly "Go on!"—

"Would you believe it Chevalier. She replied:—Pierre Philibert! Mere Christine fairly gasped, but Louise had to kiss the floor as a penance—for pronouncing a gentleman's name with such unction as she did."

"And if I did, I paid my penance heartily and loudly, as you may recollect, Louise de Beaujeu, although I confess I would have preferred kissing Pierre Philibert himself, if I had my choice!"

"Always her way! wont give in!—never! Louise Roy stands by her translation in spite of all the Greek Lexicons and nuns in the Convent!—" exclaimed Louise de Brouague.

"And so I do, and will. And Pierre Philibert is the king of men, in New France or old! Ask Amelie de Repentigny!" added she in a half whisper to her companion.

"O she will swear to it any day!" was the saucy reply of Louise de Brouague. "But without whispering it, Chevalier des Meloises!" continued she "The classes in the Convent have all gone wild in his favour since they learned he was in love with one of our late companions in School. He is the Prince Camaralzaman of our fairy tales."

"Who is that?" The Chevalier spoke tartly rather. He was excessively annoyed at all this enthusiasm in behalf of Pierre Philibert.

"Nay, I will tell no more fairy tales out of school, but I assure you if our wishes had wings the whole class of Louises would fly away to Belmont, to day like a flock of ring doves."

Louise de Brouague noticed the pique of the Chevalier, at the mention of Philibert, but in that spirit of petty torment with which her sex avenges small slights, she continued to irritate the vanity of the Chevalier, whom in her heart she rather despised.

His politeness nearly gave way. He was thoroughly disgusted with all this lavish praise of Philibert. He suddenly recollected that he had an appointment at the Palace, which would prevent him, he said enjoying the full hour of absence granted to the Greek Class of the Ursulines.

"Mademoiselle Angelique has of course gone to Belmont,

if pressing engagement prevent *you*, Chevalier," said Louise Roy. "How provoking it must be to have business to look after when one wants to enjoy life!—" The Chevalier half spun round on his heel under the quizzing of Louise's eye glass.

"No, Angelique has not gone to Belmont," replied he quite piqued. "She very properly declined to mingle with the Messieurs and Mesdames Jourdains, who consort with the Bourgeois Philibert! She was preparing for a ride, and the city really seems all the gayer by the absence of so many common place people as have gone out to Belmont."

Louise de Brouague's eyes gave a few flashes of indignation. "Fie! Chevalier, that was naughtily said of you about the good Bourgeois and his friends," exclaimed she impetuously. "Why the Governor, the Lady de Tilly and her neice, the Chevalier La Corne St Luc, Hortense and Claude Beauharnois and I know not how many more of the very elite of Society have gone to do honour to Colonel Philibert—! And as for the girls in the Convent, who you will allow are the most important and most select portion of the Community, there is not one of us but would willingly jump out of the window, and do penance on dry bread and salt fish for a month, just for one hour's pleasure at the Ball this evening. Would we not, Louises?"

Not a Louise present but assented with an emphasis, that brought sympathetic smiles upon the faces of the two young Cavaliers, who had watched all this pretty play.

The Chevalier des Meloises bowed very low. "I regret so much, ladies, to have to leave you! but affairs of State you know!—affairs of State! The Intendant will not proceed without a full board. I must attend the meeting to day at the Palace."

"O assuredly, Chevalier," replied Louise Roy. "What would become of the nation, what would become of the world, nay what would become of the *Internes* of the Ursulines, if statesmen and warriors and philosophers like you,—and the Sieurs Drouillon and La Force here"—(this in a parenthesis, not to scratch the Chevalier too deep)—"did not take wise counsel for our safety, and happiness and also for the welfare of the nation—?"

The Chevalier des Meloises took his departure under this shower of arrows.

The young La Force was as yet only an idle dangler about the city, but in the course of time became a man of wit and energy worthy of his name. He replied gaily—:

"Thanks Mademoiselle Roy. It is just for sake of the fair internes of the Convent that Drouillon and I, have taken up the vocation, of statesmen warriors and philosophers and friends. We are quite ready to guide your innocent footsteps through the streets of this perilous city, if you are ready to go."

"We had better hasten, too!" ejaculated Louise Roy, looking archly through her eye glass. "I can see Bonhomme Michel peeping round the corner of the Cote de Lery! He is looking after us, stray lambs of the fold, Sieur Drouillon!"—

Bonhomme Michel was the old watchman and factotum of the Monastry. He had a general commission to keep a sharp eye upon the young ladies, who were allowed to go out into the city. A pair of horn spectacles usually helped his vision—sometimes marred it however! when the knowing gallants slipped a crown into his hand, to put in the place of his magnifiers. Bonhomme Michel, placed all his propitiation money—he liked a pious word—in his old leathern sack which contained the redemption of many a gadding promenade through the streets of Quebec. Whether he reported, what he saw this time, is not recorded in the *Vieux Recit*, the old annals of the Convent. But as Louise Roy called him her dear old Cupid! and knew so well how to bandage his eyes, it is probable the good nuns were not informed of the pleasant meeting of the Class Louises and the gentlemen who escorted them round the city on the present occasion.

Poor Michel Bonhomme! This history would be incomplete, unless it recorded his death at a most patriarchal old age, in the monastry when to ease his good old soul at last, he piously bequeathed to it his leathern sack, filled with coins of every stamp paid him in propitiation, of so many hundred sweet stolen promenades of the lively Internes of the Convent.

The Nuns were not inexorable, when he died confessing

his fault. They received his bequest, pardoned his occasional blindness and good nature, had masses said yearly for his good old soul, long long after the memory of his honest Breton face had been forgotten by the new generations of city gallants and Internes that followed in the city of Quebec.

CHAPTER 19

"PUT MONEY IN THY PURSE"

THE Chevalier des Meloises quite out of humour with the merry Louises, picked his way with quick dainty steps down the Rue du Palais. The gay "Louises" before returning to the Convent resolved to make a hasty promenade to the walls to see the people at work upon them, and received with great contentment the military salutes of the officers of their acquaintance which they acknowledged with the courtesy of well trained Internes, slightly exaggerated, by provoking smiles and mischievous glances which had formed no part of the lessons in politeness taught them by the Nuns.

In justice be it said, however, the girls were actuated by a nobler feeling than the mere spirit of amusement. A sentiment of loyalty to France, a warm enthusiasm for their country drew them to the walls. They wanted to see the defenders of Quebec, to show their sympathy and smile approval upon them.

"Would to heaven I were a man!" exclaimed Louise de Brouague, "that I might wield a sword, a spade, any thing of use, to serve my Country—! I shame to do nothing but talk pray and suffer for it, while every one else is working or fighting."

Poor girl! she did not foresee a day, when the women of New France, would undergo trials compared with which the sword stroke that kills the strong man is as the touch of mercy, when the batteries of Wolfe would for sixty five days, shower shot and shell upon Quebec, and the South shore for a hundred miles together be blazing with the fires of devastation. Such things were mercifully withheld from their foresight, and the light hearted girls went the round of the works as gaily as they would have tripped in a ballroom.

The Chevalier des Meloises passing through the Porte du Palais, was hailed by two or three young officers of the Regiment of Bearn, who invited him into the Guard House to take a glass of wine before decending the steep hill. The Chevalier stopped willingly, and entered the well furnished quarters of the officers of the Guard where a cool flask of Burgundy presently restored him to good humour with himself and consequently with the world.

"What is up to day at the Palace" asked Captain Monredin a vivacious Navarrois. "All the *Gros Bonnets* of the Grand Company have gone down this afternoon—! I suppose you are going too, Des Meloises?—"

"Yes! They have sent for me you see on affairs of state!— what Penisault calls 'business' not a drop of wine on the board! Nothing but books and papers, bills and shipments, money paid, money received, *Doit et avoir* and all the cursed lingo of the Friponne—! I damn the Friponne, but bless her money! It pays Monredin!—It pays! better than fur trading at a lonely out post in the North West!" The Chevalier jingled a handful of coin in his pocket. The sound was a sedative to his disgust at the idea of trade, and quite reconciled him to the Friponne.

"You are a lucky dog, nevertheless, to be able to make it jingle," replied Monredin. "Not one of us Bearnois can play an accompaniment to your air of money in both pockets. Here is our famous regiment of Bearn, second to none in the Kings service, a whole year, in arrear of our pay! Gad! I wish *I* could go into 'business' as you call it, and woo that jolly Dame, La Friponne!"

"For six months we have lived on trust!—Those leeches of Jews who call themselves Christians down in the Sault au Matelot, wont cash the best orders in the Regiment for less than forty per cent discount!"

"That is true!" broke in another officer, whose rather rubicund face told of credit somewhere and the product of credit, good wine, and good meat, generally. "That is true Monredin! The old curmudgeon, of a Broker at the corner of the *Cul de Sac* had the impudence to ask me fifty per cent discount upon my drafts on Bourdeaux! I agree with Des Meloises there. 'Business' may be a good thing for them who handle it, but Devil touch their dirty fingers for me—!"

"Dont condemn all of them! Emeric," said Captain Poulariez a quiet resolute looking officer. "There is one merchant in the city who carries the principles of a gentleman into the usages of commerce. The Bourgeois Philibert gives cent per cent for good orders of the Kings officers—just to show his sympathy with the army—and his love for France."—

"Well, I wish he were paymaster of the forces that is all! and then I could go to him if I wanted to" replied Monredin.

"Why do you not go to him?" asked Poulariez.

"Why? For the same reason I suppose so many others of us do not," replied Monredin. "Colonel Dalquier endorses my orders and he hates the Bourgeois cordially, as a hot friend of the Intendant, ought to do—!—So you see I have to submit to be plucked of my best penfeathers, by that old *Fesse Mathieu,* Penisault at the Friponne!"

"How many of yours went out to the great spread at Belmont?" asked Des Meloises quite weary of commercial topics.

"Pardieu!" replied Monredin. "Except the Colonel and Adjutant, who stayed away on principle, I think every officer in the Regiment went, present company excepted who being on duty could not go, much to their chagrin. Such a glorious crush of handsome girls has not been seen they say, since our Regiment came to Quebec!"

"And not likely to have been seen before your distinguished arrival, eh! Monredin—?" ejaculated Des Meloises holding his glass to be refilled. "That is delicious Burgundy!" added he. "I did not think any one beside the Intendant had wine like that."

"That is some of La Martiniere's cargo," remarked Poulariez. "It was kind of him was it not, to remember us poor Bearnois here on the wrong side of the Atlantic—?"

"And how earnestly we were praying for that same Burgundy!" ejaculated Emeric, "when it came as if dropped upon us by Providence. Health and wealth to Captain La

Martiniere and the good frigate *Fleur de Lys*!!"

Another round followed. "They talk about those Jansenist convulsionaires at the tomb of Master Paris, which are setting all France by the ears," exclaimed Monredin, "but I say, there is nothing so contagious as the drinking of a glass of wine like that!—"

"And the glass gives us convulsions too; Monredin! if we try it too often, and no miracle about it either!" remarked Poulariez.

Monredin looked up red and puffy as if needing a bridle, to check his fast gait. "But they say we are to have peace soon. Is that true Des Meloises?" asked Poulariez. "*You* ought to know what is under the cards, before they are played."

"No! I dont know! and I hope the report is not true! Who wants peace yet? It would ruin the Kings friends in the Colony."—Des Meloises looked as statesmanlike as he could when delivering this dictum.

"Ruin the Kings friends! Who are they? Des Meloises—?" asked Poulariez with a look of well assumed surprize.

"Why the associates of the Grand Company to be sure! What other friends has the King got in New France?"

"Really! I thought he had the Regiment of Bearn for a number of them, to say nothing of the honest people of the Colony," replied Poulariez impatiently.

"The *Honnetes Gens*, you mean!" exclaimed Des Meloises. "Well Poulariez! all I have to say is, that if this colony is kept up for the sake of a lot of shop keepers, wood choppers cobblers and farmers, the sooner the King hands it over to the Devil or the English the better—!"

Poulariez looked indignant enough, but from the others a loud laugh followed this sally.—The Chevalier des Meloises pulled out his watch. "I must be gone to the Palace," said he. "I dare say, Cadet, Varin and Penisault will have balanced the ledgers by this time, and the Intendant, who is the devil for business on such occasions, will have settled the dividends, for the Quarter, the only part of the business I care about."

"But dont you help them with the work a little?" asked Poulariez.—

"Not I! I leave business to them that have a vocation for it! Besides I think, Cadet Varin and Penisault like to keep the inner ring of the company to themselves." He turned to Emeric, "I hope there will be a good dividend to night Emeric" said he. "I owe you some revenge at Piquet do I not?"

"You capoted me last night at the Taverne de Menut, and I had three aces and three kings!" exclaimed Emeric.

"But I had a quatorze, and took the fishes," replied Des Meloises.

"Well Chevalier! I will win them back to night! I hope the dividend will be good! In that way I too share in the 'business' of the Grand Company!"

"Good Bye, Chevalier! Remember me to St Blague!" This was a familiar subriquet of Bigot. "Tis the best name going!— If I had an heir for the old Chateau on the Adour, I would christen him, Bigot, for luck!"

The Chevalier des Meloises left the officers and proceded down the steep road that led to the Palace. The gardens were quiet to day. A few loungers might be seen in the magnificent alleys, pleached walks and terraces. Beyond the gardens however stretched the Kings wharves and magazines of the Friponne; these fairly swarmed with men lading, unlading ships and bateaux and piling and unpiling goods.

The Chevalier glanced with disdain at the Magazines, and flourishing his cane mounted leisurely the broad steps of the palace and was at once admitted to the Council room.

"Better late than never! Chevalier Des Meloises!—" exclaimed Bigot, carelessly glancing at him, as he took a seat at the Board, where sat Cadet, Varin Penisault and the leading spirits of the Grand Company. "You are in double luck to day. The business is over, and Dame Friponne has laid a golden egg worth a Jews tooth for each partner of the Company."

The Chevalier did not notice, or did not care for the slight touch of sarcasm in the Intendants tone. "Thanks, Bigot!" drawled he, "my egg shall be hatched to night down at Menuts. I expect to have little more left than the shell of it tomorrow."

"Well, never mind! We have considered all that, Chevalier. What one loses another gets; it is all in the family! Look here," continued he laying his finger upon a page of the ledger that lay open before him, "Mademoiselle Angelique des Meloises is now a shareholder in the Grand Company! The list of high fair and noble ladies of the Court who are members of the Company will be honoured by the addition of the name of your charming sister!"

The Chevalier's eyes sparkled with delight as he read Angeliques name on the book. A handsome sum of five digits stood to her credit. He bowed his thanks with many warm expressions of his sense of "the honour done his sister by placing her name on the roll of the ladies of the Court who honour the Company by accepting a share of its dividends."

"I hope Mademoiselle des Meloises will not refuse this small mark of our respect?" observed Bigot, feeling well assured she would not, deem it a small one.

"Little fear of that!" muttered Cadet, whose bad opinion of the sex was incorrigible. "The greedy harpies of Versailles scratch jewels out of every dunghill, and Angelique des Meloises has longer claws than any of them!—"

Cadet's ill natured remark was either unheard or unheeded. Besides he was privileged to say anything. Des Meloises bowed with an air of perfect complaisance to the Intendant, as he answered, "I will guarantee the perfect satisfaction of Angelique with this marked compliment of the Grand Company. She will I am sure, appreciate the kindness of the Intendant as it deserves."

Cadet and Varin exchanged smiles, not unnoticed by Bigot, who smiled too. "Yes Chevalier," said he, "the Company gives this token of its admiration for the fairest lady in New France. We have bestowed premiums upon fine flax and fat cattle. Why not upon beauty grace and wit, embodied in handsome women?"

"Angelique will be highly flattered Chevalier" replied he, "at the distinction. She must thank you herself, as I am sure she will."

"I am happy to try to deserve her thanks," replied Bigot, and not caring to talk further on the subject, "What news in the city this afternoon Chevalier," asked he. "How does that affair at Belmont go off?—"

"Dont know—half the city has gone I think!—At the Church door however, the talk among the merchants is, that peace is going to be made soon. Is it so very threatening, Bigot?"

"If the King wills it, it is!" Bigot spoke carelessly.

"But your own opinion Chevalier Bigot? what think you of it?"

"Amen! Amen! *quod fiat fiatur*! Seyny John the fool of Paris could enlighten you as well as I could as to what the women at Versailles may decide to do—!—" replied Bigot in a tone of impatience.

"I fear peace will be made. What will you do in that case, Bigot?" asked Des Meloises not noticing Bigots aversion to the topic.

"If the King makes it—*invitus amabo*!—as the man said who married the shrew!" Bigot laughed mockingly, "We must make the best of it, Des Meloises! and let me tell you privately I mean to make a good thing of it for myself, whichever way it turn—!—"

"But what will become of the Company should the war expenditure stop—?" The Chevalier was thinking of his dividend of five figures.

"Oh! You should have been here sooner, Des Meloises! you would have heard our grand settlement of the question in every contingency—of peace or war."

"Be sure of one thing" continued Bigot. "The Grand Company will not, like the eels of Melun, cry out before they are skinned! What says the proverb—*mieux vaut engin que force*, 'craft beats strength.' The Grand Company must prosper as the first condition of life in New France. Perhaps a year or two of repose may not be amiss to revictual and reinforce the Colony, and by that time we shall be ready to pick the lock of Bellona's temple again, and cry *vive La Guerre*! *vive La Grande Compagnie*! more merrily than ever—!"

Bigots far reaching intellect forecast the course of events, which remained so much subject to his own direction after the peace of Aix La Chapelle, a peace which in America was never a peace at all, but only an armed and troubled truce, between the clashing interests and rival ambitions of the French and English in the new world.

The meeting of the Board of Managers of the Grand Company broke up—and a circumstance that rarely happened—without the customary debauch. Bigot preoccupied with his own projects, which reached far beyond the mere interests of the Company, retired to his couch. Cadet Varin and Penisault forming an interior circle of the Friponne, had certain matters to shape for the Company's eye. The rings of corruption in the Grand Company descended narrower, and more black and precipitous down to the bottom where Bigot sat, the Demiourgos of all.

The Chevalier des Meloises was rather proud of his sister's beauty and cleverness, and in truth a little afraid of her. They lived together harmoniously enough, so long as each allowed the other his or her own way. Both took it, and followed their own pleasures, and were not usually disagreable to one another, except when Angelique commented on what she called his penuriousness and he upon her extravagance, in the financial administration of the family of the Des Meloises.

The Chevalier was highly delighted to day to be able to inform Angelique of her good fortune in becoming a partner, of the Friponne, and that too by grace of his Excellency the Intendant. The information filled Angelique with delight, not only because it made her independent of her brother's mismanagement of money, but it opened a door to her wildest hopes. In that gift, her ambition found a potent ally to enable her to resist the appeal to her heart which she knew would be made to night, by Le Gardeur de Repentigny.

The Chevalier des Meloises had no idea of his sister's own aims. He had long nourished a foolish fancy that if he had not obtained the hand of the wealthy and beautiful heiress of Repentigny, it was because he had not proposed. Something to day had suggested the thought that unless he did propose soon his chances would be nil, and another might secure the prize which he had in his vain fancy set down as his own.

He hinted to Angelique to day, that he was almost resolved

to marry, and that his projected alliance with the noble and wealthy house of Tilly could be easily accomplished, if Angelique would only do her share as a sister ought, in securing her brother's fortune and happiness.

"How?" asked she, looking up savagely, for she knew well what her brother was driving at.

"By your accepting Le Gardeur, without more delay! All the City knows he is mad in love, and would marry you any day you choose if you wore only the hair on your head, and he would ask no better fortune!"

"It is useless to advise me, Renaud!" said she, "and whether I take Le Gardeur or no, it would not help your chance with Amelie!—! I am sorry for it, for Amelie is a prize Renaud! but not for you at any price. Let me tell you, that desirable young lady will become the bride of Pierre Philibert and the bride of no other man living."

"You give one cold encouragement Sister! But I am sure, if you would only marry Le Gardeur, you could easily with your tact and cleverness induce Amelie to let me share the Tilly fortune. There are chests full of gold in the old Manor House! and a crow could hardly fly in a day, over their broad lands!—"

"Perfectly useless, Brother! Amelie is not like most girls. She would refuse the hand of a king for sake of the man she loved and she loves Pierre Philibert to his finger ends. She has married him in her heart a thousand times. I hate paragons of women, and would scorn to be one—! but I tell you brother, Amelie is a paragon of a girl without knowing it."

"Hum, I never tried my hand on a paragon. I should like to do so," replied he with a smile of decided confidence in his powers. "I fancy they are just like other women when you can catch them with their armour off."

"Yes, but women like Amelie, never lay off their armour! They seem born in it like Minerva. But your vanity will not let you believe me, Renaud! So go try her and tell me your luck—! She wont scratch you, nor scold. Amelie is a lady and will talk to you like a Queen. But she will give a polite reply to your proposal that will improve your opinions of our sex."

"You are mocking me Angelique as you always do! One never knows when you are in jest or when in earnest—even when you get angry, it is often unreal, and for a purpose! I want you to be serious for once. The fortune of the Tillys and De Repentignys is the best in New France and we can make it ours if you will help me."

"I am serious enough, in wishing you those chests full of gold and those broad lands that a crow cannot fly over in a day. But I must forego my share of them, and so must you yours Brother—!" Angelique leaned back in her chair, desiring to stop further discussion of a topic she did not like to hear.

"Why must you forego your share of the de Repentigny fortune Angelique! you could call it your own any day you chose by giving your little finger to Le Gardeur. You do really puzzle me!"

The Chevalier did look perplexed at his inscrutable sister, who only smiled over the table at him, as she nonchalantly cracked nuts and sipped her wine by drops.

"Of course I puzzle you, Renaud!" said she at last. "I am a puzzle to myself, sometimes. But you see there are so many men in the world—poor ones are so plenty, rich ones so scarce, and sensible ones hardly to be found at all, that a woman may be excused for selling herself to the highest bidder. Love is a commodity only spoken of in Romances or in the patois of milk maids now a days!"

"Zounds! Angelique, you would try the patience of all the Saints in the Calendar! I shall pity the fellow you take in! Here is the fairest fortune in the Colony, about to fall into the hands of Pierre Philibert, whom Satan confound for his assurance, a fortune which I always regarded as my own."

"It shows the folly and vanity of your sex! you never spoke a word to Amelie de Repentigny in the way of wooing in your life! Girls like her dont drop into men's arms just for the asking."

"Pshaw!—as if she would refuse me if you only acted a sisters part! But you are impenetrable as a rock, and the whole of your fickle sex could not match your vanity and caprice, Angelique."

She rose quickly with a provoked air.

"You are getting so complimentary to my poor sex Renaud," said she "that I must really leave you to yourself and I could scarcely leave you in worse company."

"You are so bitter and sarcastic upon one," replied he tartly "my only desire was to secure a good fortune for you and another for myself! I dont see for my part what women are made for, except to mar everything a man wants to do for himself, and for them."

"Certainly, every thing should be done for us, brother!— But I have no defence to make for my sex brother. I dare say we women deserve all that men think of us, but then it is impolite to tell us so to our faces. Now if I advised you Renaud! I would counsel you to study gardening, and you may one day arrive at as great distinction as the Marquis de Vandriere. You may cultivate *chou chou*, if you cannot raise a bride like Amelie de Repentigny."

Angelique knew her brother's genius was not penetrating, or she would scarcely have ventured this broad allusion to the brother of La Pompadour, who by virtue of his relationship to the Court favorite had recently been created Director of the Royal Gardens. What fancy was working in the brain of Angelique, when she alluded to him may be only surmised.

The Chevalier was indignant however at an implied comparison between himself and the plebian Marquis de Vandriere. He replied with some heat. "The Marquis de Vandriere! How dare you mention him and me together? There is not an officers mess in the army that receives the son of the fishmonger! Why do you mention him Angelique? You are a perfect riddle!"

"I only thought of something brother, that might happen if I should ever go to Paris! I was acting a charade in my fancy, and that was the solution of it—!"

"What was? You would drive the whole Sorbonne mad with your charades and fancies! But I must leave you."—

"Good bye Brother! if you will go. Think of it. If you want to rise in the world you may yet become a Royal Gardener like the Marquis de Vandriere." Her silvery laugh rang out good humouredly as he descended the stairs, and passed out of the house.

She sat down in her fauteuil. "Pity, Renaud is such a fool!" said she. "Yet I am not sure but he is wiser in his folly than I with all my tact and cleverness! which I suspect are going to make a greater fool of me than even he is!"

She leaned back in her chair in a deep thinking mood. "It is growing dark," murmured she. "Le Gardeur will assuredly be here soon in spite of all the attractions of Belmont! How to deal with him when he comes, is more than I know—! He will renew his suit I am sure!"

For a moment the heart of Angelique softened in her bosom. "Accept him I must not," said she. "Affront him I will not! cease to love him is out of my power, as much as is my ability to love the Intendant whom I cordially detest, and shall marry all the same—!" She pressed her hands over her eyes, and sat silent for a few minutes. "But I am not sure of it—! That woman remains still at Beaumanoir! will my scheming to remove her be all in vain or no?"—Angelique recollected with a shudder, a thought that had leaped in her bosom, like a young Satan engendered of evil desires. "I dare hardly look in the honest eyes of Le Gardeur after nursing such a monstrous fancy as that," said she, "but my fate is fixed, all the same! Le Gardeur will vainly try to undo this knot in my life. He must leave me to my own devices!"—To what devices she left *him*! was a thought that sprang not up in her purely selfish nature.

In her perplexity, Angelique tied knot upon knot hard as pebbles in her handkerchief. Those knots of her destiny, as she regarded them she left untied, and they remain untied to this day, a memento of her character and of those knots in her life, which posterity has puzzled itself over to no purpose, to explain.

CHAPTER 20

CROSS QUESTIONING

ANGELIQUE weary of her own reflections upon the uncertainties of fortune, summoned Lizette to arrange her toilette afresh, and amuse or rather distract her thoughts by retailing the latest gossip of the Quartier. That was Lizette's world—a stirring little world too in those days! an epitome of France itself, a Paris in miniature, where every Province from Bearn to Artois had its representatives, and the little pot of Colonial life was boiling with the rivalries, friendships, hates fears and ambitions of the Metropolis of the Kingdom, sharpened and intensified by the narrowness of the arena in which they met.

Lizette was full to day of the gossip that flew from door to door, and from gallery to gallery of the quaint old houses. Caught first by the maids, the story of the doings at Belmont was volubly retailed to the itching ears of their mistresses, and the account of the carriages and horsemen and horsewomen dresses and corteges of the fashionable people going out to honour the fete of Pierre Philibert, seemed interminable as the list of Homer's heros.

"And who may they all be, Lizette?" asked Angelique, not for information but to hear her maid's talk, for she knew well, who had been invited, who were going and who had declined to go to Belmont. Nothing happened in Quebec which did not reach Angelique's ears, and the festival at Belmont had been the talk of the city for many days.

"O, they are Bourgeoisie for the most part, my Lady, people who smell of furs, and fish and turpentine, and Lower Town—!—You see the gentlemen any day down in the Basse Ville, jingling their money in their pockets, their coats dusted

226

with flour and their knees greasy with oil, while their wives and daughters in feathers and furbelows parade through Upper Town, with all the assurance of their betters."

Lizette was a cunning Abigail, and drew her portrait to suit the humour of her mistress, whom she had heard ridiculing the festival of the *Honnetes Gens*, as she called it.

"But you know who they were, Lizette? That tongue of yours can, if it will, repeat every name dress and equipment that has gone out to Belmont to day."

"Yes, my Lady. What I did not see myself I learned from Manon Nytouche, Madame Racine's maid, who accompanied her mistress down to the house of Madame de Grandmaison, where the ladies all sat in the Balcony, quizzing the parties as they rode past on their way to Belmont."

Angelique threw herself back languidly in her chair. "Go on then. I dont care how you learned their names, but tell me who rode past?—"

"O, there were all the Brassards of course, the girls dressed like Duchesses, quite forgetting the dirty old Magazin, in *Sous Le Fort*, where their finery comes from!—And the Gravels from the *Cul de Sac*, whose large feet remind one of their grandfather the old Coureur de Bois, who acquired them tramping in the woods."

"That was well said, Lizette!" observed Angelique. "I wish the Demoiselles Gravel could hear you! Who else was there?"

"O the Huots of course, whose stiff necks and high shoulders came from their grandmother the Squaw! The Sieur Huot took her out of the wigwam, with her trousseau on her back, and a strap round her forehead, and made a city Dame of her! Marry come up! the demoiselles Huot wear furs in another fashion now! Then there were the Tourangeaus, who think themselves rich enough to marry into the Noblesse! and Cecile of course, with her hair frizzed over her forehead to hide— —" Lizette suddenly remembering she was on dangerous ground, stopped short.

"To hide what?" ejaculated Angelique rousing herself almost savagely, for she knew well why her maid hesitated.

"A mark like a red cross upon her forehead, my Lady!"

Lizette trembled a little, for she was never sure what direction the lightening would strike, when her mistress was angry.

"Ha! Ha!" laughed Angelique. "She did not get that mark in baptism, I'll be bound—! The world has a long tongue and the tip of it is in your mouth, Lizette!" continued she, leaning back in her chair quietly to her maids surprize. "Tell me now, what do people say of Cecile?"

"They say my Lady, that she would give her little finger any day for a smile from the Chevalier De Repentigny! Madame Racine says it is only to see *him* that she has gone to Belmont to day."

"Lizette, I will strike you if you pull my hair so!" exclaimed Angelique pushing her maid away with her hand, which was as prompt to deal a blow as to lavish gifts upon her dependants.

"Pardon! my Lady," replied Lizette shrewd enough to perceive the cause of her mistress's anger, and also how to allay it. "Cecile Tourangeau may look her eyes out at the Chevalier de Repentigny but I know he has no love for any woman but one, who shall be nameless!—"

"No she shall not be nameless—to me, Lizette! So tell it please." Angelique fixed her maid with a look she durst not disobey:

"It was only the other night my Lady, when the Chevalier De Repentigny, remained so late, that he said on leaving the house, 'Heaven has no door like this!—and no mansion I would inhabit without Angelique.' I would go on my knees from here to Rome for a man who loved me as Le Gardeur does my Lady!" exclaimed Lizette with a burst of enthusiasm that charmed her mistress.

Lizette knew she was saying the most agreable thing in the world to her— a thrill of pain mingled with pleasure, and a taste of sweet and bitter came upon the tongue of Angelique— she swallowed the sweet and threw off the bitter as she said with an air of gaiety:

"When a man goes on his knees for a woman Lizette, it is all over with her! is it not Lizette?"

"It would be with me, my Lady," replied the maid frankly. "But men you know are false so often, women never have them safe and sure until they are put to bed by the Sexton with a coverlet of stone on top of them!—"

"You are getting positively clever Lizette!" exclaimed Angelique clapping her hands. "I will give you a new gown for that remark of yours! What said the Chevalier de Repentigny further. Did you hear—?"

"That was all I heard my Lady, but it is plain as the spire of Charlebourg, as they say, that he does not care a pin for Cecile Tourangeau! and for her to try to make an impression on him is just as vain, Madame Racine says, as to put your finger in the water and look for the hole it has made!"

"Madame Racine's similies smack of the water side and she talks like the wife of a Stevedore!" Angelique while indulging herself in every freedom of speech, was merciless in her criticism of coarseness in others. "But go on with your beads, Lizette! who besides all those elegant Bourgeois, have gone to Belmont?—"

"O there were the Massots, of course! the young ladies in blue and white, in imitation of your last new costume my Lady."

"That shows their good taste," replied Angelique "and a deference to their betters, not always found in Lower Town, where we usually see more airs than graces—! Who besides the Massots have gone?"

"Oh, the whole tribe of the Cureux! Trust any thing going on in Quebec where they will not thrust their long noses—!"

"Oh! the Cureux, indeed!" replied Angelique, laughing till she shook, "I always laugh when I see *their* long noses come into a parlour."

"Yes, my Lady, every one does! even servants! they say they got them by smelling stock fish which they send to France by the ship load. Madame Cureux is always boasting that the Pope himself eats their stock fish in Lent."

"Well their noses are their own, and nobody envies them the possession! But all their stock fish cannot cure their ugliness!" Angelique knew the Cureux were very-rich, and it pleased her to find a good offset for that advantage.

"Nor all their money marry the demoiselles Cureux to the

noblesse!" remarked Lizette, with a touch of spite. She too did not like the Cureux for some prejudice of the servants' hall—inscrutable here.

"There you are wrong, Lizette! Money will marry any one to any body! It will marry me—enough of it!" Angelique twitched her shoulder and gave a short, bitter laugh.

"Yes, most people say so, my Lady, and I suppose it is true! But for my part, having no money, I like a bit of love to season the family potage! I would not marry Louis Le Page with his five hundred livres in his box, if I would not take him barefoot just as God made him."

"Pshaw! you talk like a fool!" Angelique moved restlessly in her chair, as if tormented with a thorn. "People of your condition are happy enough with love; you have nothing else to marry for."

"No, and for that reason Louis and I will marry," replied Lizette, seriously. "God made men wise, they say, and we women teach them to be fools."

"You are clever Lizette and worthy to be my maid," cried Angelique admiringly, "but I want to hear the rest of your gossip about Belmont. You have only mentioned the Bourgeoisie, but I know many people of condition have gone out also."

"I thought my Lady, would rather have me mention the Bourgeoisie," replied Lizette naïvely. She knew that sprinkling a little common earth upon the guests, would not displease the humour of her mistress.

"True! but I have heard enough about *them* and after all, the movements of the Bourgeoisie are of no more importance than the flight of pigeons. The *Honnetes Gens* are not all Bourgeoisie—more's the wonder! Go on Lizette with the Noblesse."

"Yes my Lady. Madame de Grandmaison held up both hands for an hour, astonished at the equipages rolling on one after another to Belmont, to visit a mere merchant, a trader, as she called the Bourgeois Philibert."

"Madame de Grandmaison forgets the old rope maker of St Malo, who spun her own family line—!" replied

Angelique tartly—she hated the Grandmaisons. "The Bourgeois Philibert is himself as well born and as proud too as the Lord de Coucy."

"And his son, the Colonel is as proud as his father, and can look as cross too when he is displeased," remarked Lizette, veering round readily to the shift of wind in her mistress' humour.

"He is the handsomest gallant in the city—but one," remarked Angelique.

"Yes my Lady," replied the facile maid. "The Chevalier de Repentigny thinks him perfection and he thinks Mademoiselle de Repentigny more than perfection! at least that was Madame Racine's opinion."

"Madame Racine's tongue would be all the better for shortening, Lizette, and yours too if you quote her sayings so much."

"Yes my Lady!—" replied the ever acquiescent maid, "and every one thought the same when she and Madame de Grandmaison joined in a cry of indignation as the Governor rode past, with that strange gentleman from Sweden, who puts flowers in a book instead of into his button hole, and pins moths and butterflies to a board. They say he is a Huguenot and would like to serve Christians in the same manner—only most people think he is mad. But he is really very nice, when you speak to him! and the Governor likes him immensely. All the maids of the Quartier say their mistresses agree on that."

"Well never mind, the strange gentleman! who besides were there—?" asked Angelique.

"O loads and loads of the most fashionable people! such as the Chavignys, the Lemoines the Lanaudieres, Duperons and De Lery's all sitting up in their carriages and looking as if the Colony belonged to them."

"A good deal of it does!" remarked Angelique with a touch of Madame de Grandmaison's irritability "But the D'Aillebousts and the Vaudreuil's—they did not go—?"

"Only the Chevalier Rigaud, my Lady, who they say always roasts a Bostonais when his soldiers are very hungry—! but I dont believe it."

"Pshaw! but tell me have the Beauharnois gone with the rest?"

"Yes, my Lady! Mademoiselle, was dressed like an angel in white, and such plumes—! Even Madame Couillard said she looked handsomer than her brother Claude."

"Oh Hortense! every one is bursting with the praises of Hortense!" exclaimed Angelique with decided pique, fanning herself impatiently. "It is because she makes herself so friendly—forward I call it—and she thinks herself so witty—! or, at least, causes the gentlemen to think so. The heir of Belmont would hardly pay her for opening her black eyes so wide—!"

Angelique was bitter and unjust. She was in truth jealous of the beauty and grace of Hortense de Beauharnois, who approached too near her own absolute kingdom, not to be looked upon otherwise than as a dangerous rival.

"Is your list ended?" Angelique got very impatient. "Of course, all the Tillys, De Repentignys, St Lucs, and their tribes from North to South, would not be absent on any such occasion as a gathering of the *Honnetes Gens* in honour of the Philiberts!"

"No my Lady, and they are all there. As Madame de Grandmaison remarked, the City has gone mad over Belmont, and every body has gone!" Lizette began counting on her fingers—"besides those I named there were the De Beaujeus, the Contrecoeurs the De Villiers, the—— —"

"For God's sake, stop!—" burst out Angelique "or go back to the Bourgeoisie and the rabble, the slops of Lower Town!"

This was a coarse speech for Angelique, but she liked sometimes to leap over the bars of politeness, and riddle society of its cinders, she said. Her supernal beauty was earth made, and she could on occasion talk coarsely, talk Argot or even smoke while comparing the points of men and horses in the penetralia of her boudoir, in the free and easy companionship of friends of her own sex.

Lizette took the hint, and gave a satirical description of a rich old merchant and his family, the Sieur Keratry, an honest Bas Breton. "They say," continued Lizette "that the

Sieur Keratry first learned the use of a pocket handkerchief, after his arrival in an Emigrant ship, and forgets to use it to this day."

"Why that is true!" laughed Angelique, restored to good humour, by the mention of the old Trader of the Sault au Matelot.

"The Bas Bretons never use anything but their sleeves and fingers! and you always recognize the honest folk of Finisterre by that unmistakable trait of Breton polish! The Sieur Keratry is true to his Province, and can never forget the primitive fashion—I hope he will practice it well at Belmont!—Bah! But I wont hear any more Lizette. I dont care who has gone, I know one who wont stay!—Mark you!" continued she, "when the Chevalier de Repentigny calls this evening show him up at once—! I am resolved he shall not remain at Belmont whoever else does—!" She held up a warning finger to her maid, "remember! and now you may go Lizette. I want to be alone."

"Yes my Lady!" Lizette would fain have continued her gossip, but she dared not. There was a flash now and then in Angelique's eyes that boded fire not far off. Lizette withdrew, somewhat perplexed about her mistress's real thoughts of persons and things, and remarked to her confidante the housekeeper, that her Lady was in a tantrum over something or other, and some body would surely suffer before tomorrow!

CHAPTER 21

BELMONT

A SHORT drive from the gate of St John, stood the old mansion of Belmont, the Country seat of the Bourgeois Philibert. A stately park, the remains of the primeval forest of oak maple and pine, trees of gigantic growth and ample shade, surrounded the high roofed many gabled house that stood on the heights of St Foye overlooking the broad valley of the St Charles. The bright river wound like a silver serpent through the flat meadows in the bottom of the valley, while the opposite slopes of alternate field and forest stretched away to the distant range of the Laurentian hills whose pale blue summits mingled with the blue sky at midday, or wrapped in mist at morn and eve were hardly distinguishable from the clouds behind them.

The bright slender spire of a village church peered up shyly from the distant woods on the mountain side, and here and there the white walls of a farm house stood out amid green meadows, or the smoke alone of a chimney rose up from orchards of apple and pear, showing where a thrifty habitant had cast his lot, under the protection of the feudal manor house that was conspicuous on more than one commanding spot in the wide landscape.

The day was charming, fresh and breezy. Summer showers had washed clean the face of Nature, and warm sunshine of almost tropical heat, which prevails in New France for a brief period, stirred all the life in animate and inanimate creation. The leaves and grass glowed in vivid green, and on every side flowers of every hue breathed out odours and seemed alive with pure delight of blooming.

The park of Belmont sweeping round to the woods of

Sillery contained a little world of wild flowers and ferns, hidden away in its sylvan recesses safe from the ploughshare, as its forests trees were safe from the woodman. Many rare and exquisite forms of floral beauty repaid the protection of the Master of Belmont. In glades half lit by struggling sun beams the ferns stood knee deep, waving their lace like tracery beautiful and delicate as the bridal veil of the Queen of fairy land. Little dells thick with shrubbery, were glowing with the rosy bells of the Linnea Borealis, and narrow leaved Kalmia first so named this day by the Count de la Galissoniere in honour of his friend Herr Kalm. The winding and in some places steep and broken paths were bordered with trailing orchises white and red and purple, ladies hair and silvery bells for garlands in fairy dances by moonlight, trillia whorling their triple glories; flowers born in the purple, like children of an Emperor,—priceless treasures of Flora in the old world, but here growing wild, the free gifts of bounteous nature. The turf of the park was thick, soft, and green as an emerald. Huge patriarchal trees, giants of the olden time stood round in solitary dignity shading the broad drives or were grouped in clusters deep and solemn as fragments of the primeval forest of which they had once formed a part.

The gardens and lawns of Belmont were stirring with gay company to day in honour of the Fete of Pierre Philibert, upon his return home from the campaign in Acadia. Troops of ladies in costumes and toilettes of the latest Parisian fashion gladdened the eye with pictures of grace and beauty, which Paris itself could not have surpassed. Gentlemen in full dress, in an age when dress was an essential part of a gentleman's distinction accompanied the ladies, with the gallantry, vivacity and politeness belonging to France, and to France alone.

Communication with the Mother Country was precarious and uncertain by reason of the war, and the blockade of the Gulf by the English cruisers. Hence the good fortune and daring of the gallant Captain Mariniere in running his frigate, the *Fleur de Lys*, through the fleet of the enemy, enabling him among other things to replenish the wardrobes of the ladies of Quebec, with latest Parisian fashions, made him immensely popular on this gala day. The kindness and affability of the ladies extended without diminution of graciousness to the little midshipmen even whom the Captain conditioned to take with him whereever he and his officers were invited. Captain Mariniere was happy to see the lads enjoy a few cakes on shore after the hard biscuit they had so long nibbled on ship board. As for himself there was no end to the gracious smiles and thanks he received from the fair guests assembled at Belmont.

At the great door of the Manor House welcoming his guests as they arrived, stood the Bourgeois Philibert dressed as a gentleman of the period in attire rich but not ostentatious. His suit of dark velvet harmonized well with his noble manner and bearing. But no one for a moment could overlook the man in contemplating his dress. The keen discriminating eye of woman overlooking neither dress nor man, found both worthy of warmest commendation, and many remarks passed between the ladies on that day, that a handsomer man and more ripe and perfect gentleman than the Bourgeois Philibert, had never been seen in New France.

His grizzled hair grew thick all over his head, the sign of a tenacious constitution. It was powdered and tied behind with a broad ribbon, for he hated peruques. His strong shapely figure was handsomely conspicuous as he stood chapeau in hand, greeting his guests as they arrived. His eyes beamed with pleasure and hospitality and his usually grave thoughtful lips, were wreathed in smiles, the sweeter because not habitually seen upon them.

The Bourgeois had this in common with all complete and earnest characters, that the people believed in him, because they saw that he believed in himself. His friends loved and trusted him to the uttermost, his enemies hated and feared him in equal measure,—but no one great or small, could ignore him, and not feel his presence as a solid piece of manhood.

It is not intellect, nor activity, nor wealth that obtains power over other men but force of Character, self control, a quiet compressed will, and patient resolve. These qualities make one man the natural ruler over other men by a title they never dispute.

The party of the *Honnetes Gens*, the "honest folks" as they were derisively called by their opponents, regarded the Bourgeois Philibert as their natural leader. His force of character made men willingly stand in his shadow. His clear intellect never at fault had extended his power and influence by means of his vast mercantile operations over half the continent. His position as the foremost merchant of New France brought him in the front of the people's battle with the Grand Company and in opposition to the financial policy of the Intendant and the mercantile assumption of the Friponne.

But the personal hostility between the Intendant and the Bourgeois had its root and origin in France, before either of them crossed the ocean to the hither shore of the Atlantic. The Bourgeois had been made very sensible of a fact vitally affecting him that the decrees of the Intendant ostensibly for the regulation of trade in New France had been sharply pointed against himself. "They draw blood!—" Bigot had boasted to his familiars as he rubbed his hands together with intense satisfaction one day, when he learned that Philibert's large trading post in Mackinaw, had been closed in consequence of the Indians having been commanded by Royal authority, excercised by the Intendant, to trade only at the Comptoirs of the Grand Company. "They draw blood!—" repeated he, "and will draw the life itself out of the Golden Dog—!" It was plain, the ancient grudge of the courtly parasite had not lost a tooth, during all those years.

The Bourgeois was not a man to talk of his private griefs or seek sympathy or even ask counsel or help. He knew the world was engrossed with its own cares. The world cares not to look under the surface of things for sake of others but only for its own sake, its own interests its own pleasures.

To day however all griefs, all resentments, were cast aside, and the Bourgeois was all joy at the return of his only son, and proud of Pierre's achievements, and still more of the honours spontaneously paid him. He stood at his door welcoming arrival after arrival, the happiest man of all the joyous company who honoured Belmont that day.—

A carriage with outriders brought the Count de la Galissoniere and his friend Herr Kalm, and Dr Gauthier, the last a rich old bachelor handsome and generous, the physician and savant, par excellence of Quebec. After a most cordial reception by the Bourgeois, the Governor walked among the guests, who had crowded up to greet him, with the respect due to the King's representative as well as to show their personal regard, for the Count's popularity was unbounded in the Colony except among the partizans of the Grand Company.

Herr Kalm was presently enticed away by a bevy of young ladies, Hortense Beauharnois leading them, to get the learned professor's opinion on some rare specimens of botany growing in the park. Nothing loath, for he was good natured as he was clever and a great enthusiast withal in the study of plants he allowed the merry talkative girls to lead him where they would. He delighted them in turn by his agreable instructive conversation which was rendered still more piquant, by the odd medly of French Latin and Swedish in which it was expressed.

The Sieur Gauthier was greeted on every side with marks of esteem and even affection. With the ladies he was an especial favorite. His sympathetic manner and ready wit won their admiration and confidence. As the first physician of the City, Dr Gauthier was to their bodies what their confessor was to their souls, indispensable to their health and comfort. The good Doctor had his specialties also, as every man of genius fails not to have. He was a good astronomer, and it was known that the science of astrology was not out of the category of his studies. *Augur, medicus, magus, omnia novit!* The middle of the eighteenth century had not quite convinced itself as the close of the nineteenth has done, that, what is what, and nothing else! Upon the good Doctor's house overlooking the *Cote aux Chiens*, was a small observatory. Its long projecting telescope was to the Habitans suggestive of magical powers. They would not be persuaded but that the good Doctor cured disceases by the *secret*, rather than by legitimate medical science, and was more beholden to the stars for his success in curing them than to the art of medicine. But that belief secured his popularity all the more!—By temperament he belonged to the merry school of the *medicins tant mieux*, whom La Fontaine immortalizes in his inimitable fable. The good Doctor laughed at the world, and was not vexed if the world laughed at him—! On one tender spot only he was very sensitive however and the quick witted ladies never ceased probing it with pins and needles— His want of a wife and still more perhaps of an heir to hand his name and fortune down to posterity.

The ladies knew he was a useful man, and they zealously strove to double his usefulness, but so far the measures taken by them were inadequate to the accomplishment of their object. To day, the Doctors feathers had been ruffled by a controversy with the learned Swede who maintained with irritating obstinacy, the fashionable theory of stay at home philosophers, in the old world, that the European race degenerates on the soil of the new.

The Doctor meeting Herr Kalm on his walk in the garden of Belmont, again rushed into the defence of the children of the soil, and roundly swore, by the three Graces! by *Lenis Lucina*! and all the powers of dittany! (He was always classical when excited.) that the progeny of New France was an improvement on the old stock. Like the Brandy of Bordeaux it acquired fresh spirit strength and bouquet by its transfer across the Atlantic.

Forgetful of the presence of the ladies who listened with open eyes and ears to his vow, the Doctor declared he would marry, and demonstrate to the utter refutation of such errors that the noble race of Gauls and Franks does not deteriorate in the New world, but its progeny strengthens as it lengthens and gathers as it grows, and that another *lustrum* should not pass over his head, before he would convince Herr Kalm himself, that European philosophy was futile in face of Canadian practice.

To be sure few of the ladies knew precisely what a *lustrum* was, but they guessed the good Doctor intended very soon to take a wife, and the news flew in as many shapes, each a complete story of itself, as there were pretty mouths to tell it all over the grounds.

"I will demonstrate!—" exclaimed the Doctor seconding his voice by active thumps of his cane upon the ground, "I will demonstrate that in New France a man of sixty is as hearty and as marriageable as a European of thirty! I will do it! I will marry!"

A laugh from the gentlemen and many conscious blushes from the ladies greeted the doctor's vow. But farther discussion of the nice point was postponed by an influx of fresh arrivals who poured into the park.

The Chevalier La Corne with his pretty daughter Agathe La Corne St Luc, the Lady de Tilly and Amelie de Repentigny, with the brothers de Villiers. The brothers had overtaken the Chevalier La Corne upon the road, but the custom of the highway in New France forbade any one passing another, without politely asking permission to do so.

"Yes, Coulon!" replied the Chevalier, "ride on!"—He winked pleasantly at his daughter as he said this. "There is I suppose nothing left for an old fellow who dates from the sixteen hundreds, but to take the side of the road, and let you pass. I should have liked however to stir up the fire in my gallant little Norman ponies against your big New England horses. Where did you get them? can they run?"

"We got them in the sack of Saratoga" replied Coulon, "and they ran well that day! but we overtook them! would Mademoiselle La Corne care if we try them now—?—"

Scarcely a girl in Quebec would have declined the excitement of a race on the high road of St Foye, and Agathe would fain have driven herself, in the race, but being in full dress to day, she thought of her wardrobe, and the company. She checked the ardour of her father, and entered the park demurely, as one of the gravest of the company.

"Happy youths! noble lads! Agathe!" exclaimed the Chevalier admiringly as the Brothers drove rapidly past them, "New France will be proud of them some day!—"

The rest of the company now began to arrive in quick succession. The lawn was crowded with guests. "Ten thousand thanks for coming!—" exclaimed Pierre Philibert as he assisted Amelie de Repentigny, and the Lady de Tilly to alight from their carriage.

"We could not choose but come to day, Pierre," replied Amelie, feeling without displeasure the momentary lingering of his hand, as it touched hers. "Nothing short of an earthquake would have kept Aunt at home," added she darting a merry glance of sympathy with her aunts supposed feelings.

"And you Amelie?"—Pierre looked into those dark eyes, which shyly turned aside from his gaze.

"I was an obedient neice, and accompanied her. It is so easy to persuade people to go where they wish to go." She withdrew her hand gently, and took his arm as he conducted the ladies into the house. She felt a flush on her cheek, but it did not prevent her saying in her frank kindly way, "I was glad to come to day, Pierre, to witness this gathering of the best and noblest in the land to honour your fete. Aunt de Tilly has always predicted greatness for you."

"And you Amelie, doubted, knowing me a shade better than your aunt?"

"No! I believed her! so true a prophet as aunt, surely deserved one firm believer!"

Pierre felt the electric thrill run through him which a man feels at the moment he discovers a woman believes in him. "Your presence here to day Amelie, you cannot think how sweet it is," said he.

Her hand trembled upon his arm. She thought nothing could be sweeter than such words from Pierre Philibert. With a charming indirectness however which did not escape him she replied, "Le Gardeur is very proud of you to day Pierre."

He laid his fingers upon her hand. It was a delicate little hand, but with the strength of an angels it had moulded his destiny and led him to the honorable position he had attained. He was profoundly conscious at this moment of what he owed to this girl's silent influence. He contented himself however with saying, "I will so strive that one day, Amelie de Repentigny shall not shame to say she too is proud of me."—

She did not reply for a moment. A tremour agitated her low sweet voice. "I am proud of you now Pierre, more proud than words can tell to see you so honoured, and proudest to think you deserve it all."

It touched him almost to tears. "Thanks Amelie. When you are proud of me, I shall begin to feel pride of myself. Your opinion is the one thing in life I have most cared for. Your approbation is my best reward."

Her eyes were eloquent with unspoken words but she thought, "If that was all!"—Pierre Philibert had long received the silent reward of her good opinion and approbation.

The Bourgeois at this moment came up to salute Amelie and the Lady de Tilly.

"The Bourgeois Philibert has the most perfect manner of any gentleman in New France," was the remark of the Lady de Tilly to Amelie, as he left them again, to receive other guests. "They say he can be rough and imperious sometimes to those he dislikes but to his friends and strangers, and especially to ladies, no breath of spring can be more gentle and balmy." Amelie assented with a mental reservation in the depths of her dark eyes, and in the dimple that flashed upon her cheek, as she suppressed the utterance of a pleasant fancy in reply to her áunt.

Pierre conducted the ladies to the great drawing room which was already filled with Company who overwhelmed Amelie and her Aunt with the vivacity of their greeting.

The conversation was light, but it sparkled with gaiety. There was a ready interchange of the current coin of society.

The Philosophers who essayed the extraction of sun beams out of cucumbers, would have found their experiment a success, in the ease with which the gay society of New France extracted social sunbeams from topics out of which graver people would have drawn only the essence of dulness and stupidity.

This cheerful temperament of the old Gallic colonists, has decended unimpaired to their posterity. The English Conquest which changed many things, could not dull the native gaiety of the French Canadians, and the grave English

Character is all the better for the dash of French vivacity and grace which leavens the new nationality that is growing up in Canada: neither purely French nor English but a happy mixture of the best elements of both.

In a fine shady grove, at a short distance from the house, a row of tables was set for the entertainment of several hundreds of the hardy dependants of the Bourgeois. For while feasting the rich the Bourgeois would not forget his poorer friends, and perhaps his most exquisite satisfaction was in the unrestrained enjoyment of his hospitality by the crowd of happy hungry fellows and their families, who under the direction of his chief Factor, filled the tables from end to end, and made the park resound with songs and merriment, Fellows of infinite gaiety with appetites of Gargantuas and a capacity for good liquour, that reminded one of the tubs of the Danaïdes. The tables groaned beneath mountains of good things, and in the center of each like Mont Blanc rising from the lower Alps, stood a magnificent Easter pie, the confection of which was a masterpiece of the skill of Maitre Guillot Gobet, the head cook of the Bourgeois, who was rather put out however when Dame Rochelle decided to bestow all the Easter pies upon the hungry voyageurs, woodmen and workmen, and banished them from the *menu* of the more patrician tables set for the guests of the mansion.

"Yet, after all!" exclaimed Master Guillot, as he thrust his head out of the kitchen door to listen to the song the gay fellows were singing, with all their lungs, in honour of the Easter pie. "After all; the fine gentlemen and ladies would not have paid my noble pies such honour as that—! and what is more the pies would not have been eaten up to the last crumb—!" Master Guillot's face beamed like a harvest moon as he chimed in with the well known ditty in praise of the great pie of Rouen

"C'est dans la ville de Rouen,
  Ils ont fait un paté si grand—
  Ils ont fait un paté si grand,
  Qu'ils ont trouvé un homme dedans!—"

Master Guillot would fain have been nearer to share in the shouting and clapping of hands which followed the saying of grace by the good Curé of St Foye, and to see how vigorously knives were handled, and how chins wagged in the delightful task of levelling down mountains of meat, while Gascon wine and Norman cider flowed from ever replenished flagons.

The Bourgeois and his son with many of his chief guests honoured for a time the merry feast out of doors, and were almost inundated by the flowing cups drank to the health and happiness of the Bourgeois and of Pierre Philibert.

Master Guillot Gobet returned to his kitchen, where he stirred up his cooks and scullions on all sides to make up for the loss of his Easter pies on the grand tables in the Hall. He capered among them like a marionette, directing here, scolding there, laughing, joking or with uplifted hands and stamping feet despairing of his underlings cooking a dinner fit for the fete of Pierre Philibert.

Master Guillot was a little fat red nosed fellow, with twinkling black eyes, and a mouth irrascible as that of a cake baker of Lerna. His heart was of the right paste however and full as a butter boat of the sweet sauce of good nature which he was ready to pour over the heads of all his fellows who quietly submitted to his dictation. But woe to man or maid servant, who delayed or disputed his royal orders—! An Indian typhoon instantly blew. At such a time, even Dame Rochelle would gather her petticoats round her, and hurry out of the storm which always subsided quickly in proportion to the violence of its rage.

Master Guillot knew what he was about however. "He did not use," he said, "to wipe his nose with a herring!—and on that day he was going to cook a dinner fit for the Pope after lent, or even for the Reverend Father de Berey himself who was the truest gourmet and the best trencher man in New France."

Master Guillot honoured his master, but in his secret soul he did not think his taste quite worthy of his cook! But he worshipped Father de Berey and gloried in the infallible judgment and correct taste of cookery possessed by the jolly

Recollet. The single approbation of Father de Berey was worth more than the praise of a world full of ordinary eating mortals who smacked their lips and said things were good, but who knew no more than one of the Cent Suisses why things were good, or could appreciate the talents of an artist of the *cordon bleu.*

Master Guillot's Easter pie had been a splendid success. "It was worthy," he said "to be placed as a crown on top of the new Cathedral of St Marie and receive the consecration of the Bishop."

Lest the composition of it should be forgotten Master Guillot had with the solemnity of a Deacon intoning the litany, ravished the ear of Jules Painchaud, his future son in law, as he taught him the secrets of its confection.

With his white cap set rakishly on one side of his head and arms a kimbo, Master Guillot gave Jules the famous recipe: "Inside of circular walls of pastry, an inch thick, and so rich as easily to be pulled down, and roomy enough within for the court of King Pepin, lay first a thick stratum of mince meat of two savoury hams of Westphalia, and if you cannot get them, of two hams of our Habitans."

"Of our habitans!" ejaculated Jules, with an air of consternation.

"Precisely! dont interrupt me!" Master Guillot grew red about the gills in an instant. Jules was silenced.—"I have said it—!—" cried he. "Two hams of our habitans! what have you to say against it, Stock Fish! Eh?—"

"O nothing, Sir," replied Jules with humility "only I thought!"—Poor Jules would have consented to eat his thought, rather than fall out with the father of his Suzette.

"You thought!" Master Guillots face was a study for Hogarth, who alone could have painted the alto tone of voice as it proceeded from his round O of a mouth. "Suzette shall remain upon my hands an old maid for the term of her natural life, if you dispute the confection of Easter pie!—"

"Now listen Jules!" continued he, at once molified by the contrite submissive air of his future son in law. "Upon a foundation of the mince meat of two hams of Westphalia or if you can not get them, of two hams of our habitans place scientifically, the nicely cut pieces of a fat turkey, leaving his head to stick out of the upper crust in evidence that Master Dindon lies buried there—! Add two fat capons, two plump partridges, two pigeons and the back and thighs of a brace of juicy hares. Fill up the whole with beaten eggs and the rich contents will resemble as a poet might say, 'fossils of the rock in golden yolks embedded and enjellied'!—Season as you would a Saint!—! Cover with a slab of pastry. Bake it as you would cook an angel, and not singe a feather. Then let it cool and eat it! And Jules! as the Reverend Father de Berey always says after grace over an Easter pie: '*Dominus vobiscum*'—!"

CHAPTER 22

"SIC ITUR AD ASTRA"

THE old hall of Belmont had been decorated for many a feast since the times of its founder the Intendant Talon, but it had never contained a nobler company of fair women and brave men, the pick and choice of their race, than to day met round the hospitable and splendid table of the Bourgeois Philibert, in honour of the Fete of his gallant son.

Dinner was duly and decorously despatched. The social fashion of New France was not for the ladies to withdraw when the wine followed the feast, but to remain seated with the gentlemen, purifying the conversation, and by their presence restraining the coarseness which was the almost universal vice of the age.

A troop of nimble servitors carried off the carved dishes and fragments of the splendid patisseries of Master Guillot, in such a state of demolition as satisfied the critical eye of the chief Cook that the efforts of his genius had been very successful. He inspected the dishes through his spectacles. He knew by what was left the ability of the guests to discriminate what they had eaten, and do justice to his skill! He considered himself a sort of pervading divinity whose culinary ideas passing with his cookery into the bodies of the guests, enabled them on retiring from the feast to carry away as part of themselves, some of the fine essence of Master Gobet himself.

At the head of his table, peeling oranges and slicing pine apples, for the ladies in his vicinity sat the Bourgeois himself, laughing jesting, and telling anecdotes with a geniality that was contagious. "The Gods are merry sometimes, says Homer, and their laughter shakes Olympus!—" was the classical remark of Father de Berey at the other end of the table. Jupiter

247

did not laugh with less loss of dignity than the Bourgeois.

The sun was setting in a sea of splendour visible through an oriel window in the great hall. His slanting golden rays caught the crisp grizzled locks of the master of the feast, and preternaturally illumined his noble face, bringing out every feature and line of it into marvellous effects, as if to make a picture which men could remember in after years,—and few of the guests did not remember to the end of their lives, the majestic and happy countenance of the Bourgeois on this memorable day.

At his right hand sat Amelie de Repentigny and the Count de la Galissoniere. The Governor charmed with the beauty and agreableness of the young Chatelaine had led her in to dinner, and devoted himself to her and the Lady de Tilly with the perfection of gallantry of a gentleman of the politest court in Europe.

On his left sat the radiant dark eyed Hortense de Beauharnois. With a gay assumption of independance Hortense had taken the arm of La Corne St Luc and declared she would eat no dinner unless he would be her Cavalier, and sit beside her! The gallant old soldier surrendered at discretion. "He laughingly consented to be her captive," he said, "for he had no power and no desire but to obey." Hortense was proud of her conquest. She seated herself by his side with an air of triumph and mock gravity, tapping him with her fan whenever she detected his eye roving round the table, compassionating she affirmed her rivals, who had failed, where she had won, in securing the youngest the handsomest and most gallant of all the gentlemen at Belmont.

"Not so fast, Hortense!" exclaimed the gay Chevalier, "You have captured me by mistake! The tall Swede. He is your man—! The other ladies all know that, and are anxious to get me out of your toils so that you may be free to ensnare the Philosopher."

"But you dont wish to get away from me?—I am your garland Chevalier, and you shall wear me to day. As for the tall Swede, he has no idea of a fair flower of our sex except to wear it at his button hole—! this way—!" added she, pulling a rose out of a vase and archly adorning the Chevaliers vest with it.

"All pretence and jealousy, Mademoiselle—! The tall Swede knows how to take down your pride, and bring you to a proper sense of your false conceit, of the beauty and wit of the ladies of New France."

Hortense gave two or three tosses of defiance to express her emphatic dissent from his opinions.

"I wish Herr Kalm would lend me his philosophic scales to weigh your sex like lambs in market," continued La Corne St Luc, "but I fear I am too old Hortense, to measure women except by the fathom, which is the measure of a man."

"And the measure of a man is the measure of an angel too! *Scriptum est*! Chevalier!" replied she. Hortense had ten merry meanings in her eye, and looked as if bidding him select which he chose. "The learned Swede's philosophy is lost upon us," continued she. "He can neither weigh by sample, nor measure by fathom, the girls of New France." She tapped him on the arm "Listen to me Chevalier!" said she. "You are neglecting me already, for sake of Cecile Tourangeau!"

La Corne was exchanging some gay badinage with a graceful pretty young lady, on the other side of the table, whose snowy forehead, if you examined it closely, was marked with a red scar, in figure of a cross, which although powdered and partially concealed by a frieze of her thick blonde hair was sufficiently distinct to those who looked for it and many did so, as they whispered to each other the story of how she got it.

Le Gardeur de Repentigny sat by Cecile talking in a very sociable manner which was also commented on. His conversation seemed to be very attractive to the young lady, who was visibly delighted with the attentions of her handsome gallant.

At this moment a burst of instruments from the musicians who occupied a gallery at the end of the hall, announced a vocal response to the toast of the King's health, proposed by the Bourgeois. "Prepare yourself for the Chorus Chevalier" exclaimed Hortense, "Father de Berey is going to lead the royal anthem."

"Vive le Roi!" replied La Corne, "no finer voice ever sang mass, or chanted God save the King—!—I like to hear the royal anthem from the lips of a churchman, rolling it out, *ore rotundo* like one of the Psalms of David; our first duty is to love God, our next to honour the King! and New France will never fail in either!—" Loyalty was ingrained in every fibre of La Corne St Luc.

"Never Chevalier. Law and Gospel rule together or fall together. But we must rise!—" replied Hortense springing up.

The whole company rose simultaneously. The rich mellow voice of the Rev. Father de Berey, round and full as the organ of St Marie commenced the royal anthem, composed by Lulli in honour of Louis Quatorze, upon an occasion of his visit to the famous convent of St Cyr in company with Madame de Maintenon.

The song composed by Madame Brinon was afterwards translated into English and words and music became by a singular transposition the national hymn of the English nation.

"God save the King," is no longer heard in France. It was buried with the peoples loyalty, fathoms deep under the ruins of the monarchy. But it flourishes still with pristine vigour in New France, that olive branch graffed on the stately tree of the British Empire. The broad chest and flexile lips of Father de Berey, rang out the grand old song in tones that filled the stately old hall.

> Grand Dieu! Sauvez le Roi!—
> Grand Dieu! Sauvez le Roi!
> Sauvez le Roi!
> Que toujours glorieux,
> Louis Victorieux,
> Voye ses ennemis
> Toujours soumis!—

The company all joined in the Chorus the gentlemen raising their cups, the ladies waving their handkerchiefs and male and female blending in a storm of applause that made the old walls ring with joy. Songs and speeches followed in quick succession cutting as with a golden blade, the hours of the dessert into quinzaines of varied pleasures.

The custom of the times had reduced speech making after dinner to a minimum. The ladies, as Father de Berey wittily remarked preferred private confession to public preaching, and long speeches without inlets for reply, were the eighth mortal sin which no lady would forgive.

The Bourgeois however felt it incumbent upon himself to express his deep thanks for the honour done his house on this auspicious occasion. And he remarked that "the doors of Belmont so long closed by reason of the absence of Pierre, would hereafter be ever open to welcome all his friends. He had that day made a gift of Belmont with all its belongings to Pierre, and he hoped—" The Bourgeois smiled as he said this, but he would not look in a quarter where his words struck home. "He hoped that some one of Quebec's fair daughters would assist Pierre in the menage of his home, and enable him to do honour to his housekeeping."

Immense was the applause that followed the short pithy speech of the Bourgeois. The ladies blushed and praised. The gentlemen cheered and enjoyed in anticipation the renewal of the old hospitalities of Belmont.

"The skies are raining plumb cakes!" exclaimed the Chevalier La Corne, to his lively companion "Joy's golden drops are only distilled in the Alembic of woman's heart! what think you Hortense? which of Quebec's fair daughters will be willing to share Belmont with Pierre—?—"

"O any of them would!" replied she. "But why did the Bourgeois restrict his choice to the ladies of Quebec, when he knew I come from the Three Rivers?"

"O, he was afraid of you, Hortense! you would make Belmont too good for this world—! what say *you*, Father de Berey. Do you ever walk on the cape—?"

The friar in a merry mood, had been edging close to Hortense. "I love of all things to air my soutane on the cape of a breezy afternoon," replied the jovial Recollet, "when the fashionables are all out, and every lady is putting her best foot foremost.—It is then I feel sure that Horace is the next best thing to the homilies:

'*Teretesque suras laudo, et integer ego!*'"

The Chevalier La Corne pinched the shrugging shoulder of Hortense, as he remarked, "Dont confess to Father de Berey, that you promenade on the Cape! But I hope Pierre Philibert will soon make his choice! We are impatient to visit him and give old Provençal the butler a run every day through those dark crypts of his where lie entombed the choicest vintages of sunny France."

The Chevalier said this waggishly, for the benefit of old Provençal, who stood behind his chair looking half alarmed at the threatened raid upon his well filled cellars.

"But if Pierre should not commit matrimony," replied Hortense, "what will become of him, and especially, what will become of us?"

"We will drink his wine all the same, good fellow that he is. But Pierre had as lief commit suicide as not commit matrimony, and who would not? Look here Pierre Philibert!" continued the old soldier, addressing him with good humoured freedom, "Matrimony is clearly your duty, Pierre. But I need not tell you so. It is written on your face plain as the way between Peronne and St Quintin! A good honest way as ever was trod by shoe leather and as old as Chinon in Touraine—! Try it soon, my boy. Quebec is a sack full of pearls!—" Hortense pulled him mischievously by the coat, so he caught her hand and held it fast in his, while he proceded, "You put your hand in the sack and take out the first that offers. It will be worth a Jew's ransom! If you are lucky to find the fairest, trust me it will be the identical pearl of great price for which the merchant, went and sold all that he had and bought it! Is not that Gospel, Father de Berey? I think I have heard something like that preached from the pulpit of the Recollets—?"

"Matter of Brimborion! Chevalier! not to be questioned by lay men—!—words of wisdom for the benefit of my poor brothers of St Francis, who after renouncing the world, like

to know that they have renounced something worth having!
But not to preach a sermon on your parable Chevalier, I will
promise Colonel Philibert, that when he has found the pearl
of great price"—Father de Berey who knew a world of secrets,
glanced archly at Amelie as he said this.—"the bells of our
monastry shall ring out such a merry peal as they have not
rung since stout Brother Le Gros broke his wind, and short
brother Bref stretched himself out half a yard, pulling the
bell-ropes on the wedding of the Dauphin."

Great merriment followed the speech of Father de Berey.
Hortense rallied the Chevalier a good old widower, upon
himself not travelling the plain way between Peronne and
St Quintin, and jestingly offered herself to travel with him
like a couple of gypsies, carrying their budget of happiness
pick a pack through the world. "Better than that!" La Corne
exclaimed, "Hortense was worthy to ride on the baggage
wagons in his next campaign! would she go?—?" She gave him
her hand. "I expect nothing else!" said she, "I am a soldier's
daughter and expect to live a soldier's wife, and die a soldier's
widow. But a truce to jest! It is harder to be witty than wise"
continued she. "What is the matter with Cousin Le Gardeur?"
Her eyes were fixed upon him, as he read a note just handed
to him by a servant. He crushed it in his hand, with a flash of
anger and made a motion as if about to tear it. But did not.
He placed it in his bosom. But the hilarity of his countenance
was gone.

There was another person seated at table whose quick eye
drawn by sisterly affection saw Le Gardeur's movement before
even Hortense. Amelie was impatient to leave her seat and go
beside him, but she could not at the moment leave the lively
circle around her. She at once conjectured that the note was
from Angelique des Meloises. After drinking deeply two or
three times Le Gardeur arose, and with a faint excuse that did
not impose on his partner, left the table. Amelie rose quickly
also, excusing herself to the Bourgeois and joined her brother
in the park where the cool night air blew fresh and inviting
for a walk.

Pretty Cecile Tourangeau had caught a glimpse of the

handwriting as she sat by the side of Le Gardeur, and guessed correctly, whence it had come, and why her partner so suddenly left the table.

She was out of humour. The red mark upon her forehead grew redder as she pouted in visible discontent. But the great world moves on, carrying alternate storms and sun shine upon its surface. The company rose from the table, Some to the Ball room, some to the park and conservatories. Cecile's was a happy disposition easily consoled for her sorrows. Every trace of her displeasure was banished and almost forgotten, from the moment the gay handsome Jumonville de Villiers invited her out to the grand Balcony, where he said, "the rarest pastime was going on!"

And rare pastime it was! A group of laughing but half serious girls were gathered round Doctor Gauthier, urging him to tell their fortunes by consulting the stars, which to night shone out with unusual brilliancy.

At that period as at the present, and in every age of the world, the female sex like the Jews of old, asks signs, while the Greeks, that is the men, seek wisdom. The time never was, and never will be, when a woman will cease to be curious, and when her imagination will not forecast the decrees of fate in regard to the culminating event of her life and her whole nature—marriage.

It was in vain, Doctor Gauthier protested his inability to read the stars without his celestial eye glasses.

The ladies would not accept his excuses. "He knew the heavens by heart" they said, "and could read the stars of destiny as easily as the Bishop his breviary."—

In truth, the worthy Doctor was not only a believer but an adept in Astrology. He had favoured his friends with not a few horoscopes and nativities, when pressed, to do so. His good nature was of the substance of butter—any one that liked could spread it over his bread. Many good men are eaten up in that way by greedy friends.

Hortense Beauharnois urged the Doctor so merrily and so perseveringly, promising to marry him herself, if the stars said so, that he laughingly gave way, but declared "he would tell

Hortense's fortune first, which deserved to be good enough, to make her fulfil her promise just made."

"She was resigned," she said, "and would accept any fate from the rank of a Queen to a cell among the old maids of St Cyr! The girls of Quebec hung all their hopes on the stars, bright and particular ones especially. They were too loving to live single, and too proud to live poor! But she was one, who would not wait for ships to land that never came, and plums to drop into her mouth, that never ripened. Hortense would be ruled by the stars, and wise Doctor Gauthier should to night, declare her fate."

They all laughed at the free talk of Hortense. Not a few of the ladies shrugged their shoulders, and looked askance at each other but all present wished they had courage to speak like her to Doctor Gauthier.

"Well! I see there is nothing else for it, but to submit to my ruling star, and that is you Hortense!" cried the Doctor. "So please stand up before me, while I take an inventory of your looks, as a preliminary to telling your fortune."—

Hortense placed herself instantly before him. "It is one of the privileges of our dry study," remarked he, as he looked admiringly on the tall charming figure and frank countenance of the girl before him.

"The Querente," said he gravely, "is tall, straight, slender, arms long, hands and feet of the smallest. Hair, just short of blackness, piercing roving eyes dark as night and full of fire. Sight quick, and temperament alive with energy wit and sense."

"O tell my fortune, not my character! I shall shame of energy, wit and sense if I hear such flattery, Doctor!—" exclaimed she shaking herself like a young eagle preparing to fly.

"We shall see what comes of it, Hortense!—!" replied he gravely, as with his gold headed cane he slowly quartered the heavens, like an ancient Augur, and noted the planets in their houses. The Doctor was quite serious now and even Hortense, catching his looks, stood very silent as he studied the Celestial aspects:—

"Carrying through ether in perpetual round
Decrees and resolutions of the Gods."—

"The Lord of the ascendant," said he "is with the Lord of
the seventh in the tenth house. The Querente therefore shall
marry the man made for her. But not the man of her youthful
hope and her first love."

"The stars are true!" continued he speaking to himself
rather than to her. "Jupiter in the seventh house denotes rank
and dignity, by marriage, and Mars in sextile foretells succesful
wars. It is wonderful, Hortense! The blood of Beauharnois
shall sit on thrones more than one! It shall rule France Italy
and Flanders; but not New France for Saturn in quintile looks
darkly upon the Twins, who rule America."

"Come, Jumonville!" exclaimed Hortense, "congratulate
Claude on the greatness awaiting the House of Beauharnois!
and condole with me that I am to see none of it myself! I do
not care for Kings and Queens in the third generation, but
I do care for happy fortune in the present for those I know
and love—! Come Jumonville! have your fortune told now, to
keep me in countenance! If the Doctor hits the truth for you,
I shall believe in him for myself."

"That is a good idea, Hortense!" replied Jumonville. "I
long ago hung my hat on the stars. Let the Doctor try if he
can find it."

The Doctor in great good humour surveyed the dark
handsome face and lithe athletic figure of Jumonville de
Villiers. He again raised his cane with the gravity of a Roman
Pontifex marking off his *Templum* in the heavens. Suddenly
he stopped. He repeated more carefully his survey, and then
turned his earnest eyes upon the young soldier.

"You see ill fortune for me, Doctor!" exclaimed
Jumonville, with bright unflinching eyes as he would look
on danger of any kind.

"The Hyleg or giver of life is afflicted by Mars in the eighth
house, and Saturn is in evil aspect in the ascendant!—" said
the Doctor slowly.

"That sounds warlike and means fighting! I suppose

Doctor—! It is a brave fortune for a soldier—! Go on!"—
Jumonville was in earnest now.

"The *pars fortunae*," continued the Doctor, gazing upward,
"rejoices in a benign aspect with Venus! Fame, true love and
immortality will be yours Jumonville de Villiers; but you will
die young under the flag of your Country, and for sake of your
King. You will not marry, but all the maids and matrons of New
France will lament your fate with tears, and from your death
shall spring up the salvation of your native land—! How I see
not. But *decretum est*, Jumonville—! ask me no more."

A thrill like a stream of electricity passed through the
company. Their mirth was extinguished, for none could
wholly free their minds from the superstition of their age. The
good Doctor sat down and wiped his moistened eye glasses.
"He would tell no more to night," he said. "He had really gone
too far making jest of earnest, and earnest of jest, and begged
pardon of Jumonville for complying with his humour."

The young soldier laughed merrily. "If fame immortality
and true love are to be mine, what care I for death? It will be
worth giving up life for, to have the tears of the maids and
matrons of New France to lament your fate. What could the
most ambitious soldier desire more?"

The words of Jumonville struck a kindred chord in the
bosom of Hortense de Beauharnois. They were stamped upon
her heart for ever. A few years after this prediction, Jumonville
de Villiers lay slain under a flag of truce on the bank of
the Monongahala, and of all the maids and matrons of New
France who wept over his grave, none shed more and bitterer
tears than his fair betrothed, bride Hortense de Beauharnois.

The prediction of the Sieur Gauthier was repeated and
retold as a strangely true tale. It passed into the traditions of
the people and lingered in their memory, generations after
the festival of Belmont was utterly forgotten.

When the great revolt took place in the English Colonies,
the death of the gallant Jumonville de Villiers was neither
forgotten nor forgiven by New France. Congress appealed
in vain for union and help from Canadians. Washington's
proclamations were trodden under foot, and his troops driven

back or captured. If Canada was lost to France partly through the death of Jumonville, it may also be said that his blood helped to save it to England. The ways of Providence are so mysterious in working out the problems of national existence that the life or death of a single individual may turn the scale of destiny over half a continent.

But all these events lay as yet darkly in the womb of the future. The gallant Jumonville who fell, and his brother Coulon who took his "noble revenge" upon Washington, by sparing his life, were to day the gayest of the gay throng who assembled to do honour to Pierre Philibert.

While this group of merry guests, half in jest half in earnest, were trying to discover in the stars the "far reaching concords" that moulded the life of each, Amelie led her brother away from the busy grounds near the mansion and took a quiet path that led into the great Park which they entered. The western horizon still retained a streak from Day's golden finger where the sun had gone down. It was very dusk under the great oaks and thick pines. But the valley was visible as it yawned darkly, beneath their feet, and the shimmering river at the bottom could be traced by the reflection of the stars that followed its course.

A cool salt-water breeze, following the flood tide that was coming up the broad St Lawrence, swept their faces as Amelie walked by the side of Le Gardeur talking in her quiet way of things familiar, and of homely interests, until she saw the fever of his blood abate, and his thoughts return into calmer channels. Her gentle craft subdued his impetuous mood, if craft it might be called, for more wisely cunning than all craft is the prompting of true affection, where reason responds like instinct to the wants of the heart.

They sat down upon a garden seat overlooking the great valley. Few of the guests had sauntered out so far, but Amelie's heart was full—she had much to say—and wanted no interruption.

"I am glad to sit in this pretty spot, Amelie" said he, at last, for he had listened, in silence to the sweet low, voice of his sister as she kept up her half sad, half glad monologue, because she saw it pleased him. It brought him into a mood in which she might venture to talk of the matter that pressed sorely upon her heart.

"A little while ago, I feared I might offend you, Le Gardeur," said she, taking his hand tenderly in hers, "if I spoke all I wished. I never did offend you that I remember, brother, did I?—"

"Never! my incomparable sister! You never did and never could. Say what you will, ask me what you like; but I fear I am unworthy of your affection Sister?"

"You are not unworthy. God gave you as my only brother— you will never be unworthy in my eyes. But it touches me to the quick to suspect others may think lightly of you, Le Gardeur!"

He flinched, for his pride was stirred, but he knew Amelie was right. "It was weakness in me," said he, "I confess it, Sister. To pour wine upon my vexation in hope to cure it, is to feed a fire with oil! To throw fire into a powder magazine were wisdom compared with my folly, Amelie. I was angry at the message I got at such a time. Angelique des Meloises has no mercy upon her lovers!—"

"O my prophetic heart! I thought as much! It was Angelique then, sent you the letter you read at table?"

"Yes, who else could have moved me so? The time was ill chosen, but I suspect hating the Bourgeois, as she does, Angelique intended to call me from Pierre's fete. I shall obey her now. But to night she shall obey me and decide to make or mar me, one way or other. You may read the letter Amelie! if you will."

"I care not to read it, Brother. I know Angelique too well not to fear her influence over you. Her craft and boldness were always a terror to the Convent. But you will not leave Pierre's fete to night?—" added she half imploringly—for she felt keenly the discourtesy to Pierre Philibert.

"I must do even that, Sister! Were Angelique as faulty as she is fair, I should only love her the more for her faults, and make them my own. Were she to come to me like Herodias with the Baptists head in a charger I should outdo Herod in keeping my pledge to her."

Amelie uttered a low moaning cry, "O my dear infatuated brother! It is not in nature for a De Repentigny to love irrationably like that! What maddening philtre have you drank to intoxicate you with a woman who uses you so imperiously? But you will not go, Le Gardeur!" added she clinging to his arm. "You are safe so long as you are with your sister. You will be safe no longer if you go to the Maison des Meloises, to night!—"

"Go, I must and shall! Amelie! I have drank the maddening philtre. I know that! Amelie! And would not take an antidote, if I had one. The world has no antidote to cure me—! I have no wish to be cured of love for Angelique, and in fine I cannot be! so let me go and receive the rod for coming to Belmont and the reward for leaving it at her summons—!" He affected a tone of levity, but Amelie's ear easily detected the false ring of it.

"Dearest brother!" said she, "are you sure Angelique returns or is capable of returning love like yours?—She is like the rest of us, weak and fickle; merely human and not at all the divinity a man in his fancy worships when in love with a woman." It was in vain however for Amelie to try to persuade her brother of that.

"What care I, Amelie, so long as Angelique is not weak and fickle to me?" answered he. "But she will think her tardy lover is both weak and fickle unless I put in a speedy appearance, at the Maison Des Meloises!" He rose up as if to depart, still holding his sister by the hand.

Amelie's tears flowed silently in the darkness. She was not willing to plant a seed of distrust in the bosom of her brother, yet she remembered bitterly and indignantly what Angelique had said of her intentions towards the Intendant. Was she using Le Gardeur as a foil to set off her attractions in the eyes of Bigot?—

"Brother!" said Amelie. "I am a woman and comprehend my sex better than you. I know Angelique's far reaching ambition and crafty ways. Are you sure, not in outward persuasion but in inward conviction that she loves you, as a woman should love the man she means to marry?"

Le Gardeur felt her words like a silver probe that searched his heart. With all his unbounded devotion, he knew Angelique too well, not to feel a pang of distrust sometimes, as she showered her coquetries upon every side of her. "It was the overabundance of her love," he said, but he thought it often fell like the dew round Gideon's fleece, refreshing all the earth about it, but leaving the fleece dry. "Amelie!" said he, "you try me hard and tempt me too, my sister, but it is useless. Angelique may be false as Cressid to other men. She will not be false to me! She has sworn it, with her hand in mine, before the Altar of Notre Dame. I would go down to perdition with her in my arms rather than be a crowned king with all the world of women to choose from and not get her."

Amelie shuddered at his vehemence; but she knew how useless was expostulation. She wisely refrained from more, deeming it her duty, like a good sister, to make the best of what she could not hinder. Some jasmins overhung the seat. She plucked a handful and gave them to him, as they rose, to return to the house.

"Take them with you Le Gardeur," said she giving him the flowers which she tied into a bouquet. "They will remind Angelique that she has a powerful rival in your sisters love."

He took them, as they walked slowly back. "Would she were liker you Amelie in all things," said he. "I will put some of your flowers in her hair to night, for your sake Sister."

"And for her own! may they be for you both an augury of good—! Mind and return home, Le Gardeur after your visit. I shall sit up to await your arrival—to congratulate you,"—and after a pause, she added, "—or to console you, brother!"

"O, no fear, sister!" replied he cheerily. "Angelique is true as steel—to me. You shall call her my betrothed tomorrow! Good by! and now go dance with all delight till morning." He kissed her and departed for the city, leaving her in the Ball room by the side of the Lady de Tilly.

Amelie related to her aunt the result of her conversation with Le Gardeur, and the cause of his leaving the fete, so abruptly. The Lady de Tilly listened with surprise and distress. "To think" said she, "of Le Gardeur asking that terrible girl to marry him—! my only hope is, she will refuse him, and if it be as I hear, I think she will!"

"It would be the ruin of Le Gardeur, if she did Aunt!—You cannot think how determined he is on this marriage."

"It would be his ruin if she accepted him!" replied the Lady de Tilly "with any other woman, Le Gardeur might have a fair chance of happiness but none with her—! More than one of her lovers lies in a bloody grave by reason of her coquettries. She has ruined every man whom she has flattered into loving her. She is without affection. Her thoughts are covered with a veil of deceit impenetrable. She would sacrifice the whole world to her vanity. I fear Amelie, she will sacrifice Le Gardeur as ruthlessly as the most worthless of her admirers."

"We can only hope for the best, Aunt, and I do think Angelique loves Le Gardeur as she never loved any other." Amelie looked into her own heart, and thought, that where love really is, the world cannot limit its possibilities.

They were presently rejoined by Pierre Philibert. The Lady de Tilly and Amelie apologized for Le Gardeur's departure. "He had been compelled to go to the city on an affair of urgency, and had left them to make his excuses." Pierre Philibert was not without a shrewd perception of the state of affairs. He pitied Le Gardeur and excused him, speaking most kindly of him in a way that touched the heart of Amelie.

The ball went on with unflagging spirit and enjoyment. The old walls fairly vibrated with the music and dancing of the gay company.

The Chevalier La Corne finding the Lady de Tilly and his Goddaughter anxious to leave before midnight, ordered their carriages and prepared to accompany them home.

The music, like the tide in the great river that night, reached its flood only after the small hours had set in. Amelie had given her hand to Pierre for one or two dances, and many a friendly, many a half-envious guess, was made as to the probable Chatelaine of Belmont.

The Governor the Lady de Tilly Amelie and many of the elder guests took courteous leave of the Bourgeois, and of Pierre, and returned about midnight to the city. But the music beat wearily under their feet before the younger and more ardent votaries of the dance could leave the splendid Ball room of Belmont. The spires of the distant churches and convents began to glitter in the grey of the morning by the time they had all reached their couches to talk or dream over the memorable fete of Pierre Philibert, the finest as all pronounced it, ever given in the old City of Quebec.

CHAPTER 23

"SO GLOZED THE TEMPTER"

THE lamps burned brightly in the Boudoir of Angelique des Meloises, on the night of the fete of Pierre Philibert. Masses of fresh flowers filled the antique Sevres Vases, sending delicious odours through the appartment which was furnished in a style of almost royal splendour. Upon the white hearth a few billets of wood blazed cheerfully, for after a hot day, as was not uncommon in New France, a cool saltwater breeze came up the great river bearing reminders of cold sea washed rocks, and snowy crevisses still lingering upon the mountainous shores of the St Lawrence.

Angelique sat idly watching the wreaths of smoke as they rose in shapes fantastic as her own thoughts. She was ill at ease and listened eagerly to every sound that came up from the street, as she watched and waited for the footstep she knew so well.

By that subtle instinct which is a sixth sense in woman she knew that Le Gardeur de Repentigny would visit her to night, and renew his offer of marriage. She tried to rehearse what she should say to him and how comport herself so as neither to affront him nor commit herself, by any rash engagement. Her fingers worked nervously together as she pondered over expressions to use and studied looks to give him, that should be neither too warm nor too cold. She meant to retain his love, and evade his proposals, and she never for a moment doubted her ability to accomplish her ends. Men's hearts had hitherto been but potter's clay in her hands, and she had no misgivings now, but she felt that the love of Le Gardeur was a thing she could not tread on without a shock to herself like the counter stroke of a torpedo to the naked foot of an Indian who rashly treads upon it as it basks in a sunny pool.

She was agitated beyond her wont, for she loved Le Gardeur with a strange selfish passion, for her own sake not for his,—a sort of love not uncommon with either sex. She had the frankness to be half ashamed of it, for she knew the wrong she was doing to one of the most noble and faithful hearts in the world. But the arrival of the Intendant, had unsettled every good resolution she had once made to marry Le Gardeur de Repentigny and become a reputable matron in Society. Her ambitious fantasies dimmed every perception of duty to her own heart as well as his, and she had worked herself into that unenviable frame of mind, which possesses a woman who cannot resolve either to consent or deny, to accept her lover or to let him go—!—

The solitude of her appartment became insupportable to her. She sprang up, opened the window and sat down in the balcony outside trying to find composure by looking down into the dark still street.

The voices of two men engaged in eager conversation, reached her ear. They sat upon the broad steps of the house, so that every word they spake reached her ear although she could scarcely distinguish them in the darkness.

These were no other than Max Grimeau and Blind Barthemy, the brace of beggars whose post was at the Gate of the Basse Ville. They seemed to be comparing the amount of alms each had received during the day, and were arranging for a supper, in some obscure haunt they frequented in the purlieus of the Lower Town, when another figure, came up, short, dapper and carrying a knapsack, as Angelique could detect by the glimmer of a lantern that hung on a rope stretched across the street. He was greeted warmly by the old mendicants.

"Sure as my old musquet! it is Master Pothier, and no body else!" exclaimed Max Grimeau, rising and giving the new comer a hearty embrace. "Dont you see Barthemy? He has been forraging among the fat wives of the South shore! What a cheek he blows! red as a peony and fat as a Dutch Burgomasters!"—Max had seen plenty of the world when he marched under Marshall de Belleisle so he was at no loss for apt comparisons.

"Yes!" replied blind Barthemy, holding out his hands to be shaken, "I see by your voice, Master Pothier, that you have not said grace over bare bones during your absence!—But where have you been this long time?"

"O, taxing the Kings subjects to the best of my poor ability in the law, and without half the success of you and Max here, who toll the gate of the Basse Ville more easily than the Intendant gets in the Kings taxes."

"Why not?" replied Barthemy with a pious twist of his neck and an upward cast of his blank orbs. "It is *pour l'amour de Dieu*! We beggars save more souls than the Curé, for we are always exhorting men to charity—! I think we ought to be part of Holy Church as well as the grey friars."

"And so we are part of Holy Church Barthemy!" interrupted Max Grimeau. "When the good Bishop washed twelve pair of our dirty feet on Maunday Thursday in the Cathedral, I felt like an Apostle, I did—! my feet were just ready for benediction! for see! they had never been washed that I remember of since I marched to the relief of Prague! But you should have been out to Belmont to day, Master Pothier!—There was the grandest Easter pie ever made in New France! You might have carried on a law suit inside of it, and lived off the estate for a year. I ate a bushel of it, I did!—"

"O the cursed luck is every day mine!" replied Master Pothier, clapping his hand upon his stomach. "I would not have missed that Easter pie, no not to draw the Pope's will! But as it is laid down in the *Coutume d'Orleans* Tit. 17, the absent lose the usufruct of their rights, *vide* also *Pothier, Des successions*, I lost my share of the pie of Belmont—!"

"Well never mind, Master Pothier," replied Max, "Dont grieve! You shall go with us to night to the *Fleur de Lys*, in the Sault au Matelot. Barthemy and I have bespoken an eel pie, and a gallon of humming cider of Normandy. We shall all be jolly as the Marguilliers of St Roch after tithing the parish!—"

"Have with you then! I am free now. I have just delivered a letter to the Intendant from a lady at Beaumanoir, and got a crown for it. I will lay it on top of your eel pie, Max!—"

Angelique from being simply amused at the conversation of the old Beggars, became in an instant all eyes and ears at the words of Master Pothier.

"Had you ever the fortune to see that lady at Beaumanoir?" asked Max, with more curiosity than was to be expected of one in his position.

"No, the letter was handed me by Dame Tremblay, with a cup of wine. But the Intendant gave me a crown, when he read it. I never saw the Chevalier Bigot in better humour! That letter touched both his purse and his feelings. But how did you ever come to hear of the lady of Beaumanoir?"

"O! Barthemy and I hear everything at the gate of the Basse Ville! My Lord Bishop and Father Glapion of the Jesuits met in the gate one day, and spoke of her, each asking the other if he knew who she was?—when up rode the Intendant, and the Bishop made free, as Bishops will you know, to question him, whether he kept a lady at the Chateau—? 'A round dozen of them, my Lord Bishop!' replied Bigot laughing. La! It takes the Intendant to talk down a Bishop! He bade my Lord not trouble himself—! The lady was under his '*tutelle*'! which I comprehended as little—as little—"

"As you do your *Nominy Dominy*!—" replied Pothier. "Dont be angry Max! if I infer that the Intendant quoted, Pigean Tit. 2.27 *Le tuteur est comptable de sa gestion.*"

"I dont care what the Pigeons have to say to it! That is what the Intendant said!" replied Max, hotly, "and *that*, for your law grimoire Master Pothier!" Max snapped his finger like the lock of his musket at Prague, to indicate what he meant by "*that*"!—

"O, *Inepte loquens*! You dont understand either law, or Latin, Max!" exclaimed Pothier shaking his ragged wig with an air of pity.

"I understand begging, and that is getting without shamming, and much more to the purpose" replied Max hotly. "Look you, Master Pothier, you are learned as three curates, but I can get more money in the Gate of the Basse Ville by simply standing still, and crying out, *Pour l'amour de Dieu*! than you with your budget of law *lingo jingo*, running up and down the country until the dogs eat off the calves of your legs, as they say in the Nivernois."

"Well, never mind what they say in the Nivernois, about the calves of my legs. *Bon coq ne fut jamais gras!* A game cock is never fat, and that is Master Pothier *dit* Robin! Lean as are my calves, they will carry away as much of your eel pie to night, as the stoutest carter's in Quebec—!"—

"And the pie is baked by this time! so let us be jogging!" interrupted Barthemy, rising. "Now give me your arm, Max! and with Master Pothier's on the other side, I shall walk to the *Fleur de Lys*, straight as a steeple.—"

The glorious prospect of supper, made all three merry as crickets on a warm hearth, and they jogged over the pavement in their clouted shoes, little suspecting they had left a flame of anger in the breast of Angelique des Meloises, kindled by the few words of Pothier, and the beggars respecting the lady of Beaumanoir.

Angelique recalled with bitterness, that the rude bearer of the note, had observed *something*, that had touched the heart and opened the purse of the Intendant. What was it? Was Bigot playing a game with Angelique des Meloises?—Woe to him and to the lady of Beaumanoir if he was—!—As she sat musing over it a knock was heard on the door of her Boudoir. She left the balcony, and reentered her room where a neat comely girl, in a servants dress, was waiting to speak to her.

The girl was not known to Angelique. But curtseying very low, she informed her that she was Fanchon Dodier, a cousin of Lizettes. She had been in service at the Chateau of Beaumanoir, but had just left it. "There is no living under Dame Tremblay," said she, "if she suspect a maid servant of flirting, ever so little, with M. Froumois, the handsome Valet of the Intendant—! She imagined I did, and such a life as she has led me! my Lady! So I came to the City, to ask advice of cousin Lizette, and seek a new place. I am sure Dame Tremblay need not be so hard upon the maids. She is always boasting of her own triumphs when she was the Charming Josephine!—"

"And Lizette referred you to me?" asked Angelique too

occupied just now to mind the gossip about Dame Tremblay which another time she would have enjoyed immensely. She eyed the girl with intense curiosity, for might she not tell her something of the secret over which she was eating her heart out.

"Yes, my Lady! Lizette referred me to you and told me to be very circumspect indeed about what I said touching the Intendant, but simply to ask, if you would take me into your service—! Lizette need not have warned me about the Intendant! for I never reveal secrets of my masters or mistresses—never! never! my lady!—"

"You are more cunning than you look nevertheless," thought Angelique. "Whatever scruple you may have about secrets, Fanchon," said she, "I will make one condition with you. I will take you into my service, if you will tell me whether you ever saw the lady of Beaumanoir?"

Angelique's notions of honour, clear enough in theory, never prevented her sacrificing them without compunction, to gain an object—or learn a secret that interested her.

"I will willingly tell *you* all I know! my Lady. I have seen her, once. None of the servants are supposed to know she is in the chateau, but of course all do—!" Fanchon stood with her two hands in the pockets of her apron, as ready to talk as the pretty Grisette who directed Laurence Sterne to the Opera Comique.

"Of course!" remarked Angelique. "A secret like that could never be kept in the Chateau of Beaumanoir!—Now tell me, Fanchon, what is she like—?—" Angelique sat up eagerly, and brushed back the hair from her ear with a rapid stroke of her hand, as she questioned the girl.—There was a look in her eyes that made Fanchon a little afraid, and brought out more truth than she intended to impart.

"I saw her this morning, my Lady! as she knelt in her oratory. The half open door tempted me to look in, spite of the orders of Dame Tremblay."

"Ah! you saw her this morning!" repeated Angelique impetuously, "how does she appear? Is she better in looks than when she first came to the Chateau or worse? she ought to be worse, much worse."

"I do not know, my lady, but as I said, I looked in the door, although forbid to do so. Half open doors are so tempting, and one cannot shut one's eyes—! Even a key hole is hard to resist when you long to know what is on the other side of it. I always found it so!"

"I dare say you did! But how does she look—?" broke in Angelique impatiently stamping her dainty foot on the floor.

"Oh, so pale my Lady! but her face is the loveliest I ever saw,—almost," added she with an after thought, "but so sad! she looks like the twin sister of the blessed Madonna in the Seminary-church, my Lady."

"Was she at her devotions, Fanchon?"

"I think not, my lady, she was reading a letter which she had just received from the Intendant."

Angelique's eyes were now ablaze. She conjectured at once that Caroline was corresponding with Bigot, and the letter brought to the Intendant by Master Pothier was in reply to one from him. "But how do you know the letter she was reading, was from the Intendant?—It could not be!" Angelique's eye brows contracted angrily, and a dark shadow passed over her face. She said "it could not be," but she felt it could be and was.

"O, but it was from the Intendant my Lady! I heard her repeat his name, and pray God to bless Francois Bigot, for his kind words. That is the Intendants name is it not my Lady—?"

"To be sure it is. I should not have doubted you, Fanchon! But Could you gather the purport of that letter? Speak truly, Fanchon! and I will reward you splendidly. What think you it was about?"

"I did more than gather the purport of it, my Lady. I have got the letter itself!" Angelique sprang up eagerly as if to embrace Fanchon. "I happened in my eagerness to jar the door. The lady imagining some one was coming, rose suddenly, and left the room. In her haste she dropped the letter on the floor. I picked it up. I thought no harm, as I was determined to leave Dame Tremblay to day. Would my Lady like to read the letter?"

Angelique fairly sprang at the offer. "You have got the letter! Fanchon! Let me see it instantly! How considerate of you to bring it! I will give you this ring for that letter!" She pulled a ring off her finger, and seizing Fanchon's hand put it on hers.

Fanchon was enchanted. She admired the ring as she turned it round and round on her finger. "I am infinitely obliged, my Lady, for your gift. It is worth a million such letters," said she.

"The letter outweighs a million rings!" replied Angelique, as she tore it open violently, and sat down to read. The first words struck her like a stone.

"Dear Caroline!" It was written in the bold hand of the Intendant, which Angelique knew very well. "You have suffered too much for my sake, but I am not unfeeling nor ungrateful. I have news for you! Your father has gone to France in search of you! No one suspects you to be here. Remain patiently where you are at present, and in the utmost secrecy, or there will be a storm that may upset us both. Try to be happy, and let not the sweetest eyes that were ever seen, grow dim with needless regrets. Better and brighter days will surely come. Meanwhile pray, pray, my Caroline! It will do you good, and perhaps make me more worthy of the love which I know is wholly mine.

Adieu

Francois"

Angelique devoured rather than read the letter. She had no sooner done, than she tore it up in a paroxysm of fury, scattering its pieces like snow flakes over the carpet, and stamping on them with her firm foot as if she would tread them into annihilation.

Fanchon was not unaccustomed to exhibitions of feminine wrath, but she was fairly frightened at the terrible rage that shook Angelique from head to foot.

"Fanchon! did you read that letter?" demanded she turning suddenly upon the trembling maid. The girl saw her mistress' cheeks twitch with passion and her hands clench as if she would strike her, if she answered—yes.

Shaking with fear, Fanchon replied faintly "No, my Lady, I cannot read."

"And you have allowed no other person to read it?"

"No, my Lady!—I was afraid to show the letter to any one.—You know, I ought not to have taken it!"

"Was no inquiry made about it?" Angelique laid her hand upon the girls shoulder who trembled from head to foot.

"Yes, my Lady, Dame Tremblay turned the chateau upside down, looking for it;—but I dared not tell her I had it—!"

"I think you speak truth, Fanchon!" replied Angelique getting somewhat over her passion—but her bosom still heaved like the ocean after a storm.

"And now mind what I say!" Her hand pressed heavily on the girls shoulder, while she gave her a look that seemed to freeze the very marrow in her bones. "You know a secret about the Lady of Beaumanoir, Fanchon! and one about me too. If you ever speak of either to man or woman or even to yourself, I will cut the tongue out of your mouth and nail it to that door post! Mind my words, Fanchon! I never fail to do what I threaten!"

"O only do not look so at me! my Lady!" replied poor Fanchon perspiring with fear. "I am sure I never will speak of it! I swear by our blessed Lady of St Foye! I will never breathe to mortal, that I gave you that letter."

"That will do—!" replied Angelique throwing herself down in her great chair, "and now, you may go to Lizette—she will attend to you. But, *remember!*"

The frightened girl did not wait for another command to go. Angelique held up her finger which to Fanchon looked terrible as a poniard. She hurried down to the servants Hall with a secret held fast between her teeth for once in her life and she trembled at the very thought of ever letting it escape.

Angelique sat with her hands on her temples staring upon the fire that flared and flickered in the deep fireplace.

She had seen a wild wicked vision there once before. It came again, as things evil never fail to come again at our bidding. Good may delay, but evil never waits. The red fire turned itself into shapes of lurid dens and caverns, changing from horror to horror, until her creative fancy transformed them into the secret chamber of Beaumanoir, with its one fair solitary inmate—Her rival for the hand of the Intendant— Her fortunate rival, if she might believe the letter brought to her so strangely. Angelique looked fiercely at the fragments of it lying upon the carpet, and wished she had not destroyed it, but every word of it was stamped upon her memory, as if branded with a hot iron.

"I see it all, now!" exclaimed she. "Bigots falseness and her shameless effrontery in seeking him in his very house!— But it shall not be!—" Angelique's voice was like the cry of a wounded panther tearing at the arrow which has pierced his flank. "Is Angelique des Meloises to be humiliated by that woman? never! But, my bright dreams will have no fulfilment, so long as she lives at Beaumanoir, so long as she lives any where!"

She sat still for a while, gazing into the fire, and the secret chamber of Beaumanoir again formed itself before her vision. She sprang up, touched by the hand of her good angel perhaps—and for the last time. "Satan whispers it again in my ear!" cried she. "St Marie! I am not so wicked as that!— Last night, the thought came to me in the dark. I shook it off at dawn of day. To night it comes again, and I let it touch me, like a lover, and I neither withdraw my hand, nor tremble! Tomorrow, it will return for the last time and stay with me! and I shall let it sleep on my pillow! The babe of sin will have been born and waxed to a full Demon, and I shall yield myself up to his embraces!—O, Bigot! Bigot! What have you not done? *C'est la faute à vous!—C'est la faute à vous!*" She repeated this exclamation, several times, as if by accusing Bigot, she excused her own evil imaginings, and cast the blame of them upon him. She seemed drawn down into a vortex, which there was no escape from. She gave herself up to its drift in a sort of passionate abandonment. The death or the banishment of Caroline were the only alternatives she could contemplate. "The sweetest eyes were ever seen—!"—"Bigot's foolish words," thought she, "and the influence of those eyes must be killed if Angelique des Meloises is ever to mount the lofty Chariot of her Ambition!—"

"Other women," she thought bitterly, "would abandon greatness for love, and in the arms of a faithful lover, like Le Gardeur, find a compensation for the slights of the Intendant."

But Angelique was not like other women. She was born to conquer men, not to yield to them! The steps of a throne glittered in her wild fancy, and she would not lose the game of her life because she had missed the first throw! Bigot was false to her, but he was still worth the winning, for all the reasons which made her first listen to him. She had no love for him, not a spark! but his name, his rank, his wealth and influence at Court, and a future career of glory there—these things, she had regarded as her own, by right of her beauty and skill in ruling men! "No rival shall ever boast she has conquered Angelique des Meloises!" cried she clenching her hands. And thus it was in this crisis of her fate the love of Le Gardeur was blown like a feather before the breath of her passionate selfishness. The golden weights pulled her down to the Nadir. Angelique's final resolution was irrevocably taken, before her eager hopeful lover appeared in answer to her summons, to recall him from the festival of Belmont.

CHAPTER 24

"SEALS OF LOVE, BUT SEALED IN VAIN"

SHE sat waiting Le Gardeur's arrival, and the thought of him began to assert its influence as the antidote of the poisonous stuff she had taken into her imagination. His presence so handsome, his manner so kind, his love so undoubted, carried her into a region of intense self satisfaction. Angelique never thought so honestly well of herself as when recounting the marks of affection bestowed upon her by Le Gardeur de Repentigny. "His love is a treasure for any woman to possess, and he has given it all to me—!" said she to herself. "There are women who value themselves wholly, by the value placed upon them by others. But I value others by the measure of myself. I love Le Gardeur, and what I love I do not mean to lose!" added she, with an inconsequence that fitted ill with her resolution regarding the Intendant. But Angelique was one to reconcile to herself all professions, however opposite or however incongruous.

A hasty knock at the door of the mansion, followed by the quick well known step up the broad stair brought Le Gardeur into her presence. He looked flushed and disordered, as he took her eagerly extended hand, and pressed it to his lips.

Her whole aspect underwent a transformation in the presence of her lover. She was unfeignedly glad to see him. Without letting go his hand, she led him to the sofa, and sat down by him. Other men had the semblance of her graciousness—and perfect imitation it was too—But he alone had the reality of her affection.

"O, Le Gardeur!" exclaimed she, looking him through and through, and detecting no flaw in his honest admiration. "Can you forgive me, for asking you to come and see me to night? and for absolutely no reason—! None in the world Le Gardeur!—but that I longed to see you! I was jealous of Belmont for drawing you away from the Maison des Meloises to night!"

"And what better reason could I have in the world, than that you were longing to see me, Angelique?—I think I should leave the door of paradise itself if you called me back, darling!—Your presence for a minute is more to me than hours of festivity at Belmont or the company of any other woman in the world."

Angelique was not insensible to the devotion of Le Gardeur. Her feelings were touched, and never slow in finding an interpretation for them, she raised his hand quickly to her lips, and kissed it. "I had no motive in sending for you but to see you Le Gardeur!" said she. "Will *that* content you? If it wont— —"

"This shall!" replied he, kissing her cheek, which she was far from averting or resenting.

"That is so like you, Le Gardeur!" replied she, "To take before it is given!" She stopped—"What was I going to say?" added she. "It was given and my contentment is perfect to have you here, by my side!" If her thoughts reverted at this moment to the Intendant, it was with a feeling of repulsion. And as she looked fondly in the face of Le Gardeur, she could not help contrasting his handsome looks, with the hard swarthy features of Bigot.

"I wish *my* contentment were perfect! Angelique But it is in your power to make it so,—will you? Why keep me for ever on the threshold of my happiness, or of my despair whichever you shall decree—? I have spoken to Amelie to night of you—!"

"O, do not press me, Le Gardeur!" exclaimed she violently agitated, anxious to evade the question she saw burning on his lips, and distrustful of her own power to refuse, "not now—! not to night—! another day, you shall know how much I love you Le Gardeur—! why will not men content themselves with knowing we love them without stripping our favours of all grace by making them duties?—and, in the end, destroying our love, by marrying us—?" A flash of her natural archness came over her face as she said this.

"That would not be your case and mine! Angelique!" replied he, somewhat puzzled at her strange speech. But she rose up suddenly, without replying, and walked to a Buffet, where stood a silver salver full of refreshments.

"I suppose you have feasted so magnificently at Belmont, that you will not care for my humble hospitalities!" said she, offering him a cup of rare wine, a recent gift of the Intendant, which she did not mention however. "You have not told me a word yet, of the grand party at Belmont.—Pierre Philibert has been highly honoured by the *Honnetes Gens* I am sure!—"

"And merits all the honour he receives!—Why were you not there too, Angelique? Pierre would have been delighted—?" replied he ever ready to defend Pierre Philibert.

"And I too! but I feared to be disloyal to the Friponne!" said she half mockingly. "I am a partner in the Grand Company, you know, Le Gardeur! But I confess Pierre Philibert is the handsomest man, except one, in New France! I own to *that*! I thought to pique Amelie one day, by telling her so, but on the contrary, I pleased her beyond measure!! She agreed without excepting even the one!—"

"Amelie told me your good opinion of Pierre, and I thanked you for it!" said he taking her hand. "And now, darling!—since you cannot with wine, words nor winsomeness, divert me from my purpose in making you declare what you think of me also, let me tell you, I have promised Amelie to bring her your answer to night—!"

The eyes of Le Gardeur shone with a light of loyal affection. Angelique saw there was no escaping a declaration. She sat irresolute and trembling, with one hand resting on his arm and the other held up, deprecatingly, but it was a piece of acting she had rehearsed to herself for this foreseen occasion. But her tongue usually so nimble and free, faltered for once in the rush of emotions that well nigh overpowered her. To become the honoured wife of Le Gardeur de Repentigny, the sister of the beauteous Amelie, the neice of the noble Lady de Tilly, was a piece of fortune to have satisfied until recently, both her heart and her ambition—! But now, Angelique was the dupe of dreams and fancies. The Royal Intendant was at her feet. France and its court splendours and court intrigues opened vistas of grandeur to her aspiring and unscrupulous ambition—she could not forgo them, and would not! She knew *that*, all the time, her heart was melting beneath the pleading eyes of Le Gardeur.

"I have spoken to Amelie and promised to take her your answer to night," said he in a tone that thrilled every fibre of her better nature. "She is ready to embrace you as her sister.—Will you be my wife, Angelique?"

Angelique sat silent—she dared not look up at him. If she had, she knew her hard resolution would melt. She felt his gaze upon her, without seeing it. She grew pale and tried to answer, No! but could not, and she would not answer, Yes!

Had Angelique looked up for one moment in those loving eyes of his which of all the world possessed a man's power over her, all might have ended in kisses and tears of joy, and this tragical history had had no foundation.

But it was not to be!—She did not look up, but her averted eyes fell down upon the glowing hearth. The vision she had so so wickedly revelled in flashed again upon her at this supreme moment. She saw in a panorama of a few seconds, the gilded halls of Versailles pass before her, and with the vision the old temptation. Wicked imaginings once admitted as guests, come in afterwards unbidden. They sit down familiarly on our hearth as masters in our house making us their servants for ever.

"Angelique!" Repeated he, in a tone full of passionate entreaty, "will you be my wife loved as no woman ever was; loved as alone Le Gardeur de Repentigny can love you?"

She knew *that*, as she weakened under his pleading, and grasped both his hands tight in hers. She strove to frame a reply, which should say yes, while it meant, No, and say, No, which he should interpret— —yes.

"All New France will honour you as the Chatelaine de Repentigny! There will be none higher as there will be none fairer than my bride—!" Poor Le Gardeur! He had a dim suspicion that Angelique was looking to France as a fitting theater for her beauty and talents.

She still sat mute and grew paler every moment. Words formed themselves upon her lips. But she feared to say them, so terrible was the earnestness of this man's love, and the no less vivid consciousness of her own. Her face assumed the hardness of marble, pale as Parian and as rigid.—A trembling of her white lips showed the strife going on within her. She covered her eyes with her hand, that he might not see the tears, she felt quivering under the full lids. But she remained mute.

"Angelique!" exclaimed he, divining her unexpressed refusal. "Why do you turn away from me? You surely do not reject me? But I am mad to think it!—Speak Darling! one word, one sign, one look from those dear eyes, in consent to be the wife of Le Gardeur, will bring life's happiness to us both!—" He took her hand and drew it gently from her eyes and kissed it, but she still averted her gaze from him. She could not look at him, but the words dropped slowly and feebly, from her lips in response to his appeal.

"I love you Le Gardeur! but I will not marry you!—" said she. She could not utter more, but her hand grasped his with a fierce pressure as if wanting to hold him fast in the very moment of refusal.

He started back as if touched by fire. "You love me, but will not marry me!—Angelique! what mystery is this? But you are only trying me! A thousand thanks for your love—the other is but a jest—! a good jest, which I will laugh at!—" And Le Gardeur tried to laugh: but it was a sad failure, for he saw, she did not join in his effort at merriment, but looked pale and trembling as if ready to faint.

She laid her hands upon his, heavily and sadly. He felt her refusal in the very touch. It was like cold lead. "Do not laugh Le Gardeur. I cannot laugh over it. This is no jest, but mortal earnest! What I say I mean! I love you, Le Gardeur! but I will not marry you—!"—

She drew her hands away as if to mark the emphasis she could not speak. He felt it like the drawing of his heart strings. She turned her eyes full upon him now, as if to look whether love of her was extinguished in him by her refusal. "I love you Le Gardeur, you know I do! but I will not—I cannot marry you, now!" repeated she.

"Now!" He caught at the straw like a drowning swimmer in a whirlpool.—"Now? I said not—Now!—but when, you please, Angelique! You are worth a man's waiting his life for!—"

"No, Le Gardeur!" she replied, "I am not worth your waiting for. It cannot be, as I once hoped it might be, but love you I do. I ever shall!" and the false fair woman kissed him fatuously. "I love you Le Gardeur but I will not marry you!"

"You do not surely mean it, Angelique!" exclaimed he. "You will not give me death, instead of life—? You cannot be so false to your own heart, so cruel to mine?—See, Angelique, my saintly sister Amelie, believed in your love, and sent these flowers to place in your hair, when you had consented to be my wife—her sister—. You will not refuse them, Angelique?—"

He raised his hand to place the garland upon her head. But Angelique turned quickly and they fell at her feet. "Amelie's gifts are not for me, Le Gardeur! I do not merit them! I confess my fault! I am, I know, false to my own heart and cruel to yours. Despise me—kill me for it if you will Le Gardeur! better you did kill me perhaps!—but I cannot lie to you, as I can to other men—! Ask me not to change my resolution for I neither can nor will—." She spoke with impassioned energy, as if fortifying her refusal by the reiteration of it.

"It is past comprehension!—" was all he could say, bewildered at her words thus dislocated from all their natural sequence of association. "Love me and not marry me! That means she will marry another!" thought he, with a jealous pang. "Tell me Angelique!" continued he after several minutes of puzzled silence. "Is there some inscrutable reason makes you keep my love and reject my hand?"

"No reason! Le Gardeur! It is mad unreason! I feel *that*—! but it is no less true. I love you but I will not marry you—!—" She spoke with more resolution now. The first plunge was over, and with it her fear and trembling as she sat on the brink.

The iteration drove him beside himself. He seized her hands, and exclaimed with vehemence, "There is a man—a rival—a more fortunate lover—behind all this! Angelique des Meloises—! It is not yourself that speaks, but one that prompts you! You have given your love to another, and discarded me! Is it not so?"

"I have neither discarded you nor loved another!" Angelique equivocated. She played her soul away at this moment with the mental reservation that she had not yet done, what she had resolved to do, upon the first opportunity:—accept the hand of the Intendant Bigot.

"It is well for that other man, if there be one!" Le Gardeur rose and walked angrily across the room two or three times. Angelique was playing a game of chess with Satan for her soul, and felt she was losing it.

"There was a sphinx in old times," said he, "that propounded a riddle, and he who failed to solve it, had to die! Your riddle will be the death of me, for I cannot solve it Angelique!—"

"Do not try to solve it. Dear Le Gardeur! remember! that when her riddle was solved, the Sphinx threw herself into the sea. I doubt that may be my fate!— —But you are still my friend Le Gardeur—!" added she, seating herself again by his side, in her old fond coquettish manner. "See! these flowers of Amelie's, which I did not place in my hair, I treasure in my bosom—!" She gathered them up and as she spoke, kissed them, and placed them in her bosom. "You are still my friend, Le Gardeur?" Her eyes turned upon him with the old look she could so well assume.

"I am more than a thousand, friends, Angelique!" replied he, "but I shall curse myself that I can remain so, and see you the wife of another!"

The very thought drove him to frenzy. He dashed her hand away, and sprang up towards the door, but turned suddenly round. "That curse was not for you, Angelique!" said he, pale and agitated. "It was for myself, for ever believing in the empty love you professed! for me. Good by! Be happy! As for me, the light goes out of my life, Angelique, from this day forth!—"

"O stop! stop! Le Gardeur. Do not leave me so!" She rose and endeavoured to restrain him, but he broke from her, and without, adieu or further parley, rushed out bareheaded in to the street. She ran to the balcony to call him back, and leaning far over it, cried out: "Le Gardeur! Le Gardeur!—" That voice would have called him from the dead could he have heard it. But he was already lost in the darkness. A few swift steps resounded on the distant pavement, and Le Gardeur de Repentigny was lost to her for ever!

She waited long on the Balcony looking over it, for a chance of hearing his returning steps, but none came. It was the last impulse of her love to save her, but it was useless. "O God!—" she exclaimed, in a voice of womanly agony. "He is gone for ever—! My Le Gardeur! my one true lover rejected by my own madness, and for what?"—She thought—for what— and in a storm of passion tearing her golden hair, over her face and beating her breast in her rage, she exclaimed: "I am wicked, unutterably bad, worse and more despicable than the vilest creature that crouches under the bushes on the batture—! How dared I, unwomanly that I am, reject the hand I worship, for sake of a hand I should loathe in the very act of accepting it? The slave that is sold in the market is better than I, for she has no choice, while I sell myself to a man, whom I already hate, for he is already false to me!—The wages of a harlot were more honestly earned than the splendour for which I barter soul and body, to this Intendant!—"

The passionate girl threw herself upon the floor, nor heeded the blood that oozed from her head bruised on the hard wood. Her mind was torn by a thousand wild fancies. Sometimes she resolved to go out like the Rose of Sharon and seek her beloved in the city and throw herself at his feet making him a royal gift of all he claimed of her.

She little knew her own wilful heart. She had seen the world bow to every caprice of hers. But she never had one principle to guide her, except her own pleasure. She was now like a goddess of earth fallen in an effort to reconcile impossibilities in human hearts, and become the sport of the powers of wickedness.

She lay upon the floor senseless, Her hands in a violent clasp. Her glorious hair torn and disordered lay over her like the royal robe of a Queen stricken from her throne, and lying dead upon the floor of her palace.

It was long after midnight, in the cold hours of the morning when she woke from her swoon. She raised herself feebly upon her elbow, and looked dazedly up at the cold unfeeling stars that go on shining through the ages making no sign of sympathy with human griefs. Perseus was rising to his meridian, and Algol her natal star alternately darkened and brightened as if it were the scene of some fierce conflict of the powers of light and darkness like that going on in her own soul.

Her face was streaked with hard clots of blood as she rose cramped and chilled to the bone. The night air had blown coldly upon her through the open lattice, but she would not summon her maid to her assistance. Without undressing she threw herself upon a couch and utterly worn out by the agitation she had undergone, slept far into the day.

CHAPTER 25

"THE HURRIED QUESTION OF DESPAIR"

Le Gardeur plunged headlong down the silent street, neither knowing nor caring whither. Half mad with grief, half with resentment, he vented curses upon himself upon Angelique, and upon the world, and looked upon Providence itself as in league with the evil powers to thwart his happiness, not seeing that his happiness in the love of a woman like Angelique was a house built on sand, which the first storm of life would sweep away.

"Holla! Le Gardeur de Repentigny! is that you?" exclaimed a voice in the night. "What lucky wind blows you out at this hour?" Le Gardeur stopped and recognized the Chevalier de Pean. "Where are you going in such a desperate hurry?"

"To the devil!" replied Le Gardeur, withdrawing his hand from De Pean's who had seized it with an amazing show of friendship. "It is the only road left open to me and I am going to march down it like a *garde du corps* of Satan—!—Do not hold me De Pean—! let go my arm! I am going to the devil, I tell you!"

"Why Le Gardeur," was the reply. "That is a broad and well travelled road—the Kings high way in fact. I am going upon it myself, as fast and merrily as any man in New France."

"Well go on it, then! march either before or after me only dont go with me, De Pean! I am taking the shortest cuts to get to the end of it, and want no one with me." Le Gardeur walked doggedly on; but De Pean would not be shook off. He suspected what had happened.

"The shortest cut I know, is by the Taverne de Menut, where I am going now," said he, "and I should like your company Le Gardeur! Our set are having a gala night of it, and

284

must be musical as the frogs of Beauport by this time!—Come along!" De Pean again took his arm. He was not repelled this time.

"I dont care where I go, De Pean!" replied he forgetting his dislike to this man, and submitting to his guidance. The Taverne de Menut was just the place for him to rush into, and drown his disappointment in wine. The two moved on in silence for a few minutes.

"Why what ails you, Le Gardeur?" asked his companion, as they walked on arm in arm. "Has fortune frowned upon the cards? or your mistress proved a fickle jade, like all her sex?—"

His words were irritating enough to Le Gardeur. "Look you De Pean!" said he stopping. "I shall quarrel with you if you repeat such remarks. But you mean no mischief I dare say, although I would not swear it—!"—Le Gardeur looked savagely.

De Pean saw it would not be safe to rub that sore again. "Forgive me! Le Gardeur!" said he, with an air of sympathy, well assumed. "I meant no harm. But you are suspicious of your friends to night, as a Turk of his harem."

"I have reason to be! and as for friends, I find only such friends as you De Pean! and I begin to think the world has no better!" The Clock of the Recollets struck two as they passed under the shadow of its wall. The brothers of St Francis slept quietly on their peaceful pillows, like sea birds who find in a rocky nook a refuge from the ocean storms. "Do you think the Recollets are happy, De Pean?" asked he turning abruptly to his companion.

"Happy as oysters at high water, who are never crossed in love except of their dinner! But that is neither your luck nor mine Le Gardeur!" De Pean was itching to draw from his companion something with reference to what had passed with Angelique.

"Well, I would rather be an oyster than a man, and rather be dead than either!" was the reply of Le Gardeur. "How soon think you will brandy kill a man, De Pean?" asked he abruptly after a pause of silence.

"It will never kill you, Le Gardeur! if you take it neat at Master Menut's. It will restore you to life, vigour and independance of man and woman. I take mine there, when I am hipped as you are Le Gardeur. It is a specific for every kind of ill fortune. I warrant it will cure and never kill you."

They crossed the Place d'Armes. Nothing in sight was moving except the sentries who paced slowly like shadows up and down the great gate way of the Castle of St Louis.

"It is still and solemn as a church yard here," remarked De Pean. "All the life of the Place is down at Menut's! I like the small hours!" added he as the chime of the Recollets ceased. "They are easily counted and pass quickly, asleep or awake. Two O clock in the morning is the meridian of the day for a man who has wit to wait for it at Menuts. These small hours are all that are worth reckoning in a man's life."—

Without consenting to accompany De Pean, Le Gardeur suffered himself to be led by him. He knew the Company that awaited him there. The wildest and most dissolute gallants of the city and garrison were usually assembled there at this hour.

The famous old hostelry was kept by Master Menut, a burly Breton, who prided himself on keeping everything full and plenty about his house—tables full, tankards full, guests full and himself very full. The house was tonight, lit up with unusual brilliance and was full of Company—Cadet, Varin, Le Mercier, and a crowd of the friends of and associates of the Grand Company. Gambling drinking, and conversing in the loudest strain on such topics as interested their class, were the amusements of the night. The vilest thought uttered in the low Argot of Paris was much affected by them. They felt a pleasure in this sort of protest against the extreme refinement of society, just as the Collegians of Oxford trained beyond their natural capacity in Morals love to fall into slang, and like Prince Hal, talk to every tinker in his own tongue.

De Pean and Le Gardeur were welcomed with open arms at the Taverne de Menut. A dozen brimming glasses were offered them on every side. De Pean drank moderatly. "I have to win back my losses of last night," said he, "and will keep my head clear." Le Gardeur however, refused nothing that was offered him. He drank with all, and drank every description of liquour. He was speedily led up into a large well furnished room where tables were crowded with gentlemen playing cards and dice, for piles of paper money which was tossed from hand to hand with the greatest nonchalance as the game ended and was renewed.

Le Gardeur plunged headlong into the flood of dissipation. He played, drank, talked Argot, and threw off every shred of reserve. He doubled his stakes and threw his dice reckless and careless whether he lost or won. His voice overbore that of the stoutest of the revellers. He embraced De Pean as his friend, who returned his compliments by declaring Le Gardeur de Repentigny to be the king of good fellows, "who had the strongest head to carry wine and the stoutest heart to defy dull care of any man in Quebec."

De Pean watched with malign satisfaction the progress of Le Gardeur's intoxication. If he seemed to flag, he challenged him afresh to drink to better fortune and when he lost the stakes, to drink again in order to spite ill luck.

But let a veil be dropped over the wild doings of the Taverne de Menut. Le Gardeur lay insensible at last upon the floor, where he would have remained had not some of the servants of the inn, who knew him lifted him up compassionately and placed him upon a couch where he lay breathing heavily like one dying. His eyes were fixed, his mouth where the kisses of his sister still lingered was partly open, and his hands were clenched rigid as a statue's.

"He is ours now!" said De Pean to Cadet. "He will not again put his head under the wing of the Philiberts!—" The two men looked at him and laughed brutally. "A fair lady whom you know, Cadet, has given him liberty to drink himself to death, and he will do it!—"

"Who is that? Angelique?" asked Cadet.

"Of course, who else—? and Le Gardeur wont be the first or last man she has put under stone sheets," replied De Pean with a shrug of his shoulder.

"*Gloria Patri, Filioque!*" exclaimed Cadet mockingly. "The

Honnetes Gens will lose their trump card! How did you get him away from Belmont, De Pean?—"

"O, it was not I. Angelique des Meloises set the trap, and whistled the call that brought him," replied De Pean.

"Like her! the incomparable witch!" exclaimed Cadet, with a hearty laugh. "She would lure the very devil, to play *her* tricks instead of his own. She would beat Satan at his best game to ruin a man."

"It would be all the same, Cadet, I fancy, Satan or she! But where is Bigot. I expected him here?—"

"O! he is in a tantrum to night and would not come—!— That piece of his, at Beaumanoir, is a thorn in his flesh and a snow ball on his spirits. She is taming him! By St Cocufin!— Bigot likes that woman!—"

"I told you that before, Cadet! I saw it a month ago, and was sure of it, on that night when he would not bring her up to show her to us."

"Such a fool, De Pean! to care for any woman—! What will Bigot do with her, think you?—"

"How should I know? Send her adrift some fine day, I suppose, down the Riviere du Loup! He will, if he is a sensible man. He dare not marry any woman without licence from La Pompadour, you know. The jolly fishwoman keeps a tight rein over her favorites! Bigot may have as many women as Solomon, the more the merrier, but woe befalls him if he marries without La Pompadour's consent!—They say she dotes herself on Bigot. That is the reason!" De Pean really believed that was the reason, and certainly there were reasons for suspecting it.

"Cadet! Cadet!" exclaimed several voices. "You are fined a basket of Champagne for leaving the table!—"

"I'll pay it," replied he, "and double it! but it is hot as Tartarus in here! I feel like a grilled salmon!" and indeed Cadet's broad sensual face was red and glowing as a harvest moon. He walked a little unsteady too, and his naturally coarse voice sounded thick. But his hard brain never gave way beyond a certain point under any quantity of liquour.

"I am going out to get some fresh air," said he "I shall walk as far as the *Fleur de Lys*. They never go to bed at that jolly old Inn!—"

"I will go with you and I," exclaimed a dozen voices.

"Come on then! We will all go to the old dog hole, where they keep the best brandy in Quebec! It is smuggled of course, but that makes it all the better."

Mine host of the Taverne de Menut, combatted this opinion of the goodness of the liquour at the Fleur de Lys. "His own Brandy had paid the Kings duties, and bore the stamp of the Grand Company," he said "and he appealed to every gentleman present on the goodness of his liquours!"

Cadet and the rest took another round of it, to please the Landlord, and sallied out with no little noise and confusion. Some of them struck up the famous song which beyond all others best expressed the gay rollicking spirit of the French Nation, and of the times of the old Regime—

Vive Henri Quatre!
Vive le Roi vaillant!
Ce diable à quatre,
A le triple talent,
De boire et de battre
et d'etre un vert galant!

When the noisy party arrived at the *Fleur de Lys*, they entered without ceremony into a spacious room, low with heavy beams, and with roughly plastered walls, which were stuck over with proclamations of Governors and the Intendants, and dingy ballads brought by sailors from French ports.

A long table in the middle of the room was surrounded by a lot of fellows plainly of the baser sort: sailors, boatmen voyageurs in rough clothes, and tuques red or blue upon their heads—every one had a pipe in his mouth, some were talking with loose loquacious tongues, some were singing. Their ugly jolly visages half illumined by the light of tallow candles stuck in iron sconces on the wall, were worthy of the vulgar but faithful Dutch pencils of Schalken and Teniers. They were singing a song as the new company came in.

At the head of the table sat Master Pothier with a black earthen jug of Norman cider in one hand, and a pipe in the other. His budget of law hung on a peg in a corner, as stuff quite superfluous at a free and easy at the Fleur de Lys.

Max Grimeau and Blind Barthemy had arrived in good time for the eel pie. They sat one on each side of Master Pothier full as ticks, and merry as grigs. A jolly chorus was in progress as Cadet entered.

The company rose and bowed to the Gentlemen who had honoured them with a call. "Pray sit down, Gentlemen! Take our chairs!" exclaimed Master Pothier officiously offering his to Cadet, who accepted it, as well as the black jug, of which he drank heartily declaring "old Norman cider suited his taste better than the choicest wine."

"We are your most humble servitors, and highly esteem the honour of your visit," said Master Pothier, as he refilled the black jug.

"Jolly fellows!" replied Cadet, stretching his legs refreshingly. "This does look comfortable!—Do you drink cider because you like it, or because you cannot afford better—?"

"There is nothing better than Norman cider, except Cognac brandy—!" replied Master Pothier, grinning from ear to ear. "Norman Cider is fit for a king, and with a lining of Brandy, is drink for a Pope! It will make a man see stars at noonday! wont it Barthemy?—"

"What! old Turn penny! are you here?" cried Cadet recognizing the old beggar of the gate of the Basse Ville.

"O, yes, your honour!" replied Barthemy with his professional whine. "*Pour l'amour de Dieu!*"

"Gad! you are the jolliest beggar I know out of the Friponne!—" replied Cadet throwing him an *ecu*.

"He is not a jollier beggar than I am your honour!—" said Max Grimeau grinning like an Alsatian over a Strasbourg pie. "It was I sang base in the ballad as you came in. You might have heard me, your honour?"

"To be sure I did. I will be sworn there is not a jollier beggar in Quebec than you Old Max—! Here is an *ecu* for you too to drink the Intendants health, and another for *you*, you roving limb of the law, Master Pothier—! Come Master Pothier! I will fill your ragged gown full as a Demi John, of brandy, if you will go on with the song you were singing."

"We were at the old ballad of the *Pont d'Avignon*, your honour," replied Master Pothier.

"And I was playing it," interrupted Jean La Marche. "You might have heard my violin! it is a good one."—Jean would not hide his talent in a napkin on so auspicious an occasion as this. He ran his bow over the strings, and played a few bars. "That was the tune, your honour!"

"Aye, that was it!—I know the jolly old song! Now go on!"— Cadet thrust his thumbs in the pockets of his laced waistcoat and listened attentively. Rough as he was, he liked the old Canadian music.

Jean tuned his fiddle afresh, and placing it with a knowing jerk under his chin, and with an air of conceit worthy of Lulli, began to sing and play the old ballad,

"A St Malo, beau port de mer,
Trois navires sont arrivés,—
Chargés d'avoine, chargés de bled;
Trois dames s'en vont les marchander!—"

"Tut!" exclaimed Varin. "Who cares for things that have no more point in them than a dumpling?—Give us a madrigal, or one of the Devils ditties from the quartier Latin!"

"I do not know a Devils ditty, and would not sing it if I did," replied Jean La Marche jealous of the ballads of his own New France. "Indians cannot swear because they know no oaths, and Habitans cannot sing devils ditties because, we never learn them But 'St Malo, beau port de mer!'—I will sing *that* with any man in the Colony."

The popular songs of the French Canadians are simple, almost infantine in their language, and as chaste in expression as the hymns of other Countries. Impure songs originate in classes who know better and revel from choice in musical slang and indecency.

"Sing, what you like! and never mind Varin, my good

fellow!—" said Cadet, stretching himself in his chair. "I like the old Canadian ballads better than all the Devils ditties, ever made in Paris. You must sing your devils ditties yourself Varin—! Our habitans wont—that is sure!—"

After an hours roystering at the Fleur de Lys, the party of gentlemen returned to the Taverne de Menut, a good deal more unsteady and more obstreperous than when they came. They left Master Pothier seated in his chair drunk as Bacchus and every one of the rest of his companions blind as Barthemy.

The gentlemen on their return to the Taverne de Menut, found De Pean in a rage. Pierre Philibert had followed Amelie to the city, and learning the cause of her anxiety and unconcealed tears, started off with the determination to find Le Gardeur.

The officer of the guard at the gate of the Basse Ville, was able to direct him to the right quarter. He hastened to the Taverne de Menut, and in haughty defiance of De Pean with whom he had high words, he got the unfortunate Le Gardeur away, placed him in a carriage, and took him home, receiving from Amelie such sweet and sincere thanks as he thought a life's service could scarcely have deserved.

"*Par Dieu*! That Philibert is a game cock, De Pean!" exclaimed Cadet, to the savage annoyance of the Secretary. "He has pluck and impudence for ten *gardes du corps*!—It was neater done than at Beaumanoir!"—Cadet sat down to enjoy a broad laugh at the expence of his friend, over the second carrying off of Le Gardeur.

"Curse him! I could have run him through! and am sorry I did not!" exclaimed De Pean.

"No, you could not, have run him through, and you would have been sorry had you tried it, De Pean!" replied Cadet. "That Philibert is not as safe as the bank of France to draw upon, I tell you! It was well for yourself, you did not try De Pean! But never mind," continued Cadet, "there is never so bad a day but there is a fair morrow after it. Make up a hand at cards with me and Colonel Trivio, and put money in your purse. It will salve your bruised feelings." De Pean failed to laugh off his ill humour. But he took Cadet's advice and sat down to play till day light.

"O, Pierre Philibert! how can we sufficiently thank you for your kindness to my dear unhappy brother?" said Amelie to him, her eyes streaming with tears and her hand convulsively clasping his, as Pierre took leave of her at the door of the mansion of the Lady de Tilly.

"Le Gardeur claims our deepest commiseration, Amelie," replied he, "you know, how this has happened—?"

"I do know, Pierre, and shame to know it. But you are so generous ever. Do not blame me for this agitation!—" She strove to compose herself, as a ship will right up for a moment in veering.

"Blame you! what a thought!—as soon blame the angels for being good! But I have a plan, Amelie, for Le Gardeur. We must get him out of the city, and back to Tilly for a while. Your noble aunt has given me an invitation to visit the Manor House. What if I manage to accompany Le Gardeur to his dear old home?"

"A visit to Tilly in your company would of all things delight Le Gardeur," said she, "and perhaps break those ties that bind him to the city."

These were pleasing words to Philibert and he thought how delightful would be her own fair presence also at Tilly.

"All the Physicians in the world will not help Le Gardeur, as will your company at Tilly!" exclaimed she, with a sudden access of hope. "But Le Gardeur needs not medicine, only— care and—"

"The love he has set his heart on, Amelie! Men sometimes die when they fail in that!" He looked at her as he said this. But instantly withdrew his eyes fearing he had been over bold.

She blushed, and only replied with absolute indirection, "O I am so thankful to you Pierre Philibert!—" But she gave him as he left, a look of gratitude and love which never effaced itself from his memory. In after years when Pierre Philibert cared not for the light of the sun nor for woman's love, nor for life itself, the tender impassioned glance of those dark eyes wet with tears, came back to him, like a break in the dark clouds, disclosing the blue heaven beyond—and he longed to be there.

CHAPTER 26

"BETWIXT THE LAST VIOLET AND THE EARLIEST ROSE"

"Do not go out to day, Brother. I want you so particularly to stay with me to day," said Amelie de Repentigny with gentle pleading voice. "Aunt has resolved to return to Tilly tomorrow, and I need your help to arrange these papers—any way I want your company, brother," added she smiling.

Le Gardeur sat feverish, nervous, and ill after his wild night spent at the Taverne de Menut. He started and reddened as his sister's eyes rested on him. He looked through the open window like a wild animal ready to spring out of it and escape.

A raging thirst was on him, which Amelie sought to assuage by draughts of water milk and tea, a sisterly attention which he more than once acknowledged by kissing the loving fingers which waited upon him so tenderly.

"I cannot stay in the house Amelie," said he. "I shall go mad if I do—! You know how it has fared with me, sweet sister—! I yesterday built up a tower of glass, high as heaven— my heaven—a woman's love. To day I am crushed under the ruins of it."

"Say not so, Brother! You were not made to be crushed by the nay of any faithless woman—!—O, why will men think more of our sex than we deserve? How few of us deserve the devotion of a good and true man!"

"How few men would be worthy of *you*, sweet Sister!" replied he proudly. "Ah! had Angelique had your heart, Amelie!—"

"You will be glad one day of your present sorrow, Brother," replied she. "It is bitter I know, and I feel its bitterness with you, but life with Angelique would have been infinitely harder to bear."

He shook his head not incredulously but defiantly at fate. "I would have accepted it," said he "had I been sure life with her had been hard as millstones! My love is of the perverse kind, not to be transmuted by any furnace of fiery trial."

"I have no answer brother, but this!" Amelie stooped and kissed his fevered forehead. She was too wise to reason in a case where she knew reason always made default.

"What has happened at the Manor House?" asked he, after a short silence, "that Aunt is going to return home sooner than she expected when she left."

"There are reports to day of Iroquois on the Upper Chaudiere, and her Censitaires are eager to return to guard their homes from the prowling savages, and what is more, you and Colonel Philibert are ordered to go to Tilly, to look after the defence of the seigneurie."

Le Gardeur sat bolt upright—his military knowledge could not comprehend an apparently useless order. "Pierre Philibert and I ordered to Tilly to look after the defence of the seigneurie! We had no information yesterday that Iroquois were within fifty leagues of Tilly. It is a false rumour raised by the good wives to get their husbands home again! Dont you think so Amelie?" asked he smiling for the first time.

"No, I dont think so, Le Gardeur! but it would be a pretty *ruse de guerre*, were it true!—The good wives naturally feel nervous at being left alone. I should, myself," added she playfully.

"O, I dont know. The nervous ones have all come with the men to the city. But I suppose the works are sufficiently advanced. The men can be spared to return home. But what says Pierre Philibert to the order despatching him to Tilly? You have seen him, since?"

Amelie blushed a little, as she replied, "Yes, I have seen him. He is well content I think, to see Tilly once more, in your company, Brother."

"And in yours, Sister! Why blush Amelie? Pierre is worthy of you!—Should he ever say to you what I so vainly said last night to Angelique des Meloises."—Le Gardeur held her tightly by the hand.

Her face was glowing scarlet. She was in utter confusion. "O stop brother, dont say such things! Pierre never uttered such thoughts to me! Never will in all likelihood!"

"But he will! and my darling sister! when Pierre Philibert shall say he loves you, and asks you to be his wife—If you love him, if you pity me, do not say him, nay—!" She was trembling with agitation and without power to reply. But Le Gardeur felt her hand tighten upon his. He comprehended the involuntary sign, drew her to him, kissed her and left the topic without pressing it further, leaving it in the most formidable shape to take deep root in the silent meditations of Amelie.

The rest of the day passed in such sunshine as Amelie could throw over her brother. Her soft influence retained him at home. She refreshed him with her conversation and sympathy—Drew from him the pitiful story of his love and its bitter ending. She knew the relief of disburthening his surcharged heart, and to none but his sister, from whom he had never had a secret until this episode in his life, would he have spoken a word of his hearts trouble.

Numerous were the visitors today at the hospitable mansion of the Lady de Tilly; but Le Gardeur would see none of them, except Pierre Philibert, who rode over as soon as he was released from his military attendance at the Castle of St Louis.

Le Gardeur received Pierre with an effusion of grateful affection, touching, because real. His handsome face so like Amelie's was peculiarly so when it expressed the emotions habitual to her, and the pleasure both felt in the presence of Pierre, brought out ressemblances that flashed fresh on the quick observant eye of Pierre.

The afternoon was spent in conversation of that kind which gives and takes with mutual delight. Le Gardeur seemed more his old self again, in the company of Pierre. Amelie was charmed, at the visible influence of Pierre over him and a hope, sprang up in her bosom, that the little artifice of beguiling Le Gardeur to Tilly, in the companionship of Pierre, might be the means of thwarting those adverse influences which were dragging him to destruction.

If Pierre Philibert grew more animated in the presence of those bright eyes, which were at once appreciative and sympathizing, Amelie drank in the conversation of Pierre, as one drinks the wine of a favorite vintage. If her heart grew a little intoxicated, what the wonder? Furtively as she glanced at the manly countenance of Pierre, she saw in it the reflection of his noble mind and independant spirit, and, remembering the injunction of Le Gardeur—for woman-like, she sought a support out of herself to justify a foregone conclusion—she thought that if Pierre asked her, she could be content to share his lot, and her greatest happiness would be to live in the possession of his love.

Pierre Philibert had taken his departure from the house of the Lady de Tilly, to make his preparations for leaving the city, next day. His father was aware of his project, and approved of it. The toils of the day were over in the house of the Chien d'or. The Bourgeois took his hat and sword, and went out for a walk upon the Cape, where a cool breeze came up fresh from the broad river. It was just the turn of tide. The full brimming waters, reflecting here and there a star, began to sparkle under the clear moon that rose slowly and majestically, over the hills of the South Shore.

The Bourgeois sat down on the low wall of the terrace to enjoy the freshness and beauty of the scene, which although he had seen it a hundred times before, never looked lovelier he thought, than this evening. He was very happy in his silent thoughts, over his son's return home. The general respect paid him on the day of his fete, had been more felt perhaps, by the Bourgeois, than by Pierre himself.

As he indulged in these meditations, a well known voice suddenly accosted him. He turned and was cordially greeted by the Count de la Galissoniere, and Herr Kalm, who had sauntered through the garden of the castle, and directed their steps towards the Cape, with intention to call upon the Lady de Tilly and pay their respects to her before she left the city.

The Bourgeois learning their intentions, said "he would accompany them, as he too owed a debt of courtesy, to the noble lady and her niece Amelie, which he would discharge at the same time."

The three gentlemen walked gravely on in pleasant conversation. The clearness of the moonlit night threw the beautiful landscape with its strongly accentuated features, into contrasts of light and shade, to which the pencil of Rembrandt alone could have done justice. Herr Kalm was enthusiastic in his admiration. Moonlight over Drachenfels on the Rhine, or the midnight sun peering over the gulf of Bothnia reminded him, of something similar, but of nothing so grand on the whole, as the matchless scene visible from Cape Diamond, worthy of its name.

Lady de Tilly received her visitors with the gracious courtesy habitual to her. She especially appreciated the visit from the Bourgeois, who so rarely honoured the houses of his friends by his welcome presence. As for his Excellency, she remarked, smiling, it was his official duty to represent the politeness of France to the ladies of the Colony. While Herr Kalm representing the Science of Europe, ought to be honoured in every house he chose to visit, she certainly esteemed the honour of his presence in her own.

Amelie made her appearance in the drawing room, and while the visitors stayed, exerted herself to the utmost, to please and interest them, by taking a ready and sympathetic part in their conversation. Her quick and cultivated intellect enabled her to do that to the delight and even surprize of the three grave learned gentlemen. She lacked neither for information nor opinions of her own, while her speech soft and womanly, gave a delicacy to her free yet modest uttrances that made her in their recollections of her in the future a standard of comparison a measure of female perfection.

Le Gardeur learning who were in the house, came down, after a while, to thank the Governor, the Bourgeois and Herr Kalm, for the honour of their visit. He exerted himself by a desperate effort to be conversible, not very succesfully however; for had not Amelie watched him with deepest sympathy and adroitly filled the breaks in his remarks, he would have failed to pass himself creditably before the

Governor. As it was, Le Gardeur contented himself with following the flow of conversation, which welled up copiously from the lips of the rest of the company.

After a while, came in Felix Baudoin in his full livery, reserved for special occasions, and announced to his Lady that tea was served. The gentlemen were invited to partake of what was then a novelty in New France. The Bourgeois in the course of the new traffic with China, that had lately sprung up in consequence of the discovery of Ginseng in New France, had imported some Chests of tea which the Lady de Tilly with instinctive perception of its utility adopted at once, as the beverage of polite society. As yet however it was only to be seen upon the tables of the refined and affluent.

A fine service of porcelaine of Chinese make, adorned her table, pleasing the fancy with its grotesque pictures then so new,—now so familiar to us all. The Chinese Garden and summer house, the fruit laden trees, and river with overhanging willows, the rustic bridge with the three long robed figures passing over it, the boat, floating upon the water and the doves flying in the perspectiveless sky—who does not remember them all?

Lady de Tilly like a true gentlewoman prized her china, and thought kindly of the mild industrious race, who had furnished her tea table with such an elegant equipage.

It was no disparagement to the Lady de Tilly, that she had not read the English poets, who sung the praise of tea. English poets were in those days an unknown quantity in French education, and especially in New France, until after the Conquest. But Wolfe opened the great world of English poetry to Canada as he recited Gray's Elegy with its prophetic line,

"The paths of glory lead but to the grave"

and as he floated down the St Lawrence, in that still autumnal night, to land his forces and scale by stealth the fatal heights of Abraham, whose possession led to the conquest of the city and his own heroic death. Then it was, the two glorious streams of modern thought and literature united in New France where they run side by side, to this day—in time to be united in one grand flood stream of Canadian literature.

The Bourgeois Philibert had exported largly to China, the newly discovered Ginseng for which at first the people of the Flowery Kingdom paid, in their Syce silver, ounce for ounce. And his Cantonese correspondant, esteemed himself doubly fortunate when he was enabled to export his choicest teas to New France in exchange for the precious root.

Amelie listened to an eager conversation between the Governor and Herr Kalm, started by the latter, on the nature, culture and use of the tea plant. They would be trite opinions now, with many daring speculations on the ultimate conquest of the tea cup over the wine cup. "It would inaugurate the third beatitude!" exclaimed the Philosopher, pressing together the tips of the fingers of both hands, "and the 'meek would inherit the earth,' so soon as the use of tea, became universal!—Mankind would grow milder as their blood was purified from the fiery products of the still and the wine press—! The life of man would be prolonged and made more valuable."

"What has given China four thousand years of existence?—" asked Herr Kalm, abruptly of the Count.

The Count, "could not tell, unless it were that the nation was dead already in all that regarded the higher life, of national existence—Had become mummified in fact, and did not know it."

"Not at all!" replied Herr Kalm. "It is the constant use of the life giving infusion of tea, that has saved China! Tea sooths the nerves. It clears the blood, expells vapours from the brain, and restores the fountain of life to pristine activity. *Ergo*: It prolongs the existence of both men and nations, and has made China the most antique nation in the world."

Herr Kalm was a devotee to the tea cup. He drank it strong to excite his flagging spirits, weak to quiet them down. He took Bohea with his facts, and Hyson with his fancy, and mixed them to secure the necessary afflatus to write his books, of science and travel. Upon Hyson he would have attempted the Iliad, upon Bohea he would undertake to square the circle, discover perpetual motion, or reform German philosophy.

The professor was in a jovial mood, and gambolled away gracefully as a Finland horse under a pack saddle laden with the learning of a dozen students of Abo, travelling home for the holidays—!

"We are fortunate in being able to procure our tea, in exchange for our useless Ginseng," remarked the Lady de Tilly, as she handed the professor a tiny plate of the leaves, as was the fashion of the day. After drinking the tea, the infused leaves were regarded, as quite a fashionable delicacy. Except for the fashion, it had not been perhaps considered a delicacy, at all.—

The observation of the Lady de Tilly set the professor off on another branch of the subject. "He had observed," he said, "the careless methods of preparing the Ginseng in New France, and predicted a speedy end of the traffic, unless it were prepared to suit the fancy of the fastidious Chinese."

"That is true, Herr Kalm," replied the Governor, "but our Indians who gather it are bad managers. Our friend Philibert, who opened this lucrative trade is alone capable of ensuring its continuance. It is a mine of wealth to New France if rightly develloped. How much made you last year, by Ginseng, Philibert?"

"I can scarcely answer," replied the Bourgeois hesitating a moment to mention what might seem like egoism. "But the half million I contributed towards the war in defence of Acadia was wholly the product of my export of Ginseng to China."

"I know it was! and God bless you for it! Philibert!" exclaimed the Governor with emotion, as he grasped the hand of the patriotic merchant. "If we have preserved New France this year, it was through your timely help in Acadia—! The King's treasury was exhausted" continued the Governor, looking at Herr Kalm, "and ruin imminent, when the noble merchant of the Chien d'Or, fed, clothed and paid the Kings troops for two months before the taking of Grand Pré from the enemy."

"No great thing in that your Excellency," replied the Bourgeois, who hated compliments to himself. "If those who have, do not give how can you get from those who have not? You may lay some of it to the account of Pierre too. He was in Acadia, you know Governor." A flash of honest pride passed over the usually sedate features of the Bourgeois at the mention of his son.

Le Gardeur looked at his sister. She knew instinctively, that his thoughts put into words would, say, He is worthy to be your father, Amelie!—She blushed with a secret pleasure, but spoke not. The music in her heart was without words, yet. But one day it would fill the universe with harmony—for her.

The Governor noticed, the sudden reticence, and half surmising the cause, remarked playfully, "The Iroquois will hardly dare approach Tilly with such a garrison as Pierre Philibert and Le Gardeur and with you my Lady de Tilly, as Commandant, and you Mademoiselle Amelie as Aide de camp!—"

"To be sure! your Excellency!" replied the Lady de Tilly. "The women of Tilly have worn swords and kept the old house before now!" she added playfully alluding to a celebrated defence of the house by a former lady of the manor at the head of a body of her censitaires. "And depend upon it we shall neither give up Tilly, nor Le Gardeur either! to whatever savages claim him, be they red or white!—"—

The Lady's allusion to his late associates did not offend Le Gardeur, whose honest nature despised their conduct while he liked their company. They all understood her and laughed. The Governor's loyalty to the Kings commission prevented his speaking his thoughts. He only remarked, "Le Gardeur and Pierre Philibert will be under your orders my Lady, and my orders are that they are not to return to the city, until all dangers of the Iroquois are over!—"

"All right! Your Excellency!" exclaimed Le Gardeur. "I shall obey my aunt." He was acute enough to see through their kindly scheming for his welfare. But his good nature and thorough devotion to his Aunt and sister and his affectionate friendship for Pierre, made him yield to the project without a qualm of regret. Le Gardeur was assailable on many sides, a fault in his character, or a weakness, which at any rate sometimes offered a lever to move him in directions opposite to the malign influences of Bigot and his associates.

The Company rose from the tea table, and moved to the drawing room, where conversation, music, and a few games of cards, wiled away a couple of hours, very pleasantly.

Amelie sang exquisitly. The Governor was an excellent musician. He accompanied her. His voice, a powerful tenor had been strengthened by many a conflict with old Boreas on the high seas, and made soft and flexible by his manifold sympathies with all that is kindly and good and true in human nature.

A song of wonderful pathos and beauty had just been brought down from the wilds of the Ottawa, and become universally sung in New France. A voyageur flying from a band of Iroquois had found a hiding place on a rocky islet in the middle of the *Sept Chutes*. He concealed himself from his foes, but could not escape and in the end died of starvation and sleeplessness. The dying man peeled off the white bark of the Birch, and with the juice of berries wrote upon it his death song, which was found long after by the side of his remains. His grave is now a marked spot on the Ottawa. *La complainte de Cadieux* had seized the imagination of Amelie. She sang it exquisitely, and to night needed no pressing to do so, for her heart was full of the new song, composed under such circumstances of woe. Intense was the sympathy of the company, as she began,

> Petit Rocher de la Haute Montagne,
> Je viens finir ici cette campagne!
> Ah! doux echos entendez mes soupirs!
> En languissant je vais bientot mourir!

There were no dry eyes as she concluded. The last sighs of Cadieux seemed to expire on her lips:

> "Rossignolet va dire à ma maitresse,
> A mes enfans, qu'un adieu je leur laisse,
> Que j'ai gardé mon amour et ma foi
> Et desormais faut renoncer à moi."

A few more friends of the family dropped in—Coulon de Villiers, Claude Beauharnois La Corne St Luc and others, who had heard of the Lady's departure and came to bid her adieu.

La Corne raised much mirth by his allusions to the Iroquois. The secret was plainly no secret to him. "I hope to get their scalps," said he, "when you have done with them and they with you Le Gardeur!"

The evening passed on pleasantly and the clock of the Recollets pealed out a good late hour before they took final leave of their hospitable hostess, with mutual goodbys and adieus which with some of them were never repeated.

Le Gardeur was no little touched and comforted by so much sympathy and kindness. He shook the Bourgeois affectionately by the hand, inviting him to come up to Tilly. It was noticed and remembered that this evening Le Gardeur clung filialy as it were, to the father of Pierre, and the farewell he gave him, was tender, almost solemn, in a sort of sadness, that left an impress upon all their minds. "Tell Pierre! but indeed he knows we start early—!—" said Le Gardeur, "and the canoes will be waiting on the Batture, an hour after sun rise."

The Bourgeois knew in a general way the position of Le Gardeur, and sympathized deeply with him. "Keep your heart up my boy!" said he on leaving. "Remember the proverb, never forget it for a moment, Le Gardeur! 'Ce que Dieu garde est bien gardé'!—"—

"Good bye, Sieur Philibert!" replied he, still holding him by the hand. "I would fain be permitted to regard you as a father, since Pierre is all of a brother to me!—"

"I will be a father and a loving one too, if you will permit me, Le Gardeur," said the Bourgeois, touched by the appeal. "When you return to the city, come home with Pierre. At the Golden Dog as well as at Belmont, there will be, open welcome, for Pierre's friend as for Pierre's self." The guests took their departure.

The preparations for the journey home, were all made, and the household retired to rest, all glad to return to Tilly. Even Felix Baudoin felt like a boy going back on a holiday.

His mind was surcharged with the endless things he had gathered up ready to pour into the sympathizing ear of Barbara Sanschagrin, and the servants and censitaires were equally eager to return, to relate their adventures in the capital when summoned on the Kings corvée to build the walls of Quebec.

CHAPTER 27

THE CANADIAN BOAT SONG

V'là l'bon vent!
V'là l'joli vent!
V'là l'bon vent!
Ma mie m'appelle!—
V'là l'bon vent,
V'là l'joli vent,
V'là l'bon vent!
Ma mie m'attend!

THE gay chorus of the voyageurs made the shores ring keeping time together with their voices while the silver spray dripped like a shower of diamonds in the bright sunshine at every stroke of their rapid paddles. The graceful bark canoes things of beauty and almost of life leaped joyously over the blue waters of the St Lawrence as they bore the family of the Lady de Tilly and Pierre Philibert with a train of censitaires back to the old Manor House.

The broad river was flooded with sunshine as it rolled majestically between the high banks crowned with green fields and woods in full leaf of summer frequent cottages and villages were visible along the shores and now and then a little church with its bright spire or belfry marked the successive parishes on either hand as the voyagers passed on, through the glorious panorama of a scene unsurpassed for beauty in the New World.

The tide had already forced its way two hundred leagues up from the ocean and still pressed irresistibly onwards surging and wrestling against the weight of the descending stream.

The wind too was favourable. A number of yachts and

306

Bateaux spread their snowy sails to ascend the river with the tide. They were for the most part laden with munitions of war for the Richelieu on their way to the military posts on lake Champlain or merchandize for Montreal to be reladen in fleets of canoes for the trading posts up the river of the Ottawas, the Great Lakes or may hap to supply the new and far off settlements on the Beautiful River and the Illinois.

The line of canoes swept past the sailing vessels with a cheer. The light hearted crews exchanged salutations and bandied jests with each other, laughing immoderately at the well worn jokes current upon the river among the rough voyageurs. A good voyage! a clear run! short portages and long rests! some enquired whether their friends had paid for the Bear and Buffalo skins they were going to buy, or they complimented each other on their nice heads of hair which it was hoped they would not leave behind as keep sakes with the Iroquois squaws.

The boat songs of the Canadian voyageurs are unique in character and very pleasing, when sung by a crew of broad chested fellows dashing their light birch bark canoes over the waters rough or smooth taking them as they take fortune cheerfully, sometimes skimming like wild geese over the long placid reaches, sometimes bounding like stags down the rough rapids and foaming saults. As might be inferred, the songs of the voyageurs differ widely from the sweet little lyrics sung in soft falsettos to the tinkling of a piano forte in fashionable drawing rooms, and called "Canadian boat songs."

The Canadian boat song is always some old ballad of Norman or Breton origin, pure in thought and chaste in expression, washed clean of all French looseness in its adaption to the pious primitive manners of the Colony that was founded as expressed in the Commission given to its discoverer Jacques Cartier, "for the increase of God's Glory and the honour of his revered name."

The boat song is usually composed of short stanzas, the closing line of each couplet or quatraine repeating itself in the beginning of the next following verse and ending with a stirring chorus, that gathers up as into a Leyden jar the life and electricity of the song, discharging it in a flash and peal of rythmic thunder, every voice joining in the refrain while the elastic paddles dip with renewed energy into the water making the canoe spring like a flying fish over the surface of lake or river.

Master Jean La Marche clean as a new pin and in his merriest mood, sat erect as the King of Yvetot in the bow of the long canoe, which held the Lady de Tilly and her family. His sonorous violin was coquettishly fixed in its place of honour, under his wagging chin, as it accompanied his voice, while he chanted an old boat song which has lightened the labour of many a weary oar on lake and river from the St Lawrence to the Rocky mountains.

Amelie sat in the stern of the canoe laving her white hand in the cool stream, which rushed past her. She looked proud and happy to day for the whole world of her affections were gathered together in that little bark.

She felt grateful for the bright sun. It seemed to have dispelled every cloud that lately shaded her thoughts on account of her brother, and she silently blessed the light breeze that played with her hair and cooled her cheek which she felt was tinged with a warm glow of pleasure in the presence of Pierre Philibert.

She spoke little and almost thanked the rough voyageurs for those incessant melodies which made conversation difficult for the time, and thus left her to her own sweet silent thoughts, which seemed almost too sacred for the profanation of words.

An occasional look or a sympathetic smile exchanged with her brother and her aunt spoke volumes of pure affection. Once or twice the eyes of Pierre Philibert captured a glance of hers which might not have been intended for him, but which Amelie suffered him to intercept, and hide away among the secret treasures of his heart. A glance of true affection brief it may be as a flash of lightning, becomes when caught by the eyes of love a real thing, fixed and imperishable for ever! A tender smile, a fond word of love's creation, contains

a universe of light and life, and immortality—small things and
of little value to others, but to him or her whom they concern
more precious and more prized than the treasures of Ind.

Master Jean La Marche, after a few minutes rest made
still more refreshing by a draught from a suspicious looking
flask, which out of respect for the presence of his mistress, the
Lady de Tilly, he said contained "milk!" began a popular boat
song which every voyageur in New France knew as well as his
prayers and loved to his very finger ends.

The canoemen pricked up their ears like troopers at the
sound of a bugle, as Jean La Marche began the famous old
ballad, of the King's son, who with his silver gun aimed at
the beautiful black duck and shot the white one, out of whose
eyes came gold and diamonds, and out of whose mouth rained
silver, while its pretty feathers scattered to the four winds were
picked up by three fair dames who with them made a bed
both large and deep—

"For poor wayfaring men to sleep."

Master Jean's voice was clear and resonant as a church
bell newly christened! and he sang the old boat song with an
energy that drew the crews of half a dozen other canoes into
the wake of his canoe and all uniting in the stirring chorus:—

"Fringue, Fringue, sur la riviere—!
Fringue, Fringue, sur l'aviron!—"

A few stanzas of this popular boat song as it was sung by
Jean La Marche and is still chanted to the oar by the Voyageurs
of the North and North West, are given in the original. The
charming simplicity of it would be lost in a translation into
another tongue, just as Josephte, the pride of a Canadian
Village, loses her natural naïveté and grace when she adopts
the fashion and language of the Bourgeoisie of Quebec and
Montreal.

Derriere chez nous
Ya—A—un étang—
    Fringue! Fringue sur l'aviron!—
Trois beaux Canards

S'en vont baignant,
     Fringue! Fringue sur la riviere!
     Fringue! Fringue sur l'aviron!

Trois beaux Canards
S'en vont baignant!
     Fringue! Fringue sur l'aviron!
Le fils du roi,
S'en va chassant.
     Fringue! Fringue sur la riviere,
     Fringue! Fringue sur l'aviron!—

Le fils du roi
S'en va chassant.
     Fringue Fringue sur l'aviron—
Avec son grand
Fusil d'argent.
     Fringue! Fringue sur la riviere!
     Fringue! Fringue sur l'aviron!—

Avec son grand
Fusil d'argent
     Fringue Fringue sur l'aviron!—
Visa le noir
Tua le blanc.
     Fringue! Fringue sur la riviere
     Fringue! Fringue sur l'aviron!—

Visa le noir
Tua le blanc.
     Fringue Fringue sur l'aviron!
O Fils du Roi
Tu es mechant.
     Fringue! Fringue sur la riviere!—
     Fringue! Fringue sur l'aviron!—

And so on, they sang for the space of half an hour, to the
end of the pleasant old ditty. Jean La Marche sang the first and

second lines solo, the crew joining in the third. He then sang the fourth and fifth, when the chorus at the conclusion was repeated by the whole company *Forte Fortissimo*, the paddles moving with renewed vigour and keeping time to the song.

The performance of Jean La Marche was highly relished by the critical boatmen and drew from them that flattering mark of approval so welcome to a vocalist, an encore, of the whole long ballad from beginning to end—!

As the line of canoes swept up the stream, a welcome cheer occasionally greeted them from the shore, or a voice on land joined in the gay refrain. They drew nearer to Tilly and their voices became more and more musical, their gaiety more irrepressible, for they were going home, and home to the Habitans as well as to their Lady, was the world of all delights.

The contagion of high spirits caught even Le Gardeur, and drew him out of himself, making him for the time forget the disappointments, resentments and allurements of the city.

Sitting there in the golden sunshine, the blue sky above him, the blue waters below, Friends whom he loved around him, mirth in every eye, gaiety on every tongue, how could Le Gardeur but smile as the music of the boatmen brought back a hundred sweet associations. Nay, he laughed and to the inexpressible delight of Amelie and Pierre who watched every change in his demeanour, united in the chorus of the glorious boat song.

A few hours of this pleasant voyaging brought the little fleet of canoes under the high bank which from its summit slopes away in a wide domain of forests, park and cultivated fields, in the midst of which stood the high pointed and many gabled Manor House of Tilly.

Upon a promontory, as if placed there for both a land and sea mark, to save souls as well as bodies, rose the belfry of the Chapel of St Michael, overlooking a cluster of white old fashioned cottages which formed the village of St Michael de Tilly.

Upon the sandy beach a crowd of women, children and old men had gathered who were cheering and clapping their hands at the unexpected return of the Lady of the Manor with all their friends and relatives.

The fears of the Villagers had been greatly excited for some days past, by exaggerated reports of the presence of Iroquois on the upper waters of the Chaudiere. They not unnaturally conjectured moreover that the general call for men on the King's Corvée to fortify the city, portended an invasion by the English, who it was rumoured, were to come up in ships from below, as in the days of Sir William Phips, with his army of New Englanders, the story of whose defeat under the walls of Quebec was still freshly remembered in the traditions of the colony.

"Never fear them!" said old Louis the one eyed Pilot. "It was in my father's day. Many a time have I heard him tell the story, how in the autumn of the good year 1690, thirty four great ships of the Bostonais came up from below, and landed an army of *ventres bleus*, of New England on the flats of Beauport! But our stout Governor Count de Frontenac came upon them in the woods with his brave soldiers, habitans and Indians and drove them pell mell back to their boats, and stripped the ship of Admiral Phips of his red flag, which, if you doubt my word—which no one does—still hangs over the high altar of the church of Notre Dame des Victoires! Blessed be our Lady! who saved our country from our ennemies, and will do so again if we do not by our wickedness lose her favour—! But the *Arbre sec*, the dry tree, still stands upon the Point de Levy, where the Boston fleet took refuge before beating their retreat down the river again, and you know the old prophecy that while that tree stands, the English shall never prevail against Quebec!—"

Much comforted by this speech of old Louis the Pilot, the Villagers of Tilly rushed to the beach to receive their friends.

The canoes came dashing into shore. Men, women and children ran knee deep into the water to meet them, and a hundred eager hands were ready to seize their prows and drag them high and dry upon the sandy beach.

"Home again! and welcome to Tilly, Pierre Philibert!" exclaimed Lady de Tilly offering her hand, "Friends like you have the right of welcome, here!"—Pierre expressed his pleasure in fitting terms and lent his aid to the noble Lady to disembark.

Le Gardeur assisted Amelie out of the canoe. As he led her across the beach he felt her hand tremble as it rested on his arm. He glanced down at her averted face and saw her eyes directed to a spot well remembered by himself, the scene of his rescue from drowning by Pierre Philibert.

The scene came before Amelie at this moment! Her vivid recollection conjured up the sight of the inanimate body of her brother, as it was brought ashore by the strong arm of Pierre Philibert and laid upon the beach. Her long agony of suspense, and her joy, the greatest she had ever felt before or since, at his resuscitation to life, and lastly her passionate vow which she made when clasping the neck of his preserver, a vow which she had enshrined as a holy thing in her heart ever since.

At that moment a strange fancy seized her that Pierre Philibert was again plunging into deep water to rescue her brother, and that she would be called on by some mysterious power to renew her vow or fulfil it to the very letter.

She twitched Le Gardeur gently by the arm and said to him in a half whisper, "It was there brother! do you remember?—"

"I know it Sister!" replied he, "I was also thinking of it. I am grateful to Pierre. Yet O, my Amelie better he had left me at the bottom of the deep river where I had found my bed. I have no pleasure in seeing Tilly any more!"

"Why not brother? Are we not all the same? Are we not all here? There is happiness and comfort for you at Tilly."

"There was once Amelie!" replied he sadly, "but there will be none for me in the future as I feel too well. I am not worthy of you Amelie."

"Come brother!" replied she cheerily. "You dampen the joy of our arrival! See! the flag is going up on the staff of the turret, and old Martin is getting ready to fire off the Culverin in honour of your arrival."

Presently there was a flash, a cloud of smoke and the report of a cannon came booming down to the shore from the Manor House.

"That was well done of Martin and the women!" remarked Felix Baudoin, who had served in his youth, and therefore knew what was fitting in a military salute. "The women of Tilly are better than the men of Beauce, says the proverb."

"Aye! or of Tilly either!" remarked Josephte Le Tardeur in a sharp snapping tone. Josephte was a short stout virago, with a turned up nose and a pair of black eyes that would bore you through like an auger. She wore a wide brimmed hat of straw overtopping curls as crisp as her temper. Her short linsey petticoat was not chary of showing her substantial ankles, while her rolled up sleeves displayed a pair of arms so red and robust that a swiss milkmaid might well have envied them.

Her remark was intended for the ear of José Le Tardeur, her husband, a lazy goodnatured fellow whose eyes had been fairly hen-pecked out of his head all the days of his married life. "Josephte's speech hit him without hurting him," as he remarked to a neighbour. "Josephte made a target of him every day. He was glad for his part that the women of Tilly were better soldiers than the men and so much fonder of looking after things! It saved the men a deal of worry and a good deal of work."

"What are you saying José?" exclaimed Felix, who only caught a few half words.

"I say Master Felix! that but for *Mere* Eve there would have been no curse upon men, to make them labour when they do not want to and no sin either, as the Curé says. We could have laid on the grass sunning ourselves all day long. Now, it is nothing but work and pray! never play, else you will save neither body nor soul. Master Felix! I hope you will remember me if I come up to the Manor House—!"

"Aye I will remember you José!" replied Felix tartly "but if labour was the curse which Eve brought into the world when she ate the apple, I am sure you are free from it! so ride up with the carts José, and get out of the way of my Lady's carriage!—"

José obeyed and taking off his cap bowed respectfully to

the Lady de Tilly as she passed leaning on the arm of Pierre Philibert, who escorted her to her carriage.

A couple of sleek Canadian horses, sure footed as goats and strong as little Elephants drew the coach with a long steady trot up the winding road which led to the Manor House.

The road unfenced and bordered with grass on each side, of the track, was smooth and well kept as became the Grande Chaussée of the Barony of Tilly. It ran sometimes through stretches of cultivated fields, green pastures or corn land ripening for the sickle of the censitaire. Sometimes it passed through cool shady woods, full of primeval grandeur, part of the great Forest of Tilly which stretched away far as the eye could reach, over the hills of the South Shore. Huge oaks that might have stood there from the beginning of the world, wide branching Elms and dark Pines overshadowed the highway, opening now and then into vistas of green fields, where stood a cottage or two, with a herd of mottled cows grazing down by the brook. On the higher ridges the trees formed a close phalanx and with their dark tops cut the horizon into a long irregular line of forest, as if offering battle to the woodman's axe that was threatening to invade their solitudes.

Half an hour's driving brought the company to the Manor House, a stately mansion gabled and pointed like an ancient Chateau on the Seine.

It was a large irregular structure of hammered stone, with deeply recessed windows mullioned and ornamented with grotesque carvings. A turret, loopholed and battlemented projected from each of the four corners of the house enabling its inmates to enfilade every side with a raking fire of musketry affording an adequate defence against Indian foes. A stone tablet over the main entrance of the Manor House was carved with the Armorial bearings of the ancient family of Tilly with the date of its erection, and a pious invocation placing the House under the special protection of St Michael de Thury, the patron saint of the House of Tilly.

The Manor House of Tilly had been built by Charles Le Gardeur de Tilly, a gentleman of Normandy, one of whose ancestors the Sire de Tilly, figures on the roll of Battle Abbey as a follower of Duke William at Hastings. His descendant Charles Le Gardeur came over to Canada, with a large body of his vassals in 1636, having obtained from the King a grant of the lands of Tilly, on the bank of the St Lawrence, "to hold in Fief and Seigneury," so ran the royal patent, "with the right and jurisdiction of Superior, Moyenne and basse justice, and of hunting, fishing and trading with the Indians throughout the whole of this royal concession, subject to the condition of *foi et hommage*, which he shall be held to perform at the Castle of St Louis in Quebec of which he shall hold under the customary duties and dues agreeably to the *coutume de Paris* followed in this country."

Such was the style of the Royal grants of Seignioral rights conceded in New France, by virtue of one of which this gallant Norman gentleman founded his settlement and built this Manor House on the shores of the St Lawrence.

A broad smooth carriage road led up to the mansion across a park dotted with clumps of evergreens and deciduous trees. Here and there an ancient patriarch of the forest stood alone, some old oak or elm, whose goodly proportions and amplitude of shade had found favour in the eyes of the Seigneurs of Tilly, and saved it from the axe of the Woodman.

A pretty brook not too wide to be crossed over by a rustic bridge, meandered through the domain peeping occasionally out of the openings in the woods as it stole away like a bashful girl from the eyes of her admirer.

This brook was the outflow of a romantic little lake that lay hidden away among the wooded hills that bounded the horizon, an irregular sheet of water a league in circumference dotted with islands and abounding with fish and waterfowl, that haunted its quiet pools. That primitive bit of nature had never been disturbed by axe or fire, and was a favorite spot for recreation to the inmates of the Manor House to whom it was accessible either by boat up the little stream, or by a pleasant drive through the old woods.

As the carriages drew up in front of the Manor House every door, window and gable of which looked like an old friend in the eyes of Pierre Philibert, a bevy of female servants, the men had all been away at the city, stood ranged in their best gowns and gayest ribbons to welcome home their mistress and Mademoiselle Amelie, who was the idol of them all.

Great was their delight to see Monsieur Le Gardeur as they usually styled their young master, with another gentleman in military costume, whom it did not take two minutes for some of the sharpeyed lasses to recognize as Pierre Philibert, who had once saved the life of Le Gardeur on a memorable occasion, and who now they said, one to another, was come to the Manor House to—to—they whispered what it was, to each other, and smiled in a knowing manner.

Women's wits fly swiftly to conclusions and right ones too on most occasions. The lively maids of Tilly told one another in whispers that they were sure Pierre Philibert was come back to the Manor House, as a suitor for the hand of Mademoiselle Amelie, as was most natural he should do, so handsome and manly looking as he was—! and Mademoiselle always liked to hear any of them mention his name. The maids ran out the whole chain of logical sequences before either Pierre or Amelie had ventured to draw a conclusion of any kind from the premises of this visit.

Behind the mansion overlooking poultry yards and stables which were well hidden from view rose a high Colombiere or pigeon house of stone, the possession of which was one of the rights which feudal law reserved to the Lord of the Manor. This Colombiere was capable of containing a large army of pigeons but the regard which the Lady de Tilly had for the cornfields of her censitaires, caused her to thin out its population to such a degree that there remained only a few favorite birds of rare breed and plumage, to strut and coo upon the roofs and rival the peacocks on the terrace with their bright colours.

In front of the mansion contrasting oddly with the living trees around it, stood a high pole, the long straight stem of a pine tree carefully stripped of its bark, bearing on its top the withered remains of a bunch of evergreens, with the fragments of a flag and ends of ribbon which fluttered gaily from it. The pole was marked with black spots from the discharge of guns fired at it by the joyous Habitans, who had kept the ancient custom of May day by planting this May pole in front of the Manor House of their Lady.

The planting of such a pole, was in New France a special mark of respect due to the feudal superior, and custom as well as politeness required that it should not be taken down until the recurrence of another anniversary of Flora, which in New France sometimes found the earth white with snow and hardened with frost, instead of covered with flowers as in the old World whence the custom was derived.

The Lady de Tilly duly appreciated this compliment of her faithful censitaires, and would sooner have stripped her park of half its live trees than have removed that dead pole with its withered crown from the place of honour in front of her mansion.

The revels of May in New France—the King and Queen of St Philip, the rejoicings of a frank loyal peasantry, illiterate in books but not unlearned in the art of life, have nearly disappeared before the levelling spirit of the nineteenth century.

The celebration of the day of St Philip has been superseded by the festival of St John the Baptist at a season of the year when green leaves and blooming flowers give the possibility of arcades and garlands in honour of the Canadian summer.

Felix Beaudoin with a wave of his hand scattered the bevy of maid servants, who stood chattering as they gazed upon the new arrivals. The experience of Felix told him that everything had of course gone wrong during his absence from the Manor House, and that nothing could be fit for his mistress' reception until he had set all to rights again himself!—

The worthy Major Domo was in a state of perspiration lest he should not get into the house before his mistress, and don his livery to meet her at the door with his white wand, and every thing *en regle* just as if nothing had interrupted their usual course of housekeeping.

The Lady de Tilly knew the weakness of her faithful old

servitor, and although she smiled to herself she would not hurt his feelings by entering the house before he was ready at his post, to receive her. She continued walking about the lawn conversing with Amelie, Pierre and Le Gardeur until she saw old Felix with his wand and livery standing at the door, when taking Pierre's arm she led the way into the house.

The folding doors were open, Felix with his wand walked before his Lady and her companions into the mansion. They entered without delay for the day had been warm and the ladies were weary, after sitting several hours in a canoe, a mode of travelling which admits of very little change of position in the voyagers.

The interior of the Manor House of Tilly presented the appearance of an old French Chateau. A large Hall with antique furniture occupied the center of the house, used occasionally as a court of justice, when the Seigneur de Tilly exercised his judicial office for the trial of offences, which was very rarely, thanks to the good morals of the people, or held a *Cour Pleniere* of his vassals on affairs of the Seigneurie for apportioning the corvées for road making and bridge building, and not the least important by any means, for the annual feast to his censitaires all on the day of St Michael de Thury.

From this Hall passages led into appartments and suites of rooms arranged for use, comfort and hospitality. The rooms were of all sizes panelled, tapestried and furnished in a style of splendour suited to the wealth and dignity of the Seigniors of Tilly. A stair of oak broad enough for a section of Grenadiers to march up it abreast, led to the upper chambers, bedrooms and boudoirs which looked out of old mullioned windows upon the lawn and gardens that surrounded the house affording picturesque glimpses of water, hills and forests far enough off for contemplation and yet near enough to be accessible by a short ride from the mansion.

Pierre Philibert was startled at the strange familiarity of every thing he saw. The passages and all their intricacies where he Le Gardeur and Amelie had hid and found one another with cries of delight, He knew where they all led to. The rooms with their antique and stately furniture, the paintings on the walls before which he had stood and gazed wondering if the world was as fair as those landscapes of sunny France and Italy, and why the men and women of the House of Tilly whose portraits hung upon the walls looked at him so kindly with those dark eyes of theirs, which seemed to follow him everywhere, and he imagined they even smiled when their lips were illumined by a ray of sunshine. Pierre looked at them again with a strange interest. They were like the faces of living friends who welcomed him back to Tilly after years of absence.

Pierre entered a well remembered appartment which he knew to be the favourite sitting room of the Lady de Tilly. He walked hastily across it to look at a picture upon the wall which he recognized again with a flush of pleasure.

It was the portrait of Amelie painted by himself during his last visit to Tilly. The young artist full of enthusiasm had put his whole soul into the work until he was himself startled at the vivid likeness which almost unconsciously flowed from his pencil. He caught the divine upward expression of her eyes, as she turned her head to listen to him and he left upon the canvass the very smile he had caught from her lips. Those dark eyes of hers had haunted his memory for ever after. To his imagination that picture had become almost a living thing. It was as a voice of his own that returned to his ear as the voice of Amelie. In the painting of that portrait Pierre had the first revelation of a consciousness of his deep love which became in the end the master passion of his life.

He stood for some minutes contemplating this portrait— so different from her in age now, yet so like in look and expression. He turned suddenly and saw Amelie. She had silently stepped up behind him and her features in a glow of pleasure took on the very look of the picture.

Pierre started—he looked again and saw every feature of the girl of twelve looking through the transparent countenance of the perfect woman of twenty. It was a moment of blissful revelation for he felt an assurance at that moment that Amelie was the same to him now as in their days of youthful companionship.

"How like it is to you yet Amelie!" said he. "It is more true than I knew how to make it!—"

"That sounds like a paradox, Pierre Philibert!" replied she with a smile. "But it means I suppose that you painted a universal portrait of me which will be like through all my seven ages. Such a picture, might be true of the soul Pierre! had you painted that, but I have outgrown the picture of my person."

"I could imagine nothing fairer than that portrait! In soul and body it is all true Amelie."

"Flatterer that you are!" said she laughing, "I could almost wish that portrait would walk out of its frame to thank you for the care you bestowed upon its foolish little original."

"My care was more than rewarded! I found in that picture the beau ideal of the beauty of life, which belonging to the soul is true to all ages."

"The girl of twelve would have thanked you more enthusiastically for that remark, Pierre than I dare do," replied she.

"The thanks are due from me not from you, Amelie! I became your debtor for a life long obligation when I learned that without genius I could do impossibilities! You taught me that paradox when you let me paint that picture."

Amelie glanced quickly up at him. A slight colour came and went on her cheek. "Would that I could do impossibilities," said she, "to thank you sufficiently for your kindness to Le Gardeur and all of us in coming to Tilly at this time."

"It would be a novelty almost a relief to put Pierre Philibert under some obligation to us, for all we owe him; would it not Le Gardeur?" continued she clasping the arm of her brother who just now came into the room. "We will discharge a portion of our debt to Pierre for this welcome visit by a day on the lake! We will make up a water party. What say you brother? The gentlemen will light fires, the ladies will make tea, and we will have guitars and songs, and maybe a dance Brother! and then a glorious return home by moonlight! What say you to my programme Le Gardeur de Repentigny? What say you Pierre Philibert?—"

Pierre admired the sisterly tact of Amelie. The projected water party was only designed for the purpose of dissipating the cloud of cares that hung over the mind of her brother. Yet if a tinge of pleasure at the presence of Pierre mingled with her joy, it was natural and pardonable.

"It is a good programme, sister! but leave me out of it. I shall only mar the pleasure of the rest. I will not go to the Lake. I have been trying ever since my return home to recognize Tilly. Everything looks to me in an eclipse and nothing bright as it once was. Not even you Amelie! Your smile has a curious touch of sadness in it, which does not escape my eyes, accursed as they have been of late seeing things they ought not to see, yet I can see that and I know it too. I have given you cause to be sad sister!—"

"Hush brother! it is a sin against your dear eyes to speak of them thus! Tilly is as bright and joyous as ever. As for my smiles if you detect in them one trace of that sadness you talk about, I will grow as melancholy as yourself, and for as little cause. Come! You shall confess before three days, brother, if you will only help me to be gay, that your sister has the lightest heart in New France."

CHAPTER 28

"CHEERFUL YESTERDAYS AND CONFIDENT TO-MORROWS"

THE ladies retired to their several rooms and after a general rearranging of toilets descended to the great parlour where they were joined by Messire La Lande the Curé of the Parish, a benevolent rosy old priest, and several Ladies from the neighbourhood with two or three old gentlemen of a military air and manner, retired officers of the Army who enjoyed their pensions and kept up their respectability at a cheaper rate in the country than they could do in the city.

Felix Beaudoin had for the last two hours kept the cooks in hot water. He was now superintending the laying of the table, resolved that notwithstanding his long absence from home, the dinner should be a marvellous success.

Amelie was very beautiful today—her face was aglow with pure air and exercise and she felt happy in the apparent contentment of her brother, whom she met with Pierre on the broad terrace of the Manor House.

She was dressed with exquisite neatness yet plainly. An antique cross of gold formed her only adornment except her own charms. That cross she had put on in honour of Pierre Philibert. He recognized it with delight as a birthday gift to Amelie which he had himself given her during their days of juvenile companionship, on one of his holiday visits to Tilly.

She was conscious of his recognition of it. It brought a flush to her cheek. "It is in honour of your visit Pierre!" said she frankly, "that I wear your gift! old friendship lasts well with me does it not? But you will find more old friends than me at Tilly who have not forgotten you."

"I am already richer than Croesus if friendship count as

riches, Amelie! The Hare had many friends but none at last. I am more fortunate in possessing one friend worth a million."

"Nay, you have the million too, if good wishes count in your favour, Pierre! You are richer—"—The bell in the turret of the Chateau began to ring for dinner, drowning her voice, somewhat.

"Thanks to the old Bell for cutting short the compliment, Pierre!" continued she laughing "You dont know what you have lost! but in compensation you shall be my cavalier and escort me to the dining room."

She took the arm of Pierre and in a merry mood which brought back sweet memories of the past, their voices echoed again along the old corridors of the Manor House as they proceeded to the great dining room where the rest of the company were assembling.

The dinner was rather a stately affair owing to the determination of Felix Beaudoin to do especial honour to the return home of the family. How the company ate, talked, and drank at the hospitable table, need not be recorded here. The good Curé, his face under the joint influences of good humour and good cheer, was full as a harvest moon. He rose at last, folded his hands and slowly repeated "*Agimus Gratias.*" After dinner the company withdrew to the brilliantly lighted drawing room where conversation, music and a few games of cards for such as liked them, filled up a couple of hours longer.

The Lady de Tilly seated beside Pierre Philibert on the sofa conversed with him in a pleasant strain, while the Curé with a couple of old dowagers in turbans, and an old veteran officer of the colonial marine, long stranded on a lee shore, formed a quartette at cards.

These were steady enthusiasts of whist and piquet, such as are only to be found in small country circles where society is scarce, and amusements few. They had met as partners or antagonists and played, laughed and wrangled over sixpenny stakes and odd tricks and honours every week for a quarter of a century and would willingly have gone on playing till the day of judgement without change of partners if they could have trumped death and won the odd trick of him!

Pierre recollected having seen these same old friends seated at the same card table during his earliest visits to the Manor House. He recalled the fact to the Lady de Tilly, who laughed and said, "her old friends had lived so long in the company of the Kings and Queens who formed the paste board Court of the kingdom of Cocagne, that they could relish no meaner amusement than one which Royalty although mad, had the credit of introducing."

Amelie devoted herself to the task of cheering her somewhat moody brother. She sat beside him leaning her hand with sisterly affection upon his shoulder, while in a low sweet voice she talked to him adroitly touching those topics only, which she knew woke pleasureable associations in his mind. Her words were sweet as manna and full of womanly tenderness and sympathy, skillfully wrapped in a strain of gaiety like a bridal veil which hides the tears of the heart.

Pierre Philibert's eyes involuntarily turned towards her, and his ears caught much of what she said. He was astonished at the grace and perfection of her language. It seemed to him like a strain of music filled with every melody of earth and heaven surpassing poets in beauty of diction, philosophers in truth, and in purity of affection all the saints and sweetest women of whom he had ever read.

Her beauty, her vivacity, her modest reticencies and her delicate tact in addressing the captious spirit of Le Gardeur, filled Pierre with admiration. He could at that moment have knelt at her feet and worshipped in her the realization of every image which his imagination had ever formed of a perfect woman.

Now and then she played on the harp for Le Gardeur, the airs which she knew he liked best. His sombre mood yielded to her fond exertions and she had the reward of drawing at last a smile from his eyes as well as from his lips. The last she knew might be simulated, the former she felt was real, for the smile of the eye is the flash of the light kindled in the glad heart.

Le Gardeur was not dull nor ungrateful. He read clearly

enough the loving purpose of his sister. His brow cleared up under her sunshine. He smiled, he laughed, and Amelie had the exquisite joy of believing she had gained a victory over the dark spirit that had taken possession of his soul,—Although the hollow laugh struck the ear of Pierre Philibert with a more uncertain sound than that which flattered the fond hopes of Amelie.

Amelie looked towards Pierre and saw his eyes fixed upon her with that look which fills every woman with an emotion almost painful in its excess of pleasure when first she meets it, that unmistakeable glance from the eyes of a man who she is proud to perceive has singled her out from all other women for his love and homage.

Her face became of a deep glow in spite of her efforts to look calm and cold. She feared Pierre might have misinterpreted her vivacity of speech and manner. A sudden distrust of herself came over her in his presence. The flow of her conversation was embarrassed and almost ceased.

To extricate herself from her momentary confusion which she was very conscious had not escaped the observation of Pierre, (—and the thought of that confused her still more—) she rose and went to the harpsichord to recover her composure by singing a sweet song of her own composition written, in the soft dialect of Provence, the *Langue d'oc* full of the sweet sadness of a tender and hopeless love.

Her voice, Amelie did not often sing, flowed in a thousand harmonies on the enraptured ears of her listeners. Even the veteran card players left a game of whist unfinished to cluster round the angelic singer.

Pierre Philibert sat like one in a trance. He loved music and, understood it passing well. He had heard all the rare voices which Paris prided itself in the possession of, but he thought he had never known what music was, till now. His heart throbbed in sympathy with every inflection of the voice of Amelie which went through him like a sweet spell of enchantment. It was the voice of a disembodied spirit singing in the language of earth, which changed at last into a benediction and good night for the departing guests who at an earlier hour than usual out of consideration for the fatigue of their hosts took their leave of the Manor House and its hospitable inmates.

The family, as families will do upon the departure of their guests, drew up in a narrower circle round the fire, that blessed circle of freedom and confidence which belongs only to happy households. The novelty of the situation kept up the interest of the day and they sat and conversed until a late hour.

The Lady de Tilly reclined comfortably in her fauteuil looking with goodnatured complacency upon the little group beside her. Amelie sitting on a stool reclined her head against the bosom of her aunt whose arm embraced her closely and lovingly, as she listened with absorbing interest to an animated conversation between her aunt and Pierre Philibert.

The Lady de Tilly drew Pierre out to talk of his travels, his studies and his military career, of which he spoke frankly and modestly. His high principles won her admiration the chivalry and loyalty of his character mingled with the humanity of the true soldier, touched a chord in her own heart, stirring within her the sympathies of a nature akin to his.

The presence of Pierre Philibert so unforseen at the old Manor House, seemed to Amelie the work of Providence, for a good and great end, the reformation of her brother. If she dared to think of herself in connection with him, it was with fear and trembling, as a saint on earth receives a beatific vision that may only be attained in Heaven.

Amelie with peculiar tact sought to entangle Le Gardeur's thoughts in an elaborate cobweb of occupation rivalling that of Arachne, which she had woven to catch every leisure hour of his, so as to leave him no time to brood over the pleasures of the Palais of the Intendant or the charms of Angelique des Meloises.

There were golden threads too, in the net work in which she hoped to entangle him—Long rides to the neighbouring Seigneuries, where bright eyes and laughing lips were ready to expel every shadow of care from the most dejected of men, much more from a handsome gallant like Le Gardeur de Repentigny, whose presence at any of these old manors put their fair inmates at once in holiday trim, and in holiday humour. There were shorter walks through the park and domaine of Tilly. Amelie intended to botanize and sketch and even fish and hunt with Le Gardeur and Pierre, although sooth to say Amelie's share in hunting would only be to ride her sure footed pony and look at her companions. There were visits to friends far and near, and visits in return to the Manor House, and a grand excursion of all to the lake of Tilly in boats. They would colonize its little island for a day, set up tents, make a Governor and Intendant, perhaps a King and Queen, and forget the world till their return home.

This elaborate scheme secured the approbation of the Lady de Tilly, who had in truth contributed part of it. Le Gardeur said "he was a poor fly whom they were resolved to catch and pin to the wall of a *Chateau en Espagne*, but he would enter the web without a buzz of opposition, on condition that Pierre would join him." So it was all settled.

Amelie did not venture again that night to encounter the eyes of Pierre Philibert. She needed more courage than she felt just now, to do that, but in secret she blessed him and treasured those fond looks of his in her heart never to be forgotten any more. When she retired to her own chamber and was alone, she threw herself in passionate abandonment before the altar in her little oratory which she had crowned with flowers, to mark her gladness. She poured out her pure soul in invocations of blessings upon Pierre Philibert and upon her brother and all the house. The golden bead of her rosary lingered long in her loving fingers that night, as she repeated over and over her accustomed prayer for his safety and welfare.

The sun rose gloriously next morning over the green woods and still greener meadows of Tilly. The atmosphere was soft and pure. It had been washed clean of all its impurities by a few showers in the night. Every object seemed nearer and clearer to the eye, while the delicious odours of fresh flowers, filled the whole air with fragrance.

The trees, rocks, waters and green slopes stood out with

marvellous precision of outline, as if cut with a keen knife. No fringe of haze surrounded them as in a drouth or in the evening when the air is filled with the shimmering of the day-dust, which follows the sun's chariot in his course round the world.

Every object great and small seemed magnified to welcome Pierre Philibert, who was up betimes this morning and out in the pure air viewing the old familiar scenes.

With what delight he recognized each favorite spot. There was the cluster of trees which crowned a promontary overlooking the St Lawrence, where he and Le Gardeur had stormed the eagles nest. In that sweep of forest, the deer used to browze and the fawns couch in the long ferns. Upon yonder breezy hill they used to sit and count the sails turning alternately bright and dark as the vessels tacked up the broad river. There was a stretch of green lawn still green as it was in his memory—how everlasting are God's colours! There he had taught Amelie to ride and holding fast ran by her side, keeping pace with her flying Indian pony. How beautiful and fresh the picture of her remained in his memory—the soft white dress she wore, her black hair streaming over her shoulders, her dark eyes flashing delight, her merry laugh rivalling the trill of the Blackbird which flew over their heads, chattering for very joy. Before him lay the pretty brook with its rustic bridge reflecting itself in the clear water as in a mirror. That path along the bank led down to the willows where the big mossy stones lay in the stream and the silvery salmon and speckled trout lay fanning the water gently with their fins as they contemplated their shadows on the smooth sandy bottom.

Pierre Philibert sat down on a stone by the side of the brook, and watched the shoals of minnows, move about in little battalions wheeling like soldiers to the right or left at a wave of the hand. But his thoughts were running in a circle of questions and enigmas for which he found neither end nor answer.—

For the hundredth time, Pierre proposed to himself the tormenting enigma harder he thought to solve than any problem of mathematics, for it was the riddle of his life. "What thoughts are truly in the heart of Amelie de Repentigny respecting me? Does she recollect me only as her brother's companion who may possibly have some claim upon her friendship but none upon her love?" His imagination pictured every look she had given him since his return. Not all! O! Pierre Philibert! The looks you, would have given worlds to catch, you were unconscious of! Every word she had spoken, the soft inflection of every syllable of her silvery voice lingered in his ear. He had caught meanings where perhaps no meaning was, and missed the key to others, which he knew were there, never perhaps to be revealed to him—! But although he questioned in the name of love and found many divine echoes in her words, imperceptible to every ear but his own, He could not wholly solve the riddle of his life. Still he hoped!—

"If love creates love, as some say it does," thought he, "Amelie de Repentigny cannot be indifferent to a passion, which governs every impulse of my being! But is there any especial merit in loving her, whom all the world cannot help admiring equally with myself? I am presumptuous to think so!—and more presumptuous still to expect after so many years of separation and forgetfulness that her heart so loving and so sympathetic, has not already bestowed its affection upon some one more fortunate than me!"

While Pierre tormented himself with these sharp thorns of doubt, and of hopes, painful as doubts, little did he think what a brave loving spirit was hid under the silken vesture of Amelie de Repentigny, and how hard was her struggle to conceal from his eyes, those tender regards which with over delicacy, she accounted censurable because they were wholly spontaneous.—

He little thought how entirely his image had filled her heart, during those years, when she dreamed of him, in the quiet cloister, living in a world of bright imaginings of her own, how she had prayed for his safety and welfare as she would have prayed for the soul of one dead, never thinking or even hoping to see him again—!

Pierre had become to her as one of the disembodied saints or angels whose pictures looked down from the wall of the Convent Chapel the bright angel of the annunciation or the, youthful Baptist, proclaiming the way of the Lord. Now, that Pierre Philibert was alive in the flesh, a man beautiful, brave, honourable and worthy of any woman's love, Amelie was frightened! She had not looked for that! And yet it had come upon her. And although trembling she was glad and proud to find she had been remembered by the brave youth who recognized in the perfect woman, the girl, he had so ardently loved as a boy.

Did he love her still? Woman's heart is quicker to apprehend all possibilities than man's. She had caught a look once or twice in the eyes of Pierre Philibert which thrilled the inmost fibres of her being. She had detected his ardent admiration. Was she offended? Far from it! and although her cheek had flushed deeply red, and her pulses throbbed hard at the sudden consciousness that Pierre Philibert admired—nay more—she could not conceal it from herself—She knew that night that he loved her—she would not have forgone that moment of revelation for all that the world had to offer.

She would gladly at that moment of discovery have fled to her own appartment, and cried for joy, but she dare not. She trembled lest his eyes, if she looked up, should discover the secret of her own. She had an overpowering consciousness that she stood on the brink of her fate, that ere long that look of his would be followed by words, blessed, hoped for words! from the lips of Pierre Philibert, words which would be the pledge and assurance to her of that love which was hereafter to be the joy—it might be the despair—but in any case the all in all of her life for ever.

Amelie had not yet realized the truth that love is the strength not the weakness of woman, and that the boldness of the man is rank cowardice in comparison with the bravery she is capable of and the sacrifices she will make for the sake of the man who has won her heart.

God locks up in a golden casket of modesty the yearnings of a woman's heart. But when the hand in which he has placed the key that opens it, calls forth her glorified affections, they come out like the strong angels and hold back the winds that blow from the four corners of the earth, that they may not hurt the man whose forehead is sealed with the kiss of her acknowledged love.

CHAPTER 29

A DAY AT THE MANOR HOUSE

AMELIE after a night of wakefulness and wrestling with a tumult of new thoughts and emotions,—no longer dreams, but realities of life—dressed herself in a light morning costume which simple as it was, bore the touch of her graceful hand, and perfect taste. With a broad brimmed straw hat set upon her dark tresses which were knotted with careless care in a blue ribbon she descended the steps of the Manor House. There was a deep bloom upon her cheeks and her eyes looked like fountains of light and gladness, running over to bless all beholders.

She enquired of Felix Beaudoin of her brother. The old Major Domo with a significant look informed her that Monsieur Le Gardeur had just ordered his horse to ride to the village. He had first called for a decanter of Cognac and when it was brought to him, he suddenly thrust it back and would not taste it. "He would not drink even Jove's nectar in the Manor House," he said, "but would go down to the village where Satan mixed the drink for thirsty souls like his! Poor Le Gardeur!" continued Felix, "You must not let him go to the village this morning! Mademoiselle!"

Amelie was startled at this information. She hastened at once to seek her brother, whom she found walking impatiently in the garden slashing the heads off the sunflowers and dahlias, within reach of his riding whip. He was equipped for a ride and waited the coming of the groom with his horse.

Amelie ran up and clasping his arm with both hands, as she looked up in his face with a smile, exclaimed, "Do not go to the village yet, Le Gardeur! Wait for us."

"Not go to the village yet! Amelie?" replied he. "Why not?

I will return for breakfast, although I have no appetite. I thought a ride to the village would give me one."

"Wait until after breakfast brother! when we will all go with you to meet our friends who come this morning to Tilly. Our cousin Heloise de Lotbiniere is coming to see you and Pierre Philibert. You must be there to welcome her. Gallants are too scarce to allow her to spare the handsomest of all, my own brother!—"

Amelie divined truly from Le Gardeur's restless eyes and haggard look, that a fierce conflict was going on in his breast, between duty and desire, whether he should remain at home or go to the village, to plunge again into the sea of dissipation out of which he had just been drawn to land, half drowned and utterly desperate.

Amelie resolved not to leave his side, but to cleave to him, and inch by inch to fight the Demons which possessed him until she got the victory.

Le Gardeur looked fondly in the face of Amelie. He read her thoughts, and was very conscious why she wished him not to go to the village. His feelings gave way, before her love and tenderness. He suddenly embraced her and kissed her cheeks while the tears stood welling in his eyes. "I am not worthy of you, Amelie!" said he. "So much sisterly care is lost on me!—"

"O say not that, Brother!" replied she, kissing him fondly in return. "I would give my life to save you, O my Brother!—"

Amelie was greatly moved and for a time unable to speak further. She laid her head on his shoulder and sobbed audibly. Her love gained the victory where remonstrance and opposition would have lost it.

"You have won the day Amelie!" said he. "I will not go to the village except with you. You are the best and truest girl in all christendom! Why is there no other like you? If there were, this curse had not come upon me, nor this trial upon you! Amelie! you are my good angel and I will try, O so faithfully try, to be guided by you! If you fail you will have at least done all, and more than your duty towards your erring brother."

"Le Brun!" cried he to the groom, who had brought his horse and to whom he threw the whip which had made such havoc among the flowers. "Lead Black Cesar to the stable again! and hark you! When I bid you bring him out in the early morning another time, lead him to me, unbridled and unsaddled with only a halter on his head, that I may ride as a clown and not as a gentleman!—"

Le Brun stared at this speech and finally regarded it as a capital joke or else as he whispered to his fellow grooms in the stable, "He believed his young master had gone mad!—"

"Pierre Philibert!" continued Amelie "is down at the Salmon pool. Let us join him Le Gardeur, and bid him good morning once more at Tilly."

Amelie, overjoyed at her victory, tripped gaily by the side of her brother, and presently two friendly hands, the hands of Pierre Philibert were extended to greet her and Le Gardeur.

The hand of Amelie was retained for a moment in that of Pierre Philibert, sending the blood to her cheeks. There is a magnetic touch in loving fingers which is never mistaken, though their contact be but for a second of time. It anticipates the strong grasp of love which will ere long embrace body and soul in adamantine chains of a union not to be broken even by death.—

If Pierre Philibert retained the hand of Amelie for one second longer than mere friendship required of him, no one perceived it, but God and themselves. Pierre felt it like a revelation—the hand of Amelie yielding timidly but not unwillingly to his manly grasp. He looked in her face. Her eyes were averted and she withdrew her hand quickly but gently, as not upbraiding him.

That moment of time flashed a new influence upon both their lives. It was the silent recognition that each was henceforth conscious of the other's special regard.

There are moments which contain the whole quintessence of our lives—our loves—our hopes—our failures, in one concentrated drop of happiness or misery. We look behind us and see that our whole past has led up to that infinitesimal fraction of time which is the consummation of the past in the present, the end of the old and the beginning of the new. We look forward from the vantage ground of the present, and the world of a new creation lies before us.

Pierre Philibert was conscious from that moment that Amelie de Repentigny was not indifferent to him—nay he had a ground of hope that in time she would listen to his pleading and at last bestow on him the gift of her priceless love.

His hopes were sure hopes, although he did not dare to give himself the sweet assurance of it, nor did Amelie herself as yet suspect how far her heart was irrevocably wedded to Pierre Philibert.

Deep as was the impression of that moment upon both of them, neither Philibert nor Amelie yielded to its influence more than to lapse into a momentary silence which was relieved by Le Gardeur, who suspecting not the cause, nay thinking it was on his account, that his companions were so unaccountably grave and still, kindly endeavoured to force the conversation upon a number of interesting topics and directed the attention of Philibert to various points of the landscape which suggested reminiscences of his former visits to Tilly.

The equilibrium of conversation was restored and the three sitting down on a long flat stone, a boulder which had dropped millions of years before out of an iceberg as it sailed slowly over the glacial ocean which then covered the place of New France, commenced to talk over Amelie's programme of the previous night—the amusements she had planned for the week, the friends in all quarters they were to visit, and the friends from all quarters they were to receive at the Manor House. These topics formed a source of fruitful comment, as conversation on our friends always does. If the sun shone hot and fierce at noontide in the dog days, they would enjoy the cool shade of the arbours with books and conversations. They would ride in the forest or embark in their canoes for a row up the bright little river. There would be dinners and diversions for the day; music and dancing for the night.

The spirits of the inmates of the Manor House could not help but be kept up by these expedients and Amelie flattered herself that she would quite succeed in dissipating the gloomy thoughts which occupied the mind of Le Gardeur.

They sat on the stone by the brook side for an hour, conversing pleasantly while they watched the speckled trout dart like silver arrows spotted with blood, in the clear pool.

Le Gardeur strove to be gay, and teased Amelie by playfully criticising her programme, and half in earnest half in jest arguing for the superior attractions of the Palace of the Intendant, to those of the Manor House of Tilly. He saw the water standing in her eyes, when a consciousness of what must be her feelings seized him. He drew her to his side, asked her forgiveness, and wished fire was set to the Palace and himself in the midst of it. He deserved it for wounding even in jest the heart of the best and noblest sister in the world.

"I am not wounded dear Le Gardeur!" replied she softly. "I knew you were only in jest. My foolish heart is so sensitive to all mention of the Palace and its occupants in connection with you, that I could not even take in jest what was so like truth."

"Forgive me, I will never mention the Palace to you again, Amelie! except to repeat the malediction I have bestowed upon it a thousand times an hour, since I returned to Tilly."

"My own Brave brother!" exclaimed she embracing him, "Now I am happy!—"

The shrill notes of a bugle were heard sounding a military call to breakfast. It was the special privilege of an old servitor of the family who had been a trumpeter in the troop of the Seigneur of Tilly, to summon the family of the Manor House in that manner to breakfast only. The old trumpeter had solicited long to be allowed to sound the reveillee at break of day, but the good Lady de Tilly had too much regard for the repose of the inmates of her house to consent to any such untimely waking of them from their morning slumbers.

The old familiar call was recognized by Philibert, who reminded Amelie of a day when Eolus, (the ancient trumpeter bore that windy soubriquet), had accompanied them on a long ramble in the forest, how the day being warm the old man fell asleep under a comfortable shade while the three children straggled off into the depths of the woods where they were speedily lost.

"I remember it like yesterday, Pierre!" exclaimed Amelie, sparkling at the reminiscence. "I recollect how I wept and wrung my hands, tired out, hungary and forlorn, with my dress in tatters and one shoe left in a miry place! I recollect moreover that my protectors were in almost as bad a plight as myself, yet they chivalrously carried the little maiden by turns or together made a Queen's chair for me with their locked hands, until we all broke down together and sat crying at the foot of a tree, reminding one another of the babes in the woods, and recounting stories of bears which had devoured lost naughty children in the forest. I remember how we all knelt down at last and recited our prayers until all at once we heard the bugle of Eolus sounding close by us.—The poor old man wild with rapture at having found us, kissed and shook us so violently, that we almost wished ourselves lost in the forest again."

The recollection of this adventure was very pleasing to Pierre. He recalled every incident of it perfectly and all three of them seemed for a while transported back into the fairy land of their happy childhood.

The bugle call of old Eolus again sounded and the three friends rose and proceeded towards the house.

The little brook,—It had never looked so bright before to Amelie—sparkled with joy like her own eyes. The Orioles and Blackbirds warbled in the bushes and the insects which love warmth and sunshine chirmed and chirruped among the ferns and branches, as Amelie, Pierre and Le Gardeur, walked home along the green footpath under the avenue of elms that led to the Chateau.

The Lady de Tilly received them with many pleasant words. Leading them into the breakfast room she congratulated Le Gardeur upon the satisfaction it afforded her to see her dear children, so she called them, once more seated round her board in health and happiness. Amelie coloured slightly and looked at her Aunt as if questioning whether she included Philibert among her children?—

The Lady de Tilly guessed her thought, but pretending

not to, bade Felix proceed with the breakfast and turned the conversation to topics more general. "The Iroquois" she said "had left the Chaudiere and gone further Eastward, so news had just been brought in by messengers to the Seigneury, and it was probable, nay certain that they would not be heard of again. Therefore Le Gardeur and Pierre Philibert were under no necessity of leaving the Manor to search for the savages, but could arrange with Amelie, for as much enjoyment as they could crowd into these summer days."

"It is all arranged Aunt!" Replied Amelie. "We have held a *Cour Pleniere* this morning, and made a code of laws for our Kingdom of Cocagne during the next eight days. It needs only the consent of our Suzeraine Lady to be at once acted upon."

"And your Suzeraine Lady gives her consent without farther questioning, Amelie! although I confess you have an admirable way of carrying your point Amelie!" said her Aunt laughing. "You resolve first what you will do and ask my approbation after."

"Yes! Aunt that is our way in the kingdom of pleasure!— as this, and we begin this morning. Le Gardeur and Pierre will ride to the Village to meet our cousin Heloise from Lotbiniere."

"But you will accompany us, Amelie!" exclaimed Le Gardeur, "I will not go else. It was a bargain!—"

"O! I did not count myself for anything but an embarrassment! of course I shall go with you Le Gardeur, but our Cousin Heloise de Lotbiniere is coming to see *you* not *me*. She lost her heart" remarked she turning to Pierre, "when she was last here, at the feast of St John and is coming to seek it again!—"

"Ah! How was that Amelie?" asked Philibert. "I remember the lovely face, the chestnut curls and bright black eyes of Heloise de Lotbiniere. And has hers really gone the way of all hearts?—"

"Of all good hearts Pierre!—but you shall hear if you will be good and listen! She saw the portraits of you and Le Gardeur one day hung in the Boudoir of my Aunt. Heloise professed that she admired both until she could not tell which she liked best, and left me to decide."

"Ah! and which of us did you give to the fair Heloise?" demanded Philibert with a sudden interest.

"Not the Abelard she wanted you may be sure Pierre!" exclaimed Le Gardeur. "She gave me and kept you! It was a case of clear misappropriation!"—

"No brother! not so!" replied Amelie hastily, "Heloise had tried the charm of the three caskets with the three names without result, and at last watched in the church porch on the eve of St John, to see the shade of her destined lover pass by, and lo! Heloise vowed she saw *me*!—and no one else pass into the church!—"

"Ah! I suppose it was you! It is no rare thing for you to visit the shrine of our Lady on the Eve of St John! Pierre Philibert do you recollect? O not as I do, dear friend—!" continued Le Gardeur with a sudden change of voice which was now filled with emotion. "It was on the day of St John you saved my poor worthless life. We are not ungrateful! She has kept the eve of St John in the church ever since in commemoration of that event!—"

"Brother! we have much to thank Heaven for," replied Amelie blushing deeply at his words, "and I trust we shall never be ungrateful for its favour and protection."

Amelie shied from a compliment like a young colt at his own shadow. She avoided further reference to the subject broached by Le Gardeur, by saying "It was me whom Heloise saw pass into the church. I never explained the mystery to her and she is not sure yet, whether it was my wraith or myself, who gave her that fright on St Johns eve! But I claimed her heart as one authorized to take it and if I could not marry her myself I claimed the right to give her to whomsoever I pleased and I gave her to you Le Gardeur! but you would not accept the sweetest girl in New France!"—

"Thanks Amelie!" replied he laughing yet wincing, "Heloise is indeed all you say, the sweetest girl in New France! But she was too Angelical for Le Gardeur de Repentigny! Pshaw! you make me say foolish things Amelie! But in penance for my slight, I will be doubly attentive to my fair Cousin de

Lotbiniere today. I will at once order the horses and we will ride down to the village to meet her."

Arrayed in a simple riding dress of dark blue, which became her as did everything else which she wore, Amelie's very attire seemed instinct with the living graces and charms of its wearer. She mounted her horse accepting the aid of Philibert to do so, although when alone she usually sprang to the saddle herself. Saluting the Lady de Tilly who waved her hand to them from the lawn, the three slowly cantered down the broad avenue of the park towards the village of Tilly.

Amelie rode well. The exercise and the pure air brought the fresh colour to her face, and her eyes sparkled with animation as she conversed gaily with her brother and Philibert.

They speedily reached the Village where they met Heloise de Lotbiniere who rushing to Amelie kissed her with effusion and as she greeted Le Gardeur looked up as if she would not have refused a warmer salutation than the kind shake of the hand with which he received her. She welcomed Philibert with glad surprise, recognizing him at once and giving a glance at Amelie, which expressed an ocean of unspoken meaning and sympathy.

Heloise was beautiful, gay, spirited, full of good humour and sensibility. Her heart had long been devoted to Le Gardeur, but never meeting with any response to her shy advances which were like the wheeling of a dove round and round its wished for mate, she had long concluded with a sigh that for her the soul of Le Gardeur was insensible to any touch of a warmer regard than sprang from the most sincere friendship.

Amelie saw and understood all this. She loved Heloise and in her quiet way had tried to awaken a kinder feeling for her in the heart of her brother. As one fights fire with fire in the great conflagrations of the prairies, Amelie hoped also to combat the influence of Angelique des Meloises, by raising up a potent rival in the fair Heloise de Lotbiniere, but she soon found how futile were her endeavours. The heart of Le Gardeur was wedded to the idol of his fancy and no woman on earth could win him away from Angelique.

Amelie comforted Heloise by the gift of her whole confidence and sympathy. The poor disappointed girl accepted the decree of fate, known to none other but Amelie, while in revenge upon herself, a thing not rare in proud, sensitive natures, she appeared in society more gay, more radiant and full of mirth than ever before. Heloise hid the asp in her bosom but so long as its bite was unseen she laughed cruelly at the pain of it, and deceived as she thought, the eyes of the world as to her suffering.

The arrival of Heloise de Lotbiniere was followed by that of a crowd of other visitors, who came to the Manor House to pay their respects to the family on their return home, and especially to greet Le Gardeur and Colonel Philibert, who was well remembered and whom the busy tongues of gossip already set down as a suitor for the hand of the young Chatelaine.

The report of what was said by so many whispering friends, was quickly carried to the ear of Amelie by some of her light hearted companions. She blushed at the accusation, and gently denied all knowledge of it, laughing as a woman will laugh who carries a hidden joy or a hidden sorrow in her heart, neither of which she cares to reveal to the world's eye. Amelie listened to the pleasant tale with secret complaisance, for despite her tremour and confusion it was pleasant to hear that Pierre Philibert loved her, and was considered a suitor for her hand. It was sweet to know that the world believed she was his choice.

She strung every one of these precious words, like a chaplet of pearls upon the strings of her heart, contemplating them, counting them over and over in secret, with a joy known only to herself and to God, whom she prayed to guide her right whatever might happen.

That something would happen ere long, she felt a premonition which at times made her grave in the midst of her hopes and anticipations.

The days passed gaily at Tilly. Amelie carried out the elaborate programme which she had arranged for the amusement of Le Gardeur as well as for the pleasures of her guests.

Every day brought a change and a fresh enjoyment. The mornings were devoted by the gentlemen to hunting, fishing, and other sports, by the ladies to reading, music, drawing, needlework or the arrangements of dress and ornaments. In the afternoons all met together and the social evening was spent either at the Manor House or some neighbouring Mansion. The hospitality of all was alike. A profusion of social feeling formed at that day a marked characteristic of the people of New France.

The Lady de Tilly spent an hour or two each day with her trusty Land Stewart or Bailli Master Coté in attending to the multifarious business of her Seigneurie. The feudal law of New France imposed great duties and much labour upon the Lords of the Manor, by giving them an interest in every man's estate, and making them participators in every transfer of land throughout a wide district of Country. A person who acquired by purchase or otherwise the lands of a Censitaire or Vassal was held to perform *foi et hommage* for the lands so acquired and to acquit all other feudal dues owing by the original holder to his Seigneur.

It was during one of these fair summer days at Tilly, that Sieur Tranchelot, having acquired the farm of the Bocage, a strip of land a furlong wide and a league, in depth with a pleasant frontage on the broad St Lawrence, The New Censitaire came as in duty bound to render *foi et hommage* for the same to the Lady of the Manor of Tilly according to the law and custom of the Seigneurie.

At the hour of noon, Lady de Tilly with Le Gardeur, Amelie and Pierre Philibert in full dress stood on a daïs in the great Hall. Master Coté sat at a table on the floor in front, with his great clasped book of Record open before him. A drawn sword lay upon the table, and a cup of wine stood by the side of it.

When all was arranged, three loud knocks were heard on the great door, and the Sieur Tranchelot dressed in his holiday costume, but bare-headed and without sword or spurs—not being gentilhomme, he was not entitled to wear them—entered the door, which was ceremoniously opened for him by the Major Domo. He was gravely led up to the daïs where stood the Lady of the Manor, by the Stewart bearing his wand of office.

The worthy censitaire knelt down before the Lady and repeating her name three times, pronounced the formula of *foi et hommage* prescribed by the Law, as owing to the Lords of the Manor of Tilly.

"My Lady de Tilly! my Lady de Tilly! my Lady de Tilly! I render you fealty and homage due to you on account of my lands of the Bocage which belong to me, by virtue of the deed executed by the Sieur Marcel before the worthy notary Jean Pothier *dit* Robin, on the day of Palms 1748, and I avow my willingness to acquit the Seigneurial and feudal *cens et rentes* and all other lawful dues whensoever payable by me,—beseeching you to be my good leige lady, and to admit me to the said fealty and homage—!"

The Lady accepted the homage of Sieur Tranchelot, remitted the customary *Lods et Ventes* or fines payable to the Seigneur, gave him the cup of wine to drink when he rose to his feet and ordered him to be generously entertained by her Major Domo and sent back to the Bocage rejoicing. So the days passed by in alternations of business and pastime, but all made a pleasure for the agreeable inmates of the Manor House.

Philibert gave himself up to the delirium of enchantment, which the presence of Amelie threw over him. He never tired of watching the fresh developments of her gloriously endowed nature. Her beauty rare as it was, grew day by day upon his wonder and admiration, as he saw how fully it corresponded to the innate grace and nobility of her mind.

She was so fresh of thought, so free from all affectation, so gentle and winning in all her ways, and sooth to say so happy in the admiration of Philibert, which she was very conscious of now. It darted from his eyes at every look, although no word of it had yet passed his lips. The radiance of her spirits flashed like sunbeams through every part of the old Manor House.

Amelie was carried away in a flood of new emotions. She tried once or twice to be discreetly angry with herself for admitting so unreservedly the pleasure she felt in Pierre's admiration. She placed her soul on a rack of self questioning torture, and every inquisition, she made of her heart returned the self same answer—"She loved Pierre Philibert!"

It was in vain she accused herself of possible impropriety—that it was bold, unmaidenly, censurable, nay perhaps sinful, to give her heart before it had been asked for, but if she had to die for it, she could not conceal the truth—that she loved Pierre Philibert! "I ought to be angry with myself" said she. "I try to be so!—but I cannot! Why?"—

"Why?" Amelie solved the query as every true woman does who asks herself why she loves one man rather than another! "Because he has chosen me out in preference to all others, to be the treasure keeper of his affections! I am proud," continued Amelie, "that he gives his love to me, to me! unworthy as I am of such preference! I am no better than others." Amelie was a true woman, proud as an Empress before other men. She was humble and lowly as the Madonna in the presence of him whom she felt was by right of love lord and master of her affections.—

Amelie could not overcome a feeling of tremour in the presence of Pierre since she made this discovery. Her cheek warmed with an incipient flush when his ardent eyes glanced at her too eloquently. She knew what was in his heart and once or twice when casually alone with Philibert, she saw his lips quivering under a hard restraint to keep in the words, the dear words, she thought, which would one day burst forth in a flood of passionate eloquence overwhelming all denial, and make her his own for ever.

Time and tide, which come to all, once in our lives,—as the Poet says—and which must be taken at their flood to lead to fortune, came at length to Amelie de Repentigny.

It came suddenly and in an unlooked for hour, the great question of questions to her as to every woman.

The hour of birth and the hour of death are in God's hand, but the hour when a woman yielding to the strong enfolding arm of a man who loves her, falters forth an avowal of her love, and plights her troth, and vows to be one with him till death, God leaves that question to be decided by her own heart. His blessing rests on her choice, if pure love guides, and reason enlightens affection. His curse infallibly follows every faithless pledge where no heart is—every union that is not the marriage of love and truth. These alone can be married and where these are absent, there is no marriage at all in the face of Heaven, and but the simulation of one on earth, an unequal yoking which if man will not sunder, God will at last where there is neither marriage nor giving in marriage but all are as his angels.

The day appointed for the long planned excursion to the beautiful lake of Tilly came round. A numerous and cheerful water party left the Manor House, in the bright cool morning to spend the day gypsying in the shady woods and quiet recesses of the little lake. They were all there! Amelie's invitation to her young friends far and near had been eagerly accepted. Half a dozen boats and canoes filled with lighthearted companions and with ample provisions for the day, shot up the narrow river and after a rapid and merry voyage, disembarked their passengers and were drawn up on the shores and islands of the lake.

That bright morning was followed by a sunny day, a happy day, warm yet breezy. The old oaks wove a carpet of shadows changing the pattern of its tissue every hour upon the leaf-strown floor of the forest. The fresh pines shed their resinous perfume on every side, in the still shade, but out in the sunshine the birds sang merrily all day.

The group of merry-makers spent a glorious day of pleasure by the side of the clear smooth lake, fishing and junketting on shore or paddling their birch canoes over its waters, among the little islands which dotted its surface.

Day was fast fading away into a soft twilight. The shadows which had been drawing out longer and longer as the sun declined lay now in all their length, like bands stretched over the green sward. The breeze went down with the sun, and the smooth surface of the lake lay like a sheet of molten gold, reflecting the parting glories of the day that still lit up the Western sky.

A few stars began to twinkle here and there. They were not destined to shine brilliantly tonight, for they would ere long be eclipsed by the splendour of the full moon which was just visible, rising in a hemisphere of light which stood like a royal pavillion on the eastern horizon. From it in a few minutes would emerge the Queen of heaven and mildly replace the vanishing glory of the day.

The company after a repast under the trees rose full of life and merriment and rearranged themselves into little groups and couples as chance or inclination led them. They trooped down to the beach to embark in their canoes for a last joyous cruise round the lake, and its fairy islands by moonlight, before returning home.

Amid a shower of lively conversation and laughter, the ladies seated themselves in the light canoes which danced like corks upon the water. The gentlemen took the paddles and expert as Indians in the use of them, swept out over the surface of the lake which was now all aglow with the bright crimson of sunset.

In the bow of one of the canoes, sat the Arion of Tilly, Jean La Marche. A flute or two accompanied his violin, and a guitar tinkled sweetly under the fingers of Heloise de Lotbiniere. They played an old air, while Jean led the chorus in splendid voice;

"Nous irons sur l'eau,
Nous y prom—promener!
Nous irons jouer dans l'isle!—"

The voices of all united in the song as the canoes swept away round a little promontory crowned with three pine trees which stood up in the blaze of the setting sun, like the three children in the fiery furnace, or the sacred bush that burned and was not consumed.

Faint and fainter, the echoes repeated the receding harmony, until at last they died away. A solemn silence succeeded. A languor like that of the Lotus eaters crept over the face of nature and softened the heart to unwonted tenderness. It was the hour of gentle thoughts, of low spoken confidences, and love between young and sympathizing souls, who alone with themselves and God, confess their mutual love, and invoke his blessing upon it.

CHAPTER 30

"FELICES TER ET AMPLIUS"

AMELIE by accident or by contrivance of her fair companions—girls are so wily and sympathetic with each other—had been left seated by the side of Philibert on the twisted roots of a gigantic oak forming a rude but simple chair fit to enthrone the king of the forest and his Dryad Queen. No sound came to break the quiet of the evening hour save the monotonous plaint of a whip-poor-will, in a distant brake and the ceaseless chirm of insects among the leafy boughs and down in the ferns that clustered on the knolls round about.

Philibert let fall upon his knee the book which he had been reading. His voice faltered. He could not continue without emotion the touching tale of Paulo and Francesca da Rimini. Amelie's eyes were suffused with tears of pity for her heart had beat time to the music of Dante's immortal verse, as it dropped in measured cadence from the lips of Philibert.

She had read the pathetic story before, but never comprehended until now, the weakness which is the strength of love—O blessed paradox, of a woman's heart—and how truly the *Commedia* which is justly called Divine, unlocks the secret chambers of the human soul.

Philibert ceased his reading and gazed fondly at her face, which she shyly averted looking away over the broad sheet of water while repeating in thought some of the Divine stanzas which lingered like the chime of silver bells upon her memory.

Amor ch'al cor gentil ratto s'apprende!—
Amor ch' a null amato amar perdona,
Questi che mai da me non fia diviso!—

"Love which is quickly caught by noble hearts!
Love that excuses no loved one from loving,
He who from me shall ne'er be sundered more!"

Love is death as well as life, separation as well as meeting.
Amelie was melted at the passionate tale and trembled she
knew not why. But she dared not for worlds at that moment
have looked up in the eyes of Pierre Philibert.

She would fain have risen, but held down as by some spell
of fascination, she kept her seat.

"Read no more Pierre!" said she, "that book is too terrible
in its beauty and in its sadness! I think it was written by a
disembodied spirit who had seen all worlds, knew all hearts
and shared in all sufferings. It sounds to me like the sad voice
of a prophet of woe."

"Amelie!" replied he. "Believe you there are women
faithful and true as Francesca da Rimini? She would not
forsake Paulo even in the gloomy regions of despair! Believe
you that there are such women?—"

Amelie looked at him with a quick confident glance. A
deep flush covered her cheek and her breath went and came
rapidly. She knew what to answer; but she thought it might
seem overbold to answer such a question. A second thought
decided her however. "Pierre Philibert would ask her no
question to which she might not answer," she said to herself.

Amelie replied to him slowly, but undoubtingly: "I think
there are such women, Pierre!" replied she. "Women who
would never, even in the regions of despair, forsake the man
whom they truly love!—No not for all the terrors recorded in
that awful book of Dante—!"

"It is a blessed truth! Amelie," replied he eagerly, and, he
thought but did not say it, "Such a woman you are! The man
who gets your love gets that which neither earth nor Heaven
nor Hell can take away!—"

He continued aloud, "The love of such a woman is truly
given away Amelie! No one can merit it! It is woman's grace
not man's deserving!—"

"I know not," said she, "it is not hard to give away God's

gifts. Love should be given freely as God gives it to us. It has no value except as the bounty of the heart, and looks for no reward but in its own acceptance."

"Amelie!" exclaimed he, passionately, turning full towards her, but her eyes remained fixed upon the ground. "The gift of such a woman's love has been the dream, the ambition of my life! I may never find it, or having found it may never be worthy of it! and yet! I must find it or die! I must find it where alone I seek it! there or nowhere! can you help me for friendship's sake, for love's sake, Amelie de Repentigny! to find that one treasure that is precious as life—which is life itself, to the heart of Pierre Philibert."

He took hold of her passive hands. They trembled in his, but she offered not to withdraw them. Indeed she hardly noticed the act in the tide of emotion which was surging in her bosom. Her heart moved with a wild yearning to tell him, that he had found the treasure he sought, that a love as strong and as devoted as that of Francesca da Rimini was her own free gift to him.

She tried to answer him but could not. Her hand still remained locked fast in his. He held to it as a drowning man holds to the hand that is stretched to save him.

Philibert knew at that moment, the hour of his fate was come. He would never let go that hand again till he called it his own, or received from it a sign to be gone for ever from the presence of Amelie de Repentigny.

The soft twilight grew deeper every moment, changing the rosy hues of the west, into a pale ashen grey, over which hung the lamp of love, the evening star which shines so brightly and sets so soon, and ever the sooner as it hastens to become again the morning star of a bright day.

The shadow of the broad spreading oak fell darker round the rustic seat where sat these two—as myriads have sat before and since, working out the problem of their lives, and beginning to comprehend each other, as they await with a thrill of anticipation the moment of mutual confidence and fond confession.

Pierre Philibert sat some minutes without speaking, he

could have sat so for ever, gazing with rapture upon her half averted countenance which beamed with such a divine beauty, all aglow with the happy consciousness of his ardent admiration, that it seemed the face of a seraph and in his heart, if not on his knees, he bent in worship, almost idolatrous at her feet.

And yet he trembled, this strong man, who had faced death in every form but this! He trembled by the side of this gentle girl, but it was for joy not for fear. Perfect love casts out fear, and he had no fear now of Amelie's love although she had not yet dared to look at him, but her little hand lay unreprovingly in his, nestling like a timid bird which loved to be there, and sought not to escape. He pressed it gently to his heart. He felt by its magnetic touch, by that dumb alphabet of love, more eloquent than spoken words, that he had won the heart of Amelie de Repentigny.

"Pierre!" said she—she wanted to say, it was time to rejoin their companions, but the words would not come. Her face was still half averted and suffused with an unseen blush as she felt his strong arm round her, and his breath, how sweet it seemed! fanning her cheek. She had no power—no will to resist him—as he drew her close, still closer to his heart.

She trembled but was happy. No eye saw but God's through the blessed twilight, and "God will not reprove Pierre Philibert for loving me," thought she, "and why should I?" She tried or simulated an attempt at soft reproof as a woman will, who fears she may be thought too fond and too easily won, at the very moment she is ready to fall down and kiss the feet of the man before her.

"Pierre!" said she, "it is time we rejoin our companions— they will remark our absence—we will go."

But she still sat there, and made no effort to go. A gossamer thread would have held her there for ever and how could she put aside the strong arm which was mightier than her own will?—

Pierre spoke now. The feelings so long pent up, burst forth in a torrent, that swept away every bond of restraint but that of love's own laws.

He placed his hand tenderly on her cheek and turned her glowing face full towards him. Still she dared not look up! She knew well what he was going to say. She might control her words but not her telltale eyes. She felt a wild joy flashing and leaping in her bosom, which no art could conceal, should she look up at this moment in the face of Pierre Philibert.

"Amelie!" said he after a pause. "Turn those dear eyes! and see and believe in the truth of mine! No words can express how much I do love you!—"

She gave a start of joy, not of surprise, for she knew he loved her, but the avowal of Pierre Philibert's love lifted at once the veil from her own feelings. She raised her dark impassioned eyes to his, and their souls met and embraced in one look both of recognition and bliss! She spake not but unconsciously nestled closer to his breast faltering out some inarticulate words of tenderness.

"Amelie!" continued he, straining her still harder to his heart. "Your love is all I ask of Heaven and of you! Give me that! I must have it, or live henceforth a man forlorn in the wide world! O say, Darling, can you—do you—care for me?—"

"Yes indeed I do!" replied she laying her arm over his neck as if drawing him towards her with a timid movement, while he stooped and kissed her sweet mouth and eyes in an ecstacy of passionate joy. She abandoned herself for a moment to her excess of bliss. "Kiss me Darling!" said he, and she kissed him more than once, to express her own great love, and assure him that it was all his own.

They sat in silence for some minutes; her cheek lay upon his as she breathed his name with many fond faltering expressions of tenderness.

He felt her tears upon his face. "You weep Amelie!" said he, starting up and looking at her cheeks and eyes suffused with moisture.

"I do!" said she, "but it is for joy! O Pierre Philibert! I am so happy! Let me weep now! I will laugh soon! Forgive me if I have confessed too readily how much I love you!—"

"Forgive you! 'Tis I need forgiveness! impetuous that I am to have forced this confession from you tonight! Those blessed words, 'Yes indeed I do!' God's finger has written them on my heart for ever. Never will I forsake the dear lips which spake them, nor fail in all loving duty and affection to you, my Amelie, to the end of my life!—"

"Of both our lives Pierre!" replied she. "I can imagine no life only death separated from you. In thought you have always been with me from the beginning—my life and yours are henceforth one."

He gave a start of joy. "And you loved me before Amelie!" exclaimed he.

"Ever and always! but irrevocably since that day of terror and joy when you saved the life of Le Gardeur and I vowed to pray for you to the end of my life."

"And during these long years in the Convent Amelie, when we seemed utterly forgotten to each other?—"

"You were not forgotten by me Pierre! I prayed for you then. Earnest prayers for your safety and happiness, never hoping for more, least of all anticipating such a moment of bliss as the present—! O my Pierre do not think me bold. You give me the right to love you without shame by the avowal of your love to me."

"Amelie!" exclaimed he kissing her in an ecstacy of pride and admiration. "What have I done, what can I ever do, to merit or recompense, such condescension as your dear words express?—"

"Love me Pierre! Always love me! that is my reward! That is all I ask, all my utmost imagination could desire!—"

"And this little hand Amelie, will be for ever mine?—"

"For ever Pierre and the heart along with it!"

He raised her hand reverently to his lips and kissed it. "Let it not be long" said he! "Life is too short to curtail one hour of happiness from the years full of trouble which are most men's lot."

"But not our lot! Pierre! not ours! With you I forbode no more trouble in this life, and eternal joy in the next!—"

She looked at him and her eyes seemed to dilate with joy. Her hand crept timidly up to his thick locks. She fondly brushed them aside from his broad forehead which she pressed down to her lips and kissed.

"Tell my Aunt, and Le Gardeur, when we return home," continued she. "They love you and will be glad, nay overjoyed to know that I am to be your—your—"

"My wife? Amelie—thrice blessed words! O say my wife!—"

"Yes! your wife, Pierre! your true and loving wife for ever."

"For ever! Yes! Love like—ours is imperishable as the essence of the soul itself, and partakes of the immortality of God, being of him and from him. The Lady de Tilly shall find me a worthy son and Le Gardeur a true and faithful brother!"

"And you, Pierre! O say it—that blessed word has not sounded yet in my ear, what shall I call you?" and she looked in his eyes, drawing his soul from its inmost depths by the magnetism of her look.

"Your husband—Your true and loving husband, as you are my wife, Amelie."

"God be praised!" murmured she in his ear, "Yes my *Husband*! the blessed Virgin has heard my prayers!" and she pressed him in a fond embrace while tears of joy flowed from her eyes! "I am indeed happy!—"

The words hardly left her lips when a sudden crash of thunder rolled over their heads and went pealing down the lake and among the islands while a black cloud suddenly eclipsed the moon shedding darkness over the landscape, which had just begun to brighten in her silvery rays.

Amelie was startled, frightened, clinging hard to the breast of Pierre, as her natural protector. She trembled and shook as the angry reverberations rolled away in the distant forests. "O Pierre!" exclaimed she, "What is that? It is as if a dreadful voice came between us forbidding our union! But nothing shall ever do that now, shall it O my love?—"

"Nothing Amelie! be comforted" replied he. "It is but a thunder storm, coming up. It will send Le Gardeur and all our gay companions quickly back to us, and we shall return home an hour sooner—that is all. Heaven cannot frown on our union, Darling."

"I should love you all the same, Pierre!" whispered she. Amelie was not hard to persuade. She was neither weak nor superstitious beyond her age and sex. But she had not much time to indulge in alarms.

In a few minutes the sound of voices was heard. The dip and splash of hasty paddles followed and the fleet of canoes came rushing into shore, like a flock of water-fowl, seeking shelter in bay or inlet from a storm.

There was a hasty preparation on all sides for departure. The camp fires were trampled out lest they should kindle a conflagration in the forest. The baskets were tossed into one of the large canoes. Philibert and Amelie embarked in that of Le Gardeur, not without many arch smiles and pretended regrets on the part of some of the young ladies for having left them on their last round of the lake.

The clouds kept gathering in the south and there was no time for parley. The canoes were headed down the stream, the paddles were plied vigorously. It was a race to keep ahead of the coming storm and they did not quite win it.

The black clouds came rolling over the horizon in still blacker masses, lower and lower, lashing the very earth with their angry skirts which were rent and split with vivid flashes of lightening. The rising wind almost overpowered with its roaring, the thunder that pealed momentarily nearer, and nearer. The rain came down in broad heavy splashes, followed by a fierce pitiless hail as if Heaven's anger was pursuing them.

Amelie clung to Philibert. She thought of Francesca da Rimini clinging to Paulo amidst the tempest of wind and the moving darkness, and uttered tremblingly the words, "O Pierre! What an omen! Shall it be said of us, as of them,

'*Amor condusse noi ad una morte*'

'Love has conducted us unto one death'?—"

"God grant we may one day say so!" replied he pressing her to his bosom. "When we have earned it by a long life of mutual love and devotion! But not now! cheer up, Darling! We are home!—"

The canoes rushed madly to the bank. The startled holiday party sprang out. Servants were there to help them. All ran across the lawn under the wildly tossing trees and in a few moments before the storm could overtake them with its greatest fury, they reached the Manor House and were safe under the protection of its strong and hospitable roof.

CHAPTER 31

"NO SPEECH OF SILK WILL SERVE YOUR TURN"

ANGELIQUE des Meloises was duly informed through the sharp espionage of Lizette as to what had become of Le Gardeur after that memorable night of conflict between love and ambition when she rejected the offer of his hand and gave herself up to the illusions of her imagination.

Still she loved Le Gardeur with such love as she was capable of, but always subordinate to her selfish vanity and it was not without many sharp pangs of contrition that she remembered her cruel rejection of one whom she admired and was proud of as the handsomest and most devoted of all men who had sought her favour.

She was sorry, yet flattered at Lizette's account of his conduct at the *Taverne de Menut*. For although pleased to think that Le Gardeur loved her to the point of self destruction, she honestly pitied him and felt or thought she felt, that she could sacrifice anything, except herself, for his sake.

Angelique pondered in her own strange fitful way over Le Gardeur. She had no thought of losing him wholly. She would continue to hold him in her silken string and keep him under the spell of her fascinations. She still admired him, nay loved him, she thought. She could not help doing so; and if she could not help it where was the blame? She would not, to be sure sacrifice for him the brilliant hopes which danced before her imagination, like fireflies in a summer night. For no man in the world, would she do that! The Royal Intendant was the mark she aimed at. She was ready to go through fire and water to reach that goal of her ambition. But if she gave the Intendant her hand it was enough! It was all she could give him, but not the smallest corner of her heart which she acknowledged to herself belonged only to Le Gardeur de Repentigny.

While bent on accomplishing this scheme by every means in her power, and which involved necessarily the ruin of Le Gardeur, she took a sort of perverse pride in enumerating the hundred points of personal and moral superiority possessed by him over the Intendant, and all others of her admirers. If she sacrificed her love to her ambition, hating herself while she did so, it was a sort of satisfaction to think that Le Gardeur's sacrifice was not less complete than her own! and she rather felt pleased with the reflection that his heart would be broken and no other woman would ever fill that place in his affections which she had once occupied.

The days that elapsed after their final interview were days of vexation to Angelique. She was angry with herself, almost, angry with Le Gardeur that he had taken her at her word,— and still more angry that she did not reap the immediate reward of her treachery against her own heart. She was like a spoiled and wilful child which will neither have a thing nor let it go. She would discard her lover and still retain his love! and felt irritated and even jealous when she heard of his departure to Tilly with his sister, who had thus apparently more influence to take him away from the city, than Angelique had to keep him there.

But her mind was especially worked upon almost to madness by the ardent professions of love, with the careful avoidance of any proposal of marriage on the part of the Intendant. She had received his daily visits with a determination to please and fascinate him. She had dressed herself with elaborate care, and no woman in New France equalled Angelique in the perfection of her attire. She studied his tastes in her conversation and demeanour, which was free beyond even her wont, because she saw that a manner bold and unconstrained took best with him. Angelique's free style was the most perfect piece of acting in the world. She laughed loudly at his wit, and heard without blushes his double entendres and coarse jests, not less coarse because spoken in the polished dialect of Paris. She stood it all, but with no more result than is left by a brilliant display of fireworks after it is over. She could read in the eager looks and manner of the Intendant that she had fixed his admiration and stirred his passions, but she knew by a no less sure intimation that she had not, with all her blandishments suggested to his mind one serious thought of marriage.

In vain she reverted to the subject of matrimony, in apparent jest but secret earnest. The Intendant quick witted as herself would accept the challenge, talk with her and caracole on the topics which she had caparisoned so gaily for him, and amid compliments and pleasantries, ride away from the point—she knew not whither—! Then Angelique would be angry after his departure, and swear—she could swear shockingly for a lady when she was angry! and vow she would marry Le Gardeur after all!—But her pride was stung not her love. No man had ever defeated her when she chose to subdue him—neither should this proud Intendant! So Angelique collected her scattered forces again, and laid closer seige to Bigot than ever.

The great ball at the Palais had been the object of absorbing interest to the fashionable society of the Capital for many weeks. It came on at last, turning the heads of half the City with its splendour which was remembered a score of years after, when faded dames and powdered dowagers recounted with nodding heads to their daughters, neices and grand-daughters the great event of their youthful prime under the old regime when they had the honour of dancing courtly minuets and lively cotillions with the gay Intendant Bigot. The old ladies never wearied of repeating with the natural exaggerations of vanity and the garrulity of old age, all the compliments he had paid their grace and beauty. More than one ancient dowager used to tell how at her first presentation at the Palace of the Intendant, Bigot had embraced her as the fashion at Court then was, and clasping her slender waist with four fingers exclaimed in ecstacy: "What a pretty handful of brunette!" or "What a charming span round of blonde!—"

The daughters and grand daughters of the old regime laughed, winked and did not wonder, that the ladies of the old times were in such ecstacies at the gallantry of the Intendant and almost ready to kill one another with envy and rivalry for his good graces!—

Nor did the memory of the old dowagers fail to recall the names of the gentlemen who were present at this famous Ball of the Palais. Rich associates of the Grand Company—Each one worth his millions—and how the girls struggled for them and pulled caps so that even the hunchback Sieur Maurin, whose hunch was said to be made of gold, was carried off by the prettiest girl in St Roch, to the despair of a score of rivals!—and the Sieur de Penissault who married so charming and complaisant a wife that she consented to be sold to the Chevalier de Levis to save the incomparable fortune of her husband from confiscation! The King's officers of both army and navy were not forgotten, at the great ball, and their laced coats, silk stockings, buckles and gold epaulettes furnished fertile subjects for hours of exposition to the narrators of the splendour of former times when gay Versailles and not dull St James set the fashions for New France.

"The Bourgeoisie were not permitted in those high caste days, as now!" said Madame de Grandmaison, "to tread upon the skirts of the Noblesse!—but had to content themselves with seats in the great gallery which ran round the Ball room of the Palais, where they could look down with admiration and envy, upon the gay scene, and feast their longing eyes upon the enchanting enjoyments of their betters!—"

Angelique shone the acknowledged Queen of the Intendant's ball. Her natural grace and beauty set off by the exquisite taste and richness of her attire threw into eclipse the fairest of her rivals. If there was one present who in admiration of her own charms, claimed for herself the first place, she freely conceded to Angelique the second. But Angelique feared no rival there. Her only fear was at Beaumanoir. She was profoundly conscious of her own superiority to all present, while she relished the envy and jealousy which it created. She cared but little what the women thought of her and boldly challenging the homage of the men obtained it as her rightful due—!

Still, under the gay smiles and lively badinage which she showered on all around as she moved through the brilliant throng, Angelique felt a bitter spirit of discontent rankling in her bosom. She was angry and she knew why, and still more angry because upon herself lay the blame! Not that she blamed herself for having rejected Le Gardeur—she had done that deliberately and for a price—but the price was not yet paid! And she had sometimes qualms of doubt whether it would ever be paid!

She who had, had her own way with all men, now encountered a man who spoke and looked like one who had, had his own way with all women, and who meant to have his own way with her!—

She gazed often upon the face of Bigot and the more she looked the more inscrutable it appeared to her. She tried to sound the depths of his thoughts, but her enquiry was like the dropping of a stone into the bottomless pit of that deep cavern of the Dark and Bloody Ground talked of by adventurous voyageurs, from the far west. It went down and down reverberating fainter and fainter as it descended and never struck the bottom. Of that nature was Angelique's questioning of the mind of Bigot. Under a glare of compliments and flattery, lay a dark unfathomable abyss of hidden purposes which defied her utmost scrutiny. She did well she thought to be angry and to nourish desperate schemes, in her heart.

That Bigot admired her beyond all other women, at the ball, was visible enough from the close and marked attention which he lavished on her as the courtly flatteries flowed like honey from his lips. She also read her preeminence in his favour from the jealous eyes of a host of rivals which watched her every movement. But Angelique felt that the admiration of the Intendant was not of that kind which had driven so many men mad for her sake. She knew Bigot would never go mad for her, much as he was fascinated! and why? Why?

Angelique while listening to his honied flatteries as he led her gaily through the ball room, asked herself again and again, why did he carefully avoid the one topic that filled her thoughts or spoke of it only in his mocking manner which tortured her to madness with doubt and perplexity.

As she leaned on the arm of the courtly Intendant, laughing like one possessed with the very spirit of gaiety, at his sallies and jests her mind was torn with bitter comparisons as she remembered Le Gardeur, his handsome face and his transparent admiration so full of love and ready for any sacrifice for her sake—and she had cast it all away for this inscrutable voluptuary! A man who had no respect for women, but who admired her person, condescended to be pleased with it and affected to be caught by the lures she held out to him, but which she felt would be of no more avail to hold him fast, than the threads which a spider throws from bush to bush on a summer morn will hold fast a bird which flies athwart them.

The gayest of the gay to all outward appearance, Angelique missed sorely the presence of Le Gardeur, and she resented his absence from the ball, as a slight and a wrong to her sovereignty which never released a lover from his allegiance.

The fair demoiselles at the Ball less resolutely ambitious than Angelique, found by degrees in the devotion of other cavaliers, ample compensation for only so much of the Intendants favour as he liberally bestowed on all the sex. But that did not content Angelique. She looked with sharpest eyes of inquisition upon the bright glances which now and then shot across the room where she sat by the side of Bigot, apparently steeped in happiness but with a serpent biting at her heart, as she felt that Bigot was really unimpressed as a stone under her most subtle manipulation.

Her thoughts ran in a round of ceaseless repetition of the question—"Why can I not subdue Francois Bigot as I have subdued every other man who exposed his weak side to my power?" and Angelique pressed her foot hard upon the floor as the answer returned ever the same—"The heart of the Intendant is away at Beaumanoir! That pale pensive lady"—(Angelique used a more coarse and emphatic word)— "stands between him and me! like a spectre as she is, and sits obstructing the path I have sacrificed so much to enter!—"

"I cannot endure the heat of the ball room! Bigot!" said

Angelique. "I will dance no more tonight! I would rather sit and catch fireflies on the terrace than chase forever without overtaking it, the bird that has escaped from my bosom!—" The Intendant ever attentive to her wishes, offered his arm to lead her into the pleached walks of the illuminated garden. Angelique rose, gathered up her rich train, and with an air of Royal coquettry took his arm and accompanied the Intendant on a promenade down the grand alley of roses.

"What favourite bird has escaped from your bosom, Angelique?" asked the Intendant, who had however a shrewd guess of the meaning of her metaphor.

"The pleasure I had in anticipation of this ball! the bird has flown I know not where or how! I have no pleasure here, at all!" exclaimed she petulantly, although she knew the Ball had really been got up mainly for her own pleasure.

"And yet Momus himself might have been your father and Euphrosyne your mother, Angelique!" replied Bigot "to judge by your gaiety to night. If you have no pleasure, it is because you have given it all away to others! But I have caught the bird you lost let me restore it to your bosom pray!" He laid his hand lightly and caressingly upon her arm—her bosom was beating wildly. She removed his hand and held it firmly grasped in her own.

"Chevalier!" said she, "the pleasure of a King is in the loyalty of his subjects, the pleasure of a woman in the fidelity of her lover!" She was going to say more but stopped. But she gave him a glance which insinuated more than all she left unsaid.

Bigot smiled to himself. "Angelique is jealous!" thought he, but he only remarked "That is an aphorism which I believe with all my heart! If the pleasure of a woman be in the fidelity of her lover, I know no one who should be more happy than Angelique des Meloises! No lady in New France has a right to claim greater devotion from a lover and no one receives it!—"

"But I have no faith in the fidelity of any lover! and I am not happy, Chevalier! far from it!" replied she with one of those impulsive speeches that seemed frankness itself, but in this woman were artful to a degree.

"Why so?" replied he "pleasure will never leave you Angelique, unless you wilfully chase it away from your side—! All women envy your beauty. All men struggle to obtain your smiles. For myself I would gather all the joys and treasures of the world and lay them at your feet, would you let me!—"

"I do not hinder you, Chevalier!" replied she with a laugh of incredulity, "but you do not do it! It is only your politeness to say that! I have told you that the pleasure of a woman is in the fidelity of her lover, tell me now Chevalier, what is the highest pleasure of a man?—"

"The beauty and condescension of his mistress! at least I know none greater!" Bigot looked at her as if his speech ought to receive acknowledgment on the spot.

"And it is your politeness to say that also! Chevalier!" replied she very cooly.

"I wish I could say of your condescension Angelique, what I have said of your beauty. Francois Bigot would then feel the highest pleasure of a man." The Intendant only half knew the woman he was seeking to deceive. She got angry.

Angelique looked up with a scornful flash! "My condescension! Chevalier! to what have I not condescended on the faith of your solemn promise that the Lady of Beaumanoir should not remain under your roof? She is still there! Chevalier! in spite of your promise!—"

Bigot was on the point of denying the fact, but there was sharpness in Angelique's tone and clearness of all doubt in her eyes. He saw he would gain nothing by denial.

"She knows the whole secret, I do believe!" muttered he. "Argus with his hundred eyes was a blind man compared to a woman's two eyes sharpened by jealousy."

"The Lady of Beaumanoir accuses me of no sin, that I repent of—!" replied he. "True! I promised to send her away; and so I will, but she is a woman, a Lady, who has claims upon me for gentle usage. If it were your case, Angelique—"

Angelique quitted his arm and stood confronting him, flaming with indignation. She did not let him finish his sentence. "If it was my case, Bigot! as if that could ever be my case, and you alive to speak of it!"

Bigot stepped backwards. He was not sure but a poniard glittered in the clenched hand of Angelique. It was but the flash of her diamond rings as she lifted it suddenly. She almost struck him.

"Do not blame me for infidelities committed before I knew you, Angelique!" said he, seizing her hand which he held forcibly in his in spite of her efforts to wrench it away. "It is my nature to worship beauty at every shrine. I have done so until I found the concentration of all my divinities in you! I could not, if I would, be unfaithful to you Angelique des Meloises!"—Bigot was a firm believer in the classical faith: that Jove laughs at love's perjuries.

"You mock me Bigot!" replied she. "You are the only man who has ever dared to do so twice."

"When did I mock you twice, Angelique?—" asked he, with an air of injured innocence.

"Now and when you pledged yourself to remove the Lady of Beaumanoir from your house. I admire your courage Bigot in playing false with me, and still hoping to win! But never speak to me more of love while that pale spectre haunts the secret chamber of the Chateau!—"

"She shall be removed, Angelique. Since you insist upon it," replied he, secretly irritated, "but where is the harm? I pledge my faith she shall not stand in the way of my love for you."

"Better she were dead than do so!" whispered Angelique to herself. "It is my due! Bigot!" replied she aloud, "You know what I have given up for your sake!—"

"Yes! I know you have banished Le Gardeur de Repentigny when it had been better to keep him securely in the ranks of the Grand Company. Why did you refuse to marry him Angelique?—"

The question fairly choked her with anger. "Why did I refuse to marry him, Francois Bigot! Do you ask me seriously that question? Did you not tell me of your own love and all but offer me your hand? giving me to understand, miserable sinner that you are! or as you think me to be! did you not pledge your own faith to me, as first in your choice. And I have done that which I had better have been dead and buried with the heaviest pyramid of Egypt on top of me—buried without hope of resurrection—than have done!—"

Bigot accustomed as he was to woman's upbraidings, scarcely knew what to reply to this passionate outburst. He had spoken to her words of love—plenty of them—but the idea of marriage had not flashed across his mind for a moment—not a word of that had escaped his lips. He had as little guessed the height of Angelique's ambition as she had the depths of his craft and wickedness, and yet there was a wonderful similarity between the characters of both—the same bold defiant spirit, the same inordinate ambition, the same void of principle in selecting means to ends—only the one fascinated with the lures of love, the other by the charms of wit, the temptations of money, or effected his purposes by the rough application of force.

"You call me rightly a miserable sinner," said he, half smiling as one not very miserable although a sinner. "If love of fair women be a sin, I am one of the greatest of sinners! and in your fair presence Angelique, I am sinning at this moment, enough to sink a ship load of saints and angels."

"You have sunk me forever in my own and the world's estimation if you mean what you say, Bigot!—" replied she unconsciously tearing in strips the fan she held in her hand. "You love all women too well ever to be capable of fixing your heart upon one!" A tear, of vexation perhaps, stood in her angry eye as she said this, and her cheek twitched with fierce emotion.

"Come Angelique!" said he soothingly. "Some of our guests have entered this alley. Let us walk down to the terrace. The moon is shining brightly over the broad river, and I will swear to you by St Picaut, my patron! whom I never deceive, that my love for all woman kind has not hindered me from fixing my supreme affection upon you."

Angelique allowed him to press her hand which he did with fervour. She almost believed his words. She could hardly imagine another woman seriously preferred to herself, when she chose to flatter a man with a belief of her own preference of him.

They walked down a long alley brilliantly illuminated with lamps of Bohemian Glass which shone like the diamonds, rubies and emeralds which grew upon the trees in the garden of Aladdin.

At every angle of the geometrically cut paths of hard beaten sea shells white as snow stood the statue of a Fawn, a Nymph or Dryad in Parian marble, holding a torch, which illuminated a great vase running over with fresh blooming flowers presenting a vista of royal magnificence which bore testimony to the wealth and splendid tastes of the Intendant.

The garden walks were not deserted. Their beauty drew out many a couple who sauntered merrily, or lovingly down the pleached avenues, which looked like the lobbies of a gorgeously decorated palace.

Bigot and Angelique moved among the guests receiving as they passed obsequious salutations, which to Angelique seemed a foretaste of royalty. She had seen the Gardens of the Palace many times before, but never illuminated as now. The sight of them so grandly decorated filled her with admiration of their owner, and she resolved that cost what it would, the homage paid to her tonight as the partner of the Intendant should become hers by right on his hearthstone as the first lady in New France.

Angelique threw back her veil that all might see her, that the women might envy and the men admire her, as she leaned confidingly on the arm of Bigot looking up in his face with that wonderful smile of hers which had brought so many men to ruin at her feet and talking with such enchantment as no woman could talk but Angelique des Meloises.

Well understanding that her only road to success was to completely fascinate the Intendant, she bent herself to the task with such power of witchery and such simulation of real passion, that Bigot wary and experienced Gladiator as he was in the arena of love, was more than once brought to the brink of a proposal for her hand.

She watched every movement of his features, at these critical moments when he seemed just falling into the snares so artfully set for him. When she caught his eyes glowing with passionate admiration, she shyly affected to withdraw them from his gaze, turning on him at times flashes of her dark eyes which electrified every nerve of his sensuous nature. She felt the pressure of his hand, the changed and softened inflections of his voice. She knew the words of her fate were trembling on his lips, and yet they did not come! The shadow of that pale hand at Beaumanoir, weak and delicate as it was, seemed to lay itself upon his lips, when about to speak to her, and snatch away the words which Angelique trembling with anticipation was ready to barter away body and soul to hear spoken.

In a shady passage through a thick greenery where the lights were dimmer and no one was near, she allowed his arm for a moment to encircle her yielding form, and she knew by his quick breath that the words were moulded in his thoughts, and were on the point to rush forth in a torrent of speech. Still they came not, and Bigot again to her unutterable disgust, shied off, like a full blooded horse which starts suddenly away from some object by the wayside, and throws his rider headlong on the ground. So again and again were dashed the ardent expectations of Angelique.

She listened to the gallant and gay speeches of Bigot, which seemed to flutter like birds round her but never lit on the ground where she had spread her net like a crafty fowler as she was, until she almost went mad with suppressed anger and passionate excitement. But she kept on replying with badinage light as his own, and with laughter so soft and silvery, that it seemed a gentle dew from Heaven, instead of the drift and flying foam of the storm that was raging in her bosom.

She read and reread glimpses of his hidden thoughts that went and came like faces in a dream, and she saw in her imagination the dark pleading eyes and pale face of the Lady of Beaumanoir. It came now like a revelation, confirming a thousand suspicions that Bigot loved that pale sad face too well, ever to marry Angelique des Meloises while its possessor lived at Beaumanoir or while she lived at all!—

And it came to that! In this walk with Bigot round the glorious garden with God's flowers shedding fragrance around them, with God's stars shining overhead above all the glitter and illusion of the thousand lamps, Angelique repeated to herself—the terrific words—"Bigot loves that pale sad face too well ever to marry me, while its possessor lives at Beaumanoir or while she lives at all!—"

The thought haunted her! It would not leave her!—She leaned heavily upon his arm, as she swept like a Queen of Cyprus through the flower bordered walks, brushing the roses and lilies with her proud train and treading with as dainty a foot as ever bewitched human eye the white paths, that led back to the grand terrace of the Palace.

Her fevered imagination played tricks in keeping with her fear. More than once she fancied she saw the shadowy form of a beautiful woman, walking on the other side of Bigot next his heart! It was the form of Caroline bearing a child in one arm and claiming by that supreme appeal to a man's heart, the first place in his affections.

The figure sometimes vanished, sometimes reappeared in the same place, and once and the last time assumed the figure and look of our Lady of St Foye, triumphant after a thousand sufferings, and still ever bearing the face and look of the Lady of Beaumanoir.

Emerging at last from the dim avenue into the full light, where a fountain sent up showers of sparkling crystals, the figure vanished and Angelique sat down on a quaintly carved seat, under a mountain ash, very tired and profoundly vexed at all things and with everybody.

A servant in gorgeous livery brought a message from the Ballroom to the Intendant.

He was summoned for a dance but he would not leave Angelique, he said, but Angelique begged for a short rest. "It was so pleasant in the garden. She would remain by the fountain. She liked its sparkling and splashing. It refreshed her. The Intendant could come for her in half an hour and she wanted to be alone. She felt in a hard unamiable mood," she said "and he only made her worse by stopping with her when others wanted him, and he wanted others!—"

The Intendant protested in terms of the warmest gallantry, that he would not leave her, but seeing Angelique really desired at the present moment to be alone, and reflecting that he was himself sacrificing too much for the sake of one Goddess, while a hundred others were adorned and waiting for his offerings, he promised in half an hour to return for her to this spot by the fountain and proceeded towards the Palace.

Angelique sat watching the play and sparkle of the fountain which she compared to her own vain exertions to fascinate the Intendant, and thought that her efforts had been just as brilliant and just as futile.

She was sadly perplexed. There was a depth in Bigot's character which she could not fathom—a bottomless abyss into which she was falling and could not save herself. Which ever way she turned the Eidolon of Caroline met her as a bar to all further progress in her design upon the Intendant.

The dim half vision of Caroline which she had seen in the pleached walk, she knew was only the shadow and projection of her own thoughts, a brooding fancy which she had unconsciously conjured up into the form of her hated rival. The addition of the child was the creation of the deep and jealous imaginings, which had often crossed her mind. She thought of that yet unborn pledge of a once mutual affection, as the secret spell by which Caroline, pale and feeble as she was, still held the heart of the Intendant in some sort of allegiance.

"It is that vile weak thing!" said she bitterly, and angrily to herself, "which is stronger than I. It is by that she excites his pity and pity draws after it the renewal of his love! If the hope of what is not yet, be so potent with Bigot, what will not the reality prove ere long? the annihilation of all my brilliant anticipations!—I have drawn a blank in life's lottery, by the rejection of Le Gardeur for his sake!—It is the hand of that shadowy babe which plucks away the words of proposal from the lips of Bigot, which gives his love to its vile mother, and leaves to me the mere ashes of his passion, words which mean nothing, which will never mean anything but insult to Angelique des Meloises, so long as that woman lives to claim the hand which but for her would be mine!—"

Dark fancies fluttered across the mind of Angelique during the absence of the Intendant. They came like a flight of birds of evil omen, ravens, choughs and owls, the embodiments of wicked thoughts. But such thoughts suited her mood and she neither chid nor banished them, but let them light and brood and hatch fresh mischief in her soul.

She looked up to see who was laughing so merrily while she was so angry and so sad, and beheld the Intendant jesting, and toying with a cluster of laughing girls who had caught him at the turn of the broad stair of the Terrace. They kept him there in utter oblivion of Angelique! Not that she cared for his presence at that moment or felt angry as she would have done at a neglect of Le Gardeur, but it was one proof among a thousand others, that gallant and gay as he was among the throng of fair guests who were flattering and tempting him on every side, not one of them herself included could feel sure she had made an impression lasting longer than the present moment, upon the heart of the Intendant.

The company had for the most part left the garden to assemble again in the brilliant ballroom, where louder as the spirit of gaiety waxed higher, rose the voluptuous strains of the orchestra, pouring out from its high gallery as from a volcano of harmony, the ravishing airs of Lulli and Destouches while the figures of the dancers glanced to and fro past the windows of the Ballroom, which opened broad and evenly upon the Terrace.

But Bigot had neither forgotten Angelique nor himself. His wily spirit was contriving how best to give an impetus to his intrigue with her, without committing himself to any promise of marriage. He resolved to bring this beautiful but exacting girl wholly under his power. He comprehended fully that Angelique was prepared to accept his hand at any moment, nay almost demanded it, but the price of marriage was what Bigot would not, dared not pay, and as a true courtier of the period he believed thoroughly in his ability to beguile any woman he chose and cheat her of the price she set upon her love.

CHAPTER 32

THE BALL AT THE INTENDANT'S PALACE

THE bevy of fair girls still surrounded Bigot on the terrace stair. Some of them stood leaning in graceful pose upon the ballusters. The wily girls knew his artistic tastes, and their pretty feet patted time to the music while they responded with ready glee to the gossiping of the gay Intendant.

Amid their idle badinage Bigot inserted an artful inquiry, for suggestion not for information, whether it was true that his friend Le Gardeur de Repentigny now at the Manor House of Tilly had become affianced to his cousin Heloise de Lotbiniere? There was a start of surprise, and great curiosity at once manifested among the ladies, some of whom protested that it could not be true, for they knew better in what direction Le Gardeur's inclinations pointed. Others more compassionate or more spiteful; with a touch of envy, said they hoped it was true!—for he had been jilted by a young lady in the City—whom they all knew!—added one sparkling Demoiselle, giving herself a twitch and throwing a side glance which mimicked so perfectly the manner of the lady hinted at, that all knew in a moment, she meant no other than Angelique des Meloises! They all laughed merrily at the conceit, and agreed that Le Gardeur de Repentigny would only serve the proud flirt right, by marrying Heloise, and showing the world how little he cared for Angelique.

"Or how much!" suggested an experienced and lively widow, Madame La Touche. "I think his marrying Heloise de Lotbiniere will only prove the desperate condition of his feelings. He will marry her not because he loves her, but to spite Angelique. I have known such things done before," added the widow seriously, and the girls whispered to one another that she had done it herself! when she married the Sieur La Touche out of shear vexation at not getting the Sieur de Marne who took another woman for her money and left the widow to light fires where she could with her charms!

The Intendant had reckoned securely on the success of his ruse. The words were scarcely spoken before a couple of close friends of Angelique found her out and sitting one on each side resting their hands on her shoulders, poured into her ears an exaggerated story of the coming marriage of Le Gardeur with Heloise de Lotbiniere!

Angelique believed them because it seemed the natural consequence of her own infidelity. False herself she had no right to expect him to be true. Still loving Le Gardeur in spite of her rejection of him, it maddened her with jealousy to hear that another had taken that place in his affections where she so lately reigned supreme and alone. She was angry with him for what she called his "faithlessness," and still more angry at herself for being the cause of it!—

Her friends who were watching her with all a woman's curiosity and acuteness were secretly pleased to see that their news had cut her to the quick. They were not misled by the affected indifference and gay laughter which veiled the resentment which was plainly visible in her agitated bosom.

Her two friends left her to report back to their companions, with many exaggerations and much pursing of pretty lips, how Angelique had received their communication. They flattered themselves they had had the pleasure of first breaking the bad tidings to her, but they were mistaken! Angelique's far reaching curiosity had touched Tilly with its antennae and she had already learned of the visit of Heloise de Lotbiniere, an old school companion of her own to the Manor House of Tilly.

She had scented danger afar off from that visit. She knew that Heloise worshipped Le Gardeur, and now that Angelique had cast him off, what more natural than that he should fall at last into her snares—so Angelique scornfully termed the beauty and amiable character of her rival. She was angry without reason and she knew it. But that made her still more angry and with still less reason.—

"Bigot!" said she impetuously, as the Intendant rejoined her when the half hour had elapsed, "You asked me a question in the Castle of St Louis, leaning on the high gallery which overlooks the cliffs! Do you remember it?—"

"I do! one does not forget easily what one asks of a beautiful woman, and still less the reply she—she makes to us," replied he looking at her sharply, for he guessed her drift.

"Yet, you seem to have forgotten both the question and the reply Bigot! Shall I repeat them?—" said she with an air of affected languour.

"Needless! Angelique! and to prove to you the strength of my memory which is but another name for the strength of my admiration, I will repeat it. I asked you that night—It was a glorious night the bright moon shone full in our faces as we looked over the shining river, but your eyes eclipsed all the splendour of the Heavens—I asked you to give me your love. I asked for it then Angelique! I ask for it now."

Angelique was pleased with the flattery even while she knew how hollow and conventional a thing it was.

"You said all that before, Bigot!" replied she, "and you added a foolish speech, which I confess pleased me that night better than now. You said that in me you had found the fair haven of your desires where your bark, long tossing in cross seas and beating against adverse winds, would cast anchor and be at rest,—the phrase sounded poetical if enigmatical, but it pleased me somehow—what did it mean Bigot? I have puzzled over it many times since, pray tell me!"

Angelique turned her eyes like two blazing stars full upon him as if to search for every trace of hidden thought that lurked in his countenance.

"I meant what I said, Angelique! that in you I had found the pearl of price which I would rather call mine than wear a king's crown."

"You explain one enigma by another. The pearl of price lay there before you and you picked it up! It had been the pride of its former owner, but you found it ere it was lost.

What did you with it Bigot?"

The Intendant knew as well as she, the drift of the angry tide, which was again setting in full upon him, but he doubted not his ability to escape. His real contempt for women was the life boat he trusted in which had carried himself and fortunes out of a hundred storms and tempests of feminine wrath.

"I wore the precious pearl next my heart as any gallant gentleman should do!" replied he blandly. "I would have worn it inside my heart could I have shut it up there."

Bigot smiled in complacent self approval at his own speech. Not so Angelique! she was irritated by his general reference to the duty of a gallant gentleman to the sex and not to his own special duty as the admirer of herself.

Angelique was like an angry Pantheress at this moment. The darts of jealousy just planted by her two friends, tore her side and she felt reckless both as to what she said and what she did. With a burst of passion, not rare in women like her, she turned her wrath full upon him, the nearest object, she struck Bigot with her clenched hand upon the breast, exclaiming with wild vehemence—

"You lie! Francois Bigot! you never wore me next your heart, although you said so! you wear the Lady of Beaumanoir next your heart. You have opened your heart to her, after pledging it to me!—If I was the pearl of price, you have adorned her neck with it—my abasement is her glory!" Angelique's tall straight figure stood up magnified with fury as she uttered this.

The Intendant stept back in surprise at the sudden attack. Had the blow fallen upon his face, such is human nature, Bigot would have regarded it as an unpardonable insult, but falling upon his breast, he burst out in a loud laugh as he caught hold of her quivering hand which she plucked passionately away from him.

The eyes of Angelique looked dangerous and full of mischief, but Bigot was not afraid or offended. In truth her jealousy flattered him, applying it wholy to himself. He was moreover a connoisseur in female temper. He liked to see the storm of jealous rage to watch the rising of its black clouds, to witness the lightening and the thunder, the gusts and whirlwinds of passion followed by the rain of angry tears, when the tears were on his account. He thought he had never seen so beautiful a Fury as Angelique was at that moment.

Her pointed epithet you lie! which it would have been death to a man to utter, made no dint on the polished armour of Bigot although he inly resolved that she should pay a woman's penalty for it.

He had heard that word from other pretty lips before; but it left no mark upon a conscience that was one stain, upon a life that was one lie. Still his bold spirit rather liked this bold utterance from an angry woman, when it was in his power by a word to change her rage into the tender cooing of a dove.

Bigot was by nature a hunter of women and preferred the excitement of a hard chase when the deer turns at bay, and its capture gave him a trophy to be proud of, to the dull conquest of a tame and easy virtue, such as were most of those which had fallen in his way.

"Angelique!" said he, "this is perfect madness—what means this burst of anger? do you doubt the sincerity of my love for you?"

"I do Bigot! I doubt it, and I deny it! So long as you keep a mistress concealed at Beaumanoir your pledge to me is false and your love an insult."

"You are too impetuous and too imperious, Angelique! I have promised she shall be removed from Beaumanoir—and she shall."

"Whither? and when?"

"To the City! and in a few days—she can live there in quiet seclusion. I cannot be cruel to her Angelique."

"But you can be cruel to me Bigot! and will be unless you exercise the power which I know is placed in your hands by the King himself."

"What is that? to confiscate her lands and goods if she had any?"

"No! to confiscate her person! Issue a *lettre de Cachet* and send her over sea to the Bastile."

Bigot was irritated at this suggestion, and his irritation was narrowly watched by Angelique.

"I would rather go to the Bastile myself!" exclaimed he, "besides the King alone issues *lettres de Cachet*. It is a royal prerogative, only to be used in matters of state."

"And matters of love Bigot!—which are matters of state in France! Pshaw! as if I did not know that the King delegates his authority and gives *Lettres de Cachet* in blank to his trusted courtiers and even to the ladies of his Court. Did not the Marquise de Pompadour send Mademoiselle Vaubernier to the Bastile for only smiling upon the King? It is a small thing I ask of you Bigot, to test your fidelity you cannot refuse me! Come!" added she with a wondrous transformation of look and manner, from storm and gloom to warmth and sunshine.

"I cannot and will not do it! Hark you Angelique I dare not do it! Powerful as I may seem, the family of that lady are too potent to risk the experiment upon. I would fain oblige you in this matter, but it would be the height of madness to do so."

"Well then Bigot, do this! if you will not do that! Place her in the Convent of the Ursulines. It will suit her and me both! No better place in the world, to tame an unruly spirit. She is one of the pious souls who will be at home there, with plenty of prayers, and penances, and plenty of sins to pray for every day."

"But I cannot force her to enter the Convent Angelique. She will think herself not good enough to go there, besides the Nuns themselves would have scruples to receive her."

"Not if *you* request her admission of Mere de la Nativité! The lady Superior will refuse no application of yours, Bigot!"

"Wont she! but she will! The Mere de la Nativité considers me a sad reprobate, and has already when I visited her parlour read me a couple of sharpest homilies on my evil ways as she called them. The venerable Mere de la Nativité will not carry coals! I assure you Angelique!—"

"As if I did not know her!" replied she impatiently. "Why, she screens with all her authority that wild nephew of hers, the Sieur Varin—! Nothing irritates her like hearing a bad report of him, and although she knows all that is said of him to be true as her breviary, she will not admit it! The *Soeurs Converses* in the laundry were put on bread and water with prayers for a week, only for repeating some gossip they had heard concerning him."

"Aye! that is because the venerable Mere Superior is touchy on the point of family—but I am not her nephew, *voilà la différence*! as the song says!—"

"Well! but you are her nephew's master and patron," replied Angelique, "and the good Mere will strain many points to oblige the Intendant of New France for sake of the Sieur Varin. You do not know her as I do, Bigot!"

"What do you advise Angelique?" asked he curious to see what was working in her brain.

"That if you will not issue a *Lettre de Cachet* you shall place the Lady of Beaumanoir in the hands of the Mere de la Nativité, with instructions to receive her into the community after the shortest probation."

"Very good Angelique! But if I do not know the Mere Superior, you do not know the Lady of Beaumanoir! There are reasons why the Nuns would not, and could not receive her at all, even were she willing to go, as I think she would be. But I will provide her a home suited to her station in the City, only you must promise to speak to me no more respecting her."

"I will promise no such thing Bigot!" said Angelique firing up again at the failure of her crafty plan for the disposal of Caroline. "To have her in the City will be worse than to have her at Beaumanoir—!—"

"Are you afraid of the poor girl Angelique? You with your surpassing beauty, grace and power over all who approach you? She cannot touch you!"

"She has touched me, and to the quick too already" she replied colouring with passion "You love that girl, Francois Bigot! I am never deceived in men! You love her too well to give her up, and still you make love to me! what am I to think?"

"Think that you women are able to upset any mans reason, and make fools of us all to your own purposes." Bigot saw the uselessness of argument, but she would not drop the topic.

"So you say, and so I have found it with others," replied she, "but not with you Bigot! But I shall have been made the fool of, unless I carry my point in regard to this lady."

"Well! trust to me Angelique! Hark you! there are reasons of state connected with her. Her father has powerful friends at Court and I must act warily—give me your hand, we will be friends! I will carry out your wishes to the furthest possible stretch of my power. I can say no more."

Angelique gave him her hand. She saw she could not carry her point with the Intendant and her fertile brain was now scheming another way to accomplish her ends. She had already undergone a revulsion of feeling and repented having carried her resentment so far, not that she felt it less but she was cunning and artful, although her temper sometimes overturned her craft and made wreck of her schemes.

"I am sorry, I was so angry Bigot, as to strike you with this feeble hand!" Angelique smiled as she extended her dainty fingers which delicate as they were had the strength and elasticity of steel.

"Not so feeble either, Angelique!" replied he laughing, "few men could plant a better blow! you hit me on the heart fairly, Angelique!—" He seized her hand and lifted it to his lips. "Had Queen Dido possessed that hand she would have held fast *pius Æneus* himself when he ran away from his engagements."

Angelique pressed the Intendants hand with a grasp that left every vein bloodless. "As I hold fast to you Bigot! and hold you to your engagements! Thank God, that you are not a woman! If you were, I think I should kill you! but as you are a man I forgive and take your promise of amendment. It is what foolish women always do."

The sound of the music and the measured tread of feet in the lively dances were now plainly heard in the pauses of their conversation.

They rose and entered the Ball room. The music ceased and recommenced a new strain for the Intendant and his fair partner, and for a time Angelique forgot her wrath in the delirious excitement of the dance.

She possessed in an eminent degree the power of hiding her ungracious moods under a mask of deceit impenetrable. With a chameleon like faculty she could assume the complexion of the company that surrounded her, when it suited her purpose to do so.

But in the dance her exuberance of spirits overflowed like a fountain of intoxicating wine. She cared not for things past or future in the extatic joy of the present.

Her voluptuous beauty lissomness and grace of movement enthralled all eyes with admiration as she danced with the Intendant, who was himself no mean votary of Terpsichore. A lock of her long golden hair broke loose and streamed in wanton disorder over her shoulders. But she heeded it not, carried away by the spirit of the dance and the triumph of present possession in the courtly Intendant. Her dainty feet flashed under her flying robe and seemed scarcely to touch the floor as they kept time to the swift throbbings of the music.

The Intendant gazed with rapture on his beautiful partner as she leaned upon his arm in the pauses of the dance and thought more than once that world would be well lost for sake of such a woman. It was but a passing fancy however, and the serious mood passed away when he was weary long before Angelique of the excitement and breathless heat of a wild Polish Dance recently first heard of in French society. He led her to a seat and left her in the center of a swarm of admirers, and passed into an alcove to cool and rest himself.

CHAPTER 33

"ON WITH THE DANCE"

BIGOT, a voluptuary in every sense, craved a change of pleasure. He was never satisfied long with one, however pungent. He felt it as a relief when Angelique went off like a laughing sprite upon the arm of De Pean. "I am glad to get rid of the women sometimes and feel like a man!" he said to Cadet, who sat drinking and telling stories with hilarious laughter to two or three boon companions and indulging in the coarsest jests and broadest scandal about the ladies at the ball, as they passed by the alcove where they were seated.

The eager persistence of Angelique in her demand for a *lettre de Cachet* to banish the unfortunate Caroline, had wearied and somewhat disgusted Bigot.

"I would cut the throat of any man in the world, for the sake of her bright eyes," said he to himself as she gave him a parting salute with her handkerchief, "but she must not ask me to hurt that poor foolish girl at Beaumanoir—! No, by St Picot! *she* is hurt enough already! and I will not have Angelique tormenting her!—What merciless creatures women are to one another, Cadet!" said he aloud.

Cadet looked up with red enflamed eyes at the remark of Bigot. He cared nothing for women himself, and never hesitated to show his contempt for the whole sex.

"Merciless creatures! do you call them Bigot? the claws of all the cats in Caen could not match the finger-nails of a jealous woman—still less her biting tongue."

"And they are all either envious or jealous I believe Cadet," replied Bigot laughing.

''Either envious or jealous?'' exclaimed Cadet contemptuously, "they are all both the one and the other!

383

Bigot, tame cats in their maudlin affections purring and rubbing against you, one moment, wild cats in their anger, flying at you and drawing blood the next—! Esops fable of the cat turned woman who forsook her bridal bed to catch a mouse, is as true of the sex as if he had been their maker."

"All the cats in Caen could not have matched Pretiosa! eh Cadet?" replied Bigot with allusion to a nocturnal adventure from which Cadet had escaped like Fabius—*discinta tunica*. "Pretiosa proved to an ocular demonstration, that no wild cat's claws can equal the nails of a jealous woman."

The Intendant's quip roused the merriment of the party, and Cadet who gloried in every shame, laughed loudest of them all.

"*Sauve qui peut!* Bigot!" ejaculated he, shaking his lusty sides. "I left some of my hair in the fingers of Pretiosa, but there was no help for it! I was as handsomely tonsured as the Abbé de Bernis! But wait Bigot until your own Pretiosa overtakes you on the road to ruin in company with—Dont twitch me Martel!—You are drunk! Bigot does not care a fig what we say!"

This was addressed to his companion who stood somewhat in awe of the Intendant, but needlessly, as Cadet well knew, for among his familiars, Bigot was the most free of boon companions. He delighted in the coarsest allusions, and was ever ready to give and take the broadest personal jibes with good humour and utter indifference to character or reputation.

The Intendant with a loud explosion of laughter sat down to the table, and holding out a long stemmed goblet of Beauvais to be filled with sparkling wine, replied gaily:

"You never spoke a truer word Cadet! though you did not know it! *My* Pretiosa yonder!" said he, pointing to Angelique, who flashed by in the dance, "would put to his trumps the best player in Paris to win the odd trick of her, and not count by honours either—!"

"But you will win the odd trick of that girl yet Bigot, and not count by honours either! or I know nothing of women," replied Cadet bluntly. "They are all alike! only some are more likely! The Pipers of Poictiers never played a spring that Angelique des Meloises would not dance to—! Look at De Pean how pleased he is with her! She is fooling him to his finger ends! He believes she is dancing with *him*, and all the time she is dancing to nobody but *you* Bigot!—"

"Well! I rather admire the way she leads De Pean such a dance! She makes a jolly fool of him, and she knows I see it too!"

"Just like them all!—full of deceit as an egg of Satan is full of mischief! Damn them all! Bigot! A man is not worth his salt in the world, until he has done with the women!"

"You are a Cynic! Cadet!" replied Bigot laughing. "Diogenes in his tub would call you brother, and ask you to share his house. But Athens never produced a girl like that. Aspasia and Thaïs were not fit to light her to bed."

"Angelique will go without a light, or I am mistaken Bigot! But it is dry talking. Take another glass of Champagne, Bigot!" Cadet with a free hand filled for Bigot and the others. The wine seemed gradually to mollify his harsh opinion of the sex.

"I know from experience Bigot," continued he after he had drank, "that every man is a fool once at least in his life time to women, and if you lose your wits for Angelique des Meloises, why she is pretty enough to excuse you. Now that is all I have got to say about her. Drink again Bigot!"

Angelique whirled again past the alcove, without looking in except by a glance so quick and subtle that Ariel herself could not have caught it. She saw the eyes of the Intendant following her motions, and her feet shot a thousand scintillations of witchery as her robe fluttered undulating round her shapely limbs revealing beauties which the freedom of the dance allowed to flash forth without censure, except on the part of a few elderly matrons who sat exchanging comments and making comparisons between the looks and demeanour of the various dancers.

"Observe the Intendant, Madame Couillard!" exclaimed Madame de Grandmaison. "He has not taken his eyes off Angelique des Meloises for the last ten minutes, and she knows it! the forward minx! She would not dance with such

zest merely to please the Chevalier de Pean, whom she hates.
I think the Intendant would look better on the floor dancing
with some of our girls, who are waiting for the honour, instead
of drinking wine and rivetting his eyes upon that piece of
assurance!—"

"I quite agree with you Madame de Grandmaison," replied
Madame Couillard, who having no daughters to bring out,
could view the matter more philosophically than her friend.
"But they say the Intendant particularly admires a fine foot
and ankle in a woman!"

"I think so, by the way he watches hers," was the tart reply,
"and she humours his taste too! Angelique is vain of her foot
as she is of her face. She once vexed the entire Convent, by
challenging them all, pupils, Nuns and postulantes to match
the perfect symmetry of her foot and leg!—She would make
the world her footstool, when she came out! she told them,
and she laughed in the face of the Venerable Mere de la
Nativité who threatened her with heavy penances to atone for
the wicked words she uttered."

"And she defies the world still as she used to defy the
Convent," replied Madame Couillard quite genteely shocked.
"Look at her now! did you ever see such *abandon* and how
the gentlemen all admire her! Well, girls have no shame
nowadays! I am glad I have no daughters, Madame de
Grandmaison!"

This was a side shot of Madame Couillard at her friend,
and it went home. Madame Couillard never scrupled to make
a target of a friend, if nothing better offered.

"Neices are just as bad as daughters! Madame Couillard!"
replied the Matron, bridling up and directing a half scornful
look at a group of lively girls who were engaged in a desperate
flirtation upon the seats farthest under the gallery, and as
they supposed well out of sight of their keen chaperone,
who saw them very well however, but being satisfied with the
company they were in, would not see more of them than the
occasion called for! Madame Couillard had set her mind upon
bestowing the care and charge of her troublesome neices
upon young de la Roque and the Sieur de Bourget—she was

therefore delighted to see her pretty brace of man-catchers running down the game so handsomely.

The black eyed girls gay as Columbines and crafty as their aunt herself, plied their gallants with a very fair imitation of the style and manner of Angelique, as the most effectual mode of ensnaring the roving fancies of their gallants. They all hated Angelique cordially for the airs they accused her of putting on, and still more for the success of her airs, but did their utmost nevertheless to copy her peculiar style, and so justified by this feminine homage, her claim to look down upon them with a sort of easy superiority, as the Queen of fashion in the gay society of the Capital.

"Angelique likes to dance with the Chevalier de Pean!" replied Madame Couillard quickly turning the conversation to less personal ground. "She thinks that his ugliness sets off her own attractions to greater advantage! That is why she dances with him—!"

"And well may she think so! for an uglier man than the Chevalier de Pean is not to be found in New France—! My daughters all think so too!" replied Madame de Grandmaison, who felt with some resentment that her own daughters had been slighted by the rich though ugly Chevalier de Pean.

"Yes, De Pean avoided them all the evening, although they looked their eyes out the way he was," thought Madame Couillard to herself, but spoke in her politest manner.

"But he is rich they say as Croesus, and very influential with the Intendant! Few girls nowadays would mind his ugliness any more than Angelique, for the sake of his wealth! But Angelique knows she is drawing the eyes of the Chevalier Bigot after her. That is enough for her! She would dance with a Hobgoblin to charm the Intendant with her pretty paces!"

"She has no shame! I would cut the feet off my girls if they presumed to run striding about as she does," replied Madame de Grandmaison with a look of scorn on lip and eyebrow. "I always taught my daughters a chaste and modest demeanour. I trained them properly when young. I used in Creole fashion to tie their ankles together with a ribbon when in the house, and never permitted them to exceed the length of two spans at a step. It is that gives that nice tripping walk which the gentlemen so much admire, and which everyone notices in my girls and in my self Madame Couillard! I learned that secret in the Antilles, where the ladies all learn to walk like angels."

"Indeed! I often wondered how the Demoiselles Grandmaisons had acquired that nice tripping step of theirs, which makes them so distinguished among the *Haut Ton* of the City!" said Madame Couillard with an imperceptible sneer. "I did not know they had been to walking school!"

"Is it not admirable? Madame Couillard! Gentlemen are often more taken by the feet than by the face."

"I dare say when the feet are the better feature of the two—! But men are such dupes, Madame de Grandmaison! some fall in love with an eye, some with a nose, or a curl, a hand an ankle and as you remark a foot—few care for a heart, for it is not seen! I know one gentleman who was caught by the waft of a skirt against his knee!" and Madame Couillard laughed at the recollection of some past incident in her own days of love making.

"A nice gait is indeed a great step in feminine education!" was the summing up of the matter by Madame de Grandmaison. "It is the first lesson in moral propriety and the foundation of all female excellence! I have impressed its importance with all my force upon the good Ursulines, as being worthy of a foremost place in their programme of studies for the young ladies entrusted to their pious care, and I have some hope of its being adopted by them. If it is future generations of our girls will walk like Angels on clouds and not step out like race horses in the fashion of Angelique des Meloises."

This was very ill natured of Madame de Grandmaison— shere envy in fact! for her daughters were at that moment attitudinizing their best in imitation of the natural freedom of Angelique's graceful movements.

Angelique des Meloises swept past the two matrons in a storm of music as if in defiance of their sage criticisms. Her hand rested on the shoulder of the Chevalier de Pean. While hating the touch of him, she had an object made her endure it—and her dissimulation was perfect. Her eyes transfixed his with their dazzling look. Her lips were wreathed in smiles, she talked continually as she danced, and with an inconsistency which did not seem strange in her, was lamenting the absence from the ball of Le Gardeur de Repentigny.

"Chevalier!" said she in reply to some gallantry of her partner. "Most women take pride in making sacrifices of themselves. I prefer to sacrifice my admirers! I like a man not in the measure of what I do for him, but what he will do for me! Is not that a candid avowal, Chevalier? You like frankness you know!"

Frankness and the Chevalier de Pean were unknown qualities together, but he was desperately smitten and would bear any amount of snubbing from Angelique.

"You have something in your mind you wish me to do!" replied he eagerly. "I would poison my grandmother if you asked me, for the reward you could give me—!"

"Yes, I have something in my mind, Chevalier! but not concerning your grandmother. Tell me why you allowed Le Gardeur de Repentigny to leave the City?"

"I did not allow him to leave the City," said he, twitching his ugly features, for he disliked the interest she expressed in Le Gardeur. "I would fain have kept him here if I could. The Intendant too had desperate need of him. It was his Sister and Colonel Philibert who spirited him away from us."

"Well! a ball in Quebec is not worth twisting a curl for in the absence of Le Gardeur de Repentigny!" replied she. "You shall promise me to bring him back to the City Chevalier, or I will dance with you no more—!—"

Angelique laughed so gaily as she said this that a stranger would have interpreted her words as all jest.

"She means it nevertheless!" thought the Chevalier. "I will promise my best endeavour, Mademoiselle" said he setting hard his teeth with a grimace of dissatisfaction which did not escape the eye of Angelique. "Moreover the Intendant desires his return on affairs of the Grand Company and has sent more than one message to him already to urge his return."

"A fig for the grand Company! remember! it is *I* desire his return, and it is my command not the Intendants, which you are bound as a gallant gentleman to obey—!"—Angelique would have no divided allegiance and the man who claimed her favours must give himself up body and soul without thought of redemption.

She felt very reckless and very wilful at this moment. The laughter on her lips was the ebullition of a hot and angry heart not the play of joyous happy spirit. Bigot's refusal of a *Lettre de Cachet* had stung her pride to the quick and excited a feeling of resentment which found its expression in the wish for the return of Le Gardeur.

"Why do you desire the return of Le Gardeur?" asked De Pean, hesitatingly. Angelique was often too frank by half and questioners got from her more than they liked to hear.

"Because he was my first admirer and I never forget a true friend, Chevalier—!—" replied she with an undertone of fond regret in her voice.

"But he will not be your last admirer," replied De Pean with what he considered a seductive leer, which made her laugh at him. "In the kingdom of love as in the kingdom of heaven the last shall be first, and the first last! May I be the last, Mademoiselle?"

"You will certainly be the last De Pean! I promise that!" Angelique laughed provokingly. She saw the eye of the Intendant watching her. She began to think he remained longer in the society of Cadet, than was due to herself.

"Thanks Mademoiselle!" said De Pean hardly knowing whether her laugh was affirmative or negative "but I envy Le Gardeur his precedence!"

Angelique's love for Le Gardeur was the only key which ever unlocked her real feelings. When the fox praised the raven's voice and prevailed on her to sing, He did not more surely make her drop the envied morsel out of her mouth than did Angelique drop the mystification she had worn so coquettishly before De Pean.

"Tell me De Pean!" said she, "is it true or no that Le Gardeur de Repentigny is consoling himself among the woods of Tilly, with a fair cousin of his, Heloise de Lotbiniere?"

De Pean had his revenge, and he took it. "It is true! and no wonder! They say Heloise is without exception the sweetest girl in New France, if not one of the handsomest."

"Without exception?" echoed she scornfully. "The women will not believe that at any rate, Chevalier! I do not believe it for one!" And she laughed in her consciousness of beauty— "do you believe it?"

"No! that were impossible," replied he "while Angelique des Meloises chooses to contest the palm of beauty."

"I contest no palm with *her* Chevalier, but I give you this rosebud for your gallant speech, but tell me, what does Le Gardeur think of this wonderful beauty? Is there any talk of marriage?"

"There is of course! much talk of an alliance!" De Pean lied, but the truth had been better for him.

Angelique started as if stung by a wasp. The dance ceased for her, and she hastened to a seat. "De Pean!" said she, "you promised to bring Le Gardeur forthwith back to the City—, will you do it?"

"I will bring him back dead or alive if you desire it! but I must have time. That uncompromising Colonel Philibert is with him. His sister too clings to him like a good angel to the skirt of a sinner. Since you desire it"—De Pean spoke it with bitterness—"Le Gardeur shall come back, but I doubt if it will be for his benefit or yours, Mademoiselle!"

"What do you mean De Pean?" asked she abruptly, her dark eyes alight with eager curiosity not unmingled with apprehension. "Why do you doubt it will not, be for his benefit or mine. Who is to harm him?"

"Nay, he will only harm himself Angelique! and by St Picot! he will have ample scope for doing it in this City! He has no other enemy but himself." De Pean felt that she was making an ox of him to draw the plough of her scheming.

"Are you sure of that, De Pean?" demanded she sharply.

"Quite sure! are not all the associates of the Grand Company his fastest friends? not one of them hurts him I am sure—!"

"Chevalier De Pean!" said she noticing the slight shrug he gave when he said this, "you say, Le Gardeur has no enemy but himself—if so, I hope to save him from himself, nothing more! therefore I want him back to the City."

De Pean glanced towards Bigot. "Pardon me Mademoiselle! Did the Intendant never speak to you of Le Gardeur's abrupt departure?" asked he.

"Never! he has spoken to you though! what did he say?" asked she with eager curiosity.

"He said that you might have detained him, had you wished, and he blamed you for his departure."

De Pean had a suspicion that Angelique had really been instrumental in withdrawing Le Gardeur from the clutches of himself and associates, but in this he erred. Angelique loved Le Gardeur at least for her own sake if not for his, and would have preferred he should risk all the dangers of the City to avoid what she deemed the still greater dangers of the Country, and the greatest of these in her opinion was the fair face of Heloise de Lotbiniere. While from motives of ambition Angelique refused to marry him herself she could not bear the thought of another getting the man whom she had rejected.

De Pean was fairly puzzled by her caprices. He could not fathom, but he dared not oppose them.

At this moment Bigot who had waited for the conclusion of a game of cards, rejoined the group where she sat.

Angelique drew in her robe and made room for him beside her, and was presently laughing and talking as free from care apparently as an Oriole warbling on a summer spray. De Pean courteously withdrew, leaving her alone with the Intendant.

Bigot was charmed for the moment into oblivion of the lady who sat in her secluded chamber at Beaumanoir. He forgot his late quarrel with Angelique, in admiration of her beauty. The pleasure he took in her presence shed a livelier beam of light across his features. She observed it and a renewed hope of triumph lifted her into still higher flights of gaiety.

"Angelique!" said he offering his arm to conduct her to a gorgeous buffet, which stood loaded with golden dishes of fruit, vases of flowers and the choicest confectionary with wine fit a feast of Cyprus. "You are happy tonight," said Bigot, "but perfect bliss is only obtained by a judicious mixture of earth and Heaven! pledge me gaily now in this golden wine Angelique and ask me what favour you will."

"And you will grant it?" asked she, turning her eyes upon him eagerly.

"Like the king in the fairy tale, even to my daughter and half of my kingdom," replied he gaily.

"Thanks for half the kingdom Chevalier!" laughed she "but I would prefer the father to the daughter!" Angelique gave him a look of ineffable meaning. "I do not desire a king to night, however. Grant me *the lettre de Cachet* and—then—"

"And then what Angelique?" He ventured to take her hand which seemed to tempt the approach of his.

"You shall have your reward! I pray you for a *lettre de Cachet*, that is all!—" She suffered her hand to remain in his.

"I cannot," he replied sharply to her urgent repetition. "Ask her banishment from Beaumanoir, her life if you like, but a *lettre de Cachet* to send her to the Bastile I cannot and will not give—!"

"But I ask it nevertheless!" replied the wilful passionate girl. "There is no merit in your love if it fears risk or brooks denial! You ask me to make sacrifices and will not lift your finger to remove that stumbling block out of my way!—A fig for such love! Chevalier Bigot!—If I were a man there is nothing in earth heaven or hell I would not do for the woman I loved!"

Angelique fixed her blazing eyes full upon him but magnetic as was their fire they drew no satisfying reply. "Who in heaven's name is this lady of Beaumanoir of whom you are so careful or so afraid?"

"I cannot tell you Angelique," said he quite irritated "She may be a run away nun, or the wife of the man in the iron mask or— —"

"Or any other fiction you please to tell in the stead of

truth! and which proves your love to be the greatest fiction of all!—"

"Do not be so angry Angelique!" said he soothingly seeing the need of calming down this impetuous spirit, which he was driving beyond all bounds. But he had carelessly dropped a word, which she picked eagerly up, and treasured in her bosom. "Her life! he said he would give me her life! Did he mean it," thought she, absorbed in this new idea.

Angelique had clutched the word, with a feeling of terrible import. It was not the first time the thought had flashed its lurid light across her mind. It had seemed of comparatively light import when it was only the suggestion of her own wild resentment. It seemed a word of terrible power, heard from the lips of Bigot. Yet Angelique knew well he did not in the least seriously mean what he said.

"It is but his deceit and flattery" she said to herself, "an idle phrase to cozen a woman! I will not ask him to explain it! I shall interpret it in my own way! Bigot has said words he understood not himself! It is for me to give them form and reality."

She grew quiet under these reflections and bent her head in seeming acquiescence to the Intendant's decision. The calmness was apparent only.

"You are a true woman Angelique!" said he "but no politician. You have never heard thunder at Versailles! Would that I dared to grant your request. I offer you my homage and all else I have to give to half my Kingdom!"

Angelique's eyes flashed fire. "It is a fairy tale after all!" exclaimed she. "You will not grant the *lettre de Cachet?*"

"As I told you before, I dare not grant that, Angelique— Any thing else— — —"

"You dare not! You the boldest Intendant ever sent to New France, and say you dare not! a man who is worth the name dare do any thing in the world for a woman if he loves her! and for such a man a true woman will kiss the ground he walks on and die at his feet if need be!" Angelique's thoughts reverted for a moment to Le Gardeur, not to Bigot, as she said this, and thought how he would do it for her sake if she asked him.

"My God! Angelique you drive this matter hard! but I like you better so, than when you are in your silkiest humours—."

"Bigot! It were better you had granted my request." Angelique clenched her fingers hard together and a cruel expression lit her eyes for a moment. It was like the glance of a Lynx seeking a hidden treasure in the ground. Her thoughts penetrated the thick walls of Beaumanoir. She suppressed her anger, however, lest Bigot should guess the dark imaginings and half formed resolution which brooded in her mind.

With her inimitable power of transformation she put on her air of gaiety again and exclaimed, "Pshaw! let it go Bigot! I am really no politician as you say! I am only a woman almost stifled with the heat and closeness of this hideous ball room. Thank God! day is dawning in the great eastern window yonder! The dancers are beginning to depart! my brother is waiting for me, I see, so I must leave you Chevalier."

"Do not depart just now, Angelique! Wait until breakfast which will be prepared for the latest guests."

"Thanks Chevalier!" said she "I cannot wait! It has been a gay and delightful ball—to them who enjoyed it."

"Among whom you were one I hope?" replied Bigot.

"Yes, I only wanted one thing to be perfectly happy!—and that I could not get! so I must console myself," said she with an air of mock resignation.

Bigot looked at her and laughed but he would not ask what it was she lacked. He did not want a scene, and feared to excite her wrath by mention of the *lettre de Cachet*.

"Let me accompany you to the carriage, Angelique!" said he, handing her cloak and assisting her to put it on.

"Willingly Chevalier!" replied she, coquettishly. "But the Chevalier de Pean will accompany me to the door of the dressing room. I promised him"—she had not, but she beckoned with her finger to him. She had a last injunction for De Pean, which she cared not that the Intendant should hear.

De Pean was reconciled by this manoeuvre. He came and Angelique and he tripped off together. "Mind De Pean! what I asked you about Le Gardeur!" said she in an emphatic whisper.

"I will not forget!" replied he with a twinge of jealousy. "Le Gardeur shall come back in a few days or De Pean has lost his influence and cunning!"

Angelique gave him a sharp glance of approval but made no remark. A crowd of voluble ladies, were all telling over the incidents of the ball, as exciting as any incidents of flood and field while they arranged themselves for departure.

The ball was fast thinning out. The fair daughters of Quebec with disordered hair and drooping wreaths, loose sandals and dresses looped and pinned to hide chance rents or other accidents of a long nights dancing were retiring to their rooms or issuing from them, hooded and mantled, attended by obsequious Cavaliers to return home.

The musicians tired out and half asleep drew their bows slowly across their violins. The very music was steeped in weariness. The lamps grew dim in the rays of morning, which struggled through the high windows. While mingling with the last strains of good night and *Bon Repos*, came a noise of wheels and the loud shouts of valets and coachmen out in the fresh air, who crowded round the doors of the Palace, to convey home the gay revellers who had that night graced the splendid Halls of the Intendant.

Bigot stood at the door bowing farewell and thanks, to the fair company. When the tall Queenly figure of Angelique came down leaning on the arm of the Chevalier de Pean, Bigot tendered her his arm which she at once accepted and he accompanied her to her carriage.

She bowed graciously to the Intendant and De Pean on her departure, but no sooner had she driven off, than throwing herself back in her carriage heedless of the presence of her brother who accompanied her home, sank into a silent train of thoughts from which she was roused with a start, when the carriage drew up sharply at the door of their own home.

CHAPTER 34

"CALLING A RAVENOUS BIRD FROM THE EAST"

ANGELIQUE scarcely noticed her brother except to bid him good night, when she left him in the vestibule of the mansion. Gathering her gay robes in her jewelled hand she darted up the broad stairs to her own appartment, the same in which she had received Le Gardeur on that memorable night in which she crossed the Rubicon of her fate, when she deliberately severed the only tie which would have bound her to virtue and honour, by seeking the happiness of Le Gardeur above all considerations of self.

There was a fixedness in her look and a recklessness in her step, that showed anger and determination. It struck Lizette with a sort of awe, so that for once, she did not dare to accost her young mistress with her usual freedom. The maid opened the door and closed it again without offering a word, waiting in the ante-room until a summons should come from her mistress.

Lizette observed that she had thrown herself onto a fauteuil after hastily casting off her mantle which lay at her feet. Her long hair hung loose over her shoulders as if parted from all its combs and fastenings. She held her hands clasped hard across her forehead and stared with fixed eyes upon the fire which burned low on the hearth, flickering in the depths of the antique fire place and occasionally sending a flash through the room which lit up the pictures on the wall seeming to give them life and movement, as if they too would gladly have tempted Angelique to better thoughts But she noticed them not, and would not at that moment have endured to look at them.

Angelique had forbidden the lamps to be lighted. It suited

397

her mood to sit in the half obscure room, and in truth her thoughts were hard and cruel, fit only to be brooded over in darkness and alone. We are influenced by an inscrutable instinct if the term may be used to make our surroundings an image of ourselves, the outward projection of our habitual thoughts, moods and passions.

The broad glare of the lamps would have been at this moment hateful to Angelique. The lurid flickering and flashing of the dim firelight resembled most her own thoughts and as her vivid fancy fastened its eye upon the embers, they seemed to change into images of all the evil things her imagination projected. She clenched her hands and raising them above her head muttered an oath between her teeth, exclaiming

"*Par Dieu*! It must be done! It must be done!" She stopped suddenly when she had said that. "What must be done?" asked she sharply of herself, and laughed a mocking laugh. "He gave me her life! He did not mean it! no! The Intendant was treating me like a petted child. He offered me her life while he refused me a *lettre de Cachet*! The gift was only upon his false lips, not in his heart! but Bigot shall keep that promise in spite of himself. There is no other way—none—!—"

In the upheaval of her troubled mind, the image of her old confessor Father Vimont, rose up for a moment with signs of warning in his lifted finger, as when he used to reprove her for venial sins and childish follies. Angelique turned away impatiently from the recollection. She would not in imagination even, lay hold of the spiritual hand, which seemed to reach forward to pluck her from the chasm, toward which she was hurrying.

This was a new world Angelique suddenly found herself in—a world of guilty thoughts and unresisted temptations, a chaotic world where black unscalable rocks, like a circle of the *Inferno* hemmed her in on every side while devils whispered in her ears the words which gave shape and substance to her secret wishes for the death of her "rival," as she regarded the poor sick girl at Beaumanoir.

How was she to accomplish it? to one unpractised in actual

deeds of wickedness, it was a question not easy to be answered, and a thousand frightful forms of evil, stalking shapes of death came and went before her imagination, and she clutched first at one then at another of the dire suggestions that came in crowds that overwhelmed her power of choice.

In despair to find an answer to the question "What must be done?", She rose suddenly and rang the bell. The door opened and the smiling face and clear eye of Lizette looked in. It was Angelique's last chance, but it was lost. It was not Lizette she had rung for. Her resolution was taken.

"My dear Mistress!" exclaimed Lizette "I feared you had fallen asleep. It is almost day!—may I now assist you to undress for bed?" Voluble Lizette did not always wait to be first spoken to by her mistress.

"No Lizette! I was not asleep; I do not want to undress! I have much to do. I have writing to do before I retire! send Fanchon Dodier here." Angelique had a forecast that it was necessary to deceive Lizette, who without a word, but in no serene humour went to summon Fanchon to wait on her mistress.

Fanchon presently came in with a sort of triumph glittering in her black eye. She had noticed the ill humour of Lizette, but had not the slightest idea why she had been summoned to wait on Angelique, instead of her own maid. She esteemed it quite an honour however.

"Fanchon Dodier!—" said she, "I have lost my jewels at the Ball! I cannot rest until I find them! You are quicker witted than Lizette. Tell me what to do to find them, and I will give you a dress fit for a lady."

Angelique with innate craft knew that her question would bring forth the hoped for reply.

Fanchon's eyes dilated with pleasure at such a mark of confidence. "Yes my lady" replied she. "If I had lost my jewels I should know what to do, but ladies who can read and write and who have the wisest gentlemen to give them counsel do not need to seek advice, where poor habitant girls go when in trouble and perplexity."

"And where is that? Fanchon, where would you go if in

trouble?"

"My lady! if I had lost all my jewels," Fanchon's keen eye noticed that Angelique had lost none of hers, but she made no remark on it. "If I had lost all mine, I should go see my Aunt Josephte Dodier. She is the wisest woman in all St Valier. If she cannot tell you, all you wish to know, nobody can."

"What! Dame Josephte Dodier, whom they call La Corriveau? Is she your aunt?" Angelique knew very well she was. But it was her cue to pretend ignorance in order to impose on Fanchon.

"Yes, ill natured people call her La Corriveau but she is my Aunt nevertheless. She is married to my Uncle Louis Dodier, but is a lady by right of her mother, who came from France, and was once familiar with all the great dames of the Court. It was a great secret why her mother left France, and came to St Valier, but I never knew what it was—people used to shake their heads and cross themselves when speaking of her, as they do now when speaking of Aunt Josephte, whom they call La Corriveau, but they tremble when she looks at them with her black evil eye as they call it. She is a terrible woman is Aunt Josephte! but O Mademoiselle! she can tell you things past, present and to come. If she rails at the world it is because she knows every wicked thing that is done in it, and the world rails at her in return but people are afraid of her all the same."

"But is it not wicked? Is it not forbidden by the Church to consult a woman like her, a sorciere!" Angelique took a sort of perverse merit to herself for arguing against her own resolution.

"Yes! my lady, but although forbidden by the Church, the girls all consult her nevertheless in their losses and crosses, and many of the men too, for she does know what is to happen, and how to do things, does Aunt Josephte—! If the clergy cannot tell a poor girl about her sweetheart and how to keep him in hand, why should she not go and consult La Corriveau who can?"

"Fanchon! I would not care to consult your Aunt. People would laugh at my consulting La Corriveau like a simple Habitant girl—what would the world say?"

"But the world need not know, my Lady. Aunt Josephte knows secrets they say, that would ruin burn and hang half the ladies of Paris. She learned those terrible secrets from her mother, but she keeps them safe in those close lips of hers, not the faintest whisper of one of them has ever been heard by her nearest neighbour. Indeed she has no gossips and makes no friends and wants none. Aunt Josephte is a safe confidante my Lady, if you wish to consult her—!—"

"I have heard she is clever, supernatural, terrible this aunt of yours! But I could not go to St Valier for advice and help. I could not conceal my movements like a plain Habitant girl."

"Indeed my Lady," replied Fanchon touched by some personal reminiscence, "A Habitant girl cannot conceal her movements any more than a great lady! A girl cannot stir a step but all the Parish is looking at her! If she goes to church and just looks across at a young man they say she went to see him! If she stays away they say she is afraid to see him! If she visits a neighbour, it is in the hope of meeting him. If she remains at home it is to wait for him. But Habitant girls do not care, my lady. If they throw the net they catch the fish— sometimes! so no matter what people say, and in revenge we talk about others as fast as others talk about us!"

"But my lady" continued Fanchon, remembering the objection of her mistress, "it is not fitting that you should go to Aunt Josephte. I will bring Aunt Josephte here to you. She will be charmed to come to the city and serve a lady like you."

"Well! no! it is not well! but ill! but I want to recover my jewels, so go for your Aunt and bring her back with you, and mind, Fanchon!" said Angelique lifting a warning finger, "if you utter one word of your errand to man or beast or to the very trees of the way side, I will cut out your tongue, Fanchon Dodier!"

Fanchon trembled and grew pale at the fierce look of her Mistress. "I will go my lady and I will keep silent as a fish!" faltered the maid "Shall I go immediately—?"

"Immediately if you will! It is almost day and you have far to go. I will send old Gujon the butler, to order an Indian

Canoe for you. I will not have Canadian boatmen to row you to St Valier, they will talk you out of all your errand, before you are half way there. You shall go to St Valier by water and return with La Corriveau by land. Do you understand? Bring her in tonight and not before midnight. I will leave the door ajar for you to enter without noise—you will show her at once to my appartment! Fanchon! Be wary and do not delay, and say not a word to mortal—!"

"I will not, my Lady, not a mouse shall hear us come in!—" replied Fanchon quite proud now of the secret understanding between herself and her mistress.

"And again! mind that loose tongue of yours! remember Fanchon, I will cut it out, as sure as you live if you betray me."

"Yes! my lady!" Fanchon's tongue felt somewhat paralysed under the threat of Angelique, and she bit it painfully as if to remind it of its duty.

"You may go now" said Angelique. "Here is money for you, give this piece of gold to La Corriveau as an earnest that I want her—! The Canotiers of the St Lawrence will also require double fare for bringing La Corriveau over the Ferry."

"No! they rarely venture to charge her anything at all, my Lady," replied Fanchon, "To be sure it is not for love, but they are afraid of her, and yet Antoine La Chance the boatman says she is equal to a Bishop for stirring up piety and more *Ave Marias* are repeated when she is in his boat than are said by the whole Parish on Sunday."

"I ought to say my *Ave Maria's* too!" replied Angelique as Fanchon left the appartment. "But my mouth is parched and burns up the words of prayer, like a furnace, but that is nothing to the fire in my heart! That girl Fanchon Dodier is not to be trusted, but I have no other messenger to send for La Corriveau. I must be wary with *her* too, and make her suggest the thing I would have done! My Lady of Beaumanoir," she apostrophized in a hard monotone "your fate does not depend on the Intendant, as you fondly imagine! Better had he issued the *lettre de Cachet*, than for you to fall into the hands of La Corriveau!—"

Day light now shot into the windows and the bright rays

of the rising sun streamed full in the face of Angelique. She saw herself reflected in the large Venetian mirror. Her countenance looked pale stern and fixed as marble. The fire in her eyes startled her with its unearthly glow—she trembled and turned away from her mirror and crept to her couch like a guilty thing, with a feeling as if she was old, haggard, and doomed to shame, for the sake of this Intendant who cared not for her, or he would not have driven her to such desperate and wicked courses as never fell to the lot of a woman before.

"*C'est sa faute*! *C'est sa faute*!" exclaimed she clasping her hands passionately together. "If she dies, it is his fault not mine! I prayed him to banish her, and he would not! *C'est sa faute*! *C'est sa faute*!" repeating these words Angelique fell into a feverish slumber broken by frightful dreams which lasted far on into the day.

CHAPTER 35

LA CORRIVEAU

THE long reign of Louis Quatorze, full of glories and misfortunes for France, was marked towards its close by portentous signs indicative of corrupt manners, and a falling state. Among these, the crime of secret poisoning suddenly attained a magnitude which filled the whole nation with terror and alarm.

Antonio Exili an Italian like many other alchemists of that period, had spent years in search of the philosopher's stone and the Elixir of life. His vain experiments to transmute the baser metals into gold, reduced him to poverty and want. His quest after these secrets had led him to study deeply the nature and composition of poisons and their antidotes. He had visited the great universities and other schools of the continent, finishing his scientific studies under a famous German chemist, named Glaser. But the terrible secret of the *Aqua Tofana* and of the *Poudre de succession*, Exili learned from Beatrice Spara, a Sicilian woman with whom he had a liaison, one of those inscrutable beings of the gentler sex, whose lust for pleasure or power is only equalled by the atrocities they are willing to perpetrate upon all who stand in the way of their desires or their ambition.

To Beatrice Spara, the secret of this subtle preparation had come down like an evil inheritance from the ancient Candidas and Saganas of imperial Rome. In the proud Palaces of the Borgias, of the Orsinis, the Scaligers and the Borromeos, the art of poisoning was preserved among the last resorts of Machiavellian state craft, and not only in Palaces but in by streets of Italian Cities, in solitary towers and dark recesses of the Appenines were still to be found the lost children of

Science, skilful compounders of Poisons, at once fatal and subtle in their operation—poisons which left not the least trace of their presence in the bodies of their victims, but put on the appearance of other and more natural causes of death.

Exili to escape the vengeance of Beatrice Spara to whom he had proved a faithless lover fled from Naples and brought his deadly knowledge to Paris, where he soon found congenial spirits to work with him in preparing the deadly *poudre de succession* and the colorless drops of the *Aqua Tofana*.

With all his crafty caution, Exili fell at last under suspicion of the Police for tampering in these forbidden arts. He was arrested and thrown into the Bastile where he became the occupant of the same cell with Gaudin de St Croix, a young nobleman of the Court, the lover of the Marchioness de Brinvilliers, for an intrigue with whom the Count had been imprisoned. St Croix learned from Exili in the Bastile the secret of the *poudre de succession*.

The two men were at last liberated for want of proof of the charges against them. St Croix set up a laboratory in his own house and at once proceeded to experiment upon the terrible secrets learned from Exili and which he revealed to his fair frail mistress, who mad to make herself his wife saw in this a means to remove every obstacle out of the way. She poisoned her husband, her father, her brother, and at last carried away by a mania for Murder administered on all sides the fatal *poudre de succession* which brought death to House, Palace, and Hospital, and filled the Capital, nay the whole kingdom, with suspicion and terror.

This fatal poison history describes either as a light and almost impalpable powder, tasteless, colorless and inodorous, or a liquid clear as a dew drop, when in the form of the *Aqua Tofana*. It was capable of causing death, either instantaneously or by slow and lingering decline at the end of a definite number of days, weeks or even months, as was desired. Death was not less sure because deferred, and could be made to assume the appearance of Dumb paralysis, wasting atrophy, or burning fever, at the discretion of the compounder of the fatal poison.

The ordinary effect of the *Aqua Tofana* was immediate death. The *Poudre de succession* was more slow in killing. It produced in its pure form a burning heat like that of a fiery furnace in the chest, the flames of which as they consumed the patient, darted out of his eyes, the only part of the body which seemed to be alive, while the rest was little more than a dead corpse.

Upon the introduction of this terrible poison into France, Death like an invisible spirit of evil glided silently about the kingdom, creeping into the closest family circles, seizing every where, on its helpless victims. The nearest and dearest relationships of life were no longer the safe guardians of the domestic hearth. The man who today appeared in the glow of health, drooped tomorrow and died the next day. No skill of the Physician, was able to save him, or to detect the true cause of his death, attributing it usually to the false appearances of disease which it was made to assume.

The victims of the *poudre de succession* were counted by thousands. The possession of wealth, a lucrative office, a fair young wife, or a coveted Husband, were sufficient reasons for sudden death to cut off the holder of these envied blessings. A terrible mistrust pervaded all classes of society. The Husband trembled before his wife, the wife before her Husband; Father and Son, brother and sister, kindred and friends of all degrees looked askance and with suspicious eyes upon one another.

In Paris, the terror lasted long. Society was for a while broken up by cruel suspicions. The meat upon the table remained uneaten. The wine undrank, men and women procured their own provisions in the market, and cooked and ate them each alone in their own appartments. Yet was every precaution in vain. The fatal dust scattered upon the pillow or a bouquet sprinkled with the *Aqua Tofana* looking bright and innocent as God's dew upon the flowers, transmitted death without a warning of danger. Nay! to crown all summit of wickedness, the bread in the hospitals of the sick, the meagre tables of the Convent, the consecrated host administered by the priest and the sacramental wine which he drank himself, all in turn were poisoned, polluted, damned by the unseen presence of the Manna of St Nicholas, as the populace mockingly called the *Poudre de succession*.

The Court took the alarm, when a gilded vial of the *Aqua Tofana* was found one day upon the table of the Duchesse de la Valiere, having been placed there by the hand of some secret rival in order to cast suspicion upon the unhappy Louise and hasten her fall already approaching.

The star of Montespan was rising bright in the East, and that of La Valiere was setting in clouds and darkness in the West. But the King never distrusted for a moment the truth of La Valiere, the only woman who ever loved him for his own sake, and he knew it, even while he allowed her to be supplanted by another infinitely less worthy, one whose hour of triumph came when she saw the broken hearted Louise throw aside the velvet and brocade of the Court, and put on the sack cloth of the barefooted and repentant Carmelite.

The King burned with indignation at the insult offered to his mistress, and was still more alarmed to find the new mysterious death creeping into the corridors of his palace. He hastily constituted the terrible *Chambre Ardente*, a court of supreme criminal jurisdiction and commissioned it to search out, try and burn without appeal all poisoners and secret assassins in the kingdom.

La Regnie, a man of Rhadamanthean justice as hard of heart as he was subtle and suspicious, was long baffled and set at naught to his unutterable rage, by the indefatigable poisoners who kept all France awake on its pillows.

History records how Gaudin de St Croix, the disciple of Exili while working in his secret laboratory at the sublimation of the deadly poison, accidentally dropped the mask of glass which protected his face. He inhaled the noxious fumes and fell dead by the side of his crucibles. This event gave Desgrais, captain of the police of Paris, a clue to the horrors which had so long baffled all his pursuit.

The correspondence of St Croix was seized. His connection with the Marchioness de Brinvilliers and his relations with Exili were discovered. Exili was thrown a second time into the Bastile. The Marchioness was arrested and put

upon her trial, before the *Chambre Ardente*, where as recorded
in the narrative of her confessor Pirol, her ravishing beauty
of feature, blue eyes, snow white skin and gentle demeanour
won a strong sympathy from the fickle populace of Paris, in
whose eyes her charms of person and manner pleaded hard
to extenuate her unparalleled crimes.

But no power of beauty or fascination of looks could move
the stern La Regnie from his judgment. She was pronounced
guilty of the death of her husband and sentenced first to be
tortured, and then beheaded and her body burnt on the Place
de Greve, a sentence which was carried out to the letter. The
ashes of the fairest and most wicked dame of the Court of
Louis XIV. were scattered to the four corners of the City which
had been the scene of her unparalleled crimes. The arch
poisoner Exili was also tried and condemned to be burnt.
The tumbril that bore him to execution was stopped on its
way by the furious rabble and he was torn in pieces by them.

For a short time the kingdom breathed freely in fancied
security, but soon the epidemic of sudden as well as lingering
deaths, from poison broke out again on all sides. The fatal
tree of the knowledge of evil, seemingly cut down with Exili
and St Croix had sprouted afresh, like a Upas that could not
be destroyed.

The poisoners became more numerous than ever.
Following the track of St Croix and La Brinvilliers they carried
on the war against Humanity without relaxation. Chief of
these was a reputed Witch and Fortune teller named La Voisin,
who had studied the infernal secret under Exili and borne a
daughter to the false Italian.

With La Voisin were associated two Priests, Le Sage and
Le Vigoureux who lived with her, and assisted her in her
necromantic exhibitions which were visited, believed in and
richly rewarded by some of the foremost people of the court.
These necromantic exhibitions were in reality a cover to
darker crimes.

It was long the popular belief in France, that Cardinal
Bonzy got from La Voisin the means of ridding himself of
sundry persons who stood in the way of his ecclesiastical

preferment, or to whom he had to pay pensions in his quality of Archbishop of Narbonne. The Duchesse de Bouillon and the Countess of Soissons, mother of the famous Prince Eugene, were also accused of trafficking with that terrible woman, and were banished from the kingdom in consequence while a royal Duke Francois de Montmorency was also suspected of dealings with La Voisin.

The *Chambre Ardente* struck right and left. Desgrais chief of the police, by a crafty ruse penetrated into the secret circle of La Voisin, and she with a crowd of associates perished in the fires of the Place de Greve. She left an illstarred daughter Marie Exili to the blank charity of the streets of Paris and the possession of many of the frightful secrets of her mother, and of her terrible father.

Marie Exili clung to Paris. She grew up beautiful and profligate. She coined her rare Italian charms, first into gold and velvet, then into silver and brocade, and at last into copper and rags. When her charms faded entirely, she began to practise the forbidden arts of her Mother and Father but without their boldness, or long impunity.

She was soon suspected, but receiving timely warning of her danger, from a high patroness at Court, Marie fled to New France in the disguise of a Paysanne one of a cargo of unmarried women sent out to the colony on matrimonial venture, as the custom then was, to furnish wives for the colonists. Her sole possession was an antique Cabinet with its contents, the only remnants saved from the fortunes of her father Exili.

Marie Exili landed in New France, cursing the old world which she had left behind, and bringing as bitter a hatred of the New, which received her without a shadow of suspicion. But under her modest peasants garb was concealed the daughter and inheritrix of the black arts of Antonio Exili and of the sorceress La Voisin.

Marie Exili kept her secret well. She played the *Ingenue* to perfection. Her straight figure and black eyes having drawn a second glance from the Sieur Corriveau, a rich habitant of St Valier who was looking for a servant among the crowd of

Paysannes who had just arrived from France, he could not escape from the power of their fascination.

He took Marie Exili home with him, and installed her in his household, where his wife soon died of some inexplicable disease which baffled the knowledge of both the Doctor and the Curate, the two wisest men in the Parish. The Sieur Corriveau ended his widowhood by marrying Marie Exili, and soon died himself leaving his whole fortune and one daughter the image of her mother, to Marie.

Marie Exili ever in dread of the perquisitions of Desgrais, kept very quiet in her secluded home on the St Lawrence, guarding her secret with a life long apprehension, and but occasionally and in the darkest ways practising her deadly skill. She found some compensation and relief for her suppressed passions in the clinging sympathy of her daughter Marie Josephte, *dit* La Corriveau, who worshipped all that was evil in her Mother and in spite of an occasional reluctance springing from some maternal instinct, drew from her every secret of her life. She made herself mistress of the whole formula of poisoning as taught by her grandfather Exili, and of the arts of sorcery practised by her wicked Grand Mother La Voisin.

As La Corriveau listened to the tale of the burning of her grandmother on the Place de Grève, her own soul seemed bathed in the flames which rose from the faggots and which to her perverted reason appeared as the fires of cruel injustice, calling for revenge upon the whole race of the oppressors of her family as she regarded the punishers of their crimes.

With such a Parentage and such dark secrets brooding in her bosom, Marie Josephte or as she was commonly called La Corriveau, had nothing in common with the simple peasantry among whom she lived.

Years passed over her, youth fled and La Corriveau still sat in her house, eating her heart out, silent and solitary. After the death of her mother, some whispers of hidden treasures known only to herself, a rumour which she had cunningly set afloat, excited the cupidity of Louis Dodier, a simple Habitant of St Valier, and drew him into a marriage with her.

It was a barren union. No child followed with God's grace

in its little hands to make a mothers feelings and soften the callous heart of La Corriveau. She cursed her lot that it was so, and her dry bosom became an arid spot of desert, tenanted by satyrs and dragons, by every evil passion of a woman without conscience and void of love.

But La Corriveau had inherited the sharp intellect and Italian dissimulation of Antonio Exili. She was astute enough to throw a veil of hypocrisy over the evil eye which shot like a glance of death under her thick black eye-brows.

Her craft was equal to her malice. An occasional deed of alms, done not for charity's sake, but for ostentation, an adroit deal of cards, or a Horoscope cast to flatter a foolish girl, a word of sympathy hollow as a water bubble, but coloured with iridescent prettiness averted suspicion from the darker traits of her character.

If she was hated, she was also feared by her neighbours, and although the sign of the cross was made upon the chair whereon she had sat in neighbours houses, her visits were not unwelcome and in the Manor House, as in the cabin of the woodman La Corriveau was received, consulted, rewarded and oftener thanked than cursed by her witless dupes.

There was something sublime in the satanic pride with which she carried with her the terrible secrets of her race, which in her own mind made her the superior of every one around her, and whom she regarded as living only by her permission, and forbearance.

For human love other than as a degraded menial, to make men the slaves of her mercinary schemes, La Corriveau, cared nothing. She never felt it, never inspired it, But looked down upon all her sex as the filth of creation and like herself incapable of a chaste feeling, or a pure thought. Every better instinct of her nature had gone out like the flame of a lamp whose oil is exhausted. Love of money remained as dregs at the bottom of her heart. A deep grudge against mankind with a secret pleasure in the misfortunes of others, especially of her own sex, were her ruling passions.

Her mother Marie Exili had died in her bed, warning her daughter not to dabble in the forbidden arts which she had taught her, but to cling to her husband and live an honest life as the only means of dying, a more hopeful death, than her ancestors.

La Corriveau heard much, but heeded little. The blood of Antonio Exili and of La Voisin beat too vigorously in her veins to be tamed down by the feeble whispers of a dying woman who had been weak enough to give way at the last. The death of her mother left La Corriveau free to follow her own will. The Italian subtlety of her race made her secret and cautious. She had few personal affronts to avenge, and few temptations in the simple community where she lived to practise more than the ordinary arts of a rural fortune teller, keeping in impenetrable shadow the darker side of her character as a born sorceress and poisoner.

Such was the woman whom Angelique des Meloises summoned to her aid in what she thought was the crisis of her life—A crisis which she had at length persuaded herself justified the only means left to get rid of her rival for the hand of the Intendant.

Her conscience which ought to have protected her had shivered under the violence of her passion like a shield of glass, but fragments of it still wounded her. She was not without some natural compunctions, for though habituated to think of sin, she had not yet been touched by crime, and she strove earnestly to blind herself to the enormity of what she had resolved, and had recourse to some sad casuistry to persuade herself, that she would be less guilty of the crime of murder if she did it by the hand of another. Moreover, she called on God, to witness that she did not mean to be a persistent sinner—far from it! She would commit but one crime, only one! just one simple breach of human and divine law. Take the life of a rival, but that done, her end attained, she would live the life of a Saint ever after! free from all further temptation, for she would be beatified by a marriage with the Intendant of New France, take precedence of all the ladies of the Colony and at last be translated to that Heaven of hope and delight, the Court of Versailles leaving far behind her, Beaumanoir and all its dark memories. What more would she have to desire in this world?

The Juggling Fiend plays with us ever thus, when we palter with conscience. A single fault seems not much, one step beyond the allowable mark does not look to be far. It will be quite a merit to stop there, and go no farther! Providence *must* be on our side and reward our abstention from further wickedness—!

Fanchon Dodier in obedience to the order of her mistress, started early in the day, to bear the message intrusted to her for La Corriveau. She did not cross the river and take the Kings Highway the rough though well travelled road on the South Shore which led to St Valier. Angelique was crafty enough amid her impulsiveness to see that it were better for Fanchon to go down by water and return by land. It lessened observation and might be important one day to baffle inquiry. La Corriveau would serve her for money, but for money also she might betray her! Angelique resolved to secure her silence by making her the perpetrator of whatever scheme of wickedness she might devise against the unsuspecting Lady of Beaumanoir. As for Fanchon, she need know nothing more than Angelique told her as to the object of her mission to her terrible aunt.

In pursuance of this design, Angelique had already sent for a couple of Indian canoemen, to embark Fanchon at the Quay of the Friponne and convey her to St Valier.

Half civilized and wholly demoralized red men, were always to be found on the beach of Stadacona as they still called the Batture of the St Charles, lounging about in blankets, smoking, playing dice, or drinking pints or quarts, as fortune favoured them or a passenger wanted conveyance in their bark canoes, which they managed with a dexterity unsurpassed by any Boatmen that ever put oar or paddle in water, salt or fresh.

These rough fellows were safe and trusty in their profession. Fanchon knew them slightly and felt no fear whatever in seating herself upon the bear skin, which carpeted the bottom of their canoe.

They pushed off at once from the shore with scarcely a

word of reply to her voluble directions, and gesticulations, as they went speeding their canoe down the stream. The turning tide bore them lightly on its bosom and they chanted a wild monotonous refrain as their paddles flashed and dipped alternately in stream and sunshine.

"Ah! Ah! Tenaouich Tenaga!
Tenaouich Tenaga, Ouich Ka!"

"Ah! Ah! Tenaouich Tenaga!
Tenaouich Tenaga! Ouich Ka!"

"They are singing about me no doubt!" said Fanchon to herself, "I do not care what people say They cannot be christians who speak such a heathenish jargon as that. It is enough to sink the Canoe; but I will repeat my pater nosters and my Ave-Maria's seeing they will not converse with me and I will pray good St Anne to give me a safe passage to St Valier!" In which pious occupation as the boatmen, continued their savage song, without paying her any attention, Fanchon with many interruptions of worldly thoughts, spent the rest of the time she was in the Indian Canoe.

Down past the green hills of the South shore, the boatmen steadily plied their paddles and kept singing their wild Indian chant. The wooded slopes of Orleans, basked in sunshine as they overlooked the broad channel, through which the canoe sped, and long before meridian the little bark was turned to shore and pulled up on the beach of St Valier.

Fanchon leaped out without assistance, wetting a foot in so doing, which somewhat discomposed the good humour, she had shown during the voyage. Her Indian boatmen offered her no help, considering that women were made to serve men and help themselves, and not to be waited upon by them.

The gallantry of Frenchmen to the sex was a thing unintelligible and absurd in the eyes of the red men, who whatever shreds of European ideas hung loosely about them, never changed their original opinions about women and hence were incapable of real civilization.

"Not that I wanted to touch one of their savage

hands!" muttered Fanchon "but they might have offered one assistance! Look there!" continued she pulling aside her skirt and showing a very trim foot wet up to the ankle. "They ought to know the difference between their red squaws and white girls of the City—! If they are not worth politeness, *we* are! but Indians are only fit to kill christians or be killed by them and you may as well courtsey to a bear in the briars as to an Indian anywhere—!"

The boatmen looked at her foot with supreme indifference, and taking out their pipes seated themselves on the edge of their canoe and began to smoke.

"You may return to the City!" said she addressing them sharply, "and pray to the Bon Dieu to strike you white—it is vain to look for manners from an Indian!—I shall remain in St Valier and not return with you!—"

"Marry me? be my squaw? Ania!" replied one of the boatmen with a grim smile, "the Bon Dieu will strike our Papooses white and teach them manners like pale faces."

"Ugh! not for all the Kings money! What! marry a red Indian and carry his pack like Fifine Perotte? I would die first! you are bold indeed Paul La Crosse to name such a thing to me—! go back to the City! I would not trust myself again in your canoe. It required courage to do so at all! But Mademoiselle selected you for my boatmen not I! I wonder she did so! when the brothers Belleau and the prettiest fellows in town are idle on the batture."

"Ania is neice to the old medicine woman in the stone wigwam—at St Valier! going to see her eh?" asked the other Boatman with a slight display of curiosity.

"Yes, I am going to visit my Aunt Dodier,—why should I not? She has crocks of gold buried in the House, I can tell you that, Pierre Ceinture—!"

"Going to get some from La Corriveau, eh? crocks of gold eh?" said Paul La Crosse.

"La Corriveau has medicines too! get some eh?" asked Pierre Ceinture.

"I am going neither for gold nor medicines but to see my Aunt, if it concerns you to know, Pierre Ceinture! which it does not!"

"Mademoiselle des Meloises pay her to go, eh? not going back ever eh?" asked the other Indian.

"Mind your own affairs Paul La Crosse! and I will mind mine! Mademoiselle des Meloises paid you to bring me to St Valier not to ask me impertinences. That is enough for you! Here is your fare—now you can return to the Sault au Matelot and drink yourselves blind with the money!"

"Very good that!" replied the Indian "I like to drink myself blind. Will do it tonight. Like to see me eh? Better that, than go see La Corriveau! The Habitans say she talks with the Devil, and makes the sickness settle like a fog upon the wigwams of the Red men. They say she can make pale faces die, by looking at them! But Indians are too hard to kill with a look—! Fire water and gun and tomahawk and fever in the wigwams only make the Indians die."

"Good! that something can make you die for your ill manners! look at my stocking!" replied Fanchon with warmth. "If I tell La Corriveau what you say of her, there will be trouble in your wigwam, Pierre Ceinture!—"

"Do not do that Ania!" replied the Indian crossing himself earnestly, "do not tell La Corriveau or she will make an image of wax and call it Pierre Ceinture, and she will melt it away before a slow fire, and as it melts my flesh and bones will melt away too! Do not tell her Fanchon Dodier!" The Indian had picked up this piece of superstition from the white Habitans, and like them thoroughly believed in the supernatural powers of La Corriveau.

"Well leave me! get back to the City, and tell Mademoiselle I arrived safe at St Valier." replied Fanchon turning to leave them.

The Indians were somewhat taken down by the airs of Fanchon, and they stood in awe of the far reaching power of her aunt from the spell of whose witchcraft, they firmly believed no hiding place even in the deepest woods could protect them. Merely nodding a farewell to Fanchon the Indians silently pushed their canoe into the stream and embarking returned to the city by the way they came.

A fine breezy upland lay before Fanchon Dodier. Cultivated fields of corn and meadow ran down to the shore. A row of white cottages formed a loosely connected street clustering into something like a village at the point where the Parish Church, stood, at the intersection of two or three roads, one of which, a narrow green track but little worn by the carts of the Habitans, led to the stone House of La Corriveau the chimney of which was just visible as you lost sight of the village spire. The road dipped down on the other side of the Hill and in the far distance beyond rose narrowed to a thread upon another hill and ran into the depths of the Forest which covered the back ground of the Landscape.

In a deep hollow, out of sight of the Village church, almost out of hearing of its little bell stood the house of La Corriveau, a square heavy structure of stone, inconvenient and gloomy, with narrow windows and an uninviting door. The pine forest touched it on one side. A brawling stream twisted itself like a live snake half round it on the other. A plot of green grass ill kept and deformed with noxious weeds, dock, fennel, thistle and foul stramonium, was surrounded by a rough wall of loose stones forming the lawn such as it was, where under a tree, seated in an armchair was a solitary woman whom Fanchon recognized as her Aunt, Marie Josephte Dodier surnamed La Corriveau.

La Corriveau in feature and person took after her grand sire Exili. She was tall and straight, of a swarthy complexion, black haired and intensely black eyed. She was not uncomely of feature, nay had been handsome, nor was her look at first sight forbidding, especially if she did not turn upon you those small basilisk eyes of hers, full of fire and glare as the eyes of a rattle snake, but truly those thin cruel lips of hers never smiled spontaneously or affected to smile upon you, unless she had an object to gain by assuming a disguise as foreign to her as light to an angel of darkness.

La Corriveau was dressed in a robe of soft brown stuff shaped with a degree of taste and style beyond the garb of her class. Neatness in dress was the one virtue she had inherited from her Mother. Her feet were small and well shod like a lady's as the envious neighbours used to say. She never in her life would wear the sabots of the peasant women, nor go barefoot as many of them did about the house. La Corriveau was vain of her feet which would have made her fortune, as she thought, with bitterness, any where, but in St Valier.

She sat musing in her chair not noticing the presence of her neice who stood for a moment looking and hesitating before accosting her. Her countenance bore when alone, an expression of malignity which made Fanchon shudder. A quick unconscious twitching of the fingers accompanied her thoughts, as if this weird woman was playing a game of Mora with the evil genius that waited on her. Her Grandsire Exili had the same nervous twitching of his fingers and the vulgar accused him of playing at Mora with the devil, who ever accompanied him, they believed.

The lips of La Corriveau moved in unison with her thoughts. She was giving expression to her habitual contempt for her sex as she crooned over in a sufficiently audible voice to reach the ear of Fanchon a hateful song of Jean Le Meung, on women—

"Toutes vous etes, serez ou futes,
    De fait ou de volonté putes!"

"It is not nice to say that, Aunt Marie!" exclaimed Fanchon coming forward and embracing La Corriveau, who gave a start on seeing her neice so unexpectedly before her. "It is not nice, and it is not true!"

"But it is true! Fanchon Dodier! If it be not nice. There is nothing nice to be said of our sex, except by foolish men! Women know one another better! But," continued she scrutinizing her neice, with her keen black eyes which seemed to pierce her through and through, "what ill wind or Satan's errand has brought you to St Valier today, Fanchon?"

"No ill wind, nor ill errand either, I hope, Aunt. I come by command of my Mistress to ask you to go to the City. She is biting her nails off with impatience to see you on some business."

"And who is your mistress who dare ask La Corriveau to

trudge to the City at her bidding?"

"Do not be angry Aunt," replied Fanchon soothingly. "It was I counselled her to send for you, and I offered to fetch you. My Mistress is a high lady who expects to be still higher, Mademoiselle des Meloises—!"

"Mademoiselle Angelique des Meloises! one hears enough of her! a high lady indeed, who will be low enough at last! A minx as vain as she is pretty, who would marry all the men in New France and kill all the women if she could have her way! what in the name of the Sabbat, does she want with La Corriveau?"

"She did not call *you* names Aunt, and please do not say such things of her or you will frighten me away before I tell my errand. Mademoiselle Angelique sent this piece of gold as earnest money to prove that she wants your counsel and advice in an important matter."

Fanchon untied the corner of her handkerchief and took from it a broad shining Louis d'or. She placed it in the hand of La Corriveau, whose long fingers clutched it like the talons of a Harpy. Of all the evil passions of this woman, the greed for money was the most ravenous.

"It is long since I got a piece of gold like that to cross my hand with Fanchon!" said she looking at it admiringly and spitting on it for good luck.

"There are plenty more where it came from, Aunt," replied Fanchon. "Mademoiselle could fill your apron with gold every day of the week if she would. She is to marry the Intendant!"

"Marry the Intendant! Ah! indeed! that is why she sends for me so urgently! I see! Marry the Intendant! She will bestow a pot of gold on La Corriveau to accomplish that match!"

"May be she would Aunt. I would myself! but it is not that she wishes to consult you about just now. She lost her jewels at the Ball and wants your help to find them."

"Lost her jewels, eh? Did she say you were to tell me that she had lost her jewels Fanchon?"

"Yes, Aunt! that is what she wants to consult you about," replied Fanchon with simplicity. But the keen perception of La Corriveau saw that a second purpose lay behind it.

"A likely tale!" muttered she, "that so rich a lady would send for La Corriveau from St Valier to find a few jewels! But it will do—! I will go with you to the City. I cannot refuse an invitation like that. Gold fetches any woman Fanchon. It fetches me always—! It will fetch you too some day, if you are lucky enough to give it the chance!"

"I wish it would fetch me now! aunt! but poor girls who live by service and wages, have small chance to be sent for in that way! We are glad to get the empty hand without the money. Men are so scarce with this cruel war, that they might easily have a wife to each finger were it allowed by the law. I heard Dame Tremblay say—and I thought her very right—the Church does not half consider our condition and necessities."

"Dame Tremblay! The Charming Josephine of Lake Beauport! She who would have been a witch and could not! Satan would not have her!" exclaimed La Corriveau scornfully. "Is she still housekeeper and bedmaker at Beaumanoir?"

Fanchon was honest enough to feel rather indignant at this speech. "Dont speak so of her Aunt! she is not bad! Although I ran away from her, and took service with Mademoiselle des Meloises, I will not speak ill of her."

"Why did you run away from Beaumanoir?" asked La Corriveau.

Fanchon reflected a moment upon the mystery of the Lady of Beaumanoir, and something checked her tongue, as if it were not safe to tell all she knew to her Aunt, who would moreover be sure to find out from Angelique herself as much as her mistress wished her to know.

"I did not like Dame Tremblay, Aunt" replied she "I preferred to live with Mademoiselle Angelique. She is a lady, a beauty, who dresses to surpass any picture in the book of modes from Paris, which I often look at on her dressing table. She allows me to imitate them, or wear her cast off dresses which are better than any other ladies' new ones. I have one of them on. Look Aunt!" Fanchon spread out very complacently the skirt of a pretty blue robe she wore.

La Corriveau nodded her head in a sort of silent approval, and remarked: "She is free-handed enough! She gives what costs her nothing and takes all she can get, and is after all a trollope like the rest of us, Fanchon! who would be very good if there were neither men nor money nor fine clothes in the world to ruin poor silly women."

"You do say such nasty things Aunt!" exclaimed Fanchon, flashing with indignation. "I will hear no more! I am going in to the house to see dear old Uncle Dodier who has been looking through the window at me for ten minutes past and dared not come out to speak to me. You are too hard on poor old uncle Dodier, Aunt," said Fanchon boldly, "if you cannot be kind to him why did you marry him?"

"Why I wanted a husband and he wanted my money that was all, and I got my bargain and his too Fanchon—!" and the woman laughed savagely.

"I thought people married to be happy Aunt," replied the girl persistently.

"Happy! such folly," replied La Corriveau. "Satan yokes people together to bring more sinners into the world and supply fresh fuel for his fires."

"My mistress thinks there is no happiness like a good match!" remarked Fanchon "and I think so too, Aunt. I shall never wait the second time of asking, I assure you, Aunt."

"You are a fool, Fanchon," said La Corriveau; "but your mistress deserves to wear the ring of Cleopatra, and to become the mother of witches and harlots for all time. Why did she really send for me?"

The girl crossed herself and exclaimed "God forbid! Aunt!—my mistress is not like that!"

La Corriveau spat at the mention of the sacred name. "But it is in her, Fanchon! It is in all of us. If she is not already, she will be! But go into the house and see your foolish uncle while I go prepare for my visit. We will set out at once Fanchon—for business like that of Angelique des Meloises cannot wait!"

CHAPTER 36

"WEIRD SISTERS"

FANCHON walked into the house to see her Uncle Dodier. When she had left, the countenance of La Corriveau put on a dark and terrible expression. Her black eyes looked downwards seeming to penetrate the very earth and to reflect in their glittering orbits the fires of the under world.

She stood for a few moments buried in deep thought with her arms tightly folded across her breast. Her fingers moved nervously as they kept time with the quick motions of her foot which beat the floor.

"It is for death and no lost jewels that girl sends for me!" muttered La Corriveau through her teeth, which flashed white and cruel between her thin lips. "She has a rival in her love for the Intendant, and she will lovingly by my help feed her with the manna of St Nicholas! Angelique des Meloises has boldness, craft and falseness for twenty women and can keep secrets like a Nun. She is rich and ambitious, and would poison half the world, rather than miss the thing she sets her mind on. She is a girl after my own heart and worth the risk I run with her. Her riches would be endless. Should she succede in her design and with her in my power nothing she has would henceforth be her own—but mine! mine! Besides" added La Corriveau her thoughts flashing back to the fate which had overtaken her progenitors—Exili and La Voisin—"I may need help myself, some day, to plead with the Intendant on my own account; who knows?"

A strange thrill ran through the veins of La Corriveau but she instantly threw it off. "I know what she wants!" added she. "I will take it with me, I am safe in trusting her with the secret of *Beatrice Spara*. That girl is worthy of it, as Brinvilliers herself—!"

La Corriveau entered her own appartment. She fastened the door and drew a bunch of keys from her bosom, and turned towards a cabinet of singular shape and Italian workmanship which stood in a corner of the appartment. It was an antique piece of furniture made of some dark oriental wood carved over with fantastic figures from Etruscan designs by the cunning hand of an old Italian workman, who knew well how to make secret drawers and invisible concealments for things dangerous and forbidden.

It had once belonged to Antonio Exili who had caused it to be made, ostensibly for the safe keeping of his Cabaliste formulas and alchemic preparations, when searching for the philosophers stone, and the Elixir of life,—really for the concealment of the subtle drugs out of which his alembics distilled the *Aqua Tofana* and his crucibles prepared the *poudre de succession*.

In the most secret place of all were deposited ready for use a few vials of the crystal liquid, every single drop of which contained the life of a man, and which administered in due proportion of time and measure killed and left no sign, numbering its victim's days, hours and minutes, exactly according to the will and malignity of his destroyer.

La Corriveau took out the vials and placed them carefully in a casket of ebony not larger than a woman's hand. In it was a number of small cellules, each filled with pills like grains of mustard seed, the essence and quintessence of various poisons, that put on the appearance of natural diseases and which mixed in due proportion with the Aqua Tofana covered the foulest murders with the lawful ensigns of the angel of death.

In that box of ebony was the sublimated dust of deadly night-shade which kindles the red fires of fever and rots the roots of the tongue. There was the fetid powder of Stramonium that grips the lungs like an asthma and Quinia that shakes its victims like the cold hand of the miasma of the Pontine Marshes. The essence of Poppies ten times distilled, a few grains of which bring on the stupor of apoplexy and the

Sardonic plant that kills its victim with the frightful laughter of madness on his countenance.

The knowledge of these and many more cursed herbs known once to Medea in the Colchian land, and transplanted to Greece and Rome with the enchantments of their use, had been handed by a long succession of sorcerers and poisoners down to Exili and Beatrice Spara until they came into the possession of La Corriveau the legitimate inheritrix of this lore of hell.

But Providence while it does not prevent the crimes which determined wickedness resolves to commit, never ceases striving against them, educing good out of evil and seeking to ameliorate man's wretched estate. It fights fire with water. It combats evil with good and error with truth. But it also permits men to fight fire with fire and out of the very armoury of Hell brings forth weapons to combat the prevailing wickedness of the time.

The researches of the Alchemists and Poisoners disclosed to them many important secrets in chemistry which in the hands of wise and good men became of prime importance in the cure of diseases, after they had been long noted for their baneful effects.

The study of the science of killing led by a reverse process to that of the science of healing. A whole school of medicine founds its claim on the principle that *similia similibus curantur*, and wise Physicians now use those terrible drugs not to take life, as the poisoners did, but as *medicamenta* to fight and conquer the malignant diseases which these deadly substances administered as poisons, simulate and appear to occasion.

Before closing the cabinet La Corriveau opened one more secret drawer and took out with a hesitating hand as if uncertain whether to do so or no, a glittering stiletto, sharp and cruel to see. She felt the point of it mechanically with her thumb; and, as if fascinated by the touch, placed it under her robe. "I may have need of it," muttered she, "either to save myself or to make sure of my work on another. Beatrice Spara was the daughter of a Sicilian Bravo, and she liked this poniard better than even the poisoned chalice."

La Corriveau rose up now well satisfied with her foresight and preparation. She placed the ebony casket carefully in her bosom, cherishing it like an only child, as she walked out of the room with her quiet tiger like tread. Her look into the future pleased her at this moment. There was the prospect of an ample reward for her trouble and risk, and the anticipated pleasure of practising her skill upon one whose position she regarded as similar to that of the great Dames of the Court, whom Exili and La Voisin had poisoned during the high Carnival of Death in the days of Louis Quatorze.

She was now ready and waited impatiently to depart.

The goodman Dodier brought the Calash to the door. It was a substantial two wheeled vehicle with a curious arrangement of springs made out of the elastic wood of the Hickory. The horse a stout Norman pony well harnessed, sleek and glossy, was hardly held in by the hand of the good man who patted it kindly as an old friend, and the pony in some sort after an equine fashion returned the affection of its master.

La Corriveau with an agility hardly to be expected from her years, seated herself beside Fanchon in the Calash and giving her willing horse a sharp cut with the lash for spite, not for need—Good man Dodier said—only to anger him—they set off at a rapid pace, and were soon out of sight at the turn of the dark pine woods, on their way to the city of Quebec.

Angelique des Meloises had remained all day in her house counting the hours as they flew by laden with the fate of her unsuspecting rival at Beaumanoir.

Night had closed in, the lamps were lit. The fire again burned red on the hearth. Her door was inexorably shut against all visitors. Lizette had been sent away until the morrow. Angelique sat alone, and expectant of the arrival of La Corriveau.

The gay dress in which she had outshone all her sex at the Ball on the previous night, lay still in a heap upon the floor where last night she had thrown it aside like the robe of innocence which once invested her. Her face was beautiful, but cruel and in its expression terrible as Medea's brooding over her vengeance sworn against Creusa for her sin with

Jason. She sat in a careless dishabille with one white arm
partially bare. Her long golden locks flowed loosely down
her back, and touched the floor as she sat on her chair, and
watched and waited for the coming footsteps of La Corriveau.
Her lips were compressed with a terrible resolution. Her eyes
glanced red as they alternately reflected the glow of the fire
within them, and of the fire without. Her hands were clasped
nervously together with a grip like iron, and lay in her lap
while her dainty foot marked the rhythm of the tragical
thoughts that swept like a song of doom through her soul.

The few compunctious feelings which struggled up
into her mind were instantly overborne by the passionate
reflection that the Lady of Beaumanoir must die! "I must,
or she must! one or other! we cannot both live and marry this
man!" exclaimed she passionately. "Has it come to this, which
of us shall be the wife, which the mistress? By God! I would
kill him too, if I thought he hesitated in his choice! but he
shall soon have no choice but one. Her death be on her own
head and on Bigots—not on mine—!"

And the wretched girl strove to throw the guilt of the sin
she premeditated upon her victim, upon the Intendant, upon
fate, and with a last subterfuge to hide the enormity of it from
her own eyes, upon La Corriveau, whom she would lead on to
suggest the crime and commit it! a course which Angelique
tried to believe would be more Venial than if it was suggested
by herself! less heinous in her own eyes, and less wicked in
the sight of God.

"Why did that mysterious woman go to Beaumanoir
and place herself in the path of Angelique des Meloises?"
exclaimed she angrily. "Why did Bigot reject my earnest
prayer, for it was earnest, for a *Lettre de Cachet* to send her
unharmed away out of New France?"

Then, Angelique sat, and listened without moving for
a long time. The clock ticked loud and warningly. There
was a sighing of the wind about the windows as if it sought
admittance to reason and remonstrate with her. A cricket sang
his monotonous song on the hearth. In the wainscot of the
room a death watch ticked its doleful omen. The dog in the

court yard howled plaintively as the hour of midnight sounded upon the Convent bell, close by.

The bell had scarcely ceased ere she was startled by a slight creaking like the opening of a door, followed by a whispering and the rustle of a woman's garments as of one approaching with cautious steps up the stair. A thrill of expectation not unmingled with fear shot through the breast of Angelique. She sprang up, exclaiming to herself, "She is come! and all the Demons that wait on murder come with her into my chamber!" A knock followed on the door. Angelique very agitated in spite of her fierce efforts to appear calm, bade them come in!

Fanchon opened the door, and with a courtsey to her mistress, ushered in La Corriveau, who walked straight into the room, and stood face to face with Angelique.

The eyes of the two women instantly met in a searching glance, that took in the whole look, bearing, dress and almost the very thoughts of each other. In that one glance each knew and understood the other and could trust each other in evil if not in good.

And there was trust between them. The evil spirits that possessed both their hearts, shook hands together and a silent league was sworn to in their souls, before a word was spoken.

And yet how unlike to human eye were these two women! How like in God's eye that sees the heart and reads the spirit, of what manner it is! Angelique, radiant in the bloom of youth and beauty, her golden hair floating about her like a cloud of glory round a daughter of the sun, Her womanly perfections which made the world seem brighter for such a revelation of completeness in every external charm.

La Corriveau, stern, dark, angular, her fine cut features were crossed with thin lines of cruelty and cunning, No mercy in her eyes, still less on her lips, none at all in her heart, cold to every humane feeling and warming only to wickedness and avarice. Still these women recognized each other as kindred spirits crafty and void of conscience in the accomplishment of their ends.

Had fate exchanged the outward circumstances of their

lives, each might have been the other easily and naturally. The proud beauty had nothing in her heart better than La Corriveau, and the witch of St Valier if born in luxury and endowed with beauty and wealth would have rivaled Angelique in seductiveness and hardly fallen below her in ambition and vanity.

La Corriveau saluted Angelique, who made a sign to Fanchon to retire. The girl obeyed somewhat reluctantly. She had hoped to be present at the interview between her Aunt and her Mistress, for her curiosity was greatly excited and she now suspected there was more in this visit than she had been told.

Angelique invited La Corriveau to remove her cloak and broad hat. Seating her in her own luxurious chair, she sat down beside her and began the conversation with the usual platitudes and common places of the time, dwelling longer upon them than need was, as if she hesitated or feared to bring up the real subject of this midnight conference.

"My lady is fair to look on. All women will admit that. All men swear to it!" said La Corriveau in a harsh voice, that grated ominously like the door of Hell which she was opening with this commencement of her business.

Angelique replied only with a smile. A compliment from La Corriveau even was not wasted upon her, but just now she was on the brink of an abyss of explanation, looking down into the pit, resolved yet hesitating to make the plunge.

"No witch or witchery but your own charms is needed Mademoiselle!" continued La Corriveau, falling into the tone of flattery, she often used towards her dupes, "to make what fortune you will in this world, what pearl ever fished out of the sea, could add a grace to this wondrous hair of yours? Permit me to touch it Mademoiselle."

La Corriveau took hold of a thick tress and held it up to the light of the lamp, where it shone like gold. Angelique shrank back as from the touch of fire. She withdrew her hair with a jerk from the hand of La Corriveau. A shudder passed through her from head to foot. It was the last parting effort of her good genius to save her.

"Do not touch it!" said she quickly, "I have set my life and soul on a desperate venture, but my hair I have devoted it to our Lady of St Foye! It is hers not mine! Do not touch it Dame Dodier!"

Angelique was thinking of a vow she had once made before the shrine of the little church of Lorette. "My hair is the one thing belonging to me that I will keep pure!" continued she, "So do not be angry with me!" she added apologetically.

"I am not angry" replied La Corriveau with a sneer. "I am used to strange humours, in people who ask my aid. They always fall out with themselves, before they fall in with La Corriveau."

"Do you know why I have sent for you at this hour, good Dame Dodier?" asked Angelique abruptly.

"Call me La Corriveau. I am not good Dame Dodier! It is an ill name and I like it best, and so should you Mademoiselle, for the business you sent me for, is not what people who say their prayers, call good! It was to find your lost jewels that Fanchon Dodier summoned me to your abode, was it not?" La Corriveau uttered this with a half suppressed smile of incredulity.

"Ah! I bade Fanchon tell you that, in order to deceive her, not you—! But you knew better La Corriveau! It was not for the sake of paltry jewels I desired you to come to the City to see me at this hour of midnight."

"I conjectured as much!" replied La Corriveau with a sardonic smile which showed her small teeth white even and cruel as those of a wild cat. "The jewel you have lost is the heart of your lover, and you thought La Corriveau had a charm to win it back, was not that it, Mademoiselle?"

Angelique sat upright, gazing boldly in the eyes of her visitor "Yes! it was that, and more than that! I summoned you for! can you not guess? You are wise La Corriveau to know a woman's desire, better than she dare avow it to herself—!"

"Ah!" replied La Corriveau returning her scrutiny with the eyes of a basilisk—a green light flashed out of their dark depths. "You have a lover, and you have a rival too! A woman more potent than yourself in spite of your beauty and your fascinations, has caught the eye and entangled the affections of the man you love! and you ask my counsel how to win him back and how to triumph over your rival! Is it not for that you have summoned La Corriveau?"

"Yes! it is that and still more than that!" replied Angelique, clenching her hands hard together and gazing earnestly at the fire with a look of merciless triumph, at what she saw there reflected from her own thoughts, distinctly as when she looked at her own face in a mirror.

"It is all that and still more than that! cannot you guess yet why I have summoned you here?" continued Angelique, rising from her seat and laying her left hand firmly upon the shoulder of La Corriveau as she bent her head and whispered with terrible distinctness in her ear.

La Corriveau heard her whisper and looked up eagerly "Yes, I know now Mademoiselle! You would kill your rival! There is death in your eye in your voice, in your heart! but not in your hand! You would kill the woman who robs you of your lover, and you have sent for La Corriveau to help you in the good work! It is a good work in the eyes of a woman to kill her rival! But why should I do that to please you? What do I care for your lover Angelique des Meloises?"

Angelique was startled to hear from the lips of another, words which gave free expression to her own secret thoughts. A denial was on her lips, but the lie remained unspoken. She trembled before La Corriveau, but her resolution was unchanged.

"It was not only to please me, but to profit yourself that I sent for you!" Angelique replied eagerly like one trying to out strip her conscience and prevent it from overtaking her sin. "Hark you! You love gold La Corriveau! I will give you all you crave in return for your help!—for help me you shall! You will never repent of it, if you do. You will never cease to regret it if you do not! I will make you rich La Corriveau or else by God! do you hear? I swear it! I will have you burnt for a Witch and your ashes strewn all over St Valier—!"

La Corriveau spat contemptuously upon the floor at the holy name. "You are a fool Angelique des Meloises! to speak thus to me! do you know who and what I am? You are a poor butterfly to flutter your gay wings against La Corriveau! and still I like your spirit! women like you are rare. The blood of Exili could not have spoken bolder than you do! You want the life of a woman who has kindled the hell fire of jealousy in your heart, and you want me to tell you how to get your revenge!"

"I do want you to do it La Corriveau, and your reward shall be great!" answered Angelique with a burst of impatience. She could beat about the bush no longer.

"To kill a woman or man were of itself a pleasure even without the profit," replied La Corriveau doggedly. "But why should I run myself into danger for you Mademoiselle des Meloises? Have you gold enough to balance the risk of it?"

Angelique had fairly overleaped all barrier of reserve now. "I will give you more than your eyes ever beheld, if you will serve me in this matter, Dame Dodier."

"Perhaps so! but I am getting old and trust neither man nor woman. Give a pledge of your good faith before you speak one word farther to me on this business, Mademoiselle des Meloises!—" La Corriveau held out her double hands significantly.

"A pledge? that is gold you want," replied Angelique, "Yes La Corriveau! I will bind you to me with chains of gold! you shall have it uncounted as I get it! Gold enough to make you the richest woman in St Valier The richest peasant woman in New France!"

"I am no peasant woman!" replied La Corriveau with a touch of pride. "I come of a race ancient and terrible as the Roman Caesars, but—pshaw! what have you to do with that? give me the pledge of your good faith and I will help you—!"

Angelique rose as instantly, and opening the drawer of an escritoire took out a long silken purse, filled with Louis d'or which peeped and glittered through the interstices of the net work. She gave it with the air of one who cared nothing for money.

La Corriveau extended both hands eagerly, clutching as with the claws of a Harpy. She pressed the purse to her thin bloodless lips and touched with the ends of her bony fingers, the edges of the bright coin visible through the silken net.

"This is indeed a rare earnest penny!" exclaimed La Corriveau. "I will do your whole bidding Mademoiselle—only I must do it in my own way. I have guessed aright the nature of your trouble and the remedy you seek. But I cannot guess the name of your false lover or that of the woman whose doom is sealed from this hour."

"I will not tell you the name of my lover!" replied Angelique. She was reluctant to mention the name of Bigot as her lover. The idea was hateful to her. "The name of the woman I cannot tell you even if I would," added she.

"How Mademoiselle? You put the death mark upon one you do not know?"

"I do not know her name. Nevertheless La Corriveau! that gold and ten times as much is yours if you relieve me of the torment of knowing that the secret chamber of Beaumanoir contains a woman whose life is death to all my hopes, and disappointment to all my plans."

The mention of Beaumanoir startled La Corriveau. "The lady of Beaumanoir!" she exclaimed, "whom the Abenaquais brought in from Acadia? I saw that lady in the woods of St Valier where I was gathering mandrakes one summer day. She asked me for some water in God's name. I cursed her silently, but I gave her milk. I had no water. She thanked me. Oh, how she thanked me! no body ever before thanked La Corriveau so sweetly as she did! I, even I bade her a good journey, when she started on afresh with her Indian guides after asking me the distance and direction of Beaumanoir."

This unexpected touch of sympathy surprised and revolted Angelique a little.

"You know her then! that is rare fortune! La Corriveau" said she, "she will remember you and you will have less difficulty in gaining access to her and winning her confidence."

La Corriveau clapped her hands laughing a strange laugh, that sounded as if it came from a deep well.

"Know her? that is all I know! she thanked me sweetly. I

said so did I not? but I cursed her in my heart, when she was gone, for I saw she was both beautiful and good, two things I hate."

"Do you call her beautiful? I care not whether she be good! that will avail nothing with *him*, but is she beautiful? La Corriveau? Is she fairer than I, think you?"

La Corriveau looked at Angelique intently and laughed. "Fairer than you! listen! It was as if I had seen a vision. She was very beautiful and very sad! I could wish it were another than she! for O! she spoke to me the sweetest, I was ever spoken to, since I came into the world."

Angelique ground her teeth with anger. "What did you do, La Corriveau? Did you not wish her dead? Did you think the Intendant or any man could not help loving her to the rejection of any other woman in the world? What did you do?"

"Do? I went on picking my mandrakes in the forest and waited for you to send for La Corriveau! You desire to punish the Intendant for his treachery in forsaking you for one more beautiful and better!"

It was but a bold guess of La Corriveau but she had divined the truth. The Intendant Bigot was the man who was playing false with Angelique.

Her words filled up the measure of Angelique's jealous hate and confirmed her terrible resolution. Jealousy is never so omnipotent as when its rank suspicions are fed and watered by the tales of others.

"There can be but one life between her and me!" replied the vehement girl! "Angelique des Meloises would die a thousand deaths rather than live to feed on the crumbs of any man's love while another woman feasted at his table. I sent for you La Corriveau to take my gold and kill that woman!"

"Kill that woman! It is easily said, Mademoiselle, but I will not forsake you were she the Madonna herself! I hate her for her goodness, as you hate her for her beauty. Lay another purse by the side of this and in thrice three days there shall be weeping in the Chateau of Beaumanoir! and no one shall know who has killed the cotquean of the Chevalier Intendant!—"

Angelique sprang up with a cry of exultation like a Pantheress seizing her prey. She clasped La Corriveau in her arms, and kissed her dark withered cheek, exclaiming, "yes! that is her name. His cotquean she is! His wife she is not, and never shall be!—Thanks! a million, golden thanks La Corriveau! if you fulfil your prophecy, in thrice three days from this hour! was it not that you said?"

La Corriveau cared not for caresses and strove to release herself as Angelique impetuously wound one of her long golden locks round her neck. "I would not let you touch my hair before," said she "I wind it round you now, in token of my love and my desire to bind you for ever to my fortunes."

"Tush! your love! save such folly for men! It is lost on me!" replied La Corriveau, releasing herself from the clasp of Angelique and unwinding the long golden tress that encircled her throat.

"Understand me!" said La Corriveau "I serve you for your money not for your liking! But I have my own joy in making my hand felt in a world which I hate and which hates me—!" La Corriveau held out her hands as if the ends of her fingers were trickling poison. "Death drops on whomsoever I send it," said she, "so secretly and so subtly that the very spirits of air cannot detect the trace of the *Aqua Tofana*."

Angelique listened with amaze yet trembled with eagerness to hear more. "What! La Corriveau have you the secret of the *Aqua Tofana* which the world believes was burnt with its possessors two generations ago, on the place de Grève?"

"Such secrets never die," replied the poisoner, "they are too precious! Few men, still fewer women, are there, who would not listen at the door of Hell to learn them! The King in his palace, the lady in her tapestried chamber, the Nun in her cell, the very beggar on the street, would stand on a pavement of fire to read the tablets which record the secret of the Aqua Tofana. Let me see your hand!" added she abruptly, speaking to Angelique.

Angelique held out her hand. La Corriveau seized it; She looked intently upon the slender fingers and oval palm.

"There is evil enough in these long sharp spatulæ of yours," said she, "to ruin the world. You are worthy to be the inheritrix of all I know! These fingers would pick fruit off the forbidden tree for men to eat, and die—! The tempter only is needed, and he is never far off! Angelique des Meloises! I may one day teach you the grand secret! Meantime, I will show you that I possess it!—"

CHAPTER 37

FLASKETS OF DRUGS, FULL TO THEIR WICKED LIPS

La Corriveau took the ebony casket from her bosom, and laid it solemnly on the table. "Do not cross yourself!" exclaimed she angrily, as she saw Angelique mechanically make the sacred sign. "There can come no blessings here! there is death enough in that casket to kill every man and woman in New France."

Angelique fastened her gaze upon the casket as if she would have drawn out the secret of its contents by the very magnetism of her eyes.—She laid her hand upon it caressingly, yet tremblingly.—Eager, yet fearful, to see its contents.

"Open it!" cried La Corriveau, "press the spring, and you will see such a casket of jewels as Queens might envy. It was the wedding gift of Beatrice Spara and once belonged to the house of Borgia. Lucrezia Borgia had it from her terrible father, and He, from the Prince of Demons."

Angelique pressed the little spring—the lid flew open and there flashed from it, a light which for the moment dazzled her eyes with its brilliancy. She thrust the casket from her in alarm, and retreated a few steps, imagining she smelt the odour of some deadly perfume.

"I dare not approach it," said she. "Its glittering terrifies me. Its odour sickens me."

"Tush! it is your sick imagination!" replied La Corriveau, "Your sickly conscience frightens you!—You will need to cast off both to rid Beaumanoir of the presence of your rival! The *Aqua Tofana* in the hands of a coward is a gift as fatal to its possessor as to its victim."

Angelique by a strong effort tried to master her fear but

436

could not. She would not again handle the casket.

La Corriveau looked at her as if suspecting this display of weakness and then drew the Casket to herself and took out a vial gilt and chased with strange symbols. It was not larger than the little finger of a delicate girl. Its contents glittered like a diamond in the sunshine.

La Corriveau shook it up, and immediately the liquid was filled with a million sparks of fire. It was the *Aqua Tofana* undiluted by mercy, instantaneous in its effect and immedicable by no antidote. Once administered, there was no more hope for its victim than for the souls of the damned who have received the final judgment. One drop of that bright water upon the tongue of a Titan would blast him like Jove's thunderbolt, would shrivel him up to a black unsightly cinder—!—

This was the poison of anger and revenge that would not wait for time and braved the world's justice. With that vial La Borgia killed her guests at the fatal banquet in her palace, and Beatrice Spara in her fury destroyed the fair Milanese who stole from her the heart of Antonio Exili.

This terrible water was rarely used alone by the poisoners but it formed the basis of a hundred slower potions which ambition, fear, avarice or hypocrisy mingled with the element of time, and coloured it with the various hues and aspects of natural disease.

Angelique sat down and leaned towards La Corriveau, supporting her chin on the palms of her hands as she bent eagerly over the table, drinking in every word as the hot sand of the desert drinks in the water poured upon it. "What is that?" said she, pointing to a vial as white as milk and seemingly as harmless.

"That!" replied La Corriveau "is the milk of mercy, It brings on painless consumption, and decay. It eats the life out of a man, while the moon empties and fills once or twice. His friends say he dies of quick decline, and so he does! ha! ha! when his enemy wills it! The strong man becomes a skeleton and blooming maidens sink into their graves blighted and bloodless, with white lips and hearts that cease gradually to beat, men know not why. Neither saints nor sacraments can arrest the doom of the milk of mercy."

"This vial," continued she, lifting up another from the casket and replacing the first, licking her thin lips with profound satisfaction as she did so. "This contains the acrid venom that grips the heart like the claws of a tiger, and the man drops down dead at the time appointed! Fools say he died of the visitation of God! The visitation of God—!" repeated she in an accent of scorn, and the foul witch spat as she pronounced the sacred name, "Leo in his sign ripens the deadly nuts of the East, which kill, when God will not—kill! He who has this vial for a possession is the Lord of life!" She replaced it tenderly. It was a favorite vial of La Corriveau.

"This one," continued she taking up another, "strikes the dead palsy, and this kindles the slow inextinguishable fires of Typhus—here is one that dissolves all the juices of the body and the blood of a mans veins runs into a lake of dropsy. This!" taking up a green vial, "contains the quintessence of mandrakes distilled in the Alembic when Scorpio rules the hour. Whoever takes this liquid" La Corriveau shook it up lovingly "dies of torments incurable as the foul disease of lust which it simulates and provokes."

There was one vial which contained a black liquid like oil. "It is a relic of the past," said she, "an heir-loom from the *Untori*, the *Ointers* of Milan. With that oil they spread death through the doomed City, anointing its doors and thresholds with the plague until the people died."

The terrible tale of the Ointers of Milan, has since the days of La Corriveau been written in choice Italian by Manzoni in whose wonderful book he that cares may read it.

"This vial" continued the Witch, "contains innumerable evils that wait upon the pillows of rejected and heart broken lovers! and the wisest Physician is mocked with lying appearances of diseases that defy his skill and make a fool of his wisdom."

"Oh! say no more!" exclaimed Angelique shocked and terrified—however inordinate in her desires, she was dainty in her ways. "It is like a Sabbat of witches to hear you talk La

Corriveau," cried she. "I will have none of those foul things which you propose. My rival shall die like a lady! I will not feast like a vampire on her dead body, nor shall you. You have other vials in the casket of better hue and flavour— what is this?" continued Angelique taking out a rose tinted and curiously twisted bottle sealed on the top with the mystic pentagon. "This looks prettier and may be not less sure than the milk of mercy in its effect. What is it?"—

"Ha! Ha!" laughed the woman with her weirdest laugh. "Your wisdom is but folly, Angelique des Meloises! You would kill and still spare your enemy! That was the smelling bottle of La Brinvilliers, who took it with her to the great Ball at the Hôtel de Ville, where she secretly sprinkled a few drops of it upon the handkerchief of the fair Louise Gauthier, who the moment she put it to her nostrils, fell dead upon the floor! She died and gave no sign, and no man knew how or why! But she was the rival of Brinvilliers for the love of Gaudin de St Croix! and in that she resembles the lady of Beaumanoir, as you do La Brinvilliers—!"

"And she got her reward! I would have done the same thing for the same reason! What more, have you to relate of this most precious vial of your casket?—" asked Angelique.

"That its virtue is unimpaired—three drops sprinkled upon a Bouquet of flowers and its odour breathed by man or woman causes a sudden swoon from which there is no awakening more in this World. People feel no pain but die smiling as if Angels had kissed away their breath. Is it not a precious toy, Mademoiselle?—"

"Oh! blessed vial!" exclaimed Angelique pressing it to her lips. "Thou art my good Angel to kiss away the breath of the Lady of Beaumanoir! She shall sleep on roses La Corriveau! and you shall make her bed."

"It is a sweet death befitting one who dies for love, or is killed by the jealousy of a dainty rival!" replied the Witch, "but I like best those draughts which are most bitter and not less sure."

"The Lady of Beaumanoir will not be harder to kill than Louise Gauthier!" replied Angelique, watching the glitter of the vial in the lamplight. "She is unknown even to the servants of the Chateau, nor will the Intendant himself dare to make public either her life or death, in his house."

"Are you sure Mademoiselle, that the Intendant will not dare to make public the death of that woman in the Chateau?" asked La Corriveau with intense eagerness. The consideration was an important link in the chain which she was forging.

"Sure? yes, I am sure by a hundred tokens!" said Angelique with an air of triumph. "He dare not even banish her for my sake, lest the secret of her concealment at Beaumanoir become known. We can safely risk his displeasure even should he suspect that I have cut the knot he knew not how to untie."

"You are a bold girl!" exclaimed La Corriveau looking on her admiringly, "you are worthy to wear the crown of Cleopatra the queen of all Gypsies and enchantresses! I will have less fear now to do your bidding for you have a stronger spirit than mine to support you."

"'Tis well La Corriveau! Let this vial of Brinvilliers bring me the good fortune I crave, and I will fill your lap with gold! If the Lady of Beaumanoir shall find death in a bouquet of flowers, let them be roses!"

"But how and where to find roses? They have ceased blooming!" said La Corriveau, hating Angelique's sentiment, and glad to find an objection to it.

"Not for her, La Corriveau! Fate is kinder than you think!" Angelique threw back a rich curtain and disclosed a recess filled with pots of blooming roses and flowers of various hues. "The roses are blooming here which will form the bouquet of Beaumanoir!"

"You are of rare ingenuity Mademoiselle!" replied La Corriveau admiringly "If Satan prompts you not, it is because he can teach you nothing either in love or stratagem."

"Love!" replied Angelique quickly, "do not name that! no! I have sacrificed all love or I should not be taking counsel of La Corriveau!"—

Angelique's thoughts flashed back upon Le Gardeur for one regretful moment. "No! it is not love" continued she "but the duplicity of a man before whom I have lowered my pride.

It is the vengeance I have vowed upon a woman for whose sake I am trifled with! It is that prompts me to this deed! But no matter, shut up the casket, La Corriveau! We will talk now of how and when this thing is to be done!"

The Witch shut up her infernal casket of ebony, leaving the vial of Brinvilliers shining like a ruby in the lamplight, upon the polished table.

The two women sat down, their foreheads almost touching together with their eyes flashing in lurid sympathy as they eagerly discussed the position of things in the Chateau. The appartments of Caroline, the hours of rest and activity were all well known to Angelique who had adroitly fished out every fact from the unsuspecting Fanchon Dodier, as had also La Corriveau.

It was known to Angelique that the Intendant would be absent from the city for some days in consequence of the news from France. The unfortunate Caroline would be deprived of the protection of his vigilant eye.

The two women sat long arranging and planning their diabolical scheme. There was no smile upon the cheek of Angelique now. Her dimples which drove men mad had disappeared. Her lips made to distil words sweeter than honey of Hybla were now drawn together in hard lines like La Corriveau's. They were cruel and untouched by a single trace of mercy.

Her golden hair swept loosely over her white robe. It might have served for the adornment of an angel; in the intensity of her feelings it seemed to curl like the fabled snakes on the head of Megæra. Her face under the influence of diabolical thoughts seemed to put on the likeness, the very features of La Corriveau! As their eyes met while contriving their wicked scheme, each saw herself reflected in the face of the other.

The hours struck unheeded on the clock in the room, and it ticked louder and louder like a conscious monitor beside them! Its slow finger had marked each wicked thought and recorded for all time, each murderous word as it passed their cruel lips.

La Corriveau held the Casket in her lap with an air of

satisfaction and sat with eyes fixed on Angelique who was now silent.

"Water the roses well Mademoiselle!" said she. "In three days I shall be here for a bouquet and in less than thrice three days I promise you, there shall be a dirge sung for the Lady of Beaumanoir."

"Only let it be done soon and surely!" replied Angelique—her very tone grew harsh. "But talk no more of it. Your voice sounds like a cry in a dark gallery that leads to Hell. Would it were done! I could then shut up the memory of it in a tomb of silence, for ever, for ever! and wash my hands of a deed done by you! not me—!"

"A deed done by you, not me!" she repeated the words as if repeating them made them true. She would shut up the memory of her crime forever! She reflected not that the guilt is in the evil intent and the sin the same before God even if the deed be never done.

Angelique was already an eager sophist. She knew better than the wretched creature whom she had bribed with money, how intensely wicked was the thing she was tempting her to do, but her jealousy maddened her, and her ambition could not let her halt in her course.

There was one thought which still tormented her. "What would the Intendant think? What would he say should he suspect her of the murder of Caroline?" She feared his scrutinizing investigation, but trusting in her power she risked his suspicions, nay remembering his words made him in her own mind an accessory in the murder.

If she remembered Le Gardeur de Repentigny at all at this moment it was only to strangle the thought of him. She shied like a horse on the brink of a precipice when the thought of Le Gardeur intruded itself. Rising suddenly she bade La Corriveau be gone about her business, lest she should be tempted to change her mind.

La Corriveau laughed at the last struggle of dying conscience, and bade Angelique go to bed. "It was two hours past midnight and she would bid Fanchon let her depart to the house of an old crone in the City who would give her a bed and a blessing in the Devil's name."

Angelique, weary and agitated, bade her begone in the devil's name if she preferred a curse to a blessing! The witch with a mocking laugh rose and took her departure for the night.

Fanchon weary of waiting had fallen asleep. She roused herself offering to accompany her Aunt in hopes of learning something of her interview with the mistress. All she got was a whisper that the jewels were found! La Corriveau passed out into the darkness and plodded her way to the house of her friend, where she resolved to stay until she accomplished the secret and cruel deed she had undertaken to perform.

CHAPTER 38

THE BROAD BLACK GATEWAY OF A LIE

The Count de la Galissoniere was seated in his cabinet a week after the arrival of La Corriveau on her fatal errand. It was a plain comfortable appartment he sat in, hung with arras and adorned with maps and pictures. It was there he held his daily sittings for ordinary despatch of business with a few such councillors as the occasion required to be present.

The table was loaded with letters, memorandums and bundles of papers tied up in official style. Despatches of Royal Ministers bearing the broad seal of France, reports from officers of posts far and near in New France lay mingled together, with silvery strips of the inner bark of the birch painted with hieroglyphics giving accounts of war parties on the Eastern Frontier and in the far West signed by the totems of Indian chiefs in alliance with France. There was a newly arrived parcel of letters from the bold enterprising Sieur de La Verendrye, who was exploring the distant waters of the Saskatchewan and the land of the Black Feet and many a missive from missionaries giving accounts of wild regions, which remain yet almost a *terra incognita* to the Government which rules over them.

The Governors Bureau in the Castle of St Louis was not an idle empty chamber in those days. It was filled with the spirits of ambition, conquest and war. From it as from the cave of Eolus, went forth storms and tempests which shook the Continent and carried the commands of Onontio the Governor to the Indian Nations of the farthest regions of North America.

At the Governor's elbow sat his friend Bishop Pontbriand with a secretary immersed in papers. In front of him was the

444

Intendant with Varin, Penisault and d'Estebe. On one side of the table, La Corne St Luc was examining some Indian despatches with Rigaud de Vaudreuil, Claude Beauharnois, and the venerable Abbé Piquet, overlooking with deep interest the rude pictorial despatches in the hands of La Corne. Two gentlemen of the law in furred gowns and bands stood waiting at one end of the room with books under their arms and budgets of papers in their hands ready to argue before the council some knotty point of controversy arising out of the concession of certain fiefs and jurisdictions granted under the Feudal laws of the Colony.

The Intendant although personally at variance with several of the gentlemen sitting at the Council table did not let that fact be visible in his countenance or allow it to interfere with the despatch of public business.

The Intendant was gay, alert and easy to day as was his wont, wholly unsuspecting the foul treason that was plotting by the woman he admired against the woman he loved. His claims were some times loftily expressed, but always courteous and firm.

Bigot never drooped a feather in face of his enemies public or private, but laughed and jested with all at table, in the exuberance of a spirit which cared for no one and only reined itself in when it was politic to flatter his Patrons and Patronesses at Versailles.

In an inner appartment whose walls were covered with tiers of books forming the private library of the Governor, might be seen through a half open door the portly form and large flaxen head of Peter Kalm.

The enthusiastic investigator of Science sat by himself at a table entrenched behind a wall of volumes which he had taken down from their shelves, and continued to pile upon the table before him as he consulted them. His broad florid face was largely visible like a full moon peering over the edge of an eastern hill.

The business of the council had begun. The mass of papers which lay at the left hand of the Governor were opened and read *seriatim* by his Secretary, and debated, referred, decided upon, or judgment postponed, as the case seemed best to the Council.

The Count was a man of method and despatch, clear headed and singularly free from prejudice, ambiguity or hesitation. He was honest and frank in council, as he was gallant on the Quarter Deck. The Intendant was not a whit behind him in point of ability and knowledge of the political affairs of the Colony and surpassed him in influence at the Court of Louis XV, but less frank for he had much to conceal, and kept authority in his own hands as far as he was able.

Disliking each other profoundly from the total divergence of their characters, opinions and habits, the Count and Intendant still met Courteously at the Council table, and not without a certain respect for the rare talents which each recognized in the other.

Many of the papers lying before them were on subjects relating to the Internal Administration of the Colony— Petitions of the people suffering from the exactions of the commissaries of the Army, Remonstrances against the late decrees of the Intendant and *arrêts* of the high Court of Justice confirming the right of the Grand Company to exercise certain new monopolies of trade.

The discussions were earnest and sometimes warm on these important questions. La Corne St Luc assailed the new regulations of the Intendant in no measured terms of denunciation, in which he was supported by Rigaud de Vaudreuil and the Chevalier de Beauharnois. But Bigot without condescending to the trouble of defending the ordinances on any sound principle of public policy, which he knew to be useless and impossible with the clever men sitting at the table, contented himself with a cold smile at the honest warmth of La Corne St Luc, and simply bade his Secretary read the orders and despatches from Versailles in the name of the Royal Ministers, and approved of by the King himself in a *Lit de Justice* which had justified every act done by him in favour of the Grand Company.

The Governor, trammelled on all sides by the powers, conferred upon the Intendant, felt unable to exercise the authority he needed, to vindicate the cause of right and justice in the Colony. His own instructions confirmed the pretentions of the Intendant and of the Grand Company. The utmost he could do in behalf of the true interests of the people and of the King, as opposed to the herd of greedy courtiers and selfish beauties who surrounded him, was to soften the deadening blows they dealt upon the trade and resources of the Colony.

A decree authorizing the issue of an unlimited quantity of paper bills, the predecessors of the assignats of the Mother Country, was strongly advocated by Bigot, who supported his views with a degree of financial sophistry which showed that he had affectively mastered the science of delusion and fraud, of which Law had been the great teacher in France, and the Mississippi Scheme, the prototype of the Grand Company, the great exemplar.

La Corne St Luc opposed the measure forcibly. "He wanted no paper lies," he said, "to cheat the husbandman of his corn and the labourer of his hire. If the gold and silver had all to be sent to France to pamper the luxuries of a swarm of idlers at the Court, they could buy and sell as they had done in the early days of the Colony—with beaver skins for livres and muskrat skins for sous. These paper bills," continued he, "had been tried on a small scale by the Intendant Hocquart, and on a small scale had robbed and impoverished the Colony. If this new Mississippi Scheme propounded by new Laws!" and here La Corne glanced boldly at the Intendant, "is to be enforced on the Scale proposed, there will not be left in the Colony one piece of silver to rub against another. It will totally beggar New France and may in the end bankrupt the Royal treasury of France itself if called on to redeem them."

"Promise is not pay!" exclaimed the old soldier, "just as hunger is not meat! He would trust no man, he would not trust himself," he added parenthetically, "with the power of making money out of rags, and of circulating lies for livres. The honest *habitans* knew the value of beaver skins in barter for their corn, but they knew no value that could be fixed on scraps of paper which might be as plentiful and would be as worthless as the leaves of the forest!"

The discussion rolled on for an hour. The Count listened in silent approbation to the arguments of the gentlemen opposing the measure, but he had received private imperative instructions from the King to aid the Intendant in the issue of the new paper money. The Count reluctantly sanctioned a decree which filled New France with worthless assignats, the non-redemption of which completed the misery of the Colony and aided materially in its final subjugation by the English.

The pile of papers upon the table gradually diminished as they were opened and disposed of. The council itself was getting weary of a long sitting, and showed an evident wish for its adjournment. The gentlemen of the law did not get a hearing of their case that day, but were well content to have it postponed, because a postponement meant new fees and increased costs for their clients. The Lawyers of old France, whom La Fontaine depicts in his lively fable, as swallowing the oyster and handing to each litigant an empty shell, did not differ in any essential point from their brothers of the long robe in New France, and differed nothing at all in the length of their bills, and the sharpness of their practice.

The breaking up of the council was deferred by the Secretary opening a package sealed with the Royal seal and which contained other sealed papers marked *special* for his Excellency the Governor. The Secretary handed them to the Count who read over the contents with deep interest and a changing countenance. He laid them down and took them up again, perused them a second time and passed them over to the Intendant, who read them with a start of surprise, and a sudden frown on his dark eyebrows. But he instantly suppressed it, biting his nether lip however, with anger, which he could not wholly conceal.

He pushed the papers back to the Count with a nonchalant air, as of a man who had quite made up his mind about them, saying in a careless manner—

"The commands of Madame La Marquise de Pompadour shall be complied with," said he. "I will order strict search to be made for the missing Demoiselle, who I suspect will be found in some camp or Fort, sharing the couch of some lively fellow, who has won favour in her bright eyes."

Bigot saw danger in these despatches, and in the look of the Governor, who would be sure to exercise the utmost diligence in carrying out the commands of the Court in this matter.

Bigot for a few moments seemed lost in reflection. He looked round the table and seeing many eyes fixed upon him, spoke boldly, almost with a tone of defiance—

"Pray explain to the Councillors the nature of this despatch, your Excellency!" said he to the Count. "What it contains is not surprising to any one who knows the fickle sex, and no gentleman can avoid feeling for the noble Baron de St Castin!"

"And for his daughter too, Chevalier!" replied the governor. "It is only through their virtues that such women are lost. But it is the strangest tale I have heard in New France!"

The gentlemen seated at the table looked at the Governor in some surprise. La Corne St Luc hearing the name of the Baron de St Castin exclaimed: "What in God's name your Excellency, is there in that despatch affecting my old friend and companion in arms, the Baron de St Castin?—"

"I had better explain," replied the Count. "It is no secret in France and will not long be a secret here."

"This letter gentlemen," continued he, addressing the Councillors, and holding it open in his hand, "is a pathetic appeal from the Baron de St Castin whom you all know, urging me by every consideration of friendship, honour and public duty, to aid in finding his daughter Caroline de St Castin, who has been abducted from her home in Acadia and who after a long and vain search for her by her Father in France, where it was thought she might have gone, has been traced to this Colony, where it is said she is living concealed under some strange alias, or low disguise."

"The other despatch" continued the Governor "is from the Marquise de Pompadour affirming the same thing, and commanding the most rigorous search to be made for Mademoiselle de St Castin. In language hardly official the Marquise threatens to make—Stock fish—that is her phrase—

of whosoever has had a hand in either the abduction or the concealment of the missing lady."

The attention of every gentleman at the table was roused by the words of the Count. But La Corne St Luc could not repress his feelings. He sprang up striking the table with the palm of his fist until it sounded like the shot of a petronel.

"By St Christopher the Strong!" exclaimed he, "I would cheerfully have lost a limb rather than heard such a tale told by my dear old friend and comrade about that angelic child of his, whom I have carried in my arms like a lamb of God many and many a time—!"

"You know gentlemen what befel her!" The old soldier looked as if he could annihilate the Intendant with the lightening of his eyes. "I affirm and will maintain that no saint in Heaven was holier in her purity, than she was in her fall! Chevalier Bigot! it is for you to answer these despatches! This is your work! If Caroline de St Castin be lost, you know where to find her!—"

Bigot started up in a rage mingled with fear—not of La Corne St Luc, but lest the secret of Caroline's concealment at Beaumanoir should become known. The furious letter of La Pompadour repressed the prompting of his audacious spirit to acknowledge the deed openly and defy the consequences; as he would have done at any less price than the loss of the favour of his powerful and jealous patroness.

The broad black gate-way of a lie stood open to receive him, and angry as he was at the words of St Luc, Bigot took refuge in it—and lied.

"Chevalier La Corne!" said he with a tremendous effort at self control. "I do not affect to misunderstand your words, and in time and place will make you account for them! but I will say for the contentment of his Excellency and of the other gentlemen at the council table, that whatever in times past have been my relations with the daughter of the Baron de St Castin, and I do not deny having shown her many courtesies, her abduction was not my work, and if she be lost, I do not know where to find her—!—"

"Upon your word as a gentleman," interrogated the

Governor, "will you declare you know not where she is to be found?"

"Upon my word as a gentleman!" The Intendant's face was suffused with passion. "You have no right to ask that! neither shall you Count de La Galissoniere! But I will myself answer the despatch of Madame la Marquise de Pompadour! I know no more, perhaps less, than yourself or the Chevalier La Corne St Luc, where to look for the daughter of the Baron de St Castin! and I proclaim here that I am ready to cross swords with the first gentleman who shall dare breathe a syllable of doubt against the word of Francois Bigot!—"—

Varin and Penisault exchanged a rapid glance partly of doubt, partly of surprise. They knew well for Bigot had not concealed from his intimate associates the fact that a strange lady, whose name they had not heard, was living in the secret chambers of the Château of Beaumanoir. Bigot never told any who she was, or whence she came. Whatever suspicion they might entertain in their own minds, they were too wary to express it. On the contrary Varin ever more ready with a lie than Bigot, confirmed with a loud oath the statement of the Intendant.

La Corne St Luc looked like a baffled lion as Rigaud de Vaudreuil with the familiarity of an old friend laid his hand over his mouth, and would not let him speak. Rigaud feared the coming challenge and whispered audibly in the ear of St Luc—

"Count a hundred before you speak La Corne! The Intendant is to be taken on his word just at present, like any other gentleman! Fight for fact not, for fancy! Be prudent La Corne! We know nothing to the contrary of what Bigot swears to."

"But I doubt much to the contrary! Rigaud!—" replied La Corne with accent of scorn and incredulity.

The old Soldier chafed hard under the bit, but his suspicions were not facts. He felt that he had no solid grounds upon which to accuse the Intendant in the special matter referred to in the letters. He was moreover although hot in temperament soon master of himself and used to the hardest discipline of self control.

"I was perhaps over hasty, Rigaud!" replied La Corne St Luc, recovering his composure; "but when I think of Bigot in the past, how can I but mistrust him in the present. However, be the girl above ground or under ground, I will, *par Dieu,* not leave a stone unturned in New France until I find the lost child of my old friend! La Corne St Luc pledges himself to that, and he never broke his word yet!"

He spoke the last words audibly, and looked hard at the Intendant. Bigot cursed him twenty times over between his teeth, for he knew La Corne's indomitable energy and sagacity, that was never at fault in finding or forcing a way to whatever he was in search of. It would not be long before he would discover the presence of a strange Lady at Beaumanoir, thought Bigot, and just as certain would he be to find out that she was the lost daughter of Baron de St Castin.

The good Bishop rose up when the dispute waxed warmest between the Intendant and La Corne St Luc. His heart was eager to allay the strife; but his shrewd knowledge of human nature and manifold experience of human quarrels, taught him that between two such men the intercession of a Priest would not at that moment be of any avail. Their own notions of honour and self respect, would alone be able to restrain them from rushing into unseemly excesses of language and act. So the good Bishop stood with folded arms looking on and silently praying for an opportunity to remind them of the seventh holy beatitude— *"Beati Pacifici!"*

Bigot felt acutely the difficulty of the position he had been placed in by the act of La Pompadour, in sending her despatch to the Governor instead of to himself. "Why had she done that?" said he savagely to himself. "Had she suspected him?"

Bigot could not but conclude, that La Pompadour suspected him in this matter. He saw clearly that she would not trust the search after this girl to him, because she knew that Caroline de St Castin had formerly drawn aside his heart and that he would have married her but for the interference of the Royal mistress. Whatever might have been done before in the way of sending Caroline back to Acadia, it could not be done now, after he had boldly lied before the Governor and the honourable Council.

One thing seemed absolutely necessary however. The presence of Caroline at Beaumanoir must be kept secret at all hazards—until—until—and even Bigot for once was ashamed of the thoughts which rushed into his mind—until—he could send her far into the wilderness, among savage tribes to remain there until the search for her was over and the affair forgotten.

This was his first thought, but to send her away into the wilderness was not easy. A matter which in France would excite the gossip and curiosity of a league or two of neighbourhood, would be carried on the tongues of Indians and Voyageurs in the wilds of North America for thousands of miles. To send her away without discovery seemed difficult. To retain her at Beaumanoir in face of the search which he knew would be made by the Governor and the indomitable La Corne St Luc, was impossible. The quandary oppressed him. He saw no escape from the dilemma; but to the credit of Bigot be it said, that not for a moment did he entertain a thought of doing injury to the hapless Caroline, or of taking advantage of her lonely condition to add to her distress, merely to save himself.

He fell into a train of sober reflections unusual to him at any time and scarcely paid any attention to the discussion of affairs at the Council table for the rest of the sitting. He rose hastily at last, dispairing to find any outlet of escape from the difficulties which surrounded him in this unlucky affair.

"With his Excellency's consent," he said, "they would do no more business that day. He was tired and would rise. Dinner was ready at the Palace, where he had some wine of the golden plant of Ay-Ay, which he would match against the best in the Castle of St Louis, if his Excellency and the other gentlemen would honour him with their company."

The Council out of respect to the Intendant rose at once. The despatches were shoved back to the Secretaries, and for the present forgotten in a buzz of lively conversation in which no man shone to greater advantage than Bigot.

"It is but a fast day your Reverence!" said he accosting

the Abbé Piquet, "but if you will come and say grace over my graceless table I will take it kindly of you. You owe me a visit you know, and I owe you thanks for the way in which you looked reproof without speaking it upon my dispute with the Chevalier La Corne. It was better than words and showed that you know the world we live in, as well as the world you teach us to live for hereafter."

The Abbé bowed low to the invitation of the Intendant. It was not tempting in itself, for he knew by report what a free table the Intendant kept, but the politic Churchman had objects of his own which he never for a moment lost sight of. He was one who as the proverb says: "would have dined with Satan for God's sake and a sinners."

"Thanks your Excellency!" said he smiling, "I have travelled uninvited, on snow shoes, a hundred leagues through the wilderness to christen or absolve a poor Indian. I cannot refuse to go a mile to say grace over your graceless table, as you please to call it! I try to be like my master St Paul—all things to all men, and I shall find myself I dare say as much at home in the Palace as in the Wigwam."

"That is right well spoken, Abbé! I like you missionaries! Your cold feet carry warm hearts! You shall be welcome at the Palace of the Intendant as you are in the Wigwam of the savage—besides I want to talk with you, Abbé on the subject of that new settlement you project at La Presentation."

"The main reason for which I accepted your invitation Chevalier! It is one great thing upon my heart just now as a minister of God to my fellow men!—"

"Well, if I cannot imitate you, I can admire you Abbé! and I promise you a clean table cloth and full opportunity to convince the Intendant of the goodness of your scheme for bringing the proud Iroquois under the dominion of the King" replied Bigot heartily and honestly too, in this matter.

The Abbé was charmed with the affability of Bigot and nourishing some hope of enlisting him heartily in behalf of his favorite scheme of Indian policy, left the Castle in his company. The Intendant also invited the Procureur du Roy and the other gentlemen of the Law who found it both politic, profitable and pleasant to dine at the bountiful and splendid table of the Palace.

The Governor with three or four most intimate friends, the Bishop, La Corne St Luc, Rigaud de Vaudreuil and the Chevalier de Beauharnois, remained in the room conversing earnestly together on the affair of Caroline de St Castin, which awoke in all of them a feeling of deepest pity for the young lady and of sympathy for the distress of her father. They were lost in conjectures as to the quarter in which a search for her might be successful.

"There is not a Fort, Camp, house, or Wigwam. There is not a hole or hollow tree in New France where that poor broken hearted girl may have taken refuge or been hid by her seducer, but I will find her out" exclaimed La Corne St Luc. "Poor girl! poor hapless girl! How can I blame her! like Magdelene if she sinned much, it was because she loved much, and cursed be either man or woman who will cast a stone at her!—"

"La Corne!" replied the Governor, "the spirit of Chivalry will not wholly pass away while you remain to teach by your example the duty of brave men to fair women—! Stay and dine with me and we will consider this matter thoroughly! Nay, I will not have an excuse to-day. My old friend, Peter Kalm, will dine with us too, he is a philosopher as perfectly as you are a soldier! So stay, and we will have something better than tobacco smoke to our wine to-day!"

"The tobacco smoke is not bad either, your Excellency!" replied La Corne, who was an inveterate smoker. "I like your Swedish friend. He cracks nuts of wisdom with such a grave air that I feel like a boy sitting at his feet glad to pick up a kernel now and then. My practical philosophy is sometimes at fault to be sure in trying to fit it to his theories. But I feel that I ought to believe many things which I do not understand."

"Well you will stay then! and you too Beauharnois and Rigaud! The Abbé Piquet has gone to say grace for the Intendant, but the Bishop will say grace over our table! We will have a feast of the Gods! Ambrosia and Nectar on tables set upon the pinnacle of Olympus!—"

The gentlemen laughed and consented to dine with the hospitable Governor, who called to his friend Peter Kalm to join them.

The Philosopher immersed in his study had not even heard the high voices of La Corne St Luc and the Intendant through the half open door of the library. His large flaxen head was bobbing up and down as he bent over the volumes, extracting this sentence and that which he duly and carefully copied into his common place book and "salted down like meat," he said, "for a rainy day and a long winter."

Kalm heard the call of the Governor however. He rose from behind his entrenchment of books. His friend's cheery voice had recalled him from the world of philosophy and speculation to the world of actual life and sociability. He rejoined the Governor and sat down at the table with them.

"Kalm!" exclaimed the cheery voice of the Count, "This is just as when we were together at Upsal in the good old times when we wore the student's white cap with black brim. You remember how the lads called you the Engineer, because you used to fortify your positions with such ramparts of quotations that they were unassailable as the walls of Midgard."

"Ah! Count!" said he, "those were indeed good times before we found out the burthen of being old and wise over much. All was bright before us then—nothing was dark behind. Every night we lay happy as birds in their nests with God's wings brooding over us. Every morning was a new revelation of light and knowledge of health, youth and joy. How proud young Linneus was of his brother giants! His Jotuns as he called us of the new philosophy! and we thought ourselves eagles, unfledged, ambitious, brood that we were! You have not forgotten our Northern speech Count?—"

"Forgotten it! no! I would not willingly forget it! Listen Kalm!" and the Governor repeated with good accent the verse of an old Swedish ballad, a great favorite once among the students at Upsal.

Sweriges mïn akter jag att lofva
Om Gud vill mig näder gifva—!

Deras dygd framföra med akt och häg
Den stund der jag mä lefva!

Swedish men I mean to praise,
God stir my heart within me!
To boast their truth and manly ways
So long as life is in me.

"That proves it Kalm!" continued the Governor enthusiastically. "I love both the old Northern land and its old northern speech, which is only fit for the mouths of frank honest men such as your brave Swedes. What says the old song of the Goths?—"

"Allsmäktig Gud, han hafver them wiss
Som Sverige äro tro!—!
Bäde nu ock förro förutam all twist
Gud gifve them ro!
Svenske män! I sagen, amen!—
Som I Sveriges rike bo!—"

"Almighty God! hold firm and fast,
Thy faithful Swedes—!
Who serve their country first and last,
In all its needs—!
Amen! Amen! Forever then,
God bless the land of Swedish men!—"

The eyes of Peter Kalm filled with moisture and his breast heaved at this cordial reference to his far off home by the Stormy Baltic. He grasped the hand of his friend. "Thank you Count! thank you Rolland Michael Barrin! I never thought to hear my dear old country so kindly spoken of in this distant land! Its praise is all the more pleasing as coming from one who knows it so well and who is so just in all he says and all he does!"

"Well, never mind!" the Count shyed off ever from a compliment. "If I were not a Frenchman I should choose to be a Swede! But the Castle bell is ringing to let the city know that his Excellency the Governor is going to dinner and during that time no body is to interrupt him with business! Business is over for today Kalm! I have kept my friends here on purpose to dine with you and eat and drink into mutual better acquaintance."

Kalm was delighted with his friend's cordial manner and with the mention of dinner for just aroused from his books, after a long and arduous study, he discovered that he had a nipping appetite. Like all wise men, Peter Kalm was a hearty eater and a sound drinker, stinting only for health and sobriety's sake. He had fixed his pin low down in the tankard of enjoyment and drank cheerfully down to it, thanking God, like a pious Swede for all good things.

The Count took his arm familiarly and followed by the other gentlemen proceeded to the dining hall where his table was spread in a style which if less luxurious than the Intendant's, left nothing to be desired by guests who were content with plenty of good cheer, admirable cooking, adroit service and perfect hospitality.

CHAPTER 39

OLYMPIC CHARIOTS AND MUCH LEARNED DUST

DINNER at the table of the Count de la Galissoniere was not a dull affair of mere eating and drinking. The conversation and sprightliness of the Host fed the minds of his guests as generously as his bread strengthened their hearts, or his wine in the Psalmist's words, made their faces to shine. Men were they, every one of them possessed of a sound mind in a sound body, and both were well feasted at this hospitable table.

The dishes were despatched in a leisurely and orderly manner, as became men who knew the value of both soul and body and sacrificed neither to the other. When the cloth was drawn and the wine flasks glittered ruby and golden upon the polished board, the old Butler came in bearing upon a tray a large silver box of tobacco, with pipes and stoppers, and a wax candle burning ready to light them, as then the fashion was in companies composed exclusively of gentlemen. He placed the materials for smoking upon the table as reverently as a Priest places his biretta upon the Altar, for the old Butler did himself dearly love the Indian weed and delighted to smell the perfume of it as it rose in clouds over his master's table.

"This is a bachelor's banquet gentlemen!" said the Governor filling a pipe to the brim. "We will take fair advantage of the absence of ladies to day and offer incense to the good Manitou who first gave tobacco for the solace of mankind."

The gentlemen were all, as it chanced, honest smokers. Each one took a pipe from the stand, and followed the Governor's example, except Peter Kalm, who more philosophically carried his pipe with him, a huge Meerchaum, clouded like a sunset on the Baltic. He filled it deliberately with tobacco, pressed it down with his finger and thumb, and leaning back in his easy chair after lighting it, began to blow such a cloud as the portly Burgomaster of Stockholm might have envied on a grand council night in the old Raadhus of the city of the Goths.

They were a goodly group of men whose frank loyal eyes looked openly at each other across the hospitable table. None of them but had travelled farther than Ulysses and like him had seen strange cities and observed many minds of men, and was as deeply read in the book of human experience as ever the crafty King of Ithaca.

The event of the afternoon, the reading of the Royal despatches had somewhat dashed the spirits of the Councillors, for they saw clearly the drift of events which was sweeping New France out of the lap of her mother country unless her policy were totally changed and the hour of need brought forth a man capable of saving France herself and with her, her faithful and imperilled colonies.

The Count was not slow to notice in the others the heavy thoughts he felt in himself, and he sought to banish them from his table by turning to other topics and drawing out some of the hidden stores of wisdom which he knew were hived up in the capacious brain of his Swedish friend.

"Kalm!" said he, leaning on his elbow in the kind familiar way that fascinated all men with the Count de la Galissoniere. "We have turned over many new leaves since we studied together in Upsal. The tide of science has ebbed and flowed several times since then."

"And some of our leaves, we have turned backwards, Count. An Era of discovery is ever followed by an Era of scepticism which lasts until men learn how to subordinate their new theories to the old eternal verities. Our age is growing more and more unbelieving every day. We light up our temples with new lamps and forget that the sun is shining over us in the heavens, as it always did."

"I believe you Kalm! The writings of Voltaire and Rousseau will bear evil fruit of which if France eat to repletion, she will become mad."

"She will become mad Count! Unbelief is in her brain and she cannot control the fiery passions in her heart! *Absit omen*! I fear an age of terrible probation awaits your noble country! The first symptom of her decay is seen in her indifference to her noble colonies. She concentrates all her thought upon herself! cares only for her own selfish interests."

The Governor reflected bitterly upon the despatches he had lately received. He knew that France was given up into the hands of extortioners and spendthrifts. Money was at the top, money at the bottom of every motive of action. The few were growing richer and richer,—the many, poorer and poorer—with a chasm opening between the two classes of society and between King and kingdom—which would one day plunge it into chaos. The colonies would go first, however.

The Count would not utter the painful thoughts which oppressed him but by an effort wrenched the conversation into another channel.

"Kalm!" said he. "We often at Upsal debated the question of the antiquity of the earth especially with reference to this New World of ours, which neither of us had then seen. What thinks Upsal now of the argument? has she ever opened the question since, from her chairs of philosophy?—"

The Swede spoke confidently in reply: "She has often done so Count, and the argument is much advanced. A new light has arisen in our intellectual heaven which promises to illuminate all philosophy with its rays."

"Aye! I have heard somewhat of that Kalm! What does the new philosophy teach?—" asked the Governor with interest expressed in every feature.

"It is less a new philosophy than a new illumination of the old" replied Kalm. "If we lay bare the foundations of things we shall see that the world is old as time and that before the creation was; time was not; only, eternity."

"Aye! that is a deep thought, and may be true! Kalm!" replied the Count reflectively.

"I believe it is true, Count, science points to revolutions and changes stretching back into the darkness of the past as far as imagination can penetrate into the darkness of the future. The infinitely swift of the celestial motions of light and gravity has its opposite and counterpart in the infinitely slow of the changes that have taken place in the formations of our earth."

"You still regard the world as very old, Kalm! It was your favorite argument at Upsal I remember."

"Then as now! Look here Count!" Kalm took a piece of coal from a little cabinet of minerals. It had been brought to the Governor by voyageurs from the western slopes of the Alleghany mountains. "Millions of ages ago," said he "in the depths, of time the sun was shining as brightly upon an earth covered with tropical vegetation as is the Equator today. This lump of coal the condensation of vegetable growths is in its last analysis nothing but the heat and light of the sun elaborated, into this concrete form. The last word of chemistry is heat and light and that only, but behind that is the cause of causes, the Love and Wisdom of God. Burn this coal, you release the long imprisoned rays of that ancient sun, and they give out the warmth and illumination of a primeval universe."

"This fern" continued the philosopher, plucking a spray from the Sevre Vase upon the table, "is the expression of a divine idea the form of some use for man's service or delight. Its tiny spores contain a principle of life capable of infinite multiplication forever. What is that life? God! who in his love and in his wisdom is in all things according to their form and use. The conservation of the universe is perpetual creation. Every moment of its existence displays as great a miracle of divine power as was shown when the earth and the heavens were first made by his *Word*. The same power which called the world from chaos alone preserves it from falling back into the same."

"I like your philosophy, Kalm!" replied the Count. "If the universe is to be regarded as the vesture of the all pervading God, it may well seem eternal, although subject to perpetual change. I can easily believe that the world is very old and has seen many many renewals of both its youth and its age."

"And may see as many more. The form of matter is destructible, but not its essence. Why?—Because in its origin it is spiritual, an emanation of the eternal logos, by which all things were made that are made. The earth is Gods footstool in a sense higher than science has yet attained the height of."

"That fern had a beginning," remarked Beauharnois who was profoundly interested in topics of this sort. "Time was when it was not. How know you, Herr Kalm! when it began?—"

"In the book of the earth whose leaves are stone, the hieroglyphics of its history were written ere man appeard to record the ages and cycles of time. Nor can his arithmatic reckon back to the period when this fern began to flourish. We may read however of the order of its creation in what the book of the beginning calls the third day. This part of America was then dry land, while Europe and Asia were still submerged under an ocean of tossing seas."

"You regard, then, the New World as really the old? Herr Kalm! and the elder born of all lands?" asked Beauharnois.

The smoke rose lightly from the philosopher's pipe and curled in silvery clouds up to the ceiling.

"Unquestionably Chevalier!" replied he blowing a fragrant gentle cloud, "I have compared North America rock with rock, plant with plant, tree with tree—fishes, birds, animals and men—all bear an Archaic type of creation, before which the creations of Europe are but as things of yesterday."

"Our Savans of the Academy have as yet made only vague guesses about these things, Kalm!" said the Count, "and I pretend not to be wiser than they, but I have heard La Corne often declare that there was something so settled and petrified in the nature of the Red men of America that he looked upon their very children as older in their instincts and ways than grown men of the white race. He has always said that the race bore the marks of an immense antiquity."

"And of an antiquity," interrupted La Corne St Luc who had listened to the conversation with fixed attention, "so old ossified, and worn out that it can never recover its spring and elasticity again. Nothing can bring back the youth of the Red men or change their ways. The very soul of the race has set and hardened in the form it will retain until it disappears from the earth."

"And yet they may say of themselves, 'We are the heirs of a lost civilization which once filled America with its wonders before the light of knowledge had dawned in any part of the old world,'" remarked Herr Kalm.

"I have seen in the tropics ruins of great cities and temples of strange Gods. I will not call them demons," continued La Corne.

"That would be unphilosophical, as well as unchristian," replied Herr Kalm, "but there is one proof of the great antiquity of the Red men which I am incapable of appreciating as well as you. The languages of these native tribes are I believe so nice in structure and exhibit such polish and smoothness of expression as can only have been acquired by ages of civilization, just as the round pebbles of the shore testify to the long continued action of the waves. An instrument of thought so perfect could not have been elaborated by wild hunters like those who now possess it."

"It is one of the wonders of the Red men, Herr Kalm!" replied La Corne. "Their languages are so far superior to themselves that they must have come down from a great ancient civilization of which they have forfeited the heritage and lost every tradition of it themselves."

"It is what I should have expected and what I have found, Chevalier," replied Kalm. "Everything appertaining to the new world proclaims its vast antiquity. Its rocks were dry land when Europe was submerged in the ocean. I have lately gazed with wonder and veneration upon the old old worn down mountains of the Laurentides, which are to all other mountains of the earth what the Pyramids of Egypt, are to all other works of man. Their very look impresses one with an idea of the hoar of an unfathomable antiquity. There we find the veritable 'bank and shoal of time' which poets only have dreamt of, the first land that emerged from the universal sea when God said 'let the waters be gathered together in one place and let the dry land appear—!' The Laurentides came into being while the old world and the rest of the new were only ideas pre-existing in the foreknowledge of the Divine Creator. There if any where, will perhaps one day be discovered the first dawn of life upon our earth."

"Our existing Flora and fauna should be also of a more antique type than those of the old world, a fact which philosophers begin to recognize, do they not?" asked Beauharnois.

"Undoubtedly! you recollect, Count!" said Kalm turning to the Governor. "Rudberg used to hold, that the horse, the elephant, the camel and the ox are not indigenous in the new world. The Buffalos that swarm on the western plains are of the same archaic type as the mammoth, while the turkey, the condor and the Llama bear the stamp of an older creation than any living creatures of Europe or Asia."

A cabinet in the room contained some well preserved specimens of fishes and shells; the Count was a great collector. Herr Kalm took from it one of those most ancient of fishes, a garpike, from Lake Ontario the last living species of a class of created beings that peopled the primeval waters of the earth before ought else that now lives had heard the fiat of the creator, to come forth.

"Yours are the oldest of waters, as well as the oldest of lands, Count!" said he. "The oldest forms of the old world are modern compared with this fish which is an idea come down to us from the depths of eternity. It tells us that that ancient world was a world of violence more perhaps than is ours now. Look at its armour of defence, its teeth of ravin, its shape for swift attack or escape. It is a terrible dream of the past! How antique must not America be, Count! to contain still living in its inland seas, this relic of primeval times!—"

"Shall we conclude then, that the native men of America are not a new but an old race, the fallen sons of a former and forgotten civilization?" asked Beauharnois, "and yet many learned men are of opinion that its primitive races came from Tartary and Japan."

"'*Non Liquet!*' If they had done so, they would not have failed to bring with them, the horse, the cow and the sheep— animals coeval with man in Asia and yet without these animals America was the scene of a great primeval civilization."

"You always believed in that, Kalm!" said the governor,

"and you liked to read Plato's account of the wonderful tale of Atlantis which was told to Solon by the Egyptian priests."

"And I believe it yet, Count! Atlantis was known to the ancient world before the building of the Pyramids, but intercourse with it, could only have been casual, else there would have been an interchange of the corn of Egypt for the maize of America. Some of the fruit trees of Asia, would have been transplanted and found flourishing at the period of its rediscovery by Columbus. I say its rediscovery—! for I claim for our Northmen, its first discovery Count!—Its civilization may have been indigenous although its sun had set long before the dawn of Asia, yet not so completely but that its reflection like a roseat sky in the west overhung Mexico and Peru, down to the period of Spanish discovery and destruction."

"It extended far beyond Mexico and Peru," replied La Corne. "In my travels over the Continent even up to the Rocky Mountains I have met with mounds and remains of ancient cities overgrown with forests and half resolved into their primal clay. Down in the deep forests of the Tropics are still more wonderful ruins of stone temples with images, carved work and inscriptions like those of Egypt which remain to prove the early civilization of America."

"Here is some confirmation of it La Corne," replied the Governor. "I received today this letter from the Sieur de La Verendrye who informs me that on the far-off rugged shores of Lake Superior he has found ancient workings in mines of copper, lead and silver, workings of times long past and by nations utterly forgotten by the present rude tribes."

"Perhaps it may be so Count," replied Kalm. "All those territories may in some remote age have formed one vast empire. The Americans like the Chinese have many languages and but one system of hieroglyphics understood by all. Those painted strips of bark upon your council table, Governor, would be read with ease by every Indian from the Northern Sea to the Gulf of Mexico."

The wine cups were replenished and in the lull of conversation fragrant columns of tobacco smoke rose and mingled gently in a silvery cloud over the heads of the group of friends.

The conversation shifted to other topics. Rigaud de Vaudreuil had kept quiet during the recent discussion. He was a soldier and a patriot, brave and honest, but he would not waste a word on antiquarian subjects which he did not understand and in his heart thoroughly despised. But he was eager to question the Northern Philosopher on his opinions respecting the war and the political signs of the times.

"You have had the privilege of a passport through England as well as her colonies Herr Kalm!" said he. "I do not ask you to tell what you saw in regard to military preparations— that would be a breach of the laws of honour as well as of hospitality, but it would be no breach of either to ask your opinion of the general policy of the English in regard to North America."

"It is to conquer New France neither more nor less!" replied Kalm, curtly. "The English Colonies never cease urging it out of fear of you, and the mother country is too ready to reap the glory of humbling her rival without regard to the consequences of such a conquest. England and her colonies in America seem as one in making this the corner stone of their policy."

"It is what we have all believed, and what for a hundred years they have tried before to do," replied Rigaud de Vaudreuil "They will succeed in it when every man worthy of the name of Canadian lies stark and stiff upon the frontiers, but not until then! I thank you, cordially, Herr Kalm!—" Rigaud shook him by the hand, for telling the truth however unpalatable. "But you spoke of the consequences of such a conquest, Herr Kalm, what do you mean by the consequences?—"

"That France will have her revenge Monsieur de Vaudreuil! I have travelled through the English colonies, with little credit to my eyes and ears if I have not convinced myself, that it is only fear of the power of France which keeps New England in subordination to the Mother Country. The spirit of the English Commonwealth of a century ago, smoulders hot in the bosoms of the old Parliamentarians of New England.

They could be true to a Cromwell—they cannot be true to a King! When the English Colonies shall have made a conquest of New France, they will speedily declare against their mother country. The commonwealth will once more contend for the mastery with the Crown! There will be war and France will then take her revenge. Every enemy of England will join her rebels to inflict upon her a mortal stab and tear from her the colonies which make her so great and powerful."

"*Par Dieu!* you speak like a prophet, Herr Kalm!" exclaimed de Vaudreuil, slapping his thigh, "that would be a revenge sweet as our conquest would be bitter. We are not ignorant in New France of the secret machinations of the disaffected republicans of New England. They have made overtures to us in times past to aid them, but we could not countenance them for we knew, that in reality they were the bitterest enemies of our King and of our church."

"They will first uproot your King with the help of England, and then overturn their own in the New World by the help of France—! The war will be long and bloody and enmities will be raised outlasting a hundred years," replied Kalm quietly. But his words had force in them.

"By St Michael! your words have the twang of truth, Herr Kalm!" interrupted La Corne St Luc, "but France if she be true to herself and to us, will never lose her dominion in the New World through the enmity of the English colonies."

"May it be so! Chevalier!" replied the Swede refilling his pipe, "The grace and polish of France are needed in the civilization of this great continent by the side of the rough energies of England. Happy the State which can unite them both. Such a one I see quickening in the womb of the future!—"

"Tell me what you see, Kalm" interrupted the Governor. "We are all philosophers to-night. A man seems to approach nearest the divine life, when he tries to live it and he feels his intellect most God like when he clearly forecasts what is to come to pass. What see you quickening in the womb of the future, Kalm?"—

"I see a time when the present English Colonies will rebel

and cast off the English yoke not because it is heavy but because it is easy and light, and does not keep down the stiff neck of a puritan democracy. I see a time when gathering up their strength to declare their independance of England they will hold out both hands to New France, then a province of England, for help. They will appeal to you, La Corne St Luc! and to you, Rigaud de Vaudreuil! and all New France to join them in rebellion against England—! and *mirabile dictu!* you shall treat their offers with disdain! and prefer to remain true to your new King and your new allegiance to which you shall have been given up by France! Nay more! Listen, Chevalier La Corne! reject my vatication if you will—! Should England having become degenerate abandon you in your extremity as France is likely to do, the last gun fired in defence of her flag will be by the hand of a French Canadian!—"

"By all the Saints in Paradise!" exclaimed La Corne St Luc! "and by all the Devils in Hell!" ejaculated Rigaud de Vaudreuil flaming up like a Volcano, "Stop your vaticinations Herr Kalm! Cassandra never predicted such things to Troy as you do to New France—! What you say is simply impossible!"

"Impossible or no, it is what I see in the not distant future," answered Kalm coolly.

"The only thing I will admit," said La Corne, "is the certainty that come what may, loyal and Catholic New France will never join hands with the heretical Puritans of New England!—"

"If we love Old England little, we love New England still less!" continued La Corne, "We should assuredly never take part with the latter against the former—! But we shall never forsake France! never!"

"But you may be cast off, La Corne! France may part with you for a mess of pottage, and buy peace with England by your Sacrifice—!"

"France! Chivalrous France! will die in her harness first!—" exclaimed La Corne with all the emphasis of incredulity.

"But France ruled not by chivalry but by courtezans, by money not by honour,—I will not pursue the black thought Chevalier La Corne! France not chivalrous may do it!—I say no more! Forgive me!" continued the Philosopher, offering his hand to La Corne. "I am only a student of man and nature, a dreamer for the most part who ought to keep his visions to himself. The Count has said that intellect is most God like when it clearly apprehends the future. It may be so, but it does not prevent the torment which accompanies like a curse every forecast of misfortune—!"

"A truce now to politics!" exclaimed the Governor. "Sufficient for the day is the Evil of it! We will not increase our miseries by adding to the present the burden of the future! Herr Kalm represents old Upsal and we will drink a health, gentlemen, a Swedish *skäl*, to his honour. Let us wash our brains clear of politics, and garnish our upper rooms for guests of a pleasanter sort."

The cups were again replenished, and, the Count setting the example, all rose and with enthusiastic energy drank a *skäl* to the health of their Swedish guest.

The Count leaned back in his chair as if recalling to mind some memories of long ago. "Six lustrums" said he, "thirty years of manhood have begun to whiten your locks and mine, Kalm! Since we finished our botanical studies at Upsal, under a youth much younger than ourselves but even then the wonder and admiration of the University, as he has since become of the world. Linneus was still a student of Olaf Celsius and Gammal Rodbeck when he opened the treasure house of nature to scholars and professors alike. Long may he wear the crown of Philosophy which the world has deservedly placed upon his head!"

"Linneus would not willingly hear that! Count," replied Kalm "He is simple as he is great, and like Newton, thinks he has only gathered a few pebbles on the shore of the vast ocean of truth which still lies unexplored before us."

"No! he would not willingly hear it, Kalm! I know" said the Governor, "but we should be ungrateful not to say it! What glorious times were those, when our only care was to learn what such men taught us! When Gammal Rodbeck put us through the same regime and courses which he never wearied of telling us he had prescribed for his brave pupil,

Charles XII."

"Yes! it quieted our grumbling at short commons during the dearth!" replied Kalm laughing at the reminder "Our groats tasted all the sweeter when we believed they had formed the bone and sinew of the arm which conquered at Narva."

The Governor plunged into a stream of reminiscences: "Our classmates are now like ourselves Kalm!" said he. "Grey headed and haply wise in the discovery that there is nothing new under the sun, and that all is vanity! Where is Crusenstolpe?—"

"Living in his ancestral Chateau in Wermland. Hunting stags, cultivating Barley and rearing a race of young Swedes to bear his name and serve their King and Country."

"And Engelshem?—" continued the Governor.

"In the army a stalwart Finland Cuirassier," replied Kalm.

"A brave fellow I warrant him!" observed the Governor "and Stroembom our Waterbull, where is he?—"

"In the navy guarding the skerries of the Baltic Coast."

"And Sternberg?—" pursued the Governor with the eagerness of a school girl asking after her classmates.

"A councillor of state at the Court of King Frederick, as he was at that of Queen Ulrica" was the reply. "I am at Abo a humble professor of philosophy and Markenshiold is preaching patriotism and religion to the Dalcarlians a needless labour! but the Dalkarls like to be told they have done their whole duty to God and the King! and dont think much of an orator who does not tell them so!"

"There was one more of our class Kalm, that wonderful youth Swedenborg. Where is he?" continued the Governor.

"Ah! he is at Stockholm in the body but as to his spirit in all the seven heavens," replied Kalm, as if not explicit enough in his answer.

"What mean you Kalm? he was the brightest genius of the University!" observed the Governor, his curiosity quite piqued.

"And is still!" replied Kalm emphatically "Few can follow to the heights where soars the spirit of Swedenborg. After exhausting the philosophy of earth he is now exploring that of heaven and hell. He is not like Dante led by the Eidolon of a Virgil or a Beatrice through scenes of intensest imagery, but in visions of divine permission sees and converses with Angels and spirits in their abodes of happiness or misery."

"You surprise me Kalm! young Swedenborg was the deepest mathematician and the closest observer of nature in our class" replied the Governor. "Olaf Celsius called him preeminently 'the philosopher' and he merited the designation! He was anything but a wild enthusiast."

"And is so yet. But you know Count, that under our Northern ice and snow smoulder hidden fires which break forth sometimes to illuminate, sometimes, to devastate the world."

"Aye Kalm!" replied the Governor with a look of frank assent. "I there recognize your Swedish genius! It is bright and cold as a winter's sun to illuminate the fields of science, but filled with irresistible impulses of a Berserkir to lift the veil and look at things never seen before by mortal man! A genius speculative and profound, but marbled with deep veins of mysticism, primordial like the spirit of the Edda and of the race of Odin! In strange ways the genius of the North reveals itself now and again, to the world's wonder and admiration."

"True Count! and our Swedish genius never revealed itself more markedly than in the soul of Swedenborg. There is no height of philosophy he has not scaled no depth of science which he has not sounded. His bold speculations are carried on with such a force of reasoning that a man can no more escape from its power than he could get out of the Maelstrom if he once trusts himself to its sweep and drift."

"And yet I do wonder, Kalm! that so crystal clear an intellect as Swedenborg's should turn towards mysticism in the face of modern philosophy and modern science which no one comprehended better than himself!—"

"*Fortasse et propter hoc!*" replied the Philosopher, "but I am unequal to judge as yet our old fellow student. He has got beyond me! I feel that clearly."

"When did you see him Kalm?" asked the Governor conjuring up to his minds eye, the handsome grave youth of his early acquaintance.

"Just before I left Stockholm on my present voyage," said Kalm. "He was in his favorite summer house in the orchard behind his residence in the Hornsgata. You know the place Count! It is there the Heavens are opened to him, and there he writes the wonders of the *Arcana Celestia* which he will one day deliver to the world."

"You surprise me Kalm! I could not have conjectured he was writing on those topics! He has left the old Philosophy then, and struck out a new path in Science and Theology."

The Governor became intensely interested in the idea of the possible devellopment or rather revelation of new truths, and a new departure in the domains of Science and Theology.

"He has struck out a new path in both Count, but it is not so much the new as the rediscovery of the old! the rejoining of the broken links of correspondence in the golden chain which once united man and nature with the spiritual world."

"You believe in it Kalm! You were always taken by that Platonic fancy of a correspondence as of soul and body between things of earth with the Divine ideas in which they originate!—"

"Nay, as I said, I know not what to believe about it yet!" replied Kalm "Swedenborg is the soul of candour, and sincere, as he is pious, humble, and enlightened. He told me wonderful things, as a brother and a philosopher who has been permitted to look at creation, not as men see it from without, but as angels may be supposed to regard it from within outwards. He has planted the germs of an entire new philosophy of spirit and matter, that may one day cover all our present systems, as the waters of a fruitful irrigation not as a destroying flood however!"

"Well Kalm! He was a noble youth, and if he has gone mad through excess of wisdom few men have had the same excuse! As for me I study philosophy in visible forms, a stone, a plant, a drop of water, a living organism of whatever kind. The three kingdoms of nature are my book, and reason is its commentary. I look no farther! Theology I love, but leave that to its divinely appointed teacher, *Credo in Sanctam Excelsiam Catholicam!* As my fathers before me believed, I also hope to be saved in that faith, as I trust it has saved them. I seek not to reconcile religion and science, as you do, Kalm!"

The count, as he said this glanced at the Bishop who looked approvingly at him. Bishop Pontbriand made small allowance for the aberrations of genius. The path of life was in his view so plain that a wayfarer, though a fool need not stumble over any rocks of philosophy, for none was to be found in it.

"No wise man," said the Bishop "tries to judge God! we take him as he has revealed himself, and can know with certainty no further. We cannot judge even men justly, let alone the things of creation which he left to be named by us as they were named by Adam, who gave all things their names just as he understood their nature and learned their qualities—but it is only the earthly, not the divine ideas they express which we can interpret."

"I bow with deference to the good Bishop" remarked Kalm. "We differ in signs and tokens only. The sea has many waves upon its surface but in its depths it is all one abiding peace and uniformity. But you know Count that in Sweden we question the sphinx as deeply as she questions us. We take nothing for granted and acknowledge no authority but divine truth expounded by reason. We ask what man is made for? whence he comes? and wither he goes? We lift the stones of Science one by one. We see what they rest upon and get if we can at the very foundations of things questioning even God himself, whom we study in his works, as well as in his word."

"But our old fellow student at Stockholm," replied the Count, "is he establishing a new faith, a new religion, a new philosophy Kalm?"

"Far from it! He is only kneading into the world's effete beliefs a leaven of new principles which will in time, in a century or two, or three, perhaps—bring science and theology into perfect harmony and accord with each other."

"What would Diderot and Voltaire say to this?—" remarked the Count, "but I say with the Athenians, we will hear thee again on this matter Kalm!—"

"Hark!" exclaimed the Bishop lifting his hand, "the

Angelus is ringing from tower and belfry, and thousands of knees are bending with the simplicity of little children in prayer without one thought of theology or philosophy—! Every prayer rising from a sincere heart asking pardon for the past and grace for the future is heard by our Father in heaven, think you not it is so Herr Kalm?—"

"It is doubtless so, and I thank God it is so, my Lord Bishop!" replied the Philosopher. "Salvation is by the grace of God, a truth rarely apprehended, and never comprehended, but by those who receive it like little children."

"May we receive it so!" replied the Bishop.

A few moments were passed by the gentlemen at table by reciting silently the customary invocation during the ringing of the Angelus. When it was over the company resettled themselves at the table. The cups were again replenished.

The Governor was warned by an ill-suppressed yawn from Rigaud de Vaudreuil that the conversation on his old classmates at Upsal had been void of interest to the old soldier, who hated philosophers as a brood of scoffing skeptics, who were pulling down religion and would one day pull down the King and all France together.

The silvery smoke rose again in thin clouds to the ceiling and the conversation shifted to other topics, by chance, in appearance, but really by a slight and unobserved artifice of the Count, who kindly led it to a subject in which Rigaud would shine.

There is some topic upon which every one is able to descant upon, and feel his strength. It is a pleasure to watch a taciturn man get into the saddle and rattle away in a dust of conversation when he knows the road and has no fear of a dismount.

Rigaud de Vaudreuil was taciturn as an Indian, but seated in his war saddle he let the world see he could ride and also talk. His friends loved him for his honesty and his modesty. Nothing was more delightful than to draw out Rigaud de Vaudreuil on Military topics which few could talk better about than he, and none illustrated by braver deeds.

He grew eloquent tonight telling what had been done

by the King's troops and Loyal Indians in defence of the Colony, and what remained unaccomplished through the remissness of the Court and the division of authority in New France, where the Governor controlled the campaign, the Commander-in-chief led the army, and the Intendant held the sinews of war. "The King expects victories" said he, "and at ten prices of our blood, and we gain them for him. But the King's courtiers, the King's mistresses and all the crowd of sycophants who surround the throne, demand lawless tribute of the remnant of our wealth. New France in the hands of Bigot is wrung of the last drop of its blood, and the last doit of its treasure. The pay of our soldiers is withheld, as in Acadia, where our victorious troops had to pillage their own countrymen for bread. Was it not so, La Corne?" added he, turning to his old friend and comrade.

The smoke was rising thick and ominous as from a furnace about the head of La Corne St Luc. He took his pipe from his lips and snapping it in two, replied, "It is too true Rigaud! New France is doomed to fall like Acadia and will be broken like that! unless a new fire of patriotism be kindled in French hearts at home, unless the nation be governed by Statesmen and on principles of honour and duty, not by trulls, spendthrifts and philosophs!—"

"You are an historian Herr Kalm!" continued La Corne, "I want you to write this in your book, that if New France be ever lost its fall will be due neither to the strength of the English, nor to the want of patriotism in our people, but because of the cowardice of wealth, the decay of loyalty, the loss of the sentiment of national pride and greatness in the mother Country! If France loses her Empire in America it will be because she has not spirit to keep what her sons so bravely won! When a nation once prefers its money to its blood, its peace to its honour, its doom is sealed! It will ere long have neither blood nor money nor honour to offer for its miserable existence—the best of its life's blood will go off to other lands. Its money will be extorted from it in tribute to nations daring enough to demand it and its honour will be sunk forever in the ocean of national degradation."

La Corne St Luc in these few words reflected the sentiments of nearly every officer of intelligence in the colony. They felt themselves half abandoned and wholly disregarded by the mother country whose policy the shrewdest of them began to see was influenced by the anti-colonial teachings of Voltaire who afterwards kindled bonfires to celebrate the defeat of Montcalm and the loss of her greatest Colony.

Strange to say after the lapse of more than a century, a race of Englishmen has sprung up, as the successors of the Encyclopedists of France, but who argue to deaf ears, let us hope, that wealth is the only greatness of a nation, and that the way for England to keep great is to rid herself of her Colonies, to alienate millions of her most loyal subjects, to break up the mightiest elements of national strength by dividing her Empire, and casting the fragments of it into the lap of her enemies. There are English Voltaires and Diderots who believe in national pusillanimity and teach it! They are like the man followed by wolves who cast out of his sledge, one child after another in hopes of assuaging the hunger of his pursuers! and saving his own ignoble life at the expense of every feeling of duty and manhood to his children.

Voltaire and the philosophs set up a graven image of liberty which they called England, which true in itself was false in their conception of it, and degraded by the factious use they made of their ideal. Just so these English successors of Voltaire set up a graven image which they call America! and grovel at its feet with a worship, half of idolatry half of fear but wholly degenerate from the brave, independent, and manly spirit of the English nation.

The sad forebodings of Colonists like La Corne St Luc did not prevent the desperate struggle that was made for the preservation of French dominion in the next war. Like brave and loyal men they did their duty to God, and their Country preferring death and ruin in a lost cause to surrendering the flag which was the symbol of their native land. The spirit if not the words of the old English Loyalist was in them—

For Loyalty is still the same,
Whether it win or lose the game,
True as the dial to the sun,
Although it be not shone upon.

New France after gathering a harvest of glory such as
America had never seen reaped before, fell at last through
the neglect of her mother country. But she dragged down the
nation in her fall and France would now give the apple of her
eye for the recovery, never to be, of "the acres of snow!" which
La Pompadour so scornfully abandoned to the English.

These considerations lay in the lap of the future however.
They troubled not the present time and company. The glasses
were again replenished with wine or watered as the case might
be, for the Count de la Galissoniere and Herr Kalm, kept
Horatian time and measure drinking only three cups to the
Graces, while La Corne St Luc and Rigaud de Vaudreuil drank
nine full cups to the Muses, also fearing not the enemy that
steals away men's brains. Their heads were helmeted with
triple brass, and impenetrable to the heaviest blows of the
thyrsus of Bacchus. They drank with impunity as if garlanded
with parsley and while commending the Bishop who would
drink naught save pure water, they rallied mercilessly Claude
Beauharnois who would not drink at all.

In the midst of a cheerful sound of merriment the door
of the cabinet opened and the servant in waiting announced
the entrance of Colonel Philibert.

All rose to welcome him. Pierre looked anxious and
somewhat discomposed, but the warm grasp of the hands
of so many true friends made him glad for the moment.

"Why Pierre!" exclaimed the Count. "I hope no ill wind
has blown you to the City so unexpectedly! You are heartily
welcome however! and we will call every wind good that blows
our friends back to us again!—"

"It is a cursed wind that blows me back today," replied
Philibert sitting down with an air of disquiet.

"Why what is the matter, Pierre?" asked the Count "My
honoured Lady de Tilly and her lovely niece are they well?—"

"Well! your Excellency, but sorely troubled. The devil has tempted Le Gardeur again and he has fallen! He is back to the city—Wild as a savage and beyond all control."

"Good God! it will break his sister's heart!" said the Governor sympathizingly. "That girl would give her life for her brother! I feel for her, I feel for you too Pierre!" Philibert felt the tight clasp of the Governor's hand as he said this. He understood well its meaning. "And not less do I pity the unhappy youth who is the cause of such grief to his friends." continued he.

"Yes, your Excellency! Le Gardeur is to be pitied as well as blamed—he has been tried and tempted beyond human strength."

La Corne St Luc had risen and was pacing the floor with impatient strides. "Pierre Philibert!" exclaimed he, "Where is the poor lad? He must be sought for and saved yet. What Demons have assailed him now? Was it the serpent of strong drink that bites men mad or the legion of fiends that rattle the dice box in their ears? or was it the last temptation which never fails when all else has been tried in vain—a woman?—"

"It was all three combined. The Chevalier de Pean visited Tilly on business of the Intendant—In reality I suspect to open a communication with Le Gardeur, for he brought him a message from a lady, you wot of, which drove him wild with excitement. A hundred men could not have restrained Le Gardeur after that. He became infatuated with De Pean and drank and gambled all night and all day with him at the village Inn, threatening annihilation to all who interfered with him. Today he suddenly left Tilly and came with De Pean to the City."

"De Pean!" exclaimed La Corne "the spotted snake! A fit tool for the Intendant's lies and villainy! I am convinced he went not on his own errand to Tilly! Bigot is at the bottom of this foul conspiracy to ruin the noblest lad in the Colony!—"

"It may be," replied Philibert, "but the Intendant alone would have had no power to lure him back. It was the message of that artful syren which has drawn Le Gardeur de Repentigny again into the whirlpool of destruction."

"Aye, but Bigot set her on him like a retriever to bring back the game!—" replied La Corne fully convinced of the truth of his remark.

"It may be," answered Philibert, "but my impression is, that she has influenced the Intendant rather than he her in this matter."

The Bishop listened with warm interest to the account of Philibert. He looked a gentle reproof but did not utter it, at La Corne St Luc and Philibert, for their outspoken denunciation of the Intendant. He knew—none knew better—how deserved it was! but his ecclesiastical rank placed him at the apex of all parties in the colony and taught him prudence in expressing or hearing opinions of the King's representatives in the Colony.

"But what have you done Pierre Philibert," asked the Bishop, "since your arrival? have you seen Le Gardeur?—"

"No, my Lord; I followed him and the Chevalier to the City. They have gone to the Palace whither I went and got admittance to the cabinet of the Intendant. He received me in his politest and blandest manner. I asked for an interview with Le Gardeur. Bigot told me that my friend unfortunately at that moment was unfit to be seen, and had refused himself to all his city friends. I partly believed him for I heard the voice of Le Gardeur in a distant room amid a babble of tongues and the rattle of dice. I sent him a card with a few kind words, and received it back with an insult, deep and damning scrawled upon it. It was not written however in the hand of Le Gardeur, although signed by his name. Read that your Excellency!" said he throwing a card to the Count. "I will not repeat the foul expressions it contains. Tell Pierre Philibert what he should do to save his honour and save his friend! Poor wild infatuated Le Gardeur! never wrote that! never! They have made him sign his name to he knew not what!—"

"And by St Martin!" exclaimed La Corne, who had looked at the card, "Some of them shall bite dust for that! As for Le Gardeur, poor boy, overlook his fault, pity him, forgive him! He is not so much to blame Pierre! as those plundering thieves of the Friponne, who shall find that La Corne St Luc's sword is longer by half an ell, than is good for some of their stomacks!—"

"Forbear, dear friends!" said the Bishop "It is not the way of Christians to talk thus!"

"But it is the way of gentlemen," replied La Corne, impatiently, "and I always hold that a true gentleman is a true Christian! But you do your duty, my Lord Bishop! in reproving us and I honour you for it, although I may not promise obedience. David fought a duel with Goliath and was honoured by God and man for it, was he not?"

"But he fought it not in his own quarrel, La Corne!" replied the Bishop gently. "Goliath had defied the armies of the living God and David fought for his King, not for himself."

"*Confiteor*! my Lord Bishop! but the logic of the heart is often truer than the logic of the head, and the sword has no *raison d'etre*, except in purging the world of scoundrels."

"I will go home now! I will see your Excellency again on this matter," said Pierre, rising to depart.

"Do Pierre! my utmost services are at your command," said the Governor, as the guests all rose too. It was very late.

The hour of departure had arrived. The company all rose, and courteously bidding their Host good night proceeded to their several homes, leaving him alone with his friend Kalm.

They two at once passed into a little museum of minerals, plants, birds and animals where they sat down eager as two boy students. The world, its battles and its politics were utterly forgotten as they conversed far into the night and examined with the delight of new discoverers the beauty and variety of nature's forms that exist in the New World.

CHAPTER 40

THE COUTUME DE PARIS

THE Chevalier De Pean had been but too successful in his errand of mischief to the Manor house of Tilly.

A few days had sufficed for this accomplished ambassador of Bigot to tempt Le Gardeur to his ruin and to triumph in his fall.

Upon his arrival at the Seigneurie, De Pean had chosen to take up his quarters at the Village inn in preference to accepting the proffered hospitality of the Lady de Tilly, whom however he had frequently to see, having been craftily commissioned by Bigot with the settlement of some important matters of business relating to her Seigneurie, as a pretext to visit the Manor House and linger in the village long enough to renew his old familiarity with Le Gardeur.

The visits of De Pean to the Manor House were politely but not cordially received. It was only by reason of the business he came upon that he was received at all. Nevertheless he paid his court to the Ladies of the Manor, as a gentleman anxious to remove their prejudices and win their good opinion.

He once and but once essayed to approach Amelie with gallantry, a hair breadth only beyond the rigid boundary line of ordinary politeness, when he received a repulse so quick, so unspoken and invisible that he could not tell in what it consisted, yet he felt it like a sudden paralysis of his powers of pleasing. He cared not again to encounter the quick glance of contempt and aversion which for an instant flashed in the eyes of Amelie, when she caught the drift of his untimely admiration.

A woman is never so Rhadamanthean in her justice and so quick in her execution of it, as when she is proud and happy in her love for another man. She is then indignant at every suggestion implying any doubt of the strength, purity, and absoluteness of her devotion.

De Pean ground his teeth in silent wrath at his quiet but unequivocal, repulse, and vowed a bitter vow that Amelie should ere long repent in sackcloth and ashes for the wound inflicted upon his vanity and still more upon his cupidity.

One of the day dreams of his fancy was broken never to return. The immense fortune and high rank of the young Chatelaine de Repentigny had excited the cupidity of De Pean for a time, and although the voluptuous beauty of Angelique fastened his eyes, he would willingly have sacrificed her for the reversion of the lordships of Tilly and Repentigny.

De Pean's soul was too small to bear with equanimity the annihilation of his cherished hopes. As he looked down upon his white hands, his delicate feet and irreproachable dress and manner, he seemed not to comprehend that a true woman like Amelie cares nothing for these things in comparison with a manly nature that seeks a woman for her own sake by love, and in love, and not for the accessories of her fortune. For such a one she would go barefoot if need were, while golden slippers would not tempt her to walk with the other.

Amelie's beau ideal of manhood was embodied in Pierre Philibert, and the greatest King in Christendom, would have wooed in vain at her feet much less an empty pretender like the Chevalier De Pean.

"I would not have treated any gentleman so rudely," said Amelie in confidence to Heloise de Lotbinière, when they had retired to the privacy of their bedchamber. "No woman is justified in showing scorn of any man's love if it be honest and true, but the Chevalier De Pean is false to the heart's core, and his presumption woke such an aversion in my heart, that I fear my eyes showed less than ordinary politeness to his unexpected advances."

"You were too gentle, not too harsh, Amelie!" replied Heloise, with her arm round her friend. "Had I been the object of his hateful address I should have repaid him in his own false coin. I would have led him on to the brink of the precipice of a confession and an offer, and then I would have dropped him as one drops a stone into the deep pool of the Chaudière."

"You were always more bold than I, Heloise! I could not do that for the world," replied Amelie "I would not willingly offend even the Chevalier De Pean! moreover I fear him and I need not tell you why, darling! That man possesses a power over my dear brother that makes me tremble, and in my anxiety for Le Gardeur, I may have lingered as I did yesterday, too long in the parlour when in company with the Chevalier de Pean, who mistaking my motive may have supposed that I hated not his presence so much as I truly did."

"Amelie, your fears are my own!" exclaimed Heloise pressing Amelie to her side. "I must, I will tell you! O loved sister of mine! let me call you so!—to you alone I dare acknowledge my hopeless love for Le Gardeur and my deep and abiding interest in his welfare."

"Nay do not say, hopeless! Heloise!" replied Amelie kissing her fondly. "Le Gardeur is not insensible to your beauty and goodness. He is too like myself not to love you."

"Alas! Amelie! I know it is all in vain, I have neither beauty nor other attractions in his eyes. He left me yesterday to converse with the Chevalier de Pean on the subject of Angelique des Meloises, and I saw by the agitation of his manner, the flush upon his cheek, and the eagerness of his questioning, that he cared more for Angelique, notwithstanding her reported engagement with the Intendant, than he did for a thousand Heloises de Lotbinières!—"

The poor girl, overpowered by the recollection, hid her face upon the shoulder of Amelie and sobbed as if her very heart were breaking, as in truth it was.

Amelie so happy and secure in her own affection, comforted Heloise with her tears and caresses. But it was only by picturing in her imagination her own state, should she be so hapless as to lose the love of Pierre Philibert, that she could realize the depth of misery and abandonment which filled the bosom of her fair companion.

She was moreover struck to the heart by the words of Heloise, regarding the eagerness of her brother to get word of Angelique. "The Chevalier de Pean might have brought a message, perhaps a love token from Angelique to Le Gardeur, to draw him back to the City," thought she. If so, she felt instinctively that all their efforts to redeem him would be in vain, and that neither sister's love nor Pierre's remonstrances would avail to prevent his return. He was the slave of the lamp and Angelique its possessor!

"Heaven forbid! Heloise!" she said faintly, "Le Gardeur is lost if he return to the City, now. Twice lost! lost as a gentleman, lost as the lover of a woman who cares for him only as a pastime and as a foil to her ambitious designs upon the Intendant! Poor Le Gardeur! What happiness might not be his in the love of a woman, noble minded as himself! What happiness were he yours, O Darling Heloise!"—She kissed her pallid cheeks wet with tears which lay by hers on the same pillow, and both remained silently brooding over the thoughts which spring from love, and sorrow.

"Happiness can never be mine, Amelie!" said Heloise after a lapse of several minutes. "I have long feared it, now I know it. Le Gardeur loves Angelique—he is wholly hers and not one little corner of his heart is left for poor Heloise to nestle in! I did not ask much Amelie! but I have not retained the little interest I believed was once mine! He has thrown the whole treasure of his life at her feet. After playing with it she will spurn it for a more ambitious alliance! O Amelie!" exclaimed she with vivacity, "I could be wicked! heaven forgive me! I could be cruel and without pity, to save Le Gardeur from the wiles of such a woman!—"

The night was a stormy one. The East wind which had lain in a dead lull through the early hours of the evening rose in all its strength at the turn of the tide. It came bounding like the distant thud of a cannon. It roared and rattled against the windows and casements of the Manor House, sounding a deep bass in the long chimneys and howling like souls in torment, amid the distant woods.

The rain swept down in torrents as if the windows of

heaven were opened to wash away the world's defilements. The stout walls of the Manor House were immovable as rocks, but the wind and the rain and the noise of the storm struck an awe into the two girls. They crept closer together in their bed. They dared not separate for the night. The storm seemed too much the reflex of the agitation of their own minds, and they lay clasped in each others arms mingling their tears and prayers for Le Gardeur until the gray dawn looked over the eastern hill and they slept.

The Chevalier de Pean was faithful to the mission upon which he had been despatched to Tilly. He disliked intensely the return of Le Gardeur to renew his old ties with Angelique but it was his fate, his cursed crook, he called it, ever to be overborne by some woman or other, and he resolved that Le Gardeur should pay for it with his money and be so flooded by wine and debauchery that Angelique herself would repent that she had ever invited his return.

That she would not marry Le Gardeur was plain enough to De Pean, who knew her ambitious views regarding the Intendant, and that the Intendant would not marry her was equally a certainty to him, although it did not prevent De Pean's entertaining an intense jealousy of Bigot.

Despite discouraging prospects, he found a consolation in the reflection that failing his own vain efforts to please Amelie de Repentigny for sake of her wealth, the woman he most loved for sake of her beauty and spirit, would yet drop like a golden fleece into his arms, either through spite at her false lover or through love of himself. De Pean cared little which,—for it was the person not the inclination of Angelique, that carried away captive the admiration of the Chevalier De Pean.

The better to accomplish his crafty design of abducting Le Gardeur, De Pean had taken up his lodging at the village inn. He knew that in the polite hospitalities of the Manor House he could find few opportunities to work upon the susceptible nature of Le Gardeur, that too many loving eyes would there watch over his safety, and that he was himself suspected and his presence only tolerated on account of the business which had ostensibly brought him there. At the Inn, he would be free to work out his schemes sure of success, if by any means and on any pretense he could draw Le Gardeur thither, and rouse into life and fury the sleeping serpents of his old propensities, the love of gaming and love of wine, and the love of Angelique.

Could Le Gardeur be persuaded to drink a full measure to the bright eyes of Angelique des Meloises and could he when the fire was kindled be tempted once more to take in hand the box more fatal than that of Pandora, and place fortune on the turn of a die, De Pean knew well that no power on earth would stop the conflagration of every good resolution and every virtuous principle in his mind. Neither aunt, nor sister, nor friend, could withold him then! He would return to the City, where the Grand Company had a use to make of him, which he would never understand until it was too late for aught but repentance.

De Pean pondered long upon a few words he had one day heard drop from the lips of Bigot, which meant more, much more than they seemed to imply, and they flitted long through his memory like bats in a room seeking an outlet into the world ominous of some deed of darkness.

De Pean imagined that he had found a way to revenge himself upon Le Gardeur and Amelie, each for thwarting him in a scheme of love or fortune. He brooded long and malignantly how to hatch the plot which he fancied was his own but which had really been conceived in the deeper brain of Bigot, whose few seemingly harmless words had dropped into the ear of De Pean casually as it were, but, which Bigot knew would take root and grow in the congenial soul of his secretary and one day bring forth terrible fruit.

The next day was wet and autumnal, with a sweeping east wind which blew raw and gustily over the dank grass and dropping trees that edged the muddy lane of the Village of Tilly.

The water courses were full and yellow with the washing of frequent showers. The sky was dark—the heavily laden clouds scarcely rose above the level of the horizon, and trailed their ragged skirts of mist over the tree tops and hillsides—while the river hardly visible in the fog mingled a hoarse roar of waves from its stony beach, with the continuous noise of the wind and the rain on shore.

The grey church upon the point of Tilly was shrouded in still greyer mist. The sound of the Vesper bell rung by the lonely Sexton was scarcely heard in the village, and few obeyed its summons that day, preferring a penance for not going to Church to the risk of a wet skin and draggled garments. It was not easy in such weather to ascend the miry road up the steep hill worthy to be called the hill Difficulty which led from the low lying village to the Parish Church.

The few houses in the village were very quiet. All the little world of life had taken refuge indoors or under cover. The steaming cattle shivered together under sheds and in fence corners. The strutting poultry had long since drooped their wet feathers and perched disconsolate enough in barn and stable. Even the lately clamorous ducks and geese seemed to have had enough of it, and stood in one-legged quiet contemplation of the little pools of water foaming and bubbling about them which would be pools of delight for many a day to come.

The figure of a woman with a shawl or cloak thrown hastily over her head stepping lightly through the mud as she hurried to or from a neighbour's house, was the only sign of inhabitants about the village except at the oldfashioned Inn with its low covered gallery and swinging sign of the Tilly arms.

There flitting round the door, or occasionally peering through the windows of the tap room with pipes in their mouths and perchance a tankard in their hands, were seen the elders of the village, boatmen, and habitans making use or good excuse of a rainy day for a social gathering in the dry snug chimney corner of the Tilly arms.

In the warmest corner of all, his face aglow with fire light and good liquor, sat Master Pothier *dit* Robin with his gown tucked up to his waist as he toasted his legs and old gamashes in the genial warmth of a good fire.

Opposite him bursting with stories of the late riot in the

City and of the destruction of his fiddle by the Intendant, sat Jean La Marche nursing a new violin on his lap tenderly as a ten days old baby, and taking the word out of everybody's mouth as was his custom, in his goodnatured eagerness to have his say whoever was speaking, a feat rather difficult to night for Master Pothier was tremendous on a string of talk. His law phrases and dog latin sometimes overrode the voluble recitals of Jean, who had his revenge however, for when fairly outtalked and hard pressed by argument, he would take out his violin and striking up a lively air bring all the listeners to his side and force Master Pothier to a new trial.

Half a dozen worthies of the village in red Breton caps were, at once audience and chorus to Master Pothier and Jean La Marche; Censitaires of the house of Tilly, proud of their Lady, cheerful payers of all her feudal dues and equally fond of disputing them point by point, for the sake of a good wrangle, with their Lady's steward, the grave and consequential Master Coté.

The arrival of Master Pothier in the course of his rounds as a travelling notary, was an event quite as interesting to the men as the arrival of the cheerful old Recollets was to the women of the village of Tilly.

Master Pothier with his budget of law papers had hardly installed himself in his old seat in the chimney corner before the news of his arrival was flying round the Seigneurie, and a dozen of would be litigants, were drawing themselves up an inch taller in the prospect of a good bout at cheap law with neighbours as fond of it as themselves.—

A year's accumulations of petty quarrels and verbal contracts waiting to be put in black and white as they expressed it, were ready for the manipulation of Master Pothier. Sick men had deferred dying until the travelling notary came round to draw their wills. Impatient couples were not allowed by prudent parents to marry, no matter how high the torch of Cupid was flaring, until a proper contract on thick paper with a good blotch of sealing wax upon it, had been duly executed under the notarial hand of Master Pothier.

The old notary knew well how to extract his fees from the

close fisted Habitans, notwithstanding their inveterate habit of driving hard bargains for their law as for any other commodity they dealt in.

"How much, Master Pothier will you charge me for scribbling off an *acte de damnation?*" asked Louis Du Sol. He meant to say an *acte de donation*, of, "a reasonable pig," in return for the use of a little field down by the mill. Master Pothier understood him all the same, and probably thought there was usually not much difference in either the thing or the name.

"With a seal upon it, Master Louis?—" asked Master Pothier with a very judicial air.

"Yes, Master Pothier, with a seal upon it, all complete."

Master Pothier rubbed his wig for a minute, very gravely. "It will cost you five livres to make a tight and sure '*Acte de damnation'*" said he. "A middling one with not more than two or three holes to creep out at will cost you three livres. A very common one that will hold nothing and nobody, I will give you for a frank. So you take your choice Master Louis—!" The Habitant thought the cheap and common one good enough to give away—at any rate it left his hands as free as the other party's to the contract, to raise a glorious cavil, and so lead to the luxury of a lawsuit over the "*acte de damnation.*"

Conversation in the presence of Master Pothier ever took a litigious turn. His wallet smelled of law as naturally as a Doctor's smells of drugs.

The Censitaires of Tilly were happy in their feudal relations with the noble Lady of the manor, but true Normans as they were, they loved to exercise their wits, upon quibbles, and points of the *coutumes* of Paris and Rouen, which applied to their land tenures and other dealings with their Lady.

They admitted cheerfully their obligations to pay *cens* and *rentes*, some five farthings per arpent, for lands in the Lordship of Tilly, which the Lady of the Manor had as regularly returned to them, for several years past, on account of the hard times in the Colony; but that did not prevent their envying the lot of the happier Censitaires of Brille who annually on their rent day, went in procession to the chateau of their Lord, with their largest wagon drawn by six horses, superbly harnessed, conveying one pepper corn to their Lord as the full rent due for their lands and who had to treat his loyal vassals with a great feast into the bargain!

The *banality* of the old mill of Tilly which ground the corn of the Seigneurie for nothing, except a few handfuls out of each *Minot*, given as toll to the miller, was a standing subject of controversy among the sharp wits of the village, as to whether the handfuls were single as some argued, or double as claimed by old Joachim the miller.

The Lady of the Manor kept down her stock of doves in the great colombiere, feeding them carefully at home to prevent their flying abroad to pick in the cornfields of the Habitans; but the number she *might* keep and the number her censitaires *might* be required to feed, formed a problem in feudal arithmetic that often filled the table top and the inn door itself, with chalk marks of interminable calculations equalled at last by the landlord's score of mugs of cider drank to the health of the good Lady of the manor, while they were disputing her rights.

"My Lady may, by the *Coutume* of Rouen," exclaimed Master Pothier, "build a colombiere that will feed all the Seigneury as well as eat it up. It is her right and as our good Lady she may exercise it if she will."

"You may as well tell me Master Pothier!" replied Jean La Marche as the defender of popular rights, "that the *Droit de Grenouillage* is in the Manor of Tilly as it is in the Lordship of Marais Le Grand!"

"I do tell you so Jean La Marche!" replied Master Pothier. "It is inherent in all Norman Fiefs! only there are no frog ponds at Tilly, else would the vassals be bound to beat them with long poles all the night preceeding the marriage of their Lord, crying;

'Pa! Pa! rainotte, Pa!
Notre Seigneur dort, que Dieu gâ!'

to enable their Lord to sleep soundly and be strong and vigorous for the morrow."

"Aye that is a sensible custom! one can sympathize with that!" replied Jean. "Were you ever married Master Pothier?—"

"I married! Jean La Marche!" Master Pothier gave a scornful laugh. "Ha! Ha! The idea! No! No! I know too much law for that! What? When there is not a seigneur in New France, but has the right of *Jambage* inherent in his Lordship by the ancient coutumes of Normandy, and for aught I could plead in bar would exercise it in case Master Pothier took a wife! No Jean La Marche! you may marry and I shall be happy to write you a marriage contract, as broad as your wedding sheet, but do not ask me to adorn my brows with even invisible antlers!—"

"Aye but they say our Seigneurs have lost the right of *Jambage*, more the pity say our penniless maids, who never married without a nice dower in the good old times!" replied Jean looking round the company for support in his regret.

"Bah!" exclaimed Nicholas Houdin a staring Habitant "I have lived in Tilly three score years and I never heard that our noble seigneurs had the right of *Jambage*."

"It was the *possibilities* of the law, Master Houdin!" replied Pothier,"not its actuality, I referred to."

Nicholas Houdin not comprehending the law latin, as he regarded the reply of Master Pothier, said "Oh! yes!" and resumed his stare of wonder at the vast learning of the worthy notary.

"Well, we need not mind about *Jambage* in Tilly, where we are ruled by a lady and not by a lord! I drink her health before all the company" exclaimed Jean La Marche, suiting "the action to the word and the word to the action," as well as if he had received advice from Hamlet.

"I join in the health of the noble Lady with all my heart!" replied Master Pothier, "but you do not catch me with that hook, Jean La Marche! A lady may depute her right of *Jambage* to her heir in the barony, as is proved by Arrêts of the Court of Bourges—respect the law therefore Jean La Marche!—"

"I do Master Pothier! and I want some of it for myself. You know my poor Fifine took a cold and died last winter. She has left a buxom sister in the flesh whom I wish to marry. The Curé says: no! The woman says Oh!—Now what says the law? Is it permissible to marry your wife's sister?—"

Master Pothier pricked up his ears like a war horse at the sound of a trumpet. Here was a case to come down upon! The rustics clustered round, for everybody in the village knew poor Jean's wants and wishes. The men jeered him, the women sympathized with him. Master Pothier put on his old cap *à Mortier* and cried out, "Do you want to be hanged Jean La Marche? Marry your wife's sister and you will be condemned to be trussed up by all the laws of the Imperium!—"

"What! do you mean to say they will hang me, Master Pothier, if I marry my wife's sister? The Sexton says it would be polygamy even in the church yard for a man to have two wives, would it?—"

"Hang you? Yes! and Polygamy is a hanging matter, and your case for merely thinking of it, is first cousin to the Gallows."

"I dont believe it, Master Pothier! Who are your Authorities?"—Jean had learned the names of sundry famous law Doctors from his frequent discussions with Master Pothier.

"My Authorities? Listen, Jean La Marche!" and Master Pothier launched into a musical descant of great authorities on the subject:

"'Si vous consultez nos Auteurs,—
Legislateurs et Glossateurs,—
Jason, Aliciat, Cujas,
Le grand homme si capable!—
La polygamie est un cas,
Est un cas pendable!—'

If that will not hang you Jean La Marche, you are not worth hanging! and that is my opinion as well as Molieres for which I charge you a round of Norman cider for this fair company!—"

The opinion of Master Pothier was received with tumultuous applause. Jean was overwhelmed but in revenge swore he would sing his best song the famous old *apologie du Cidre*, a Norman Ditty of the fourteenth century which had been brought to the Colony in the ships of Samuel Champlain.

"Now fill all your mugs!" cried he "and be in time with the Chorus. I will prove to you that cider is better than law any day!—"

Jean twanged his fiddle and handling his bow like a genuine virtuoso, began the jolly old ballad:—

De nous se rit le Francois
Mais quoi qu'il en die,
Le cidre de Normandie
Vaut bien son vin quelquefois!

Coule à val! et loge! loge!
Il fait grand bien à la gorge!

Ta bonté O cidre beau!
De te boire me convie,
Mais pour le moins je te prie
Ne me trouble le cerveau!

Coule à val! et loge! loge!
Il fait grand bien à la gorge!—

Voisin ne songe en proces!
Prends le bien qui se presente!
Mais, que l'homme se contente,
Il en a toujours assez!

Coule à val et loge! loge!
Il fait grand bien à la gorge!—

The *Apologie du cidre* was sung in Jean's best timbre and chorussed *con amore* by the company with a rattling accompaniment of pewter mugs and hard knuckles rapping on the oak table.

Master Pothier threw up his hands in extasy repeated the chorus and proposed a double round in honour of the Lady de Tilly, and the fair young chatelaine, Mademoiselle Amelie. It was drank with enthusiasm.

"I want now" continued Master Pothier "to drink the health and happiness of the young seigneur de Repentigny and a long law suit and a short purse to the censitaire who will not join in it."

"Hush! Master Pothier! dont name the young Seigneur" interjected Jean La Marche, "he is in the parlour yonder, playing dice and drinking hot wine, with the Chevalier De Pean and two other big dogs of the Friponne."

"The Chevalier de Pean! The Secretary of the Intendant! is he here?" asked Master Pothier discreetly lowering his voice. "What brings him to Tilly?"

"Some Devil's business of the Friponne, I warrant!" whispered Jean. "I kept aloof for a week fearing he was making inquiries about the riot but finding all right and being very thirsty, I could not stay away from the Tilly Arms any longer. Do you know the Chevalier de Pean, Master Pothier?—"

"Know him! I know every dog of high and low degree in the Capital."

"He is a gay, lively fellow! but he has an eye to cheat man and woman or I am no judge! What do you think, Master Pothier?—" asked Jean.

"What do I think?" repeated Master Pothier, taking a serious pull at the tankard and slowly shaking his head as he echoed the question. "I think he is worthy to be secretary to Caius Verres himself." Master Pothier had not quite lost the tincture of his humanities learned at the old school of Arles.

"Who is that? Master Pothier!" Jean had a prodigious respect for learning, and the more in proportion to the less he knew of it.

"Caius Verres!" replied Master Pothier as cautious as a fox. "He was a Roman and should be spoken of in the Roman tongue he was Intendant of Sicily *populatae vexatae funditus evarsaeque Provinciae!* like this poor New France of ours and that is my opinion."

Honest Jean was perfectly content with Master Pothier's explanation. It was Latin like what he heard at mass and therefore to be taken on trust with implicit confidence. The rest of the company were of the same mind, for not one of them thought it necessary to ask Master Pothier for an interpretation of his learned opinion of the Intendant.

CHAPTER 41

A WILD NIGHT INDOORS AND OUT

MASTER Pothier leaned back his head and twirled his thumbs for a few minutes without speaking or listening to the babble around him, which had now turned upon the war and the latest sweep of the Royal commissaries for corn and cattle. "Did you say Jean La Marche," said he, "that Le Gardeur de Repentigny was playing dice and drinking hot wine with the Chevalier de Pean and two big dogs of the Friponne?—"

"I did." Jean spoke with a choking sensation. "Our young Seigneur has broken out again wilder than ever and is neither to hold or bind any longer!—"

"Aye!" replied Master Pothier reflectively, "the best bond I could draw would not bind him more than a spider's thread! They are stiff necked as bulls, these De Repentignys! and will bear no yoke but what they put on of themselves! Poor lad! Do they know at the Manor House he is here drinking and dicing with the Chevalier de Pean?—"

"No! Else all the rain in Heaven would not have prevented his being looked after by Mademoiselle Amelie and My Lady," answered Jean. "His friend, Pierre Philibert who is now a great officer of the King, went last night to Batiscan on some matter of the army, as his groom told me. Had he been here, Le Gardeur would not have spent the day at the Tilly Arms as we poor Habitans do when it is washing day at home."

"Pierre Philibert!" Master Pothier rubbed his hands at the reminder. "I remember him Jean!—A hero like St Denis! It was he who walked into the Chateau of the Intendant and brought off young De Repentigny as a cat does her kittens."

"What in his mouth, Master Pothier?—"

"None of your quips Jean! Keep cool!—" Master Pothier's

497

own face grew red. "Never ring the coin thats a gift, and do not stretch my comparisons like your own wit to a bare thread. If I had said in his mouth, what then? It was by word of mouth I warrant you, that he carried him away from Beaumanoir. Pity he is not here to take him away from the Tilly Arms!—"

Master Pothier rose, and looked through the window against which the rain was beating furiously. The gloom of approaching night began to mingle distant objects together but on the edge of the hill cutting the grey sky the tall pines stood out distinctly and bowed their tops in the wind which was scattering the mist before sunset, with promise perhaps of a fair day for tomorrow. But as yet there was no lull in the driving rain. The eye of Master Pothier traced with a dubious glance the steep road leading up the hill. It was lost in darkness long before it reached the summit.

Master Pothier reflected on the long league to the Manor House behind the hill then upon the rain and the coming darkness, and turning to the glowing fire, the dry chimney corner, the good liquor and the good company, he resumed his seat solidly, took out his pipe and began doggedly to smoke as if he did not mean to stir out of his warm corner any more that night.

But it was no use. Master Pothier was very fidgety. The sound of voices, the rattle and clash of the dice box in the distant parlour reached his ear, amidst the laughter and gabble of the common room. He tried the tankard and drank deep draughts to compose his mind, and fancying he was drowsy, drank again to rouse himself up and keep awake.

"A man may as well walk on it, as sit on it!" said he. "The cause is decided against me! and I must pay the costs! Jean La Marche will you go with me to the Manor House tonight?—"

"To the Manor House!" replied Jean very thickly for he too had been trying to float his thoughts by giving them plenty of liquor to swim in. "The way is as long as a Christmas Carol and the rain will spoil my fiddlestrings, but I will not refuse you, Master Pothier! those dogs of the Friponne are barking louder and louder! They will devour Le Gardeur before morning. I will go with you. Give me your hand old Robin! But I find it hard to rise with a heavy seat like this under me."

With a mutual pull, Master Pothier and Jean taking hold of hands managed to get upon their legs, and with some lurching and unsteady squaring they stretched themselves into their great coats. With a jug of Santa Crux rum as sea stores, the two good natured fellows more willing than capable, set out arm in arm on a tramp through the rain and darkness to the Manor House.

Sooth to say they never reached it!—for stopping to rest and refresh themselves by the wayside in a hut tenanted by an old boon companion, they were welcomed with such empressment and hospitality that once seated by his fire Master Pothier took out his jug and Jean La Marche his violin for a tune to cheer them on their tramp.

Minutes ran on to hours, hours stretched to the third watch. The jug was exhausted. Jean's elbow flagged. The long ballad of the King's son with original variations was never finished. They forgot their mission and dropped down one by one upon the hearth. The host and his guests all slept till day.

When they woke up, the bright sun was shining, the storm was all gone. Master Pothier and Jean with some effort recollected—how—why—and when they had got to the hut of Roger Bontemps! A sense of honest shame crept over them. They were debating whether to go on to the Manor House or sneak back to the village, when a groom rode up who had been sent at dawn of day to the Tilly Arms, and he was returning with the intelligence that Le Gardeur had embarked that morning in a canoe with the Chevalier de Pean and his companions and gone to the city.

The night had been a hard one in the little inn. The Habitans and fishermen reduced to comparative quiet by the departure of Master Pothier and Jean La Marche, with their money spent and credit difficult, left by ones and twos to trudge or reel home as best they could. Some of them were suddenly sobered by the prospect of the lecture that they knew was simmering for them in the mind of the good wife who with gathered brows was rocking herself on her stool before the dying fire, nursing her wrath like a cross baby in her bosom, ready to throw it at the head of the good man as he came reeling into his cottage.

In proportion as the common room of the inn grew quiet by the departure of its guests, the parlour occupied by the gentlemen became more noisy and distinct in its confusion. The song, the laugh, the jest and jingle of glasses mingled with the perpetual rattle of dice or the thumps which accompanied the play of successful cards.

Paul Gaillard the host, a timid little fellow not used to such high imperious guests only ventured to look into his parlour when summoned for more wine. He was a born censitaire of the House of Tilly and felt shame and pity as he beheld the dishevelled figure of his young Seigneur shaking the dice box and defying one and all to another cast for love, liquor or whole handfuls of uncounted coin.

Paul Gaillard had ventured once to whisper something to Le Gardeur, about sending his Calash to the Manor House hoping that his youthful master would consent to be driven home. But his proposal was met by a wild laugh from Le Gardeur and a good humoured expulsion from the room.

He dared not again interfere, but contented himself with waiting until break of day to send a message to the Lady de Tilly informing her of the sad plight of his young Master.

De Pean with a great object in view had summoned Le Mercier and Emeric de Lantagnac from the city, potent topers and hard players, to assist him in his desperate game for the soul, body and fortune of Le Gardeur de Repentigny.

They came willingly. The Intendant had laughingly wished them *Bon Voyage!* and a speedy return with his friend Le Gardeur, giving them no other intimation of his wishes nor could they surmise that he had any other object in view than the pleasure of again meeting a pleasant companion of his table and a sharer of their pleasures.

De Pean had no difficulty in inticing Le Gardeur down to the Village Inn, where he had arranged that he should meet by mere accident as it were, his old city friends.

The bold generous nature of Le Gardeur who neither suspected nor feared any evil, greeted them with warmth.

They were jovial fellows he knew, who would be affronted if he refused to drink a cup of wine with them. They talked of the gossip of the City, its coteries and pleasant scandals and of the beauty and splendour of the Queen of Society, Angelique des Meloises.

Le Gardeur with a painful sense of his last interview with Angelique, and never for a moment forgetting her reiterated words, "I love you Le Gardeur but I will not marry you," kept silent whenever she was named, but talked with an air of cheerfulness on every other topic.

His one glass of wine was soon followed by another. He was pressed with such cordiality that he could not refuse. The fire was rekindled, at first with a faint glow upon his cheek, and a sparkle in his eye but the table soon overflowed with wine, mirth and laughter. He drank without reflection and soon spoke with warmth and looseness from restraint.

De Pean resolved to excite Le Gardeur to the utmost, would not cease alluding to Angelique. He recurred again and again to the splendour of her charms and the fascination of her ways. He watched the effect of his speech upon the countenance of Le Gardeur, keenly observant of every expression of interest excited by the mention of her.

"We will drink to her bright eyes," exclaimed De Pean, filling his glass until it ran over, "first in beauty and worthy to be first in place in New France—yea or Old France either! And He is a heathen who will not drink this toast!—"

"Le Gardeur will not drink it! neither would I in his place!" replied Emeric de Lantagnac too drunk now to mind what he said. "I would drink to the bright eyes of no woman who had played me the trick Angelique has played upon Le Gardeur."

"What trick has she played upon me?" repeated Le Gardeur with a touch of anger.

"Why, she has jilted you, and now flies at higher game and nothing but a prince of the blood will satisfy her!—"

"Does she say that? or do you invent it?" Le Gardeur was almost choking with angry feelings.

Emeric cared little what he said, drunk or sober. He replied gravely:—

"Oh, all the women in the city, say that she says it—! But you know Le Gardeur, women will lie of one another faster than a man can count a hundred by tens."

De Pean, while enjoying the vexation of Le Gardeur, feared that the banter of Emeric might have an ill effect on his scheme. "I do not believe it Le Gardeur!" said he, "Angelique is too true a woman to say what she means, to every jealous rival. The women hope she has jilted you. That counts one more chance for them you know! Is not that feminine arithmetic! Le Mercier?" asked he.

"It is at the Friponne!" replied Le Mercier laughing. "But the man who becomes debtor to Angelique des Meloises will never if I know her be discharged out of her books even if he pays his debt."

"Aye, they say she never lets a lover go or a friend either!" replied De Pean. "I have proof to convince Le Gardeur that Angelique has not jilted him. Emeric reports women's tattle nothing more."

Le Gardeur was thoroughly roused. "*Par Dieu!*" exclaimed he, "my affairs are well talked over in the City I think! Who gave man or woman the right to talk of me thus?"

"No one gave them the right," said De Pean. "But the women claim it indefeasibly from Eve who commenced talking of Adam's affairs with Satan the first time her man's back was turned."

"Pshaw! Angelique des Meloises is as sensible as she is beautiful! she never said that! No Par Dieu! she never said to man or woman that she had jilted me, or gave reason to others to say so!—"

Le Gardeur in his vexation poured out with nervous hand a large glass of pure brandy and drank it down. It had an instant effect. His forehead flushed and his eyes dilated with fresh fire. "She never said that!" Repeated he fiercely! "I would swear it on my Mothers head. She never did!—and would kill any man who would dare affirm it of her!—"

"Right! the way to win a woman is never to give her up!" answered De Pean. "Hark you Le Gardeur! All the City knows that she favoured you more than any of the rest of her legion of admirers. Why are you moping away your time here at Tilly when you ought to be running down your game in the City?"

"My Atalanta is too fleet of foot for me, De Pean," replied Le Gardeur "I have given up the chase. I have not the luck of Hippomanes."

"That is she is too fast!" said De Pean mockingly. "But have you thrown a golden apple at her feet to stop your runaway nymph?—"

"I have thrown myself at her feet De Pean! In vain!" said Le Gardeur gulping down another cup of brandy.

De Pean watched the effect of the deep potations which Le Gardeur now poured down to quench the rising fires kindled in his breast. "Come here Le Gardeur," said he, "I have a message for you which I would not deliver before, lest you might be angry."

De Pean led him into a recess of the room, "You are wanted in the city" whispered he. "Angelique sent this little note by me. She put it in my hand as I was embarking for Tilly. She blushed redder than a rose as she did so. I promised to deliver it safely to you."

It was a note quaintly folded in a style Le Gardeur recognized well, inviting him to return to the city. Its language was a mixture of light persiflage and tantalizing coquettry. She was dying of the dullness of the city. The late Ball at the Palace had been a failure lacking the presence of Le Gardeur. Her house was forlorn without the visits of her dear friend, and she wanted his trusty counsel in an affair of the last importance to her welfare and happiness.

"That girl loves you and you may have her for the asking," continued De Pean as Le Gardeur sat crumpling the letter up in his hand. De Pean watched his countenance with the eye of a basilisk.

"Do you think so?" asked Le Gardeur eagerly "but no, I have no more faith in woman. She does not mean it!—"

"But if she does mean it! Would you go Le Gardeur?—"

"Would I go?" replied he rising up excitedly. "Yes! I would go to the lowest pit in hell for her! but why are you taunting me, De Pean?"

"I taunt you! Read her note again! She wants your trusty counsel in an affair of the last importance to her welfare and happiness. You know what is the affair of last importance to a woman! Will you refuse her now Le Gardeur?—"

"No! *Par Dieu!* I can refuse her nothing! no not if she asked for my head, although I know it is but mockery."

"Never mind! Then you will return with us to the city? We start at daybreak."

"Yes, I will go with you De Pean! You have made me drunk and I am willing to stay drunk till I leave Amelie and my Aunt and Heloise, up at the Manor House. Pierre Philibert, he will be angry that I leave him,—but he can follow and they can all follow! I hate myself for it De Pean! But Angelique des Meloises is to me more than creature or Creator. It is a sin to love a woman as I love her De Pean!—"

De Pean fairly writhed before the spirit he had evoked. He was not so sure of his game, but that it might yet be lost. He knew Angelique's passionate impulses and he thought that no woman could resist such a devotion as that of Le Gardeur.

He kept down his feelings however. He saw that Le Gardeur was ripe for ruin. They returned to the table and drank still more freely, dice and cards were resumed, fresh challenges were thrown out, Emeric and Le Mercier were already deep in a game. Money was pushed to and fro. The contagion fastened like a plague upon Le Gardeur who sat down at the table drew forth a full purse, and pulling up every anchor of restraint set sail on the flood tide of drinking and gaming which lasted without ceasing until break of day.

De Pean never lost sight for a moment of his scheme for the abduction of Le Gardeur. He got ready for departure, and with a drunken rush and a broken song the four gallants with unwashed faces and disordered clothes, staggered into their canoe and with a shout bade the boatmen start.

The hardy canotiers were ready for departure. They headed their long canoes down the flowing river, dashed their paddles into the water, just silvered with the rays of the rising sun and shot downstream towards the city of Quebec.

De Pean elate with his success did not let the gaiety of the party flag for a moment during their return. They drank sang and talked Balderdash and indecencies in a way to bring a look of disgust upon the cheeks of the rough boatmen.

Le Gardeur from an innate cleanness of soul and imagination, intoxicated as he might be, never defiled his lips with impurities, although he drank and rioted to match the wildest of his companions. Emeric de Lantagnac and he sat supporting one another drinking unmeaning healths to all the bright eyes in the City, which they were going to see, and joining in the wild chorus of the Boatmen who strove vainly to drown the noise of their drunken passengers.

Much less sober than when they left Tilly the riotous party reached the Capital. The canotiers with rapid strokes of the paddle passed the high cliffs and guarded walls and made for the quay of the Friponne, De Pean forcing silence upon his companions as they passed the *Sault au Matelot*, where a crowd of idle boatmen hailed them with volleys of raillery which only ceased when the Canoe was near enough for them to see whom it contained. They were instantly silent. The rigorous search made by order of the Intendant after the late rioters and the summary punishments inflicted upon all who had been convicted, inspired a careful avoidance of offence towards Bigot and the high officers of his Staff.

De Pean landed quietly, few caring to turn their heads too often towards him. Le Gardeur wholly under his control staggered out of the canoe and taking his arm was dragged rather than led up to the Palace, where Bigot greeted the party with loud welcome. Appartments were assigned to Le Gardeur as to a most honoured guest in the Palace. Le Gardeur de Repentigny was finally and wholly in the power of the Intendant.

Bigot looked triumphant and congratulated De Pean on the success of his mission. "We will keep him now!" said he. "Le Gardeur must never draw a sober breath again until we have done with him!—"

De Pean looked knowingly at Bigot. "I understand!" said he "Emeric and Le Mercier will drink him blind and Cadet, Varin and the rest of us will rattle the dice like hail. We must pluck the pigeon to his last feather before he will feel desperate enough to play your game Chevalier."

"As you like De Pean about that!" replied Bigot, "only mind that he does not leave the palace—! His friends will run after him. That accursed Philibert will be here. On your life do not let him see him! Hark you, when he comes make Le Gardeur affront him by some offensive reply to his inquiry. You can do it!—"

De Pean took the hint and acted upon it by forging that infamous card in the name of Le Gardeur, and sending it as his reply to Pierre Philibert.

CHAPTER 42

MERE MALHEUR

La Corriveau eager to commence her work of wickedness took up her abode at the house of her ancient friend Mere Malheur whither she went on the night of her first interview with Angelique.

It was a small house built of uncut stones with rough stone steps and lintels, a peaked roof and low overhanging eaves, hiding itself under the shadow of the cliff, so closely that it seemed to form part of the rock itself.

Its sole inmate an old crone, who had reached the last degree of woman's ugliness and woman's heartlessness, Mere Malheur, sold fair winds to superstitious sailors and good luck to hunters and voyageurs. She was not a little suspected of dabbling in other forbidden things. Half believing in her own impostures she regarded La Corriveau with a feeling akin to worship, who in return for this devotion imparted to her a few secrets of minor importance in her diabolic arts.

La Corriveau was ever a welcome guest at the house of Mere Malheur, who feasted her lavishly, and served her obsequiously but did not press with undue curiosity to learn her business in the city. The two women understood one another well enough not to pry too closely into each other's secrets.

On this occasion La Corriveau was more than usually reserved and while Mere Malheur eagerly detailed to her all the doings and undoings that had happened in her circle of acquaintance, she got little information in return. She shrewdly concluded that La Corriveau had business on hand which would not bear to be spoken of.

"When you need my help, ask for it without scruple, Dame

507

Dodier!" said the old crone. "I see you have something on hand that may need my aid. I would go into the fire to serve you, although I would not burn my finger for any other woman in the world and you know it!—"

"Yes! I know it! Mere Malheur!" La Corriveau spoke with an air of superiority, "and you say rightly. I have something on hand which I cannot accomplish alone, and I do need your help! although I cannot tell you yet how or against whom."

"Is it a woman or a man? I will only ask that question Dame Dodier!" said the Crone turning upon her a pair of green inquisitive eyes.

"It is a woman, and so of course you will help me! Our sex for the bottom of all mischief Mere Malheur! I do not know what women are made for except to plague one another for the sake of worthless men!"

The old crone laughed a hideous laugh, and playfully pushed her long fingers into the ribs of La Corriveau. "Made for! Quotha? men's temptation to be sure, and the beginning of all mischief!"

"Pretty temptations you and I are, Mere Malheur!" replied La Corriveau with a scornful laugh.

"Well, we were pretty temptations once! I will never give up that! You must own Dame Dodier! we were both pretty temptations once!—"

"Pshaw! I wish I had been a man for my part!" replied La Corriveau impetuously. "It was a spiteful cross of fate to make me a woman!—"

"But Dame Dodier! I like to be a woman, I do! a man cannot be half as wicked as a woman, especially if she be young and pretty!" said the old woman laughing till the tears ran out of her bleared eyes.

"Nay, that is true Mere Malheur! The fairest women in the world are ever the worst! fair and false! Fair and false! They are always so. Not one better than another. Satan's mark is upon all of us!" La Corriveau looked an incarnation of Hecate as she uttered this calumny upon her sex.

"Aye! I have his mark on my knee! Dame Dodier!" replied the Crone. "See here! It was pricked once in the high court of Arras! but the fool judge decided that it was a mole and not a witch mark. I escaped a red gown that time however! I laughed at his stupidity and bewitched him for it in earnest! I was young and pretty then! He died in a year! and Satan sat on his grave in the shape of a black cat until his friends set a cross over it. I like to be a woman I do. It is so easy to be wicked and so nice! I always tell the girls that, and they give me twice as much as if I had told them to be good and nice, as they call it. Pshaw! *nice!* If only men knew us as we really are!"

"Well I do not like women, Mere Malheur!" replied La Corriveau. "They sneer at you and me, and call us witch and sorceress, and they will lie, steal, kill and do worse themselves for sake of one man today, and cast him off for sake of another tomorrow! Wise Solomon found only one good woman in a thousand. The wisest man now, finds not one in a worldful! It were better all of us were dead! Mere Malheur! But pour me out a glass of wine for I am tired of tramping in the dark to the house of that gay lady, I told you of."

Mere Malheur poured out a glass of choice Beaune from a demi jeanne, which she had received from a roguish sailor who had stolen it from his ship.

"But you have not told me who she is, Dame Dodier?" replied Mere Malheur refilling the glass of La Corriveau.

"Nor will I, yet. She is fit to be your mistress and mine, whoever she is, but I shall not go again to see her."

And La Corriveau did not again visit the house of Angelique. She had received from her precise information respecting the movements of the Intendant. He had gone to the Trois Rivieres on urgent affairs and might be absent for a week.

Angelique had received from Varin, in reply to her eager question for news, a short falsified account of the proceedings in the council relative to Caroline, and of Bigot's indignant denial of all knowledge of her.

Varin as a member of the council dared not reveal the truth, but would give his familiars, half hints, or tell to others elaborate lies when pressed for information. He did not in this case even hint at the fact that a search was to be made for Caroline. Had he done so Angelique would herself have given secret information to the Governor, to order the search of Beaumanoir and thus got her rival out of the way without trouble, risk or crime.

But it was not to be. The little word that would have set her active spirit on fire to aid in the search for Caroline was not spoken, and her thoughts remained immoveably fixed upon her death.

But if Angelique had been misled by Varin, as to what had passed at the council, Mere Malheur through her intercourse with a servant of Varin, had learned the truth. An eavesdropping groom had overheard his master and the Intendant conversing on the letters of the Baron and of La Pompadour. The man told his sweetheart, who coming with some stolen sweetmeats to Mere Malheur told her, who in turn was not long in imparting what she had heard to La Corriveau.

La Corriveau did not fail to see that should Angelique discover that her rival was to be searched for, and taken to France if found, she would at once change her mind, and Caroline would be got rid of without need of her interference. But La Corriveau had got her hand in the dish. She was not one to lose her promised reward or miss the chance of so cursed a deed by any untimely avowal of what she knew.

So Angelique was doomed to remain in ignorance until too late. She became the dupe of her own passions and the dupe of La Corriveau who carefully concealed from her a secret so important.

Bigot's denial in the Council weighed nothing with her. She felt certain that the lady was no other than Caroline de St Castin. Angelique was acute enough to perceive that Bigot's bold assertion that he knew nothing of her bound him in a chain of obligation never to confess afterwards ought to the contrary. She eagerly persuaded herself that he would not regret to hear that Caroline had died by some sudden and to appearance natural death, and thus relieved him of a danger, and her of an obstacle to her marriage.

Without making a full confidante of Mere Malheur, La Corriveau resolved to make use of her in carrying out her diabolical scheme. Mere Malheur had once been a servant at Beaumanoir. She knew the house and in her hey day of youth and levity had often smuggled herself in and out by the subterranean passage which connected the solitary watch tower with the vaults of the Chateau. Mere Malheur knew Dame Tremblay who as the Charming Josephine had often consulted her on the perplexities of a heart divided among too many lovers.

The memory of that fragrant period of her life was the freshest and pleasantest of all Dame Tremblay's experience. It was like the odour of new mown hay, telling of early summer, and frolics in the green fields. She liked nothing better than to talk it all over in her quiet room with Mere Malheur, as they sat opposite one another at her little table, each with a cup of tea in her hand well laced with brandy which was a favorite weakness of them both.

Dame Tremblay was in private neither nice nor squeamish as to the nature of her gossip. She and the old fortune teller, when out of sight of the rest of the servants, had always a dish of the choicest scandal fresh from the City.

La Corriveau resolved to send Mere Malheur to Beaumanoir under the pretence of paying a visit to Dame Tremblay, in order to open a way of communication between herself and Caroline. She had learned enough during her brief interview with Caroline in the forest of St Valier, and from what she now heard respecting the Baron de St Castin to convince her that this was no other than his missing daughter.

"If Caroline could only be induced to admit La Corriveau into her secret chamber, and take her into her confidence, the rest—All the rest," muttered the Hag to herself, with terrible emphasis, "would be easy! and my reward sure! But that reward shall be measured in my own bushel not in yours, Mademoiselle des Meloises when the deed is done!—"

La Corriveau knew the power such a secret would enable her to exercise over Angelique. She already regarded the half of her reputed riches as her own. "Neither she nor the Intendant will ever dare neglect me after that!" said she. "When once Angelique shall be linked in with me by a secret compact of blood, the fortune of La Corriveau is made! If the death of this girl be the elixir of life to you, it shall be the touchstone of fortune forever to La Corriveau!—"

Mere Malheur was next day despatched on a visit to her old gossip Dame Tremblay. She had been well tutored on every point what to say and how to demean herself. She bore a letter to Caroline written in the Italian hand of La Corriveau, who had learned to write well from her mother Marie Exili.

The mere possession of the art of writing was a rarity in those days, in the class among whom she lived. La Corriveau's ability to write at all, was a circumstance as remarkable to her illiterate neighbours as the possession of the black art which they ascribed to her, and not without a strong suspicion that it had the same origin.

Mere Malheur in anticipation of a cup of tea and brandy with Dame Tremblay, had dressed herself with some appearance of smartness, in a clean striped gown of Linsey. A peaked Artois hat surmounted a broad frilled cap which left visible some tresses of coarse grey hair and a pair of silver earings which dangled with every motion of her head. Her shoes displayed broad buckles of brass and her short petticoat showed a pair of stout ankles enclosed in red clocked stockings. She carried a crutched stick in her hand by help of which she proceeded vigorously on her journey.

Starting in the morning, she trudged out of the City towards the ferry of Jean Le Nocher, who carefully crossed himself and his boat too as he took Mere Malheur on board. He wafted her over in a hurry as something to be got rid of as quickly as possible.

Jean would not even have accepted his fare from her, had not Dame Babet, always at hand, noticed his hesitation. She stepped promptly up and took the coin from the hand of Mere Malheur. Dropping it in her capacious pocket, she remarked to her husband: "You are always a fool Jean! Good money never smells! besides we will pay it to the church as a christening fee, and that will make it clean as the face of St Catherine."

Mere Malheur although accustomed to slights and scorns

when she appeared in public, was provoked at the remark of Babet. She struck her stick violently into the ground and lifting up a bony finger exclaimed, "Devil fly away with you Dame Babet! A bad witch was spoiled when you became the wife of an honest man! Your red cheeks will be as white as chalk before you get another, when you lose him!"

"Look here!—" continued she, drawing with the end of her stick the figure of a pentagram upon the sand, "when that mark is rubbed out and gone, look out for a misfortune! I do not cause it, mind you! I only predict it! So now Dame Babet, good speed to my journey and bad luck to your staying at home!—"

The old Crone wheeled round and dinting her stick hard into the ground at every step, moved away quickly, leaving Jean stupified with terror and Babet flaming with anger as she clapped her hands and vociferated, "Aroint you for a witch! Mere Malheur! May you go up to the moon in the flames of a tarbarrel! Bad speed to your journey for good it cannot be!—"

"She has left the Devils mark on the sand, Babet!" said Jean disconsolately "Shall we rub it out or get the Curé to sprinkle it with holy water? There will be sure to come some misfortune to somebody after that!—"

"Well! if the misfortune only does not come to us! and she did not say it would, Jean, we need not cry tears! But let the mark remain Jean, and the Curé shall rub it out and avert the bad luck she has threatened." Babet was less brave over the witch mark than she pretended to be.

Jean felt uneasy, and agreed with Babet, that it were best to preserve the mark as long as possible, seeing that bad luck was to accompany its disappearance. He ran to the cottage and brought out a tub which he turned carefully over the pentagram to prevent its being obliterated before the arrival of the Curé who was to be informed of this strange proceeding of Mere Malheur.

The old crone went on her way cursing and laughing by turns, as she passed up the long hill of Charlebourg. She rested herself for a time under the old tree in front of the Couronne de France where two or three Habitans sat enjoying a mug of cider, and who promptly moved from their seat to make room for her.

She sat down looking at them with her bleared eyes, until they shied off one by one leaving her alone, with the stout Landlady Dame Bedard, and her pretty daughter Zoe, who at once plunged into conversation with the old woman, and finally demanded that she should tell Zoe's fortune, and what was to happen after her marriage with Antoine La Chance.

Mere Malheur satisfied the curiosity of the mother and daughter by a circumstantial lie of the object of her present journey, and having had her hand duly crossed with a piece of silver She told Zoe's fortune in a way that suffused her maiden cheeks with happy blushes, and made her cry out, "That Mere Malheur, no matter what folks said, was the dearest and trustiest old woman in the land! That she believed every word told by her would come true! and that time would make it true!—"

Zoe for a long time would not tell her mother, what the fortune teller had said; but when she did, both mother and daughter laughed and looked as happy as Godmothers at a Christening.—

Mere Malheur although but half trusted by La Corriveau instinctively guessed something of the nature of her black errand and was as impatient for its accomplishment as if the ill had been all of her own contriving.

Mere Malheur tramped on like a heavy gnome through the fallen and flying leaves of the woods of Beaumanoir, caring nothing for the golden hazy sky, the soft balmy air or the varicoloured leaves scarlet yellow and brown of every shade and tinge that still hung upon the Autumnal trees.

A frosty night or two had ushered in the summer of St Martin as it was called by the Habitans—The Indian summer, that brief time of glory and enchantment which visits us like a gaudy herald to announce the approach of the winter king. It is nature's last rejoicing in the sunshine, and the open air, like the splendour and gaiety of a maiden devoted to the cloister, who for a few weeks is allowed to flutter like a bird of Paradise amid the pleasures and gaieties of the world, and then comes the end. Her locks of pride are shorn off. She veils her beauty and kneels a nun on the cold stones of her passionless cell, out of which even with repentance, there comes no deliverance.

Mere Malheur's arrival at Beaumanoir was speedily known to all the servants of the Chateau. She did not often visit them, but when she did, there was a hurried recital of an ave or two to avert any harm, followed by a patronizing welcome and a rummage for small coins to cross her hand withal, in return for her solutions of the grave questions of love, jealousy, money and marriage which fermented secretly or openly in the bosoms of all of them. They were but human beings, food for imposture and preyed on by deceivers! The visit of Mere Malheur was an event of interest in both kitchen and laundry of the Chateau.

Dame Tremblay had the first claim however upon this singular visitor. She met her at the back door of the Chateau and with a face beaming with smiles and dropping all dignity, exclaimed,

"Mere Malheur! upon my life! welcome! you wicked old soul! you surely knew I wanted to see you! come in and rest! you must be tired unless you came on a broom! ha! ha! come to my room and never mind anybody!—"

This last remark was made for the benefit of the servants who stood peeping at every door and corner not daring to speak to the old woman in the presence of the Housekeeper, but knowing that their time would come, they took patience.

The housekeeper giving them a severe look, proceeded to her own snug appartment, followed by the crone, whom she seated in her easiest chair and proceeded to refresh with a glass of Cognac, which was swallowed with much relish and wiping of lips, accompanied by a little artificial cough. Dame Tremblay kept a carafe of it in her room to raise the temperature of her low spirits and vapours to summer heat. Not that she drank—far from it! but she liked to sip for her Stomach's sake.

"It is only a thimble full, I take now and then," she said. "When I was the Charming Josephine, I used to kiss the cups I presented to the young gallants and I took no more than a fly!

but they always drank bumpers from the cup I kissed!" The old Dame looked grave as she shook her head, and remarked: "but we cannot be always young and handsome, can we Mere Malheur?—"

"No Dame! but we can be jolly and fat, and that is what we are! you dont quaff life by thimble fulls, and you only want a stout offer to show the world that you can trip as briskly to Church yet, as any girl in New France."

The humour of the old crone convulsed Dame Tremblay with laughter, as if some invisible fingers were tickling her wildly under the armpits.

She composed herself at last and drawing her chair close to that of Mere Malheur, looked her inquiringly in the face and asked: "what was the news?—"

Dame Tremblay was endowed with more than the ordinary curiosity of her sex. She knew more news of City and Country than anyone else, and she dispensed it as freely as she gathered. She never let her stock of gossip run low, and never allowed man or woman to come to speak with her without pumping them dry of all they knew! A secret in anybody's possession set her wild to possess it, and she gave no rest to her inordinate curiosity until she had fished it out of even the muddiest waters.

The mystery that hung about Caroline was a source of perpetual irritation to the nerves of Dame Tremblay. She had tried as far as she dared by hint and suggestion to draw from the Lady some reference to her name and family, but in vain. Caroline would avow nothing and Dame Tremblay completely baffled by a failure of ordinary means to find out the secret, bethought herself of her old resource in case of perplexity, Mere Malheur.

For several days she had been brooding over this mode of satisfying her curiosity, when the unexpected visit of Mere Malheur set aside all further hesitation about disobeying the Intendant's orders, not to inquire or allow any other person to make inquisition respecting Caroline.

"Mere Malheur! you feel comfortable now!" said she. "That glass of Cognac has given you a colour like a peony!"

"Yes! I am very comfortable now, Dame! your cognac is heavenly! It warms without burning. That glass is the best news I have to tell of today."

"Nay, but there is always something stirring in the City! Somebody born, married or dead. Somebody courted, won, lost or undone! Somebody's name up. Somebody's reputation down! tell me all you know Mere Malheur! and then I will tell you something will make you glad you came to Beaumanoir today! Take another sip of cognac and begin!—"

"Aye Dame, that is indeed a temptation!" She took two deep sips and holding her glass in her hand, began with loose tongue to relate the current gossip of the City, which although already known to Dame Tremblay, an ill natured version of it from the lips of her visitor seemed to give it a fresh seasoning and a relish which it had not previously possessed.

"Now Mere Malheur! I have a secret to tell you," said Dame Tremblay in a low confidential tone. "A dead secret! mind you, which you had better be burnt than reveal. There is a lady, a real lady if I ever saw one living in the Chateau here in the greatest privacy. I and the Intendant only see her. She is beautiful and full of sorrow as the picture of the blessed Madonna. What she is I may guess, but who she is I cannot conjecture, and would give my little finger to know!—"

"Tut, Dame!" replied Mere Malheur with a touch of confidence. "I will not believe any woman could keep a secret from you! But this is news indeed, you tell me! A lady in concealment here? and you say you cannot find her out! Dame Tremblay?—"

"In truth I cannot. I have tried every artifice but she passes all my wit and skill. If she were a man I would have drawn her very teeth out with less difficulty, than I have tried to extract the name of this Lady. When I was the Charming Josephine of Lake Beauport I could wind men like a thread round which finger I liked, but this is a tangled knot which drives me to despair to straighten it out."

"What do you know about her, Dame? tell me all you suspect!—" said Mere Malheur.

"Truly," replied the Dame without the least asperity, "I

suspect the poor thing like the rest of us is no better than she should be, and the Intendant knows it and Mademoiselle des Meloises knows it, too, and to judge by her constant prayers and penitence she knows it herself, but will not say it to me!"

"Aye! Dame, but this is great news, you tell me!" repeated Mere Malheur, eagerly clutching at the opportunity thus offered for the desired interview. "But what help do you expect from me in the matter?—"

Mere Malheur looked very expectant at her friend, who continued: "I want you to see that lady, under promise of secresy mark you! and look at her hands and tell me who and what she is."

Dame Tremblay had an unlimited faith in the superstitions of her age.

"I will do all you wish Dame, but you must allow me to see her alone," replied the Crone who felt she was thus opening the door to La Corriveau.

"To be sure I will! that is if she will consent to be seen, for she has in some things a spirit of her own! I am afraid to push her too closely! The mystery of her is taking the flesh off my bones, and I can only get asleep by taking strong possets Mere Malheur! Feel my elbow! feel my knee! I have not had so sharp an elbow or knee since Goodman Tremblay died! and he said I had the sharpest elbow and knee in the City! but I had to punch him sometimes to keep him in order! But set that horrid cap straight Mere Malheur! while I go ask her if she would like to have her fortune told. She is not a woman if she would not like to know her fortune, for she is in despair I think with all the world, and when a woman is in despair, as I know by my own experience, she will jump at any chance, for spite, if not for love, as I did when I took the Sieur Tremblay by your advice Mere Malheur!"

Dame Tremblay left the old crone making hideous faces in a mirror, as she rubbed her cheeks and mouth with the corner of her apron and proceeded to the door of Caroline's appartment. She knocked gently and a low soft voice bade her enter.

Caroline was seated on a chair by the window, knitting her

sad thoughts into a piece of work which she occasionally lifted from her lap with a sudden start as she broke the train of her reflections.

She was weighing over and over her thoughts, like gold in a scale, by grains and pennyweights. A few kind words lately spoken to her by Bigot, when he ran in to bid her adieu before departing on his journey to the Trois Rivières, seemed a treasure inexhaustible as she kept on repeating them without end. The pressure of his hand had been warmer, the tone of his voice softer, the glance of his eye more kind and he looked pityingly, she thought, upon her wan face, when he left her in the gallery, and with a cheery voice and a kiss, bade her take care of her health, and win back the lost roses of Acadia.

These words passed through her mind with unceasing repetition and a white lining of light was visible on the edge of the dark cloud which hung over her. "The roses of Acadia will never bloom again!" thought she sadly. "I have watered them with salt tears too long and all in vain! O Bigot! I fear it is too late, too late!" Still his last look and last words reflected a faint ray of hope and joy upon her pallid countenance.

Dame Tremblay entered the appartment and while busying herself on pretence of setting it in order, talked in her garrulous way of the little incidents of daily life in the Chateau, and finished by a mention, as it were casual, of the arrival of the wise woman of the city, who knew everything, could interpret dreams and tell by looking in a glass or in your hand things past, present and to come.

"A wonderful woman!" Dame Tremblay said, "a perilous woman too! not safe to deal with, but for all that, every one runs after her, and she has a good or bad word for every person who consults her. For my part," continued the Dame, "she foretold my marriage with the Goodman Tremblay, long before it happened, and she also foretold his death to the very month it happened. So I have reason to believe in her as well as to be thankful!—"

Caroline listened attentively to the Dame's remarks. She was not superstitious, but yet not above the beliefs of her age, while the Indian strain in her lineage and her familiarity with the traditions of the Abenaquais inclined her to yield more than ordinary respect to dreams.

Caroline had dreamed of riding on a coal black horse seated behind the veiled figure of a man, whose face she could not see, who carried her like the wind away to the ends of the earth and there shut her up in a mountain for ages and ages until a bright angel cleft the rock and clasping her in his arms bore her up to light and liberty in the presence of the Redeemer and of all the host of heaven.

This dream lay heavy on her mind. For the veiled figure she knew was one she loved, but who had no honest love for her. Her mind had been brooding over the dream all day and the announcement by Dame Tremblay of the presence in the Chateau of one who was able to interpret dreams, seemed a stroke of fortune if not an act of Providence.

She roused herself up and with more animation than Dame Tremblay had yet seen in her countenance requested her to send up her visitor that she might ask her a question.

Mere Malheur was quickly summoned to the appartment of Caroline, where Dame Tremblay left them alone.

The repulsive look of the old crone sent a shock through the fine nervous organization of the young girl. She requested Mere Malheur to be seated however, and in her gentle manner questioned her about the dream.

Mere Malheur was an adept in such things, and knew well how to humour human nature, and lead it to put its own interpretations upon its own visions and desires, while giving the credit of it to herself.

Mere Malheur therefore, interpreted the dream according to Caroline's secret wishes. This inspired a sort of confidence and Mere Malheur seized the opportunity to deliver the letter from La Corriveau.

"My Lady!" said she, looking carefully round the room to note if the door was shut and no one was present. "I can tell you more than the interpretation of your dream. I can tell you who you are and why you are here—!"

Caroline started with a frightened look and stared in the face of Mere Malheur. She faltered out at length. "You know who I am and why I am here! Impossible! I never saw you before!—"

"No my Lady you never saw me before, but I will convince you that I know you—you are the daughter of the Baron de St Castin. Is it not so?" The old crone looked frightfully knowing as she uttered these words.

"Mother of Mercies! What shall I do?" ejaculated the alarmed girl. "Who are you to say that?—"

"I am but a messenger my Lady! listen! I am sent here to give you secretly this letter from a friend, who knows you, better than I, and who above all things desires an interview with you as she has things of the deepest import to communicate."

"A letter! O! what mystery is all this? A letter for me! Is it from the Intendant?—"

"No, my Lady. It is from a woman!" Caroline blushed and trembled as she took it from the old Crone.

A woman! It flashed upon the mind of Caroline that the letter was important. She opened it with trembling fingers anticipating she knew not what direful tidings when her eyes ran over the clear handwriting.

La Corriveau had written to the effect that she was an unknown friend desirous of serving her in a moment of peril. "The Baron de St Castin had traced her to New France and had procured from the King instructions to the Governor to search for her everywhere, and to send her to France. Other things of great import," the writer said, "she had also to communicate, if Caroline would grant her a private interview in the Chateau."

"There was a passage leading from the old deserted watch tower to the vaulted chamber," continued the letter, "and the writer would without further notice come on the following night to Beaumanoir, and knock at the arched door of her chamber about the hour of midnight, when if Caroline pleased to admit her she would gladly inform her of very important matters relating to herself, to the Intendant and to the Baron de St Castin, who was on his way out to the Colony to conduct in person the search for his lost daughter."

The letter concluded with the information, "that the Intendant had gone to the Trois Rivières, whence he might not return for a week and that during his absence the Governor would probably order a search for her to be made at Beaumanoir."

Caroline held the letter convulsively in her hand as she gathered its purport, rather than read it. Her face changed colour from a deep flush of shame to the palest hue of fear, when she comprehended its meaning and understood that her father was on his way to New France to find out her hiding place.

"What shall I do! O! what shall I do!" exclaimed she wringing her hands for very anguish regardless of the presence of Mere Malheur, who stood observing her with eyes glittering with curiosity but void of every mark of womanly sympathy or feeling.

"My father! my loving father!" continued Caroline "my deeply injured father! coming here with anger in his face to drag me from my concealment! I shall drop dead at his feet for very shame! O that I were buried alive with mountains piled over me to hide me from my father! What shall I do? Whither shall I go? Bigot! Bigot! why have you forsaken me?—"

Mere Malheur continued eying her with cold curiosity but was ready at the first moment to second the promptings of the evil spirit contained in the letter.

"Mademoiselle!" said she. "There is but one way to escape from the search to be made by your father, and the Governor. Take counsel of her who sends you that friendly letter. She can offer you a safe hiding place until the Storm blows over. Will you see her my Lady?—"

"See her? I who dare see no one! Who is she that sends me such strange news? Is it truth? do you know her?" continued she looking fixedly at Mere Malheur, as if in hope of reading on her countenance some contradiction of the matter contained in the letter.—

"I think it is all true my Lady!" replied she with mock humility. "I am but a poor messenger however, and speak not myself of things I do not know, but she who sends me will tell you all."

"Does the Intendant know her?—"

"I think he told her to watch over your safety during his absence. She is old and your friend, will you see her?—" replied Mere Malheur, who saw the point was gained.

"O yes! yes! tell her to come! Beseech her not to fail to come! or I shall go mad! O woman! you too are old and experienced and ought to know, can she help me in this strait think you?" exclaimed Caroline clasping her hands in a gesture of entreaty.

"No one is more able to help you," said the Crone. "She can counsel you what to do and if need be, find means to conceal you from the search that will be made for you."

"Haste then and bid her come tomorrow night! why not tonight?" Caroline was all nervous impatience. "I will wait her coming in the vaulted chamber, I will watch for her as one in the valley of Death watches for the angel of deliverance! Bid her come, and at midnight tomorrow she shall find the door in the secret chamber open to admit her."

The eagerness of the illfated girl to see La Corriveau, outran every calculation of Mere Malheur. It was in vain and useless for her to speak further on the subject. Caroline would say no more. Her thoughts ran violently in the direction suggested by the artful letter. "She would see La Corriveau tomorrow night, and would make no more avowals to Mere Malheur," she said to herself.

Seeing no more was to be got out of her, the crone bade her a formal farewell, looking at her curiously as she did so, and wondering in her mind if she would ever see her again! For the old creature had a shrewd suspicion that La Corriveau had not told her all her intentions with respect to this singular girl.

Caroline returned her salute still holding the letter in her hand. She sat down to peruse it again and observed not Mere Malheur's equivocal glance as she turned her head for the last time upon the innocent girl, doomed to receive the midnight visit from La Corriveau.

CHAPTER 43

"OUTVENOMS ALL THE WORMS OF NILE"

"THERE is death in the pot!" the crone muttered as she went out. "La Corriveau comes not here on her own errand either! That girl is too beautiful to live and to some one her death is worth gold! It will go hard but La Corriveau shall share with me the reward of the work of tomorrow night!"

In the long Gallery she encountered Dame Tremblay ready to eat her up, as she told La Corriveau afterwards, in the eagerness of her curiosity to learn the result of her interview with Caroline.

Mere Malheur was wary and accustomed to fence with words. It was necessary to tell a long tale of circumstances to Dame Tremblay but not necessary nor desirable to tell the truth. The old crone, therefore, as soon as she had seated herself in the easy chair of the housekeeper and refreshed herself by twice accepting the Dame's pressing invitation to tea and cognac, related with uplifted hands, and shaking head a narrative of bold lies regarding what had really past during her interview with Caroline.

"But who is she? Mere Malheur! Did she tell you her name? Did she show you her palm?—"

"Both! Dame, both! She is a girl of Ville Marie who has run away from her parents for love of the gallant Intendant, and is in hiding from them. They wanted to put her into the Convent to cure her of love. The Convent always cures love Dame, beyond the power of philters to revive it!" and the old crone laughed inwardly to herself as if she doubted her own saying.

Dame Tremblay dissented heartily from this opinion. "It would not have cured me, when I was the charming Josephine

524

of Lake Beauport!" said she, "they once talked of sending *me* to the convent! But Law! all the young gentlemen in the City would have filled the parlour to see me on every visiting day. There is nothing they admire so much as a pretty nun, Mere Malheur! But you have not told me all about my Lady. What did she say? Does she expect the Intendant to marry her? Is she to be mistress and all of the Chateau?—"

"She is the mistress of the Chateau now, Dame!" replied Mere Malheur. "The Intendant will refuse her nothing and I believe he will marry her! There! that is all I know."

"No, you know more! Did she not tell you how jealous she was of that bold faced Angelique des Meloises, who they say is resolved to marry the Intendant whether he will or no?"

"No! she mentioned not her name, but she loves the Intendant and fears every woman as a rival, and with reason—!" chuckled Mere Malheur.

"Aye! Does she not!" replied Dame Tremblay. "She fears Angelique des Meloises more than poison! but she would not of course tell you as she tells me. But did she not tell you her name, Mere Malheur?—"

"No! Girls of that kind and in her condition have generally lost their name without finding another," said the old crone with a mocking laugh.

"Well, I cannot laugh at her!" replied Dame Tremblay kindly. "If her good name is gone it was for love not for hate! It is only your women without hearts who laugh at those who have them. If all the world laugh at her I will not. She is a dear angel, and I love her. When I was the charming Josephine— — — —"

"Aye! We are all dear Angels some time or other Dame! and the world is full of fallen ones!—" interrupted the crone with a leer, as if some far off reminiscence revisited her fancy.

"When I was the charming Josephine of Lake Beauport—I was going to say, but you always interrupt me Mere Malheur!— no one could say black was my nail or if they did; they lied!" exclaimed the Dame with a little heat, but presently reflecting that Mere Malheur had received all her tender confessions and knew all her secrets concerning more than a score of admirers, she burst out laughing and pouring out the old crone another cup, bade her, "go down stairs and tell the fortunes of the idle girls in the kitchen, who were not putting a hand to a single thing in the house, until she settled their curiosity, about the worthless men, who filled their heads and caused them to empty their pockets of their last coin to bestow it on ribbons, combs and fortune-tellers! Such ridiculous things are girls now-a-days with their high heels and paint and patches that one cannot tell the mistress from the Lady's maid any more!—When I was the Charming Josephine— — — —"

Mere Malheur cut short the impending story by getting up and going at once to the kitchen, where she did not dally long with the girls, "but fed them with big spoonfuls of good fortune" she said, "and sent them to bed happy as expectant brides, that night."

The crone eager to return to La Corriveau with the account of the successful interview with Caroline, bade Dame Tremblay a hasty but formal farewell and with her crutched stick in her hand trudged stoutly back to the city.

Mere Malheur while the sun was yet high reached her cottage under the rock where La Corriveau was eagerly expecting her at the window. The moment she entered the masculine voice of La Corriveau was heard asking loudly:

"Have you seen her Mere Malheur? Did you give her the letter? never mind your hat! tell me before you take it off!" The old crone was tugging at the strings and La Corriveau came to help her.

"Yes! she took your letter" replied she impatiently "She took my story like spring water. Go at the stroke of twelve tomorrow night and she will let you in Dame Dodier! but will she let you out again? ah!" The crone stood with her hat in her hand, and looked with a wicked glance at La Corriveau.

"If she will let me in, I can let myself out, Mere Malheur," replied La Corriveau in a low tone. "But why do you ask that?—"

"Because I read mischief in your eye, and see it twitching in your thumb, and you do not ask me to share your secret!—Is it so bad as that, Dame Dodier?—"

"Pshaw! You are sharing it! Wait and you will see your share of it! But tell me Mere Malheur! how does she look, this mysterious lady of the Chateau?—" La Corriveau sat down and placed her long thin hand on the arm of the old crone.

"Like one doomed to die! because she is too good to live! Sorrow is a bad pasture for a young creature like her to feed on, Dame Dodier!—" was the answer, but it did not change a muscle on the face of La Corriveau.

"Aye! but there are worse pastures than sorrow for young creatures like her, and she has found one of them," she replied coldly.

"Well! as we make our bed so must we lie on it! Dame Dodier! that is what I always tell the young silly things who come to me asking their fortunes and the proverb pleases them. They always think the bridal bed must be soft and well made, at any rate."

"They are fools! better make their death bed than their bridal bed! But I must see this piece of perfection of yours, tomorrow night, Dame! The Intendant returns in two days and he might remove her. Did she tell you that?"

"No! He is a devil more powerful than the one we serve Dame! I fear him—!"

"Tut! I fear neither devil nor man. It was to be at the hour of twelve? Did you not say at the hour of twelve, Mere Malheur?—"

"Yes! go in by the vaulted passage and knock at the secret door. She will admit you! But what will you do with her Dame Dodier? Is she doomed? could you not be gentle with her, Dame?"

There was a fall in the voice of Mere Malheur—an intonation partly due to fear of consequences, partly to a fibre of pity which—dry and disused—something in the look of Caroline had stirred like a dead leaf quivering in the wind.

"Tut! Has she melted your old dry heart to pity Mere Malheur? ha! ha! who would have thought that! and yet I remember she made a soft fool of me for a minute in the wood of St Valier!"—La Corriveau spoke in a hard tone as if in reproving Mere Malheur, she was also reproving herself.

"She is unlike any other woman I ever saw," replied the crone ashamed of her unwonted sympathy. "The devil is clean out of her as he is out of a church."

"You are a fool Mere Malheur. Out of a church! quotha!" and La Corriveau laughed a loud laugh, "why I go to church myself and whisper my prayers backwards, to keep on terms with the Devil, who stands nodding behind the altar, to every one of my petitions—! That is more than some people get in return for their prayers!" added she.

"I pray backwards in church too, Dame! but I could never get sight of him there as you do—! Something always blinds me!" and the two old sinners laughed together at the thought of the Devil's litanies they recited in the church.

"But how to get to Beaumanoir? I shall have to walk as you did Mere Malheur. It is a vile road and I must take the byway through the forest. It were worth my life to be seen on this visit!" said La Corriveau conning on her fingers the difficulties of the by path, which she was well acquainted with however.

"There is a moon after nine by which hour you can reach the wood of Beaumanoir," observed the Crone "are you sure you know the way Dame Dodier?—"

"As well as the way into my gown! I know an Indian Canotier who will ferry me across to Beauport and say nothing. I dare not allow that prying knave Jean Le Nocher or his sharp wife to mark my movements."

"Well thought of Dame Dodier!—You are of a craft and subtlety to cheat Satan himself at a game of hide and seek!—" The crone looked with genuine admiration almost worship at La Corriveau, as she said this, "but I doubt he will find both of us at last Dame! when we have got into our last corner!"

"Well, *Vogue la Galère!*" exclaimed La Corriveau starting up. "Let it go as it will! I shall walk to Beaumanoir and I shall fancy I wear golden garters and silver slippers to make the way easy and pleasant! But you must be hungry Mere, with your long tramp! I have a supper prepared for you so come and eat in the Devils name! or I shall be tempted to say grace *in Nomine Domini*, and choke you—!—"

The two women went to a small table and sat down to

a plentiful meal of such things as formed the dainties of persons of their rank of life, upon the table stood the dish of sweetmeats which the thievish maid servant had brought to Mere Malheur with the grooms story of the conversation between Bigot and Varin a story which could Angelique have got hold of, it would have stopped at once her frightful plot to kill the unhappy Caroline.

"I were a fool to tell her that story of the groom's" muttered La Corriveau to herself, "and spoil the fairest experiment of the *Aqua Tofana* ever made, and ruin my own fortune too! I know a trick worth two of that!" And she laughed inwardly to herself, a laugh which was repeated in Hell and made merry the ghosts of Beatrice Spara, Exili and La Voisin.

A bottle of brandy stood between La Corriveau and Mere Malheur, which gave zest to their repast, and they sat long exchanging vile thoughts in viler language mingled with ridicule, detraction and scandal of all their dupes and betters.

All next day La Corriveau kept closely to the house, but she found means to communicate to Angelique, her intention to visit Beaumanoir that night.

The news was grateful yet strangely moving to Angelique. She trembled and turned pale not for ruth but for doubt and dread of possible failure or discovery.

She sent by an unknown hand to the house of Mere Malheur, a little basket containing a bouquet of roses so beautiful and fragrant that they might have been plucked in the Garden of Eden.

Angelique loved flowers, but her hands shook with a palsy of apprehension and an innate feeling of repugnance as she reflected on the purpose for which her beautiful roses were given. She only recovered her composure after throwing herself on a sofa and plunging headlong into the day dreams which now made up the sum of her existence.

La Corriveau carried the basket into an inner chamber, a small room, the window of which never saw the sun, but opened against the close overhanging rock which was so near, that it might be touched with the hand. The dark damp wall of the cliff shed a gloomy obscurity in the room even at midday.

The small black eyes of La Corriveau glittered like poniards as she opened the basket, and taking out the bouquet found attached to it by a ribbon, a silken purse containing a number of glittering pieces of gold. She pressed the coins to her cheek, and even put them between her lips, to taste their sweetness, for money she loved beyond all things. The passion of her soul was avarice. Her wickedness took its direction from the love of money and scrupled at no iniquity for the sake of it.

She placed the purse carefully in her bosom and took up the roses regarding them with a strange look of admiration, as she muttered, "They are beautiful and they are sweet! Men would call them innocent! They are like her who sent them fair without and as yet, like her who is to receive them fair within." She stood reflecting for a few moments and exclaimed as she laid the bouquet upon the table,

"Angelique des Meloises! you send your gold and your roses to me because you believe me to be a worse demon than yourself! but you are worthy to be crowned tonight with these roses as Queen of Hell and mistress of all the witches that ever met in Grand Sabbat at the Palace of Galienne where Satan sits on a throne of gold—!"

La Corriveau looked out of the window and saw a corner of the rock, lit up with the last ray of the setting sun. She knew it was time to prepare for her journey.

She loosened her long black and grey elfin locks and let them fall dishevelled over her shoulders. Her thin cruel lips were drawn to a rigid line, and her eyes were filled with hell fire, as she drew the casket of ebony out of her bosom and opened it with a reverential touch as a devotee would touch a shrine of relics. She took out of it a small gilded vial of antique shape containing a clear bright liquid which as she shook it up seemed filled with a million sparks of fire.

Before drawing the glass stopper of the vial La Corriveau folded a handkerchief carefully over her mouth and nostrils to avoid inhaling the volatile essence of its poisonous contents. Then holding the bouquet with one hand at arms length, she sprinkled the glowing roses with the transparent liquid from the vial which she held in the other hand, repeating in a low harsh tone the formula of an ancient incantation which was one of the secrets imparted to Antonio Exili by the terrible Beatrice Spara.

La Corriveau repeated by rote as she had learned from her mother, the illomened words, hardly knowing their purport beyond that they were something very potent, and very wicked, which had been handed down through generations of poisoners and witches from the times of heathen Rome—

"Hecaten Voco!
Voco Tisiphonem!
Spargens Avernales aquas,
Te morti devoveo—, Te diris ago!"

The terrible drops of the *Aqua Tofana* glittered like dew on the glowing flowers, taking away in a moment all their fragrance, while leaving all their beauty unimpaired. The poison sank into the very heart of the roses whence it breathed death from every petal and every leaf, Fair to see as she who had sent them, but fatal to the approach of lip or nostril, fit emblem of her unpitying hate and remorseless jealousy!

La Corriveau wrapped the bouquet in a medicated paper of silver tissue, which prevented the escape of the volatile death and placing the roses carefully in the basket, prepared for her departure to Beaumanoir.

CHAPTER 44

"QUOTH THE RAVEN: 'NEVERMORE!'"

IT was the Eve of St Michael. A quiet autumnal night brooded over the forest of Beaumanoir. The moon in her wane had risen late and struggled feebly among the broken clouds that were gathering slowly in the East indicative of a storm. She shed a dim light through the glades and thickets, just enough to discover a path where the dark figure of a woman made her way swiftly and cautiously towards the Chateau of the Intendant.

She was dressed in the ordinary costume of a peasant woman, and carried a small basket on her arm, which, had she opened it, would have been found to contain, a candle and a bouquet of fresh roses, carefully covered with a paper of silver tissue, nothing more. An honest peasant woman would have had a rosary in her basket, but this was no honest peasant woman and she had none.

The forest was very still. It lay steeped in quietness. The rustling of the dry leaves under the feet of the woman, was all she heard, except when the low sighing of the wind, the sharp bark of a fox, or the shriek of an owl broke the silence, for a moment, and all was again still.

The woman looked watchfully round as she glided onwards. The path was known to her, but not so familiarly as to prevent the necessity of stopping every few minutes to look about her and make sure she was right.

It was long since she had travelled that way, and she was looking for a land mark, a grey stone that stood somewhere not far from where she was, and near which she knew that there was a footpath, that led not directly to the Chateau but to the old deserted watchtower, of Beaumanoir.

That stone marked a spot not to be forgotten by her, for it was the memorial of a deed of wickedness now only remembered by herself and by God. La Corriveau cared nothing for the recollection. It was not terrible to her, and God made no sign. But in his great book of account, of which the life of every man and woman forms a page, it was written down and remembered.

On the secret tablets of our memory which is the book of our life every thought, word and deed, good or evil is written down, indelibly and for ever, and the invisible pen goes on writing day after day, hour after hour, minute after minute, every thought even the idlest, every fancy the most evanescent, nothing is left out of our book of life which will be our record in judgment—! When that book is opened and no secrets are hid, what son or daughter of Adam is there, who will not need to say?—"God be merciful!"

La Corriveau came suddenly upon the grey stone. It startled her, for its rude contour standing up in the pale moonlight, put on the appearance of a woman. She thought she was discovered, and she heard a noise. But another glance reassured her. She recognized the stone, and the noise she had heard was only the scurrying of a hare among the dry leaves.

The Habitans held this spot to be haunted by the wailing spirit of a woman in a grey robe, who had been poisoned by a jealous lover. La Corriveau gave him sweetmeats of the manna of St Nicholas, which the woman ate from his hand, and fell dead at his feet in this trysting place, where they met for the last time. The man fled to the forest hunted by a remorseful conscience, and died a retributive death. He fell sick and was devoured by wolves. La Corriveau alone of mortals held the terrible secret.

La Corriveau gave a low laugh as she saw the pale outline of the woman, resolve itself into the grey stone. "The dead come not again!" muttered she, "and if they do she will soon have a companion to share her midnight walks round the Chateau—!" La Corriveau had no conscience. She knew not remorse and would probably have felt no great fear had that pale spirit really appeared at that moment to tax her with wicked complicity in her murder.

The clock of the Chateau struck twelve. Its reverberations sounded far into the night, as La Corriveau emerged stealthily out of the forest. Crouching on the shady side of the high garden hedges she reached the old watchtower, which stood like a dead sentinel at his post on the flank of the Chateau.

There was an open doorway, on each side of which lay a heap of fallen stones. This was the entrance into a square room, dark and yawning as a cavern. It was traversed by one streak of moonshine which struggled through a grated window set in the thick wall.

La Corriveau stood for a few moments looking intently into the gloomy ruin, then casting a sharp glance behind her, she entered. Tired with her long walk through the forest, she flung herself upon a stone seat to rest, and to collect her thoughts for the execution of her terrible mission.

The dogs of the Chateau barked vehemently as if the very air bore some ominous taint; but La Corriveau knew she was safe. They were shut up in the court yard and could not trace her to the tower. A harsh voice or two and the sound of whips presently silenced the barking dogs, and all was still again.

She had got into the tower unseen and unheard. "They say there is an eye that sees everything," muttered she, "and an ear that hears our very thoughts. If God sees and hears, he does nothing to prevent me from accomplishing my end! and He will not interfere tonight! No! not for all the prayers she may utter, which will not be many more!—! God!—if there be one—lets La Corriveau live and will let the lady of Beaumanoir die—!—"

There was a winding stair of stone narrow and tortuous in one corner of the tower. It led upwards to the roof and downwards to a deep vault which was arched and groined. Its heavy rough columns supported the tower above and divided the vaults beneath. These vaults had formerly served as magazines for provisions and stores for the use of the occupants of the Chateau upon occasions when they had to retire for safety from a sudden irruption of Iroquois.

La Corriveau after a short rest got up with a quick

impatient movement. She went over to an arched doorway upon which her eyes had been fixed for several minutes. "The way is down there!" she muttered, "now for a light!—"

She found the entrance to the stair open. She passed in closing the door behind her so that the glimmer might not be seen by any chance stroller, and struck a light. The reputation which the tower had of being haunted made the servants very shy of entering it even in the daytime, and the man was considered bold indeed who came near it after dark.

With her candle in her hand La Corriveau descended slowly into the gloomy vault. It was a large cavern of stone a very habitation of darkness which seemed to swallow up the feeble light she carried. It was divided into three portions separated by rough columns.

A spring of water trickled in and trickled out of a great stone trough, ever full and over flowing with a soft tinkling sound, like a clepsydra measuring the moments of eternity. The cool fresh living water diffused throughout the vaults an even mild temperature the year round. The gardeners of the Château took advantage of this and used the vault as a favorite store room for their crops of fruit and vegetables for winter use in the Chateau.

La Corriveau went resolutely forward as one who knew what she sought and where to find it, and presently stood in front of a recess containing a wooden panel similar to that in the Chateau, and movable in the same manner. She considered it for some moments muttering to herself as she held aloft the candle to inspect it closely and find the spring by which it was moved.

La Corriveau had been carefully instructed by Mere Malheur in every point regarding the mechanism of this door. She had no difficulty in finding the secret of its working. A slight touch sufficed when the right place was known. She pressed it hard with her hand. The panel swung open and behind it gaped a dark narrow passage leading to the secret chamber of Caroline.

She entered without hesitation, knowing whither it led. It was damp and stifling. Her candle burned dimmer and dimmer in the impure air of the long shut up passage. There were however, no other obstacles in her way. The passage was unincumbered. But the low arch scarcely over her own height, seemed to press down upon her as she passed along as if to prevent her progress. The fearless wicked heart bore her up, nothing worse than herself could meet her, and she felt neither fear at what lay before her, nor remorse at what was behind.

The distance to be traversed was not far, although it seemed to her impatience to be interminable. Mere Malheur with her light heels could once run through it in a minute, to a tryst in the old tower. La Corriveau was thrice that time in groping her way along it before she came to a heavy iron ribbed door set in a deep arch, which marked the end of the passage.

That black, forbidding door was the dividing of light from darkness, of good from evil, of innocence from guilt. On one side of it in a chamber of light sat a fair girl confiding, generous and deceived, only through her excess of every virtue. On the other, wickedness fell and artful, was approaching with stealthy footsteps through an unseen way, and stood with hand upraised to knock, but incapable of entering in, unless that unsuspecting girl removed the bar.

O Caroline de St Castin! martyr to womanly love, and the victim of womanly hate! amid all the tossing thoughts that agitate your innocent breast, is there not one to suggest a fear, or a suspicion of fear of the strange woman who comes in such mysterious fashion to the door of your last place of refuge, except the grave?

Alas no! Caroline sat waiting, counting the minutes one by one as the finger passed over the dial of the clock, impatient yet trembling she knew not why, to hear the promised knock upon the fatal door.

She had no suspicion of evil. Her guardian angel had turned aside to weep. Providence itself for the nonce seemed—but only seemed—to have withdrawn its care. It may be the sooner to bear this lost lamb into its fold of rest and peace. But not the less did it seem for ends inscrutable to have delivered her over to the craft and cruelty of her bitter enemy.

As the hour of midnight approached, one sound after another died away in the Chateau. Caroline who had sat counting the hours and watching the spectral moon as it flickered among the hazy clouds, withdrew from the window, with a trembling step, like one going to her doom.

She descended to the secret chamber where she had appointed to meet her strange visitor and hear from strange lips the story that would be told her.

She attired herself with care, as a woman will in every extremity of life. Her dark raven hair was simply arranged and fell in thick masses over her neck and shoulders. She put on a robe of soft snow white texture and by an impulse she yielded to, but could not explain, bound her waist with a black sash like a strain of mourning in a song of innocence. She wore no ornaments save a ring the love gift of Bigot which she never parted with but wore with a morbid anticipation that its promises would one day prove true. She clung to it as a talisman that would yet conjure away her sorrows and it did! but alas! in a way little anticipated by the constant girl!—A blast from Hell was at hand to sweep away her young life and with it all her earthly troubles.

She took up a guitar, mechanically as it were, and as her fingers wandered over the strings a bar or two of a strain sad as the sigh of a broken heart, suggested an old ditty she had loved formerly when her heart was full of sunshine and happiness when her fancy used to indulge the luxury of melancholic musings, as every happy, sensitive and imaginative girl will do, as a counterpoise to her highwrought feelings.

In a low voice sweet and plaintive as the breathings of an Æolian harp, Caroline sang:

"A linnet sat upon the thorn
At Evening chime,
Its sweet refrain fell like the rain
Of summer time.
Of summer time when roses bloomed,
And bright above,

A rainbow spanned my fairy land
Of hope and love!
Of hope and love! O linnet cease
Thy mocking theme!
I neer picked up love's golden cup
In all my dream!
In all my dream, I missed the prize
Should have been mine!
And dreams wont die! though fain would I
And make no sign!"

The lamps burned brightly shedding a cheerful light upon the landscapes and figures woven into the tapestry, behind which, was concealed the black door that was to admit La Corriveau.

It was oppressively still. Caroline listened with mouth and ears for some sound of approaching footsteps until her heart beat like the swift stroke of a hammer as it sent the blood throbbing through her temples with a rush that almost overpowered her.

She was alone, and lonely beyond expression. Down in these thick foundations no sound penetrated to break the terrible monotony of the silence around her except the dull solemn voice of the bell striking the hour of midnight.

Caroline had passed a sleepless night after the visit of Mere Malheur, sometimes tossing on her solitary couch, sometimes starting up in terror. She rose and threw herself despairingly on her knees, calling on Christ to pardon her, and on the Mother of Mercies to plead for her, sinner that she was, whose hour of shame and punishment had come!—

The mysterious letter brought by Mere Malheur, announcing that her place of concealment was to be searched by the Governor, excited her livliest apprehension. But that faded into nothingness in comparison with the absolute terror that seized her at the thoughts of the speedy arrival of her father in the Colony.

Caroline overwhelmed with a sense of shame and contrition pictured to herself in darkest colours, the anger of her father at the dishonour she had brought upon his unsullied name.

She sat down, she rose up, she walked her solitary room, and kneeled passionately on the floor covering her face with her hands, crying to the Madonna for pity and protection.

Poor self accuser! The hardest and most merciless wretch who ever threw stones at a woman was pitiful in comparison with Caroline's inexorable condemnation of herself.

Yet her fear was not on her own account. She could have kissed her father's hand and submitted humbly to death itself if he chose to inflict it, but she trembled most at the thought of a meeting between the fiery Baron and the haughty Intendant. One or other or both of them she felt instinctively must die, should the Baron discover that Bigot had been the cause of the ruin of his idolized child.

She trembled for both, and prayed God that she might die in their stead, and the secret of her shame never be known to her fond father.

A dull sound like footsteps shuffling in the dark passage, behind the Arras, struck her ear. She knew her strange visitant was come. She started up clasping her hands hard together as she listened, wondering who and what like she might be?— She suspected no harm, for who could desire to harm her who had never injured a living being? Yet there she stood on the one side of that black door of doom, while the calamity of her life stood on the other side like a tigress ready to spring through. Caroline thought nought of this, but rather listened with a sense of relief to the stealthy footfalls that came slowly along the hidden passage. Perhaps it is well that for the most part the catastrophies and sorrows of life overtake us without long warning. Life would be intolerable had we to forsee as well as to endure the pains of it!

A low knock twice repeated on the thick door behind the arras, drew her at once to her feet. She trembled violently as she lifted up the tapestry—something rushed through her mind telling her not to do it! Happy had it been for her never to have opened that fatal door!—

She hesitated for a moment, but the thought of her father

and the impending search of the Chateau, flashed suddenly upon her mind. The visitant whoever she might be, professed to be a friend and could she thought have no motive to harm her.

Caroline with a sudden impulse pushed aside the fastening of the door, and uttering the words *Dieu! protege moi*! stood face to face with La Corriveau.

The bright lamp shone full on the tall figure of the strange visitor and Caroline whose fears had anticipated some uncouth sight of terror, was surprised to see only a woman dressed in the simple garb of a peasant with a little basket on her arm enter quietly through the secret door.

The eyes of La Corriveau glared for a moment with fiendish curiosity upon the young girl who stood before her like one of God's angels. She measured her from head to foot, noted every fold of her white robe, every flexure of her graceful form, and drank in the whole beauty and innocence of her aspect with a feeling of innate spite, at ought so fair and good. On her thin cruel lips there played a smile as the secret thought hovered over them in an unspoken whisper, "She will make a pretty corpse! Brinvilliers and La Voisin never mingled drink for a fairer victim than I will crown with roses tonight!—"

Caroline retreated a few steps frightened and trembling as she encountered the glittering eyes and sinister smile of La Corriveau. The woman observed it and instantly changed her mien, to one more natural and sympathetic, for she comprehended fully the need of disarming suspicion and of winning the confidence of her victim to enable her more surely to destroy her.

Caroline reassured by a second look at her visitor, thought she had been mistaken in her first impression. The peasant's dress, the harmless basket, the quiet manner assumed by La Corriveau as she stood in a respectful attitude, as if waiting to be spoken to, banished all fear from the mind of Caroline and left her only curious to know the issue of this mysterious visit.

What La Corriveau had planned was not a deed of violence

although she had brought with her an Italian stiletto of sharpest steel, the same which Beatrice Spara had left sticking in the heart of Beppa Farinata whom she found in the chamber of Antonio Exili. But it was only at the last extremity La Corriveau meant to resort to its use. She had brought it more to protect her own life if in danger, than to take that of her victim.

She had resolved on a quieter and surer plan to kill the innocent unsuspecting girl. She would visit her as a friend, a harmless peasant woman, moved only for her safety. She would catch her attention in a network of lies, she would win her confidence by affected sympathy, cheer her with bright hopes and leave her dead with the bouquet of roses like a bridal gift in her hand! No one should know whence came the unseen stroke. No one should suspect it, and the Intendant who would not dare in any event to promulgate a syllable of her death, nay, he should himself believe that Caroline de St Castin had died by the visitation of God.

It was an artful scheme wickedly conceived and mercilessly carried out, with a burst of more than its intended atrocity. La Corriveau erred in one point. She did not know the intensity of the fires that raged in her own evil bosom.

Providence for some inscrutable end seemed for the moment to have withdrawn its care from the secret chamber of Beaumanoir, and left this hapless girl to die by blackest treachery unseen and unknown, but not forgotten by those who loved her and who would have given their lives for her safety.

CHAPTER 45

"A DEED WITHOUT A NAME"

CAROLINE profoundly agitated rested her hands on the back of a chair for support, and regarded La Corriveau for some moments without speaking. She tried to frame a question of some introductory kind, but could not. But the pent up feelings came out at last in a gush straight from the heart.

"Did you write this?" said she falteringly to La Corriveau and holding out the letter so mysteriously placed in her hand by Mere Malheur. "O! tell me is it true?—"

La Corriveau did not reply except by a sign of assent and standing upright, waited for further question.

Caroline looked at her again wonderingly. That a simple peasant woman could have indited such a letter, or could have known ought respecting her father, seemed incredible.

"In heaven's name tell me who and what you are!" exclaimed she "I never saw you before!"

"You have seen me before," replied La Corriveau quietly.

Caroline looked at her amazedly, but did not recognize her. La Corriveau continued "Your father is the Baron de St Castin, and you lady, would rather die than endure that he should find you in the Chateau of Beaumanoir, ask me not how I know these things, you will not deny their truth, as for myself I pretend not to be other than I seem."

"Your dress is that of a peasant woman, but your language is not the language of one. You are a lady in disguise visiting me in this strange fashion." said Caroline puzzled more than ever. Her thoughts at this instant reverted to the Intendant. "Why do you come here in this secret manner?" asked she.

"I do not appear other than I am," replied La Corriveau,

542

evasively "and I am come in this secret manner because I could get access to you in no other way."

"You said that I had seen you before. I have no knowledge or recollection of it," remarked Caroline looking fixedly at her.

"Yes! you saw me once in the wood of St Valier. Do you remember the peasant woman who was gathering mandrakes when you passed with your Indian guides, and who gave you milk to refresh you on the way?—"

This seemed like a revelation to Caroline. She remembered the incident and the woman. La Corriveau had carefully put on the same dress she wore that day.

"I do recollect!" replied Caroline as a feeling of confidence welled up like a living spring within her. She offered La Corriveau her hand. "I thank you gratefully!" said she. "You were indeed kind to me that day in the forest, and I am sure you must mean kindly by me now."

La Corriveau took the offered hand but did not press it. She could not for the life of her, for she had not heart to return the pressure of a human hand. She saw her advantage however, and kept it through the rest of the brief interview.

"I mean you kindly Lady!" replied she softening her harsh voice as much as she could, to a tone of sympathy, "and I come to help you out of your trouble."

For a moment that cruel smile played on her thin lips again, but she instantly repressed it. "I am only a peasant woman," repeated she again, "but I bring you a little gift in my basket to show my good will." She put her hand in her basket but did not withdraw it at the moment, as Caroline thinking little of gifts but only of her father, exclaimed—

"I am sure you mean well! But you have more important things to tell me of than a gift. Your letter spoke of my father! What in God's name have you to tell me of my father?—"

La Corriveau withdrew her hand from the basket and replied, "He is on his way to New France in search of you! He knows you are here, lady!—"

"In Beaumanoir? O it cannot be! No one knows I am here!—" exclaimed Caroline clasping her hands in an impulse of alarm.

"Yes, more than you suppose Lady, else how did I know? Your father comes with the King's letters to take you hence and return with you to Acadia or to France." La Corriveau placed her hand in her basket, but withdrew it again. It was not yet time.

"God help me then!" exclaimed Caroline shrinking with terror. "But the Intendant! what said you of the Intendant?—"

"He is ordered *de par le Roy* to give you up to your father, and he will do so if you be not taken away sooner by the Governor." Caroline was nigh fainting at these words.

"Sooner! how sooner?—" asked she faintly.

"The Governor has received orders from the King to search Beaumanoir from roof to foundation stone, and he may come tomorrow Lady and find you here!"

The words of La Corriveau struck like sharp arrows into the soul of the hapless girl.

"God help me then!" exclaimed she, clasping her hands in agony. "O! that I were dead and buried where only my Judge could find me at the last day! for I have no hope, no claim upon man's mercy!—The world will stone me dead or living! and alas! I deserve my fate! It is not hard to die! but it is hard to bear the shame which will not die with me!—"

She cast her eyes upwards despairingly, as she uttered this and did not see the bitter smile return to the lips of La Corriveau, who stood upright cold and immovable before her, with fingers twitching nervously, like the claws of a Fury, in her little basket, while she whispered to herself, "Is it time? is it time?" but she took not out the bouquet yet.

Caroline came still nearer with a sudden change of thought and clutching the dress of La Corriveau, cried out: "O woman! is all this true? how can you know all this to be true of me and you a stranger?—"

"I know it of a certainty, and I am come to help you. I may not tell you by whom I know it. Perhaps the Intendant himself has sent me!" replied La Corriveau with a sudden prompting of the spirit of evil, who stood beside her. "The Intendant will hide you from this search if there be a sure place of concealment in New France."—

The reply shot a ray of hope across the mind of the agonized girl. She bounded with a sense of deliverance. It seemed so natural that Bigot so deeply concerned in her concealment should have sent this peasant woman to take her away, that she could not reflect at the moment how unlikely it was! nor could she in her excitement read the lie upon the cold face of La Corriveau.

She seized the explanation with a grasp of despair, as a sailor seizes the one plank which the waves have washed within his reach when all else has sunk in the sea around him.

"Bigot sent you?" exclaimed Caroline raising her hands while her pale face was suddenly suffused with a flush of joy. "Bigot sent you to conduct me hence to a sure place of concealment! O! blessed messenger! I believe you now!" Her excited imagination outflew even the inventions of La Corriveau. "Bigot has heard of my peril and sent you here at midnight to take me away to your forest home until this search be over! Is it not so? Francois Bigot did not forget me in my danger, even while he was away!"

"Yes, Lady, the Intendant sent me to conduct you to St Valier to hide you there in a sure retreat until the search be over," replied La Corriveau calmly eying her from head to foot.

"It is like him! He is not unkind when left to himself! It is so like the Francois Bigot I once knew! But tell me woman what said he further? did you see him? did you hear him? tell me all, all he said to you—!"

"I saw him lady and heard him," replied La Corriveau taking the bouquet in her fingers, "but he said little more than what I have told you. The Intendant is a stern man, and gives few words, save commands to those of my condition. But he bade me convey to you a token of his love. You would know its meaning he said. I have it safe lady in this basket—shall I give it to you?—"

"A token of his love! of Francois Bigot's love to me! are you a woman and could delay giving it so long? Why gave you it not at first? I could not have doubted you then! O give it me and be blessed as the welcomest messenger that ever came to Beaumanoir."

La Corriveau held her hand a moment more in the basket. Her dark features turned a shade paler although not a nerve quivered as she plucked out a parcel carefully wrapped in silver tissue. She slipped off the cover, and held at arms length towards the eager expectant girl the fatal bouquet of roses, beautiful to see as the fairest that ever filled the lap of Flora.—

Caroline clasped it with both hands, exclaiming in a voice of exultation, while every feature radiated with joy, "It is the gift of God! and the return of Francois' love! All will yet be well!—"

She pressed the glowing flowers to her lips with passionate kisses, breathed once or twice their mortal poison, and suddenly throwing back her head with her dark eyes fixed on vacancy, but holding the fatal bouquet fast in her hands, fell stone dead at the feet of La Corriveau!

A weird laugh terrible and unsuppressed, rang round the walls of the secret chamber, where the lamps burnt bright as ever, but the glowing pictures of the tapestry never changed a feature. Was it not strange that even those painted men should not have cried out, at the sight of so pitiless a murder?—

Caroline lay amid them all, the flush of joy still on her cheek, the smile not yet vanished from her lips. A pity for all the world could it have seen her, but in that lonely chamber, God's eye alone pitied her.

But now a more cruel thing supervened. The sight of Caroline's lifeless form instead of pity or remorse, roused all the innate furies that belonged to the execrable race of La Corriveau. The blood of generations of poisoners and assassins boiled and rioted in her veins. The Spirits of Beatrice Spara and of La Voisin inspired her with new fury. She was at this moment like a pantheress that has brought down her prey and stands over it to rend it in pieces.

Caroline lay dead, dead, beyond all doubt, never to be resuscitated, except in the resurrection of the Just! La Corriveau bent over her and felt her heart. It was still. No sign of breath flickered on lip or nostril.

The poisoner knew she was dead, but something still woke her suspicions as with a new thought, she drew back and looked again at the beauteous form before her. Suddenly, as if to make assurance doubly sure, she plucked the sharp Italian stiletto from her bosom and with a firm heavy hand plunged it twice into the body of the lifeless girl!—"If there be life there!" she said, "It too shall die! La Corriveau leaves no work of hers half done!—"

A faint trickle of blood in red threads, ran down the snow white vestment, and that was all! The heart had forever ceased to beat, and the blood to circulate. The golden bowl was broken and the silver cord of life loosed for ever and yet this last indignity would have recalled the soul of Caroline, could she have been conscious of it. But all was well with her now! not in the sense of the last joyous syllables she spoke in life, but in a higher holier sense, as when God interprets our words and not men. All was well with her now!—

She had got peace now, she slept in her beauty and innocence as one waiting in a happy dream to be carried off by a flight of Angelic messengers, to that only heaven of rest, which had lately been so often revealed to her in dreams and visions at the foot of the cross.

The passage of the dark water had been short, perhaps bitter, perhaps sweet. God only knows how sweet or how bitter that passage is. We only know that it is dark and looks bitter, but whether sweet or bitter the black river must be traversed alone, alone by every one of us!—A dark journey away from the bright sun and the abodes of living men! Happy he who can take with him the staff of faith to support him in the solitary ford where no help is more from man. Happy she who can carry love in death and meet death in love, for her love goes with her like a lamp shining on the way of the faithful spirit which returns to God.

The gaunt iron visaged woman knelt down upon her knees gazing with unshrinking eyes, upon the face of her victim, as if curiously marking the effect of a successful experiment, of the *Aqua Tofana*. It was the first time she had ever dared to administer that subtle poison in the fashion of La Borgia.

"The *Aqua Tofana* does its work like a charm!" muttered she. "That vial was compounded by Beatrice Spara and is worthy of her skill and more sure than her stiletto! I was frantic to use that weapon, for no purpose than to redden my hands with the work of a low Bravo!—"

A few drops of blood were on the hand of La Corriveau. She wiped them impatiently upon the garment of Caroline where it left the impress of her fingers on the snowy muslin. No pity for her pallid victim who lay with open eyes looking dumbly upon her, no remorse for her act touched the stony heart of La Corriveau.

The clock of the Chateau struck one. The solitary stroke of the bell reverberated like an accusing voice, through the house, but failed to awaken one sleeper to a discovery of the black tragedy that had just taken place under its roof.

That sound had often struck sadly upon the ear of Caroline as she prolonged her vigil of prayer through the still watches of the night. Her ear was dull enough now to all earthly sound—! But the toll of the bell reached the ear of La Corriveau, rousing her to the need of immediately effecting her escape, now that her task was done.

She sprang up and looked narrowly round the chamber. She marked with envious malignity the luxury and magnificence of its adornments. Upon a chair lay her own letter sent to Caroline by the hands of Mere Malheur. La Corriveau snatched it up. It was what she sought. She tore it in pieces and threw the fragments from her, but with a sudden thought as if not daring to leave even the fragments upon the floor, she gathered them up hastily and put them in her basket, with the bouquet of roses, which she wrested from the dead fingers of Caroline in order to carry it away and scatter the fatal flowers in the forest.

She pulled open the drawers of the escritoire, to search for money but finding none, was too wary to carry off ought else. The temptation lay sore upon her to carry away the ring from the finger of Caroline. She drew it off the pale wasted finger but a cautious consideration restrained her. She put it on again, and would not take it.

"It will only lead to discovery!" muttered she, "I must take nothing but myself and what belongs to me away from Beaumanoir and the sooner the better!—"

La Corriveau with her basket again upon her arm, turned to give one last look of fiendish satisfaction at the corpse which lay like a dead angel slain in God's battle. The bright lamps were glaring full upon her still beautiful but sightless eyes, which wide open looked even in death reproachfully yet forgivingly upon their murderess.

Something startled La Corriveau in that look. She turned hastily away, and relighting her candle passed through the dark archway of the secret door, forgetting to close it after her, and retraced her steps along the stone passage until she came to the watch tower where she dashed out her light.

Creeping round the tower in the dim moonlight she listened long and anxiously at door and window to discover if all was still about the Chateau. Not a sound was heard, but the water of the little brook gurgling in its pebbly bed, which seemed to be all that was awake on this night of death.

La Corriveau emerged cautiously from the tower and crept like a guilty thing under the shadow of the hedge, and got away unperceived, by the same road she had come. She glided like a dark spectre through the forest of Beaumanoir and returned to the city to tell Angelique des Meloises that the arms of the Intendant were now empty and ready to clasp her as his bride, that her rival was dead and she had put herself under bonds forever to La Corriveau as the price of innocent blood.

La Corriveau reached the city in the grey of the morning. A thick fog lay like a winding sheet upon the face of Nature. The broad river, the lofty rocks, every object great and small were hidden from view.

To the intense satisfaction of La Corriveau, the fog concealed her return to the house of Mere Malheur, whence after a brief repose and with a command to the old crone to ask no questions yet, she sallied forth again to carry to Angelique the welcome news that her rival was dead.

No one observed La Corriveau as she passed in her peasant dress through the misty streets, which did not admit of an object being discerned ten paces off.

Angelique was up. She had not gone to bed that night and sat feverishly on the watch expecting the arrival of La Corriveau.

She had counted the minutes of the silent hours of the night, as they passed by as in a terrible panorama, she pictured to her imagination the successive scenes of the tragedy which was being accomplished at Beaumanoir.

The hour of midnight culminated over her head, and looking out of her window at the black distant hills in the recesses of which she knew lay the Chateau, her agitation grew intense. She knew at that hour La Corriveau must be in the presence of her victim. Would she kill her? Was she about it now? The thought fastened on Angelique like a wild beast, and would not let go. She thought of the Intendant and was filled with hope. She thought of the crime of murder and shrunk now that it was being done.

Angelique was not wholly bad, far from it. Her reckless ambition, hot passions and cold heart had led her blindly where she now found herself, the principal in a deed of murder which by no subterfuge could she now conceal from herself, she was more guilty of, than the wicked instrument she had made use of.

All night long had she tossed and disquieted herself in an agony of conflicting emotions. The thought of the murder was not absent for one moment from her mind. By turns she justified it, repented of it, hoped for it, condemned it and wished for it again! Believing it done, she wished it undone. Fearing it undone she was ready to curse La Corriveau and her stars that it was not done! Her mind was like water ready to rush through any floodgate that chance opened to her. But no gate opened except the one she had deliberately put into the keeping of La Corriveau!—

It was in this mood she waited and watched for the return of her bloody messenger. She heard the cautious foot on the stone steps. She knew by a sure instinct whose it was, and rushed down to admit her.

They met at the door, and without a word spoken, one

eager glance of Angelique at the dark face of La Corriveau drank in the whole fatal story. Caroline de St Castin was dead! Her rival in the love of the Intendant was beyond all power of rivalry now! The lofty doors of ambitious hope stood open. What to admit, the Queen of beauty and of society? No! but a murderess, who would be ever haunted with the fear of justice! It seemed at this moment as if the lights had all gone out in the Palaces and royal Halls, where her imagination had so long run riot, and she saw only dark shadows and heard inarticulate sounds of strange voices babbling in her ear. It was the unspoken words of her own troubled thoughts and the terrors newly awakened in her soul!

Angelique seized the hand of La Corriveau not without a shudder. She drew her hastily up to her chamber and thrust her into a chair. Placing both hands upon the shoulders of La Corriveau she looked wildly in her face, exclaiming in a half exultant, half piteous tone: "Is it done? Is it really done? I read it in your eyes! I know you have done the deed! O! La Corriveau!"

The grim countenance of the woman relaxed into a half smile of scorn and surprise at the unexpected weakness which she instantly noted in Angelique's manner.

"Yes! It is done!" replied she, coldly, "and it is well done! But, by the manna of St Nicholas!" exclaimed she, starting from the chair and drawing her gaunt figure up to its full height, while her black eyes shot daggers, "you look, Mademoiselle, as if you repented its being done! Do you?"

"Yes! No! No, not now!" replied Angelique, touched as with a hot iron. "I will not repent now it is done! that were folly, needless, dangerous, now it is done! But is she dead? Did you wait to see if she were really dead? People look dead sometimes and are not! Tell me truly, and conceal nothing!"

"La Corriveau does not her work by halves, Mademoiselle, neither do you; only you talk of repentance after it is done, I do not! that is all the difference! Be satisfied; The lady of Beaumanoir is dead! I made doubly sure of that, and deserve a double reward from you!"

"Reward! You shall have all you crave! But what a secret

between you and me!" Angelique looked at La Corriveau as if this thought now struck her for the first time. She was in this woman's power. She shivered from head to foot. "Your reward for this days work is here!" faltered she, placing her hand over a small box. She did not touch it. It seemed as if it would burn her. It was heavy with pieces of gold. "They are uncounted," continued she. "Take it. It is all yours—!—"

La Corriveau snatched the box off the table, and held it to her bosom. Angelique continued in a monotonous tone as one conning a lesson by rote, "Use it prudently. Do not seem to the world to be suddenly rich! It might be inquired into. I have thought of everything during the past night, and I remember I had to tell you that, when I gave you the gold!—Use it prudently! Something else too, I was to tell you, but I think not of it at this moment."

"Thanks and no thanks! Mademoiselle!" replied La Corriveau in a hard tone. "Thanks for the reward so fully earned. No thanks for your faint heart that robs me of my well earned meed of applause for a work done so artistically, and perfectly, that La Brinvilliers or La Borgia herself might envy me, a humble paysanne of St Valier!—"

La Corriveau looked proudly up as she said this, as if she felt herself to be anything but a humble paysanne. She nourished a secret pride in her heart over the perfect success of her devilish skill in poisoning.

"I give you whatever praise you desire," replied Angelique mechanically. "But you have not told me how it was done. Sit down again!" continued she with a touch of her imperative manner, "and tell me all! and every incident of what you have done."

"You will not like to hear it! Better be content with the knowledge that your rival—She was a dangerous and a beautiful one." Angelique looked up at this. "Better be content to know that she is dead without asking any more."

"No! you shall tell me everything," replied Angelique impatiently. "I cannot rest unless I know all."

"Nor after you do know all will you rest!" replied La Corriveau slightingly, for she despised the evident trepidation of Angelique.

"No matter! you shall tell me! I am calm now!" Angelique made a great effort to appear calm, while she listened to the tale of tragedy in which she had played so deep a part.

La Corriveau observing that the gust of passion was blown over, sat down in the chair opposite Angelique, and placing one hand on the knee of her listener, as if to hold her fast began the terrible recital.

A flood of words pent up in her bosom, sought for utterance to a listening sympathetic ear. La Corriveau was a woman in that respect, and although often moody and silent, a great occasion made her pour out her soul in torrents of speech like fiery lava. She spoke powerfully and terribly.

She gave Angelique a graphic, minute and not untrue account of all she had done at Beaumanoir, dwelling with fierce unction on the marvellous and sudden effects of the *Aqua Tofana*, not sparing one detail of the beauty and innocent looks of her victim, and repeating with a mocking laugh the deceit she had practised upon her with regard to the bouquet, as a gift from the Intendant.

Angelique listened to the terrible tale, drinking it in with eyes, mouth and ears. Her countenance changed to a mask of ugliness wonderful in one by nature so fair to see. Cloud followed cloud over her face and eyes as the dread recital went on and her imagination accompanied it by vivid pictures of every phase of the diabolical crime.

When La Corriveau described the presentation of the bouquet as a gift of Bigot, and the deadly sudden effect which followed its joyous acceptance, the thoughts of Caroline in her white robe, stricken as by a thunderbolt, shook Angelique with terrible emotion. But when La Corriveau coldly and with a bitter spite at her softness, recounted with a sudden gesticulation and eyes piercing her through and through the strokes of the poniard upon the lifeless body of her victim, Angelique sprang up, clasped her hands together and with a cry of woe fell senseless upon the floor.

"She is useless now!" said La Corriveau rising and spurning Angelique with her foot. "I deemed she had courage to equal her wickedness. She is but a woman after all! doomed to be the slave of some man through life while aspiring to command all men. It is not of such flesh that La Corriveau is made!—"

La Corriveau stood a few moments reflecting what was best to be done.

All things considered, she decided to leave Angelique to come to of herself, while she made the best of her way back to the house of Mere Malheur with the intention which she carried out, of returning to St Valier with her precious reward that very day.

CHAPTER 46

"LET'S TALK OF GRAVES AND WORMS AND EPITAPHS"

ABOUT the hour that La Corriveau emerged from the gloomy woods of Beauport on her return to the City the night of the murder of Caroline, two horsemen were battering at full speed on the highway that led to Charlebourg. Their dark figures were irrecognizable in the dim moonlight. They rode fast and silent like men having important business before them which demanded haste. Business which both fully understood and cared not now to talk about.—

And so it was! Bigot and Cadet after the exchange of a few words about the hour of midnight, suddenly left the wine, the dice, and the gay company at the palace, and mounting their horses rode, unattended by groom or valet in the direction of Beaumanoir.

Bigot under the mask of gaiety and indifference had felt no little alarm at the tenor of the Royal despatch, and of the letter of the Marquise de Pompadour, concerning Caroline de St Castin.

The proximate arrival of Caroline's father in the Colony, was a circumstance ominous of trouble. The Baron was no trifler and would as soon choke a king as a beggar to revenge an insult to his personal honour, or the honour of his house.

Bigot cared little for that however. The Intendant was no coward and could brave and brazen a thing out with any man alive. But there was one thing which he knew he could not brazen out or fight out, or do anything but miserably fail in, should it come to the question.

He had boldly and wilfully lied at the Governor's council table, sitting as the King's councillor among gentlemen of honour, when he declared that he knew not the hiding place

555

of Caroline de St Castin. It would cover him with eternal
disgrace as a gentleman to be detected in such a flagrant
falsehood. It would ruin him as a Courtier in the favour of the
great Marquise, should she discover that in spite of his denials
of the fact, he had harboured and concealed the missing lady
in his own Chateau!—

Bigot was sorely perplexed over this turn of affairs and
uttered a thousand curses upon all concerned in it, excepting
upon Caroline herself, for although vexed at her coming to
him at all, he could not find it in his heart to curse her.
But cursing or blessing availed nothing, now that time was
pressing, and he must act.

That Caroline would be sought after in every nook and
corner of the land, he knew full well, from the character of La
Corne St Luc, and of her father. His own Chateau would not
be spared in the general search, and he doubted if the secret
chamber would remain a secret from the keen eyes of these
men. He surmised that others knew of its existence besides
himself—old servitors and women who had passed in and out
of it in times gone by. Dame Tremblay who did know of it was
not to be trusted in a great temptation. She was in heart the
charming Josephine still, and could be bribed or seduced by
any one who bid high enough for her confidence.

Bigot had no trust whatever in human nature. He felt he
had no guarantee against a discovery farther than interest
or fear barred the door against inquiry. He could not rely
for a moment upon the inviolability of his own house. La
Corne St Luc would demand to search it, and he bound by his
declarations of noncomplicity in the abduction of Caroline,
could offer no reason for refusal without rousing instant
suspicion, and La Corne was too sagacious not to fasten upon
the minutest trace of Caroline, and follow it up to a complete
discovery.

She could not therefore remain longer in the Chateau—
this was absolute—and he must at whatever cost and whatever
risk remove her to a fresh place of concealment, until
the storm blew over, or some other means of escape from
the present difficulty offered themselves, in the chapter of

accidents, which Bigot had more faith in, than in any chapter of the old or new Testament, which only taught him to do right and trust God.

In accordance with this design, Bigot under pretence of business had gone off the very next day after the meeting of the Governor's Council in the direction of the Three Rivers, to arrange with a band of Montagnais whom he could rely upon, for the reception of Caroline in the disguise of an Indian girl, with instructions to remove their wigwams immediately and take her off with them to the wild romantic valley of the St Maurice.

The old Indian Chief eager to oblige the Intendant, had assented willingly to his proposal promising the gentlest treatment of the Lady, and a silent tongue concerning her.

Bigot was impressive in his commands upon these points, and the chief pledged his faith upon them, delighted beyond measure by the promise of an ample supply of powder, blankets and provisions for his tribe, while the Intendant added an abundance of all such delicacies as could be forwarded for the use and comfort of the Lady.

To carry out this scheme, without observation, Bigot needed the help of a trusty friend, one whom he could thoroughly rely upon to convey Caroline secretly away from Beaumanoir, and place her in the keeping of the Montagnais, as well as to see to the further execution of his wishes for her concealment and good treatment.

Bigot had many friends, men living on his bounty, who ought only to have been too happy to obey his slightest wishes, friends bound to him by disgraceful secrets, common interests, and mutual risks. But he could trust none of them with the secret of Caroline de St Castin.

He felt a new and unwonted delicacy in regard to her. Her name was dear to him, her fame even was becoming dearer. To his own surprise it troubled him now, as it had never troubled him before. He would not have her name defiled in the mouths of such men, as drank his wine daily and nightly and disputed the existence of any virtue in woman.

Bigot ground his teeth, as he muttered to himself: "They

might make a mock of whatever other woman they pleased—
he himself could outdo them all in coarse ribaldry of the
sex—but they should not make a mock and flash obscene
jests at the mention of Caroline de St Castin! They should
never learn her name. He could not trust one of them with
the secret of her removal, and yet some one of them must
perforce be entrusted with it!"—

He conned over the names of his associates one by
one, and one by one condemned them all, as unworthy of
confidence in a matter, where treachery might possibly be
made more profitable than fidelity. Bigot was false himself to
the heart's core, and believed in no man's truth!

He was an acute judge of men. He read their motives, their
bad ones especially, with the accuracy of a Mephistophiles and
with the same cold contempt for every trace of virtue.

"Varin was a cunning knave," he said, "ambitious of the
support of the church, communing with his aunt the superior
of the Ursulines, whom he deceived, and who was not without
hope of himself one day rising to be Intendant. He would
place no such secret in the keeping of Varin!"

"Penisault was a sordid dog. He would cheat the
Montagnais of his gifts, and so discontent them with their
charge. He had neither courage nor spirit for an adventure.
He was in his right place superintending the counters of the
Friponne! He despised Penisault while glad to use him in the
basest offices of the Grand Compagny."

"Le Mercier was a pickthank angling after the favour
of La Pompadour, a pretentious knave as hollow as one of
his own morters. He suspected him of being a spy of hers
upon himself! Le Mercier would be only too glad to send La
Pompadour red hot information of such an important secret
as that of Caroline!—and She would reward it as good service
to the King and to herself."

"Deschenaux was incapable of keeping a secret of any kind
when he got drunk or in a passion, which was every day. His
rapacity reached to the very altar. He would rob a church and
was one who would rather take by force than favour. He would
strike a Montagnais who would ask for a blanket more than

he cheated him with. He would not trust Deschenaux."

"De Pean the quiet fox! was wanted to look after that desperate gallant Le Gardeur de Repentigny, who was still in the palace, and must be kept there by all the seductions of wine, dice, and women—until we have done with him! De Pean was the meanest spirit of them all. He would kiss my foot in the morning and sell me at night for a handful of silver!" said Bigot. "Villians every one of them! who would not scruple to advance their own interests with La Pompadour by his betrayal in telling her such a secret as that of Caroline's."

"De Repentigny had honour, and truth in him and could be entirely trusted if he promised to serve a friend. But Bigot dared not name to him a matter of this kind. He would spurn it. Drunk as he was, he was still in all his instincts a gentleman, and a soldier. He could only be used by Bigot through an abuse of his noblest qualities. He dared not broach such a scheme to Le Gardeur de Repentigny!"

Among his associates there was but one who in spite of his brutal manners and coarse speech, perhaps because of these, Bigot would trust as a friend, to help him in a serious emergency like the present.

Cadet the Commissary General of New France, was faithful to Bigot as a fierce bull dog to his master. Cadet was no hypocrite, nay, he may have appeared to be worse than in reality he was. He was bold and outspoken, rapacious of other men's goods and as prodigal of his own—clever withal, fearless and fit for any bold enterprise. He ever allowed himself to be guided by the superior intellect of Bigot, whom he regarded as the prince of good fellows, and swore by him, profanely enough, on all occasions, as the shrewdest head and the quickest hand to turn over money in New France.

Bigot could trust Cadet. He had only to whisper a few words in his ear to see him jump up from the table where he was playing cards, dash his stakes with a sweep of his hand into the lap of his antagonist—a gift or a forfeit he cared not which, for not finishing the game! In three minutes Cadet was booted with his heavy riding whip in his hand ready to mount his horse and accompany Bigot "To Beaumanoir or to Hell!"

he said, "if he wanted to go there."

In the short space of time, while the grooms saddled their horses, Bigot drew Cadet aside and explained to him the situation of his affairs, informing him in a few words, who the lady was, who lived in such retirement in the Chateau, and of his denial of the fact before the council and Governor. He told him of the letters of the Baron de St Castin and of La Pompadour respecting Caroline and of the necessity of removing her at once far out of reach before the actual search for her was begun.

Cadet's large eyes flashed in genuine sympathy with Bigot and he laid his heavy hand upon his shoulder and uttered a frank exclamation of admiration for his ruse to cheat La Pompadour and La Galissoniere both.

"By St Picot!" said he, "I would rather go without dinner for a month, than you should not have asked me, Bigot, to help you out of this scrape! What if you did lie to that fly catching beggar at the Castle of St Louis, who has not conscience to take a dishonest stiver, from a cheating Albany Dutchman—! and what if you did lie? Better lie to him than tell the truth to La Pompadour about that girl—! Egad! Madame Fish would serve you as the Iroquois served my fat clerk at Chouagen! make roast meat of you if she knew it! Such a pother about a girl! Damn the women! always! I say Bigot! a man is never out of hot water when he has to do with them!"—

Cadet was a habitual scorner of women. He was always glad to shun them or get rid of them, but on the present occasion he saw clearly that Bigot's position was fatally compromised unless he got well out of this affair of Caroline de St Castin.

Striking Bigot's hand hard with his own, he promised, "wet or dry, through flood or fire, to ride with him to Beaumanoir, and take the girl, or lady! he begged the Intendant's pardon! and by such ways as he alone knew, he would in two days place her safely among the Montagnais and order them at once if he ordered them, pull up stakes and remove their wigwams to the *Tuque* of the St Maurice where Satan himself could not find her! And the girl might remain there for seven years without ever being heard tell of, by any white person in the

Colony!"

Bigot and Cadet rode rapidly forward until they came to the dark forest where the faint outline of road barely visible, would have perplexed Bigot to have kept it alone in the night. But Cadet was born in Charlebourg he knew every path, glade, and dingle in the forest of Beaumanoir and rode on without drawing bridle.

Bigot in his fiery eagerness had hitherto ridden foremost. Now Cadet led the way dashing under the boughs of the great trees that overhung the road. The tramp of their horses woke the echoes of the woods. But they were not long in reaching the park of Beaumanoir.

They saw before them the tall chimney stacks, and the high roofs and the white walls of the Chateau looking spectral enough in the wan moonlight, ghostly, silent and ominous. One light only was visible in the Porter's lodge. All else was dark, cold and sepulchral.

The old watchful porter at the gate was instantly on foot to see who came at that hour, and was surprised enough at sight of his master and the Sieur Cadet, without retinue or even a groom to accompany them.

They dismounted and tied their horses outside the gate. "Run to the Chateau Marcele, without making the least noise," said Bigot. "Call none of the servants, but rap gently at the door of Dame Tremblay. Bid her rise instantly, without waking anyone. Say the Intendant desires to see her. I expect guests from the City."—

"I have to lie even to servants!" said Bigot indignantly. "No one knows what inquiries may be made! No weed that grows is so prolific in multiplication as a lie! A weed will fill the world, and a lie will fill the universe with its progeny, unless it be checked or choked to death."

"Well!" said Cadet, "I do not care to lie often, Bigot! because truth hits your enemy harder than lies—! When it does not, I see no harm in a round shot of a lie, if it will hurt him more!—"

The porter returned with the information that Dame Tremblay had got up, and was ready to receive His Excellency.

Bidding old Marcele take care of the horses, they walked across the lawn to the Chateau, at the door of which stood Dame Tremblay hastily dressed, courtseying and trembling at this sudden summons to receive the Intendant and the Sieur Cadet.

"Good night Dame!" said Bigot in a low tone, "Conduct us instantly to the Grand Gallery!"

"O your Excellency!" replied the Dame, courtseying at every sentence, "I am your humble servant at all times, Day and night as it is my duty and my pleasure to serve my Master—!"

"Well then!" replied Bigot impatiently, "let us go in and make no noise."

The three, Dame Tremblay leading the way with a candle in each hand, passed up the broad stair and into the Gallery communicating with the apartments of Caroline. The Dame set her candles on the table and stood with her hands across her apron, in a submissive attitude waiting for the orders of her master.

"Dame!" said he, "I think you are, a faithful servant I have trusted you with much! Can I trust you with a greater matter still?—"

"O, Your Excellency! I would die to serve so noble and generous a Master! It is a Servants duty!—"—

"Few servants think so! nor do I! But you have been faithful to your charge respecting this poor lady within, have you not Dame?" Bigot looked as if his eyes searched her very vitals.

"O Lord! O Lord!" thought the Dame turning pale. "He has heard about the visit of that cursed Mere Malheur, and has come to hang me up for it in the Gallery!" She stammered out in reply, "O yes! I have been faithful to my charge about the lady, Your Excellency! I have not failed willfully or negligently in any point I assure you!—I have been at once careful and kind to her as you bade me to be, Your Excellency! Indeed I could not be otherwise to a live angel in the house like her!—"

"So I believe Dame!" said Bigot in a tone of approval, that quite lifted her heart. This spontaneous praise of Caroline touched him somewhat, "You have done well! Now, can you keep another secret Dame?—"

"A secret! and entrusted to me by Your Excellency!" replied she in a voice of wonder, at such a question. "The marble statue in the grotto is not closer than I am, your Excellency! I was always too fond of a secret ever to part with it! When I was the charming Josephine of Lake Beauport I never told even in confession, who they were who—"

"Tut! I will trust you Dame, better than I would have trusted the charming Josephine. If all tales be true! You were a gay girl Dame, and a handsome one, in those days I have heard!" added the Intendant with well planned flattery.

A smile and look of intelligence followed this sally, both from the Dame and from Bigot, while Cadet had much to do to keep in one of the hearty horse laughs he used to indulge in, and which would have roused the whole Chateau.

The flattery of the Intendant quite captivated the Dame. "I will go through fire and water to serve Your Excellency, if you want me," said she. "What shall I do to oblige your Excellency?"—

"Well, Dame you must know then, that the Sieur Cadet and I have come to remove that dear lady from the Chateau to another place, where it is needful for her to go for the present time, and if you are questioned about her, mind you are to say she never was here and you know nothing of her!—"

"I will not only say it," replied the Dame with promptness, "I will swear it, until I am black in the face if you command me your Excellency! Poor dear lady! may I not ask where she is going?—"

"No! she will be all right! I will tell you in due time. It is needful for people to change sometimes you know Dame—! You comprehend that! You had to manage matters discreetly when you were the charming Josephine! I daresay you had to change too sometimes? Every woman has an intrigue once at least, in her life time. But this lady is not clever like the charming Josephine. Therefore we have to be clever for her!"

The Dame laughed prudently yet knowingly at this, while Bigot continued: "Now you understand all? Go to her chamber, Dame! Present our compliments with my regrets for disturbing her, at this hour. Tell her that the Intendant and the Sieur Cadet desire to see her on important business."

Dame Tremblay with a broad smile all over her countenance at her master's jocular allusions to the charming Josephine, left at once to carry her message to the chamber of Caroline.

She passed out, while the two gentlemen waited in the Gallery, Bigot anxious but not doubtful of his influence to persuade the gentle girl to leave the Chateau, Cadet cooly resolved that she must go whether she liked it or no! He would banish every woman in New France to the *Tuque* of the St Maurice, had he the power in order to rid himself and Bigot of the eternal mischief and trouble of them!—

Neither Bigot nor Cadet spoke for some minutes after the departure of the Dame. They listened to her footsteps as the sound of them died away in distant rooms, where one door opened after another as she passed on to the secret chamber.

"She is now at the door of Caroline," thought Bigot as his imagination followed Dame Tremblay on her errand. "She is now speaking to her! I know Caroline will make no delay to admit us!" Cadet on his side was very quiet and careless of ought save to take the girl, and get her safely away before day break.

A few moments of heavy silence and expectation passed over them. The howl of a distant watch dog was heard and all was again still. The low monotonous ticking of the great clock at the head of the gallery made the silence still more oppressive. It seemed to be measuring off eternity, not time.

The hour, the circumstance, the brooding stillness, waited for a cry of murder to ring through the Chateau, waking its sleepers and bidding them come and see the fearful tragedy that lay in the secret chamber.

But no cry came. Fortunately for Bigot it did not! The discovery of Caroline de St Castin under such circumstances would have closed his career in New France, and ruined him forever in the favour of the Court.

Dame Tremblay returned to her master and Cadet with the information "that her lady was not in her bed chamber, but had gone down as was her wont, in the still hours of the night, to pray in her oratory in the secret chamber, where she wished never to be disturbed."

"Well Dame!" replied Bigot, "you may now retire to your own room! I will go down to the secret chamber myself. These vigils are killing her!—poor girl! If your lady should be missing in the morning, remember Dame! that you make no remark of it. She is going away tonight with me and the Sieur Cadet and will return soon again! so be discreet and keep your tongue well between your teeth, which I am glad to observe," remarked he with a smile, "are still sound and white as ivory!"

Bigot wished by such flattery to secure her silence, and he fully succeeded. The compliment to her teeth was more agreeable than would have been a purse of money. That caught the Dame by a hook there was no escape from.

Dame Tremblay courtseyed very low, and smiled very broadly to display her really good teeth of which she was extravagantly vain. She assured the Intendant of her perfect discretion and obedience to all his commands.

"Trust to me Your Excellency!" said she with a profound courtesy "I never deceived a gentleman yet, except the Sieur Tremblay, and he good man was none! When I was the charming Josephine and all the gay gallants of the City used to flatter and spoil me, I never deceived one of them! never! I knew that all is vanity in this world. But my eyes and teeth were considered very fine in those days your Excellency!—"

"And are yet Dame! Zounds! Lake Beauport has had nothing to equal them since you retired from business as a beauty. But mind my orders, Dame! keep quiet and you will please me! Good night Dame!—"

"Good night Your Excellency! good night your Honour!" replied she, flushed with gratified vanity. She left Bigot vowing to herself that he was the finest gentleman and the best judge of a woman in New France! The Sieur Cadet she could not like. He never looked pleasant on a woman, as a gentleman ought to do!—

The Dame left them to themselves and went off trippingly in high spirits to her own chamber, where she instantly ran to the mirror to look at her teeth!—and make faces in the glass, like a foolish girl in her teens.

Bigot out of a feeling of delicacy not usual with him, bid Cadet wait in the Anteroom while he went forward to the secret chamber of Caroline. "The sudden presence of a stranger might alarm her," he said.

He descended the stair and knocked softly at the door calling in a low tone, "Caroline! Caroline!" No answer came! He wondered at that, for her quick ear used always to catch the first sound of his footsteps while yet afar off.

He knocked louder, and called again her name. Alas! he might have called forever! that voice would never make her heart flutter again or her eyes brighten at his footstep that sounded sweeter than any music as she waited and watched for him, always ready to meet him at the door.

Bigot anticipated something wrong! and with a hasty hand pushed open the door of the secret chamber and went in! A blaze of light filled his eyes! A white form lay upon the floor. He saw it and he saw nothing else! She lay there with her unclosed eyes looking, as the dead only look at the living. One hand was pressed to her bosom, the other was stretched out, holding the broken stem and a few green leaves of the fatal bouquet which La Corriveau had not wholly plucked from her grasp.

Bigot stood for a moment stricken dumb and transfixed with horror, then sprang forward and knelt over her with a cry of agony. He thought she might have fallen in a swoon, he touched her pale forehead, her lips, her hands He felt her heart It did not beat. He lifted her head to his bosom. It fell like the flower of a lily broken on its stem, and he knew she was dead. He saw the red streaks of blood on her snowy robe, and he knew she was murdered!—

A long cry like the wail of a man in torture burst from him. It woke more than one sleeper in the distant chambers of the Chateau, making them start upon their pillows to listen for another cry, but none came. Bigot was a man of iron. He retained self possession enough to recollect the danger of rousing the house.

He smothered his cries in suffocating sobs. But they reached the ear of Cadet who foreboding some terrible catastrophe, rushed into the room where the secret door stood open. The light glared up the stair. He ran down and saw the Intendant on his knees holding in his arms the half raised form of a woman which he kissed and called by name, like a man distraught with grief and despair.

Cadet's coarse immovable nature stood him in good stead at this moment. He saw at a glance what had happened. The girl they had come to bear away, was dead! How? he knew not. But the Intendant must not be suffered to make an alarm. There was danger of discovery on all sides now, and the necessity of concealment, was a thousand times greater than ever. There was no time to question, but instant help was needed. In amaze at the spectacle before him, Cadet instantly flew to the assistance of the Intendant.

He approached Bigot without speaking a word although his great eyes expressed a look of sympathy never seen there before. He disengaged the dead form of Caroline tenderly from the embrace of Bigot, and laid it gently upon the floor, and lifting Bigot up in his gigantic arms, whispered hoarsely in his ear, "Keep still Bigot! keep still! not one word! Make no alarm! This is a dreadful business! but we must go to another room to consider, calmly, calmly mind! what it means, and what is to be done!—"

"O Cadet! Cadet!" moaned the Intendant still resting on his shoulder. "She is dead! dead! when I just wanted her to live! I have been hard with women but if there was one I loved, it was her who lies dead before me! Who? Who has done this bloody deed to me?—"

"Who has done it to her you mean! You are not killed yet, old friend! but will live to revenge this horrid business!—" answered Cadet with rough sympathy.

"I would give my life to restore hers!" replied Bigot despairingly. "O, Cadet! you never knew what was in my heart about this girl! and how I had resolved to make her reparation for the evil I had done her!—"

"Well I can guess what was in your heart—! Bigot! come

old friend, you are getting more calm. You can walk now! Let us go up stairs to consider what is to be done about it. Damn the women! they are man's torment whether alive or dead!—"

Bigot was too much absorbed in his own tumultuous feelings to notice Cadet's remark. He allowed himself to be led without resistance to another room, out of sight of the murdered girl, in whose presence he knew calm council was impossible.

Cadet seated Bigot on a couch and sitting beside him, bade him be a man and not a fool! He tried to rouse Bigot by irritating him, thinking in his coarse way, that, that was better than maudlin over him, as he considered it, with vain expressions of sympathy.

"I would not give way so!" said he, "for all the women in and out of Paradise! and you are a man Bigot!—Remember you have brought me here and you have to take me safely back again out of this den of murder!"

"Yes! Cadet!" replied Bigot rousing himself up at the sharp tone of his friend. "I must think of your safety, I care but little for my own, at this moment. Think for me!"

"Well then, I will think for you! and I think this Bigot! that if the Governor finds out this assassination done in your house and that you and I have been here at this hour of night with the murdered girl, By God! he will say we have done it! and the world will believe it! so rouse up! I for one do not want to be taxed with the murder of a woman, and still less to be hung innocently for the death of one. Damn the women! I would not risk my little finger for all the women alive—! let alone my neck for a dead one!"

The suggestion was like a sharp probe in his flesh. It touched Bigot to the quick. He started up, on his feet! "You are right, Cadet! It only wants that accusation to make me go mad! But my head is not my own, yet! I can think of nothing but her lying there, dead in her loveliness and in her love! Tell me what to do and I will do it!—"

"Aye now you talk reasonably! Now, you are coming to yourself! Bigot. We came to remove her alive from here did we not? We must now remove her dead! She cannot remain where she is at the risk of certain discovery tomorrow."

"No! the secret chamber would not hide such a secret as that!" replied Bigot recovering his self possession. "But how to remove her? We cannot carry her forth without discovery!" Bigots practical intellect was waking up to the danger of leaving the murdered girl in the Chateau.

Cadet rose and paced the room with rapid strides, rubbing his forehead and twitching his moustache violently. "I will tell you what we have to do, Bigot! *Par Dieu!* We must bury her where she is! down there, in the vaulted chamber!"

"What bury her!" Bigot looked at him with intense surprise.

"Yes! we must bury her in that very chamber Bigot! We must cover up somebody's damnable work to avert suspicion from ourselves! A pretty task for you and me Bigot, *Par Dieu!* I could laugh like a horse if I were not afraid of being over heard!—"

"But who is to dig a grave for her? surely not you or I!" replied Bigot with a look of dismay.

"Yes! Gentlemen as we are, you and I must do it, Bigot! Zounds! I learned to dig and delve when I was a stripling at Charlebourg, and in the trenches at Louisbourg, and I have not yet forgotten the knack of it! But where to get spades Bigot? You are master here, and ought to know.—"

"I! how should I know? It is terrible Cadet! to bury her as if we had murdered her! Is there no other way?—"

"None! We are in a cahot and must get our cariole out of it as best we can! I see plainly we two shall be taxed with this murder Bigot! if we let it be discovered. Besides utter ruin awaits you from La Pompadour if she find out you ever had this girl at Beaumanoir in keeping! Come! Time for parley is past! Where shall we find spades?—We must to work Bigot!"

A sudden thought lighted up the eyes of the Intendant who saw the force of Cadets suggestion strange and repulsive as it was. "I think I know!" said he. "The gardeners keep their tools in the old tower and we can get there by the secret passage and return."

"Bravo!" exclaimed Cadet, encouragingly "Come show the

way, and we will get the tools in a trice! I always heard there was a private way under ground to the old tower. It never stood its master in better stead than now! Perhaps never worse, if it has let in the murderer of this poor girl of yours!—"

Bigot rose up, very faint and weak. Cadet took his arm to support him, and bidding him be firm and not give way again at sight of her dead body, led him back to the chamber of death. "Let us first look around a moment" said he, "to find, if possible some trace of the hellish assassins."

The lamps burned brightly shedding a glare of light over every object in the secret chamber.

Cadet looked narrowly round, but found little trace of the murderers. The drawers of the escritoire stood open with their contents in great disorder, a circumstance which at once suggested robbers. Cadet pointed it out to Bigot with the question—

"Kept she much money Bigot?—"

"None that I know of. She asked for none, poor girl! and I gave her none, though I would have given her the King's treasury had she wished for it."

"But she might have had money when she came, Bigot?—" continued Cadet, not doubting but robbery had been the motive for this murder.

"It may be, I never questioned her," replied Bigot. "She spoke never of money. Alas! all the money in the world was as dross in her estimation. Other things than money occupied her pure thoughts."

"Well! it looks like robbers! They have ransacked the drawers and carried off all she had, were it much or little," remarked Cadet still continuing his search.

"But why kill her? O Cadet!—why kill the gentle girl? who would have given them every jewel in her possession for the bare asking!—"

"Nay, I cannot guess," said Cadet. "It looks like robbers, but the mystery is beyond my wit to explain! What are you doing, Bigot!"

Bigot had knelt down by the side of Caroline. He lifted her hand first to his lips, then towards Cadet, to show him the stalk of a rose from which the flower had been broken and which she held with a grip so hard that it could not be loosened from her dead fingers.

The two men looked long and earnestly at it, but failed to make a conjecture even, why the flower had been plucked from that broken stalk, and carried away for it was not to be seen in the room.

The fragment of a letter lay under a chair. It was a part of that which La Corriveau had torn up and missed to gather up again with the rest. Cadet picked it up and thrust it in his pocket.

The blood streaks upon her white robe and the visible stabs of a fine poniard rivited their attention. That, that was the cause of her death they doubted not, but the mute eloquence of her wounds spoke only to the heart. It gave no explanation to the intellect. The whole tragedy seemed wrapped in inexplicable mystery.

"They have covered their track up well!" remarked Cadet. "Hey! but what have we here?" Bigot started up at the exclamation. The door of the secret passage stood open. La Corriveau had not closed it after her when making her escape. "Here is where the assassins have found entrance and exit! Egad! More people know the secret of your Chateau than you think, Bigot!—"

They sprang forward, and each seizing a lamp, the two men rushed into the narrow passage. It was dark and still as the Catacombs. No trace of anything to the purpose could they perceive in the vaulted subterranean way to the turrett.

They speedily came to the other end, the secret door there stood open also. They ascended the stairs in the tower but could see no trace of the murderers. "It is useless to search farther for them at this time," remarked Cadet, "perhaps not safe at any time! but I would give my best horse to lay hands on the assassins at this moment!"

Gardener's tools lay round the room. "Here!" exclaimed Cadet, "is what is equally germane to the matter, and we have no time to lose."

He seized a couple of spades and a bar of iron and bidding

Bigot go before him with the lights, they returned to the chamber of death.

"Now for work! This sad business must be done well, and done quickly!" exclaimed Cadet. "You shall see that I have not forgotten how to dig, Bigot!—"

Cadet threw off his coat and setting to work, pulled up the thick carpet from one side of the chamber. The floor was covered with broad smooth flags, one of which he attacked with the iron bar, raised the flag stone and turned it over, another easily followed and very soon a space in the dry brown earth was exposed, large enough to make a grave.

Bigot looked at him in a sort of dream. "I cannot do it! Cadet! I cannot dig her grave!" and he threw down the spade which he had taken feebly in his hand.

"No matter Bigot! I will do it! Indeed you would only be in my way. Sit down while I dig, old friend! *Par Dieu*! this is nice work for the Commissary General of New France! with the Intendant overseeing him!—"

Bigot sat down, and looked forlornly on, while Cadet with the arms of a Hercules, dug and dug throwing out the earth without stopping, for the space of a quarter of an hour, until he had made a grave, large and deep enough to contain the body of the hapless girl.

"That will do!" cried he leaping out of the pit. "The sexton of Charlebourg could not have made a nicer bed to sleep in! Our funeral arrangements must be of the briefest, Bigot! So come help me to shroud this poor girl, who I hope will forgive her rough undertaker for doing his best to make a woman comfortable in her last bed!—"

Cadet found a sheet of linen and some fine blankets upon a couch in the secret chamber. He spread them out upon the floor, and motioning to Bigot, without speaking, the two men lifted Caroline tenderly and reverently upon the sheet. They gazed at her for a minute in solemn silence, before shrouding her fair face, and slender form in their last winding sheet. Bigot was overpowered with his feelings yet strove to master them, as he gulped down the rising in his throat, which at times almost strangled him.

Cadet eager to get his painful task over, took from the slender finger of Caroline a ring, a love gift of Bigot, and from her neck a golden locket containing his portrait and a lock of his hair. A rosary hung at her waist—this Cadet also detached, as a precious relic to be given to the Intendant by and by. There was one thread of silk woven into the coarse hempen nature of Cadet.

Bigot stooped down and gave her pale lips and eyes, which he had tenderly closed, a last despairing kiss before veiling her face, with the winding sheet as she lay, white as a snowdrift, and as cold. They wrapped her softly in the blankets and without a word spoken, lowered the still lissom body into its rude grave.

The aweful silence was only broken by the spasmodic sobs of Bigot as he leaned over the grave to look his last upon the form of the fair girl whom he had betrayed and brought to this untimely end! "*Mea Culpa! Mea Maxima Culpa!*" said he beating his breast. "O Cadet! we are burying her like a dog! I cannot, I cannot do it!—"

The Intendant's feelings overcame him again, and he rushed from the chamber, while Cadet glad of his absence for a few moments, hastily filled up the grave and replacing with much care, the stone slabs over it, swept the debris into the passage, and spread the carpet again smoothly over the floor. Every trace of the dreadful deed was obliterated in the chamber of murder.

The secret chamber looked again as if nothing strange or horrible had happened in it—just so the sea, when its smooth waters close over a man who sinks into its cold bosom. A splash, a few circles of agitation, all is over—and out of sight!—

Cadet acutely thoughtful of everything at this supreme moment would leave no ground of suspicion for Dame Tremblay when she came in the morning to visit the chamber. She would think that her lady was gone away with her master, as mysteriously as she had come, and no further inquiry would be made after her. In this Cadet was right.

Buried in this unconsecrated earth, with no requiem sung for her last repose, no prayer, no sprinkling save the tears which dropped heavily from the eyes of Bigot, and which could she have been conscious of, Caroline would have prized more than the waters of Jordan poured over her grave—!—No bell tolled for her. There was no chant of priest or lifting of the Sacrament for the dead, but unknelled, uncoffined, and unknown save to God only, and these two men, Caroline de St Castin slept and still sleeps in the dust of the deep foundations of the Chateau of Beaumanoir.

It was necessary for Cadet and Bigot now to depart by the secret passage to the tower. The deep toned bell of the Chateau struck three. Its solemn voice seemed to bring with it the cold shuddering breath of approaching morn.

"We must now be gone! Bigot! and instantly!" exclaimed Cadet. "Our night work is done! Let us see what day will bring forth! You must see to it tomorrow, Bigot!—that no man or woman alive ever again enter this accursed chamber of death!—"

Cadet fastened the secret door of the stair and gathering up his spades and bar of iron left the chamber with Bigot who was passive as a child in his hands. The Intendant turned round and gave one last sorrowful look at the now darkened room as they left it. Cadet and he made their way back to the tower, and sallied out into the open air which blew fresh and reviving upon their fevered faces, after escaping from the stifling atmosphere below.

They proceeded at once towards their horses and mounted them but Bigot felt deadly faint and halted under a tree, while Cadet rode back to the Porters lodge, and roused up old Marcele to give him some brandy, if he had any. "As of course he had," said Cadet. "Brandy was a gate porter's inside livery, the lining of his laced coat, which he always wore." Cadet assumed a levity which he did not really feel.

Marcele fortunately could oblige the Sieur Cadet. "He did line his livery a little, but very lightly, as his honour would see!" said he bringing out a bottle of cognac, and a drinking cup.

"It is to keep us from catching cold!" continued Cadet in his jocular way, "is it good?" He placed the bottle to his lips and tasted it.

Marcele assured him it was good as gold.

"Right!" said Cadet throwing Marcele a Louis d'or, "I will take the bottle to the Intendant to keep him from catching cold too! Mind, Marcele! you keep your tongue still or else—!" Cadet held up his whip, and bidding the porter "good night!" rejoined Bigot.

Cadet had a crafty design in this proceeding. He wanted not to tell Marcele that a lady was accompanying them, but not to let him perceive that they left Beaumanoir without one. He feared that the old Porter and Dame Tremblay might possibly compare notes together, and the Housekeeper discover that Caroline had not left Beaumanoir with the Intendant.

Bigot sat faint and listless in his saddle when Cadet poured out a large cup full of Brandy and offered it to him. He drank it eagerly. Cadet then filled and gulped down a large cup full himself, then gave another to the Intendant and poured another and another for himself until he said "he began to feel warm and comfortable! and got the damnable taste of gravedigging out of his mouth—!—"

The heavy draught which Cadet forced the Intendant to take relieved him somewhat, but he groaned inwardly and would not speak. Cadet respected his mood, only bidding him ride fast. They spurred their horses, and rode swiftly unobserved by any one, until they entered the gates of the palace of the Intendant.

The arrival of the Intendant or of the Sieur Cadet at the Palace at any untimely hour of the night excited no remark whatever, for it was the rule, rather than the exception with them both.

Dame Tremblay was not surprised next morning to find the Chamber empty and her lady gone.

She shook her head sadly. "He is a wild gallant is my master! No wilder ever came to Lake Beauport, when I was the charming Josephine and all the world ran after me! But I can keep a secret, and I will! This secret I must keep at any rate by the Intendant's order! and I would rather die than be railed at by that fierce Sieur Cadet! I will keep the Intendant's secret! safe as my teeth which he praised so handsomely and so justly!"

And she did keep it, until years after the conquest of Canada when Bigot was atoning in the Bastile for high misdemeanours and maladministration as Intendant of New France. Then did a garrulous old woman, use to babble before her death about the charming Josephine of Lake Beauport and tell what she knew, not much after all, of the fate of the unhappy lady, who had either been spirited away or buried alive in the secret chamber of Beaumanoir.

The fact that Caroline never returned to the Chateau and that the search for her was so long and so vainly carried on by La Corne St Luc and the Baron de St Castin caused the Dame to suspect at last, that some foul play had been perpetrated— but she dared not speak openly.

The old woman's suspicions grew with age into certainties when at last she chanced to talk with her old fellow servant Marcele the gatekeeper and learned from him, that Bigot and Cadet had left the Chateau alone on that fatal night. Dame Tremblay was more perplexed than ever. She talked she knew not what, but her talk passed into the traditions of the Habitans. It became a popular belief that a beautiful woman, the mistress of the powerful Intendant Bigot had been murdered and buried in the Chateau of Beaumanoir.

The secret chamber was immediately after the tragedy disfurnished and shut up by order of the Intendant. Dame Tremblay sedulously avoided it. She believed it haunted.

It was never visited save by Bigot who in his after career of pretorian riot and extravagance sometimes broke off from his companions, in the height of their revelry rode out to Beaumanoir and descending to the gloomy chamber, flung himself despairingly upon the cold stone that he had sculptured with the solitary letter *C*, which covered the dust of the one woman who had ever loved Francois Bigot for his own sake! The only one, who, had she been spared might by her sweet influences have made a better and a nobler man of him— —and who knows? might have checked his career of extravagance and corruption, and turned his undoubted talents to the benefit instead of to the ruin of New France!

Caroline de St Castin had she lived, might have averted the conquest of the Colony, which was mainly lost through the misgovernment of Bigot and his waste of all the public resources that should have contributed to the defence of New France. But it was not to be! No other influence for good remained after the death of the unfortunate Caroline.

The storms of six score Winters have howled among the ruins of Beaumanoir, of Chateau Bigot, as it is now popularly called by the Habitans, who look still upon its crumbling walls with feeling of awe, as a place accursed in the history of their Country.

All has gone to ruin. The Chateau itself is a pile of destruction. Its very stones have been carted away by the peasantry, save a few stern old gables that still brave the elements, and its thick massive foundations that still preserve an outline of the great wicked edifice. The secret chamber itself lies uncovered to the sun, God's light streams upon it! Green grass and wild flowers tangle among its stone heaps! The bird builds its nest and the hare makes its form, and rears its young above the grave of Caroline, now lost under a mass of debris and ruin!—

Old grey men still living, remember a period before the final delapidation of the Chateau, when daring visitors who ventured down into the deep vaults, could still see the solitary tombstone with its one mysterious initial letter *C* carved upon it—all that was left upon earth to perpetuate the memory of the beautiful and unfortunate Caroline de St Castin.

CHAPTER 47

SILK GLOVES OVER BLOODY HANDS

ALL the way back to the Palace, Bigot had scarcely spoken a word to Cadet. His mind was in a tumult of wildest conjectures, and his thoughts ran to and fro like hounds in a thick brake darting in every direction to find the scent of the game they were in search of. When they reached the Palace, Bigot without speaking to any one passed through the anterooms to his own apartment and threw himself dressed and booted as he was upon a couch, where he lay like a man stricken down by a mace by some unseen hand.

Cadet had coarser ways of relieving himself from the late unusual strain upon his rough feelings. He went down to the billiard room and joining recklessly in the game that was still kept up, by De Pean, Le Gardeur and a number of wild associates, strove to drown all recollections of the past night at Beaumanoir, by drinking and gambling with more than usual violence until far on in the day.

Bigot never slept nor wished to sleep—the image of the murdered girl lying in her rude grave was ever before him with a vividness so terrible that it seemed he could never sleep again. His thoughts ran round and round like a millwheel, without advancing a step towards a solution of the tragedy.

He summoned up his recollections of every man and woman he knew in the colony, and asked himself regarding each one, the question, "Is it he who has done this? Is it she, who has prompted it? and who could have a motive and who not, to perpetrate such a bloody deed."—

One image came again and again before his minds eye as he reviewed the list of his friends and enemies. The figure of Angelique appeared and reappeared intruding itself between

578

every third or fourth personage, which his memory called up, until his thoughts fixed upon her with the maddening inquiry, "Could Angelique des Meloises have been guilty of this terrible deed?—"

He remembered her passionate denunciation of the Lady of Beaumanoir, her fierce demand for her banishment by a *lettre de Cachet*. He knew her ambition and recklessness, but still versed as he was, in all the ways of wickedness and knowing the inexorable bitterness of envy and the cruelty of jealousy in the female breast, at least in such women as he had for the most part had experience of, Bigot could hardly admit the thought that one so fair as Angelique, one who held him in a golden net of fascination, and to whom he had been more than once on the point of yielding, could have committed so great a crime.

He struggled with his thoughts like a man amid tossing waves, groping about in the dark for a plank to float upon, but could find none. Still in spite of himself, in spite of his violent asseverations that "it was *impossible!*" In spite of Cadet's plausible theory of robbers, which Bigot at first seized upon as the likeliest explanation of the mystery, the thought of Angelique ever returned back upon him like a fresh accusation.

He was deeply moved, and at last almost alarmed at the persistence with which the reflection of her face went and came now far, now near like the phantasm of a magic lantern that haunted his most secret thoughts.

He could not accuse her yet, though something told him he might have to do so at last. He grew angry at the ever recurring thought of her, and turning his face to the wall like a man trying to shut out the light, resolved to force disbelief in her guilt until clearer testimony than his own suspicions should convict her of the death of Caroline.

And yet in his secret soul he dreaded a discovery that it might turn out as he feared. But he pushed the black thought aside, he would wait and watch for what he feared to find.—

The fact of Caroline's concealment at Beaumanoir and her murder at the very moment when the search was about to be made for her, placed Bigot in the cruellest dilemma. Whatever his suspicions might be, he dared not by word or sign avow any knowledge of Caroline's presence, still less of her mysterious murder in his Chateau. Her grave had been dug she had been secretly buried out of human sight and he was under bonds as for his very life, never to let the dreadful mystery be discovered.

So Bigot lay on his couch, for once, a weak and a frightened man, registering vain vows of vengeance against persons unknown, vows which he knew at the moment were empty as bubbles because he dared not to move hand or foot in the matter to carry them out or make open accusation against any one of the foul crime. What thoughts came to Bigot's subtle mind were best known to himself, but something was suggested by the mocking Devil who was never far from him, and he caught and held fast the wicked suggestion with a bitter laugh. He then grew suddenly still and said to himself, "I will sleep on it!" and pillowing his head quietly not on sleep but on thoughts deeper than sleep, he lay till day.

It was long before Angelique came to herself from the frightful swoon into which she had fallen at the feet of La Corriveau, and who had left her lying as one dead upon the floor of her chamber. Fortunately for Angelique, it was without discovery. Not one of the servants of the house came in while she lay in that condition. A weakness so strange to Angelique's usual hardihood, would have become the city's talk before night; would have set all the idle tongues in Quebec conjecturing or inventing reasons for it. It would have reached the ear of Bigot: as every spray of gossip did and set him thinking more savagely than he had yet done as to the possible complicity of Angelique with the murder of Caroline.

Angelique who had never in her life swooned before, felt when she awoke like one returning to life from death. She opened her eyes wondering where she was, and half remembering the things she had heard, as things she had seen, looked anxiously round the chamber for La Corriveau. She rose up with a start, when she saw she was gone, for Angelique recollected suddenly that La Corriveau now held the terrible secret which concerned her life and peace, for evermore.

The thing she had so long wished for, and prayed for, was at last done! Her rival was out of the way!—But she also felt that if the murder was discovered her own life was forfeit to the law, and the secret was in the keeping of the vilest of women!—

A mountain, not of remorse but of apprehension overwhelmed her for a time. But Angelique's mind was too intensely selfish, hard and superficial to give way to the remorse of a deeper nature. Her feelings such as they were played like flame on the surface of her heart, but never warmed it to the core. She was incapable of real regret and would regard the world well lost for sake of herself. Her nature was too artificial to take the tragedy very deeply to heart. No Furies would ever sit on her pillow accusing her of midnight murder, and she would go through life forgetting, in the enjoyment of a brilliant career, the bloody episode of Caroline de St Castin.

Still the tidings of Caroline's death gave her a shock. It was her first plunge into positive crime, and she trembled for the consequences. She who had never shunned man or woman before, felt like hiding herself now.

She was angry at her own cowardice, but she feared the suspicions of Bigot. There was ever something in his dark nature which she could not fathom, and deep and crafty as she knew herself to be, she feared that he was more deep and more crafty than herself.

"What if he should discover her hand in this bloody business?—" The thought drove her frantic, until she fancied she repented of the deed! But it was self delusion. She did not repent. She only feared punishment for herself. Then she tried to pray, but prayer stuck in her throat and then she cursed her folly not her cruelty. She was too hard hearted for that. Her words came in a flow of invective against Bigot, for not removing Caroline from Beaumanoir, and against Caroline for having come there at all! She cursed La Corriveau for shaping the evil desires of her heart into instruments of murder—the poison and the dagger—and she cursed herself for paying so terrible a price for the bare possibility, not the certainty of becoming the wife of Bigot!

Had it brought a certainty, this crime, then—why then,— she had found a compensation for the risk she was running! for the pain she was enduring which she tried to believe was regret and pity for her victim. Her anxiety redoubled when it occurred to her that Bigot remembering her passionate appeals to him for the removal of Caroline, might suspect her of the murder, as one alone having a palpable interest in it.

"But Bigot shall never believe it even if he suspect it!" exclaimed she at last, shaking off her fears. "I have made fools of many men for my pleasure. I can surely blind one for my safety, and after all, whose fault is it but Bigot's? He would not grant me the *lettre de cachet*, nor keep his promise for her removal! He even gave me her life! but he lied! He did not mean it! He loved her too well and meant to deceive me and marry her! and *I* have deceived him and shall marry him! that is all!" and Angelique laughed a hysterical laugh, such as Dives in his torment may sometimes give way to.

"La Corriveau has betrayed her trust in one terrible point," continued she. "She promised a death so easy, that all men would say that Caroline de St Castin had died of heart break only, or by God's visitation! a natural death! The foul witch has used her stiletto and made a murder of that which without it had been none! Bigot will know it, must know it, even if he dare not reveal it! for how in the name of all the saints is it to be concealed?—"

"But my God! this will never do!" continued she starting up, "I look like very guilt!" She stared fiercely in the mirror at her hollow eyes, pale cheeks and white lips. She scarcely recognized herself. Her bloom and brightness had vanished for the time.

"What if I have inhaled some of the poisoned odour of those cursed roses?" thought she, shuddering at the supposition, but she reassured herself that it could not be. "Still my looks condemn me! The pale face of that dead girl is looking at me out of mine! Bigot if he sees me will not fail to read the secret in my looks!"

She glanced at the clock. The morning was far advanced towards noon. Visitors might soon arrive. Bigot himself might come. She dared not deny herself to him. She would deny herself to no one today! She would go everywhere and see every body! and show the world if talk of it should arise that she was wholly innocent of that girl's blood!

She would wear her brightest looks, her gayest robe her hat and feathers the newest from Paris. She would ride out into the City, go to the Cathedral, show herself to all her friends and make every one say or think that Angelique des Meloises had not a care or trouble in the world to day.

She rang for Fanchon, impatient to commence her toilette, for when dressed she knew that she would feel like herself once more, cool and defiant. The touch of her armour of fashionable attire would restore her confidence in herself, and enable her to brave down any suspicion in the mind of the Intendant. At any rate it was her only resource, and Angelique was not one to give up even a lost battle, let alone one half gained, through the death of her rival.

Fanchon came in haste at the summons of her mistress. She had long waited to hear the bell, and began to fear she was sick or in one of those wild moods which had come over her occasionally since the night of her last interview with Le Gardeur.

The girl started at sight of the pale face and paler lips of her mistress. She uttered an exclamation of surprise. But Angelique anticipating all questions, told her: "She was unwell but would dress and take a ride out in the fresh air and sunshine to recruit."

"But had you not better see the Physician? my Lady, you do look so pale today, you are really not well!—"

"No, but I will ride out!" and, she added in her old way "perhaps Fanchon I may meet some one who will be better company than the Physician! *Qui sait?*"—and she laughed with an appearance of gaiety which she was far from feeling, and which only half imposed on the quick witted maid who waited upon her.

"Where is your Aunt, Fanchon? When did you see Dame Dodier?" asked she, really anxious to learn what had become of La Corriveau.

"She returned home this morning my Lady! I had not seen her for days before, but supposed she had already gone back to St Valier, but Aunt Dodier is a strange woman, and tells no one her business."

"She had perhaps other lost jewels to look after besides mine!" replied Angelique mechanically yet feeling easier upon learning the departure of La Corriveau.

"Perhaps so, my Lady. I am glad she is gone home, I shall never wish to see her again."

"Why?" asked Angelique sharply, wondering if Fanchon had conjectured anything of her Aunts business.

"They say she has dealings with that horrid Mere Malheur, and I believe it" replied Fanchon with a shrug of disgust.

"Ah! Do you think Mere Malheur knows her business or any of your Aunt's secrets, Fanchon?—" asked Angelique thoroughly roused.

"I think she does, My Lady. You cannot live in a chimney with another, without both getting black alike and Mere Malheur is a black witch as sure as Aunt is a white one," was Fanchon's reply.

"What said your Aunt on leaving?" asked her mistress.

"I did not see her leave my Lady. I only learned from Ambroise Gariepy that she had crossed the river this morning to return to St Valier."

"And who is Ambroise Gariepy, Fanchon? You have a wide circle of acquaintance for a young girl, I think!"—Angelique knew the dangers of gossiping too well, not to fear Fanchon's imprudences.

"Yes, my Lady!" replied Fanchon with affected simplicity "Ambroise Gariepy keeps the *Lion Vert* and the ferry upon the South Shore—he brings me news and sometimes a little present from the pack of the Basque peddlers. He brought me this comb my Lady!" Fanchon turned her head to show her mistress a superb comb in her thick black hair, and in her delight at talking of Ambroise Gariepy, the little Inn of the Ferry and the cross that leaned like a failing memory over the grave of his former wife, Fanchon quite forgot to ease her mind further on the subject of La Corriveau nor did Angelique resume the dangerous topic.

Fanchon's easy shallow way of talking of her lover, touched a sympathetic chord in the breast of her mistress. Grand passions were grand follies in Angelique's estimation which she was less capable of appreciating than even her maid, but flirtation and coquetry, skin deep only, she could understand and relished beyond all other enjoyments. It was just now like medicine to her racking thoughts to listen to Fanchon's shallow gossip.

"She had done what she had done," she reflected, "and it could not be undone! why should she give way to regret and lose the prize for which she had staked so heavily? She would not do it!—No *Par Dieu!* She had thrown Le Gardeur to the fishes for sake of the Intendant, and had done that other deed!" She shied off from the thought of it, as from an uncouth thing in the dark,—and began to feel shame of her weakness at having fainted at the tale of La Corriveau.

The light talk of Fanchon while dressing the long golden hair of her mistress and assisting her to put on a new riding dress and the plumed hat fresh from Paris which she had not yet displayed in public, did much to restore her equanimity.

Her face had however not recovered from its strange pallor. Her eager maid anxious for the looks of her mistress insisted on a little rouge, which Angelique's natural bloom had never before needed. She submitted,—"for she intended to look her best today" she said, "who knows whom I shall fall in with?—"

"That is right my Lady!" exclaimed Fanchon admiringly "No one could be dressed perfectly as you are and be sick! I pity the gentlemen you meet today that is all! There is murder in your eye, my Lady!—"

Poor Fanchon believed she was only complimenting her mistress and at other times her remark would only have called forth a joyous laugh. Now the word seemed like a sharp knife. It cut,—and Angelique did not laugh. She pushed her maid forcibly away from her, and was on the point of breaking out into some violent exclamation, when recalled by the amazed look of Fanchon, she turned the subject adroitly and asked, "Where is my brother?—"

"Gone with the Chevalier de Pean to the Palace, my Lady!—" replied Fanchon trembling all over and wondering how she had angered her mistress.

"How know you that, Fanchon?" asked Angelique recovering her usual careless tone.

"I overheard them speaking together, my lady. The Chevalier De Pean said that the Intendant was sick, and would see no one this morning."

"Yes? and what then?" Angelique was struck with a sudden consciousness of danger in the wind, "are you sure they said the Intendant was sick?" asked she.

"Yes! my Lady, and the Chevalier De Pean said that he was less sick than mad, and out of humour to a degree he had never seen him before!—"

"Did they give a reason for it? that is for the Intendants sickness or madness?" Angelique's eyes were fixed keenly upon her maid, to draw out a full confession.

"None my Lady! only the Chevalier des Meloises said he supposed it was the news from France, which sat so ill on his stomach."

"And what then Fanchon? You are so long of answering!" Angelique stamped her foot with impatience.

Fanchon looked up at the reproof so little merited and replied quickly, "The Chevalier de Pean said, It must be that for he knew of nothing else. The gentlemen then went out and I heard no more."

Angelique was relieved by this turn of the conversation. She felt certain that if Bigot discovered the murder he would not fail to reveal it to the Chevalier de Pean who was understood to be the depositary of all his secrets. She began to cheer up under the belief that Bigot would never dare accuse anyone of a deed which would be the means of proclaiming his own falseness and his duplicity towards the King and the Marquise de Pompadour.

"I have only to deny all knowledge of it," said she to herself. "Swear to it if need be! and Bigot will not dare go farther in the matter. Then will come my time, to turn the tables upon him, in a way he little expects! Pshaw!" continued she, glancing at her gay hat in the mirror and with her own dainty fingers setting the feather more airily to her liking. "Bigot is bound fast enough to me, now that she is gone—! and when he discovers that I hold his secret he will not dare meddle with mine!—"

It is recorded that the Athenians ignorantly worshipped the true deity, under the name of the Unknown God. Angelique like many in modern times worshipped heathen deities, in the name of the true. The Goddess ignorantly worshipped by Angelique, and who received the first offerings of her heart, was Venus Victrix, in the form of herself, and no woman of Greece or Rome was ever more devout in the homage she paid to the heathen shrine.

Angelique, measureably reassured and hopeful of success in her desperate venture, descended the steps of her mansion and gathering up her robes lightly mounted her horse which had long been chafing in the hands of her groom waiting for his mistress.

She bade the man remain at home until her return, and dashed off down the Rue St Louis drawing after her a hundred eyes of admiration and envy.

"She would ride down to the *Place d'Armes*," she thought where she knew, that before she had skirted the length of the Castle wall, half a dozen gallants would greet her with offers of escort, and drop any business they had in hand for the sake of a gallop by her side.

She had scarcely passed the monastry of the Recollets when she was espied by the Sieur La Force, who too was as quickly discerned by her, as he loitered at the corner of the Rue St Anne, to catch sight of any fair piece of mischief that might be abroad that day from her classes, in the convent of the Ursulines.

"Angelique is as fair a prize as any of them," thought La Force as he saluted her with Parisian politeness, and with a request to be her escort in her ride through the City.

"My horse is at hand! and I shall esteem it such an honour!" added La Force smiling, "and such a profit too," added he! "My credit is low in a certain quarter! you know where!" and he laughingly pointed towards the convent. "I desire to make *her* jealous, for she has made me madly so, and no one can aid in an enterprize of that kind better than yourself Mademoiselle des Meloises!"

"Or more willingly, Sieur La Force!" replied she laughing. "But you overrate my powers I fear."

"O! by no means!" replied La Force "there is not a lady in Quebec, but feels in her heart, that Angelique des Meloises can steal away her lover when and where she will. She has only to look at him across the street and presto! change! he is gone from them as if by magic! But will you really help me Mademoiselle?"

"Most willingly Sieur La Force! for your profit, if not for your honour! I am just in the humour for tormenting somebody this morning! So get your horse and let us be off."

Before La Force had mounted his horse, a number of gaily dressed young ladies came in sight full sail down the Rue St Anne, like a fleet of rakish little yachts, bearing down upon Angelique and her companion.

"Shall we wait for them La Force?" asked she, "They are from the convent—!"

"Yes, and *she* is there too! The news will be all over the City in an hour, that I am riding with you," exclaimed La Force in a tone of intense satisfaction.

Five girls just verging on womanhood perfect in manner and appearance—as the Ursulines knew well how to train the young olive plants of the Colony—walked on demurely enough, looking apparently straight forward but casting side glances from under their veils which raked the Sieur La Force and Angelique with a searching fire, that nothing could withstand, La Force said, but which Angelique remarked, was simply, "impudence, such as could only be found in Convent girls!"

They came nearer. Angelique might have supposed they

were going to pass by them, had she not known too well their sly ways. The foremost of the five, Louise Roy whose glorious hair was the boast of the city, suddenly threw back her veil and disclosing a charming face, dimpled with smiles and with a thousand mischiefs lurking in her bright grey eyes, sprang towards Angelique, while her companions, all Louises of the famous class of that name, also threw up their veils and stood saluting Angelique and La Force with infinite merriment.

Louise Roy quizzing La Force through a coquettish eye glass which she wore on a ribbon round her pretty neck, as if she had never seen him before, motioned to him in a queenly way as she raised her dainty foot, giving him a severe look, or what tried to be such,—but was in truth an absurd failure.

He instantly comprehended her command, for such it was, and held out his hand upon which she stepped lightly and sprang up to Angelique, embracing and kissing her with such cordiality, that if it were not real, the acting was perfect! At the same time Louise Roy made her understand that she was not the only one who could avail herself of the gallant attentions of the Sieur La Force—!—

In truth Louise Roy was somewhat piqued at the Sieur La Force, and to punish him made herself as heavy as her slight figure would admit of. She stood perched up as long as she could, and actually enjoyed the tremour which she felt plainly enough in his hand as he continued to support her, and was quite disposed to test how long he could or would hold her up, while she conversed in whispers with Angelique.

"Angelique!" said she, "they say in the convent that you are to marry the Intendant! Your old Mistress Mere St Louis is crazy with delight. She says she always predicted you would make a great match!"

"Or none at all, as Mere St Helene used to say of me! but they know every thing in the Convent do they not?" Angelique pinched the arm of Louise as much as to say, "of course it is true!" "But who told you that Louise?" asked she.

"O, every bird that flies! But tell me one thing more—they say the Intendant is a Bluebeard who has had wives without number—! Nobody knows how many or what became of them, so of course he kills them! Is that true?—"

Angelique shrank a little, and little as it was the movement was noticed by Louise. "If nobody knows what became of them, How should I know, Louise?" replied she. "He does not look like a Bluebeard, does he?"

"So says Mere St Joseph, who came from the Convent at Bordeaux, you know, for she never tires telling us. She declares that the Chevalier Bigot was never married at all, and she ought to know that surely, as well as she knows her beads, coming from the same City as the Intendant, knowing his family as she does."

"Well Louise!" replied Angelique impatiently. "But do you not see the Sieur La Force is getting tired of holding you up so long with his hand—for Heaven's sake get down!"

"I want to punish him for going with you, and not waiting for me!" was the cool whisper of Louise "but you will ask me Angelique to the wedding will you not? if you do not," continued she, "I shall die!", and delaying her descent as long as possible she commenced a new topic concerning the hat worn by Angelique.

"Mischief that you are! get down! The Sieur La Force is my Cavalier for the day, and you shall not impose on his gallantry that way! He is ready to drop!" whispered Angelique.

"One word more! Angelique!" Louise was delighted to feel the hand of La Force tremble more and more under her foot.

"No! *not a word*—get down!"

"Kiss me then and good bye! Cross thing that you are! Do not keep him all day, or all the class besides myself will be jealous!" replied Louise not offering to get down.

Angelique had no mind to allow her cavalier to be made a horse block of, for anybody but herself! She jerked the bridle and making her horse suddenly pirouette compelled Louise to jump down. The mischievous little fairy turned her bright laughing eyes full upon La Force and thanked him for his great courtesy, and with a significant gesture, as much as to say, he was at liberty now, to escort Angelique, having done penance for the same, rejoined her expectant companions, who had laughed heartily at her manoeuvre.

"She paints!" was Louise's emphatic whisper to her companions, loud enough to be heard by La Force for whom the remark was partly intended. "She paints! and I saw in her eyes that she has not slept all night! She is in love! and I do believe it is true, she is to marry the Intendant!—"

This was delicious news to the Class of Louises, who laughed out like a chime of silver bells, as they mischievously bade La Force and Angelique *Bon Voyage!* and passed down the *Place d'Armes* in search of fresh adventures to fill the budgets of fun, budgets which on their return to the convent, they would open under the very noses of the good nuns, (who were not so blind as they seemed, however), and regale their companions with a spicy treat, in response to the universal question ever put to all who had been out in the world, "What is the news?"

La Force, compliant as wax to every caprice of Angelique, was secretly fuming at the trick played upon him, by the mischief of the convent, as he called Louise Roy, for which he resolved to be revenged even if he had to marry her! He and Angelique rode down the busy streets receiving salutations on every hand. In the great Square of the market place Angelique pulled up in front of the Cathedral.

Why she stopped there, would have puzzled herself to explain. It was not to worship, not to repent of her heinous sin. She neither repented nor desired to repent. But it seemed pleasant to play at repentance and put on imaginary sackcloth. She would try at any rate to say in church the prayers which had choked her at home.

Angelique's brief contact with the fresh sunny nature of Louise Roy, had sensibly raised her spirits. It lifted the cloud from her brow, and made her feel more like her former self. The story half told in jest, by Louise, that she was to marry the Intendant, flattered her vanity and raised her hopes to the utmost. She liked the City to talk of her in connection with the Intendant.

The report had already become the City's talk and she knew that it was not strange to the ears of the Intendant himself, for at the *Taverne de Menut*, only a few nights ago, her name had been toasted upon their knees by Bigot and the wild gallants of his train. She had been spoken of freely over their cups, and Bigot had not denied, but cheered louder than the rest, when she was named as the future bride of the Intendant.

Angelique remembered this as she entered the Cathedral, and began to think it was not so unfortunate after all, that she had taken counsel of La Corriveau.

The image of Beaumanoir grew fainter and fainter as she knelt down upon the floor, not to ask pardon for her sin but to pray for immunity for herself and the speedy realization of the great object of her ambition and her crime! She almost persuaded herself that the death of Caroline taking it all in all, had been an act of especial grace in answer to her ardent prayers, to the unknown Goddess Venus Victrix.

The pealing of the organ rising and falling in waves of harmony, the chanting of choristers, and the voice of the Celebrant during the service in honour of St Michael and all the angels, touched her sensuous nature, but failed to touch her conscience. She admired, she felt the harmony, saw the glory of the Archangel, and forgot the mortal angel lying in her bloody shroud under the cold flags of the secret chamber of the Chateau where she hoped full soon to be the regent and mistress.

A crowd of worshippers were kneeling upon the floor of the Cathedral, unobstructed in those days by seats and pews, except on one side where rose the stately *Bancs* of the Governor and the Intendant, on either side of which stood a sentry with ported arms and over head upon the wall blazed the Royal Escutcheons of France.

Angelique whose eyes roved incessantly about the church, turned them often towards the gorgeous *Banc* of the Intendant, and the thought intruded itself to the exclusion of her prayers, "When shall I sit there with all these proud ladies forgetting their devotions through envy of my good fortune?—"

She conjured up an image of herself sitting on the royal *Banc* and her nimble fancy flashed for a moment with a woman's interest, upon the colour of the robe, the fashion of her hair and her head-dress, upon that momentous day—a momentous day indeed to her if it ever came! A still more momentous thing if the day never came! Either way to gain the world she had lost her soul. Happy if she did not lose the world too, by the loss of her life, should the dark deed at Beaumanoir ever be laid to her charge.

Bigot did not appear in his place at church today. He was too profoundly agitated and sick, and lay on his bed till evening, revolving in his astute mind, schemes of vengeance possible and impossible, to be carried out should his suspicions of Angelique become certainties of knowledge and fact. His own safety was at stake. The thought that he had been outwitted by the beautiful, designing, heartless girl, the reflection that he dare not turn to the right hand nor to the left, to inquire into this horrid assassination, which if discovered would be laid wholly to his own charge, drove him to the verge of distraction.

The Governor and his friend Peter Kalm occupied the Royal *Banc*. Lutheran as he was, Peter Kalm was too philosophical and perhaps too faithful a follower of Christ to consider religion as a matter of mere opinion, or of form, rather than a humble dependence upon God the father of all, with faith in Christ and the conscientious striving to love God and his neighbour.

A short distance from Angelique, two ladies in long black robes and evidently of rank were kneeling with downcast faces and hands clasped over their bosoms in a devout attitude of prayer and supplication.

Angelique's keen eye which nothing escaped needed not a second glance to recognize the unmistakable grace of Amelie de Repentigny and the nobility of the Lady de Tilly.

She started at sight of these relatives of Le Gardeur's but did not wonder at their presence, for she already knew that they had returned to the city immediatly after the abduction of Le Gardeur by the Chevalier de Pean.

Startled, frightened and despairing, with aching hearts but unimpaired love, Amelie and the Lady de Tilly had followed

Le Gardeur, and reoccupied their stately house in the City, resolved to leave no means untried, no friends unsolicited, no prayers unuttered to rescue him from the gulf of perdition into which he had again so madly plunged.

Within an hour after her return, Amelie accompanied by Pierre Philibert had gone to the Palace to seek an interview with her brother. They were rudely denied. "He was playing a game of piquet for the championship of the Palace with the Chevalier de Pean, and could not come if St Peter let alone Pierre Philibert stood at the gate knocking!—"

This reply had passed through the impure lips of the Sieur de Lantagnac before it reached Amelie and Pierre. They did not believe it came from their brother. They left the Palace with heavy hearts after long and vainly seeking an interview, Philibert resolving to appeal to the Intendant himself and call him to account at the swords point if need be for the evident plot in the Palace to detain Le Gardeur from his friends.

Amelie dreading some such resolution on the part of Pierre returned next day alone to the palace to try once more to see Le Gardeur.

She was agitated and in tears at the fate of her brother. She was anxious too over the evident danger which Pierre seemed to court, for his sake and she would not hide the truth from herself, for her own sake too, and yet she would not forbid him. She felt her own noble blood stirred within her to the point that she wished herself a man to be able to walk sword in hand into the Palace and confront the herd of revellers who she believed had plotted the ruin of her brother.

She was proud of Pierre while she trembled at the resolution which she read in his countenance of demanding as a soldier and not as a suppliant the restoration of Le Gardeur to his family.

Amelie's second visit to the Palace had been fruitless as her first. She was denied admittance with the profoundest regrets on the part of De Pean who met her at the door and strove to exculpate himself from the accusation of having persuaded Le Gardeur to depart from Tilly, and of keeping him in the palace against the prayers of his friends.

De Pean remembered his presumption as well as his rejection by Amelie at Tilly, and while his tongue ran smooth as oil in polite regrets that Le Gardeur had resolved not to see his sister to day, her evident distress filled him with joy which he rolled under his tongue as the most delicate morsel of revenge he had ever tasted.

Bowing with well affected politeness, De Pean attended her to her carriage and having seen her depart in tears returned laughing into the palace remarking as he mimicked the weeping countenance of Amelie, that "the *Honnetes Gens* had learned it was a serious matter to come to the burial of the virtues of a young gentleman like Le Gardeur de Repentigny!"

On her return home, Amelie threw herself on the neck of her Aunt, repeating in broken accents, "My poor Le Gardeur! My brother! He refuses to see me Aunt! He is lost and ruined in that den of all iniquity and falsehood."

"Be composed Amelie!" replied the Lady de Tilly, "I know it is hard to bear, but perhaps Le Gardeur did not send that message to you. The men about him are capable of deceiving you to an extent you have no conception of, you who know so little of the worlds baseness."

"O Aunt it is true! He sent me this dreadful thing and I took it, for it bears the handwriting of my brother."

She held in her hand a card one of a pack. It was the deathcard of superstitious lookers into futurity. Had he selected it because it bore that reputation or was it by chance?—

On the back of it, he had written or scrawled in a trembling hand yet plainly, the words, "Return home Amelie! I will not see you! I have lost the game of life and won the card you see. Return home dear sister! and forget your unworthy and ruined brother Le Gardeur—!"

Lady de Tilly took the card and read and reread it, trying to find a meaning it did not contain, and trying not to find the sad meaning it did contain.

She comforted Amelie as best she could, while needing strength herself to bear the bitter cross laid upon them both, in the sudden blighting of that noble life of which they had been so proud.

She took Amelie in her arms, mingling her own tears with her's, and bidding her not despair, "A sisters love," said she, "never forgets, never wearies, never despairs." They had friends too powerfull to be withstood even by Bigot and the Intendant would be compelled to loosen his hold upon Le Gardeur. She would rely upon the inherent nobleness of the nature of Le Gardeur himself, to wash itself pure of all stain, could they only withdraw him from the seductions of the Palace. "We will win him from them, by counter charms Amelie! and it will be seen that virtue is stronger than vice to conquer at last, the heart of Le Gardeur."

"Alas! Aunt!" replied the poor girl, her eyes suffused with tears "neither friend nor foe will avail to turn him from the way he has resolved to go. He is desperate and rushes with open eyes upon his ruin. We know the reason of it all! There is but one, who could have saved Le Gardeur if she would! She is utterly unworthy of my brother, but I feel now it were better Le Gardeur had married even her, than that he should be utterly lost to himself and us all! I will see Angelique des Meloises myself. It was her summons brought him back to the city. She alone can withdraw him from the vile companionship of Bigot and his associates at the Palace."

Angelique had been duly informed of the return of Amelie to the city and of her fruitless visits to the Palace to see her brother.

It was no pleasure but a source of angry disappointment to Angelique that Le Gardeur in despair of making her his wife, refused to devote himself to her as her lover. He was running wild to destruction, instead of letting her win the husband she aspired to, and retain at the same time the gallant she loved and was not willing to forego.

She had seen him at the first sober moment after his return from Tilly in obedience to her summons. She had permitted him to pour out again his passion at her feet. She had yielded to his kisses when he claimed her heart, and hand, and had not refused to own the mutual flame that covered her cheek with a blush at her own falseness. But driven to the wall by his impetuosity she had at last killed his reviving hopes by her repetition of the fatal words "I love you Le Gardeur but I will not marry you!—"

Let justice be done to Angelique. It was hard even for her to repeat those words, but her resolution once taken could not be overthrown. There was no base of real feeling in her nature upon which to rest the lever that moves other women to change with pardonable inconsistencies. Angelique was by impulse true, by deliberate calculation false and immovable.

It was in vain that Le Gardeur pleaded with her. He touched her sympathy the nearest that any mortal man could do, but her sympathy was a hard polished surface. Her heart was impenetrable to true love. It was cold as marble and empty of all save idols of vanity frivolity and utter selfishness. It could reflect love as from a mirror but never felt its true warmth stirring within.

Angelique was seized with a sudden impulse to withdraw from the presence of Amelie in the Cathedral, before being discovered by her. She was half afraid, that her former school companion would speak to her on the subject of Le Gardeur. She could not brazen it out with Amelie who knew her too well, and if she could, she would gladly avoid the angry flash of those dark pure eyes which looked through and through you like the eyes of Gods cherubim which see within and without.

Amelie was to the imagination of Angelique an embodiment of spiritual forces which she could never comprehend, but which she knew to be irresistible in any combat with falsehood and deceit. On more than one occasion Angelique's hardihood had quailed and broken down before the quiet moral strength of Amelie de Repentigny.

The organ was pealing the last notes of the doxology and the voices of the choristers seemed to reecho from the depths of eternity the words "*in sæcula sæculorum*," when Angelique rose up suddenly to leave the church.

Her irreverent haste caused those about her to turn their heads at the slight confusion she made, Amelie among the rest, who recognized at once the countenance of Angelique somewhat flushed and irritated, as she strove vainly with the help of La Force to get out of the throng of kneeling people who covered the broad floor of the Cathedral.

Amelie deemed it a fortunate chance to meet Angelique so opportunely just when her desire to do so was strongest. She caught her eye, and made her a quick sign to stay, and approaching her seized her hands in her old affectionate way.

"Wait a few moments Angelique!" said she, "until the people depart. I want to speak to you alone. I am so fortunate to find you here."

"I will see you outside Amelie! The Sieur La Force is with me and cannot stay." Angelique dreaded an interview with Amelie.

"No, I will speak to you here. It will be better here in Gods temple than elsewhere. The Sieur La Force will wait for you if you ask him, or shall I ask him?" A faint smile accompanied these words of Amelie which she partly addressed to La Force.

La Force to Angeliques chagrin, understanding that Amelie desired him to wait for Angelique outside at once offered to do so.

"Or perhaps," continued Amelie, offering her hand, "the Sieur La Force whom I am glad to see will have the politeness to accompany the Lady de Tilly while I speak to Mademoiselle des Meloises."

La Force was all compliance. "He was quite at the service of the Ladies," he said politely, "and would esteem it an honour to accompany the noble Lady de Tilly."

The Lady de Tilly at once saw through the design of her niece. She acceded to the arrangement and left the Cathedral in company with the Sieur La Force whom she knew as the son of an old and valued friend.

He accompanied her home while Amelie holding fast to the arm of Angelique until the church was empty of all but a few scattered devotees and penitents, led her into a side chapel separated from the body of the church by a screen of carved work of oak, wherin stood a small altar and a reliquary with a picture of St Paul.

The seclusion of this place commended itself to the

feelings of Amelie. She made Angelique kneel down by her side before the altar. After breathing a short silent prayer for help and guidance, she seized her companion by both hands and besought her "in Gods name to tell her what she had done to Le Gardeur who was ruining himself both soul and body?"

Angelique, hardy as she was, could ill bear the searching gaze of those pure eyes. She quailed under them for a moment, afraid that the question might have some reference to Beaumanoir, but reassured by the words of Amelie that her interview had relation to Le Gardeur only, she replied,

"I have done nothing to make Le Gardeur ruin himself soul or body, Amelie! Nor do I believe he is doing so. Our old Convent notions are too narrow to take out with us into the world. You judge Le Gardeur too rigidly, Amelie!—"

"Would that were my fault Angelique!" replied she earnestly "but my heart tells me he is lost unless those who led him astray remit him again into the path of virtue whence they seduced him."

Angelique winced, for she took the allusion to herself, although in the mind of Amelie it referred more to the Intendant. "Le Gardeur is no weakling to be led astray" replied she. "He is a strong man to lead others not to be led as I know better than even his sister!—"

Amelie looked up inquiringly, but Angelique did not pursue the thought nor explain the meaning of her words.

"Le Gardeur," continued Angelique "is not worse, nay with all his faults is far better than most young gallants who have the laudable ambition to make a figure in the world such as women admire. One cannot hope to find men saints and we women be such sinners! Saints would be dull companions. I prefer mere men, Amelie!"

"For shame Angelique! to say such things before the sacred shrine!" exclaimed Amelie indignantly stopping her. "What wonder that men are wicked when women tempt them to be so! Le Gardeur was like none of the gallants you compare him with. He loved virtue and hated vice, and above all things he despised the companionship of such men as now detain him at the Palace. You first took him from me, Angelique! and I ask you to give him back to me. Give me back my brother, Angelique des Meloises!" Amelie grasped her by the arm in the earnestness of her appeal.

"I took him from you!" exclaimed Angelique hotly. "It is untrue! Forgive my saying so Amelie! I took him no more than did Heloise de Lotbiniere or Cecile Tourangeau! Will you hear the truth? He fell in love with me and I had not the heart to repulse him, nay, I could not, for I will confess to you, Amelie as I often avowed to you in the Convent, I loved Le Gardeur, the best of all my admirers! and by this blessed shrine!" continued she laying her hand upon it, "I do still! If he be, as some say he is, going too fast, for his own good or yours or mine, I regret it, with my whole heart! I regret it as you do! can I say more?"

Angelique was sincere in this. Her words sounded honest and she spoke with a real warmth in her bosom such as she had not felt in a long time.

Her words impressed Amelie favorably. "I think you speak truly Angelique!" replied she, "when you say, you regret Le Gardeur's relapse into the evil ways of the Palace. No one that ever knew my noble brother could do other than regret it! But O Angelique! Why with all your influence over him did not you prevent it? Why do you not rescue him now? a word from you would have been of more avail than the pleading of all the world beside!"

"Amelie you try me hard," said Angelique uneasily conscious of the truth of Amelie's words, "but I can bear much for the sake of Le Gardeur! Be assured that I have no power to influence his conduct in the way of amendment except upon impossible conditions! I have tried and my efforts have been vain as your own!"

"Conditions!—" replied Amelie, "what conditions?—but I need not ask you! He told me in his hour of agony of your inexplicable dealing with him, and yet not so inexplicable now! Why did you profess to love my brother leading him on and on to an offer of his hand, and then cruelly reject him adding one more to the list of your heartless triumphs? Le

Gardeur de Repentigny was too good for such a fate from any woman, Angelique!" Amelie's eyes shed tears of indignation as she said this.

"He was too good for me!" said Angelique drooping her eyes. "I will acknowledge that, if it will do you any good Amelie! But can you not believe that there was a sacrifice on my part as well as on his or yours?—"

"I judge not between you Angelique! or between the many chances wasted on you, but I say this O Angelique des Meloises! You wickedly stole the heart of the noblest brother in New France to trample it under your feet—!"

"Fore God! I did not Amelie!" she replied indignantly "I loved and do love Le Gardeur de Repentigny, but I never plighted my troth to him. I never deceived him! I told him I loved him but I could not marry him! and by this sacred cross," said she placing her hands upon it "It is true! I never trampled upon the heart of Le Gardeur. I could kiss his hands, his feet with true affection as ever loving woman gave to man but my duty—my troth—my fate—was in the hands of another!—"

Angelique felt a degree of pleasure in the confession to Amelie of her love for her brother. It was the next thing to confessing it to himself, which had been once the joy of her life, but it changed not one jot her determination to wed only the Intendant—unless—yes! her busy mind had to day called up a thousand possible and impossible contingencies that might spring up out of the unexpected use of the stiletto by La Corriveau. "What if the Intendant suspecting her complicity in the murder of Caroline should refuse to marry her? Were it not well in that desperate case to have Le Gardeur to fall back upon? He would take her at a word, nay she flattered herself, that he would take her believing her denial of guilt against the conviction of all the world."

If the golden arrow missed the target, she would hit it with the silver one, and her mind misgave her sometimes, that it might be almost as pleasant to marry the man she loved for his own sake, as the man she wanted for sake of his rank and riches.

Amelie watched nervously the changing countenance

of Angelique. She knew it was a beautiful mask covering impenetrable deceit, and that no principle of right kept her from wrong, when wrong was either pleasant or profitable. A man had better trust his naked hand in the mouth of a wolf than his true heart in the keeping of Angelique.

The conviction came upon Amelie like a flash of inspiration, that she was wrong in seeking to save Le Gardeur by seconding his wild offer of marriage to Angelique. A union with this false and capricious woman would only make his ruin more complete and his latter end worse than the first. "She would not urge it," she thought.

"Angelique!" said she, "If you love Le Gardeur you will not refuse your help to rescue him from the Palace. You cannot wish to see him degraded as a gentleman because he has been rejected by you as a lover."

"Who says I wish to see him degraded as a gentleman? and I did not reject him as a lover! not finally that is! I did not wholly mean it. When I sent to invite his return from Tilly It was out of friendship, love if you will Amelie, but from no desire that he should plunge into fresh dissipation."

"I believe you Angelique! You could not if you had the heart of a woman who loved him ever so little desire to see him fall into the clutches of men who with the wine cup in one hand and the dice box in the other, will never rest untill they ruin him body soul and estate."

"Before God! I never desired it and to prove it, I have cursed De Pean to his face and erased Lantagnac from my list of friends, for coming to show me the money he had won from Le Gardeur while intoxicated. Lantagnac brought me a set of pearls which he had purchased out of his winnings. I threw them in the fire and would have thrown him after them had I been a man! fore God! I would! Amelie! I may have wounded Le Gardeur but no other man or woman shall injure him with my consent!"

Angelique spoke this in a tone of sincerity that touched somewhat the heart of Amelie, although the aberrations and inconsistencies of this strange girl, perplexed one to the utmost to understand what she really felt.

"I think I may trust you Angelique, to help me to rescue him from association with the Palace," said Amelie gently almost submissively, as if she half feared a refusal.

"I desire nothing more!" replied Angelique. "You have little faith in me. I see that!" Angelique wiped her eyes, in which a shade of moisture could be seen "but I am sincere in my friendship for Le Gardeur. The Virgin being my witness, I never wished his injury even when I injured him most. He sought me in marriage and I was bound to another!"

"You are to marry the Intendant they say! I do not wonder and—yet I do wonder at your refusing my brother even for him—!"

"Marry the Intendant! Yes it is what fools and some wise people say. I never said it myself, Amelie."

"But you mean it nevertheless and for no other would you have thrown over Le Gardeur de Repentigny."

"I did not throw him over!" she answered indignantly. "But why dispute? I cannot Amelie say more even to you! I am distraught with cares and anxieties and know not which way to turn."

"Turn here! where I turn in my troubles Angelique!" replied Amelie moving closer to the altar. "Let us pray for Le Gardeur." Angelique obeyed mechanically and the two girls prayed silently for a few moments but how differently in spirit and feeling. The one prayed for her brother. The other tried to pray, but it was more for herself—for safety in her crime and success in her deep laid scheming. A prayer for Le Gardeur mingled with Angelique's devotions giving them a colour of virtue. Her desire for his wellfare was sincere enough and she thought it disinterested of herself to pray for him.

Suddenly Angelique started up as if stung by a wasp, "I must take leave of you, my Amelie!" said she. "I am glad I met you dear! I trust you understand me now, and rely on my being as a sister to Le Gardeur, to do what I can to restore him perfect to you and the good Lady de Tilly."

Amelie was touched. She embraced Angelique, and kissed her, yet so cold and impassive she felt her to be, a shiver ran through her as she did so. It was as if she had touched the dead, and she long afterwards thought of it. There was a mystery in this strange girl, that Amelie could not fathom nor guess the meaning of. They left the Cathedral together. It was now quite empty, save of a lingering penitent or two kneeling at the shrines. Angelique and Amelie parted at the door, the one eastward the other westward, and carried away by the divergent currents of their lives, they never met again.

CHAPTER 48

THE INTENDANT'S DILEMMA

"DID I not know for a certainty that she was present till midnight at the party given by Madame de Grandmaison I should suspect her *by God!*" exclaimed the Intendant as he paced up and down his private room in the Palace, angry and perplexed to the uttermost over the mysterious assassination at Beaumanoir. "What think you Cadet?—"

"I think that proves an *alibi!*" replied Cadet stretching himself lazily in an armchair and smoking with half shut eyes. There was a cynical mocking tone in his voice which seemed to imply that although it proved an *Alibi* it did not prove innocence to the satisfaction of the Sieur Cadet.

"You think more than you say Cadet! Out with it! Let me hear the worst of your suspicions. I fancy they chime with mine," said the Intendant in quick reply.

"As the bells of the Cathedral with the bells of the Recollets!" drawled out Cadet. "I think she did it, Bigot! and you think the same! but I should not like to be called upon to prove it nor you either! not for the sake of the pretty witch, but for your own."

"I could prove nothing, Cadet! She was the gayest and most lighthearted of all the company last night at Madame de Grandmaison's! I have made the most particular inquiries of Varin and Deschenaux. They needed no asking but burst out at once into praise and admiration of her gaiety and wit. It is certain she was not at Beaumanoir."

"You often boasted you knew women better than I, and I yielded the point in regard to Angelique," replied Cadet, refilling his pipe. "I did not profess to fathom the depth of that girl but I thought you knew her! Egad! She has been too clever for you Bigot! She has aimed to be the Lady Intendant and is in a fair way to succeed! That girl has the spirit of a war horse. She would carry any man round the world! I wish she would carry me! I would rule Versailles in six weeks with that woman, Bigot!—"

"The same thought has occurred to me, Cadet, and I might have been entrapped by it, had not this cursed affair happened! La Pompadour is a simpleton beside Angelique des Meloises! My difficulty is to believe her so mad as to have ventured on this bold deed."

"Tis not the boldness, only the uselessness of it, would stop Angelique!—" answered Cadet shutting one eye with an air of lazy comfort.

"But the deceitfulness of it! Cadet! A girl like her could not be so gay last night with such a bloody purpose on her soul. Could she think you?"

"Couldnt she! Tut! Deceit is every woman's nature! Her wardrobe is not complete unless it contains as many lies for her occasions as ribbons for her adornment."

"You believe she did it then? What makes you think so Cadet?" asked Bigot eagerly, drawing near his companion.

"Why she and you are the only persons on earth who had an interest in that girls death! she to get a dangerous rival out of the way, you to hide her from the search warrants sent out by La Pompadour. You did not do it, I know, *ergo*, she did! Can any logic be plainer? That is the reason I think so Bigot!"

"But how has it been accomplished Cadet? Have you any theory? She can not have done it with her own hand!"

"Why there is only one way that I can see. We know she did not do the murder herself—therefor she has done it by the hand of another! Here is proof of a confederate Bigot! I picked this up in the secret chamber."

Cadet drew out of his pocket the fragment of the letter torn in pieces by La Corriveau. "Is this the handwriting of Angelique?—" asked he.

Bigot seized the scrap of paper read it, turned it over and scrutinized it, striving to find resemblances between the writing and that of every one known to him. His scrutiny was in vain.

"This writing is not Angelique's," said he. "It is utterly unknown to me! It is a woman's hand, but certainly not the hand of any woman of my acquaintance, and I have letters and billets from almost every lady in Quebec! It is proof of a confederate however, for listen, Cadet! It arranges for an interview with Caroline poor girl! It was thus she was betrayed to her death. It is torn, but enough remains to make the sense clear. Listen!"

"At the arched door about midnight—if she pleased to admit her she would learn important matters concerning herself, the Intendant and the Baron de St Castin—speedily arrive in the Colony— — —"

"That throws light upon the mystery Cadet! A woman was to have an interview with Caroline at midnight! Good God! Cadet! not two hours before we arrived! and we deferred starting in order that we might rook the Seigneur de Port Neuf! too late! too late! O! cursed word that ever seals our fate when we propose a good deed!" and Bigot felt himself a man injured and neglected by providence.

"'Important matters relating to herself'," repeated Bigot reading again the scrap of writing. "'The Intendant and the Baron de St Castin—speedily to arrive in the Colony.' No one knew but the sworn councillors of the Governor that the Baron de St Castin was coming out to the Colony! A woman has done the deed! and she has been informed of the secrets spoken in Council by some councillor present on that day at the Castle. Who was he? and who was she?—" questioned Bigot excitedly.

"The argument runs like water down hill, Bigot But *Par Dieu!* I would not have believed that New France contained two women of such mettle as the one to contrive, the other to execute a masterpiece of devilment like that!—"

"Since we find another hand in the dish, it may not have been Angelique after all!" remarked Bigot. "It is hard to believe one so fair and free spoken, guilty of so dark and damnable a crime." Bigot would evidently be glad to find himself in error touching his suspicions.

"Fairest without, is often foulest within Bigot!" answered Cadet doggedly. "Open speech in a woman is often an open trap to catch fools! Angelique des Meloises is free spoken and open handed enough to deceive a conclave of Cardinals! But she has the lightest heels in the City. Would you not like to see her dance a Ballet de Triomphe on the broad flag stone I laid over the grave of that poor girl? If you would, you have only to marry her, and she will give a ball in the secret chamber!"

"Be still Cadet! I could take you by the throat, for suggesting it! but I will make her prove herself innocent," exclaimed Bigot angry at the cool persistence of Cadet.

"I hope you will not try it to day, Bigot!" Cadet spoke gravely now. "Let the dead sleep and let all sleeping dogs and bitches lie still! Zounds! We are in greater danger than she is! You cannot stir in this matter without putting yourself in her power. Angelique has got hold of the secret of Caroline and of the Baron de St Castin! What if she clear herself by accusing you? The King would put you in the Bastile for the magnificent lie you told the Governor and La Pompadour would send you to the Place de Greve when the Baron de St Castin returns with the bones of his daughter dug up in your Chateau!—"

"It is a cursed dilemma!" Bigot fairly writhed with perplexity, "and dark as the bottomless pit turn which way we will. Angelique knows too much! that is clear!—It were a charity if it were a safe thing, to kill her too, Cadet!—"

"Not to be thought of Bigot! She is too much in every man's eye, and not stowed away in a secret corner like her poor victim! A dead silence on every point of this cursed business is our only policy, our only safety!—" Cadet had plenty of common sense in the rough, and Bigot was able to appreciate it.

The Intendant strode up and down the room clenching his hands in a fury. "If I were sure! sure! she did it, I would kill her by God! such a damnable cruel deed as this would justify any measure of vengeance," exclaimed he savagely.

"Pshaw! not when it would all rebound upon yourself. Besides if you want vengeance take a man's revenge upon a woman. You can do that! It will be better than killing her, much more pleasant and quite as effectual—!—"

Bigot looked as Cadet said this, and laughed "You would send her to the *Parc aux cerfs*, eh Cadet? Par Dieu! She would sit on the throne in six months!"

"No, I do not mean the *Parc aux cerfs*, but the Chateau of Beaumanoir! But you are in too ill humour to joke to day Bigot!" Cadet resumed his pipe and an air of nonchalance.

"I never was in a worse humour in my life! Cadet! I feel that I have a padlock upon every one of my five senses, and I cannot move hand or foot in this business."

"Right! Bigot! Do not move hand or foot eye or tongue in it! I tell you, the slightest whisper of Caroline's life or death in your house, reaching the ears of Philibert, or La Corne St Luc will bring them to Beaumanoir with warrants to search for her. They will pick the Chateau to pieces stone by stone. They will drag Caroline out of her grave and the whole country will swear you murdered her! and that I helped you! and with appearances so strong against us, that the mothers who bore us would not believe in our innocence! Damn the women! The burying of that girl was the best deed I did for one of the sex in my life! but it will be the worst, if you breathe one word of it to Angelique des Meloises, or to any other person living! I am not ready to lose my head yet Bigot! For sake of any woman, or even for you!—"

The Intendant was staggered by the vehemence of Cadet, and impressed by the force of his remarks. It was hard to sit down quietly and condone such a crime, but, he saw clearly the danger of pushing inquiry in any direction without turning suspicion upon himself! He boiled with indignation. He fumed and swore worse than his wont, when angry. But Cadet looked on quietly smoking his pipe waiting for the storm to calm down.

"You were never in a womans clutches so tight before Bigot!" continued Cadet. "If you let La Pompadour suspect one hair of your head in this matter, she will spin a cart rope out of it that will drag you to the Place de Greve."

"Reason tells me that what you say is true, Cadet," replied

Bigot gloomily.

"To be sure! but is not Angelique a clever witch to bind Francois Bigot neck and heels in that way, after fairly outwitting and running him down—?"

Cadet's cool comments drove Bigot beside himself. "I will not stand it by St Maur! She shall pay for all this! I who have caught women all my life, to be caught by one thus! She shall pay for it!—"

"Well make her pay for it by marrying her!" replied Cadet. "*Par Dieu!* I am mistaken if you have not got to marry her in the end! I would marry her myself if you do not—only I should be afraid to sleep nights! I might be put under the floor before morning if she liked, another man better!—"

Cadet gave way to a feeling of hilarity at this idea, shaking his sides so long and heartily that Bigot caught the infection, and joined in with a burst of sardonic laughter.

Bigots laughter was soon over, he sat down at the table again and being now calm considered the whole matter over point by point with Cadet who coarse and unprincipled, was a shrewd councillor in difficulties.

It was determined between the two men that nothing whatever should be said of the assassination. Bigot should continue his gallantries to Angelique and avoid all show of suspicion in that quarter. He should tell her of the disappearance of Caroline, who had gone away mysteriously as she came, but profess absolute ignorance as to her fate.

Angelique would be equally cautious in alluding to the murder. She would pretend to accept all his statements as absolute fact. Her tongue if not her thoughts would be sealed up in perpetual silence on that bloody topic. Bigot must feed her with hopes of marriage and if necessary set a day for it far enough off, to cover all the time to be taken up in the search after Caroline.

"I will never marry her Cadet!" exclaimed Bigot, "but will make her regret all her life she did not marry me!—"

"Take care Bigot! It is dangerous playing with fire—you dont half know Angelique!"

"I mean she shall pull the chesnuts out of the fire for

me with her pretty fingers, even if she burn them," remarked Bigot gruffly.

"I would not trust her too far! In all seriousness you have but a choice of two things, Bigot, marry her or send her to the convent!—"

"I would not do the one, and I could not do the other, Cadet!" was Bigot's prompt reply to this suggestion.

"Tut! Mere Migeon de la Nativité will respect your *lettre de cachet*, and provide a close comfortable cell for this pretty penitent in the Ursuline's," said Cadet.

"Not she! Mere Migeon gave me one of her parlour lectures once, and I care not for another! Egad, Cadet! She made me the nearest of being ashamed of Francois Bigot of any one I ever listened to! Could you have seen her with her veil thrown back, her pale face still paler with indignation, her black eyes looking still blacker beneath the white fillet upon her forehead, and then her tongue Cadet! Well, I withdrew my proposal and felt myself rather cheapened in the presence of Mere Migeon."

"Aye! I hear she is a clipper when she gets a sinner by the hair! What was the proposal you made to her Bigot?" asked Cadet smiling as if he knew.

"Oh! It was not worth a livre to make such a row about! I only proposed to send a truant damsel to the Convent, to repent of *my* faults! that was all! Mere Migeon fired up. She would not be gaoler for the King! she said. It was in vain, I talked of La Valiere, and threatened her with the bishop. She set me at defiance and bade me go marry the girl instead of trying to make a nun of her!—"

"But you carried your point. Did you not? She took her in at last!"

"Not for my account Cadet! Poor Lucille went in at last of her own accord. The sympathizing nuns all cried over her and pleaded upon their knees to the Mere Superior so long and so hard that she relented and took her in, but Mere Migeon indignantly refused the dowry I offered with her. My little nun is now as happy as a lamb in a meadow! and I think as innocent! for it was all my fault, Cadet! was that adventure."

"You could never say that of Angelique, Bigot!" replied Cadet, laughing "Egad! she will fool any man faster than he can make a fool of her! but I would try Mere Migeon notwithstanding. She is the only one to break in this wild filly and nail her tongue fast to her prayers!"

"It is useless trying! they know Angelique too well! She would turn the convent out of the windows in the time of a Novaine! They are all really afraid of her!" replied Bigot.

"Then you must marry her or do worse, Bigot. I see nothing else for it," was Cadets reply.

"Well I will do worse if worse can be! For marry her I will not!—" said Bigot stamping his foot upon the floor.

"It is understood then Bigot! not a word, a hint, a look is to be given to Angelique regarding your suspicions of her complicity in this murder—?"

"Yes it is understood! The secret is like the Devils Tontine. He catches the last possessor of it."

"I expect to be the last then, if I keep in your company, Bigot!—" remarked Cadet.

Cadet having settled this point to his mind reclined back in his easy chair and smoked on in silence while the Intendant kept walking the floor anxiously because he saw farther than his companion, the shadows of coming events.

Sometimes he stopped impatiently at the window beating a tattoo with his nails on the polished casement as he gazed out upon the beautiful parterres of autumnal flowers beginning to shed their petals around the gardens of the palace. He looked at them without seeing them. All that caught his eye was a bare rose bush, from which he remembered he had plucked some white roses, which he had sent to Caroline to adorn her oratory, and he thought of her face more pale and delicate than any rose of Provence that ever bloomed. His thoughts ran violently in two parallel streams side by side, neither of them disappearing for a moment, amid the crowd of other affairs that pressed upon his attention—the murder of Caroline and the perquisition that was to be made for her in all quarters of the Colony. His own safety was too deeply involved in any discovery that might be made respecting her, to allow him to drop the subject out of thought for a moment.

By imposing absolute silence, upon himself in the presence of Angelique touching the death of Caroline, he might impose a like silence upon her whom he could not acquit of the suspicion of having prompted the murder; but the certainty that there was a confederate in the deed, a woman too, judging by the fragments of writing picked up by Cadet, tormented him with endless conjectures.

Still he felt, for the present secure from any discovery on that side; but how to escape from the sharp inquisition of two men like La Corne St Luc and Pierre Philibert? and who knew how far the secret of Beaumanoir was a secret any longer? It was known to two women at any rate, and no woman in Bigot's estimation of the sex would long keep a secret which concerned another and not herself.

"Our greatest danger Cadet! lies there!" continued the Intendant stopping in his walk, and turning suddenly to his friend. "La Corne St Luc and Pierre Philibert are commissioned by the Governor to search for that girl! They will not leave a stone unturned, a corner unransacked in New France. They will find out through the Hurons and my own servants that a woman has been concealed in Beaumanoir. They will suspect if they do not discover who she was. They will not find her on earth and will look for her under the earth, and by St Maur! it makes me quake to think of it Cadet! for the discovery will be utter ruin! They may at last dig up her murdered remains in my own Chateau! As you said the Bastile and the Place de Greve would be my portion and ruin yours, and that of all our associates."

Cadet held up his pipe as if appealing to heaven—: "It is a cursed reward for our charitable nights work, Bigot!" said he "Better you had never lied about the girl! We could have brazened it out or fought it out with the Baron de St Castin or any man in France!—That lie will convict us if found out!"

"Pshaw! the lie was a necessity," answered Bigot impatiently. "But who could have dreamed of its leading us such a dance as it has done! *Par Dieu!* I have not often lied except to women and such lies do not count! But I had better have stuck to truth in this matter, Cadet. I acknowledge that now."

"Especially with La Pompadour! She is a woman. It is dangerous to lie to her at least about other women."

"Well Cadet! It is useless blessing the Pope or banishing the devil! We are in for it. And we must meet La Corne St Luc and Pierre Philibert as warily as we can! I have been thinking of making safe ground for us to stand upon, as the trappers do on the great Prairies by kindling a fire in front to escape from the fire in the rear!"

"What is that Bigot? I could fire the Chateau, rather than be tracked out by La Corne and Philibert!—" said Cadet sitting upright in his chair.

"What burn the Chateau!" answered Bigot. "You are mad Cadet! No! but it were well to kindle such a smoke about the eyes of La Corne and Philibert that they will need to rub them to ease their own pain instead of looking for poor Caroline."

"How Bigot! will you challenge and fight them? That will not avert suspicion but increase it!" remarked Cadet.

"Well, you will see! A man will need as many eyes as Argus to discover our hands in this business."

Cadet started without conjecturing what the Intendant contemplated. "You will kill the bird that tells tales on us Bigot, is that it?" asked he.

"I mean to kill two birds with one stone Cadet! hark you; I will tell you a scheme shall put a stop to these perquisitions by La Corne and Philibert—the only two men I fear in the Colony. And at the same time deliver me from the everlasting bark and bite of the Golden Dog."

Bigot led Cadet to the window and poured in his ear the burning passions which were fermenting in his own breast. He propounded a scheme of deliverance for himself and of crafty vengeance upon the Philiberts which would turn the thoughts of every one away from the Chateau of Beaumanoir and the missing Caroline, into a new stream of public and private troubles. Amid the confusion of which he would escape, and his present dangers be overlooked and forgotten in a great Catastrophe that might upset the Colony but at any rate it would free Bigot from his embarrassments and perhaps inaugurate a new reign of public plunder and the suppression of the whole party of the *Honnetes Gens*.

CHAPTER 49

"I WILL FEED FAT THE ANCIENT GRUDGE I BEAR HIM"

THE treaty of Aix La Chapelle so long tossed about in the storm of war was finally signed in the beginning of October. A swift sailing Goelette of Dieppe brought the tidings to New France and in the early nights of November from Quebec to Montreal bonfires on every headland blazed over the broad river. Churches were decorated with evergreens and *Te Deums* sung in gratitude for the return of peace and security to the Colony.

New France came out of the struggle scathed and scorched as by fire, but unshorn of territory or territorial rights, and the glad Colonists forgot and forgave the terrible sacrifices they had made, in the universal joy their country, their religion, language and laws were still safe, under the Crown of France with the white banner still floating over the Castle of St Louis.

On the day after the arrival of the Dieppe Goelette bringing the news of peace, Bigot sat before his desk amid his despatches and letters from France when the Chevalier De Pean entered the room with a bundle of papers in his hand brought to the Palace by the chief clerk of the Bourgeois Philibert for the Intendants signature.

The Bourgeois in the course of his great commercial dealings got possession of innumerable orders upon the Royal Treasury which in due course had to be presented to the Intendant for his official signature. The signing of these Treasury orders in favour of the Bourgeois never failed to throw Bigot into a fit of ill humour.

On the present occasion he sat down muttering ten thousand curses upon the Bourgeois, as he glanced over the papers with knitted eyebrows and teeth set hard together. He

616

signed the mass of orders and drafts made payable to Nicholas Philibert and when done threw into the fire the pen which had performed so unwelcome an office.

Bigot sent for the chief clerk who had brought the bills and orders and who waited for them in the ante chamber. "Tell your master, the Bourgeois," said he, "that for this time and only to prevent loss to the foolish officers, the Intendant has signed these army bills, and that if he purchase more in defiance of the sole right of the Grand Company I shall not sign them. This shall be the last time tell him!"

The Chief Clerk, a sturdy grey haired Malouin, was nothing daunted by the angry look of the Intendant. "I shall inform the Bourgeois of your Excellency's wishes" said he, "and— —."

"Inform him of my commands!—" exclaimed Bigot sharply. "What! have you more to say? But you would not be the Chief Clerk of the Bourgeois without possessing a good stock of his insolence!—"

"Pardon me, your Excellency!" replied the Chief Clerk "I was only going to observe, that His Excellency the Governor and the Commander of the forces, both have decided that the officers may transfer their warrants to whom soever they will."—

"You are a bold fellow, with your Breton speech! but by all the Saints in Saintonge, I will see whether the Royal Intendant or the Bourgeois Philibert shall control this matter! And as for you— —"

"*Tut!* *Cave canem!*—let this cur go back to his master!" interrupted Cadet, amused at the coolness of the Chief Clerk. "Hark you fellow!" said he "present my compliments, the Sieur Cadet's compliments, to your master, and tell him, I hope he will bring his next batch of army bills himself, and remind him that it is soft falling at low tide out of the window of the Friponne!"

"I shall certainly advise my master not to come, himself, Sieur Cadet!—" replied the Chief Clerk, "and I am very certain of returning in three days with more army bills, for the signature of his Excellency the Intendant."

"Get out you fool!" shouted Cadet laughing at what he regarded the insolence of the Clerk "You are worthy of your master!" and Cadet pushed him forcibly out of the door and shut it after him with a bang that resounded through the palace.

"Don't be angry at him Bigot! he is not worth it," said Cadet. "'Like master like man!' as the proverb says. And after all I doubt whether the furred law cats of the Parliament of Paris would not uphold the Bourgeois on an appeal to them from the Golden Dog."

Bigot was excessively irritated, for he was lawyer enough to see that Cadet's fear was well founded. He walked up and down his cabinet venting curses upon the heads of the whole party of the *Honnetes Gens*, the Governor and commander of the forces included.

The Marquise de Pompadour too came in for a full share of his maledictions, for Bigot knew that she had forced the signing of the treaty of Aix la Chapelle influenced less by the exhaustion of France than by a feminine dislike to camp life, which she had shared with the King and a resolution to withdraw him back to the gaieties of the Capital where he would be wholly under her own eye and influence.

"She prefers love to honour, as all women do," remarked Bigot "and likes money better than either! The Grand Company pays the fiddlers for the Royal fetes at Versailles! While the Bourgeois Philibert skims the cream off the trade of the Colony! While Peace will increase his power and influence double what it already is!"

"Egad Bigot!" replied Cadet who sat near him smoking a large pipe of tobacco "you speak like a preacher in Lent! We have hitherto buttered our bread on both sides, but the company will soon I fear have no bread to butter! I doubt we shall have to eat your decrees which will be the only things left in the possession of the Friponne!—"

"My decrees have been hard to digest for some people who think they will now eat us! Look at that pile of orders, Cadet, in favour of the Golden Dog—!"

The Intendant had long regarded with indignation

the ever increasing trade and influence of the Bourgeois Philibert, who had become the great banker as well as the great merchant of the Colony able to meet the Grand Compagny itself upon its own ground and fairly divide with it the interior as well as the exterior commerce of the Colony.

"Where is this thing going to end?" exclaimed Bigot, sweeping from him the pile of bills of exchange that lay upon the table. "That Philibert is gaining ground upon us every day! he is now buying up army bills and even the Kings officers are flocking to him with their certificates of pay and drafts on France, which he cashes at half the discount charged by the company!"

"Give the cursed papers to the clerk and send him off, De Pean!" said Bigot.

De Pean obeyed with a grimace, and returned.

"This thing must be stopped and shall!" continued the Intendant savagely.

"That is true, your Excellency!" said De Pean. "We have tried vigorously to stop the evil, but so far in vain. The Governor and the *Honnetes Gens* and too many of the Officers themselves countenance his opposition to the company. The Bourgeois draws a good bill upon Paris and Bourdeaux they are fast finding it out!"

"The Golden Dog is drawing half the money of the Colony into his coffers, and he will blow up the credit of the Friponne some fine day, when we least expect it, unless he be chained up!" replied Bigot.

"*A Mechant Chien court bien*! says the proverb and so say I," replied Cadet. "The Golden Dog has barked at us for a long time. *Par dieu!* he bites now! Ere long he will gnaw our bones in reality as he does in effigy, upon that cursed tablet in the Rue Buade."

"Every dog has its day! and the Golden Dog has nearly had his, Cadet! But what do you advise?—" asked Bigot.

"Hang him up with a short rope and a shorter shrift Bigot! You have warrant enough if your Court friends are worth half a handful of chaff."

"But they are not worth half a handful of chaff, Cadet!

If I hung the Bourgeois there would be such a cry raised among the *Honnetes Gens* in the Colony, and the whole tribe of Jansenists in France, that I doubt whether even the power of the Marquise could sustain me."

Cadet looked quietly truculent. He drew Bigot aside. "There are more ways than one to choke a dog, Bigot," said he. "You may put a tight collar outside his throat or a sweetened roll inside of it. Some course must be found, and that promptly. We shall before many days have La Corne St Luc and young Philibert like a couple of stag hounds in full cry at our heels about that business at the Chateau! They must be thrown off that scent, come what will, Bigot!"

The pressure of time and circumstance was drawing a narrower circle round the Intendant. The advent of peace would he believed, inaugurate a personal war against himself. The murder of Caroline was a hard blow and the necessity of concealing it irritated him with a sense of fear, foreign to his character.

His suspicion of Angelique tormented him day and night. He had loved Angelique in a sensual admiring way without one grain of real respect. He worshipped her one moment as the Aphrodite of his fancy. He was ready to strip and scourge her the next as the possible murderess of Caroline. But Bigot had fettered himself with a lie, and had to hide his thoughts under degrading concealments. He knew the Marquise de Pompadour was jealously watching him from afar. The sharpest intellects and most untiring men in the Colony were commissioned to find out the truth regarding the fate of Caroline. Bigot was like a stag brought to bay. An ordinary man would have succumbed in despair but the very desperation of his position stirred up the Intendant to a greater effort to free himself. He cared nothing for the morality or immorality of any course, if it only ensured success and brought safety!—

He walked gloomily up and down the room absorbed in deep thought. Cadet who guessed what was brooding in his mind made a sign to De Pean to wait and see what would be the result of his cogitations.

Bigot gesticulating with his right hand and his left, went on balancing as in a pair of scales the chances of success or failure in the blow he meditated against the Golden Dog, a blow which would scatter to the winds the inquisition set on foot to discover the hiding place of Caroline.

He stopped suddenly in his walk, striking both hands together as if in sign of some resolution arrived at in his thoughts.

"De Pean!" said he, "Has Le Gardeur de Repentigny shown any desire yet to break out of the palace?—"

"None your Excellency! He is fixed as a bridge to fortune. You can no more break him down than the *Pont Neuf* at Paris. He lost last night a thousand at cards and five hundred at dice, then drank himself dead drunk until three o'clock this afternoon. He has just risen. His valet was washing his head and feet with brandy when I came here."

"You are a friend that sticks closer than a brother De Pean. Le Gardeur believes in you as his guardian angel, does he not?" asked Bigot with a sneer.

"When he is drunk he does," replied De Pean, "when he is sober I care not to approach him too nearly! He is a wild colt that will kick his groom when rubbed the wrong way and every way is wrong when the wine is out of him!"

"Keep him full then!" exclaimed Bigot, "you have groomed him well, De Pean! but he must now be saddled and ridden to hunt down the biggest stag in New France!"

De Pean looked hard at the Intendant, only half comprehending his allusion, "You once tried your hand with Mademoiselle de Repentigny did you not?" continued Bigot—

"I did, your Excellency? but that bunch of grapes was too high for me. They are very sour now."

"Sly fox that you were? Well, do not call them sour yet, De Pean. Another jump at the vine and you may reach that bunch of perfection!" said Bigot, looking hard at him.

"Your Excellency overrates my ability in that quarter and if I were permitted to choose—"

"Another and a fairer maid would be your choice. I see, De Pean, you are a connoisseur in women. Be it as you wish!

manage this business of Philibert discreetly and I will coin the Golden Dog into doubloons for a marriage portion for Angelique des Meloises? You understand me now?"

De Pean started. He hardly guessed yet what was required of him, but he cared not in the dazzling prospect of such a wife and fortune, as were thus held out to him.

"Your Excellency will really support my suit with Angelique?" De Pean seemed to mistrust the possibility of such a piece of disinterestedness on the part of the Intendant.

"I will not only commend your suit, but I will give away the bride and Madame De Pean shall not miss any favour from me which she has deserved as Angelique des Meloises," was Bigots reply, without changing a muscle of his face.

"And your Excellency will give her to me?" De Pean could hardly believe his ears.

"Assuredly you shall have her if you like," cried Bigot "and with such a dowry as has not been seen in New France—!"

"But who would like to have her at any price?" muttered Cadet to himself with a quiet smile of contempt. Cadet thought De Pean a fool for jumping at a hook baited by a woman, but he knew what the Intendant was driving at and admired the skill with which he angled for De Pean! "But Angelique may not consent to this disposal of her hand" replied De Pean, with an uneasy look. "I should be afraid of your gift unless she believed that she took me, and not I her."

"Hark you De Pean! You do not know what women like her are made of, or you would be at no loss how to bait your hook! You have made four millions they say out of this war, if not more!"

"I never counted it your Excellency, but much or little I owe it all to your friendship," replied De Pean with a touch of mock humility.

"My friendship! Well, so be it! It is enough to make Angelique des Meloises Madame De Pean when she finds she cannot be Madame Intendant. Do you see your way now De Pean!"

"Yes! your Excellency, and I cannot be sufficiently grateful for such a proof of your goodness!"

Bigot laughed a dry meaning laugh. "I hope you will always think so of my friendship De Pean! If you do not, you are not the man I take you to be! Now for our scheme of deliverance!—"

"Hearken De Pean!" continued the Intendant fixing his dark fiery eyes upon his secretary. "You have craft and cunning to work out this design and good will to haste it on. Cadet and I considering the necessities of the Grand Company have resolved to put an end to the rivalry and arrogance of the Golden Dog. We will treat the Bourgeois"—Bigot smiled meaningly—"not as a trader with a baton, but as a gentleman with a sword!—for although a merchant the Bourgeois is noble and wears a sword which under proper provocation he will draw, and remember he can use it too! He can be tolerated no longer by the gentlemen of the Company. They have often pressed me in vain to take this step but I now yield. Hark De Pean! The Bourgeois must be *insulted, challenged* and *killed*! by some gentleman of the company, with courage and skill enough to champion its rights! But mind you! it must be done *fairly*, and in *open day* and without my knowledge or approval! Do you understand?"

Bigot winked at De Pean and smiled furtively as much as to say: "You know how to interpret my words!"

"I understand your Excellency! and it shall be no fault of mine if your wishes which chime with my own be not carried out before many days. A dozen partners of the Company will be proud to fight with the Bourgeois if he will only fight with them."

"No fear of that De Pean! Give the devil his due. Insult the Bourgeois and he will fight with the seven champions of christendom! so mind you get a man able for him! for I tell you De Pean, I doubt if there be over three gentlemen in the Colony who could cross swords fairly and successfully with the Bourgeois."

"It will be easier to insult and kill him in a chance medley than to risk a duel!" interrupted Cadet, who listened with intense eagerness, "I tell you Bigot! Young Philibert will pink any man of our party if there be a duel! and, he will insist on fighting it for his father. The old Bourgeois will not be caught, but we shall catch a tartar instead in the young one."

"Well duel or chance medley be it! I dare not have him assassinated," replied the Intendant, "he must be fought with in open day and not killed in a corner. Eh! Cadet am I not right?—"

Bigot looked for approval from Cadet, who saw that he was thinking of the secret chamber at Beaumanoir.

"You are right Bigot! He must be killed! in open day and not in a corner. But who have we among us capable of making sure work of the Bourgeois?"

"Leave it to me," replied De Pean! "I know one partner of the company who if I can get him in harness will run our chariot wheels in triumph over the Golden Dog."

"And who is that?" asked Bigot eagerly.

"Le Gardeur de Repentigny!" exclaimed De Pean with a look of exultation.

"Pshaw! he would draw upon us more readily! Why he is bewitched with the Philiberts," replied Bigot.

"I shall find means to break the spell long enough to answer our purpose, your Excellency!" replied De Pean. "Permit me only to take my own way with him."

"Assuredly take your own way De Pean! A bloody scuffle between De Repentigny and the Bourgeois would not only be a victory for the Company but would break up the whole party of the *Honnetes Gens*!"

The Intendant slapped De Pean on the shoulder and shook him by the hand. "You are more clever than I believed you to be De Pean! You have hit on a mode of riddance which will entitle you to the best reward in the power of the company to bestow."

"My best reward will be the fulfilment of your promise, your Excellency," answered De Pean.

"I will keep my word De Pean! By God you shall have Angelique with such a dowry as the company can alone give! or if you do not want the girl, you shall have the dowry without the wife!"

"I shall claim both, your Excellency but—"

"But what? confess all your doubts De Pean!"

"Le Gardeur may claim her as his own reward!" De Pean guessed correctly enough the true bent of Angelique's fancy.

"No fear! Le Gardeur de Repentigny drunk or sober is a gentleman. He would reject the Princess d'Elide were she offered on such conditions as you take her on! He is a romantic fool. He believes in womens virtue and all that stuff!"

"Besides if he kill the Bourgeois he will have to fight Pierre Philibert before his sword is dry!" interjected Cadet. "I would not give a Dutch stiver for Le Gardeur's bones five hours after he has pinked the Bourgeois!—"

The prospect, nay the certainty of a second duel between Le Gardeur and Pierre Philibert, should the Bourgeois be killed, satisfied all the doubts of De Pean, who felt himself secure in the reversion of Angelique and the rich dowry promised by the Intendant.

They were now all eager to set on foot the diabolical scheme of murder. These thorough men of the age, glossed over it as a legitimate compromise between honour and necessity. The Bourgeois was to be killed but in a way to reflect no discredit either upon the contrivers of his death or upon the unwitting instrument selected to accomplish it.

An open duel in form was not to be thought of, because in that they would have to fight the son and not the father, and the great object would be frustrated. But the Bourgeois might be killed in a sudden fray, when blood was up and swords drawn when no one, as De Pean remarked, would be able to find an *I* undotted or a *T* uncrossed in a fair record of the transaction which would impose upon the most critical judge as an honorable and justifiable act of self defence.

This was Cadets real intent, and perhaps Bigots, for the Intendant's thoughts lay at unfathomable depths, and were not to be discovered by any traces upon the surface. No divining rod could tell where the springs lay hid which ran through Bigot's motives.

Not so De Pean. He meditated treachery and it were hard to say, whether it was unnoted by the penetrating eye of Bigot.

The Intendant however did not interfere farther either by word or sign, but left De Pean to accomplish in his own way the bloody object they all had in view, namely the death of the Bourgeois and the break up of the *Honnetes Gens*. De Pean while resolving to make Le Gardeur the tool of his wickedness, did not dare to take him into his confidence. He had to be kept in absolute ignorance of the part he was to play in the bloody tragedy until the moment of its denouement arrived. Mean time he must be plyed with drink, maddened with jealousy, made desperate with losses and at war with himself and all the world, and then the whole fury of his rage should by the artful contrivance of De Pean, be turned without a minutes time for reflection, upon the head of the unsuspecting Bourgeois.

To accomplish this successfully a woman's aid was required, at once to blind Le Gardeur and to sharpen his sword.

In the interests of the company Angelique des Meloises was at all times a violent partizan. The Golden Dog and all its belongings were objects of her open aversion. But De Pean feared to impart to her his intention to push Le Gardeur blindly into the affair. She might fear for the life of one she loved. De Pean reflected angrily on this, but he determined she should be on the spot. The sight of her and a word from her, which De Pean would prompt at the critical moment, would decide Le Gardeur to attack the Bourgeois and kill him! and then!—what would follow? De Pean rubbed his hands with extacy at the thought that Le Gardeur would inevitably bite the dust under the avenging hand of Pierre Philibert, and Angelique would be his beyond all fear of rivals.

CHAPTER 50

THE BOURGEOIS PHILIBERT

THE Bourgeois Philibert after an arduous day's work was enjoying in his armchair a quiet siesta in the old comfortable parlour of his city home.

The sudden advent of peace had opened the seas to commerce and a fleet of long shut up merchantmen were rapidly loading at the quays of the Friponne as well as at those of the Bourgeois, with the products of the Colony for shipment to France before the closing in of the St Lawrence by ice. The summer of St Martin was lingering soft and warm on the edge of winter, and every available man, including the soldiers of the garrison, were busy loading the ships to get them off in time to escape the hard nip of winter.

Dame Rochelle sat near the window, which today was open to the balmy air. She was occupied in knitting and occasionally glancing at a volume of Jurieu's hard Calvinistic divinity which lay upon the table beside her. Her spectacles reposed upon the open page where she had laid them down while she meditated, as was her custom, upon knotty points of doctrine, touching free will, necessity, and election by grace, regarding works as a garment of filthy rags in which publicans and sinners who trusted in them were burned while in practice the good soul was as earnest in performing them as if she believed her salvation depended exclusively thereupon.

Like many of the Huguenots, despite a narrow and partial creed, her life of pure morality made smooth a hundred inconsistencies of belief. The Dame found in practice no difficulty in reconciling contradictions of doctrine which to less earnest Christians seemed impossible to be harmonized. She had long ago received the blessing pronounced upon

627

the pure in heart, that they should see God. It is the understanding which is of the heart that alone comprehends spiritual facts, and sees spiritual truths, as the presence of summer light and warmth bring the flowers out of the dark earth, and fill it with abundance.

Dame Rochelle had received a new lease of life by the return home of Pierre Philibert. She grew radiant almost gay, at the news of his betrothal to Amelie de Repentigny and although she could not lay aside the black puritanical garb she had worn so many years, her kind face brightened from its habitual seriousness. The return of Pierre broke in upon her quiet routine of living, like a prolonged festival. The preparation of the great house of Belmont for his young bride completed her happiness.

In her anxiety to discover the tastes and preferences of her young mistress, as she already called her, Dame Rochelle consulted Amelie on every point of her arrangements, finding her own innate sense of the beautiful quickened by contact with that fresh young nature. She was already drawn by that infallible attraction which every one felt in the presence of Amelie.

"Amelie was too good and too fair" the Dame said "to become any mans portion but Pierre Philibert's!" The Dame's Huguenot prejudices melted like wax in her presence, until Amelie almost divided with Grande Marie, the saint of the Cevennes, the homage and blessing of Dame Rochelle.

Those were days of unalloyed delight which she spent in superintending the arrangements for the marriage which had been fixed for the festivities of Christmas.

It was to be celebrated on a scale worthy of the rank of the heiress of Repentigny, and of the wealth of the Philiberts. The rich Bourgeois in the gladness of his heart, threw open all his coffers and blessed with tears of happiness the money he flung out with both hands to honour the nuptials of Pierre and Amelie.

The summer of St Martin was shining over the face of nature. Its golden beams penetrated the very heart of the Bourgeois, and illumined all his thoughts. Winter might not be far off, but with peace in the land, its coming, if rough, was welcome. Storms and tempests might be under the horizon, but he saw them not, and heeded them not. His chief care in life was now to see Pierre married, and secure in the love of Amelie De Repentigny. After that the Bourgeois was ready to bid a hard world farewell, and say with devout Simeon, "*Nunc dimittis servum tuum! Domine! in pace!*"

The Bourgeois was profoundly happy during these few brief days of Indian Summer. As a Christian he rejoiced that the long desolating war was over. As a colonist he felt a pride that unequal as had been the struggle, New France remained unshorn of territory and by its resolute defence had forced respect from even its enemies. In his eager hope, he saw commerce revive and the arts and comforts of peace take the place of war and destruction! The husbandman would now reap for himself the harvest he had sown, and no longer be crushed by the exactions of the Friponne.

There was hope for the Colony. The iniquitous regime of the Intendant, which had pleaded the war as its justification, must close, the Bourgeois thought, under the new conditions of peace. The hateful monopoly of the Grand Company must be overthrown by the constitutional action of the *Honnetes Gens*, and its condemnation by the parliament of Paris to which an appeal would presently be carried, it was hoped, would be secured.

The King was quarreling with the Jesuits. The Molinists were hated by La Pompadour and he was certain His Majesty would never hold a *Lit de Justice* to command the registration of the decrees issued in his name by the Intendant of New France after they had been in form condemned by the parliament of Paris. Such formed the subjects of the meditations of the Bourgeois.

Dame Rochelle continued plying her needles quietly as she meditated by turns upon the page of Jurieu by turns upon the marriage of Pierre Philibert, illustrating the one by the other, and proving to her own perfect content that this marriage had been from all time predestinate, and that the doctrine of her favorite divine never received a more striking demonstration of its truth than in the life long constancy of Pierre and Amelie to their first love.

The Bourgeois still reclined very still on his easy chair. He was not asleep. In the day time he never slept. His thoughts like the Dames reverted to Pierre. He meditated the repurchase of his ancestral home in Normandy, and the restoration of its ancient honours for his son.

Personal and political enmity might prevent the reversal of his own unjust condemnation, but Pierre had won renown in the recent campaigns. He was favoured with the friendship of many of the noblest personages in France, who would support his suit for the restoration of his family honours, while the all potent influence of money the open sesame of every door in the Palace of Versailles, would not be spared to advance his just claims.

The crown of the Bourgeois' ambition, would be to see Pierre restored to his ancestral Chateau as the Count de Philibert, and Amelie as its noble Chatelaine dispensing happiness among the faithful old servitors and vassals of his family, who in all these long years of his exile never forgot their brave old Seigneur who had been banished to New France.

His reflections took a practical turn, and he enumerated in his mind the friends he could count upon in France to support, and the enemies who were sure to oppose the attainment of this great object of his ambition. But the purchase of the chateau and lands of Philibert was in his power. Its present possessor, a needy courtier, was deeply in debt, and would be glad, the Bourgeois had ascertained, to sell the estates for such a price as he could easily offer him.

To sue for simple justice in the restoration of his inheritance would be useless. It would involve a life long litigation. The Bourgeois preferred buying it back at whatever price, so that he could make a gift of it at once to his son, and he had already instructed his bankers in Paris to pay the price asked by its owner, and forward to him the deeds which he was ambitious to present to Pierre and Amelie on the day of their marriage.

The Bourgeois at last looked up from his revery. Dame

Rochelle closed her book waiting for her masters commands.

"Has Pierre returned Dame?" asked he.

"No master, he bade me say he was going to accompany Mademoiselle Amelie to Lorette."

"Ah! Amelie had a vow to our Lady of St Foye, and Pierre I warrant desired to pay half the debt! What think you Dame, of your Godson? Is he not promising?" The Bourgeois laughed quietly as was his wont sometimes.

Dame Rochelle sat a shade more upright in her chair. "Pierre is worthy of Amelie and Amelie of him," replied she gravely, "Never were two out of heaven more fitly matched. If they make vows to the lady of St Foye they will pay them as religiously as if they had made them to the Most High, to whom we are commanded to pay our vows."

The good old Huguenot would have censured a vow to our Lady of St Foye in any other but Amelie and Pierre.

"Well, Dame, some turn to the east and some to the west to pay their vows, but the holiest shrine is where true love is, and there alone the oracle speaks in response to young hearts. Amelie sweet modest flower that she is pays her vows to our lady of St Foye, Pierre his to Amelie. I will be bound Dame! There is no saint in the Calendar so holy in his eyes as herself!"

"Nor deserves to be master! Theirs is no ordinary affection. If love be the fulfilling of the law, all law is fulfilled in these two, for never did the elements of happiness mingle more sweetly in the soul of a man and a woman than in Pierre and Amelie!—"

"It will restore your youth Dame, to live with Pierre and Amelie," replied the Bourgeois. "Amelie insists on it, not because of Pierre, she says, but for your own sake. She was moved to tears one day Dame, when she made me relate your story."

Dame Rochelle put on her spectacles to cover her eyes which were fast filling, as she glanced down on the black robe she wore, remembering for whom she wore it.

"Thanks master! It would be a blessed thing to end the remaining days of my mourning in the house of Pierre and

Amelie! but my quiet mood suits better the house of my master, who has also had his heart saddened by a long long day of darkness and regret."

"Yes, Dame, but a bright sunset, I trust awaits it now. The descending shadow of the dial goes back a pace on the fortunes of my house! I hope to welcome my few remaining years with a gayer aspect and a lighter heart than I have felt since we were driven from France. What would you say to see us all reunited once more in our old Norman home?"

The Dame gave a great start, and clasped her thin hands. "What would I say, master? O! to return to France and be buried in the green valley of the Côte D'or by the side of him, were next to rising in the resurrection of the just at the last day—!—"

The Bourgeois knew well whom she meant by *him*. He reverenced her feeling, but continued the topic of a return to France. "Well Dame I will do for Pierre what I would not do for myself. I shall repurchase the old Chateau, and use every influence at my command to prevail on the King to restore to Pierre the honours of his ancestors. Will not that be a glorious end to the career of the Bourgeois Philibert?—"

"Yes! Master but it may not end there, for you! I hear from my quiet window many things spoken in the street below. Men love you so, and need you so, that they will not spare any supplication to bid you stay in the Colony, and you will stay and die as you have lived so many years under the shadow of the Golden Dog! Some men hate you too, because you love justice and stand up for the right. I have a request to make, Dear Master!"

"What is that Dame?" asked he kindly, prepared to grant any request of hers.

"Do not go to the market tomorrow," replied she earnestly.

The Bourgeois glanced sharply at the Dame who continued to ply her needles. Her eyes were half closed in a semi trance, their lids trembling with nervous excitement. One of her moods rare of late was upon her, and she continued—

"O my dear master, you will never go to France! but Pierre

shall inherit the honours of the house of Philibert!"

The Bourgeois looked up contentedly. He respected, without putting entire faith in Dame Rochelle's inspirations: "I shall be resigned" he said "not to see France again, if the Kings Majesty wills it, as a condition, that he restore to Pierre the dignity, while I give him back the domain of his fathers."

Dame Rochelle clasped her hands hard together and sighed. She spake not but her lips moved in prayer as if deprecating some evil danger, or combatting some presentiment of trouble.

The Bourgeois watched her narrowly not that his hard worldly wisdom considered the moods of devout Quietism, in which she believed she had intuitions of coming events, as other than the natural operations of a wonderfully sensitive and apprehensive nature. Still in his experience he had found that her fancies if not supernatural were not unworthy of regard as the sublimation of reason by intellectual processes of which the possessor was unconscious.

"You again see trouble in store for me, Dame!" said he smiling, "but a merchant of New France setting at defiance the decrees of the royal Intendant, an exile seeking from the King the restoration of the Lordship of Philibert may well have trouble on his hands."

"Yes, master, but so far I only see trouble like a misty cloud which as yet has neither form nor colour of its own, but only reflects red rays as of a setting sun. No voice from its midst tells me its meaning, I thank God for that! I like not to anticipate evil that may not be averted!"

"Whom does it touch? Pierre or Amelie, me or all of us?" asked the Bourgeois.

"All of us Master! How could any misfortune do other than concern us all! What it means I know not. It is most like the wheel seen by the Prophet full of eyes within and without, like Gods providence looking for his elect."

"And finding them?—"

"Not yet Master, but ere long! *finding* all ere long!" replied she in a dreamy manner. "But go not to the market tomorrow."

"These are strange fancies of yours Dame Rochelle! Why

caution me against the market tomorrow? It is the day of St
Martin. The poor will expect me! and if I go not, many will
return empty away."

"They are not wholly fancies, Master. Two gentlemen of
the Palace passed to day and looking up at the tablet one
wagered the other on the battle tomorrow between Cerberus
and the Golden Dog. I have not forgotten wholly my early
lessons in classical lore," added the Dame.

"Nor I Dame! I comprehend the allusion! but it will not
keep me from the market. I will be watchful however, for I
know that the malice of my enemies is at this time greater
than ever before."

"Let Pierre go with you and you will be safe!" said the
Dame half imploringly.

The Bourgeois laughed at the suggestion and began
good humoredly to rally her on her curious gift and on
the inconvenience of having a prophetess in his house to
anticipate the evil day.

"Philip the Evangelist," said she, "had four daughters in
his house, virgins who did prophecy, and it is not said he
complained of it master!" replied the Dame with a slight smile.

"But Philip had apostolic grace to support him under it
Dame!" said the Bourgeois smiling. "I think with the preacher
It is best not to be wise overmuch, I would not look too far
before or after."

Dame Rochelle would not say more. She knew that to
express her fears more distinctly would only harden the
resolution of the Bourgeois. His natural courage would make
him court the special danger he ought to avoid.

"Master!" said she, suddenly casting her eyes in the street,
"there rides past one of the gentlemen who wagered on the
battle between Cerberus and the Golden Dog."

The Bourgeois had sufficient curiosity to look out. He
recognized the Chevalier De Pean, and tranquilly resumed
his seat with the remark, that "that was truly one of the heads
of Cerberus which guards the Friponne, a fellow who wore
the collar of the Intendant and was worthy of it! the Golden
Dog had nothing to fear from him—!—"

Dame Rochelle full of her own thoughts followed with her eyes the retreating figure of the Chevalier De Pean whom she lost sight of at the first turn as he rode rapidly to the house of Angelique des Meloises.

Since the fatal eve of St Michael, Angelique had been tossing in a sea of conflicting emotions, sometimes brightened by a wild hope of the Intendant, sometimes black with fear of the discovery of her dealings with La Corriveau.

It was in vain she tried every artifice of female blandishment and cunning to discover what was really in the heart and mind of Bigot. She had sounded his soul, to try if he entertained a suspicion of herself but its depth was beyond her power to reach its bottomless darkness, and to the last she could not resolve whether he suspected her or not of complicity with the death of the unfortunate Caroline.

She never ceased to curse La Corriveau for that felon stroke of her mad stiletto, which changed what might have passed for a simple death by heartbreak into a foul assassination.

The Intendant she knew, must be well aware that Caroline had been murdered, but he had never named it, or given the least token of consciousness that such a crime had been committed in his house.

It was in vain that she repeated with a steadiness of face, which sometimes imposed even on Bigot, her request for a *Lettre de Cachet* or urged the banishment of her rival until the Intendant one day with a look which for a moment annihilated her, told her that her rival had gone from Beaumanoir and would never trouble her any more.

What did he mean? Angelique had noted every change of muscle, every motion of lip and eyelash as he spake, and she felt more puzzled than before.

She replied however with the assurance she could so well assume, "Thanks Bigot! I did not speak from jealousy. I only asked for justice and the fulfilment of your promise to send her away."

"But I did not send her away! She has gone away I know not whither! Gone! do you mind me Angelique? I would give half my possessions to know who helped her to *escape*—yes! that is the word,—from Beaumanoir."

Angelique had expected a burst of passion from Bigot. She had prepared herself for it by diligent rehearsal of how she would demean herself under every possible form of charge from bare innuendo to direct impeachment of herself.

Keenly as Bigot watched Angelique, he could detect no sign of confusion in her. She trembled in her heart but her lips wore their old steady smile. Her eyes opened widely, looking surprise, not guilt, as she shook him by the arm and coquettishly pulled his hair, asking if he thought that, "she had stolen away his lady love?—"

Bigot though only half deceived, tried to persuade himself of her innocence, and left her after an hour's dalliance with a half belief that she did not really merit the grave suspicions he had entertained of her.

Angelique feared however that he was only acting a part. What part? It was still a mystery to her and likely to be; she had but one criterion to discover his real thoughts. The offer of his hand in marriage, was the only test she relied upon to prove her acquittal in the mind of Bigot, of all complicity with the death of Caroline.

But Bigot was far from making the desired offer of his hand. That terrible night in the secret chamber of Beaumanoir was not absent from his mind an hour. It could never be forgotten least of all in the company of Angelique, whom he was judging incessantly; either convicting or acquitting her in his mind, as he was alternately impressed with her well acted innocent gaiety or stung by a sudden perception of her power of deceit, and unrivalled assurance.

So they went on from day to day, fencing like two adepts in the art of dissimulation, Bigot never glancing at the murder, and speaking of Caroline as gone away to parts unknown, but as Angelique observed with bitterness, never making that a reason for pressing his suit, while she assuming the role of innocence and ignorance of all that had happened at Beaumanoir, put on an appearance of satisfaction, or pretending still to fits of jealousy grew fonder in her demeanour and acted as though she assumed, as a matter of course, that Bigot would now fulfil his hopes of speedily making her his bride.

The Intendant had come and gone every day unchanged in his manner, full of spirits and gallantry, and as warm in his admiration as before, but her womanly instinct told her there was something hidden under that gay exterior.

It was in vain that she exerted her utmost powers of pleasing, dressed herself to his voluptuous tastes, put on an appearance of gaiety she was far from feeling sat with him, walked with him, rode with him, and in every way drew him off and on like her glove.

Bigot accepted every challenge of flirtation and ought to have declared himself twenty times over, but he did not—he seemed to bring himself to the brink of an avowal only to break into her confidence, and surprize the secret she kept so desperatly concealed.

Angelique met craft by craft, duplicity by duplicity, but it began to be clear to herself that she had met with her match, and although the Intendant grew more pressing as a lover, she had daily less hope of winning him as a husband.

The thought was maddening. Such a result admitted of a twofold meaning. Either he suspected her of the death of Caroline, or her charms which had never failed before with any man, failed now to entangle the one man she had resolved to marry.

She cursed him in her heart, while she flattered him with her tongue, but by no art she was mistress of, neither by fondness nor by coyness, could she extract the declaration she regarded as her due and was indignant at not receiving. She had fairly earned it by her great crime! She had still more fully earned it, she thought, by her condescensions. She regarded Providence as unjust in withholding her reward, and for punishing as a sin that which for her sake ought to be considered a virtue.

She often reflected with regretful looking back upon the joy which Le Gardeur de Repentigny would have manifested over the least of the favours which she had lavished in vain upon the inscrutable Intendant. At such moments she cursed her evil star, which had led her astray to listen to the promptings of ambition and to ask fatal counsel of La Corriveau.

Le Gardeur was now in the swift downward road of destruction. This was the one thing that caused Angelique a human pang. She might yet fail in all her ambitious prospects and have to fall back upon her first love, when even that would be too late to save Le Gardeur or to save her!—

De Pean rode fast up the Rue St Louis, not unobservant of the dark looks of the *Honnetes Gens* or the familiar nods and knowing smiles of the partizans of the Friponne whom he met on the way.

Before the door of the mansion of the Chevalier Des Meloises he saw a valet of the Intendant holding his masters horse and at the broad window, half hid behind the thick curtains sat Bigot and Angelique engaged in badinage and mutual deceiving, as De Pean well knew.

Her silvery laugh struck his ear as he drew up. He cursed them both, but fear of the Intendant and a due regard to his own interests, two feelings never absent from the Chevalier De Pean, caused him to ride on, not stopping as he had intended.

He would ride to the end of the grand Allée, and return. By that time the Intendant would be gone and she would be at liberty to receive his invitation for a ride tomorrow when they would visit the Cathedral and the market.

De Pean knew enough of the ways of Angelique to see that she aimed at the hand of the Intendant. She had slighted and vilipended himself even, while accepting his gifts and gallantries. But with a true appreciation of her character he had faith in the ultimate power of money, which represented to her as to most women, position, dress, jewels, stately houses, carriages and above all the envy and jealousy of her own sex.

These things De Pean had wagered on the head of Angelique against the wild love of Le Gardeur, the empty admiration of Bigot, and the flatteries of the troop of idle gentlemen who dawdled around her.

He felt confident that in the end victory would be his and

the fair Angelique would one day lay her hand in his as the wife of Hugues de Pean!—

De Pean knew that in her heart she had no love for the Intendant, and the Intendant no respect for her. Moreover, Bigot would not venture to marry the Queen of Sheba without the sanction of his jealous patroness at Court. He might possess a hundred mistresses if he liked, and be congratulated on his *bonnes fortunes*, but not one wife, under the penalty of losing the favour of La Pompadour who had chosen a future wife for him out of the crowd of Intrigantes who fluttered round her, basking like butterflies in the sunshine of her demi-regal splendour.

Bigot had passed a wild night at the Palace among the partners of the Grand Company, who had met to curse the peace, and drink a speedy renewal of the war! Before sitting down to their debauch however they had discussed with more regard to their peculiar interests than to the principles of the Decalogue the condition and prospects of the company.

The Prospect was so little encouraging to the associates that they were glad when the Intendant bade them cheer up, and remember that all was not lost that was in danger! Philibert would yet undergo the fate of Acteon and be torn in pieces by his own dog! Bigot as he said this glanced from Le Gardeur to De Pean, with a look and a smile which caused Cadet, who knew its meaning to shrug his shoulders and inquire of De Pean privatly, "Is the trap set?—"

"It is set!" replied De Pean in a whisper. "It will spring tomorrow and catch our game I hope."

"You must have a crowd and a row mind! This thing, to be safe, must be done openly," whispered Cadet in reply.

"We will have both a crowd and a row! never fear! The new preacher of the Jesuits who is fresh from Italy and knows nothing of our plot is to inveigh in the market against the Jansenists and the *Honnetes Gens*. If that does not make both a crowd and a row, I do not know what will."

"You are a deep Devil De Pean! So deep that I doubt you will cheat yourself yet," answered Cadet gruffly.

"Never fear Cadet! Tomorrow night shall see the Palace

gay with illumination and the Golden Dog in darkness and despair."

CHAPTER 51

A DRAWN GAME

LE Gardeur was too drunk to catch the full drift of the Intendants reference to the Bourgeois under the metaphor of Acteon torn in pieces by his own dog. He only comprehended enough to know that something was intended to the disparagment of the Philiberts and firing up at the idea, swore loudly that "neither the Intendant nor all the Grand Company in mass should harm a hair of the Bourgeois' head!—"

"It is the Dog!" exclaimed De Pean, "which the company will hang—not his master, nor your friend his son nor your friend's friend the old Huguenot witch! We will let them hang themselves when their time comes but it is the Golden Dog we mean to hang at present Le Gardeur!"

"Yes! I see!" replied Le Gardeur looking very hazy, "hang the Golden dog as much as you will! but as to the man that touches his master, I say he will have to fight *me* that is all!" Le Gardeur after one or two vain attempts succeded in drawing his sword, and laid it upon the table.

"Do you see that De Pean! That is the sword of a gentleman and I will run it through the heart of any man who says he will hurt a hair of the head of Pierre Philibert, or the Bourgeois or even the old Huguenot witch as you call Dame Rochelle, who is a lady and too good to be either your Mother Aunt or cater Cousin, in any way, De Pean!"

"By St Picot! You have mistaken your man! De Pean!" whispered Cadet. "Why the deuce did you pitch upon Le Gardeur to carry out your bright idea?—"

"I pitched upon him because he is the best man for our turn, but I am right! You will see I am right! Le Gardeur is the pink of morality when he is sober. He would kill the devil when he is half drunk. But when wholly drunk he would storm paradise and sack and slay like a German Reiter. He would kill his own grandfather. I have not erred in choosing him."

Bigot watched this by play with intense interest. He saw that Le Gardeur was a two edged weapon just as likely to cut his friends as his enemies, unless skilfully held in hand and blinded as to when and whom he should strike.

"Come Le Gardeur! put up your sword!" exclaimed Bigot coaxingly, "we have better game to bring down to night than the Golden Dog. Hark! they are coming! open wide the doors and let the blessed peacemakers enter—!"

"The Peacemakers!" ejaculated Cadet. "The cause of every quarrel among men since the creation of the world! What made you send for the women, Bigot?"

"O! not to say their prayers, you may be sure, old Misogynist! but this being a gala night at the Palace, the girls and fiddlers were ordered up by De Pean, and we will see you dance fandangoes with them until morning Cadet."

"No you wont! Damn the women! I wish you had kept them away, that is all. It spoils my fun Bigot—!"

"But it helps the company's! here they come!"

Their appearance at the door caused a hubbub of excitement among the gentlemen who hurried forward to salute a dozen or more of women dressed in the extreme of fashion who came forward with plentiful lack of modesty and a superabundance of gaiety and laughter.

Le Gardeur and Cadet did not rise like the rest, but kept their seats. Cadet swore the Intendant had spoiled a jolly evening by inviting the women to the palace.

These women had been invited by De Pean, to give zest to the wild orgie that was intended to prepare Le Gardeur for the plot of tomorrow that was to compass the fall of the Bourgeois. They sat down with the gentlemen, listening with peals of laughter to their coarse jests, and tempting them to wilder follies. They drank, they sang, they danced, and conducted or misconducted themselves in such thorough shameless fashion that Bigot, Varin and other experts of the court, swore that the *petits appartemens* of Versailles or even the Royal fetes at the *Parc aux cerfs* could not surpass the high life and jollity of the Palace of the Intendant.

In that wild fashion Bigot passed the night previous to his present visit to Angelique. The Chevalier De Pean rode the length of the Grand Allée and returned. The valet and horse of the Intendant were still waiting at the door, and De Pean saw Bigot and Angelique still seated at the window engaged in a lively conversation and not apparently noticing his presence in the street as he sat pulling hairs out of the mane of his horse, "with the air of a man in love," as Angelique laughingly remarked to Bigot.

Her quick eye which nothing escaped had seen De Pean the first time he passed the house. She knew he had come to visit her and seeing the horse of the Intendant at the door had forborne to enter. That would not have been the way with Le Gardeur, she thought. He would have entered all the readier had even the Dauphin held her in conversation.

Angelique was woman enough to like best the bold gallant that carries the female heart by storm and puts the parleying garrison of denial to the sword, as the Sabine women admired the spirit of their Roman captors and became the most faithful of wives.

De Pean clever and unprincipled, was a menial in his soul, as cringing to his superiors, as he was arrogant to those below him.

"Fellow!" said he, to Bigot's groom, "How long has the Intendant been here—?"

"All the afternoon Chevalier," replied the man, respectfully uncovering his head.

"Hum! and have they sat at the window all the time?"

"I have no eyes to watch my master!" replied the groom. "I do not know."

"Oh!" was the reply of De Pean as he suddenly reflected that it were best for himself also not to be seen watching his master too closely. He uttered a spurt of ill humour and continued pulling the mane of his horse through his fingers.

"The Chevalier De Pean is practicing patience to day! Bigot," said she, "and you give him enough time to excercise it!"

"You wish me gone Angelique!" said he rising, "the Chevalier De Pean is naturally waxing impatient, and you too!—"

"Pshaw!" exclaimed she, "he shall wait as long as I please to keep him there."

"Or as long as I stay! He is an accommodating lover and will make an equally accommodating husband for his wifes friend, someday!" remarked Bigot laughing.

Angeliques eye flashed out fire! but she little knew how true a word Bigot had spoken in jest! She could have choked him for mentioning her in connection with De Pean, but remembering she was now at his mercy it was necessary to cheat and cozen this man by trying to please him.

"Well if you must go, you must, Chevalier! Let me tie that string." continued she, approaching him in her easy manner. The knot of his cravat was loose. Bigot glanced admiringly at her slightly flushed cheek and dainty fingers as she tied the loose ends of his rich Steinkirk, together.

"Tis like love!" said she, laughing. "A slip-knot that looks tied until it is tried—!"

She glanced at Bigot expecting him to thank her, which he did with a simple word. The thought of Caroline, flashed over his mind like lightning at that moment. She too as they walked on the shore of the Bay of Minas, had once tied the string of his cravat when for the first time he read in her flushed cheek and trembling fingers, that she loved him. Bigot hardy as he was and reckless, refrained from touching the hand or even looking at Angelique, at this moment.

With the quick perception of her sex, she felt it, and drew back a step, not knowing but the next moment might overwhelm her with an accusation! But Bigot was not sure, and he dared not hint, to Angelique more than he had done.

"Thanks for tying the knot! Angelique" said he at length. "It is a hard knot mine, is it not, both to tie and to untie?—"

She looked at him, not pretending to understand any meaning he might attach to his words. "Yes it is a hard knot to tie is yours, Bigot! and you do not seem particularly to thank me for my service. Have you discovered the hidden place of your fair fugitive yet?" She said this just as he turned to depart. It was the feminine postscript to their interview.

Bigot's avoidance of any allusion to the death of Caroline was a terrible mark of suspicion less in reality however than it seemed.

Bigot although suspicious could find no clue to the real perpetrators of the murder. He knew it had not been Angelique herself in person, he had never heard speak of La Corriveau, not the smallest ray of light penetrated the dark mystery.

"I do not believe she has left Beaumanoir Bigot!" continued Angelique "or if she has, you know her hiding place! Will you swear on my book of hours that you know not where she is to be found—?"

He looked fixedly at Angelique for a moment, trying to read her thoughts but she had rehearsed her part too often and too well, to look pale or confused. She felt her eye brow twitch but she pressed it with her fingers believing Bigot did not observe it, but he did.

"I will swear and curse both if you wish it! Angelique" replied he. "Which shall it be?"

"Well do both! swear at me and curse the day that I banished Le Gardeur de Repentigny for your sake! Francois Bigot! If the lady be gone, where is your promise?"

Bigot burst into a wild laugh, as was his wont, when hard pressed. He had not to be sure made any definite promise to Angelique but he had flattered her with hopes of marriage, never intended to be realized.

"I keep my promises to ladies as if I had sworn by St Dorothy!" replied he.

"But your promise to me Bigot! will you keep it or do worse?" asked she impatiently.

"Keep it or do worse! What mean you Angelique?" he looked up in genuine surprize. This was not the usual tone of women towards him.

"I mean that nothing will be better for Francois Bigot than to keep his promise, nor worse, than to break it to Angelique des Meloises—!" replied she with a stamp of her foot, as was her manner when excited.

She thought it safe to use an implied threat, which at any rate might reach the thought that lay under his heart like a centipede under a stone which some chance foot turns over.

But Bigot minded not the implied threat, he was immoveable in the direction she wished him to move—he understood her allusion but would not appear to understand it lest worse than she meant, should come of it.

"Forgive me Angelique!" said he with a sudden change from frigidity to fondness, "I am not unmindful of my promises. There is nothing better to myself than to keep them, nothing worse than to break them. Beaumanoir is now without reproach and you can visit it without fear of ought but the ghosts in the gallery."

Angelique feared no ghosts, but she did fear that the Intendants words implied a suggestion of one which might haunt it for the future if there were any truth in tales.

"How can you warrant that Bigot?" asked she dubiously.

"Because Pierre Philibert and La Corne St Luc have been with the Kings warrant and searched the Chateau from crypt to attic without finding a trace of your rival."

"What Chevalier! searched the Chateau of the Intendant?"

"*Par bleu*! Yes! I insisted upon their doing so, not however till they had gone through the Castle of St Louis, they apologized to me for finding nothing! What did they expect to find think you?—"

"The Lady, to be sure! O Bigot!" continued she, tapping him with her fan, "if they would send a commission of women to search for her, the secret could not remain hid!—"

"No, truly, Angelique! If you were on such a commission and discovered the secret of her—?"

"Well Bigot! I would never betray it if I knew it," answered she promptly.

"You swear to that, Angelique?—" asked he, looking full in her eyes, which did not flinch under his gaze.

"Yes! on my book of hours as you did," said she.

"Well there is my hand upon it, Angelique! I have no secret to tell respecting her, and she has gone I cannot tell whither."

Angelique gave him her hand on the lie. She knew he was playing with her, and she with him a game of mutual deception, which both knew to be such, and yet they must, circumstanced as they were, play it out to the end, which end she hoped would be her marriage with this arch deceiver! A breach of their alliance was as dangerous as it would be unprofitable to both.

Bigot rose to depart with an air of gay regret at leaving the company of Angelique to make room for De Pean, "who" he said "would pull every hair out of his horses mane if he waited much longer!"

"Your visit is no pleasure to you Bigot" said she looking hard at him, "you are discontented with me and would rather go than stay—!"

"Well Angelique! I am a dissatisfied man to day. The mysterious disappearance of that girl from Beaumanoir is the cause of my discontent. The defiant boldness of the Bourgeois Philibert is another! I have heard to day that the Bourgeois has chartered every ship that is to sail to France during the remainder of the Autumn. These things are provoking enough. But they drive me for consolation to you, but for you I should shut myself up in Beaumanoir, and let everything go helter skelter to the Devil—!"

"You only flatter me and do not mean it!" said she as he took her hand with over-empressment as perceptible to her, as was his occasional coldness.

"By all the saints! I mean it," said he. But he did not deceive her. His professions were not all true. But how far they were true was a question that again and again tormented her, and set her bosom palpitating as he left her room with his usual courteous salute.

"He suspects me! He more than suspects me!" said she to herself, as Bigot passed out of the mansion and mounted his horse to ride off. "He would speak out plainer if he dared avow, that that woman was in truth the missing Caroline de St Castin!" thought she with savage bitterness.

"I have a bit in your mouth there Francois Bigot that will
forever hold you in check! That missing demoiselle no one
knows as you do, where she is! I would give away every jewel
I own to know what you did with the pretty piece of mortality
left on your hands by La Corriveau! Foul witch!" continued
she. "It was she made a murder of a natural death! and led me
into this cursed coil. But for that poniard stroke the Intendant
would have been mine to day! I could wear sackcloth for spite
when I reflect on it—! I feel to the very ends of my finger nails
that Satan has put this crook in my lot to thwart my legitimate
hopes!—"

Thus soliloquized Angelique for a few moments looking
gloomy and beautiful as Medea, when the step of De Pean
sounded up the broad stairs.

With a sudden transformation as if touched by a magic
wand, Angelique sprang forward all smiles and fascinations to
greet his entrance.

The faculty of a woman to read a man is said to be a sixth
sense of the sex. If so the faculty of appearing other than she
is, and of preventing a man from reading her, is assuredly a
seventh sense. Angelique possessed both to perfection.

All women have that faculty, but never one surpassed
Angelique in the art of transformation. None knew better than
she how to suit her rare powers of fascination to the particular
man she desired to please, or the mood she desired to take
advantage of.

The Chevalier De Pean had long made distant and timid
pretensions to her favour, but he had been overborne by a
dozen rivals. He was incapable of love in any honest sense but
he had immense vanity. He had been barely noticed among
the crowd of Angeliques admirers. "He was only food for
powder," she had laughingly remarked upon one occasion,
when a duel on her account seemed to be impending between
De Pean and the young Captain de Tours, and beyond doubt
Angelique would have been far prouder of him shot for her
sake in a duel, than she was of his living attentions.

She regarded him as a lady regards her pet spaniel. He
was most useful to fetch and carry, to stand on his hind feet

and turn the whirligig of her fancy when she had no better company.

She was not sorry however, when he came in today after the departure of the Intendant. It kept her from her own thoughts which were bitter enough when alone. Moreover she never tired of any amount of Homage and admiration come from what quarter it would.

De Pean staid long with Angelique. How far he opened to her the details of the plot to create a riot in the market place that afternoon, can only be conjectured, by the fact of her agreeing to ride out at the hour designated, which she warmly consented to do, as soon as De Pean informed her that Le Gardeur would be there, and might be expected to have a hand in the tumult raised against the Golden Dog. The conference over, Angelique speedily dismissed De Pean. She was in no mood for flirtation with him. Her mind was taken up with the possibility of danger to Le Gardeur in this plot which she saw clearly was the work of others, and not of himself, although he was expected to be a chief actor in it.

CHAPTER 52

"IN GOLD CLASPS LOCKS IN THE GOLDEN STORY"

LIFE is divided into triads of epochs, Youth, Manhood and Age—Birth, Marriage and Death. Each epoch has its own progress from morning to noon and from noon to night, as if our moral and physical states retained in their changes an image and reflection of the great never ending ever beginning revolutions of the Sun.

The Father rejoices in his children. They will live upon the earth after him, and in their eyes he will still see the pleasant light of day. Man turns towards the woman whom he has selected from among the many possible women, whom he might have loved, and she calls herself for a while, perhaps forever, blessed among women.

Love is like a bright river. It springs from the fresh fountains of the heart—it flows on between fair and everwidening banks until it reaches the ocean of eternity, and happiness.

The days illumined with the brightest sunshine are those which smile over the heads of a loving pair who have found each other and with tender confessions and mutual avowals plighted their troth and prepared their little ark for sailing together down the changeful stream of time.

So it had been through the long Indian summer days, with Pierre Philibert and Amelie de Repentigny. Since the blessed hour they plighted their troth, in the evening twilight upon the shore of the little Lake of Tilly, they had showed to each other in the hearts confessional, the treasures of true human affection, holy in the eyes of God and man.

One mind, one hope, and one desire possessed them to be all in all to one another, to study each others inmost character,

650

an easy task when instead of concealment each loved to guide the other to a perfect understanding.

When Amelie gave her love to Pierre she gave it utterly and without a scruple of reservation. It was so easy to love Pierre, so impossible not to love him. Nay she remembered not the time it was otherwise, or when he had not been first and last in her secret thoughts as he was now in her chaste confessions, although whispered so low, that her approving angel hardly caught the sound as it passed into the ear of Pierre Philibert.

Amelie's devotion was like that of a holy woman of old. The image of Pierre mingled in her prayers inspiring them with a fervour deeper than she dreamt of. She thanked God for the love of the one man out of all the world, who had won her virgin heart, one whom she could look up to with pride for his manhood, with reverence for his greatness of soul and in return for his love counted the devotion of her whole life as inadequate to repay it.

A warm soft wind blew gently down the little valley. The Lairet, wound and rippled over its white glossy pebbles murmuring a quiet song down in its hollow bed. Tufts of spiry grass clung to its steep banks and a few wild flowers peeped out of nooks among the brown fallen leaves that lay upon the still green sward on each shore of the little rivulet.

Pierre and Amelie had been tempted by the beauty of the Indian summer to dismount and send their horses forward to Belmont in charge of a servant while they walked home by way of the fields, to gather the last flowers of Autumn which Amelie said lingered longest in the deep swales of the Lairet.

A walk in the Golden sunshine with Amelie alone amid the quiet fields, free to speak his love and she to hear him, and be glad, was a pleasure Pierre had dreamt of but never enjoyed since the blessed night when they plighted their troth to each other by the Lake of Tilly.

The betrothal of Pierre and Amelie had been accepted by their friends on both sides, as a most fitting and desirable match, but the manners of the age with respect to the unmarried, did not admit of that freedom in society which prevails at the present day.

They had seldom met save in the presence of others and except for a few chance but blissful moments, Pierre had not been favoured with the company all to himself of his betrothed.

Amelie was not unmindful of that, when she gave a willing consent today to walk with him along the banks of the Lairet, under the shady elms, birches, and old thorns that overhung the path by the little stream.

She felt with the tender compassion of a woman for the man she loves, that he had longed for more of her society than the custom of the time permitted him to enjoy, and although rigid and precise in her ideas of duty Amelie could not persuade herself against her own heart not to grant him this propitious hour to converse with ease and freedom.

The happy present was intoxicating as sweet wine and the still more happy future loomed up before her imagination like a fairy land, where she was to dwell forever. To talk of it to day was a foretaste of bliss for them both not to be denied, so leaning on the arm of Pierre, she sauntered along the banks of the Lairet conversing with innocent animation and that entire trust which their relationship to each other permitted.

Pierre was now her betrothed. Amelie happy and confiding regarded her lover as her other self. She loved him too well to affect any unreal thought or feeling and when his eager admiring eyes met hers, she blushed but would not refuse to let him perceive that he was loved with the tenderness and devotion of her whole being. She then felt that Pierre loved her as his own soul and in the fulness of her gratitude resolved that as her past life had been one prayer for his happiness so her future would be one neverceasing effort to repay his love.

"Pierre!" said she smiling, "our horses are gone and I must now walk home with you right or wrong! My Old Mistress in the Convent would shake her head if she heard of it! but I care not who blames me today, if you do not, Pierre!—"

"Who can blame you, Darling? what you do is ever wisest and best in my eyes, except one thing, which I will confess now that you are my own, I cannot account for."

"I had hoped Pierre, there was no exception to your admiration. You are taking off my angel's wings already and leaving me a mere woman!" replied she merrily.

"It is a woman I want you to be Darling, a woman not faultless but human as myself, a wife to hold to me and love me despite my faults not an angel too bright and too perfect to be my other self."

"Dear Pierre!" said she pressing his arm. "I will be that woman to you, full enough of faults to satisfy you! an angel I am not, and cannot be, nor wish to be! untill we go together to the spirit land! I am so glad I have a fault for which you can blame me if it makes you love me better! Indeed I own to many, but what is that one fault Pierre! which you cannot account for—?"

"That you should have loved a rough soldier like me Amelie, that one so fair and perfect in all the graces of womanhood with the world to choose from, should have permitted Pierre Philibert to win her loving heart of hearts!—"

Amelie looked at him with a fond expression of reproach, "Does that surprise you Pierre? You rough soldier! You little know and I will not tell you the way to a womans heart! but for one blindfolded by so much diffidence to his own merits, you have found the way very easily! Was it for loving you that you blamed me? What if I should recall the fault?" added she laughing.

Pierre raised her hand to his lips kissing devotedly the ring he had placed upon her finger. "I have no fear of that Amelie! The wonder to me is, that you could think me worthy of the priceless trust of your happiness."

"And the wonder to me," replied she, "is that your dear heart ever burdened itself with my happiness! I am weak in myself and only strong in my resolution to be all a loving wife should be to you, my Pierre. You wonder how you gained my love? Shall I tell you! You never gained it! It was always yours before you formed a thought to win it! You are now my betrothed Pierre Philibert, soon to be my husband. I would not exchange my fortune to become the proudest Queen that ever sat on the throne of France—!—"

Amelie was very happy to day. The half stolen delight of walking by the side of Pierre Philibert was enhanced by the hope that the fatal spell that bound Le Gardeur to the palace had been broken and he would yet return home, a new man.

Le Gardeur had that morning in a moment of recollection of himself, and of his sister, addressed a note to Amelie asking pardon for his recent neglect of home and promising to come and see them on St Martins day.

He had heard of her betrothal to Pierre. "It was the gladest news" he said "that had ever come to him in his life. He sent a brothers blessing upon them both, and claimed the privilege of giving away her hand to the noblest man in New France, Pierre Philibert!—"

Amelie showed the precious note to Pierre. It only needed that to complete their happiness for the day. The one cloud that had overshadowed their joy in their approaching nuptials, was passing away, and Amelie was prouder in the anticipation that Le Gardeur, restored to himself, sober and in his right mind, was to be present at her wedding and give her away, than if the whole court of France with thousands of admiring spectators were to pay her Royal honours.

It was very pleasant under the brown trees and bushes that fringed the little brook. The gentle wind rustled the fallen leaves that strewed the earth. Scarcely a sound else mingled with the low sweet tones of love and confidence which fell from the lips of Pierre and Amelie as they loitered in the secluded pathway.

The summer birds were nearly all gone. The few that remained in the bushes no longer sang as in the genial days of June, but chirped sad notes hopping, solitary here and there, as if they knew that the season of joy was passing away, and the dark days of winter were at hand.

But nothing of this noted, Pierre and Amelie. Wrapped in the entrancement of each others presence, they only observed nature so far as it was the reflex of their own happy feelings. Amelie unconsciously leaned as she had often dreamed of doing upon the arm of Pierre, who held her hand in his, gazing on her half averted face, catching momentary glances of her dark eyes which she cast down abashed under the fondness which she felt was filling them with tears of joy.

They sauntered on towards a turn of the stream where a little pool lay embayed like a smooth mirror reflecting the grassy bank. Amelie sat down under a tree while Pierre crossed over the brook to gather on the opposite side, some flowers which had caught her eye.

"Tell me which Amelie?" exclaimed he, "for they are all yours! You are Flora's heiress with right to enter into possession of her whole Kingdom!—"

"The water lillies! Pierre those! and those! and those! they are to deck the shrine of Notre Dame des Victoires. Aunt has a vow there and tomorrow it must be paid, I too!"

He looked up at her with eyes of admiration "a vow let me share in its payment, Amelie," said he.

"You may! but you shall not ask me what it is, there now! do not wet yourself farther! You have gathered more lilies than we can carry home!"

"But I have my own thank offering to make to Notre Dame des Victoires, for I think I love God even better for your sake Amelie," said he.

"Fie Pierre! say not that! and yet I know what you mean! I ought to reprove you, but for your penance you shall gather more lilies for I fear you need many prayers and offerings to expiate—" She hesitated to finish the sentence.

"My Idolatry! Amelie!" said he completing her meaning.

"I doubt it is little better Pierre! If you love me as you say, but you shall join in my offering and that will do for both. Please pull that one bunch of lilies and no more or Our Lady of Victory will judge you harder than I do!—"

Pierre stept from stone to stone over the placid pool gathering the Golden Lillies while Amelie clasped her hands and silently thanked God for this happy hour of her life.

She hardly dared trust herself to look at Pierre except by furtive glances of pride and affection, but as his form and features were reflected in an image of manly beauty in the still pool, she withdrew not her loving gaze from his shadow, and leaning forward, towards his image

"A thousand times she kissed him in the brook,
Across the flowers with bashful eyelids down!"

Amelie had Royally given her love to Pierre Philibert.
She had given it without stint or measure and with a depth
and strength of devotion of which more facile natures know
nothing.

Amelie was incapable of trifling with the semblance of
love. She was a stranger to the frivolous coquettry which
formed a study and was a science with most of her sex. She
had loved Pierre Philibert from the first awakening of her
affections. She loved him now with a passion which in her
heart she thought it no shame to feel for her betrothed. She
had confessed much to Pierre of her love, but shrank with
virgin modesty from trying to make him comprehend all the
strength and greatness of it, yet the mere overflowing of her
heart had seemed to him like the rich flood of the glorious
Nile that covers all the land enriching it with the harvests of
Egypt, but even he had no clear conception of the magnitude
and purity of that affection which lay like a great silence down
in the still depths of her being.

It was a world of womans love which God alone its
creator could fathom. Pierre got a glimpse of it through that
wondrous look of her dark eyes, which was like the opening
of heaven, and a sudden revelation of the spiritual Kingdom.
He was lost in admiration not unmingled with awe as of a
vision of something most holy and so it was! So is every true
woman's love. It is a holy and sacred thing in the sight of God
and should be of man.

Pierre with his burthen of Golden lilies came back over
the brook, and seated himself beside her, his arm encircled
her and she held his hand firmly clasped in both of hers.

"Amelie!" said he, "I believe now in the power of fate
to remove mountains of difficulty, and cast them into the
sea. How often while watching the stars wheel silently over
my head as I lay pillowed on a stone, while my comrades
slumbered round the camp fires, have I repeated my prayer
for Amelie De Repentigny. I had no right to indulge a hope of

winning your love. I was but a rough soldier, very practical and not at all imaginative. 'She would see nothing in me' I said, and still I would not have given up my hope for a Kingdom."

"It was not so hard after all, to win what was already yours Pierre! was it?" said she with a smile and a look of unutterable sweetness, "but it was well you asked, for without asking you would be like one possessing a treasure of gold in his field without knowing it, although it was all the while there and all his own. But not a grain of it would you have found, without asking me, Pierre."

"But having found it, I shall never lose it again, darling!" replied he, pressing her to his bosom.

"Never, Pierre, it is yours for ever!" replied she her voice trembling with emotion, "love is I think the treasure in heaven which rusts not and no thief can steal."

"Amelie!" said he after a few minutes silence "some say men's lives are counted not by hours but by the succession of ideas and emotions. If it be so, I have lived a century of happiness with you this afternoon! I am old in love Amelie!—"

"Nay I would not have you old in love, Pierre! love is the perennial youth of the soul. Grand Mere St Pierre who has been fifty years an Ursuline and has now the visions which are promised to the old in the latter days, she tells me that in Heaven those who love God and one another grow ever more youthful—the older the more beautiful! Is not that better than the philosophers teach Pierre?—"

"Better than all teaching of Philosophy are your words Amelie. Grand Mere St Pierre has discovered a truth that the academy of Sciences cannot reach. The immortality of Tithonus was full of decrepitude and decay, a body without a soul, but the immortality that springs from love and goodness is a fountain of everlasting youth, because the source of it is divine. I can well believe you Amelie! The more years the angels count under the skies of heaven, the more beautiful and youthful they grow for ever! It is a sweet thought. I thank you for it darling! Had De Soto loved as we do, Amelie! he would have found in the heart of love, the fountain of life he sought for! You see Darling," continued he as he pressed her fondly to his side, "I am an apt scholar of the Ursuline philosophy."

"You must not jest Pierre at the expense of our philosophy," replied she smiling, "there is more in it than man thinks! I sometimes fancy only women can understand it!—"

"Nay! I jest not! but believe it with my whole soul! How could I do otherwise with its proof radiating from those dear eyes of yours, bright enough to enlighten the wisest men with a new revelation."

He drew her closer and Amelie permitted him to impress a kiss on each eyelid as she closed it. Suddenly she started up:

"Pierre!" said she, "you said you were a soldier and so practical. I feel shame to myself for being so imaginative and so silly. I too would be practical if I knew how. This was to be a day of business with us was it not Pierre?"

"And is it not a day of business, Amelie? or are we spending it like holiday children wholly on pleasure! But after all love is the business of life and life is the business of eternity. We are transacting it to day Amelie! I never was so seriously engaged as at this moment nor you either, darling! tell the truth!—"

Amelie pressed his hands in hers. "Never Pierre! and yet I cannot see the old brown woods of Belmont rising yonder upon the slopes of St Foye without remembering my promise not two hours old, to talk with you today about the dear old mansion."

"That is to be the nest of as happy a pair of lovers as ever went to housekeeping, and I promised to keep soberly by your side as I am doing," said he mischievously twitching a stray lock of her dark hair, "and talk with you on the pretty banks of the Lairet, about the old mansion."

"Yes Pierre! that was your promise, if I would walk this way with you. Where shall we begin—?"

"Here Amelie!" replied he kissing her tenderly. "Now the congress is opened! I am your slave of the wonderful lamp ready to set up and pull down the world at your bidding. The old mansion is your own. It shall have no rest until it become within and without a mirror of the perfect taste and fancy of its lawful mistress."

"Not yet Pierre! I will not let you divert me from my purpose by your flatteries! The dear old home is perfect, but I must have the best suite of rooms in it for your noble father and the next best for good Dame Rochelle. I will fit them up on a plan of my own and none shall say me nay—that is all the change I shall make."

"Is that all? and you tried to frighten the slave of the lamp with the weight of your commands! a suite of rooms for my father and one for good Dame Rochelle. Really and what do you devote to me Amelie."

"O! all the rest with its mistress included! for the reason that what is good enough for me is good enough for you Pierre!" said she gaily.

"You little Economist! why one would say you had studied housekeeping under Madame Painchaud."

"And so I have! You do not know what a treasure I am Pierre!" said she laughing merrily. "I graduated under *Mes Tantes* in the kitchen of the Ursulines and received an *accessit* as *bonne Menagere* which in secret, I prize more than the crown of honour they gave me."

"My fortune is made, and I am a rich man for life!" exclaimed Pierre clapping his hands "Why I shall have to marry you like the girls of Acadia with a silver thimble on your finger and a pair of scissors at your girdle, emblems of industrious habits, and proofs of a good houswife!—"

"Yes Pierre! and I will comb your hair to my own liking! Your valet is a rough groom!" said she taking off his hat and passing her fingers through his thick fair locks.

Pierre although always dressed and trimmed like a gentleman really cared little for the petit maitre fashions of the day. Never had he felt a thrill of such exquisite pleasure as when Amelies hands arranged his rough hair to her fancy.

"My blessed Amelie!" said he with emotion pressing her fingers to his lips, "Never since my mother combed my boyish locks has a woman's hand touched my hair, until now!—"

The sun was gradually going down the last slope of day. The western sky glowed like a sea of fire reflecting its rays in the brook that glided so smoothly at their feet. A few cattle stood quietly in the water full and happy, chewing their cud and waiting for the voice of the cowboy to call them home to the milking. The shadows were growing longer upon the hill sides. The broad meadows were tremulous with the gentle evening breeze. The earth was bathed in golden light and so still, that no sound was heard save the occasional chirp of a bird and the quiet ripple of the stream over the pebbles, as it flowed past at their feet.

The hour, the secluded nook, the calmness every where inclined the heart to confidence and tenderness grave but not sad.

Pierre and Amelie talked reverently of their marriage which was to open to them the portals of a new life, when hand in hand they would walk together their allotted pathway through the world and at the end of that pathway out of the world, into the eternal.

The apostle has in a few words epitomized the meaning of love which all think they understand, and but few reach the knowledge of. A selfish man and a selfish woman love selfishly for their own sakes, but with true men and true women Love as St Paul says, "is without dissimulation in honour preferring one another."

Amelie de Repentigny and Pierre Philibert had this in common, their love had rooted itself deeply in secret and in absence long before its glorious blooming. It was without dissimulation and in honour did they truly prefer one another.

Its days of fruition alas, never came! But why anticipate? Sufficient for the day is the evil thereof. Happily the day is not sufficient for the good! and the good endures for ever! Their love never received its consummation on earth, but for all that it did not fail to receive it in heaven!

Amelie felt that touch of sadness which is never absent from the highest happiness. It is the thin veil which shadows the brightness of the vision before the eyes of mortals.

Leaning her head fondly against the shoulder of Pierre, she bade him repeat to her again—to her who had not forgotten one word or syllable of the tale he had told her before—the story of his love.

She listened with moistened eyelids and heaving bosom as he told her again of his faithfullness in the past, his joys in the present, and his hopes in the future! She feared to look up lest she should break the charm, but when he had ended she turned to him passionately and kissed his lips and hands murmuring: "Thanks my Pierre! I will be a true and loving wife to you!—"

He strained her to his bosom, and held her fast as if fearful to let her go—!

"Her image at that last embrace
Ah little thought he twas the last!—"

Something cast its shadow over them, but they heeded it not. Heeded nothing but the presence of each other—! These blissful moments were never forgotten by them. Happen what would, Pierre and Amelie were united in love forever! The sun was going down in clouds of glory. The whole west changed into a temple, dazzling with effulgence, and hung with the drapery of golden clouds. The temple of Solomon with its lofty gates glittering in the morning sun was but a feeble reflex of the gates of heaven open at this moment, as if to let in the pair who stood glorified in that hour of beauty and happiness.

The vision closed! Dim twilight crept into the Valley. It was time to return home. Pierre and Amelie, full of joy in each other, grateful for the happiest day in their lives, hopeful of tomorrow and many morrows after it, and mercifully blinded to what was really before them, rose from their seat under the great spreading elm. They slowly retraced the path through the meadow, leading to the bridge, and reentered the highway which ran to the City, where Pierre conducted Amelie home.

CHAPTER 53

THE MARKET PLACE ON ST MARTIN'S DAY

THE smoky fog which hung heavily over the City, on the morning of St Martin lifted suddenly as the bells of the Cathedral ceased to chime. The sound of the organ, the chanting of litanies within the sacred edifice mingled with the voices and din of the great market hard by.

The sun shone large and ruddy through the hazy atmosphere of the Indian Summer. A warm breeze swept over the great square singing the requiem of Autumn, among the dark boughs where only a yellow leaf here and there dangled and fluttered in the wind. The rest of Summer's foliage lay heaped in nooks and corners of the streets whither it had been swept by the autumnal gales. The first frost had come and gone like the pinch of love tingeing the deciduous trees with a flush of fire but leaving the dark pine woods and evergreens still darker amid the passing glory.

The market place then as now, occupied the open square lying between the great Cathedral of Ste Marie and the College of the Jesuits. The latter a vast Edifice, occupied one side of the square. Through its wide portal a glimpse was had of the gardens and broad avenues of ancient trees, sacred to the meditations and quiet exercises of the Reverend Fathers who walked about in pairs according to the rule of their order, which rarely permitted them to go singly.

The market place itself was lively this morning with the number of carts and stalls ranged on either side of the bright little rivulet which ran under the old Elms that intersected the square, the trees affording shade and the rivulet drink for man and beast.

A bustling loquacious crowd of Habitans and Citizens

wives and maid servants were buying, selling, exchanging compliments, or complaining of hard times. The market place was full but all were glad at the termination of the terrible war, and hopeful of the happy effect of peace in bringing plenty back again to the old market.

The people bustled up and down, testing their weak purses against their strong desires to fill their baskets with the ripe Autumnal fruits and the products of field and garden, river and *basse cour* which lay temptingly exposed in the little carts of the Market men and women who on every side extolled the quality and cheapness of their wares.

There were apples from the Cote de Beaupré small in size but impregnated with the flavour of honey, pears, grown in the old orchards about Ange Gardien, and grapes worthy of Bacchus from the Isle of Orleans with baskets of the delicious bilberries that cover the wild hills of the north shore, from the first wane of Summer until late in the autumn.

The drain of the war had starved out the Butchers stalls, but Indians and hunters took their places for the nonce with an abundance of game of all kinds, which had multiplied exceedingly during the years that men had taken to killing Bostonais and English instead of deer and wild turkies.

The market abounded with the products of the chase by land and water. Wild geese, swans and Canards, on their passage from the Bay of Hudson and a thousand northern Lakes paid heavy toll on the battures of the *Isle Aux Grues* and on the Canardiere, where they congregated in screaming thousands before the closing in of Winter upon the St Lawrence.

Fish was in especial abundance. The blessing of the old Jesuits still rested on the waters of New France, and the Fish swarmed metaphorically, with money in their mouths.

There were piles of speckled trout fit to be eaten by Popes and Kings, taken in the little pure lakes and streams tributary to the Montmorency, Lordly Salmon that swarmed in the tidal weirs along the shores of the St Lawrence, and huge Eels thick as the arm of the fisher who drew them up from their rich river beds.

In the early days of the Colony these luscious eels formed the main staple of diet to the Citizens of Quebec, who by reason of the scarcity of domestic animals, kept a sort of Lent the year round, but always with abundant thankfulness and fear of God, saving their souls while they filled their bellies and depending on the grace of Providence literally for their daily food.

There were sacks of meal ground in the Banal mills of the Seigneuries for the peoples bread, but the old tinettes of yellow butter the pride of the good wives of Beaupré and Lauzon, were rarely to be seen and commanded unheard of war prices! The hungry children who used to eat tartines of bread buttered on both sides, were now accustomed to the cry of their frugal mother, as she spread it thin as if it were gold leaf: "Mes Enfans! take care of the butter!—"

The commissaries of the Army, in other words the agents of the Grand Company had swept the settlements far and near of their herds and the Habitans soon discovered that the exposure for sale in the market of the products of the dairy, was speedily followed by a visit from the purveyors of the Army, and the seizure of their remaining Cattle.

Roots and other esculents of field and garden were more plentiful in the market among which might have been seen the newly introduced potato a vegetable long despised in New France, then endured, and now beginning to be liked and widely cultivated as a prime article of sustinance.

Immense was the petty trafficking done that morning in the market of the Upper Town, amid the jangling of the church bells and a babble of cheerful voices such as may still be heard on the self same spot on a market day with but little change of language or even of subject in the market talk of the people frequenting it.

At the upper angle of the square stood a lofty cross or holy Rood overtopping the low roofs of the shops and booths in its neighbourhood. About the foot of the cross was a platform of timber raised a few feet from the ground giving a commanding view of the whole market place.

A crowd of habitans were gathered round this platform

listening, some with exclamations of approval, not unmingled on the part of others with sounds of dissent, to the fervent address of one of the Jesuit Fathers from the College who with Crucifix in hand was preaching to the people upon the vices and backslidings of the times.

Father Glapion the Superior of the order in New France, a grave saturnine man and several other Fathers, in close black cassocks and square caps, stood behind the preacher, watching with keen eyes the faces of the auditory as if to discover who were for and who were against the sentiments and opinions promulgated by the preacher.

The storm of the great Jansenist Controversy which rent the Church of France from top to bottom had not spared the Colony, where it had early caused trouble, for that controversy grew out of the Gallican liberties of the national Church and the right of national participation in its administrations and appointments. The Jesuits ever fiercely contested these liberties. They boldly set the Tiara above the Crown, and strove to subordinate all opinions of Faith, morals, education and ecclesiastical government to the infallible judgment, of the Pope alone.

The Bishop and Clergy of New France had laboured hard to prevent the introduction of that mischevious controversy into the Colony, and had for the most part succeeded in preserving their flocks if not themselves from its malign influence. The growing agitation in France however made it more difficult to keep down troublesome spirits in the Colony and the idea got abroad not without some foundation, that the Society of Jesus had secret Commercial Relations with the Friponne. This report fanned the mouldering fires of Jansenism into a flame visible enough and threatening enough to the peace of the Church.

The failure and bankruptcy of Father Vallette's enormous speculations in the West Indies had filled France with bad debts and protested obligations, which the Society of Jesus repudiated but which the Parliament of Paris ordered them to pay. The excitement was immense all over the Kingdom and the Colonies and on the part of the order, it became a fight for existence.

The Jansenists and Molinists had long disputed the five theological propositions in terms that filled the vocabulary of invective with new coined words of polemical warfare and which afterwards supplied the fiery orators of the Revolution with an armoury of sharpest weapons. In fine, the pens and tongues of the rival Controversialists set the whole Kingdom by the ears.

The position of the order was becoming daily more critical in France. They were envied for their wealth and feared for their ability and their power. The secular clergy were for the most part against them. The Parliament of Paris in a violent decree had declared the Jesuits to have no legal standing in France. The rising minister, the Duc de Choiseul was bent upon suppressing them for their opposition to the modern philosophy. Voltaire and his followers, a growing host, thundered at them from the one side. The Vatican in a moment of inconsistency and ingratitude, thundered at them from the other. They were in the midst of Fire, and still their ability and influence over individual consciences, and especially over the female sex prolonged their power for fifteen years longer. When Louis XV driven to the wall by the Jansenists, issued his memorable decree declaring the Jesuits to be Rebels, traitors and stirrers up of mischief, the King confiscated their possessions, proscribed their persons, and banished them from the kingdom as enemies of the state.

The dissolution of the order in France, was naturally followed by its dissolution in Canada, and the great College of Quebec, which had sent out scholars to teach the people, missionaries to convert the Heathen, and martyrs to die for their faith in every part of North America subject to France became a barrack for English soldiers and such it continues to this day. The cross carved over the ancient gate-way, with the sacred letters IHS and the crown of thorns surmounting the weather vane upon the top of its highest pinnacle, alone remain to show the original purpose of that imposing structure but these trials were yet to come. The first rumbling of the distant storm was as yet only heard in New

France.

Padre Monti, an Italian newly arrived in the Colony, was a man very different from the venerable Vimont and the Jogues and the Lallements, who had preached the Evangel to the wild tribes of the Forest and rejoiced when they won the crown of martyrdom for themselves.

Monti was a bold man in his way, and ready to dare any bold deed in the interests of religion which he could not dissociate from the interests of his order. He stood up erect and commanding upon the platform under the holy rood while he addressed with fiery eloquence and Italian gesticulation the crowd of people gathered round him.

The subject he chose was an exciting one. He enlarged upon the coming of Anti-Christ, and upon the new philosophy of the age, the growth of Gallicanism in the Colony, with its schismatic progeny of Jansenists and *Honnetes Gens*, to the discouragement of true religion and the endangering of immortal souls.

His covert allusions and sharp innuendoes were perfectly understood by his hearers, and signs of dissentient feeling, were rife among the crowd. Still the people continued to listen on the whole respectfully, for whatever might be the sentiment of old France with respect to the Jesuits they had in New France inherited the profound respect of the Colonists, and deserved it.

The preacher, the better to excite the sympathy and enlist the prejudices of the people launched out into a long allegory of the suffering of Faith, which he discribed, as Christ laid on the way side, stripped, wounded and half dead, like the man who went down to Jericho and fell among thieves.

Priest and Levite meaning the Jansenists and secular clergy, passed him by, and went on the other side. The good Samaritans meaning the Jesuit Fathers had had compassion on him, bound up his wounds, pouring in oil and wine and took him to the Inn, the Church, where they left him in charge of the Host, with two pence, the tithes and offerings of the faithful, to take care of him with a promise to repay whatever was spent more.

"There were three crosses raised on Calvary" continued the preacher, "one for the impenitent thief who railed and was damned, one for the penitent thief who confessed his sin and supped with his Lord in Paradise, but Christ's cross is alone enough for us—let us embrace and kiss that!"

The preacher turned round and clasped the Holy rood in his arms after the fervid manner of Italians and all his hearers crossed themselves and repeated amen! He waited for the space of a *miserere,* and went on.

"This is all we need to live by, and die by. Oh! my Brothers! But do we live by it? We crucify our Lord daily by our trespasses and sins! but do we also Crucify the thieves in our own midst? The Jansenists who rob God of his honours and man of the merits of his works? who cry Grace! Grace! when they should cry work and pray! pray and work and earn as faithful labourers, Gods hire if it be only a penny in the eleventh hour!—"

"The *Honnetes Gens* rob God of his dues, and the Kings subjects of their hearts, crying peace! peace! and withhold the tribute money of Cæsar, the Kings dues and taxes and appeal to the Parliament of Paris not to register the decrees of the Royal Intendant! The Jansenists and the *Honnetes Gens* sit on high seats and are protected and cherished in Kings houses! Yea! in Castles!" The preacher glanced over his shoulder at the pinnacles of the Castle of St Louis visible above the housetops which intervened between it and the market place.

"No wonder Charity waxeth cold in the rich and the spirit of disobedience increaseth in the poor! these are pregnant signs of the consummation of the age, in which, if the days be not shortened, your house shall soon be left to you desolate!—"

"The Jansenists and *Honnetes Gens* sit day after day in their seats like so many Pilates asking, 'what is Truth?' and disputing the decrees of the Church, with threats to refer them to the Parliament of private judgment! *Serpentes ad serpentes! O Genimina Viperarum! Quomodo fugietis a Judicio Gehennae?* O! Generation of vipers! How will you escape the damnation of Hell?"

"These are things, O my hearers! to call down upon our heads the sword of St Michael more terrible than the sword of the English."

"The Scribes and Pharisees of Jansenism no longer sit in Moses' seat, to dispute the *droit* and the *fait* from the bocage of Port Royal, which is covered with the ruins of their house and overgrown with nettles docks and all evil weeds, the product of their five heresies, condemned like tares to everlasting fire by the *anathema* of the Vatican—! But they disappear as Religieux, to reappear as politicians and *Honnetes Gens*! In the seditious parliaments of Paris and Rouen, and, among the Bourgeois of the Colonies, like the Golden Dog, they threaten, to bite the good shepherds who take care of the flock of Christ!"

A commotion and cries of dissent broke from a portion of the crowd, but the intrepid Jesuit went on.

"The Jansenists build not the tombs of the prophets but only the tomb of the anti-prophet, Diacre Paris, of St Medard, where the uncanonized saint, amid Convulsions of men and women, wrought his two only miracles! The man who came to the tomb to pray for the restoration of his one broken leg, was carried out with two! and the woman, whom the uncanonized saint cured of an issue went blind instead! The prayers of St Paris are naught—God only heard them to their confusion!"

A loud laugh followed this sally of the preacher, not at the irreverence of the remark but at the defeat of the Jansenists, which showed that half the crowd of hearers at least, had no sympathy with the teachings of Port Royal.

The laugh however was met with many indignant denials, from another portion of the crowd, of the preachers version of the miracles at the tomb of Diacre Paris. One side seemed as determined to believe, as the others were to dispute the genuineness of the miracles asserted to have been wrought there: a point which at the moment divided France itself into two uncompromising theological camps to the intense delight of the Savans and philosophers, who ridiculed both sides and religion itself.

The King ordered the tomb to be walled up, and no one

to be allowed to approach it. This measure gave occasion to the famous Jansenist pasquinade written over the gate of the Cemetery of St Medard—

"De par le roi! Defence à Dieu,
De plus operer en ce lieu!—"

A few gentlemen some in military some in fashionable civil attire, strolled up towards the crowd, but stood somewhat aloof and outside of it. The market people pressed closer and closer round the platform, listening with mouths open and eager eyes to the sermon storing it away in their retentive memories which would reproduce every word of it, when they sat round the fire-side in the coming Winter Evenings.

One or two Recollets stood at a modest distance from the crowd still as statues with their hands hid in the sleeves of their grey gowns, shaking their heads at the arguments and still more at the invectives of the Preacher! for the Recollets were accused, wrongfully *perhaps*, of studying the Five propositions of Port Royal, more than beseemed the humble followers of St Francis to do, and they either could not, or would not repel the accusation.

The Jesuits were not a little feared by the other religious orders, for their intellectual superiority, their subtle spirit and untiring perseverance which by high ways or by ways never failed to achieve its objects. The Recollets were loved and not feared at all. Too much familiarity with all classes especially with the poor while it did not lessen the value of their labours, rubbed off some of the respect that was their due.

A proverb was current in the Colony, that a fine penknife was needed to carve a Jesuit, a Priest required a sharp chisel, but an axe was good enough to block out a Recollet! yet despite this homely opinion of the good brothers of St Francis, they came closer to the people's hearts than any other of the Religious orders.

"Padre Monti deserves the best thanks of the Intendant for his Sermon," remarked the Sieur D'Estebe to Le Mercier who accompanied him.

"And the worst thanks of his Excellency the Count! It was

bold of the Italian to beard the Governor in that manner! But
La Galissoniere is too great a philosoph to mind a Priest!" was
the half scoffing reply of Le Mercier.

"Is he? I do not think so Le Mercier! I hate them myself
but egad! I am not philosoph enough to let them know it! one
may do so at Paris, but not in New France! besides the Jesuits
are just now our fast friends, and it does not do to quarrel
with your supporters!—"

"True D'Estebe! We get no help from the Recollets! Look
yonder at Brothers Ambrose and Daniel. They would like to
tie Padre Monti neck and heels with the cord of St Francis and
bind him over to keep the peace towards Port Royal! but the
grey gowns are afraid of the black robes. Padre Monti knew
they could not catch the ball when he threw it! The Recollets
are all afraid to hurl it back!"

"Not all!" was the reply. "The Reverend Father de Berey
would have thrown it back with a vengeance! But I confess Le
Mercier! the Padre is a bold fellow to pitch into the *Honnetes
Gens*, the way he does! I did not think he would have ventured
upon it here, in the market in face of so many Habitans who
swear by the Bourgeois Philibert."

"O! it was quite time to check the prevailing murmurs of
discontent and give the *Honnetes Gens* a hint, to moderate their
hostility! Besides the Jansenists are lifting their heads again in
France, saucy as ever and we are sure to feel the effect of it
here. Dont you think so D'Estebe?"

"Yes!" replied Le Mercier. "They say the Parliament of Paris
and half the Court, are Jansenists on all fours! and that the
overthrow of the Jesuits is a settled thing among the leading
philosophs of Versailles! De Choiseul is the head and tail of
the plot! His itching fingers long to touch the money bags of
the Society of Jesus!"

"It will be doomsday with the order, if De Choiseul gets
the upper hand!" continued Le Mercier, "nor are we much
better off here! The Count has been fuming like the Kitchen
Chimney of the Castle, ever since he got wind of that affair at
Ville Marie!—"

"What affair! Le Mercier?" asked D'Estebe.

"Why, that affair of the comptoirs of the Demoiselles Desaulniers at Sault St Louis. De Choiseul is making a handle of it, I assure you!"

"Oh! I heard of *that* from the Intendant! What a fruitful text to preach from! If the Recollets only had wit and courage! how they might retort eh? Le Mercier! But how did it leak out? That secret was supposed to be water and fire proof! Those cursed old maids must have babbled as women will—!"

"No! the Demoiselles Desaulniers were tight as wax! They never told the secret. It was the Bourgeois Philibert! The Golden Dog who nosed it out as he does every thing else to our disadvantage!—"

This was in allusion to an immense Fur trading establishment carried on in the mission at Sault St Louis, in the name of a couple of Maiden Ladies of Montreal, the real owners of the establishment being certain Jesuit Fathers, who the better to secure their influence over the Iroquois of Caughnawaga and stop their secret dealings with the English, erected these comptoirs at Sault St Louis in the name of the Demoiselles Desaulniers.

The Grand Company encouraged this establishment, caring nothing for the religious considerations of the Jesuits, but hoping to secure the support of the order by allowing them a secret share in the Fur trade.

During the war no controversy had been raised respecting that establishment but with the advent of peace, the sparks of discontent were blown speedily into a flame.

Upon the arrival of the Marquis de Jonquières as Governor in place of the Count de la Galissoniere a fierce controversy began with the College of Jesuits in regard to the comptoirs of the Demoiselles Desaulniers.

The end of it was that the Marquis de Jonquières summarily decided all points according to his own view of the matter, and closed up the establishment by a royal decree.

This affair caused immense feeling and unpleasantness, and was afterwards brought up in judgment against the order in connection with their avowed commercial speculations in the West Indies, the failure of which aggravated the theological quarrel with the Jansenists and led to the suppression of the whole order in France, and her Colonies.

The bold denunciations by the Preacher against the *Honnetes Gens* and against the people's friend and protector the Bourgeois Philibert caused a commotion in the crowd of Habitans who began to utter louder and louder exclamations of dissent and remonstrance. A close observer would have noticed angry looks and clenched fists in many parts of the crowd, pressing closer and closer round the platform.

The signs of increasing tumult in the crowd did not escape the sharp eyes of Father Glapion, who seeing that the hot blooded Italian was overstepping the bounds of prudence in his harangue, called him by name, and with a half angry sign brought his sermon suddenly to a close! Padre Monti obeyed with the unquestioning promptness of an automaton. He stopped instantly, without rounding the period or finishing the sentence that was in his mouth.

His flushed and ardent manner changed to the calmness of marble, as lifting up his hands with a devout *oremus*, he uttered a brief prayer and left the puzzled people to finish his speech and digest at leisure his singular Sermon.

"I do not care for the Jansenists! Our Curé says they are no better than Calvinists," remarked an old staid Habitant to his neighbour. "A good deed without a word spoken is a better prayer for a Christian man, than a ship load of sermons like the Padre's! but lo! they are all going back into the College!"

"High time!" was the reply, "High time! broken heads would have been plentiful as potatoes in the market, had he continued to denounce the *Honnetes Gens* and the Golden Dog! If he had only continued to belabour the Jansenists, nobody could feel sorry. They can be kicked for they have few friends. I mock at St Paris! but neither do I believe in the Friponne!—!"

"You say right, neighbour! The Jesuits are too learned for you and me! I am more afraid than fond of them! It would be long before a plain honest Recollet would bid us distrust the *Honnetes Gens*, the peoples friends, or warn us against the bite of the Golden Dog—!"

"Pray, say not so, Jean Huot!" said a quiet voice, while a gentle hand twitched his sleeve. It was the Recollet Brother Daniel. "We only teach you to fear God, to honour the King and respect those in authority to be no brawlers but gentle, showing all meekness to all men. Our good Brothers the Jesuits teach you the same things, only they set greater store by the wise head than by the loving heart! unlike us poor Recollets who have only wisdom enough to know that charity never faileth, while knowledge vanisheth away! for though we have faith to remove mountains, and have not charity, we are nothing!"

The soft words of Brother Daniel, fell like oil upon the troubled waters. The angry crowd relaxed its pressure round the Holy Rood and dispersed through the market carrying to every cart, stall and group of people a feeling of uneasiness, as if the troubles of the day were not over. The sermon had excited the people and where ever a cluster of Habitans or Citizens got together, the Padre's bold attack upon the Governor and the *Honnetes Gens* was discussed with heat and acrimony.

The market was now thronged with people busily making their little purchases and paying out their money with a careful hand for the hard times severely pinched the purses and baskets of the poor.

CHAPTER 54

"BLESSED THEY, WHO DIE DOING THY WILL!"

It was the practice of the Bourgeois Philibert to leave his counting room, and walk through the market place, not for the sake of the greetings he met, although he received them from every side, nor to buy or sell on his own account, but to note with quick sympathising eye the poor and needy and relieve their wants.

Especially did he love to meet the old, the feeble, the Widow and the Orphan, so numerous from the devastation of the long and bloody war.

He knew the poor even better than the rich. It was his delight to call them by name, to fill their empty baskets with good things, and send them home rejoicing, and not thanking him for it too much! He carefully taught them, that he was only a poor Steward of his Lord's goods, and Christ bade all men be loving and helpful to each other.

The Bourgeois had another daily custom which he observed with unfailing regularity. His table in the House of the Golden Dog, was set every day with twelve covers and dishes for twelve guests, "the twelve apostles," as he gaily used to say, "whom I love to have dine with me and who come to my door in the guise of poor hungry and thirsty men, needing meat and drink, strangers to be taken in, and sick wanting a Friend." If no other guests came he was always sure of the apostles to fill his table and while some simple dish sufficed for himself he ordered the whole banquet to be given away to the poor. His choice wines which he scarcely permitted himself to taste were removed from his table and sent to the Hotel Dieu, the great Convent of the Nuns Hospitalières for the use of the sick in their charge, while the Bourgeois returned thanks with a heart more content than if Kings had dined at his table.

To-day, was the day of St Martin, the anniversary of the death of his wife, who still lived in his memory, fresh as upon the day he took her away as his Bride from her Norman home. Upon every recurrence of that day, and upon some other special times and holidays, his bounty was doubled and the Bourgeois made preparations as he jocularly used to say "not only for the twelve apostles but for the seventy diciples as well—!"

He had just dressed himself with scrupulous neatness in the fashion of a plain Gentleman as was his wont without a trace of foppery. With his stout gold headed cane in his hand he was descending the stair to go out as usual to the market, when Dame Rochelle accosted him in the hall:—

Her eyes and whole demeanour wore an expression of deep anxiety, as the good Dame looked up in the face of the Bourgeois:—

"Do not go to the Market today Dear Master!" said she beseechingly, "I have been there myself and have ordered all we need for the due honour of the day."

"Thanks good Dame! for remembering the blessed anniversary! but you know I am expected in the Market! and it is one of my special days. Who is to fill the baskets of the poor people who feel a delicacy about coming for alms to the door unless I go. Charity fulfils its mission best, when it respects the misfortune of being poor in the persons of its recipients. I must make my round of the market good Dame."

"And still Dear Master! go not to-day! I never asked you before! I do this time. I fear some evil this morning!—"

The Bourgeois looked at her inquiringly. He knew the good Dame too well not to be sure she had some weighty reason for her request:—

"What particularly moves you to this singular request Dame Rochelle?" asked he.

"A potent reason Master! but it would not weigh a grain with you, as with me! There is this morning a wild spirit afloat. People's minds have been excited by a Sermon from one of the College Fathers. The friends of the Intendant are gathered in force, they say, to clear the Market of the *Honnetes Gens*. A disturbance is impending! That Master, is one reason! My other is a presentiment that some harm will befall you if you go to the Market in the midst of such excitement."

"Thanks good Dame!" replied the Bourgeois calmly, "both for your information and your presentiment! But they only furnish an additional reason why I should go and try to prevent any disturbance among my fellow Citizens."

"Still, Master! you see not what I see! and hear not what I hear! and would not believe it, did I tell you! I beseech you go not to-day—!" exclaimed she imploringly, clasping her hands in the eagerness of her appeal.

"Good Dame," replied he, "I deeply respect your solicitude, but I could not, without losing all respect for myself as a Gentleman, stay away out of any consideration of impending danger. I should esteem it my duty all the more to go, if there be danger! which I cannot believe."

"O! that Pierre were here to accompany you! But at least take some servants with you Master!" implored the Dame persisting in her request.

"Good Dame! I cannot consult fear when I have duty to perform, besides, I am in no danger. I have enemies enough I know, but he would be a bold man who would assail the Bourgeois Philibert in the open market place of Quebec!—"

"Yet there may be such a bold man, Master!" replied she. "There are many such men who would consider they did the Intendant and themselves good service by compassing your destruction!—"

"May be so, Dame! but I should be a mark of scorn for all men if I evaded a duty small or great through fear of the Intendant—or any of his friends."

"I knew my appeal would be in vain Master but forgive my anxiety. God help you! God defend you!"

She looked at him fixedly for a moment. He saw her features were quivering with emotion and her eyes filled with tears.

"Good Dame!" said he kindly taking her hand, "I respect your motives and will so far show my regard for your forecast of danger as to take my sword, which after a good conscience is the best friend a gentleman can have to stand by him in peril. Please bring it me."

"Willingly Master! and may it be like the sword of the Cherubim to guard and protect you to day!"

She went into the great Hall for the rapier of the Bourgeois, which he only wore on occasions of full dress and ceremony. He took it smilingly from her hand, and throwing the baldrick over his shoulder bade Dame Rochelle good-bye, and proceeded to the Market.

The Dame looked earnestly after him until he turned the corner of the great Cathedral, when wiping her eyes, she went into the house and sat down pensively for some minutes.

"Would that Pierre had not gone to St Anns, to-day!" cried she. "My Master! my noble good Master! I feel there is evil abroad for him in the market to day!" She turned as was her wont in time of trouble to the open Bible that ever lay upon her table and sought strength in meditation upon its sacred pages.

There was much stir in the market when the Bourgeois began his accustomed walk among the stalls, stopping to converse with such friends as he met and especially with the poor and infirm who did not follow him—He hated to be followed—but who stood waiting his arrival at certain points which he never failed to pass. The Bourgeois knew that his poor alms-men would be standing there, and he would no more avoid them than he would avoid the Governor.

A group of girls very gaily dressed loitered through the market, purchasing bouquets of the last of Autumnal flowers, and coquetting with the young men of fashion who chose the market place for their morning promenade, and who spent their smiles and wit freely, and sometimes their money upon the young ladies they expected to find there.

This morning the Demoiselles Grandmaison and Hebert, were cheapening immortelles and dry flowers to decorate their Winter vases, a pleasant fashion not out of date in the city at the present day.

The attention of these young ladies was quite as much

taken up with the talk of their cavaliers as with their barganing, when a quick exclamation greeted them from a lady on horseback, accompanied by the Chevalier De Pean. She drew bridle sharply in front of the group, and leaning down from her saddle gave her hand to the Ladies bidding them good morning, in a cheery voice which there was no mistaking, although her face was invisible behind her veil. It was Angelique Des Meloises more gay and more fascinating than ever.

She noticed two gentlemen in the group. "O pardon me, Messieurs Le Mercier and D'Estebe!" said she, "I did not perceive you, my veil is so in the way!" She pushed it aside coquettishly and gave a finger to each of the gentlemen who returned her greeting with extreme politeness.

"Good morning! say you Angelique" exclaimed Mademoiselle Hebert. "It is good noon. You have slept rarely! How bright and fresh you look, Darling—!"

"Do I not?" laughed Angelique in reply. "It is the morning air and a good conscience make it! Are you buying flowers? I have been to Sillery for mine!" said she, patting her blooming cheeks with the end of her riding whip. She had no time for further parley, for her attention was suddenly directed by De Pean, to some stir upon the other side of the market, with an invitation to her to ride over and see what was the matter. Angelique at once wheeled her horse to accompany De Pean.

The group of girls felt themselves eclipsed and overborne by the queenly airs of Angelique and were glad when she moved off, fearing that by some adroit manoeuvre she would carry off their Cavaliers. It needed but a word as they knew, to draw them all after her—!

Angelique under the lead of De Pean, rode quickly towards the scene of confusion where men were gesticulating fiercely and uttering loud angry words, such as usually precede the drawing of swords and the rush of combatants.

To her surprise, she recognized Le Gardeur De Repentigny, very drunk, and wild with anger in the act of leaping off his horse with oaths of vengeance against some one whom she could not distinguish in the throng.

Le Gardeur had just risen from the gaming table where he had been playing all night—he was maddened with drink and excited by great losses, which in his rage he called unfair.

"Colonel St Remi had rooked him at Piquet," he said, "and refused him the chance of an honorable gamster to win back some part of his losses. His antagonist had left the Palace like a sneak! and he was riding round the City to find him and horsewhip him if he would not fight like a man!" Le Gardeur was accompanied by the Sieur de Lantagnac who by splendid dissipation had won his whole confidence. Le Gardeur when drunk thought the world did not contain a finer fellow than Lantagnac, whom he thoroughly dispised when sober.

At a hint from De Pean the Sieur de Lantagnac had clung to Le Gardeur that morning like his shadow, had drank with him again and again, exciting his wrath against St Remi, but apparently keeping his own head clear enough for whatever mischief De Pean had put into it.

They rode together to the Market place hearing that St Remi was at the sermon. Their object as Le Gardeur believed, was to put an unpardonable insult upon St Remi by striking him with his whip, and forcing him to fight a duel, with Le Gardeur or his friend. The reckless De Lantagnac asserted loudly "he did not care a straw which!—"

Le Gardeur and De Lantagnac rode furiously through the market, heedless of what they encountered or whom they ran over, and were followed by a yell of indignation from the people who recognized them as gentlemen of the Grand Company.

It chanced that at that moment, a poor almsman of the Bourgeois Philibert, was humbly and quietly leaning on his crutches, listening with bowing head and smiling lips, to the kind inquiries of his benefactor as he received his accustomed alms.

De Lantagnac rode up furiously, followed by Le Gardeur. De Lantagnac recognized the Bourgeois who stood in his way, talking to the crippled soldier. He cursed him between his teeth and lashed his horse with intent to ride him down, as if by accident.

The Bourgeois saw them approach and motioned them to stop, but in vain. The horse of De Lantagnac only swerved in his course, and without checking his speed, ran over the crippled man who instantly rolled in the dust, his face streaming with blood, from a sharp stroke of the horse shoe upon his forehead.

Immediately following De Lantagnac, came Le Gardeur lashing his horse and yelling like a demon to all to clear the way.

The Bourgeois was startled at this new danger, not to himself. He thought not of himself, but to the bleeding man lying prostrate upon the ground. He sprang forward to prevent Le Gardeur's horse going over him.

He did not in the haste and confusion of the moment, recognize Le Gardeur, who inflamed with wine and frantic with passion, was almost past recognition by any who knew him in his normal state, nor did Le Gardeur in his frenzy, recognise the presence of the Bourgeois, whose voice calling him by name with an appeal to his better nature, would undoubtedly have checked his headlong career.

But it was not to be! the terrible game of life where each man is like a pawn on the world's chess board, the game played by the spirits of good and evil, was played to-day for the life of the Bourgeois Philibert and the good lost and the evil won!

The moment was critical. It was one of those points of time where the threads of many lives and many destinies cross and intersect each other and thence part different ways, leading to life or death, happiness or despair for ever.

Le Gardeur spurred his horse madly over the wounded man, who lay upon the ground, but he did not hear him, he did not see him! Let it be said for Le Gardeur if aught can be said in his defence, "he did not see him!" His horse was just about to trample upon the prostrate cripple lying in the dust, when his bridle was suddenly and firmly seized by the hand of the Bourgeois, and his horse wheeled round with such violence that rearing back upon his haunches, he almost threw his rider headlong.

Le Gardeur not knowing the reason of this sudden

interference and flaming with wrath leaped to the ground, just at the moment when Angelique and De Pean rode up:—

Le Gardeur neither knew nor cared at that moment who his antagonist was. He saw but a bold presumptious man who had seized his bridle and whom it was his desire to punish on the spot.

De Pean recognized the stately figure and fearless look of the Bourgeois, confronting Le Gardeur. The triumph of the Friponne was at hand! De Pean rubbed his hands with extacy as he called out to Le Gardeur his voice ringing above the din of the crowd "*Achevez le*! finish him! Le Gardeur!—"

Angelique sat upon her horse fixed as a statue and pale as marble, not at the danger of the Bourgeois, whom she at once recognized, but out of fear for her lover, exposed to the menaces of the crowd who were all on the side of the Bourgeois. The flash and suddeness of the catastrophe came and went leaving its irreparable train of ruin behind it—like a thunderbolt that splits the wall of a palace, and strikes the King in the midst of his honours, so the good Bourgeois was stricken in the midst of his good works!

Le Gardeur leaped down from his horse and advanced with a terrible imprecation upon the Bourgeois, and struck him with his whip. The brave old merchant had the soul of a marshal of France. His blood boiled at the insult, he raised his staff to ward off a second blow, and struck Le Gardeur sharply upon the wrist, making his whip fly out of his hand. Le Gardeur instantly advanced again upon him, but was pressed back by the Habitans, who rushed to the defence of the Bourgeois. Then came the tempter to his ear, a word or two! and the fate of many innocent lives was decided in a moment!—

Le Gardeur suddenly felt a hand laid upon his shoulder and heard a voice, a woman's voice, speaking to him, in passionate tones.

Angelique had forced her horse into the thick of the crowd. She was no longer calm nor pale with apprehension, but her face was flushed redder than fire, and her eyes those magnetic orbs, which drove men mad, blazed upon Le

Gardeur with all their terrible influence. She had seen him struck by the Bourgeois, and her anger was equal to his own.

De Pean saw the opportunity. "Angelique" exclaimed he! "the Bourgeois strikes Le Gardeur! what an outrage! Can you bear it?"

"Never!" replied she, "neither shall Le Gardeur!"

With a plunge of her horse she forced her way close to Le Gardeur and leaning over him laid her hand upon his shoulder and exclaimed in a voice choking with passion *"Comment Le Gardeur! vous souffrez qu'un Malva comme ca vous abime de coups? et vous portez l'epée!—"* "What Le Gardeur! you allow a ruffian like that to load you with blows, and you wear a sword?"

It was enough! that look, that word, would have made Le Gardeur slaughter his father at that moment!—

Astonished at the sight of Angelique and maddened by her words as much as by the blow he had received, Le Gardeur swore he would have revenge upon the spot!! With a wild cry and the strength and agility of a panther, he twisted himself out of the grasp of the Habitans, and drawing his sword before any man could stop him, thrust it to the hilt through the body of the Bourgeois, who not expecting this sudden assault, had not put himself in an attitude of defence to meet it.

The Bourgeois fell dying by the side of the bleeding man who had just received his alms, and in whose protection he had thus risked and lost his own life.

"Bravo! Le Gardeur!" exclaimed De Pean! "that was the best stroke ever given in New France! The Golden Dog is done for! and the Bourgeois has paid his debt to the Grand Company!"

Le Gardeur looked up wildly, "Who is he De Pean?" exclaimed he, "what man have I killed?"

"The Bourgeois Philibert! who else?" shouted De Pean with a tone of exultation.

Le Gardeur uttered a wailing cry. "The Bourgeois Philibert! have I slain the Bourgeois Philibert? De Pean lies! Angelique!" said he suddenly, turning to her. "I would not kill a sparrow belonging to the Bourgeois Philibert! O tell me, De

Pean lies!—"

"De Pean does not lie! Le Gardeur," answered she frightened at his look. "The Bourgeois struck you first, I saw him strike you first, with his staff! you are a gentleman, and would kill the King if he struck you like a dog with his staff! Look! where they are lifting him up. You see it is the Bourgeois and no other!—"

Le Gardeur gave one wild look and recognized the well known form and features of the Bourgeois. He threw his sword on the ground, exclaiming "Oh! Oh! unhappy man that I am! It is parricide! parricide to have slain the Father of my Brother Pierre! Oh! Angelique des Meloises! You made me draw my sword and I knew not who it was or what I did?"

"I told you Le Gardeur and you are angry with me! But see! Hark! what a tumult is gathering we must get out of this throng! or we shall all be killed as well as the Bourgeois! Fly Le Gardeur. Fly! Go to the Palace!—"

"To hell sooner. Never shall the Palace see me again!—" exclaimed he, madly. "The people shall kill me if they will, but save yourself Angelique! De Pean! lead her instantly away from this cursed spot or all the blood is not spilt that will be spilt to day. This is of your contriving De Pean!—" cried he, looking savagely as if about to spring upon him!

"You would not harm me or her, Le Gardeur!" interrupted De Pean, turning pale, at his fierce look.

"Harm her! you fool! No! but I will harm you if you do not instantly take her away, out of this tumult. I must see the Bourgeois! Oh! God! if he be dead!—"

A great cry now rang through the Market place. "The Bourgeois is killed! The Grand Company have assasinated the Bourgeois!" Men ran up from every side shouting and gesticulating. The news spread like wild fire through the city and simultaneously, a yell for vengeance, rose from the excited multitude.

The Recollet Brother Daniel, had been the first to fly to the help of the Bourgeois. His grey robe was dyed red with the blood of the best friend and protector of their monastry. But death was too quick for even one prayer to be heard or uttered by the dying man.

The grey Brother made the sign of the Cross upon the forehead of the Bourgeois who opened his eyes once, for a moment, and looked in the face of the good Friar while his lips quivered with two inarticulate words: "Pierre! Amelie!" That was all! His brave eyes closed again forever from the light of the sun! The good Bourgeois Philibert was dead! "Blessed are the dead who die in the Lord!" repeated the Recollet, "even so says the spirit for they rest from their labours!"

De Pean had foreseen the liklihood of a popular commotion. He was ready to fly on the instant, but could not prevail on Angelique to leave Le Gardeur, who was kneeling down by the side of the Bourgeois, lifting him in his arms and uttering the wildest accents of grief as he gazed upon the pallid immovable face of the friend of his youth.

"That is the assassin! and the woman, too!" cried a sturdy Habitant. "I heard her bid him draw his sword upon the Bourgeois!"

The crowd for the moment believed that De Pean had been the murderer of Philibert.

"No! not him! It was the other! It was the Officer who dismounted! The drunken officer! who was he? where is he—?" cried the habitant, forcing his way into the presence of Le Gardeur, who was still kneeling by the side of the Bourgeois, and was not seen, for a few moments, but quickly he was identified. "That is he!" cried a dozen voices. "He is seeing if he has killed him! By God—!"

A number of men rushed upon Le Gardeur who made no defence but continued kneeling beside the Recollet Brother Daniel, over the body of the Bourgeois! He was instantly seized by some of the crowd. He held out his hands and bade them "take him prisoner, or kill him on the spot if they would, for it was he who had killed the Bourgeois!"

Half a dozen swords were instantly drawn as if to take him at his word when the terrible shrieks of Angelique pierced every ear. The crowd turned in astonishment to see who it was on horseback that cried so terribly: "Do not kill him! Do not kill Le Gardeur de Repentigny!" She called several citizens by name and entreated them to help to save him. By her sudden interference Angelique caused a division in the crowd. Le Gardeur rose up to his feet and many persons recognized him with astonishment and incredulity, for no one could believe that he had killed the good Bourgeois, who was known to have been the warm friend of the whole family of De Repentigny.

De Pean taking advantage of the sudden shift of feeling in the crowd and anxious for the safety of Angelique, seized the bridle of her horse to drag her forcibly out of the press; telling her that: "her words had been heard and in another instant the whole mob would turn its fury upon her and in order to save her life she must fly—!"

"I will not fly De Pean! You may fly yourself, for you are a coward! They are going to kill Le Gardeur and I will not forsake him! They shall kill me first!"

"But you must! You shall fly! hark! Le Gardeur is safe for the present. Wheel your horse round and you will see him standing up yonder quite safe! The crowd rather believes it was I who killed the Bourgeois, and not Le Gardeur!—I have a soul and body to be saved as well as he."

"Curse you soul and body! De Pean! You made me do it! You put those hellish words in my mouth! I will not go until I see Le Gardeur safe!—"

Angelique endeavoured frantically to approach Le Gardeur but could not, but as she looked over the surging heads of the people, she saw Le Gardeur standing up surrounded by a ring of agitated men who did not appear however to threaten him with any injury—nay, looked at him more with wonder and pity, than with menace of injury.

He was a prisoner, but Angelique did not know it or she would not have left him. As it was, urged by the most vehement objurgations of De Pean and seeing a portion of the crowd turning their furious looks towards herself as she sat upon her horse unable either to go or stay, De Pean suddenly seized her rein and spurring his own horse, dragged her furiously in spite of herself out of the tumult and rode headlong to the Casernes of the Regiment of Bearn where they took refuge for the moment, from the execrations of the populace.

The hapless Le Gardeur became suddenly sobered and conscious of the enormity of his act. He called madly for death, from the raging crowd. He held out his hands for chains to bind a murderer, as he called himself! But no one would strike him, or offer to bind him. The wrath of the people was so mingled with blank astonishment at his demeanour, his grief and his despair were so evidently genuine and so deep, that many said he was mad! and more an object of pity than of punishment.

At his own reiterated command he was given over to the hands of some soldiers and led off followed by a great crowd of people to the main guard of the Castle of St Louis, where he was left a prisoner, while another portion of the multitude gathered about the scene of the tragedy, surrounded the body of the Bourgeois which was lifted off the ground and borne aloft on men's shoulders followed by wild cries and lamentations to the house of the Golden Dog, the House which he had left but half an hour before, full of life, vigour and humanity looking before and after as a strong man looks who has done his duty and who feels still able to take the world upon his shoulders and carry it, if need were.

The sad procession moved slowly on amid the pressing agitated crowd, which asked and answered a hundred eager questions in a breath. The two poor Recollet Brothers Daniel and Ambrose, walked side by side after the bleeding corpse of their friend, and stifled their emotions by singing in a broken voice, that few heard but themselves, the words of the solitary hymn of St Francis d'Assisi, the founder of their order:—

"Praised be the Lord! by our sweet Sister, Death!
From whom no man escapes however he try.
Woe to all those who yield their parting breath,
In mortal sin—! But blessed those who die,
Doing Thy will in that decisive hour—!
The second Death oer such shall have no power!
Praise, blessing and thanksgiving to My Lord!
For all he gives and takes be he adored!—"

Dame Rochelle heard the approaching noise and tumult. She looked out of the window, and could see the edge of the crowd in the market place, tossing to and fro, like breakers upon a rocky shore. The people in the streets were hurrying towards the market. Swarms of men employed in the magazines of the Bourgeois, were running out of the Edifice towards the same spot.

The Dame divined at once that something had happened her master. She uttered a fervent prayer for his safety. The noise grew greater, and as she reached out of the window to demand of passers by "what was the matter?" a voice shouted up, that "the Bourgeois was dead! that he had been killed by the Grand Company, and they were bringing him home!—"

The voice passed on, and no one but God heeded the long wail of grief, that rose from the good Dame as she fell upon her knees in the door way, unable to proceed further. She preserved her consciousness however.

The crowd now swarmed in the streets about the doors of the House. Presently were heard the shuffling steps of a number of men in the Great Hall, bearing the body of the Bourgeois into the large room, where the sunshine was playing so gloriously.

The crowd impelled by a feeling of reverence stood back. Only a few ventured to come into the house.

The rough habitans who brought him in, laid him upon a couch and gazed for some moments in silent awe upon the noble features so pale and placid which now lay motionless before them.

Here was a man fit to rule an empire, and who did rule the half of New France! who was no more now, save in the love and gratitude of the people, than the poorest piece of human clay in the potter's field! The great leveller had passed his rule over him as it passes it over everyone of us. The dead lion was less now than the living dog, and the Golden Dog itself was henceforth only a memory, and an epitaph forever of the tragedy of this eventful day!

"O my Master! My good noble Master!" exclaimed Dame Rochelle, as she roused herself up and rushed to the chamber of the dead. "Your implacable enemies have killed you at last! I knew it! O! I knew that your precious life would one day pay the penalty of your truth and justice! And Pierre! O where is he, on this day of all days of grief and sorrow?"

She wrung her hands at the thought of Pierre's absence today and what a welcome home awaited him—!—

The noise and tumult in the street continued to increase. The friends of the Bourgeois poured into the house among them the Governor and La Corne St Luc, who came with anxious looks and hasty steps to inquire into the details of the murder.

The Governor after a short consultation with La Corne St Luc, who happened to be at the Castle, fearing a riot and an attack upon the magazines of the Grand Company ordered the troops immediately under arms, and despatched strong detachments under the command of careful and trusty officers, to the palace of the Intendant, and the great warehouses of the Friponne, and also into the Market-place and to the residence of the Lady de Tilly, not knowing in what direction the fury of the populace might direct itself.

The orders were carried out in a few minutes, without noise or confusion. The Count with La Corne St Luc whose countenance bore a concentration of sorrow and anger wonderful to see, hastened down to the House of Mourning. Claude Beauharnois and Rigaud de Vaudreuil followed hastily after them. They pushed through the crowd that filled the Rue Buade, and the people took off their hats while the air resounded with denunciations of the Friponne and appeals for vengeance upon the assassin of the Bourgeois.

The Governor and his companions were moved to tears at the sight of their murdered friend, lying in his bloody vesture, which was open to enable the worthy Doctor Gauthier who had run in all haste to examine the still oozing wound. The Recollet Brother Daniel still knelt in silent prayer at his feet, while Dame Rochelle with trembling hands arranged the drapery decently over her dead Master, repeating to herself:—

"It is the end of trouble! and God has mercifully taken him away before he empties the vials of his wrath upon this New

France and gives it up for a possession to our enemies! What, says the prophet? 'The righteous perisheth and no man layeth it to heart, and merciful men are taken away, none considering that the righteous are taken away from the evil to come!—'"

The very heart of La Corne St Luc seemed bursting in his bosom, and he choked with agony as he placed his hand upon the forehead of his friend, and reflected that the good Bourgeois had fallen by the sword of his Godson, the old man's pride, Le Gardeur de Repentigny!

"Had death come to him on the broad common road of mortality, had he died like a soldier in the battle field," exclaimed La Corne, "I would have had no spite at Fate! But to be stabbed in the midst of his good deeds of alms, and by the hand of one whom he loved—Yes! by God! I will say it! and by one who loved him! Oh! it is terrible Count! Terrible and shameful to me as if it had been the deed of my own son!"

"La Corne! I feel with you the grief and shame of such a tragedy! But there is a fearful mystery in this thing, which we cannot yet unravel. They say the Chevalier de Pean dropped an expression that sounded like a plot—! I cannot think Le Gardeur de Repentigny would deliberately and with forethought have killed the Bourgeois!—"

"On my life he never would! He respected the Bourgeois, nay loved him, for the sake of Pierre Philibert as well for his own sake! Terrible as is his crime! he never committed it out of malice or aforethought! He has been himself the victim of some hellish plot, for a plot there has been. This has been no chance medly Count!" exclaimed La Corne St Luc impetuously.

"It looks like chance medly, but I suspect more than appears on the surface," replied the Governor. "The removal of the Bourgeois decapitates the party of the *Honnetes Gens*, does it not?"

"Gospel is not more true! The Bourgeois was the only merchant in New France capable of meeting their monopoly, and fighting them with their own weapons! Bigot and the Grand Company will have everything their own way now!"

"Besides there was the old feud of the Golden Dog!"

continued the Governor. "Bigot took its allusion to the Cardinal as a personal insult to himself. Did he not La Corne?"

"Yes! and Bigot knew he deserved it equally with his Eminence! whose arch tool he had been!" replied La Corne. "By God! I believe Bigot has been at the bottom of this plot! It would be worthy of his craft!"

"These are points to be considered, La Corne! But such is the secrecy of these men's councils that I doubt we may suspect more than we shall ever be able to prove." The Governor looked much agitated.

"What amazes me, Count is not that the thing should be done! but that Le Gardeur should have done it!" exclaimed La Corne, with a puzzled expression.

"That is the strangest circumstance of all, La Corne!" observed the Governor. "The same thought has struck me. But he was mad with wine they say, and men who upset their reason do not seldom reverse their conduct towards their friends. They are often cruellest to those whom they love best."

"I will not believe but that he was made drunk purposely to commit this crime." exclaimed La Corne striking his hand upon his thigh. "Le Gardeur in his senses would have lost his right hand sooner than have raised it against the Bourgeois!"

"I feel sure of it! His friendship for Pierre Philibert to whom he owed his life was something rarely seen nowadays!" remarked the Count.

La Corne felt a relief in bearing testimony in favour of Le Gardeur. "They loved one another like brothers" said he "and more than brothers. Bigot had corrupted the habits, but could never soil the heart or lessen the love of Le Gardeur for Pierre Philibert, or his respect for the Bourgeois, his father!—"

"It is a mystery La Corne! I cannot fathom it! but there is one more danger to guard against," said the Governor meditatively, "and we have sorrow enough already among our friends.—"

"What is that, Count?" La Corne stood up erect as if in mental defiance of a new danger.

"Pierre Philibert will return home to night," replied the

Governor. "He carries the sharpest sword in New France! A duel between him and Le Gardeur would crown the machinations of the secret plotters in this murder. He will certainly revenge his father's death even upon Le Gardeur."

La Corne St Luc started at this suggestion! but presently shook his head. "My life upon it!" said he. "Le Gardeur would stand up to receive the sword of Pierre through his heart, but he would never fight him! Besides the unhappy boy is a prisoner!"

"We will care well for him and keep him safe. He shall have absolute justice La Corne, but no favour."

An officer entered the room to report to the Governor that the troops had reached their assigned posts and that there was no symptom of rioting among the people in any quarter of the city.

The Governor was greatly relieved by these tidings. "Now, La Corne!" said he, "we have done what is needful for the public. I can spare you! for I know where your heart yearns most to go, to offer the consolations of a true friend."

"Alas, Yes!" replied La Corne sadly "Men weep tears of water but women tears of blood! What is our hardest grief compared with the overwhelming sorrow and desolation that will pass over my poor God-daughter Amelie de Repentigny, and the noble Lady de Tilly at this doleful news?"

"Go, comfort them, La Corne! and the angel of consolation go with you!—" The Governor shook him by the hand and wished him God speed.

La Corne St Luc instantly left the house. The crowd uncovered and made way for him as they would have done for the Governor himself, as with hasty strides he passed up the Rue du Fort and on towards the cape where stood the mansion of the Lady de Tilly.

"O Rigaud! what a day of sorrow this is!" exclaimed the Governor to De Vaudreuil, on their return to the Castle of St Louis. "What a bloody and disgraceful event to record in the annals of New France!—"

"I would give half I have in the world could it be forever blotted out!" replied De Vaudreuil. "Your friend Herr Kalm has left us fortunately before he could record in his book for all Europe to read that men are murdered in New France to sate the vengeance of a Royal Intendant, and fill the purses of the greatest company of thieves that ever plundered a nation."

"Hark Rigaud! Do not say such things!" interrupted the Governor, "I trust it is not so bad as that! But it shall be seen into, if I remain Governor of New France! the blood of the noble Bourgeois shall be required at the hands of all concerned in his assassination. The blame of it shall not rest wholly upon that unhappy Le Gardeur. We will trace it up to its very origin and fountainhead—!"

"Right Count! You are true as steel! but mark me! If you begin to trace this assassination up to its origin and fountainhead, your letters of recall will be despatched by the first ship that leaves France after the news reaches Versailles!—" Rigaud looked fixedly at the Count as he said this.

"It may be so, Rigaud!" replied the Count sadly,—"strange things take place under the regime of the strange women who now rule the Court. Nevertheless while I am here, my whole duty shall be done in this matter! justice shall be meted out with a firm and impartial hand no matter who shall be incriminated."

The Count de la Galissoniere at once summoned a number of his most trusted and most sagacious councillors together—the Intendant was not one of those summoned—to consider what steps it behoved them to take to provide for the public safety and to ensure the ends of Justice in this lamentable tragedy.

CHAPTER 55

"EVIL NEWS RIDES POST"

THE sunbeams never shone more golden through the casement of a lady's bower, than on that same morning of St Martin's through the window of the chamber of Amelie de Repentigny as she sat in the midst of a group of young ladies holding earnest council over the dresses and adornments of herself and companions who were to be her bridesmaids at the altar on her marriage with Pierre Philibert.

Amelie had risen from pleasant dreams. The tender flush of yesterday's walk on the banks of the Lairet lingered on her cheek all night long, like the rosy tint of a midsummer's sunset. The loving words of Pierre floated through her memory like a strain of divine music, with the sweet accompaniment of her own modest confessions of love which she had so frankly expressed.

How full and ample seemed all that Pierre had said to her. His words had been glorified in her fervid imagination, while she reflected tremulously over her own expressions, lest they might have seemed either too forward or too cold.

A girl who has yielded her heart to a lover finds it not easy to satisfy herself. If too fond she fears he may despise her; if too reserved he may doubt her affection. But when the words of betrothal have been spoken, and its precious pledges given, a true woman is like Sara in the presence of Abraham, bowing herself and in spirit calling him Lord. She exalts him in her fancy to a height of worthiness that justifies the worship of her entire being; to love, honour and obey seems to her less a duty than a passionate delight.

Amelie's spirits overflowed with happiness. She had dreamed last night of Elysian fields. But, even the heavenly

694

landscape had resembled the sloping shores of the Lake of Tilly or the winding banks of the pastoral Lairet.

Clothed in shining robes with a garland of flowers upon his head which she had placed there as a sign that he was king of her heart and the ruler of her destiny, Pierre had seemed to lead her by the hand while choirs of happy angels sang their marriage song, and blessed their union for ever and ever.

Amelie's chamber was vocal with gaiety and laughter, for with her today were the chosen friends and lifelong companions, who had ever shared her love and confidence.

There were Hortense Beauharnois happy also in her recent betrothal to Jumonville de Villiers, Heloise de Lotbiniere so tenderly attached to Amelie, and whom of all her friends, Amelie wanted most to call by the name of sister, Agathe the fair daughter of La Corne St Luc, so like her father in looks and spirit, and Amelie's cousin Marguerite de Repentigny, the reflection of herself in feature and manners.

There was rich material in that chamber for the conversation of such a group of happy girls. The bridal trousseau was spread out before them, and upon chairs and couches lay dresses of marvellous fabric and beauty, muslins and shawls of India and Cashmere, and the finest products of the looms of France and Holland. It was a trousseau fit for a Queen and an evidence at once of the wealth of the Lady de Tilly, and of her unbounded love for her niece Amelie. The gifts of Pierre were not mingled with the rest, nor as yet had they been shown to her bridesmaids. Amelie kept them for a pretty surprise upon another day.

Upon the table stood a golden casket of Venetian workmanship, the carvings of which represented the marriage of Cana in Galilee. It was stored with priceless jewels which dazzled the sight and presented a constellation of starry gems, the like of which had never been seen in the New World. It was the gift of the Bourgeois Philibert who gave this splendid token of his affection and utter contentment with Amelie, as the bride of his son and heir.

Amelie regarded these things with the natural pleasure of a pure and noble girl. She was a true woman and loved beautiful things simply because of their beauty, but she valued their richness only because it was a proof of the love of those whom she most valued and most delighted to please.

Without that ennobling sentiment all the precious gifts in the world would have seemed to her no better than dross and fairy glamour of sticks and straw.

She was supremely happy, and gay beyond her wont, as she sat this morning amidst her fair companions, dressed in a white robe soft and pure as a fresh snowwreath. Her black tresses drooped carelessly over her neck. Her wonderful eyes dark with excessive light, shot proud and happy glances at her companions, but their tenderest expression was the inward look she cast upon the image of Pierre in her own heart. Feelings long suppressed were now revealed, with shyness indeed, but no shame, and all the world might know if it liked that Amelie had given the rich treasure of her love to Pierre Philibert.

She wore that day for her only ornament, a golden cross, the birthday gift of Pierre, and a brooch the gift of Le Gardeur. On her finger was a ring, the pledge of her betrothal, which she never afterwards removed for a moment, in all her subsequent life.

These five girls equal in age and almost in beauty, so like, yet so dissimilar, had all been companions at School and formed together the fairest circle of society in the Capital.

In the ease of frankest intimacy, they met in the chamber of their friend sitting on chairs or stools or kneeling upon the floor as chance or fancy dictated, while they settled the details of their wedding garments, with as much seriousness as the Diplomats at Aix-La-Chapelle had recently settled the great treaty of peace for Europe—And why not?—

Woman's Kingdom comes closer to the human heart than a King's! Her accession to her throne, is to her, and to the man she marries an event of more lasting importance than any other revolution in mundane things.

It is her prerogative to govern the household where a man lays up the riches of his life. She is Queen there wearing the crown, and no true man disputes her right of ruling her kingdom *Jure Divino.*

Hortense Beauharnois knelt in graceful abandon at the feet of Amelie, resting her arms upon the lap of her friend, holding her by the hand as she twisted the betrothal ring round and round her slender finger.

"We little thought of this in the Convent, at least you did, not Amelie!" said she with an arch look, laying her finger, on which was a ring given her by Jumonville de Villiers, by the side of Amelie's finger, as if to compare them.

"It is a charming ring yours, Hortense! and one which any woman might be proud to wear!" said Amelie in a low voice, as she caressed the finger of her friend.

"I am proud of it!" replied Hortense in a whisper. "Except your Pierre I know no gentleman in the world like Jumonville."

"You think he resembles Pierre?" said Amelie.

"In his noble ways he does, if not in his looks. He has not Pierre's stature nor steel blue Norman eyes, but he is as handsome in his own way, and as brave and generous. He is, I admit proudly—Dark complexioned to a fault!"

"What fault Hortense!" asked Amelie, pressing her hand and smiling in sympathy with her friend.

"Nay, he has no fault, unless loving me so much be one! Would I were more worthy of him! but I will try to be a worthy wife to Jumonville. I am sure I shall be a loving one! You too are proud and happy today, Amelie!"—

"Yes, I almost tremble at it!" replied Amelie gravely. "I am so very happy darling, that I almost fear it may be the forerunner of some misfortune. But Pierre comes home tonight, not to go away again without me! do you understand? And Le Gardeur has written me the kindest letter! My brother will yet be his own noble self again. O Hortense! you cannot comprehend the happiness that thought brings me!—"

"Yes! I can imagine it, were Claude and not Le Gardeur the returning prodigal! Dear Le Gardeur! Shall I own to you Amelie? It was fortunate that Jumonville returned when he did, or I know not what might have happened to me! It might have been my lot to become the rival of Heloise, and like her be triumphed over by Angelique."

"Fortunately you escaped!" whispered Amelie. "Poor Heloise! she would have been comforted somewhat had you been her rival instead of Angelique! for she loves Le Gardeur so unselfishly that she would rejoice in his happiness, even at the hands of another."

"Alas! Poor me! I could not boast such angelic resignation. It is wicked to confess it, Amelie! But if Jumonville would not have let me be the cause of his happiness, I fear I should not have liked to hear of another making him happy!—Is not that very selfish and very wicked—? though it is very natural!" said Hortense with honest emphasis.

"Ah! you do not know yourself! Hortense! you are better than that although I fear most women would do as you say," replied Amelie, caressing her hand.

"Well, never mind! you and I are fortunate Amelie! we shall never be put to the test! Pierre Philibert though the pattern of courtesy to our sex has never given a second look at any girl in the city—since he saw you!—"

"And Jumonville?—" asked Amelie archly.

"O! he is a gallant of the first water! He admires all ladies so generally and only one so particularly that I have no room for jealousy. But I should die Amelie were he unfaithful."

"To you, he could not be, Darling! nor I think to any one who trusted in him."

"You two engaged ones! are so selfish in your happiness, that I protest against any more whisperings of mutual congratulations!" exclaimed the lively Marguerite de Repentigny, who sat in the midst of a foaming sea of silks and muslins, veils and orange blossoms, eagerly discussing with the bridesmaids the respective merits of each toilette.

"I wish," interrupted the pretty Agathe La Corne St Luc, "you would both get married and have done with it! It is provoking to see you two so insufferably happy and we looking on and—and—"—

"Languishing! Agathe!" replied Hortense springing up and embracing her. "I will be your bridesmaid dear! when among all your admirers you can decide which you will take."

"Thanks Hortense! I could not have a fairer one. But my prince has not arrived yet to claim his bride! My husband shall be a king in my eyes, even were he a beggar in the eyes of others. But if not a king he shall be an officer, for I shall never marry out of the army!—"

"You remember our school-girl play," continued Agathe archly—

"Je voudrais bien me marier,
Mais j'ai grand'peur de me tromper—!
Je voudrais bien d'un officier—!
Je marcherais à pas carrés—
Dans ma jolie chambrette!"

Agathe holding up her pretty chin and fluttering her dress as she sang this merry doggrel, marched with a mock military step to and fro across the floor, wearing a garland of orange blossoms, and a veil upon her head, and with such an air of mimicry, taking off first Amelie and then Hortense, that the whole bevy of girls laughed and screamed with delight, while Agathe continued her promenade singing the drollest impromptus her wit suggested.

The sun of St Martin shone gloriously through the casement, shedding an aureole of golden light over the group of fair girls. A stream of slanting rays shot into the little oratory so that it looked to the eye of Amelie like the ladder of heaven, where the Patriarch saw angels ascending and descending upon it.

As she gazed at the singular appearance she recited a silent prayer of thanks to God for her happiness, while Heloise in a still more spiritual mood, laid her hand upon the shoulder of Amelie, and also watched the wonderful play of light flaming round the cross and thinking thoughts she had never given utterance to except in her own secret musings.

The girls were startled in the midst of their glee by the sudden dashing past of a horseman, who rode in a cloud of dust, followed by a wild strange cry as of many people shouting together in lamentation and anger.

Amelie and Heloise looked at each other with a strange

feeling, but sat still, while the rest rushed to the balcony where they leaned eagerly over it to catch sight of the passing horseman and discover the meaning of the loud and still repeated cry.

The rider had disappeared round the angle of the cape, but the cry from the city waxed still louder, as if more and more voices joined in it.

Presently men on horseback and on foot, were seen hurrying towards the Castle of St Louis, and one or two shot up the long slope of the Place d'Armes galloping towards the mansion of the Lady de Tilly talking and gesticulating in the wildest manner.

"In God's name, what is the matter, Monsieur La Force?" exclaimed Hortense as that gentleman rode furiously up and checked his horse violently at the sight of the ladies upon the balcony.

Hortense repeated her question. La Force took off his hat and looked up puzzled and distressed. "Is the Lady de Tilly at home?" inquired he eagerly.

"Not just now! She has gone out, but what is the matter in Heaven's name?" repeated she, as another wild cry came up from the city.

"Is Mademoiselle Amelie home?" again asked La Force with agitated voice.

"She is home! Heavens! have you some bad news to tell her, or the Lady de Tilly?—" breathlessly inquired Hortense.

"Bad news for both of them, for all of us! Hortense! but I will not be the bearer of such terrible tidings. Others are following me, ask them? O Hortense! prepare poor Amelie for the worst news that ever came to her."

The Sieur La Force would not wait to be further questioned. He rode off furiously.

The bridesmaids all turned pale with affright at these ominous words, and stood looking at each other and asking what they could mean—!

Amelie and Heloise caught some of the conversation between Hortense and La Force. They sprang up and ran to the balcony just as two of the servants of the house came rushing up with open mouths, staring eyes, and trembling with excitement. They did not wait to be asked what was the matter, but as soon as they saw the ladies, they shouted out the terrible news, as the manner of their kind is, without a thought of the consequences, "that Le Gardeur had just killed the Bourgeois Philibert in the Market place! and was himself either killed or a prisoner! and the people were going to burn the Friponne and hang the Intendant under the tablet of the Golden Dog, and all the city was going to be destroyed—!"

The servants having communicated this piece of wild intelligence, instantly rushed into the house and repeated it to the household, filling the mansion in a few moments with shrieks and confusion.

It was in vain Hortense and Agathe La Corne St Luc strove to withhold the terrible truth from Amelie. Her friends endeavoured with kindly force and eager exhortations to prevent her coming to the balcony, but she would not be stayed. In her excitement she had the strength of one of God's angels, she had caught enough of the speech of the servants to gather up its sense into a connected whole. In a moment of terrible enlightenment that came like a thunderbolt driven through her soul, she understood the whole significance of their tidings.

Her hapless brother maddened with disappointment, drink and desperation had killed the father of Pierre! the father of her betrothed husband! his own friend and hers! Why or how was a mystery of amazement—!

She saw at a glance all the ruin of it! Her brother a murderer, the Bourgeois a bleeding corpse! Pierre her lover and her pride lost—lost—to her forever! the blood of his father rising up between them calling for vengeance upon Le Gardeur, and invoking a curse upon the whole house of Repentigny—!—

The heart of Amelie but a few moments ago expanding with joy and overflowing with the tenderest emotions of a loving bride, suddenly collapsed and shrivelled like a leaf in the fire of this unlooked for catastrophe.

She stared wildly and imploringly in the countenances

of her trembling companions, as if for help, but no human help could avail her. She spake not, but uttering one long agonizing scream fell senseless upon the bosom of Heloise de Lotbinière, who herself nigh fainting, bore Amelie with the assistance of her friends to a couch where she lay unconscious of the tears and wailing that surrounded her.

In the absence of the Lady de Tilly Marguerite de Repentigny with the presence of mind so characteristic of her family, ordered the servants to their duties and the doors to be shut against all visitors from the city, numbers of whom were hurrying up to the Cape, bearing the doleful tidings, and anxious to sympathize with their distress.

Madame Couillard, Madame de Grandmaison and other neighbours near and far, vainly knocked at the door of the mansion—Marguerite was inexorable. She would not have Amelie gazed, upon or made a subject of comment or of curiosity or even sympathy to the idle gossips of the City.

Marguerite with her weeping companions remained in the chamber of Amelie watching eagerly for some sign of returning consciousness, and assiduously administering such restoratives as were at hand.

Their patience and tenderness were at last rewarded. Amelie gave a flutter of reviving life. Her dark eyes opened and stared wildly for a moment at her companions, with a blank look until they rested upon the veil and orange blossoms on the head of Agathe, who had put them on in such a merry mood and forgotten in the sudden catastrophe to take them off again.

The sight of the bridal veil and wreath seemed to rouse Amelie to consciousness. The terrible news of the murder of the Bourgeois by Le Gardeur flashed upon her mind and she pressed her burning eyelids hard shut with her hands as if not to see the hideous thought.

Her companions wept, but Amelie found no relief in tears, as she murmured the name of the Bourgeois, Le Gardeur and of Pierre.

They spoke softly to her in tones of tenderest sympathy, but she scarcely heeded them, absorbed as she was, in deepest thought, and still pressing her eyes shut, as if she had done with day and cared no more to see the bright sunshine that streamed through the lattice. The past, present and future of her whole life started up before her in terrible distinctness, and seemed concentrated in one present spot of mental anguish.

Amelie came of an heroic race, stern to endure pain as to inflict it, capable of unshrinking fortitude and of desperate resolves. A few moments of terrible contemplation decided her forever, changed the whole current of her life, and overthrew as with an earthquake, the gorgeous palace of her maiden hopes and long cherished anticipations of love and happiness as the wife of Pierre Philibert.

She saw it all! there was no room for hope! no chance of averting the fatal doom that had fallen upon her! Her life as she had long pictured it to her imagination was done and ended! Her projected marriage with Pierre Philibert— It was like sudden death! In one moment the hand of God had transported her from the living to the dead world of woman's love!—A terrible crime had been perpetrated, and she innocent as she was, must bear the burthen of punishment.

She had but one object now to live for, to put on sackcloth and ashes and wear her knees out in prayers before God, imploring forgiveness and mercy upon her unhappy brother and expiate the righteous blood of the just man who had been slain by him.

She rose hastily and stood up. Her face was beautiful as the face of a marble Niobe but as pale and as full of anguish.

"My loving bridesmaids!" said she, "It is now all over with poor Amelie de Repentigny! Tell Pierre!" and here she sobbed, almost choking in her grief. "Tell Pierre not to hate me for this blood that lies on the threshold of our house! Tell him how true and faithfully I was preparing to devote myself to his happiness as his bride and wife. Tell him how I loved him and I only forsake him because it is the inexorable decree of my sad fate! Not my will but my cruel misfortune! But I know his noble nature. He will pity not hate me. Tell him it will even rejoice me where I am going, to know that Pierre Philibert still loves me! I cannot, dare not ask him to pardon Le Gardeur! I dare not pardon him myself! But I know Pierre will be just and merciful to my poor brother, even in this hour of doom!"

"And now," continued she, speaking with a terrible energy. "Put away these bridal deceits! they will never be worn by me! I have a garb more becoming the bridal of death, more fitting to wear by the sister of—O God! I was going to say, of a murderer!—"—

Amelie with a wild desperation gathered up the gay robes and garlands and threw them in a heap in the corner of the chamber. "My glory is departed!" said she, "O Hortense! I am punished for the pride I took in them! Yet it was not for myself but for the sake of *him* I took pride in them! Bestow them I pray you upon some more happy girl who is poor in fortune but rich in love, who will wear them at her bridal instead of the unhappy Amelie."

The group of girls beheld her, while their eyes were swimming with tears. "I have long, long kept my bridal veil in my closet," she went on, "and knew not it was to be mine!" Opening a wardrobe she took out a long black veil. It had belonged to her grand aunt the Nun Madelaine de Repentigny, and was kept as an heir loom in her family.

"This," said she, "shall be mine till death! Embrace me, O my sisters, my bridesmaids and companions! I go now to the Ursulines to kneel at the door and crave admittance to pass a life of penitence for Le Gardeur and of prayer for my beloved Pierre."

"O Amelie! think what you do!" exclaimed Hortense Beauharnois. "Be not hasty! Take not a step that cannot be recalled. It will kill Pierre!—"

"Alas! I have killed him already," said she, "but my mind is made up! dear Hortense! I love Pierre, but O! I could never look at his face again without shame, that would burn like guilt. I give myself henceforth to Christ, not for my own sake, but for his, and for my unhappy brother's! Do not hinder me, dear friends! and do not follow me! May you all be happy in your happiness, and pray for poor Amelie whom fate has stricken so hard and so cruelly in the very moment of her brightest hope! and now let me go—alone—and God bless you all—! bid my aunt to come and see me" added she. "I cannot even wait her return."

The girls stood weeping round her, and kissed and embraced her over and over. They would not disobey her request to be allowed to go alone to the convent, but as she turned to depart she was clasped round the neck by Heloise de Lotbinière, exclaiming that she should not go alone! that the light of the world had gone out, for her as well as for Amelie! and she would go with her—!—

"But why Heloise would you go with me to the Convent?" asked Amelie sadly. She knew but too well, why?—

"O my cousin! I too would pray for Le Gardeur! I too!— but no matter! I will go with you Amelie! If the door of the Ursulines open for you, it shall open for Heloise de Lotbinière, also!"

"I have no right to say nay, Heloise! nor will I!" replied Amelie embracing her, "you are of my blood and lineage—and the lamp of Repentigny is always burning in the holy chapel to receive broken-hearted penitents, like you and me—!"

"O Heloise! Do not you also, leave us! Stay till tomorrow!" exclaimed the agitated girls amazed at this new announcement.

"My mind is made up, it has long been made up!" replied Heloise. "I only waited the marriage of Amelie before consummating my resolution to enter the convent. I go now to comfort Amelie, as no other friend in the world can comfort her. We shall be more content in the midst of our sorrows, to be together."

It was in vain to plead with or to dissuade them. Amelie and Heloise were inexorable and eager to be gone. They again kissed their companions, with many tears bidding them a last farewell, and the two weeping girls hiding their heads under their veils left the bright mansion that was their home, and proceeded with hasty steps towards the Convent of the Ursulines.

CHAPTER 56

THE URSULINES

CLOSELY veiled, acknowledging no one, looking at no one, and not themselves recognized by any, but clinging to each other for mutual support, Amelie and Heloise traversed swiftly the streets that led to the Convent of the Ursulines.

At the doors and in the porches and galleries of the old fashioned houses, women stood in groups discussing eagerly the wild reports that were flying to and fro through the city, and looked up and down the streets for further news of the tragedy in the Market-place. The male part of the population had run off and gathered in excited masses round the mansion of the Golden Dog, which was suddenly shut up and long streamers of black crape were hanging at the door.

Many were the inquisitive glances and eager whisperings of the goodwives and girls, as the two ladies deeply veiled in black passed by with drooping heads and handkerchiefs pressed against their faces, while more than one quick ear caught the deep suppressed sobs that broke from their bosoms. No one ventured to address them however, although their appearance caused no little speculation as to who they were and whither they were going.

"They look broken-hearted poor things!" exclaimed good Madame Bissot to her next door neighbour in the Rue des Jardins. "Some friends of the Bourgeois, or perhaps they are making for the Convent. They are high ladies I warrant by their dress, and certainly sweeter figures I never saw. Did you Madame Hamel?"

"Never!" replied Madame Hamel eagerly, "I do wonder who they can be! It is plain to see they are bound for the Ursulines. I have lived in the Rue des Jardins, maid and wife thirty years Madame Bissot, and I have never been mistaken in the appearance of a girl taking her broken heart to the Convent to lay it upon the tomb of Mere Marie de l'Incarnation!"

Madame Bissot was at no loss for an explanation. "That is because our sex is all feeling, Madame Hamel!" said she. "I was all feeling myself when I was a girl! They say that the tomb of Mere Marie has a rare secret for consoling the troubles of the heart! But is it not queer, Madame Hamel! that whenever a girl loses her lover she always wants to fly to the Convent? You remember pretty Madelaine des Meloises, how she ran barefoot to the Ursulines, leaping out of bed at midnight when news came of the death of that young officer to whom she was betrothed! She has found consolation in the Cloister; for you know how she sings like a nightingale ever since! as we all can hear any day at Vespers, if we chose to listen, as I always do."

"Yes! It is very queer!" replied Madame Hamel "but my goodman always says, 'girls' feelings, men's failings, and love's foolings, keep life alive!' Nothing can overtake a girl on the run from a disappointment, or to a wedding! A man who is jilted never delays helping himself to a second cake, if he be at all hungry for matrimony." Madame Hamel had been thrice married and was therefore an authority on the subject.

"Indeed, a man has little chance to escape a second cake now a days," replied Madame Bissot, "and it is well they can stand a first, second and even third course of matrimony. This cruel war has left men as scarce as gold and as valuable, while the women are plenty as hops and as cheap! How fortunate it is that peace has been made! for it began to be prophesied that the day was coming in New France when seven women would take hold of one man, and wear their own clothes too, for the sake of being called by his name!—What a dreadful prospect. Think of me with the seventh part of a man, Madame Hamel!—"

"It is a sad reflection Madame Bissot! and me with my ten daughters upon my hands! What to do with them, in any way decent and respectable except make nuns of them, I do not know! I ought to have been grandmother by this time! Here am I but seventeen years older than my eldest daughter! I wish some of my girls would run away to the Convent too before they do worse. I see no chance of marrying them—!"

"It is a bad prospect" replied Madame Bissot! "as I heard a gentleman of the Castle—It was the Sieur Lemoine—remark the other day, as I was going to church. 'The women,' he said, 'would have the Colony all to themselves by and by if the war continued, and we should have to fight the English, with an army of Amazons' so he called them, which I take to be some strange tribe of savages. But look! Madame Hamel! those two ladies are really crossing over to the Convent. I knew I was not mistaken! Who can they be?"

Whether the legitimate curiosity of the good gossips of the Rue des Jardins was ever gratified on this point, the record sayeth not. But Amelie and Heloise almost fainting under their sorrow, stood upon the broad stone step which formed the threshold that separated the world they were entering into from the world they were leaving.

The high gables and old belfry of the Monastery stood bathed in sunlight. The figure of St Joseph that dominated over the ancient portal held out his arms and seemed to welcome the trembling fugitives into the house with a gesture of benediction.

The sun darted a stream of rays into the deep porch, illuminating its gloomy interior. The golden shafts shot through the open wicket, forming upon the stone floor within a square of light emblazoned with the figure of a cross projected from the bars of the wicket.

The two ladies paused upon the stone steps. Amelie clasping her arm round Heloise whom she pressed to her bosom said, "Think before you knock at this door and cross this threshold for the last time, Heloise! You must not do it for my sake, Darling!—"

"No Amelie!" replied she sadly. "It is not wholly for your sake. Would I could say it were! Alas! If I remained in the world, I could even now pity Le Gardeur, and follow him to the world's end, but it must not, cannot be! Do not seek to dissuade me, Amelie, for it is useless."

"Your mind is made up then, to go in with me, my Heloise!—" said Amelie with a fond questioning look.

"Fully, finally and for ever!" replied she with energy that left no room for doubt. "I long ago resolved to ask the community to let me die with them! My object, dear sister, is like yours, to spend my life in prayers and supplications for Le Gardeur, and be laid when God calls me to his rest by the side of our Aunt Mere Madelaine de Repentigny, whose lamp still burns in the Chapel of the Saints, as if to light you and me to follow her footsteps."

"It is for Le Gardeur's sake I too, go!" replied Amelie, "to veil my face from the eyes of a world I am ashamed to see, and to expiate, if I can, the innocent blood that has been shed! But the sun shines very bright for those to whom his beams are still pleasant!" said she looking round sadly, as if it was for the last time she bade adieu to the sun which she would never again behold under the free vault of heaven.

Heloise turned slowly to the door of the Convent. "Those golden rays that shine through the wicket," said she, "and form a cross upon the pavement within, as we often observed with school-girl admiration, are the only rays to gladden me now! I care no more for the light of the sun; I will live henceforth in the blessed light of the lamp of Repentigny! My mind is fixed and I will not leave you Amelie! 'Where thou goest I will go, where thou lodgest I will lodge—thy people shall be my people and thy God my God.'"

Amelie kissed her cousin tenderly. "So be it, then, Heloise! Your heart is broken as well as mine! We will pray together for Le Gardeur, beseeching God to pity and forgive."

Amelie knocked at the door twice, before a sound of light footsteps was heard within. A veiled nun appeared at the little wicket and looked gravely for a moment upon the two postulants for admission, repeating the formula usual on such occasions—

"What seek you, my sisters?"

"To come in and find rest, good Mere des Seraphins!" replied Amelie to whom the portière was well known. "We desire to leave the world and live henceforth with the community in the service and adoration of our blessed Lord, and to pray for the sins of others as well as our own."

"It is a pious desire, and no one stands at the door and knocks but it is opened! Wait my sisters I will summon the Lady Superior to admit you."

The nun disappeared for a few minutes, her voice was heard again as she returned to the wicket—: "The Lady Superior deputes to Mere Esther the privilege on this occasion of receiving the welcome postulants of the house of Repentigny."

The portière retired from the wicket, the heavy door swung noiselessly back, opening the way into a small ante-chamber, floored with smooth flags, and containing a table and a seat or two. On either side of the interior door of the ante chamber was a turn stile or tourelle, which enabled the inmates within to receive anything from the outside world without being themselves seen. Amelie and Heloise passed through the inner door, which opened as of its own accord as they approached it, with trembling steps and troubled mien.

A tall nun of commanding figure but benign aspect received the two ladies with the utmost affection, as well known friends, but without the gush of empressment that would have marked their reception by a Lady of French origin.

The venerable Mere Esther in look, temperament as well as in birth, was English, although in language and ideas wholly French of the best type. She was gentle and sedate as became a woman of pure cold and holy thoughts, that set no store by the world, and never had done so! She had left it at the age of fifteen and lived the quiet life of an Ursuline for the space of thirty-four years.

The news of the commotion in the City had been at once conveyed to the Convent, and the Lady Superior doubting the discretion and calmness of Mere St Gertrude, to communicate with the outer world on that day of excitement, had deputed Mere Esther to receive the postulants.

Mere Esther wore a black robe sweeping the ground. It was bound at the waist by a leathern girdle. A black veil fell on each side of the snowy fillet that covered her forehead, and half covered the white wimple upon her neck and bosom.

Her hair was invisible, being cut short and wholly hidden in the ungainly fashion of the spouses of Christ, as if the heavenly Bridegroom loves not the beauty he creates in woman.

The flowing locks that fall under the ruthless shears at the consecration of a nun, are never permitted to grow long again. Why? It were hard to tell, unless to mortify the natural pleasure of a woman in the beauty of her hair in which abides so much of her strength, as the strength of Samson abode in his.

Esther Wheelwright had in her childhood undergone a fate not uncommon in those hard days of war upon the English frontiers. Her father's house had been stormed and pillaged and herself carried off captive by a war party of Abenaquis. She had lived among the savages several years until she was discovered and rescued by a Jesuit missionary, who brought her to the Castle of St Louis, where her beauty amiability and misfortunes inlisted so strongly the sympathies of the Governor, the first Marquis de Vaudreuil, that he adopted her as his own child, and sent her to the Ursulines to be educated with his own daughter.

But the memories of her captivity were ineffaceable from the mind of the young English girl. Her friends in New England were in time apprised of her safety. They sent messengers to solicit her return home, but after a hard struggle between natural affection and her duty as she conceived it to be, Esther chose to remain in New France, where grateful for her deliverance from the Abenaquis, she resolved to consecrate her life to Christ and good works. In the language of the enthusiastic Jesuit who had rescued her from the savages, "the fair Esther mounted the throne as the bride not of a mighty Ahasuerus on earth, but of a mightier King of Kings in heaven." She became an Ursuline and in conjunction with the Venerable Superior Mere Migeon de la Nativité governed the community for a lifetime prolonged beyond the ordinary allottment of humanity.

The beautiful portrait of her mother sent to persuade the young girl to return home haunted her night and day, and would not leave her. Its image only ceased to torment her when the facile hand of Mere des Anges, the great artiste of the Convent, drew a halo of glory round the head and transformed the worthy English mother into the fairest Madonna of the Monastery, where it still remains the precious adornment of a reliquary in the Convent Chapel to this day.

Mere Ste Gertrude in whose bosom all feminine curiosity was not quite extinct, would have been content to remain at the wicket to look out as from a safe rock at the tossing sea in the city, and bless her immunity from the dangers and troubles of the world. But Mere Esther was assistant Superior, and the habit of obedience which was a second nature to Mere Ste Gertrude, caused her to rise at once and with a humble salute retire into the interior of the house to help the faithful Marthas, *my Aunts* as the *Soeurs Converses* were styled, in their multiferous labours in the Convent kitchen. Mere Ste Gertrude as a penance for her tacit and momentary spirit of disobedience spent the rest of the day at the self-imposed task of washing linen in the Laundry to the edification of the pious nuns to whom she confessed her guilt, and declared her penance.

Mere Esther at the first sight of the veil thrown over the heads of Amelie and Heloise, and the agitation of both, knew at once that the time of these two girls like that of many others had come! Their arrival was a repetition of the old, old story of which her long experience had witnessed many instances. These two sorrowing girls sought refuge from the storms of the world. They had been wrecked and cast half drowned upon the rock of ages as Mere Esther regarded it, where she herself had found a quiet and restful harbour for so many years.

"Good Mother!" exclaimed Amelie throwing her arms round the nun, who folded her tenderly to her bosom, although her face remained calm and passionless. "We are come at last! Heloise and I wish to live and die in the Monastery! Good Mother Esther! will you take us in?"

"Welcome both!" replied Mere Esther kissing each of them on the forehead. "The Virgins who enter in with the bridegroom to the marriage are those whose lamps are burning! The lamp of Repentigny is never extinguished in the Chapel of Saints, nor is the door of the Monastery ever shut against one of your house."

"Thanks Good Mother! But we bring a heavy burthen with us. No one but God can tell the weight and the pain of it—!" said Amelie sadly.

"I know Amelie, I know! but what says our blessed Lord? 'Come unto me all you that are weary and heavy laden and I will give you rest.'"

"I seek not rest, good Mother," replied she patiently, "but a place for penance to melt Heaven with prayers for the innocent blood that has been shed today that it be not recorded for ever against my brother!—O Mere Esther! You know my brother Le Gardeur! how generous and kind he was! You have heard of the terrible occurrence in the Market-place?"

"Yes I have heard!" said the Nun. "Bad news reaches us ever soonest. It fills me with amazement that one so noble as your brother, should have done so terrible a deed!—"

"O Mere Esther!" exclaimed Amelie eagerly. "It was not Le Gardeur in his senses who did it. No! he never knowingly struck the blow that has killed me as well as the good Bourgeois! Alas! he knew not what he did—! But still he has done it! And my remaining time left on earth must be spent in sackcloth and ashes, beseeching God for pardon and mercy for him."

"The community will join you in your prayers, Amelie!" replied Mere Esther who stood wrapt in thought for a few moments. "Heloise!" said she, addressing the fair cousin of Amelie, "I have long expected you in the monastery. You struggled hard for the world and its delights, but God's hand was stronger than your purposes! When he calls, be it in the darkest night, happy is she who rises instantly to follow her Lord—!"

"He has indeed called me, O Mother! and I desire only to

become a faithful servant of his tabernacle forever—! I pray good Mere Esther for your intercession with the Mere de la Nativité! The venerable Lady Superior used to say we were dowerless brides, we of the House of Lotbinière!—"

"But you shall not be dowerless, Heloise!" burst out Amelie. "You shall enter the Convent with as rich a dowry as ever accompanied an Ursuline."

"No Amelie! If they will not accept me for myself, I will imitate my aunt the *admirable Queteuse*, who being like me a dowerless postulante begged from house to house throughout the City for the means to open to her the door of the Monastery."

"Heloise!" replied Mere Esther, "this is idle fear. We have waited for you knowing that one day you would come! and you will be most welcome—dowered or not—!—"

"You are ever kind Mere Esther, but how could you know, I should come to you?—" asked Heloise with a look of inquiry.

"Alas, Heloise! We know more of the world and its doings than is well for us! Our Monastery is like the ear of Dionysius, not a whisper in the City escapes it! O Darling! We knew you had failed in your one great desire upon earth and that you would seek consolation where it is only to be found, in the arms of your Lord—!—"

"It is true Mother! I had but one desire upon earth and it is crushed—! one little bird that nestled awhile in my bosom, and it has flown away! The event of today has stricken me and Amelie alike, and we come together to wear out the stones of your pavement praying for — — the hapless brother of Amelie."

"And the object of Heloise's faithful love!" replied the nun with a tender sympathy. "O! how could Le Gardeur de Repentigny refuse a heart like yours, Heloise for the sake of that wild daughter of levity, Angelique des Meloises?—"

"Mother! speak not of it! He did not refuse my heart. He knew not I loved him, and Angelique is more beautiful and clever than I am or ever was."

"You are early learning the lesson of self depreciation Heloise!—But you have what Angelique has not, a true heart and guileless lips. Ste Angele will rejoice at two such followers. But come! I will conduct you to the Venerable Lady Superior who is in the garden conversing with Grande Mere St Pierre, and your old friend and mistress, Mere Ste Helene."

The news of the tragedy in the Market-place had been early carried to the Convent by the ubiquitous Bonhomme Michel, who was out that day on one of his multiferous errands in the service of the community.

The news had passed quickly through the Convent, agitating the usually quiet Nuns, and causing the wildest commotion among the classes of girls who were assembled at their morning lessons in the great school room. The windows were clustered with young comely heads looking out in every direction, while nuns in alarm streamed from the long passages to the lawn where sat the Venerable Superior Mere Migeon de la Nativité, under a broad ash tree sacred to the Convent by the memories that clustered round it. The Ste Therese of Canada, Mere Marie de l'Incarnation, for lack of a better roof in the first days of her mission, used to gather round her under that tree, the wild Hurons as well as the young children of the Colonists, to give them their first lessons in religion and letters.

Mere Esther held up her finger warningly to the nuns not to speak, as she passed onward through the long corridors, dim with narrow lights and guarded by images of saints, until she came into an open square flagged with stones. In the walls of this court, a door opened upon the garden into which a few steps downward conducted them.

The garden of the monastry was spacious and kept with great care. The walks meandered round beds of flowers and under the boughs of apple trees, and espaliers of ancient pears and plums.

The fruit had long been gathered in, and only a few yellow leaves hung upon the autumnal trees, but the grass was still green on the lawn, where stood the great ash tree of Mere Marie de l'Incarnation. The last hardy flowers of Autumn lingered in this sheltered spot.

In these secluded alleys the quiet recluses usually walked

and meditated in peace, for here man's disturbing voice was never heard.

But today a cluster of agitated nuns gathered round the great ashtree and here and there stood groups of black and white veils. Some were talking while others knelt silently before the guardian of the house, the image of St Joseph which overlooked this spot, considered particularly sacred to prayer and meditation.

The sight of Mere Esther followed by the well-known figures of Amelie and Heloise caused every head to turn with a look of recognition, but the nuns were too well disciplined to express either surprise or curiosity in the presence of Mere Migeon, however much they felt of both. They stood apart at a sign from the lady Superior leaving her with a nun attendant on each side to receive Mere Esther and her two companions.

CHAPTER 57

THE LAMP OF REPENTIGNY

MERE Migeon de la Nativité was old in years but fresh in looks and alert in spirit. Her features were set in that peculiar expression of drooping eyelids and placid lips which belongs to the Convent, but she could look up and flash out on occasion with an air of command derived from high birth and a long exercise of authority as superior of the Ursulines, to which office the community had elected her as many trienniums as their rules permitted.

Mere Migeon had been nearly half a century a nun and felt as much pride as humility in the reflection. She liked power which however she exercised wholly for the benefit of her subjects in the convent and wore her veil with as much dignity as the Queen her crown. But if not exempt from some traces of human infirmity she made amends by devoting herself night and day to the spiritual and temporal welfare of the community, who submitted to her government with extreme deference and unquestioning obedience.

By her side stood two faithful and trusty members of the *Conseil des Sages* of the Monastery, whom she never failed to consult in all emergencies, although she always followed at last, the wise suggestions and firm guiding hand of Mere Esther her coadjutrice in the government.

One of these a very aged nun, was the famous Grande Mere Genevieve de St Pierre, the worthy daughter of a remarkable man, the Seigneur de Boucherville ennobled for his defence of Three Rivers against an army of Iroquois in 1653. Grande Mere St Pierre counted nearly fourscore years of age at this time, threescore of which she had passed in the Cloister. She was still strong in mind and vigorous of body as became her father's daughter, and she reached a still greater age before she succumbed at last to the siege of nearly a century of years.

At her feet kneeling with elbow reposed on the lap of the Venerable Grande Mere St Pierre was a fair delicate woman, Mere Charlotte de Muy de Ste Helène granddaughter of the same stock of the Seigneur de Boucherville, and who if she had not inherited the strong bodily attributes of her race, had succeeded to the literary talents of her Grand Sire, and shone among the nuns as the annalist of the Convent and of the Colony.

The histories of the Convent and of the Colony are so intermingled in those years of war and suffering that in the records of the ancient Monastery they became almost as one.

Mere Ste Helène had succeeded to many of the blessings poured out upon her race in the "adieux" of Grand Père Boucher, whose last testament reminds one of dying Jacob's patriarchal blessing of his twelve sons. She was a woman of keen intellect, remarkable power of observation, and facile expression. Under her snow white wimple, beat as warm a heart for her country as ever stirred under the robe of a statesman or the gorget of a soldier.

It is difficult in these days of quiet and security to realize the vivid emotions excited in the Convent by the bloody progress of the war with England, and by the handwriting upon the wall which to some of the nuns already foreshadowed the downfall of New France.

The annals of the Cloister intended only to record the warfare of the Church and the triumphs of Faith, are intermingled by the pen of Mere Ste Helène, with vivid pictures of the war, and filled with proofs of the irrepressible sympathies of the nuns, with their fathers, brothers and countrymen in arms against the English, to preserve that New France so dear to them all.

With what sorrow that old recital, the *Vieux Récit*, records the defeats and disasters of the French arms! with what joy and exultation their Victories! But through good report and bad, the graphic pen of Mere Ste Helène went on to the end of her book and the end of her life.

When the seven years war broke out, Mere Ste Helène was still the annalist of the old Monastery. Her spirit watched eagerly from the dim Cloister the movements of the armies of Montcalm on the Frontiers. Her joyous pen records in strains of triumph the victories of Chouagen and of Carillon—! But as the war progressed, she saw like others, with dismay, that the Colony was abandoned by France to its own feeble and ever diminishing resources. The circle of fire narrowed closer and closer round the Capital, and when at last Quebec itself was surrounded by the English, when Wolfe was pouring shot and shell for sixty days without intermission upon the devoted city, she knew that all was lost. The heart of the patriotic nun broke, and in the very hour, when the heroic Montcalm was lowered into his grave, which was a cavity made by the bursting of a bomb, in the Convent Chapel, Mere Ste Helene breathed her last with the despairing agonizing cry—"*Le pays est à bas!*" The Country is down! The end of her life, and of her history and of New France were finished at one fatal blow! Mere Migeon closed the eyes of the dead nun with a kiss, saying, "*Requiescat in pace!* Mere Ste Helene broke no vow in loving her native land—!—"

But these sad events lay as yet in the womb of the future. The peace of Aix-La-Chapelle promised for the present an era of rest and recuperation to the wasted colony. The pen of Mere Ste Helene had just recorded the emotions of joy and thankfulness which animated the community upon the peace just concluded with the English.

Mere Migeon had directed the two sorrowing ladies, to be brought into the garden where she would receive them under the old tree of Mere Marie de l'Incarnation.

She rose with affectionate eagerness as they entered and embraced them one after the other, kissing them on the cheek and calling them "her little prodigals returning to the house of their father and mother! after feeding on the husks of vanity in the gay world which was never made for them. We will kill the fatted calf in honour of your return Amelie! will we not Mere Esther?" said the Lady Superior addressing Amelie, rather than Heloise.

"Not for me, reverend Mere! you shall kill no fatted calf real or symbolical for me!" exclaimed Amelie. "I come only to hide myself in your Cloister, to submit myself to your most austere discipline. I give up all, O my Mere! I have given up all! None but God can know what I have given up, forever!—"

"You were to have married the son of the Bourgeois, were you not, Amelie?" asked the Superior who as the aunt of Varin and by family ties connected with certain leading spirits of the Grand Company had no liking for the Bourgeois Philibert— her feelings too had been wrought upon by a recital of the sermon preached in the Market-place that morning.

"O speak not of it! Good Mere! I was betrothed to Pierre Philibert—and how am I requiting his love? I should have been his wife but for this dreadful deed of my brother! The Convent is all that is left to me now."—

"You are a brave girl!" said Grande Mere St Pierre, "and worthy of your race! Such as you and Heloise are the salt that saves the world, and brings blessings upon the Monastery."

Mere Ste Helene had already recognized and embraced the two girls. "I have recorded many dear names in our annals," said she, "but none with the gladness I shall have in recording yours! My pleasure is doubled because it is so unexpected. You sow in sorrow but you shall reap in joy."—

"I fear it may never be," replied Amelie, "but I may at least find quiet and time for prayer. I know that ere long I shall find rest. The sword has passed through my soul also!"

"Your aunt called herself the humble handmaid of Mary, and the lamp of Repentigny will burn all the brighter trimmed by a daughter of her noble house," remarked Mere Migeon.

"By two daughters! Good Mere! Heloise is equally a daughter of our house," replied Amelie with a touch of feeling.

"Was to have been her sister!" whispered a young novice in a white veil to another who had gradually approached near enough to the old ash tree to hear what was said. "Heloise was to have been the bride of Le Gardeur de Repentigny!"

"No! It was Angelique des Meloises for whom Le Gardeur ran wild, they say. He would have married her, but she jilted him!—" replied another eagerly.

"No! You are both wrong!" whispered a third little novice. "It was Angelique was to have married the Intendant!"

"But she refused Le Gardeur all the same! as I know from the best authority. My sister was at the Intendant's ball, and overheard part of a conversation between her and the Intendant!" interrupted a fourth little novice with sparkling black eyes and flushed cheek "and they do say he has a wife all the time at the Chateau of Beaumanoir!—"

"No! she is not his wife! My Aunt de Grandmaison heard something, from Madame Varin," replied another.

"And Madame Varin knows that the Intendant is not married!" rejoined another novice warmly. Their voices now mingled in sweet confusion, jangling like silver bells as they all talked together.

Mere St Charles the grave mistress of the novices was never far away from her young charge. She listened quietly to the end of the conversation, and then confronted the little group with a reproving look, that caused them to blush redder than peonies at being caught indulging in such worldly conversation as about balls and marriages.

"Come with me to the Chapel, dear children!" said Mere St Charles. "We must all repent our faults, you for permitting your thoughts to take delight in such vain worldly things, I for not keeping better watch over your youth and inexperience. Well that our Venerable Zelatrice, Mere St Louis did not overhear you, instead of your old indulgent Mere St Charles."

"We should have caught it in earnest then! But is it wrong to speak of marriage, good Mere?" asked Marie Cureux, a girl somewhat older and bolder than the rest. "My father and mother were married therefore it cannot be wrong to marry and the Church marries people therefore it cannot be sinful! Besides, we only whispered!—"

"The sinful thought Marie, is worse than the whispered word! and both the word and the thing are forbidden to us," replied the Nun.

"We are sad sinners then!" remarked Demoiselle Bedard, a pretty cousin of Zoe Bedard of Charlebourg, a wild young creature, who when she was at last broken in, became an exemplary nun, and in time the most bustling *Tante* of the Convent Kitchen! where she left a receipt for making that famous *potage du Couvent*, which the old Baroness de Longueil said was the next thing to the sacrament, and used to send to the Convent for a bowl of it every day.

"Well! Well! My children!" continued Mere St Charles, "never more speak even in whispers of gentlemen, or of marriages except your own, when you become the brides of Heaven."

"Amen! Mere St Charles, we will try!" said the humbled novices who with drooping heads and hands clasped in a penitential manner followed meekly their mistress, and proceeded to the Chapel to repent of their grievous fault.

Mere Esther whispered a few words in the ear of the Superior, bidding her concede every request of Amelie and Heloise, and returned to the wicket to answer some other hasty call from the troubled city.

Messengers despatched by Bonhomme Michel followed one another at short intervals, bringing to the Convent exact details of all that occurred in the streets, with the welcome tidings at last, that the threatened outbreak had been averted by the prompt interposition of the Governor and troops— comparative quietness again reigned in every quarter of the city.

Le Gardeur de Repentigny had voluntarily surrendered himself to the guard and given up his sword being overwhelmed with remorse for his act. He had been placed, not in irons as he demanded, but as a prisoner in the strong ward of the Castle of St Louis.

"I pray you Reverend Mere Superior," said Amelie, "permit us now to go into the Chapel of Saints, to lay our hearts as did our kinswoman Madelaine de Repentigny at the feet of our Lady of Grand Pouvoir!"

"Go my children, and our prayers shall go with you!" replied the Superior. "The Lamp of Repentigny will burn brighter than ever to night to welcome you."

The Chapel of Saints was held in reverence as the most

sacred place in the Monastery. It contained the shrines and relics of many saints and martyrs. The devout nuns lavished upon it their choicest works of embroidery painting and gilding in the arts of which they were eminent. The old Sacristaine was kneeling before the altar as Amelie and Heloise entered the Chapel.

An image of the Virgin occupied a niche in the chapel wall and before it burned the silver lamp of Repentigny which had been hung there two generations before, in memory of the miraculous call of Madelaine de Repentigny and of her victory over the world.

The high bred and beautiful Madelaine had been the delight and pride of Ville Marie. Stricken with grief by the death of a young officer to whom she was affianced, she retired to Quebec and knelt daily at the feet of our Lady of Pouvoir beseeching her for a sign if it was her will, that she should become an Ursuline.

The sign was given and Madelaine de Repentigny at once exchanged her gay robes for the coarse black gown and veil, and hung up this votive lamp before the Madonna, as a perpetual memorial of her miraculous call.

Seven generations of men have passed away since then. The house of Repentigny has disappeared, from their native land. Their name and fame lie buried in oblivion, except in that little Chapel of the Saints, where their lamp still burns brightly as ever! The pious nuns of St Ursule as the last custodians of the traditions of New France, preserve the sole memorial of the glories and misfortunes of the noble house: The lamp of Repentigny.

Amelie and Heloise remained long in the Chapel of Saints, kneeling upon the hard floor as they prayed with tears and sobs for the soul of the Bourgeois and for God's pity and forgiveness upon Le Gardeur.

To Amelie's woes was added the terrible consciousness that by this deed of her brother, Pierre Philibert was torn from her forever. She pictured to herself his grief, his love, his despair, perhaps his vengeance and to add to all she his betrothed bride had forsaken him and fled like a guilty thing without waiting to see whether he condemned her.

An hour ago, Amelie had been the envy and delight of her gay bridesmaids. Her heart had overflowed like a fountain of wine intoxicating all about her with joy at the hope of the speedy coming of her bridegroom. Suddenly the idols of her life had been shattered as by a thunder bolt, and lay in fragments round her feet.

The thought came upon her like the rush of angry wings. She knew that all was over between her and Pierre! The Cloister and the veil were all that were left now to Amelie de Repentigny.

"Heloise! dearest sister!" exclaimed she, "my conscience tells me I have done right, but my heart accuses me of wrong to Pierre! of falseness to my plighted vows in forsaking him! and yet not for heaven itself would I have forsaken Pierre! Would that I were dead! O what have I done, Heloise! to deserve such a chastisement as this from God?"

Amelie threw her arms round the neck of Heloise, and leaning her head on her bosom wept long and without restraint, for none saw them save God and the old Sacristaine, who observed without seeming to observe, as she knelt silently counting the beads of her rosary, and repeating mechanically the formula of prayers attached to them.

"Mere Ste Vierge! pray for me!" continued Amelie suddenly apostrophizing the old nun, who now regarded her fixedly from under the white fillet that covered her dark eyebrows. "I am unworthy to pray for myself! I plighted my troth before God and all the Saints to marry Pierre Philibert! and today I forsake him in order to atone by a life of sacrifice for the innocent blood that lies upon the house of Repentigny! Mere Ste Vierge! you are wise in the way of salvation. Tell me if my sin against Pierre, be not greater than any prayer or penance can expiate—?"

Mere Ste Vierge looked at her pityingly and not without a trace of wonder, for the old Sacristaine had been so long under the veil, that the very name of human love sounded to her like a word of an unknown tongue. It called up no blessed association and woke no sympathy or only the most remote, in her cold saintly bosom.

"The sin would have been greater, Amelie!" said she quietly, without changing a muscle of her placid face, "had you disobeyed the call of the heavenly voice. It seems to you harsh and cruel, but the divine rods have no efficacy unless they sting! Fast and pray! and soon they will not sting at all, and you will rejoice in the stripes of your Lord! In the cloister you will forget your earthly bridegroom, in the joys of your heavenly one!"

"Never, Good Mere! I can never forget Pierre Philibert! I pledged my word to him and have broken it—! I must now bury in my heart out of human sight the love which I cannot redeem with my hand!—"

The Sacristaine shook her head in disapproval. "The fashions of this world pass away," said she. "It is hard to purge the affections of all earthly dross, but a daughter of Ste Angele must forsake father and mother, brethren and sisters, houses and lands, in a word all the world for Christ's sake, and to inherit eternal life! For thirty years I have fed this sacred lamp of your house, and now the heiress herself of Repentigny, comes to take my place!—*Laus Deo!*"

"O Mere! you do not know and cannot understand how great a sorrow has befallen Amelie!" exclaimed Heloise heroically, concealing the wound in her own bosom.

"I do know and I do understand!" replied the nun. "I was twenty when the Lord caught me in his net, and drew me from the waters of vanity and sin, but I set at defiance even my Lord, until he sent the angel of death to the house of him I loved, to subdue me by the loss of my sole earthly hope!"

Amelie was touched by the words of the nun, which seemed a reflection of her own thoughts. She raised her hand and kissed it.

"Mere Ste Vierge!" said she, "forgive me. Sorrow makes us selfish, and we think there are no troubles but our own! Let me follow in your footsteps! O, Mere! they say you subject yourself to the severest discipline of fasting, prayer and vigils; teach me I pray you, teach me the hardest service in this house. I will perform it!"

"Amelie de Repentigny! think! before you offer to follow in my footsteps! Can you fast all day and stand with naked feet all night upon the cold floor of the Sanctuary? Can you with bruised knees traverse the *via crucis* hour after hour from midnight until the bell rings for matins? Can you begin the work of the day at the first hour and resolutely keep on till the last, and yet never feel that you are aught but an unprofitable servant of your Lord?—"

The Sacristaine might have added, but refrained, through fear of seeming proud of her self-humiliation, that she wore the coarsest sackcloth under her black robe, and it was even whispered among the nuns that her shoulders were scarred with the self-inflicted scourge.

"Alas! Mere if your venial sins call for such chastisement, what penance is not due from me for the sin of my brother, which I desire to expiate by suffering—?" replied Amelie sadly.

The Sacristaine let her hands fall in her lap, and looked at her admiringly:

"Daughter" said she, "rejoice in your tribulation! What says blessed St Thomas? 'Temptations and trials are profitable although they be troublesome and grievous, for in them we are humbled, purified and exalted.'"

"Alas Mere!" replied Amelie "I am humbled beyond all humiliation, and wish only to hide myself from every mortal eye."

"Amelie," said the Nun impressively, "If thou carry thy cross willingly it will carry thee, and bring thee to thy desired end!"

"I know it Mere! else I had not come to this place!—"

"Listen!" interrupted the nun, raising her pale, thin finger as the swelling strain of the organ floated up from the chapel. The soft voices of the nuns mingled in plaintive harmony as they sang the hymn of the Virgin:—

"Eia, Mater! Fons amoris!—
Me sentire vim doloris,
Fac, ut tecum lugeam!"

"Listen again!" continued the nun, "They who sow in tears

shall reap in joy but only in paradise!"

Again came the soft pleading notes of the sacred hymn:

"Quando Corpus Morietur,
Fac ut animae donetur,
Paradisi gloria! Amen!—"

The harmony filled the ears of Amelie and Heloise, like the lap of the waves of eternity upon the world's shore. It died away, and they continued praying before our Lady of Grand Pouvoir, while the Sacristaine kept on reciting her appointed litanies and supplications half unmindful of their presence.

The silence was suddenly broken. Hasty steps traversed the little chapel. A rush of garments caused Amelie and Heloise to turn round and in an instant they were both clasped in the passionate embrace of the Lady de Tilly, who had arrived at the Convent.

"My dear children, my poor stricken daughters!" exclaimed she kissing them passionately and mingling her tears with theirs, "What have you done to be dashed to the earth by such a stroke of divine wrath?—"

"O! Aunt! pardon us for what we have done!" exclaimed Amelie, "and for not asking your counsel, but alas! it is God's will and doing! I have given up the world! do not blame me, Aunt!"

"Nor me, Aunt!" added Heloise. "I have long known that the Cloister was my sole heritage, and I now claim it."

"Blame you, darlings! O Amelie! in the shame and agony of this day I could share the Cloister with you myself for ever!— but my work is out in the wide world, and I must not withdraw my hand!"

"Have you seen Le Gardeur? O Aunt! have you seen my brother?" asked Amelie, seizing her hand passionately.

"I have seen him, and wept over him!" was the reply. "O Amelie! great as is his offence—his crime—yes! I will be honest calling it such, no deeper contrition could rend his heart had he committed all the sins forbidden in the Decalogue! He demands a Court-Martial to condemn him at once to death, upon his own self accusation and confession of the murder of the good Bourgeois."

"O Aunt! and he loved the Bourgeois so! It seems like a hideous dream of fright and nightmare! that Le Gardeur should assail the father of Pierre Philibert and mine that was to be!—"

At this thought the poor girl flung herself upon the bosom of the Lady de Tilly, convulsed and torn by as bitter sobs as ever drew human pity.

"Le Gardeur! Le Gardeur! Good God! what will they do with him? Aunt! Is he to die?" cried she imploringly, as with streaming eyes she looked up at her Aunt.

"Listen Amelie! Compose yourself and you shall hear. I was in the Church of Notre Dame des Victoires, when I received the tidings. It was long before the messenger found me. I rose instantly and hastened to the house of the Bourgeois where its good master lay dead in his bloody vesture. I cannot describe the sad sight, Amelie! I there learned that the Governor and La Corne St Luc had been to the house of the Bourgeois and had returned to the Castle."

"O Aunt! did you see him? Did you see the good old Bourgeois? and you know he is dead—!—"

"Yes Amelie! I saw him, and could have wished my eye-sight blasted forever after. Do not ask me more."

"But I must, dear Aunt! did you see? O why may I not yet utter his dear name? Did you see Pierre?"

"Yes! Amelie! Pierre came unexpectedly home while I was weeping over the dead corpse of his father. Poor Pierre! my own sorrows were naught to his silent grief! It was more terrible than the wildest outburst of passion I ever saw!—"

"And what did he say? O Aunt! tell me all! do not spare me one word however bitter! Did he not curse you? Did he not curse me? And above all, Le Gardeur? O he cursed us all! he heaped a blasting malediction upon the whole house of Repentigny, did he not?—"

"Amelie be composed! do not look at me so wildly with those dear eyes and I will tell you—!" Her Aunt tried to sooth her with fond caresses.

"I will be composed! I am calm! Look now, Aunt! I am

calm!" exclaimed the grief stricken girl, whose every nerve was quivering with wild excitement.

The Lady de Tilly and Heloise forced her to sit down while each held forcibly a hand to prevent an access of Hysteria. Mere Ste Vierge rose and hastily left the Chapel to fetch water.

"Amelie! the nobleness of Pierre Philibert is almost beyond the range of fallible mortals," said the Lady de Tilly. "In the sudden crash of all his hopes, he would not utter a word of invective against your brother. His heart tells him that Le Gardeur has been made the senseless instrument of others in this crime."

"A thousand thanks! dearest Aunt, for your true appreciation of Pierre! I know he deserves it all! and when the veil covers my head forever from the eyes of men, it will be my sole joy to reflect that Pierre Philibert was worthy, more than worthy of my love! But what said he further? Aunt O tell me all!"

"He rose from his knees beside the corpse of his father," continued the Lady "and seeing me kneeling raised me and seated me in a chair beside him. He asked me where you were? and who was with you to support and comfort you in this storm of affliction? I told him, and he kissed me, exclaiming, 'O Aunt! Mother! What shall I do—!—'"

"O Aunt! did Pierre say that? Did he call you Aunt, and Mother? and he did not curse me at all? Poor Pierre!" and she burst out into a flood of tears, which nothing could control.

"Yes Amelie! His heart is bleeding to death with this dreadful sword-stroke of Le Gardeur's," said the Lady de Tilly after waiting till she recovered somewhat.

"And will he not slay Le Gardeur? Will he not deem it his duty to kill my brother and his?" cried she. "He is a soldier and must!—"

"Listen Amelie! There is a divinity in Pierre that we only see revealed in the noblest of men—he will not slay Le Gardeur. He is his brother and yours, and will regard him as such. Whatever he might have done in the first impulse of anger, Pierre will not now seek the life of Le Gardeur. He knows too well whence this blow has really come. He has been deeply touched by the remorse and self-accusation of Le Gardeur."

"I could kiss his feet! my noble Pierre! O Aunt! Aunt! What have I not lost!—But I was betrothed to him was I not?" She started up with a shriek as of mortal agony. "They never can recall that!" she cried wildly. "He was to have been mine! He is still mine, and forever will be mine! Death will reunite what in life is sundered! Will it not, Aunt?—"

"Yes, be composed darling! and I will tell you more, nay do not look at me so Amelie!" the Lady de Tilly stroked her cheek and kissed the dark eyes that seemed flaring out of their sockets with maddening excitement.

"When I had recovered strength enough to go to the Castle to see the Count, Pierre supported me thither. He dared not trust himself to see Le Gardeur, who from his prison sent message after message to him to beg death at his hand."

"I held a brief conference with the Governor, La Corne St Luc and a few gentlemen, who were hastily gathered together in the Council Chamber. I pleaded long, not for pardon, not even for Le Gardeur could I ask for pardon, Amelie!" exclaimed the just, and noble woman, "but for a calm consideration of the terrible circumstances which had surrounded him in the Palace of the Intendant, and which had led directly to this catastrophe."

"And what said they? O be quick, Aunt! Is not Le Gardeur to be tried by martial law and condemned at once to death?—"

"No Amelie! The Count de la Galissoniere with the advice of his wisest consellors, among whom is your Godfather and others, the dearest friends of both families, have resolved to send Le Gardeur to France, by the *Fleur de Lys*, which sails tomorrow. They do this in order that the King may judge of his offence, as also to prevent the conflict that may arise between the contending factions in the Colony, should they try him here. This resolution may be wise or not—I do not judge—but such is the determination of the Governor and Council to which all must submit."

Amelie held her head between her palms for some moments. She was violently agitated, but she tried to consider as best she might, the decision with regard to her brother.

"It is merciful in them!" she said, "and it is just! The King will judge what is right in the sight of God and man! Le Gardeur was but a blind instrument of others in this murder, as blind almost as the sword he held in his hand. But shall I not see him Aunt, before he is sent away?"

"Alas no! The Governor while kind, is inexorable on one point. He will permit no one after this to see Le Gardeur, to express either blame or approval of his deed, or to report his words. He will forbid you and me and his nearest friends from holding any communication with him before he leaves the Colony. The Count has remitted his case to the King and resolved that it shall be accompanied by no self accusations which Le Gardeur may utter in his frantic grief. The Count does this in justice as well as mercy, Amelie!—"

"Then I shall never see my brother more in this world! Never!" exclaimed Amelie, supporting herself on the arm of Heloise. "His fate is decided as well as mine, and yours too, O Heloise!—"

"It may not be so hard with him as with us, Amelie!" replied Heloise, whose bosom was agitated with fresh emotions at every allusion to Le Gardeur. "The King may pardon him, Amelie!" Heloise in her soul hoped so and in her heart prayed so.

"Alas! If we could say God pardoned him!" replied Amelie, her thoughts running suddenly in a counter current. "But my life must be spent in imploring God's grace and forgiveness all the same, whether man forgive him or no."

"Say not my life, but our lives, Amelie! We have crossed the threshold of this house together for the last time! We go no more out to look upon a world fair and beautiful to see, but so full of disappointment and wretchedness to have experience of!"

"My daughters!" interrupted the Lady de Tilly, "another time we will speak of this! Harken Amelie! I did not tell you that Pierre Philibert came with me to the gate of the Convent to see you! He would have entered but the Lady Superior refused inexorably to admit him even to the bars."

"Pierre came to the Convent! to the Convent!" repeated

Amelie with a fond iteration, "and they would not admit him! Why would they not admit him? But I should have died of shame to see him! They were kind in their cruelty. Poor Pierre! he thinks me still worthy of some regard—!" She commenced weeping afresh.

"He would fain have seen you, darling!" said her Aunt. "Your flight to the Convent—He knows what it means— overwhelms him with a new calamity!—"

"And yet it cannot be otherwise! I dare not place my hand in his now for it would redden it! But it is sweet amid my affliction to know that Pierre has not forgotten me, that he does not hate me, nay that he loves me still! although I abandon the world and him who to me was the light of it! Why would they not admit him?—"

"Mere Migeon is hard as she is just Amelie! I think too she has no love for the Philiberts. Her nephew Varin has all the influence of a spoilt son over the Lady Superior."

Amelie scarcely regarded the last remark of her Aunt, but repeated the words, "hard and just! Yes, it is true, and hardness and justice are what I crave in my misery! The flintiest couch shall be to me a bed of down! the scantiest fare, a royal feast! the hardest penance, a life of pleasure!—Mere Migeon cannot be more hard nor more just to me than I would be to myself!"

"My poor Amelie! My poor Heloise!" repeated the Lady stroking their hair and kissing them both alternately, "be it as God wills! When it is dark every prospect lies hid in the darkness, but it is there all the same, though we see it not! but when light returns every thing is revealed! We see nought before us now, but the image of our Lady of *Grand Pouvoir* illumined by the lamp of Repentigny, but the sun of righteousness will yet arise with healing on his wings for us all! But O my children! let nothing be done hastily, rashly, or unbecoming the daughters of our honourable house."

CHAPTER 58

"LOVELY IN DEATH"

THE chant of vespers had long ceased. The angelus had rung its last summons to invoke a blessing upon life and death, at the close of the day. The quiet nuns filed off from their frugal meal in the long refectory and betook themselves to the community or to their peaceful cells. The troop of children in their charge had been sent with prayers to their little couches in the Dormitory, sacred to sleep and happy dreams.

Candles flickered through the long passages as veiled figures slowly and noislessly passed towards the Chapel to their private devotions. Scarcely a footfall reached the ear, nor sound of any kind, except the sweet voice of Mere Madelaine de St Borgia. Like the flow of a full stream in the still moonlight, she sang her canticle of praise to the guardian of the House, before she retired to rest—

"Ave, Joseph! Fili David Juste!
Vir Mariae de qua natus est Jesus!—"

Lady de Tilly sat listening as she held the hands of her two neices thinking how merciless was Fate and half rebelling in her mind against the working of Providence. The sweet song of Mere St Borgia fell like soft rain upon her hard thoughts, and instilled a spirit of resignation amid the darkness, as she repeated the words "*Ave Joseph*—!" She fought bitterly in her soul against giving up her two lambs, as she called them to the cold scant life of the Cloister, while her judgment saw but too plainly, that nought else seemed left to their crushed and broken spirits. But she neither suggested their withdrawal from the Convent, nor encouraged them to remain.

In her secret thought, the Lady de Tilly, regarded the

Cloister as a blessed refuge for the broken hearted, a rest for the weary and overladen with earthly troubles, a living grave, which such may covet and not sin, but the young, the joyous, the beautiful and all capable of making the world fairer and better she would inexorably shut out! Christ calls not these from the earthly paradise, but the afflicted, the disappointed, the dispairing: those who have fallen helplessly down in the journey of life, and are of no further use in this world—these he calls by their names and comforts them. But for those rare souls who are too cold for ought but spiritual joys, he reserves a peculiar if not his choicest benediction.

The Lady de Tilly pondered these thoughts over and over in the fulness of pity for her children! she would not leave the convent at the closing of the Gates for the night, but remained the honoured guest of Mere Migeon, who ordered a chamber to be prepared for her in a style that was luxurious, compared with the scantily furnished rooms allotted to the Nuns.

Amelie prevailed, after much entreaty upon Mere Esther, to intercede with the Superior for permission to pass the night with Heloise in the cell that had once been occupied by her pious kinswoman Mere St Agathe.

"It is a great thing to ask!" replied Mere Esther as she returned with the desired boon, "and a greater still to obtain it! But Mere Migeon is in a benevolent mood to night, for the sake of no one else, would she have granted a dispensation of the rule of the House."

In truth the venerable Superior was overjoyed by the arrival of so distinguished a postulante as Amelie de Repentigny. She regarded it as a special answer to her fervent and frequent prayers for the restoration to the Community of the prosperity they had enjoyed before the War. The Lady Superior refused Amelie nothing.

The two postulantes were conducted by Mere Esther through a long passage, on one side of which opened the doors of the chambers of the Nuns, each cell with its solitary tenant asleep, after repeating her pious *memorare* or awake and reciting it over again.

Mere Esther stopped before a closed door, over which was

painted in black letters, the sacred text, "Come unto me, all ye that labour and are heavy laden and I will give you rest."—

"This was the cell of the faithful handmaid of Mary, your beloved Aunt, Mere St Agathe—!" remarked Mere Esther as she opened the door.

"I know it!" replied Amelie. "It is a narrow haven, but it will hold my small and shattered bark! The spirit of my kinswoman lingers here and will help me to learn the hard lesson of resignation."

"Our Lord who wept at Bethany will weep with you my children!" replied Mere Esther, kissing the young postulantes as she bade them, "good night!" and left them, with tears of true womanly sympathy upon her aged cheek.

"I feel a cold breath, as it were a greeting from the spirit of our kinswoman," said Amelie, as she entered the little room, which revealed in the light of the lamp she carried, a couch of spotless drapery, but hard as the bed of an anchorite, a chair or two of wood, a plain table upon which lay a few books of devotion and in a little recess, a picture of the weeping Madonna, wrought in silk, a masterpiece of needlework from the hands of Mere St Agathe.

"The embroidering of that, saved her life!" whispered Amelie holding up the lamp as she knelt reverently before it, "for in that she wrought the grief of her soul for the loss of Julian Lemoine! It is a picture of her agony for his death upon the field of battle! But she is now happy with Julian! think you not so, Heloise?"

"I pray so! nay I believe it, Amelie! but Aunt Agathe's fate was enviable compared with ours! to lose the dead is hard, but it may be borne; but to lose the living and live on and remember daily our loss who can endure that, Amelie?"

The lamp shed a melancholy radiance over the suggestive picture. The two girls knelt together and wept and prayed for hours uncounted by themselves. Only God counted them, and put all their tears in his bottle, as the Hebrew Prophet quaintly describes, the tender care of the Lord for his children of affliction.

Lady de Tilly held that night long and serious conference

with Mere Migeon and Mere Esther upon the event which
had driven her neices to the Cloister, promising that if, at the
end of a month, they persisted in their resolution, she would
consent to their assumption of the white veil, and upon the
completion of their noviciate when they took the final vows,
she would give them up with such a dower, as would make all
former gifts of the house of Repentigny and Tilly, poor in the
comparison.

Mere Migeon was especially overjoyed at this prospect of
relieving the means of her house, which had been so terribly
straitened of late years. The losses occasioned by the war
had been a never ending source of anxiety to her and Mere
Esther, who however kept their troubles as far as possible to
themselves, in order that the cares of the world might not
encroach too far upon the minds of the community. Hence
they were more than ordinarily glad at this double vocation
in the house of Repentigny. The prospect of its great wealth
falling to pious uses they regarded as a special mark of Divine
providence and care for the House of St Ursule.

"O Mere Esther! Mere Esther—!" exclaimed the Lady
Superior. "I feel too great a satisfaction in view of the rich
dower of these two girls—! I need much self examination to
weed out worldly thoughts! alas! alas! I would rather be the
humblest Aunt in our kitchen than the Lady Superior of the
Ursulines! Blessed old Mere Marie used to say: 'A good turn
in the kitchen, was as good as a prayer in the Chapel.'"

Mere Esther reflected a moment, and said, "We have long
found it easier to pray for souls than to relieve bodies! I
thank good St Joseph for this prospective blessing upon our
Monastry."

During the long and wasting war, Mere Migeon had seen
her poor Nuns reduced to grievous straits which they bore
cheerfully however, as their share of the common suffering of
their country. The *cassette* of St Joseph wherein were deposited
the oboli for the poor, had long been emptied. The image
of St Joseph *au blé* that stood at the head of the great stair,
and kept watch over the store room of corn and bread,
had often guarded an empty chamber. St Joseph *au labeur*

overlooking the great kitchen of the Convent had often been deaf to the prayers of "My Aunts", who prepared the food of the Community. The meagre tables of the refectory had not seldom been the despair of the old Depositaire Mere St Louis, who devoutly said her longest grace over her scantiest meals—!

"I thank St Joseph for what he gives, and for what he withholds, yea, for what he takes away," observed Mere St Louis to her special friend and gossip Mere St Antoine, as they retired from the Chapel. "Our years of famine are nearly over—! The day of the consecration of Amelie de Repentigny, will be to us the marriage of Cana—! Our water will be turned into wine! I shall no longer need to save the crumbs, except for the poor at our gate."

The advent of Amelie de Repentigny was a circumstance of absorbing interest to the nuns, who regarded it as a reward for their long devotions and prayers for the restoration of their house to its old prosperity. We usually place Providence upon our side, when we have consciously done ought to merit the good fortune that befalls us.

And now, days came and went, went and came as Time the inexorable ever does, regardless of human joys or sorrows. Amelie weary of the world was only desirous of passing away from it, to that sphere where Time is not, and where our affections and thoughts alone measure the periods of Eternity—for Time there, is but the shadow that accompanies the joys of angels or the woes of sinners, not the reality. It is time here, eternity there.

The two postulantes seemed impressed with the spirit that to their fancies lingered in the cell of their kinswoman Mere St Agathe. They bent their gentle necks to the heaviest yoke of spiritual service, which their Superior would consent to lay upon them.

Amelie's inflexible will made her merciless towards herself. She took pleasure in the hardest of self imposed penances, as if the racking of her soul by incessant prayers, and wasting of her body by vigils and cruel fastings were a vicarious punishment borne for the sake of her hapless brother.

She could not forget Pierre, nor did she ever try to forget him. It was observed by the younger Nuns, that when by chance or design, they mentioned his name, she looked up, and her lips moved in silent prayer, but she spoke not of him, save to her Aunt and to Heloise. These two faithful friends alone knew, the inexpressible anguish with which she had heard of Pierre's intended departure for France.

The shock caused by the homicide of the Bourgeois and the consequent annihilation of all the hopes of her life in a happy union with Pierre Philibert, was too much for even her naturally sound and elastic constitution. Her health gave way irrecoverably! Her face grew thin and wan without losing any of its spiritual beauty, as her soul looked through its ever more transparent covering, which daily grew more and more ætherialized, as she faded away. A hectic flush, like a spot of fire came and went for a time, and at last settled permanently upon her cheek. Her eyes, those glorious orbs filled with unquenchable love, grew supernaturally large and brilliant with the flames that fed upon her vital forces. Amelie sickened and sank rapidly. The vulture of quick consumption had fastened upon her young life—!—

Mere Esther and Mere Migeon shook their heads. They were used to broken hearts, and knew the infallible signs which denote an early death in the young and beautiful. Prayers and masses were offered for the recovery of Amelie but all in vain—! God wanted her! He alone knew how to heal that broken heart.—It was seen that she had not long to live. It was known she wished to die!

Pierre heard the tidings with overwhelming grief. He had been permitted but once, to see her for a few brief moments which dwelt upon his mind for ever. He deferred his departure to Europe in consequence of her illness, and knocked daily at the door of the Convent to ask after her, and leave some kind message or flower which was faithfully carried to her by the friendly Nuns who received him at the wicket. A feeling of pity and sympathy for these two affianced and unfortunate lovers, stole into the hearts of the coldest Nuns, while the Novices and the romantic Convent girls, were absolutely wild over the melancholy fate of Pierre and Amelie.

He long solicited in vain for another interview with Amelie, but until it was seen that she was approaching the end, it was not granted him. Mere Esther interceded strongly with the Lady Superior, who was jealous of the influence of Pierre with her Young Novice. At length, Amelie's prayers overcame her scruples. He was told one day that Amelie was dying, and wished to see him for the last time, in this world.

Amelie was carried in a chair to the bars to receive her sorrowing lover. Her pale face retained its statuesque beauty of outline, but so thin and wasted! "Pierre will not know me!" whispered she to Heloise, "but I shall smile at the joy of meeting him, and then he will recognize me—!"

Her flowing veil was thrown back from her face. She spake little, but her dark eyes were fixed with devouring eagerness upon the door by which she knew Pierre would come in. Her aunt supported her head upon her shoulder while Heloise knelt at her knee and fanned her with sisterly tenderness and whispered words of sisterly sympathy in her ear.

Pierre flew to the convent at the hour appointed. He was at once admitted, with a caution from Mere Esther to be calm and not agitate the dying girl. The moment he entered the great parlour, Amelie sprang from her seat, with a sudden cry of recognition, extending her poor thin hands through the bars towards him. Pierre seized them, kissing them passionately, but broke down utterly at the sight of her wasted face and the seal of death set thereon.

"Amelie! My darling Amelie!" exclaimed he, "I have prayed so long to see you and they would not let me in."

"It was partly my fault, Pierre!" said she fondly, "I feared to let you see me! I feared to learn that you hate as you have cause to do the whole house of Repentigny! And yet you do not curse me. Dear Pierre!"

"My poor angel! you break my heart! I curse the house of Repentigny—! I hate you!—Amelie you know me better—!"

"But your good father! the noble and just Bourgeois! O! Pierre! what have we not done to you and yours!"

She fell back upon her pillow, covering her eyes with her

semi transparent hands, bursting as she did so into a flood of passionate tears, and passing into a dead faint.

Pierre was wild with anguish. He pressed against the bars. "For God's sake let me in!" exclaimed he, "she is dying—!"

The two quiet nuns who were in attendance, shook their heads at Pierre's appeal to open the door. They were too well disciplined in the iron rule of the house to open it without an express order from the Lady Superior or from Mere Esther. Their bosoms abounding in spiritual warmth, responded coldly to the contagion of mere human passion. Their ears unused to the voice of man's love tingled at the words of Pierre. Fortunately Mere Esther ever on the watch came into the parlour, and seeing at a glance, the need of the hour, opened the iron door and bade Pierre come in. He rushed forward and threw himself at the feet of Amelie, calling her by the most tender appellatives, and seeking to recall her to a consciousness of his presence.

That loved familiar voice overtook her spirit already winging its flight from earth, and brought it back for a few minutes longer. Mere Esther, a skilful nurse administered a few drops of cordial, and seeing her dying condition sent instantly for the Physician and the Chaplain.

Amelie opened her eyes and turned them inquiringly round the group until they fastened upon Pierre. A flush of fondness suddenly suffused her face, as she remembered how and why he was there! She threw her arms round his neck and kissed him, many times, murmuring, "I have often prayed to die thus, Pierre! close to you, my love! close to you! in your arms and Gods—! where you could receive my last breath and feel in the last throb of my heart, that it is wholly yours—!"

"My poor Amelie!" cried he pressing her to his bosom. "You shall not die! courage darling! It is but weakness, and the air of the Convent! you shall not die."

"I am dying now, Pierre," said she falling again upon her pillow "I feel I have but a short time to live! I welcome death, since I cannot be yours! But, O! the unutterable pang of leaving you my dear love!—"

Pierre could reply only by sobs and kisses. Amelie was

silent for a few moments as if revolving some deep thought in her mind.

"There is one thing Pierre! I have to beg of you," said she falteringly as if doubting his consent to her prayer. "Can you—will you accept my life for Le Gardeur's? If I die for *him*, will you forgive my poor bloodstained and deluded brother—and your own—?—Yes Pierre!" repeated she as she raised his hand to her lips, and kissed it, "your brother as well as mine! will you forgive him, Pierre?"

"Amelie! Amelie!" replied he with a voice broken with emotion. "Can you fancy other, than that I would forgive him? I forgave Le Gardeur from the first. In my heart I never accused him of my father's death. Alas! he knew not what he did!—He was but a sword in the hands of my father's enemies. I forgave him then, darling! and I forgive him wholly now, for your sake and his own—!"

"My noble Pierre!" replied she putting out her arms towards him. "Why might not God have suffered me to reward such divine goodness—? Thanks, my love! I now die content with all things, but parting with you!" She held him fast by his hands, one of which she kept pressed to her lips. They all looked at her expectingly, waiting for her to speak again. For her eyes were wide open and fixed with a look of ineffable love upon the face of Pierre, looking like life after life was fled. She still held him in her rigid clasp, but she moved not. Upon her pale lips a smile seemed to hover. It was but the shadow left behind of her retreating soul. Amelie de Repentigny was dead! The angel of death had kissed her lovingly, and unnoticed of any, she passed with him away!

The watchful eye of the Lady de Tilly was the first to see that Amelie's breath had gone so quietly that no one caught her latest sigh. The Physician and Chaplain rushed hurriedly into the chamber, but too late—! The Great Physician of souls had already put his beloved to sleep—the blessed sleep whose dream is of love on earth, and whose waking is in heaven! The great high Priest of the sons and daughters of men had anointed her with the oil of his mercy, and sent his blessed angels to lead her to the mansions of everlasting rest.

The stroke fell like the stunning blow of a hammer upon the heart of Pierre. He had indeed foreseen her death, but tried in vain to realize it. He made no outcry, but sat still wrapped in a terrible silence as in the midst of a desert. He held fast her dead hands and gazed upon her dead face until the heartbreaking sobs of Heloise and the appeals of Mere Esther, roused him from his stupor.

He rose up, and lifting Amelie in his arms, laid her upon a couch tenderly and reverently as a man touches the holiest object of his religion. Amelie was to him a sacrament, and in his manly love he worshipped her more as a saint than as a woman, a creation of heavenly more than of earthly perfections.

Pierre bent over her and closed for the last time those dear eyes which had looked upon him so pure and so lovingly. He embraced her dead form and kissed those pallid lips, which had once confessed her unalterable love and truth for Pierre Philibert.

The agitated Nuns gathered round them at the news of death in the Convent. They looked wonderingly and earnestly at an exhibition of such absorbing affection. They were for the most part in tears. With some of these gentle women, this picture of true love broken in the midst of its brightest hopes woke sympathies and recollections, which the watchful eye of Mere Migeon promptly checked as soon as she came into the parlour.

The Lady Superior saw that all was over and that Pierre's presence was an uneasiness to the Nuns, who glanced at him with eyes of pity, and womanly sympathy. She took him kindly by the hand, with a few words of condolence, and intimated that as he had been permitted to see the end, he must now withdraw from these forbidden precincts, and leave his lost treasure to the care of the Nuns who take charge of the dead.

CHAPTER 59

"THE MILLS OF GOD GRIND SLOWLY"

Pierre was permitted to see the remains of his affianced bride interred in the Convent Chapel. Her modest funeral was impressive from the number of sad sympathizing faces which gathered round her grave. The quiet figure of a Nun was seen morn and eve, for years and years after, kneeling upon the stone slab that covered her grave, laying upon it her daily offering of flowers, and if the name of Le Gardeur mingled with her prayers, it was but a proof of the unalterable affection of Heloise de Lotbiniere known in religion as Mere St Croix.

The Lamp of Repentigny shed its beams henceforth over the grave of the last representative of that noble house, where it still shines to commemorate their virtues and perpetuate the memory of their misfortunes. But God has long since compensated them for all.

Lady de Tilly was inconsolable over the ruin of her fondest hopes. She had regarded Pierre as her son, and intended to make him and Amelie joint inheritors with Le Gardeur, of her immense wealth. She desired still to bequeath it to Pierre, not only because of her great kindness for him, but as a sort of self imposed amercement upon her house for the death of his father.

Pierre refused. "I have more of the world's riches already than I can use," said he, "and I value not what I have, since she is gone for whose sake alone I prized them. I shall go abroad to resume my profession of arms, not seeking yet not avoiding an honorable death, which may reunite me to Amelie, and the sooner the more welcome!—"

"O God that rules the world!" was an exclamation often

743

repeated by the noble Lady, in those sad days. "What a wreck of happiness is ours—! I cannot resign myself to it! and I ask vainly, vainly, what we have done to bring upon our heads such a heavy judgment as this?"

"The ways of Providence are justified by faith, not by fallible reason which is too short sighted to see the ends of things!" was the reply of the Reverend Father de Berey, who often visited her in her affliction. "We see but in part, we know but in part. The righteous perisheth and I see the wicked in great power spreading like a green Bay tree. But mark the end! 'The end of the upright man is peace, the end of the wicked shall be cut off,' saith God. Let us never forget amid our repinings at Providence that God reigneth over all!—The end that we see is not the end that God sees. Man's ends are but beginnings in the eternal scheme of human destiny. God's ends are not on earth, but in that spiritual world, where Eternity takes the place of Time, where our sharp, may be our unmerited trials here, are amply recompensed in the full plan of Divine beneficence hereafter. 'Darkness lasteth through the night, but Joy cometh in the morning!'"—

The habitual gaiety of the Superior of the Recollets dropped like a mask from his face in the presence of a real sorrow, and he stood revealed in his true character of a grave earnest Christian teaching in all seriousness, the duty of resignation amid the trials of this world and a lively faith in the certainty of God's ways being justified in the world to come.

Lady de Tilly sought by assiduous devotion to the duties of her life and station, distraction from the gnawing cares that ever preyed upon her. She but partially succeeded. She lived through the short peace of Aix La Chapelle and shared in the terrible sufferings of the seven years war that followed in its wake. When the final conquest of New France overwhelmed the Colony to all appearances in utter ruin, she endowed the Ursulines with a large portion of her remaining wealth and retired with her nearest kinsmen to France. The name of Tilly became extinct among the noblesse of the Colony. But it still flourishes in a vigorous branch upon its native soil of

Normandy.

Pierre Philibert passed a sad winter in arranging and settling the vast affairs of his father, before leaving New France. In the spring following the death of Amelie, he passed over to the old world bidding a long and last adieu to his native land.

Pierre endeavoured manfully to bear up under the load of recollections and sorrows which crushed his heart, and made him a grave and melancholy man before his time. He rejoined the army of his Sovereign, and sought danger—his comrades said for danger's sake—with a desperate valour that was the boast of the army. But few suspected that he sought death, and tempted Fate in every form.

His wish was at last accomplished, as all earnest absorbing wishes ever are. He fell valorously, dying a soldier's death upon the field of Minden, his last moments sweetened by the thought that his beloved Amelie was waiting for him on the other side of the dark river, to welcome him with the bridal kiss promised upon the banks of the Lake of Tilly. He met her joyfully in that land where love is real and its promises are never broken!—

The death of the Bourgeois Philibert affecting so many fortunes was of immense consequence to the Colony. It led to the ruin of the party of the *Honnetes Gens*, the supremacy of the Grand Company and the final overthrow of New France.

The power and extravagance of Bigot, after that event, grew without check or challenge. The departure of the virtuous La Galissoniere left the colony to the weak and corrupt administrations of La Jonquiere and De Vaudreuil. The latter made the castle of St Louis as noted for its venality, as was the Palace of the Intendant. Bigot kept his high place through every change. The Marquis de Vaudreuil gave him free course, and it was more than suspected shared with the corrupt Intendant in the plunder of the Colony.

These public vices bore their natural fruit, and all the efforts of the *Honnetes Gens* to stay the tide of corruption were futile. Montcalm after reaping successive harvests of victories, brilliant beyond all precedent in North America, died a sacrifice to the insatiable greed and extravagance of Bigot and his associates, who while enriching themselves starved the army, and plundered the colony of all its resources. The fall of Quebec and the capitulation of Montreal were less owing to the power of the English, than to the corrupt misgovernment of Bigot and Vaudreuil, and the neglect of the court of France of her ancient and devoted colony.

Le Gardeur after a long confinement in the Bastille where he incessantly demanded trial and punishment for his rank offence of the murder of the Bourgeois, as he ever called it, was at last liberated, by express command of the King, without trial, and against his own wishes. His sword was restored to him, accompanied by a Royal order bidding him upon his allegiance return to his Regiment, as an officer of the King, free from all blame for the offence laid to his charge. Whether the killing of the Bourgeois was privately regarded at Court as good service, was never known. But Le Gardeur true to his loyal instincts obeyed his King, rejoined the army and once more took the field.

Upon the outbreak of the last French war in America he returned to New France, a changed and reformed man, an ascetic in his living, and although a soldier, a monk in the rigour of his penitential observances. His professional skill and daring were conspicuous among the number of gallant officers upon whom Montcalm chiefly relied to assist him in his long and desperate struggle against the ever increasing forces of the English. From the Capture of Chouaguen and the defence of the Fords of Montmorency, to the last brave blow struck upon the plains of St Foye, Le Gardeur de Repentigny fulfilled every duty of a gallant and desperate soldier. He carried his life in his hand and valued it as cheaply as he did the lives of his ennemies—!

He never spoke to Angelique again!—once he met her full in the face upon the perron of the Cathedral of St Marie. She started, as if touched by fire, trembled, blushed, hesitated and extended her hand to him in the old familiar way, with that look of witchery in her eyes, and that seductive smile upon her lips, which once sent the hot blood coursing madly in his veins. But Le Gardeur's heart was petrified now!—He cared for no woman more, or if he did, his thought dwelt with silent regret upon that pale Nun in the Convent of the Ursulines, once Heloise de Lotbiniere, who he knew was wasting her young life in solitary prayers for pardon for his great offence.

His anger rose fiercely at the sight of Angelique, and Le Gardeur forgot for a moment that he was a gentleman, a man who had once loved this woman. He struck her a blow, and passed on! It shattered her last illusion. The proud guilty woman still loved Le Gardeur, if she loved any man. But she felt she had merited his scorn. She staggered, and sat down on the steps of the Cathedral, weeping the bitterest tears her eyes had ever wept in her life. She never saw Le Gardeur again.

After the conquest of New France, Le Gardeur retired with the shattered remnant of the army of France back to their native land. His Sovereign loaded him with honours, which he cared not for. He had none to share them with, now—! Lover, sister, friends all were lost and gone! But he went on performing his military duties with an iron rigour and punctuality that made men admire while they feared him. His life was more mechanical than human. Le Gardeur spared neither himself nor others. He never married—never again looked with kindly eye upon a woman. His heart was proof against every female blandishment. He ended his life in solitary state and greatness, as Governor of Mahé in India, many years after he had left his native Canada.

One day in the year of grace 1777 another Council of war was sitting in the great chamber of the Castle of St Louis, under a wonderful change of circumstances! An English governor, Sir Guy Carleton, presided over a mixed assemblage of English and Canadian officers. The royal arms and colours of England had replaced the emblems and ensigns of France upon the walls of the Council Chamber, and the red uniform of her army was loyally worn by the old but still indomitable La Corne St Luc, who with the De Salaberrys, the De Beaujeus, Duchesnays, de Gaspes, and others of noblest name and lineage in New France, had come forward as loyal subjects of England's crown to defend Canada against the armies of the English Colonies now in rebellion against the King.

The noblesse and people of New France, all that was best and of most esteem in the land, gave their allegiance loyally and unreservedly to England, upon their final abandonment by the Court of France. They knew they had been coldly, deliberately, cruelly deserted by their King, and the colony utterly ruined by the malversations of their Governor and Intendant.

Montcalm had appealed vainly, again and again for help. He fought his last campaign with the letter of the Marshal De Belle Isle in his pocket, refusing the reinforcements he had so earnestly requested, and coldly bidding him make "the best fight he could, to save the Kings honour and his own."—

The Canadians neither forgot nor forgave the bonfires of Voltaire, nor the flatterers who congratulated La Pompadour, on the loss of those "acres of snow in Canada."—But the honour and much of the strength of France were lost with them. "When the house is on fire, nobody minds about the stables!" was the heartless sarcasm of Berreyer, Minister of Marine and Colonies, to De Bougainville, deputed to make a last desperate appeal for aid, to the Mother Country, which caused the indignant delegate to reply to Berreyer, that: "his answer was worthy of a horse!—"

Still, the rending of the old ties of nationality had been terrible, and the fond Habitans long looked and prayed for the return of their *bonnes Gens*, from France, who never came—! Canada had been left to its fate. The people of the Colony settled down by degrees as loyal and faithful subjects of England.

When the conquest of New France by England, had its counterstroke in the revolt of the English colonies, the Canadians were immovable from their new allegiance. They turned a deaf ear to the appeals of Congress and to the proclamations of Washington, inciting them to revolt, and especially scorned the seductive offers of La Fayette and D'Estaing to join in the league with the Americans.

The Canadians saw with resentment, French fleets and armies, despatched to America, to aid the Bostonais, a fraction of which force sent in the hour of need, would have saved New

France from conquest!—The assistance which had been so brutally denied to her own children, France now gave lavishly to their hereditary enemies who had for over a century been trying to conquer Canada.

Through causes rooted deeply in the history of New France the Canadians had ever regarded the English Colonists in America as their enemies far more than the English themselves. And therefore, when driven to a choice between the two, they remained true to England, and their wise choice has been justified to this day!

The patriotic Bishop Briand exhorted the people in season and out of season to stand by their King and Country! The Clergy everywhere preached damnation against all who took not up arms to oppose the invasion of Arnold and Montgomery! Some of them like the warlike Curé Bailly, actually took the field and fell in defence of the Colony—! The officers and leaders of the Canadians who had fought in the old wars so gallantly for France, now donned the English uniform, and led their countrymen to the defence of Quebec, with the same valour and with better success, than when opposing Wolfe and Murray. The death of Jumonville de Villiers was gloriously avenged!—

"Read that, La Corne!" said Sir Guy Carleton, handing him a newspaper just received from England. "An old friend of yours, if I mistake not, is dead—! I met him once in India. A stern saturnine man he was! but a brave and able commander—! I am sorry to hear of his death, but I do not wonder at it. He was the most melancholy man I ever saw!—"

La Corne took the paper and gave a start of intense emotion as he read an obituary notice as follows:

"East Indies!—Death of the Marquis De Repentigny! The Marquis Le Gardeur de Repentigny, general of the army and Governor of Mahé, died last year in that part of India which he had by his valour and skill preserved to France. This officer had served in Canada with the reputation of an able and gallant soldier—."

La Corne was deeply agitated,—his lips quivered and tears gathered in the thick grey eye lashes that formed so prominent a feature of his rugged but kindly face. He concluded his reading in silence, and handed the paper to De Beaujeu, with the single remark—: "Le Gardeur is dead!—poor fellow! He was more sinned against than sinning—! God pardon him for all the evil he meant not to do—! Is it not strange, that she who was the cursed cause of his ruin, still flourishes like the Queen of the Kingdom of brass? It is hard to justify the ways of Providence, when wickedness like hers prospers and virtues like those of the brave old Bourgeois find a bloody grave—! My poor Amelie too! poor girl, poor girl!" La Corne St Luc sat silent a long time immersed in melancholy reflections.

The Canadian officers read the paragraph which revived in their minds also sad recollections of the past. They knew that, by *her*, who had been the cursed cause of the ruin of Le Gardeur and of the death of the Bourgeois, La Corne referred to the still blooming widow of the Chevalier de Pean, the leader of fashion and gaiety in the capital now, as she had been thirty years before, when she was the celebrated Angelique des Meloises.

Angelique had played desperately her game of life with the juggling fiend of Ambition, and had not wholly lost. Although the murder of Caroline de St Castin, pressed hard upon her conscience and still harder upon her fears, no man read in her face the minutest asterisk that pointed to the terrible secret buried in her bosom, and never discovered. So long as La Corriveau lived, Angelique never felt safe, but fear was too weak a counsellor, for her to pretermit either her composure or her pleasures. She redoubled her gaiety and her devotions, and that was the extent of her repentance! The dread secret of Beaumanoir was never revealed. It awaited, and awaits still, the judgment of the final day of accompt.

Bigot in his heart suspected her of complicity with the bloody deed, but proof failed, nor could he ever detect upon her countenance or in her words, watch as he would, one sign of the guilt, she kept so well concealed from his eye.— He was never quite satisfied however with her innocence, and although so deeply smitten by her beauty and fascinations, he would not marry her.

Angelique had intrigued and sinned in vain. She feared Bigot knew more than he really did in reference to the death of Caroline, and oft while laughing in his face, she trembled in her heart when he played and equivocated with her earnest appeals to marry her—! Wearied out at length with waiting for his decisive yes or no, Angelique mortified by wounded pride and stung by the scorn of Le Gardeur on his return to the Colony, suddenly accepted the hand of the Chevalier de Pean, and as a result, became the recognized mistress of the Intendant, imitating as far as she was able the splendour and the guilt of La Pompadour and making the palace of Bigot, as corrupt if not as brilliant as that of Versailles.

Angelique lived thenceforth a life of splendid sin. She clothed herself in purple and fine linen, while the noblest ladies of the land were reduced by the war, to rags and beggary. She fared sumptuously while men and women died of hunger in the streets of Quebec. She bought houses and lands and filled her coffres with gold out of the public treasury, while the brave soldiers of Montcalm starved for want of their pay. She gave fetes and banquets while the English were thundering at the gates of the Capital. She foresaw the eventual fall of Bigot and the ruin of the country, and resolved that since she had failed in getting himself, she would make herself possessor of all that he had! and she got it!—

The fate of Bigot was a warning to public Peculators and oppressors. He returned to France soon after the surrender of the Colony, with Cadet, Varin Penisault and others of the Grand Company, who were now useless tools and were cast aside by their Court friends. The Bastile opened its iron doors to receive the godless and wicked crew, who had lost the fairest Colony of France, the richest jewel in her crown. Bigot and the others, were tried by a special commission, were found guilty of the most heinous malversations of office, and sentenced to make full restitution of the plunder of the King's treasures, to be imprisoned until their fines and restitutions were paid and then banished from the kingdom for ever.

History has so far utterly failed to tell us with certainty what was the end of Bigot. Singular as it may seem a man who played so important a part in Canada, found no one to record his death, or to write his epitaph. It is believed that by favour of La Pompadour, his heavy sentence, was commuted, and he retained a sufficiency of his illgotten wealth, to enable him under a change of name, to live in ease and opulence at Bordeaux where he died.

Angelique had no sympathy for Bigot in his misfortunes, no regrets save that she had failed to mould him more completely to her own purposes, flattering herself that had she done so, the fortunes of the war and the fate of the Colony might have been different. What might have been, had she not ruined herself and her projects by the murder of Caroline, it were vain to conjecture! But she who had boldly dreamed of ruling King and Kingdom, by the witchery of her charms and the craft of her subtle intellect, had to content herself with the name of De Pean, and the shame of a lawless connection with the Intendant.

She would fain have gone to France to try her fortunes when the Colony was lost, but La Pompadour forbade her presence there under pain of her severest displeasure. Angelique raved at the inhibition, but was too wise to tempt the wrath of the royal mistress, by disobeying her mandate. She had to content herself with railing at La Pompadour, with the energy of three Furies, but she never ceased to the end of her life to boast of the terror which her charms had exercised over the great favorite of the King.

Rolling in wealth and scarcely faded in beauty, Angelique kept herself in the public eye. She hated retirement, and boldly claimed her right to a foremost place in the Society of Quebec. Her great wealth and unrivalled power of intrigue enabled her to keep that place down to the last decade of the last century. A generation ago, very old men and women still talked, of the gorgeous carriages and splendid liveries of the great "Dame De Pean," whom they had seen in their childhood, rolling in state along the broad avenue of St Foye, the admiration envy and evil example of her sex! Many people shook their heads and whispered queer stories of her past life, in the days of the Intendant Bigot, but none knew the worst of her. The forgotten chamber of Beaumanoir kept its terrible secret till long after she had disappeared from the scene of her extravagant life. The delight of Angelique was in the eyes of men, and the business of her life was to retain their admiration down to the last years of an incorrigible old age.

The fate of La Corriveau her confederate in her great wickedness, was peculiar and terrible. Secured at once by her own fears as well as by a rich yearly allowance paid her by Angelique, La Corriveau discreetly bridled her tongue over the death of Caroline, but she could not bridle her own evil passions in her own household.

One summer day of the year following the conquest of the Colony, the goodman Dodier was found dead in his house at St Valier. Fanchon who knew something and suspected more, spoke out. An investigation into the cause of death of her husband resulted in the discovery, that he had been murdered by pouring melted lead into his ear while he slept! La Corriveau was arrested as the perpetrator of the atrocious deed.

A special court of Justice, was convened in the great hall of the Convent of the Ursulines, which in the ruinous state of the city after the seige, and bombardment, had been taken for the headquarters of General Murray. Mere Migeon and Mere Esther, who both survived the conquest, effected a prudent arrangement with the English general, and saved the Convent from all further encroachment by placing it under his special protection.

La Corriveau was tried with all the fairness if not with all the forms of English law. She made a subtle and embarrassing defence, but was at last fairly convicted of the cruel murder of her husband. She was sentenced to be hung and gibbetted in an iron cage, upon the hill of Levis, in sight of the whole city of Quebec.

La Corriveau made frantic efforts during her imprisonment to engage Angelique to intercede in her behalf, but Angelique's appeals were fruitless before the stern administrators of English law. Moreover Angelique, to be true to herself, was false to her wicked confederate. She cared not to intercede too much, or enough to insure success—! In her heart she wished La Corriveau well out of the way! that all memory of the tragedy of Beaumanoir might be swept from the earth, except what of it remained hid in her own bosom. She juggled with the appeals of La Corriveau, keeping her in hopes of pardon until the fatal hour came, when it was too late, for La Corriveau to harm her by a confession of the murder of Caroline.

The hill of Levis where La Corriveau was gibbetted, was long remembered in the traditions of the Colony. It was regarded with superstitious awe by the Habitans. The ghost of La Corriveau long haunted, and in the belief of many, still haunts the scene of her execution. Startling tales, raising the hair with terror, were told of her round the fire sides in winter, when the snow drifts covered the fences, when the north wind howled down the chimney, and rattled the casements of the cottages of the habitans—How all night long in the darkness she ran after belated travellers, dragging her cage at her heels, and defying all the exorcisms of the church to lay her evil spirit—!

Singularly enough, after the ancient gibbet had rotted down, and three generations of men had passed over the forgotten spot, where her bones and her cage had been buried together, out of human sight, a Habitant of Levis, digging in the earth, discovered the horrid cage, rusted and decayed with its long interment. It was taken up, and exhibited in the city as a curiosity, though few remembered its story. Finally it was bought at a great price by a collector of relics—the ghastlier the better—, and deposited in the public Museum at Boston in New England, where it remains dissociated from the terrible memories which were connected with it—! A young lady of Quebec, acquainted with the legends of her country and whose quick eyes nothing escapes, discovered not long ago the horrible thing, covered with the dust and oblivion of Time, the last relic, that remains of the memory of La Corriveau!—

The House in St Valier, the scene of her atrocious crime, was burnt to the ground on the night she was gibbetted, by the indignant habitans to whom it had ever been an object of supreme terror. With it, were consumed the relics of the laboratory of Antonio Exili, and the deadly secret of the *Aqua Tofana*, a secret, which it is hoped, modern chemistry will not rediscover, but let it remain for ever, among the lost arts of an ancient and evil world—!—

Our Tale is now done. It ends in all sadness as most true tales of this world do! There is in it neither poetic nor human Justice. Fain would we have had it otherwise, for the heart longs for happiness as the eye for light! But truth is stronger as well as stranger than fiction, and while the tablet of the *Chien d'or* overlooks the Rue Buade, while the Lamp of Repentigny burns in the ancient chapel of the Ursulines, while the ruins of Beaumanoir cover the dust of Caroline de St Castin, and Amelie sleeps her long sleep by the side of Heloise de Lotbiniere, the writer has neither courage nor power to deviate from the received traditions, in relating the story of the Golden Dog.

END

Explanatory Notes

Some of these explanatory notes have to do with people and events associated with British, French, and North American history, particularly in the eighteenth century. Others identify quotations from and references to British, Canadian, French, German, Greek, Italian, Roman, and Swedish literature and popular culture. As might be expected, William Shakespeare is the most frequently quoted author. Still others deal with citations from and allusions to the Bible, Catholic rituals, and Christian saints. The Bible, in fact, provides the largest number of citations and allusions from a single source. The notes are keyed to the text by page and line numbers. A person or event is normally annotated only when first mentioned. When the publication from which Kirby drew his information is known, then this item is cited.

1.2-6   *"In questo ... che conoscinto"*] Alessandro Manzoni, *I Promessi Sposi*, Revised Edition, 1840–42. Kirby took this quotation from an edition of this revision issued in Brussels in 1843, a copy of which he owned, and from which he probably translated the lines into English. A modern version reads, "And to tell the truth, our object in relating this story is not only to set the stage for our characters, but also to give an adequate picture—to the best of our ability and within the limits of our space—of a period in our country's history which, although famous enough in a general way, is very little known in detail." See Alessandro Manzoni. *The Betrothed.* Trans. Bruce Penman. London: Penguin Books, 1972, p. 564.

3.14   *Peter Kalm*] Pehr (Peter) Kalm, a Swedish-born "professor of ... natural history," visited Quebec in August and September 1749. In his account of his travels in North America from 1748 to 1751, which Kirby read in Forster's English translation, Kalm commented on the "extraordinary goodness" that Roland-Michel Barrin de La Galissonière, "a nobleman of uncommon qualities," showed him during his stay in the city. See "Kalm, Pehr." *DCB.* Vol. 4, pp. 406–08, and Peter Kalm.

Travels Into North America. Trans. John Rein[h]old Forster. Vol. 3. London: Printed for the Editor; And Sold by T. Lowndes, 1771, p. 97.

3.14   *Count de la Galissoniere*] From 1747 until 1749, when he left Quebec, Roland-Michel Barrin de La Galissonière, an officer in the French navy who then held the rank of captain, was "commandant general of New France." During this time he also acted as governor general in the place of the Marquis de La Jonquière who had been appointed to this position in 1746, but who did not arrive in New France for three years. While he lived in Quebec, La Galissonière took a keen interest in the "natural history" of North America. See "Barrin De La Galissonière, Roland-Michel." *DCB.* Vol. 3, pp. 26–32.

3.18   *Louis XV.*] He was King of France from 1715 to 1774.

4.31–34   *His ... repulse of Admiral Byng ... led to the death of that ... officer who was shot by sentence of Court Martial*] In May 1756 Roland-Michel Barrin de La Galissonière, who had been promoted "to the rank of lieutenant-general" in the French navy the previous year, commanded the ships that fought off the island of Minorca with the British fleet under John Byng, an admiral in the Royal Navy who had been governor of Newfoundland in the 1740s. Byng's defeat in the battle led to a court martial where he was found guilty of "negligence" and "condemned to death." Despite efforts to save his life, Byng "was executed by a firing squad" in March 1757. See "Barrin De La Galissonière, Roland-Michel." *DCB.* Vol. 3, pp. 26–32, and "Byng, John." *DCB.* Vol. 3, pp. 91–92.

5.26   *Linneus*] Carl Linnaeus, who was a professor of medicine at the University of Uppsala from 1741 until his death in 1778, "exerted an influence in his fields—botany and natural history—that has had few parallels in the history of science." Pehr (Peter) Kalm, who attended the University in the 1740s, was one of Linnaeus' most famous students. There is no evidence that Roland-Michel Barrin de La Galissonière ever studied in Sweden, however. See "Linnaeus (or Von Linné), Carl." *Dictionary Of Scientific Biography.* Vol. 8. Ed. Charles Coulston Gillispie. New York: Charles Scribner's Sons, 1973, pp. 374–81.

5.32   *the term 'Gods footstool'*] That is, the earth. Compare Matthew
5:34–35, in which Jesus, teaching his disciples, said:

> But I say unto you, Swear not at all; neither by
> heaven; for it is God's throne:
> Nor by the earth; for it is his footstool.

See *IB.* Vol. 7. 1951, p. 300.

6.2–3   *an empire ... Caesar wrested from Ambiotrix*] In 53 B.C. Julius
Caesar waged a campaign of total destruction against Ambiorix,
a leader of the Eburones, who had annihilated a Roman army
at Atuatuca (Tongeren [Tongres], Belgium) the previous year.
Although Ambiorix "was never caught," his defeat was an
important step in Caesar's conquest of Gaul. See T. Rice Holmes.
Caesar's Conquest Of Gaul. Second Edition. 1911; rpt. Oxford:
Oxford University Press, and London: Humphrey Milford, 1931,
p. 128.

7.18–20 *Jacques Cartier ... first winter in Canada ... guests of ... Donacana*]
In September 1535 Jacques Cartier "decided to lay up his ships
in the river Sainte-Croix (Saint-Charles), at the mouth of the
stream called Lairet," about three kilometres from what is now
the city of Quebec. Cartier had been led to this harbour by
Donnacona, the Iroquois who was "chief of Stadacona." In his
relation of his voyage to Canada in 1535–36, Cartier described
this site as "ung affourcq d'eaulx fort beau et plaisant auquel
lieu y a une petite riviere et hable de basre marinant de deux à
troys brasses." He added, "Aupres d'icelluy lieu y a ung peuple
dont est seigneur le *dit* Donnacona et y est sa demeurance qui se
nomme Stadaconé." See Jacques Cartier. *Relations.* Ed. Michel
Bideaux. Montréal: Les Presses de l'Université de Montréal,
1986, p. 138; "Cartier, Jacques." *DCB.* Vol. 1, pp. 165–72; and
"Donnacona." *DCB.* Vol. 1, pp. 275–77.

7.24   *the Intendant*] Appointed "intendant of New France" in February
1748, François Bigot "arrived at Quebec" on 26 August of
that year. He held this position, which included the direction
of "trade, finance, industry, food supplies, prices, policing,
and other such matters," until France surrendered the colony
to Great Britain in 1760. After his return to France Bigot
was arrested for his role in the so-called *affaire du Canada,*

"imprisoned in the Bastille for two years," found guilty of the charges of graft and corruption brought against him, and banished "from France forever." He died at Neuchâtel, Switzerland, in 1778. See "Bigot, François." *DCB*. Vol. 4, pp. 59–71.

8.23–24 *the Bishop*] In 1740 Henri-Marie Dubreil de Pontbriand was named bishop of the Roman Catholic diocese of Quebec by Louis XV of France. Consecrated in France in April 1741, he "took possession of his see" at Quebec the following August. He served as bishop of the diocese until his death in Montreal in June 1760. See "Dubreil De Pontbriand, Henri-Marie." *DCB*. Vol. 3, pp. 192–99.

8.32 *the Marshal de Saxe*] During the War of the Austrian Succession (1740–48), Maurice de Saxe, Count de Saxe and, from 1743, Marshal of France, was "Commander-in-Chief of the French armies in Flanders" that routinely defeated the Austrian, British, and Dutch forces sent to fight them. See Skrine, Francis Henry. *Fontenoy And Great Britain's Share in the War of the Austrian Succession 1741–48*. Edinburgh And London: William Blackwood And Sons, 1906, p. 136.

8.36–37 *a peace ... at Aix La Chapelle*] As a result of negotiations that lasted several months, a treaty to end the War of the Austrian Succession was concluded at Aix-la-Chapelle (Aachen, Germany) on 18 October 1748. According to Article V of this treaty, all "*the Conquests*" made during the war "*in* Europe, *or the* East *or* West-Indies, *or in any other Part of the World whatsoever*" were to be restored. See *The Definitive Treaty Of Peace and Friendship, Between His* Britannick *Majesty, the Most* Christian *King, and the* States General *of the United Provinces. Concluded at* Aix la Chapelle ... *Published by Authority*. London: Printed by Edward Owen, in Warwick-Lane, 1749, p. 10.

9.23 *Rigaud de Vaudreuil*] In 1748 François-Pierre de Rigaud de Vaudreuil, the son of a former "governor general of New France" and a major in "the colonial regulars," was "named king's lieutenant in the Government of Quebec" by Roland-Michel Barrin de La Galissonière. Two years before Rigaud de Vaudreuil had led a raiding party that captured and razed Fort Massachusetts (Williamstown, Massachusetts) and on "the way back ... burned some 200 buildings along the Kaskékoué" (Hoosic) River. See "Rigaud De Vaudreuil, François-Pierre De." *DCB.* Vol. 4, pp. 660–62.

9.27 Probatum est] That is, "It has been tried and proved." See *A Dictionary Of Latin And Greek Quotations, Proverbs, Maxims And Mottos.* Ed. H. T. Riley. London: George Bell And Sons, 1909, p. 345.

10.9–14 *the Chevalier de Beaujeu ... defeating an army ten times more numerous than his*] In February 1747 Daniel-Hyacinthe-Marie Liénard de Beaujeu, a native of Montreal who was an "officer in the colonial regular troops," was one of the leaders of "300 Canadians and Indians" who "attacked 500 New Englanders billeted in Grand Pré," Nova Scotia, "and forced their surrender after bloody fighting." Beaujeu was killed in July 1755 during a battle in which the British were defeated near the Monongahela River a few miles from Fort Duquesne (Pittsburgh, Pennsylvania). Major-General Edward Braddock, the "commander in chief" of the British forces in North America, also died as a result of wounds that he received there. The loss of this battle on the Monongahela, usually interpreted as a classic confrontation between rigid regular soldiers and flexible colonial and native troops, dealt a very heavy blow to British prestige in the Thirteen Colonies. See "Braddock, Edward." *ANB,* and "Liénard De Beaujeu, Daniel-Hyacinthe-Marie." *DCB.* Vol. 3, pp. 400–02.

10.17–22 *Jumonville de Villiers ... his brother Coulon De Villiers ... Washington ... 1754*] In May 1754 Joseph Coulon de Villiers de Jumonville, one of several brothers who served as officers in "the colonial regulars," was killed near Fort Duquesne (Pittsburgh, Pennsylvania), when he and his men were attacked by militiamen under the command of George Washington from the British colony of Virginia. Jumonville had been "dispatched" from Fort Duquesne "to discover if Washington had in fact invaded French-claimed territory. Were this to be the case he was to ... deliver a formal summons to Washington calling on him to withdraw." According to the French, Jumonville "was struck down while trying to proclaim his official summons." Two months later, in July 1754, Jumonville's brother, Louis Coulon de Villiers, led another French force from Fort Duquesne that attacked Washington and his men at "Fort Necessity (near Farmington, Pa.)," a "crude log redoubt" where they "had taken refuge," and forced them to surrender. The terms of capitulation permitted the "Americans" to go back "to their country in safety with the honours of war" in return for their agreement to certain conditions, which they never observed. See "Coulon De Villiers, Louis." *DCB.* Vol. 3, pp. 148–49, and "Coulon De Villiers De Jumonville, Joseph." *DCB.* Vol. 3, pp. 150–51.

10.29   *the Sieur De Lery, the Kings Engineer*] Gaspard-Joseph Chaussegros de Léry, an officer in the French army and an engineer, arrived in Canada in 1716 "to prepare plans of existing fortifications at Quebec and to recommend those required to protect the city from attack." This undertaking eventually "led to a permanent appointment as chief engineer" of the colony, "a post he held until his death" in 1756. See "Chaussegros De Léry, Gaspard-Joseph." *DCB.* Vol. 3, pp. 116–19.

10.31   *Vauban's genius*] Sébastien le Prestre de Vauban, an engineer in the French army during the second half of the seventeenth century, was famous for building forts and conducting sieges. In *Siècle de Louis XIV* (1751), François-Marie Arouet de Voltaire described Vauban, who became "maréchal de France" in 1703, as "l'un de ces grands hommes et de ces génies qui parurent dans ce siècle pour le service de Louis XIV," and as "le meilleur ingénieur de l'Europe." Kirby, who owned a copy of this history published in 1823, was probably echoing Voltaire's assessment of "le génie de Vauban." See "Vauban (Sébastien Le Prestre De)." *BU*, and *Siècle.* Vol. 1, pp. 116, 155, and 315.

10.36–11.3 *Claude de Beauharnois, brother of a former Governor of the Colony ... the ancestor of ...Hortense de Beauharnois ... her son Napoleon III. ... of France*] Claude de Beauharnois de Beaumont et de Villechauve, a "French naval officer," was the brother of Charles de Beauharnois de La Boische, "governor general of New France" from 1726 until 1747. Through his "eldest son, François," Claude de Beauharnois was also the great-grandfather of Hortense-Eugénie de Beauharnais, who married Louis Bonaparte, the brother of Napoléon I of France. Their son Louis-Napoléon Bonaparte ruled France as

Napoléon III from 1852 to 1870. Claude de Beauharnois died in 1738. His son Charles-Claude de Beauharnois, however, served as an army officer in Canada from 1734 until sometime after 1749. The Beauharnois "have frequently been confused." See "Beauharnois De Beaumont Et De Villechauve, Claude De." *DCB*. Vol. 2, pp. 52–53, and "Beauharnois De La Boische, Charles De." *DCB*. Vol. 3, pp. 41–51.

11.7–13   *the Chevalier La Corne St Luc … fresh from … the capture of an army of New Englanders*] In the winter of 1747 Louis de La Corne, "known as the Chevalier de La Corne," a captain "in the colonial regular troops," took over the "command of a party of … Canadians and Indians" during an attack on a force of British troops from New England at Grand Pré, Nova Scotia. Under "La Corne's leadership … a large number of the enemy were killed, wounded, or taken prisoner." In *Le Chien d'or* Kirby conflates the career of Louis de La Corne, who drowned in 1761, with that of his brother Luc de La Corne, "known as … La Corne Saint-Luc," who died in Montreal in 1784. Because of their participation "in military and commercial endeavours which took them to the same battlefields south of Lake Champlain and the same fur-trading territories in the west," the two brothers "were often confused." See "La Corne, Louis … De." *DCB*. Vol. 3, pp. 331–32, and "La Corne, Luc De." *DCB*. Vol. 4, pp. 425–29.

11.15–16   *Father De Berey the Superior of the Recollets*] Claude-Charles Berey Des Essarts, a native of Montreal who took the name of Félix when he entered the Recollets in the 1730s, became the superior of this order in Canada in 1775. A military chaplain with the French army in North America during the Seven Years' War, he spent some time in the 1740s as a priest at Beauport. In *Mémoires* (1866), Philippe-Joseph Aubert de Gaspé described "le père de Bérey" as having "des allures et des goûts tant soit peu soldatesques," and as being known for "ses saillies, ses bons mots, ses reparties vives." Kirby owned a copy of this publication. See Philippe-Joseph Aubert de Gaspé. *Mémoires*. Ottawa: G. E. Desbarats, 1866, pp. 63–64.

11.31   *Father Glapion the Superior of the Jesuits*] Augustin-Louis de Glapion, a Jesuit priest, was "superior general" of the Jesuits in Canada from 1763 until his death in 1790. Although he "taught

... at the Jesuit college" in Quebec for several years in the 1740s, in 1748 he was studying "philosophy and theology" in his native France. See "Glapion, Augustin-Louis De." *DCB.* Vol. 4, pp. 297–99.

13.13–15　*Sieur De St Denis ... from Beauport*] Antoine Juchereau Duchesnay was seigneur of Beauport from 1720 until 1772, when he died leaving his son, who bore the same name, a "huge estate." The elder Antoine's grandfather was Nicolas Juchereau de Saint-Denis; he had been "ennobled" in 1692 "for his services as a colonizer and soldier" in New France. See "Juchereau De Saint-Denis, Nicolas." *DCB.* Vol. 1, pp. 401–02, and "Juchereau Duchesnay, Antoine." *DCB.* Vol. 5, pp. 462–64.

14.12–16　*Wolfe ... on the beach of Beauport*] On 31 July 1759 James Wolfe, "major-general and commander-in-chief of the land forces for the expedition against Quebec," launched "a frontal assault" on the French army encamped on the north shore of the St. Lawrence just to the east of the city of Quebec. His attack "on the Beauport lines" resulted in "a bloody reverse" in which "over 200" British soldiers were killed. In Andrew Bell's translation of the third edition of François-Xavier Garneau's *Histoire Du Canada* (1859), Wolfe, "a young officer full of talent, who was consumed with a desire to distinguish himself by brilliant feats of arms," was described as being "in great chagrin" at this "check," because of which he "saw vanish, in a moment, all his proud illusions of glory." Kirby owned a copy of Bell's translation. See Bell. Vol. 2, pp. 235 and 243, and "Wolfe, James." *DCB.* Vol. 3, pp. 666–74.

14.28–29　*the Easter eggs hard as agates*] In Philippe-Joseph Aubert de Gaspé's *Mémoires* (1866), Alexis and Marc, two Recollet brothers who were visiting the Aubert de Gaspés in Saint-Jean-Port-Joli, Lower Canada, recalled the time that the Recollets at their monastery in Quebec, served eggs "durs comme des diamants" for eleven days in a row, all became ill. They finally surmised that a stranger, "qui ne craignait ni Dieu, ni diable," helped by "quelques mauvais sujets," had hard-boiled all the eggs gathered from the people for the monastery during the last two weeks of Lent. In this, and in the following anecdote about the Recollets, Kirby is most probably taking his material from his copy of *Mémoires*. See Philippe-Joseph Aubert de Gaspé. *Mémoires*. Ottawa: G. E. Desbarats, 1866, pp. 77 and 79.

15.5 Catuli Catulorum] That is, literally, puppies of puppies.

15.9–12 *father Ambrose ... the poor dogs of Quebec ... in his kitchen*] In *Mémoires* (1866), Philippe-Joseph Aubert de Gaspé listed the duties of the dog owned by the Recollet order in Quebec, including the job of turning the spit in the kitchen of the monastery two times a day. The work being very hot, the Recollets' dog "avait souvent la finesse de s'évader vers l'heure où sa présence aurait été la plus requise." When he disappeared, "le frère Ambroise," the Recollets' cook, had to find "un substitut" from among the dogs of the city. See Philippe-Joseph Aubert de Gaspé. *Mémoires*. Ottawa: G. E. Desbarats, 1866, pp. 75 and 82.

15.33–34 *the Lordship or Seigneurie of Tilly*] In 1700 Pierre-Noël Legardeur de Tilly, an officer "in the colonial regular troops," bought the seigneury of Villieu on the south shore of the St. Lawrence nearly opposite the city of Quebec. Pierre-Noël died in 1720 and his widow in 1739; their heirs held the estate, which had been renamed Tilly, until August 1748, when it was sold. Pierre-Noël Legardeur de Tilly was the eldest son of Charles Legardeur de Tilly, who in 1636 had emigrated from Normandy with his brother Pierre Legardeur de Repentigny. Although by the mid-eighteenth century the descendants of the two brothers were cousins of varying degrees, Kirby may have been encouraged to link these relatives more closely because of J. B. A. Ferland's remark in *Cours D'Histoire Du Canada* (1865) that in 1636 "Les LeGardeur de Repentigny et de Tilly" were one of "deux grandes familles" who established themselves "dans la colonie." Kirby owned a copy of this history. See "Legardeur De Tilly, Pierre-Noël." *DCB*. Vol. 2, p. 387, and J. B. A. Ferland. *Cours D'Histoire Du Canada. Seconde Partie 1663–1759*. Québec: Augustin Coté, 1865, p. 6.

17.1 *Le Gardeur*] Pierre-Jean-Baptiste-François-Xavier Legardeur de Repentigny was the great-great-grandson of Pierre Legardeur de Repentigny, the Norman who emigrated to New France in 1636. His father was Jean-Baptiste-René Legardeur de Repentigny; his mother, Marie-Catherine Juchereau de Saint-Denis. In January

1748, when he wounded "fatally ... with his sword" Nicolas Jacquin *dit* Philibert, Legardeur, aged twenty-eight, was an officer in the French "colonial regular troops," his parents were both dead, and he did not have a sister. Legardeur, whose sentence "to be decapitated" was remitted in 1749, "went to France" after the fall of Quebec "and settled at Tours. In 1769 he entered the service of the Compagnie des Indes as adjutant general and commander of the troops." He died in India in 1776. See "Legardeur De Repentigny, Pierre-Jean-Baptiste-François-Xavier." *DCB*. Vol. 4, pp. 448–49.

17.6–7   *Mere Marie de l'Incarnation*] Marie Guyart Martin, a native of Tours, "took her vows" as "an Ursuline nun under the name Marie de l'Incarnation" in 1633. In 1639 she left France for Quebec, where she founded the Ursulines, one of whose main aims was to educate the young women of New France. See "Guyart, Marie." *DCB*. Vol. 1, pp. 351–59.

17.17   *Angelique des Meloises*] In *Les Ursulines De Québec, Depuis Leur Établissement Jusqu'à Nos Jours*, Angélique Renaud D'Avène Des Méloizes, born in 1722, was listed among the students "Qui Se Sont Trouvées Au Pensionnat" at the Ursuline Convent in Quebec "De 1700 À 1739." A "personne très-remarquable pour sa beauté, ses agréments et son esprit," Angélique "married Michel-Jean-Hugues Péan, adjutant at Quebec," in 1746. In 1760, after "the capitulation of Montreal," she "accompanied Bigot and her husband to France." She died in Blois in 1792. See "Renaud D'Avène Des Méloizes, Angélique." *DCB*. Vol. 4, pp. 659–60, and *Ursulines*. Vol. 2. 1864, pp. 171 and 176.

18.14–18   *the gallant defence of a fort ... by a former lady of her house, who ... saved the lives of all from the fire and scalping knife*] Possibly Kirby was referring to Marie Perrot Jarret de Verchères, the wife of the seigneur of Verchères. In 1690, with "only three or four men," she defended the seigneury on the south shore of the St. Lawrence just east of Montreal for "two days" against the Iroquois. The story of Marie and her daughter, Marie-Madeleine Jarret de Verchères, who repeated in 1692 "the role her mother had played so well" two years before, "was not well known" in the nineteenth century. Kirby most likely took his allusion from Philippe-Joseph Aubert de Gaspé, the great-great-grandson of

Marie and the great-grandson of Madeleine. He mentioned these "Dames de Verchères" who "défendirent un fort attaqué par les sauvages, et les repoussèrent" in both *Les Anciens Canadiens* (1864) and *Mémoires* (1866). Kirby owned a copy of each volume. See Philippe-Joseph Aubert de Gaspé. *Les Anciens Canadiens.* Second Edition. Québec: G. Et G. E. Desbarats, 1864, p. 255; Jane Brierley, trans. *A Man of Sentiment: The Memoirs of Philippe-Joseph Aubert de Gaspé 1786–1871.* Montréal: Véhicule Press, 1988, p. 449; and "Jarret De Verchères, Marie-Madeleine." *DCB.* Vol. 3, pp. 308–13.

19.3–5   *King Francis used to say, that a court without ladies, was a year without a spring or a summer without roses*] Compare the memoirs composed by Pierre de Bourdeilles, "seigneur de l'abbaye De Brantôme," in the three decades before his death in 1614. Commenting on the numerous women who frequented the court of Francis I during his reign from 1514 to 1547, Brantôme wrote that the French king considered that "toute la décoration d'une court estoit des dames. ... Comme de vray, une court sans dames, c'est un jardin sans aucunes belles fleurs." See "Brantôme (Pierre De Bourdeilles, seigneur de l'abbaye De)." *BU,* and *Oeuvres Complètes De Pierre De Bourdeille Seigneur De Brantôme.* Ed. Ludovic Lalanne. Vol. 3: *Grands Capitaines François.* Paris: Chez Mme Ve Jules Renouard, 1867, p. 127.

19.15   *Agathe*] Louis de La Corne, "known as the Chevalier de La Corne," did not have a daughter. In the fall of 1748 Luc de La Corne, "known as ... La Corne Saint-Luc," had two daughters, one of them Geneviève-Élisabeth, who was a few weeks old. In 1769 she married Charles-Louis Tarieu de Lanaudière and, thus, became the aunt of Philippe-Joseph Aubert de Gaspé. He described her as the "fille de M. de Saint-Luc" in *Les Anciens Canadiens* (1864) and as the "fille du chevalier de Saint-Luc" in *Mémoires* (1866). Kirby, following his copy of each of these volumes, was probably modelling Agathe on Geneviève-Élisabeth. See Philippe-Joseph Aubert de Gaspé. *Les Anciens Canadiens.* Second Edition. Québec: G. Et G. E. Desbarats, 1864, p. 273; Philippe-Joseph Aubert de Gaspé. *Mémoires.* Ottawa: G. E. Desbarats, 1866, p. 42; "La Corne, Louis ... De." *DCB.* Vol. 3, pp. 331–32; and "La Corne, Luc De." *DCB.*

Vol. 4, pp. 425–29.

20.5–6   *Colonel Philibert*] In the fall of 1748 Pierre-Nicolas Jacquin *dit* Philibert, "the eldest" son of Nicolas Jacquin *dit* Philibert, was eleven years old. In "Le Chien d'Or—The Golden Dog," a sketch in *Maple Leaves: A Budget Of Legendary, Historical, Critical, And Sporting Intelligence* (1863), James MacPherson Le Moine depicted "Pierre Nicolas Philibert" in 1760 as an "austere but beautiful" man of "twenty-three summers," who, "studious and reserved in his habits," was preparing to leave for "old France to obtain a commission in the army." Kirby developed the character of Colonel Philibert from this sketch in Le Moine's volume, which he first read in 1865, and a copy of which he owned. See "Jacquin, *dit* Philibert, Nicolas." *DCB*. Vol. 3, pp. 304–05, and *Maple Leaves*, p. 32.

20.19   *Cadet*] From 1745 until 1756 Joseph-Michel Cadet, a native of Quebec who became "the last purveyor general to the French forces in Canada and a rich and powerful businessman," provided "all the meat required by the crown" at Quebec. During these years he also "carried on with his own butchering business" and "ventured into other commodities, milling flour and selling it to ships' captains, buying ships' cargoes and re-selling them, and dealing in fish, fur, and general shipping." See "Cadet, Joseph-Michel." *DCB*. Vol. 4, pp. 123–28.

20.19   *Varin*] In 1747 Jean-Victor Varin de La Marre, who had arrived in Quebec in 1729 as "chief scrivener of the Marine in Canada," was appointed "commissary of the Marine and subdelegate of the intendant in Montreal." There, engaging over the next few years "in commercial transactions in which his private interests were clearly, and improperly, in conflict with the interests of the state," he became a very rich man. See "Varin De La Marre, Jean-Victor." *DCB*. Vol. 4, pp. 749–51.

20.19   *De Pean*] In 1745 Michel-Jean-Hugues Péan, an "officer in the colonial regular troops" in New France, was appointed "adjutant of the town and Government of Quebec." Especially after the arrival of François Bigot in 1748, Péan used "his privileged position" to become "a veritable middleman between suppliers and the intendant." He "participated in all the undertakings and all the contracts, and influenced the recommendations and appointments made by" Bigot. As a result, Péan was "one of the most prominent," and wealthiest, men in New France. In 1746 he married Angélique Renaud d'Avène Des Méloizes. After his return to France in 1760, Péan was tried for corruption in the so-called *affaire du Canada*, but in the end "no hint of dishonour attached to his name." He died in Cangey in 1782. See "Péan, Michel-Jean-Hugues." *DCB*. Vol. 4, pp. 614–17.

20.20 *the Friponne*] Literally, this was "a warehouse, part of which" encroached "upon the king's land," that Pierre Claverie, who arrived in Canada from France "around 1745," had built in Quebec in the early 1750s. There, working closely with François Bigot and his associates, Claverie sold "to the state at top price," often many times over, the supplies that the Intendant had deliberately ordered in "inadequate quantities" from the French court. "Exasperated at seeing their sales decline, the Quebec merchants nicknamed the establishment 'La Friponne' ('the Rogue')." In *Cours D'Histoire Du Canada* (1865), J. B. A. Ferland provided a detailed description of this "vaste maison avec des magasins" built "près du palais de l'intendant," which concluded with the comment that the profits of this business being "très-considérables . . . , le peuple donna à cette maison le nom de *Friponne*." Kirby may have taken his information about the Friponne from his copy of Ferland's work. See "Claverie (Clavery), Pierre." *DCB*. Vol. 3, pp. 124–25, and J. B. A. Ferland. *Cours D'Histoire Du Canada. Seconde Partie 1663–1759*. Québec: Augustin Coté, 1865, p. 533.

21.6–7 *the old Bourgeois . . . tablet of the Golden Dog*] Nicolas Jacquin *dit* Philibert, a native of the Vosges region of France, was the Quebec merchant who died in January 1748 as a result of his "violent altercation" with Pierre-Jean-Baptiste-François-Xavier Legardeur de Repentigny. His house bore on its "façade" the lines that "gave rise to the legend of the Golden Dog." This inscription had most likely been placed on the house by the "surgeon" Timothée Roussel when he had it built in 1688. See "Roussel, Timothée." *DCB*. Vol. 1, p. 583, and "Jacquin, *dit* Philibert, Nicolas." *DCB*. Vol. 3, pp. 304–05.

21.8 *the Cardinal*] This is most likely Hercule-André de Fleury, a Roman Catholic priest who became the tutor of Louis XV in

1717. In 1726 he was elevated to the rank of cardinal and made "ministre d'État." From this year until his death in 1743, he functioned as the King's prime minister and, therefore, was the most influential politician in France. Kirby would have read about "le Cardinal" in Mouffle d'Angerville's *Vie Privée De Louis XV* (1781), passages from which he copied into his notebooks. See "Fleury (Hercule-André De)." *DBF,* and *Vie Privée.* Vol. 2, p. 104.

21.34   *the gay refrain of* La Belle Canadienne] That is, probably, "Vive la Canadienne, / Vole, mon coeur, vole," the opening lines of "Vive La Canadienne." In *Chansons Populaires Du Canada* (1865), Ernest Gagnon called this song a kind of "hymne national," but noted that the first couplet was the only one that was generally known. Kirby owned a copy of Gagnon's volume. See *Chansons,* pp. 4 and 6.

25.20   *horses* en fleche] That is, "horses harnessed one behind the other." See *The Concise Oxford French Dictionary. Second Edition. French-English.* Ed. H. Ferrar. Oxford: Clarendon Press, 1980, p. 228.

27.15–16   *Her face ... worthy ... of a Titian*] During the Renaissance Tiziano Vecellio (Titian), "considered the greatest painter of the Venetian school," painted Madonnas and Venuses as well as contemporary women in radiant flesh-coloured tones and, often, with blonde hair. Although it is impossible to know if Kirby had a particular painting in mind when he composed this passage, the portrait of "Violante," now in the Kunsthistorisches Museum in Vienna, with her long, golden hair, dark eyes, chiselled features, and fine, bare shoulders, could be a model for his description of Angelique des Meloise. See "Titian [Vecellio, Tiziano]." Grove's. Vol. 31, pp. 31–45.

27.23–24   *Renaud d'Avesne des Meloises*] Nicolas-Marie Renaud D'Avène Des Méloizes, a native of the city of Quebec, descended from "a distinguished *épée* family in Nivernais (France)." An "officer in the colonial regular troops" and the "seigneur" of Neuville, from the mid 1730s until two years before his death in 1743, he was involved "in the manufacture of roofing tile" in New France. "In the end," however, his name became "distinguished in Canadian history not for his entrepreneurship," which was unusual, but on account of his oldest child, Angélique. See "Renaud D'Avène Des Méloizes, Nicolas-Marie." *DCB*. Vol. 3, pp. 549–51.

27.32–33   *Louise de La Valiere ... Fontainebleau*] In 1661 Louise-Françoise de la Baume le Blanc de la Vallière, a beautiful teenager, became the mistress of Louis XIV of France. The "intimité de leur liaison" began at the King's palace at Fontainebleau. See "Vallière (Louise-Françoise De La Baume Le Blanc De La)." *BU*.

30.19   *the haughty Francoise de Lantagnac*] Probably Geneviève-Françoise Adhémar de Lantagnac, whose family "may be traced back to the time of the first crusade." The daughter of Gaspard Adhémar de Lantagnac, a native of Monaco who served in New France as an "officer in the colonial regular troops," in 1744 Geneviève-Françoise began her noviciate at the Ursuline Convent in Quebec where she had previously studied, "et après les épreuves ordinaires, elle prit l'habit de l'Ordre sous le nom de St. Henri." Neither she nor any of her five sisters, who also "devoted their lives to serving others through religious orders," appears to be associated with a duel. See "Adhémar De Lantagnac, Gaspard." *DCB*. Vol. 3, p. 5, and *Ursulines*. Vol. 3. 1866, p. 100.

33.14–16   *as pretty a fable as La Fontaine related of the*, Avare qui avait perdu son tresor] Compare Jean de La Fontaine, *Fables Choisies*, 1668, Book 4, Fable 20, "L'Avare Qui A Perdu Son Trésor." In this fable, which illustrates that "L'usage seulement fait la possession," La Fontaine told the story of a miser whose buried treasure was stolen. When he lamented his loss, a passerby commented that since the "homme en pleurs" was not using this money, it had as much value to him as a stone. See *Fables De La Fontaine Illustrées. . . . Nouvelle Édition*. Tours: Ad Mame Et Cie, Imprimeurs-Libraires, 1851, pp. 138–39. Kirby owned a copy of this printing of La Fontaine's work.

33.17   *the knight errant Fortunatus*] A poor man who received an inexhaustible purse from Fortune, he appears in several works of Renaissance literature. In *The Pleasant Comedie of Old Fortunatus* (1600), which was first played in 1599, Thomas Dekker, for example, presented him as an "olde hoarie wandring Knight" to whom Fortune offered one of "Wisedome, strength, health, beautie, long life, and riches." Having chosen riches, Fortunatus was fated to "dwell with cares and quickly die." See *The Dramatic Works Of Thomas Dekker.* Ed. Fredson Bowers. Cambridge: At The University Press, 1962. Vol. 1, pp. 117, 122, and 125.

33.31   *Aunt Mere St Borgia*] Marie-Madeleine Renaud d'Avèsne Des Méloises, Angelique's aunt, took the name Mère St. François de Borgia when she became an Ursuline nun at the Convent in Quebec. By the time she died in her late twenties in 1725, she had become known for her beautiful voice, which was "si digne de chanter les louanges du Seigneur." See *Ursulines.* Vol. 2. 1864, p. 219.

35.8–9   *Joseph in Egypt, next to Pharoah in authority*] Compare Genesis 41: 40–41. Joseph, sold into slavery in Egypt, interpreted Pharoah's dream and was, thus, set by him to rule "over all the land of Egypt." Only "in the throne" would the Pharoah be "greater" than Joseph. See *IB.* Vol. 1. 1952, p. 778.

35.19   *the Marquise De Pompadour*] Jeanne-Antoinette Poisson, the wife of Guillaume Lenormand, "seigneur d'Etioles," became the mistress of Louis XV in 1745; in the same year she was created "marquise de Pompadour." From then until her death in 1764, she maintained her great influence over the King and, through him, the French nation. See "Pompadour (Jeanne-Antoinette Poisson, marquise De)." *BU.*

37.6   *Caroline*] Kirby takes many details of his story about Caroline and François Bigot from James MacPherson Le Moine's account of "A Visit to Chateau-Bigot. 4th June, 1863," published in *Maple Leaves: A Budget Of Legendary, Historical, Critical, And Sporting Intelligence* (1863), a copy of which he owned. In Le Moine's version, however, Caroline was "an Algonquin beauty ... a child of love borne on the shores of the great Ottawa river: a French officer was her sire, and the powerful Algonquin tribe of the Beaver claimed her mother." She and Bigot had met, furthermore, one night in the woods near Beaumanoir. See *Maple Leaves,* p. 16.

41.1   *I know a hawk from a handsaw*] William Shakespeare, *Hamlet,* II.ii.379. Hamlet, in conversation with Rosencrantz and Guildenstern, explains, "I am but mad north-north-west. When the / wind is southerly I know a hawk from a hand-saw." See *Shakespeare,* p. 1157.

47.25–27   *a ... volume ... of the* Coutume de Paris *and ... an odd tome of Pothier, ... prime authority in the law*] The *Coutume de Paris* was the legal code of New France in 1748; by the time Kirby was composing *Le Chien d'or*, however, the laws of Quebec concerning civil matters included citations from such French legal authorities as Robert-Joseph Pothier. Described as "le plus célèbre jurisconsulte que la France ait produit," he published his first work, on the *Coutumes d'Orléans*, in 1740; throughout the 1760s he issued several volumes on the laws governing contracts in France. Kirby, who owned a copy of the *Code Civil Du Bas-Canada* (1866), in which Pothier is frequently cited, probably took his name from this volume. See "Pothier (Robert-Joseph)." *BU*.

49.6–20   *Ricard ... page 970 ... 'Donations ... marriage.' Bourdon*] Jean-Marie Ricard was "un des plus célèbres avocats du parlement de Paris." Perhaps his most influential work was *Traité des donations entre vifs et testamentaires*, first published in 1652, in which Article 970 reads, "Qu'une des qualités nécessaires de la donation entre-vifs, est d'être irrévocable." This Article is cited as "1 Ricard, part. 1, No. 970," in Article 783 of the *Code Civil Du Bas-Canada* (1866): "Toute donation entrevifs stipulée révocable suivant la seule volonté du donateur est nulle. Cette disposition ne s'applique pas aux donations faites par contrat de mariage." In *Le Chien d'or* Kirby not only translated these sentences from his copy of the *Code Civil*, but he also probably took the name Bourjon, transcribed as Bourdon, from it. François Bourjon, a French lawyer whose *Droit commun de la France et la Coûtume de Paris réduite en principes*, first published in 1747, was "an attempt to formulate a common law for France," is also frequently cited in this section of the *Code Civil* on "Donations Entrevifs Et Testamentaires." See "Ricard (Jean-Marie)." *BU*; *Code Civil Du Bas-Canada*. Ed. Joseph-Edouard Lefebvre de Bellefeuille. Montréal: Beauchemin & Valois, 1866, p. 180; Jean-Marie Ricard. *Traité des Donations Entre-Vifs et Testamentaires* .... Volume 1. Riom: Chez Martin Dégoutte, 1783, p. 247; and David M. Walker. "Bourjon, François." *The Oxford Companion To Law*. Oxford: Clarendon Press, 1980, p. 146.

52.8–11   *that nose ... fiery as Bardolphs, with hardly a cool spot for a fly to rest his foot upon*] Compare, for example, William Shakespeare, *Henry V*, II.iii.40–42. The Boy, speaking of Sir John Falstaff who has just died, says, "Do you not remember, 'a saw a flea stick / upon Bardolph's nose, and 'a said it was a black soul / burning in hell?" Throughout the Shakespearean plays in which Bardolph appears, there are various references to his "fiery" face. See *Shakespeare*, p. 945.

55.7   *If fools only carried cruppers! as Panurge says*] Compare Thomas Urquhart's translation of François Rabelais' *Gargantua and Pantagruel*, Book Three (1546), Chapter 38. Panurge, proclaiming with his master Pantagruel the virtues of Triboulet, a French fool, says, "If all fools carried cruppers." Kirby owned a copy of the 1849 Bohn edition of Urquhart's work. See *Rabelais*. Vol. 2, p. 121.

55.11   *hunc!, hanc! hoc!*] That is, the masculine, feminine, and neuter forms of the accusative case of the demonstrative pronoun "*this*" in Latin. See, for example, B. C. Taylor and K. E. Prentice. *Living Latin*. Toronto: Clarke, Irwin, 1950, p. 260.

56.19   de usis et fructibus] That is, literally, in Latin, *concerning uses and fruits*. In *Code Civil Du Bas-Canada* (1866), a copy of which Kirby owned, the legal concept of usufruct is defined as "le droit de jouir des choses dont un autre a la propriété, comme le propriétaire lui-même, mais à la charge d'en conserver la substance." See *Code Civil Du Bas-Canada*. Ed. Joseph-Edouard Lefebvre de Bellefeuille. Montréal: Beauchemin & Valois, 1866, p. 99.

57.2–6   *The Chateau ... built ... by the Intendant Jean Talon*] Jean Talon was "intendant of New France" from 1665 to 1668 and again from 1670 to 1672. During these years he acquired several properties in and near the city of Quebec, including from 1667 to 1670 the "domaine" or the "fief des Islets," which fronted on the St. Charles River, and where by 1668 he had built "a large house, a barn, and other buildings." This property was "created a barony" in 1671, at which time it was enlarged by the gift of Louis XIV of "the communities of Bourg-Royal, Bourg-la-Reine, and Bourg-Talon." In suggesting that Talon may have built "the old chateau" of Beaumanoir on these newly-acquired properties before he left New France in 1672, Kirby is following James MacPherson Le Moine's account of "A Visit to Chateau-Bigot. 4th June, 1863," published in *Maple Leaves: A Budget Of Legendary, Historical, Critical, And Sporting Intelligence* (1863). Kirby owned a copy of this volume. See Thomas Chapais. *The Great Intendant: A Chronicle of Jean Talon in Canada 1665–1672.* Toronto: Glasgow, Brook, 1914, p. 47; Thomas Chapais. *Jean Talon Intendant De La Nouvelle-France (1665–1672).* Québec: Imprimerie De S.-A. Demers, 1904, p. 502; "Talon, Jean." *DCB.* Vol. 1, pp. 614–32; and *Maple Leaves,* p. 9.

57.12 *Louis XIV.*] He was King of France from 1643 to 1715.

57.14–22 *Within ... Beaumanoir had ... Joliet recounted ... his ... travels, and ... Marquette confirmed the ... rumours ... of a wonderful river ... that flowed ... into the Gulf of Mexico. Here ... had ... La Salle taken counsel of ... Talon, when he set off to explore the ... Mississippi ... and claim it ... as the possession of France*] During his second term as intendant of New France, Jean Talon "set in motion a veritable exploration programme" designed to extend French territory throughout North America. In the fall of 1670, for example, shortly after his "return to the colony" in August of that year, Talon sent René-Robert Cavelier de La Salle, who had arrived in Quebec from his native France in 1667, "southward" to find a way by water to the Gulf of Mexico. Five years later Talon had apparently heard nothing of La Salle's explorations. Before he left for France in November 1672, therefore, he "chose Louis Jolliet," a native of Quebec and a graduate of the Jesuit seminary there, who had traded for furs around Sault-Ste-Marie, to follow the "'beautiful river'" that was already known as the Mississippi to see where it flowed. Jolliet left Quebec in October 1672 to winter most probably in Michilimackinac, from where he set out in May 1673 with Jacques Marquette, a Jesuit missionary who had come from France in 1666. They "entered the Mississippi" in June 1673 and sailed down it "to a point near the modern boundary of Arkansas and Louisiana" before they turned back in "mid-July." It was almost ten years later when La Salle led an expedition down the Mississippi that arrived at its mouth at the Gulf of Mexico, where, on 9 April 1682, he "took solemn possession of Louisiana" in the name of France. See "Cavelier

De La Salle, René-Robert." *DCB.* Vol. 1, pp. 172–84; "Jolliet, Louis." *DCB.* Vol. 1, pp. 392–98; "Marquette, Jacques." *DCB.* Vol. 1, pp. 490–93; and "Talon, Jean." *DCB.* Vol. 1, pp. 614–32.

59.24–25 *the cow of Montmorency*] That is, Montmorency Falls. In a notebook Kirby recorded, "La Vache de Montmorency / La Chute." See OTAR, Kirby, F–1076, Miscellaneous Manuscripts, MU1646, D–18, Note-book kept by Kirby containing . . . excerpts from various historical publications relating to the history of New France, p. 19.

60.4–14 *the song . . . heard . . . in Paris . . . "Pour des vins . . . La Faridondé!—"*] Pierre-Jean de Béranger, "Le Scandale," ll. 25–32. The poem, probably written in the 1820s and sung to the "Air: *La farira dondaine, gai!,"* was one of many by Béranger on "Le vin, . . . la haine du trône et de l'autel" that made him popular in liberal and republican circles in France in the nineteenth century. Kirby's version of the stanza differed only in its chorus from the rendition in *Chansons De De Béranger* (1832). In this volume, a copy of which Kirby owned, the last four lines read, "Bon! / La farira dondaine, / Gai! / La farira dondé!" See *Chansons De De Béranger.* Bruxelles: J. P. Meline, 1832. Vol. 1, pp. 192–93, and "Béranger (Pierre-Jean De)." *DBF.*

60.17–18 ore rotundo] Compare Horace, *The Art of Poetry,* l. 323, in which the poet explained that "to the Greeks," the Muse "gave speech in well-rounded phrase" ("ore rotundo"). See Horace, *Satires, Epistles And Ars Poetica.* Trans. H. Rushton Fairclough. London: William Heinemann, and Cambridge: Harvard University Press, 1970, pp. 476–77.

60.28–31 *They would . . . drag me into the Hall, to make sport for the Philistines, and I am not . . . Samson . . . I could not pull the Chateau down upon their heads*] Compare Judges 16:23–30. Samson, a judge of the Israelites and an "enemy" of the Philistines, having been captured by them, was led into a "house . . . full of men and women," including "all the lords of the Philistines," to make "sport" for them. Placed between "the pillars whereupon the house" stood, Samson used his immense, and newly-returned, strength to pull it down and kill "all the people that *were* therein. So the dead which he slew at his death were more than *they* which he slew in his life." See *IB.* Vol. 2. 1953, pp. 796–97.

62.5–7   *the past orgies of the Regency, and the present ... of Croissy and ... Versailles*] In 1715, because of the minority of Louis XV, Philippe, duc d'Orléans, a nephew of Louis XIV, became Regent of France. His rule, which lasted until 1723, was marked by a general liberalization of manners. This trend continued under Louis XV, who frequently left his private apartments at Versailles, the so-called "petits appartemens," for his residence at Choisy. In linking both the regency and the two chateaux with licentious behaviour, Kirby was following *Vie Privée De Louis XV* (1781), to which he referred many times in his notebooks. Citing "V. P," he wrote, for example, "Le Duc d'Orleans mourut dans les bras de ... sa maitresse ... Dec 1. 1723," and "Chateau de Choisy sur les bords du Seine ... palais de plaisir de Louis XV et Madame de Mailly," one of his many mistresses. See OTAR, Kirby, F–1076, Miscellaneous Manuscripts, MU1646, D–18, Note-book kept by Kirby containing ... excerpts from various historical publications relating to the history of New France, pp. [2] and 5, and *Vie Privée*. Vol. 2, p. 50.

62.25   *the King and Queen*] These are, most likely, Louis XV and his Queen, Marie Leszczyńska, daughter of Stanislaw I of Poland. They married in 1725.

62.25–28   *Montespan ... Maintenon ... Louise de la Valiere, the only mistress of Louis XIV who loved him for his own sake*] Françoise-Athénaïs de Rochechouart de Mortemart, marquise de Montespan, succeeded Louise-Françoise de la Baume le Blanc, duchesse de la Vallière, as mistress of Louis XIV. Madame de Montespan was herself replaced as the King's mistress by Françoise d'Aubigné, marquise de Maintenon. In stating that Louise de la Vallière was the only mistress who loved Louis XIV "uniquement pour lui-même," Kirby is following his copy of the 1823 printing of François-Marie Arouet de Voltaire's *Siècle de Louis XIV* (1751). See *Siècle*. Vol. 1, p. 403.

62.28–30   *portrait ... in the Chapel of the Ursulines of Quebec where ... Louise is represented as St Thaïs*] Kirby is probably thinking of "Sainte Thaïs et Saint Paphnuce," an oil painting by an unknown artist, which may date from the seventeenth century, that the Ursulines acquired in the 1820s. The painting shows the hermit Paphnuce standing before Thaïs, a former Egyptian prostitute who had returned to her Christian faith, as she emerges from the cave where she has spent three years in solitary penitence. Kirby was most likely drawn to make the connection between Thaïs and Louise de la Vallière through his reading of *Les Ursulines de Québec, Depuis Leur Établissement Jusqu'à Nos Jours*. A section entitled "Les Ursulines Font Des Pénitences Extraordinaires Pour Obtenir La Conversion De Madame De La Vallière" describes how for "plus de douze ans, nos Mères offrirent à Dieu leurs prières pour obtenir" the conversion and penitence of Louis XIV's mistress. See *Ursulines*. Vol. 1. 1863, pp. 303–07.

63.24–25   *the ravishing strains of Lulli and Destouches*] Jean-Baptiste Lully (Lulli), a native of Florence, became through his scores for such works as Jean-Baptiste Poquelin *dit* Molière's *Le Bourgeois Gentilhomme* (1670) not only the favorite composer of Louis XIV but also "the master of French music." One of his successors as a musician at the French court was André-Cardinal Destouches, who composed numerous scores for the Royal Academy of Music and the Paris Opéra in the first three decades of the eighteenth century. Kirby is following the description of French musicians in his 1823 copy of François-Marie Arouet de Voltaire's *Siècle de Louis XIV* (1751), in which Lulli is called "le père de la vraie musique en France" and Destouches one of his many "imitateurs." Louis XIV is said to have remarked that "Destouches was the only musician who did not make him miss Lully." Lully died in 1687, Destouches in 1749. See Spire Pitou. *The Paris Opéra: An Encyclopedia of Operas, Ballets, Composers, and Performers*. Vol. 1: *Genesis and Glory, 1671–1715*. Westport, Connecticut: Greenwood Press, 1983, pp. 208 and 258, and *Siècle*. Vol. 2, pp. 449–50.

64.33–65.4   *Le Mercier ... De Breard ... Penisault ... Perrault, D'Estebe Morin and Vergor, all creatures of the Intendant ... partners of the "Grand Company of associates trading in New France"*] These men were all business associates of François Bigot in what their contemporaries called in the 1750s the "Grande Société," and, with the exception of Vergor, they were all tried in Paris in the early 1760s for various fiduciary improprieties in New France during Bigot's time as intendant. In 1748, however, they were just beginning their partnerships. In that year François-Marc-Antoine Le Mercier, who had come to New France "in 1740 as a cadet in the colonial regular troops," was an "artillery officer" in Quebec. Jacques-Michel Bréard arrived in New France with Bigot in August 1748 as "controller of the Marine at Quebec with supervision over finances, stores, construction, and recruiting"; in July 1748, before leaving France, he became a partner with Bigot "in a transatlantic trading company." Louis Pennisseaut, who had arrived in New France "around 1747," was in 1748 "dividing his time between Quebec and Montreal" as a "merchant-trader." Paul Perrault, the only one of these men born in New France, farmed at Deschambault and headed "his community's militia." Guillaume Estèbe, who had emigrated to New France in the late 1720s, was a prosperous "merchant-trader" and "entrepreneur" in Quebec; "a councillor of the Conseil Supérieur" of the colony since 1736 and the seigneur of La Gauchetière since 1744, he formed a business partnership with Bréard in November 1748. When François Maurin, a hunchback who gained the reputation of being the ugliest man in New France, arrived in the colony sometime before 1756, he worked "as a clerk for some Montreal merchants." Louis Du Pont Duchambon de Vergor, an "officer in the colonial regular troops" who had served with Bigot in Louisbourg, where they had become close friends, had in 1748 recently been "posted to Canada." See "Maurin, François." *DCB*. Vol. 3, pp. 441–42; "Perrault ..., Paul." *DCB*. Vol. 3, pp. 510–11; "Bréard, Jacques-Michel." *DCB*. Vol. 4, pp. 90–92; "Du Pont Duchambon de Vergor, Louis." *DCB*. Vol. 4, pp. 249–51; "Estèbe, Guillaume." *DCB*. Vol. 4, pp. 263–64; "Le Mercier ..., François-Marc-Antoine." *DCB*. Vol. 4, pp. 458–61; "Pennisseaut ..., Louis." *DCB*. Vol. 4, pp. 621–22; and Guy Frégault. *François Bigot Administrateur français*. 1948; rpt. Montréal: Guérin, 1994. Vol. 2, p. 194.

65.11–16   *a number of dissolute Seigneurs, and gallants of fashion ... the class ... described by Charlevoix ... as "Gentlemen ... versed in the ... modes of spending money, but ... at a loss how to obtain it"*] This is apparently Kirby's summary translation of the last paragraphs of the third letter of *Journal D'Un Voyage Fait Par Ordre Du Roi Dans L'Amérique Septentrionnale* (1744), the reworked version of a diary that the "Jesuit priest" Pierre-François-Xavier de Charlevoix had kept when he spent "two and a half years" in North America from 1720 to 1722. In this letter, dated October 1720, Charlevoix, who in 1748 was "procurator in Paris for the Jesuit missions and Ursuline convents in New France and Louisiana," commented on the "*character*" of the "*inhabitants*" of Quebec and "*the manner of living in the* French *colony*"; he also compared the apparent richness of the Canadians, which was actually "une pauvreté cachée par un air d'aisance," with the real wealth of "des Anglois nos Voisins." Kirby wrote in a notebook, "Charlevoix says—1720. English accumulate wealth but do not know how to enjoy it. Canadians understand thoroughly the most elegant and agreable modes of spending money but at same time are greatly at a loss how to obtain it." See Charlevoix. *Histoire De La Nouvelle France*. Vol. 3: *Journal D'Un Voyage*. Paris: Chez la Veuve Ganeau, 1744, p. 80; Charlevoix. *Journal Of A Voyage To North-America*. London: R. and J. Dodsley, 1761. Vol. 1, p. 99; "Charlevoix, Pierre-François-Xavier De." *DCB*. Vol. 3, pp. 103–10; and OTAR, Kirby, F–1076, Miscellaneous Manuscripts, MU1646, D–19, Twenty-four small note-books filled with miscellaneous notations by Kirby, n. pag..

66.22   *the Gabelle*] That is, literally, the tax on salt. Under the "Ancien Régime" salt was not only taxed in most of France, but it was also often sold at a fixed price by a dealer who held a monopoly. As a result of this system, and the severe punishments, including being sent to the galleys and being put to death, meted out to those who tried to circumvent this tax, during the eighteenth century "la gabelle" became ever more "insupportable." It was, in fact, abolished in 1790 by the Revolutionary government. See "Gabelle." *Grand Dictionnaire Encyclopédique Larousse*. Paris: Librairie Larousse, 1983. Vol. 5, p. 4620.

67.7–9   *When we skin . . . eels we dont begin at the tail! . . . the habitans would . . . like the eels of Melun cry out before they were hurt*] Compare Thomas Urquhart's translation of François Rabelais' *Gargantua and Pantagruel*, Book Five (1564), Chapter 22, which relates "*How Queen Whim's officers were employed*," including some who "began to flay eels at the tail; neither did the eels cry before they were hurt, like those of Melun." Kirby most likely adapted this passage from his copy of the 1849 Bohn edition of Urquhart's work. See *Rabelais*. Vol. 2, pp. 468–69.

67.24–27 *the gentlemen of Beauce ... breakfast by gaping ... It will make them spit clean*] Compare Thomas Urquhart's translation of François Rabelais' *Gargantua and Pantagruel*, Book One (1532), Chapter 26, in which the felling of a forest "a little above Orleans" by the huge tail of "Gargantua's mare" is described. "But all the breakfast the mare got that day, was but a little yawning and gaping, in memory whereof the gentlemen of Beauce do as yet to this day break their fast with gaping, which they find to be very good, and do spit the better for it." Kirby summarized this passage, probably from his copy of the 1849 Bohn edition of Urquhart's work, in a notebook as "Gentlemen of Beauce break their fast with gaping which they find to be good & spit the better for it." See OTAR, Kirby, F–1076, Miscellaneous Manuscripts, MU1646, D–19, Twenty-four small note-books filled with miscellaneous notations by Kirby, n. pag., and *Rabelais*. Vol. 1, pp. 152–53.

67.38–68.1 *the chief Baker of Pharaoh, who got hanged*] Compare Genesis 40. When Joseph was a prisoner of "the king of Egypt," he interpreted a dream for Pharaoh's baker, who was imprisoned for offending his master, and, thus, foretold that "within three days" Pharaoh would "hang" him "on a tree." And on "the third day" the King "hanged the chief baker." See *IB*. Vol. 1. 1952, pp. 769–72.

68.5–6 *Amantium irae ... Latin for love*] Compare Publius Terentius Afer, *Incipit Andria*, 166 B.C., III. 555, in which Chremes commented to Simo that "amantium irae amoris integratiost," or "lovers' quarrels are love's renewal." See "The Lady of Andros." *Terence*. Trans. John Sargeaunt. London: William Heinemann, and Cambridge: Harvard University Press, 1959. Vol. 1, pp. 60–61.

68.9–18 *a favorite ditty of the day ... Il y en aura*] That is, apparently, "C'est Le Bon Vin Qui Danse." In *Chansons Populaires Du Canada* (1865), a copy of which Kirby owned, Ernest Gagnon provided another version of this round, which began, "Ce n'est point du raisin pourri, / C'est le bon vin qui danse!" See *Chansons*, pp. 220–21.

69.2   *the Sieur Deschenaux*] In 1748 Joseph Brassard Deschenaux was "secretary to the intendant." Although born "at Quebec ... into a family of modest means," through his membership in "the Grande Société" he "amassed a fortune." As a result, in the 1760s and 1770s he was able to buy several seigneuries. These included "the seigneuries of La Livaudière and Saint-Michel" that he bought from Michel-Jean-Hugues Péan and the seigneury of Neuville that he acquired from Nicolas Renaud d'Avène Des Méloizes. See "Brassard Deschenaux, Joseph." *DCB*. Vol. 4, pp. 87–89.

70.32–33   *hard to please as Villiers Vendome whom the King himself could not satisfy*] In *Siècle de Louis XIV* (1751), François-Marie Arouet de Voltaire recounted an anecdote about a man called Villiers-Vendôme, a companion of the "duc de Vendôme" and "un de ces hommes de plaisirs qui se font un mérite d'une liberté cynique." A resident at Versailles, he loudly and repeatedly condemned the King's tastes in music, painting, architecture, and gardening. After Villiers-Vendôme criticized one of his projects yet again, Louis XIV remarked laughingly, "On ne peut pas plaire à tout le monde." Kirby undoubtedly took this story from his copy of the 1823 printing of Voltaire's work. See *Siècle*. Vol. 2, p. 44.

71.14   *Cleopatra's pearls*] Compare Pliny, *Natural History*, Book 9, Section 58. Pliny, discussing *"Pearls of exceptional value,"* relates the story of "two pearls that were the largest in the whole of history," and that were "owned by Cleopatra, the last of the Queens of Egypt," who wore them as earrings. Wagering with Mark Antony about the cost of "a single banquet," Cleopatra "took one earring off and dropped the pearl" in "vinegar, the strong rough quality of which can melt pearls." When the pearl dissolved, Cleopatra "swallowed" the drink that was then worth "10,000,000 sesterces" and, thus, won the bet. See Pliny. *Natural History*. Vol. 3. Trans. H. Rackham. Cambridge: Harvard University Press, and London: William Heinemann, 1967, pp. 242–47.

71.26–27   *St Picot ... St Benoit*] Kirby most likely took these—and other, similar—names from his copy of the 1849 edition of Thomas Urquhart's translation of François Rabelais' *Gargantua and*

Pantagruel. In Book Three (1546), Chapter 29, for example, Panurge rejected Pantagruel's proposal to invite to "dinner a divine, a physician, and a lawyer" so that they could discuss Panurge's "project ... of marriage" with the statement, "By Saint Picot ... we never shall do any good that way." In Book Five (1564), Chapter 46, Friar John swore, "How, marry! by St. Bennet's boot, / And his gambadoes, I'll ne'er do't." See *Rabelais.* Vol. 2, pp. 75–76 and 539.

71.28   *the King of Yvetot*] This is probably a reference to the very popular "Le Roi d'Yvetot" by Pierre-Jean de Béranger, the first song in the first volume of *Chansons De De Béranger* (1832), a copy of which Kirby owned. Dated "Mai 1813" and sung to the "Air: *Quand un tendron vient en ces lieux,*" "Le Roi d'Yvetot" described a "bon petit roi" who took "le plaisir" for his law, and who toured his realm on a donkey. See *Chansons De De Béranger.* Bruxelles: J. P. Maline, 1832. Vol. 1, pp. 1–3.

71.38–   *a macaronic verse of Moliere ... "Bene, ... friponnat!"*] Compare
72.12   Jean-Baptiste Poquelin *dit* Molière, *Le Malade Imaginaire. Comédie Mêlée De Musique Et De Danse,* 1673, Troisième Intermède. In this interlude that concludes Molière's last comedy, a chorus sings the following version of each of the verses quoted by Kirby: " *Bene, bene, bene, bene respondere. / Dignus, dignus est entrare / In nostro docto corpore,*" and " *Vivat, vivat, vivat, vivat, cent fois vivat / Novus Doctor, qui tam bene parlat! / Mille, mille annis et manget et bibat, / Et seignet et tuat!*" The subject of this interlude was "une cérémonie burlesque" admitting a man as a medical doctor. See *Molière.* Vol. 9. 1925, pp. 439, 445, and 451.

73.30–31   *the persecuted Jansenists in the Parliament of Rouen*] In the late seventeenth and early eighteenth centuries, French Roman Catholics who accepted the ideas of Cornelius Jansen about the need for God's grace to save humanity from its natural evil and perversity were both banished and imprisoned. According to François-Marie Arouet de Voltaire in *Siècle de Louis XIV* (1751), one reason for this harassment was that the "querelles du jansénisme" covered not only religious controversies among Roman Catholics in France but also political tensions between provincial parliaments and Louis XIV. The "parlement of Normandy at Rouen," for example, often "distinguished itself

... by its recalcitrance in the face of the royal will"; it was also strongly influenced by Jansenism, which "had put down substantial roots in parts of Normandy." For his interpretation of these events Kirby may have been following his copy of the 1823 printing of Voltaire's *Siècle.* See Dale Van Kley. *The Jansenists and the Expulsion of the Jesuits from France 1757–1765.* New Haven and London: Yale University Press, 1975, p. 175, and *Siècle.* Vol. 2, p. 224.

75.27–28   *belle Gabrielle*] That is, Gabrielle d'Estrées, the mistress of Henri IV, whom he made "marquise de Montceaux" in 1595. After her death in 1599, she became the subject of several popular songs. One had the lines, "Sa belle Gabrielle / Fut dans ces lieux." Another, repeating rumours that the marquise had been poisoned, stated that she died from smelling "un bouquet / de trois roses jolies." See Henri Davenson. *Le Livre Des Chansons Ou Introduction A La Connaissance De La Chanson Populaire Française.* Neuchâtel: Éditions De La Baconnière, 1946, pp. 212–14, and "Estrées (Gabrielle D')." *DBF.*

76.5–9   *King ... nobles of Persia ... Queen Vashti, to show her beauty to ... his court*] Compare Esther 1:1–2:17. In "Shushan the palace" King Ahasuerus entertained at a "feast" that lasted "seven days" the "power of Persia and Media, the nobles and princes of the provinces." During this feast, where "drinking *was* according to the law," the king commanded his servants to "bring Vashti the queen before the king with the crown royal, to show the people and the princes her beauty," but she "refused to come." As a result of her disobedience, Vashti was deposed, and Esther was made "queen instead." See *IB.* Vol. 3. 1954, pp. 834–44.

78.4–5   *"Lamb of God ... have mercy upon me!—"*] Compare "O Lamb of God, that takest away the sin / of the world, have mercy upon us," the lines said in "*the Communion time*" in "The Order For The Administration Of The Lord's Supper Or Holy Communion" according to *The Book of Common Prayer.* See *The Book Of Common Prayer.* Toronto: The Anglican Book Centre, 1959, p. 84.

78.25–28   *Caroline ... an Acadienne of ... noble family, whose head ... had married the beautiful daughter of the high chief of the Abenaquis*] Jean-Vincent d'Abbadie de Saint-Castin, a "French officer" who became "the third Baron de Saint-Castin" in 1674, married Pidianske or Pidiwamiska, whose "Christian name" was Marie-Mathilde, "the daughter of the great Penobscot chief Madokawando," according to Roman Catholic rite in 1684. He and his wife, who was apparently "very pretty," settled in Acadia among the Abenakis and had several children, including Bernard-Anselme d'Abbadie de Saint-Castin, who became "the fourth Baron de Saint-Castin" on his father's death in 1707, and Joseph d'Abbadie de Saint-Castin, who "inherited the title of Baron de Saint-Castin" when Bernard-Anselme died in 1720. Joseph, who was still alive in the late 1740s, probably died childless. Bernard-Anselme had three daughters born in the second decade of the eighteenth century; none was named Caroline, however. See "Abbadie De Saint-Castin, Bernard-Anselme D'." *DCB*. Vol. 2, pp. 3–4; "Abbadie De Saint-Castin, Jean-Vincent D'." *DCB*. Vol. 2, pp. 4–7; and "Abbadie De Saint-Castin, Joseph D'." *DCB*. Vol. 3, p. 3.

82.7–8   *the Regent Duke of Orleans and Cardinal du Bois*] Guillaume Dubois, the Duke's former tutor who became a cardinal in 1721, made himself "indispensable" to Philippe during his regency. Dubois was also often accused of corrupting the "prince" by surrounding him with "comédiennes" and "prostituées" and plunging him into shameful "débauches." See "Orléans (Philippe, duc D')." *BU*, and "Dubois (Guillaume, cardinal)." *DBF.*

85.3–4   *Quintin Corentin, where nobody gets anything they want*] Most probably, Quimper-Corentin, a city in southwest Britanny. In Jean de La Fontaine's "Le Chartier Embourbé" (1668), the "pauvre homme" is described as being stuck in the country near "un certain canton de la basse Bretagne, / Appelé Quimper-Corentin," where "le Destin" sends people whom it wishes to enrage. See *Fables De La Fontaine Illustreés ... Nouvelle Édition*. Tours: Ad Mame Et Cie, Imprimeurs-Libraires, 1851, p. 185. Kirby owned a copy of this printing of La Fontaine's work.

85.11–12   *splay footed as St Pedauque of Dijon*] Compare Thomas Urquhart's translation of François Rabelais' *Gargantua and Pantagruel*, Book 4 (1548), Chapter 41, in which the battle between Pantagruel and his companions and the Chitterlings is interrupted by the appearance of a "flying hog" with "feet ... of the splay kind, like those of geese, and as Queen Dick's used to be at Thoulouse, in the days of yore." A note on "*La Royne Pedaucque. Pié d'oie*: Goose-foot" explained, "At Toulouse there is a bridge called Queen Pedauque's bridge. Menage says, that the statue of that queen, with goose feet, is to be seen at Dijon, in the porch of St. Benigne's church, and at Nevers, in the cathedral church there; and asserts, that she was called Pedauque, because of her splay-footedness." Kirby presumably took this simile from his copy of the 1849 Bohn edition of Urquhart's work. See *Rabelais.* Vol. 2, p. 313.

85.23–26   *a hunting refrain of Louis XIV. "Sitot ... pour elle!—"*] In *Siècle de Louis XIV* (1751), François-Marie Arouet de Voltaire recorded two "bagatelles" attributed to Louis XIV; one, allegedly composed when he wished to go hunting, included the line "Sitôt qu'il voit sa chienne, il quitte tout pour elle." Kirby most likely took this song from his copy of the 1823 printing of Voltaire's work. See *Siècle.* Vol. 2, p. 42.

87.8   *the Fleur de Lys*] In *Vie Privée De Louis XV* (1781), Mouffle d'Angerville listed ships in the French navy for the year 1756; these included "*La Fleur-de-lys*," which carried "30" cannons and was captained by "Mariniere." Kirby copied this information from *Vie Privée* into a notebook as "La Fregatte — Le Fleur de Lys — 30 canons Capitaine Mariniere à Quebec." See OTAR, Kirby, F–1076, Miscellaneous Manuscripts, MU1646, D–18, Note-book kept by Kirby containing ... excerpts from various historical publications relating to the history of New France, p. [12], and *Vie Privée.* Vol. 3, p. 55.

89.8   *poculum*] That is, in Latin, cup or goblet.

90.16–20   *Pothier's imagination fell into a vision ... of his favorite text ... "rise ... kill and eat!—"*] Compare Acts 10:9–13, in which Peter

fell into a trance,

And saw heaven opened, and a certain vessel descending unto him, as it had been a great sheet knit at the four corners, and let down to the earth:

Wherein were all manner of four-footed beasts of the earth, and wild beasts, and creeping things, and fowls of the air.

And there came a voice to him, Rise, Peter; kill, and eat.

See *IB.* Vol. 9. 1954, p. 136.

94.5–6   *the ships of ... Champlain*] From 1603 until his death in 1635, Samuel de Champlain, "the founder of Canada," crossed "the Atlantic 21 times." He established "a habitation" at Quebec in 1608. See "Champlain, Samuel De." *DCB.* Vol. 1, pp. 186–99.

94.28–30   *Peter Kalm ... says: "The peasant women all wear their hair in ringlets, and nice they look!"*] In his account of his travels in North America from 1748 to 1751, which Kirby read in Forster's English translation, Pehr (Peter) Kalm commented at least twice on the curled hair of the "ladies in *Canada.*" In July 1749, for example, he described the "*French*" women in "*Canada*" as "handsome," "well bred, and virtuous," and "very fond of adorning their heads, the hair of which is always curled." See Peter Kalm. *Travels Into North America.* Trans. John Rein[h]old Forster. Vol. 3. London: Printed for the Editor; And Sold by T. Lowndes, 1771, pp. 55–56 and 280.

97.35–36   "*Ah! ... à l'ognon!—*"] Compare "Frit À L'Huile," the first lines of which read:

> Mon père à fait bâtir maison,
> Ah! ah! ah! frit à l'huile,
> L'a fait bâtir à trois pignons,
> Fritaine, friton, friton, poëlon,
> Ah! ah! ah! frit à l'huile, frit au beurre et à l'ognon.

Kirby most likely adapted his version from his copy of Ernest Gagnon's *Chansons Populaires Du Canada* (1865). See *Chansons,* p. 64.

100.18–19   *Madame de Grandmaison and Madame Couillard*] Both families were well known in Quebec in the 1740s. Paul Mallepart de Grand Maison, *dit* Beaucour, a "soldier" and "painter," came "to New France around 1720 in the colonial regular troops." By 1747 he and his wife, born Marguerite Haguenier, were living in "the parish of Notre-Dame de Québec" while he did paintings for various churches in the area. Guillaume Couillard de Lespinay came "to Canada about 1613" and, therefore, "was one of the first to settle permanently in the colony." The "son-in-law of Louis Hébert," Guillaume and his wife Guillemette "had 10 children, and because of the numerous descendants of these children Couillard appears in the genealogy of almost all the old French-Canadian families." The Couillards themselves acquired both the seigneury of Saint-Joseph or Lespinay and that of Rivière-du-Sud. In 1743, for example, Charles Couillard de Beaumont and his wife Marie Couillard Després sold "une partie" of the seigneury of Rivière-du-Sud. See F.-J. Audet. "La seigneurie de la Riviere du Sud." *Recherches Historiques*, 7 (1901), 117–19; "Couillard De Lespinay, Guillaume." *DCB*. Vol. 1, pp. 236–37; and "Mallepart De Grand Maison, *dit* Beaucour, Paul." *DCB*. Vol. 3, pp. 422–23.

101.32   *Bigot . . . a . . . relative of the Count de Marville*] François Bigot was a "cousin" of Charles-Jean-Baptiste Fleuriau de Morville. In the 1720s, when Bigot was beginning his career in France in "the Marine administration," the Comte de Morville was "secrétaire d'État à la Marine" and then Secretary of State for Foreign Affairs. See "Fleuriau De Morville (Charles-Jean-Baptiste)." *DBF*, and "Bigot, François." *DCB*. Vol. 4, pp. 59–71.

107.2–4 *voila la différence . . . the refrain of a song . . . popular both in New France and in old, at that period*] The song, modelled on a French folk song, was composed in 1758 apparently to celebrate the victory of the French over the English at Fort Carillon (Ticonderoga, New York). Its two refrains, "Voilà la ressemblance" and "Voilà la différence," highlighted similarities and differences between the two nations, although "Le Français" always turned out to be better than "l'Anglais" as, for example, in the following stanza:

> Le Français comme l'Anglais
> Prétend soutenir ses droits
> Voilà la ressemblance;
> Le Français par équité,
> L'Anglais par duplicité,
> Voilà la différence.

See Hubert Larue. "Les Chansons Historiques Du Canada." *Le*

Foyer Canadien, 3 (1865), 5–72.

108.34–36 *Penelope's web ... pulled in pieces at night ... woven through the day*] Compare Homer, *The Odyssey*, Book Two. Penelope, in order to avoid choosing a new husband when Odysseus failed to return to Ithaca after the Trojan wars, tricked her "suitors" by making them agree not to "press" her "nuptials" until she had completed her weaving of "a web of amplest size / And subtlest woof." When they "With her request complied," Penelope spent "Three years" weaving "the ample web" by day, "and by the aid / Of torches" unravelling "it again at night." See, for example, *The Works Of William Cowper*. Vol. 13: *The Odyssey Of Homer. Translated Into English Blank Verse ... Vol. I*. London: Baldwin And Cradock, 1837, pp. 29–30. Kirby owned a copy of Cowper's translation of Homer issued in Philadelphia in 1838.

109.34–36 *Coulon de Villiers ... marched into the New England camp, and made widows*] Nicolas-Antoine Coulon de Villiers, a "captain in the colonial regular troops" in Quebec, led the "assault" in February 1747 on the "over 500 New England troops" who were wintering in Acadia at Grand Pré. When Villiers' "left arm was shattered by a musket ball," Louis de La Corne, "the Chevalier de La Corne," took command of the "party of ... Canadians and Indians" who "killed, wounded," or took prisoner "a large number" of the British soldiers. See "Coulon De Villiers, Nicolas-Antoine." *DCB*. Vol. 3, pp. 149–50, and "La Corne, Louis ... De." *DCB*. Vol. 3, pp. 331–32.

113.11–12 *Henry of Navarre*] That is, "bon roi Henri," Henri IV, King of France from 1589 to 1610. A leader of the Huguenots before he converted to Roman Catholicism in 1593, he was instrumental in bringing about the Edict of Nantes (1598), which guaranteed liberty of conscience and equality of rights to both Protestants and Roman Catholics in France. See "Henri IV." *DBF*.

113.20–21 *the old latin grace:* "Benedic Domine nos et haec tua dona,"] That is, "Bless us, O Lord, and these thy gifts."

113.38–   *apples ... delicious as those that comforted the Rose of Sharon*]
114.1   Compare The Song of Songs 2:1–5, in which "the rose of Sharon" sings, "Stay me with flagons, comfort me with apples: for I *am* sick of love." See *IB*. Vol. 5. 1956, pp. 112–14.

116.14–15 *the Devils cave ... in the Ottawa Country*] That is, almost

certainly, the Wakefield Cave. In a paper read before the Ottawa
Natural History Society in November 1868, James Alexander
Grant described the recently discovered "Wakefield Cave" as
"the largest cavern in the entire Dominion of Canada." Kirby
probably based his account of the cave on that of his friend
Benjamin Sulte, who related his visit to the "caverne de
Wakefield" in a pamphlet published in 1875, a copy of which
he gave to Kirby. See James Alexander Grant. *Superficial Geology
Of The Valley Of The Ottawa, And The Wakefield Cave.* Ottawa:
Hunter, Rose, 1869, p. 15, and Benjamin Sulte. *La Caverne De*
Wakefield *Comté D'Ottawa.* Montreal: Burland-Desbarats, 1875,
p. 27 et passim.

117.38–   *that glorious Psalm ... Toto pectore ... Amabo ... in a version*
118.17   *made for Queen Mary of France and Scotland*] George Buchanan,
Paraphrase of Psalm 116, ca. 1565, ll. 1–8. These lines
correspond to the first verse of Psalm 116, "I love the LORD,
because he hath heard my voice *and* my supplications." The
first edition of *Paraphrasis Psalmorum Davidis Poetica,* published
most likely "in the winter of 1565," was dedicated to Mary I of
Scotland. Kirby owned a copy of this work published in Glasgow
in 1750. Buchanan functioned as Mary's "Latin court poet"
when she returned to Scotland after her reign as Queen of
France ended with the death of her husband, François II, in
1560. See *IB.* Vol. 4. 1955, p. 610, and I. D. McFarlane. *Buchanan.*
London: Gerald Duckworth, 1981, pp. 229 and 255.

122.30–31   *My father has killed the fatted calf for his returned prodigal*] Compare
Luke 15:11–32, where, in the parable of the prodigal son, Jesus
tells the story of a "younger" son who took "the portion of goods"
given to him by his father, travelled "into a far country, and there
wasted his substance with riotous living." When, hungry and
penniless, he returned home, his father ordered his servants to
"bring hither the fatted calf, and kill *it*; and let us eat, and be
merry." See *IB.* Vol. 8. 1952, pp. 270–80.

123.30–32   *Richelieu ... and ... Colbert*] In 1627 Armand-Jean du Plessis,
Cardinal Richelieu, Louis XIII's powerful prime minister from
1624 to 1642, "established the 'Compagnie des Cents-Associés
for trade in Canada,' and made over New France to it,
'with full seigneurial rights of ownership and justice.'" In

the 1660s Jean-Baptiste Colbert, Louis XIV's most important minister, not only reorganized the government of the colony but also undertook a program of populating it with French settlers. About "three-quarters" of these came "from west of a line between Bordeaux," in the old Aquitaine, and Soissons, in Île-de-France. "The foremost provinces were Normandy and Île-de-France, followed by Poitou, Aunis, Brittany, and Saintonge." See *Historical Atlas Of Canada*. Vol. 1: *From the Beginning to 1800*. Ed. R. Cole Harris. Toronto: University of Toronto Press, 1987, Plate 45, and André Vachon. "The Administration of New France." *DCB*. Vol. 2, pp. xv–xxv.

123.38–
124.2
Louis Buade de Frontenac ... with his fair Countess ... "The Divine"] Louis de Buade de Frontenac et de Palluau was "governor-general of New France" from 1672 to 1682, and again from 1689 until his death in 1698. In 1648 he married Anne de La Grange, who "was noted for her rare physical beauty." According to *Les Ursulines De Québec, Depuis Leur Établissement Jusqu'à Nos Jours*, she was called "la divine" because of her "esprit." See "Buade De Frontenac Et De Palluau, Louis De." *DCB*. Vol. 1, pp. 133–42, and *Ursulines*. Vol. 1. 1863, p. 508.

124.2–4
Vaudreuil ... and Beauharnois] Philippe de Rigaud de Vaudreuil, who emigrated to Canada in 1687, was "governor of Montreal" from 1699 until 1703, when he became "governor general of New France." He died in Quebec in October 1725 in "his 23rd" year in this position. Charles de Beauharnois de la Boische succeeded Vaudreuil as "governor general of New France" in February 1726. Although New France was once again in crisis when Beauharnois left "for France in October 1747," during his tenure as governor general he had achieved a period of relative stability both within and without the colony. See "Rigaud De Vaudreuil, Philippe De." *DCB*. Vol. 2, pp. 565–74, and "Beauharnois De La Boische, Charles De." *DCB*. Vol. 3, pp. 41–51.

124.8
Laval] François de Laval was "vicar apostolic in New France" from 1658 to 1674, and the "first bishop of Quebec" from 1674 to 1688. During these three decades, in addition to building the Roman Catholic church in Quebec, he established "the seminary of Quebec," the "Petit Séminaire," and "at

Saint-Joachim a trades school, as well as a primary school where children would learn reading and arithmetic." See "Laval, François De." *DCB.* Vol. 2, pp. 358–72.

124.22–26   *three Ecclesiastics ... the Abbé Metavet ... Pere Oubal ... and his confrere La Richardie*] Jean-Claude Mathevet, a Sulpician priest who arrived in Canada in 1740, spent many years from 1746 on "ministering" to the Algonquins (Algonkins) at "the Lac-des-Deux Montagnes mission" (Oka, Quebec). A "specialist in the Algonkin language, in which he wrote a grammar (dated 1761), sermons, a sacred history, and a life of Christ," he "was held in the highest esteem" by the Algonquins, who called him "Ouakoui-the sky." The so-called "missionary to the Abenakis" was Sébastien Rale, whose name either Kirby or his copyists apparently mistranscribed as "Oubal." A Jesuit priest who arrived at Quebec in 1689, except for a few years, from 1694 until he was killed during an "attack" by a "New England force" in 1724, he served "the Abenakis at Norridgewock on the Kennebec River" in what is now Maine. During this time he also prepared an "Abenaki-French dictionary." Armand de La Richardie, another Jesuit priest, came to Canada in 1725. Except for two years (1746–48), when he "returned to Canada for a rest cure," from 1728 until 1751 he was missionary to the Hurons in and around what is now Windsor, Ontario. See "Rale (Râle, Rasle, Rasles), Sébastien." *DCB.* Vol. 2, pp. 542–45; "La Richardie, Armand De." *DCB.* Vol. 3, pp. 355–56; and "Mathevet, Jean-Claude." *DCB.* Vol. 4, pp. 521–22.

124.30   *Abbé Piquet*] François Picquet, a Sulpician priest, arrived from France in 1734. In 1749, with the goal of winning "over to France all Indians living to the south of the Great Lakes," he "founded the post of La Présentation" (Ogdensburg, New York), from where he worked throughout most of the next decade "to wean the Six Nations from their alliance with the English." In portraying this "célèbre sulpicien," including calling him the "missionnaire du roi" and "l'apôtre des Iroquois," Kirby is following Joseph Tassé's "L'Abbé Picquet," published in the *Revue canadienne* in 1870. Kirby owned the relevant volume of this periodical. See "Picquet, François." *DCB.* Vol. 4, pp. 636–38, and Joseph Tassé. "L'Abbé Picquet." *Revue Canadienne,* 7 (1870),

5–23 and 102–18.

125.14 "Manibus date lilia plenis"] Virgil, *Aeneid*, Book VI, l. 883. When Aeneas visits Anchises in the Elysium fields, his father tells him of the unhappy "fate" of Marcellus, son of the Emperor's sister Octavia, who was to become Emperor but who died young. Anchises adds, "Grant me to scatter in handfuls lilies" ("manibus date lilia plenis") and, thus, "perform an unavailing duty." According to Joseph Tassé in "L'Abbé Picquet," who is himself quoting Félix Martin's *De Montcalm En Canada* (1867), a pole bearing the Latin "inscription" was planted at "le fort Choueguen" (Oswego, New York) to mark its surrender to the French in 1756; Picquet had taken part in the French siege of this English fort. See Félix Martin. *De Montcalm En Canada Ou Les Dernières Années De La Colonie Française (1756–1760)*. Paris: Laroche, 1867, p. 42; Joseph Tassé. "L'Abbé Picquet." *Revue Canadienne*, 7 (1870), 5–23 and 102–18; and Virgil. *Eclogues. Georgics Aeneid I–VI*. Trans. H. Rushton Fairclough. Rev. G. P. Goold. Cambridge and London: Harvard University Press, 1999, pp. 594–97.

128.23–24 *De Lery, a solid ... officer of Engineers*] Gaspard-Joseph Chaussegros de Léry, the son of Gaspard-Joseph Chaussegros de Léry, the "chief engineer" of Canada, served "in the colonial regular troops" as "an assistant engineer." By the time he achieved the rank of "ensign in 1748," he had already "carried out engineering duties" at various places in the colony, including Quebec. See "Chaussegros De Léry, Gaspard-Joseph." *DCB*. Vol. 4, pp. 145–47.

134.11–12 *the revocation of the Edict of Nantes*] In April 1598 Henri IV proclaimed the Edict of Nantes, which gave French Protestants "limited freedom of worship." Louis XIV revoked this Edict "in the Edict of Fontainebleau" in October 1685. Despite their being prohibited from leaving France, many thousands of Huguenots subsequently emigrated to such places as England, Holland, and what was then the Dutch colony of the Cape of Good Hope (South Africa) with the result that France suffered "considerable economic damage." See James B. Collins. *The State in Early Modern France*. Cambridge: Cambridge University Press, 1995, pp. 103–04.

134.17–18 *the ... civil war of the Cevennes*] The Protestant uprising in
the Cévennes began in 1702. Although most of the fighting
occurred over the next three years, various dates are used for the
end of the religious troubles in this region of France. In *Histoire
Des Troubles Des Cévennes Ou De La Guerre Des Camisars, sous le regne
de* Louis *le Grand* (1760), for example, Antoine Court concluded
his history in 1711, when new leaders who had the people's
trust arose in the area and, therefore, "sauvèrent la France"
from events that sooner or later would have destroyed her. See
Antoine Court. *Histoire Des Troubles Des Cévennes.* Villefranche:
Chez Pierre Chretien, 1760, Vol. 3, p. 401.

135.2–3 *Her ... studies were ... the Hymns of Marot and the sermons
of the famous Jurieu*] In the 1530s and 1540s Clément Marot,
a French poet who had Protestant leanings, made "metrical
translations of the Psalms," which were "much admired" and
sung, especially by the Huguenots. Pierre Jurieu, a "French
Calvinist controversialist," became particularly well known
among the Huguenots for his *Lettres pastorales.* Published from
1686 to 1689, after the revocation of the Edict of Nantes, they
described "the sufferings of the French Protestants." In citing
Marot and Jurieu, Kirby was probably following his copy of the
1823 printing of *Siècle De Louis XIV* (1751); in his chapter on
Calvinism François-Marie Arouet de Voltaire mentioned both
"les psaumes de Marot" and "Le ministre Jurieu ... un des
plus ardents" Protestant prophets who incited the rebellion in
the Cévennes. See "Marot, Clément." *The Oxford Companion To
French Literature.* Ed. Paul Harvey and J. E. Heseltine. Oxford:
At The Clarendon Press, 1959, pp. 456–57; "Jurieu, Pierre." *The
Oxford Dictionary Of The Christian Church.* Ed. F. L. Cross. London:
Oxford University Press, 1957, pp. 755–56; and *Siècle.* Vol. 2,
pp. 168 and 180.

135.3–6 *She had listened to ... Grande Marie, and ... been breathed upon,
on ... Mount Peira by the Huguenot Prophet De Serre*] In *Histoire
Des Troubles Des Cévennes Ou De La Guerre Des Camisars, sous le
regne de* Louis *le Grand* (1760), Antoine Court recorded that
in January 1704 a celebrated Huguenot prophetess, called "la
Grande Marie" because of her height, was captured; she was
executed in Nîmes on 6 March of the same year. In *Siècle De*

Louis XIV (1751), François-Marie Arouet de Voltaire named "la grande Marie" as the "prophétesse" who inspired and helped Jean Cavalier, an important leader of the Camisards. Kirby most likely took her name and that of "de Serre" from his 1823 copy of *Siècle*. Voltaire described the latter as "un vieil huguenot" who prophesied on a mountain in "Dauphiné" called "Peira," and who passed on the gift of prophecy by breathing upon others. See Antoine Court. *Histoire Des Troubles Des Cévennes.* Villefranche: Chez Pierre Chretien, 1760, Vol. 2, p. 216, and *Siècle*. Vol. 2, pp. 181 and 185.

135.31–33 *old Simeon . . . cried . . .* "Domine! nunc dimittis"] Compare Luke 2:29. Simeon, a "just and devout" man in Jerusalem unto whom "the Holy Ghost" had revealed "that he should not see death, before he had seen the Lord's Christ," was drawn "by the Spirit" to the temple when Mary and Joseph "brought in the child Jesus, to do for him after the custom of the law." Simeon took Jesus "in his arms, and blessed God." He said:

> Lord, now lettest thou thy servant depart in peace, according to thy word:
> For mine eyes have seen thy salvation,
> Which thou hast prepared before the face of all people;
> A light to lighten the Gentiles, and the glory of thy people Israel.

See *IB.* Vol. 8. 1952, pp. 60–61.

136.4–5 *Beniah . . . the host of Solomon*] Compare 1 Kings 4:4. During the reign of King Solomon, "Benaiah the son of Jehoiada *was* over the host"; that is, he "was in command of the army." See *IB.* Vol. 3. 1954, p. 45.

136.33–34 *the Cardinal, and the Princess de Carignan*] In *Vie Privée De Louis XV* (1781), Mouffle d'Angerville described "la Princesse de Carignan" as the mistress of Cardinal de Fleury and explained how she used her influence to create the circumstances that persuaded Louis XV to take as his mistress the Countess of Mailly. Kirby, having read this account in *Vie Privée*, copied into his notebook, "La Comtesse de Mailly, maitresse du Roi à force d'un complot entre Cardinal Fleuri et la Princesse de Carignan sa maitresse. 1737 VP." The princess of Carignan was most likely Victoire-Marie-Anne, daughter of the Duke of Savoy and wife of Victor-Amédée of Savoy, prince of Carignan. See OTAR, Kirby, F–1076, Miscellaneous Manuscripts, MU1646, D–18, Note-book kept by Kirby containing ... excerpts from various historical publications relating to the history of New France, p. [4], and *Vie Privée.* Vol. 2, p. 26.

137.24   *Vengeance is mine saith the Lord*] Compare Romans 12:19. In his epistle to the Romans, Paul writes, "Dearly beloved, avenge not yourselves, but *rather* give place unto wrath: for it is written, Vengeance *is* mine; I will repay, saith the Lord." See *IB.* Vol. 9. 1954, p. 594.

139.18–19   *the defence of Prague under the Marshal de Belleisle*] During the War of the Austrian Succession, Charles-Louis-Auguste Fouquet, the Count, later Duke, of Belle-Isle and "maréchal de France," commanded the troops that defended Prague when it was besieged in 1742. Unable to make "une longue défense," Belle-Isle and his army finally retreated from Prague in December 1742. See "Belle-Isle (Charles-Louis-Auguste Fouquet, duc De)." *DBF.*

146.38   *the ... Count de Lusignan*] Paul-Louis Dazemard de Lusignan, a "captain in the colonial regular troops" who was born at Champlain, Quebec, in 1691, commanded "at Baie-des-Puants" (Green Bay, Wisconsin) from 1743 to 1747, and at "Fort Saint-Frédéric" (Crown Point, New York) from 1749 to 1758. He served at Carillon (Ticonderoga, New York) sometime in the 1750s. At least one nineteenth-century source, however, located him there before 1749. In *Le Panthéon Canadien* (1858), Maximilien Bibaud stated that after returning from the west "en Canada en 1739," Lusignan "commanda à Carillon, puis à St. Frédérick, où il était en 1749." See Maximilien Bibaud. *Le Panthéon Canadien.* Montreal: Cérat Et Bourguignon, 1858, p. 173, and "Dazemard ... De Lusignan, Paul-Louis." *DCB.* Vol. 3, pp. 168–69.

147.28   *Fontenoy*] The battle of Fontenoy (now in Belgium) was fought on 11 May 1745 between the English and their allies and the French, who were finally victorious. In *Précis Du Siècle De Louis XV* (1768), François-Marie Arouet de Voltaire provided a detailed account of this battle, which, he claimed, decided the outcome of the War of the Austrian Succession. He also praised the British infantry who opposed the French forces as "si réunie, si disciplinée et si intrépide." Kirby owned a copy of an 1823 printing of this work. See François-Marie Arouet de Voltaire. *Précis Du Siècle De Louis XV.* Paris: Chez Mme Veuve Dabo, 1823, p. 116.

148.34   *Voltaire*] François-Marie Arouet de Voltaire, who through the influence of "madame de Pompadour" held several appointments, including "le brevet d'historiographe de France," at the French court in the mid 1740s, was known as a free thinker who was particularly hostile to the Roman Catholic clergy and their role in the affairs of the state. See "Voltaire (François-Marie Arouet De)." *BU.*

151.12–14   *The late victory at Lawfelt ... the Duke of Cumberland*] On 2 July 1747 the French defeated an army commanded by William Augustus, Duke of Cumberland, son of King George II, at Laffeldt, Belgium. Kirby recorded this event in a notebook as "Battle of Lawfelt July 1747." See OTAR, Kirby, F–1076, Miscellaneous Manuscripts, MU1646, D–18, Note-book kept by Kirby containing ... excerpts from various historical publications relating to the history of New France, p. 17.

151.25   *the Count de Maurepas*] Jean-Frédéric Phelippeaux, "comte de" Maurepas, was "the secretary of state for the Marine" in France from the 1720s to the late 1740s and, thus, Louis XV's "representative and spokesman for colonial affairs." See "Maurepas (Jean-Frédéric Phelippeaux)." *BU,* and André Vachon, "The Administration of New France." *DCB.* Vol. 2, pp. xv–xxv.

152.22–23   *Lange Vaubernier*] Marie-Jeanne Aimart de Vaubernier, a Paris prostitute who adopted the name "mademoiselle Lange," became the mistress of Louis XV in the 1760s after the death of the marquise de Pompadour. From the time of her marriage to Guillaume du Barry, Vaubernier was known as Madame La Comtesse du Barry. In 1793, sentenced to death by the "tribunal révolutionnaire," she uttered "des cris perçants" as she was led to the guillotine. Kirby recorded in a notebook that "Mad Lange Vaubernier dit du Barry succeded Mad de

Pompadour—guillotined 1793 she cried on way, Life, life, life, for my repentance—life for all my devotion to the republic—life for all my riches to the nation." See "Barry (Marie-Jeanne Aimart De Vaubernier, Comtesse Du)." *BU*, and OTAR, Kirby, F–1076, Miscellaneous Manuscripts, MU1646, D–19, Twenty-four small note-books filled with miscellaneous notations by Kirby, n. pag..

153.16   *the fall of Montcalm*] Louis-Joseph de Montcalm, "promoted lieutenant-general ... in the French army" and "given command of all the military forces in Canada" in 1758, "received a mortal wound" as he retreated from the battle of the Plains of Abraham on 13 September 1759. He died the following day in Quebec. See "Montcalm, Louis-Joseph De." *DCB*. Vol. 3, pp. 458–69.

153.34–35   *The loss of the fleet of ... Jonquiere*] In May 1747 Jacques-Pierre de Taffanel de La Jonquière, a "rear-admiral" in the French navy who had been "appointed governor general of New France" in 1746, left France for Quebec in command of "a division ... of three frigates and two ships of the line." On 14 May 1747 La Jonquière and his ships fought a battle with a British squadron off the coast of Spain. All "the French warships" were captured, and "La Jonquière, who had been wounded, was taken prisoner" to England, where he remained until "he was liberated by the peace of Aix-la-Chapelle." See "Taffanel De La Jonquière, Jacques-Pierre De." *DCB*. Vol. 3, pp. 609–12.

155.11–15   *men whose names were ... familiar, or ... glorious ... Celeron de Bienville ... Le Gardeur de St Pierre*] In 1748 Pierre-Joseph Céloron de Blainville, an "officer in the colonial regular troops" who was praised for his leadership abilities, commanded a convoy of "troop reinforcements and supplies" that "rushed to Detroit to quell an insurrection of western tribes that threatened to drive the French out of the west." The next year he led "an expedition through the Ohio valley to assert" French "claims to the region, to map the route, and to drive out the English traders." In naming him "Céleron de Bienville" and in associating him with important accomplishments in New France, Kirby is following his copy of Andrew Bell's translation of the third edition of François-Xavier Garneau's *Histoire Du Canada* (1859). Jacques Le Gardeur de Saint-Pierre, another "officer in the colonial regular troops" who "was promoted captain" in 1748, was also known for his service in the west as well as for his expertise in "Indian affairs." From 1747 to 1749 he commanded "at the strategic post of Michilimackinac, where he could influence events in the entire Upper Lakes area." He was "killed in the battle of Lac Saint-Sacrement" (Lake George, New York) in 1755. See Bell. Vol. 2, p. 116; "Céloron De Blainville, Pierre-Joseph." *DCB*. Vol. 3, pp. 99–101; and "Legardeur De Saint-Pierre, Jacques." *DCB*. Vol. 3, pp. 374–76.

155.21   *the terms of* uti possidetis] That is, as you now possess. In international law the "phrase is sometimes referred to as a principle under which property not expressly provided for in a treaty terminating hostilities is to remain in the hands of the party who happened to have possession of it when hostilities ended." See David M. Walker. "*Uti possidetis*." *The Oxford Companion To Law*. Oxford: Clarendon Press, 1980, p. 1269.

156.22–23   *his wife ... a love gift to the Duc de Choiseul*] According to Mouffle d'Angerville in *Vie Privée De Louis XV* (1781), it was Louis Pennisseaut whose "jolie femme" had "le bonheur" to please the Duc de Choiseul, and who, thus, saved both her husband and his "gains frauduleux" when the "crime des Canadiens" was tried in Paris in the late 1760s. Kirby had this passage reproduced for him from a copy of d'Angerville's book in the "Can. Parl. Libr." Etienne-François de Choiseul, who became "duc" de Choiseul in 1760, was the most powerful minister in France during the 1760s. See "Choiseul ... (Étienne-François De)." *DBF*; OTAR, Kirby, F–1076, Miscellaneous Manuscripts, MU1646, D–19, Twenty-four small note-books filled with miscellaneous notations by Kirby, n. pag.; and *Vie Privée*. Vol. 4, p. 78.

164.30   *Hocquart*] Gilles Hocquart, a member of a "wealthy" French family "with influence in the magistracy and government bureaucracy as well as in finance," was appointed "financial commissary and acting intendant in New France" in 1729 and "promoted intendant" of the colony the following year. He held this post until François Bigot replaced him in 1748. Hocquart married Anne-Catherine de La Lande in Brest, France, in 1750, when he was in his fifties. See "Hocquart, Gilles." *DCB*. Vol. 4, pp. 354–65.

168.7   *Mons Froumois*] Louis Froumois was the "véritable nom" of François Bigot's "valet de chambre." Kirby may have taken this name from the copy of Joseph Marmette's *L'Intendant Bigot* that Benjamin Sulte sent him in August 1872 shortly after its publication. In a note to the text of this historical novel, Marmette explained that he was able to identify Bigot's servant from the account books of his ancestor Jean Taché. A rich merchant in Quebec, he had fought "contre la coterie Bigot." See Joseph Marmette. *L'Intendant Bigot.* Montreal: George E. Desbarats, 1872, p. 13.

171.15–16   *the prayer of millions—"Ave Maria gratia plena"*] That is, "Hail Mary, full of grace." This is the opening line of "the Hail Mary," a salutation to the Virgin Mary that was traditionally repeated three times in the Angelus, "a short practice of devotion" in Roman Catholic liturgy "in honour of the Incarnation," which was itself said "three times each day, morning, noon, and evening, at the sound of the bell." See "Angelus." *Catholic.* Vol. 1. 1907, pp. 486–87.

171.19–20   "Mea culpa! Mea maxima culpa!"] That is, "By my fault, my most grievous fault." This is a line from the "Confiteor" (the "Confession of Sins"), one of the prayers said at the foot of the altar at the beginning of the Roman Catholic mass as it was celebrated in the eighteenth and nineteenth centuries. See, for example, J. Feder. *Missel* quotidien *Des Fidèles.* Tours: Maison Mame, 1961, p. 796.

172.4   *quietly as the waters of Shiloh*] Compare Isaiah 8:6, in which the Lord, speaking to the prophet, says that the people of Judah refuse "the waters of Shiloah that go softly" and "melt in fear" before their enemies. See *IB.* Vol. 5. 1956, p. 223.

174.2–3   *the Chevalier des Meloises*] In 1748 Nicolas Renaud d'Avène Des Méloizes, Angelique's nineteen-year-old brother, held a commission as "second ensign" in the French "colonial regular troops." He continued to serve in North America until, having been taken prisoner by the British in 1760, he was sent "on parole to France." There, for "a short time" in the 1760s, "he was suspected of complicity in Intendant Bigot's malfeasance, but no evidence could be brought against him." See "Renaud

D'Avène Des Méloizes, Nicolas." *DCB*. Vol. 5, p. 711.

174.27–28 *Her arms bare to the elbows would have excited Juno's jealousy, and Homer's verse*] Compare William Cowper's translation of Homer's *The Iliad*, Book One, in which Juno, the "consort" of Jove, of whose power she is jealous, is described at various points as "white-armed." See, for example, *The Works Of William Cowper.* Vol. 11: *The Iliad Of Homer. Translated Into English Blank Verse . . . Vol. I.* London: Baldwin And Cradock, 1837, pp. 5, 11, and 24–26. Kirby may have taken his details about Juno (Hera), wife of Jove (Zeus), from his copy of Cowper's translation of Homer.

175.10 *a* Precieuse] Literally, a woman who frequented—and held—salons in seventeenth-century France where good manners and fine language were practised and discussed. Kirby may be taking his sense of "précieuse" from the definition given by Pierre-René Auguis in his introduction to the first volume of his edition of the works of Jean-Baptiste Poquelin *dit* Molière. In his "Notice Biographique Sur La Vie Et Les Écrits De Molière," Auguis explained that in the 1600s women who aspired "au bon ton" took "le nom de *précieuses*," and that in *Les Précieuses Ridicules* (1659), which was included in Volume One of Auguis' edition, Molière satirized "les fausses précieuses," those who took manners and language to ridiculous extremes. Kirby owned a copy of this volume. See Pierre-René Auguis, ed. *Oeuvres Complètes De Molière . . . Précédées D'Une Nouvelle Vie De Molière.* Paris: Froment, 1823. Vol. 1, p. 29.

175.18–21 *Vanloo . . . Le Brun*] The van Loos were a "family of artists of Flemish origin" who painted in France in the seventeenth and eighteenth centuries. Kirby recorded in a notebook that "Jean Vanloo mourut à Paris 1746," a reference to Jean-Baptiste van Loo, who actually died in Aix-en-Provence, France, in 1745. The best known of these artists was Carle (Charles-André) Vanloo. In 1737, the year he was appointed a "professor at the Académie Royale" in Paris, he painted "*Rest on the Hunt*" to hang in a dining room at Fontainebleau. The picture, which shows a hunting party having lunch while their attendants and horses, a symbol of passion, wait, was traditionally said to represent Louis XV on an outing with three women, all of whom were his mistresses. Charles Le Brun was the

"French painter and designer" who "dominated 17th-century French painting." Confirmed as "Premier Peintre" of Louis XIV in 1664, he was responsible for the transformation of the interior of Versailles. Although no painting of Antony and Cleopatra is attributed to him, he frequently represented classical subjects. See "Le Brun, Charles." Grove's. Vol. 19, pp. 19–25; "Loo, van." Grove's. Vol. 19, pp. 644–49; and OTAR, Kirby, F–1076, Miscellaneous Manuscripts, MU1646, D–18, Note-book kept by Kirby containing ... excerpts from various historical publications relating to the history of New France, p. 17.

184.25–26 *likeDelilah ... the seven locks of his strength*] Compare Judges 16:19. Samson, the Nazarite, having lied to Delilah three times about the source of his strength, finally confessed that it lay in his hair. "And she made him sleep upon her knees; and she called for a man, and she caused him to shave off the seven locks of his head; and she began to afflict him, and his strength went from him." See *IB*. Vol. 2. 1953, p. 795.

185.36 *Professor Vallier*] François-Elzéar Vallier, a French priest who arrived in Quebec in 1729, was "appointed ... superior of the seminary of Quebec" in 1734, a post he held until his death in 1747. He was known for his intelligence, his learning, and his ability as a teacher. See "Vallier, François-Elzéar." *DCB*. Vol. 3, pp. 638–39.

186.25–37 *the new Hymn ... "Soutenez, grande Reine, / ... Protegez nos remparts!—"*] This was the final stanza of a cantata, sung to the tune of "*Or, nous dites Marie*" and addressed to the Virgin Mary, composed to celebrate the victory of the French over the British at the battle on the Monongahela River near Fort Duquesne (Pittsburgh, Pennsylvania) in July 1755. Its author, according to Hugolin Lemay, was probably the chaplain at Fort Duquesne, "un récollet sans doute." Kirby's version, which he most likely copied from *Les Ursulines De Québec, Depuis Leur Établissement Jusqu'à Nos Jours*, replaced "nos" with "vos" in the phrases "vos lis" and "vos remparts"; otherwise, his words are identical to those in *Ursulines*. See Hugolin Lemay. *Vieux papiers, Vieilles chansons*. Montréal: Imprimerie des Franciscains, 1936, p. 108, and *Ursulines*. Vol. 2. 1864, p. 281.

188.2   *"SPLENDIDE MENDAX"*] Horace, *Odes*, Book III, Ode 11, l. 35. The phrase described a daughter of Danaus, who, "splendide mendax," or "magnificently deceitful," to "her scheming father," saved her husband from him and her wicked sisters. See *Odes And Epodes*, pp. 174–75.

188.15–16 *a... picture from... Vanloo of the... Marquise de Pompadour*] Both Carle (Charles-André) Vanloo and his nephew Louis-Michel van Loo painted her portrait. Carle Vanloo's *"La belle jardinière,"* which depicted Madame de Pompadour carrying a basket of flowers, was produced "probably as early as 1754–5." See Colin Jones. *Madame De Pompadour Images Of A Mistress*. London: National Gallery, 2002, p. 68.

190.29–30 *women are... ready to sail in the Ships of Tarshish, so long as the cargo is, gold, silver, ivory, apes and peacocks*] Compare I Kings 10:22, which states that among King Solomon's possessions was "a navy of Tharshish" that came "once in three years... bringing gold, and silver, ivory, and apes, and peacocks." See *IB*. Vol. 3. 1954, p. 100.

193.10   *Le Nostre*] André Le Nôtre, "architecte et dessinateur des jardins du roi," was the creator of the formal French garden, a dominant landscape design in the seventeenth century and beyond. His most famous achievement was the park and gardens of Louis XIV's palace at Versailles. See "Lenôtre (André)." *BU*.

195.29–30 *mistress of my heart, and home as the song says*] There are many variations of all, or part, of this phrase. Compare, for example, John Brougham, *Jane Eyre. A Drama, In Five Acts*, IV.iii, in which Rochester describes Jane Eyre as "sole mistress of this heart and home." The play was first performed in New York City in 1856. See John Brougham. *Jane Eyre*. New York: Samuel French, n.d., p. 26. French's American Drama, The Acting Edition, No. 136.

200.17–19 *an Amant Magnifique ... 'Quelque ... venir un jour!—'*] *Les Amants Magnifiques*, a comedy by Jean-Baptiste Poquelin *dit* Molière first performed before Louis XIV in 1670, dealt with two lovers who courted the same princess. Molière's *La Princesse D'Élide*, first performed before Louis XIV in 1664, was an earlier version of the same theme. In this play, when the princess finally falls in love and agrees to marry, a chorus sings in the comedy's sixth and last interlude the lines about the irresistible power of "l'Amour." See *Molière*. Vol. 4. 1878, p. 218.

205.14   *Le Vasseur*] The Levasseurs were "the great family of craftsmen in wood" that "left its particular stamp on artistic production" in Quebec, especially in the eighteenth century. Several members of this family, including Noël Levasseur, worked on the cathedral in Quebec. His most famous creation, however, "one of the major pieces of carving in French Canada," in which he was assisted by his sons François-Noël and Jean-Baptiste-Antoine and "perhaps ... their cousin Pierre-Noël" Levasseur, was the retable, shaped like an arch, in the Ursuline chapel. According to *Les Ursulines De Québec, Depuis Leur Établissement Jusqu'à Nos Jours*, in the 1730s "Le Sieur Le Vasseur, sculpteur, travailla pendant quatre années à ce rétable." See "Levasseur, Noël." *DCB*. Vol. 2, pp. 430–32; "Levasseur, Pierre-Noël." *DCB*. Vol. 3, pp. 397–98; and *Ursulines*. Vol. 2. 1864, p. 110.

207.25–26   *Mademoiselle de Brouague*] Louise Martel de Brouague was the daughter of François Martel de Brouague and Louise Mariauchau d'Esgly; born in Quebec in 1738, she was ten in 1748. In 1753 she married Gaspard-Joseph Chaussegros de Léry, who, apparently with his wife, "had the distinction of being the first Canadian seigneur to be presented to King George III" after New France was officially ceded to the British in 1763. This event was recounted in *Les Ursulines De Québec, Depuis Leur Établissement Jusqu'à Nos Jours*, "Le Roi, charmé de ce bel échantillon de ses nouveaux sujets Canadiens, s'écria en apercevant Mme. de Léry: 'If all the ladies of Canada are as handsome, I have indeed made a conquest!' c'est-à-dire: 'Si toutes les dames Canadiennes vous ressemblent, la conquête en vaut la peine!'" Kirby, citing as his source "Ursulines 3 224," and mistakenly giving Louise her mother's name, summarized the relevant paragraphs in a notebook, "Louise Marichau d'Esglis belle et d'un esprit vif, fut mariée à Jos. Gaspard Chaussegros de Lery. Cette femme fut presentée a George III, qui dit—If all the ladies of Canada are as handsome, I have indeed made a conquest.—Si toutes les dames Canadiennes vous ressemblent, la conquete en vaut la peine!" See "Chaussegros De Léry, Gaspard-Joseph." *DCB*. Vol. 4, pp. 145–47; OTAR, Kirby, F–1076, Miscellaneous Manuscripts, MU1646, D–19, Twenty-four small note-books filled with miscellaneous notations by Kirby, n. pag.; and *Ursulines*. Vol. 3. 1866, pp. 224–25.

207.34–35 *the famous class of 'the Louises,'*] Les Ursulines De Québec, Depuis Leur *Établissement Jusqu'à Nos Jours* records that, about "l'époque de la conquête," a class "presque toute formée de *Louise*" attended the Convent. Among the sixteen students named Louise were "Louise de Brouague" and "Louise de Beaujeu." This passage appeared in *Ursulines* just before that discussing Louise de Brouague's marriage and her presentation to George III. See *Ursulines*. Vol. 3. 1866, p. 224.

208.5 *Mere des Seraphins*] Jacqueline Juchereau de Saint-Denis was one of the "12 children" of Nicolas Juchereau de Saint-Denis, who "possessed vast domains" in New France, including "properties at Quebec, Beauport, and the Île d'Orléans," and his wife Marie-Thérèse Giffard. Jacqueline made her "profession religieuse" as an Ursuline in 1687. As "Mère Marie des Séraphins" she was for many years "maîtresse générale des classes" before she died in 1722. She was known for her "bon coeur." See "Juchereau De Saint-Denis, Nicolas." *DCB*. Vol. 1, pp. 401–02, and "La Novice De 1686." *Ursulines*. Vol. 1. 1863, pp. 447–49.

208.34 *Louise Roy*] A "Lse. Roy," that is, Louise Roy, was recorded in the "Liste De La Plupart Des Élèves Qui Se Sont Trouvées Au Pensionnat De 1700 À 1739" published in *Les Ursulines De Québec, Depuis Leur Établissement Jusqu'à Nos Jours*. A note in the same work recorded that "Les familles Roy" were common in Quebec and Montreal as "marchands, artisans etc.," and that "leurs enfants ont fréquenté nos classes." See *Ursulines*. Vol. 2. 1864, p. 174, and *Ursulines*. Vol. 3. 1866, p. 335.

208.35–36 *She was light and sprightly as Titania*] Compare William Shakespeare, *A Midsummer Night's Dream*, V.i.391–400. Oberon and Titania, the "*King and Queen of Fairies*," order "*their* TRAIN" to "Sing, and dance ... trippingly." Oberon asks "Every elf and fairy sprite" to "Hop as light as bird from brier," while Titania says, "Hand in hand, with fairy grace, / Will we sing." See *Shakespeare*, p. 246.

209.32 *Louise de Beaujeu*] Born in 1748, Julie-Louise Liénard de Beaujeu de Villemonde was the daughter of Louis Liénard de Beaujeu de Villemonde, an "army and militia officer and seigneur," and Louise-Charlotte Cugnet, who "died giving" her birth. In 1765 she married Antoine Juchereau Duchesnay, who "inherited" several seigneuries, including that of Beauport, just months before her death in 1773. See "Juchereau Duchesnay, Antoine." *DCB*. Vol. 5, pp. 462–64, and "Liénard De Beaujeu De Villemonde, Louis." *DCB*. Vol. 5, pp. 498–99.

209.37–38 *the proper name of the Anax Andron ... in the Iliad*] Agamemnon is described as "King of men" in the opening lines of Homer's *The Iliad*. See, for example, *The Works Of William Cowper*. Vol. 11: *The Iliad Of Homer. Translated Into English Blank Verse ... Vol. I*. London: Baldwin And Cradock, 1837, p. [3]. Kirby owned a copy of Cowper's translation of Homer.

210.3   *Mere Christine*] She is most likely based on Catherine Doherty, Mère Sainte Christine, who was the "maîtresse générale" of the non-resident students at the Ursuline Convent in Quebec. Of Irish background, she became a correspondent of Josephine Lowe, who attended the Convent school from 1863 to 1869, and who sent Kirby information about the Ursulines. Sister Marie Marchand, of the Ursulines of Quebec, kindly provided the details about both Josephine Lowe's attendance at the Convent and Catherine Doherty.

210.21   *Prince Camaralzaman*] Compare "*The Story of the amours of Camaralzaman, Prince of the Isles of the Children of Khaledan; and of Badoura, Princess of China*," *Arabian Nights Entertainments: Consisting Of One Thousand and One Stories*. In the English translation of Antoine Galland's French version of these stories, the only son of Schahzaman, the king of Khaledan, is described as "so beautiful" that he was given "the name of Camaralzaman; *i.e*. The Moon of the Age." This translation, frequently reprinted, was the standard version of the *Thousand and One Nights* from its first publication in the early eighteenth century until well into the nineteenth century. See, for example, *Arabian Nights Entertainments: Consisting Of One Thousand and One Stories. ... The Fourteenth Edition*. Edinburgh: Printed by and for Colin Macfarquhar, and sold by the Booksellers in town and country, 1772. Vol. 2, p. 161.

211.7   *the Messieurs and Mesdames Jourdains*] Compare *Le Bourgeois*

Gentilhomme (1670) by Jean-Baptiste Poquelin *dit* Molière. The chief character in this "Comédie-Ballet" is Monsieur Jourdain, a wealthy merchant who longs to be a "gentilhomme," and who, therefore, allows himself to be duped and robbed by the "gens de qualité" and their servants. The sensible bourgeois in the play, including Madame Jourdain, recognize Monsieur Jourdain's folly and scorn his desire to be a gentleman; for them the term "gentilhomme," in fact, seems to authorize "le vol." See *Molière.* Vol. 8. 1923, pp. 51 and 142.

211.35–36   *the Sieurs Drouillon and La Force*] In 1748 Pierre-Jacques Druillon de Macé, born in 1727, was a student in France. The next year, however, he abandoned his "advanced legal studies for a military career." Appointed an "officer in the colonial regular troops," he served in New France until 1760, when he returned to his native Blois. He "is remembered chiefly for his part in the Jumonville affair." Wounded and taken prisoner in May 1754, when the French troops under Joseph Coulon de Villiers de Jumonville were attacked by George Washington "near present-day Jumonville," Pennsylvania, his "complaints" about his "maltreatment during his detention in Virginia" became "part of the accelerated Anglo-French diplomatic war of 1755–56." René-Hippolyte Laforce, who turned twenty in 1748, was also "taken prisoner and sent to Virginia" for his part in "the Jumonville affair" of 1754. After his release he fought as a French naval officer in his native New France. From the mid 1770s he held various military appointments in the British North American colony of Quebec. See "Druillon De Macé, Pierre-Jacques." *DCB.* Vol. 4, pp. 226–27, and "Laforce, René-Hippolyte." *DCB.* Vol. 5, pp. 470–71.

212.13–14   *Bonhomme Michel*] According to *Les Ursulines De Québec, Depuis Leur Établissement Jusqu'à Nos Jours,* Bonhomme Michel served the Convent in Quebec from 1747, when he arrived from France, until his death in 1788. For more than thirty years he was the foreman, a true "*Factotum,*" who watched over the Convent day and night. In his description of this good man, Kirby is translating and paraphrasing the entry about him in *Ursulines.* See "L'Héritage Du Bonhomme Michel." *Ursulines.* Vol. 3. 1866, pp. 185–88.

212.26–27 *the* Vieux Recit, *the old annals of the Convent*] The *Vieux Récit*
contains the records constructed from memory that replaced
the journals and other items held by the Ursulines that were
destroyed by fire and other disasters. The entry on "L'Héritage
Du Bonhomme Michel" in *Les Ursulines De Québec, Depuis Leur
Établissement Jusqu'à Nos Jours* is based on "les données du Récit"
and quotes directly from it. See *Ursulines.* Vol. 3. 1866, p. 185.

214.2   *"PUT MONEY IN THY PURSE"*] William Shakespeare, *Othello,*
I.iii.339–40, et passim. Iago, planning to destroy Othello, advises
Roderigo to "Put money in thy purse" so that he can win the love
of Desdemona when she tires of "the Moor." See *Shakespeare,*
pp. 1210–11.

214.27–30 *the batteries of Wolfe . . . fires of devastation*] From mid July 1759
to the battle on the Plains of Abraham on 13 September of the
same year, James Wolfe, "commander of the British expedition
that took Quebec," carried out "a policy of terror" as part of his
campaign to defeat the French in Canada. His strategy included
bombarding Quebec from batteries that he had constructed at
"Pointe-Lévy (Lauzon)" on the south shore of the St. Lawrence
opposite the city and laying "waste the south shore" of the
colony "from Kamouraska to Pointe-Lévy." These "devastations,
in which more than 1,400 houses" were burned "in the rural
districts" and much of Quebec was destroyed, are described in
Andrew Bell's translation of the third edition of François-Xavier
Garneau's *Histoire Du Canada* (1859), a copy of which Kirby
owned. See Bell. Vol. 2, pp. 237–39, and "Wolfe, James." *DCB.*
Vol. 3, pp. 666–74.

216.4–5   *Captain Poulariez*] Also called "Poulariès" (Johnstone) and
"Poulardier" (Bell), he served as an officer in the Royal
Roussillon regiment in New France in the 1750s and 1760s.
According to J. B. A. Ferland in the second part of
Cours D'Histoire Du Canada (1865), for example, in 1757
"M. de Poulariez" was "alors capitaine des grenadiers de
Royal-Roussillon." In his "Memoires" James Johnstone, "known
as the Chevalier de Johnstone," described him as "un Officier
ferme, d'une Bravoure Phlegmatique, rempli d'honneur, et
d'un rare Mérite." In his spelling of Poulariez's name and
his identification of him as a captain in the grenadiers, Kirby

followed Ferland's *Cours D'Histoire*, a copy of which he owned. In a notebook, however, Kirby wrote that "M. Poulariez" was "Capt des grenadiers du Regt de Béarn." See Bell. Vol. 2, p. 283; "Johnstone, James." *DCB*. Vol. 4, pp. 400–01; J. B. A. Ferland. *Cours D'Histoire Du Canada. Seconde Partie 1663–1759*. Québec: Augustin Coté, 1865, p. 547; James Johnstone. "Memoires de M. le Chev. De Johnstone." *Ninth Series, Historical Documents*. Quebec: Literary And Historical Society Of Quebec, 1915, p. 150; and OTAR, Kirby, F–1076, Miscellaneous Manuscripts, MU1646, D–18, Note-book kept by Kirby containing . . . excerpts from various historical publications relating to the history of New France, p. 15.

216.14   *Colonel Dalquier*] Jean d'Alquier de Servian, an "officer in the French regular troops," served in New France from 1755 to 1760. In 1748 he was commissioned "captain of grenadiers," the rank he held when he arrived in Quebec "as a member of the second battalion of Béarn." He "was promoted lieutenant-colonel" and commander of this battalion in 1757. See "Alquier (Dalquier) De Servian, Jean D'." *DCB*. Vol. 3, p. 12.

217.2–3   *Jansenist convulsionaires at the tomb of Master Paris*] Before he died in 1727, François de Pâris, a deacon in the Roman Catholic church who followed the Jansenist "ideals of piety and interior religiosity," had "devoted many hours daily to the performance of some pious or charitable act on behalf of his less fortunate neighbors" in "an area of considerable poverty and very high population density" in Paris. After his death his tomb in the cemetery of the church of Saint-Médard was the site of apparently miraculous cures that came to be accompanied by forms of convulsions. These happenings attracted so many people and caused so much controversy that the cemetery was closed to the public in 1732. The next day the "pasquinade Jansénienne: De par le Roi, défense à Dieu, / De plus opérer en ce lieu" appeared on the cemetery's walls. Kirby made several entries about "M. Paris, Diacre inhumé à St Medard . . . un St Jansenist," as he summarized in a notebook the passage about this Parisian from Mouffle d'Angerville's *Vie Privée De Louis XV* (1781). See B. Robert Kreiser. *Miracles, Convulsions, And Ecclesiastical Politics In Early Eighteenth-Century*

Paris. Princeton: Princeton University Press, 1978, pp. 85–87; OTAR, Kirby, F–1076, Miscellaneous Manuscripts, MU1646, D–18, Note-book kept by Kirby containing ... excerpts from various historical publications relating to the history of New France, pp. 3–[4]; and *Vie Privée*. Vol. 1, pp. 172–76.

220.9   *Amen! Amen!* quod fiat fiatur!] Compare Thomas Urquhart's translation of François Rabelais' *Gargantua and Pantagruel*, Book Three (1546), Chapter 14, in which Panurge, giving his interpretation of his dream of horns being driven into his head by a "wanton, toying girl," states, "*Amen, Amen, Fiat, fiatur*," or "Amen, Amen, What will be, will be." Kirby was probably recalling this phrase in his copy of the 1849 Bohn edition of Urquhart's work. See *Rabelais*. Vol. 2, pp. 2–3.

220.9–10   *Seyny John the fool of Paris*] Compare Thomas Urquhart's translation of François Rabelais' *Gargantua and Pantagruel*, Book Three (1546), Chapter 37, in which Pantagruel recounts a "verdict, award, and arbitrement" made by "Seyny John, the noted fool of Paris." Kirby most likely took this character from his copy of the 1849 edition of Urquhart's work. See *Rabelais*. Vol. 2, pp. 114–17.

220.16   invitus amabo] Ovid, *The Amores*, Book 3, 11b, l. 35. The poet, struggling with a "fickle heart" that is torn between "love" and "hate," explains, " I will hate, if I have strength; if not, I shall love unwilling," or "invitus amabo." See Ovid. *Heroides And Amores*. Trans. Grant Showerman. Cambridge: Harvard University Press, and London: William Heinemann, 1963, pp. 490–91.

224.15   *the Marquis de Vandriere*] The brother of "la marquise de Pompadour," Abel-François Poisson, known in the 1740s as the "marquis de Vandières," held at that time "a largely honorific post involving protection of the royal forests." In 1751 he became "*directeur des Bâtiments, Arts et Manufactures du Roi*," a position that included "the commissioning and management of artistic work at all the royal palaces and supervision over state manufactories." In a notebook Kirby, epitomizing Mouffle d'Angerville's description of Madame de Pompadour's brother in *Vie Privée De Louis XV* (1781), recorded that the "Marquis de Vandriere" was "frere de Pompadour directeur des Jardins, arts et batimens." See "Marigny (Abel-François Poisson, marquis

De Menars et De)." *BU*; Colin Jones. *Madame De Pompadour Images Of A Mistress.* London: National Gallery, 2002, pp. 40–42; and OTAR, Kirby, F–1076, Miscellaneous Manuscripts, MU1646, D–19, Twenty-four small note-books filled with miscellaneous notations by Kirby, n pag..

226.28   *Bourgeoisie*] People by the name of those mentioned as going to Belmont lived in Quebec in the 1740s, including several who were merchants and tradesmen. In the 1744 census of the city, for example, the merchant Philippe d'Ailleboust de Cerry is listed as a "négociant" aged "40," and the blacksmith Louis Cureux dit Saint-Germain as a "forgeron" aged "45." Cureux lived with his wife, eight children, four "Domestiques nègres," and one apprentice. See "Le Recensement De Québec, En 1744." *Rapport De L'Archiviste De La Province De Québec Pour 1939–1940.* Québec: Redempti Paradis, 1940, pp. 118 and 140.

231.3   *the Lord de Coucy*] For "more than four hundred years," from the tenth to the fifteenth centuries, the de Coucys, whose castle was located in Picardy, held "one of the four great baronies of France." Their family motto was

> *Roi ne suis,*
> *Ne prince ne duc ne comte aussi;*
> *Je suis le sire de Coucy.*

> (Not king nor prince,
> Duke nor count am I;
> I am the lord of Coucy.)

See Barbara W. Tuchman. *A Distant Mirror: The Calamitous 14th Century.* New York: Alfred A. Knopf, 1978, pp. [3]–4.

232.37   *the Sieur Keratry*] No merchant called Keratry appeared in "Le Recensement De Québec, En 1744." Kératry, however, was the name of "une ancienne famille de noblesse bretonne" who held land in the Finistère region of Britanny. When Kirby was composing *Le Chien d'or,* the most famous member of this family was probably Émile-Hilarion Kératry, who as "préfet de police" in Paris in 1870 drove the German invaders from the city during the Franco-Prussian war. See "Kératry (Auguste-Hilarion De)." *DBF,* and "Kératry (Émile-Hilarion)." *DBF.*

238.4   *Dr Gauthier*] Jean-François Gaultier ("Gautier, Gauthier, or Gaulthier"), a French medical doctor, took up the well-paid position of "king's physician" in Quebec in 1742. During the years he spent in the city, he was also "the regular physician of the Hôtel-Dieu and the seminary of Quebec." The "foremost naturalist in Canada," Gaultier acted as Pehr (Peter) Kalm's "guide" during his visit to the colony in 1749. To recognize these services "Kalm dedicated to him the genus *Gaultheria,* ... wintergreen." Aged forty in 1748, Gaultier married in 1752. See "Gaultier ..., Jean-François." *DCB.* Vol. 3, pp. 675–81.

238.31   Augur, medicus, magus, omnia novit] Compare Decimus Junius Juvenal, *Satire III*, l. 77. The poet, criticizing those Romans who imitate Greeks, says that they play "any character you please," including "augur ... medicus magus: omnia novit," that is, "augur, doctor or astrologer:— / 'All sciences.'" See *Juvenal And Persius.* Trans. G. G. Ramsay. London: William Heinemann, and Cambridge: Harvard University Press, 1965, pp. 36–37.

239.3–5   *the merry school of the* medicins tant mieux, *whom La Fontaine immortalizes in his ... fable*] Compare Jean de La Fontaine, *Fables Choisies,* 1668, Book 5, Fable 12, "Les Médecins." In this fable Tant-pis and Tant-mieux, both medical doctors, visited a sick man. Tant-pis predicted his death, while Tant-mieux, the optimist of the two, hoped that the patient would recover. When, after following the instructions of Tant-pis, he died, the former was triumphant because he had foreseen the sick man's end. Tant-mieux was also satisfied, however, because he could say that, had his instructions been obeyed, the dead man would be "plein de vie." See *Fables De La Fontaine Illustrées ... Nouvelle Édition.* Tours: Ad Mame Et Cie, Imprimeurs-Libraires, 1851, p. 157. Kirby owned a copy of this printing of La Fontaine's work.

239.22   Lenis Lucina] That is, gentle Lucina, the goddess identified with both birth and light. Horace's "Carmen Saeculare" ("Hymn For A New Age") (17 B.C.), ll. 13–16, for example, reads:

> rite maturos aperire partus
> lenis, Ilithyia, tuere matres,
> sive tu Lucina probas vocari

seu Genitalis,

or "You whose gentle function it is to open the way for births in due season, protect our mothers, o Ilithyia, or Lucina if you prefer that name, or Genitalis." See *Odes And Epodes*, pp. 262–63.

240.25   *the sack of Saratoga*] According to Andrew Bell's translation of the third edition of François-Xavier Garneau's *Histoire Du Canada* (1859), a copy of which Kirby owned, for "three years" beginning in "the autumn of 1745," French forces made "twenty-seven successive raids" on "the frontiers of the British plantations" in North America "from Boston to Albany." On one of these, usually dated as having occurred in November 1845, they attacked Fort Saratoga (Schuylerville, New York). "Saratoga was taken, and its people massacred." See Bell. Vol. 2, p. 107.

242.29–30 *The Philosophers who essayed the extraction of sun beams out of cucumbers*] Compare Jonathan Swift, *Gulliver's Travels*, 1726, Part III, Chapter 5. Captain Lemuel Gulliver, visiting the metropolis of Lagado, was taken on a tour of "*the grand Academy of Lagado*." There he met a "Projector" who "had been Eight Years upon a Project for extracting Sun-Beams out of Cucumbers, which were to be put into Vials hermetically sealed, and let out to warm the Air in raw inclement Summers." In "Eight Years more" he was certain "that he should be able to supply the Governors Gardens with Sun-shine at a reasonable Rate." In a notebook Kirby recorded this passage as "The philosophers of the academy of Lagado, extracted sun beams from cucumbers." See OTAR, Kirby, F–1076, Miscellaneous Manuscripts, MU1646, D–19, Twenty-four small note-books filled with miscellaneous notations by Kirby, n. pag., and Jonathan Swift. *Gulliver's Travels 1726*. Ed. Herbert Davis. Oxford: Basil Blackwell, 1965, p. 179.

243.32–37 *the well known ditty in praise of the great pie of Rouen "C'est dans la ville de Rouen ... un homme dedans!—"*] That is, "C'est Dans La Ville De Rouen." Kirby reproduced the first two lines of each of the first two stanzas of the version of this song in Ernest Gagnon's *Chansons Populaires Du Canada* (1865), a copy of which he owned. See *Chansons*, p. 119.

245.4   *the Cent Suisses*] The "Hundred Swiss," mercenary soldiers who often came from the ranks of "the despised peasants of tiny

Switzerland," acted as the French king's "personal guard" in the eighteenth century. Kirby, citing Mouffle d'Angerville's *Vie Privée De Louis XV* (1781), recorded in a notebook that "Les cent Suisses etaient de grands mangeurs." See J. Christopher Herold. *The Swiss Without Halos.* New York: Columbia University Press, 1948, pp. 52 and 55, and OTAR, Kirby, F–1076, Miscellaneous Manuscripts, MU1646, D–18, Note-book kept by Kirby containing ... excerpts from various historical publications relating to the history of New France, p. [6].

245.18–19 *roomy enough . . . for the court of King Pepin*] Compare the nursery rhyme, well known in the nineteenth century:

> Little King Pippin he built a fine hall,
> Pie-crust and pastry-crust that was the wall;
> The windows were made of black pudding and white,
> And slated with pancakes, you ne'er saw the like.

Pippin (Pepin) is most likely named after Pepin, "dit *le Bref*," the first Carolingian king of the Franks, who died in 768. See "Pepin, dit *le Bref*." *BU,* and *The Oxford Dictionary Of Nursery Rhymes.* Ed. Iona and Peter Opie. Oxford: At The Clarendon Press, 1966, p. 352.

245.32 *Hogarth*] William Hogarth, the "English painter and engraver," was known for his comic depiction of the people and places of eighteenth-century London. See "Hogarth, William." *Grove's.* Vol. 14, pp. 636–43.

246.12 'Dominus vobiscum'] That is, "The Lord be with you." An "ancient form of devout salutation," this clause is used at various places in the liturgy of the Roman Catholic church. See "Dominus Vobiscum." *Catholic.* Vol. 5. 1909, p. 114.

247.2 *"SIC ITUR AD ASTRA"*] Virgil, *Aeneid,* Book IX, l. 641. When Ascanius (Iulus), the son of Aeneas, killed an enemy for the first time, Apollo blessed him with the words, "sic itur ad astra," or "So man scales the stars." See Virgil. *Aeneid VII–XII Appendix Vergiliana.* Trans. H. Rushton Fairclough. Rev. G. P. Goold. Cambridge and London: Harvard University Press, 2000, pp. 158–59.

247.29–30 *The Gods are merry sometimes, says Homer, and their laughter shakes*

Olympus] Compare, for example, Homer, *The Iliad,* Book One, ll. 739–40. After Vulcan had soothed his mother Juno's wrath at her husband Jove, "Heaven rang with laughter inextinguishable / Peal after peal." See *The Works Of William Cowper.* Vol. 11: *The Iliad Of Homer. Translated Into English Blank Verse . . . Vol. I.* London: Baldwin And Cradock, 1837, p. 27. Kirby owned a copy of Cowper's *Homer.*

249.14 Scriptum est] That is, It is written. A clause from the Latin Bible, probably its best-known use is Luke 4:4. Jesus, tempted by the devil to turn stone into bread, replied, "It is written, That man shall not live by bread alone, but by every word of God." See *IB.* Vol. 8.1952, p. 85.

250.5 *the Psalms of David*] The "one hundred and fifty religious poems" of the Psalter were frequently recited or sung in the liturgy of the Roman Catholic church. See *IB.* Vol. 4. 1955, p. 3.

250.13–20 *the royal anthem, composed by Lulli in honour of Louis Quatorze, upon . . . his visit to the famous convent of St Cyr . . . with Madame de Maintenon. The song composed by Madame Brinon . . . translated into English . . . became . . . the national hymn of the English nation*] There are various accounts of the origin of "God Save the King (Queen)," the British national anthem. One of them, the so-called "St. Cyr legend," has as its most prominent source *Souvenirs De La Marquise De Créquy De 1710 A 1803* (1834). Attributed to Renée-Caroline-Victoire de Froullay, who became la marquise de Créquy when she married "Louis-Marie, marquis de Créquy," and who in her widowhood kept a salon in Paris in the mid eighteenth century, its author was actually "Maurice Cousin, qui cachait une modeste origine sous le nom de comte de Courchamps." In *Souvenirs* the narrator recalled a scene at the convent-school in St. Cyr when the young noblewomen who were students there greeted Louis XIV and Madame de Maintenon by singing in unison "une sorte de motet, ou plutôt de cantique national et glorieux, dont les paroles étaient de Mme de Brinon et la musique du fameux Lully." Marie de Brinon was the first principal of the school, which had been founded in 1686 by the King at the urging of Madame de Maintenon. Kirby probably took this anecdote directly or indirectly from Cousin's work, which was widely published in French and translated into English in the nineteenth century. In a notebook Kirby entered, "'Grand Dieu Sauvez le Roi'—Music par Lulli—chante par les elèves de St Cyr—Lorsque le roi rendait visite avec Mme de Maintenon. Les paroles par Mme Brinon." See Maurice Cousin. *Souvenirs De La Marquise De Créquy De 1710 A 1803.* New Edition. Paris: Garnier Frères, [1855]. Vol. 1, p. 130; "Créquy (Renée-Caroline-Victoire De Froullay, épouse de Louis-Marie De)." *DBF*; OTAR, Kirby, F–1076, Miscellaneous Manuscripts, MU1646, D–18, Note-book kept by Kirby containing ... excerpts from various historical publications relating to the history of New France, p. [30]; and Percy A. Scholes. *God Save the Queen! The History And Romance Of The World's First National Anthem.* London, New York, and Toronto: Oxford University Press, 1954, p. 293.

250.28–34 *Grand Dieu ... soumis!*—] Compare the same lines in the version of "God Save the King (Queen)" in *Souvenirs De La Marquise De Créquy De 1710 A 1803* (1834):

> Grand Dieu, sauvez le Roi!
> Grand Dieu, vengez le Roi!
>   Vive le Roi!
> Qu'à jamais glorieux,
> Louis victorieux
> Voye ses ennemis
> Toujours soumis!

See Maurice Cousin. *Souvenirs De La Marquise De Créquy De 1710 A 1803.* New Edition. Paris: Garnier Frères, [1855]. Vol. 1, pp. 130–31.

252.1–3 *Horace ...* 'Teretesque suras laudo, et integer ego!'] Compare Horace, *Odes*, Book II, Ode 4, ll. 21–22, in which the poet advised Phocian Xanthias not to "be ashamed ... of loving a servant." He added that he himself admired "her ... shapely legs—though quite disinterested, of course" ("teretesque suras / integer laudo"). See *Odes And Epodes*, pp. 103–05.

252.23–24 *plain as the way between Peronne and St Quintin! A good honest way as ever was trod by shoe leather*] Compare Thomas Urquhart's translation of François Rabelais' *Gargantua and Pantagruel*, Book Five (1564), Chapter 26, in which the voyagers "*came to the Island of Odes, where the ways go up and down.*" One of the ways they see is "the old way between Peronne and St. Quentin, which seemed ... a very good, honest, plain way, as smooth as a carpet, and as good as ever was trod upon by shoe of leather." Kirby most probably modelled his passage on that in his copy of the 1849 Bohn edition of Urquhart's work. See *Rabelais.* Vol. 2, p. 481.

252.30–32   *the ... pearl ... for which the merchant ... sold all that he had and bought it*] Compare Matthew 13:45–46. Jesus, explaining the parables to his disciples, said:

> Again, the kingdom of heaven is like unto a merchantman, seeking goodly pearls:
> Who, when he had found one pearl of great price, went and sold all that he had, and bought it.

See *IB.* Vol. 7. 1951, p. 420.

252.35   *Brimborion*] Compare Thomas Urquhart's translation of François Rabelais' *Gargantua and Pantagruel,* Book One (1532), Chapter 21, in which Gargantua's life in Paris is described. Among his activities "he went to church" every morning, where he "mumbled" nonsensical "breborions," or litanies. Kirby probably adopted this usage of brimborion (breborion) from his copy of the 1849 Bohn edition of Urquhart's work. See *Rabelais.* Vol. 1, p. 170.

256.1–2   *"Carrying ... Gods."*] William Wordsworth, *The Excursion,* 1814, Book IV, ll. 697–700. The Wanderer, describing "Chaldean Shepherds," recounted that they

> Watched, from the centre of their sleeping flocks,
> Those radiant Mercuries, that seemed to move
> Carrying through Ether, in perpetual round,
> Decrees and resolutions of the Gods.

See William Wordsworth. *The Excursion.* Ed. Sally Bushell, James A. Butler, and Michael C. Jaye. Ithaca and London: Cornell University Press, 2007, p. 150.

257.3   pars fortunae] That is, part of fortune. An astrological concept, "it signifies the physical health and material wellbeing of the body, as well as the potential for growth of the soul." See "Astrology on the Web." 15 March 2005, http://www.

astrologycom.com/parts.html.

257.10   decretum est] That is, it is decreed. A clause from "Roman law," it carried the connotation of an unalterable decision. See David M. Walker. "Decree." *The Oxford Companion To Law.* Oxford: Clarendon Press, 1980, p. 343.

258.13–14   *"far reaching concords"*] Ralph Waldo Emerson, "Musketaquid," 1847, l. 63. The poet, "content with these poor fields," recalls how "The gentle deities / Showed" him "Far-reaching concords of astronomy / Felt in the plants and in the punctual birds." See Ralph Waldo Emerson. *Poems.* Boston and New York: Houghton, Mifflin, 1904, pp. 141–44.

259.36–37   *Herodias ... the Baptists head in a charger ... Herod*] Compare Matthew 14:3–11. On his birthday Herod, who had imprisoned John the Baptist, offered to give "the daughter of Herodias," who had pleased him by dancing before him, whatever "she would ask," and "she, being before instructed of her mother, said, Give me here John Baptist's head in a charger." Although "the king was sorry," he, nevertheless, commanded that John be beheaded. "And his head was brought in a charger, and given to the damsel: and she brought *it* to her mother." See *IB.* Vol. 7. 1951, pp. 427–28.

261.6–7   *the dew round Gideon's fleece, refreshing all the earth ... but leaving the fleece dry*] Compare Judges 6:39–40. Gideon, demanding proof that God had chosen him to save Israel from the Midianites, asked the Lord to send him a sign by means of "a fleece of wool":

> let it now be dry only upon the fleece, and upon all the ground let there be dew.
>
> And God did so that night: for it was dry upon the fleece only, and there was dew on all the ground.

See *IB.* Vol. 2. 1953, p. 737.

261.9   *false as Cressid*] Compare William Shakespeare, *Troilus and Cressida,* V.ii.178. Troilus, after witnessing Cressida's unfaithfulness to him with Diomedes, exclaimed, "O Cressid! O false Cressid! false, false, false!" See *Shakespeare,* p. 486.

264.2   *"SO GLOZED THE TEMPTER"*] John Milton, *Paradise Lost,* 1667, Book IX, l. 548. Satan, in the form of a serpent, having found Eve alone in the garden of Eden, flattered her with comments on her "celestial beauty." "So glozed the Tempter" as he prepared to entice Eve to eat of the tree of "knowledge of good and evil." See John Milton. *Paradise Lost. A Poem.* Boston: Published At The Water Street Bookstore, 1833, pp. 203–04 and 207. Kirby owned a copy of this printing.

266.29–31 Coutume d'Orleans *Tit. 17, the absent lose the usufruct of their rights,* vide *also* Pothier, Des successions] Robert-Joseph Pothier dealt with the rights of succession when "une personne est absente" in "Titre XVII. *Des Droits de Successions,*" Item 37, in *Coutumes D'Orléans* (1760). In Chapter 3, Section 1, Number 1, of "Traité Des Successions" (1778), he also discussed these rights when no news had been heard of an inheritor for "un temps assez considérable." Kirby most likely took this information from his copy of *Code Civil Du Bas-Canada* (1866), in which Chapter 2, Item 93, discussed the rights of other beneficiaries of a will to take provisional possession of the legacy of a person whose whereabouts had been unknown "depuis [cinq] ans." This item referred to "Pothier, *Intr. à la Cout. d'Orl.,* tit. 17, No. 37. *Id., Des Successions,* c. 3, s. 1, § 1." See *Code Civil Du Bas-Canada.* Ed. Joseph-Edouard Lefebvre de Bellefeuille. Montréal: Beauchemin & Valois, 1866, p. 24; Robert-Joseph Pothier. *Coutumes Des Duché, Bailliage Et Prévôté D'Orléans. Nouvelle Édition.* Paris: Chez Debure, and Orléans: Chez la Veuve Rouzeau-Montaut, 1780, pp. 575 and 585; and Robert-Joseph Pothier. *Œuvres Posthumes De M. Pothier.* Vol. 2. Paris: Chez De Bure, 1778, p. 123.

267.24–25 *Pigean Tit. 2.27* Le tuteur est comptable de sa gestion] Compare the section on "Du Compte De La Tutelle" in *Code Civil Du Bas-Canada* (1866), in which Item 308 states, "Le tuteur est comptable de sa gestion lorsqu'elle finit," and cites "2 Pigeau, 27." Eustache-Nicolas Pigeau described the "*Compte de tutelle*" in *La Procédure Civile Du Châtelet De Paris* (1779). Kirby obviously followed his copy of *Code Civil Du Bas-Canada* for his discussion of the responsibility of a guardian to account for the management of a ward's estate when the latter's majority is attained. See *Code Civil Du Bas-Canada.* Ed. Joseph-Edouard Lefebvre de Bellefeuille. Montréal: Beauchemin & Valois, 1866,

p. 67, and Eustache-Nicolas Pigeau. *La Procédure Civile Du Châtelet De Paris, Et De Toutes Les Jurisdictions Ordinaires Du Royaume.* Paris: Chez la Veuve Desaint, 1779. Vol. 2, p. 27.

267.31   Inepte loquens] That is, inept or foolish speech.

269.23–25   *the pretty Grisette who directed Laurence Sterne to the Opera Comique*] Compare Laurence Sterne, *A Sentimental Journey Through France And Italy By Mr. Yorick,* 1768, in which Yorick, visiting Paris, asked a seamstress, whom he described as "the handsomest grisset" he had ever seen, which way to "turn to go to the Opera comique." See Laurence Sterne. *A Sentimental Journey through France and Italy And Continuation of the Bramine's Journal.* Ed. Melvyn New and W. G. Day. Gainesville: University Press of Florida, 2002, pp. 69–70.

275.2   *"SEALS OF LOVE, BUT SEALED IN VAIN"*] William Shakespeare, *Measure for Measure,* IV.i.6. Mariana, Angelo's betrothed, and a boy enter singing a song, the last two lines of which are, "But my kisses bring again, bring again, / Seals of love, but seal'd in vain, seal'd in vain." See *Shakespeare,* p. 572.

282.31–32   *she resolved to go out like the Rose of Sharon and seek her beloved in the city*] Compare The Songs of Songs, 3:2. The Rose of Sharon, having failed to find her lover in her bed, sings, "I will rise now, and go about the city in the streets, and in the broad ways I will seek him whom my soul loveth: I sought him, but I found him not." See *IB.* Vol. 5. 1956, p. 118.

284.2   *"THE HURRIED QUESTION OF DESPAIR"*] George Gordon Byron, Lord Byron, "The Bride of Abydos. A Turkish Tale," 1813, Canto II, Stanza 27, l. 662. When Zuleika's death was made known to her father Giaffir, the narrator reports, "Hark — to the hurried question of Despair! / 'Where is my child?' — an Echo answers — 'Where?'" See Lord Byron. *The Complete Poetical Works.* Vol. 3. Ed. Jerome J. McGann. Oxford: At The Clarendon Press, 1981, p. 145.

286.33–34   *like Prince Hal, talk to every tinker in his own tongue*] Compare William Shakespeare, *1 Henry IV,* II.iii.17–20. Henry, Prince of Wales, tells his gentleman-in-waiting Edward Poins about his drinking adventures in Eastcheap, "To conclude, I am so good a proficient in one quarter of an hour, that I can drink with any tinker in his own language during my life." See *Shakespeare,*

p. 858.

287.38   Gloria Patri, Filioque] That is, "Glory to the Father and to the
Son." The opening words of the "*Gloria Patri*," or the "Lesser
Doxology," they are said "at the end of the Psalms and hymns
in the offices" of various Christian churches. See, for example,
"*Gloria.*" *A Dictionary of Biblical Tradition in English Literature.*
Ed. David Lyle Jeffrey. Grand Rapids, Michigan: William B.
Eerdmans, 1992, p. 310.

289.14–22   *the famous song . . . Vive Henri Quatre . . . un vert galant*] Kirby's
rendering of the first stanza of this song celebrating Henri IV
replaced the more usual "ce roi" with "le Roi" in the line, "Vive
ce roi vaillant!" See, for example, J. B. Weckerlin. *La Chanson
Populaire.* Paris: Firmin-Didot, 1886, p. 37.

289.36   *Schalken and Teniers*] Godfried Schalcken (1643–1706), a "Dutch
painter and etcher," was known for his paintings of candle-lit
scenes. David Teniers II, also named David Teniers the Younger
(1610–90), a native of Antwerp, achieved recognition as a
painter "of peasant scenes" that were often set "in a smoky,
half-darkened interior." The Wallace Collection in London, for
example, owns a Schalcken entitled "Girl Threading a Needle
by Candlelight" and one Teniers called "Boors Carousing" and
another called "Gambling Scene at an Inn." See "Schalcken,
Godfried." Grove's. Vol. 28, pp. 49–50; "Teniers." Grove's.
Vol. 30, pp. 460–64; and "The Wallace Collection." 25 April 2005,
http://www.wallacecollection.org.

291.5   *the old ballad of the* Pont d'Avignon] There are many versions
of "Sur Le Pont D'Avignon," including the famous "ronde
enfantine," which begins, "Sur le pont d'Avignon, / On y danse,
on y danse." Kirby, however, was most likely referring to the
version of the song in Ernest Gagnon's *Chansons Populaires Du
Canada* (1865), a copy of which he owned. Its opening stanza
reads:

> Sur le pont d'Avignon,
> Sur le pont d'Avignon,
> Trois dames s'y promènent,
>   Ma dondaine,
> Trois dames s'y promènent,

Ma dondé.

See Henri Davenson. *Le Livre Des Chansons Ou Introduction A La Connaissance De La Chanson Populaire Française.* Neuchâtel: Éditions De La Baconnière, 1946, p. 319, and *Chansons,* p. 94.

291.18–22 *the old ballad "A St Malo . . . les marchander!—"*] Compare Ernest Gagnon's version of "A Saint-Malo, Beau Port De Mer" in *Chansons Populaires Du Canada* (1865). Kirby reproduced the first line of each of the first four stanzas from the song in his copy of this volume. See *Chansons,* pp. 24–25.

292.36 *Colonel Trivio*] On 19 February 1759 Lieutenant-Colonel Trivio, who commanded a battalion of the "régiment de Berry," witnessed the marriage of the regiment's drum-major on the Ile d'Orléans. On 28 April 1760, still stationed in New France, he was slightly wounded at the battle that took place "devant Québec" at Ste. Foye. See Cyprien Tanguay. *A Travers Les Registres.* Montréal: Librairie Saint-Joseph, 1886, p. 168.

294.2 *"BETWIXT THE LAST VIOLET AND THE EARLIEST ROSE"*] Frances Anne (Fanny) Kemble, "Sonnet [To Harriet St. Leger]," 1866, l. 14. The narrator, recollecting "the happy time / When you and I held converse dear together," concludes, "And as I date it still, our love arose / 'Twixt the last violet and the earliest rose." See Frances Anne Kemble. *Poems.* London: Edward Moxon, 1866, p. 143.

298.6–7 *contrasts of light and shade, to which the pencil of Rembrandt alone could have done justice*] Rembrandt van Rijn, the celebrated seventeenth-century "Dutch painter, draughtsman and etcher," was known for the "dramatic lighting" in his paintings and the "powerful chiaroscuro effects" that he achieved in his drawings and etchings. See "Rembrandt (Harmensz.) van Rijn." Grove's. Vol. 26, pp. 152–79.

299.29–34 *Wolfe . . . recited Gray's Elegy with its prophetic line . . . that . . . autumnal night*] There is a tradition, frequently repeated, that James Wolfe, "commander of the British expedition that took Quebec in 1759," recited "in a low voice to the officers by his side 'Gray's Elegy in a Country Church-yard'" as they "dropt down" the St. Lawrence River on the night of 12–13 September 1759 on their way to the Battle of the Plains of Abraham the next morning. The line quoted by Kirby, line 36 of Thomas Gray's "Elegy Written in a Country Church Yard" (1751), is the fourth line of the ninth stanza:

The boast of heraldry, the pomp of pow'r,
And all that beauty, all that wealth e'er gave,
Awaits alike th'inevitable hour.
The paths of glory lead but to the grave.

See "Wolfe, James." *DCB.* Vol. 3, pp. 666–74; Thomas Gray. *The Complete Poems Of Thomas Gray.* Ed. H. W. Starr and J. R. Hendrickson. Oxford: At The Clarendon Press, 1966, p. 38; and George Warburton. *The Conquest Of Canada.* London: Richard Bentley, 1849. Vol. 2, pp. 333–34.

300.13–16 *the third beatitude ... 'meek would inherit the earth,'*] Compare Matthew 5:5. Jesus, teaching his disciples, gives them the "*Third Beatitude,*" "Blessed *are* the meek: for they shall inherit the earth." See *IB.* Vol. 7. 1951, p. 282.

303.21–22 La complainte de Cadieux] In *Chansons Populaires Du Canada* (1865), Ernest Gagnon recounted the story of Cadieux and provided the words and music of his "*complainte.*" Kirby probably summarized the section on "Petit Rocher De La Haute Montagne" from his copy of Gagnon's work; in *Le Chien d'or* Amelie sings the first stanza and the penultimate ninth stanza of this "*chant de mort.*" See *Chansons,* pp. 199–207.

306.3–10 *V'là l' bon vent! ... Ma mie m'attend!*] Kirby most likely took this version of "V'Là L'Bon Vent" from his copy of Ernest Gagnon's *Chansons Populaires Du Canada* (1865). Gagnon described this chorus, sung by lumbermen on the Ottawa River, as a "composition canadienne." See *Chansons,* p. 21.

307.33–35 *the Commission ... to ... Jacques Cartier, "for ... his revered name"*] Compare the "*Commission for his Third Voyage*" given to Jacques Cartier on "17 October 1540" by Francis I, "Roy de France," that instructs the explorer to carry out the King's intention "à faire chose aggréable à Dieu nostre createur et redempteur et qui soict à l'augmentacion de son sainct et sacré nom." See *A Collection Of Documents Relating To Jacques Cartier And The Sieur De Roberval.* Ed. H. P. Biggar. Ottawa: Public Archives Of Canada, 1930, pp. 128–29.

309.11–12 *the famous old ballad, of the King's son*] Compare "En Roulant Ma Boule" in Ernest Gagnon's *Chansons Populaires Du Canada* (1865). Kirby, using his copy of Gagnon, repeated the latter's version of "Le fils du roi," except that he replaced "En roulant ma boule roulant" with an equally well-known French-Canadian chorus, "Fringue, fringue sur la rivière, / Fringue, fringue, sur l'aviron." See *Chansons*, pp. 12–15.

312.9–11 *Sir William Phips . . . his army of New Englanders, the . . . defeat under the walls of Quebec*] William Phips, a native of "what is now the state of Maine," who had been knighted by James II of England for retrieving "over £207,600" from "a sunken treasure-ship" in 1687, arrived at Quebec "with about 32 ships . . . and somewhat more than 2,000 Massachusetts militiamen" in mid October 1690. Although there were several skirmishes between "the New Englanders" and "the French," Phips, having failed in his attempt to capture the city, sailed for Boston in the last week of the month. See "Phips, Sir William." *DCB*. Vol. 1, pp. 544–46.

312.21–23 *his red flag . . . hangs over the high altar of the church of Notre Dame des Victoires*] According to Andrew Bell's translation of the third edition of François-Xavier Garneau's *Histoire Du Canada* (1859), on 16 October 1690 a shot from the "batteries of the lower town" of Quebec "brought down the flag of Phipps' own vessel." This flag, fished out of the St. Lawrence by the French, was later hung, not in the church of Notre Dame des Victoires, but in the Roman Catholic cathedral of Notre Dame du Québec, where "it remained till that edifice was consumed, during the siege of 1759." Kirby, who probably took this story from his copy of Bell, may have deliberately changed the location of the flag to Notre Dame des Victoires because one of the victories commemorated in its name was that of the French over William Phips. See Bell. Vol. 1, pp. 355–56.

315.36–37 *Charles Le Gardeur de Tilly*] Charles Legardeur de Tilly, a native of Thury-Harcourt, Normandy, immigrated to Quebec "in 1636," where he "became a person of importance and influence." In "1652, with other associates, he received the Cap-des-Rosiers seigneury" in the Gaspé region of the colony. He died poor, however, in Quebec in 1695, five years before his son Pierre-Noël Legardeur de Tilly bought the seigneury of Villieu that was renamed Tilly. See "Legardeur De Tilly, Charles." *DCB*. Vol. 1, pp. 447–48.

315.38– *the Sire de Tilly ... Hastings*] "Raoul de Tilly," from "near Caen,"
316.1 Normandy, is listed on the "Battle Abbey Rolls" as one of the "companions who supposedly accompanied William," Duke of Normandy (William the Conqueror, William I of England), at the Battle of Hastings in 1066. Battle Abbey, where the original roll, no longer extant, was reputedly kept, was founded by William "on the field of Hastings as an act of contrition and as a memorial to the dead." See "The Battle Abbey Roll Timekeeper." 3 May 2005, http://members.tripod.com/ ~midgley/battleroll.html, and David Bates. "William I [*known as* William the Conqueror] (1027/8–1087)." *ODNB* [http://www.oxforddnb.com/view/article/29448, accessed 3 May 2005].

316.4–14 *"to hold in Fief and Seigneury," ... Such was the style of the Royal grants of Seignioral rights conceded in New France*] Compare, for example, the original title-deed to the seigneury of Tilly granted by "Sa Majesté" Louis XIV in 1672 to "le sieur de Villieu." It stated, among other clauses, that he was to enjoy his land "en fief et seigneurie ... à la charge de la foy et hommage" that he was to render "au chateau St.-Louis de Quebec." The land was to be governed according to "la Coutume de Paris." See "*Titres du Fief de Tilly*." *Pièces Et Documents Relatifs A La Tenure Seigneuriale.* Quebec: Imprimerie De E. R. Fréchette, 1852, p. 128.

318.21–22 *the day of St Philip ... superseded by the festival of St John the Baptist*] The first of May was traditionally associated in the Roman Catholic church with the feast of Philip "the Apostle"; the twenty-fourth of June, with that of St. John the Baptist. The celebration of "Saint-Jean-Baptiste" in Quebec, at first "primarily religious" although with nationalist overtones, began in earnest in the 1840s. See "Philip, Saint, Apostle." *Catholic*. Vol. 11. 1911, p. 799, and "Fête nationale du Québec." 4 May 2005, http://en.wikipedia.org.

323.2–3 *"CHEERFUL YESTERDAYS AND CONFIDENT TO-MORROWS"*] William Wordsworth, *The Excursion*, 1814, Book VII, ll. 573–75. The "Solitary," seeing "a Peasant of the lowest class," described him as "A Man ... of cheerful yesterdays / And confident to-morrows." See William Wordsworth. *The Excursion*. Ed. Sally

Bushell, James A. Butler, and Michael C. Jaye. Ithaca and London: Cornell University Press, 2007, p. 244.

323.6   *La Lande*] An old Norman family, La Landes had been in New France since the seventeenth century. A "Mlle. . . . de La Lande," for example, was a student at the Ursuline Convent in Quebec before it burned in 1686. "*Marie-Anne*" Lalande, the daughter of Léonard Lalande of Lachine, married Jean-Baptiste Le Gardeur De Repentigny in 1732. See Cyprien Tanguay. *Dictionnaire Généalogique Des Familles Canadiennes.* Vol. 5. Montréal: Eusèbe Senécal, 1888, p. 98, and *Ursulines.* Vol. 1. 1863, p. 326.

324.1   *The Hare had many friends but none at last*] Compare John Gay, "Fable L.: *The* Hare *and many* Friends," 1727. Illustrating the moral, "who depend / On many, rarely find a friend," the fable recounts the story of a "Hare" whose "care was, never to offend, / And ev'ry creature was her friend." Chased by the hunter's hounds, however, she is refused help by "the horse," "the stately bull," "the goat," the "sheep," and "the trotting calf," who, the last to leave her, bids her "Adieu. / For see the hounds are just in view." See John Gay. *Poetry And Prose.* Ed. Vinton A. Dearing and Charles E. Beckwith. Oxford: At The Clarendon Press, 1974. Vol. 2, pp. 368–70.

324.22   "Agimus Gratias"] That is, "we give thanks." Compare the "Grace after meals" that begins "Àgimus tíbi grátias, omnípotens Déus" ("We give you thanks, almighty God"). See "Agimus tibi gratias." 9 May 2005, www.IPASource.com.

331.2–4   *pictures . . . the wall of the Convent Chapel . . . the annunciation . . . the . . . Baptist, proclaiming the way of the Lord*] On 22 April 1869, when she was a student at the Ursuline Convent in Quebec, Josephine Lowe sent Kirby a list of the "Paintings In the Church of the Ursuline Convent," which included her notation of "The Annunciation, sculpture on the two doors near the altar." According to Luke 1, "the angel Gabriel" announced to Mary that she should "conceive . . . and bring forth a son, and . . . call his name JESUS." John the Baptist, the son of Mary's cousin Elisabeth, was to "go before the face of the Lord to prepare his ways." See *IB.* Vol. 8. 1952, pp. 26–48, and OTAR, Kirby, F–1076, The Josephine Lowe Correspondence, MU1638, A–17, ALS, Josephine Lowe to Kirby, 22 April 1869.

334.5   *Heloise de Lotbiniere*] Heloise de Lotbiniere does not appear to
be an historical figure. Louis-Théandre Chartier de Lotbinière,
sometimes dubbed "the 'father of the Canadian magistrature'"
because of his role in the early judicial systems of New France,
however, emigrated "to Canada" in 1651. A member of a noble
French family of "ancient lineage," his descendants, including
several girls educated at the Ursuline Convent in Quebec, played
key roles in the colony for several generations. The seigneury
of Lotbinière, which had been granted to René-Louis Chartier
de Lotbinière, Louis-Théandre's son, in 1672, was located not
far from the seigneury of Tilly on the south shore of the St.
Lawrence River. See "Chartier De Lotbinière, Louis-Théandre."
DCB. Vol. 1, pp. 201–03.

340.4   *Abelard*] Pierre Abélard, a French "philosophe et théologien"
who was "a key figure" in "what is generally called the
Twelfth-Century Renaissance," had a passionate love affair with
Héloïse, "a young girl" who was the niece of "one of the canons"
of Notre Dame Cathedral in Paris. Their relationship, which
included a son, a secret marriage, Abélard's castration, and
Héloïse's becoming a nun, was chronicled in Abélard's "*Historia
calamitatum*: Abelard to a Friend: The Story of His Misfortunes,"
written about 1132, and in a series of letters that he and Héloïse
exchanged when she was "abbesse du Paraclet" in Quincey,
France, in the 1130s. See "Abélard, Pierre." *DBF*; "Héloïse."
DBF; and Betty Radice, trans. *The Letters of Abelard and Heloise*.
Harmondsworth, Middlesex: Penguin Books, 1974, pp. 9 and
66.

340.8   *the charm of the three caskets with the three names*] Compare
William Shakespeare, *The Merchant of Venice*, I.ii.27–33. Nerissa,
Portia's "*waiting-woman*," justifies Portia's late father's will and
its strictures on her choice of a husband, "Your father was ever
virtuous, and holy men at their death have good inspirations;
therefore the lott'ry that he hath devis'd in these three chests of
gold, silver, and lead, whereof who chooses his meaning chooses
you, will no doubt never be chosen by any rightly but one who
you shall rightly love." In the play the Prince of Morocco, the
Prince of Arragon, and Bassanio, whom Portia loves and who
chooses correctly, are the three suitors who try the test. See

Shakespeare, pp. 256–57.

340.9–10   *watched ... her destined lover pass by*] There are various superstitions and traditions associated with the festival of St. John the Baptist on 24 June. That of seeing one's future husband in a church porch is more usually connected to Halloween, however. In the county of Yorkshire, England, for example, it was believed that "Should you want to know who will be married during the year, repair to the church porch ... on All Hallows' Eve and at midnight, and the votaries of Hymen will come trooping into the church." See A. R. Wright. *British Calendar Customs: England*. Vol. 3: *Fixed Festivals June-December, Inclusive*. Ed. T. E. Lones. London: William Glaisher, and Glasgow: John Wylie, 1940, p. 117.

343.13   *Master Coté*] In the first half of the eighteenth century there was a large family named Coté in "St-Antoine-Tilly." See Cyprien Tanguay. *Dictionnaire Généalogique Des Familles Canadiennes*. Vol. 3. Montréal: Eusèbe Senécal, 1887, p. 142.

344.14   *the day of Palms 1748*] That is, Palm Sunday, 7 April 1748, according to "the Gregorian calendar ('New Style')" in use in France and her colonies in the 1740s. See "The Calendar." *The Oxford Companion To English Literature*. Ed. Margaret Drabble. Oxford: Oxford University Press, 1985, pp. 1126–47.

345.32–34   *Time and tide ... lead to fortune*] Compare William Shakespeare, *Julius Caesar*, IV.iii.218–19. After the murder of Julius Caesar, Brutus, arguing that "There is a tide in the affairs of men, / Which taken at the flood, leads on to fortune," persuades Cassius to battle Mark Antony and Octavius Caesar at Philippi. See *Shakespeare*, p. 1127.

347.22   *Arion*] A "Greek lyric poet ... said to have been born at Methymna in Lesbos, but largely a figure of legend," Arion is supposed to have created "the dithyram." He is also "connected with the birth of tragedy." See "Arī'on." *The Oxford Companion To Classical Literature. Second Edition*. Ed. M. C. Howatson. Oxford and New York: Oxford University Press, 1989, p. 54.

347.25–29   *an old air ... "Nous irons ... dans l'isle!—"*] That is, "A Saint-Malo, Beau Port De Mer." In Ernest Gagnon's *Chansons Populaires Du Canada* (1865), from his copy of which Kirby is most likely quoting, the chorus reads, "Nous irons sur l'eau / Nous y prom' promener, / Nous irons jouer dans l'île." See *Chansons*, p. 24.

347.32–34 *like the three children in the fiery furnace, or the sacred bush that . . . was not consumed*] Compare Daniel 3:12–27 and Exodus 3:2. In the first, Nebuchadnezzar, the king of Babylon, "cast" Shadrach, Meshach, and Abednego, three young Jews whom he had "set over the affairs of the province of Babylon," into a "burning fiery furnace" heated "one seven times more than it was wont to be" when they refused to "worship the golden image" that he had erected; they emerged, however, unscathed from the fire. In the second, "the Angel of the LORD appeared unto" Moses "in a flame of fire out of the midst of a bush: and he looked, and, behold, the bush burned with fire, and the bush *was* not consumed." See *IB.* Vol. 6. 1956, pp. 399–404, and *IB.* Vol. 1. 1952, p. 871.

347.37 *A languor like that of the Lotus eaters*] Compare Alfred Tennyson, "The Lotus-Eaters," 1832, ll. 5–6, in which the Greek mariners, returning from their victory at Troy, "came unto a land" where "All round the coast the languid air did swoon, / Breathing like one that hath a weary dream." Kirby's copy of Tennyson's poems seems to have been one from an issue of the edition published by Ticknor and Fields in 1867. See *The Poetical Works Of Alfred Tennyson, Poet Laureate. Complete Edition.* Boston: Ticknor And Fields, 1867, p. 39.

349.2 *"FELICES TER ET AMPLIUS"*] Horace, *Odes*, Book I, Ode 13, l. 17. The first-person narrator, addressing Lydia, states, "Thrice blest and more than thrice" ("felices ter et amplius") are "those who are held fast by an unbreakable bond." See *Odes And Epodes*, pp. 50–51.

349.14 *the . . . tale of Paulo and Francesca da Rimini*] Compare Dante Alighieri, *The Divine Comedy: Inferno*, Canto 5, ll. 73–142. Dante, led by the poet Virgil, descends to the second circle of the Inferno where he sees several "carnal sinners," including Paolo Malatesta and Francesca da Rimini, who recounts the tale of their doomed love. "According to the accepted story," which is supposed to have occurred in thirteenth-century Italy, "Francesca, betrothed to Gianciotto for political reasons, fell in love with his younger brother Paolo, . . . and shortly after the marriage was surprised with him" by her husband, "who immediately killed them both." Kirby owned a copy of the edition of *La Divina Commedia* published by Truchy in Paris in 1841. See Dante Alighieri. *The Divine Comedy. Inferno.* Trans. Charles S. Singleton. *1: Italian Text and Translation.* Second Printing with Corrections. Princeton: Princeton University Press, 1977, pp. 46–57, and Dante Alighieri. *The Divine Comedy. Inferno.* Trans. Charles S. Singleton. *2. Commentary.* Princeton: Princeton University Press, 1970, p. 84.

349.27– 350.3　Amor ... *"Love ... more!"*] Dante Alighieri, *The Divine Comedy: Inferno*, Canto 5, ll. 100, 103, and 135. The second of these lines, which are all part of Francesca's account of her love for Paolo, reads in most versions, "Amor, ch'a nullo amato amar perdona." Kirby probably translated these lines from his copy of the 1841 Paris edition of *La Divina Commedia.* See Dante Alighieri. *The Divine Comedy. Inferno.* Trans. Charles S. Singleton. *1: Italian Text and Translation.* Second Printing with Corrections. Princeton: Princeton University Press, 1977, pp. 52–55.

356.29–30　'Amor ... *one death*'] Dante Alighieri, *The Divine Comedy: Inferno*, Canto 5, l. 106. Kirby probably translated this line, in which Francesca describes the fatal consequences of her love for Paolo, from his copy of the 1841 Paris edition of *La Divina Commedia.* See Dante Alighieri. *The Divine Comedy. Inferno.* Trans. Charles S. Singleton. *1: Italian Text and Translation.* Second Printing with Corrections. Princeton: Princeton University Press, 1977, pp. 52–53.

358.2　"*NO ... TURN*"] Algernon Charles Swinburne, *The Queen-Mother*, 1860, II.i. Catherine De Medici chides her son Charles IX of France for questioning her decision to instigate a massacre of Protestants on 24 August 1572, the festival of St. Bartholomew, "Nay, there's no speech of silk will serve your turn, / You must be whole with me or break." See Algernon Charles Swinburne. *The Queen-Mother And Rosamond.* London: Edward Moxon, 1860, p. 49.

361.11–13　*the Sieur de Penissault who married ... a wife ... sold to the Chevalier de Levis*] In 1753 Louis Pennisseaut married Marie-Marguerite Lemoine, *dit* Monière, the daughter of Alexis Lemoine, *dit* Monière, a Montreal merchant. Beautiful and charming, she became "the mistress" of François de Lévis, the French "army officer" who was the "second in command" and then the commander of the French "army in Canada" from 1756 to 1760. According to Louis-Léonard Aumasson de Courville's memoir of events in Canada from 1749 to 1760, this "fort jolie femme" had previously been the mistress of Michel-Jean-Hugues Péan, the husband of Angélique Renaud d'Avène Des Méloizes. Madame Pennisseaut won "the Duc de Choiseul's favour" after she and her husband went to live in France in 1760. See Louis-Léonard Aumasson de Courville. *Mémoires Sur Le Canada, Depuis 1749 Jusqu'à 1760.* Québec: T. Cary, 1838, p. 86; "Lévis, François ... De, Duc de Lévis." *DCB.* Vol. 4, pp. 477–82; and "Pennisseaut ..., Louis." *DCB.* Vol. 4, pp. 621–22.

362.17–18   *that deep cavern of the Dark and Bloody Ground*] Kentucky, known for its "magnificent caves," carries this "nickname," which dates from the eighteenth century and "refers to the Indian battles, between Creek, Shawnee, Chickasaw, Cherokee and other tribes, that took place along the Cumberland River in Kentucky and Tennessee." See "Kentucky." 29 July 2005, http://www.netstate.com/states/intro/ky_intro.htm.

374.27   *La Touche*] Étienne Pézard de La Tousche (Touche), a French "soldier," whose "arrival in Canada is generally dated as 1661," became "a prominent inhabitant of New France." In 1664 he was granted the seigneury of Champlain in the district of Trois-Rivières, a fiefdom that his descendants held until the late eighteenth century. In *Les Ursulines De Québec, Depuis Leur Établissement Jusqu'à Nos Jours*, "M. Pezard de Latouche," probably his daughter, is listed as a student at the Convent after the fire in 1686. See "Pézard De La Tousche Champlain, Étienne." *DCB.* Vol. 1, p. 543, and *Ursulines.* Vol. 1. 1863, p. 332.

379.28   *Mere de la Nativité*] Marie-Anne de Branssat *dite* de la Nativité, a native of Montreal, "joined the Ursulines in Quebec in 1702.... Elected superior in 1735 and re-elected in 1738, she served again from 1744 to 1750 and from 1753 to 1760." In the 1750s she wrote several letters in which she discussed the affairs of her "neveu" Jean-Victor Varin de La Marne, François Bigot's associate. Her name had been given to Kirby by Josephine Lowe, a student at the Ursulines in 1869. In a letter dated "17 Mars/69," she wrote, "La Superior en 1748 était La Mère de la Nativité." See

"Migeon De Branssat . . . , Marie-Anne." *DCB.* Vol. 4, pp. 535–36; OTAR, Kirby, F–1076, The Josephine Lowe Correspondence, MU1638, A–17, ALS, Josephine Lowe to Kirby, 17 March 1869; and "Mission providentielle de la Mère Marie Anne Migeon de la Nativité." *Ursulines.* Vol. 3. 1866, pp. 110–19.

381.23–24 *Queen Dido . . . pius Æneus*] Virgil, *Aeneid*, Book IV, l. 393. After dallying for some time with Dido, Queen of Carthage, "loyal" ("pius") Aeneas, "though longing to soothe and assuage her grief and by his words turn aside her sorrow, with many a sigh, his soul shaken by his mighty love, yet fulfils Heaven's bidding and returns to the fleet" to prepare to sail for Italy. See Virgil. *Eclogues. Georgics. Aeneid I–VI.* Trans. H. Rushton Fairclough. Rev. G. P. Goold. Cambridge and London: Harvard University Press, 1999, pp. 448–49.

383.2 *"ON WITH THE DANCE"*] George Gordon Byron, Lord Byron, *Childe Harold's Pilgrimage*, Canto 3, 1816, Stanza 22, l. 192. The poet, describing a ball in Brussels in June 1815 interrupted by the sounds of a nearby battle between Great Britain and her allies and France, notes that at first the revellers determined to go "On with the dance!" See Lord Byron. *The Complete Poetical Works.* Vol. 2: *Childe Harold's Pilgrimage.* Ed. Jerome J. McGann. Oxford: At The Clarendon Press, 1980, p. 84.

384.3–4 *Esops fable of the cat turned woman*] There are various versions of this fable, which is usually attributed to Aesop. A "new translation," however, replaces the cat with a weasel who is changed by "the blessed goddess Aphrodite" into "a beautiful woman." She marries "a handsome young man," but while "the wedding feast was in progress, a mouse ran by. The bride leaped up from her richly decorated couch and began to run after the mouse, thus bringing an end to the wedding. After having played his little joke, Eros took his leave: Nature had proved stronger than Love." See "Aphrodite and the Weasel." *Aesop's Fables.* Trans. Laura Gibbs. New York and Oxford: Oxford University Press, 2002, pp. [v] and 166.

384.6 *Pretiosa*] Compare John Ford, Thomas Dekker, Thomas Middleton, and William Rowley, *The Spanish Gypsy*, written in 1623, in which Preciosa (or Pretiosa) is the name assumed by Constanza, the daughter of the "Corregidor of Madrid," when

she is disguised as "a young Spanish Gypsy girl." Preciosa is said
to have "such absolute beauty, / Dexterity of wit, and general
qualities, / That Spain reports of her, not without admiration."
See Thomas Middleton. *The Collected Works*. Ed. Gary Taylor and
John Lavagnino. Oxford: Clarendon Press, 2007, pp. 1727 and
1732.

384.8   *Fabius–discinta tunica*] Horace, *Satires*, Book I, Satire 2, l. 132.
The poet, describing the perils of committing adultery with
a married woman, explains that when her husband returns
unexpectedly, "With clothes dishevelled" ("discincta tunica")
and "bare of foot, I must run off, dreading disaster in purse
or person or at least repute." He adds, "To be caught is an
unhappy fate: this I could prove, even with Fabius as umpire."
Fabius was a "writer on Stoicism ... said to have been detected
in adultery." See Horace. *Satires, Epistles And Ars Poetica*. Trans.
H. Rushton Fairclough. London: William Heinemann, and
Cambridge: Harvard University Press, 1970, pp. 28–29.

384.17   *the Abbé de Bernis*] François-Joachim de Pierre Bernis, a young
abbé who frequented "le meilleur monde" in Paris, and
who was admitted to the Académie française in 1744 in
recognition of his poetry, became a close friend of Madame
de Pompadour and lived at the Louvre in the late 1740s
"dans l'intimité du roi et de sa maîtresse." After serving in
various diplomatic posts, he was named "secrétaire d'État aux
Affaires étrangères" in 1757. Kirby recorded in a notebook
that the "Abbé de Bernis" was an "homme aimable poli"
and "tres bien" with Madame de Pompadour: "Il la tenait
compagnie durant les voyages de Louis XV. Il l'avait initié à
la politique. Elle le fit ministre des affaires etrangeres." See
"Bernis (François-Joachim De Pierre, cardinal De)." *DBF*, and
OTAR, Kirby, F–1076, Miscellaneous Manuscripts, MU1646,
D–18, Note-book kept by Kirby containing ... excerpts from
various historical publications relating to the history of New
France, p. [12].

385.15   *Aspasia and Thaïs*] Aspasia, a native of Miletus, was "the mistress
of the Athenian statesman Pericles." She lived with him "from
some time in the 440s until his death in 429 BC" and bore him
a son, also called Pericles. "She had the reputation of being a

woman of intellect" who often influenced "Pericles' political actions." Thaïs was a "Greek courtesan" who is said to have accompanied Alexander the Great to Persia and "incited" him to burn Persepolis when in 330 B.C. it fell to the Greeks. In "Alexander's Feast; Or The Power Of Musique. An Ode, In Honour of St. Cecilia's Day" (1697), to which Kirby may be alluding, John Dryden portrayed her as "The Lovely *Thais*" who lit Alexander on his way to the destruction of the Persian city and who, thus, "like another *Hellen*, fir'd another *Troy*." See John Dryden. *The Poems Of John Dryden*. Ed. James Kinsley. Vol. 3. Oxford: At The Clarendon Press, 1958, pp. 1428–33, and "Alexander the Great" and "Aspā'sia." *The Oxford Companion To Classical Literature. Second Edition.* Ed. M. C. Howatson. Oxford and New York: Oxford University Press, 1989, pp. 24–27 and 67.

385.26   *Ariel*] Compare, for example, William Shakespeare, *The Tempest*, V.i.21. Ariel, a spirit that is "but air," helps Prospero perform his magic. See *Shakespeare*, p. 1632.

390.32–34 *the fox praised the raven's voice and prevailed on her to . . . drop the envied morsel out of her mouth*] Compare Aesop, "*The Fox and the Raven.*" In this fable a "raven seized a piece of cheese and carried his spoils up to his perch high in a tree." A fox, "planning a trick" to get the raven to drop his food, cried:

> "O raven, the elegant proportions of your body are remarkable, and you have a complexion that is worthy of the king of the birds! If only you had a voice to match, then you would be first among the fowl!" The fox said these things to trick the raven and the raven fell for it: he let out a great squawk and dropped his cheese. . . . The fox then grabbed the cheese.

See *Aesop's Fables*. Trans. Laura Gibbs. New York and Oxford: Oxford University Press, 2002, pp. 53–54.

393.10–11 *the king in the fairy tale . . . daughter and . . . kingdom*] Compare Jacob Ludwig Carl and Wilhelm Carl Grimm, "The Valiant Little Tailor," 1812–15. A "little tailor" who wears "a girdle" that says "'Seven at one stroke!'" is promised the King's "only daughter to wife, and half of his kingdom as a dowry" if he kills "two giants." Although the King attempts to renege on his promises, in the end the tailor marries the King's daughter and receives half his kingdom. "So the little tailor was and remained a king to the end of his life." See *The Complete Grimm's Fairy Tales*. 1944; rpt. New York: Random House, 1972, pp. 112–20.

393.36–37 *the man in the iron mask*] There are many stories about "*l'homme au masque de fer*," including François-Marie Arouet de Voltaire's in *Siècle de Louis XIV* (1751). According to this account, in the early 1660s "un prisonnier inconnu" whose face was hidden by a mask with iron springs came to live in a château on an island off Provence. Transferred to the Bastille in Paris in 1690, he died there in 1703. Although he was always treated with great respect, his identity remained a "secret de l'Etat." Kirby undoubtedly read about this mysterious man in his copy of the 1823 printing of Voltaire's history. See *Siècle*. Vol. 1, pp. 390–93.

397.2 *"CALLING A RAVENOUS BIRD FROM THE EAST"*] Compare Isaiah 46:11, in which God reminds the Israelites that He will do his "pleasure: Calling a ravenous bird from the east, the man that" will execute his "counsel from a far country." See *IB*. Vol. 5. 1956, p. 542.

398.23–24 *her old confessor Father Vimont*] Barthélemy Vimont, "priest, Jesuit, missionary," arrived in Quebec in 1639 as "superior" of the Jesuit mission in Canada and, apart from one return to France in the 1640s, remained there until 1659. During his sojourn in Quebec, he ministered to parishes in and around the city; his name is also associated with the Ursuline Convent. He may have been Kirby's model, therefore, for Angelique's confessor. See "Vimont, Barthélemy." *DCB*. Vol. 1, p. 665.

400.5 *Josephte Dodier*] In 1763 Marie-Josephte Corriveau, "known as La Corriveau," born in Saint-Vallier de Bellechasse, "near Quebec," in 1733, was found guilty of "murdering Louis Dodier, her second husband," a farmer in Saint-Vallier, whom she had married two years before. Hanged in the spring of 1763, her corpse was exposed in an "iron cage" at "Pointe-Lévy (Lauzon)," Quebec, for about a month. In "Marie Josephte Corriveau,—A Canadian Lafarge," which appeared in *Maple Leaves: A Budget Of Legendary, Historical, Critical, And Sporting Intelligence* (1863), James MacPherson Le Moine repeated several traditions associated with this woman, including the one "which our old friend, M. DeGaspé, has introduced with happy effect in his late work 'Les Anciens Canadiens.'" Kirby took details about La Corriveau from both his copy of *Maple Leaves* and his copy of *Les Anciens Canadiens*, which was originally published in 1863. He also recorded in a notebook that "La Corriveau was tried by Court Martial ... in the convent of the Ursulines—the table used is still preserved in the Salle des quarante pieds." See "Corriveau (Corrivaux), Marie-Josephte." *DCB*. Vol. 3, pp. 142–43; *Maple Leaves*, pp. 68–74; and OTAR, Kirby, F–1076, Miscellaneous Manuscripts, MU1646, D–18, Note-book kept by Kirby containing ... excerpts from various historical publications relating to the history of New France, n. pag.

404.9   *Antonio Exili*] Egidio Exili, an Italian "in the service of the former Queen Christina of Sweden," was imprisoned in the Bastille from 2 February to 27 June 1663, at which point "he was escorted to Calais so that he could sail to England." Although he was never charged with any crime, he became known in France as a poisoner who spread his "funestes secrets" throughout Paris and, thus, was one of the sources of the so-called "Affair of the Poisons" in seventeenth-century France. Kirby, who copied into a notebook an entry on "Exili Aqua Tofana St Croix et La Marquise de Brinvilliers 1676," most likely took at least some details about these notorious events from his copy of the 1823 printing of François-Marie Arouet de Voltaire's *Siècle de Louis XIV* (1751). See OTAR, Kirby, F–1076, Miscellaneous Manuscripts, MU1646, D–18, Note-book kept by Kirby containing ... excerpts from various historical publications relating to the history of New France, n. pag.; Anne Somerset. *The Affair Of The Poisons: Murder, Infanticide And Satanism At The Court Of Louis XIV*. London: Weidenfeld and Nicolson, 2003, p. 10; and *Siècle*. Vol. 1, p. 429.

404.17   *Glaser*] Christophe Glaser, "a Swiss chemist based in Paris," had "by 1663 ... not only become 'apothecary-in-ordinary' to both King Louis XIV and his brother, the Duc d'Orléans, but he had also been appointed resident lecturer at the Royal Botanical Gardens in Paris." Some years later, probably after his death, he was implicated in the so-called "Affair of the Poisons."

Kirby is probably following his copy of the 1823 printing of François-Marie Arouet de Voltaire's *Siècle de Louis XIV* (1751), which describes Glaser as "un apothicaire allemand" with whom Egidio Exili had worked for a long time. See Anne Somerset. *The Affair Of The Poisons: Murder, Infanticide And Satanism At The Court Of Louis XIV.* London: Weidenfeld and Nicolson, 2003, p. 12, and *Siècle.* Vol. 1, p. 429.

404.19   *Beatrice Spara*] Compare, for example, Charles Mackay's *Memoirs Of Extraordinary Popular Delusions* (1841), which was issued at least four times between its first publication and 1869. In his chapter on "The Slow Poisoners" Mackay describes Hieronyma Spara (La Spara) as "an old woman," a "reputed witch and fortune-teller," who "acted as president" of "a society of young wives" that was formed in seventeenth-century Rome and that met at her house there allegedly to plan the poisoning of unsatisfactory husbands. La Spara, who was accused of supplying "the wonderful elixir" that was the poison, was eventually hanged. See *Memoirs.* Vol. 2, pp. 344–45.

404.25–26 *the . . . Candidas and Saganas of imperial Rome*] Compare Horace, *Satires*, Book I, Satire 8. The poet, in the guise of a scarecrow, states that it is "the witches who with spells and drugs vex human souls" that "cause" him "care and trouble." He explains further, "My own eyes have seen Canidia walk with black robe tucked up, her feet bare, her hair dishevelled, shrieking with the elder Sagana. . . . Then they began to dig up the earth with their nails, and to tear a black lamb to pieces with their teeth; the blood was all poured into a trench, that therefrom they might draw the sprites, souls that would give them answers." See Horace. *Satires, Epistles And Ars Poetica.* Trans. H. Rushton Fairclough. London: William Heinemann, and Cambridge: Harvard University Press, 1970, p. 99.

404.26–27 *the Borgias, . . . the Orsinis, the Scaligers and the Borromeos*] All powerful Italian families, they played key roles in church and state, especially in the Renaissance. Cesare Borgia, for example, "the natural son of Rodrigo Borgia (Pope Alexander VI) and Vannozza Cattanei," carved "out a principality in the Romagna and the Marches" at the end of the fifteenth century through a variety of methods, including, most likely, that of poisoning two

Orsinis, members of a "Roman family, noted for its power and wealth ... from the 12th to the 16th century." Although Cesare ultimately lost his principality, in *Il principe* (*The Prince*) (1515), Niccolò Machiavelli presents him as a model of a successful ruler. The Scaligeri family held "the lordship of Verona from 1277 to 1387," while the Borromeos, "a distinguished noble family of Milan," included St. Charles Borromeo and his cousin Federico Borromeo, both Roman Catholic priests who became cardinals and archbishops of Milan. See *The New Century Italian Renaissance Encyclopedia*. Ed. Catherine B. Avery. New York: Meredith Corporation, 1972, pp. 150, 158, 690, and 850.

405.13–15 *Gaudin de St Croix ... the Marchioness de Brinvilliers*] Jean-Baptiste Godin "dit *Sainte-Croix*," a French army officer, became the lover of Marie-Madeleine D'Aubray, marquise de Brinvilliers, in the early 1660s. Having learned the art of poisoning, apparently during the time he spent in the Bastille because of his affair with Madame de Brinvilliers, from 1666 to 1670 Godin helped his mistress to poison her father and her two brothers. Godin died in 1672, possibly from inadvertently breathing poisons in his laboratory. For her crimes the marquise was beheaded and her body "brûlé" in Paris in 1676. Kirby is most likely following the account of these events in his copy of the 1823 printing of François-Marie Arouet de Voltaire's *Siècle de Louis XIV* (1751), in which Godin is described as a young man "d'une trop belle figure" and Madame de Brinvilliers as "jeune, belle et sensible." See "Brinvilliers (Marie-Madeleine D'Aubray, marquise De)." *DBF*; "Godin (Jean-Baptiste)." *DBF*; and *Siècle*. Vol. 1, p. 429.

407.1 *the Manna of St Nicholas*] Compare Charles Mackay, *Memoirs Of Extraordinary Popular Delusions* (1841). In his chapter on "The Slow Poisoners" Mackay introduces "a hag, named Tophania," who "resided first at Palermo and then at Naples," and who sold a poison "similar to that manufactured" by Hieronyma Spara. Tophania "sent large quantities of it to all parts of Italy in small vials, with the inscription 'Manna of St. Nicholas of Barri.'" She "artfully gave this name to her poison to elude the ... custom-house officers, who, in common with everybody else, had a pious respect for St. Nicholas de Barri" and the "wonderful oil" that was said to ooze from his tomb and to effect miraculous cures. See *Memoirs*. Vol. 2, pp. 346–47.

407.24 *La Regnie*] In 1667 Nicolas-Gabriel La Reynie was appointed the first chief of police for Paris, a post that he held for thirty years. In the early 1680s he also presided over the special court, "dite 'chambre ardente,'" that was constituted to prosecute those allegedly involved in "l'Affaire des poisons." See "La Reynie (Nicolas-Gabriel)." *DBF.*

407.32 *Desgrais*] According to several nineteenth-century sources, including Charles Mackay's *Memoirs Of Extraordinary Popular Delusions* (1841), François Desgrez (Desgrais), a police officer in Paris, went to Liège, Belgium, to carry out the arrest of the marquise de Brinvilliers after she had taken shelter in a convent there. A man not "to be baffled," Desgrez lured her out of her refuge by pretending to be a lover. She "came, and found herself, not in the embrace of a gallant, but in the custody of a policeman." See *Memoirs*. Vol. 2, p. 359.

408.2   *Pirol*] Edme Pirot, a respected theologian who was "docteur et professeur de Sorbonne," was the marquise de Brinvilliers' confessor during the last few days of her life in 1676. In his account of her "derniers moments," which was first published in 1883, he described her as having very thick chestnut hair, a "rond & assez beau" face, soft and beautiful blue eyes, and skin that was "extraordinairement blanche." See "Pirot (Edme)." *BU*, and G. Roullier. *La Marquise De Brinvilliers Récit De Ses Derniers Moments (Manuscrit Du P. Pirot, Son Confesseur) Notes Et Documents Sur Sa Vie Et Son Procès*. Paris: Alphonse Lemerre, 1883. Vol. 1, p. 77.

408.27 *La Voisin*] Catherine Des Hayes Monvoisin, known as La Voisin, was a prominent midwife, fortune-teller, and, probably, abortionist in Paris in the 1660s and 1670s. According to Charles Mackay in his chapter on "The Slow Poisoners" in *Memoirs Of Extraordinary Popular Delusions* (1841), she also sold poisons, particularly "to women who wanted to get rid of their husbands." In connecting her as someone who knew the "secrets" of Egidio Exili and who made money "de la curiosité des ignorants" among all ranks of society, Kirby is following his copy of the 1823 printing of François-Marie Arouet de Voltaire's *Siècle de Louis XIV* (1751). There is no evidence to suggest, however, that La Voisin had a daughter by Exili. For her crimes she was burned alive in the Place de la Grève in Paris in 1680. See *Memoirs.* Vol. 2, p. 363, and *Siècle.* Vol. 1, pp. 430–31.

408.30–31 *Le Sage and Le Vigoureux*] Adam Coeuret, "dit Dubuisson puis Lesage," was the lover of Catherine Des Hayes Monvoisin and participated with her in her magic and other activities in the 1660s and 1670s. Arrested in 1679 during the so-called "Affair of the Poisons," he testified against his now ex-mistress. He remained in prison until at least 1683. In calling both Lesage and Levigoureux, another accomplice, priests, and in stating that they were burned along with La Voisin "à la Grève" in Paris in 1680, Kirby is following his copy of the 1823 printing of François-Marie Arouet de Voltaire's *Siècle de Louis XIV* (1751). He also entered in a notebook that "La Voisin & Levigoureux" were "executed on the Place de Greve 22 Feb 1680" and that "30 accomplices" were "executed—many fled." See "Coeuret (Adam)." *DBF*; OTAR, Kirby, F–1076, Miscellaneous Manuscripts, MU1646, D–18, Note-book kept by Kirby containing ... excerpts from various historical publications relating to the history of New France, n. pag.; and *Siècle.* Vol. 1, p. 435.

408.36–37 *Cardinal Bonzy*] Pierre Bonzi, a native of Florence, who became "archevêque de Toulouse" in 1669 and "de Narbonne" in 1673, was made a cardinal of the Roman Catholic church in 1672. In his chapter on "The Slow Poisoners" in *Memoirs Of Extraordinary Popular Delusions* (1841), Charles Mackay reports that "Cardinal de Bonzy" was linked "by the gossips of the day" to "M. de Penautier, treasurer of the province of Languedoc, and Receiver-general for the clergy," who was accused of poisoning "the late Receiver-general, in order to obtain his appointment":

> The Cardinal's estates were burthened with the payment of several heavy annuities; but, about the time that poisoning became so fashionable, all the annuitants died off, one after the other. The Cardinal, in talking of these annuitants, afterwards used to say, "Thanks to my star, I have outlived them all!" A wit, seeing him and Penautier riding in the same carriage, cried out, in allusion to this expression, "There go the

Cardinal de Bonzy and his *star*!"

See "Bonzi (Pierre V, card. De)." *DBF*, and *Memoirs*. Vol. 2, pp. 361–62.

409.2   *The Duchesse de Bouillon*] Marie-Anne Mancini, born in Rome, married Godefroi-Maurice de La Tour d'Auvergne, the third Duke of Bouillon, in 1662. Living mostly in Paris in the late 1670s, "'par curiosité,' elle entra en relations avec la Voisin ... sans doute pour s'instruire dans la magie." Accused by her enemies, however, of wishing to poison her husband, she was brought before the "chambre ardente," and, although never found guilty, she was "exilée à Nérac" in 1680. In *Siècle de Louis XIV* (1751), François-Marie Arouet de Voltaire related that Nicolas-Gabriel La Reynie asked "la duchesse de Bouillon" during her interrogation if she had seen the devil as a result of her dealings with Catherine Des Hayes Monvoison and her accomplices. The Duchess, known for her wit, replied that she was seeing him at that very moment, that he was "fort laid et fort vilain," and that he was "déguisé en conseiller d'Etat." Kirby followed his copy of the 1823 printing of Voltaire's work for his information not only on the Duchess of Bouillon but also on the Countess of Soissons, Prince Eugène, and François de Montmorency. See "Bouillon (Godefroi-Maurice De La Tour D'Auvergne, 3e duc De)." *DBF*, and *Siècle*. Vol. 1, p. 432.

409.3   *the Countess of Soissons*] Olympe Mancini, a sister of Marie-Anne Mancini, married Eugène-Maurice de Savoie, the Count of Soissons, in 1657. A one-time favourite of Louis XIV, she was implicated in the so-called "Affair of the Poisons" for having "des relations fréquentes avec la Voisin." In 1680, however, before she could be arrested, she fled to Brusssels. In *Siècle de Louis XIV* (1751), François-Marie Arouet de Voltaire reports that the King condescended to tell "cette princesse" that if she felt herself guilty, she should leave Paris. She replied that she was "très innocente, mais qu'elle n'aimait pas à être interrogée par la justice." See "Soissons (Olympe Mancini, comtesse De)." *BU*, and *Siècle*. Vol. 1, p. 432.

409.3–4   *Prince Eugene*] The son of the Count and Countess of Soissons, Eugène-Maurice de Savoie and his wife Olympe Mancini,

Eugène de Savoie-Carignan, called Prince Eugène, left France in the 1680s when "Louis XIV lui refusa un régiment" and fought for the rest of his life on behalf of Austria. During the War of the Spanish Succession (1701–14), he and John Churchill, the first Duke of Marlborough, the other great general of their generation, defeated the French at such battles as Blenheim (1704) and Oudenarde (1708). See "Eugène (François De Savoie, appelé *le prince*)." *BU.*

409.6   *Francois de Montmorency*] François-Henry de Montmorency-Bouteville, a French army officer who became "duc de Luxembourg" when he married in 1661 and a "maréchal de France" in 1675, was implicated in "l'affaire des poisons." Arrested and kept in the Bastille for "14 mois," he was finally released in 1680 without any charges being proved. In *Siècle de Louis XIV* (1751), François-Marie Arouet de Voltaire, who discusses the case of this "duc, pair et maréchal de France" and "grand capitaine" at some length, alleges that the "accusations" against him were as "improbables" as they were "atroces." See "François-Henry De Montmorency-Bouteville." *DBF,* and *Siècle.* Vol. 1, pp. 432–33.

409.37   *the Sieur Corriveau*] Joseph Corriveau was "a farmer" who lived at Saint-Vallier de Bellechasse, "near Quebec." His wife was Marie-Françoise Bolduc, by whom he is said to have had several children, including Marie-Josephte, "known as La Corriveau." In April 1763 Joseph "was found guilty of the murder" of Louis Dodier, La Corriveau's second husband. This judgement was reversed, however, when it was proved that it was Marie-Josephte alone who had committed the crime. See "Corriveau (Corrivaux), Marie-Josephte." *DCB.* Vol. 3, pp. 142–43.

414.6–9   *"Ah! Ah! ... Ouich Ka!"*] Compare "Tenaouiche Tenaga, Ouich' Ka!" in *Chansons Populaires Du Canada* (1865). Kirby's lines, which he undoubtedly took from his copy of Gagnon's work, represent the chorus of this song. Gagnon calls "ces mots étranges" gibberish and suggests that they are "l'*imitation* de sauvage, comme savent en faire tous les jeunes enfants." See *Chansons,* pp. 123–25.

414.15   *St Anne*] The "traditional name of the mother of the Blessed

Virgin Mary," she "became one of the most popular saints" in the Roman Catholic church. Since the seventeenth century the "principal patron of the province of Quebec," she is particularly worshipped at "the shrine of St. Anne de Beaupré." See "Anne, Saint." *Catholic.* Vol. 1. 1907, pp. 538–39.

418.19–22 *a . . . song of Jean Le Meung . . . "Toutes . . . putes!"*] Compare Jean de Meun, *Le Roman de la Rose,* c. 1275, ll. 9159–60, "Toutes estes, serez ou fustes / De fait ou de voulenté, pustes!" A version of these lines in modern French reads, "Vous êtes toutes, vous serez ou vous fûtes, en acte ou en intention, des putes!" An English translation of these lines, which includes them in a section spoken by a "Jealous Husband," renders them as "All women are, have been, and e'er will be, / In thought if not in deed, unvirtuous." See Guillaume de Lorris and Jean de Meun. *Le Roman De La Rose.* Ed. Armand Strubel. Librairie Générale Française, 1992, pp. 546–47, and Guillaume de Lorris and Jean de Meun. *The Romance Of The Rose.* Ed. Charles W. Dunn. Trans. Harry W. Robbins. New York: E. P. Dutton, 1962, pp. 183 and 185.

421.24 *the ring of Cleopatra*] Compare the Greek epigram attributed to either Asclepiades or Antipater of Thessalonica, "I AM Drunkenness, the work of a skilled hand, but I am carved on the sober stone amethyst. The stone is foreign to the work. But I am the sacred possession of Cleopatra: on the queen's hand even the drunken goddess should be sober." Although this Cleopatra has often been equated with the "queen of Egypt" who was Mark Antony's mistress, the author and the date of composition of this epigram and, therefore, the identity of Cleopatra are disputed. In "Cleopatra's Ring," for example, Kathryn J. Gutzwiller argues that the lines refer to Cleopatra, "the daughter of Philip II" of Macedon and "the sister of Alexander the Great," who was "murdered at Sardis about 308 B.C." The author, then, would be Asclepiades from whom this Queen Cleopatra most likely "commissioned" the ring to strengthen her association with "the worship of Dionysus" and, thus, her claim through a possible "male heir . . . to the throne of Macedon." See *The Greek Anthology.* Vol. 3. Trans. W. R. Paton. London: William Heinemann, and New York:

G. P. Putnam's Sons, 1917, pp. 406–07 and 450, and Kathryn
J. Gutzwiller. "Cleopatra's Ring." *Greek, Roman, And Byzantine Studies*, 36 (1995), 383–98.

422.2 *"WEIRD SISTERS"*] William Shakespeare, *Macbeth*, I.iii.32. The *"Three* Witches, *the Weïrd Sisters,"* waiting "to meet with Macbeth" on "the heath," chant:

> The weïrd sisters, hand in hand,
> Posters of the sea and land,
> Thus do go, about, about,
> Thrice to thine, and thrice to mine,
> And thrice again, to make up nine.
> Peace, the charm's wound up.

See *Shakespeare*, pp. 1312 and 1314.

424.4 *Medea*] In Greek mythology the daughter of the "king of Colchian Aia" and the sometime wife of Jason, Medea, "the archetypal example of the scheming, barbarian woman," was known for "her mastery of drugs and potions," including poisons. See "Medea." *The Oxford Classical Dictionary. Third Edition*. Ed. Simon Hornblower and Antony Spawforth. Oxford and New York: Oxford University Press, 1996, p. 944.

424.25 similia similibus curantur] That is, *like cures like*. This was a basic principle expounded by Samuel Hahnemann, a German "docteur en médecine" and chemist, when he founded homeopathy, an alternative system of medicine, in the late eighteenth century. After his book on the subject, first published in German in 1810, appeared in English in 1833 as *Organon of Homeopathic Medicine*, homeopathy became popular in North America. Hahnemann died in Paris in 1843. See "Hahnemann (Samuel-Chrétien-Frédéric)." *BU.*

436.17–18 *Lucrezia Borgia . . . her terrible father*] Lucrezia Borgia was "the natural daughter of Rodrigo Borgia," Pope Alexander VI, and his mistress Vannozza Cattanei. Her brother was Cesare Borgia. Although she herself was accused "of the most depraved crimes," she appears to have been "a submissive pawn in the schemes of her father and her brother," both of whom were known for their corruption. In Lorenzo L. Da Ponte's *A History Of The Florentine Republic* (1833), a copy of which Kirby owned, Alexander VI, for example, is described as a man of "unhallowed ambition," the worst "in the long line of papal tyrants," and as "one who had been in his life a scourge to his fellows." See Lorenzo L. Da Ponte. *A History Of The Florentine Republic: And Of The Age And Rule Of The Medici.* New-York: Collins and Hannay, 1833. Vol. 2, pp. 147–48 and 163, and "Borgia, Lucrezia." *The New Century Italian Renaissance Encyclopedia.* Ed. Catherine B. Avery. New York: Meredith Corporation, 1972, pp. 155–58.

438.24–29 *the* Untori, *the* Ointers *of Milan ... Manzoni*] In 1629–30 the plague killed about three-quarters of the population of Milan. One reason alleged for the spread of this pestilence was that people were "anointing" various objects in the city with "poisonous" unguents. The story of these so-called ointers was incorporated by Alessandro Manzoni in his historical novel *I Promessi Sposi* (1827 ff.), a copy of which, issued in Brussels in 1843, Kirby owned. See Alessandro Manzoni. *The Betrothed.* Trans. Bruce Penman. London: Penguin Books, 1972, pp. 579, 581, et passim.

441.22–23 *sweeter than honey of Hybla*] Compare William Shakespeare, *1 Henry IV*, I.ii.41. Henry, Prince of Wales, chatting with Sir John Falstaff, replies to the latter's question about the "hostess of the tavern" being "a most sweet wench" that she is "As the honey of Hybla." Hybla is a region in Sicily known for the quality of its honey. See *Shakespeare*, p. 849.

441.28–29 *the fabled snakes on the head of Megæra*] Megaera, associated with jealousy, was one of the Greek furies who punished crimes, including murder. These "goddesses" were frequently depicted as being "wreathed with snakes." See "Furies." *The Oxford Companion To Classical Literature. Second Edition.* Ed. M. C. Howatson. Oxford and New York: Oxford University Press, 1989, pp. 240–41.

444.17–18 *the ... Sieur de La Verendrye*] Pierre Gaultier de Varennes et de La Vérendrye, an army "officer, fur-trader, explorer" born in New France in 1685, made several voyages to "search for the western sea" in the 1730s and 1740s. Although neither he nor his sons, who often accompanied him on his travels, ever arrived at the Pacific, they did develop the notion that one route "for reaching that ocean" was "to utilize the Saskatchewan River." In

1748–49 La Vérendrye planned "another western expedition, this time up the Saskatchewan," but he died in Montreal before he could leave on his journey. In Andrew Bell's translation of the third edition of François-Xavier Garneau's *Histoire Du Canada* (1859), "Pierre-Gauthier de Varennes, sieur de la Vérendrye," is described as "an enthusiastic explorer" and "a gentleman who had trafficked much with the tribes of the west, and gained much information among them of the countries that lay beyond." Kirby, summarizing in a notebook the section about the La Vérendryes from his copy of Bell, records that in "1734 M de la Verendrye explores the far north west his sons in 1752 claim right to continue explorations—Intendant Bigot sets claims aside and ... trades himself." See Bell. Vol. 2, p. 76; "Gaultier De Varennes Et De La Vérendrye, Pierre." *DCB*. Vol. 3, pp. 246–54; and OTAR, Kirby, F–1076, Miscellaneous Manuscripts, MU1646, D–18, Note-book kept by Kirby containing ... excerpts from various historical publications relating to the history of New France, n. pag..

447.13–14 *Law ... and the Mississippi Scheme*] In 1717 John Law, a native of Scotland who became "effectively chief minister and minister of finance" of France in early 1720, organized the "Compagnie d'Occident" or, as it was later renamed, the "Compagnie des Indes" that "had exclusive rights to exploit the French colony in Louisiana." This "Mississippi System," or scheme, which became a kind of "'giant holding company'" for the French national debt, finally collapsed in July 1720. The result was that those who had not sold their shares in the company at an inflated price when it appeared to be prospering lost all the money that they had invested. Kirby recorded in a notebook that "La compagnie du Mississipi" was "formed by Law" in "1717." See OTAR, Kirby, F–1076, Miscellaneous Manuscripts, MU1646, D–18, Note-book kept by Kirby containing ... excerpts from various historical publications relating to the history of New France, p. 1, and Richard Bonney. "Law, John (*bap.* 1671, *d.* 1729)." *ODNB* [http://www.oxforddnb.com/view/article/16150, accessed 13 November 2005].

448.15–17 *The Lawyers ... whom La Fontaine depicts ... as swallowing the oyster*] Compare Jean de La Fontaine, *Fables Choisies*, 1668,

Book 9, Fable 9, "L'Huitre Et Les Plaideurs." In this fable, which warns people to beware of lawyers and their fees that often leave the litigants with nothing, La Fontaine told the story of two "pèlerins" who found an oyster on a beach. Unable to decide who should have it, they choose "Perrin Dandin," a judge, to arbitrate their case. He swallows the oyster, presents each litigant with a shell, and orders "chacun" to go "en paix ... chez soi." See *Fables De La Fontaine Illustrées ... Nouvelle Édition.* Tours: Ad Mame Et Cie, Imprimeurs-Libraires, 1851, pp. 278–79. Kirby owned a copy of this printing of La Fontaine's work.

450.7   *St Christopher the Strong*] A "martyr, probably of the third century" A.D., St. Christopher is known for his "extraordinary size and strength." The protector of travellers, his task was "carrying people, for God's sake, across a raging stream." His burdens included "a child who continually grew heavier, so that it seemed ... as if he had the whole world on his shoulders." The child later revealed himself as Jesus. See "Christopher, Saint." *Catholic.* Vol. 3. 1908, pp. 728–29.

452.26–27   *the seventh holy beatitude—"Beati Pacifici!"*] Compare Matthew 5:9. Jesus, teaching his disciples, gives them the seventh beatitude, "Blessed *are* the peacemakers: for they shall be called the children of God." See *IB.* Vol. 7. 1951, p. 286.

454.18–19   *like ... St Paul—all things to all men*] Compare I Corinthians 9:22. Paul explains in his letter to the Corinthians that in order to win people to "the gospel of Christ," he is "made all things to all *men,* that" he "might by all means save some." See *IB.* Vol. 10. 1953, pp. 103–04.

455.16   *Magdelene ... loved much*] Compare Luke 7:47. Jesus, explaining to "the Pharisee" why he has allowed "a woman in the city," a sinner who is often identified as Mary Magdalene, "to wash his feet with tears" and to anoint them "with the ointment" that she has brought in "an alabaster box," says, "Her sins, which are many, are forgiven; for she loved much." In English literature from the late eighteenth century, the "name Magdalene becomes a noun, indicating a repentant prostitute or an unwed mother." See "Mary Magdalene." *A Dictionary of Biblical Tradition in English Literature.* Ed. David Lyle Jeffrey. Grand Rapids, Michigan: William B. Eerdmans, 1992, pp. 486–89, and *IB.* Vol. 8. 1952, pp. 142–45.

456.33–   *the verse of an old Swedish ballad* ... *So long as life is in me*] "Slaget
457.6   vid Bränkyrka 1518" ("Battle at Brännkyrken 1518"), ll. 1–4. The
           song commemorates a victory of the Swedes over the Danes at
           Brannkyrken (Stockholm), Sweden, in 1518. The translation of
           its opening lines was probably Kirby's. See *Svenska Folk-Visor.* Ed.
           Erik Gustaf Geijer and Arvid August Afzelius. Vol. 2. Stockholm:
           Zacharias Haeggström, 1816, pp. [302]–304. Kirby owned a copy
           of this anthology that he autographed "William Kirby 1858." It is
           now held by the Queen's University Library, Kingston, Ontario.

457.10–23 *the old song of the Goths* ... *"Almighty God!* ... *bless the land
           of Swedish men!—"*] "Gothlands Visan" ("The Gotland Song"),
           1444, ll. 163–68. The lines quoted and most likely translated by
           Kirby are the last stanza of this patriotic song that encouraged
           the Swedes in their war with the Danes. See *Svenska Folk-Visor.*
           Ed. Erik Gustaf Geijer and Arvid August Afzelius. Vol. 2.
           Stockholm: Zacharias Haeggström, 1816, pp. 279–86. Kirby's
           copy of this anthology, which he autographed in 1858, is now
           owned by the Queen's University Library, Kingston, Ontario.

459.6–7   *his bread* ... *made their faces to shine*] Compare Psalm 104:15, in
           which the singer, praising the power of God, says that He brings
           forth "wine *that* maketh glad the heart of man, *and* oil to make
           his face to shine, and bread *which* strengtheneth man's heart."
           See *IB.* Vol. 4. 1955, p. 554.

460.36   *Rousseau*] The ideas of Jean-Jacques Rousseau, like those of his
           older contemporary François-Marie Arouet de Voltaire, were
           influential in shaping literary, political, and social events in
           France, including the French Revolution, in the late eighteenth
           and early nineteenth centuries. In the 1740s, however, Rousseau
           had done little to suggest "l'importance du rôle philosophique
           et littéraire" that he was to play. See "Rousseau (Jean-Jacques)."
           BU.

461.2   Absit omen] That is, May the omen be absent. See
           "absit omen." *Oxford English Dictionary Online.* 10 July 2011,
           http://www.oed.com.proxy.library.carleton.ca.

464.32   *the* ... *'bank and shoal of time'*] William Shakespeare, *Macbeth,*
           I.vii.6. Macbeth, contemplating Duncan's murder, muses that if
           "this blow / Might be the be-all and the end-all—here, / But

here, upon this bank and [shoal] of time, / We'ld jump the life to come." See *Shakespeare*, p. 1317.

464.34–35 *God said 'let the waters ... appear—!'*] Compare Genesis 1:9. On the second day of God's creation of the world, He "said, Let the waters under the heaven be gathered together unto one place, and let the dry *land* appear: and it was so." See *IB*. Vol. 1. 1952, p. 472.

465.7 *Rudberg*] That is, probably, Olof Rudbeck. In 1655 he was "appointed assistant professor in the Medical Faculty of Uppsala University" and remained there until he died in 1702. As a young man, studying "animal anatomy," he "performed a number of systematic dissections and vivisections of calves, sheep, cats, and dogs" that allowed him to conduct research "on the lymphatic system." In the 1670s he "took up the notion that Sweden was the cradle of civilization, Plato's lost Atlantis," an idea that he "developed" in a "four-volume work ... commonly called *Atlantica*" that was "published in Swedish and Latin" between 1679 and 1702. Since *Atlantica* "achieved considerable European notoriety," Kirby may be basing his ideas about the age of North America on those of Rudbeck. See "Rudbeck, Olof." *Dictionary Of Scientific Biography*. Vol. 11. Ed. Charles Coulston Gillispie. New York: Charles Scribner's Sons, 1975, pp. 586–88.

465.34 'Non Liquet!'] That is, "It is not clear." A term in English "civil law," it "means the failure of a party to discharge a material burden of proof." See David M. Walker. "*Non liquet.*" *The Oxford Companion To Law*. Oxford: Clarendon Press, 1980, p. 885.

466.1–2 *Plato's account ... of Atlantis ... told to Solon by the Egyptian priests*] Compare Plato, *Timaeus*. The Greek Solon, one of "the wisest of men," is told by an Egyptian priest, "a prodigiously old man," the story of "a confederation of kings" from the "island of Atlantis" who "by one single onslaught" attempted to conquer both Greece and Egypt and their surrounding territory. The "invaders" were "defeated," however, chiefly by "the manhood" of Athens. Later "there occurred portentous earthquakes and floods, and one grievous day and night ... the whole body" of Greek "warriors was swallowed up by the earth, and the island of Atlantis in like manner was swallowed up by the sea and vanished." In *Timaeus* the "tale," passed down from Solon by the "great-grandfather" and then the "grandfather" of Critias, is related by the last to Socrates, Timaeus, and Hermocrates. See Plato. *Timaeus Critias Cleitophon Menexenus Epistles.* Trans. R. G. Bury. Cambridge: Harvard University Press, and London: William Heinemann, 1966, pp. 29–33 and 41–43.

468.1   *Cromwell*] Oliver Cromwell, a leader of the Parliamentarians during the Civil War in England in the 1640s, and "the third to append his name to the death warrant" of Charles I, became "the single most powerful man in England" after "the king's head was cut off on 30 January 1649." The "lord protector of England, Scotland, and Ireland" from 1653 until his death in 1658, in the late 1630s, already "a radicalized puritan," he had "powerful links through the families of his father and of his wife … to some of the leading figures who had emigrated to New England." See John Morrill. "Cromwell, Oliver (1599–1658)." *ODNB* [http://www.oxforddnb.com/view/article/6765], accessed 26 November 2005.

468.22   *St Michael*] That is, Michael the Archangel. One "of the principal angels," his "offices" included fighting "against Satan," rescuing "the souls of the faithful from the power of the devil," acting as "the champion" of Christians, and calling "away from earth" and bringing "men's souls to judgment." See "Michael the Archangel." *Catholic.* Vol. 10. 1911, pp. 275–77.

469.8   mirabile dictu] Virgil, *Georgics*, Book 2, l. 30. The poet, describing the cultivation of trees, explains, "When the trunks are cleft … an olive root thrusts itself from the dry wood"; he interjects, "how wondrous the tale!" ("mirabile dictu"). See Virgil. *Eclogues. Georgics. Aeneid I–VI.* Trans. H. Rushton Fairclough. Rev. G. P. Goold. Cambridge and London: Harvard University Press, 1999, pp. 138–39.

469.19   *Cassandra*] The daughter of Priam, king of Troy, and a prophetess, she "proclaimed the downfall of Troy, but was believed by no one." In William Shakespeare's *Troilus and Cressida*, II.ii, for example, she is called "mad" and is portrayed as "*raving [with her hair about her ears]*" and calling repeatedly, "Cry, Troyans, cry!" as she predicts "with prophetic tears" Troy's destruction. See *Shakespeare*, p. 462, and Virgil. *Aeneid VII–XII*

Appendix Vergiliana. Trans. H. Rushton Fairclough. Rev. G. P. Goold. Cambridge and London: Harvard University Press, 2000, p. 541.

470.9   *Sufficient ... is the Evil of it*] Compare Matthew 6:34. Jesus, teaching his followers, counsels, "Take therefore no thought for the morrow: for the morrow shall take thought for the things of itself. Sufficient unto the day *is* the evil thereof." See *IB.* Vol. 7. 1951, p. 324.

470.24–25   *Olaf Celsius and Gammal Rodbeck*] Olof Celsius, "professeur de théologie et de langues orientales" at the University of Uppsala, made a name for himself as a distinguished botanist; he was particularly known for his identification of Biblical plants. Olof Rudbeck, also "a competent botanist and zoologist," succeeded his father and namesake as "professor of medicine at Uppsala" in 1691. Both men became "influential promoters" of the work of Carl Linnaeus after he "went on to the University of Uppsala" in 1728. See "Celsius (Olaus)." *BU*; "Linnaeus (or Von Linné), Carl." *Dictionary Of Scientific Biography.* Vol. 8. Ed. Charles Coulston Gillispie. New York: Charles Scribner's Sons, 1973, pp. 374–81; and "Rudbeck, Olof." *Dictionary Of Scientific Biography.* Vol. 11. Ed. Charles Coulston Gillispie. New York: Charles Scribner's Sons, 1975, pp. 586–88.

470.30–32   *Newton ... the vast ocean of truth*] Sir Isaac Newton, the great "natural philosopher and mathematician," is reported "a short time before his death" to have said, "I do not know what I may appear to the world, but to myself I seem to have been only like a boy playing on the sea-shore, and diverting myself in now and then finding a smoother pebble or a prettier shell than ordinary, whilst the great ocean of truth lay all undiscovered before me." See David Brewster. *Memoirs of the Life, Writings, And Discoveries of Sir Isaac Newton.* 1855; rpt. New York and London: Johnson Reprint Corporation, 1965. Vol. 2, p. 407, and Richard S. Westfall. "Newton, Sir Isaac (1642–1727)." *ODNB* [http://www.oxforddnb.com/view/article/20059, accessed 2 December 2005].

471.1   *Charles XII*] King of Sweden from 1697 to 1717, from the age of four Charles was tutored by Norcopensis, "the Uppsala professor of *Eloquentiae*" who was ennobled as Nordenhielm. In

1700 Charles' army defeated the Russians at Narva, Estonia, a "fortified town" that was then "in the Swedish province of Ingria." See R. M. Hatton. *Charles XII of Sweden*. London: Weidenfeld and Nicolson, 1968, pp. 44 and 644.

471.8–9   *there is nothing new . . . all is vanity*] Compare Ecclesiastes 1:2 and 1:9. The "Preacher, the son of David, king in Jerusalem," says, "Vanity of vanities ... all *is* vanity," and "*there is* no new *thing* under the sun." See *IB*. Vol. 5. 1956, pp. 26–29.

471.21–22 *King Frederick ... Queen Ulrica*] Princess Ulrika Eleonora, the sister of Charles XII of Sweden, became queen of Sweden in 1719 after her brother's death late in the previous year. In 1720 she ceded the throne to her husband Frederick von Hessen-Kassel who, thus, became Frederick I of Sweden. He reigned until his death in 1751.

471.29   *Swedenborg*] Emanuel Swedenborg, a Swedish "scientist, Biblical scholar, and mystic" who had studied "classics and Cartesian philosophy at Uppsala," developed "the doctrine of correspondence," a "variation of the Platonic theory of the relations between the world of ideas and the world of senses." After undergoing in the mid 1740s "a profound spiritual experience," Swedenborg "directed his reasoning exclusively toward the interpretation of Scripture according to" his doctrine. "His first exegetic work" was *Arcana Coelestia* (*Heavenly Arcana*), eight volumes of which were published in London between 1749 and 1756. As a result of his studying in Cincinnati, Ohio, with Alexander Kinmont, "an early Swedenborgian," Kirby "acquired a lifelong interest in the philosophical and religious principles of" this Swede, many of whose works, including several volumes of *Arcana Coelestia,* he owned. See "Kirby, William." *DCB*. Vol. 13, pp. 551–54; "Swedenborg, Emanuel." *The Encyclopedia of Philosophy*. Vol. 8. Ed. Paul Edwards. New York: The Macmillan Company & The Free Press, 1967, pp. 48–51; and Alfred Habegger. *The Father: A Life of Henry James, Sr.* New York: Farrar, Straus and Giroux, 1994, p. 214.

472.16–20 *a Berserkir ... the Edda ... Odin*] An Old Norse name given to two manuscripts, one called the Prose Edda and the other the Poetic Edda, the Edda contained "the mythology, the ethical conceptions, and the heroic lore of the ancient North," including tales about Odin, the chief god in the Norse pantheon, who, among his other attributes, "inspired the frightful *berserkers*, maddened warriors who rushed naked into the midst of the fray." Kirby, who had a long-standing interest in things Scandinavian, owned at least two volumes relevant to the Edda; they are now among the "96 Volumes from the Scandinavian Section" of his "Private Library" held by the Queen's University Library, Kingston, Ontario. See Arthur Cotterell. "Odin." *A Dictionary Of World Mythology.* Oxford and Melbourne: Oxford University Press, 1986, pp. 172–75; Lee M. Hollander, ed. *The Poetic Edda.* Austin: University of Texas Press, 1962, p. xv; and *William Kirby's Library.* Special Collections, Douglas Library, Queen's University, 1978.

472.33 Fortasse et propter hoc] That is, literally, *Perhaps and because of this.*

473.37–38 Credo ... Catholicam] Compare the "Apostles' Creed," "*Credo in ... sanctam ecclesiam catholicam,*" or " I believe in ... The holy Catholic Church." See *The Book Of Common Prayer.* Toronto: The Anglican Book Centre, 1959, p. 10.

474.35 *Diderot*] The most famous work of the French "philosophe" Denis Diderot is the *Encyclopédie,* a multi-volume dictionary of universal knowledge published from the 1750s to the 1770s that he edited and to which he, as well as François-Marie Arouet de Voltaire, contributed many articles. Although the *Encyclopédie* represents much of the thinking of the eighteenth-century Enlightenment, many of Diderot's more audacious ideas had already been expressed in his *Pensées philosophiques* (1746), in which he attacked Christianity and advocated "la religion naturelle." See "Diderot (Denis)." *DBF.*

474.36–37 *the Athenians ... on this matter*] Compare Acts 17:32. The Athenians, having listened to Paul preach about the teachings of Jesus, reacted in various ways, "And when they heard of the resurrection of the dead, some mocked: and others said, We will hear thee again of this *matter.*" See *IB.* Vol. 9. 1954, p. 237.

477.9–16 *Englishmen ... enemies*] Kirby's particular "arch Lucifer" in regard to these ideas was Goldwin Smith. A "writer, journalist, and controversialist" who was "regius professor of modern history at Oxford" from 1858 to 1866, Smith moved to Toronto in 1871. There he continued to develop his beliefs, already outlined in such works as *The Empire. A Series Of Letters Published In "The Daily News," 1862, 1863* (1863), that Great Britain should emancipate its colonies "as rapidly as possible"; that, because of its lack of "cultural homogeneity" due to the French Canadians, "Canada could never become a genuine nation"; and that, therefore, "its destiny lay in union with the United States." Although *Canada And The Canadian Question,* his "most famous expression" of these convictions, did not appear until 1891, they had already been articulated in newspaper and periodical articles published in Canada in the 1870s. See "Smith, Goldwin." *DCB.* Vol. 13, pp. 968–74, and OONA, MG29, E29, Denison Papers, Vols. 3 and 4, p. 1781, ALS, Kirby to Charles Taylor Denison, 20 February 1890.

477.18–19   *the man followed by wolves who cast out of his sledge, one child after another*] Compare *The Englishwoman In Russia,* 1855, Chapter 12. The anonymous author relates a "dreadful anecdote" about "a peasant woman" whose sled was attacked by wolves as with her three children she crossed "the forest that stretched for many miles between her isba and the neighbouring village." Each time "the hungry savage beasts" closed upon the sled, she threw out one of her children until they were all "devoured" by the "famished" animals. When "the miserable mother" reached the village, she was instantly murdered by "the horror-stricken peasant" who first heard her story. In 1866 Kirby borrowed the copy of *The Englishwoman In Russia* owned by the Niagara Mechanics' Institute. See *The Englishwoman In Russia; Impressions Of The Society And Manners Of The Russians At Home. By A Lady, Ten Years Resident In That Country.* London: John Murray, 1855, pp. 174–76.

477.36–
478.4   *the words of the old English Loyalist ... For Loyalty ... shone upon*] Samuel Butler, *Hudibras,* Part 3, 1678, Canto 2, ll. 173–76. Describing "the royalists" towards the end of the English Commonwealth in the 1650s, Butler writes that "though out-number'd, overthrown, / And by the fate of war run down," they remained dutiful and faithful:

> For loyalty is still the same,
> Whether it win or lose the game;
> True as the dial to the sun,
> Although it be not shin'd upon.

See Samuel Butler. *Hudibras. A Poem.* London: Thomas Allman, 1836, pp. 274–75. Kirby owned a copy of this edition.

478.9   *"the acres of snow!"*] Compare François-Marie Arouet de Voltaire, *Candide,* 1759, Chapter 23. Approaching the coast of England, Candide asks his companions if England is as foolish as France. Martin replies that the English display "une autre espèce de folie." He explains that "ces deux nations" are at war "pour quelques arpents de neige vers le Canada," and that they are spending "pour cette belle guerre" much more than "tout le Canada" is worth. See *Les Oeuvres Complètes De Voltaire.* Vol. 48: *Candide ou l'optimisme.* Ed. René Pomeau. Oxford: The Voltaire Foundation, 1980, p. 223.

480.34   *St Martin*] That is, most probably, Martin of Tours. A Roman soldier who converted to Christianity, he preached "the Gospel in the central and western parts of Gaul" before he became Bishop of Tours in about 376 A.D. One of the "greatest saints" of the Roman Catholic church in France, his feast is celebrated on 11 November. See "Martin of Tours." *Catholic.* Vol. 9. 1910, pp. 732–33.

481.9–13   *David fought ... with Goliath ... not for himself*] Compare I Samuel 17. David, "the son of ... Jesse the Beth-lehemite," offered to fight "a champion ... of the Philistines, named Goliath," who had challenged the Israelites for "forty days." Coming "in the name of the Lord of hosts, the God of the armies of Israel," David "prevailed over the Philistine with a sling and with a stone, and smote the Philistine, and slew him." See *IB.* Vol. 2. 1953, pp. 970–80.

485.8–9   *the slave of the lamp and ... its possessor*] Compare *"The story of Aladdin; or, the Wonderful Lamp,"* a tale incorporated into Antoine Galland's French version of the *Arabian Nights* stories that was first published in the early eighteenth century. In the English translation of Galland, which became the standard version of the *Thousand and One Nights* until well into the nineteenth century, when Aladdin, a native of China, rubs the lamp to which he has been directed by his fake uncle "The African Magician," a genie appears and demands, "What wouldst thou have? I am ready to obey thee as thy slave, and slave of all those who have that lamp in their hands; I, and the other slaves of the lamp." See, for example, *Arabian Nights Entertainments: Consisting Of One Thousand and One Stories. . . . The Fourteenth Edition.* Edinburgh: Printed by and for Colin Macfarquhar, and sold by the Booksellers in town and country, 1772. Vol. 3, pp. 240 and 255.

488.10   *the hill Difficulty*] Compare John Bunyan, *The Pilgrim's Progress,* 1678. The dreamer sees the pilgrim Christian come to the bottom of a hill up which there were three ways, "but the narrow way lay right up the hill, and the name of the going up the side of the hill is called *Difficulty.*" Christian, who took this way up the hill, "fell from running to going, and from going to clambering upon his hands and knees, because of the steepness of the place." See John Bunyan. *The Pilgrim's Progress.* London: William Tegg, 1862, pp. 49–50. Kirby owned a copy of this imprint.

491.26–35 *the* Droit de Grenouillage ... *'Pa! ... gâ!'*] Kirby, apparently following the chapter "On some very Peculiar Feudal Institutions" in his copy of *Maple Leaves: A Budget Of Legendary, Historical, Critical, And Sporting Intelligence* (1863), paraphrases James MacPherson Le Moine's description of "the famous *Droit de Grenouillage*" as the right of "the landed aristocracy" to compel "their serfs to turn out on the wedding night of the lord of the manor, to beat the frog ponds, in order that his lordship's rest might not be disturbed by the noisy croakings of the frogs." This custom was also followed by "certain jolly friars ... whenever they resided in their domains." Le Moine adds that during this "operation" the "peasants" were "expected to croak out" the "cabalistic formula" of "Pâ! Pâ! rainotte, Pâ! (silence, frogs, silence!) / Voici monsieur l'abbé que Dieu gâ. (Near you rests monsieur l'abbé whom may heaven watch over)." See *Maple Leaves,* pp. 57–58.

492.7   *the right of* Jambage] Also known as the "*Droit du Seigneur,*" this includes the right, which, in fact, may never have existed, of a feudal lord to have sexual intercourse with a vassal on her wedding night. In his chapter "On some very Peculiar Feudal Institutions" in *Maple Leaves: A Budget Of Legendary, Historical, Critical, And Sporting Intelligence* (1863), James MacPherson Le Moine mentions several "*arrêts* and passages" that have to do with this custom, including one from "la Cour de Bourges." Kirby is probably following his copy of this volume. See *Maple Leaves*, p. 60.

492.29–31 *suiting ... Hamlet*] Compare William Shakespeare, *Hamlet*, III.ii.17–18. Hamlet, instructing the players, tells them to "Suit the action to the word, the word to the action." See *Shakespeare*, p. 1161.

493.23–30 *a musical descant ... 'Si vous consultez ... un cas pendable!—'*] Compare Jean-Baptiste Poquelin *dit* Molière, *Monsieur De Pourceaugnac*, 1669, II.xi. Monsieur de Pourceaugnac, accused of polygamy, is taken to consult two lawyers who sing a song on the subject that includes several lines similar to those recited by Master Pothier:

> *Si vous consultez nos auteurs,*
> *Législateurs et glossateurs,*
>
> ...
>
> *Jason, Alcial, et Cujas,*
> *Ce grand homme si capable,*
> *La polygamie est un cas,*
> *Est un cas pendable.*

See *Molière*. Vol. 7. 1922, pp. 316–18.

493.36–37 *the ... apologie du Cidre*] "Apologie Du Cidre" is usually attributed to Olivier Basselin, a native of Vire, Normandy, who lived in the fifteenth century. A "bon vivant," Basselin is supposed to have composed several songs for the drapers of Vire; these, which came to be known as "vau-de-vires," mark the beginnings of the vaudeville tradition. Kirby prints a version of the first, second, and fourth stanzas of this drinking song. See "Basselin (Olivier)." *DBF*, and *Vaux-De-Vire D'Olivier Basselin Et De Jean Le Houx*. Paris: Adolphe Delahays, 1858, pp. 40–41.

495.25 *Caius Verres*] The son of a Roman senator, from 73 to 71 B.C. Caius Verres was governor of Sicily. The next year, when he returned to Rome, he was tried for corruption at the request of the Sicilians. In the speech in which he argued his fitness to prosecute the case against Verres, Cicero explained that the "charge against Gaius Verres" was "that during a period of three years" he had "laid waste the province of Sicily" by plundering "Sicilian communities," stripping "bare Sicilian homes," and pillaging "Sicilian temples." See Cicero. *The Verrine Orations ... In Two Volumes.* Trans. L.H.G. Greenwood. London: William Heinemann, and Cambridge: Harvard University Press, 1959, Vol. 1, pp. 10–11.

495.32–33 populatae ... Provinciae] Cicero, "Speech Delivered Against Quintus Caecilius Niger (Maintaining Cicero's Own Greater Fitness To Prosecute Verres)," III, 7. Cicero, arguing his case for prosecuting Caius Verres, states that trying the former governor of Sicily would "contribute" to "the general safety and prosperity" of all Romans, for "Populatae, vexatae, funditus eversae provinciae" ("Our provinces have been ravaged and plundered and utterly ruined"). See Cicero. *The Verrine Orations ... In Two Volumes.* Trans. L.H.G. Greenwood. London: William Heinemann, and Cambridge: Harvard University Press, 1959, Vol. 1, pp. 8–9.

497.27 *St Denis*] In the third century A.D., Denis, known "for his virtuous life ... and firm faith," was sent by the Pope to Gaul on the "difficult mission" of restoring the "Church of Gaul" to "its former flourishing condition." Settling near Paris, he and his two companions made "countless conversions," but they were eventually arrested, tortured, and beheaded. Denis, whose feast is celebrated on 9 October, became the patron saint of France. See "Denis, Saint." *Catholic.* Vol. 4. 1908, p. 721.

509.14–15 *Wise Solomon found only one good woman in a thousand*] Compare Ecclesiastes 7:27–28. The "Preacher," who is frequently identified with King Solomon, seeks "a good (wise) man" or woman, but he concludes, "one man among a thousand have I found; but a woman among all those have I not found." See *IB.* Vol. 5. 1956, p. 68.

512.36-37 *St Catherine*] Most likely Catherine of Alexandria, she was "the object of a very popular devotion" in both England and France for many centuries. Frequently represented as the bride of Christ, she was usually depicted with the wheel on which she was "condemned to die." The feast day of this "patroness of young maidens" is November 25. See "Catherine of Alexandria, Saint." *Catholic.* Vol. 3. 1908, pp. 445–46.

524.2   *"OUTVENOMS ALL THE WORMS OF NILE"*] William Shakespeare, *Cymbeline*, III.iv.35. Pisano, lamenting Posthumus Leonatus' letter in which he wrongly accuses his wife Imogen of adultery, says of "slander" that its "tongue / Outvenoms all the worms of Nile." See *Shakespeare*, p. 1539.

530.21–22   *the Palace of Galienne where Satan sits on a throne of gold*] Compare Sir Walter Scott, *Letters on Demonology and Witchcraft*, 1830. In Letter VII Scott discusses "the persecution of witches" that "broke out in France" in the seventeenth century, in particular in the area of Bordeaux, where Satan was alleged to have "held his *cour plénière* before the gates" of the city "and in the square of the palace of Galienne." At these events he was supposed to sit on "a sort of gilded throne." See Sir Walter Scott. *Complete Works Of Sir Walter Scott ... In Seven Volumes.* Vol. 1: *Letters On Demonology And Witchcraft.* New York: Conner and Cooke, 1833, p. 42. Kirby owned a copy of this edition.

531.10–13   *"Hecaten ... ago!"*] Literally, "I call on Hecate! / I call on Tisiphone! Sprinkled water from Lake Avernus, / I curse you to death—, I drive you mad!" In making up this incantation Kirby has adapted lines from two works by Horace. "Hecaten vocat altera, saevam altera Tisiphonen" ("One witch calls on Hecate, the other on fell Tisiphone"), *Satires*, Book I, Satire 8, ll. 33–34, names the spirits whom Canidia and Sagana, two Roman witches, evoke. "Spargens Avernalis aquas" ("sprinkled water from Lake Avernus"), Epode 5, l. 26, describes Sagana sprinkling water from Lake Avernus "all through the house" as part of her preparation to murder her young victim. See *Odes And Epodes*, pp. 282–83, and Horace. *Satires, Epistles And Ars Poetica.* Trans. H. Rushton Fairclough. London: William Heinemann, and Cambridge: Harvard University Press, 1970, pp. 98–99.

532.2   *"QUOTH THE RAVEN: 'NEVERMORE!'"*] Edgar Allan Poe, "The Raven," 1845, l. 48 et passim. Variations of this line form the refrain of this "melancholy, melodramatic, reflective lyric of love and sorrow." See *The Complete Works Of Edgar Allan Poe*. Ed.

James A. Harrison. Vol. 7: *Poems*. New York: AMS Press, 1965, pp. 94–100 and 212.

542.2   *"A DEED WITHOUT A NAME"*] William Shakespeare, *Macbeth*, IV.i.49. The witches, meeting Macbeth for the second time, reply to his question "What is't you do?" that they are executing "A deed without a name." See *Shakespeare*, p. 1329.

555.2   *"LET'S TALK OF GRAVES AND WORMS AND EPITAPHS"*] William Shakespeare, *Richard II*, III.ii.145. King Richard, finding himself abandoned, says, "Let's talk of graves, of worms, and epitaphs." See *Shakespeare*, p. 822.

582.20   *Dives in his torment*] Compare Luke 16:19–31. Jesus, teaching his disciples, related the parable of the rich man, "often called 'Dives,' the word with which the Vulg[ate] translated the adjective 'rich,'" and "a certain beggar named Lazarus." When Lazarus died, he "was carried by the angels into Abraham's bosom," but when Dives died, he went to hell where he was "in torments." See *IB*. Vol. 8. 1952, pp. 288–93.

584.26   *Gariepy*] Members of the Gariépy family first came to Quebec from France in the seventeenth century. "Marie M. Gariépy," for example, was a student at the Ursuline Convent in Quebec just after its fire in 1686. See *Ursulines*. Vol. 1. 1863, p. 327.

587.15   *Venus Victrix*] That is, Victorious Venus. One of several personae of the goddess Venus, she "became one of the major divinities" of the Roman Empire. See "Venus." *The Oxford Classical Dictionary. Third Edition*. Ed. Simon Hornblower and Antony Spawforth. Oxford and New York: Oxford University Press, 1996, p. 1587.

589.29   *Mere St Louis*] Geneviève de La Grange de St. Louis, the daughter of Jean Léger de La Grange, "ship's captain, merchant, and privateer," and his first wife, Louise Fauvel, entered the Ursuline Convent in Quebec in 1708, when she was fifteen, and served until her death in 1776. Superior from 1740 to 1744, she also acted as "maîtresse particulière des pensionnaires"; in this role she was much loved by her students and much admired for her skills as a teacher. See "Léger De La Grange, Jean." *DCB*. Vol. 2, pp. 387–88, and *Ursulines*. Vol. 3. 1866, p. 359.

589.32   *Mere St Helene*] The daughter of Nicolas Daneau de Muy, an officer in the French "colonial regular troops," and his wife, Marguerite Boucher, Charlotte Daneau de Muy de Sainte

Hélène "entered the noviciate of the Ursulines of Quebec" in 1716. The "annalist" of "the community during the Seven Years' War," she died on 14 September 1759 and was, thus, the "dernière Ursuline qui s'empara du ciel sous la domination française en Canada." See "Daneau De Muy, Nicolas." *DCB.* Vol. 2, pp. 168–69; "Daneau De Muy, Charlotte, *dite* de Sainte-Hélène." *DCB.* Vol. 3, p. 161; and *Ursulines.* Vol. 2. 1864, p. 359.

590.6   *Mere St Joseph*] This is possibly a reference to Marie-Dorothée Jeryan (or Jordan). Originally from New England, she had been captured by the Abenakis, from whom she was "ransomed and converted" in 1720 by Joseph Aubery, a Jesuit priest then serving in Acadia. As "Mère de St. Joseph" she was a nun at the Ursuline Convent in Quebec for almost forty years. Her death occurred on 14 September 1759 shortly before that of Charlotte Daneau de Muy de Sainte Hélène. See "Aubery . . . , Joseph." *DCB.* Vol. 3, pp. 23–25, and "Une captive du Seigneur deux fois expatriée." *Ursulines.* Vol. 2. 1864, pp. 358–59.

597.34   "in sæcula sæculorum,"] That is, "*world without end.*" These are the last words in the doxology that is frequently recited in the rituals of Catholic churches. In *The Book of Common Prayer*, for example, the "Gloria Patri" reads, "Glory be to the Father, and to the Son, / and to the Holy Ghost; / As it was in the beginning, is now, and ever shall be, / world without end." See *The Book Of Common Prayer*. Toronto: The Anglican Book Centre, 1959, p. 10.

607.17–18 *the Seigneur de Port Neuf*] That is, most likely, Eustache Lambert Dumont, "the younger," a lieutenant "d'une compagnie des troupes du détachement de la marine." He bought "the barony of Portneuf, a substantial property on the north shore of the St Lawrence River" between Quebec and Trois Rivières from Charles Legardeur de Croisille in 1741. Legardeur de Croisille's wife and sister-in-law, the daughters of Pierre Robineau de Bécancour, Baron de Portneuf, had inherited the seigneury from their uncle Jacques Robinau when he died in 1715. Portneuf had originally been granted in 1636 to Jacques Leneuf de La Poterie, a native of Normandy whose wife was Marguerite Legardeur de Tilly, the "sister of Pierre Legardeur de Repentigny and of Charles Legardeur de Tilly." In 1671

Leneuf de La Poterie passed the estate to his son-in-law René Robinau de Bécancour, the "chief road officer of New France"; the seigneury was raised "to the status of a barony" in 1681. See "Leneuf De La Poterie, Jacques." *DCB.* Vol. 1, p. 467; "Robinau De Bécancour, René." *DCB.* Vol. 1, pp. 574–76; "Legardeur De Croisille, Charles." *DCB.* Vol. 3, p. 374; and Pierre-Georges Roy. *Inventaire Des Ordonnance[s] Des Intendants De La Nouvelle-France Conservées Aux Archives Provinciales De Québec.* Beauceville: L'"Eclaireur," 1919. Vol. 3, p. 20.

610.6   *St Maur*] That is, most likely, Maurus, "son of Equitius, a nobleman of Rome." A "disciple of St. Benedict," he has been "described as a model of religious virtues, especially of obedience." He is supposed to have founded the abbey at Saint-Maur-sur-Loire in the sixth century. See "Maurus, Saint." *Catholic.* Vol. 10. 1911, p. 72.

616.2   *"I WILL FEED FAT THE ANCIENT GRUDGE I BEAR HIM"*] William Shakespeare, *The Merchant of Venice,* I.iii.47. Shylock, expressing his hatred for Antonio, the Venetian merchant, because "he is a Christian," decides, "If I can catch him once upon the hip, / I will feed fat the ancient grudge I bear him." See *Shakespeare,* p. 258.

617.28   Cave canem] Compare, for example, Gaius Petronius Arbiter, *Satyricon,* Chapter 27. Encolpius, the narrator of Petronius' novel, reports that in Trimalchio's house "a great dog on a chain was painted on the wall, and over him was written in block capitals 'BEWARE OF THE DOG'" ("Cave canem"). See *Petronius.* Trans. Michael Heseltine. Rev. E. H. Warmington. Cambridge and London: Harvard University Press, 1997, pp. 48–49.

623.31–32 *the seven champions of christendom*] These are "Saint *George* of England, Saint *Dennis* of Fraunce, Saint *James* of Spaine, Saint *Anthonie* of Italie, Saint *Andrew* of Scotland, Saint *Pattricke* of Ireland, and Saint *David* of Wales." See Richard Johnson. *The Seven Champions of Christendom (1596/7).* Ed. Jennifer Fellows. Aldershot, England: Ashgate Publishing, 2003, p. [1].

625.6   *the Princess d'Elide*] Compare Jean-Baptiste Poquelin *dit* Molière, *La Princesse D'Élide Comédie Galante,* 1664. The daughter of a wealthy prince "d'humeur galante et magnifique," the "princesse d'Élide" is described as so beautiful and charming that, despite her pride, she has attracted many lovers. See *Molière*. Vol. 4. 1878, pp. 143 and 145.

629.26   *The Molinists*] This is probably a reference to the followers of Luis de Molina, "one of the most learned and renowned theologians of the Society of Jesus," who in the late sixteenth century published his ideas on "the difficult problem of reconciling grace and free will." These ideas, which came to be known as "Molinism," emphasized "the unrestrained freedom of the will, without detracting in any way from the efficacy, priority, and dignity of grace." Their adoption by the Society of Jesus brought this order into further conflict with other orders of the Roman Catholic church and increased the Jesuits' unpopularity in Europe. See "Molina, Luis De." *Catholic*. Vol. 10. 1911, pp. 436–37, and "Molinism." *Catholic*. Vol. 10. 1911, pp. 437–41.

633.32–33   *the wheel . . . full of eyes*] Compare Ezekiel 10:9–12. The prophet, describing his vision of "the four wheels by the cherubim," says that "they four had one likeness, as if a wheel had been in the midst of a wheel." He adds, "And their whole body, and their backs, and their hands, and their wings, and the wheels, *were* full of eyes round about, *even* the wheels that they four had." See *IB*. Vol. 6. 1956, p. 116.

634.19–20   *Philip the Evangelist . . . had four daughters . . . who did prophecy*] Compare Acts 21:8–9. Luke the apostle reports that they "that were of Paul's company" travelled to Caesarea. There they "entered into the house of Philip the evangelist . . . and abode with him." This "same man," he adds, "had four daughters, virgins, which did prophesy." See *IB*. Vol. 9. 1954, p. 278.

634.23–24   *the preacher . . . wise overmuch*] Compare Ecclesiastes 7:16, in which "the Preacher" advises, "Be not righteous over much, neither make thyself over wise." See *IB*. Vol. 5. 1956, p. 66.

639.5   *the Queen of Sheba*] Compare I Kings 10:1–10. The queen of Sheba, hearing of Solomon's fame, "came to Jerusalem with a very great train, with camels that bare spices, and very much gold, and precious stones." When she had "communed" with him and seen evidence of his wealth and wisdom, she gave the king of Israel "a hundred and twenty talents of gold, and of spices very great store, and precious stones." At the time of the visit "Sheba was the great trading community of southwestern Arabia." See *IB*. Vol. 3. 1954, pp. 96–98.

643.20   *the Sabine women*] Compare Livy, "Ab Urbe Condita" ("From The Founding Of The City"), Book I, Sections 9–13. Livy recounts the story of the Sabine "maidens," who, being invited to Rome with their families, were then seized and carried off by "young Romans" whom they had previously spurned. Eventually, however, their "sense of injury" gave "place to affection." When their Sabine fathers attacked their Roman husbands, therefore, they begged both sides to stop fighting. "Then the leaders came forward to make a truce, and not only did they agree on peace, but they made one people out of the two." See *Livy In Fourteen Volumes*. Vol. 1: *Books I and II*. Trans. B. O. Foster. Cambridge: Harvard University Press, and London: William Heinemann, 1967, pp. 33–51.

645.30–31 *St Dorothy*] Probably Dorothea, "virgin and martyr," she is usually "represented with an angel and a wreath of flowers." Her feast day is 6 February. See "Dorothea, Saint." *Catholic*. Vol. 5. 1909, pp. 135–36.

650.2   *"IN GOLD CLASPS LOCKS IN THE GOLDEN STORY"*] William Shakespeare, *Romeo and Juliet*, I.iii.92. Lady Capulet, extolling the virtues of Paris as a possible husband for Juliet, says, "That book in many's eyes doth share the glory, / That in gold clasps locks in the golden story." See *Shakespeare*, p. 1063.

656.1–2 *"A thousand ... eyelids down!"*] Alice Cary, "The Fatal Arrow," ll. 19–20. The narrator, in love with her father's "fair-haired harvester," and wrongly convinced that he loves her, confesses, "A thousand times I kissed him in the brook, / Across the flowers,—with bashful eyelids down." See Alice and Phoebe Cary. *Early And Late Poems Of Alice And Phoebe Cary*. Boston and New York: Houghton, Mifflin And Company, 1887, p. 245. Alice Cary's poems also appeared in periodicals before she died in 1870.

657.14–15 *the treasure ... which ... no thief can steal*] Compare Matthew 6:19–20. Jesus, teaching his disciples, instructs them not to lay up for themselves "treasures upon earth, where moth and rust doth corrupt, and where thieves break through and steal." Instead, he advises, "lay up for yourselves treasures in heaven, where neither moth nor rust doth corrupt, and where thieves do not break through nor steal." See *IB*. Vol. 7. 1951, pp. 317–18.

657.21   *Grand Mere St Pierre*] Geneviève Boucher, "*dite* de Saint-Pierre," the daughter of Pierre Boucher ("Grand-Père Boucher"), "seigneur de Boucherville," and his wife Jeanne Crevier, served as an Ursuline nun in Quebec from 1694 to 1766. Called "Le Mathusalem" of the Ursulines, she fulfilled all the principal roles of the Convent, including those of "maîtresse des novices" and "supérieure," and was considered the "'perfect Ursuline.'" See "Boucher, Geneviève, *dite* de Saint-Pierre." *DCB*. Vol. 3, pp. 78–79, and "Le Mathusalem de notre Histoire, ou la digne fille du Grand-Père Boucher." *Ursulines*. Vol. 3. 1866, pp. 94–97.

657.36   *De Soto*] Hernando de Soto, a "Spanish conquistador and explorer," acquired great wealth through his activities in Central America and Peru. He died in 1542 in what is now Arkansas after spending several years in "the American Southeast." The Spanish explorer whose name is associated with "the 'fountain of youth,'" however, is Juan Ponce de León. Having failed to discover this "*Fons Juventutis*," either on the island of Bimini in the Bahamas or in Florida, he died in Cuba in 1521. See "Soto, Hernando de." *ANB*, and "Ponce de León, Juan." *Catholic*. Vol. 12. 1911, p. 228.

660.21–23   *Love... "is... preferring one another"*] Compare Romans 12:9–10. Paul, instructing the Romans about the nature of love, writes, "*Let* love be without dissimulation. Abhor that which is evil; cleave to that which is good," and "*Be* kindly affectioned one to another with brotherly love; in honor preferring one another." See *IB*. Vol. 9. 1954, pp. 586 and 588.

661.11–12   *"Her image ... the last!—"*] Compare Robert Burns, "A Song," 1789, ll. 15–16. The poet, recalling his final parting from his beloved Mary "by the winding Ayr," says that he cannot forget "Thy image at our last embrace, / Ah, little thought we 'twas our last!" See Robert Burns. *The Poems And Songs Of Robert Burns*. Ed. James Kinsley. Vol. 1: *Text*. Oxford: At The Clarendon Press, 1968, p. 493.

665.17–   *The Jesuits ... enemies of the state*] In this passage Kirby is partly
666.26   following the chapter on the "*Assassinat du roi de Portugal. Jésuites chassés du Portugal, et ensuite de France*" in his copy of

an 1823 printing of *Précis Du Siècle De Louis XV* (1768), in
which François-Marie Arouet de Voltaire discusses, among other
issues relating to the Jesuits and their expulsion from France
by Louis XV in the 1760s, the priest "nommé la Valette." The
head of the Jesuit mission in Martinique, and its "plus fort
commerçant," he became "une banqueroute de plus de trois
millions." In a notebook Kirby not only records this incident,
but he also adds:

> The Parliament of Paris inimical to the Jesuits
> continued the war against the Society, & declared it
> had no legal standing in France. The Duc de Choiseul
> prime minister determined to suppress them as being
> opposed to modern philosophy....
>
> 5 mai 1758: La loi les declara rebelles ... et
> ordonna qu'ils fussent chassés de ses etats....
>
> The Parliament of Paris declara la Société dissoute.

See OTAR, Kirby, F–1076, Miscellaneous Manuscripts, MU1646,
D–18, Note-book kept by Kirby containing ... excerpts from
various historical publications relating to the history of New
France, pp. [18]–19, and François-Marie Arouet de Voltaire.
Précis Du Siècle De Louis XV. Paris: Chez Mme Veuve Dabo, 1823,
pp. 325–32.

666.2–3   *the five theological propositions*] The "five propositions" attributed
to Cornelius Jansen (or Jansenius), which were condemned by
Pope Innocent X in 1653, were:

> (1) "Some commandments of God are impossible
> for the just by reason of their present forces no matter
> what intentions they have or what efforts they make,
> for they lack the grace by which these commandments
> are made possible for them."
>
> (2) "In the state of fallen nature one can never
> resist interior grace."
>
> (3) "To merit or sin in the state of fallen nature it
> is unnecessary for man to possess a liberty opposed to
> (psychological) necessity, but it suffices that he possess
> a liberty opposed to [physical] constraint."

(4) "The semi-Pelagians conceded the necessity of an interior prevenient grace for all actions, even for the beginning of faith, but they were heretics to the extent that they wished this grace to be such that the will of man could resist or obey it."

(5) "It is a semi-Pelagian error to maintain that Jesus Christ died and shed his blood for all men generally."

See Dale Van Kley. *The Jansenists and the Expulsion of the Jesuits from France 1757–1765.* New Haven and London: Yale University Press, 1975, pp. 12–13.

667.2–4   *Padre Monti ... was ... different from ... the Jogues and the Lallements*] Isaac Jogues, a Jesuit priest, arrived from France in 1636 to minister to the Hurons and later to the Iroquois. He was murdered by the latter ten years after "at Ossernenon (Auriesville, N.Y.)." Gabriel Lalemant, another French Jesuit priest, arrived as a missionary to the Hurons in 1646 shortly before Jogues' martyrdom. Captured by the Iroquois "at the Saint-Louis mission," he was killed by them at "the little town of Saint-Ignace (half-way between Coldwater and Vasey, in the county of Simcoe, Ontario)." Both Jogues and Lalemant were canonized by the Roman Catholic church in 1930. Padre Monti does not appear to be an historical character. See "Jogues, Isaac." *DCB.* Vol. 1, pp. 387–90, and "Lalemant, Gabriel." *DCB.* Vol. 1, pp. 412–13.

667.29–30   *the man who ... fell among thieves*] Compare Luke 10:25–37. Jesus, responding to "a certain lawyer" who asked what he should "do to inherit eternal life," replies with the parable of the good Samaritan. A "certain *man* went down from Jerusalem to Jericho, and fell among thieves," who "stripped ... and wounded *him*," and left "*him* half dead." Passed by a priest and a Levite, both of whom ignored him, he was finally rescued by "a certain Samaritan" who "bound up his wounds, ... and brought him to an inn, and took care of him." See *IB.* Vol. 8. 1952, pp. 192–97.

668.33   *Pilates asking, 'what is Truth?'*] Compare John 18:38. Pontius Pilate, the governor of the Roman province of Judea, judging Jesus, repeatedly asks him if he is a king. "Jesus answered, Thou sayest that I am a king. To this end was I born, and for this cause came I into the world, that I should bear witness unto the truth. Every one that is of the truth heareth my voice." And Pilate, perplexed, "saith unto him, What is truth?" See *IB*. Vol. 8. 1952, pp. 769–70.

668.35–36   Serpentes ... Gehennae?] That is, Matthew 23:33, "*Ye* serpents, *ye* generation of vipers, how can ye escape the damnation of hell?" This question forms part of Jesus' denunciation of the scribes and Pharisees. See *IB*. Vol. 7. 1951, p. 539.

672.1–2   *the comptoirs of the Demoiselles Desaulniers at Sault St Louis*] Marguerite, Marie-Anne, and Marie-Madeleine Desauniers, three sisters from Montreal, ran a store at the Jesuit mission of "Sault-Saint-Louis (Caughnawaga)" from 1726 to 1751. During these years, but especially in the 1740s, the sisters "were suspected of smuggling with the English in Albany, New York, under cover of honest trade with the Indians." One of their accomplices was supposedly Jean-Baptiste Tournois, the Jesuit priest who had served at Sault-Saint-Louis since 1741, and who "was named superior of the mission" in 1744. In 1751, after the store was finally closed by order of the French government, Tournois was forced "to return to France." The Desauniers sisters left for France at the same time. See "Tournois, Jean-Baptiste." *DCB*. Vol. 3, pp. 627–28.

673.19   oremus] That is, *let us pray*. An "invitation to pray," it is "said before collects and other short prayers" in the liturgy of the Roman Catholic church. See "Oremus." *Catholic*. Vol. 11. 1911, p. 295.

674.8–11   *charity ... nothing*] Compare I Corinthians 13:2 and 8. Paul, defining love, writes, "And though I have *the gift of* prophecy, and understand all mysteries, and all knowledge; and though I have all faith, so that I could remove mountains, and have not charity, I am nothing," and "Charity never faileth: but whether *there be* prophecies, they shall fail; whether *there be* tongues, they shall cease; whether *there be* knowledge, it shall vanish away." See *IB*. Vol. 10. 1953, pp. 169–70, 185, and 187.

678.34   *Hebert*] Louis Hébert, the "first officer of justice in New France" and the "first Canadian settler to support himself from the soil," arrived in Quebec with his wife and children in 1617. By the eighteenth century Hébert was a common name in the colony. In 1744, for example, "Angélique Hébert" lived on the "Rue Saint-Charles" in the city of Quebec. See "Hébert, Louis." *DCB*. Vol. 1, pp. 367–68, and "Le Recensement De Québec, En 1744." *Rapport De L'Archiviste De La Province De Québec Pour 1939–1940*. Québec: Redempti Paradis, 1940, pp. 57 and 65.

685.7–9   *"Blessed ... labours!"*] Compare Revelation 14:13, in which John records, "And I heard a voice from heaven saying unto me, Write, Blessed *are* the dead which die in the Lord from henceforth: Yea, saith the Spirit, that they may rest from their labors; and their works do follow them." See *IB*. Vol. 12. 1957, p. 473.

687.28–37   *the solitary hymn ... "Praised ... adored!—"*] Francis of Assisi, "The Canticle of Brother Sun," 1225–26. The last lines of the poem, composed by Francis of Assisi and sung to him just before his death in 1226, read in a modern translation of the original "Umbrian dialect":

> All praise be yours, my Lord, through Sister Death,
>   From whose embrace no mortal can escape.
> Woe to those who die in mortal sin!
> Happy those She finds doing your will!
> The second death can do no harm to them.
> Praise and bless my Lord, and give him thanks,
>   And serve him with great humility.

See St. Francis of Assisi. *Writings And Early Biographies*. Ed. Marion A. Habig. Chicago: Franciscan Herald Press, 1973, pp. 129–31.

690.2–4   *'The righteous ... evil to come!—'*] Compare Isaiah 57:1. The prophet, condemning the faithlessness of the Israelites and predicting their punishment by God, states, "The righteous perisheth, and no man layeth *it* to heart: and merciful men *are* taken away, none considering that the righteous is taken away from the evil *to come*." See *IB*. Vol. 5. 1956, p. 663.

694.2   *"EVIL NEWS RIDES POST"*] John Milton, *Samson Agonistes*, 1671, l. 1538. The Chorus, hearing the noise when Samson pulls down the theatre on his Philistine captors and himself, but not yet knowing its cause, comments, "Of good or bad so great, of bad

the sooner; / For evil news rides post, while good news baits."
See John Milton. *The Works Of John Milton.* Gen. Ed. Frank Allen
Patterson. New York: Columbia University Press, 1931. Vol. 1,
Part 2, p. 392.

694.25   *a true woman ... like Sara in the presence of Abraham*] Compare
Genesis. Sarah, the wife of Abraham who bore him his son Isaac
in his old age, and who died when she "was a hundred and
seven and twenty years old," is portrayed in Genesis as a true
"wife and comrade" who "had gone through many experiences
with" her husband "always in fidelity." Very beautiful as a young
woman, she "had her obvious faults, but she had character and
great distinction—a woman who could be jealous, but who had
passionate devotion to those she loved." See *IB.* Vol. 1. 1952,
pp. 646 and 648.

695.30–31   *the marriage of Cana in Galilee*] Compare John 2:1–11. Jesus and
his disciples join his mother at "a marriage in Cana of Galilee."
When she tells him that there is "no wine," Jesus makes it out
of the water that he has ordered the servants to pour into "six
waterpots of stone, ... containing two or three firkins apiece."
With this "beginning of miracles" Jesus "manifested forth his
glory; and his disciples believed on him." See *IB.* Vol. 8. 1952,
pp. 490–94.

697.1   Jure Divino] That is, *By divine right.* See Henry Campbell Black.
Black's Law Dictionary ... Fifth Edition. St. Paul, Minnesota: West
Publishing Company, 1979, p. 765.

699.8–12   *"Je voudrais ... ma jolie chambrette!"*] Compare the version of
"Je Ne Veux Pas D'Un Habitant" in Ernest Gagnon's *Chansons
Populaires Du Canada* (1865). From his copy of Gagnon's
anthology Kirby reproduced the first two lines of the first stanza
and the first three lines of the eighth and final stanza with one
variation in spelling—"jolie" instead of "joli'" in the third line
of the last stanza—and minor variations in punctuation. See
Chansons, pp. 264–66.

699.24–26   *the ladder of heaven, where the Patriarch saw angels ascending and
descending upon it*] Compare Genesis 28:12. Jacob, travelling
"from Beersheba ... toward Haran," stopped to rest "all night"
at "a certain place." There "he dreamed, and behold a ladder set
up on the earth, and the top of it reached to heaven: and behold

the angels of God ascending and descending on it." Above the
ladder, furthermore, stood "the LORD," who promised to be
always with Jacob and his "seed." See *IB*. Vol. 1. 1952, pp. 688–90.

704.23–24 *the Nun Madelaine de Repentigny*] Marie-Jeanne-Madeleine
Legardeur de Repentigny, "*dite* de Sainte-Agathe," the aunt
of the historical Pierre-Jean-Baptiste-François-Xavier Legardeur
de Repentigny and the fictional Amelie, "asked to be admitted
to the Ursuline order of Quebec" in 1717 after her fiancé,
supposedly a cousin, whom Kirby names Julian Lemoine, died.
It took her some time, however, to accept fully her vocation
as a nun, a state that she accomplished only when "she placed
her trust in Notre-Dame du Grand Pouvoir." To commemorate
"her gratitude towards the Madonna," she had the so-called
lamp of Repentigny, a perpetual lamp, installed in the chapel
of the Convent in 1724. "Mother Sainte-Agathe," whose family
was related to the Lemoines, died in 1739. Kirby most likely
took her story from "La Lampe Qui Ne S'Éteint Pas" and "Les
deux Lampes de N. D. du Grand-Pouvoir—La Mère M. Mad. de
Repentigny de Ste. Agathe," sections in *Les Ursulines De Québec,
Depuis Leur Établissement Jusqu'à Nos Jours*. See "Legardeur De
Repentigny, Marie-Jeanne-Madeleine, *dite* de Sainte-Agathe."
DCB. Vol. 2. p. 385, and *Ursulines*. Vol 2. 1864, pp. 132–37 and
234–36.

706.24–28 *Madame Bissot ... Madame Hamel*] Although neither character
appears to be historical, families named Bissot and Hamel
lived in and around Quebec in the eighteenth century.
François-Joseph Bissot, for example, "merchant and navigator"
and "bourgeois of Quebec," and his wife Marie Lambert
Dumont Bissot lived in the city with their "6 daughters and
3 sons" for most of their adult lives. He died in 1737, she
in 1745, but their children remained in the area. See "Bissot,
François-Joseph." *DCB*. Vol. 2, pp. 65–66.

709.25–27 *'Where thou ... my God.'*] Compare Ruth 1:16. Naomi, a widow,
leaves Moab to return to her native Bethlehem in Judah with
her two daughters-in-law. When she urges them not to go with
her, one leaves, but the other, Ruth, "said, Entreat me not to
leave thee, *or* to return from following after thee: for whither
thou goest, I will go; and where thou lodgest, I will lodge: thy

people *shall be* my people, and thy God my God." See *IB*. Vol. 2. 1953, p. 837.

710.9   *Mere Esther*] Esther Wheelwright, "(rebaptized Marie-Joseph), *dite* de l'Enfant-Jésus," was captured by the Abenakis in 1703 when she was seven and rescued from them by Vincent Bigot, a Jesuit priest, who took her to Quebec. She became "Esther-Marie-Joseph de l'Enfant-Jésus," an Ursuline nun, in 1713. The superior of the Ursuline Convent in Quebec "from 1760 to 1766, and from 1769 to 1772," she died in 1780. During her years as a nun her family in "Wells, Massachusetts (now Maine)" made various efforts to see her and to persuade her to return home. According to Charlotte Alice Baker, in 1754 a nephew visited her in Quebec and "gave to his aunt a miniature portrait of her mother," who was "a blonde with hazel eyes and an oval face." This miniature, retouched "by the addition of a veil and drapery, and enclosed in a richly embossed frame," is still "cherished as a Madonna" by the Ursulines of Quebec. Kirby's source for this story was most likely *Les Ursulines De Québec, Depuis Leur Établissement Jusqu'à Nos Jours*. Its version seems to date the receipt of the picture to shortly "après la profession de Mlle. Wheelwright" in 1713; otherwise its account is similar to Baker's. See Charlotte Alice Baker. *True Stories Of New England Captives Carried To Canada During The Old French And Indian Wars*. Cambridge, 1897, pp. 60 and 68; "Wheelwright, Esther." *DCB*. Vol. 4, pp. 764–66; and *Ursulines*. Vol. 2. 1864, p. 88.

710.34   *Mere St Gertrude*] She was the daughter of Jacques Le Picard Du Mesnil de Norrey, a French naval officer, and his wife, Marie-Renée Chorel de Saint-Romain, *dit* d'Orvilliers, a "merchant's daughter" from Trois-Rivières, Quebec. After her father came to Canada in 1684, he was made a "captain in the colonial regular troops" and, from 1706 until his death in 1713, the "garrison adjutant (*major des troupes*) of the troops in Canada." Named after her mother, Marie-Renée "Norey du Mesnil de Ste. Gertrude" was one of several daughters of prominent Montreal families who were novices in the Ursuline Convent in Quebec around 1720. Frequently ill and, therefore, unable to hold a regular office, she was known for her "humilité." She died in 1751. See "Le Picard Du Mesnil De

Norrey, Jacques." *DCB.* Vol. 2, pp. 415–17, and *Ursulines.* Vol. 2. 1864, pp. 350–51.

711.32–35 *the language of the ... Jesuit ... "the fair Esther ... Kings in heaven"*] Vincent Bigot, the Jesuit priest and "missionary to the Abenakis" who "had rescued" Esther Wheelwright from their hands, preached the sermon when she became an Ursuline. In this discourse, which appeared in an abridged form in *Les Ursulines De Québec, Depuis Leur Établissement Jusqu'à Nos Jours,* he exclaimed, "N'êtes-vous pas, ma chère Soeur, une autre petite Esther, à qui une dure captivité va ouvrir le chemin au trône, non pas du puissant Assuérus; mais du Maître d'Assuérus, du Maître des monarques, de l'immortel Epoux des Vierges!" Kirby's lines are a translation of this passage. According to Esther 2:1–17, Ahasuerus, whose kingdom extended from India to Ethiopia, took the "fair and beautiful" Esther, the niece of Mordecai the Jew, for his queen after he had deposed Queen Vashti. Esther and her uncle were later able to liberate the Jews throughout Ahasuerus' huge empire. See "Bigot, Vincent." *DCB.* Vol. 2, pp. 64–65; *IB.* Vol. 3. 1954, pp. 839–44; and *Ursulines.* Vol. 2. 1864, pp. 81–82.

712.4 *Mere des Anges*] Marie Le Maire des Anges was a French Ursuline who arrived in Quebec from the "Grand Couvent de Paris" in 1671. Superior of the Convent from 1694 to 1700, and again from 1712 until her death in 1717, she played an energetic role in the enlargement and decoration of its buildings. According to "La Mère Marie Le Maire des Anges dernière professe du Grand Couvent de Paris," her obituary in *Les Ursulines De Québec, Depuis Leur Établissement Jusqu'à Nos Jours,* her "plus douce récréation" was to make "des beaux ornements" to decorate altars and other places not only at the Ursuline Convent in Quebec but also in many churches in New France. See *Ursulines.* Vol. 2. 1864, pp. 210–12.

713.11–12 *'Come ... rest'*] Compare Matthew 11:28. Jesus, teaching, invites his audience, "Come unto me, all *ye* that labor and are heavy laden, and I will give you rest." See *IB.* Vol. 7. 1951, p. 389.

714.9 *the* admirable Queteuse] Marie-Angélique Mariauchau d'Esgly (d'Esglis) was the daughter of François Mariauchau d'Esgly, a French soldier who first "came to New France in 1689" and held several important military positions in the colony until his death in 1730, and his wife, Louise-Philippe Chartier de Lotbinière. Educated at the Ursuline Convent in Quebec, Marie-Angélique wished to become a nun there, but she realized that her father lacked the necessary "ressources pécuniaires" to provide a dowry. When he died, in fact, he "was buried in the paupers' cemetery" of "the Hôtel-Dieu of Quebec." She, thus, went begging for money "de porte en porte" in Quebec and, thereby, showed such virtue that "tous, grands et petits, en restèrent dans l'admiration et s'empressèrent d'assister la noble demoiselle." Known as "Mère Herman de St. Eustache," she made her profession as an Ursuline in 1733 and served in the Convent until her death in the 1750s. See "Mariauchau D'Esgly (d'Esglis), François." *DCB.* Vol. 2, pp. 456–57, and "Une admirable queteuse." *Ursulines.* Vol. 2. 1864, pp. 351–54.

715.1   *Ste Angele*] Angela Merici, a native of "Desenzano, a small town on the southwestern shore of Lake Garda" in what is now Italy, established a school there in the late fifteenth century to instruct "young girls in the rudiments of the Christian religion." This institution led not only to another in Brescia but also to Angela's choosing "twelve virgins" to found "the order of the Ursulines" there in 1535. Her feast day is 27 January, the day she died in Brescia in 1540. See "Angela Merici, Saint." *Catholic.* Vol. 1. 1907, pp. 481–82.

715.17–18 *Ste Therese*] Teresa Sanchez Cepeda Davila y Ahumada, born in Avila to a wealthy Castilian family, joined the Carmelites there in the 1530s. Unhappy with their lax rules, however, after "many troubles and much opposition" she "founded the convent of Discalced Carmelite Nuns of the Primitive Rule of St. Joseph at Avila" in 1562. This establishment, in which the nuns lived in conditions of poverty, hardship, and solitude, was the model for several others begun by Teresa before her death in 1582. As well as a reformer, she was also an author and a mystic. Her feast day is 15 October. See "Teresa of Jesus, Saint." *Catholic.* Vol. 14. 1912, pp. 515–17.

717.27   *the Seigneur de Boucherville*] Pierre Boucher was the father of fifteen children, including Geneviève, the much admired Ursuline nun, born to Jeanne Crevier, his second wife.

"Interpreter, soldier, governor of Trois-Rivières, royal judge, founder and seigneur of Boucherville," he successfully defended "the post of Trois-Rivières" when it was besieged by the Iroquois in 1653 and, thus, helped bring an end to their frequent attacks on the French settlements. Ennobled in 1661, by the mid 1660s he "had become the dominant figure in the colony." When he died at Boucherville in "1717 at the age of 95 years," he left a "spiritual testament... entitled 'My last wishes.'" "Les adieux du Grand-Pere Boucher" is partially reprinted in the section on him and his family in *Les Ursulines De Québec, Depuis Leur Établissement Jusqu'à Nos Jours*, the source that Kirby most probably followed for his information on this "vénérable patriarche" and his family. See "Boucher, Pierre." *DCB*. Vol. 2, pp. 82–87, and "Si L'On Aime Ses Parents Au Monastère." *Ursulines*. Vol. 2. 1864, pp. 89–101.

718.16–17 *dying Jacob's patriarchal blessing of his twelve sons*] Compare Genesis 49:1–28. Before he died, Jacob called his sons together and blessed each from Reuben, his "firstborn," to Benjamin, his youngest, who "shall raven *as* a wolf: in the morning he shall devour the prey, and at night he shall divide the spoil." And "these *are* the twelve tribes of Israel: and this *is it* that their father spake unto them, and blessed them; every one according to his blessing he blessed them." See *IB*. Vol. 1. 1952, pp. 818–23.

719.5 *the victories of Chouagen and of Carillon*] The French captured Chouaguen (Oswego, New York) on Lake Ontario in August 1756, a result that the annalist of the Ursulines called both "prodigieux" and unexpected. The French also successfully defended Fort Carillon (Ticonderoga, New York) on Lake Champlain against an English attack in July 1758 and, thus, achieved, in the annalist's words, a "brillante victoire." See *Ursulines*. Vol. 2. 1864, pp. 290 and 307.

721.16 *Mere St Charles*] The daughter of Charles Perthuis, a Quebec "merchant," and his wife, Marie-Madeleine Roberge, whom he married in 1697, Madeleine-Geneviève Perthuis entered the Ursuline Convent in Quebec in the early 1720s. As "Mère Geneviève Perthuis de St. Charles," she played various roles there, including those of "maîtresse des novices, et maîtresse-générale," until her death in 1761. See "Perthuis,

Charles." *DCB.* Vol. 2, pp. 520–21, and *Ursulines.* Vol. 2. 1864, p. 342.

722.4   *the old Baroness de Longueil*] Most probably this is a reference to Marie-Charles-Joseph Le Moyne de Longueuil, "fourth baroness of Longueuil." Born in Montreal, she studied at the Ursuline Convent in Quebec in the 1770s and lived in the city intermittently after she married David Alexander Grant in 1781, and after she was widowed in 1806. Known "as a pious and charitable woman," she sent "quelques barils" of apples every year to "les enfants du Vieux Monastère." She was also parsimonious, particularly as she aged. In Montreal, for example, she used to pull her buggy "un vieux cheval" that had formerly belonged to a baker, and that children repeatedly halted by crying "*Bread* (pain)" as it passed in the street. "Madame la Baronne" died in 1841 a month before her eighty-fifth birthday. See "Le Moyne De Longueuil, Marie-Charles-Joseph, Baronne de Longueuil (Grant)." *DCB.* Vol. 7, pp. 500–01; Alexandre Jodoin and Joseph Louis Vincent. *Histoire De Longueuil Et De La Famille De Longueuil.* Montréal: Imprimerie Gerhardt-Berthiaume, 1889, pp. 368–69; and "Mlle. de Longueuil ou 'La Baronne.'" *Ursulines.* Vol. 3. 1866, pp. 236–39.

724.24   *Mere Ste Vierge*] Marie-Louise Gaillard was the daughter of Guillaume Gaillard, "businessman, seigneur of the Île d'Orléans and member of the Conseil Supérieur," and his first wife, Marie-Catherine Neveu (Nepveu). In 1712 Marie-Louise entered the Ursuline Convent in Quebec where she took the name "Mère ... de la Ste. Vierge." Superior of the Ursulines for a brief period in 1735, she also acted as "maîtresse-générale des pensionnaires" and as "sacristine" in the chapel dedicated to the Virgin Mary, which was her special charge. She died in 1764. See "Gaillard, Guillaume." *DCB.* Vol. 2, pp. 234–35, and "Heureuses sympathies de deux soeurs." *Ursulines.* Vol. 3. 1866, pp. 121–23.

725.21   Laus Deo] That is, *Praise be to God.* See *A Dictionary Of Latin And Greek Quotations, Proverbs, Maxims And Mottos.* Ed. H. T. Riley. London: George Bell And Sons, 1909, p. 201.

726.19–22   *What says ... Thomas? 'Temptations ... exalted'*] Thomas a

Kempis, *The Imitation of Christ,* 1418, Book 1, Chapter 13. There have been many English translations of this work. Compare, for example, that by John Wesley, in which the relevant passage reads, "Temptations are often very profitable to men, though they be troublesome and grievous; for in them a man is humbled, purified, and instructed." First published in 1735, Wesley's translation was frequently reprinted in the eighteenth and nineteenth centuries. See Thomas A Kempis. *The Christian's Pattern; Or, A Treatise On The Imitation Of Christ.* Trans. John Wesley. Halifax: Milner And Sowerby, 1862, p. 20.

726.33– *the hymn of the Virgin:—"Eia, Mater! ... Paradisi gloria! Amen!—"*]
727.5   That is, the "Stabat Mater Dolorosa," a hymn that "was well known ... by the end of the fourteenth century." Kirby reproduced the first stanza and the seventh and last stanza of the version traditionally associated with Morning Prayer in the liturgy of the Roman Catholic church. An English translation of these stanzas reads, "O Mother, fountain of love, / make me feel the power of sorrow, / that I may grieve with you," and "When my body dies, / grant that to my soul is given / the glory of paradise. Amen." See "Stabat Mater." *Catholic.* Vol. 14. 1912, pp. 239–40, and "The Stabat Mater: Latin with literal English translation." http://www.shrinesf.org/stabatmater.htm.

733.2   "*LOVELY IN DEATH*"] Edward Young, *Night The Third. Narcissa,* 1742, l. 104. The poet, lamenting the loss of his "beautiful" and "young" Narcissa, states, "Like blossom'd Trees o'erturn'd by vernal Storm, / Lovely in Death the beauteous Ruin lay." See Edward Young. *Night Thoughts.* Ed. Stephen Cornford. Cambridge: Cambridge University Press, 1989, p. 75.

733.15–18 *her canticle ... "Ave ... Jesus!—"*] That is, the "Ave Joseph" prayer. Its opening lines read, in English, "Hail Joseph! son of David, just! / Husband of Mary of whom is born Jesus!" The lines themselves are variations of Matthew 1:16, "And Jacob begat Joseph the husband of Mary, of whom was born Jesus," and Matthew 1:20, in which "the angel of the Lord" addressed Joseph "in a dream" as "Joseph, thou son of David." From its founding "St. Joseph" was regarded as "le premier et principal gardien" of the Ursuline Convent in Quebec. See *IB.* Vol. 7. 1951, pp. 252–53 and 255, and *Ursulines.* Vol. 1. 1863, pp. 307 and 311.

734.36   memorare] That is, "the beautiful prayer to the Blessed Virgin" Mary. Popularized in the seventeenth century by Claude Bernard, a "French ecclesiastic known as 'the poor priest,'" and "sometimes attributed to him but certainly of an earlier date," the prayer reads in a modern English version:

> Remember, O most gracious Virgin Mary, that never was it known that anyone who fled to your protection, implored your help or sought your intercession was left unaided. Inspired with ... confidence, I fly to you, O virgin of virgins, my Mother. To you I come, before you I stand, sinful and sorrowful. O Mother of the Word Incarnate, despise not my petitions, but in your mercy, hear and answer me. Amen.

In *Les Ursulines De Québec, Depuis Leur Établissement Jusqu'à Nos Jours*, it is recorded that after the Convent burned down in 1686, several Ursulines took shelter at the Hôtel-Dieu. On their arrival there they sang "le *Memorare* à la Ste. Vierge," their "Mère et principale Supérieure, la suppliant" to take care of them. See "Bernard, Claude." *Catholic*. Vol. 2. 1907, p. 496; "Memorare." http://www.catholic-forum.com/SAINTS/pray0423.htm; and *Ursulines*. Vol. 1. 1863, pp. 432–33.

735.10   *Our Lord ... wept at Bethany*] Compare Luke 19:28–43. Jesus, "ascending up to Jerusalem," came "nigh to ... Bethany, at the mount called the *mount* of Olives." There he "sent two of his disciples" to fetch a colt on which to ride into Jerusalem. "And when he was come near, he beheld the city, and wept over it." For, he said, "the days shall come upon thee, that thine enemies shall cast a trench about thee, and compass thee round, and keep thee in on every side." See *IB*. Vol. 8. 1952, pp. 334–41.

735.34–37   *God ... put all their tears in his bottle, as the Hebrew Prophet ... describes ... affliction*] Compare Psalm 56:8–9. David, complaining about his enemies, says to God, "Thou tellest my wanderings: put thou my tears into thy bottle: *are they* not in thy book?" Then he adds, "When I cry *unto thee*, then shall mine enemies turn back: this I know; for God *is* for me." See *IB*. Vol. 4. 1955, p. 294.

737.9   *Mere St Antoine*] She is most likely based on Marie-Anne

Buteau de Ste. Agnès, the daughter of Antoine Buteau, "riche propriétaire de la paroisse de St. Joachim," and his wife, Anne Cloutier. Anne-Marie entered the Ursuline Convent of Quebec as a teenager and served in various capacities until her death in 1781 "dans la 83e année de son âge." In "Notre Héritière de St. Joachim dans sa pieuse et utile carrière," the section about her in *Les Ursulines De Québec. Depuis Leur Établissement Jusqu'à Nos Jours*, she is described as being constantly at the side of "Mères St. Louis et de l'Enfant Jésus . . . tant aux observances régulières que dans le détail des travaux communs." See *Ursulines*. Vol. 3. 1866, pp. 365–67.

743.2   *"THE MILLS OF GOD GRIND SLOWLY"*] Henry Wadsworth Longfellow, "Poetic Aphorisms From The Sinngedichte Of Friedrich Von Logau . . . Retribution," ca. 1836, l. 1. The complete aphorism reads:

> Though the mills of God grind slowly, yet
> they grind exceeding small;
> Though with patience he stands waiting,
> with exactness grinds he all.

See Henry Wadsworth Longfellow. *The Poetical Works of Longfellow. Cambridge Edition*. Introd. George Monteiro. Boston: Houghton Mifflin, 1975, p. 616.

744.8–20   *We see . . . 'Darkness . . . in the morning!'*] A pastiche of various Biblical phrases, this speech includes several from Psalm 37. Among these are "I have seen the wicked in great power, and spreading himself like a green bay tree," "Mark the perfect *man*, and behold the upright: for the end of *that* man *is* peace," and "the end of the wicked shall be cut off." The final sentence, "Darkness lasteth through the night, but Joy cometh in the morning," is a version of Psalm 30:5, "weeping may endure for a night, but joy *cometh* in the morning." See *IB*. Vol. 4. 1955, pp. 160 and 192–99.

745.15   *Minden*] Fought in August 1759 during the Seven Years' War, the battle of Minden (Germany) pitched a "37,000-strong Anglo-Hanoverian force" against "a French army of 44,000." The conflict "lasted for about five hours," during which the French, who were defeated, lost "between 7,000–10,000 men."

See "Minden, battle of." *The Oxford Companion To Military History.* Ed. Richard Holmes. Oxford: Oxford University Press, 2001, p. 589.

745.28   *De Vaudreuil*] Pierre Rigaud de Vaudreuil de Cavagnial, who began calling himself "the Marquis de Vaudreuil" in the early 1740s, was the son of Philippe de Rigaud de Vaudreuil, Marquis de Vaudreuil, the "governor general of New France" from 1703 until his death in 1725. After serving as governor of Louisiana from 1742 to 1753, the Quebec-born Pierre was appointed "governor general of New France" in 1755. The last to hold that position, in September 1760 in Montreal he negotiated the terms of "the capitulation of Canada, Acadia, and the western posts as far south as the Illinois" to the British. Shortly thereafter he sailed for France. Implicated along with François Bigot, with whom he had "good" relations, in the so-called *affaire du Canada*, he spent time in the Bastille in 1762. Although the next year he was "exonerated by the judges" who investigated "the huge bills that had accrued" for the defence of the colony, he was often "depicted ... in a bad light," especially for his failure to control Bigot's expenditures. See "Rigaud De Vaudreuil De Cavagnial, Pierre De." *DCB.* Vol. 4, pp. 662–74.

746.26–28 *the defence of ... Montmorency, to ... St Foye*] These were French victories in North America during the Seven Years' War. The French dislodged the British from the base of Montmorency Falls, Quebec, in July 1759, and they defeated the British force sent out from Quebec at nearby Ste. Foye in April 1760 and, thus, "gloriously avenged" the French defeat on the Plains of Abraham the previous September. See Bell. Vol. 2, p. 285.

747.29   *Sir Guy Carleton*] Guy Carleton, "army officer and colonial administrator," served as "'Lieutenant Governor and Administrator' of Quebec" from 1766 to 1768, and then from that year until 1778 as "'Captain General and Governor in Chief'" of the colony. As "Baron Dorchester" he returned as "commander-in-chief" and "governor-in-chief" of the British North American provinces of Quebec, Nova Scotia, and New Brunswick in 1786. He held these positions until 1796, when he "left Canada for good." See "Carleton, Guy." *DCB.* Vol. 5, pp. 141–55.

747.34–37 *the De Salaberrys, the De Beaujeus, Duchesnays, de Gaspes ...*
loyal subjects of England's crown] A member of each of
these seigneurial families fought with the British when
the Americans invaded Canada in 1775–76. Pierre-Ignace
Aubert de Gaspé, "JP, seigneur, politician, and militia officer,"
while "still a student" at "the Petit Séminaire" in Quebec,
"responded to the call by Governor Guy Carleton ... to
take up arms against the American troops under Richard
Montgomery and Benedict Arnold." Ignace-Michel-Antoine
d'Irumberry de Salaberry, "army and militia officer, seigneur,
politician, JP, and office holder," helped "defend Fort St
Johns (Saint-Jean-sur-Richelieu)" in 1775. Antoine Juchereau
Duchesnay, "army and militia officer, seigneur, and politician,"
also "volunteered ... for the defence of Fort St Johns.... He was
taken prisoner on 1 Nov. 1775 and spent 18 months as a captive
in New England." And in "March 1776, with the Americans
besieging Quebec," Louis Liénard de Beaujeu de Villemonde,
"army and militia officer and seigneur," at Carleton's request
raised "a relief force among the Canadians along the south shore
of the St Lawrence below Quebec." See "Juchereau Duchesnay,
Antoine." *DCB*. Vol. 5, pp. 462–64; "Liénard De Beaujeu De
Villemonde, Louis." *DCB*. Vol. 5, pp. 498–99; "Aubert De
Gaspé, Pierre-Ignace." *DCB*. Vol. 6, pp. 16–17; and "Irumberry
De Salaberry, Ignace-Michel-Louis-Antoine D'." *DCB*. Vol. 6,
pp. 345–46.

748.9–10 *the letter of the Marshal De Belle Isle*] Charles-Louis-Auguste
Fouquet, the Duke of Belle-Isle, was named "secrétaire d'État
au département de la Guerre" for France in March 1758. In
February 1759 he informed the French general Louis-Joseph
de Montcalm that "reinforcements must not be expected" in
Quebec. He added in the same letter, which is quoted in
Andrew Bell's translation of the third edition of François-Xavier
Garneau's *Histoire Du Canada* (1859):

"not only would additional troops be a means of
aggravating the evils of the dearth which has too long
afflicted the colony, but the chances are great that, if
sent thither, they would be captured by the British on

their way to you; and as the king cannot pretend to send forces in any equal proportion to those which the British can oppose to ours, the only result of our increasing the latter would be, that the cabinet of London would augment theirs in an over-proportion, so as to maintain the superiority which Britain has acquired in that part of your continent."

Kirby may be paraphrasing this passage from his copy of Bell. See Bell. Vol. 2, p. 225, and "Belle-Isle (Charles-Louis-Auguste Fouquet, duc De)." *DBF.*

748.17–22 *"When ... stables!" ... Berreyer ... De Bougainville ... "his ... horse!—"*] In 1758 Louis-Antoine de Bougainville, a French army officer who had come to Quebec in 1756 "as aide-de-camp" to Louis-Joseph de Montcalm, returned to France to "report on the lamentable state of the colony" and to "ask for aid." At a meeting he and Nicolas-René Berryer, who had been named "ministre de la Marine" in November 1758, are supposed to have exchanged the insults repeated by Kirby. He also recorded them in a notebook as "Dit Berreyer Ministre de la Marine 1757 à De Bougainville qui demandait des secours pour la Nouvelle France—'Monsieur quand le feu est a la Maison on ne s'occupe pas des ecuries!' & De Bougainville riposta—'On dirait du moins que vous parlez comme un cheval.'" Kirby may have taken this passage from *Les Ursulines De Québec, Depuis Leur Établissement Jusqu'à Nos Jours* where these words "d'insulte" are added as a note to the description of De Bougainville's "audience à Versailles." See "Berryer (Nicolas-*René*)." *DBF*; "Bougainville, Louis-Antoine De." *DCB*. Vol. 5, pp. 102–06; OTAR, Kirby, F–1076, Miscellaneous Manuscripts, MU1646, D–18, Note-book kept by Kirby containing ... excerpts from various historical publications relating to the history of New France, p. 23; and *Ursulines*. Vol. 2. 1864, p. 317.

748.34–35 *the seductive offers of La Fayette and D'Estaing*] Both Marie-Joseph-Paul-Yves-Roch Gilbert du Motier Lafayette, "French soldier and statesman," and Jean-Baptiste-Charles-Henri-Hector d'Estaing, "French general and admiral," fought with the rebels in the American Revolution. In 1778 Lafayette, "major general in the Continental army," led "an abortive expedition to invade Canada." D'Estaing's "two expeditions" in 1778 and 1779 "were the only instances of direct French intervention in the American Revolution during the first twenty-eight months of the Franco-American alliance." Both men also worked to persuade Canadians "to take part in the struggle." In May 1779, for example, "a proclamation" issued by "the Comte d'Estaing" that "urged Canadians to rise against Britain" was distributed throughout Quebec. In Andrew Bell's translation of the third edition of François-Xavier Garneau's *Histoire Du Canada* (1859), it is reported that "Count d'Estaing, chief admiral of the French fleet cruising on the American seaboard in 1778, had no more success than other appellants.... His words, wafted from the Ocean, found no responsive echo in Canadian cottages." Likewise Lafayette's "reproachful saying ... to the Canadian officers kept prisoners at Boston" was ineffective. See "Estaing, Comte d.'" *ANB*; "Lafayette, Marquis de." *ANB*; Bell. Vol. 3, p. 34; and "Cazeau, François." *DCB*. Vol. 5, pp. 173–74.

749.11 *Bishop Briand*] Jean-Olivier Briand, a French priest who came as a missionary to Quebec in 1741, was the Roman Catholic bishop of Quebec from 1766 to 1784. During the American Revolution Briand "urged his faithful to repulse" the American invaders and "issued a pastoral letter supporting Carleton's proclamation concerning the re-establishment of the militia," an action that was not popular with many residents of the colony. See "Briand, Jean-Olivier." *DCB*. Vol. 4, pp. 94–103.

749.14–15 *Arnold and Montgomery*] In 1775 Richard Montgomery, a former British army officer who had "sold his commission and emigrated" to New York in 1772, "was appointed a brigadier-general in the newly formed Continental Army." In this capacity he invaded Canada with a force that captured "in succession Fort Chambly, Fort St Johns, Montreal, and Sorel" and eventually attacked Quebec in "a blinding snowstorm" on "the night of 30–31 December" 1775. In this attack Montgomery was joined by Benedict Arnold, "army officer and merchant," who had led his troops to Quebec through Maine. Montgomery was killed in this action; Arnold was wounded. The Americans continued to lay siege to Quebec until the following spring, but their failure to capture the city marked a turning point in their hope of Canada's becoming the fourteenth colony to revolt against the British. See "Montgomery, Richard." *DCB.* Vol. 4, pp. 545–50, and "Arnold, Benedict." *DCB.* Vol. 5, pp. 28–36.

749.15   *Curé Bailly*] Charles-François Bailly de Messein, born near Montreal, "was ordained priest" in 1767. In 1776 he was a director of "the Petit Séminaire" in Quebec, where he taught "rhetoric and *belles-lettres.*" He also served the parish of Saint-Pierre on the south shore of the St. Lawrence, where, in the spring of 1776, he "was shot in the abdomen and taken prisoner" when he, "'*a zealous Royalist,*'" and other "volunteers" loyal to Great Britain were attacked by a group of Americans and their Canadian supporters. Called "un belliqueux curé" by James Macpherson Le Moine in *Album Canadien* (1870), Bailly was consecrated as the "coadjutor" Roman Catholic "bishop of Quebec" in 1789. See "Bailly De Messein, Charles-François." *DCB.* Vol. 4, pp. 41–44, and James MacPherson Le Moine. *Album Canadien, Histoire, Archéologie—Ornithologie.* Québec: Des Presses Mécaniques Du *Canadien,* 1870, pp. [61]–65.

749.21   *Murray*] James Murray, "army officer and colonial administrator," served under James Wolfe "at the siege of Quebec" in 1759. He "commanded the left wing of the battle line on the Plains of Abraham," and, after Wolfe's death, he was left "in charge of Quebec during the winter of 1759–60." He, thus, led the British troops at "the battle of Sainte-Foy" in April 1760 and during the French siege of Quebec that followed and that ended only with "the arrival of a British squadron in May" of that year. Murray "became governor of the District of Quebec" in October 1760 and "governor of the province" of Quebec in 1763, a position that he held until 1766. See "Murray, James." *DCB.* Vol. 4, pp. 569–78.

749.30–36   *an obituary notice . . . "East Indies . . . gallant soldier—."*] In its issue for 19 June 1777, the *Quebec Gazette / Gazette de Québec* reported under the heading "Indes Orientalles":

> Le Marquis Legardeur Repentigny, Brigadier des armées du Roi, Gouverneur de Mahé, est mort l'année dernière dans cette partie de l'Inde, qu'il avoit par

sa valeur et sa bonne conduite conservé contre les entreprises d'un Prince du païs. Cet Officier avait servi en Canada sa patrie avec toute la réputation qu'un vrai Militaire doit acquérir.

This notice, identified as having appeared in "la *Gazette de Québec* en l'année 1777," was reprinted in *Les Ursulines De Québec, Depuis Leur Établissement Jusqu'à Nos Jours*, from which Kirby may have taken it. Pierre-Jean-Baptiste-François-Xavier Legardeur de Repentigny "was made commandant at Mahé, India," in 1774 and "colonel of the Régiment de Pondichéry" in 1775. He died in Pondicherry in May 1776. See "Legardeur De Repentigny, Pierre-Jean-Baptiste-François-Xavier." *DCB*. Vol. 4, pp. 448–49; *Quebec Gazette / Gazette De Québec*, 19 June 1777, p. [3]; and *Ursulines*. Vol. 2. 1864, p. 137.

754.26–30 *It was ... deposited in the public Museum at Boston in New England*] In his chapter on "Marie Josephte Corriveau" in *Maple Leaves: A Budget Of Legendary, Historical, Critical, And Sporting Intelligence* (1863), a copy of which Kirby owned, James MacPherson Le Moine recalled that "a rusty iron cage," supposed to have been La Corriveau's, "was exhibited" in Quebec in 1850 before it was sold for "a handsome amount ... to the prince of modern humbugs, in whose museum the 'Point Levy relic' ... remained on view for a long time, where, next to the woolly horse, ... it attracted considerable attention." In *Les Anciens Canadiens* (1863), a copy of which Kirby also owned, Philippe-Joseph Aubert de Gaspé asserted that the cage was sold to the "Musée Barnum, à New York, où on doit encore la voir." P. T. Barnum's American Museum, established in late 1841 and "located from 1845 to 1865 at the corner of Broadway and Ann Street in lower Manhattan," displayed various "sensational" attractions, including the "Woolly Horse," that could be viewed for "a twenty-five cent admission" fee. Barnum, the ultimate "showman," sometimes exchanged exhibits with Moses Kimball's similar Boston Museum, which existed from 1841 to 1903. The cage, which has apparently disappeared, could, thus, have been displayed at both these places of popular entertainment. See "Barnum, P. T." *ANB*; Philippe-Joseph

Aubert de Gaspé. *Les Anciens Canadiens.* Second Edition. Québec: G. Et G. E. Desbarats, 1864, p. 373; "The 'Barnum Museum' Archive." 10 July 2011, http://www.lostmuseum.cuny. edu/archives/museum.htm; and *Maple Leaves*, p. 69.

Description of Manuscript Copy-text

The manuscript copy-text for the CEECT edition of *Le Chien d'or* is the manuscript of the novel held in the William Kirby Collection at the Archives of Ontario in Toronto, Ontario (OTAR, Kirby, F-1076, Miscellaneous Manuscripts Compiled or Copied by Kirby, MU1643-1644, D-12, Boxes 10 and 11). In the *Inventory of the William Kirby Collection*, the finding aid for this collection, the entry for this item reads, "An original manuscript copy of The Golden Dog. Some of the chapters are badly mutilated."[1] The entry describing this item on its microfilm also reads, "An original manuscript of The Golden Dog." It adds, "At one point, some of the chapters suffered water damage and although conservation was undertaken on the manuscript, (1982), parts of the text are either hard to read or in some cases are missing."[2] This manuscript was the copy-text for the Lovell, Adam, Wesson and Company impression of the first edition of the novel published in 1877. It represents, however, several stages in its composition, its preparation for printing by the Lovells' Lake Shore Press at Rouses Point, New York, and its conservation by the Archives of Ontario. The following paragraphs describe characteristics of the manuscript that denote each of these stages. See also "Page of Manuscript Copy-text" (clxxiii).

Because of the damage sustained by the manuscript before it came into the possession of the Archives of Ontario, and because of the way it was conserved by this institution, it is impossible to ascertain the exact number of leaves that the manuscript copy-text contained. The best guess is that it had about 1035 leaves approximately 339 mm. in height by 210 mm. in width. These leaves, comprised of wood-pulp paper, were sewn together in a series of twelve notebooks, or, to use Kirby's term, volumes. On the recto of the first leaf of each notebook, Kirby usually recorded, in pen or pencil, some combination of the number of the notebook, the title of his novel, his name, and his address. On the recto of the leaf numbered 114, for example, he has written in pencil, "Vol 2 | No 2 | Le Chien d'or | W Kirby | Niagara." With the exception of the final leaves of the manuscript copy-text, the text of the novel was entered on the verso of each leaf. When it was necessary, the recto of a leaf was used by Kirby to indicate revisions to his text. Their placement in the text was often signaled by an "X" at the relevant spot on the facing verso. Each verso that contained the text and each recto that held Kirby's revisions were numbered. The number on each verso normally appeared at its top left-hand corner; the number on each inscribed recto, at the top right-hand corner. The number on these rectos was usually formed by adding "$1/2$" to the number on the previous verso. On the recto opposite the leaf that has "949" on its verso, for instance, Kirby has written "949$1/2$" in the top right-hand corner; further down this recto, roughly opposite the spot on verso 949 where the addition should go, he has entered "from page 949," marked an "X," and added a paragraph symbol and five lines of text. Their placement on the verso of leaf 949 is signaled on this verso both by a line, an "X," and the words "To page 949$1/2$."

The numbers and the text on the first 405 leaves of the manuscript copy-text are written in Kirby's hand. These leaves constitute Chapters 1 to 26 of *Le Chien d'or* (3–305) and represent the reduction of the length of the text of the novel and, thus, the recasting that its author undertook in 1875–76. The text on leaves 406 to 1007 of this manuscript has been transcribed by five different copyists: Hannah Lowe (leaves 406 to 507 and 597 to 804); Mrs. Lowe, the mother of Hannah and Josephine (leaves 508 to 596); Josephine Lowe (leaves 805 to 897); Mrs. Kirby (leaves 898 to 938); and Mary Torrance (leaves 939 to 1007). These leaves constitute Chapters 27 to 57 of the novel (306–732). They also represent roughly 636 leaves, numbered [743] to 1409, of an earlier, longer version of *Le Chien d'or*, probably that which existed after the author revised the last section of the novel in 1874–75. In his own hand Kirby has crossed out the previous numbers on these leaves and renumbered them sequentially. The text on the final leaves of the manuscript copy-text, also in Kirby's hand, constitutes the last two chapters of the novel, Chapters 58 and 59 (733–55), and represents the shortened conclusion that Kirby prepared in 1874–75. These leaves also represent twenty-four leaves of a previous manuscript and, thus, carry an older sequence of numbers; that is, 1410 to 1428, 1431, 1437, and 1438. Between leaves 1431 and 1437 there are two leaves on which this older sequence of numbers is not visible. As in the copied section of the manuscript, Kirby has crossed out these higher numbers and written over or beside them the new sequence of numbers beginning at 1008 and ending at 1038. The text on the seventeen leaves numbered 1008 to 1024 is written on the verso of each leaf. On the last seven leaves the text is written on both the recto and the verso of each leaf. These leaves, thus, carry the numbers 1025 to 1038. No recto or verso, however, is numbered 1036.

Throughout the manuscript copy-text there are revisions in Kirby's hand both on the verso of the leaves and on their facing rectos. Many of these involve changes in a word or a short phrase. On the verso of leaf 437, for example, in the sentence "The flow of her conversation became embarrassed and nearly ceased," Kirby has crossed out both "became" and "nearly." This sentence, thus, reads in its revised form, "The flow of her conversation was embarrassed and almost ceased" (326). Other revisions are more extensive. One of the most complicated also begins on the verso of leaf 437 when Kirby directs the compositor to "page 437 1/2"; that is, the recto of leaf 438. On this he has added several lines, including a song that begins "A linnet sat upon a thorn" and ends "And make no sign!" Kirby has noted at the top of the recto of leaf 734, numbered "733 1/2," however, "NB following song was misplaced in a previous chapter. The compositor will please place it here with accompanying paragraph." He has then recopied the song about the linnet, this time attributing its performance to Caroline de St Castin rather than to Amelie de Repentigny (537).

These leaves contain as well the additions made by Kirby in 1876 at the request of the Lovells. These include the quotations marks around "the conversational parts" to which in his letter dated Montreal, 12 July 1876, John Lovell asked Kirby to attend,[3] and the "subject heading for each chapter" that John Wurtele Lovell required in his letter written from Rouses Point on 17 August 1876.[4] Although in his haste to comply he missed some and misplaced others, Kirby did his best to place quotation marks around the characters' speeches throughout the manuscript copy-text. On the verso of leaf 44, for example, he added in pencil the needed punctuation around Amelie de Repentigny's shocked reply to Angelique des Meloises' statement that she meant "to win and wear" (35) the Intendant Bigot, " 'Fie, Angelique! Such a libel on our sex!—you know better. But you cannot love him?' " (35). On the same verso, however, Kirby forgot to add the quotation marks at the end of Amelie's question about the truth of the rumour "that the Intendant" had "a wife whom he" kept "in the seclusion of Beaumanoir" (36). After he received John Wurtele Lovell's request of 17 August for chapter titles, Kirby began adding them directly on the relevant leaves in the two notebooks that contained the final part of the text of the novel and that were sent on 22 August 1876 to the Lovells for printing. The first title in the manuscript, "The Market Place on St Martin's Day," appears on the verso of leaf 898 at the beginning of Chapter 53 (662); Kirby has entered this heading in ink. On the recto of this leaf, which constitutes the title-page of the eleventh notebook, and on which Kirby has entered in ink "Vol 11 / The Chien d'Or / W Kirby / Niagara," he has also written in pencil, possibly at the same time as he was adding the titles in August 1876, "The first 40 pages of this are transcribed in a difficult hand rather. I hope the compositor will not have much difficulty in making it out—as I do not want to delay you by" having it recopied; the bottom of this leaf has been destroyed, and, therefore, Kirby's last words are no longer there.

Since it was the copy-text for the Lovell, Adam, Wesson impression of *Le Chien d'or*, the manuscript contains evidence of its preparation for printing and its composition at the press established in 1874 at Rouses Point, New York, by the Lovell Printing and Publishing Company. Particularly at the beginning of the manuscript, someone, most likely at the press, has underlined or marked with an "X" French words, French-sounding words, and foreign-sounding words. On the verso of leaf 6, for example, the word "Laurentides" (7) has been underlined, while on the verso of leaf 8 the phrase "Cote à Bonhomme" (8) has been signaled by an "X." The name of each of the twenty-three employees who composed the manuscript has been written in each time s/he began typesetting the text. One of them, Nelson Valentine, whose name appears as "Valentine" on the top of the verso of leaf 852, had been working in "The Composing Room" along with "nearly a hundred workmen... , including a number of girls," from the time that the Lovells opened their "great printing establishment" on Lake Champlain.[5]

The number of almost every one of the over two hundred galleys that comprised the proofs of the Lovell, Adam, Wesson impression of the first edition is also recorded in the manuscript. On the bottom of the verso of leaf 807, for instance, "End gal 161" is written."Gall 162" appears at the top of the verso of leaf 808. The end of galley 161 and the beginning of galley 162 coincide with a line break in the 1877 impression. Galley 161 concludes with the phrase "of my brother." (595), while galley 162 opens with the phrase "She held" (595). The first phrase appears on page 533, line 19, and the second on page 533, line 20, in the Adam, Lovell, Wesson impression. The last galley noted, "gal 201," commences about two-thirds down on the recto numbered 1027 with "and the colony utterly ruined" (748). In the 1877 impression these words begin line 6 on page 672. On recto 1027 there is also a compositor's stint mark in the form of an opening square bracket before the galley number.

At some point this manuscript was returned to its author. It remained in the possession of the Kirby family until Kirby's grandson and namesake sold it, along with other material, to the Niagara Parks Commission in 1944. In 1951 this manuscript was transferred with other documents in the Kirby Collection to the Archives of Ontario. By this time leaves were missing, and those that did exist had sometimes survived either in fragments and / or with severe water and other damage. The Archives conserved the manuscript of *Le Chien d'or* in 1982.

When the manuscript was conserved, the notebooks were disbound. The manuscript now exists, therefore, in single leaves or in double adjoining leaves. Each leaf appears to have been treated using a heat-seal adhesive and tissue paper. Before the heat-sealing was carried out, possibly all the leaves but certainly the damaged ones were brushed to remove such accretions as dirt and mould. These leaves are now kept in forty-one file folders numbered 1 to 41. Small pieces of leaves that could not be placed in their proper sequence in the manuscript when its conservation was complete are kept in File Folder No. 42. These folders are located in Boxes 10 and 11 of the William Kirby Collection at the Archives of Ontario.

ENDNOTES

[1] D. F. McOuat, *Inventory of the William Kirby Collection* (Toronto: Archives of Ontario, 1953, rev. 1977), p. 11.

[2] OTAR, Kirby, Microfilm Reel 12.

[3] OTAR, Kirby, F-1076, Correspondence with Publishers, MU1635, A-6, ALS, John Lovell to Kirby, 12 July 1876.

[4] OTAR, Kirby, F-1076, Correspondence with Publishers, MU1635, A-6, ALS, John Wurtele Lovell to Kirby, 17 August 1876.

[5] "Lakeshore Press. The Monster Printing House at Rouses Point," *Plattsburgh Sentinel,* 3 September 1875, p. 1.

Bibliographical Description of Published Copy-text

A bibliographical description of the Lovell, Adam, Wesson and Company impression of the first edition of *Le Chien d'or* published in 1877, one of the two copy-texts used to prepare the CEECT edition of Kirby's novel, follows. This transcription presents an ideal copy of the Adam, Lovell, Wesson impression and, thus, includes the blank leaf that was an integral part of the preliminary gathering and the eight-page publisher's advertisement and the blank leaf that were an integral part of the final gathering. Some copies of this impression, however, were bound without the preliminary blank leaf and without the advertisement, and some of these copies were printed on cheap pulp paper. In this transcription the differences between the size and type of capitals have not been noted, and the form (thin / thick, swelled, etc.) and length (short, full measure, etc.) of rules have not been specified. For further details about this impression, see Elizabeth Brady, "A Bibliographical Essay On William Kirby's *The Golden Dog* 1877–1877," *Papers of the Bibliographical Society of Canada* 15 (1976), 24–48, and Thomas B. Vincent, *Bibliofiles: A bibliographical database of Canadian authors, their publications and editions*, http://www.bibliofiles.ca.

Title-page:

THE | CHIEN D'OR | THE GOLDEN DOG | A LEGEND OF QUEBEC | BY | WILLIAM KIRBY | [illustration of the Golden Dog tablet (500 × 750 mm.)] | NEW YORK AND MONTREAL: | LOVELL, ADAM, WESSON & COMPANY. | 1877.

Size of leaf:

185 × 125 mm.

Paper:

White, woven, unwatermarked, all edges cut

Collation:

8°, π⁴ 1–43⁸ [$1 signed], 348 leaves, pp. *1–2 i–v* vi *1* 2–9 *10* 11–79 *80* 81–678 1–8 *9–10*

In all the copies examined the number 116 is placed at the bottom of p. 116 instead of at the top left-hand corner, and p. 212 is misnumbered p. 112.

Contents:

pp. [1–2] blank; p. [i] title-page; p. [ii] printer's imprint; p. [iii] dedication; p. [iv] blank; pp. [v]–vi "CONTENTS."; pp. [1]–9 "CHAPTER I. | MEN OF THE OLD REGIME."; pp. [10]–14 "CHAPTER II. | THE WALLS OF QUEBEC."; pp. 14–24 "CHAPTER III. | A CHATELAINE OF NEW FRANCE."; pp. 24–34 "CHAPTER IV. | CONFIDENCES."; pp. 34–46 "CHAPTER V. | THE ITINERANT NOTARY."; pp. 46–53 "CHAPTER VI. | BEAUMANOIR."; pp. 53–67 "CHAPTER VII. | THE INTENDANT BIGOT."; pp. 67–79 "CHAPTER VIII. | CAROLINE DE ST. CASTIN."; pp. [80]–86 "CHAPTER IX. | PIERRE PHILIBERT"; pp. 86–92 "CHAPTER X. | AMELIE DE REPENTIGNY."; pp. 92–105 "CHAPTER XI. | THE SOLDIER'S WELCOME."; pp. 105–115 "CHAPTER XII. | THE CASTLE OF ST. LOUIS."; pp. 116–129 "CHAPTER XIII. | THE CHIEN D'OR."; pp. 129–140 "CHAPTER XIV. | THE COUNCIL OF WAR"; pp. 141–153 "CHAPTER XV. | THE CHARMING JOSEPHINE."; pp. 153–167 "CHAPTER XVI. | ANGELIQUE DES MELOISES."; pp. 167–182 "CHAPTER XVII. | SPLENDIDE MENDAX."; pp. 182–190 "CHAPTER XVIII. | THE MEROVINGIAN PRINCESS."; pp. 190–201 "CHAPTER XIX. | PUT MONEY IN THY PURSE."; pp. 201–208 "CHAPTER XX. | CROSS QUESTIONING."; pp. 208–220 "CHAPTER XXI. | BELMONT."; pp. 220–235 "CHAPTER XXII. | SIC ITUR AD ASTRA."; pp. 235–245 "CHAPTER XXIII. | SO GLOZED THE TEMPTER."; pp. 245–253 "CHAPTER XXIV. | SEALS OF LOVE, BUT SEAL'D IN VAIN."; pp. 253–262 "CHAPTER XXV. | THE HURRIED QUESTION OF DESPAIR."; pp. 262–272 "CHAPTER XXVI. | BETWEEN THE LATEST VIOLET AND THE EARLIEST ROSE."; pp. 273–288 "CHAPTER XXVII. | THE CANADIAN BOAT SONG."; pp. 288–296 "CHAPTER XXVIII. | CHEERFUL YESTERDAYS AND CONFIDENT TO-MORROWS."; pp. 296–310 "CHAPTER XXIX. | A DAY AT THE MANOR HOUSE."; pp. 310–318 "CHAPTER XXX. | FELICES TER ET AMPLIUS."; pp. 318–332 "CHAPTER XXXI. | "NO SPEECH OF SILK WILL SERVE YOUR TURN.""; pp. 332–340 "CHAPTER XXXII. | THE BALL AT THE INTENDANT'S PALACE."; pp. 340–353 "CHAPTER

XXXIII. | "ON WITH THE DANCE.""; pp. 353–359 "CHAPTER XXXIV. | "CALLING A RAVENOUS BIRD FROM THE EAST.""; pp. 359–376 "CHAPTER XXXV. | LA CORRIVEAU."; pp. 376–388 "CHAPTER XXXVI. | WEIRD SISTERS."; pp. 388–395 "CHAPTER XXXVII. | "FLASKETS OF DRUGS, FULL TO THEIR WICKED LIPS.""; pp. 395–408 "CHAPTER XXXVIII. | THE BROAD BLACK GATEWAY OF A LIE."; pp. 408–430 "CHAPTER XXXIX. | OLYMPIC CHARIOTS AND MUCH LEARNED DUST."; pp. 430–443 "CHAPTER XL. | THE COUTUME DE PARIS."; pp. 443–452 "CHAPTER XLI. | A WILD NIGHT INDOORS AND OUT."; pp. 452–468 "CHAPTER XLII. | MERE MALHEUR."; pp. 468–475 "CHAPTER XLIII. | OUTVENOMS ALL THE WORMS OF NILE."; pp. 475–484 "CHAPTER XLIV. | QUOTH THE RAVEN: "NEVERMORE!""; pp. 484–495 "CHAPTER XLV. | A DEED WITHOUT A NAME."; pp. 496–517 "CHAPTER XLVI. | "LET'S TALK OF GRAVES AND WORMS AND EPITAPHS.""; pp. 517–541 "CHAPTER XLVII. | SILK GLOVES OVER BLOODY HANDS."; pp. 541–551 "CHAPTER XLVIII. | THE INTENDANT'S DILEMMA."; pp. 551–561 "CHAPTER XLIX. | "I WILL FEED FAT THE ANCIENT GRUDGE I BEAR HIM.""; pp. 561–573 "CHAPTER L. | THE BOURGEOIS PHILIBERT."; pp. 573–581 "CHAPTER LI. | A DRAWN GAME."; pp. 581–592 "CHAPTER LII. | "IN GOLD CLASPS LOCKS IN THE GOLDEN STORY.""; pp. 592–604 "CHAPTER LIII. | THE MARKET PLACE ON ST. MARTIN'S DAY."; pp. 604–621 "CHAPTER LIV. | "BLESSED THEY WHO DIE DOING THY WILL.""; pp. 622–633 "CHAPTER LV. | EVIL NEWS RIDES POST."; pp. 633–642 "CHAPTER LVI. | THE URSULINES."; pp. 643–657 "CHAPTER LVII. | THE LAMP OF REPENTIGNY."; pp. 658–667 "CHAPTER LVIII. | "LOVELY IN DEATH THE BEAUTEOUS RUIN LAY.""; pp. 667–678 "CHAPTER LIX. | "THE MILLS OF GOD GRIND SLOWLY.""; pp. 1–8 "LOVELL, ADAM, WESSON & CO.'S | RECENT AND FORTHCOMING PUBLICATIONS."; pp. [9–10] blank

Printer's imprint reads "LAKE CHAMPLAIN PRESS, | ROUSES POINT, N. Y."

Dedication reads "TO | MISS RYE, | IN ADMIRATION OF HER INTELLIGENT AND WOMANLY PERSEVERANCE | IN THE GOOD WORK TO WHICH SHE DEVOTES HER LIFE—THE RESCUE | FROM POVERTY AND VICE OF DESTITUTE CHILDREN—THIS BOOK

IS | RESPECTFULLY INSCRIBED BY THE AUTHOR. | NIAGARA ONTARIO, | January, 1877."

In the list of "Contents," p. vi, "inn" should be "in" in "XLI. A wild night inn doors and out," and "feet" should be "feed" in "LXIX. "I will feet fat the ancient grudge I bear him.""

There is no period after "PIERRE PHILIBERT" on p. [80] and after "THE COUNCIL OF WAR" on p. 129.

"END." appears on p. 678.

"LE CHIEN D'OR (THE GOLDEN DOG): A Novel founded on a | Legend of Quebec. By William Kirby, Niagara. 1 vol. Crown | 8 vo. Cloth. *In preparation.* " appears on p. 2 of "LOVELL, ADAM, WESSON & CO.'S | RECENT AND FORTHCOMING PUBLICATIONS."

Head-title:

"THE CHIEN D'OR." appears on p. [1].

Running-titles:

"*CONTENTS.*" appears on p. vi. Except on pp. [10], [80], and 116 (chapter breaks) "*THE CHIEN D'OR.*" appears on each verso from pp. 2–678 (the apostrophe is missing on p. 108, the period is missing on pp. 132 and 260, and "*THE*" is misprinted "*TEE*" on p. 470). On the advertisement of Lovell, Adam, Wesson's publications "*LOVELL, ADAM, WESSON & CO'S.*" appears on p. 2; "*LOVELL, ADAM, WESSON & COS*" on p. 4; "*LOVELL, ADAM, WESSON & CO'S*" on p. 6; and "*LOVELL, ADAM, WESSON & CO.*" on p. 8. On each recto "*MEN OF THE OLD REGIME.*" appears from pp. 3–9; "*THE WALLS OF QUEBEC.*" from pp. 11–13; "*A CHATELAINE OF NEW FRANCE.*" from pp. 15–23; "*CONFIDENCES.*" from pp. 25–33; "*THE ITINERANT NOTARY.*" from pp. 35–45; "*BEAUMANOIR.*" from pp. 47–51; "*THE INTENDANT BIGOT.*" from pp. 53–65; "*CAROLINE DE ST. CASTIN.*" from pp. 67–79; "*PIERRE PHILIBERT.*" from pp. 81–85; "*AMELIE DE REPENTIGNY.*" from pp. 87–91; "*THE SOLDIER'S WELCOME.*" from pp. 93–103; "*THE CASTLE OF ST. LOUIS.*" from pp. 105–115; "*THE CHIEN D'OR.*" from pp. 117–131 (pp. 129 and 131 should read "*THE COUNCIL OF WAR.*"); "*THE COUNCIL OF WAR.*" from pp. 133–139; "*THE CHARMING JOSEPHINE.*" from pp. 141–151 (the period is missing on p. 149); "*ANGELIQUE DES MELOISES.*" from pp. 153–167 (p. 167 should read "*SPLENDIDE MENDAX.*"); "*SPLENDIDE*

MENDAX." from pp. 169–181; "*THE MEROVINGIAN PRINCESS*." from pp. 183–189; "*PUT MONEY IN THY PURSE*." from pp. 191–199; "*CROSS QUESTIONING*." from pp. 201–207; "*BELMONT*." from pp. 209–219; "*SIC ITUR AD ASTRA*." from 221–233; "*SO GLOZED THE TEMPTER*." from pp. 235–243; "*SEALS OF LOVE, BUT SEAL'D IN VAIN*." from pp. 245–251 (the comma is missing on pp. 249 and 251); "*THE HURRIED QUESTION OF DESPAIR*." from pp. 253–261; "*"BETWEEN THE LATEST VIOLET, ETC.*"" from pp. 263–271 (the "*ETC.*" on pp. 263 and 265 is "*&C.*" on pp. 267–271); "*THE CANADIAN BOAT SONG*." from pp. 273–287; "*CHEERFUL YESTERDAYS, ETC.*" from pp. 289–295; "*A DAY AT THE MANOR HOUSE*." from pp. 297–309; "*FELICES TER ET AMPLIUS*." from pp. 311–317; "*"NO SPEECH OF SILK," ETC.*" from pp. 319–331; "*THE BALL AT THE INTENDANT'S PALACE*." from pp. 333–339; "*"ON WITH THE DANCE.*"" from pp. 341–351; "*"CALLING A RAVENOUS BIRD," ETC.*" from pp. 353–371 (pp. 359–371 should read "*LA CORRIVEAU*."); "*LA CORRIVEAU*." from pp. 373–375; "*WEIRD SISTERS*." from pp. 377–387; "*"FLASKETS OF DRUGS, &C.*"" from pp. 389–393; "*THE BROAD BLACK GATEWAY OF A LIE*." from pp. 395–407; "*OLYMPIC CHARIOTS, ETC.*" from pp. 409–429; "*THE COUTUME DE PARIS*." from pp. 431–441; "*A WILD NIGHT INDOORS AND OUT*." from pp. 443–451; "*MERE MALHEUR*." from pp. 453–467; "*OUTVENOMS ALL THE WORMS OF NILE*." from pp. 469–473; "*QUOTH THE RAVEN: 'NEVERMORE!'*"" from pp. 475–483; "*A DEED WITHOUT A NAME*." from pp. 485–495; "*"LET'S TALK OF GRAVES," ETC.*" from pp. 497–515; "*SILK GLOVES OVER BLOODY HANDS*." from 517–539; "*THE INTENDANT'S DILEMMA*." from pp. 541–549; "*"I WILL FEED FAT THE ANCIENT GRUDGE, &C.*"" from pp. 551–559; "*THE BOURGEOIS PHILIBERT*." from pp. 561–571; "*A DRAWN GAME*." from pp. 573–579; "*"IN GOLD CLASPS," ETC.*" from pp. 581–589 (the period is missing from "*ETC*" on p. 589); "*"IN CLASPS OF GOLD," ETC.*" on p. 591; "*THE MARKET PLACE ON ST. MARTIN'S DAY*." from pp. 593–603; "*"BLESSED THEY WHO DIE," ETC.*" from pp. 605–621 (the comma after "*DIE*" is a period on p. 605); "*EVIL NEWS RIDES POST*." from pp. 623–631; "*THE URSULINES*." from pp. 633–641; "*THE LAMP OF REPENTIGNY*." from pp. 643–657; "*"LOVELY IN DEATH," ETC.*" from 659–665; "*"THE MILLS OF GOD GRIND SLOWLY.*"" from pp. 667–677 (a single closing quotation mark follows "*SLOWLY.*" on pp. 667 and 673); "*RECENT AND FORTHCOMING PUBLICATIONS*." on p. 3, and

"*RECENT PUBLICATIONS AND RE-ISSUES.*" on pp. 5 and 7 of Lovell, Adam, Wesson's advertisement.

Casing:

The casing is in diagonal, fine rib-cloth, deep blue in colour. The front cover is black- and gilt-stamped: [black rule] | [double black rule] | [on black ornamental background gilt-stamped Golden Dog tablet (22 × 31 mm.)] | LE CHIEN D'OR [gilt, fancy] | [gilt rule] | WILLIAM KIRBY [gilt, fancy] | [double black rule] | [black rule]. The spine is also black- and gilt-stamped: [black rule] | [black ornamental rule] | LE [gilt] | CHIEN D'OR [gilt] | (THE GOLDEN DOG) [gilt] | [gilt rule] | WM. KIRBY. [gilt] | [black ornament] | [gilt publisher's device] | [black ornamental rule] | [black rule]. The back cover is blind-stamped with the same pattern of rules at head and tail as the front cover.

Copies Examined:

AEU PS8471 I65 G6 1877

BVAU Koerner Library PR9221 I82 G6 1877

This copy has on p. [ii], as well as the printer's imprint, the following copyright notice: "Entered According to Act of Parliament, in the year one thousand and seventy- | seven, by WILLIAM KIRBY, Niagara, in the office of the Minister of Agriculture | and Statistics of the Dominion of Canada." The copy, which has been rebound, is missing both the preliminary blank leaf in the first gathering and the concluding blank leaf in the last gathering.

CEECT

This copy has a ticket marked "HENDERSON & CO. | *Stationers,* | OTTAWA." pasted on the top left-hand corner of the brown endpaper stuck to the back of the front cover. In 1877 this firm was located at 20 Sparks Street.

OKR 2 copies

Both copies are uncatalogued. One copy is flagged as "Special Collections Watters (no call number)." The other copy, which formerly belonged to Elizabeth Brady, is autographed on the title-page by "J. M. Le Moine," that is, James MacPherson Le Moine. This copy was microfilmed for CEECT.

OONL PS8471 I73 G16 1877 Reserve

This copy is autographed by Kirby on the recto of a front free fly-leaf "To Mrs D Servos | with compliments | of W Kirby | Niagara | March 1877." Mrs. Servos was the former Mary Torrance, one of the transcribers of the manuscript copy-text used in the CEECT edition.

OONL PS8471 I78G6 1877 c.2

This copy, which has been rebound, is missing gatherings 24 and 25, pp. 369–400. It was microfilmed for CEECT.

OTAR, Kirby, F-1076, Kirby Library, MU1675, L-65, Box 41

This copy is autographed on its title-page by "William Kirby," Kirby's grandson, and by "Maria S. Rye / Niagara." This may, in fact, be the copy that Rye received from the author in March 1877 when she was visiting England. Throughout this copy Kirby has entered corrections.

Published Versions of the Work

Information about the published versions of *Le Chien d'or* is available in Elizabeth Brady's "A Bibliographical Essay on William Kirby's *The Golden Dog* 1877–1977," *Papers of the Bibliographical Society of Canada* 15 (1976), 24–48, and in Thomas B. Vincent's *Bibliofiles: A bibliographical database of Canadian authors, their publications and editions,* http://www.bibliofiles.ca/. Their data have been incorporated as needed in the "Editor's Introduction" and in other apparatus in this edition. The "Editor's Introduction" also includes previously unpublished information that pertains to projected editions of Kirby's novel as well as to such matters as the sales and reception of the printed versions of this work.

Unrecoverable Manuscript Readings:
Readings from Published Copy-text

This list records, with three exceptions, material taken from the 1877 Lovell, Adam, Wesson and Company impression of the first edition of *Le Chien d'or* that replaces material that is either missing or unrecoverable in the manuscript copy-text of the CEECT edition. Each entry is keyed to the CEECT edition by page and line number. The material not adopted from the 1877 edition is "La Friponne" (72.34) and "From" (72.35), both supplied by the editor, and "continued" (469.28), a change written by Kirby into Maria Susan Rye's copy of the Lovell, Adam, Wesson impression of the first edition to correct "replied" in this edition. These three entries are marked with an asterisk, *. The material in square brackets, [], denotes punctuation, words, and partial words that are decipherable in the manuscript copy-text. When appropriate in passages of more than six words, ellipsis dots, ..., have been used to shorten the entry.

5.6	[gr]aceful	68.15	la!
5.7	marked by	68.19	in
6.19	the fog	69.4	his [fingers] dabbled
7.9	chase	69.5	but he [did] not notice
7.10	regions.	70.30	as he was
8.32	a	70.31	still held his
10.14	own.	71.36	"now
20.38	never	71.37	breath
42.32	[reflectively].	71.37	chorus[!—"]
56.7	[me];	71.38	led off a macaronic
57.21	seen	72.1	made merry the orgies
60.21	"knock at	72.5	glasses accompanied
60.22	in	72.6	as the company stood
63.16	a	72.7	with a grand burst at
65.18	splendid	72.9	cent fois vivat!
65.20	embodied	72.10	bene parlat!

72.11	manget et bibat	81.16	[sympathy]. She
72.33	The toast of	81.16	a look
72.33–34	applause, followed by	81.17	he [must]
72.34	La Friponne *	81.17	words
72.35	From *	81.18	He was still
73.24	in purgatory	81.19	his
73.28	man	82.2	to those
74.13	rest	82.3	for me
74.14	perruque	82.5	at
74.15	and	82.6	The
74.15	where	82.6	as Hebes and
74.16	to come and	82.7	on
75.4	Will	82.29	was not I
75.6	please. There	82.30	is always a
75.32	[nevertheless]. "She	82.30–31	the [wine] overfl[ows,]
75.32–33	to look even		as I am
75.33	she has not slept	82.31	I would not
75.34	din."	82.31	to him!
76.22	at	82.31–32	Caroline, I have
76.23	was a	82.32	my
76.23–24	an eye in her	82.32	jeer me finely
76.24	inquisitively at her	82.33	[with]out
	master	82.33	thought
76.25	cap, and threw back	82.34	this
77.20	was	82.34–35	Do up
77.21	could	83.18	me Queen Vashti?
77.22	spared in its	83.19	prophet than he knew,"
77.23	and [beside]	83.19–20	she with ineffable
78.16	delicacy[,]		sadness. "Queen
78.16	and eyes	83.20–29	refused to . . . replied
78.20	as		he, really
79.7	as himself possessed	88.35	a
79.8	sincere a	94.30	look!"
80.23	became	118.1	Toto
80.27	fancy was	122.5	"To
80.28	of cruelty and injustice.	122.5	[gutters] of
80.29	she was ready to	122.7	to
81.15	the	122.8	says

124.18–19	who [were]	136.6	"Grand merci for
127.19	grim	136.7	Bourgeois smiling
128.11	The	136.33–34	Princess de Cari[gnan]
128.37	is	136.34	of the
129.1	"La	136.35	"I think not, Deborah.
129.23	a	136.35	that
129.23	Corne's	136.36	*du Roi* in my
129.24	of	170.32	on
129.25	"The	171.37	[on].
129.25–26	of the	173.25	nowadays
130.11	sound and	175.32	the [talk]
130.12	they	175.33	to [listen]
131.23	sad	177.9	real
131.24	Above	179.34	of
131.24	couchant	180.21	it
131.25	man, is	181.9	fingers
132.22	navies	181.37	forth
132.23	were	182.25	[folly].
132.24	Bourgeois upon the	183.13	[to] his
132.25	the royal forges	183.14	Angelique;
132.26	a product worth	184.3	towards
132.27	the Chinese for their	184.4	not
133.19–20	A man keenly	184.28	said she.
133.20	in resentments	185.17	all
133.21	the fullest	185.17	and devoted woman.
134.10	Dame Rochelle, the	187.8	hoofs
134.11	[re]vocation of the	187.9	[pavement].
134.12	glorious work	188.27	which
134.13	persecution and	188.28	living.
134.14	elect of her population,	192.22	experience of his own.
134.15	name of religion.	193.13	[morning].
135.7	not without	195.20	of
135.8	gift she had	197.27	[France]."
135.9	intuitions of the	229.27–	"Oh! the Cureux,
135.10	emanations of her	230.18	indeed!" ... to be
135.11	the foresight of a pure		fools."
136.3–4	hand, and to be over	356.15	headed
136.4	Jehoiada, over the	358.30	it

358.31	him,		420.12–13	Tremblay say—and …
360.14	and			necessities."
361.28	natural		420.22	["]Why did
362.16	was like		420.22	asked
376.29	[me]!"		420.24	Fanchon
377.23	[heart].		420.24–25	the Lady of
383.15	in		420.25	tongue[,]
383.16	said		420.37–38	nodded her head …
383.18	No,			She gives
385.18	filled		421.6	[more]!
386.6	[Grandmaison],"		421.21	"and I think so too,
389.23–24	features, for he … if I		421.22–26	never wait … for me?"
	could.		421.33	des Meloises
389.36	of		422.6	and to
391.8	it?"		422.7	the under
391.10	beauty.["]		422.8	She stood
395.4	a		422.8–9	with her
396.7	any incidents of		422.9	fingers
409.8	left.		422.10	the
409.10	crowd		422.24–27	her thoughts … who
410.24	which [rose]			knows?"
417.22	was		423.4	Italian
417.23	her		423.21–22	and left no sign,
417.28	of feature, … look			numbering
419.34	say		423.22	victim's days, hours and
419.34	tell me			minutes,
419.35	had lost		423.23	to the will … his
419.35	Fanchon?"			destroyer.
419.36	"Yes,		423.32	In that
419.36	you		423.32	of deadly
419.37	[simplicity]. But the		423.33	of fever
419.38	that		423.34	the [fetid]
420.10	[money]. Men are		423.35	lungs
420.10	cruel war, that they		424.11	commit,
420.11	have a wife to each		424.12	striving against them,
	finger			educing
420.11–12	allowed … heard		424.12–14	and seeking …
				combats

424.21	for
424.23	The study of
424.23	by
424.24	to
424.32	to do so or no, a
424.33–37	cruel to see. . . . Beatrice Spara was
425.8	great
425.9	Voisin
425.10	of Death
425.20–21	and giving
425.21–24	with the lash . . . [Good] . . . [out] . . . [the] . . . Quebec.
425.33	The gay
425.33	all her sex
425.34	still
425.35	like the
425.36	her.
426.10	doom through her
426.11	The few
426.11–13	feelings . . . reflection that the
426.22	with
426.22	of it from
426.23	whom she
426.24	a
426.36	cricket sang
426.37–	on the hearth. . . .
427.2	bell, close by.
427.11	efforts to
427.13	to
427.24–27	women! . . . hair floating about
427.38	Had
428.13–15	La Corriveau . . . and began
428.23	from

428.37	her from head to
428.38–	of her good genius
429.2	. . . but my
429.13	["]Do you
429.13	hour,
429.26	replied La Corriveau
429.27	teeth
429.28	as those of a wild
429.28–30	lost is the heart . . . Mademoiselle?"
429.37	rival
429.38	in spite
430.2	man you
430.3	it not
430.16	[rival]!
430.17	in your voice, in your
430.18	not in your hand! . . . woman who
430.19–20	your lover, . . . good work!
430.28	"It was
430.28	that I
430.29	one
431.4	have
431.5	life
431.5	fire of
431.6	you want me to tell you
431.7	[revenge]!"
431.8–10	"I do want you . . . no longer.
431.19	of your
431.20	to me on
431.23	"A pledge?
431.24	you to me
431.38	pressed
432.1	and touched with
432.1–2	fingers, the edges of the

432.2	through the silken net.
432.3	"This is ... exclaimed
432.25–26	[me]. Oh,
432.26–29	ever before ... [sweetly] ... [Indian] ... Beaumanoir."
433.12	did you
433.14	Intendant or any man
433.14–15	to the rejection of any
433.15–16	in the world? ... mandrakes in the
433.24	is never
433.37	the cotquean of the
434.1–3	Angelique sprang up ... kissed her dark
434.11	she
434.12	my love
434.12	[to] my
434.24	[trembled] with
434.25	have you the
434.26	which the world believes
434.27	its possessors ... on
434.29–31	"Such secrets ... listen at the
434.37	it;
434.38	and
435.1	long sharp
435.2	world.
436.7	every
436.9	Angelique
436.9–10	casket as if she would
436.10–13	its contents ... [magnetism] ... contents.
436.24	dare
437.3–4	out a
437.4	with

437.4–5	It was not ... of a
437.5–6	[girl]. Its contents ... diamond in
437.7	La Corriveau shook ... immediately the
437.17	world's
437.18	her [guests]
437.32	replied
437.32–33	["]is the milk ... [painless] ... the life
437.34–36	a man, ... when his
438.19	when [Scorpio] rules
438.20	this
438.21	"dies of torments incurable as
438.21–22	of lust which it
438.23	There was one ... black liquid
438.31	["]This
439.7	of
439.9	"Ha! Ha!"
439.10	"Your wisdom
439.10–14	You would kill ... the handkerchief
440.8	"Sure? yes,
440.9–12	[triumph]. "He dare ... to untie."
440.38	duplicity
440.38–	[pride]. It is ...
441.1	I have
441.1–3	whose sake ... the casket, La
441.26	Her golden hair
441.27	have served for the adornment
441.27–28	angel; in the intensity of

441.28–30	it seemed to ... the very
442.1	now
442.17–21	deed be never ... and her
443.10	way to the house of
443.11–12	the secret and cruel deed
444.31	with a secretary
444.31–	the Intendant with
445.1	Varin, Penisault
445.2–8	of the table, ... [with] ... their hands
445.36	business
445.37	which lay at
445.38–	read *seriatim* ... [and]
446.3	... despatch, clear
446.33	read
446.33–34	in [the] ... Royal Ministers,
446.34–35	the King ... which
446.35–	act done ... right
447.1	and justice
447.29	New
447.30	on
447.31	"Promise is not pay!"
447.32–37	hunger ... as plentiful
448.23	*special* for his
448.24–29	[Governor]. The [Secretary] ... dark eyebrows.
449.11	knows the
449.12	can avoid ... [the] noble
449.14–16	"And for his ... New France!"
450.23	the deed
450.24	he would have done

450.24–28	price ... and lied.
451.14	from his intimate
451.14–17	a strange lady, ... suspicion
452.1–7	of self control. ... pledges himself
452.28	Bigot
452.28–31	of the position ... suspected him?"
453.17-21	St Luc, ... taking advantage of
454.4–5	the Chevalier ... It was
454.5–9	and showed ... [hereafter]." ... he knew
454.30	full opportunity
454.31–32	the goodness ... bringing
454.32	under the dominion
454.33	[King]" replied
454.33–37	too, in this ... invited
455.22–26	with me ... wine to-day!"
456.14	the
456.15	down at the table with them.
456.16	the Count,
456.16	is
456.17–18	we were together ... cap with
456.18–21	[brim]. You remember ... quotations that
457.2	Den
457.3–6	Swedish men ... in me.
457.29–30	one who knows it
457.30	is so ... and
457.32	"Well, never mind!" the Count

457.32–	from ... during	463.34	ossified, and
458.2	that time	463.34	its spring
459.23	"We will	463.35	[again]. Nothing ...
459.24–25	and offer incense to		[bring] ... back the
459.25–29	who first ...	463.35	the [Red]
	Governor's example,	463.36–	or change ...
460.19	Count	464.1	[say] of
460.20	thoughts he felt in	464.23	"It is what I
	himself, and	464.23–27	I have ... [replied
460.21–23	from his ... [turning]		Kalm]. ... [lately] ...
	to [other] ... some		veneration
	[of] ... [brain] ...	465.10–11	turkey, the condor
	friend.	465.11	the stamp
461.8	that ... into the	465.12–14	Europe ... specimens
461.9–12	extortioners and	465.14–15	and shells; ... Herr
	spendthrifts. ... of	465.15	from it ... ancient
	society	465.15	a
461.13–14	kingdom ... in[to] ...	465.35	the cow and
	however.	465.36	man in Asia
461.36–37	[Count], ...	465.37	America was the scene
	revolutions and	465.37–	civilization." ...
461.37	back into the darkness	466.2	[Plato's] ... [Atlantis]
	of		... told to
461.38–	imagination ... in[to	466.22–23	of America." ...
462.2	the] ... [The] ...		confirmation
	[counterpart] ...	466.23–24	La Corne," ...
	infinitely		Governor[.]
462.23	capable	466.24	the Sieur de
462.24–25	[forever]. What ...	466.24–26	me ... shores [of] ...
	wisdom is in		lead and
462.25–29	and use. The	467.8	war
	conservation ... his	467.18	to
	Word. The	467.19	and her
463.10	began to	467.21	seem as
463.11	of the order ... what	467.21–23	making ... [stone] ...
463.12	calls the third day.		[policy."] ... and what
463.12–16	of America ... [as] ...	467.24–25	to do,[" replied] ...
	elder born		Vaudreuil

467.25	succeed in it when
467.26	the name of
468.7	and tear
468.8	which
468.8–9	so ... [powerful."] ... Kalm!["]
468.10–11	his thigh, ... bitter.
468.12	in New France
468.12	secret
468.13	republicans
468.33	to-night. A
468.34	the divine
468.34	to live ... [and] ... his
468.35	like when ... what
468.36–38	come ... [quickening] ... [Kalm?"—] ... time
469.19	such ... [Troy] ... do to
469.20–21	is ... [impossible!"] ... it
469.21–25	future," ... [Kalm] ... hands
469.25–27	Puritans ... [England!—"] ... Old England
469.28	continued *
470.11	we will
470.11–12	health, [gentlemen,] ... honour.
470.12–16	our brains ... the example,
470.16	with enthusiastic
470.17	health of their
470.37–38	never wearied of telling us
470.38– 471.2	brave ... XII[."] ... it
471.2	at short commons

471.3	laughing at
471.3–4	"Our [groats] tasted all
471.4	had formed
471.5	which conquered at
471.24–25	Dalcarlians [a] needless
471.25	Dalkarls
471.25	be told they
471.26	whole duty
471.26	and the King[!]
471.27	an orator
471.28	"There was one more
471.28–29	Kalm, that wonderful youth
471.29	continued
471.30	"Ah! he is at
472.14	genius! It is
472.15	as a ... illuminate
472.15–17	science, ... [impulses] ... man!
472.18	and profound, but
472.19	of [mysticism,]
472.19	of the Edda and
473.4	there the
473.4	him, and
473.5	writes the
473.5	he will one
473.7	"You
473.7	I could not have
473.8	writing on those
473.9	then, and
473.36	[farther]! Theology I love, but
473.37–38	its ... [Sanctam] ... my
473.38	also hope
474.1–2	saved in ... [them.] ... to
474.3	The count, as he said

474.3–4	who looked approvingly at	477.3	half abandoned and
474.4	made small	477.4	country
474.28	"But our old	477.5	began to see was
474.28–29	Stockholm," replied the Count,	477.5	[anti-colon]ial
474.29	a new faith, ... religion,	477.26	a graven [image] which they
474.30	Kalm?"	477.27	and ... [at] ... with
474.31	"Far from	477.27–28	of idolatry [half] ... but
474.31	effete	477.28	from [the] brave,
474.32	will in time, in	477.28–29	and manly [spirit] of the
474.33	bring	477.30	The sad
475.16	The	477.31	was
475.16–17	an ill-suppressed yawn from	478.17	that
475.17	that the conversation	478.18	men's brains.
475.18	had been	478.19	triple brass, and
475.18–19	old [soldier,] who	478.19–20	the ... [blows] ... thyrsus
475.19	skeptics, who	478.20	[im]punity
475.20	one day	478.21	and [while com]mending
475.21	together[.]	478.22	save
476.12-13	as in [Acadia,] where our	478.22	Claude
476.14	own countrymen	478.23	all[.]
476.14–15	it not so, La Corne?" added he, turning	479.4	["]Good
476.15–16	old ... comrade[.] ... smoke	479.5	"That girl
476.16	as from	479.6	I feel for [her,]
476.17	Corne	479.6–7	Pierre[!" Philibert] felt the tight
476.18	and	479.8	well its
476.37	enough	479.9	unhappy
477.1	La Corne	479.9	to his
477.1	few words [reflected] the	479.31	"De Pean[!]"
477.2	of [intelligence] in the colony.	479.31	"[the spotted] snake! A fit
		479.32	Intendant's lies [and] ... am

479.33	not on [his] own errand
479.33–34	of this
479.34	in the
480.17	"No, my Lord;
480.17	and the [Chevalier] to
480.18	have [gone] ... [Palace] ... I
480.19	cabinet of the
480.20	politest and
480.20	an interview
480.21	that
481.3	["]Forbear,
481.3	"It is
481.3–4	way of Christians
481.5	"But it is
481.5	Corne,
481.6	gentleman is
481.7	duty, my
481.8	you for it,
481.27	the
481.27	examined
481.28	new
481.28	beauty and variety
481.29	forms ... [exist] ... World[.]
482.25	yet
482.25	of his powers
482.26	not again to encounter
483.18	in
483.19	nature that seeks a
483.19–20	sake ... in love,
484.9	for Le Gardeur,
484.9–10	did yesterday, too
484.10	when in company with the
484.35–36	be so hapless as to
484.36	Philibert, that she

485.21	I know
485.22	he is
485.22–23	one little corner of his
486.8	gray
486.9	and
486.32	design
486.33	had
486.33	at the village inn.
486.34	the polite hospitalities
487.20	an out[let]
487.21	ominous of
488.7	a penance for not
488.8	risk ... and
488.8–9	It ... such
489.19	Pothier in the course of
490.4	will you charge
490.5	*acte de damnation?"*
490.29	they were, they loved to
490.29	quibbles,
490.30	*coutumes* of Paris and Rouen,
490.31	other dealings with
491.17	inn door itself,
491.17	calculations
491.18	landlord's score of mugs
492.8–9	aught I could plead
492.9	case Master Pothier
492.10	Marche! you may marry
492.33–34	with that hook,
492.34	may depute her
492.35	heir in the barony,
493.20	the names
493.21	discussions with Master Pothier.
493.22	Listen, Jean La Marche!"
494.8	die,

494.10	vin quelquefois!	602.28	list of
495.3	to the censitaire	602.29	intoxicated.
495.4	in it."	602.31	fire
495.5	name the young	603.18	[dispute]? I
495.27	Jean had a	603.19	and [anxieties]
495.28	for ... pro[portion]	603.19	way
495.29	knew of it.	604.7	never met [again].
497.24	would	608.18	put
497.24	Tilly Arms as	608.19	lie
497.25	do when it is washing	608.19	La
498.14	It	608.30	is
498.16	the long league to	608.31	to
498.17	the hill	609.6	I do not
498.38	[Robin]! But	609.6	but the
499.1	rise ... like	609.7	in
499.22	the	610.17	at the
499.23	of honest shame	610.18	considered
499.24	were debating whether	610.19	Cadet
	to	611.32	in at
499.24–25	or sneak back	611.33	own
500.30	other intimation	611.33	cried
500.31	could they surmise that	611.34	long and
500.31	object in view than	611.35	took her
501.13	faint	612.22	the
501.14	in his eye	612.22–23	farther [than] his
501.14–15	with wine, mirth	612.23	of coming
501.15	drank without	612.35	of
501.16	warmth and	612.35	the
501.34	will satisfy	613.9	he felt, for the
502.19	["] *Par Dieu!*	613.9–10	any ... [on] ... but
502.20	are well talked	613.10	the sharp [inquisition]
503.6–7	"But have you		of two
515.11	of [them.]	613.11	and [Pierre] Philibert?
551.10–	inarticulate sounds	613.12–13	the secret [of] ...
552.1	... La Corriveau		[longer]? ... was
561.21	[them].	613.13	any
563.26	where	613.14	long
591.15	is	613.37	[done]!

613.38	But I	620.6	["]There are more
614.1	this matter, [Cadet]. I	620.6–7	choke … may
614.3	a woman.	620.7–8	outside … sweetened
614.25	mean to kill	620.8	it. Some course must
614.25–26	Cadet! [hark] you; I will	620.10	and young
614.26	put a [stop] to these	620.10–11	full cry
614.27	and … [the] … I	621.17	are a
614.28	And at the same time	621.18	his guardian angel, does he
614.28	everlasting	621.20	drunk he does,"
614.29	Dog[."]	621.21	him too
616.15	the Crown [of] France	621.24–	"Keep him … on the
616.16	still floating over the Castle	622.9	part of the Intendant.
618.1	what he	622.32	with a touch of
618.2	"You are	622.34	friendship!
618.4	a	622.35	Angelique des
618.6	"Don't be	622.35	De Pean when she finds
618.6–7	not … "'Like	622.36	your
618.7	the proverb says. And	622.36–37	De Pean!"
618.9	Paris	622.38	cannot
618.19	of	623.23	Bigot
618.19	to camp	623.23	furtively
618.20	and a	623.24	know how [to] interpret my
618.21	him back to the	623.25	["]I [understand] … [Excellency!] … it
618.21	where he		
618.22	own eye and	623.26	if your
618.34	the [possession]	623.26	be not
619.8	gaining	623.36	in a
619.9	buying [up] army	623.37	with
619.9	are	624.10	["]You are right
619.10	him with	624.10–11	in open day and not
619.10–11	and drafts [on] France, which	624.11	have … of
619.11	the discount	624.12–13	the Bourgeois[?"] … De
619.11	the		
619.13–17	"Give … the Intendant savagely.	624.13–14	know … [get] … harness

624.14–15	our ... [triumph] over the	627.14	them ... winter.
624.23	own way	627.21–22	works as a
624.24	scuffle	627.22–23	and [sinners] who
624.37	have	628.6	of life by
625.1–2	"I ... [Excellency] ... doubts	628.7–8	home ... [Pierre] ... [radiant] ... [at] the
625.3	"Le Gardeur may claim	628.8	his ... [to] ... Repentigny
625.3	his own reward[!]"	628.9–11	she ... [not] ... [garb] ... [face] ... The
625.4	correctly enough the true bent of	628.11–13	broke in ... house
625.5	de ... is	628.23–24	Dame's Huguenot
625.13	of a [second] duel	628.36	of St
625.14	Pierre [Philibert,] should	628.36–38	over ... [of nature]. ... [beams] ... [of] ... and
625.26	would be	628.38–	his ... [Winter]
625.26–27	might be killed	629.1	... but
625.27	fray, when blood was up	629.1–4	in the land, ... secure
625.28	when ... De Pean	629.14	of peace
625.28–29	be ... record of the	629.16	had
625.30	would impose upon the	629.30–31	after ... parliament of
625.31	as an honorable and justifiable	629.31–32	[sub]jects ... meditations of
626.14	accomplish this	629.33	Dame Rochelle continued plying her
626.14–15	woman's ... once to		
626.15–17	and to ... company	629.33–34	as she ... the page
626.18	was ... violent	629.34–38	by turns [upon] ... favorite
626.18–19	Dog ... were		
626.19–20	aversion. ... im[part]	630.22–24	His reflections ... enemies
627.6	seas		
627.7–8	merchantmen [were] rapidly loading	630.24–25	sure ... this great
		630.25–28	his ambition. ... [a] ... and would
627.8–9	quays ... [as] well ... with	630.28–29	Bourgeois ... a price
627.9–11	Colony ... [to] France [before] ... warm	630.35	to him
		630.36	present to
627.12	edge ... man,	631.11	two out of
627.13	soldiers ... loading the		

631.12–18	If ... [vows."] ...
	[censured] ... shrine
632.4	["]Yes, Dame, but a
	bright sunset,
632.4	awaits it
632.5–9	descending ... [dial]
	... [a] ... [house] ...
	[gayer] ... home?"
632.17	will do
632.35–36	nervous excitement.
	One of
632.36–37	her, and she
	continued—
632.38–	dear master, ... [but]
633.1	... [house] ...
	Philibert! ["]
633.8–9	prayer as
633.9	danger, or
633.24–27	"Yes, ... [see] ... [rays]
	... [tells] ... like
633.27–28	anticipate evil that may
	not be averted!"
634.15–17	began ... house to
634.18–20	day. ... said he
635.3	to the
635.27–28	with ... [moment] ...
	rival
635.28–29	Beaumanoir ... her
	any
636.15	really merit the grave
636.16–17	entertained ... that he
636.17–19	acting ... his real
637.5	in his manner,
637.5	and as warm in
637.6	her womanly instinct
637.7–8	hidden ... powers
637.33–34	her reward, and for
637.34	which ... ought to

637.36	She often reflected
	with regretful
637.36–38	the joy [which] ...
	lavished
638.13–14	way. ... mansion of
638.15	a valet of the Intendant
638.16	at the ... hid
637.17	sat ... engaged in
638.18	mutual ... well knew.
639.3	knew that in
639.3–4	the Intendant, and the
	Intendant
639.4–5	Moreover, Bigot would
	not venture
639.5–6	of Sheba ... of
639.6–9	at Court. ... La
645.19	bel[ieving]
648.31	[admirers].
649.19	in it.
650.30	them
654.35	[feelings].
655.13	be paid, I too!"
660.3	and
660.16	through
661.31	where Pierre
683.6	[Gardeur]!"
685.10	of
685.34	to
687.15	the scene
689.30–31	to tears at
689.31–32	his bloody vesture,
690.3	to
690.23	the Bourgeois,
690.24	as well
690.25	he never com[mitted]
690.33	not?"
691.19	best."
691.20–21	purposely to

691.22	his thigh.	693.2	that men
691.22	would have	693.3	vengeance of a
691.23	it against	693.3–4	of the greatest
691.27–28	of Le Gardeur.		company
691.29	than brothers.	693.4	[nation]."
691.29	but	693.5	the
692.10	[safe]. He	693.6	shall
692.11	[favour]."	693.7	blood
692.12–13	to the Governor that	693.10	upon
692.13–14	and that there was no	693.11	origin
692.19	a true friend."	722.13–18	followed … troubled
692.21	[blood]!		city.

Emendations in Copy-texts

This list records all the emendations made in this edition of *Le Chien d'or* to its copy-texts—the manuscript and the Lovell, Adam, Wesson and Company impression of the first edition published in 1877—except those changes noted in the introduction. Each entry in this list is keyed to the CEECT edition by page and line number. In each entry the reading of the CEECT edition is given before the square bracket,] , the source of this reading before the semi-colon, ; . The reading that has been emended appears after the semi-colon, the source of this reading after the greater than symbol, > . When the reading is not in the copy-text, then the word "*omitted*" appears after the semi-colon. The wavy dash, ~, indicates that the same word (and nothing else) appears in both the CEECT edition and the copy-text. When appropriate in passages of more than six words, ellipsis dots, . . . , have been used to shorten the entry. In these entries A represents the manuscript copy-text; B, the Lovell, Adam, Wesson impression; C, the copy of this impression signed by Maria Susan Rye that Kirby corrected; D, the copy of the impression of the first edition issued by Richard Worthington in 1878 that Kirby corrected; E, the 1897 edition prepared by L. C. Page and Company; and Ed, the editor. Thus, for example, the entry "4.19 statesman.] B; ~ > A" indicates that at page 4, line 19, "statesman." appears in the CEECT edition and in the Lovell, Adam, Wesson impression (B), but that the period after "statesman" was missing in the manuscript copy-text (A).

1.1–12	PREFACE . . .	7.18	Jacques] B; Jaques > A
	understood.] D; *omitted*	7.25	France.] B; ~ > A
	> A	8.24	man.] B; ~ > A
3.2	MEN OF THE OLD	8.31	Governor.] Ed; ~ > A
	REGIME] B; *omitted*	9.30	end] B; ~. > A
	> A	9.30	fire."] B; fire! ~." > A
4.19	statesman.] B; ~ > A	10.2	soldier.] B; ~ > A
5.1	years.] B; ~ > A	10.13	defeating] E; and ~
5.7	eyes] B; eye > A		> A
7.1	as] B; *omitted* > A	11.30	Colony.] B; ~ > A

12.3	morning.] B; ~ > A	29.18	across] B; accross > A
13.2	THE WALLS OF QUEBEC] B; *omitted* > A	30.6	replied Angelique, laughing.] B; *omitted* > A
15.25	Recollets."] B; ~ > A	30.15	exclaimed Amelie.] B; *omitted* > A
16.3	proportion] B; porportion > A	30.25	de] B; *omitted* > A
17.23	the] B; *omitted* > A	30.31	perjuries.] Ed; ~ > A
17.28	XV.] B; XV > A	31.2	Francoise] B; Marie > A
18.2	A CHATELAINE OF NEW FRANCE] B; *omitted* > A	31.4	Francoise'] B; Marie's > A
18.29	of her husband] C; *omitted* > A	31.7	you] B; *omitted* > A
		31.18	not] B; *omitted* > A
19.4	without] B; with > A	31.38	by] B; in > A
20.2	brother—] Ed; ~ > A	32.5	fascinate] B; facinate > A
20.6	Beaumanoir."] B; ~" > A	32.5	an] B; an ~ > A
23.8	Philibert.] B; ~ > A	32.13	Philosopher] B; Philospher > A
23.19	hesitation] B; hestitation > A	32.15	But] B; but ~ > A
23.29	she] B; *omitted* > A	32.16	than] B; than ~ > A
24.2	Amelie.] B; ~ > A	32.23	on] B; on ~ > A
24.26	him,] B; ~, and the more she questioned herself > A	33.32	was Angelique's flippant reply.] B; *omitted* > A
24.28	temples] B; tembles > A	33.33	She] B; She ~ > A
		34.7	since."] B; ~ > A
24.36	needlessly.] B; ~ > A	34.10	Angelique.] B; ~ > A
25.12	him.] B; ~ > A	34.11–12	the same] B; same the > A
25.17	King.] B; ~ > A		
26.15	Angelique] B; althougth ~ > A	34.25	replied Amelie.] B; *omitted* > A
27.14	knees.] B; ~ > A	35.20	replied Angelique warmly.] B; *omitted* > A
27.26	companions,] B; ~ > A		
27.31	with] B; *omitted* > A	36.1	the] B; *omitted* > A
29.2	CONFIDENCES] B; *omitted* > A	36.15	Beaumanoir] B; Beamanoir > A

37.11	consciousness] B; conciousness > A	54.23	fluttering] B; fluttered > A
37.15	but] B; but ~ > A	54.30	Honour] Ed; Honor > A
37.32	De Pean] B; him > A		
38.13	it.] B; ~ > A	55.4	awkward] B; akward > A
40.2	THE ITINERANT NOTARY] B; *omitted* > A	55.15	*Hunc! hanc! hoc!*] B; *omitted* > A
40.5	the St] B; St > A	58.9	while] B; *omitted* > A
40.9	occasions.] B; ~ > A	58.34	all] B; All > A
40.29	he] B; *omitted* > A	59.25	Montmorency."] B; ~" > A
41.34	oppressed.] B; ~ > A		
41.37	commodities] B; commodoties > A	60.6	Paris.] B; ~ > A
43.2	Huguenot] B; Hugenot > A	60.18	*ore rotundo*] C; *os rotundum* > A
43.20	gazed.] B; ~ > A	60.35–61.1	knocked loudly upon the door again and again! he tried it at last,] B; *omitted* > A
44.20	a] B; a ~ > A		
45.8	storm.] B; ~ > A		
45.32	sways] C; sway > A	62.2	THE INTENDANT BIGOT] B; *omitted* > A
46.1	unconsciously] B; unconconsciously > A	62.24	bore] B; were > A
46.9	Tilly.] B; ~ > A	63.5	Bacchus] B; Bachus > A
48.30	*vifs*] B; *vivs* > A	63.7	satyrs.] B; ~ > A
48.36	*pour*] C; *par* > A	63.8	cups] B; Cups > A
49.12	everybody] B; everbody > A	63.12	carpet.] B; ~ > A
49.12	in] B; in ~ > A	64.24	Quebec.] B; ~ > A
49.25	over] C; with > A	65.1	D'Estebe] B; D Estelle, > A
49.38	ends.] B; ~ > A		
50.38	they] B; I ~ > A	66.34	exclaimed] B; Exclaimed > A
51.30	seigneuries.] B; ~ > A	67.17	Beauce] B; Beaucé > A
52.11	without burning] B; *omitted* > A	67.21	Beauce!"] B; Beaucé! > A
54.2	BEAUMANOIR] B; *omitted* > A	67.25	Beauce] B; Beaucé > A
54.7	seldom.] B; ~ > A	67.26	Poitou.] B; ~ > A
54.22	leaping] C; leaped > A	67.28	Beauce] B; Beaucé > A

67.29	Beauce] B; Beaucé > A	86.7	brows.] Ed; ~ > A
67.33	Beauce] B; Beaucé > A	88.29	grasped] C; had ~ > A
67.37	Beauce] B; Beaucé > A	89.17	he] B; he ~ > A
68.3	Beauce] B; Beaucé > A	89.28	palm.] Ed; ~ > A
68.5	Beauce] B; Beaucé > A	91.2	PIERRE PHILIBERT]
68.7	Bacchus] B; Bachus		B; *omitted* > A
	> A	91.4	occasionally] B;
69.22	Deschenaux'] B;		occasionly > A
	Dechenaux' > A	92.8	—his] B; ~ > A
69.24	Deschenaux] B;	93.7	Philibert] B; he > A
	Dechenaux > A	93.24	panegyric] B; panygyric
69.25	imprecation] B;		> A
	emprecation, > A	93.34	hostelry] B; hotelry
69.32	Deschenaux] B;		> A
	Dechenaux > A	94.17	Antoine] C; Jean > A
69.36	Deschenaux] B;	94.24	to] B; to ~ > A
	Dechenaux > A	94.31	a] B; a ~ > A
70.19	Deschenaux.] Ed; ~	97.33	to] B; to ~ > A
	> A	98.2	AMELIE DE
70.24	Deschenaux] B;		REPENTIGNY] B;
	Dechenaux > A		*omitted* > A
71.4	detected] B; dedected	98.4	d'Armes] B; d'Arms,
	> A		> A
71.6	be] B; *omitted* > A	98.20	the] B; *omitted* > A
71.7	Intendant.] B; ~ > A	99.20	discomposure.] B; ~
71.25	admission] B;		> A
	addmission > A	99.30	brothers] B; brother's
76.7	to] B; *omitted* > A		> A
77.2	CAROLINE DE ST	100.4	*fleur de lys*] B; *fleur* de
	CASTIN] B; *omitted* > A		lys > A
77.14	descended] B;	100.7	Occasionally] B;
	decended > A		Occassionaly > A
80.38	Occasionally] B;	101.2	no] B; *omitted* > A
	Occasionly > A	102.20	disparagingly] B;
83.6	days at] B; das at > A		dispargingly > A
85.3	he] B; *omitted* > A	105.2	THE SOLDIER'S
85.23	commenced] B;		WELCOME] B; *omitted*
	commence > A		> A

106.34   we] B; ~ we > A

107.16   executing] B; excuting > A

109.10   were] B; were ~ > A

109.19   exclaimed La Corne.] B; *omitted* > A

109.22   too," said Philibert.] B; too. > A

109.35   marched] B; mched > A

110.17   manifested.] B; ~ > A

110.27   integrity.] B; ~ > A

110.34   Amelie.] B; ~ > A

112.5   An] Ed; ~ an > A

113.1   black] B; *omitted* > A

113.19   hands] B; hand > A

113.33   censitaires] B; censitairs > A

115.18   subject] B; subjet > A

116.2   and said] B; *omitted* > A

116.22   Francois] Ed; Francis > A

116.29   reached] B; rached > A

116.29   father!"] B; ~?" > A

116.33   the estate] B; it > A

117.7   hills.] B; ~ > A

117.38   Psalm: the 116th] B; Psalm > A

118.17   Queen Mary] B; a Queen > A

119.2   THE CASTLE OF ST LOUIS] B; *omitted* > A

121.5   cleanse] B; clease > A

121.17   sovereign] B; soverign > A

121.33   Council."] B; ~" > A

122.9   the] B; the ~ > A

122.19   it] B; It > A

122.31   prodigal.] B; ~ > A

123.12   to] B; *omitted* > A

123.26   sovereignty] B; sovreignty > A

123.27   colony.] B; ~ > A

123.36   discoverer] B; discover, > A

124.2   loveliness] B; lovliness > A

124.5   confederacy] B; confedracy > A

125.4   Mississippi] B; Mississipi > A

125.11   Mississippi] B; Mississipi > A

125.23   Confederacy] B; Confedracy > A

125.28   their own] B; the own > A

126.34   servants."] B; ~ > A

127.26   a] Ed; a ~ > A

128.11   with] B; with ~ > A

128.15   of] B; *omitted* > A

129.10   Remi] Ed; Remy > A

131.2   THE CHIEN D'OR] B; *omitted* > A

131.18   every] B; in ~ > A

134.24   her] B; his > A

135.12   Calvinists] B; faithful > A

135.17   to England] B; *omitted* > A

137.9   a] B; I > A

137.31   multitude] B; mutitude > A

138.22   this] B; his > A

139.20   Barthemy] Ed; Bartemy > A

139.24	Barthemy] Ed; Bartemy > A
139.38	Barthemy] Ed; Bartemy > A
140.5	of] B; of ~ > A
140.9	of the] B; of > A
140.13	laughing] B; laughhing > A
141.30	threatening] B; theatening > A
143.2	THE COUNCIL OF WAR] B; *omitted* > A
143.14	Excellency] B; Exellency > A
144.18	traitors.] B; ~ > A
145.37	at] B; at ~ > A
145.38	comparatively] B; comparitively > A
146.16	instigators] B; istigators > A
146.37	in] B; In > A
147.12	question.] B; ~ > A
147.14	Majesty] B; Majesty's > A
147.33	France.] B; ~ > A
147.36	Lusignan.] B; ~ > A
148.11	he] B; *omitted* > A
148.14	added he angrily.] B; *omitted* > A
148.19	Louisbourg] B; Louisburg > A
148.35	it] B; It > A
149.14	looks] C; glances > A
149.19	grave] B; ~, > A
150.4	Chippewas] B; Chippawas > A
150.4	great] B; Great > A
150.5	lakes] B; Lakes > A
151.14	Fontenoy.] B; ~ > A
151.28	I] B; *omitted* > A
152.1	by peace] B; *omitted* > A
152.6	to] B; *omitted* > A
152.12	Gallican] C; Gallic > A
152.22	Lange] B; Langé > A
152.30	guillotine] B; guilliotine, > A
153.21	raised] B; *omitted* > A
153.30	its walls] B; them > A
154.35	Province.] B; ~ > A
154.38	English.] B; ~ > A
155.22	it] B; It > A
156.35	Bigot.] B; ~ > A
156.36	by] B; *omitted* > A
157.2	nonchalantly] B; nonchalently, > A
157.10	by] B; by ~ > A
157.12–13	said Bigot, sententiously!] B; *omitted* > A
157.33	a] B; *omitted* > A
157.38	Meloises] B; Meloise > A
158.7	of] B; *omitted* > A
159.2	THE CHARMING JOSEPHINE] B; *omitted* > A
159.28	Tremblay] B; Trembly, > A
160.1	enter.] B; ~ > A
164.18	recital] B; reital > A
164.34	draw] B; draws > A
166.11	is] B; ~ a > A
166.24	Tremblay] B; Trembly > A

167.1	Tremblay] B; Trembly > A	180.2	prodigal] B; prodical > A
168.4	to] B; to ~ > A	181.25	*preux Chevalier*] C;
169.5	So] B; so ~ > A		*Chevalier preux* > A
169.25	Froumois] B; Fromois > A	183.8	question.] B; ~ > A
		183.30	an] B; an ~ > A
170.17–22	like this ... to the bright beyond.] B; like that, on the distant shore of Minas. The trees were glorified with golden light, the waters overlaid with a broad path of shimmering sun light, like a street of the Holy City. The thrush and oriole twittered their even song, before seeking their nests. > A	184.9	I] B; I ~ > A
		185.8	horizon;] B; ~ > A
		185.36	Vallier.] B; ~ > A
		185.38	to] B; and > A
		186.6	shuddered] B; shuddred > A
		188.2	"SPLENDIDE MENDAX"] B; *omitted* > A
		188.4	fragments] B; fragment > A
		189.30	at the palace] B; *omitted* > A
		189.30	sups] B; breakfasts > A
170.25	gave the pledge] B; oath > A	191.20–21	If Le Gardeur be entangled] B; ~ ~ ~ ~ ~ If Le Gardeur be entagled > A
170.29	highest crest] B; high crests > A		
170.36	lattices] B; latties > A	192.11	his] B; was ~ > A
171.21	Sinners;] B; ~ > A	193.7	the summer] B; summer > A
173.2	ANGELIQUE DES MELOISES] B; *omitted* > A	194.5	empressement] B; empressment. > A
173.8	a lover] B; *omitted* > A	194.23	scarce] B; scarc > A
173.20	house.] B; ~ > A	196.23	her] B; *omitted* > A
173.24	its] B; its ~ > A	196.28	be!":] B; ~!": her > A
175.35	the] B; *omitted* > A	196.38	Mademoiselle] B; ~! > A
176.25	and] B; and ~ > A		
176.34	reality.] B; ~ > A	197.22	if] B; If > A
177.1	procrastinate] B; proscratinate > A	197.34	and] B; and ~ > A
		198.17	*appartemens*] Ed; *appartmens* > A
177.8	was] B; *omitted* > A		

198.28	sat erect] B; stood up > A
199.35	Hieroglyphics] B; Hieroglythics > A
201.5	than] B; that > A
202.25	she] B; *omitted* > A
203.23	a] B; *omitted* > A
203.28	as] B; and ~ > A
204.3	with] B; *omitted* > A
205.2	THE MEROVINGIAN PRINCESS] B; *omitted* > A
206.2	by] B; by ~ > A
206.12	Intendant] B; Intendants > A
207.5	gesticulations] B; geticulations > A
207.31	could] B; to > A
208.28	contrivances] B; contivances > A
209.28	of] B; *omitted* > A
209.38	Iliad] B; Illiad > A
211.14	Tilly] B; Tillie > A
212.23	liked] B; like > A
212.35	to it] C; *omitted* > A
214.2	"PUT MONEY IN THY PURSE"] B; *omitted* > A
214.22–23	or fighting] B; *omitted* > A
215.31	au] B; a > A
216.12	Poulariez] B; Poularliez > A
216.19	went] Ed; ~ gone > A
216.34	Poulariez] B; Poularliez > A
217.12	Poulariez] B; Poularliez > A

217.19	Poulariez] B; Poularliez > A
217.24	Poulariez] B; Poularliez > A
217.26	Poulariez] B; Poularliez > A
217.30	Poulariez] B; Poularliez > A
217.38	Poulariez] B; Poularliez > A
218.22	with] B; with ~ > A
219.19	Meloises] B; Meloise > A
220.16	King] B; Kings > A
221.22	to be] B; to ~ ~ > A
221.31	own] B; owns > A
221.33	not] B; *omitted* > A
222.11	advise] B; adise > A
223.4	Tillys] B; Tillies > A
223.17	smiled] B; ~ at > A
223.20	sometimes.] B; ~ > A
223.23–24	is a] B; is > A
224.31	that] Ed; *omitted* > A
225.19	remove] B; remover > A
225.32	explain] B; ~ them > A
226.2	CROSS QUESTIONING] B; *omitted* > A
226.15	the] B; the ~ > A
229.29	parlour] Ed; parlor > B
231.34	irritability] B; irritibility > A
233.17	go] B; *omitted* > A
234.2	BELMONT] B; *omitted* > A
234.12	to] B; to ~ > A
234.15	behind] B; that ~ > A

236.3	conditioned] B; condititioned > A	258.13	were trying] B; sought > A
236.12	ostentatious] B; ostantatious. > A	258.13–14	"far reaching concords"] B; far reaching influences > A
237.32	cares not] C; cared not > A		
237.38	door] B; gate > A	258.15	busy grounds near the mansion] B; illumined grounds > A
238.31	*Augur, medicus, magus, omnia novit!*] B; *omitted* > A		
		258.16	took] B; turned down > A
240.6	marriageable] B; marriagable > A	258.16	that led] B; *omitted* > A
240.12	with] B; with ~ > A	258.16–17	which they entered] B; *omitted* > A
240.33	one of] B; one > A		
241.2	de] B; to > A	258.23–24	A cool ... faces as] B; A fresh salt breeze swept their faces bringing memories of sea-washed capes and mountain tops stretching far away down the mighty St Lawrence. > A
241.27	is," said he.] B; is." > A		
242.11	her] B; ~ of > A		
243.4	mixture] B; mixuture > A		
243.6	for] B; for ~ > A		
245.30	Suzette] B; Susette > A		
246.10	cool and] B; ~ ~ and > A		
247.2	"SIC ITUR AD ASTRA"] B; *omitted* > A	259.4–5	Le Gardeur,] B; *omitted* > A
248.1	Bourgeois.] B; ~ > A	260.22	her] B; her ~ > A
248.22	captive] B; capitive > A	260.28	darkness.] B; ~ > A
249.1	vest] B; vest ~ > A	261.14	shuddered at his vehemence; but she] B; *omitted* > A
249.14	she] B; *omitted* > A		
249.37	Bourgeois.] B; ~ > A		
250.3	or] C; nor > A	261.24	things," said he.] B; things. > A
250.21	heard] B; herad > A		
252.35	be] C; *omitted* > A	262.6	might] B; might he ~ > A
254.8	Cecile's] B; Cecil's > A		
255.9	her mouth] B; their mouths > A	262.27–28	of the] B; of the ~ ~ > A
257.19	care] B; cared > A	263.2	the] B; the ~ > A
257.19	will be] B; was > A		

264.2	"SO GLOZED THE TEMPTER"] B; *omitted* > A
265.22	darkness.] B; ~ > A
265.24	Barthemy] Ed; Bartemy > A
265.28	came up,] B; *omitted* > A
266.1	Marshall] Ed; Marsall > A
267.5	lady] B; ~? > A
267.6	be] B; *omitted* > A
267.32	his] B; his ~ > A
268.4	in] B; in ~ > A
268.35	Tremblay] B; Trembly > A
269.2	have] B; *omitted* > A
269.6	Lizette] B; Lizitte > A
269.10	Intendant] B; secret > A
270.7	say] B; *omitted* > A
270.9	is] B; is ~ > A
270.9	loveliest] B; lovliest > A
270.37	Tremblay] B; Trembly > A
271.19	us both] B; me > A
275.2	"SEALS OF LOVE, BUT SEALED IN VAIN"] C; *omitted* > A
275.4	antidote] B; andidote > A
275.27	it was] B; *omitted* > A
276.9	or] B; or ~ > A
276.23	a] B; a ~ > A
276.31	press me,] B; ~, ~ > A
282.19	bad, worse and more] B; bad," cried she. "More > A
283.11	alternately] B; alteranately > A
283.13	on] B; in > A
284.2	"THE HURRIED QUESTION OF DESPAIR"] B; *omitted* > A
284.17	I] B; I ~ > A
286.26	Le] Ed; *omitted* > A
286.34	Hal] B; Hall > A
287.4	were] B; where > A
288.4	Pean.] B; ~ > A
288.30	You] B; Your > A
289.1	*Lys.*] B; ~ > A
289.4	the] B; *omitted* > A
289.6	it] B; *omitted* > A
289.10	he appealed] B; He appealed > A
289.27	French] B; Fench > A
289.36	Teniers.] B; ~ > A
289.37	in.] B; ~ > A
290.7	chorus] C; song > A
291.14	liked] B; like > A
292.32	as safe] B; a safe > A
293.17	Le] B; of ~ > A
294.2	"BETWIXT THE LAST VIOLET AND THE EARLIEST ROSE"] C; *omitted* > A
294.12	raging] B; ragaing > A
295.4	fiery] B; *omitted* > A
295.24	it] B; to > A
295.28	sufficiently] B; sufficently > A
296.1	in] B; in ~ > A
297.17–18	in the house of the Chien d'or] B; *omitted* > A

297.26	lovelier] B; lovlier > A	315.19	horizon] B; horizen > A
298.17	to] B; the > A		
298.22	the] B; the ~ > A	316.38	servants,] B; ~ > A
298.27	gentlemen.] B; ~ > A	317.18	ran] B; run > A
300.5	Kingdom] B; Kindom > A	319.21	for the] B; ~ ~ the > A
		321.19–20	do," replied she.] B; do. > A
300.14	Philosopher] B; Philosoper > A	323.2–3	"CHEERFUL YESTERDAYS AND CONFIDENT TO-MORROWS"] B; *omitted* > A
300.15	inherit] B; inhereit > A		
300.25	it.] B; ~ > A		
300.37	Iliad] B; Illiad, > A		
301.26	the] B; the ~ > A		
302.26	her] B; stood ~ > A	325.26	Le] B; La > A
302.30	return to] B; ~ ~ to > A	325.31	and] B; an > A
		326.9	an] B; a ~ > A
302.37	was] B; was ~ > A	326.16	manner.] B; ~ > A
304.18	minds.] B; ~ > A	328.4	Amelie] Ed; She ~ > A
304.38	Felix] B; Filex > A	330.7	have] B; have ~ > A
306.2	THE CANADIAN BOAT SONG] B; *omitted* > A	333.2	A DAY AT THE MANOR HOUSE] B; *omitted* > A
306.16	Lawrence] B; Laurence > A	333.16	a] B; a ~ > A
306.17	censitaires] B; censitaries > A	333.25	sunflowers] D; tulips > A
306.23	successive] B; sucessive > A	335.20	adamantine] B; adamantined > A
307.17	squaws.] B; ~ > A	338.3	reminiscence] E; reminscence > A
307.35	honour] Ed; honor > A		
308.10	honour] Ed; honor > A	338.27	love] B; ~, > A
308.13	Lawrence] B; Laurence > A	340.26	Heloise] B; Heloises > A
309.33	Derriere] B; Deriere > A	341.30	friendship] C; ~, and regard > A
313.9	The] B; It ~ > A	344.1	not] B; *omitted* > A
314.5	Beauce] B; Beaucé > A	344.20–21	remitted the customary *Lods et Ventes* or fines payable to the
314.24	José] B; Jose > A		
314.38	José] B; Jose > A		

	Seigneur,] C; *omitted*	372.26	Destouches] B;
	> A		Destouche > A
346.1	of] B; of ~ > A	374.2	THE BALL AT THE
346.24	by] B; *omitted* > A		INTENDANT'S
349.2	"FELICES TER ET		PALACE] B;
	AMPLIUS"] B; *omitted*		*omitted* > A
	> A	378.6	the] B; the ~ > A
349.20	of love] B; *omitted* > A	379.1	Angelique.] B; ~ > A
349.28	*Amor ch' a null amato*	381.30	amendment.] B; ~ > A
	amar perdona,] B;	381.35	They] B; The > A
	omitted > A	381.37	in] B; in ~ > A
350.2	Love that excuses no	383.2	"ON WITH THE
	loved one from loving,]		DANCE"] B; *omitted*
	B; *omitted* > A		> A
353.14	both] B; and > A	384.1	tame] B; *omitted* > A
353.28	minutes;] B; ~ > A	385.29	fluttered] B; fluttered
353.30	tenderness.] B; ~ > A		~ > A
353.36	too] B; *omitted* > A	387.31	Intendant] B; ~! > A
356.10	canoes.] B; ~ > A	388.9	imperceptible] B;
358.2	"NO SPEECH OF SILK		imperceptable > A
	WILL SERVE YOUR	391.24	a] B; *omitted* > A
	TURN"] B; *omitted* > A	392.16	have] B; *omitted* > A
358.4	espionage] B;	392.20	she] B; Angelique ~
	espoinage > A		> A
360.24	faded] B; Faded > A	393.2	a] Ed; an > A
360.30	exaggerations] B;	393.6	wine] B; *omitted* > A
	exagerations > A	393.32	their] B; there > A
360.36	or] B; *omitted* > A	394.11	comparatively] B;
361.4	of the] B; of the ~ ~		comparitively > A
	> A	394.32	sent] B; seen > A
361.10	Roch] B; Rochs > A	395.14	and] B; *omitted* > A
361.34	superiority] B;	397.2	"CALLING A
	superiorty > A		RAVENOUS BIRD
362.3	spirit] B; spirt > A		FROM THE EAST"] B;
365.17	of] B; it ~ > A		*omitted* > A
368.5	Aladdin] B; Alladin	398.13	them] B; her hands
	> A		> A
369.18	they] B; ~ the > A	399.10	taken.] B; ~ > A

399.34	but ladies] B; but ladies ~ ~ > A
401.3	Paris. She] B; Paris she > A
401.12	Fanchon] B; Lizette > A
401.23	Fanchon] B; Lizette > A
403.10	*sa faute*] C; *la faute à lui* > A
403.10	*sa faute*] C; *la faute à lui* > A
403.12–13	*sa faute*] C; *la faute à lui* > A
403.13	*sa faute*] C; *la faute à lui* > A
404.2	LA CORRIVEAU] B; *omitted* > A
404.4	by] C; ~ a > A
404.18	*succession*] B; *sucession* > A
405.17	*succession*] B; *sucession* > A
405.26	*poudre de succession*] B; *poudre* de succession > A
405.32	capable] B; capable ~ > A
405.32	instantaneously] B; instantaineously > A
405.35	could] C; it ~ > A
405.37	compounder] B; ~. > A
406.2	*succession*] B; *sucession* > A
407.2	*succession*] B; *sucession* > A
407.8	in] B; the > A
408.2	narrative] B; narative > A
408.14	unparalleled] B; unparalled > A
409.32	her] B; the ~ > A
411.14	iridescent] B; irridescent > A
412.2	of] B; of ~ > A
413.6	on] B; *omitted* > A
414.21	their paddles] B; their ~ ~ > A
416.17	die] B; ~ who > A
416.34	spell] C; power > A
420.14	Tremblay] B; Trembly > A
421.14	savagely.] B; ~ > A
421.16	persistently.] B; ~ > A
421.32	I] B; *omitted* > A
422.2	"WEIRD SISTERS"] B; *omitted* > A
424.15	armoury] C; armour > A
427.16	a] B; a ~ > A
429.20	half] Ed; have > A
430.4	summoned] B; summon > A
431.14	the] B; the ~ > A
432.19	disappointment] B; dissapointment > A
433.2	for] Ed; face ~ > A
433.37	cotquean] Ed; couchquean > B
436.2	FLASKETS OF DRUGS, FULL TO THEIR WICKED LIPS] B; *omitted* > A
436.15	Queens] B; Queen's > A

436.21   brilliancy.] B; ~ > A

437.1   casket.] B; ~ > A

437.26   sat down and] B; now > A

438.16   dissolves] B; disolves > A

438.33   is] D; are > A

439.22   asked Angelique.] B; *omitted* > A

442.8   tone] C; voice > A

444.2   THE BROAD BLACK GATEWAY OF A LIE] B; *omitted* > A

444.18   La] Ed; *omitted* > A

445.5   despatches] Ed; dispatches > B

445.31   a] B; a ~ > A

446.24   St Luc] Ed; de ~ ~ > A

446.32   St Luc] Ed; de ~ ~ > A

446.36   favour] Ed; favor > B

447.16   St Luc] Ed; de ~ ~ > A

447.23   Hocquart] Ed; Hoquart > A

449.16   New France] Ed; ~-~ > B

450.25   favour] Ed; favor > B

451.9   proclaim] B; proclain > A

455.28   an] B; in > A

456.13   him] C; *omitted* > A

459.2   OLYMPIC CHARIOTS AND MUCH LEARNED DUST] B; *omitted* > A

459.6   strengthened] B; strengthed > A

460.11   crafty] B; craft > A

465.7   the] B; as ~ > A

470.2   to] B; to him ~ > A

470.12   honour] Ed; honor > B

473.33   study] B; sudy > A

476.22   Statesmen] B; Statemen > A

476.32–33   its peace] B; Its peace > A

477.1   Corne] Ed; Corné > B

477.17   pusillanimity] B; pusilanimity > A

477.20   pursuers] B; pursurers > A

479.36   back.] B; ~ > A

482.2   THE COUTUME DE PARIS] B; *omitted* > A

482.8   Seigneurie] B; Signeurie > A

484.10   parlour] Ed; parlor > A

485.35   windows] B; window > A

486.11   had] B; has > A

489.6   of talk] B; *omitted* > A

489.37   executed] B; excuted > A

491.29   so] B; say > A

493.4   pricked] B; picked > A

493.25   consultez] C; conseillez > A

494.1   Samuel Champlain] C; Jacques Cartier > A

497.2   A WILD NIGHT INDOORS AND OUT] B; *omitted* > A

497.26   Pothier] B; *omitted* > A

498.8   objects] B; object > A

502.8   you.] B; ~ > A

502.33   he fiercely!] Ed; ~! ~ > A

503.24	city.] B; ~ > A		532.2	"QUOTH THE RAVEN: 'NEVERMORE!'"] B; *omitted* > A
504.6	although] B; athough > A			
504.23	Le Mercier] B; Mericier > A		532.18	lay] C; was > A
504.33	boatmen] B; boatman > A		533.6	the life of] B; *omitted* > A
507.2	MERE MALHEUR] B; *omitted* > A		533.10	indelibly] B; indilibly > A
507.8	lintels] B; lintles > A		533.22	scurrying] E; scurring > A
507.15	things.] B; ~ > A		534.37	Iroquois.] B; ~ > A
507.18	arts.] B; ~ > A		535.18	an] B; a ~ > A
507.23	to pry too] B; too pry to > A		538.26	terror.] B; ~ to throw > A
508.35	an] B; in > A		542.2	"A DEED WITHOUT A NAME"] B; *omitted* > A
510.13	Baron] B; King > A			
511.12	fields.] B; ~ > A		546.3	the] B; *omitted* > A
511.21	La] B; Le > A		555.1	46] B; 45 > A
512.2	elixir] B; elixer > A		555.2	"LET'S TALK OF GRAVES AND WORMS AND EPITAPHS"] B; *omitted* > A
512.9	of the] B; in the > A			
514.34	winter king] C; Winter King > A			
515.1	off] B; of > A		556.1	eternal] B; eteranal > A
517.22	Madonna.] B; ~ > A			
518.2	des] C; de > A		556.3	favour] Ed; favor > A
518.24	sharpest] B; sharp > A		558.26	the] B; th > A
518.35	of her] B; of her ~ ~ > A		558.27	Mercier] D; Mericier > A
520.33	to] B; and ~ > A		558.27	favour] Ed; favor > A
522.8	colour] Ed; color > A		558.30	Mercier] D; Mericier > A
522.24	second] B; seccond > A			
524.2	"OUTVENOMS ALL THE WORMS OF NILE"] B; *omitted* > A		559.1	Deschenaux] B; Dechenaux > A
527.30–33	There … wind.] B; *omitted* > A		560.7	Baron de St Castin] Ed; King > A
529.25	bouquet] B; boquet > A		560.27	to] B; *omitted* > A

567.33 answered Cadet with rough sympathy.] B; *omitted* > A

568.26–27 to be hung] C; hang > A

568.34 loveliness] B; lovliness > A

572.17 Commissary] B; commissary > A

575.24 they] B; the > A

575.28 the] B; this > A

576.17 Marcele] B; Marcel > A

576.18 and] B; and ∼ > A

577.7 storms] B; storm > A

578.1 47] B; 46 > A

578.2 SILK GLOVES OVER BLOODY HANDS] B; *omitted* > A

578.3 *omitted*] Ed; It was long before Angelique came to herself, from the swoon in which she had been left lying on the floor by La Corriveau. Fortunately for her, it was without discovery none of the servants happened to come to her room during its continuance—else a weakness so strange to her usual hardihood would have become the City's talk before night, and set all its idle tongues conjecturing or inventing a reason for it. It would have reached the ears of Bigot as every spray of gossip did, and set him thinking too more savagely than he was yet doing, as to the causes and occasions of the murder of Caroline. > A

579.33 convict] B; convicted > A

582.10 palpable] B; palapable > A

583.9 Paris.] B; ∼ > A

585.11 Fanchon's] B; Fanchon > A

585.24 equanimity] B; equamity. > A

587.13–14 The Goddess ignorantly worshipped] B; The Goddess ignorantly worshipped ∼ ∼ ∼ ∼ > A

587.31 Recollets] B; Recollèts > A

587.34 Anne] Ed; Ann > A

588.20 a] B; A > A

589.29 Louis] B; Louise > A

591.12 their] C; all ∼ > A

593.28 their] B; there > A

594.33 had] B; was ∼ > A

595.19 deceiving] B; deceiveing > A

595.25 futurity.] B; ∼ > A

596.4 she, "never] B; "∼ ∼ > A

597.2 repetition] B; repitition > A

597.18	Cathedral] B; Cathredal > A
597.20	speak] D; not ~ > A
598.21	"the] B; "The > A
598.29	Cathedral] B; Cathredal > A
602.10	than] B; than ~ > A
602.10	first.] B; first > A
602.36	aberrations] B; abberations > A
603.10	to] B; too > A
603.16	Repentigny."] B; ~ > A
603.27	success] B; sucess > A
603.28	devotions] B; devotion > A
604.3	Cathedral] B; Cathredal > A
605.1	48] B; 47 > A
605.2	THE INTENDANT'S DILEMMA] B; *omitted* > A
605.3	certainty] B; certainity > A
606.2	succeed] B; suceed > A
606.6	occurred] B; ocurred > A
606.21	Cadet?"] B; ~ > A
606.31	confederate] B; confedrate > A
607.6	confederate] B; confedrate > A
607.22	writing.] B; ~ > A
610.28	statements] B; statments > A
610.36	fire—] Ed; ~ > A
612.27	of the] B; of the ~ ~ > A
612.28	seeing them.] B; ~ ~ > A
613.6	certainty] B; certanity > A
613.14	Bigot's] B; Bigot > A
613.19	commissioned] B; comissioned > A
614.9	Prairies] B; Praires > A
614.11	rather] B; rather ~ > A
614.19	suspicion] B; suspision > A
614.28	And] Ed; and > B
616.1	49] B; 48 > A
616.2	"I WILL FEED FAT THE ANCIENT GRUDGE I BEAR HIM"] B; *omitted* > A
616.17	Goelette] B; Goellette > A
616.24	innumerable] B; inumerable > A
617.1	Nicholas] B; Nicholaus > A
617.3	performed] B; preformed > A
618.23	prefers] B; perfers > A
620.30	succumbed] B; sucumbed > A
620.33	success] B; sucess > A
621.2	success] B; sucess > A
622.27	De] D; de > A
623.34	successfully] B; sucessfully > A
623.35	Bourgeois.] B; ~ > A
625.20	legitimate] B; legitmate > A
626.8	denouement] B; denoument > A

627.2   THE BOURGEOIS
         PHILIBERT] B; *omitted*
         > A
628.25   Grande] B; Grand > A
629.15   husbandman] B;
         husbandmen > A
629.21   monopoly] B; monoply
         > A
630.26   chateau] Ed; château
         > B
632.4   now.] B; ~ > A
632.12   Côte] B; Coté > A
633.1   honours] Ed; honors
         > B
633.24   so far] C; as yet > B
633.25   colour] Ed; color > B
634.6   Cerberus] B; Ceberus
         > A
634.32   Cerberus] B;
         Cerberous > A
634.36   Cerberus] B; Ceberus
         > A
635.6   of] B; *omitted* > A
635.18   heartbreak] B;
         hearbreak, > A
636.1   possessions] B;
         posessions > A
636.10   surprise] B; suprise > A
636.38   jealousy] B; jealously,
         > A
637.9   voluptuous] B;
         voluptous > A
637.38   favours] Ed; favors > B
638.11   familiar] B; familar > A
638.17   badinage] B;
         bandinage > A
638.26   Cathedral] B;
         Cathredal > A

638.33   jealousy] B; jealously
         > A
639.9   favour] Ed; favor > B
641.1   51] B; 49 > A
641.2   A DRAWN GAME] B;
         omitted > A
641.9   Bourgeois'] B; ~ > A
642.3   choosing] B; chosing
         > A
642.38   the *petits*] B; *petits* > A
643.15   forborne] B; foreborne
         > A
644.7   accommodating] B;
         accomadating > A
644.8   accommodating] B;
         accomadating > A
646.31   commission] B;
         comission > A
647.18   Beaumanoir] B;
         Beauminor > A
647.24   Beaumanoir] B;
         Beaumnoir > A
647.28   occasional] B;
         occassional > A
647.30   professions] B;
         proffessions > A
648.1   there] B; their > A
649.6   amount] B; ammount
         > A
650.1   52] B; 50 > A
650.2   "IN GOLD CLASPS
         LOCKS IN THE
         GOLDEN STORY"] B;
         omitted > A
650.6   physical] B; physcial
         > A
650.30   One mind,] B; one,
         mind > A

650.30	possessed] B; posessed > A
652.12	precise] B; percise > A
652.13	to] B; ~ to > A
652.21	to] B; too > A
652.24	affect] B; effect > A
653.20	surprise] B; suprise > A
655.10	possession] B; posession > A
655.12	Aunt has] B; I have > A
655.30	Victory] B; Vicotry > A
657.7	possessing] B; posessing > A
657.8	and] B; and ~ > A
657.17	succession] B; sucession > A
658.3	our] B; the ~ > A
658.5	fancy] C; think > A
658.19	and life] B; *omitted* > A
659.24	of] B; ~ a > A
659.25	at your] B; at you > A
661.12	Ah] B; A > A
662.1	53] B; 51 > A
662.5	chime.] B; ~ > A
662.16	but] C; and ~ > A
663.27	screaming] B; screaning > A
664.14	it were] B; were > A
664.20	purveyors] B; purveyers > A
664.21	of] B; of the ~ > A
664.27	Immense] B; Immence > A
665.6	Glapion] E; Goupion > A
665.13	had] B; and ~ > A
665.19	education] B; ededucation > A

666.18	inconsistency] B; inconsistancy > A
666.33	day.] C; ~! > A
667.9	dissociate] B; dissosciate > A
667.20	dissentient] B; dessentient > A
667.30	Jericho] B; Jerico > A
668.13	honours] Ed; honors > A
669.10	politicians] B; politicans > A
670.3	Cemetery] B; Cemetry > A
671.2	Galissoniere] Ed; Gallissonière > A
671.9	Recollets] B; Recollects > A
671.22	to] B; to ~ > A
672.5	Recollets] B; Recollects > A
672.6	Mercier] B; Mericier > A
672.17	of] B; of ~ > A
672.28	Jonquières] B; Jonquiers > A
672.29	Galissoniere] Ed; Gallissonière > A
672.30	comptoirs] B; comptoires > A
674.3	honour] B; honor > A
675.2	54] B; 52 > A
675.5	received] B; recieved > A
676.7	preparations] B; pereparations > A
676.20	honour] Ed; honor > A
677.1	they] Ed; thay > A

677.34	moment.] B; ~ > A	704.23	Madelaine] B; Marie
678.19	pages.] B; ~ > A		> A
679.11	Mercier] B; Mericier	706.1	56] B; 54 > A
	> A	707.6–7	I was] B; I was ~ ~ > A
679.12	perceive] B; percieve	712.31	she] B; ~ had > A
	> A	714.7	ever] B; ~ was > A
679.14	politeness.] B; ~ > A	715.25	until] B; intil > A
680.8	Le] B; La > A	715.36	Autumn] B; ~— > A
680.32	received] B; recieved	716.9	well-known] C;
	> A		well-know > A
681.13	Le] B; the ~ > A	717.1	57] B; 55 > A
683.9	and] B; *omitted* > A	718.19	Under] B; under > A
683.10	*souffrez*] B; *soufrez* > A	718.26	foreshadowed] B;
683.17	received] B; recieved		forshadowed > A
	> A	718.34	*Récit,*] B; *Rècit),* > A
683.25	received] B; recieved	720.3	to hide] B; to ~ ~ > A
	> A	720.8	the] B; *omitted* > A
684.22	he,] B; *omitted* > A	722.30	Castle] B; ~. > A
685.14	of] B; of ~ > A	724.3	overflowed] C;
689.29	the Bourgeois] B;		overflown > A
	Bourgeois Philibert	724.5	bridegroom.] B; ~; > A
	> A	724.26	that] B; the > A
689.32	Gauthier] B; ~ to > A	726.16	sadly.] B; ~ > A
689.33	to] B; *omitted* > A	727.22	me] B; aunt > A
691.30	lessen] B; lessened > A	730.26	Galissoniere] D;
694.2	55] B; 53 > A		Gallissonière > A
694.4	morning of] B; ~ ~ of	732.6	her] B; his > A
	> A	733.1	58] B; 56 > A
695.25	The] B; The ~ > A	734.7	in] B; in ~ > A
698.31	the bridesmaids] B; the	736.13	as far as] B; as far > A
	~ ~ > A	736.38	often] B; ofted > A
699.9	grand'peur] C; grand	737.26	there,] C; ~ > A
	peur > A	737.27–28	reality. It is time here,
699.27	at] B; at ~ > A		eternity there.] B;
700.23	Mademoiselle] D;		reality it is here. > A
	Madamoiselle > A	737.29	that] B; that ~ > A
700.37	They] B; She > A	739.19	whispered] Ed;
701.21	a] B; a ~ > A		whispering > A

740.38	could] B; could ∼ > A	752.1	in] B; in ∼ > A
741.24	upon] B; upon ∼ > A	752.9	completely] B;
743.1	59] B; 57 > A		completly > A
744.8	visited] B; visted > A	753.4	the business … to
744.31	Chapelle] B;		retain] B; she found
	Chappelle, > A		her sole delight in
745.27	Galissoniere] Ed;		retaining > A
	Gallissoniere > A	753.32	the hill] B; the ∼ ∼ > A
748.5	cruelly] B; crully > A	754.6	when it] B; when it ∼ ∼
748.13	neither] B; nether > A		> A
750.6	flourishes] B; flourishs	754.15	covered] C; cover > A
	> A	754.16	howled] C; howls > A
751.8	the hand] B; hand > A	754.16	rattled] C; rattles > A
751.35	imprisoned] B;	754.33–34	not long ago] B; *omitted*
	imprisioned > A		> A

Line-end Hyphenated Compounds
in Manuscript Copy-text

The compound or possible compound words that appear in this list were hyphenated at the end of a line in the manuscript copy-text used for this edition of *Le Chien d'or*. They have been resolved in the CEECT edition in the manner indicated below. In order to decide how to resolve these words, examples of their use within the lines of the manuscript copy-text were sought, and the spelling that appeared there adopted. In cases where the spelling of compound or possible compound words within the lines was inconsistent, the spelling most frequently used has been adopted. When these compounds or possible compounds appeared only at the end of the line in the manuscript copy-text, the *Oxford English Dictionary* was consulted for examples of how they were spelled in the eighteenth and nineteenth centuries. Their resolution was based on this information. The words in this list are keyed to the CEECT edition by page and line number. At 22.26 the second "Goodby" was hyphenated at the end of the line in the manuscript copy-text.

14.3	Lord-Governor	472.8	anything
22.26	Goodby	512.3	touchstone
60.32	ill-grounded	607.33	masterpiece
92.13	sunbeam	638.25	tomorrow
100.15	preoccupied	658.28	housekeeping
207.22	goodby	667.14	Anti-Christ
219.27	unnoticed	680.8	horsewhip
244.15	uplifted	696.30	Aix-La-Chapelle
314.17	hen-pecked	726.13	self-inflicted
376.5	overlooks	730.27	Godfather
438.24	heir-loom		
464.37	pre-existing		

Historical Collation

This list records variant readings that affect meaning between the manuscript copy-text of Kirby's *Le Chien d'or* and the Lovell, Adam, Wesson and Company impression of the first edition of this novel, but that have not been incorporated into the CEECT edition. Each entry in this list is keyed to the CEECT edition by page and line number. In each entry the reading in the manuscript copy-text and in the CEECT edition is given before the square bracket,], the variant reading in the 1877 impression after it. Thus the entry "3.24 on] upon" indicates that at page 3, line 24 "on" appears both in the CEECT edition and in the manuscript copy-text, but that the reading is "upon" in the Lovell, Adam, Wesson impression. The two exceptions occur in the entry for page 98, lines 19–20, where the word "the" before "river" does not appear in the manuscript copy-text, and in the entry for page 224, line 31, where the word "that" does not appear in the manuscript copy-text. In each entry the emendation is printed in square brackets, []. When appropriate in passages of more than six words, ellipsis dots, . . . , have been used to shorten the entry. In the entries the wavy dash, ~, signifies that the same word (and nothing else) as in the CEECT edition appears in the variant reading.

3.24	on] upon	9.14	their fields] her fields
4.12	dangers] danger	9.34	looking] pointing
4.37	generous] as ~	9.36	those] these
6.18	masts] mast	10.30	fortifications]
6.22	companion]		fortification
	companions	11.4	the ancient] their
6.35	alone] and ~		ancient
7.12	populous] dotted	11.11	had] *omitted*
7.26	its] the	14.16	on] upon
8.36	a] *omitted*	14.18	sight] the ~
9.1	on] upon	14.33	at] in
9.4	destiny] supremacy	14.36	Anne's] Anne
9.12	cruel] such	14.38	in] at

15.19	appear] shall ~	29.8	on] upon
15.27	laughing] merrily	29.21	look] to ~
15.33	mistress] Lady	30.9	on] upon
16.1	to be] as if	31.13	triumphs] triumph
16.9	tamed] tame	32.3	Philosoph]
16.32	that] which		philosopher
16.37	succeed] ~ him	32.31	he] as ~
16.38	only] *omitted*	33.4	on] upon
17.17	Angelique] to ~	33.14	and] *omitted*
17.18	the] girls	33.23	dared] dare
18.12	the] that ~	33.35	and she] She
19.5	or] and	34.21	on] of
19.22	afresh] deeply	34.24	idol] ideal
21.19	the] being ~	35.12	on the] upon the
21.36	on] upon	35.15	so dissolute,] *omitted*
24.6	of] her ~	35.18	too] *omitted*
24.9	frontiers] frontier	35.18	a] *omitted*
24.19	illumined] illuminated	35.21	Court] Count
25.8	victrix] a victim	35.34	on] upon
25.14	and] *omitted*	35.36	bitterly] scornfully
25.16	and] *omitted*	36.3	these] them
25.22	rich gay] gayest	36.38	down] *omitted*
25.23	a] the	37.6	She started up] *omitted*
25.30	the Lady] that Lady	37.16	took not] scarcely took
26.2	we] you	37.30	a hint] from a hint
26.8	you] *omitted*	38.22	has] must have
26.10	and I would] I should	39.10	that] her
26.11	frown] smile	39.16	in] on
26.18	say] speak	40.8	that] which ~
26.38	at last found] found at	40.24	on] upon
	last	41.8	to] of
27.1	and] or	41.13	on] upon
27.11–12	show mankind the	42.1	will continue]
	possibilities of		continues
	feminine perfection]	42.22	on] ~ to
	realize the dreams of a	42.24	Satans] Satan
	Titian or a Giorgione	42.34	at] of
27.21	over many] for many	42.36	and] ~ the

43.23	Anne] Annes	56.34	spread] lay ~
43.30	on] upon	58.8	Its] The
43.35	up] upon	58.10	song] songs
43.36	a tall] an old	58.12	peered] appeared
44.2	on] upon	58.15	and] with
44.3	the grass] grass	58.20	air] wind
44.4	tipped] dressed	59.22	underlying] lying under
44.15	all] were		
44.16	airs] air	60.1	waving] waiving
44.35	richest] proudest	60.20	on] upon
45.5	thought] the ~	61.2	the door] it
45.25	preeminence] prominence	62.5	past] wild
		63.9	on] upon
45.30	logic] by ~	64.14	men and true] and true men
45.38	soul] being		
46.7	on] upon	65.31	horloge] clock
47.31	on] upon	65.38	hazily] lazily
48.6	advocate] advocates	66.13	bottom] bottoms
48.26	his pen] the pen	66.14	glass] glasses
49.5	fast] as ~	66.25	till] until
49.10	please] read, ~	66.31	really] and ~
49.23	and] *omitted*	67.1	clean] as ~
49.23	not] is ~	67.10	politic] polite
52.5	easy] as ~	67.33	plenty] ~ of corn
52.10	cool] *omitted*	68.4	at Varin] to Varin
52.28	leave off] get out	68.16	Tire] Vive
52.38	and] *omitted*	68.23	on] upon
53.1	church] house	68.26	toast on] toast upon
54.31	intricate] as ~	69.23	if] though
55.12	Latin] Satan's	69.25	fierce] a ~
55.17	Master] *omitted*	69.31	them] those
55.24	finds] find	69.32	fury] frenzy
55.29	to get] get	70.15	finger] fingers
55.32	more] a ~	70.32	hard] as ~
55.34	twinkled] trembled	71.4	on] upon
55.34	brow] brows	71.18	minutes] moments
56.1	gowns] robes	71.37	will] who ~
56.6	there] and ~	72.24	ship on] ship upon

73.8	at us] by	87.10	on] upon
73.8	day] by ~	87.11	thoughts] mind
73.22	panders] panderers	88.2	do] *omitted*
73.34	Magazin] Magazine	88.23	the] this
75.6	what] ~ toast	88.30	dress] clean
75.15	desires] desire	89.8	the more] more
75.29	you] that ~	89.13	our cheeks not] not
75.36	says] say		our cheeks
76.23	ruddy] a ~	89.24	the] *omitted*
76.28	pursed] pressed	89.27	into] in
77.6	distressed] disturbed	90.7	and plenty] with plenty
77.11	touched] and ~	90.7	empty] to ~
78.21	strain] stain	90.9	on alone] along
79.2	courtiers] courtesies	90.10	and fit] fit
79.6	was] had	90.13	contract of marriage,
79.16	no] nor		or] marriage contract,
79.17	no] nor	90.14	will] last ~
79.26	over] ever	90.14	greatest] ~ of
80.26	and] ~ over	94.25	shod] clad
81.13	on] upon	94.26	duchesse] Duchess,
81.19	the] *omitted*	95.19	at] up ~
81.25	worst] his ~	97.31	Ah] Oh
81.31	on] upon	98.19	the high] upon ~ ~
82.1	still, still] still	98.19–20	closing the view on the
82.6	Pshaw] Why		farther side of [the]
82.8	Cardinal] the ~		river] the farther side
82.10	grand fetes] great feasts		of the river closing the
82.22	on] upon		view
82.28	in] on	99.19	up] upon
83.3	in] into	99.36	on] upon
83.14	lout] beast	100.20–21	and costume] costume
85.4	they want] he wants	100.33	upon] on
85.23	Cadet] he	101.20	say.] ~ or—
85.25	chienne] Chien	101.23	them] *omitted*
85.26	elle] ellene	101.26	on] upon
86.16	on] upon	102.16	accent] sound
86.22	Tut] ~, tut	102.19	mistress] minister
86.27	of] at	102.22	that] *omitted*

102.27–28	with well bred phrases	113.1	lofty] *omitted*
	their disappointment]	113.10	A] and a
	their disappointment	113.12	on] upon
	under well bred	113.29	finest] the ~
	phrases	113.35	coral] corals
102.28	a] *omitted*	115.15	Le Gardeur] he
104.1	itself] *omitted*	115.21	on] upon
104.5	that] this	116.1	of of] of
104.16	keener] a ~	116.4	would] should
104.25	memory] mind	116.23	a] that ~
105.8	and] *omitted*	116.33	to him] *omitted*
105.27	twitching] twisting	117.22	if] and
106.25	dear] *omitted*	117.26	on] upon
107.5	hesitation] ~ and tone	117.38	into] in
107.21	on] upon	118.18	and hope] hope
107.29	it] that ~	120.1	called Philibert at
107.30	life] heart		once] at once called
107.34	as] and		Philibert
108.11	find myself] be	121.14	reply] to ~
108.22	thanking him] very	122.4	present] same
	grateful	122.12	in] of
108.23	would] should	122.33	next day] to-morrow,
108.25	would] should	122.38	on] upon
108.28	acquaintance]	123.12	The] These
	acquaintances	123.29	escutcheon] throne
108.35	all] what	124.12	striking] more ~
109.18	bob-tail] bobtailed	124.24	These] There
109.32	fire side] firesides	124.28	these] the
109.36	most] the ~	124.33	disputes] dispute
109.36	a] the	124.35	On] Upon
109.37	is] was	125.22	caused] created
110.2	best] the ~	125.25	on their] upon their
110.15	the] *omitted*	125.37	the way] that way
110.15	on] upon	126.4	on] upon
111.6	fresh] new	126.8	late] *omitted*
112.5	An] as an	126.19	have also] also have
112.9	inquiring] inquired	126.29	aright] right
112.10	begging] begged	126.30	almost of] of utmost

126.38	protected] defended	138.26	and] to
127.22–27	The Secretary …	138.27	this] the
	Council table.] *omitted*	138.30	and cry] or cry
127.31	Therefore] and	139.8	hardy] sturdy
	therefore	139.29	led] leads
128.21	on] upon	140.24	of execration] and
129.2	farther] further		execrations
129.7	in] something ∼	140.33	image] idol
132.10	in piles] piled up	141.2	dashing] darting
133.12	strongly] and ∼	142.17	on] upon
133.27	quickly] rapidly	143.1–2	CHAPTER 14 / THE
133.35	appearance] exterior,		COUNCIL OF WAR]
133.35	kindest] kindliest		*omitted*
134.6	bespoke] betrayed	143.7	tramping] trampling
134.8	retained] still ∼	145.14	defend] excuse
134.8	intonations] intonation	146.16	on] upon
134.18	war] wars	146.17	matter] dispute
134.21	the] his	146.18	The Council]
134.27	on] upon		CHAPTER 14 / THE
134.30	On] In		COUNCIL OF WAR ∼
135.8	child] girl		∼
135.17	abroad] *omitted*	146.20	marks] looks
135.17	finally] *omitted*	146.20	on] in
135.23	She] and she	146.30	Their] English
136.9	serving in] being over	146.33	to erect] the erection
136.16	and] *omitted*		of
136.20	sadness] shadows	147.8	within] *omitted*
136.20	but] *omitted*	147.13	falls] fall
136.23	so] and ∼	147.13	enemies] enemy's
136.23	and the] The	147.18	the] be ∼
136.24	pleasure] rejoicing	147.31	that] *omitted*
137.7	enemies] as ∼	148.3	prize] prizes
137.17	turned and] *omitted*	149.16	eye] eyes
137.29	a] such ∼	150.29	on] in
137.32	was] had	151.4	served] and ∼
138.21	will sing] shall sing	151.5	thus] this
138.23	announcement]	151.12	suddenly end] end
	reception		suddenly

151.31	to] *omitted*	161.38	on] upon
151.35	in] involved ~	162.12	very] *omitted*
153.2	that] *omitted*	162.22	Quebec] the city
153.3	caused] had ~	162.36	icy] *omitted*
153.5	Still] Therefore	163.17	Their] Men's
153.9	corrupt] a ~	163.26	The women] but the women
153.11	the other was ever ready with his sword to risk] he was ready with his sword in the other to give	163.31	opinions] opinion
		164.21	women] us ~
		164.36	it] ~ is
153.15	last] final	165.1	amaze] amazement
153.16	when] and ~	165.11	am] was
153.17	and] *omitted*	165.17	her] *omitted*
153.20	eyes] eye	165.22	If] As if
153.30	on] upon	165.22	do] did
153.35	much] greatly	165.22	I] but ~
153.37	our] the	166.28	asked] added
154.9	upon] on	166.34	I had] ~ ~ had
154.29	another] or ~	167.11	at Beauport,] where he lies.
154.34	relative] the ~		
156.14	as lief] like to	167.16	they] and ~
156.14–15	I would] and ~ ~	167.25	as if] *omitted*
156.26	got] asked	167.27	and are] and fast
156.27	Get] Ask	167.28–29	where it is] which are
157.3	holds] binds	167.29	secret] dull
157.11	ill] bad	168.18	sayings] savings
159.5	She] as she	168.36	good] best
159.16	Spurn] only spurn	169.21	talking] telling
159.23	and the whole] Everything	169.21	past] my ~
		169.23	got] has ~
160.19	Governor] Governor's	169.24	angered] has ~
160.29	men and] *omitted*	169.33	on] in
161.3	quite feelingly—of you] of you quite feelingly	169.34	at] out
		170.13	that] *omitted*
161.6	was] were	170.29	a] as ~
161.13	replied] continued	171.9	fisher] fishers
161.19	body] lady	171.11	the oar] his oar
		171.11	sounds] sound

171.31	Yet] and yet	183.11	ever] that ~
171.33	air and harmony] melody	184.2	on] upon
		184.7	every] your
171.36	voices of angels were] voice of an angel was	184.19	That] this
		184.19	She kissed] said she, kissing
173.6	and] *omitted*		
173.15	until] till	184.22	drank] have ~
173.23	now] *omitted*	184.23	question] questions,
174.26	falbelas] furbelows	184.24	fond] soft
174.28	and] or	185.4	upon] on
174.34	rich] *omitted*	185.8	on] in
175.14	paintings] painting	185.8	was driving] had driven
175.26	one was] was one	185.19	in] of
175.31	choirs] choir	185.33	one] that
175.32–33	and men] Men	185.38	some] which ~
176.9	sake] the ~	186.1	turns] changes
176.15	devoured by] saturated with	186.6	drew] pressed
		186.13	and all] All
176.26	in his] into his	186.16	rose] arose
177.17	a] the	186.20	de] *omitted*
177.35	for supremacy] and ~ ~	186.26	this] the
		186.26	service] occasion
178.16	whole] *omitted*	186.28	for] to
178.31	our] an	187.7	the horses] his horse's
179.19	bell] clock	187.15	but] and
179.22	Piquet] patrol	187.19	waters] water
179.26	rang] clattered	187.20	save] rescue
179.28	portico] steps	187.24	woke] awoke
180.1	replied] repeated	188.10	have] to ~
180.21	in] from	189.4	patroness] friends
180.32	lightly] fondly	189.7	would] might
181.22	gave] give	189.8	would] might
181.23	passing] pressing	189.13	all] those
182.1	or] *omitted*	189.18	and] *omitted*
182.12	She] The	189.25	on] upon
182.13	and closed] closed	189.35	card] hold
182.25	were] was	191.4	draw the herring] fight and win
182.27	smaller] small		

191.8	who] *omitted*
191.22	home] at ∼
191.26	like] as
191.27	women] ∼ do
192.29	show] shows
193.3	suddenly] *omitted*
193.7	alone sitting] sitting alone
193.15	had] she ∼
193.17	not] nor
193.24	fancies] images
193.30	will] shall
194.18	replied Bigot, feeling] Bigot, felt
194.22	of] *omitted*
194.30	further] farther
196.37	scanned] seen
197.3	accomplishing] accomplished
197.12	called] had ∼
197.32	dazed] dazzled
197.34	gorgeous] as ∼
198.3	was] were
198.17	of Choisy] *omitted*
198.26	Chevalier] the ∼
198.27	and] or
199.2	choose] chose
199.35	hard] as ∼
199.36	said Bigot rather] Bigot was quite
200.28	and] *omitted*
201.1	No!] *omitted*
201.3	that] it
201.35	you] yourself
202.29	now] fully
202.33	year] month
202.38	did] has
203.1	a] *omitted*

203.25	with] between
204.2	and] a
205.4	compared] in comparison
205.10	swelling] which swelled
205.10	and] *omitted*
206.19	upon] of
206.29	attire outside] outside attire
207.3	on] upon
207.28	which however] The business, however,
208.5	interceded] who ∼
208.35	light] pretty,
209.14	little] *omitted*
209.14	lips] pretty ∼
210.5	as she did] *omitted*
210.8	had] had ∼
210.11	and nuns] *omitted*
210.32	rather] *omitted*
211.1	engagement] engagements
212.9	and philosophers] philosophers
212.15	fold] flock
214.7	and] They
215.27	of] with
215.36	meat] dinners
216.2	them] those
216.19	went] have gone
216.24	went] *omitted*
216.33	remarked] replied
216.37	Emeric] Monredin
217.26	kept] to be ∼
218.7	exclaimed Emeric.] *omitted*
218.10	will] shall
218.20	the] these

218.21	magazines] the ~	234.21	the feudal] a feudal
218.22	lading, unlading] loading and unloading	234.22	on] upon
		234.29	breathed] breathing
219.17	greedy harpies] game fowls	234.29	and] *omitted*
		235.3	forests] forest
220.9	Seyny] Seigny	235.5	Master] Manor
220.19	myself] ourselves	235.9	bells] cups
220.20	turn] turns	235.12	and broken] hill-side
221.38	was] had	235.14	whorling] whirling
222.9–10	and he] He	236.8	guests] ladies
222.24	sake] the ~	236.21	thick] thickly
222.25	loved] loves,	236.25	arrived] approached
222.37	a] you ~	236.37	power] most ~
224.11	brother] none	236.37	other] *omitted*
224.13	if] as	237.1	other men] others
224.28	There is] There's	237.27	itself] yet
224.31	of something brother, [that] might happen] something might happen, brother	237.35	all griefs, all resentments] cares, griefs, and resentments
		237.38	his] the
225.6	even] ever	238.33–34	nothing else] that only
225.24	He] but he	239.1	them] *omitted*
226.16	Caught] as caught	239.6	On] In
226.23	maid's] maid	239.13	were] had been
227.19	Magazin] magazine	239.24	Brandy] wines
227.22	de] du	239.37–38	very soon to take a wife] to take a wife very soon
227.25	was] were		
228.3	mark] cross		
228.28	does] ~ you	240.4	voice] words
228.35	Lizette] *omitted*	240.4	active] solid
228.37	with] all over ~	240.9	farther] further
228.38	women never have] A woman never has	240.33	company] guests
		240.35	drove] rode
229.9	on] upon	242.37	many] so ~
229.10	in] into	243.17	Mont] Mount
232.6	the] *omitted*	243.27	the] his
233.17	and] *omitted*	245.5	artist] artiste
234.17	and] while	245.36	molified] modified

245.38	a] the	266.27	hand] hands
246.11	And] ~ then	267.21	trouble] to ~
247.10	fashion] fashions	267.28	finger] fingers
248.6	into] with	267.35	shamming] cheating
249.16	us] me	268.8	the stoutest carter's]
250.24	graffed] grafted		those of the stoutest
251.31	come] came		carter
251.36	soutane] gray gown	268.14	and] as
252.36	the benefit of] *omitted*	268.17	and the beggars]
253.7	stout] fat		*omitted*
253.15	pack] back	268.23	to] *omitted*
253.27	table] the ~	268.33	I] that ~
253.33	times] time	270.12	Seminary-church]
254.22	and when] when		Seminary Chapel
254.34	his] their	270.17	the] that ~
255.12	the] this	271.7	on] *omitted*
255.14	all] many	271.15	not] neither
255.36	now] *omitted*	271.20	that] *omitted*
257.28	grave] fate	271.28	done] perused it
258.11	assembled] had ~	271.29	carpet] floor
258.26	homely] home	272.3	Shaking] Shrinking
258.33	Few] None	272.24	will] shall
258.34	wanted] wished	273.3	transformed] formed
259.14	stirred] touched	273.35	which there was no
259.26	and] *omitted*		escape from] from
259.31	the Convent] her		which there was no
	companions		escape
260.3	irrationably]	274.14	and] his
	irrationally	274.21	golden weights]
261.15	from more] *omitted*		weights of gold
261.21	bouquet] wreath.	274.23–24	to recall] recalling
261.24	liker] like	275.7	self] *omitted*
261.30	cheerily] cheeringly	275.17	to reconcile] who
264.10	bearing] bringing		reconciled
265.1	treads] steps	275.27	and] ~ a
265.27	in some] at some	276.7	door of paradise] gate
266.3	hands] hand		of heaven
266.7	taxing] fleecing	276.24	in] on

277.2	and] nor	288.38	out] *omitted*
277.22	opinion] opinions	289.9	own] *omitted*
278.6	pleading] passionate	289.26	the] *omitted*
278.20–21	so so] so	290.2	jug] mug
278.23	vision] ~ came	290.3	a corner] the corner
278.25	come in] enter	290.3	stuff] *omitted*
278.26	hearth] hearths	290.12	jug] mug
278.26	servants] slaves	290.17	jug] mug
279.4–5	the no less vivid	291.13	in the pockets] into the
	consciousness] no less		armholes
	vivid the consciousness	291.26	it] one
280.9	I ever] and ever	291.29	we] they
280.32	minutes] moments	291.30	learn] learned
280.33	makes] that ~	292.35	morrow] to-morrow
281.17	old] olden	292.35	Make] so make
281.26	treasure] ~ them	293.1	till day light] for the
281.27	and] *omitted*		remainder of the night
282.8	swift] rapid	293.4	streaming] tremulous
282.14	womanly] mortal	293.11	compose] steady
282.38	become] became	293.26	But] *omitted*
283.10	was rising] had risen	294.4	gentle] a ~
283.15	streaked] stained	294.6	and] *omitted*
284.6	and upon] upon	294.6	any] and ~
285.1	time] hour	294.9	Taverne] Tavern
285.24	two] the hour	294.23	us] ~ do
286.26	friends of] friends	295.5	Amelie] and ~
286.29	thought] thoughts	295.29	The] and the
286.30	was] were	296.5	asks] ask
286.38	will] must	296.24	released] relieved
287.9	threw] cast	297.14	had taken] took
287.20	in order] *omitted*	297.14	from] early ~
287.28	open] opened	297.28	The] and the
287.37	shoulder] shoulders	298.26	that] so
288.14	likes] loves	298.27	for] *omitted*
288.23	keeps] holds	298.31	perfection] perfections
288.24	have] keep	299.13	affluent] the ~
288.28	were reasons] was	299.26	read the] read
	reason	299.33	and as] As

300.1	run] have ~	320.22	caught from] seen
300.38	German] the ~		upon
302.20	house] château	321.15	found] find
303.7	He] and	321.16	the beau] my beau
303.34	leur] leurs	321.22–23	when I learned that]
304.10	goodbys] good wishes		wher
304.18	their] *omitted*	321.28	in] for
304.33	open] ever	321.36	will light] shall light
306.12	keeping] as they kept	321.36	will make] shall make
306.12	together] *omitted*	322.20	will] shall
306.12	voices] oars	324.20	influences] influence
307.7	Beautiful River] Belle	324.38	change] a ~
	Rivière	325.6	who] that
307.32	adaption] adaptation	325.11	leaning] resting
307.32	pious] *omitted*	325.17	hides] covers
307.35	revered] reverend	325.36	light] joy
308.12	has] had	326.16	A sudden] Sudden
308.17	were] was	326.25	and hopeless]
308.26	those] their		impassioned
309.22	canoe and] music,	326.26	Amelie did not often
309.31	fashion] fashions		sing] tremulous in its
309.34	Ya—A—un] Ya—t—un		power
312.14	day] days	327.27	attained] realized
312.16	Bostonais] Bostonians	327.29	occupation]
312.19	in] from		occupations
312.27	Levy] Levis	328.4	Amelie] where she
313.9	scene] whole ~	328.30	prayer] prayers
314.29	laid] lain	331.26	on] upon
315.9	land] lands	334.1	will] shall
316.38	bevy] body	334.35	have at least done] at
317.14	was] had		least have done
318.18	nearly] wholly	335.5	and] *omitted*
318.24	arcades] arches	335.27	quickly] quietly
319.7	Felix] and ~	335.31	other's special regard]
319.22	all] *omitted*		special regard of the
320.2	walls] wall		other
320.20	caught] had ~	336.1	creation] revelation
320.21	he] *omitted*	336.5	pleading] pleadings

336.32	conversations] conversation	356.33	not] *omitted*
337.11	was] were	356.35	rushed] pushed
338.11	woods] wood	358.11	her] the
338.13	all at once] suddenly	359.32	was] were
339.3	so] the	360.4	intimation] intuition
339.15	farther] further	360.10	topics] topic
339.20	as this] *omitted*	360.26	event] events
340.24	his] its	362.21	Of that nature] Equally
340.26	me] I		futile
341.9	three] ~ friends	362.27	close and] *omitted*
342.29	strung] threaded	362.28	on] upon
344.7	repeating] repeated	362.28	as] and
344.24	alternations] alternation	362.28	flowed] that ~
345.1	emotions] emotion	362.30	which] who
345.4	on] upon	363.27	as] for
346.24–25	a happy day] of blue skies	363.27	unimpressed] unimpressible
346.30	group] groups	363.36–37	sits obstructing] obstructs
347.6	visible] at hand	364.15	really been] been really
350.1	which is ... noble hearts] that doth quickly seize the gentle heart	364.35	any] my
		365.37	was] were
		366.21	chamber] chambers
		366.37–38	did you not pledge] that you pledged
350.3	sundered] parted	367.9	had] *omitted*
350.35	is] ~ a	367.22	forever] *omitted*
351.21	locked fast] fast locked	367.31	brightly] bright
351.23	moment] ~ that	367.36	hardly] scarcely
351.27	deeper] ~ and deeper	368.1	of] for
351.31	bright] brighter	368.14	lobbies] corridors
351.32	oak] tree	368.19	Palace] Palais
351.34	problem] problems	369.26	almost went] went almost
352.10	of] for		
352.33	would] could	370.36	and] *omitted*
352.34	which] that	376.7	she—she] she
354.22	pride] joy	377.18	him] ~ as
356.30	unto] into	377.25	neck] *omitted*

378.6	to a] for a	393.18	pray] ask
378.11	lie] fraud	393.38	in] me ∼
378.26	she] you ∼	394.6	eagerly up] up eagerly
379.15	are] is	394.20	reality] meaning
380.7	*difference*] *différance*	394.27	give] ∼ you
381.7	furthest] farthest	395.3	humours] humor
381.24	*pius*] *omitted*	395.7	Her thoughts] It
382.15	in] of	395.14	hideous] horrid
382.20	world] the ∼	395.28	mention] ∼ again
382.21	and] *omitted*	396.6	no] ∼ further
382.22	when] and	396.14	return] accompany
384.1	Bigot] *omitted*		them
385.4	finger] very ∼	397.19	onto] into
385.29	undulating] and	397.21	if] it
	undulated	399.37	trouble] ∼ and
387.33	run] step		perplexity
388.1	that nice] the nice	401.21	no matter] it matter's
388.3	that] the		not
388.8	*Ton*] *tons*	402.2	will] would
388.11	Madame] You see, ∼	402.3	are] were
388.14	de] *omitted*	404.5	portentous signs] a
388.22	de] *omitted*		portentous sign
388.27	the] *omitted*	404.6	crime] crimes
388.28	I] *omitted*	404.19	woman] *omitted*
388.32	de] *omitted*	404.27	and] *omitted*
388.34–35	the natural freedom	405.23	this] these
	of] *omitted*	405.29	either as] as either
389.1	made] which ∼	406.30	each alone] *omitted*
389.14	qualities] quantities	407.26	set at naught to his
390.9	joyous] a ∼,		unutterable rage] to
391.3	wonder!] ∼," said he,		his unutterable rage,
391.7	her] the		set at naught
391.16	but] and	408.7	looks] look
391.37	hurts] will hurt	408.8	La] Le
392.36	beam] glow	409.27	remnants] remnant
393.2	a] the	409.27	fortunes] fortune
393.4	a] for ∼	409.32	But] that
393.4	said Bigot] are you not	411.1	make] create

411.9	under] from ~	424.18	disclosed] had ~
411.18	neighbours houses] a	424.24	A] and a
	neighbor's house	424.25	claim on] practice,
411.26	and] or		upon
411.29	But] She	425.5	pleased] was pleasant
412.7	the] *omitted*		to
412.21	violence] blows	425.16	hardly] lightly
413.6	abstention] abstinence	425.16	in] *omitted*
414.8–9	"Ah! Ah! . . . Ouich	425.28	closed] now ~
	Ka!"] *omitted*	425.29	on] upon
414.24	to] in ~	426.2	partially] partly
415.7	may] might	426.25	was] were
415.13	and] I	427.22	both] each of
415.26	are] were	427.28	Her] with her
417.2	meadow] meadows	427.32	were] *omitted*
417.3	formed] forming	427.33	none] and ~
417.4	clustering] clustered	428.6	vanity] power
417.12	covered] formed	428.26	pit] dark ~
418.8	alone] she was ~	429.15	It] mine
418.37	dare] dares to	429.20	half] *omitted*
419.1	trudge] go	429.33	to] you
419.13	or] for	430.8	when] if
420.32	look] looked	430.12	from her seat] *omitted*
420.33	allows] allowed	431.2	and] but
420.34	are] were	431.11	man] a ~
421.4	ruin] tempt	431.15	fairly] now ~
421.17	replied La Corriveau]	431.15	barrier] barriers
	omitted	431.15	now] *omitted*
421.30	not] ~ so	431.21	La] Le
422.4	had left] was gone	432.7	or] nor
422.22	design] designs	432.23	where] when
423.2	fastened] locked	432.33	and] *omitted*
423.3	and] behind her	433.2	for] *omitted*
423.12	Cabaliste] cabalistic	433.13	not] ~ not
423.26	cellules] flaskets	433.30	feasted] feasts
423.37	distilled] sublimated	436.26	sick] weak
424.4	known once to] once	436.31	by] with
	known to	437.3	and then] She then

437.10	immedicable by no]	462.23	spores] pores
	not medicable by any	463.30–31	the race bore] our
437.20	stole] had stolen		Indians bear
438.1	saints nor sacraments]	464.11	as well] so well
	saint nor sacrament	465.7	hold] remark
438.30	cares] will	465.8	in] to
438.32	evils] griefs	465.9	The Buffalos that
438.34	diseases] disease		swarm on] but that the
440.7	in] of		buffaloes of
440.15	Gypsies] the ~	466.6	for] and
440.15	will] shall	466.24	this] a
441.33	and] as	466.24	La] *omitted*
442.9	in] from	466.28	tribes] ~ that occupy
444.7	ordinary] the ~		the country
444.20	accounts] account	466.35	Sea] Seas
445.14	or] nor	468.4	the] *omitted*
445.16	alert] *omitted*	468.14	could] would
445.19	claims] opinions	471.21	A] *omitted*
445.19–20	courteous and firm]	471.31	as if not] hardly
	courteously as well as	473.8	the old] *omitted*
	firmly	473.12	a] of ~
446.12	Count] Governor	473.27	planted the germs]
448.12	gentlemen] gentleman		opened the flood-gates
449.20	is] what ~	473.30	flood] deluge
450.6	fist] hand	474.7	was] were
452.8	yet] *omitted*	474.12	he] are
452.16	Baron] the ~	474.15	earthly] earthy
454.25	new] *omitted*	474.16	we can interpret]
454.27	one] the ~		science interprets
455.32	it to] *omitted*	474.20	Count] Bishop
456.12	cheery] well known	475.12	table by] table in
456.13	had] *omitted*	475.28	upon] *omitted*
456.25	their] our	475.37	illustrated] had ~
457.14	twist] twiss	476.7	and] *omitted*
460.17–18	with her] *omitted*	476.17	about] above
462.12	vegetation] vegetations	476.30	loses] lose
462.12	is] upon	476.31	spirit] had ~
462.16	that is] there is	476.35	life's blood] life-blood

477.2	officer] man	497.12	or] nor
477.10	but] *omitted*	498.1	thats] that is
477.22	philosophs]	498.15	long] *omitted*
	philosophers	498.20	solidly, took out]
477.26	set] have ~		stolidly, refilled
478.17	also] *omitted*	498.36	those] these
478.22	mercilessly] gayly	499.9–10	rest and] *omitted*
478.24	sound] concert	499.16	elbow] elbows
479.29	came] has come	499.26	he] *omitted*
480.3	remark] opinion	500.10	his] the
480.34	had] *omitted*	500.19	Le] La
483.4	his quiet] this quiet	501.16	restraint] all ~
483.11	a] some	502.1	that she says] she said
483.20	for] by	502.14	pays] pay
483.20	her fortune] wealth	502.22	said De Pean] *omitted*
	and position	502.28	reason to] reason for
483.37	address] addresses	503.9	In] And in
487.11	would] could	503.18–19	She blushed] and
487.21	world] night		blushed
487.32	dank] dark	503.36	rising] *omitted*
487.33	dropping] drooping	504.5	asked] ~ me
487.37	and] They	504.16	had] *omitted*
488.8	draggled] drabbled	504.19	a] *omitted*
488.20	delight] ~ to them	504.29	lost sight for a
488.23	stepping] tripping		moment] for a
488.37	good] bright		moment lost sight
489.7	sometimes] *omitted*	505.21	punishments]
489.14	Censitaires] they were		punishment
	all ~	505.22	inspired] had ~
489.15	all] *omitted*	507.10	part] a ~
489.29	accumulations]	508.7	do] *omitted*
	accumulation	509.13	sake of one] the ~ ~ ~
490.3	dealt in] needed	509.19	Beaune] Beaume
490.19	frank] franc	511.7	on] upon
492.32	the noble] our noble	511.13	quiet] snug
492.35	of] in	513.38	a mug] their mugs
493.15	wives] ~ lying there	514.30	still] *omitted*
493.28	Le] Ce	515.26	took] had

515.34	sip] ~ a little	531.18	Fair to see] leaving
516.14	was] is		them fair
516.24	about] round	531.20	emblem] emblems
517.35	straighten it out]	531.23	placing] replacing
	unravel it	534.5	hedges] ~, until
518.4	but] ~ too well and	535.17	moments] movements
518.5	repeated] replied	536.32	promised] expected
518.21	asleep] sleep	537.5	hazy] drifting
518.34	as she] She	537.18	prove true] be fulfilled
518.35	and] as she	537.24	a strain] the strain
519.2	she] something	537.27	indulge] ~ in
519.4	thoughts] in ~	537.31	sang] ~ her
519.7	seemed] They ~		Minne-song
519.8–9	without end] to herself	537.32	the] a
519.15	lining] border	538.5	love's] the
519.24	it] if ~	538.27	on her] upon her
519.25	could] who ~	539.3	room] chamber
520.18	her visitor] the visitor	539.13	other] the ~
520.27	giving] ~ all	540.31	look] glance
520.35–36	you who] who	540.35	fear] fears
521.38	for] after	543.1	am] *omitted*
523.19	in] of	543.12	wore] had worn
523.29	would] should	544.24	upwards despairingly]
523.35	head] eyes		despairingly upward
525.26	those] us	544.32	all this] this all
525.30	are] were	545.9	a grasp] the grasp
526.9	Lady's] *omitted*	545.11	sea] seas
526.17	the] her	545.28	all, all] all
526.31	ah] eh	545.31	what] *omitted*
526.33	can] shall	545.38	could] should
526.34	La] *omitted*	545.38	me] to ~
527.20	that] about him	546.26	God's eye alone] no eye
527.21	He] Bigot	547.28	he] is ~
530.14	and] *omitted*	548.8	on] upon
530.28	hell] red	549.1	will] would
531.6	purport] meaning	549.20	and] She
531.17	heart] hearts	550.6	by] ~ her
		551.6	ever] for ~

552.4	days] night's	562.17	for] *omitted*
552.22	as if] for	562.28	and] ~ he
552.35–36	replied Angelique impatiently] *omitted*	562.32	point] one ~
		563.11	look] a ~
553.11	often] usually	563.11–12	followed this sally, both from the Dame and from Bigot] between the Dame and Bigot followed this sally
553.25	by] with		
553.32	recounted] described		
554.9	precious] infamous		
555.17	and of] and at		
555.22	king] prince	563.33	life time] ~ and wants a change
555.25	brave and] *omitted*		
556.7	and] He	563.37	my] our
556.11	now that time] now Time	564.15	distant] the ~
		564.37	her lady] the lady
556.23	confidence] *omitted*	565.3	now] *omitted*
556.28	it] *omitted*	565.12	silence] fidelity
556.32	minutest] remotest	565.14	That] It
557.10	romantic] remote	565.15	by] with
557.29	common] and ~	565.17	display] show
557.30	mutual risks] pleasures	566.1	make] made
558.26	Compagny] Company	566.32	knew] saw
560.11	large] cynical	567.8	immovable] and ~
560.13	for] at	567.21	gigantic] stout
560.20	and what if you did lie] Where was the harm in it	567.29	her] she
		568.7	he] Cadet
		568.19	but] *omitted*
560.29	de St] St. de	568.24	done] alone ~
560.34–35	if he ordered them] without an hour's delay, to	568.27	Damn the women!] *omitted*
		569.9	have] ~ got
561.9	Now Cadet] Cadet now	570.32	them] *omitted*
561.28	have] hate	571.10	in] into
561.32	checked or choked to death] choked in time	572.18	Intendant] Royal ~
		572.28	woman] ~ lie
561.36	him] the	572.32	motioning] motioned
562.4	the Sieur] Sieur	573.29	all] and ~
562.8–9	at every sentence] *omitted*	573.30	thoughtful] thinking
		573.33	would] should

573.33	was] had	578.11	by some] from some
574.2	waters] water	578.19	never] neither
574.22	and] They	578.23	tragedy] mystery of her death
574.33	very] *omitted*		
574.37	jocular] peculiar	578.27	have] ~ had
575.8	but] also	579.34	it] *omitted*
577.9	look still] still look	579.35	thought] thoughts
577.10	feeling] feelings	580.11	to] *omitted*
577.25	letter] the ~	580.18	on sleep] in sleep
578.3	ALL] It was long before Angélique came to herself from the swoon in which she had been left lying on the floor by Le Corriveau. Fortunately for her it was without discovery. None of the servants happened to come to her room during its continuance, else a weakness so strange to her usual hardihood would have become the city's talk before night, and set all its idle tongues conjecturing or inventing a reason for it. It would have reached the ears of Bigot as every spray of gossip did, and set him thinking, too, more savagely than he was yet doing, as to the causes and occasions of the murder of Caroline. ~	580.19	on] in
		580.20–31	It was long ... murder of Caroline.] *omitted*
		580.36	round] around
		580.36	chamber] table
		581.13	regret] remorse
		581.16	ever] *omitted*
		582.10	one] the ~
		582.20	torment] torments
		582.23	that Caroline de St Castin had] the Lady of Beaumanoir
		583.4	dared] dare
		583.12	to day] *omitted*
		584.8	had] has
		584.22	Aunt] my ~
		584.38	at] of
		586.31	the] *omitted*
		586.37	his duplicity] duplicity
		587.2	go] to ~
		587.20	lightly] daintily
		587.33	discerned] discovered
		588.2	is] it
		588.3	added] said
		588.15	them] her
		590.10	coming] for ~
		590.10	knowing] and ~
		590.12	replied] interrupted
578.4	wildest] the ~	591.9	the] their

591.14	world] city	618.27	While] This
593.23	a] of	618.28	already is] is already
594.19	returned] went back	619.22	they] and ~
594.33	fruitless] as ~	619.28	*bien*] *lien*
595.22	and] *omitted*	619.33	its] his
597.15	felt] feel	621.16	with] in
600.2	you] ~ now	622.17	such] *omitted*
601.2	shed] swam in	622.20	by] with
601.9	O] *omitted*	623.2	hope] truly ~
601.19	was] were	623.8	haste] hasten
601.32	conviction] accusation	624.17	Le] La
602.22	who loved] loving	625.32	for] but
602.31	in] into	625.35	springs] secret spring
602.37	one] her	625.36	through] under
603.7	being] be	626.25	would] should
603.33	dear] here	627.23	burned] damned
603.33	rely] will ~	629.8	these] those
605.30	depth] depths	629.18	Colony] country
608.21	returns] returned	632.26	as] where
608.28	not] cannot be	633.5	wills it, as] makes it
609.8	and] with	633.10	trouble] evil
611.1	even] until	633.13	of coming events, as]
611.4	a] the		were
611.20	a clipper] clipper	633.14	operations] result
611.32	for] on	633.32	most] now
613.1	thought] his ~	634.2	and] *omitted*
613.7	fragments] fragment	634.22	apostolic] evangelical
613.24	and] they	635.7	black] darkened
613.30	appealing] appealingly	635.31	motion] curve
614.5	banishing] banning	636.9	steady] practised
614.24	asked] added	636.15	a] the
616.3–4	in the storm] on the	636.29	with] by
	waves	639.33	of] about
616.14	joy] ~ that	642.2	Reiter] Ritter
616.18	amid] reading	642.28	the Intendant] that De
617.8	and] but		Pean
617.33	window] windows	642.38	at] of
618.12	see] know	643.3	passed] had ~

643.12	escaped] could escape	658.1	Ursuline] Grande
643.13	knew] ~ that		Mère's
643.19	that] who	658.22	his hands in hers] her
644.38	is] *omitted*		hands in his
645.9	speak] her ~	658.34	tenderly] fondly
646.32	and discovered] to	658.37	become] becomes
	search for	659.29	fingers] finger
647.2	and] *omitted*	660.30	and] for
647.4	and] as	661.6	hands] his ~
647.27	over-empressment] an	661.19	clouds] palaces
	~	662.4	morning] day
648.14	stairs] stair	662.23	meditations]
649.3	when] that		meditation
649.9	to her] *omitted*	663.3	but] and
650.3	and] *omitted*	664.10	Beaupré] Beauport
650.15	It] when it	665.38	and on] On
650.19	illumined] illuminated	666.33	continues] continued
650.22	ark] bark	666.33	this] our
651.10	a holy woman] holy	666.38	heard] beginning to be
	Sarah		~
651.19	white] brown	667.28	of the] on the
651.22	brown] sere	667.33	Samaritans] Samaritan
651.26	Belmont] the city	668.4–5	is alone] alone is
652.30	would] should	668.21–22	the Royal Intendant]
653.15	loved] taken		our lawful authorities
654.5	that morning] only	669.4	Pharisees] the ~
	yesterday	669.34	the] that
654.28	were] had	670.35	his] this
654.30	solitary] solitarily	671.14	could] would
655.31	placid pool] gentle	671.25	effect] effects
	brook	671.38	Le] *omitted*
655.36	an image] a shadow	671.38	asked] added
656.18	clear] full	672.18	stop] to ~
656.20	being] soul	672.23	hoping] hoped
656.22	fathom] measure	675.8	relieve] to ~
656.28	be] ~ in the sight	675.14	and send] to send
657.15	no] which ~	675.26	fill] empty
657.23	she] *omitted*	676.13	stair] stairs

677.7	and] to	706.10	looked] looking
678.3	me] to ~	707.21	A] But a
678.9	baldrick] belt	707.22	be] is
679.16	good] a ~	708.31	clasping] clasped
680.14	drank] drunk	708.32	said] and ~
681.2	only] just	708.33	this] the
681.3	his] its	709.9	Aunt] noble ~
681.5	horse] horse's	709.11	her] in ~
682.19	good] *omitted*	709.15	his] its
684.29	rang] ran	709.16	was] were
685.21	him] he	709.17	would] should
685.27	seeing] looking	710.28	that] who
686.2	division] diversion	710.34	St] *omitted*
686.19	believes] believe	710.35	that] this
686.26	but could] and could	710.36	the postulants] all
686.27	saw] could see		visitors
687.26	after] before	711.15	frontiers] frontier
688.33	it passes] he passes	711.16	captive] a ~
689.18	warehouses] warehouse	712.8	reliquary] shrine
690.11	in] on	712.18	multiferous]
690.26	or] *omitted*		multifarious
692.4	revenge] avenge	713.13	patiently] sadly
694.8–9	at the altar] *omitted*	713.31	who] *omitted*
695.1	Lake of] Lake de	714.31	a] *omitted*
695.11	There] These	715.6	Michel] Michael
695.31	of] at	715.7	multiferous]
696.38	man] ~ ever		multifarious
697.24	a worthy] a good	715.31	espaliers] by ~
698.6	hands] hand	718.13	became] become
698.35	and—and—] and—	719.33	and calling them]
701.20	In] and in		*omitted*
702.36	of] *omitted*	720.4	give] have given
703.1	thought] despair	721.26	Venerable] severe
703.24	prayers] prayer	722.3	left] has ~
703.34	true] truly	722.19	Michel] Michael
704.20	my] a	723.10	of her] her
705.3	hope] hopes	723.27	the sole] that sole
705.6	round] around	724.10	now] *omitted*

725.13	redeem] reward	736.36	the head of] *omitted*
726.31	chapel] convent ~	737.5	grace] graces
726.34	Eia] Pia	737.12	of] at
727.21	counsel] consent	737.18	place] count
727.26	darlings] darling	737.31	St Agathe] Madelaine
728.12	I] It	738.22	They] for they
728.24	dear] *omitted*	740.24	flush] flash
728.36	those] these	740.34	again] back
729.3	forced] made	741.4	falteringly] faltering
729.34	revealed] *omitted*	741.29	passed] had ~
730.4	as] *omitted*	742.21	They] and
730.23	this] the	742.32	these] those
731.33	interrupted] exclaimed	744.6	ends] end
731.37	bars] parlor	744.13	repinings] repining
732.1	a] *omitted*	745.19	its] where ~
732.12	loves me still] still loves	745.23	the supremacy] to ~ ~
	me	745.26	The] and the
732.15	hard] as ~	746.5	neglect of] neglect by
732.28	light] the day	746.17	his] the
733.2	DEATH] ~ THE	746.22	rigour] vigor
	BEAUTEOUS RUIN	747.21–22	never again] and ~ ~
	LAY	748.6	their Governor and]
733.8	prayers] prayer		his
733.19	her] *omitted*	748.20	aid] help
734.7	those] they	749.19	to] in
734.11	if] though	750.25	discovered] ~ it
734.21	St Agathe] Madelaine	751.18	coffres] coffers
734.26	rule] rules	753.16	her] the
735.4	St Agathe] Madelaine	753.24	effected] had ~
735.8	will] it ~	754.12	La] Le
735.21	St Agathe] Madelaine	754.15	when the north] and
735.25	picture] memorial		the north
735.28	Agathe's] Madelaine's	754.16	casements] casement
735.38	long] a ~	754.23	forgotten] accursed

Appendix

Dedication of 1877 Lovell, Adam, Wesson and Company Impression of
First Edition

TO

MISS RYE,

IN ADMIRATION OF HER INTELLIGENT AND WOMANLY PERSEVERANCE

IN THE GOOD WORK TO WHICH SHE DEVOTES HER LIFE—THE RESCUE

FROM POVERTY AND VICE OF DESTITUTE CHILDREN—THIS BOOK IS

RESPECTFULLY INSCRIBED BY   THE AUTHOR.

NIAGARA ONTARIO,
January, 1877.